SPECIES IMPERATIVE

SURVIVAL

MIGRATION

REGENERATION

JULIE E. CZERNEDA

DAW BOOKS, INC.

DONALD A. WOLLHEIM, FOUNDER

375 Hudson Street, New York, NY 10014

ELIZABETH R. WOLLHEIM
SHEILA E. GILBERT
PUBLISHERS

www.dawbooks.com

Introduction

To my mind, the *Species Imperative* trilogy that's gathered here for the first time in one volume for you is one of the best examples around of just how immensely appealing great character-driven science fiction can be when it weaves a complex, expansive plot around some of the most charming, if often dangerous, beings of various sorts that you can imagine.

These novels mix solid science, both not-too-distant and wildly extrapolative, with beautiful writing that tugs us along lyrically through a most interesting time period in the life of the very appealing Dr. Mackenzie Connor, who thinks of herself as an ordinary hard-working biologist spending many a happy year studying the spawning habits of salmon along the Pacific Coast of Canada. The story takes place in the near future, when Earth has made contact with star-faring civilizations and the more adventuresome humans are able to travel to other planets for reasons scientific or political. But Mac, as she likes to be known, has avoided paying the slightest attention to those other worlds and other beings and, instead, spends her time deeply immersed in her research. And then, a little late to the party, Mac finds herself embroiled in a great interstellar struggle between civilizations and worlds.

Like the charming character that she has created for us, Julie Czerneda herself came late to the party, and that's part of the amazement that underlies this terrific trilogy. *Species Imperative* displays so much control, such perfect balance between that grand sweep of alien conflicts and the tight focus on spawning salmon in pristine northern streams, that it can't be possible, we think, that this ambitious and, in its own way, profound story is the work of an author who had only been publishing novels for a few years when she produced *Species Imperative*.

Thing is, from her first novel in 1997 to 2004's *Survival*, the first of the *Species Imperative* novels, Julie produced six other novels, working her way most successfully back and forth through two great series, *The Clan Chronicles* and *The Web Shifters*.

Why the hurry? Why such a pace? Well, as she will tell you, while she had enjoyed a fine career as a scientist and a science writer and editor, Julie had long held a secret desire to write novels and there was a trunk full of those books in various stages of incompletion. When she got the chance in the mid-1990s, she took it, and got busy working on those novels and others. Praise followed. That same year as her debut novel she was a finalist for the John W. Campbell Award for Best New Writer and DAW Books wisely signed her up for more novels, among them the splendid trilogy you are about to embark on.

Without giving too much away about the wonders you are about to encounter in *Species Imperative*, suffice it to say that you will meet a self-effacing and reluctant hero, a sidekick who's as serious about having fun as she is about saving the universe, a bevy of complex and weird and wonderful and downright utterly believable alien species that allow Julie full range to show how imaginative a biologist can be when it comes to creating life forms.

It's all about as seductively charming and thrilling as it could possibly be. Somehow these three novels are both enormous in scale and comprise together one of the great space sagas of the past few decades even as they are warm, intimate, understanding, and sympathetic portrayals of characters from the instantly recognizable to the amazingly difficult to fathom.

Worlds and species are at war, billions are dying as whole planets are decimated, great battles are taking place even as complex spying and careful negotiations involving the future of mankind (and a lot of other species) are occurring. And yet, somehow, Julie Czerneda manages to mix in enough charm to leaven the tragedy and give us hope in the middle of sorrow.

How does she do this? It's an amazing juxtaposition, really, the balance of the intimate with the grand, the deeply personal with the worldly, and all of it wrought in a writing style that is lyrical and convincing and heart-thumping by turn.

In short, this is, indeed, the good stuff, the really really good stuff. Sit back, get comfortable, and enjoy yourself.

Rick Wilber

—Rick Wilber is a novelist and short-story writer whose next novel, *Arrival* (2015), is volume one in a trilogy based on his long-running series of S'hudonni Empire stories that have run in *Asimov's Science Fiction* magazine and elsewhere. He has recently edited the anthologies *Future Media* and *Field of Fantasies: Baseball Tales of the Strange and Supernatural*. His novelette "Something Real" won the 2012 Sidewise Award for Best Alternate History-Short Form.

For Roger. . .

Always.

★ ★ ★

I dedicate this special edition to those readers who fell in love with Mac's story
because they too treasure life in all its myriad forms.

Biogeeks Unite!

Acknowledgments

The story of "Mac" and the Interspecies Union epitomizes all I love about writing, being a writer, and this world of ours. Imagine my joy when DAW Books chose to celebrate the 10th anniversary of Mac's story with this beautiful new omnibus edition! Thank you, Sheila Gilbert and all those at DAW, with special hugs for Joshua Starr, Katie Hoffman, and, of course, G-Force Design.

Though at first we wondered . . . could it all fit?

Yes! With some ingenuity, every word is here, plus a wonderful introduction by Rick Wilber. Rick is more than my friend and extremely talented writer, he's a shining beacon of how to use words and science fictional thought to better ourselves and our world. Thank you, Rick, 'tis an honour!

Much as I've loved Luis Royo's stunning covers for the separate books, for the omnibus we needed something new. I'm delighted we went to the marvellous Kenn Brown of Mondolithic Studios. The result is magic, Mac-approved.

I've done my utmost to reflect what is known now, from shorelines to eyeballs to the antics of New Zealand's keas. My sincere gratitude to the following individuals for their expertise (any factual errors are mine): Erin Kenny, Kaila Krayewski, Nahanni River Adventures, Doranna Durgin, Dr. Isaac Szpindel, J. Kim McLean, Nathan Azinger, Kevin Maclean, Dr. Sally Leys, Dr. Scott Hinch, and Lance Lones.

There are real people whose names appear in these pages, though any resemblance to the actual person is unintentional except for the good bits: Professor Jabulani Sithole (a gift from our Jennifer), John Ward, Lee Fyock, Frank Wu, Cathy Palmer-Lister, Wendy Carlson, Lara Herrera, Robert Herrera, Bobbie Barber, Carol Gaupp, Sam Schrant, Sebastian Jones, Doug Court, Kevin Maclean, and, of course, the ever-heroic Michael Gillis.

Writing's half the process. There was reading to be done! My thanks to those who willingly read draft, in whole or bleeding bits: Jihane Billacois, Jana Paniccia, Ruth Stuart, Kristen Britain, Doranna Durgin, Nalo Hopkinson, Janet BF Chase, Janny Wurts, and, most of all, Jennifer Czerneda (I must have sent you the same pages ten times).

As always, I'd help from family, all the way. Scott, thanks for letting me talk out the dark details of plot. And, Jennifer? Thanks forever for 'Mac.' I'd like to take this chance to thank my Poppa and Uncle Gordon, because they're in here, as real as can be. And, at last, to acknowledge with all my heart Dr. R.J.F. Smith (Jan), who introduced me to fisheries biology and left us far too soon.

The best part of writing this ten years later? I've the opportunity to single out a special group of readers—nay, friends! "Biogeeks" are avowed fans of Mac and the biology in my books, and I love you more than salmon. Thanks for letting me include your names. (If you know you belong here, and aren't, I've made arrangements below. Clever, yes?)

Biogeeks Unite!

Adrianne Middleton, Agatha Phan Bernal, Alan Petrillo, Alison Sinclair, Andrea Gawlas Hirsh, Ann Morris, Anna Zorawski, Antonia Hughes, "BF" Chase, Bill Ryan, Bob Milne, Carl Floren, Carolyn Charron, Caryn Cameron, Cathy Chance, Cheryl Strazdins, Cindy Londeore, Claire Eamer, Cyn Wise, Damien Warman, David DeGraff, David Lott, David-Glenn Anderson, Denise Wiles, Ed Parton, Elaine Parent, Elizabeth Farley-Dawson, Erin Stirling, Franciska Incze ("arky"), Gerald Vargas, Ginette Cyr, Guy Stewart, Heather Dryer, Helen Merrick, Henri Reed, J. Kim McLean, Jacqueline Starink, James Alan Gardner, Jason Simcoe, Jeanette Glass, Jeffrey Allan Boman, Jenna Fischer, Jennifer Seely, Jihane Billacois, Jim C. Hines, Jim Proctor, Jim Wagner, John Miller, Judy Angsten, Julie Page, Kendall Morris, Kris Burger, Krista Cobb, Lance Lones, Lawren Louli, Layne Olson, LeAmber Raven, Linda Carrigan, Liz Bennefeld, Lyn SE, Maria Urton, Marleen Beaulieu, Marni Leigh, Melissa Linde, Mike Young, Misa Yny, Monique Murphy, Natalie Reinelt, Paul Goat Allen, Paula Johanson, Paula McCaskill-Whitehouse, Paula S. Jordan, Rachel Blackman, Rachael Jael Wiles, Rachel McDonald, Reynard Spiess, Robert J. Sawyer, Rosalind M. Green-Holmes, Roxanne Hubbard, Sally McLennan, Sciffy Snugglemonster, Scott Czerneda, Sean Emerson, Shannan Palma, Shayne Shark, Sheri Smith Moreau, Stephen Ragan, Susan Lehman, Tanja Wooten, Torbjørn Rasch Pettersen, Tracey Lackey, Veronica Jones, Wayne Carey, Wendy Shark, Wesley Struebing, Zel Hamster, and...

Don't forget me. I'm a biogeek too! ——————————————————————————

SURVIVAL

How do we know

why we act

as we do?

The root causation

of civilization

eludes me.

*(Earliest recorded wall inscription,
Progenitors' Chamber, Haven.)*

- Portent -

THE DROP glistened, green and heavy, as it coalesced at the leaf's tip. The drop trembled, then tumbled. It fell into the calm water of the pond below, sending a ring of ripples outward, its green diffusing until invisible. Mute.

Another fell. Then another. Within moments, there were drops forming and flowing to the tips of thousands of leaves, each drop falling free in turn, the sum etching the pond's surface, staining its clarity an ominous turquoise. Released from their burden, the leaves stirred the air as they sprang upward, only to be bent again under more of the green liquid. Below, the pond blurred and grew, consuming its banks.

Yet more fell.

The leaves themselves began to blur, their sharp edges washing away, the softer tissues dissolving with each new drop until skeleton veins rattled with the beat of false green.

More.

Ferns lining the pond's edge rotted as the floodwater reached their base, fronds having no time to curl into death as they toppled and sank. The trees themselves began to blur, their bark no match for this new and hungry rain, their branches weakening first where the green drops collected in fork and crook, so they cracked and fell, landing with a splash.

The drops continued for hours.

Until all that remained was a green lake, cupped by lifeless stone.

Then the mouths began to drink.

MEETINGS AND MISSION

"MY MONEY'S on the plant."

The antique clay pot on the windowsill ignored Mac's comment, preoccupied with containing the immense aloe that folded its lower thick leaves over the pot's rim like grasping fingers and burst roots from beneath so the combination tilted in its saucer. There weren't cracks . . . yet. But the plant would win. Time, toughness, and a single-minded refusal to accept barriers to its growth. Mac approved.

Not that she *had time on her side.*

Her "pot" was this waiting room, her discomfort in it undoubtedly a pleasure to the man whose offices filled the remaining two-thirds of this floor. Mac was convinced those who ran the Wilderness Trusts shared a disdain for those who required roofs and meetings, begrudging any budget toward such things—even for their own staff. This building was shabby, the neighborhood matched, and the floor space was probably donated. The waiting room? Bland, square, and furnished to test the resolve of anyone waiting. The carpet gave off a stifling aroma, a combination of stale body and damp fiber. The only window had been frosted for no imaginable reason except to prevent gazing at anything but the imprisoned aloe on its sill. The reader on the side table? Never worked. There was a framed piece of art on the wall not occupied by window or closed, forbidding door. As this was an aerial view of a dense forest, with the words: "Leave Me Alone!" blazoned in threatening yellow across the center, Mac's eyes automatically avoided it.

Dr. Mackenzie Connor, just "Mac" to anyone she cared about, avoided the mainland's cities, including this one, just as automatically. Her preferred environment was at the ocean's edge, where the tallest structures were snow-covered peaks. It wasn't hard to confine her excursions to the halls and labs of academia, with the occasional foray into shopping or visits with her dad. At one time, she'd even been able to avoid entanglement in the many layers of bureaucracy and politics that governed Earth and her solar system. During elections, Mac would ask Kammie, who was as political as they came, which representatives were most likely to keep or raise funding levels for their work and would vote accordingly. It kept her life simple.

Until Mac encountered the politics of the Trusts. One Trust in particular. The one whose Oversight Committee consisted solely of the man sitting on the other side of that door.

Mac glared at it, well aware that Charles Mudge III knew to the second how long he could make her wait before she'd throw something.

There was an Oversight Committee for each of the Wilderness Trusts beading the western coast of the Pacific, from the Bering Strait to Tierra del Fuego. Their mandate, like such Trusts elsewhere on Earth, was identical and straightforward: keep the Anthropogenic Perturbation Free Zones, Classes One through Fifteen, exactly that: off-limits to Humans or Human activity.

As an evolutionary biologist, Mac approved. To become a Trust, these fortunate patches of nature had to have been undisturbed for a minimum of two hundred years—some perhaps for the extent of Human history. They were standards against which to compare restoration and preservation efforts elsewhere, not to mention a source of biodiversity for the rest of the planet. Earth had come a long way since relieving her Human population pressure by moving much of it, and her heavy industry, offworld. She had a long way left to go, and the rules protecting the Trusts were part of that journey.

Unfortunately, as senior coadministrator of Norcoast Salmon Research Facility, located just offshore of the Wilderness Trust that encompassed the shoreline and forested hills surrounding Castle Inlet, Mac found herself in the unexpected position of asking for those rules to be, if not broken, then seriously bent.

Mac sighed and went back to the room's only chair, the seat's padding warm from the last time she'd sat on it. She liked rules. They helped people behave in a reasonable manner, most of the time. Unfortunately, other living things tended to run rampant over rules, blurring boundaries and refusing to conveniently exist in isolation. Case in point: Castle Inlet. Norcoast's mandate—her mandate—from Earthgov was to conduct ongoing studies of the metapopulations of local salmonide species, a valued Human food source as well as a crucial portion of the energy and nutrient web of the area. Fine, but that meant more than counting fish in the ocean and waterways. Salmon were essential to the surrounding forest and its life, their bodies carrying nutrients from the ocean depths to land. The forest organisms, in turn, were essential to the vigor and health of the waterways the salmon needed in order to reproduce. Researchers at Norcoast thus required access to the land as well as water. Earthgov, through the Office of Biological Affairs, had readily granted Norcoast's scientists that access.

Legally, that should have been it. However, a clause in the Wilderness Trust charter granted each Oversight Committee the power to ban any specific encroachment it deemed detrimental to the life therein. Which put Mac in this same chair, watching the aloe fight its pot, twice each year. Once to deliver, in person, the details of all research proposals for the coming field season, complete with Norcoast's planned precautions to avoid any anthropogenic interference with the Trust lands.

Once a year, in other words, to beg permission to continue their life's work from Charles Mudge III.

As if that wasn't demeaning enough, Mac was also required to report, in person, any and all slips in those precautions, no matter how minor, that may have occurred during the course of the field season, these to be included in the Oversight Committee's annual catalog of outside, undue influence.

Once a year, in other words, to grovel and confess their sins to Charles Mudge III.

Today's meeting would be one of the former: begging. Mac winced. Regardless of having plenty of practice, she wasn't good at it. Arm wrestling, verbal or otherwise, was more her style.

It had only been an hour and thirteen minutes since she'd arrived. Too soon to be pacing and scowling, though Mac admitted to temptation. To keep still, she pulled out her imp—a tougher-than-standard version of the ubiquitous Interactive Mobile Platform carried by almost everyone on or off Earth—from the ridiculous little sack she'd been forced to carry. No pockets. She laid the stubby black wand on her left palm and tapped her code against its side with a finger of the other hand. In answer, a miniature version of her office workscreen appeared in midair, hovering at the exact distance from her eyes that she preferred.

Just as Mac was about to review the access request she knew by heart, she glanced at the black, unblinking vidbot hovering at the ceiling. Pursing her lips, she disengaged the 'screen and put the imp away.

Privacy wasn't an option on the mainland.

Not that she'd anything to hide, Mac assured herself. *It was the principle of the thing.*

Time. Time. Time. She folded her hands to resist the urge to fiddle with her hair. It was, unusually, tucked up and tidy. As was she, dressed in her mainland business suit and borrowed shoes. There'd been the expected startled looks from those at Base when she'd left this morning. Dr. Connor, professor and friend to an ever-changing group of grad students every summer—when not investigating the evolutionary impact of diversity within migratory populations—typically went about her business in clothing with useful pockets, her hip-length hair in a braid knotted into a loose pseudo-pretzel, and her feet bare or in waterproof boots with decent tread.

A fashion statement she wasn't, even now. Mac had reluctantly taken her father's advice after graduating, investing in The Suit for those all-important tenure interviews. Ironically, she'd landed her first choice without it: Norcoast, where she'd been a student herself.

Which made The Suit a decade and a half out-of-date. *If she waited long enough,* Mac thought pragmatically, *its short jacket and pleated pants would come back in style.* The dark blue weave was, in her estimation, timeless, if a trifle warm for this time of year.

The dress shoes were Kammie's, Mac's not having survived being worn through waves and sand one memorable night. Dr. Kammie Noyo was the other coadministrator at Norcoast and loaned her favorite shoes with the clear expectation that Mac wouldn't mess up the applications of Kammie's own lab and students. Mac squinted down her legs and flexed one ankle, wondering who in their right mind would design footwear to topple the wearer down the first set of stairs she might encounter.

But it would be worth the shoes and Suit. Worth the wait. Worth whatever it took. *It had better be,* Mac amended, time crawling over her skin. This meeting was unusual and an alteration in routine never sat well with Mudge. She'd been here, as always, midwinter to confirm his permission—however grudging—for this field season's projects. However, thanks to Emily's—Dr. Emily Mamani's— recent accomplishments in the Sargasso Sea, Mac had seen an opportunity to move her own work up by three years, maybe more. With that motivation, she'd chanced Mudge's temper and scrambled to get the changed request to him by spring, hoping for permission before the early fall salmon runs—her target— approached the continental shelf. But with the damnable timing of bureaucracy in general, suspicious timing from an organization and individual that surely understood that much of the natural world it was supposed to protect from Human interference, she was in this waiting room when she should have been calibrating sensors at Field Station Six.

The salmon were coming.

And Emily was late. Emily, who could charm a clearance from Earth customs, let alone a curmudgeon who called himself a committee.

Mac scowled at the empty room. Emily, her coresearcher and friend, was never late for the start of their field season. The first time *would* have to be this one, when so much was at stake.

The plant caught her attention and Mac transferred her scowl to its pot, willing the aloe to grow faster and shatter the damn thing. She contemplated helping it along by tossing pot and plant at the door. *Satisfying, if hardly beneficial to her own cause.*

With impeccable timing, the door in question abruptly opened wide enough to let a slice of face and one pale eye peer into the room. "Dr. Connor," said a voice with clear disapproval. "You're still here."

"Yes, I am," Mac confirmed. "You'd think I had nothing else to do but wait, wouldn't you?"

"The office is about to close for the day. I suggest you come back tomorrow."

The thin smile stretching Mac's lips was the one which gave inadequately prepared students nightmares, but all she said was: "You're new here, aren't you?"

The opening remained a slit, as though the person on the other side, older and female by the voice, preferred a barrier between herself and imagined hordes in the waiting room. "I've been here since last fall, Dr. Connor," complete with sniff. "You really should go—"

Mac felt a twinge of remorse. Not at forgetting the woman—she tended to focus on Mudge, not the receptionists who appeared and vanished like shoe styles—but last fall had been the Incident. The Oversight Committee, namely Mudge, had been outraged by the report of a near-attack by a grizzly, an episode he treated, with intolerable smugness, as incited by the grad student in question. He'd claimed the student had grossly interfered with the animal's normal movements through the forest—a serious charge, possibly enough to cancel Norcoast's access.

Upon hearing this, Mac had forced her way past the futile protests of a pimpled young man into Mudge's office, there dumping a bucket of distinctly ripe salmon on his desk. The so-called incitement had been no more than a similarly fragrant sample on its way back to the lab. The bear, needless to say, had willingly followed the scent and student. The Wilderness Trust didn't control the air.

She'd made her point, but Mac hadn't wished to cost someone their job. *Still.* Mudge seemed to have a limitless supply of new staff. She leaned back comfortably and gazed at the eyeball in the door slit. "You can go home, if you like."

The door closed. Mac sighed and raised an eyebrow at the vidbot's lens. "The game's getting old," she told it, in case anyone was watching.

"Norcoast."

"Oversight."

"Counting this—this change of yours, Norcoast, there are three more applications from your facility than last year."

No apologies, no pleasantries. Not even names, as though to Mudge their roles mattered more than their own existence. Mac couldn't disagree.

She ran a finger along the edge of the bare, gleaming white table separating them, gathering her patience around her.

The man with authority to grant or refuse the land-based portion of Norcoast's research was florid in face and manner, with a body determined to stress the midline of his clothing. *How many underestimated him?* Mac wondered. *Their mistake, not hers.* Charles Mudge III's lineage could be traced back to the earliest wave of loggers to settle the Pacific coast and, beyond any doubt, he was obsessed with its forests. Castle Inlet's forests in particular, since it was partly his great grandmother's doing that so many of its slopes had remained pristine enough to qualify for Trust status. Mudge vehemently opposed any Human presence in the Trust.

Mac was here, as she had been each of the past fourteen years—in The Suit—to arrange just that. "I turned down twenty from my staff," she replied calmly. "We understand the restrictions, Oversight. We follow them."

Mudge looked rumpled and aggrieved, not that Mac could recall seeing him otherwise. Now he scowled at her, his round face creased with wear and sun.

His cheeks and chin sported the beginnings of a beard, mottled in gray, red, and black despite the brown hue of what hair struggled to cap his shiny head. "You'd better. Castle Inlet gains Class Two rating in fifty-one years, three months, and two days. *If* it survives your scientists. And you know what that means. No exemptions, none. I plan to be there on that day, Norcoast, to see your people ousted permanently."

Mac hid her dismay. The active lifespan of a Human was lengthening with each generation—on Earth, anyway—so it was entirely possible she and Mudge would continue these meetings into the next century. *Sit in that waiting room another hundred times?* For a moment, she seriously considered delegating the job, something she'd never done—even to Emily the charming. Then Mac looked into Mudge's small and anxious eyes, read the determined defensiveness of his hunched shoulders and lowered head, and gave a slow, respectful nod.

"I'll be there," she promised. "Norcoast will be overjoyed to see the Castle Inlet Wilderness Trust reach its four hundredth birthday unspoiled. We aren't at odds on that, Oversight, by any measure. Now, about my application?"

She knew better than to hope for a curt "yes" and an end to waiting. Sure enough, Mudge tugged his own imp from a chest pocket and set an enlarged workscreen between them, one that reached to the ends of the table and almost touched the ceiling. Proposals and precautions formed chains of text in the air, most glowing red and trailing comments like drops of gore. She'd been afraid of this. He'd complain about everything possible all over again, a knight defending the virtue of his forest against the pillages of field research.

Elbows on the table, Mac propped her chin in her hands and plastered an attentive look on her face.

Good odds the aloe plant would escape before she did.

The hired skim deposited Mac on the deserted pier, in time to watch the second-last northbound transport lev rise and bank out over the harbor. The driver was apologetic and willing to take her somewhere else; Mac paid him and sent him away.

She didn't mind this kind of waiting, the kind where the city lights played firefly over the dark waters of the bay, skims darting from building to building in such silence the lapping of waves against the pylons rang in her ears. She took her time walking to the pier's end and discovered a small series of crates there, a couple stacked atop one another. Taking off Kammie's dress shoes with a groan of relief, Mac placed them carefully on a lower crate. She climbed the stack, sat on the topmost, and dangled her bare feet over its edge, admiring the view. She had time, all right. The final t-lev of the night would be late; its driver lingering at each stop so as not to strand anyone.

Meanwhile, the cool sea air held pulses of city heat, scented with late summer flowers. Mac half closed her eyes to puzzle at the scents, letting the tension of her meeting with Mudge escape with every exhalation, feeling her bones melt. Castle Inlet was too far north for plants that couldn't take a little bluster and gale with their winter. *Bluster.* She smiled to herself. Mudge had certainly done enough of that, but even he'd found nothing in her changed request that would impact his precious Trust. *Not for want of trying.* In his own way, he was as tough as the aloe.

Mac's hands strayed to her hair, tugging free the mem-ribbons making it behave. Loose, the stuff drifted down her back and arms until Mac swept it forward over her right shoulder and began to braid, fingers moving in the soothing, familiar pattern.

The meeting hadn't been a disaster. *Chalk one up for diplomacy,* Mac decided proudly. It sounded better than saying she'd managed to keep her temper. They'd had their share of confrontations in the past; times when she and Mudge had shouted at one another until both were hoarse. Once, he'd walked out in a fury. Only once, since Mac had proved herself willing and able to camp in his office for as long as it took. Today? He'd agreed to her request, confirmed all but one of the existing permissions, insisted on onerous but doable increases in their precautions, and been, all in all, reasonable. For Mudge.

Now one of Kammie's grad students would have to travel up the coast to find a new study site. Mac could live with that, being finished with Kammie's shoes for six months. *Flexibility was worth learning,* she grinned to herself. Mac always included one or more projects she knew Mudge wouldn't allow. It let them both get some satisfaction out of the day. She'd been surprised he'd passed it in the first place.

Leaning back on her hands, Mac smiled peacefully at the city outlining itself against the night. *Not a bad meeting at all.*

The voice startled her out of an almost doze, an hour later. "I can't believe you wore that thing again!"

Mac turned awkwardly and too quickly, almost falling off the crate into the bay. "Emily? What the—" Smiling so broadly it hurt her cheeks, she clambered down, her bare feet landing in a puddle of cold seawater. It didn't dim her joy one iota. "About time—"

The glows lining the pier's edge were sufficient to put color to the tall slim woman standing in front of her, touching a gold shimmer from a dress that was most likely the latest rage in Paris, sliding warm tan over the skin, and lifting red along the scarf supporting Emily's left forearm. *A sling?*

"What have you done to yourself?" Mac demanded, drawing back from the relieved hug she'd planned to offer.

"This?" Emily raised her left arm. The scarf fell back to show a flash of white. "Little collision between the edge of a stage, a dance floor, and yours truly."

Mac took Emily's left hand and pulled it gently into the light. "A cast?" she said worriedly, looking up. "A bit archaic, isn't it?"

"I had a reaction to the bone-knitting serum. Just have to heal up the old-fashioned way. Don't worry." The fingers in Mac's hold wriggled themselves free. "Won't slow me down."

"You're late, you know."

"Glad to see you, too, Mac."

Mac grinned. Looking beyond Emily, she could see a trio of skims parked near the entrance to the pier, figures unloading boxes. "That your gear? Is it—is it ready?"

"You find me your salmon run, and I'll tell you who's in it. Name, rank, and DNA sequence."

A shiver of anticipation ran down Mac's spine. "I've such a good feeling about this, Em," she said. "What we'll accomplish—what we'll learn—" Mac stopped, embarrassed by the passion in her voice. "Great to have you back."

Emily stilled—or was it merely a pause in the waves tasting the pier? Mac decided she'd imagined it, for her friend went on briskly: "Before you publish our results, Dr. Connor, mind calling in a t-lev on Norcoast's tab? I'd rather not stand out here all night."

Mac pointed to the nearby crates. "Have a seat. Public transit will be arriving soon enough. While we wait, you can show me the upgrades to your DNA Tracer."

A laugh and a shake of Emily's head greeted her words. "Don't you want to know what I've been up to these last few weeks?"

Mac moved Kammie's shoes so Em could sit without climbing, joining her on the crate. "Nope. Not if it involves ridiculous prices for clothes, seedy bars, or places I've never heard of," she stated firmly. "Or anything about men," she added, to forestall Emily's usual list of adventures. "Salmon, girl. That's why you're back in the Northern Hemisphere." Mac pulled out her imp, chewing her lower lip as she activated the workscreen and hunted for the latest schematic.

The city lights faded behind the radiance of the three-dimensional image floating in front of the pair, its network of wiring and data conduits peeled back to show the innermost workings of the device. Emily reached over and traced a series of components with one finger, turning them blue within the image.

"Happy now?"

"I will be when we know it works in the field," Mac muttered, eyes devouring the modified image. "We'll set up right away."

"After I settle in, you mean."

"Settle?" Mac sputtered. "You're late, remember? We're moving out at dawn. The tents and my gear are already at the field station."

"Kammie's right. You're a damned workaholic," Emily bumped her good shoulder into Mac's. "A day at Base to unpack. Two." The display gleamed in her dark eyes. "Not to mention a chance to look over this year's crop."

Mac bumped her back. "The students are busy. As we'll be. The run won't wait—" She glanced at Emily's injured arm and sighed. "One day. We can run some sims . . ."

"Muchas gracias," Emily said dryly. "I trust you'll let me eat sometime in there?"

Grinning, Mac let the plaintive request be answered by the hum of the approaching t-lev.

No more barriers, she thought with triumph. *No more delays. Nothing but the work.*

Life didn't get much better.

- 2 -

SUCCESS AND SURPRISE

"**B**AH! THERE'S no sex in this one either."

The offending book sailed over Mac's head, landed with a bounce, then began slithering down the massive curve of rock. She lunged for it, scraping both knees on wet granite in the process, and somehow managed to hook one finger in the carrystrap before the book sailed off the rock for the river several meters below. Sitting back, she caught her breath before glowering at Em. "At last we have the truth about Dr. Emily Mamani Sarmiento, consummate professional researcher from Venezuela, holder of more academic credentials than I knew existed. She's nothing but a randy teenager in disguise."

"Nice catch."

Mac's lips pressed together, then twitched into a grin. "And she's impossible."

Emily tilted the brim of her rain hood enough to show Mac a raised eyebrow. "What I am is stuck on this rock, reduced to watching you, my dear Dr. Mackenzie Connor, also holder of innumerable awards which don't pay rent, chase lousy books that have no sex in them. Remind me again why I agreed to such suffering."

Mac snorted, busy sorting through their pile of waterproof bags for one to protect the latest of Emily's rejects. Lee would not be pleased to find a member of his novel collection soaked and nonfunctional. *Ah.* There was the one from the sandwiches, consumed hours past. She shook the bag, and book, to remove most of the raindrops, before unzipping the one to shove in the other.

Mac made sure the bag was securely wedged in a crevice before turning her attention back to the river. She tucked her throbbing knees against her chest, and put her chin on a spot that seemed unscraped, her rain cape channeling the warm drizzle into tiny rivulets that converged on her bare feet. She wiggled her toes, playing with the water.

"I don't see why there has to be sex in everything you read," Mac commented absently, her eyes sweeping the heave of dark water below with the patience of experience. She could relax now. They'd delayed at Base for two days, not one, while Emily fussed over her equipment, settled into her quarters, and charmed "her" new students. Mac's anxious complaints hadn't hurried her fellow scientist in the least.

Hard now to complain about Emily's lack of speed, after five days camped with no sign of salmon whatsoever. Em had been insufferably smug the first day; bored and smug the second; simply bored by the third. Mac was rather enjoying her discomfort.

"And I don't see why it has to rain here every hour of the day," that worthy countered predictably. "This is worse than the Amazon."

A bright little head suddenly popped out of the river depths, patterned in bold white and rich chestnut. The Harlequin bobbed for an instant in the midst of the maelstrom, the water's froth seeming to entertain it. Then it dove again, seeking its prey in the rapids. Mac smiled to herself. "The sun was out this morning," she reminded Emily.

"Oh. Was that the sun? Tell my sleeping bag. Which, for your information, barely achieved damp status before we had to haul the gear back into the tents." A rustle of synthrubber as Emily came to sit beside her. *With their hoods and capes, the two of them,* Mac decided, *must look like small yellow tents themselves.*

Emily was quiet for about thirty seconds. "How long before they get here?"

"When we see them—right there." Mac pointed downstream, where the river wrapped itself around the base of a wall of rock and disappeared.

Below their toes, and the generous outcrop of granite beneath them, the Tannu River was over forty meters wide, in its mid-reach already swollen, powerful, and swift as it sped down the west side of the Rocky Mountains to the Pacific Coast. Along its surface, mist competed with the unceasing rain: some tossed where the river did its utmost to dislodge boulders and tumble gravel, some curling up along the eddies where the ice-cold glacial meltwater met the warm, saturated late-August air. The river always won. It had carved the sides of its valley into downward sheets of sheer rock, anchored at their base by the lushness of riparian rain forest, itself a thin line of green stitched to the water's edge by the pale gray of fallen tree trunks. The river's edge was a perilous place to grow.

Yet grow here life did, with a tenacity and determination Mac had long ago taken as personal inspiration. Cloud clung to the forests; the forest clung to any nonvertical surface, lining cliff tops as well as valley floors. Where trees couldn't survive, lichens and mosses latched themselves to rock face and crevice, nourishing the mountain goats who danced along the perpendicular cliffs.

The mountains' own relentless push skyward added force to the river. The river gladly tore at the mountains. Life thrived in the midst of geologic conflict. It was, Mac firmly believed, the most wonderful place on Earth.

And the ideal location for Field Station Six.

"I don't think it will be much longer, Em," she assured her, relenting. "This afternoon, if I'm any judge."

What Emily muttered to that was too low to compete with the river. Its thunder overwhelmed the rustle of leaves in the trees and the beat of rain on

Tracer. Something in Quechua, Mac judged, and likely bawdy as could be. She'd have to ask for a translation later, over some celebratory beer.

They were a good match. Mac smiled, grateful for every step of the process that had drawn Dr. Emily Mamani from one ocean and hemisphere to another, to come here and join her at Norcoast. There were never guarantees a scientist's personality would be as welcome as his or her abilities. Being trapped together for a field season brought out the worst in people; Mac had endured the consequences many times before. But Em had not only fit right in, she'd single-handedly turned the facility into a place where Saturday night meant a party about to happen.

To the surprise of everyone else at Norcoast, rowdy, raucous Emily had become the perfect foil to Mac's more reserved approach to life. Within moments of meeting, they'd recognized a kindred passion for the work; within a week, it was as if they'd always known one another. *Perhaps,* Mac admitted to herself, *it was because they were both such complete frauds in public:* herself wary of showing her intensity, Emily disguising hers with jokes and flirtation.

By now, in their third northern field season together, there was no one Mac would rather have share this moment. She hummed along, doing her best to follow the melody. The drumming of rain against hood, cape, and console was her private percussion section.

After a few moments, Mac activated her imp. The imp had a ten-year power supply of its own—and the ability to tap into local supplies, such as those maintained around most cities—but not so the consoles or Tracer. No need to verify the power feed from Norcoast's broadcast generators; it was obviously reaching them, as it would be other researchers in the field and at sea.

What concerned Mac were their results. The 'screen now hovering over the console mirrored the one in her office at Base, winking with tallies that showed the data stream making the return trip as steady, the system flawlessly making and sending copies. *She'd have it all.*

Reassured, Mac let her shoulders relax and rubbed a wet hand over her face, putting the device away. "Ready to anchor it, Em?"

"Not yet. I want to make sure we don't get some lateral drift with that wind. It's not much up here, but there's a funneling effect closer to the surface I have to watch—*ai caramba!*—like that. How's the feed? Still okay?"

Mac gave a quick glance. "Nominal. This looks to be just the initial group. I'll heat some soup while you make sure we're stable. There won't be time for a break later."

"Now this is why I keep telling you we should have brought along that helpful grad student of yours, John. Wonderful cook."

Mac patted her console fondly before heading for the tents nestled against the cliff face. "I hadn't noticed it was his cooking you liked," she tossed over her shoulder. The fact that the good-looking John Ward blushed so abundantly had been a bonus, as far as Em was concerned, likely the reason he'd requested Field Station Four this year. Emily's admiration tended to be outspoken and results-oriented.

"So I like men who are— Mac, get back here! Hurry!"

"What is it? What's wrong?" She returned to her console as quickly as she dared on the rain-slicked stone. "The wind . . . What the hell?" Blinking rapidly, then rubbing her hand over the screen didn't change the wrong-scale image now among the salmon. The display red-flagged its code.

Unknown.

"You get whales up here?" Em asked shakily.

"No, but we get idiots." Mac hadn't felt this infuriated since she'd found someone fishing a headwater lake with explosives, nets, and a truck. She left her console to go as close to the bluff's edge as she dared, then judged the distance. Grabbing a piece of jagged rock, she threw it with all the force she possessed.

Close enough. Bubbles exploded on the surface, startling the ducks into flight. A shape appeared shortly afterward, bouncing up and down in the current. Before it could be swept downstream, a repeller activated to hold it in place, a telltale ring of vibrating water plainly visible. Offended salmon burst from the river in all directions as their lateral line sense reacted to the output from the device, dropping back to scatter into the depths.

Any chance of calling this a natural, undisturbed run was gone. Emily didn't need to be told. Mac watched the Tracer's curtain snap out of existence, Emily's 'bots left hovering above the river as if lost.

Meanwhile, the begoggled head was turning from side to side as if hunting the source of the rock. Mac gritted her teeth and fought the urge to hunt for something else to throw. Something heavier—or at least pointy.

"You've got to be kidding." Emily came to stand beside her. The rain conveniently eased into a light drizzle so they had a clearer view, but the diver floating below still hadn't thought to look up. "How'd that *cabrón* get this far without setting off an alarm?"

Mac thrust her arm downstream, as if her finger could impale what was coming toward them. "Like that." The big skim moved above the water's surface, though close enough that spray from the rapids splashed over its cowling. It was heading for the diver. "Best bring in the 'bots before it bumps into one."

With a growl better suited to one of the grizzlies they'd watched yesterday, Emily went to her console. Mac watched the 'bots break formation, a couple swooping near the diver's head so he—or she—ducked back under for a moment, then they all rose until level with the rock shelf. Like a string of beads, the tiny, and very expensive, devices came to rest at Emily's feet. One-handed, she began tucking them inside her console's locker without another word.

Silence, from Dr. Mamani, was not a good sign.

Feeling herself beginning to shake from head to foot wasn't good either. Mac made herself take slow, steady breaths through her nose, fighting back both disappointment and fury, forcing her heart to calm itself. They might—*might*—be able to salvage something if they could get the river cleared of interlopers before the big runs started to arrive—likely by tonight. She'd have more chance of that if she wasn't throwing more rocks, tempting as it was.

Especially at a skim bearing the insignia of her own research facility, hovering beside the diver. *They'd brought him, all right.* They were already lowering the harness of hooked cables that would connect to one of the high-end commercial dive rigs. Interference from those who knew better was worse than unwitting trespass.

Mac turned away, uninterested in the details of extricating her problem, refusing to speculate and have her blood pressure rise even further toward rock throwing. She spent the next few minutes locking down her console, its screen again mute and empty of code.

She was on her knees, struggling with the cover fasteners on the river side of the device, when a deep hum announced the skim had set down on the ledge. Mac ignored both the arrival and the sound of footsteps that followed, including the unfamiliar voice saying: "Dr. Connor, I presume?"

When she was good and ready, Mac rolled her head to gaze at a pair of soaking wet, though shiny, men's shoes, better suited to an office than lichen-coated, bepuddled granite. Her eyes traveled up a pair of damp beige dress pants, were unsurprised to encounter a suit jacket of the same color and condition topped by a conservative yet fashionable—and damp—cravat, and finally stopped at a face she didn't know.

And didn't care to know. Even through the rain, she could smell a bureaucrat. Sure enough, he had a portable office slung under one arm, doubtless jammed with communication gear and clearances someone, somewhere, thought gave him the right to ruin her observations.

The bureaucrat offered her his hand. Mac stared at the manicured fingers until they curled up and got out of her way.

She rose to her feet, shoving her rain hood to her shoulders, and looked around for someone with answers. *There.* A familiar figure stood beside the skim. Tie McCauley, her stalwart chief of operations and the man who single-handedly kept all Norcoast equipment running through budget-pinching and Pacific storms. Catching her eye on him, he simply raised both arms and let them drop at his sides.

That wasn't good.

Mac found herself forced to look to the bureaucrat after all. Up at the bureaucrat. He was taller than he'd appeared at first glance, despite what seemed a permanent slouch. An ordinary, almost pleasant face, bearing rain-spattered glasses and hair that looked to have been actually in the river, so neither eyes nor hair showed their true color. Drips were running down both sides of his face, which bore an expression that could only be described as anxious.

That expression made Mac swallow what she intended to say, replacing it with a much milder: "Do you realize you've seriously disrupted our work?"

"I know, Dr. Connor. It is Dr. Connor?" At her nod, he continued, "Believe me, we wouldn't have come if it hadn't been so important to the Honorable Delegate—"

A booming voice interrupted. "That would be me, Mackenzie Connor."

Mac's eyes widened as if that could somehow help her mind fit the figure now climbing from the skim into the reality of a field camp in the coastal ranges. He—she assumed it was a he—waved off Tie's offer of assistance. *Just as well,* Mac thought numbly, *since their visitor looked to outmass the chief several times over.*

The diving suit, and distance, had helped disguise the nonhuman. Now, his head free and his body wrapped in what appeared to be bands of brightly colored silk, there was no escaping that she was standing three meters from a Dhryn.

Mac had seen the news report on the t-lev from Vancouver. Dhryn—the only oxy-breathing species within the Interspecies Union to never set foot—or more accurately, pods—on Earth, had sent a representative.

Here?

She licked rain from her lips and recaptured the hair strayed from her braid, pushing it behind one ear. "We're honored," she said at last, after a quick look to Emily, who could only shrug and roll her eyes. The Dhryn finished piling himself out of the skim, which rocked as if in relief, and stood before her.

Xenobiology wasn't something Mac had cared to study—there being more than a lifetime's worth of Earth biology to learn, in her opinion—still, she couldn't help but be intrigued by her first, up-close look at an alien.

The Dhryn seemed a sturdy creature, capable of standing erect in Earth gravity—assuming a 45 degree angle from stern to head was erect. Mac thought it likely, given the placement of limbs, seven in number, appeared useful in that stance. Three limbs were paired opposite each other. These were jointed similarly to human arms, although movement at those joints suggested a more free turning ball-and-socket arrangement than an elbow, and the musculature implied greater strength. A heavier gravity world, perhaps.

She really should read more.

The seventh limb, originating high and central from the chest, was—perplexing. It appeared to have several more joints, giving it an almost tentacle-like nature. Instead of the trio of grasping fingers at its tip, like the other six arms, the seventh had something more like scissors, with a hard, chitonous material lining the inner surfaces. As if her attention to this limb was impolite, the Dhryn tucked it under one of his other arms, but gave no other sign her inspection was at all unwelcome.

Legs and feet were one and the same, the being balanced on two elephant-like limbs. The limbs appeared to spread at their bases, ever so slightly. Perhaps the bottoms were adhesive.

The body might have been mammalian, what she could see of it past the gaudy bands; hairless, but with a thick, blue-toned skin that had a sheen, as if waxed. There were dark, pitlike ovals scattered over the body's surface. *Glands? Or sense organs,* Mac debated with herself, unwilling to rush to conclusions.

The head sat between narrow shoulders, and bore thick bony ridges that overhung the two large eyes. Their pupils were shaped like figure eights lain on their sides, black and lustrous, embedded within an oval iris of yellow that spread over the rest of what Mac could see of the eye. The nose and ears were also shaped by curved rises of bone beneath the skin, protected and also likely augmented in their function by those shapes. The mouth was unexpectedly small and tidy, with a pair of thin lips coated with what appeared to be pink lipstick. Now that she paid attention, there were signs of colored pigment applied, quite subtly, to accentuate the shape of eyebrow and nose ridges. There were tiny rings embedded along the top of each ear.

Mac found herself disarmed by a giant bearlike being who'd applied makeup to go diving with salmon, and warned herself—again—against drawing any conclusions at all.

"Mackenzie Connor." The creature's low voice made her jump. From the way her skin shivered, it could well be uttering additional tones below her hearing range, possibly infrasound. "I deeply regret if my curiosity has interfered with your research. I had heard of the wonders of diving with the spawning run. It was never my intention to disrupt your fine work."

Reminded, Mac couldn't help but scowl. "I hope you were bagged," she said, eyes flicking to Tie.

That worthy managed to look offended and embarrassed at the same time, protesting: "Hey, Mac. You think I'd let him in without? There was no chemical contamination. The repeller was on auto—to hold him for pickup. The water's pristine."

"It had better be." Mac shuddered to think of the confusion downstream if the dissolved odors of the Tannu River this year contained added Essence of Dhryn.

"I repeat, Mackenzie Connor. I intended no disruption—"

"Intended or not, Mr.— What do I call you?" The bureaucrat leaned forward, as if this was a question he'd like answered as well.

A graceful, if ponderous, tilt of the head. "Having not yet served in *grathnu*, Mackenzie Connor, I regret I can offer only one name for your use. Please do not be offended."

The Dhryn's face conveyed emotion that matched her human interpretation of his words, the edges of both eyes and mouth flexible enough to turn downward as if in regret. Mac felt chilled. *How much was true similarity in thought processes—how much coincidence—and how much the mimicry of an accomplished diplomat?*

"One name's fine," she said warily.

The Dhryn angled his body more upright, spreading six arms in what appeared a ritual gesture. The seventh was now out of sight under the silk bands. "Brymn is all my name."

The ensuing pause was silent except for the background roar of the Tannu, the intermittent patter of raindrops, and Mac's own breathing. The Dhryn didn't move. Finally, Mac slid her eyes to the bureaucrat and frowned meaningfully. *This was his problem.*

The man seemed very careful not to smile. Instead, he took a step closer, to stand beside Mac, and said, spreading out his own arms: "I take the name of Brymn into my keeping. Nikolai Piotr Trojanowski is all my name."

The Dhryn clapped all six hands together and bowed in the bureaucrat's direction. "I take the name Nikolai Piotr Trojanowski into my keeping. A very fine name, sir." The lips parted, revealing a row of small, even, and brilliantly white teeth, each curved like a rose petal. "Most pleasing."

Emily, not one to miss a cue, spoke up. "Emily Mamani Sarmiento is all my name."

Tie pointedly leaned back against the skim. Mac presumed he planned to stay out of this. *Wise man.*

"I have the name Emily Mamani Sarmiento in my keeping," Brymn acknowledged with another hearty multiple clap. "Most impressive. You are very accomplished for one so young."

Emily smiled. Mac wrinkled her nose at her. The clouds were sinking into the treetops and a return to heavier rain was only moments away. *They had no time for this*—but Brymn had turned to her expectantly. She sighed. "Fine. You can call me—" The bureaucrat with the mouthful of names caught her eye and shook his head very slightly, as if he guessed she planned to say "Mac" and be done with it.

Mac weighed her impatience against what was probably informed advice, given the bureaucrat had come with the alien and knew about this ceremonial exchange of names. "Mackenzie—" she hid a wince, "—Winifred Elizabeth Wright Connor is all my name." From the choked sounds coming from Emily, the "Winifred" would soon be all around Base.

"Magnificent!" The Dhryn clapped, then reared almost vertically, its tiny mouth stretching in what looked like a human smile—or a reasonable facsimile. "I most proudly take the name Mackenzie Winifred Elizabeth Wright Connor into my keeping. An honor, as I expected it would be. Please, accept my invitation to dine together this evening. We have much to share with one another."

Mac scrubbed her bare toes against wet granite, just to verify her surroundings. A line of four eagles flew by, barely visible among the clouds, and she wondered what they thought of this intrusion into their world. *She was,* she decided, *quite sure what she thought.*

"Thank you, Mr. Brymn—"

"Brymn."

"Brymn. A kind offer, but I can't leave this field station. Dr. Mamani and I are in the midst of the most important phase of our work. By the end of the month, I should have time to—"

The Dhryn let out a plaintive wail, not loud but certainly piercing. At the same time, he closed his eyes tightly and began rocking back and forth. There seemed little doubt of his suffering.

"Excuse us," Mac told the decidedly inattentive alien. She grabbed the bureaucrat by one arm and hauled him as far away from Brymn as the rock outcrop allowed.

"What the hell is going on here, Mr. Trojanowski?"

"To quote Brymn, I'm most impressed." The corner of his mouth twitched. "Most people have trouble with my name."

"I've heard all I want about names for one day," Mac warned. "What I want is to hear how quickly you're going to get this—this—intruder off my river! And you, too," she added, just to be clear. "We'll be damned fortunate if we can re-install the Tracer before the rain hits."

"Isn't it raining now?" He glanced upward with almost comic dismay.

"This?" Mac snorted. "Not hardly."

He used a finger to wipe the drops from his glasses; they were immediately replaced. "I'll take your word for it, Dr. Connor. As for leaving—believe me, I'd like nothing better. The IU's going to rake me over the coals as it is. Our distinguished guest is supposed to be attending a state dinner in his honor at the Consulate, not snorkeling with fish in the middle of—" He broke off and looked around as if startled by a sudden thought. "Where are we, anyway?"

Obviously not deep enough in the bush to save her from desk jockeys, Mac thought with disgust. "Where you shouldn't be, Mr. Trojanowski. Just shut him up and take him away." The Dhryn's keening hadn't abated. In fact, Mac thought it had climbed a notch or two in volume.

The bureaucrat hugged his bag to his chest and leaned down to say very quietly, "He doesn't exactly listen to me, Dr. Connor."

Mac narrowed her eyes. "Then he'll listen to me, Mr. Trojanowski. I guarantee it."

His bleated "I wouldn't—" was left behind as Mac walked back to confront the unhappy Dhryn, but the man caught up to her. "Please, Dr. Connor. We can't have an interspecies incident. Brymn is the first of his kind to visit Earth—"

"And I don't care if he's the last." Mac pulled out her imp and used it to poke the Dhryn in the middle of his widest band of rose-colored silk.

Brymn's eyes shot open and his wailing ended in an exaggerated "whhooff" of air leaving his mouth. Before anything else came out, Mac put her hands on her hips and said firmly: "Leave. Now." She put away her imp and hoped it still worked; she went through several a year as it was. "I have work to do and you are interfering."

Without another word, the Dhryn turned and clambered back into the skim. Tie jumped in after him, possibly afraid the creature would take off with the team's vehicle.

Not surprisingly, the bureaucrat was staring at Mac, his mouth working as though unsure what expression would be safe. He did take a cautious step out of range.

As Mac feared, the rain chose the least convenient moment to turn from drizzle to blinding sheets that made it hard to breathe. She tugged her hood over her head and waved impatiently to the sodden figure still hesitating in front of her. Emily was already splashing toward her console. "Good-bye, Mr. Trojanowski."

The fool was digging into his office pouch. As Mac prepared to tell him where he could file his paperwork, she saw what he was pulling out.

It was an envelope, in the unmistakable blue and green reserved for documents pertaining to the safety and security of humanity. Such an envelope must be accepted by any person; refusing such an envelope was treason against the Human species. Its contents were both secret and vital.

Mac had only seen them in movies featuring spies and intergalactic warfare. She'd half-believed they were nothing more than a handy plot device.

Her hands lifted to accept the envelope, closing over what wasn't rain-coated paper, but instead felt like thin metal, heat-stealing and sharp. Her name suddenly crawled over its surface in mauve-tinted acknowledgment.

Did she imagine a flash of sympathy on Nikolai Trojanowski's face before he turned to join Brymn in the skim?

Mac watched the vehicle lift, then drop to the river's surface, vanishing into the rain. Beneath, dorsal fins sliced the heaving darkness of the river and bodies twisted to leap through the foam. The Harlequins landed on the shore, walking in single file to plunge into the river. Left alone, life on the Tannu sought its own rhythm, heedless of Human affairs.

Emily shook her cape as she approached, adding her spray to the deluge. "Well, that broke the boredom . . ." Her voice trailed away as she spotted the envelope. *"Ai."*

Mac's hands wanted to drop the thing but couldn't. "Lock us down, Dr. Mamani," she ordered, wondering at the steadiness of her own voice. "I expect the other shoe to drop will be— Ah, yes. Base sending a pickup."

On cue, a shape formed itself from rain and mist: the transport lev from Norcoast, angling for a landing that wouldn't crush either tent or console.

"It seems someone thinks we're finished here," Mac said, giving the t-lev a short nod that had nothing to do with agreement.

And everything to do with challenge.

3

ARRIVAL AND ANNOYANCE

ON HER OFFICE wall, Mac had a satellite image of Hecate Strait, its intense blue kept from the Pacific by the lush green arms of the Queen Charlotte Islands, the Haida Gwaii. To the east, the strait tried to sneak its waters into the snow-capped Rockies, wrapping around islands and through inlets like fingers grabbing for a hold, thwarted by the growing bones of a continent. Rivers, like tears of sympathy, leaked through the mountains to join the strait.

From an eagle's perspective, the midst of the strait might be the center of the Pacific, especially during storm winds. The submerged mountains forming the Queen Charlottes hid their tips below the horizon; the continent was nowhere to be seen. Mariners treated the area with respect. Whales sang here.

But approach the coast and the landscape shot skyward again, as if the ocean waves constantly pushed the rock to heaven and forest anchored cliff to cloud. On clear days, the scale changed again, as the mountain ranges laughed down at forest, cliff, and ocean. Victor and goal in one.

As the eagle flew, the coast was a labyrinth of deep cut channels that bent, fractured, and found one another again. There were hidden coves of water so still the bird's reflection chased it. Along every shore, the bleached remains of giant trees competed with splintered bits of mountain, a rubble reshaped every spring.

Every spring, the Norcoast Salmon Research Facility, or Base, as its staff of scientists, techs, and students preferred to call it, came back to life.

Base floated within the southwest curl of Castle Inlet, a peaceful intrusion of humanity consisting of a half dozen pods, various docks, and landing pads linked by walkways. The pods were domes, their mottled grays, mauves, and browns matched to the exposed rock of the shoreline in the hope they'd resemble tiny islands themselves. It might have worked, if there had been forests of cedar and fir on the flattened roofs instead of aerials, solar collectors, skylights, and the occasional deck chair. Though the practice was discouraged, students tended to hang their laundry from the balconies surrounding each pod, further dispelling the illusion of blending with nature.

The walkways were also employed to dry both wet towels and fish specimens. On those rare occasions when the sun encouraged such effort, they formed
the favored spot for people to dry out as well, making it impossible to walk from
pod to pod with any speed.

Not that speed was the point. Norcoast's researchers worked by nature's time-
table, not their own, and endurance mattered more than haste. As the Coho,
Pink, Chinook, and King salmon arrived from the Pacific, feeding on the immense schools of pilchard converging in Hecate Strait, survey crews hovered
overhead in aqualevs, sleeping over their monitors, if at all. Those studying the
impacts of oceanic predation slept at Base, but only at the whim of orca pod,
shark, and seal. Easy to know the predator researchers. Preds were the ones running along the walkways with still-lathered hair or wearing pajamas under their
rain gear, a consequence of wearing wrist alarms activated by remotes listening
at the entrances to the Sound as well as the various inlets.

A few at Base lived by Human hours, in order to process data from their compatriots with the commercial harvesters. To compensate for that luxury, Harvs
wound up cooking for the rest, being more likely to be awake and functional
when supplies had to be ordered and received.

They were doubtless all awake now, Mac thought grimly. She'd tucked the envelope from Trojanowski under her clothes, where it molded with unsettling comfort against her skin. There'd been no time or privacy to read its contents. She
and Emily had sealed their equipment against weather, bear, and packrat.
There'd been the required clarification for the t-lev's crew—namely that Mac
had no intention of letting them dismantle and remove Field Station Six, no
matter what fool had ordered it. The crew, in turn, wisely professed themselves
exceedingly content to remove only the two scientists and their personal gear.

At the very last moment, Mac had remembered to pluck the bag with Lee's
book from its soggy crevice.

Now, as the t-lev sank within the arms of the inlet and approached the north
landing pad, Mac heard Emily click her tongue against her teeth. "We've company
waiting."

"I see." The rain hadn't stopped, so the figures lining the walkway to the pad
wore either rain gear or bathing suits. Only one carried an umbrella. "Trojanowski," Mac concluded, pointing down. "Knew he was a tourist."

"Nice butt, though," Emily countered. "Not that you noticed."

Mac snorted. "The day I check out someone like—" She shut her mouth and
smiled despite herself. "You are impossible."

"Of course. Now that we have both formed our opinions of the meddlesome
Nikolai, what's next?"

The t-lev took its time coming to rest, the pilot knowing exactly the reaction
he'd get from onlookers if he so much as rocked the landing pad, let alone
dumped anyone in the inlet. Mac leaned back on the bench, gazing at Emily.

They were both filthy as well as barefoot, with streaks of gray mud running
from toes to thighs. Em's knees were only muddy; hers were scraped and bloody,

like some kid coming in from street hockey. Their rain gear was clean enough; underneath, though, their clothing was, to put it kindly, ripe. Emily's hair was so black as to have blue highlights; she wore it short and snug, a style that not only accentuated the fine lines of her neck and high cheekbones, but also forgave a few days of living in the bush. It really wasn't fair. Mac tried to poke a finger through hers but couldn't reach her scalp. Despite the braid, the stuff had reached the point of feeling like lichen. Tangles were doubtless the least of what rode her head.

"What's next?" Mac repeated, contemplating the disturbing message lying against her stomach and the expectant crowd below.

"A shower."

Mac and Emily, backpacks on their shoulders and the rest of their gear to follow when the t-lev was unloaded, disembarked with every intention of simply walking past those waiting. The first person they encountered, the bureaucrat, seemed to grasp that point. He met Mac's warning scowl with no more than a searching look, then stepped aside, holding his umbrella high so she and Emily could pass without having to duck under it. Annoyingly, he was impeccably clean and dry, wearing what had to be the twin of the suit and cravat he'd had on at the field station. His eyes, now visible through clear dry lenses, were hazel; his hair was light brown, thick, and prone to curl. *Doubtless,* Mac thought, *Emily would have something to say about both.*

For her part, she was grateful not to be delayed, more determined than ever to set her own pace regardless of the business at hand. She needed privacy to read the message. Not to mention the fact that she wasn't going to conduct any business whatsoever without a shower. But as easily walk on water as evade the curiosity of grad students. As they pressed closer instead of giving way, Emily thoughtfully let her lead.

As if she could simply push past them all. Mac sighed, taking in the intensity on those young faces, and slowed her pace. Jumping in the water and swimming to the next pod would only encourage them to do the same, probably turning it into a race pitting Preds against Harvs, with the rest cheering. She'd seen it happen more than once.

Of course, the instant they knew they had her attention, questions began flying from every direction, interspersed with hugs of welcome and offers to carry her bag. Mac returned the hugs as quickly as was polite, held on to her bag, and kept up a running patter of answers. She reassured Cecily and Stanislaus that the other field stations were running as usual, then achieved two full steps before having to stop and tell Roman that no, this didn't mean there would be weekend passes to Prince Rupert or any other shoreline destination with restaurants. A glower and five steps brought her face-to-face with Jeanine Duvois, who looked about to cry.

"What's wrong?" Mac asked involuntarily.

The sudden hush wasn't reassuring.

"I didn't have any choice, Dr. Connor. They made me do it."

"Do what?"

Definitely close to tears. "You won't hold it against me, please? I know my grades aren't the best, but I've been trying—"

"Hold what against you?" Mac demanded.

A hiccup and a wild-eyed glance around for nonexistent help. "I—I helped move the Dhryn into your quarters this morning, Dr. Connor."

"The Honorable Delegate needs a fair amount of space," said an unapologetic and by-now familiar voice in her ear. "Yours were the biggest available, Dr. Connor. I'm sure you understand."

Grad students had a finely honed instinct for when to become invisible, while staying close enough to catch the juicy details. The light slap of seawater against the floats underfoot was suddenly louder than the rain.

Mac gritted her teeth and stared longingly at Pod Three, where her admittedly spacious quarters waited, complete with shower and clean clothes. "What about my things?" she demanded, turning to glare at Trojanowski.

The bureaucrat eased back a step, a move that put him against the railing. "The furnishings are satisfactory," he assured her warily. "Brymn is very accommodating about such things."

"Your personal stuff is piled in the main hall," Jeanine sniffled in Mac's ear. "Beside the spare generator. We didn't have time to do anything more with it."

First Brymn in her *river, the envelope, being summarily dragged back to Base, and now this?* Ignoring Emily's alarmed protest, Mac planted both hands against the dry fabric of Trojanowski's suit and shoved with all her might. The bureaucrat was over the rope rail of the walkway and into the water before he could do more than tighten his grip on his umbrella.

As the students cheered, Mac resumed walking to the pods. No one else got in her way. Emily kept up, making a few strangled noises as if testing her voice.

"What?" Mac growled.

"Think he can swim?"

"Think I care?"

"Point taken." Another few steps. "You realize the poor man probably lost his glasses." Em lifted her cast. "We old-fashioned types are at such disadvantage."

"He had a spare suit. He'll have spare glasses," Mac said, resisting a twinge of remorse. She paused at the intersection of the walkways to Pods Three and Two, then resignedly turned away from "home." "Mind if I borrow your shower?"

"And some clothes, no doubt. I've a nice little number in red that should fit."

The walkway became a ramp, shifting gently underfoot as they climbed in synchrony. There was another splash in the distance. Mac presumed either the bureaucrat was being rescued or her helpful students had tossed him in again. "Base coveralls will do. You were issued three pairs, remember?"

Emily made a sound of disgust. "Fit for scrubbing bilge."

"That could be what I'm doing."

"Not with what you're carrying."

Mac wiped her hand dry on her shorts before slapping it on the entry pad. "We don't know what I'm carrying," she said in a low voice as the door opened. "We don't know anything yet—but I intend to get some answers. And my quarters back."

"No argument here. No offense, but having you for a roomie would seriously cramp my lifestyle."

"Spare me the details, please."

Each pod had two floors above sea level and one below. The submerged space was used for wet labs and as bays for the underwater research equipment and vehicles. The first floor above the surface was divided into dry labs and offices, while the uppermost held residences and lounges.

Pod Six, the newest addition to Norcoast, was the only exception to this plan. Larger and broader than the others, its interior was hollow and flooded, an isolated chunk of ocean protected from the elements. Entire schools of fish could be herded inside, scanned, then released. They'd even housed a lost baby humpback whale until acoustic and DNA samples could locate his mother and aunts.

Pod Two was reserved for visiting researchers, like Emily, so its walls were free of the bulletins, vids, and outright graffiti that adorned the student habitats: Pods Four and Five. Pod One held the fabrication and repair shops, while Pod Three held Norcoast's administration and archives—as well as Mac's year-round home.

Until now. Mac let Emily lead the way up the stairs that ringed the inside of the pod's transparent outer wall. Mac found it perfectly appropriate that the stunning view of inlet, coast, and mountain was opaqued by rain.

"His being here has to be a secret," Emily said, halfway up.

"Brymn's? What makes you say that?"

Emily rapped the wall with her knuckles. "No tiggers mobbing a crowd; I didn't see any vidbots either."

The "tiggers" were the automated warn offs that discouraged kayakers and other adventurers from venturing into Castle Inlet. They looked more like herring gulls than the real thing, which added to the shock effect when they flew over a trespasser's head and began intoning the hefty fines and other penalties for entering a restricted wildlife research zone, or worse, the Wilderness Trust itself. If ignored, a tigger would deposit an adhesive dropping containing a beacon to summon the law. If someone were foolish enough to try and evade the dropping— or shoot at the tigger? Suffice it to say there were other droppings in its arsenal, and a flock was a serious threat.

Vidbots didn't belong here either, though they were a familiar nuisance in cities. The little aerial 'bots were the eyes and ears of reporters—local, planetary, and, for all Mac knew, they reached other worlds as well.

"That doesn't mean it's a secret," she protested, unhappy at the thought of more conspiracy. The envelope was bad enough. "Maybe a Dhryn visiting a salmon research station isn't news, Em."

At the top of the stairs Emily palmed the door open. They passed into a corridor with thick carpet, blissfully soft and dry underfoot. The ceiling was clear, though patterned by now driving sheets of rain. Supplementary lighting glowed along the base of the walls and around each residence door. Norcoast provided superb accommodations for its guest experts, even though they rarely had time to use them before heading into the field. It looked good on the prospectus.

It had looked good to Mac, her master's thesis on St. Lawrence salmon stocks under her belt and her new professor willing to send her west to Norcoast's pods for the season. Mind you, her first quarters hadn't quite been like Emily's.

Tie had been the one to welcome Mac to Norcoast, although it hadn't seemed much of a welcome at the time. Mac hadn't known what to make of him. The tool belt over torn shorts said one thing; the casual first-name basis with which he greeted everyone another. As he'd led her down sidewalks that bobbed alarmingly, he'd lectured her dolefully on the proper care of equipment she'd never used in her life, seeming convinced scientists and students were equally inept with any technology and it being his thankless duty to make sure it all worked regardless.

At the residence pod, Tie had broken the unpleasant news that Mac would share her living quarters with four other students, the new pod being delayed in construction, that delay caused by other individuals also hopelessly inept with any technology whatsoever. Mac hadn't dared venture an opinion.

"You'll miss all this, soon enough," Tie had pronounced as he'd watched her thread her way among the shoes, bags, and general paraphernalia of the others to reach the bed with the least number of books stacked on it. Hers, supposedly.

Mac had desperately wanted to appear dignified and knowledgeable; she was closer to homesick and anxious. "Miss what?" she'd asked. "Why?"

"A bed. A roof." Tie had laughed at her expression. "They didn't tell you? A tent and sleeping on the ground. That's the routine here, while the rivers are free of ice. You live with the salmon."

Mac brought herself to the present with a shake of her head. *Tie had been right, as usual. What was she doing, worrying about something as trivial as where she slept? Must be getting old.*

"Brymn isn't news?" Emily scoffed, as if unaware Mac's thoughts had wandered. "I'd say he's more newsworthy than that delicious graphic opera star you entertained here last year. Weren't you the one telling me you had to call in the coast patrol to get rid of the reporters who followed him?"

"Two years ago," Mac corrected, waiting for Emily to unlock her door. "And there was no entertaining involved. He claimed to be making whale documentaries and had heard about our work. I offered him a tour."

"Tour." The word oozed innuendo. "Really."

"Dibs on the shower," Mac said quickly, taking advantage of her smaller size to squeeze by Emily and dash for the washroom.

There were times to linger over the sheer hedonism of hot water after living under field conditions. This wasn't one of them. Mac hit the air dry the instant her hand skimmed the last clumps of lather from her head, bending over so the jets meant to dry her skin did double duty on her hair. The locks were still damp enough to stick to her fingers when she shut off the shower and stepped out, her other hand snagging the navy blue Norcoast coveralls Emily had found for her.

They fit, in the way shapeless, untailored, thoroughly practical clothes did. Mac rolled up the cuffs at ankle and wrist, securing each by pinching the mem-fabric in their hems. She'd had everything else she needed, including dry sandals, in her backpack.

"Your turn, Em." Mac kicked her 'pack into Emily's living room, her hands busy sorting her hair into its customary braid, twisting the result into a knot to lie at the base of her neck. "Don't dawdle."

Emily was stretched out on the couch, one arm trailing on the floor as if she'd melted into the furniture, the other, with its cast, resting on the couch back. She lifted her head from a cushion, her expression one of complete disbelief. "What did you do? Skip the soap? I just got comfy—"

"I know. Sorry." Mac pulled the envelope from a pocket, its dark blue veined with green like some exotic shell. Her name, in lighter mauve, looked ridiculous. "This shouldn't wait much longer. And—" Mac paused, then gave words to the unease she'd felt since first touching it, an unease she'd postponed acknowledging as long as she could. "I don't want to read this alone."

"Of course not," Emily agreed, rising to her feet in one smooth motion. She took a step toward the washroom, then stopped, looking at Mac. Her eyes dropped suggestively to the envelope.

"Fine," Mac said, just as relieved. "I'll open it now." She chose to sit cross-legged on the carpet. Emily joined her.

"Do you know how?"

Mac turned the envelope over, running a fingertip along each edge. There were no seams. It might have been a wafer of mother-of-pearl, solid to the core. "Any ideas?"

"Not I." Emily leaned forward, studying their problem. "I won't touch it either. Not with your name on it. Maybe you should call our friend Nikolai."

Mac remembered the searching look the bureaucrat had given her—the way he'd obviously decided not to talk to her. "He expected me to have opened it already," she concluded out loud. "So there's nothing high tech about it." Before she could hesitate, Mac grabbed the envelope in both hands and ripped it in half.

A tiny multifolded sheet slipped from the portion of the envelope in her right hand, landing on her leg. Mac put the halves aside and picked up the sheet, opening it slowly. Mem-paper, if a far finer, thinner version than those in Lee's books. The sheet was smooth between her fingers as she angled it to read:

TO:　　　　Dr. Mackenzie Connor, Norcoast Salmon Research Facility, British Columbia, Earth.

FROM:　　Muda Sa'ib XIII, Secretary General, Ministry of Extra-Sol Human Affairs, Narasa Prime.

Dear Dr. Connor:

Our Ministry has been advised of a potential Category Zeta threat. This is a hazard to life on an intersystem, planetary scale. The appropriate agencies representing all signatories of the Interspecies Union have been notified and have agreed to share any findings in this matter.

This threat, if confirmed, could affect a portion of space which includes over three hundred Human worlds and even more extraplanetary habitats. It could impact Earth herself. This threat must therefore be considered as a threat to our species' survival, authorizing the most extreme measures, should they be necessary.

Among the investigations being conducted is one by a Dhryn scientist who has requested access to your facility and your research, claiming it has relevance to our mutual concern. While he has not yet explained that relevance, citing its preliminary and speculative nature, his request has, of course, been granted. We expect you will offer him all possible assistance.

We ask that you keep this information, and any findings you and the Dhryn obtain, confidential until such time as our Ministry reaches a conclusion concerning the existence of this threat and what action, if any, should be taken. While we hold little expectation for this particular line of investigation, we have nonetheless assigned a diplomatic liaison to you, who has identified himself by giving you this message. Through him, you may communicate with my office at any time.

It is our sincere hope and belief that this threat will turn out to be spurious, another rumor to be dispelled as quickly and quietly as possible. If not, we will rely on you to provide your assistance, however and as long as required.

Thank you, Dr. Connor.

See Attachment

"You look as though you've eaten some of Ward's scrambled eggs. It can't be that bad."

Mac shook her head, more to postpone Emily's questions than in answer. "It doesn't say much of anything," she puzzled. "There's more attached." A light tap on the page and the memo was replaced by a list of reports. *This mem-sheet was definitely more sophisticated than those in Lee's novels.* "Grab your shower, Em," she suggested, looking up to meet her friend's eyes. "This is going to take a while to read."

The other woman didn't budge. "Not until you tell me if we're all going to die before the weekend. If so, I've got plans to make first."

"I think your weekend is safe."

"Not good enough."

Mac's lips quirked. "Fine. It's from the Ministry of Extra-Sol Human Affairs—"

"Whoa." Emily's eyebrows rose. "That's weird. Earthgov, I expected. The Consulate, I could see. Any alien entering our air has to go through them. But the Ministry? To state the obvious, they don't deal with Earth at all."

She was right, of course. Mac knew that much history. Humanity's spread throughout its own solar system had produced another layer of governance, to speak for the differing needs of those living without gravity or biosphere. The Ministry, as most now called it, had served as the conduit for both complaint and accommodation. As the populations living off the planet had increased, so had the Ministry.

In a way, that exponential growth had prepared humanity for its next great leap outward. A mere 150 years after the first Human birth on Mars, Humans gained the technology to expand to the stars. Oh, it wasn't theirs. *Very little,* Mac thought ruefully, *from imp to broadcast power, was.* When the first non-Human probe arrived, with its standard invitation from the Interspecies Union to build and maintain transects to bypass normal space, and thus participate in its economic community of other intelligences, humanity hadn't hesitated an instant. The Ministry, for its part, moved outward with every Human starship and colonist, a familiar safety net—and occasionally useful bureaucratic aggravation—for those brave souls venturing into the true unknown. Mind you, it turned out that much of the galaxy in Earth's vicinity was very well known and populated, so over the last century, the Ministry had quietly evolved into a convenient way of keeping Earth's far-flung offspring in touch with home.

Meanwhile, the Interspecies Union, or IU, hadn't left that home alone. It had requested, and been granted, property on Earth to build a Consulate. In New Zealand, in fact, due to the variety of climates readily available. There, visitors of any biological background could be welcomed, briefed on local customs, checked for transmissibles, and sent off to conduct whatever business they deemed worth doing on the Human home world. Little about Earth wasn't of interest to someone or something, although Saturn's moons boasted more alien traffic on an annual basis.

In return, Humans continued to feast on the combined technology of thousands of other races, many more advanced in one field or another, the whole benefiting from the cross-pollination of ideas. The IU wasn't composed of fools. Not entirely, anyway. There were always stories—

Not that Mac paid attention to stories about aliens or their business, content to use the latest tools and stay within her field and species. *Until now.*

"You'll see why it comes from the Ministry, Em," Mac said soberly, then read the rest of the message out loud. When done, she added thoughtfully: "I'm not downplaying the threat, but this part about Brymn coming to me? Does it sound like a plea for some diplomatic nuisance-sitting to you?"

"Oh, as if diplomacy is your strong suit," Emily quipped, but looked only faintly reassured. "You read the rest while I clean up. Then I want to know everything else that's in there. Deal?"

Mac hesitated. A little late, her conscience was bothering her. "The message said confidential."

Emily flashed a grin. "So don't tell Tie. You know he spreads gossip faster than the com system—"

"Be serious, Em."

A sudden, very sober look from those dark brown eyes. "I'm nothing but serious, Mac. A possible 'Category Zeta' threat? We can't let word of this spread in any way. You probably shouldn't have told even me—but now that I'm in it, I'm damned if I'll sit by and wonder what's going on overhead."

Mac acknowledged the truth of that with a single nod. "We need to talk to Brymn. Go shower. I'll start going through this."

"On my way, boss." Emily shed clothing as she went, apparently determined to challenge Mac's speed.

Once the door closed, Mac stretched out on her stomach, laying the memsheet on the floor in front of her. Unconfirmed rumor or crackpot notion, Em was right—this scale of threat had to be taken seriously until proven otherwise. Obviously, she and Em weren't the only ones to think so.

She was, however, the only one to poke the scientist she was supposed to help in the midriff, shoo him from her field station, then attempt to drown the man sent by the Secretary General to assist them both.

Not the most auspicious start to their relationship.

Resisting a quite remarkable level of guilt, Mac began to read.

Mac tapped the com. "Dr. Connor to Pod Three, please." While she waited, she frowned at Emily, who'd settled on her outfit of choice with unusual alacrity and was now resplendent in a black evening jumpsuit that oozed sophistication and personal style. She'd given up on the sling and wrapped the cast in matching fabric. At the moment, the other biologist was holding out a similar garment in red, a gleam in her eye. *Over my dead body,* Mac mouthed at her.

"Pod Three."

No mistaking that voice. "Tie? What are you doing on coms?"

"Oh, it's you. Hi, Mac. Yeah. Everyone else has headed for the gallery to get a good seat—I pulled short straw, having met our guest. Should be quite the affair. Why aren't you down there yourself?"

Emily shook the red jumpsuit suggestively; Mac stuck out her tongue. So much for her hope to arrange a private meeting with—and apology to—both

Brymn and Mr. Trojanowski before supper. "We'll be there shortly," she said. "I wanted to check that everything was on schedule." Emily rolled her eyes.

"On schedule?" Tie's laugh was a bark worthy of a sea lion. "No problem. It's been the Pied Piper and his rats around here. Last I saw, that Dhryn was walking through Admin, collecting people as he went. Cooks will have to hustle to be ready, that's my guess."

Disrupting everyone else's research, Mac thought, changing her mind about the apology as she closed the connection. "Let's go."

"Dressed like—that. You can't be serious. Now that we know it's for supper—"

"Supper?" Mac raised both eyebrows. "Em, it's Pizza Tuesday."

Emily appeared to struggle with the concept, then spat out something frustrated in Quechan. "You're meeting with a scientist of another species and a representative of the Ministry of Extra-Sol Human Affairs! What kind of impression will you make in those?"

Mac brushed nonexistent dust from her borrowed coveralls. "No worse than I've made already. You impress them. I want to get this over with so we can get back to work."

The rejected jumpsuit sailed across the room to drape itself over the couch. "So you've made up your mind about this so-called threat to humanity." Emily's voice was studiously neutral. She'd read the reports after Mac and had had nothing—yet—to say.

Not knowing what to do with the pieces of the secret envelope, Mac had slipped them over the refolded mem-sheet, intending to save all three. To her astonishment, the two halves had immediately mended themselves into an unblemished whole, once more winking with her name. The envelope now seemed to burn a hole in Mac's hip pocket. "What threat?" she asked. Mac walked over to the window wall and stood peering out through the droplets, then refocused on them. With a finger, she traced imaginary patterns between drops picked at random, touching each as she recited the list from memory. "A group of climbers disappears from a mountain on Thitus Prime. A cruise barge on Regellus drifts ashore, empty. Balloonists never land on N'not'k. An eco-patrol vanishes from a forest in Ascendis. A harvesting crew isn't seen again on Ven Twenty-Nine—"

"Don't forget the Dhryn."

"Ah." Mac left her finger on one particularly large drop. "The Dhryn misplace an entire field trip's worth of students on their Cryssin colony." She let her hand fall to her side and faced Emily. "Don't get me wrong, Em. I sympathize with everyone involved. These are all tragedies. But nothing from the Secretary General explains why a handful of missing person reports put Brymn in my quarters and our population survey on hold."

"There's more missing than these people. Information on our Nikolai, for one."

Mac blinked. "What information?"

"Exactly. There isn't anything in the message about either Brymn or Trojanowski. Why?" Emily lowered her voice. "Or was it there—and someone tampered with it?"

For an instant, Mac seriously considered the notion. Then she laughed. "You, my dear Dr. Mamani, have read far too many books of the wrong sort. It isn't there, because it isn't necessary. Brymn will enlighten us tonight on his credentials and, hopefully, why he's here at all. As for our 'field operative'?" Mac paused, then shook her head. "To land this choice assignment, he's either offended the wrong people or is lousy at his job. Or both. In any event, there's no reason to believe we'll be stuck with them long enough for their backgrounds to matter."

Emily's long fingers played with the oversized emerald of her necklace, a family heirloom she never bothered to lock away, confident no one would believe she'd wear something so rare and expensive at Base. Mac had to concede her logic, even though she couldn't help occasionally translating the bauble's worth into an upgrade to the docking pads.

She knew the signs. "I take it you disagree, Em."

"You did take note of the locations and dates," Emily said in an odd voice. "The disappearances do not appear random."

"It's not like you to jump to conclusions from so small a sample—"

"It's not like you to put your own convenience ahead of the data."

"My—" Mac closed her mouth over the protest and stared at Emily. Rain drummed on the ceiling and walls like so many impatient fingers. "Is that what I'm doing?" she asked finally.

Emily raised one eyebrow and waited.

"Damn."

"We each have our failings at times. We won't mention your fashion sense, *sí?*"

Mac pulled out the envelope and waved it in the air. "Just show me what I missed."

"I can tell you. All of the locations are along the Naralax Transect." Perhaps sensing Mac's confusion, Emily shook her head, then drew a line in the air between them. "You never travel, do you? There are thousands of transects maintained by the Interspecies Union—"

"No-space corridors," Mac said dryly. "A.k.a. instant travel between connected solar systems. I may not gallivant like some, but I do know a bit about what's outside the atmosphere. So where does this Naralax Transect go?"

"Your ignorance is astounding."

Mac raised one brow. "I prefer to think of it as selective. So—are you going to tell me if there's anything special about the Naralax or continue to berate my choice of sciences?"

Emily shook her head in resignation. "Special? Depends on your definition. Home, for some. A dozen Human colonies. A few hundred non-Human systems, including our friend Brymn's. A record, of sorts. Our most distant trading partner, Thitus Prime, is reached via the Naralax. Beyond Thitus, the Naralax extends—oh—a few systems more." Emily's light tone gave no warning. "One famous. The Hift System. The rest, infamous."

"The Chasm." As she uttered the words, Mac felt the hairs lifting on the back of her neck.

"Ah, she does know something. Yes, the Naralax is the only transect that

extends into the Chasm. There's a special destination for you, if you're a pros-
pector, archaeologist, or tourist with a taste for the macabre."

Oh, she knew about the Chasm. Every biologist, every religious order—probably
every being who learned of it—worried over its very existence at some point in
their lives. "There's nothing in the Chasm," Mac said. Except for system after
system containing life-capable planets, all completely without life.

Oh, it had been there once. It had—disappeared—three thousand years ago.
That much, and only that, they knew.

She shook off a chill. *Stuff of fables.* "Don't tell me," Mac continued, raising
her voice into a falsetto. "Chasm Ghouls have kidnapped all these beings and are
on their way to Earth next. We're the only ones who can save the day." Before
Emily could do more than begin to look offended, Mac relented. "That was
uncalled for—"

"That's for sure—"

"I am grateful for any insights you have, Em. Frankly, if it were up to me alone,
I'd stuff this message down your Nikolai's throat and let him look after our guest."

"Thus causing an interspecies' incident before supper?" Emily said, the corners
of her lips curving up. "One would think you enjoyed notoriety. The vidbots
would be here before dessert." Her smile faded. "Mac. The locations and dates
matter because they occur as if whomever or whatever was behind the disappearances is traveling the Naralax from Thitus Prime toward Human-dominated
space. The affected Dhryn colony is only systems away from our outermost settlement. If this pattern continues, the next beings to disappear may well be Human.
I'd say that's valid reason for the Ministry and us to take this seriously."

"Serial murders. Mysterious disappearances. They happen all the time," Mac
protested, stuffing the message back in her pocket. "We're talking thousands of
worlds. Trillions of beings. Standards of morality that vary from incomprehensible to those that would make an alpha shark swim deep and fast. Let alone species like the Ehztif and Setihak . . . Sethilak . . . or however you say the damn
name—you know, the ones who eat one another given half a chance and a dark
alley. With all that, what makes these few incidents so significant?"

"Your first question for our dinner guests, I presume," Emily said, gesturing
to the door. Then her slim hand turned palm up, stopping Mac before she could
take a step. "The hair. At least the hair. Please, Mac."

"You've got to be kid—"

"Think of it as camouflage."

"You're going to be a pest about this, aren't you?"

"I'm right and you know it." Before Mac could move out of reach, Emily had
grabbed her braid's end and tugged smartly. Hair, still damp enough to smell
faintly of soap, cascaded over Mac's shoulder and threatened to cover one eye.
"There," Emily pronounced with satisfaction.

Mac shook her head to settle the mass down the center of her back, shoving
the strand over her left eye behind her ear. "Happy now?"

Emily's wolfish smile wouldn't have looked out of place on one of the Haida
totems that still startled visitors to the shore. "I will be."

- Portent -

THE FIRST drop plunged into the fine sand, coalescing grains into a tiny, glistening ball, green against the dusky red of the dune. The ball slipped downslope very slightly, drawing a shallow line behind.

More drops fell, more balls formed, more lines clawed at the massive upcurve of the dune.

More. Drops struck already dampened balls, shattering them into smaller, darker portions that spread the green tint, the lie of life, across the sand.

Each impact sent its vibration coursing through the dune, the sum of all the drops a siren call to those who spread sensory hairs and waited for opportunity.

Serrated claws pushed through the sand, their owners as eager to sip from the rare cloudburst as they were to hunt others with the same intention. Slender whiskers trembled in search of imminent danger as other, barely larger creatures were drawn into the evening air. Writhing nodes of worms collected beneath what should have been the moisture they needed to reproduce.

It was not.

More drops fell, dissolving claw tip and whisker, searing away fur and flesh, melting everything they touched or that touched them into more balls of sand.

As the balls slipped downslope, the mouths were waiting.

4

ENCOUNTER AND ENLISTMENT

T HE GALLERY was on the main level of Pod Three, located there by practicality, since Three was the only residence pod in operation year-round.
There were smaller cafeterias within the other residential pods, where students
and staff could make their own meals. Most came here, saying they preferred the
convenience and camaraderie of eating together. As a former student herself,
Mac knew it had more to do with having someone else wash dishes.

The gallery was large enough to accommodate everyone on Base, but Mac
had never seen this many filled tables on a late summer afternoon. *Was no one but
Tie working?* Hopefully no ongoing experiments—besides hers and Emily's—
were being ruined by neglect.

Not that she blamed the excited crowd. Most students had been here since
spring thaw and novelty was a treasure. Their "guest" was the former, if not
necessarily the latter.

He was sitting at the head table already—or rather beside it. Someone had
done some quick work to modify a second table for the Dhryn so it sloped at an
angle parallel to the alien's normal posture. Holes had been cut in the tabletop to
support a variety of bowls and other utensils. The table leaned in the other direction as well, there being only enough room on the raised dais that held the head
table for one end of it. Mac hoped the Dhryn could manage. The head table was
supposedly for the research leaders, but was usually commandeered by whichever students got there first. The dais' elevation gave those sitting there the best
view of the wallscreen during hockey games and other events.

No students up there now, Mac noted, wending her way through a maze of
chairs, bags, and long, and some quite hairy, legs. She nodded and smiled in
greeting, but didn't stop to chat with anyone, reasonably sure Emily would prod
her in the back to get to where she was expected. Mac would have happily sat
with the students, but there were two empty places beside the Dhryn.

The rest of the seats were already taken by Mac's fellow lead scientists: Lee
Fyock, Martin Svehla, Kammie Noyo, Jirair Grebbian. The order in which they

sat had nothing to do with relative seniority. Mac's and Kammie's work was year-round, which was why they split the administrative duties for Norcoast. The rest arrived each spring with their own teams of scientists, techs, and students, cluttering up available space and demanding more than their share of equipment. Once the resulting waves stopped crashing about, everyone slipped into research mode. The only command structure, as such, lay between the students and their supervisors and, by early summer, that typically degenerated, leaving only a group of individuals focused on their work.

There was, however, an unspoken acknowledgment that lovestruck Lee could sit beside Emily—who tolerated his attention because he lent her books—and Jirair, who tended to wander absently from any meal halfway through, always had an end seat. The other researchers would be either sitting with their students, in the field, or in a few cases, taking their meals in their lab. There were always some who remained blissfully oblivious to anything outside their work.

Mac glanced around the room. Trojanowski was conspicuously absent. She nodded to her bright-eyed colleagues as she took the seat closest to the Dhryn's table. No doubt they were brimming with curiosity. Mac paused to admire the cutlery, not having seen this many pointy objects on display in the gallery since Jirair's students had built a ceiling-high castle from sea urchin husks and left the remains to fumigate the entire pod. Emily sat beside her.

The room, which had been buzzing with voices and the tinkle of utensils as students experimented with theirs, fell silent.

"Welcome, Mackenzie Winifred Elizabeth Wright Connor!" The Dhryn's deep boom shook the windows. "Welcome, Emily Mamani Sarmiento!"

Definitely infrasounds under there, Mac told herself, now obliged to look directly at her guest for the first time since poking him in the whatever.

The Dhryn had reapplied his makeup, adding sequins along his ear ridges. The bands of silk wrapping his torso were now bright crimson, a color that went rather well with the Dhryn's mottled blue skin. There were gilded bobbles hanging from those bands showing above the sloped tabletop. *Dressed for the occasion.* As were, Mac registered belatedly, everyone else who possibly could be. Even the students were in their civvies, looking en masse like a riotous garden of floral shirts punctuated by the inevitable black T-shirts. No coveralls in sight.

Mac could feel Emily's *I told you so.* She sat a little straighter, taking what comfort she could in being clean. At least her hair wasn't trying escape its usual asymmetrical lump at the back of her head. Despite her cast, Emily had managed to pull the mass upward into a tight French braid, leaving only the length down Mac's back free to cause trouble. While it felt as though something with little claws and attitude was sitting on the top of her head, even Mac had to admit she looked more dignified than usual. Maybe she should wear it like this for her next meeting with Mudge, which now seemed by far the simpler half of her life.

"It is we who welcome you, Honorable Delegate," Mac responded, unsure if she was supposed to use his name in public, since even the Secretary General hadn't used it in the message. As she sought frantically for anything else to say, well aware the entire room was listening, she found herself transfixed by the alien's gold-irised eyes. They seemed to hold a great sadness, despite the polite smile the Dhryn wore.

Could the disappearances of the Dhryn on Cryssin have involved individuals close to Brymn? His family, perhaps? Mac hadn't the slightest idea what a Dhryn family unit might be, but she trusted her instincts. *Whatever reason brought Brymn to her,* she decided, *it was something personal.* "We will help you," she promised quietly, "if we can."

Brymn's lips formed a small, closed circle. A bead of glistening yellow moisture trembled at the opening of one large nostril. Even as Mac hoped this was an indication of a positive emotional response and not a virus, the Dhryn flung his uppermost arm around her shoulders. "I knew I was right to come here. *Slimienth om glathu ra!* Thank you, Mackenzie Winifred Elizabeth Wright Connor! Thank you, all!" Brymn's voice vibrated the glasses on the table.

With each "thank you," the arm squeezed tighter. Forget bruising. Mac began to seriously worry if her bones could take the pressure. She managed a little squeak of protest which the Dhryn fortunately understood. Or he was about to let her go anyway. She was, Mac decided, saved from damage either way.

The buzzing of voices started up again as the students spotted the food trolleys being wheeled from the back. The buzz rose to near-deafening levels. *An extreme reaction to pizza, even from this group.* Mac squinted, trying to make out what was coming.

"'My treat.' Is that the expression?" One of the advantages of multiple limbs was apparent as Brymn gestured grandly in all directions at once. "There was to be a grand supper at the Consulate for me tonight. I insisted the food be sent here instead. This is acceptable?"

From the exclamations of rapture spreading across the gallery, Mac had no doubts at all. "Thank you. Although I hope this won't cause you any difficulties." She wondered what a formal meal would be like at the IU Consulate and was ashamed when the first image in her mind was feeding time at an old-fashioned zoo.

"Difficulties, no." The Dhryn tilted forward conspiratorially. "But I suspect the consular staff would like to serve me for supper," he told her in what was presumably his notion of a whisper.

She almost smiled. "Here's hoping that doesn't happen."

"Indeed," Brymn agreed, leaning upright again. "I imagine there could be considerable discomfort involved!"

Mac chewed her lower lip for a second, then decided. She turned in her chair to more directly face the alien. "I want to apologize for—for—"

"What? Not letting me bully you?" His small lips could fashion quite an infectious grin. "Dear Mackenzie Winifred Elizabeth Wright Connor, I'm lucky you don't work for the Consulate, or there'd be no treat on these tables tonight!"

"Why, you—" Mac shook her head, then found herself smiling. "You had me worried, I'll admit."

Brymn picked up two water-filled glasses, passing one to her. "To mutual understanding," he offered, lifting his glass to hers.

"Psst." Emily's breath tickled her ear. "Check out Seung and the rest of the Preds."

As she sipped her water, Mac let her eyes drift across the tables. They'd doubtless been arranged in tidy rows before the students arrived and "modified" their environment. Now, they were clearly in clusters by research preference.

The Harvs were near the back wall. *She was slipping,* Mac told herself, not to have noticed those who should have been in the kitchen to help prepare food were sitting with the rest. Missies, catch-all slang for other, miscellaneous topics, filled the bulk of the room, subclustered by interests in benthic organisms, competition, long-term climatic trends, water or soil chemistry, and so on.

The Preds had claimed a group of five tables to the far right of Dhryn's table, aligned so they could run for the nearest exit if whales sang into their hydrophones. They were busy tossing buns to—or at—the occupants of one of their tables.

Clad in a black T-shirt, likely a loan from a student, and hefting a bun himself, Nikolai Trojanowski had blended remarkably well. Mac appreciated the effectiveness of Emily's radar for the new and male. She took another sip as she studied him. At least he had his glasses.

Coincidence, perhaps, that Trojanowski chose that moment to glance at the head table and catch her eyes. From this distance, Mac couldn't make out his expression. Not that she wanted to. Her face and neck flooded with heat as she remembered everything from the prickly softness of his suit under her hands to the splash when the poor man hit the water.

Make an impression indeed.

"What a wonderful color change," Brymn commented. *It begged the question of whether his vision included the infrared or the color red,* Mac thought glumly.

"She's very good at it," Emily said, leaning over the table to speak past Mac as if that worthy wasn't there and glaring.

"Is there significance? A hormonal state, perhaps?"

Mac aimed a kick under the table at her oh-so-amused friend, then decided against further physical reactions for the time being. "I'm a little warm," she assured Brymn, then went on quickly. "What's your preferred ambient temperature?"

"This is comfortable. A warmer and drier climate would be agreeable. Not that I'm complaining, but does it always rain here?"

The boisterous agreement from all within earshot seemed to startle the Dhryn, but he recovered quickly and waved his upper arms again in what Mac took for pleased acknowledgment. She edged her chair closer to Emily's, in case the Dhryn needed more room for such self-expression.

"Do you not have technology to modify your climate?" Brymn asked. "If this isn't what you prefer yourselves, wouldn't that be the obvious course? It is the first installation on any Dhryn colony."

"We do. There are control mechanisms in place to reduce the intensity of storms that threaten lives, or to end excessive drought in agricultural zones. Otherwise? No, we leave Earth pretty much as she is and complain about the weather." The trolley for the head table was now behind Mac. She sniffed appreciatively, leaning to one side to let the waiter-of-the-day, a skim-tech named Turner-Jay, deposit a steaming plate in front of her. Mac's eyes widened. *If this was the appetizer, they were in for a five-star feast.* Her stomach rumbled.

"Now you and I can leave." Brymn's low voice was almost lost beneath the clatter of knife and fork. She hadn't known he could speak so quietly.

Mac swallowed the saliva filling her mouth and looked at the Dhryn in disbelief. "Leave?" she echoed.

"A good time to speak privately is when others feast, is it not?"

She had to concede no one appeared interested in them at the moment. Even Trojanowski had his head bowed over Brymn's "treat." *Which now seemed something other than generosity.*

"As you wish." Mac folded her napkin beside her plate and inhaled the rich aroma one last time before standing.

The rain had stopped. Not only that, but the clouds were lifting, revealing foothills and shoreline, a hint of gray-mauve cliff, and, to the southwest, a glow where the sun would kiss the sea in another two hours. A westerly breeze chuckled through the pods and walkways, teased Emily's braidwork, then left to stir up waves in the distant heart of the inlet. Mac drew the smell of sea and forest into her nostrils, savored it, then promised her stomach something more substantial later.

There could be leftovers.

She led the way down the ramp from Pod Three to the walkway, glancing back to be sure her otherworldly companion could negotiate passages designed for Humans and their gear. Brymn moved like someone cautious of his balance, wise given the tendency of the walkway to rock from side to side under his greater mass. He could also have been unhappy about the ocean underfoot.

A valid conclusion, given his next request. "Could we go onshore, Mackenzie Winifred Elizabeth Wright Connor?"

"Call me Mac."

"Amisch a nai!"

Whatever the words meant, it wasn't something happy. Mac stopped and turned, her fingers wrapping around the rope rail. She narrowed her eyes as she stared up at him. "You aren't planning to make that abominable noise again, I hope."

The Dhryn was holding onto the ropes on both sides, using all six available hands. His seventh limb remained tucked under a red band. *Just as well,* Mac thought, remembering its sharp digits. Not helpful for rope grabbing, that was certain. "Are you all right?" she asked. "Should we go back inside?" Her stomach growled eagerly.

"I am well, Mackenzie Winifred Elizabeth Wright Connor. I will be even better if we can hold our discussion somewhere more private. And onshore."

Mac weighed the pleading note in the Dhryn's voice and the message in her pocket against the rules she'd have to bend, then shrugged. *It shouldn't be a problem.* She pointed down the walkway to Pod One. "Land's that way."

Norcoast's floating pods, like most of the homesteads, harvester processing plants, and other buildings along the coast, were kept upright and in place with anchors; ballast kept them submerged at the desired depth. In winter, Pods Three and Six remained as they were, protected from ice floes and storm winds by inflated barriers. Similar barriers, placed beneath, were used to lift the other pods free of the water until spring. The experience tended to startle those students who'd lingered through late fall to write up their theses and hadn't paid attention to the move-out date in their calendars. Someone always had to be plucked from a rooftop.

The complex of pods was linked to shore by one walkway, also removed from service during the winter months. Mudge, in his persona as Oversight Committee, had tried and failed to prevent a physical connection to the lands of the Wilderness Trust.

But it was access that could, and would, be rescinded at the first sign of complacency. All of the protective restrictions could be summed up by one phrase: no avoidable contact. Any unavoidable contact, such as the walkway holdfasts on shore, had been carefully planned for minimum impact and thoroughly documented so future researchers would be aware of all perturbations made to the area.

Which had led to some unique features in design and construction.

"It's perfectly safe," Mac assured the Dhryn when they reached the transition between the interpod walkway and the segment leading toward land. The former was built from slats of mem-wood, grown so that each piece would fit into the next like a giant puzzle and could be dismantled as easily. The shoreward walkway was something else again.

Seeing it, Brymn came to an abrupt halt, gripping the rope rails again. "Mackenzie Winifred Elizabeth Wright Connor," he rumbled somewhat breathlessly. "I do not wish to doubt, but are you sure?"

"I'm sure. We roll heavy equipment along it all the time." Mac stepped forward, trusting the anxious Dhryn would follow.

Trust was essential. To the eye, there was nothing between her feet and the white hiss of incoming surf four meters below. At least it wasn't high tide and the water almost underfoot. She did a little shuffle step, the effect as though she danced in air. "There's a bit of spring, but it's solid," she assured the Dhryn. The walkway material was a membrane, completely permeable to visible light, radiation, even water droplets—another way of reducing the impact of human structures on the shore's inhabitants. Mac could taste the spray on her lips and wondered what Dhryn thought of salt.

There was a railing of the same substance, continuing from the rope but invisible. Brymn found it by virtue of moving his hands forward two at a time, so he never had to completely let go. First one leg and footpod gingerly tested the walkway, then the other. "This is quite—remarkable," he said, his small mouth pursed as if in concentration.

Then he released his grips and sprang up into the air, dropping down with a bass *"Whoop!"* to meet the flex of the walkway, for all the world like her nephew on his backyard trampoline. Arms flailing for balance as the walkway pitched, Mac managed to find and grab the rail herself. "What—?"

The Dhryn's massive legs bent backward at a hitherto unseen joint, absorbing the energy from the walkway so it settled. "My apologies, Mackenzie Winifred Elizabeth Wright Connor." His eyes blinked slightly out of sync. "We have a *symlis*—a fable—of individuals who jump on air. I couldn't resist."

Play? Another congruence between their species? Mac filed the possibility away for later examination. *Much later.* "I take it you don't have a problem with heights."

Three arms waved in an extravagant gesture that, in a Human, dared her to do her worst.

The walkway carried them up and over the shore as it rose from the sea, the dark wet stone beneath giving way to a confusion of pale tree bones laced with drying strings of kelp. Crabs scuttled along, seeking shadows. A real gull, prospecting among the rocks, tilted its head to center one bright black eye on the spectacle of Human and Dhryn passing overhead, walking on air. That much interference couldn't be helped, although a low-level repeller kept flying things from collision or perch on the walkway itself. *Or web-building*, Mac mused, rather fond of the strands that glistened throughout the rest of the complex, beaded with crystal after every fog.

An artificial web faced them now, strung between the holdfasts as a token barrier. The tiggers pretending to roost in the staggered rows of forest ahead were the true guardians of the place, active night and day, programmed to accost anyone whose profile didn't appear in their data files. Given their lack of attention to Brymn, Mac concluded Tie had taken care of that detail. *Or Trojanowski.*

She pressed her palm over the lock on the right-hand pillar, then keyed in this season's code, waiting for Norcoast to send confirmation. The web folded itself away, a course of lights from beneath their feet briefly illuminating the choices currently in place: a path leading along the inner arm of the inlet, one rising to the treetops ahead, and a third swinging high over the rock to the left. The first two flashed red, indicating they had been reserved for specific projects. The last shone green.

In spite of everything, Mac grinned as she clawed wisps of hair from her eyes. She wasn't sure how much privacy Brymn wanted for their conversation, but she'd take any excuse to climb the inlet's outreaching arm. It had been two seasons since this particular area had been accessible. "Follow me."

The walkway was more rigid here, taut and formed into a series of steps. Each rise courteously drew itself in the air with a flash of green along its edge as they approached. Mac, curious, stood aside at the second step to let the alien take the lead. He didn't hesitate, lifting his ponderous foot the required amount to clear the illuminated line. *So.* The Dhryn's large eyes perceived at least that color.

Mac held tight to the railing as the walkway took them beyond the protection of the inlet's stone arm and they met the westerly wind straight off the Pacific. In the fall, those winds would shift east and intensify into storms. They were strong enough now. Her coveralls flapped against her skin and Emily's braid gave up the fight for dignity. Mac grabbed her suddenly free hair with one hand, turning to check on the Dhryn.

His eyes were no longer golden yellow and black. A membrane, perhaps an inner eyelid, now covered each. The result was as if his eyes had been plucked from their sockets and replaced with gleaming blue marbles. His silks, plastered tightly to his body by the wind, showed no signs of coming loose. Mac was mildly disappointed, having wondered what might be revealed of the alien's anatomy. Brymn waved her on.

Mac nodded, not bothering to talk over the rustling of her clothes, and led the way.

The outer side of the inlet's protective arm boasted a different shoreline, one that plunged like a knife into the ocean. Immense fingers of kelp, knuckled by shiny round bladders, stroked the waves into a dark, smooth rhythm. Salmon would be slipping through that underwater forest, drawn by the tastes of home flooding mouth and nostrils.

Mac could smell them, over the tang of cedar and fir.

The tide was on the move, too, its powerful eddies fighting the wind and each other with a roar and crash. Mac squinted, hoping to spot the sharp upright fins of orcas in the distance and seeing only the deceptive edges of waves to the horizon. She should have brought her 'scope.

They weren't here to sightsee. "Let me go first here," she advised Brymn, making sure the alien paid attention. He seemed as caught by the view as she'd been.

Four steps down, one after the other limned in black as the walkway compensated for the light now striking low and from the west. At the bottom, a mem-wood platform waited on pylons, complete with built-in bench and rails. From the way the wind stopped when they reached it, it must be surrounded by a curtain of the membrane that formed the walkway.

Probably Svehla's work. The joke around Base was that the talented carpenter would build everyone's retirement cottage instead of ever retiring himself. Mac explored the small area, then ran her hand along the rail on the ocean side. Regular holes marked where Preds had fastened their recorders and 'scopes.

Brymn came up beside her. She forced herself to stay still, even though his bulk intimidated this close. "Private enough?" she asked.

"Private and most spectacular. Thank you, Mackenzie Winifred Elizabeth Wright Connor."

She gritted her teeth. His continued use of her full name was becoming supremely annoying. *At least he didn't have a discernible body odor,* she reminded herself, trying to look on the bright side. She turned away from the Pacific to stare up at her visitor, noticing that his eyes had returned to normal. "Now. Why me?"

The Dhryn pursed his small mouth. "Sit. Please."

Mac walked over to the bench and obeyed, but hugged her knees to her chest so she could rest her arms on top. "I'm sitting."

He faced her, then slowly settled his backside to the platform by bending his legs at their uppermost joint. His two lower hands pressed against the wood, arms stiffening to form a secure tripod. "Ah. I've wanted to do this all day."

"You didn't have to use a chair," Mac noted dryly.

A cavalier wave. " 'When visiting a species . . .' You know the rest of the expression, I'm sure. Still, it does the body good." Before Mac could attempt to swing the conversation back to the note in her pocket, Brymn grew serious, his voice lowering in depth until she felt it through the bench. "Evolutionary units."

Mac blinked. "Pardon?"

Brymn looked worried. "You are the Mackenzie Winifred Elizabeth Wright Connor who has published extensively on that topic, are you not? There can't be two Humans with that same name, surely."

"Yes. To being the one, that is." Mac frowned. "I thought you were investigating the disappearances."

"I am. You've read the report, I see."

An eagle skimmed past them, the head and spine of a salmon locked in its talons. Mac suddenly empathized with the fish. "Forgive me, Brymn, if I seem confused, but I don't see any connection between my research and these missing people. Tragic as those losses are," she added hastily.

"People?" he echoed, eye ridges rumpling. "Far more than people are missing, Mackenzie Winifred Eliz—"

Enough was enough! "Please. Stop doing that. Humans rarely use their complete names. Never in conversation. Call me Mac." As Brymn opened his mouth again, Mac pointed at him and shook her finger warningly. "Mac."

"It would be highly disrespectful for me to omit any of your earned names. *Amisch a nai.*"

His distress was palpable. Mac rubbed her chin on her forearm. "A compromise to keep me sane," she offered. "Call me Mac when it's just you and me. Like this. No one else need know."

"If you insist." Brymn's lips pressed tightly together for an instant, as if over a bad taste. "Mac."

"Perfect. See how nice and quick that is?" Mac lifted her head. "So. What else was missing?"

"Everything."

"Equipment, transports—" she hazarded.

He shook his head. "Those remained, though damaged. Everything alive. Everything that had been alive. Gone."

Mac sat up, her feet thumping down on the platform. "Over how large an area?"

"The largest discovered so far involved almost twenty square kilometers. A valley. Scoured clean to the overburden. Even the soil was empty of life or its remains."

"Like the worlds in the Chasm," Mac said, her lips numb.

"Like the worlds in the Chasm," the Dhryn repeated. He rocked back and forth, his ridged nostrils flared. "So I come to you, Macken—Mac—because those aware of these disasters have good reason to believe we are all in the gravest of dangers. And I believe your work may hold a key to our survival."

Mac shook her head, sending hair tumbling over one shoulder. Automatically, her hands began braiding the tangled mass into order. She wished she could do the same with her thoughts. *Why hadn't the so-secret report contained this information? How could such a thing still be secret at all?* She focused on what she did know. "I work with salmon. An Earth species."

A low hooting sound. Frustrating, not knowing if it was laughter, a sob, or alien flatulence. *She had to read more.* "Your interest is in a bigger question, is it not? One that applies to all living things. What is the minimum genetic diversity required in a population to respond to evolutionary stress? What is that evolutionary unit for a species, a community? For a world?"

"You can't simply extrapolate . . ."

Brymn rose to his feet. "Do you deny the importance, Mac, of knowing how many of us must continue to live, if our species are to survive the doom threatening us all?"

The Dhryn had a distinct flare for melodrama, Mac decided. Her eyes narrowed in suspicion. "Exactly what do you do, Brymn?"

"I study the remains of the past, to better understand what may be to come."

"A—paleontologist?"

Another low hoot. *Surprise or humor,* Mac concluded. "No, no. An archaeologist. I thought you might have heard of me. Read my work? I'm quite famous in some circles."

"I study salmon," Mac found herself emphasizing, as if the words anchored her to something saner than this conversation. "I don't get outside my field much."

"You study life! That's why I need your expertise."

"Why come all the way here—to me?" she asked reasonably. "Why not work with a Dhryn biologist? Surely some of your scientists are working on the same questions."

The Dhryn became utterly still, his large eyes regarding her with what Mac could only interpret as a wistful expression. Then he said in a voice only slightly louder than the slap of water on rock: "This is something you need to know, Mac, but I can only tell you if you agree to keep it in the strictest confidence. Not even my assigned companion, Nikolai Piotr Trojanowski, may learn this. May I tell you?"

As if she'd refuse? Mac gave one quick nod.

"I am ashamed to admit there are no Dhryn biologists. The study of living things has been forbidden throughout our history. It remains so. I would be re-fused *grathnu,* Mackenzie Winifred Elizabeth Wright Connor, should any of my lineage learn I was speaking to you about such things, or that I had read and understood any of your work."

Mac tried to wrap her brain around an entire civilization without biology and failed. "What about medicine? Doctors?"

Brymn sat down again. "*Nie rugorath sa nie a nai.* It translates roughly as: 'A Dhryn is robust or a Dhryn is not.' There are other such sayings. Suffice it to say there are no sick Dhryn."

"Agriculture?"

"We consume varieties of what you would call fungi, Mac. Long ago, our leaders conveniently ruled that what is grown for this purpose is not alive. Today, these organisms are considered components of a chemical manufacturing pro-cess. Their study is part of engineering, not life science as you know it." He paused, seemingly thoughtful. "Truly, we don't have many scientists at all. The most proper study for a Dhryn is what it means to be Dhryn. Our brightest minds are urged to become artists, historians, or perhaps analysts. Our advances in applied science and technology, like many of yours, are purchased from those who possess that cultural priority."

Fascinated, Mac started to reply, then abruptly signaled the Dhryn to silence.

Anywhere else along the coast, the sound of gulls would signal the arrival of a harvester, or a run of pilchard or candlefish. They'd gather and bark in their hundreds over the bubbles of a humpback's fishing trap.

They wouldn't sound like these gulls. This vocal outrage was too regular in pitch and pacing, a deliberate mismatch to nature so these calls wouldn't distract or lure the real thing. *Tiggers.*

"Is something wrong, Mac?" Brymn asked.

"Wait here."

Mac ran up the steps, her hands shoving her braid under her collar. As she left the protection of the membrane, the wind gave her a too-helpful push. She grabbed at where the rail should be but missed it, the result being a drunken stagger to the next step. Of course, the Dhryn would be watching all of this grace in motion.

She found her footing and continued to the top of the rise.

The reason for the outrage was clear enough. A solitary figure was climbing the walkway toward her. Brown hair and a black T-shirt. The glint of glasses as the head angled up. *Trojanowski.* He dared wave at her, as if they'd arranged to meet.

The bureaucrat wasn't the target of the milling tiggers, however. They were massed over a flotilla of kayaks attempting to dock near Pod Two. Attempting, because the tiggers were programmed to prevent that as well, so they were fly-ing directly at the faces of those paddling before dropping their tags. Mac could almost feel sorry for them.

Almost. She scowled. "Tourists."

Or worse. The gleefully clashing colors of life jackets and kayaks might shout summer rental, but Mac didn't forget Emily's prediction that the media would be interested in her guest. *Guests,* she sighed to herself, glaring at the man below.

"Guests?" Brymn boomed in her ear.

Mac gave a yip of surprise at having her thoughts echoed in a deep bass. Either the Dhryn could tiptoe, or the wind flapping her coveralls had overwhelmed whatever noise the creature had made.

She recovered, indicating Trojanowski, who'd turned to watch the show in the inlet. "I don't understand how he got in—takes the gate code and confirmation. No one at Base would give it to him without asking me first."

Brymn "sat" beside her, putting his head on a level with hers. "Nikolai Piotr Trojanowski was assigned to me at the Consulate, upon my arrival. We have not been traveling together long enough for me to assess his technical capabilities. I think we must assume they are considerable, given the importance of my investigation." There was a note of what would be pride in a Human voice.

Mac came close to telling the Dhryn the assessment of his investigation expressed in the Secretary General's note, then changed her mind. She'd defended her share of research that seemed esoteric and irrelevant to the layperson. The uncommon, unpopular questions were, in her experience, worth asking. More than once she'd seen them generate new schools of thought and previously unimagined applications.

More than once, she'd poured time and energy into an idea that turned out to be riddled with holes, but she preferred that risk over the chance of missing something significant. She would make her own judgment about Brymn's investigation.

And about something else. "Let's not assume anything about Mr. Trojanowski, Brymn, until we know him better," she suggested. "Keep things between the two of us for now. We can continue our discussion later—come to my office when you get a chance."

"Then, Mac, we are truly *lamisah*—allied?"

Yesterday, Mac would have laughed at anyone who said she'd be standing here, talking to an alien—an archaeologist, yet—about an alliance that included keeping secrets from a representative of her own government. *Hell,* she told herself ruefully, *she'd have laughed off any suggestion she wouldn't be deep in observations at Field Station Six right now.*

She gazed at the inlet, seeing how the clouds had lifted so they draped languidly over the white shoulders of the coastal peaks, the sun intensifying the necklace of forest green below, begemmed by the gold and oranges of early turning trees. The glittering blues, blacks, and greens of the ocean, stirred by the breeze, refused to reflect that glory, as if more interested in the life surging beneath its waves. The pods, full of humanity probably now enthralled by dessert trays; the kayaks, filled with the curious . . .

Yesterday, she would have scoffed at any threat to this place.

"*Lamisah,* Brymn," Mac agreed, wrapping her arms around herself, as if the wind had grown cold.

5

DINNER AND DISCORD

"SO THEY are the damned media!" Mac lowered her voice with an effort. She hadn't thought her life could become any more complicated, but Trojanowski's confident nod left no doubt.

"I recognized a couple of faces from press gatherings at the Consulate," he told her. "Someone must have leaked the Honorable Delegate's itinerary. First Dhryn on Earth, you know."

"Must be a slow news week," Mac muttered under her breath. Louder, "I'll call the coast police to—"

"I don't advise it, Dr. Connor. That would only fuel their interest. They'd be back tomorrow, in larger numbers."

Trojanowski had escorted her and Brymn back to Pod Three, which had meant passing the crowd of angry, miserable-looking kayakers, their bodies and heads splattered with tigger droppings, their boats trapped between Norcoast skims. The Dhryn had seemed fascinated by all the shouting, although they didn't stay in range long.

Mac had caught Trojanowski waving at Tie, who'd been standing in one of the skims. Tie had offered back an unusually cheerful "thumbs-up."

So. The bureaucrat must have delayed in following her and Brymn, presumably to give Tie instructions on how to deal with the intruders. Mac wasn't sure if she approved of Mr. Trojanowski ordering her staff around.

She did realize she didn't have much say in the matter.

Now, standing outside the closed door to her own quarters, which presently housed a large, blue alien, Mac did her best to regain some control of the situation. "If I'm not to call the police, Mr. Trojanowski, what are you suggesting? That I leave them in their kayaks to keep swearing at my staff?"

"And what kind of reports would they make about the Honorable Delegate's trip, Dr. Connor, or your facility?" He lifted his hands and shoulders, as if asking her to admit defeat. "I've made arrangements for them to stay here overnight. I'll be setting up interviews with the Honorable Delegate in a couple of hours. Hopefully, that will satisfy them."

"A couple of hours?" *So much for Brymn coming to her office later.*

Trojanowski's eyes twinkled behind their lenses. "They'll need time to shower first, don't you think?"

Tigger glue. It had a deliberately pungent odor. Mac's lips twitched involuntarily at the image. "A soak in solvent's more useful." She conceded the inevitable with a shrug of her own. "Seems you have this well in hand, Mr. Trojanowski. But I'd better not meet one of them—or hear they've interfered with anyone's work."

Trojanowski gave a crisp bow. "Leave it with your diplomatic liaison, Dr. Connor. That's why I'm here."

"Among other reasons," she dared add. The corridor outside her quarters was deserted. "I've read the message."

"And you have questions," he guessed. "Let me walk you to your office, Dr. Connor. If that's where you were heading?"

Mac sighed. She'd hoped to go back to the gallery and hunt leftovers, but the large central hall was undoubtedly filling up with filthy media eager for a target. They'd probably spilled into the lower corridors already. "I'd better check in with the Admin staff first—smooth whatever feathers were ruffled by our visitors and see what, if anything, the Oversight Committee has to say on the subject." *Not in a hurry to find that out,* Mac decided. "We can go on the terrace and take the stairs," she suggested.

"Excellent idea." He held up the pouch he'd been carrying, the one that held his portable office. Mac was beginning to believe he slept with the thing. "I've enough for two."

"I beg your pardon?"

Trojanowski refused to explain, leading the way to the terrace door and holding it for her.

Mac licked a crumb from her lower lip and smiled blissfully. "That was—that was great. Thank you." *Who'd have guessed?* Yet here she was, halfway down the stairs curving around Pod Three, legs outstretched, back comfortably against the wall, sitting shoulder to shoulder with Nikolai Trojanowski to share his stolen supper. Strips of savory duck, asparagus tips, salmon puffs, the list went on and on, each having appeared like magic from his pouch, each disappearing in what Mac had to admit was one of the most relaxed and companionable meals she'd had in a long time.

The view didn't hurt. Mac gazed contentedly out at Pods Five and Six, their curves catching the setting sun, the opposite halves deep in shadow so they looked more like natural islands than usual. The waves beyond were gilded as well. "Pod Six is the newest," she informed him, pointing to it. Their conversation had proved as easy as the meal, on her part, anyway. Answering questions about her home was always a pleasure. Mac only hoped she wasn't overdoing it. "Not that it's that new—I spent a summer there doing a special project."

"Salmon acoustics with Professor Sithole."

Mac looked at Trojanowski in surprise. "We didn't publish anything. How did you know?"

He grinned. "The wonders of record keeping, Dr. Connor. You received a grant to work with him. Money leaves tracks, as the expression goes."

A satisfied stomach helped calm Mac's initial reaction to being "tracked," but there was still an edge to her: "Professional snoop, are you?"

"I like to know who I'm dealing with," he admitted, unrepentant. "So tell me. Did you enjoy listening to your salmon?"

Mac looked back at Pod Six. Her voice grew wistful. "Of course. But I did it to work with Jabulani—Dr. Sithole—while Norcoast still had him. He could do incredible things with sound. Which is why he moved to bigger and better labs years ago."

Trojanowski was rooting around in his pouch. "Looks like we're done," he announced. "I'll have to run this through the sonic shower."

"I still can't believe you took the butter," she commented, watching him smear the last of it on his half of a bun.

"I wasn't the only one," Trojanowski said cheerfully. "Those students of yours probably stripped the table. Besides, I had time as well as opportunity. Your Dr. Mamani wasn't in a hurry to let me get up and follow you."

"Em?" Mac laughed. "You're lucky you escaped. Few men—" She stopped, remembering who she was with. Outside in familiar surroundings, the casualness of sitting on mem-wood, even his borrowed black T-shirt and pants fooled her, as if Trojanowski was just another student. Nicely snug shirt and pants, as Emily would doubtless notice. Mac blushed and pulled her knees to her chest. *He wasn't a student; she didn't notice such things.* "I meant to apologize for pushing you off the walkway," she said, to cover the moment and because she meant it.

His shrug brushed her shoulder. "No need. I'd have lost my temper, too. I regret we came at such a crucial time in your work, Dr. Connor." A pause while they both watched an eagle circle high above the pod. When it was little more than a black speck, he went on: "I hear you left your equipment at the river. Does that mean you'll be able to continue?"

Mac stared out across the inlet, at the mountains beyond. The mouth of the Tannu was hidden from sight behind tree-coated islands. Her salmon would find it, no trouble at all. They could be there now, in their hundreds of thousands, in their millions.

But what she'd learned from Brymn—what might be happening—that mattered, too. "How soon I go back depends on what you want from me, doesn't it?"

Trojanowski closed the pouch and stood, reaching down one hand to pull Mac to her feet. She had the impression her question troubled him. "It isn't what I want—or the Ministry," he began. "Brymn's the one who asked for you, Dr. Connor. He hasn't told us why. Did he tell you? That is why he insisted on your missing supper, wasn't it? To talk to you without me."

Mac didn't answer immediately, distracted by the way he'd kept her hand in his. *Social quandaries weren't her strength.* Should she tug her hand free, in case he'd simply forgotten to let go, or leave it there, in case he wanted to hold it even longer—which led to another complicated series of possibilities she really didn't need to consider under the circumstances. *What if he thought* she *was holding on to* him *and was going through the same choices?* No, definitely he was the one holding. Her hand was just lying there, innocent of any intention.

"Dr. Connor?" Trojanowski gave her an odd look.

What would Emily do?

Mac eased her hand back the tiniest amount, not hard enough to say she was offended, but enough to remind him it was there. He let go, his hand staying palm up between them for an instant longer, as if surprised to be empty.

Mac wrapped her fingers around the railing and coughed her voice back into existence. "Brymn's obviously familiar with my work. Some of it, at least. But nothing he said explained how it might help investigate these terrible disappearances. I don't see any relevance."

"Frankly, neither do I. I've sent a complete set of his publications to your office. Maybe you can find a link we can't."

Mac gave him a dismayed look. "Brymn is an archaeologist. I study salmon." *Why did she have to keep explaining that?*

"You'll be back to your fish sooner, Dr. Connor, if you can establish that Brymn's line of investigation is—invalid. If he even has one."

The sun was dipping into the ocean. Where the pod wall shadowed the terrace, lights began to glow along the underside of the railing, more outlining the steps of the stairs. It reflected in his glasses, hiding his eyes.

"And you won't have to baby-sit," Mac said, sure she was right.

"We both have other duties being neglected, Dr. Connor. I have to consider the possibility that the Honorable Delegate is, intentionally or not, playing tourist at our expense."

"What if Brymn is on to something significant?"

Trojanowski gave an expansive gesture, including the inlet and pods. "We are here," he reminded her, "in hopes he is. What else did he tell you?"

The impromptu feast had brought them closer. *Such moments never lasted,* Mac told herself. "I can't say," she said firmly.

She might have thrown a switch. Trojanowski frowned, his voice sharp and officious. "Can't—as in won't?"

Mac nodded.

"You must know that's not an option, Dr. Connor. The Ministry expects your full cooperation." Trojanowski took the next step and turned to face her, his hand on the railing below hers. The move effectively blocked her path down the stairs.

It also started her temper rising. *She hated being trapped.*

"I told you, Mr. Trojanowski: I can't say," Mac pressed her lips together, then settled for: "It was nothing that would matter to you."

"Let me be the judge of that, please. It's my job, Dr. Connor." No antagonism, no threat. Just an implacable purpose sheathed in courtesy.

He wasn't a Charles Mudge she could outshout or bluff.

Honesty, then, Mac decided. "I'm sorry, Mr. Trojanowski. But Brymn asked me to promise I wouldn't share our discussion. I did and I won't."

"I see." He took his hand from the rail, and backed down another step, giving her room, not a sense that he was giving up. She hadn't expected he would. "It's not possible to fulfill every promise we make, Dr. Connor," he said reasonably. "In this case, I think you must realize—"

"I keep my word, Mr. Trojanowski," Mac interrupted stiffly. "Don't you?"

He turned his head to look out over the inlet. The sun was almost down. Mac doubted he could see much more than the silhouettes of ocean and land against the dusk-washed clouds. *Or,* she wondered abruptly, *was he looking at something else entirely?*

"I don't give it, Dr. Connor," he said at last. "Not anymore." Then he met her eyes. His own were warm behind their lenses, their hazel darker in the changing light. "That doesn't mean you should stop. For now, I'll rely on your judgment to know what to pass along from Brymn."

"I didn't do this to cause a problem," Mac said uncomfortably. "Brymn was anxious, embarrassed. It was the only way to reassure him he could talk to me." She frowned. "But that's exactly what you wanted. Brymn and I, away from anyone else. Otherwise, you would have stopped us before we left the gallery."

His lips quirked. "You've got me there, Dr. Connor."

"Hmmph." Mac shook her head. "You could have just said so."

"We weren't on the best of terms earlier today." Definitely a grin—an infectious one. "I confess to fearing you'd toss me in the drink again, Dr. Connor."

Mac snorted. Skims were unloading by Pod Five and she stepped down to stand beside him at the rail to watch. "You mentioned other duties," she ventured, a peace offering of sorts. "What do you do when you aren't looking after traveling aliens and delivering scary envelopes to unsuspecting biologists?"

"Oh, that's pretty much my full-time job." His voice was deeper when amused, feathered a bit along the edges. Mac rather liked the sound.

"There you are!"

Of all the voices Mac hadn't wanted to hear at this moment, Emily's cheerful call was at the top of the list. *What were the odds?* Trojanowski turned to give the approaching woman a pleasant smile. As turning put him closer to Mac, something Emily acknowledged with a sly look the moment she reached them, all Mac could do was hope the darkening sky would hide any blush. "Hi, Em."

Gone was the sophisticated jumpsuit Emily had worn to supper with Brymn. Now her sandals kicked aside panels of a wild floral print skirt as she came up the stairs to join them, the fabric gathered in a knot low on one bare hip. Her top was a relatively conservative yellow shirt, with huge buttons shaped like letters spelling 'YUM' down the front. The same word was scrawled on her cast.

Camouflage, Mac judged it. Emily dressed as she wanted to be seen. This version was the "brain-on-hold" party animal. The question remained, was it for the media, Brymn, or the man standing beside her? *Could be all three.*

"And you must be what's been keeping our Mac busy. I don't believe we've been properly introduced." Em proffered her right hand to Trojanowski, eyes sliding up and down his lean frame with obvious approval. "I see you're nice and dry."

"Nikolai Trojanowski, at your service, Dr. Mamani." He touched his fingertips to hers, but didn't take her hand. Instead, he bowed his head briefly.

Emily narrowed her eyes. *Assessment,* Mac decided. "So formal. Emily, please."

"My duty as liaison requires formality, Dr. Mamani."

Mac knew that glint in those dark eyes. *Trouble.* To forestall it, she nodded at the stairs. "I'd better get going. I've some—reading—waiting for me."

"Kitchen first," Emily ordered brusquely. "You will help me make sure Mac gets something in her stomach, won't you . . . Mr. . . . Trojanowski?"

"Already taken care of," he said.

"Really?"

"I really need to get going." Mac suited action to words, hurrying down the remaining flight of stairs. She reached the walkway at the pod base before the other two could catch up, and headed around its curve to the entrance, only to halt in dismay. The main door was open to the night air and presently filled with strangers.

Nothing for it but to reach the Admin office the back way, which meant going back upstairs. Mac spun around, only to collide forcibly with those coming behind her.

No one was hurt. In fact, Emily laughed, loudly enough to attract attention from Pod One, let alone the curious horde waiting by the door, doubtless equipped with vids and recorders. Mac hurriedly shook off the hands that had saved her from bouncing on her rump and pushed by both of them.

"Hey, Mac. Mac! Slow down. I'm sorry!"

Already on the third step, Mac glanced back. Emily was hurrying after her, but she'd expected that. Her friend was typically—and charmingly—contrite after embarrassing her. Trojanowski was there too. He pointed to the entrance. "They'll be gone any minute, Dr. Connor. Mr. McCauley's there—I assume to take them to their quarters. We can just wait, if you like."

She would like to run up the stairs and avoid any chance of being interviewed. Instead, Mac sighed and sat down where she was. *Mature behavior was expected from the co-administrator of a world-class research facility.* It was a lovely night, now that the breeze had died away. "Good idea."

Trojanowski sat one step below hers, leaning back against the pod wall. Emily picked the same step, but closer to the railing. *The ensuing silence could only,* Mac decided, *be called painful.*

There were reasons, she thought grimly, *to avoid social interactions.*

Trojanowski spoke first. "I understand you're quite the traveler, Dr. Mamani."

"I like to go places," Emily said, imbuing the phrase with more than one meaning. *No chance she'd tone down the innuendo,* Mac knew. Not in this mood. She leaned back on the rail support to listen, only to sit up straight again as Emily went on: "Not like our Mac, here."

"What?"

"C'mon, Mac. You know it's true. Your idea of an exotic landscape is anything with traffic control. You haven't been *anywhere*."

"I just got back from Vancouver, thank you very much," Mac retorted.

"I make my case," Emily crowed. "Mr. Trojanowski, you work with the Interspecies Union. I'm sure you're a very well-traveled man yourself." *Amazing—or was it appalling?* Mac debated numbly—*what that sultry voice could do with a phrase.* "Did you know you were in the presence of a woman who's never left her continent, let alone her planet? Nor plans to?"

That again? "I'm perfectly happy here," Mac replied somewhat testily. Emily was forever trying to convince her to travel offworld. She should have known it wouldn't stop because they had company. Of sorts.

Polite company, at least. "Not everyone enjoys space flight," Trojanowski pointed out. "I take it you do, Dr. Mamani?"

A broad smile. "I'm the adventurous sort. But then again, I like knowing what's around me. But not our Mac. Oh, no."

"Drop it, Em," Mac said under her breath, doing her best to glare without being obvious.

Emily ignored her, words coming more quickly as she warmed to her topic. "What if I told you, Mr. Trojanowski, that you are in the presence of a woman—a biologist!—whose willing experience with non-Human intelligence can be summed up by a handful of entertainment vids and news clips, until the arrival of our being in blue? Who can't name the three systems closest to ours . . . who has absolutely no interest in any intelligent species but her own!" Emily stopped, the "Y" button on her shirt threatened by her deepened breathing. The light from the railing shone in her hair, but didn't reach her face.

Mac knew what was happening, if not why. For whatever reason, Emily didn't like Trojanowski—or was it his questions—and was tossing Mac between them as a diversion. *Which would have been fine, except—* Mac stopped the thought. "Are you quite finished?" she asked instead.

Emily tossed her head. "Not yet. Mr. Trojanowski is an expert—the kind we never see on Norcoast. I want to hear his opinion of such a person."

He didn't seem to notice Mac's discomfort. "My opinion? There isn't anyone alive who doesn't have something left to learn." He brought up one knee and rested his arm on it. "And I submit that the opposite is true. There's no one alive without something they'd like to unlearn—to forget. Wouldn't you agree, Dr. Mamani? Care to us give an example—something recent, perhaps?"

Check and challenge.

"We're talking about Dr. Connor, not me. Come on. You must see the waste. The least you can do is help me yank Mac's head out of her river—make her see there's a universe nearby."

"I am sitting right here," Mac protested. "On the off chance you decide to talk to me, instead of about me."

Whatever had Emily in such fine and difficult form, it was more than

Trojanowski. Em turned and stared up at her, her eyes shockingly brilliant, as if moist with tears. "I've tried talking to you, Mac," she said, her voice low and intense. "I've tried for three years and you haven't heard a word I've said. Not a word. I might as well be shouting in a vacuum. And it's going to be too late, Mac, by the time you wake up. Too damned late for anything."

With that, she stood and walked away, skirt whirling around her long legs.

Mac froze, torn between following Emily and demanding an explanation, and the patent need to explain to the now silent man beside her on the stairs that this wasn't what Emily was like.

Until this minute, anyway. *What was going on?*

Mac decided she didn't want to know. "Mr. Trojanowski. Let me apologize for Emily. Dr. Mamani. She's usually more—" *tactful wasn't really the word,* "—considerate."

The railing light caught the lenses of his glasses, the curls in his hair. Nothing more. "Was she right about you?"

Did it matter what he thought? Mac hesitated, then again decided on honesty. She wasn't ashamed of her way of life. "I frustrate her because I made a choice long ago. You talked about having more to learn. Well, there's more to learn, right here, about this world, than I could fit into a dozen lifetimes. So I chose to focus. That's all. But Emily believes I'm deliberately ignoring what she considers important."

Another quiet question. "Are you?"

"Maybe. To some extent, yes." Mac patted the mem-wood stair by her foot. "What happens here is my business. If I believed it mattered to what I do here, I'd pay attention to other sentients. I tend to treat politics and—social situations—the same way." Mac sighed. "Come to think of it, that gets Emily angry, too."

"Yet you're good friends."

"The best!" Mac shook her head. "But stubborn. Em tries to improve me. I'm the way I am." Nervously, she unknotted her braid and began to undo it. *She had to know.* "Are you sorry you brought your Honored Delegate to someone with her head stuck in a river?"

"Not when I consider that in less than a day, Dr. Connor, you've learned his name and gained his confidence, all while sacrificing your own work to help investigate a possible threat to our species. Dr. Mamani would be impressed by that, don't you think?"

For an instant, Mac thought he somehow knew she'd shown Emily the message, then she realized Trojanowski was simply being kind. "Emily will be fine," she said confidently. "Ten minutes from now you'll never know she'd been angry."

"What about you?"

"Me?" Mac watched a spider starting to spin her web under the railing, taking advantage of the light. Were personal questions part of his job? *Probably.* "I can hold a grudge a while," Mac said lightly. Permanently was more like it.

"I'd never have guessed."

She laughed. "You?"

Trojanowski put one hand over his heart. "They set civil servants to run on neutral—didn't you know?"

Like a signal, the bar of light marking the door dimmed and brightened as people walked through it. Mac could see small groups heading to Pods Four and Five. "Tie's putting them in with the students," she observed. "I wish them luck getting any sleep."

"I'd better grab a few for interviews now. Brymn's eager, at any rate."

They walked around the curve to the entrance, finally deserted. Before she opened the door, Mac stopped to look up at him. "I'll read his publications over tonight," she said. "Maybe I'll find something there."

"Here's hoping. Good night, Dr. Connor."

"Good night. And thank you. For the meal and your company." Mac reached out her hand. "I enjoyed both."

Maybe it was the growing darkness that dislocated time. Maybe it was lapping of waves and distance-muted voices that created a bubble of stillness around them. Maybe that's what made it seem they'd known each other much longer than a day. Whatever the reason, Mac somehow wasn't at all surprised when Trojanowski not only took her hand in his, but lifted it to his lips.

"As did I, Dr. Connor," he said quietly, his breath warm on her fingers.

- 6 -

STUDY AND SUSPENSE

"AND...?"

"That's all of it."

Emily's eyebrows disappeared under her bangs. "You've got to be kidding. A doom like the Chasm spreading through known space, and all Brymn told you was how ashamed he was at his kind's lack of scientists? Nothing more?"

"I told you, Em," Mac said, digging the knuckles of two fingers into a tight spot on her neck. "We were interrupted. Brymn shut up tighter than a drum when Trojanowski reached us. After that—well, we took him to my quarters to temporarily protect the Honorable Delegate from the less than honorable intentions of the world media. Reasonable, I suppose."

"Considering what it's been like dealing with seventeen of them covered in tigger spots, three claiming we tried to drown them, and one locking himself to the nearest vidphone?" Emily grinned suddenly. "I'd want to be protected, too."

"As if you'd need it. Brymn will come here when he can. Which may not be until tomorrow. Till then . . ." Mac dropped her imp into its slot, then put her bare feet up on her desk and leaned back her chair. She toggled off her deskside privacy mode and the workscreen formed in the air before her eyes. The 'screen adjusted its distance and brightness according to the level of eye fatigue it detected. It compensated for ambient light as well, tilting to avoid competing with any beams of sunlight coming into Mac's office—not a problem at this hour. All well and good, Mac decided, except that the optimum distance grew slightly every year, as the 'screen tactfully compensated for the aging of human eyes. At the rate it was traveling down her legs, it would be hovering over her toes before she retired.

The Admin office had been surprisingly peaceful, under the circumstances; Mudge as well, apparently uninformed about the kayak invasion. Mac saw no reason to enlighten him, since none had approached shore. On returning to her office, Mac hadn't been surprised to find Emily already waiting, eager to talk about Brymn. Back to her normal, cheerful self as if nothing had happened.

If there was an explanation to come, Mac wasn't going to hold her breath waiting for it.

She began calling up data, then asked absently: "Is he unlocked yet? The reporter?"

"No one was rushing, let's put it that way. Let me see." As Emily was peering over her shoulder, Mac sent a duplicate 'screen to hover over the other chair in her office.

Her friend took the hint and the seat, body passing through the 'screen while her head swiveled to keep reading its display. "Dhryn physiology. Why? Planning to poison him? A little drastic over missing the salmon run."

Mac ignored her, busy scanning down what turned out to be a disappointingly brief list of references. She called each up in turn.

Emily read along. "Great. Now we know they pay their dues to the IU on time, have colonies on forty-eight intensely dreary planets, and prefer their privacy. No other species says bad things about them. No one says good things about them. How boring can a race be?"

"Surely not this boring." Mac was keying in other parameters without success, her curiosity engaged. "Odd. We seem to have found out more for ourselves than has been recorded about the Dhryn. You know what little that is. You'd think there'd at least be dietary info . . ."

"Well, Brymn's supper was wonderful. Shame you missed it."

"Didn't," Mac said absently. " 'Cept the dessert."

"Maybe there's something in the stas-unit?"

"I cleaned it out before we left for the field. You do remember what happened last year . . ."

Em wrinkled her nose in disgust. "I still say you should have made that a project for one of the pathology postdocs. Maybe I should send to the kitchen? Can't have you starve, Mac."

"Emily. I'm not hungry." At the knowing smile greeting this, Mac rolled her eyes and sat back, knowing Em would persist until satisfied. "Fine. For your information, Dr. Mamani, Mr. Trojanowski grabbed what he could of supper before following us onshore. We sat on the terrace and he kindly shared it with me before you showed up. That's all."

"Oh-ho. That's not all by a long shot, Mac." Emily perched on Mac's desk. "I want details."

"Asparagus, duck, little puffy things—"

"Not those details."

Mac felt herself flush. "We just sat and ate cold leftovers. There are no 'details.' "

"*Ai!* You're blushing!" Emily planted her hands on the desktop and leaned forward, her face pushing through Mac's 'screen. The image retreated in self-defense. "C'mon, Mac. Spill it."

Avoiding Emily in this mood was like jumping out of the way of a crashing t-lev. *You might survive, but there'd be a wreck to clean up.* Mac sighed her surrender.

"It was nice. He was nice. I enjoyed his company—when we weren't talking shop."

"Not to mention those pants."

"I didn't notice," Mac insisted.

Emily laughed and sat up. "You are hopeless, girl."

"I am not. In fact—" She closed her mouth in time. Emily arched one eyebrow interrogatively, but Mac shook her head. "Okay, I'm hopeless," she agreed. *She didn't want Emily's opinion of how the evening had ended.*

Then, something about that evening, or that afternoon, niggled at Mac. She narrowed her eyes in thought. "Emily, Brymn didn't eat supper."

"*Ai.* Changing the subject?" With a wave of her hand, Emily gave up the chase and returned to her seat. "You think Brymn avoided eating deliberately? Interesting. I'd love a skin sample."

"And you accuse me of trying to start an interspecies' incident?"

Emily chuckled. "I said I'd love a sample—not that I'd attack the Honorable Delegate with a scalpel. Sentients tend to be sensitive about their inner workings. I worked with a Sythian once who cremated her mandible trimmings in a ceramic pot every night, just in case—"

"Spare me." The moment the words were out, Mac regretted them. The last thing she wanted was to set Emily off again tonight.

Sure enough, a disapproving finger wagged in her direction. "Tsk, tsk. You see? You stick yourself to one planet and one biosystem, and this is the price. Do you know why you shouldn't put a Nerban and a Frow in the same taxi?" Em didn't bother to wait for Mac's reply, saying triumphantly: "Such ignorance of our fellow beings."

"I'm a salmon researcher, not a taxi driver," Mac muttered to herself.

"Seung could help, you know. He taught an intro xeno-sentient course on the mainland last winter."

Mac shook her head. "I don't need a course—"

"You need something, Mackenzie Connor." Emily's eyes were flashing again.

"Okay, Emily. I'll bite. Why is this suddenly more of an issue with you than usual? Why now?" Deliberately calm, Mac steepled her fingertips in front of her, studying her friend's angry face over that barrier. "What aren't you telling me?"

"You're the one with the Ministry envelope in her pocket. You're the one an alien traveled through three systems to meet. And you ask me why I think you should be paying attention!"

"I'm paying attention now," Mac said reasonably. "How did you know Brymn went through three systems?"

"Unlike you, Mac, I know what it takes to travel to and from this ball of dirt. I know the questions to ask and where to get answers. So while you were getting dewy-eyed with your bureaucrat, I was checking on them both."

Mac refused to take the bait, or offense. Emily on the warpath was a person who got results. "What did you find out?"

Emily's smile was wicked. "Your supper thief isn't in any Earth-bound birth record. From his accent, slight as it is, I'd put him as no more local than a Jovian moon. I've a query out with the Ministry for details, but I wouldn't hold out hope for any answers. A man of mystery still, your Nikolai." She slowly licked her full lower lip. "Adds a certain spice, doesn't it?"

"Is that all you learned?"

"About Trojanowski." Emily's left hand made a fist. Her right opened, palm up. "Our Dhryn archaeologist, on the other hand, is anything but a mystery. Departed his colony to hunt relics from other species—a pastime I suspect was of no particular interest to his own kind, since Brymn hasn't been home since. It has gained him some acclaim from other pot-hunters. He's sought after for lecture tours by a variety of system universities—one of which he canceled to come here. He's an accomplished linguist—shaming those of us who only learn Instella." Emily paused and her face turned serious. "Nothing I found says he's a crackpot."

"I never said he was." Mac refocused on her 'screen. "Here. Trojanowski sent me Brymn's publications."

The list of publications attributed to their guest filled each 'screen, then kept scrolling.

"Prolific fellow, isn't he?"

"How do you want to split it?" Mac asked.

"We have to read all that?" Emily saw Mac's expression and rolled her eyes. "We have to read all that. Fine. I'll start at the beginning. You start at the end. We should be done some time next year, given you have no social life and mine will be over."

"I'd put students on it, but . . ."

Emily had already settled deeper into the chair and called up her own 'screen, transferring the list from Mac's doppelganger with a finger-touch in midair. "I know," she said soberly. "End of the species. Need to know. All that, too."

Mac remembered her reaction to Brymn's news about the disappearances, the hollow feeling in her chest even now when she considered the Chasm and its sterilized worlds. "If it's true, we can't risk panic," she said, hearing the echo of it in her own voice.

"It won't come to that," Emily insisted. "We aren't alone, Mac. I keep telling you that. Others are working on this—have been working on it." She held up two fingers and pinched them together. "We Humans just have our small parts to play. After that? It will be over and you'll be back with your fish before you know it. Have some faith in your wise old friend Em."

"We'll both be back," Mac corrected. "If you think I'm running that device of yours on my own, Dr. 'Wise Old Friend,' while you cavort with sex-crazed manatees . . ."

Emily didn't smile as Mac expected. "Have some faith, Mac," she repeated. "You know I'll do whatever I can to help you."

With the Tracer—or something else? Mac knew from experience that cryptic statements, from Emily, were never invitations to pry further. She shook her head and leaned forward again, peering at the 'screen. "I trust you to help me read as much of this as humanly possible before I see Brymn again, Em. If you don't mind?"

The room quieted as both became absorbed in their work.

Or tried to. *Concentrating would have been easier,* Mac thought, staring at the text, *if Emily had answered her question.*

Why the frustration, the outright anger, now?

It hadn't taken long before they found a problem in having Mac read the most recent articles first. Later articles referred to those before, some to the point of being completely incomprehensible—to a nonarchaeologist—on their own. Mac redivided the list so Emily was reading the dozens Brymn had published in the prestigious *Journal of Interspecies Archaeology*. She took everything else.

"Everything else" was an eclectic mix, at first appearing random. Letters to the Editor in *About Things Past*. Essays in collected works on topics ranging from statistical analysis to the emergence of interstitial recording technology, many dealing with findings from Chasm sites. Articles scattered in more than twenty different publications. Even a popular treatment, a vid script that had somehow found its way into a documentary series shown on transstellar liners, entitled: *Bringing the Past to Life.*

Then Mac noticed two commonalities. Although Emily had said Brymn was a linguist, these publications were in Instella, the multispecies' language that had to be learned by any member of the Interspecies Union who wished to leave their world. It was taught as a matter of course in Human schools; the same held true for the other species in the Union, to the best of Mac's admittedly meager knowledge. It made sense: a shared language was crucial to understanding.

But Brymn had spoken to her in English. She hadn't paid attention to that until now. Em was right to chide her for being blind to things outside her field. Mac bit her lip. *What else had she missed?*

There was nothing particularly unusual in Brymn publishing in Instella. It was the language of choice for any scientist addressing a multispecies audience. What puzzled Mac was the lack of any reference to publications in Dhryn. Did this mean there were none—or merely that Dhryn didn't permit cataloging of work in their language?

The second nonrandom characteristic was quality. Brymn hadn't exaggerated when he said his work had been noticed in "some circles." With the exception of the vid script, all the listings Mac called up were in peer-reviewed, academic journals. Their Dhryn was taken very seriously by colleagues on many worlds. Just not by the Secretary General of the Ministry of Extra-Sol Human Affairs.

Or by his own species? Mac suddenly wondered if the Dhryn had the same prohibition on archaeology as they did on biology.

The workscreen winked out of existence, replaced by a soft green message at least two hands' width high: "Can no longer compensate for fatigue."

Mac didn't argue. It wouldn't do any good. In a fit of self-protectiveness, she'd programmed the 'screen to ignore any requests to reinitialize for thirty minutes. It would doubtless take longer than that to find the password to change it.

She was startled to find the room dark except for the glow around the door-frames. The automatics had kicked in night illumination levels when she hadn't set the ambient to increase. There was just enough for Mac to see Emily was sound asleep in her chair, head twisted back at an angle impossible for anyone with a shorter neck, the sloppy old sweater she'd always borrowed around her shoulders. Every third breath was that soft little snore Em denied utterly when awake. Her 'screen was gone. It would have turned itself off after detecting her eyes had been closed for more than a few minutes.

So much for Brymn paying a visit. The media must have tied him up longer than she'd expected.

Keying on a low light, Mac stood and stretched, easing the kinks out of her spine. *Some,* she decided, *felt permanent.*

They probably were. Winter months, Mac lived in her office, analyzing data from past seasons, writing proposals for the next, daydreaming. It was her environment, her life, that surrounded her. She could forgive Brymn taking her quarters. They weren't as personal as this room.

She'd had the wall removed between the dry lab and her office space the first year, replacing the window side two-thirds of that barrier with what Tie affectionately referred to as the lousiest garden he'd ever seen. It had begun as a series of old barrels, cut in half, some on tables and some on the floor. Mac was in the habit of stuffing interesting local vegetation into her backpack, roots and all. Whatever survived her collecting method would be thrust into the nearest empty bit of soil in one of the barrels and more or less left to its own devices.

They were also abandoned to the local weather. The second winter, Mac had installed a microclimate around her growing collection. Far from creating a greenhouse, she linked the humidity, temperature, and daylight controls to those being experienced at any given moment along the shore of the spawning beds at Field Station One, some 700 kilometers northeast and 1100 meters higher than the pod. Even the wind conditions were replicated, making it not unusual for visitors to her office to be startled by a self-contained blizzard in the corner.

Tonight, the ceiling-high mass of young cottonwood, sedges, and orchids was peaceful save for the rustle of dying leaves. Field Station One's seasons, mirrored by those in Mac's garden, rushed ahead of those at Base. The urgency drew her closer to the living things she studied, who had to anticipate change or die.

Mac retracted the invisible barrier so she could feel the same soft breeze against her face. She closed her eyes and drew in the scent of soil and living things. A faint tinge of corruption on the back of her palate. Perhaps a lingering piece of salmon. She tossed a few corpses in each fall, challenging the air scrubbers. Or had one of the newer arrivals decided to rot instead of grow? *Fair enough*.

The patch of wilderness indoors wasn't the only unusual aspect of Mac's workspace. She'd had a load of stream-washed gravel delivered at the start of her fourth winter at Base. Instead of gaming or doing puzzles in the gallery, she'd coaxed the few other full-time staff into spending their evenings re-creating a spawning bed by gluing the stones to her floor. The result snaked through her office, its authentically irregular swath owing a fair amount to the number of beers consumed during its creation.

Needless to say, the cleaning staff wouldn't go near it.

Mac loved it. She'd meander along it barefoot, while the winter storms coated the pods with sleet, imagining the depressions she felt with her toes were redds, the holes scoured in the gravel by female salmon. The spawning bed ended at her garden, where overflow from rain spilled over the last few stones. When the garden froze, water eased drop by drop from under an icy rim, glazing each pebble.

Mac had a small warning buoy she'd salvaged to put on the icy patch, in case a visitor was careless when walking.

Almost everything else about her office was standard fare: chairs, desks, lamps, shelves, and tables. Posters, maps, and doors on two walls. The third wall and outer half of the ceiling were part of the pod exterior and could be made transparent or opaque at will. Wide doors led through the wall to the terrace that ringed the pod; fair-weather shortcut to her neighbors, impassable hazard during winter storms.

There was, however, one other feature unique to this room. Mac watched its shadows dancing over Emily's sleeping face and looked up with a smile.

The transparent portion of the ceiling was festooned with wooden salmon, hanging so that they moved with every breath of air. When she'd first come to live on the west coast, Mac had found herself drawn to the stylized carvings of the Haida, their use of large, white-rimmed eyes and realistic form. She'd bought a few pieces, then commissioned more, with different species, different sexes.

All this, so she could stand on the gravel of a spawning bed, and gaze up at the starry sky past the silhouettes of dozens of salmon as they swam through the air, while hearing a breeze stir the vegetation onshore.

All this, so she could daydream about life and its needs.

A flash of brighter light played over her eyes. Squinting in protest, Mac wheeled in time to see the door to the corridor close behind the Dhryn.

Instead of speaking, he rose to stand almost upright, his eyes fixed on the ceiling. *Not the first time a visitor's had that reaction*, Mac smiled to herself.

She took advantage of his fascination to go to Emily and shake the other biologist awake. "Waasaa? I'm reading . . . oh." The incoherent muttering faded as Em saw who was there. She glanced quickly at Mac's desk. Mac understood. Em was checking both 'screens were off. *Not that Brymn should object to their reading his research—but still.*

Brymn probably wouldn't have noticed if they'd strewn his publications over the floor. He kept staring as he said: "This—This is what it was like, Mackenzie Winifred Elizabeth Wright Connor. When I swam in the river."

"You should have visited me here first, then," Mac observed, her mouth twisted in a wry smile. "I wouldn't have had to throw a rock at your head." She went to the wall control and raised the ambient lighting.

Brymn's torso returned to its more customary orientation. He gave a pair of low hoots. "That was you?"

"Mac isn't subtle," Emily explained, rubbing her left arm beneath the cast as she stood. She noticed Brymn's attention. "Arm's asleep."

"A figure of speech," Mac clarified, distracted by what the alien would make of creatures whose body parts rested at differing times.

"Ah." The sound was noncommittal. "I have brought this for you, Mackenzie Winifred Elizabeth Wright Connor." Brymn held out a small bag.

Mac took it, surprised by the weight.

"I regret you did not get to enjoy the supper provided by the Consulate," the alien explained. "So I obtained for you the food item which received the most praise."

"Thank you." Touched, Mac opened the bag and looked inside. At first, she couldn't guess what the gooey brown mass could be, then she sniffed. Chocolate. Rum. She stuck her finger in and brought out a trace to put on her tongue. "Soufflé?" she hazarded. *What remained of one, anyway.* Emily stifled a giggle.

"Yes! It is a masterpiece, I'm told."

Was. Mac closed the bag and gently put it on her desk. "You are very kind. I'll save it for later." Either Dhryn weren't concerned about microorganisms in their food or—given the lack of life science—this one didn't know what several hours at room temperature could produce.

Her stomach expressed its interest in chocolate, regardless. She ignored it. "How did the interviews go?"

"Interviews?" Brymn crisscrossed six of his arms. "Torture. Oh, not torture for me." Another series of hoots. "For them! I have discovered a skill of being utterly boring on any topic."

Emily laughed. "I like you, Brymn."

The Dhryn gave one of his tilting upward bows. "I am most gratified, Emily Mamani Sarmiento."

Mac frowned. "I thought Mr. Trojanowski was going to help you with the interviews."

"As did I. But he said he had to attend to other urgent business, leaving me surrounded in my own quarters." *My quarters,* Mac couldn't help but think. Brymn lifted his topmost elbows in what appeared an approximation of a Human shrug. "Perhaps the Consulate set these media persons to punish me. I believe they are still upset about the supper. Don't worry. I've attended many a lecture that put me to sleep. All I did was emulate the worst of those. Several individuals stopped recording after the first hour." He seemed pleased with himself.

Would he be as pleased to learn she'd shared his secrets with Emily? *Time to find out,* Mac decided. The two biologists had discussed how to handle the situation. They'd found no better approach than honesty, no matter its consequences. "Brymn. Emily is my closest colleague and friend. I trust her with my work." Emily's eyebrow lifted and Mac hurried on before her friend's irrepressible nature asserted itself. "Please accept her as your *lamisah,* as you did me."

The alien's arms unfolded and he sat rather abruptly. It didn't seem to bother him that he sat on the gravel of Mac's pseudo-spawning bed. "Why would I not?" he replied, sounding puzzled.

"Good," Emily said much too cheerfully. "Because Mac's already told me everything."

Before Brymn could respond to that, Mac stepped closer to the alien, hoping the earnestness of her words and expression translated into something comparable within his ridged blue forehead. "I can't work alone on this, Brymn," she told him. "I'll need Emily to cover for me if I have to take time away from my duties at Norcoast. More than that. I need her to talk to—to bounce ideas against. I can't know how you think. I don't know Trojanowski well enough. If you want my best, that includes her."

Brymn didn't stand, but he did reach one pale blue hand toward each of them. He'd found time to repaint his fingernails lime-green. "Then we three shall be *lamisah.*" When the two women put their hands in his, he gave a heavy sigh. "I suppose this means Mac will insist I call you 'Em' in private. *Amisch a nai.*" There was, however, an upturn to his lips, as if the Dhryn was attempting humor.

Brymn's hand was warmer than Mac had expected, softer in the palm than it had looked. There were three digits, equally opposed so the hand would spread like a flower. Each digit was flattened, with a faint ridging along its sides, knuckled in three locations like Mac's own. A nail, manicured, smooth, and presently green, covered the end portion.

His grip was gentle. She squeezed more firmly, assessing the bone and muscle beneath the skin. A powerful hand.

Under careful control. Brymn tightened his own grip only slightly before releasing her hand. His eyes blinked. This time Mac confirmed her impression that the right blinked a fraction of a second earlier than the left. "We don't have much time, my *lamisah,* to speak in private," Brymn said. "Is this place secure from eavesdropping?"

Emily perched on Mac's desk, swinging one long leg. "Who'd want to listen to Mac whistle to herself?" she asked. "You do," when Mac opened her mouth to object. "Off-key. Gets worse when you're happy."

Which she wasn't at the moment. *Eavesdropping?* "There are no vidbots or recorders running in my office, if that's what you mean."

Brymn looked around the room, his arms gesticulating nervously. "Then we must take the chance. There is little time."

"Little time? You've just arrived—" Mac paused. "Something's happened."

"Another incident. I received the news before the first interview."

"Along the Naralax?" Emily asked, eyes intent. "Closer to Human systems?"

The Dhryn nodded. "Yes. You have observed the pattern of the raiding parties, then."

"Raiding parties?" Mac put one hand on her desk, assuring herself it was nearby in case the room seemed to shift underfoot again. "No one's said anything about raiding parties."

Another one-two blink. "What else could the attacks be but the advance assaults of an invading species?"

Mac glanced at Emily and received that patented "let him run till he chokes" look. It usually applied to one of the grad students spouting a hypothesis, or a prospective date spouting a better-than-average line.

In this case, Mac understood the message. *They needed to know more before deciding if Brymn was to be believed.* "Who do you think is involved?" she asked.

"Who destroyed the worlds within the Chasm?" Brymn countered. The salmon hanging above their heads vibrated. The Dhryn's voice must have included another of the infrasound tones. Mac wondered what information it would have conveyed to those who could hear it. She had to bring an infrasound detector to their next conversation.

Emily looked skeptical. "There's no consistent evidence to prove the destruction wasn't a natural disaster—a plague or some unknown type of cosmic event."

"No?" Brymn looked around, the conspiratorial movement exaggerated by his ponderous body. Any other time Mac might have smiled. "I have that evidence. That is why They pursue me. That is why They pursue all Dhryn."

They? Smile gone, Mac felt the hairs rising on the back of her neck. "Who pursues—" A loud chime interrupted her question and startled Brymn to his feet.

"It's my dad," Mac said hastily, glancing at the clock on her desk. "I had no idea it was so late—excuse me."

Emily moved out of Mac's way as she went around her desk and activated the vid 'screen. "Hi, Dad," she said somewhat lamely.

"Hi, Princess." Her father, Norman Connor, had been smiling. He looked past her, and his smile faded. "Aren't you supposed to be camped along the river by now? What's wrong?"

Mac narrowed the field of view she was transmitting, in case the Dhryn became curious. "A little delay involving Emily's Tracer," she told him, ignoring Emily's sniff. "Nothing we can't resolve, but it means we're stuck at Base a while longer. How's everything with you?"

"Oh, the usual. Your uncle and I had to watch those knuckleheads blow an early lead again. You'd think they'd pick up some better pitchers. He says hello, by the way. The geraniums are filling up the balcony. My neighbor brought over some rainbow trout this morning. Next time you visit I'll have to cook you some."

"You're on." Mac's stomach voiced its opinion. "Pardon," she muttered.

"You could eat more than once in a while," her father noted, the twinkle back in his eyes. "That's what you tell me."

"We've had a busy day."

"Your visitor?" Mac's shock must have shown on her face, because her father laughed. "I do watch the news, Kitten. A Dhryn on Earth? It was the second lead, right after that freighter disaster over the Arctic this morning. What's he like?"

Numbly, Mac widened the transmitted field to include her entire office. "Dad, meet Brymn."

The alien opened his arms, keeping the seventh safely tucked away, and gave one of his bows. "I am honored to be introduced to the Progenitor of Mackenzie Winifred Elizabeth Wright Connor."

Norman Connor widened his own field, so they could see his slight form stand and bow. Geraniums in every color imaginable filled the background. *Calling from his balcony, then.* "The honor is mine, sir. I trust my daughter is treating you well. Lovely place she has there."

"Indeed. I have been most impressed. She must have already performed several fine and unforgettable acts to serve in *grathnu* so often for your betterment and pride."

Mac and Emily exchanged blank looks, but Norman Connor didn't hesitate. Parenting three very different if talented offspring easily took the place of diplomatic training. "Thank you. Yes, she's been a treasure."

"I, alas, have yet to so honor my Progenitors." The Dhryn's nostrils oozed yellow fluid. "I yearn for the opportunity, but it has eluded me."

Mac's father smiled reassuringly. "Don't worry, Brymn. I'm sure your time will come. You are the first of your kind to visit Earth—surely an accomplishment."

"Unfortunately, I come under a cloud, Progenitor of Mackenzie Winifred Elizabeth Wright Connor. A dreadful cloud of foreboding and doom."

Mac wasn't sure what was more alarming: Brymn bonding with her father or what the alien was saying over a completely unsecured transmission. Before either could go further, she spoke up. "We have to get back to our meeting, Dad. I'll call you tomorrow, if that's okay?"

Her father nodded. "Any time after four, dear. The pool tournament's underway this week." He hesitated. Mac understood—he was alarmed by what Brymn had said, but didn't want to ask without privacy.

"Don't worry," she said. "Emily and I are looking after things."

Emily waved from the background. "She means I'm doing the work, as usual."

"Good for you, Em. Keep her out of trouble."

If there was more to the words than usual, if there was worry in his eyes, Mac could do nothing about it now. "I'll call," she promised. "Bye, Dad."

"Bye, Princess."

The 'screen disappeared. Mac couldn't take her eyes from where it had been.

"Thank you."

"What?" She dragged her attention back to Brymn.

His lips were trembling. "Thank you. I had no doubts of you before, Mackenzie—Mac. But to share the regard of your Progenitor with another is the highest courtesy among Dhryn. I am truly touched." Yellow fluid dripped to the floor and his eyes blinked repeatedly.

Congruence or coincidence? Mac had no guideline but her own reactions. The alien seemed sincerely moved. Gingerly, she patted one of Brymn's arms, feeling warm, rubbery skin. "Dad was pleased to meet you, too, Brymn." *Except for the "doom" part,* she added to herself, with a stern reminder to call her father.

Now, Mac thought. *Down to business.* She opened her mouth to ask Brymn more about his conjecture when Emily asked in an alarmed whisper: "What was that?"

"What was what?" Mac snarled, beginning to feel as though she was in a badly written spy thriller.

Emily was staring out the window into the dark. "That."

This time, Mac felt the tiny series of jolts through her feet. Relieved, she grinned at Emily. "'That' was Hector. You should know the feel of him by now." The nightly routine of the elderly humpback whale who visited the inlet included a good belly rub along the pod floats.

"I do," Emily said softly, before Mac could explain to Brymn. "It's not him." She pressed her face against the window. "It's *him*." This with triumph and a slap on the control that opened the door to the outside terrace.

The night air rushing into the room sent salmon careening into one another, their wooden bodies meeting in a cacophony of musical notes. With a protest of her own, Mac followed Emily as she ran outside. "What do you think you're doing?"

Emily stopped, her hands gripping the rail, her head swinging from left to right and back again. "He was right here," she insisted.

"Who?" Mac fought to keep her voice down, uncomfortably aware of passersby on the walkway below.

"I saw a man, standing on the terrace, looking in. I swear it was him. Trojanowski."

"You saw his face?" There was no moon, and the only lighting was that which spilled from occupied rooms and traced the undersides of the railing. Mac could barely see Emily's silhouette against the glow from her office.

"Since when did I need a face to recognize someone?" Emily countered.

"Even if you saw someone—and it was him—this is public space. Anyone can walk here. It's a nice night for a stroll, Em."

It was, too. Warm and still, fragrant with forest and ocean. The sound of conversation and laughter drifted from somewhere nearby. Farther, but no less clear across the placid water, the unmistakable *chuff* of a whale blowing out air. Mac took a deep, calming breath. "We're all tired," she began.

"And you think I'm imagining things." There was real hurt in Emily's voice.

"I hope you are," Mac said honestly. "I've as much as I can handle going through my mind right now. I don't need visions of skulking bureaucrats before I try to catch some sleep."

Mac couldn't see Emily's face, but her quick hug around Mac's shoulders said enough. "Understood. As for sleeping? Sure you don't want to come back to my place? I've the couch."

"There's a mattress on the way," Mac assured her. "Tie promised to look after it. Anyway, we'd better get back inside and talk to our troubled friend."

Easier said than done. The Dhryn was gone.

"Think he was spooked by Trojanowski?" Emily asked once they were back inside. "Or whoever it was I saw?"

Mac held her tongue. Little good now to accuse Emily of scaring away their guest—*and they could be both be wrong.* "He might have needed a bathroom, for all we know."

This drew the rueful smile she'd hoped to see. "Well, he knows where to find one. Or us. Meanwhile, you get that sleep. You look ready to drop on your face."

"Thanks."

"Hey, I tell it like I see it," Emily said. Picking up the sweater from the chair, she started for the door, then paused, looking over her shoulder at Mac. There was a question in her dark eyes.

"Do I believe any of this?" Mac said for her, and shrugged. "I'm not ready to decide without more information. Tomorrow we'll talk to Brymn—and I'll talk to Mr. Trojanowski." She forestalled Emily's complaint with a raised hand. "I'll ask if he was peeking in the window, don't worry. I hope he wasn't," she went on uneasily. "I'd rather he didn't learn how much you know about all this, not yet anyway."

"If you're trying to protect me from fallout over that message—"

"I was thinking more along the lines of keeping you my secret weapon, Dr. Mamani."

The gleam of Emily's teeth was nothing short of predatory. "I had no idea you were so devious, Dr. Connor."

"Grant proposals," Mac explained wryly. They shared a smile, then Mac yawned.

"I can take a hint," Emily said. "Seriously, Mac. You should take me up on that couch."

"No, thanks. I'm going to read a bit more anyway. And since when did you want me hanging around your quarters at night?" Mac stared at her friend. "This isn't so you can berate me for another few hours, is it? Because I've had enough for one night, Em. I really have."

Emily reached out and gently tugged Mac's braid where it draped over her shoulder. "I know. I should have left it alone. Sorry." Then she seemed to search Mac's face, or for some odd reason was trying to memorize it. "You'll be okay," she said finally, in a strange voice. "When push comes to shove, you do the right thing, Mac. I should remember that more often."

"And the right thing is to send you to bed," Mac said kindly. "You're babbling. Go get some sleep." She gave Em a quick hug, then pushed her toward the
door. "See you at breakfast." Mac went to her desk and activated her 'screen,
fighting a yawn.

She was startled to look up and see Emily hadn't left. She'd stopped, one hand
on the door frame, and was watching her. "Now what?"

"Promise me something, Mac."

Mac called up the next publication with a stroke through the 'screen. "If
you'll go to bed—anything," she muttered.

"Promise you'll forgive me."

"I forgive you. Now go."

"No, not now. Not today. Promise you will forgive me."

The qualification was not reassuring. Mac leaned around the 'screen to get a better
look at Em. "What are you planning to do?"

"Just—just give me a one-shot 'get out of trouble with Mac' card, okay? It'll
help me sleep."

Mac was disturbed by the wildness in Emily's eyes, the same look she'd get
before disappearing for days with some stranger she'd picked up at a bar, or before challenging one of the students to a drinking contest he couldn't possibly
win.

Then, with a sinking feeling, Mac thought she understood. "You saw him
kiss my hand, didn't you? Em—"

The other woman leaned her back on the doorframe, cradling her cast and
sweater against her chest. "Actually, no. I missed that. Who knew pushing a man
into the ocean would have a plus side?"

"Then what?" Mac let her exasperation show. "You aren't making any sense."

Emily rubbed her eyes with her right hand. "Forget it, Mac. You're right. I'm
overtired. See you in the morning." She turned with almost boneless grace and
left.

Mac hurried to the door, catching it before it closed. Her friend was already
halfway down the night-dimmed corridor. "Emily."

Her name stopped her, but Emily didn't turn around.

"I don't know what's bothering you, Em, but you don't need me to make a
promise," Mac told her. "There's nothing you could do I wouldn't forgive.
You're my friend. That's what it means."

A whisper. "Thanks, Mac."

And Emily walked away.

The triumphant arrival of two students bearing a mattress pad and bedding startled Mac from a cramped curl in the armchair, where she'd moved to read more
of Brymn's publication list and had fallen asleep instead. With apologies and an
endearing lack of coordination, the pair insisted on making up her bed. Mac

dimly remembered shooing them out the door, then tripping her way on to the promised comfort.

By that point, anything flat would have worked.

So she was vaguely surprised some unknown time later to find herself lying flat on her back, wide awake. It was dark, without even stars glowing overhead. Darker than it should be. The light rimming the doorframes was gone, as were the pinpricks of green and red from the indicators on various gauges she should be able to see in her lab.

Power failure?

She must be dreaming. Norcoast didn't have power failures. It broadcast its own power and there were backups and redundant systems galore—more than most major medical centers—necessities in an environment subject to hurricane winds and the vagaries of summer students.

Her stomach mentioned breakfast.

Not dreaming, Mac decided, coming fully awake. Instinct kept her still.

Something *scurried* across the ceiling.

Mac's heart began to pound. She fought to keep her breathing quiet and even, as if she still slept.

She wasn't alone.

She had no idea what else was in the room with her.

Scurry, scurry.

Not a mouse or Robin's pet monkey, Superrat. The movement she heard had more in common with something insect or crablike. *No.* Too large for anything of that nature.

Skitter, scurry.

Silence. Sweat trickled maddeningly down Mac's neck and chest, but she didn't dare move to wipe it away. She'd always loved the dark; now, it had a weight, a suffocating thickness.

Her fingers walked across the floor, found a sandal, then threw it.

Water hitting a red-hot pan made that kind of hard *spit!* and *pop!* Right after those sounds, Mac heard the door to the terrace open and close.

The door?

Mac lunged to her feet, stumbling in the direction that should lead to the same door, her hands outstretched. Desk edge. *Feel along it.* Desk end. The door should be straight ahead. Two steps. *Nothing.*

She froze in place, then stretched out one foot. It touched the smooth irregularity of gravel and she sagged with relief, knowing where she was. A turn and three steps to the right. The door control was under her hand. Mac followed the cold night air outside.

Overcast. Not raining, but moisture immediately condensed on her lips and eyelids, beaded her hair. The morning fog was forming. *Dawn couldn't be far off.* Mac blinked, trying to see anything.

Again, her ears were her best sense. *Scurry . . . spit! Pop!* From the roof, this time, as if her unwanted visitor had climbed the curve of the pod wall. *Why not?*

Mac thought numbly. It had been running along her ceiling. She hadn't imagined it.

Whatever it *was.*

She knew one thing. It wasn't getting away from her that easily.

Back inside, hands groping in the dark. Mac found her desk, pulled open the second drawer, and grabbed the candle lantern she kept in there. There were matches in the base. She closed her eyes to slits before striking one and lighting the candle. The wick caught, burning brightly. Mac waited until the flame was steady before lowering the glass shield. "Thanks, Dad," she whispered. The lantern had been a birthday gift.

Mac played the lantern's light over the interior of her office, shaking her head in disbelief. Trails of clear, glistening slime, a half meter in width, lay over the floor, walls, and ceiling. Some passed between the suspended salmon, a couple over her desk. Mac lowered the beam to the floor, following a trail that led over the bed where she'd slept. She checked her legs. Sure enough, the material below her knees shone with slime.

"I'm getting well and truly sick of alien biology," Mac muttered, using a clean section of blanket to wipe her pant legs.

She ignored the confused pile of her belongings stacked against the far wall, refugees from her purloined quarters, hurrying instead to the storage cupboard. Putting the lamp where it would shine on the cupboard's contents, Mac pulled out what she wanted. Slicker. Hiking boots. That really old wool sweater that had belonged to her brother William which she kept for winter nights when she was too busy to head upstairs to her quarters. Warm, too big, and itchy as could be.

Mac tried to activate her imp. Nothing, despite its supposed decade-worth of stored power. "Neat trick," she told her quarry, tossing the device aside.

It took Mac only seconds to bundle up—a side effect of innumerable excursions in the dead of winter to chip off ice and help unload surface or air transports. They'd never listened to her recommendation to bring in supplies underwater, where weather wasn't a factor.

Back out the door to the terrace. Mac opened the lantern and blew out her candle, tucking the unit into a pocket, then stood perfectly still, listening.

She knew her responsibility. To catch whatever had invaded her office and Norcoast—or at least get close enough to identify it. The too-convenient power failure had to be a ruse by the creature; waking up the rest of Base's inhabitants would only add a crowd of confused students, sure to get in her way.

Scurry.

Fainter. *The sound was different.* "Gotcha," Mac said to herself, making the connection. It was on the walkway below.

She ran along the terrace, guided by memory and one hand on the pod wall, heading for the stairs. Stealth wasn't as important as speed, but speed wouldn't matter if she broke her neck in the dark.

Her feet knew every centimeter, every rise and fall along the walkways.

A whiff of roses. *Dr. Reinhold's rooftop planter.* She was passing Pod Two.

Scurry . . . scurry. It wasn't stopping. Mac wasn't surprised. Her boots made a solid drumming on the walkway. She wanted it that way. *Keep her quarry moving, panicked.* With luck, she'd corner it against one of the pod doors.

Ambush seemed unlikely—given its reaction to her sandal. Mac was sure her visitor was a thief or spy. Maybe even one of the media, sliming around for a story. She should have asked if all had been Human. *Not a question that would have occurred to her yesterday.*

Whether it knew her plan or not, the creature wasn't cooperating. Mac kept stopping to listen; the susurrations continued to move straight ahead. Not to a launch pad and waiting escape vehicle, as she'd feared, but retracing the path she and Brymn had taken that afternoon.

Toward land.

Mac kept her fingertips sliding along the top of the right-hand rail, moving as quickly as she dared through the darkness. There were sounds behind her now—perplexed voices as people began questioning one another about the power failure. A glow of new lights reflected on the water, candles and lanterns caught on each upward swell, enough to etch out the darker line of the walkway in front of Mac's feet, so she risked starting to run.

If the creature reached land first, it might be trapped by the web gate.

If it wasn't, it would have the entire coastal forest and a continent beyond in which to lose her.

- Portent -

THE FIRST drop hissed into the snow, its remains a crater, stained green, like a dead eye staring back at the sky.

Another embedded eye. Another.

The pristine snowfield became pocked with green, rotting under unseasonable rain. Rivulets began to form, eating deeper as they flowed.

More drops fell.

Beneath the snow, those asleep in their shells knew only the regular, once-weekly beating of their hearts, dreamed only of the coming warmth, when their world danced closer to its partner sun. Under the open fronds of the Nirltrees, they would teach their offspring. It had always been thus. It would always be thus. The Great Sleep was their salvation, the snow their protection.

They were wrong.

The green rivulets melted deeper and deeper. Soon, they flowed over what seemed a bed of immense pebbles, each regular in form and smooth, as if polished.

The pebbles were seamed, the edges held by ligaments laced together like so many fingers in prayer. Admirable defense against cold and predator, but the ligaments rotted away as the rivulets touched them. The halves of every pebble fell open, exposing the flesh within, flesh that dissolved in the flood before it could awake to scream.

The shells melted almost as quickly, washed away with the dormant stumps of the Nirltree grove, even the roots of the trees dissolving as the green drops penetrated the frozen soil. Drops and rivulets joined into a widening river, washing away the snow, dissolving all life that had sheltered beneath it, scouring the mountainside until all that remained was rock.

Where the river flowed into a cirque, becoming a limpid pool of green, mouths gathered.

And began to drink.

CHASE AND CONFRONTATION

MAC SMACKED her hand against the lock on the pillar. Of course it didn't respond. No confirmation signal for her code could come from Norcoast until Base's power was restored. The webbing of the gate remained in place, a default that would have pleased Mac immensely had her quarry seen fit to be delayed by it.

But no. She'd arrived at the gate between the holdfasts to find herself alone. *Maybe.*

Remembering how easily the creature had hidden in her office, Mac put her back to the pillar and stared outward until her eyes burned. Warm yellow marked activity around the pods. Someone had already strung a series of lanterns along the walkway leading to Pod Three, probably anticipating breakfast. Which would rely on the ingenuity of those on duty if the power remained off. Mac wasn't worried. Enough students had stashed grills in their rooms to cook for the entire crew, if need be.

She willed herself silent, wanting to hear what was around her.

Waves licked the rocks. The fog was condensing in the forest, producing a combination of drip and sigh as leaves released their burdens. A cone dropped on the moss. A salmon leaped and splashed in the inlet. *All sounds she knew.* Mac listened for the unfamiliar and was rewarded.

A low, regular *thrumming.* If she hadn't lived here for years, Mac would have dismissed it as the call of an insect, perhaps a large cricket rubbing its legs together.

Even as she became convinced she was hearing the creature breathing, she realized the sound was coming from over her head.

Mac swallowed, then took one step forward and turned around, keeping her movements slow and cautious. "I know you're up there," she said, hoping her Instella wasn't completely rusty. "Come down and talk to me."

Spit! Pop! The same noises as when she'd thrown her sandal. *Surprise?* Mac peered upward, wondering if she was imagining being able to see the outline of the holdfast pillar against the trees. Dawn must be fighting its way over the mountains. The fog would delay true light another hour yet. "I won't hurt you," she ventured, hoping for the same attitude.

"Dr. Connor!" The call came from Base, echoed by a series of anxious voices. Someone had probably gone to alert her about the power failure, Mac realized, and discovered the condition of her office.

She was reasonably sure shouting in answer would cost her any chance of seeing her visitor. There was definitely more light every minute now. *If she could only keep the creature here . . .*

It might have had the same thought. *Scurry . . . thump!* The odd clattering of its movement on the pillar ended in a rapid rustling through the underbrush. It had climbed over the gate and left the walkway for the forest floor.

"Damn it!" Mac smacked her hand against the lock again. *Nothing.*

"It broke the rules first, Oversight," she muttered, then felt her way to the edge of the walkway membrane and sat, boots dangling in midair. The walkway guide lights inside the Trust would stay off, since no access code had been confirmed to the gate. But, with the sort of luck Mac was coming to expect tonight, the repeller field was still active, being powered—like the tiggers—from an inland broadcast source owned by the Wilderness Trust. As she sat down, the field vibrated unpleasantly through her pelvis and up her spine, setting her teeth on edge, but its intensity was meant to discourage bats, wasps, and jays, not an adult and determined woman.

And probably a foolish one, too, Mac told herself, but that didn't stop her from jumping into the dark.

Scritch . . . whoosh.

Mac let out the breath she'd unconsciously held while striking the match. She lit her small lantern, then carefully wrapped the tip of the spent match in wet moss before tucking it into an upper pocket. *Minimal presence,* she reminded herself. The light was more welcome than she wanted to admit.

Its tiny flickering reminded her of another hunt through the dark.

Her dad hadn't been sure about bringing a very young Mackenzie on his owl survey. Her older brothers had talked him into it, probably so they needn't feel any guilt over choosing not to come. Mac hadn't cared about their reasons; she'd been hoping to go as long as she could remember. After all, what was the fun of staying in town with her aunts while the rest of her family went camping in the dark and perilous northern forests?

Not that they were either, but at seven, Mac had been nothing if not imaginative. To her, trees traded stories about you behind your back and, if they didn't like you, they would move to confuse your path. Moss-covered stones were worse. The little ones would try to trip you. The big ones would wait until you passed before turning into something else, something with long, thin fingers and sharp nails, something that snacked on children who didn't know the magic words. Mac was very proud of her ability to make up such words, each having proved most effective on past walks through the park near her aunts' house.

She'd been ready for anything the northern forest could offer. Until her father lost himself.

"Poppa?" Mac had been sure he was outside their tent, putting up the pack for the night, but he'd been nowhere in sight. She'd stopped shouting immediately, careful not to draw the attention of tree or stone. In this wilder forest, both were larger and stranger than any she'd seen before. *Where could he be?* She'd noticed her father was easily distracted. Why the very first day, he'd sat transfixed by the huge eyes of a large white owl, until she'd had to grab his hand to remind him he had a daughter to feed.

Glow in hand, she'd set off to find him, careful to say a magic word each time she passed a threatening stone, careful not to step on the exposed roots of trees and give them reason to spread dislike about her.

Mac had walked all night, longer than she'd ever walked in her life, a girl on a heroic quest. Her glow had dimmed until the moonlight was brighter, if only in clearings where there were more stones. Her voice had grown hoarse, then faded to a whisper, but she'd kept uttering the magic words, knowing she had to keep herself safe if she was to help her father.

And when she'd finally found him, surprisingly close to their campsite, his own voice had been strained to a whisper, his face pale and lined with fear. Tight in his arms, feeling him shake, Mac had decided not to scold him for getting lost. It could happen to anyone, alone in a dark forest.

Mac shook her head, smiling at the memory. *Gossiping trees and hungry stones?* At least she hadn't made up her visitor, invisible or not. She glanced up. The drop hadn't been far. If she stretched, she could brush the bottom of the walkway with her fingertips. It didn't show to her light.

It didn't matter. Mac needed to see the forest floor, not where she'd been. She hurried over moss-covered stones, grateful for her boots, holding the lantern low. *There.* A couple of meters past the holdfast pillar, lines of moss had been peeled up in a series of loops, as if the tines of a large fork had scooped them from the soil. Mac refused to speculate what body parts would leave such a mark, instead raising her lantern to look for more tracks. If the thing could climb from tree to tree, she'd never be able to follow it.

Another rip in the moss. Another beyond that. They led her to a row of similar marks scoring the top of an immense nurse log that loomed like a tanker out of the mist. Mac set her lantern on top and clambered over, her hands sinking into the decaying wood. She whispered an apology to Charles Mudge III under her breath as a clump broke free under her boot.

She wiggled on her belly over the log, no doubt damaging the tiny saplings growing there, and retrieved her lantern to hunt for more tracks. *There.* Leading upward. Away from Base.

Where they didn't belong, Mac thought, welcoming the anger that warmed her body. Bad enough she was ripping through the vegetation.

At least she was from this planet!

Hiking through a coastal rain forest was never a straight-line affair at best, even in full daylight. Myriad tiny streams, ice-cold and swift, flowed down every crease in the rock. The rocks themselves were the jagged shoulders of a new mountain range, untamed by time and unsympathetic to anyone who chose to climb them. Hunched over the spot of light from her lantern, moving from one track to the next, Mac felt as though she crawled across the forest floor like a slug.

The slope increased in jagged steps, but luckily never so steep that Mac couldn't follow the creature's spoor. Still, she often had to plant one foot firmly, then reach with her free hand for a branch that wouldn't come loose. Then pull. Her shoulders began to burn.

Abruptly, the tracks ended. Mac hunted with her lantern for a few moments, careful not to move too far from the last impression. *Nothing.* Finally, she sank to her knees to rest and consider what to do next. *How long until dawn?* she wondered, and closed the front of the lantern to assess the light.

Dawn might be touching the mountaintops by now, but not here. She hadn't expected it yet, not under the fog-laden mammoth trees and certainly not deep within this fold of land. "But what's this?" Mac breathed, staring at the ground. A faint, green fluorescence shone from under her knees, leading up the next rise. *The slime,* Mac exulted, surging to her feet.

Now she raced against the dawn. The fluorescence remained visible, barely, for mere seconds after her lantern activated it. She proceeded in sprints now, waving her light to memorize the terrain as well as energize the slime, then covering it so she could run along the glowing path.

Up the path was more accurate. The landscape had become punishingly vertical. Mac prided herself on her conditioning; even so, she struggled to make any speed. The footing was wet and slick, so her boots slid backward with every step. Progress was measured in altitude gained, not the number of strides it took. Achievement? How quickly she could stand after a fall that slammed her against tree trunks, not the number of times she slipped.

"I've got you now," she whispered to herself.

Every so often, Mac snatched leaves and licked the moisture from their surfaces. The lifting fog had condensed in the upper canopy, drops runneling down every branch and dripping from leaf tips. This time of year, it wouldn't be long before real rain followed, so dehydration wasn't a problem. The hollow feeling in her gut she could ignore. A good thing she'd shared leftovers with Trojanowski last night.

Her growing ability to see her surroundings was something else again. Mac blinked and stopped, leaning against a redwood wider than her last apartment. She blew out the candle and tucked the lantern away.

Not quite bright enough for color, but her dark-adapted eyes could easily discern the shapes of tree, log, and rock from the background mist. The slime's faint glow could no longer compete with the rising sun. *The morning rain would wash it away soon anyway,* Mac thought resignedly. She tightened the collar of her slicker, but left the hood down. She'd have to listen for her quarry now.

It helped that most birds were finished singing for the season. A few twittered sleepily around her. A squirrel complained about intruders in the distance. *That way.* Mac lifted her head from its rest against the tree like a hound taking point. She was willing to gamble the intruder was hers.

Crack.

From *behind,* down the hill. Mac pressed herself against the redwood again.

It might be nothing. Forests cracked and snapped all the time. She waited, hardly breathing. The squirrel continued to chatter furiously, not far at all. She could be gaining on the creature at last.

To take advantage of that meant moving. Mac shoved away from the shelter of the tree, feeling every muscle protest, and began to climb toward the outraged squirrel.

The clearing was new. Mac didn't need a vegetation survey map to tell her, she'd been able to smell the sap and bruised leaves, the spicy tang of freshly cut—or rather freshly smashed—cedar well before she'd reached it.

Poor Mudge would be horrified.

As she'd expected, the fog had slipped from under the forest canopy to make room for the rain that replaced it, the kind of steady, soaking deluge that promoted the lush growth of fern and moss and mocked even the best slicker's ability to keep a body dry. Mac shivered spasmodically as she crouched under the partial shelter of a leaning nurse log, distracting herself with daydreams of hot showers, hot towels, and hot sunshine.

She hadn't found her quarry. *Not yet.* But this had to be its destination. The clearing had been made either for or by a landing craft. Within the past day, she guessed. The broken vegetation was still green and unwilted. Dark exposed soil marked a too-regular series of depressions, now filling with rainwater.

Mac refused to believe she'd arrived too late. There'd been no sound or flash, no vibration. Even a t-lev on hush would have stirred the treetops on its way down.

Crack.

Only Mac's eyes shifted to search the wall of green and brown to her left. The contrast to the clearing, despite the low cloud and rain, was enough to darken the forest beyond into night.

Rabbit or deer, she told herself, licking water from her lips. *Grizzlies weren't so careless.*

A scrap of moss floated down past her eyes, like the tuft of a feather dislodged from a bird. Mac froze.

Scurry . . . scurry. The log above her vibrated. More moss fell. Mac launched herself from the shelter that now felt like a trap, looking around frantically for any sign of it. *Nothing*. She was alone. "The fun's worn off," she muttered, heart still pounding with shock. Louder. "Look—I just want to talk to you—"

"Get down—!"

The shout, in a man's voice, was lost in the roar of an engine where no engine existed. Mac stared into the empty clearing, hearing what she couldn't see. Wind from nowhere buffeted her, driving the rain sideways into her face. She staggered back, grabbing at branches to keep her footing.

But there was nothing there!

A blinding flash of light as heat struck her, both preludes to a wind that shoved her backward. Mac threw her arms in front of her face and turned with the force, throwing herself to the ground. The roar grew louder, then, as suddenly as it had started, ceased.

Mac spat out a mouthful of fern and dirt as she pushed herself up to sit. She opened and closed her eyes, fighting to see past the fiery specks blurring her vision.

"Are you all right?"

Her ears might be ringing, but she recognized the voice now. *Trojanowski?* She didn't waste time in "hows" or "whys." "Did you see what—who—it was?" Mac demanded.

"No." A wealth of self-disgust in the word.

Mac swore under her breath and fought her way to her feet, grateful to find her eyes sore but functioning. He was standing a couple of meters away, looking not at her but at the presumably now-empty clearing. There were new scars in the ground as if whatever had landed had put down feet. "An invisible ship?" she said in wonder. "Who has such technology?"

"Good question," he said, taking what looked to be an unusually small scanner from a pocket and walking into the opening.

So, Mac thought. *His device wasn't keyed to Norcoast's power broadcast, or Norcoast was up and running again*. She was inclined to believe the latter. A technology that could hide a ship from view? Once the need had passed, they'd probably restored power to the inlet with a nod—if they had heads and bendable necks. *No guarantees on either point.*

Mac followed, studying the man, not the place. Bureaucrat? Diplomatic flunky? *Not likely*. The glasses were gone, as was the apologetic slouch. This version of Nikolai Piotr Trojanowski was all business, stepping easily over the uneven surface, dressed in a jacket and pants that might have been made from the forest, their camouflage so perfect Mac found him hard to see even this close. He wore a pack on his shoulders and her stomach chose that moment to remind her about breakfast.

Mac fought for patience. Her eyes were improving by the minute; they weren't helping her make sense of any of this. "Anything?" she asked, watching him scowl at his device.

Trojanowski might not have heard. He made an adjustment, then crouched to pass his scanner close to the dark soil exposed in one of the scars.

With a shiver, Mac pulled her slicker tighter to her neck and followed. The rain had eased to the mist-in-your-face variety that could last all day. The sun was high enough now to add pastel colors to the trees and ground, if not send its warmth through the clouds. *Pleasant enough weather, if you weren't already soaking wet.* She tried again. "Do you know what it wanted?"

That drew a look. "You should go—" he began to say, then, perversely: "Don't move." He took three quick strides to stand in front of her. Mac fought the impulse to back away as he raised the scanner to the side of her face. His expression was cold, clinical.

This wasn't the man who'd laughed and shared his supper with her, who'd held her hand, who'd kissed her fingers like some centuries-past gallant. Yesterday might have been something she'd dreamed.

"What is it?" she asked, reaching up with one hand. "What's wrong?" The question was about more than her face.

"Don't touch your skin, Dr. Connor." He put away the device. "Minor flash burn. You didn't move fast enough."

Mac's fingers hovered near her cheeks. "I don't feel any pain," she said doubtfully.

He raised an eyebrow. "I suspect that's temporary. You'd better go and have it treated."

Go? Given the effort involved in retracing her steps downslope and in the rain, Mac was in no hurry. She looked Trojanowski over from head to boot-encased foot. No stains. No rips. Unlike her poor abused slicker. It meant he had transport of his own. *And something else.* "You didn't follow me," she deduced. "You were already here. Waiting. I want to know why."

His eyes narrowed, their hazel turning almost green. Mac supposed intimidating looks were part of his training. She was too full of adrenaline to be impressed. "Same side, remember?" she told him. "Protecting the species. Working with Brymn to solve this mysterious threat." She tilted her head back and gave him her own intimidating look. "Or are we?"

"You know the Secretary General assigned me to accompany the Honorable Delegate—"

"'Accompany,'" Mac repeated, interrupting him. "Or was that a convenient excuse to come here? I don't think you or the Secretary General are paying any attention to Brymn's work at all. I think you are here because you expected this!" She waved somewhat wildly at the clearing, lacking any better idea of what *this* was.

"Is that why you're here, Dr. Connor?" *Oh, he was good.* The return accusation was sharp and slick.

Mac would have stomped her foot if it would have done more than splatter mud. "Look, this—thing—woke me. I followed it—"

"You what? Did you see it?" Trojanowski demanded. "Did you see anything?"

Mac shook her head. "Only its tracks . . . Hey!" She found herself talking to his back. His moving-away-from-her, you-are-irrelevant-and-dismissed back. She spat a rude phrase Emily had taught her and forced her tired legs in pursuit. "Wait! What did you expect to find here?"

That stopped him in the middle of the clearing. His eyebrows drew together as he glared down at her. "I didn't expect to find you."

Mac bristled. "What was I supposed to do, Mr. Trojanowski? The thing was in my office. It ran away when I woke up."

"Woke up? So, you were asleep in your office," he rephrased as if trying to make sense of what she was telling him, "and, when a 'thing' you couldn't see woke you, you chased it up here. Alone."

"I didn't see a choice. Someone had to follow it, find out what it wanted—"

"What if it had wanted you dead?"

Mac shook her head, soaking wet hair falling in her eyes. She tucked it behind an ear, careful of her numb skin. "Then I would have been dead," she said reasonably. "It wanted something else. What?"

"In your office," he echoed, in the same skeptical tone he'd used for "alone." His look became intense, as though he could somehow read the answer in her face, burned or otherwise. It was like being transfixed by a spotlight—an unfriendly one at that. "Why your office? And how could you possibly follow it here . . . unless you already knew where to go." Clear threat now. "Which brings us back to the key question. How did you know to come here, Dr. Connor?"

"And who the hell are you, Mr. Trojanowski, to stand here and ask me questions of any kind?" Mac retorted, despite feeling that arguing with a man who secretly skulked in the forest in camouflage gear wasn't necessarily wise. "You aren't who you pretend to be, that's for sure. Let me finish," she snapped, but quietly when he opened his mouth.

A wary nod.

"You're the one who handed me the message that dragged me away from my work, remember? You're the one who brought that Dhryn—and the media—into my life. You want to know why some weird, invisible alien was running across my ceiling in the middle of the night? Well, that makes two of us."

Trojanowski pursed his lips and considered her. She did the same, waiting. *He remained a contradiction,* Mac decided. The camouflage gear and pack, how naturally he wore them, his sudden shift in personality . . . clearly he'd been trained to handle situations other than ferrying diplomatic messages to biologists. For all she knew, he was some kind of spy, like those in Em's old movies, if less glamorous.

But Trojanowski's face didn't suit the man-of-action mode. When he was thinking, as now, little perplexed lines formed at the corners of his eyes and mouth. *He doesn't like mysteries,* she thought abruptly. *Neither did she.* So Mac wasn't surprised when his very next words addressed another. "How did you find your way through the dark, Dr. Connor? Please."

Mac put her hand in her pocket. He tensed and she blinked at him. "It's only a lantern," she said before pulling it out, in case he needed reassurance. "Combustible. A candle." She offered the lantern to him and he took it, giving her an inscrutable look. "Whatever—whoever—was in my office left a trail of slime that fluoresced under its light. The glow didn't last long; just enough that I could follow it. No mystery, Mr. Trojanowski."

He handed the lantern back. "Quick thinking."

His praise was unexpected. Mac had begun to believe "foolhardy" and "stupid" were better descriptions of what she'd done. "Fair's fair," she suggested, replacing the lantern in her pocket. "How did you know to be here?"

Trojanowski frowned, *but not, this time, at her,* Mac thought. "There was a collision yesterday, northeast of here, involving a low-orbit freighter. All hands were lost. No evidence of what it collided with until this—" he nodded at the flattened clearing, "—appeared on the monitors. I was contacted to check it out as soon as I could get away from Brymn. I played a hunch and stayed."

"Do all diplomatic liaisons check out freighter crashes and holes in the forest canopy?"

"Not all." He had the grace to look embarrassed, a reminder of the man she'd met yesterday. "I'm not supposed to get caught like this, Dr. Connor. I'd planned a quiet investigation, no one the wiser."

"Why the pretense? I mean, it's not as if Base is full of—" She closed her mouth into a grim line.

"Spies?" Trojanowski's expression matched her own. "I'd say my precautions were well advised, given your visitor."

"Who was it? What was it? You know, don't you?"

"Even if I did, Dr. Connor," he said with what seemed sincere regret, "I couldn't tell you. Secrecy is more important than ever now." With that, he turned and walked away.

"Oh, no, you don't!"

Mac caught up with the bureaucrat-cum-spy at the opposite side of the clearing, where he'd started removing a camouflage net from what turned out to be a one-person lev. "We aren't done here, Trojanowski," she told him fiercely. "Not by a long shot."

"Duty calls. I'm sure you know the way back." In one easy motion, Trojanowski straddled the seat and activated the lev. There was barely a whisper of engine noise. *Not your average off-the-lot weekend toy,* Mac thought, unsurprised. Probably maneuverable enough to fly under the canopy, out of sight. "Good day, Dr. Connor," he said, donning a black helmet and visor.

Mac stepped away as the lev lifted, contemplating several things, including what she'd transmit to Trojanowski's boss before the day ended. Her foot caught in a fragment of toppled cedar and she fell on her rump within its branches. *Perfect.* As she sat there, she glared up at the lev, which was now almost at tree height, and added a few others to the list to "speak to" about Mr. Trojanowski.

A breeze free to roam the new clearing slipped through her hair, scented with bruised leaves. Leaves bruised by the intruder in her office. Mac said "Damn," to herself, but squirmed to her feet. Once standing, she cupped her hands around her mouth and shouted: "I heard it."

The lev paused, then plunged groundward to rest over her head. Mac swallowed hard, but stood her ground. Trojanowski flipped up his visor and looked down, his expression noncommittal. "What did you hear?"

"Not words I could understand. Other sounds. When it was in my office, when I was following it, I heard——"

"That's enough. Stop," he ordered, emphasizing the command with a raised hand.

Mac obeyed, but pressed her lips together and scowled fiercely.

Trojanowski's expression became slightly more conciliatory. "Please don't take offense, Dr. Connor. You're right—this is important and I'll want your full report, but we need an audio expert to help reconstruct the sounds. Please don't talk to anyone else about what you think you heard until then—not even yourself. Premature verbalizing can distort recall. In Humans, at least."

He probably thought he was making sense, but Mac wasn't inclined to listen. Her toes were icicles, her legs ached, and her face was beginning to burn along the right side, from chin to forehead. "Then I suggest you call a transport to get me home."

"Call—? Does the concept of secrecy hold any meaning whatsoever to you?" Trojanowski actually sounded frustrated, likely the closest to an honest emotion he'd shown her since she'd arrived. "No one can know we've been up here."

Somehow, she doubted he was worried about the Wilderness Trust Oversight Committee. "Our 'visitors' already do," Mac pointed out.

"Which is more than enough. This isn't a debate, Dr. Connor. I'm very sorry, but you'll have to go back the way you came. I'll contact you as soon as I can."

Mac prided herself on keeping her temper. She found nothing productive or appealing in the furies the more volatile Emily would unleash without warning at targets ranging from slow drivers to political leaders. Now, however, she put her fists on her hips, stared up at Trojanowski, and let fly: "You're right. This isn't a debate, Mr. Trojanowski. You will arrange for me to be transported back to Base, or the moment I get back I'll be in touch with the Secretary General and everyone else I can find." She drew a shuddering breath, but kept going. "I'm sure some of the media are still around."

He lowered the lev until it brushed the ground, making it easier for her to read his expression. Not anger. *Regret.* Mac felt her blood chill as he spoke.

"You leave me no choice, Dr. Connor. One word about any of this—our encounter, what you chased, what happened here—and I'll have you arrested and removed from your facility as a threat to the species. And before you ask, yes, the Ministry of Extra-Sol Human Affairs has that authority, as an agency of the Interspecies Union. There would be no recourse or question. You would disappear."

What could she say to that? Mac stared at him, feeling as though her feet were sinking. *Which could well be,* part of her acknowledged.

He leaned forward. "I don't want to do that to you. But I will, if I have to—no matter how beautiful your eyes are at sunset. Your word, Dr. Connor, please, that you won't tell anyone."

Mac could only nod. Trojanowski's face was replaced by the black sheen of his visor. The lev shot toward the forest and vanished.

Her eyes were beautiful?

A squirrel complained furiously and Mac snorted, feeling—she wasn't sure what she felt. Angry, maybe. "Losing your temper never helps," she advised the squirrel. "Trust me."

She'd been about as effectual as the tiny creature. *Worse,* Mac realized with dismay, *she'd been wrong.* Trojanowski hadn't lied. There were secrets to protect, even if she hated being part of them. And it was her fault, no one else's, that she was part of them now.

She could already hear Emily's voice, providing a scathingly complete list of why she, Mac, should leave secrets and the pursuit of invisible aliens to professionals.

Like Trojanowski.

"Then she'll want to know how he looked without glasses," Mac told the squirrel. "Sorry, Em. I forgot to notice." *But he'd noticed her eyes.*

She made her way back through the clearing, dodging shattered stumps and piles of leafy debris. This couldn't possibly be overlooked by the Wilderness Trust and their satellite monitors.

"Who am I kidding?" Mac grumbled, about to step over another scar in the ground. "He probably has authority over Mudge, too. I'm so far out of my league it's . . ."

She paused. This scar was another that was too regular, forming an indentation longer than it was wide. Unlike the others, it was marked along one edge in a pattern of narrow scrapes similar to the one Mac had seen near the pillar, where the creature had dropped to the ground.

Mac sank on her heels to look out across the clearing. The other large depressions she'd judged the imprints of landing gear were at even distances from this one. She twisted on her heels to check behind her. The log where she'd crouched under the alien was in a direct line from this point. "I'll be . . ." she breathed. "This must have been the hatch."

They'd literally watched the creature enter its ship, and seen nothing.

Mac whistled between her teeth. "Now, that's camouflage." She unzipped the right-hand pocket of her slicker and shoved its contents—tissues, pencil remnants, and an unused t-lev ticket—into the left with the lantern. Taking a piece of torn bark, she removed soil from the longest of the scrapes, putting as much into her empty pocket as she could fit. *A little present for Kammie.*

Mac smiled, wincing as it stretched the tender skin of her cheek. Now to see if Trojanowski's fancy scanner was as good as one of the top soil chemists on Earth.

Maybe she wasn't a professional whatever, with a fancy lev and helmet, Mac told herself. *But she was used to looking for answers—and finding them.*

The shadows cast by ruined branches and trampled ground abruptly lost their edges. The forest, already dim under the canopy, became as inviting as the door of an unlit basement and Mac heard the rain approaching through the trees. "Perfect," she said aloud, then pulled her hood over her head in time to keep her hair only damp, and stood.

Time to go home.

"Why sneak around my . . . *omphf* . . . office?" Mac muttered to herself as she slid down the next dip on her rump, grabbing whatever handholds she could find. It might not be dignified, but between the rain-slick slopes and her growing fatigue, she judged it safer than trying to climb down on her feet.

On reaching the next patch that was more or less level, she levered herself to her feet, casting an eye to what lay ahead. A choice between vertical rock or slightly less than vertical rock covered in wet roots. "This was all so much easier on the way up—and in the dark, so I couldn't see what an idiot I was." *Time to catch her breath.* Mac leaned on the nearest tree to mull the question troubling her. "Em," she decided, "your radar was off for once." She gave a lopsided grin, avoiding the damaged side of her face. The figure on the terrace last night hadn't been Trojanowski—he'd been here. But if the spy on the terrace had been the creature—or its more visible accomplice—then its search of her office later made an ironic kind of sense.

Mac shook her head. Had it thought the bag with the soufflé contained some secret Brymn had brought her? "Well, that must have been a shock," she told the finger-long banana slug climbing the bark near her ear. An unhappy thought, an accomplice on Base, but it would have been easy enough. After all, they'd been invaded by fifteen kayak-loads of local media folk disguised as badly dressed tourists. *Even* she *could have infiltrated that group.*

Trojanowski's insistence on secrecy, however uncomfortable it made her trip home, suddenly seemed more reasonable.

The thought of more spies wandering around Base got Mac moving again, not to mention a distinct longing for the simple things in life. Although Mac couldn't make up her mind. "Shower, then breakfast," she decided, checking for the next foothold. "No. Strip and sleep, then shower. No. Breakfast, then more answers from that Dhryn."

She'd have plenty of time to work out the order. The return trip was less straightforward than the one up. For one thing, the trails she and the creature had left had been obliterated by the rain. For another, landmarks looked remarkably different viewed from above. *Oh, she wasn't lost.* Mac knew the overall shape of the landscape well enough to be sure she was heading toward the arm's inner curve, not the Pacific side. She intended to follow the ridge that led to the arm's tip, which should bring her out of the forest near one of the three walkways or perhaps the gate itself.

"With luck, Oversight will never know I was here," she reassured herself before starting her next, cautious descent. Mac wasn't proud of such a hope. She hung on tight, reaching with her boots for a foothold, and promised herself that despite Trojanowski's oath of secrecy she'd document every bruised leaf for Mudge, in case a researcher ever climbed this ridiculous excuse for a—

As if paying attention, the root clutched in her right hand chose that moment to pop free of the rock, ripping away with it an appalling number of connecting rootlets, ferns, and moss clumps. Mac wedged her boot in a crack in time to save herself from joining them at the bottom of the tiny cliff. "Oops," she said, staring down at what was undeniable proof of anthropogenic interference.

Then again, she could hope that Mr. Trojanowski had every bit of the authority he claimed when threatening her. He'd need it. The amount of damage she'd done climbing up and back would be enough to rescind Norcoast's land access permanently. It wouldn't matter that the alien ship had smacked a hole the size of a transport lev in the forest.

She *was supposed to know better.*

"Aliens," Mac muttered darkly.

Hours later, Mac pressed her hand to the door release of Pod Three with a relief so close to pain she couldn't tell the difference. She'd half expected to find the walkways crowded despite the driving rain, but she'd staggered to the pod without seeing anyone but a family of orcas, breaching in the inlet. All she wanted from life at this moment was a roof and dry floor. And to get her boots off, if humanly possible. Everything and everyone else could wait.

Unfortunately, everyone else was waiting inside Pod Three.

Mac blinked stupidly at the sight that greeted her as the door opened. The corridor was lined three deep with people on each side, most shouting in confused, though joyful, unison when they saw her.

One shout penetrated the rest. "Mac! Where the hell have you been? We've got search parties out—the police—"

It took a second before Mac could put a name to the almost hysterical voice. *Kammie? The unflappable?* She winced with guilt as that worthy burst through the crowd toward her, arms flailing and eyes wild. "Ah. Sorry to alarm everyone," Mac said. "I'm fine. I'll explain later." *Once she found the energy to dream up a plausible story.* "Was Brymn okay through the excitement?"

"Brymn? Excitement?" Kammie seemed stuck on repeat.

Another voice interjected helpfully: "Still snoring."

Mac found herself grateful for the support of the doorframe. "Glad someone was."

The rising babble of concerned, relieved voices made it impossible to carry on a conversation. Several hands took over the work of the frame and her sagging muscles, guiding Mac forward into the blissfully dry and warm, if noisy, building. *But why were they all here?* She fought to stand still so she could search their faces, dismayed by what she saw.

And by who she didn't see.

"Em?"

She might have dropped a stone into a tidal pool, the way silence rippled outward from her question. The few faces turned her way seemed those of strangers.

"Where's Emily Mamani?" Mac demanded, shaking free of her caretakers.

Kammie, who looked to have aged a decade since yesterday, stared up at her. "We'd hoped she was with you, Mac."

- 8 -

DISPUTE AND DECISION

IT WAS A nightmare from which no one would let her wake. Mac turned herself into an automaton, answering questions in the order they arrived, steeling herself against any emotion, hers or those around her. As if authorizing a barnacle survey, she sent divers to search under the pods, and skims to follow the tide. As if making arrangements for the delivery of fresh fruit, she called Emily's younger sister and gave the story as it stood: *Emily is missing. There's been no contact from a kidnapper. Yes, you'll be kept informed.*

Mac didn't mention the slime coating every surface of Emily's quarters, the smashed furniture, or the blood. Kammie's report had been graphic. She'd been the only one inside Em's quarters and, given what she'd seen, it was no wonder she'd immediately called the local police. They'd ordered Em's quarters and Mac's office sealed. A forensics team had arrived and set up at dawn, their warn offs extending to corridor and terrace.

Mac had no doubt Trojanowski would be allowed to cross; she could not.

There was nothing more for her to do but wait.

She didn't do that well.

As if she'd lost her dearest friend, those around her lowered their voices and hovered when they obviously had other places to be. To be rid of them, Mac finally agreed to be escorted to the Base nurse.

Because she refused to believe she'd lost her dearest friend, Mac left the nurse· the moment her face was treated for its burn.

Now, she stood before the door to her quarters, seeking answers in the only place left. *Emily had tried to warn her. Emily had known there was danger, that something was coming, that this wasn't about risks to aliens at distances Mac couldn't imagine, but to* them, *here, now.*

Emily had been afraid, last night. She'd asked not to be alone and Mac hadn't understood even that much.

What kind of friend was she?

It wasn't locked. Mac hesitated, afraid Brymn wouldn't be able to help, afraid of losing hope. Recognizing the weakness, she raised her fist and knocked.

No answer.

Mac pressed her palm on the entry. For no reason she could name, she let the door open fully before she took a step inside.

Her hands covered her mouth, a painful pressure on the mem-skin now coating her burn.

They'd said Brymn was snoring. She should have realized that none of them would know if a Dhryn snored in the first place.

From somewhere, Mac found the strength to snap the paralysis holding her in the doorway, taking three slow steps into the room. The form hanging in the middle of her living room was Brymn. She could tell that much by the patches of blue skin showing between the glistening threads wrapped around him, if little more. The threads led upward to form a thick knot stuck to the ceiling.

He was alive. That much was clear from the regular, low moaning. *It did sound a bit like snoring,* Mac decided numbly.

By rights, she should call the police immediately.

Instead, Mac locked the door behind her, then went to the com, leaning her back against the wall beside it. "Dr. Connor. Is Mr. Trojanowski back yet?"

"What are you doing out of bed?" Tie was back on com duty—a rock in a storm.

Mac rolled her head toward the familiar voice, her problem solver when skims failed to run or pods developed a list, but said only: "Trojanowski."

Tie knew better than to argue. "Yes, he's back. He's been with the forensics guys. I'll hunt him up for you, Mac."

"Thanks. I'll be in my—in Brymn's quarters."

"There's been no more word about Dr. Mamani," he said, almost making it a question.

"Keep me posted, Tie."

Mac stayed propped against the wall beside the com, studying the Dhryn. The one eye she could see was closed. Unconscious—*or pretending to be.* The netting that held him had an artificial look, but she was no expert.

Emily had told her to take that xeno course from Seung.

Mac wasn't a fool. She understood she was experiencing shock, made worse by physical exhaustion. She understood her calm was a brittle coating over emotions she wasn't ready to face. It didn't matter, as long as it let her find Emily.

Then, she'd let herself feel.

Meanwhile, there was the problem posed by the netted Dhryn. Mac examined the threads. They looked sticky as well as moist. Stepping closer at last, she could see that each length had adhered to whatever it touched, puckering his skin into thick, tight creases.

"Explains the moaning," she said to herself. His silks were on the floor, but laid out neatly, as if the Dhryn had been undressed before the attack. It wasn't that his assailants had been tidy. Other than the fabric, the contents of Mac's quarters showed the same disarray as Emily's.

The same trails of slime coated ceiling and walls.

A knock on the door.

"Who is it?" she asked without moving.

"Trojanowski. You sent for me, Dr. Connor. I've been trying to find you—" A pause. "May I come in?"

"Are you alone?"

"Yes." Another pause. "What's that noise?"

"The Honorable Delegate."

His voice lowered a notch. "What's going on, Dr. Connor? Let me in."

Mac crossed her arms and stood beside the hanging Dhryn to wait.

Seconds later, her locked door opened. Trojanowski took a quick step in, then another to one side, slapping the door closed behind him. "Practiced that, have you?" Mac commented, noticing he was back to his student garb: T-shirt and jeans, complete with glasses. *The so-harmless look didn't play well anymore.*

"What the—?" His expression went from shocked to guarded. "Is he conscious?"

"I don't know." The "I don't care" was in her tone.

"Have you tried to find out?"

"I don't know anything about alien physiology, remember? I called you."

He took what looked like a pen from his pocket and used it to poke one of the threads holding Brymn.

"What's that?" Mac asked. "A weapon?"

"It's a pen."

"Oh." She wasn't sure why she was surprised. *Too many old movies with Em.*

His lips quirked to one side. "This," he pulled a black flattened disk from the same pocket, "is a weapon." It disappeared against the palm of his left hand. Then he raised that hand and pointed two fingers at the ceiling, where the threads combined into the holdfast.

A narrow beam of intense blue shot up. Where it touched the threads, they shriveled and broke apart, to become bits of soot drifting through the air. Trojanowski played the beam over the massive knot, flaking away more and more until Brymn's body shifted downward a few centimeters.

He stopped and put away the weapon. "He's going to fall. Help me put the mattress under him."

"That's my bed," Mac protested, although she moved to help. "Was my bed," she amended. It looked as though someone had attempted to shred the surface of the mattress, then glue it back together with slime.

They flipped it over before dragging it under the Dhryn. It was the work of seconds for Trojanowski to cut him down completely. *He fell like a salmon*, Mac decided, *limp but firm.*

Once Brymn was down, Trojanowski used his strange weapon to singe the ends of the threads wrapped around the being, careful not to ignite the mattress itself. Mac stood back and watched, her arms wrapped around her middle. She didn't remember breakfast. She thought she'd gulped something handed to her while she'd been at her desk. Her stomach wasn't happy about it.

Ungrateful organ.

Each singed thread continued to flake away along its entire length, as if losing some inner cohesion. Where they'd adhered to Brymn, the small dark pits of his skin oozed a clear liquid, presumably the source of an almost palpable odor, musklike and with a hint of sulfur, that began to fill the room. Mac took tiny breaths through her nose. *She'd smelled and seen worse.* Walking on bloated salmon corpses in July came to mind. No matter how carefully you put your feet, one would always pop.

"Good thing you checked on him," Trojanowski said, continuing to work. He'd been watching her, too. She'd seen his eyes slip her way every few seconds, their expression inscrutable. "I might not have for another hour or so—might have been too late."

"I wanted—how long until he wakes up? Until he can answer questions?"

The last thread fell away. "No idea. Is there any clean bedding? A blanket?"

Mac pointed to a cupboard. Trojanowski rummaged inside and returned with a sheet, which he laid over Brymn with care.

Then, he looked at her. "I'm sorry about your friend, Dr. Mamani." His eyes were presently more hazel than green, lending them an unexpected softness. Mac doubted she could look away of her own volition. She also doubted she could so much as flex her fingers without throwing up.

She managed to force words through her tight lips. "What are you doing to find her?"

Mac had the impression he was taken aback by the question. "The police will do all they can," he said after that almost imagined hesitation.

"You brought *him* here," she managed to say. "That—thing—followed. This is your fault. You have to find Emily." Tears welled up in her eyes. *She hated tears.* "You should have been protecting us—not—not—"

"Dr. Connor, you should be lying down. Wait." Trojanowski shut up and dropped to his knees beside the Dhryn. "Listen," he urged, waving her closer with one hand.

Mac copied his position, finding it all too easy to answer to gravity. *He was right.* The moaning had changed. She leaned forward, wary of her body's wobble.

The alien was muttering one word, over and over again.

"*Nai . . . Nai . . . Nai . . . Nai . . .* "

"Nothing . . . Nothing . . ." Trojanowski translated under his breath.

Oddly enough, that was the last thing Mac heard before Brymn's midsection rose from the mattress to smack her in the face.

"I don't bloody well care who you are, mate. You can't come in here like—"

From the thickening of his Aussie accent, the nurse, Dan Mandeville, was ready to do battle. Considering he stood slightly over two meters and was built, in Em's terms, like an antique forklift, that couldn't be a good thing. Mac's eyelids felt glued shut, but she found her voice somehow. "It's okay, Mandy. I'm awake."

"Then only for a moment. The woman needs rest!" A door closed with sufficient force to vibrate through the floor.

Her arm felt strangely heavy. Somehow, Mac brought her hand to her face, and scrubbed her eyelids until they cracked open. "What happened?" she asked, less than surprised to find herself flat on her back in what passed for a hospital room on Base.

Trojanowski pulled over a stool and sat beside her bed. "You passed out on me. They brought you here."

Wonderful. Mac tried to rise to her elbows, but the room tilted in the oddest way so she dropped back down. "Emily?" she demanded.

He shook his head.

"How long?"

"They've finished serving breakfast—not that anyone here seems to have much appetite."

She'd returned midday of what was now yesterday. *Nothing she could do about time already wasted.* Mac assessed herself, finding a musty taste at the back of her mouth. She remembered it from some minor surgery a couple of years ago. Mandy must have given her a sedative. *Hopefully, it was wearing off by now.*

Mac rolled on her side and swung her legs over the bed, using the momentum to pull herself upright. She hung on to the mattress with both hands, waiting patiently for the universe to finish sloshing back and forth. It helped to focus on her visitor.

There were dark smudges under Trojanowski's eyes and a grim set to his mouth. The plain black T-shirt and jeans he wore glistened in streaks. Slime from the rooms. *So he hadn't slept yet.* "Brymn?" she asked, resisting a certain amount of remorse. "Is he all right?"

"I don't know." Trojanowski gave a half shrug, clearly frustrated. "The experts at the Consulate were no help. Said to leave him alone until he recovered. They did offer to pick up his body, if he dies."

"'A Dhryn is robust, or a Dhryn is not,'" Mac quoted. At his questioning look, she shrugged. "Something Brymn told me."

"This Dhryn better survive." He studied her. "What about you? You look awful."

"I'll do," Mac answered curtly.

"Good. Because I have some questions."

"About last night?"

"No. Dr. Mamani."

Even behind the glasses, there was something in his eyes that made her swallow, a distancing, as if he felt the need to somehow protect himself—or was it her?

Mac shifted on the bed, then realized part of her discomfort was an IV wrap around her upper arm. She ripped it free, in case the device was delivering more sedative.

Why was her arm bare?

Mac stared down at herself. Bad enough her legs and feet, swinging freely above the floor, were bare, too, her toes and ankles decorated with lovely red blotches from her boots. *But this?*

Someone had dressed her in an orange, knee-length flannel nightgown, trimmed with purple lace and covered in vivid yellow spots. Spots with eyeballs and tiny, pointy teeth.

Where was dignity when you needed it?

"This is not mine," Mac assured Trojanowski, determined to straighten at least that much out. She knew better than to check her hair.

The corner of his mouth deepened, producing a dimple in one cheek. *Emily would probably notice something like that.* Mac's eyes started to fill and she blinked fiercely. "Ask your questions."

"Could Dr. Mamani have followed you that night?" he asked, his voice carefully neutral. "Become lost?"

Mac felt a thrill of hope. *Em lost in the woods would be an irritable, grumpy, miserable Em, but a living one.* Then she thought it through, and shook her head. "It was pitch-black around the pods. Even if she'd somehow seen me heading for shore, the gate wasn't working. Anyway, Em—Dr. Mamani—is a techhead. She'd have gone straight to the main power node to see what was wrong before looking for me."

He pressed his lips together, then nodded as if she'd confirmed his own conclusions. "A slim chance, at best. I had the police run scans for her genetic markers on the bridge and up the slope a considerable distance. Nothing."

Mac ignored the implications of the police doing what he asked, too dumbfounded by the concept of teams of non-Base personnel romping at will through the Wilderness Trust. "The Oversight Committee—" she began.

Trojanowski's face had a way of becoming still that sent a small shiver down her spine. "The Committee has no objections to any investigation we choose to conduct," he finished in a voice that left no doubt at all in Mac's mind about objections made and summarily squashed. She felt mildly envious. "In fact, this entire inlet—land, sea, air, and orbit—is now under the direct jurisdiction of the Ministry of Extra-Sol Human Affairs, although we'd prefer not to share that with the media. You can understand."

"I don't need to understand, as long as it means you are hunting for Emily."

"Oh, we're doing that."

His statement should have been reassuring. Mac wasn't sure why she abruptly didn't feel reassured at all. She narrowed her eyes. "What—who was in my office, Mr. Trojanowski? Who took Emily?" Despite her effort to remain calm, her voice failed her after: "Why—?"

A glint from his glasses. "Why did they take her and not you?"

It was the right question. The one she'd been asking herself over and over again since learning Emily was gone. Mac loosened her clenched hands and made her fingers toy with the purple lace crossing her thighs. "If you're asking me an opinion," she answered slowly, "I have none. I threw a sandal at it."

Trojanowski's eyebrows lifted. "Hardly a deterrent."

"It worked," she pointed out the obvious. "The thing ran out the door. It ran from me all the way to its ship."

"Dr. Connor—"

Shivering at the memory, Mac drew one leg up under the other and pulled the blanket around her shoulders. "I prefer Mac."

"Mac." Trojanowski didn't smile. He took off his glasses—which Mac doubted served any useful function beyond camouflage—and leaned forward, elbows on his knees. "I don't know what you've been told about the condition of her quarters, but Dr. Mamani—Emily—must have put up a significant struggle. We found her blood—" Mac had no idea what suddenly showed on her face, but Trojanowski shifted in mid-sentence. "Trust me. If they'd been after you, you'd be missing, too."

Mac stared at her feet. Red and sore, but no real blisters. There were the inevitable pine bits between her toes. Socks seemed irrelevant. With her luck, whoever had undressed her would forget to pull both socks and liners from her boots. *They'd take days to dry.*

"We can do this later." A reluctant compassion.

She raised her eyes to his. "No need. I'm worried about my friend and I'm angry. Neither affect my ability to participate in whatever will help find her— and those who took her. Please continue, Mr. Trojanowski."

"As you wish." He straightened, replaced his glasses on his nose, and took out a disappointingly ordinary imp which he made a point of consulting.

"I'm okay," Mac insisted.

He peered at her over his glasses, a curl of brown hair sliding down over one eyebrow. An artfully harmless look Mac didn't believe for an instant. "What do you know of Emily's life outside her work?"

Startled, Mac began to frown. "I don't see the relevance—"

"Please just answer the question." He passed her a bottle of water from the side table.

Emily's life outside of work? Mac opened the bottle and took a long drink, then another. "If you mean her life on Base," she answered warily, "the usual. During the research season, we're either at a field camp or here. Emily—" *Might as well be honest,* she told herself bitterly, *he probably has it all in some damned dossier . . . Emily's wealth of lovers, her own solitary years.* "Emily tends to be more social than I—" Her blush made the burn along her cheek throb and Mac ended with a lame: "You'd have to ask around."

He didn't seem to notice her embarrassment. *That didn't mean he hadn't,* Mac thought. "What about off-season, when she's not here with you?"

"She makes time for her—family." Mac knew if she said "sister," she'd hear Maria's voice again, those horrid flat tones reciting a number for the office, another for her friend, a litany of ways Mac could reach her at any time with news. *Would call her, as if the numbers were like magic, drawing answers from the air.* Mac coughed to clear her throat. "Em heads out to the Sargasso Sea for a month or two to work on her Tracer. It's a remote biosensor—do you want details?"

"I've been briefed. It's impressive technology, but not the concern at the moment."

"What is?"

His eyes were hooded. "Just keep going, please, Mac. What else does Emily do? Does she take vacations? Travel?"

Mac didn't bother arguing that hopping between the north Pacific to the south Atlantic twice a year was traveling, since he apparently didn't think so. "She mentioned shopping in Paris. A visit to Pietermaritzberg. That's near the southern tip of—"

"I know where it is. Did Emily tell you about going anywhere else? Even a hint? Think, Mac. This could be important."

"Nowhere else." Mac's left foot was asleep under her right thigh, and she was feeling a somewhat inconvenient desire to visit the washroom. Nonetheless, she narrowed her eyes at her questioner. "You were asking her about traveling. You know something," she accused. "What aren't you telling me?"

"Thank you for your time, Dr. Connor." Trojanowski stood, a fluid motion that belied the weariness on his face. *He doesn't move like that in public,* Mac thought, wondering what else the man was trained to hide. "I'm expecting the audio reconstructionist shortly after lunch. We'll resume our conversation then." As if they were finished, he headed for the door.

Not again, Mac vowed to herself. "This isn't the top of a mountain," she snapped. "I'll decide when we're done, Mr. Trojanowski—if that's even your real name." Mac jumped off the bed with every intention of following him out that door if he dared open it, obnoxious orange nightie or not.

Well, that's what she'd planned to do, but to Mac's chagrin, her legs crumpled beneath her. As if he had eyes in the back of his head, Trojanowski spun around with disturbing grace, reaching out to steady her before she could fall.

For a moment, they stood face-to-face, his fingers wrapped securely around her elbows, his forearms like warm, sturdy rails under hers, supporting a considerable amount of her weight. His breath stung the burn on her cheek as his eyes searched hers. *For what?* Mac wondered, suddenly more perplexed than angry.

Then, as if impelled by something he saw, the man she'd once thought nothing more than a messenger said in a low and urgent voice: "Mac, listen to me. Listen carefully. The best thing you can do right now is be yourself. Be the reclusive scientist. Be the private, careful person who doesn't let anyone close. Anyone." His fingers tightened with the word. "The only reason you're here and you're safe is because you weren't in your quarters last night. Do you understand me? They found poor Brymn—but I believe they came for you."

"For me? Why?" Involuntarily, Mac's hands closed on his arms, not for comfort, but to hold him there, to demand more answers. "What about the intruder in my office?"

"I wish I knew." Trojanowski hesitated, then went on: "My guess is that one of them was to search your office and he, she, it was to run if discovered. You were lucky."

"Emily wasn't." Mac stared at him, aghast. "Brymn wasn't. I must go and see him—"

"He's being monitored. Meanwhile, you," the spy said sternly, "will stay here." Before Mac could protest, he used his grip on her arms to heft her up on the bed and sit her there. "Get some rest. I don't want that rugby player you call a nurse chasing me down the hall."

As the room was elongating on two axes, Mac didn't even attempt to nod. "You'll call me when your audio expert arrives, Mr. Trojanowski," she told him firmly.

He looked back at her, his hand on the doorplate. "It is my real name," he said, without smiling. "But I prefer Nik."

Then he was gone.

Mac lay back, legs dangling over the side of the bed, her head spinning far too much for safe passage anywhere but horizontal. *He'd been briefed on more than Emily's Tracer.* She'd rarely heard a more precise summary of her life.

Her fingertips followed the lingering heat from his skin along the underside of her arms. *Nik, was it?* Did "Nik" think she'd missed his implications? Of course not. Mac doubted a single word came out of that man he didn't fully intend to say. So there was something she didn't know and he did about where Emily had been, something connected to invisible aliens and Brymn's being here, something that meant she, Mac, wasn't to become close to anyone. She was to keep up her guard.

Good advice, regardless of its source. "Against you, too, Mr. Nik," she muttered, sitting up more cautiously this time. The local representative of the Ministry of Extra-Sol Human Affairs might have access to a dossier of her work, life, and likely even a psych profile. *He didn't know her.*

Not if he thought he could put her aside.

Mac achieved vertical with no more than a momentary wobble. "Must thank our Mandy for whatever he pumped into me," she told the room. Not that there'd been anything wrong with her body a few calories and some sleep hadn't cured.

As for her mind and heart, well, her dossier should have warned Trojanowski that Dr. Mackenzie Connor was a person of action, not mood. Worrying about Emily meant finding Emily. Finding Emily meant getting to her feet and back into the game.

Now.

- Portent -

ISHT HAD hidden.

It was *isht*'s only duty, to scramble into the smallest, darkest place *isht* could find. Quickly. Without hesitation. Without thought.

That place should have been the one of soft warmth, the one filled with the rhythmic rush of sound, moist with the sweet satisfying taste of *aisht* or perhaps the bitter tang that meant *isht* had mistakenly climbed into *oeisht*. Any *oeisht* would have forgiven *isht,* would have willingly provided shelter.

Isht shivered in *isht*'s hiding place, hearing nothing, tasting dust.

Time passed, unmarked by light. *Isht* vibrated *isht*'s distress, unfelt by *aisht* or *oeisht*.

Isht's thoughts couldn't form abstracts such as hope or despair. There was only the duty to hide, the need to breathe and seek nourishment, the urgency of survival. Slowly but inevitably, survival warred with duty.

Isht couldn't stay here and live.

The moment came when, trembling, *isht* climbed upward, one clawhold at a time. *Isht* reached the slit through which *isht* had first passed into the place and stopped to listen. Nothing.

The slit led sharply downward, a twist *isht*'s narrow form negotiated with ease. Then, *isht* was outside the place, clinging with all its might, looking for help.

Isht was accustomed to climbing from *aisht* to find *ishtself* in a new and amazing world. This was different.

Isht vibrated with fear.

The world wasn't new; it was gone. *Isht* clung, its grip the only safety.

What had been *isht*'s home was now a skeleton of metal and glass.

What had been a farm was now an ocean reaching in every direction *isht* could see. It filled *isht*'s home, lapping at the column of *isht*'s hiding place like a tongue seeking *isht*'s taste.

A shadow sent *isht* scrambling into the smallest, darkest place *isht* could find.

Isht heard the mouths begin to drink.

9

MEETINGS AND MISCHIEF

M AC GRASPED the terrace rail and leaned back, turning her face to the sun as if she were a flower. It prickled the mem-skin covering her burned cheek and seared bright dots beneath her closed eyelids. She hadn't expected a gift like this, one of those unabashedly perfect days, where the sky was saturated with blue and the breezes, full of cedar and salt, slipped over skin and hair like a warm caress.

It would do them all good. Mac pulled herself upright to look down at the walkways filled with students and their gear. Several teams were loading their skims; others were loafing on towels, waiting their turn. Business as usual in the latter half of the research season.

Or not. On her way to meet with Kammie, having delayed only to exchange the obnoxious nightie for clothing that was actually hers for a change, Mac had quietly asked Tie to head up to Field Station Six with a couple of volunteers to dismantle her and Emily's equipment. It would be brought back and stored for use next year.

She couldn't bear to think otherwise.

Now, Mac headed left along the terrace, the long way around, since the section outside her office was still off limits.

Dr. Kammie Noyo's office and lab was on the opposite side of the pod from hers, affording a stunning view past the tip of the inlet to the open ocean. Not that you could see it from inside. Rumor in the student pods was that the venerable chemist had opaqued her window wall because she was afraid of water.

Mac knocked perfunctorily on the door, propped open to the sunshine with an earthenware pot containing a surprised cactus, and walked inside.

Rumor, as usual, was untrustworthy. *Afraid of water?* Mac shook her head at the notion. Kammie Noyo was a deepwater sailor and had picked this very office for its view. Unfortunately, all that was left of the view was through her open door. She'd covered her walls with shelves to hold her growing collection of soil samples, adamantly refusing to move so much as a single precious vial out of her sight. "You never knew when you'd need one to compare," she'd say in her cheerful voice, hands shoved into her brilliant white lab coat. The window wall? Permanently opaqued simply to protect the samples from daylight.

Mac let her eyes adjust to the interior lighting, then followed voices through the empty office to the lab to find Kammie, hands in her lab coat, holding court with her latest crop of postdocs. They were a matched set: three gangly young-sters who had faith the pale fuzz on their chins would be worthy beards by the end of the research season and their theses would change the world. Months working with Kammie, whose head barely topped Mac's ear, had given them a distinctly stooped posture. Kammie professed herself pleased with their individ-uality and brilliance. Mac still couldn't tell them apart, but she trusted Kammie's judgment.

She needed it more than ever now.

Quite sure Kammie had seen her—the woman's peripheral vision was leg-endary—Mac waved to show she could wait, then went back into the office. She punched her codes into Kammie's desk interface to bring up her own main workscreen, directly linked to Norcoast's, then found a chair with fewer period-icals than usual, and sat carefully on top. Everyone at Base, starting with the cleaning staff, knew better than to mess with Dr. Noyo's furniture-based filing system.

Mac leveled her bottom with a careful wiggle, grumbling automatically over the chemist's continued fondness for paper, then tapped the air where her work-screen had decided to float. She brought out her imp and initialized its personal 'screen—smaller, self-contained, and able to reference only data carried within the imp itself. Layering one over the other, Mac got to work.

Kammie bustled in half an hour later. "Sorry to keep you waiting, Mac," she apologized cheerily in her soft, high-pitched voice. "The boys had an interesting problem." She stretched to tuck a small aluminum vial box back into its place on a shelf behind her desk, then, as if struck by a thought, she stayed there, tracing the labels of its neighbors with her fingers.

"You okay?" Mac asked, glancing up through her 'screens. Unlike yesterday, when she'd been so distraught in the hall of Pod Three, the other woman ap-peared back to normal, hair smoothly coiffed, round face wearing the patented half smile that Kammie joked she'd inherited from a wise grandfather.

"I'm supposed to be asking you that, aren't I?" Smile fading, Kammie turned and sank into her chair. Whatever she'd left on it raised her to just the right height for her desk. Her almond-shaped eyes were troubled as she called up her own 'screen in preparation for their briefing. "I'm worried about my students. Is it wrong to send them back to work so soon?"

"Look at us." Mac poked a finger through her 'screen. "I'd say it's the only productive thing we can do, Kammie. And Em—you know she'd be the first person to take our heads off for moping around."

The chemist looked wistful. "No argument there. So. What can I do for you, Mac?"

"This." With a slide of her hand through the air, Mac sent her Admin codes, schedules, everything she had pending on Base to Kammie's 'screen. "I want you to take over for me, Kammie. Indefinitely."

"You're kidding. I'm in the middle of—"

"I'm very serious, Kammie. I need you to look after all the admin, not just your half."

Kammie Noyo leaned back in her chair, studying Mac over her steepled fingers. "No offense, dear lady, but didn't you just say work was the only productive thing we can do? I don't see you, of any of us, taking a break right now." Kammie's delicate eyebrows met. "Which means you're up to something. What?"

Mac almost smiled. She'd never joined Kammie's seafaring adventures or visited her extensive family; she was well aware that Kammie, for her part, considered Mac an eccentric workaholic who must be reminded at regular intervals that others had real lives. But when it came to what mattered, each knew the other very well indeed. "I was a witness."

Kammie's eyes widened. "Your office?" she breathed, moving forward again. "You were there? But—"

"I chased one of them out of it. Don't give me that look, Kammie Noyo. It seemed perfectly safe at the time. And turned out to be, except for some sore muscles. As a result, while I don't know how much help I can be to the— investigation," Mac had trouble with the word. "There's no doubt I'm going to be called away from my duties. In fact, I may be asked to leave Base without notice. We've been disrupted enough. I won't let my absence jeopardize anyone's work. I won't have the entire season lost."

Norcoast had never lost a season, although it had been a near thing the year of the "almost perfect" storm. Mac watched Kammie remember it. How could she not? To anyone who'd been there, it had seemed like the end of the world.

The storm had slid toward them from the southwest, a late October mass of subtropical moisture and wind the weather controllers had decided to leave alone. The tides would be unusually high, but the storm track was northward, so the predicted surge was minimal. Such storms had immense natural value, stirring the depths of the ocean to bring up nutrients, and flushing rivers as it drove up the coast. Coastal communities had been warned to prepare for several days of heavy rain and strong sustained winds. Many had viewed the chance to experience a major storm as a rare adventure. It was dubbed the "almost perfect" storm by those who didn't know better.

Some at Norcoast had been eager to document the storm's impact on marine life. Mac had viewed it as a major inconvenience. She'd been working on her postdoc, lingering at Base through the fall months to help ready the pods for the winter, store samples and data, and generally earn her keep while waiting for her next projects to be approved. But nothing was going to get done outdoors until the storm passed through.

It was more than inconvenient. The first day, 15 centimeters of rain fell, carried on winds that hit 100 kilometers per hour. Weather controllers admitted they'd let a hurricane slip through their net and began remedial efforts. Too little, too late. The second day, gusts reached 289 kilometers per hour, blowing down trees like sticks in sand, and another 30 centimeters of rain landed on the coast. The third day 20 centimeters fell . . . The fourth . . .

There was no need to pack up the pods for winter. The original four that had made up Norcoast's Base had been nestled against the mainland at the mouth of the Tannu, protected by surrounding islands from wave action, but directly in the path of both landslide and flood.

Students, staff, and scientists had huddled together on transport levs to watch the pods tip and sink within a thick soup of snapped trees, gravel, mud, rock, and water. Then they'd gone to work. It hadn't mattered what your credentials or research plans that winter. Everyone had pitched in to ensure the first replacement pod was constructed and anchored—in a new, safer location—in time for the spring salmon runs. They'd succeeded. In Mac's estimation, that winter's catchall phrase had come to define Norcoast: "we'll get it done."

The new pods in their new location had weathered far worse since without incident. *It remained to be seen,* Mac thought, *if its people continued to have that kind of determination.*

Mac waited anxiously as Kammie, never one to make a snap decision, scrolled through the data on her 'screen without changing her expression from that slight frown. With her in charge, the others should be able to continue. Mac didn't have students of her own this summer, other than a shared project with John Ward. Kammie could stand in her place as his adviser, if need be. "Well?" she asked finally.

The frown was replaced by a somewhat surprised look. "Of course, Mac. I was only checking who from Wet could assist with your stuff. John looks available."

Mac and Kammie split the administrative duties of Base along practical lines: dry versus wet. Dry included those researchers who worked on land, but also those who conducted aerial surveys, retrieved remote sensing data, or worked primarily in the labs at Base. Kammie's highly technical criterion was that her people never had wet socks. Wet was thus everyone else, and Mac's responsibility.

"He can be," Mac admitted with an inner wince, although Kammie was right. The bulk of Ward's analysis work could be left for the coming winter. *His reaction, though?* she grimaced. Mac knew he'd arranged classes at Berkeley, in California, but this would mean he'd have to stay on Base another six months. *Surfing, skiing. Both sports where you rode on something flat, right?* Mac keyed the message to John Ward's workscreen before she could change her mind. "Anything else?"

"Why does that sound final? I will be able to contact you—I won't," Kammie corrected herself as Mac shook her head. "Well." She sat a little straighter. "In that case, I'll go under the premise you'll approve anything I decide."

"Within the operating budget," Mac cautioned, but with distinct relief. She hadn't felt the weight of keeping up with the concerns of Base and its researchers until this moment, when it was no longer hers to carry. "I'll do my best to keep you informed, Kammie. I—I never wanted to dump all this on you."

Kammie made a rude noise. "Tell me that next spring when you fly off to a field station and leave me to settle the new arrivals."

With a chuckle, Mac got to her feet. "There's one more thing." She put away her imp, 'screens winking from sight, and drew out a vial, identical to any of the thousands in the boxes lining the walls around her.

Kammie rose and came around her desk, hand reaching out as if the tiny thing were a magnet. "What's this?"

As much truth as she dared, Mac thought. "There may be something unique about this soil," she said. The idea that such secrecy could be for Kammie's protection didn't help. "I'd like to know what you think of it. Between us for the time being, please."

From the speed with which the tiny chemist withdrew her fingers, Mac might have offered her poison. "Oh, no, you don't. If this is something that could help find Emily, it should go to the forensics—"

"No. No. Nothing like that," Mac insisted. *Did lying become easier with practice?* She could ask "Nik" Trojanowski, doubtless an expert. "It's something I've been carrying around in my pocket for you." *All too easy to sound frustrated.* "I'd like to know at least something of my work is getting done."

Kammie's transparent features eased from skeptical to sympathetic. She took the vial. "Not a problem, Mac. Sorry I jumped on you. You leave this with me. I'll get on it right away." A smile. "Well, after I deal with the 'A for At Once' on the list you dumped on me. What kind of category name is that anyway?"

"I thought it was more tactful than 'A for Annoying.'"

A laugh that made Kammie wipe her eyes. "Oh, dear. I suppose there're more gems waiting in here. Thanks a lot, Mac."

Mac rested her hand on the other woman's shoulder and squeezed gently. "Thank you, Kammie."

Kammie's fingers, callused and warm, captured hers. "They'll find her, Mac," she promised, eyes brimming with tears that now had nothing to do with laughter. "And she'll be okay. Emily's smart and she's tougher than any of us. You know she is."

All Mac could do was nod.

During lunch, while a police officer from nearby Kitimat stood at the gallery entrance and politely resisted all attempts by incoming Pred students to inspect his weaponry, Mac sat alone. *Literally.* The gallery's tables were deserted, its few visitors opting for a bag lunch to take outside while the sun still shone.

The privacy was welcome. Mac alternated absentminded bites of her sandwich with glances at the small 'screen hovering over her plate. She'd finished copying what she and Emily had found into her imp, whether about Brymn or his species. Now, as she awaited her summons from Trojanowski, she reviewed the list of everything else she'd grabbed, in case she had to abandon her resources at Base for any length of time.

"Anyone reading this would consider me certifiable," Mac mumbled around a mouthful of fluffy barbequed salmon and bun. One of the distinct advantages to eating in the gallery were the samples brought in by the Harvs; any extras turned up on the grill.

Oh, her list did include reasonable, logical things: summaries of the most recent Chasm research, a simplified spatial geography of the Naralax Transect complete with traveler "must see" suggestions, and a copy of Seung's course materials on xenobiology. Mac could no longer afford the luxury of thinking in Earth-only terms.

Emily'd tried to tell her.

She'd tucked the more eyebrow-raising entries under the heading "Groceries:" reported sightings of Chasm Ghouls; the latest popular theories, scholarly or not, on the existence of the Chasm; a report on the feasibility of invisibility from one of last year's exchange students, inspired by another too-close encounter with grizzlies; occurrences of invisible aliens on Earth—more than Mac had ever dreamed—and, last but not least, Emily Mamani's personal logs.

Mac took a sip of tea, her hands wrapped around the mug to seek its warmth. It had only taken a quick call. Maria had sent Emily's logs without question, although she'd admitted to denying their existence to "those officials who have no right coming to my home, prying into private family business when they should be looking for my sister." Knowing Emily's passionate temper, as quick to fade as it was to flare, Mac guessed Maria had regretted her lack of cooperation the moment the "officials" left. It probably relieved her conscience to send the logs to Mac. Certainly they all believed in doing anything that could help the investigation. . . .

That damn word again. Mac knew why she hated it. You investigated a crime that had already happened, searching for the culprits, not the victim. But she couldn't deny that finding the culprits seemed the only way to find Emily.

The only way Mac accepted, ignoring the fact that search teams were still out, following the tide, scouring the shoreline, and bumping around underneath the pods.

As for the logs? She'd received them directly on her imp, keeping them away from Norcoast's systems. *Now?* Mac flicked a finger through the 'screen to turn it off. She sipped more tea, gazing out the window at the novel spectacle of white-capped mountains cutting into a blue sky, unable to deny what troubled her most. *Was there something in those logs Emily would prefer not be known, even by a friend?*

She'd asked Mac for forgiveness. And now Trojanowski's questions about Emily were like splinters Mac couldn't reach to pull out.

Thinking about him made her impatient as well as uneasy. Mac pushed to her feet, tucked away her imp, and grabbed her lunch tray to take back to the kitchen.

"There you are, Dr. Connor!"

Think of the devil, Mac said to herself. Outwardly, she gave a polite nod, waiting as Trojanowski, again resplendently civil in suit and cravat, came walking toward her. Then Mac saw he was accompanied by a very dark, very round man in an ancient yellow rain suit who began smiling the instant she did.

Mac dropped her tray on the table with a clatter. "Jabulani!" She launched herself into his arms, her hands barely reaching around his sides. Almost as quickly, she pulled back, needing to feast her eyes on one of the dearest, most brilliant, people she knew.

Jabulani Sithole had hardly aged. His tight curls had silvered before they'd met, she remembered fondly. His dark eyes still twinkled. *And the raincoat.* Jabulani had decided long ago the only way to beat the coast weather was to always dress for its worst. Sweat pearled his brow and beaded his generous nose, but Mac knew from experience nothing would pry the heavy coat and sweater from the man if he thought they'd be going outside again soon. "I can't believe you're here."

"You said he could do incredible things with sound," Trojanowski said, standing to one side.

"Did you really?" Jabulani planted a kiss on Mac's forehead. "You were always kind, Mackenzie dear. A treasure."

"Because I kept you in sandwiches," she corrected, with a fond smile, "so you'd let me listen to my salmon."

Jabulani turned to Trojanowski. "Even then, so young, she called them 'hers.' Is it any wonder she's in charge now?" His voice softened and he gazed down at her, wide mouth losing its smile. "Mackenzie, I am so sorry—"

Before the sympathy of her old friend could do more than mist her eyes, Mac patted Jabulani once more to make sure he was real, then said simply: "If anyone can replicate what I heard, Jabulani, it's you." *If she could bear to relive that night with anyone, it was him.* She shot Trojanowski a look of gratitude. "Thank you."

He nodded, once. "If you're ready, Dr. Connor? Dr. Sithole? We should start as soon as possible."

Mac caught Jabulani's longing look at her tray and snorted affectionately. *Some things never changed.* "We can pick up a bag in the kitchen," she assured him.

The audio lab was in Pod Six, relocated there during the sojourn of the lost whale so researchers could interpret the baby's linguistic heritage and find its family; left there because the lab's space had been "mistakenly" reapportioned between its former neighbors in Pod Four almost overnight. The unspoken rule at Base held that a clear bench was a bench ready for a new owner.

Audio hadn't protested. Pod Six was hollow, fixed to the ocean floor year-round, and everything above the waterline was now unofficially theirs. Every year since, new projects had grafted themselves to the interior of the dome wall, supported by whatever means the researchers could afford or create. Despite appearances, to date only one had come loose and fallen into the water, fortunately not harming the students who'd been using that platform for a moment's indiscretion, nor unduly disturbing the otters who'd again found their way inside.

Mac led the way into Pod Six. The access door from the walkway opened on a small platform offering a choice of stairs, one set dropping down to the inner ring that floated directly on the ocean, the other newer and curving up along the wall itself.

She sensed her companions' wonder and stopped obligingly, fond of the place herself. Six was, well, unique.

From the outside, its domelike walls had the same curved, reddish stone appearance as those of the other pods, albeit with no terraces or antennae to foil the illusion. From the inside, it was a bubble of calm floating in the midst of Castle Inlet, any wave that traveled past damped to the hint of a swell. The walls, except for some necessary supports and the audio platforms, were almost transparent. They opaqued under the rare full sun to keep the ambient light level no brighter than that at a depth of ten centimeters underwater outside the dome, save for spot lighting on stairs and platform. This didn't bother the audio researchers. The interior air temperature was matched to an outside standard as well, something they did complain about—particularly when they arrived in early spring to work space close to the freezing point—but to no avail.

The floating inner ring was currently a jumble of diving gear, sample cases, and other gear, a maze busily negotiated by upward of three dozen researchers at any given time. Some waved up at them; most were too busy to notice the new arrivals. This week, Pod Six was temporarily entertaining an entire school of smolts, a combination of young salmon born last year and the year before, their bodies busy adapting to life in salt water. Varied species as well. They couldn't stay in even this huge space for long, some being eager to head to the open ocean, others destined for the mouths of estuaries and the rich feeding there. The race was on to learn as much as possible before the eight great sea doors of the pod opened to release them again.

Abruptly, someone shouted and began running along the ring in pursuit of something sinuous and brown. "I see the otters are still up to their tricks," Jabulani noted with amusement as the student below stopped and threw up her hands in patent disgust.

"Brains enough for trouble," Mac agreed. The boisterous river otters weren't just after the conveniently trapped smolts. They enjoyed chewing on synthrubber fittings and made toys out of anything they could tip into the water. Mac didn't doubt the animals were well aware that inside the pod they were safe from anything but the insincere ire of a few researchers.

"Which way, Dr. Connor?"

Trojanowski shouldn't need to remind her they weren't here to watch otters. Mac flushed and took the stairs up two at a time. "You can use Denise's setup, Jabulani," she said over her shoulder.

"Perfect!" Despite the makeshift construction, Jabulani's weight didn't budge the stairs as he rumbled eagerly behind her. "I hadn't dared hope she was still here, too."

"You kidding? She takes fewer off-Base trips than I do."

"Hold on a minute—"

Mac stopped on the staircase, her head below the first and largest side platform. The ones farther up overhung the water itself, but here the inward curve of the wall was barely detectable. She peered around Jabulani's thick shoulder to meet Trojanowski's gathering scowl. "Dr. Pillsworthy has the equipment," she informed him, understanding immediately. "And she can help."

"Dr. Pillsworthy does not have clearance—"

"Fine." Mac shrugged and waved the two men back down the stairs. "We'll have to leave Base, then."

"Dr. Connor—" Trojanowski didn't budge. "We must make the recording as soon as possible."

"And I can guarantee you we won't be allowed anywhere near her equipment unless Denise stays, clearance or not. She won't let a soul, not me, not even Jabulani here, use it without her present."

"Is there anyone here who—? No, forget I asked." The patently exasperated Trojanowski actually ran one hand over his face before using it to gesture that she should continue climbing to the platform. "Lead on."

Mac hid her smile by turning obediently to face the platform.

A few steps later, they crowded together on what was no more or less than an extension tacked onto the existing staircase. The extension itself hung out over the water to form the floor for what looked like, and was, a converted t-lev cargo compartment now bolted to the wall. Someone had painted "aUDiOcel-lAR" on the dingy gray door.

"Nice touch," Jabulani noted, pointing to a painted window filled with a cluster of desperate faces trapped behind what appeared to be hockey sticks.

"We ran out of beer in the play-offs two years ago," Mac explained. She pressed her hand on the doorplate to request entry. No use calling ahead to Denise; the audiophile detested the existing com and refused to use it, relying on runners or insisting on in-person visits. Mac had, in her first year as coadministrator, asked Denise to submit a budget proposal for the ideal system. Since that moment of weakness, Mac had agreed Pod Six wasn't too far to walk. Nor was a little company too much for someone as dedicated to her lab as Denise was to ask.

Not that Denise Pillsworthy was a gracious host, Mac grinned to herself as a strident "Who is it?" came through the wall.

To let Jabulani go first, Mac squeezed against Trojanowski. "Trust me," she hissed, when he would have argued.

"One guess, Sweet Thing!" Jabulani shouted.

The door opened immediately. "It can't be—"

"Me!"

"Jabby!"

Jabulani disappeared inside the audio lab as if inhaled by a whale. Mac followed, Trojanowski right on her heels, to find the older man sitting on a stool, cradling a cooing Denise Pillsworthy in his ample lap, yellow raincoat and all.

Denise stopped cooing only long enough to toss out: "Hi, Mac! Who's that?" before continuing to pepper Jabulani's chubby cheeks with kisses.

"Dr. Connor." From behind, low and amused. "Is everyone who works here so—so—"

"Close?" Mac suggested. *He might be amused, but she wasn't.* "You form friendships for life working in a place like Norcoast—or enemies," she added, being honest.

Quieter still. "I'm not your enemy, Mac."

"I didn't say you were. That doesn't make us friends," she replied evenly. Before he could continue whispering, Mac raised her voice to carry over the giggles. "Save it for later, okay? We don't have time to spare."

Jabulani's head lifted. "Ah, Little Mackenzie is right, Sweet Thing. We have some reconstructions to record—to help find your missing friend."

Denise surged to her feet, poking at her hair. "You could have told me," she grumbled. "Honestly, Jabby, you never get to the point. We're on it, Mac. What do you need, Jabby?"

As the two audiophiles began to talk a language all their own, Mac leaned on the nearest bit of equipment that wasn't blinking madly to itself. The lab was lined with cases and wires, the technology an eclectic mix of old and new— much like its operator. Denise, gray-haired and bone-thin, wore a sleeveless, eye-piercing pink sweater over a brown woven skirt of indeterminate hemline, but three pairs of state-of-the-art headsets swung around her long neck and her ears were studded with implants. Her pale blue eyes were almost buried beneath lids colored to match her sweater, but her hands were those of a concert pianist, long-fingered and strong, callused by years of slipping over guitar strings and old-fashioned wire.

Trojanowski had his own preparations to make. While Denise and Jabulani assembled equipment, he closed and locked the lab door, then came over to lean beside Mac. "Where were you when you first heard your visitor?" Before she could say anything, he brought out an imp and sent its 'screen to hover in front of her face. "Show me."

Mac found herself staring into a view of her office, generated as if taken from above, in daylight. It hadn't been searched—it had been destroyed. Her garden was a pile of vegetation, dirt, and broken barrels. The stones had been pried from her floor. The salmon models were heaped in a corner, most broken.

Nothing was untouched.

The forensics team. Trojanowski. *Or both.* She realized numbly they must have been hunting for clues to her intruder. Everything still glistened with slime, as if the material had hardened into a permanent coating. *Had they found anything else?*

She must have uttered a protest, for the image winked out of existence. "I'm sorry, Mac," she heard Trojanowski say. "I didn't think of how it would look. I should have warned you—"

"It's only a room," she replied coolly. "Show me again." When the image reappeared, Mac swallowed and ignored everything but the task at hand. She put her finger on the mattress in front of her desk. "Here. The first time." Trojanowski reached over to lock the display. "I was out on the terrace the second time." He provided that image. Mac showed where she'd stood, then: "The walkway to the shore, the mem-wood section—and in front of the gate."

He locked in her locations for each, then nodded. "I have the time of the power shutdown, of course, but do you know when you first woke up and heard it?"

"Not much before dawn," Mac guessed. "The fog was starting to condense in the trees, but there wasn't any light on the horizon that I could see. The mountains, clouds," she shook her head apologetically. "It's hard to say. But only minutes passed before there were people moving about—lanterns going up near Pod Three behind me."

"Shortly after five, then," he said, giving a small, tight smile at her look. "The police did extensive interviews and we've cross-referenced every statement. The only time line I didn't have was yours." The 'screen reoriented itself in front of Trojanowski and he stroked through it several times. "Dr. Sithole will incorporate the appropriate environmental parameters into his reconstructions."

"You've worked with him before," Mac guessed.

His eyes sought the other man. Mac couldn't read their expression. "No, but I'm familiar with the process." Trojanowski looked down at her again and said quietly: "They won't need to know anything about the creature's—appearance— or its actions, just how it sounds, so please watch what you say."

"Or you'll have to lock us all up?"

"Hopefully not."

"I was joking," Mac protested.

His lips quirked, but all Trojanowski said was: "It might be a while yet. Keep your mind busy while you wait."

"No problem." Mac pulled out her imp and headed for the nearest stool. "I brought plenty to read."

Mac made it through five of Brymn's publications before Jabulani called them to the studio at the far end of the lab, learning little more than a respect for the Dhryn's grasp of nonlinear analysis. Trying to follow his reasoning for the dating of certain Chasm artifacts had taken her mind completely off what they were trying to do.

Standing in front of the cubicle where she was supposed to re-create the sounds of the alien, however, Mac began to wonder if she hadn't made a mistake not trying to remember the sounds beforehand. "I didn't hear speech," she told them doubtfully.

"You can't know that," Denise said firmly, pulling a headset over her ears. "There was a time people didn't believe orcas had local dialects."

"Any information might help," Trojanowski added, coming to stand beside her. "Do your best. That's all."

Jabulani smiled confidently and waved her inside. "Easy as can be, Little Mackenzie. You give me a starting point—whatever you can recall," he said as Mac stepped into the small soundproofed room in the back corner of the lab. "I'll echo it back. Each time I do, you tell me how to make what you hear now more like what you heard then. Ask me anything and I can do it. I am a genius," he added with a sly wink.

She couldn't argue with him there. Mac took the only seat, a built-in bench. Two strides in any direction and she'd bump into a padded wall. When Jabulani closed the door, it blended into wall as well. Before she could react to the closeness of the space, his rich voice filled it. "We're ready to start. Your first sound, Mackenzie."

"Give me a minute," she asked.

How to start? Experimentally, she scratched her fingernails on the bench surface. *Definitely* not *that sound.* Mac tried sitting absolutely still, only to have her ears fill with the pounding of her heart, the air through her lungs. After a few seconds, she was convinced she could hear her stomach digesting the salmon sandwich.

She couldn't "hear" anything else. "It's too quiet," she complained, feeling foolish.

"Understood. Stand by."

Five slow breaths later, Mac abruptly realized she could hear the ocean under the pod supports. *Tide moving through,* she judged, finding that odd for the middle of the afternoon until she caught on to the trick. "Clever," she complimented Jabulani, who must have checked the charts for conditions that night.

"A genius, am I. Keep listening."

The ocean faded into background, in part because Mac was so accustomed to the sound in her life that she herself tuned it out. Overlaying it came the babble of water over stone, with a touch of wind through drying leaves. *Her garden.* He even replicated the clink of her suspended salmon touching one another as they swayed in their hangers.

"Try lying down." Trojanowski's voice. "The way you were when the sound woke you in your office."

True, the floor space wasn't much larger than her mattress had been. Mac laid down, then, remembering, rolled on her back. "Turn out the lights, please."

Darkness pressed against her face. She drew it into her lungs, imagining the scents of her office. "The power was off when I woke up."

The water and wind from her garden died away. Only the lapping of the ocean and the occasional snick of salmon to salmon remained.

Mac concentrated. *Where to start?* "Rain on a skim cover," she suggested.

The room filled with an irregular drumming on metal and plastic.

"Softer." It quieted. "Only from the upper left of the room—and sharper, crisper."

Not bad, Mac thought, listening to the result.

"Now, short little bursts, not continuous." Jabulani obliged. "Vary the— the—" she hunted for a word and growled to herself.

"Pardon?"

"Sorry. I don't know how to describe it. It was as if the thing moved across different surfaces, so the noise changed in small segments, but very quickly."

This time, a sequence of sounds played through. Mac shook her head, although they couldn't have seen her in the dark even if there had been a window. "Stop!"

She listened to the silence and the echo came back through her memory. "Not rain. Ice pellets. Sleet."

The modified sound played again. *Skitter skitter.*

"That's it!" Mac shouted, sitting up in the dark. "Soften the edge on the last third." *Skitter . . . scurry!* "Yes. Yes. More of that ending sound. The other happened in between."

She listened to *scurry . . . skitter . . . scurry* and hugged herself tightly. Like this, in the dark, it was as if the alien had somehow crawled in with her.

Had it?

They wouldn't have seen it.

Mac controlled her imagination. "Okay," she said rather breathlessly, "you've got the first sound. It made that frequently. I believe it was from its movement. Body parts or maybe feet."

"Leave those determinations for later," Trojanowski ordered. "Can you give Dr. Sithole direction and volume?"

They played with the sound until Mac felt dizzy, but she was reasonably sure they'd mapped it as she'd heard it that night in her room. "Sound number one done," she said, standing up and fumbling her way to the bench.

"Ready for number two?" Trojanowski asked.

"Yes. A bit of light please," she asked.

"Whatever you say, Little Mackenzie."

The illumination came from the ceiling and floor—rose pink. Mac spared a moment to wonder what Denise had been thinking.

"This might be easier," she said hopefully. "A drop of water hitting a hot pan."

Splot . . . hiss.

"Or it might not." She leaned against the wall and closed her eyes. "A much hotter pan. Cut out the sound of the drop landing. It's what happens afterward."

Spit . . . Sizzle.

"Close. Keep the 'spit.' Lose the 'sizzle.' Add—add popcorn popping."

"Popcorn?" Trojanowski's voice.

"Try this, Mackenzie."

Spit . . . pop!

Now that she heard the combination again, Mac realized there had been an-other sound sandwiched between the louder two. Maddeningly, she could only tell something was missing, but had no idea what. "It's right as far as you have it," she told Jabulani finally. "There should be more to it, but I can't remember."

"No problem, Mackenzie. Locations and direction." They mapped the sound in her office.

"One more, Dr. Connor, unless you've remembered more than three."

Mac rubbed her neck. "Yes, I have. The first sound, the scurrying. It changed when the alien was traveling along the walkway. More of a 'shuh' to each scurry. Not as sharp."

Jabulani nailed it in one. Mac was relieved.

"The last sound." She looked up. The ceiling was low enough to touch if she were standing. "It's what I heard when—" she swallowed hard. "—when it was hanging onto the pillar at the gate, right over my head. I was worried I'd lost it, so I was standing with my back against the pillar to listen. I heard what I thought was its breathing."

"How did you feel at that moment?"

"Feel?" Trojanowski's tangential question surprised her. Mac took a moment to consider before answering. "Triumphant, I suppose. I thought I'd cornered it, could talk to it. But when I tried, it made sound number two—the spit/pop—then took off into the woods." She shrugged to herself. "At that point, I switched back to feeling annoyed."

"You never felt in any danger."

"No. Why would I? It was running away from me. What are you getting at?" Mac wasn't sure she liked being cross-examined by a disembodied voice.

"I don't know. But it could matter to the interpretation of what we re-create here. Thank you. Please continue with the last sound." His voice sharpened. "Doctors! When you're ready?"

Mac stifled a laugh, well able to imagine what was going on—not that the two couldn't restrain themselves, but they'd enjoy Trojanowski's discomfiture.

He shouldn't have worn the suit.

"Are you ready?

"Impress us, Genius-Man." Mac, cross-legged on the audio lab floor, grinned up at Jabulani. He might have stripped off his raincoat and sweater, but the crowded space had been warmed by bodies and busy equipment to the point where even her shirt was sticking to her skin. The big man's well-worn khakis were drenched in sweat, but he was smiling from ear to ear. Denise played a tiny fan over the back of his neck, alternating with her own flushed face.

Trojanowski, Mac decided, sneaking another incredulous look, *couldn't possibly be Human.* His suit and ridiculous cravat were immaculate. There wasn't a drop of moisture on his skin. It made it impossible to argue with his insistence on keeping the door closed and locked. He repaid her look with a raised eyebrow, saying: "Oh, I'm ready, too."

"I've tweaked it so we should hear the creature as if it were here, with us."

Mac braced herself. "Go ahead, Jabulani."

They listened together, Mac watching Trojanowski for any reaction to the sounds filling the lab. His expression showed intense interest, nothing more. *As if he'd let his face reveal anything he didn't want it to,* Mac reminded herself.

The final sound. The *thrumming.* Mac's hands tightened around her knees in frustration. "I was so close," she said.

"Too close," Trojanowski commented grimly. "Move the sound files to my imp, please, Dr. Sithole. Thank you for your work."

Mac stirred herself. "Denise, erase any copies or records. This never happened, okay?"

"I'll do no such—"

Jabulani cupped Denise's angry face in his big hands and kissed her lightly on the nose, but there was nothing light in his voice. "Yes, you will, Sweet Thing. For all our sakes. Trust me."

Denise pulled away and began smacking switches to power down the lab, muttering something that sounded like *"same old government covercrap."* Mac pretended not to hear as she got to her feet and stretched.

Trojanowski studiously ignored the agitated audio researcher as well, getting the files from Jabulani and pocketing his imp. "Time to go," he announced briskly. "Thank you again, Dr. Pillsworthy."

Before Denise could utter whatever was about to spill from her thinned lips, Mac interjected: "This could help us find Em."

Denise's fingers fussed at the nubs of her implants. "Not arguing with that, Mac," she said grudgingly, then scowled at Jabulani. "It's erasing records I don't countenance and you know it, Jabby."

"Of course I do, but sometimes it's necessary to protect those—"

Trojanowski went to the door and unlocked it, as if to avoid further argument. Mac, drawn by the rush of cool, ocean-scented air as the door opened, followed close behind. She was almost through the doorway to the platform when his hand shot back to hold her in place. "Shhh."

Mac knew better than to ask. Instead, she strained her every sense to catch what had alarmed him.

The platform was empty except for themselves. *Amazing,* Mac told herself, as the hairs on her neck rose, *how between one breath and the next, a place you knew as home could feel like a trap.* She could barely see over the rail to the stairway and down, but the activity below seemed normal enough, a reassuring cacophony of footsteps, equipment, and voices rising to where they stood. Mac lifted her gaze along the wall's curve. The next platforms were behind this one, out of her sight.

Meanwhile, Trojanowski was turning his head, so slowly and smoothly that Mac hadn't caught the movement until she glanced back at him, turning it so he could look toward her . . .

No, she thought, her heart pounding in her ears, *so he could look* above *her.*

A low, regular, *familiar* thrumming, from overhead and behind. Mac held her breath as Trojanowski completed his movement, his eyes tracking upward. She'd have taken more comfort from his calm expression, if his face hadn't been deathly pale.

His eyes lowered to hers; in the platform's lighting they seemed dark pits behind their lenses. *Back inside,* he mouthed.

She'd been wrong, he hadn't stopped moving for an instant. His shoulders were almost perpendicular to her now and she could see one of his hands pulling something out of his suit coat.

Mac eased her weight to the foot still inside the doorframe. It flashed through her mind to argue that they had a chance to capture it, to demand answers—as quickly, she remembered the two unknowing people behind her in the audio lab, and the dozens working below on the ring, and hoped Nikolai Trojanowski was as good with his weapon as he was at secrets.

Scurry . . . skitter . . .

Flash!

Even as Trojanowski drew and fired, Mac heard footsteps behind her and threw herself around to stop Jabulani and Denise from coming out the door. Fortunately, they were so startled by the sight of Trojanowski and his weapon that they halted of their own accord, both shouting questions. "Stay there!" Mac ordered, whirling back to see what was happening.

"Did you—?" She shut her mouth on the words, seeing Trojanowski rush to lean over the rail.

"I don't know. It fell," he added unnecessarily as she came up beside him and could see for herself the commotion below. "Or jumped."

This side of the floating ring was being lifted and dropped with a smack by waves originating where the water was still churned white from an impact. Students and their supervisors were scrambling to keep equipment from bouncing into the ocean, yelling questions at one another. A couple jumped in, ruining whatever experiments were underway, but obviously concerned someone might be drowning.

Trojanowski's elbow bumped Mac's as he put his weapon away.

"Shouldn't we stop them?" Mac demanded, worrying about the would-be rescuers.

"They won't find it," her companion predicted.

He was right.

10

SEARCH AND SHOCKS

THERE WERE clouds forming on the horizon. Mac hugged herself tightly and watched them blur the line where wave met sky in a spectrum of heaving gray and black. Where she stood, outside Pod Six, the midafternoon sun scoured to a hard-edged gleam every section of mem-wood walkway, every rail, every ripple of ocean surrounding them all.

It did nothing to expose an invisible foe.

"They worried they'd have to stop looking at dusk," Trojanowski announced. "Then someone volunteered to rig lights." He'd removed his coat and cravat sometime in the last hour, pressing the mem-fabric of his shirt sleeves to hold them above his elbows. Mac hadn't seen him put his hands into the water, but they dripped on the walkway as he approached her.

As "they" referred to a cobbled-together team of enthused students and supervisors using skims and whatever diving gear was at hand to search the water within and around the pod, Mac was less than impressed. "You told me yourself there's no point," she protested, pressing her lips together. Finally: "I should stop this."

"And how will you explain why?" he asked mildly, shaking droplets from his fingertips and squinting at the line of skims. "Too many heard something fall in the water. A stubborn bunch you have here."

Enough was enough. Mac took a deep breath, then said: "I won't bother with explanations. They can be as stubborn as they want at home, where I don't have to worry about them. I'm going to order Base evacuated."

The look he shot her at this was anything but mild. "No. Under no circumstances are you to do that, Dr. Connor. That would be—"

"What? An act of treason against my species?" He might be taller by a head, but Mac had no trouble glaring at him. "I have no problem being bait for our intruder, Mr. Trojanowski, if that's what it takes. I draw the line at risking the people of this facility in any way."

He met her glare with a resigned sigh. "I know. But—"

Just then, a skim swooped to a stop above the water in front of them, disgorging a pair of soaking wet and begoggled students who waved happily as they jumped onto the walkway. Between them they carried a seaweed-coated length of pipe, with links of chain dangling from each end, that they dropped at Mac's feet. "Look what we found, Mac!" one exclaimed with glee. "Part of the old goal post!" Without waiting for an answer, they dove back in their skim and headed for the others.

Mac nudged the pipe with the toe of her shoe. "Well, you've been missing a while," she scolded, to keep her voice free of either laughter or sob. Then, to the silent man beside her: "These people have no idea what we're up against. Even if they did, they'd still try to help. We can't protect them here. You know that as well as I do."

"Dr. Connor. Mac. Walk with me, please," he said, a command more than invitation. "I've some things to tell you that shouldn't be overheard."

"Is one going to be a damned good reason why I shouldn't send my people to safety—right now?"

"You'll have to judge that for yourself."

Without another word, Trojanowski led Mac to the very end of the walkway, away from searchers and spectators, to where the mem-wood slats broadened into a platform that ramped down on either side to meet the now-empty slips of Norcoast's small skim and t-lev fleet. He stood with the sun and the end rail at his back. *To hide his expression or illuminate her own?*

"Well, this should be private enough," Mac commented, raising her voice to be heard above the slap of water and the raucous chatter of gulls roosting on the slips. She adjusted out of habit to the sway of the walkway as it rode the incoming swells, then tapped her foot smartly on the mem-wood. "Or is it? We've no way to know, do we?"

"No way to know," he agreed, but didn't seem unduly concerned by this or the shifting surface underfoot. He rubbed his hands together as if to finish drying them, then spread them wide apart. "But this isn't the first time. It's been like chasing a ghost, Mac. No images on record. A few traces of slime that contain no genetic information or cells. No clues, beyond the type of encounter we've just had. We call them 'Nulls,' for want of anything better."

"So there have been other—encounters," Mac said, finding his word choice unsettling. *What would they call murder? A meeting?* "Where? Was anyone else taken? Harmed? What—"

"Nothing as tangible as this, until now," he answered, cutting her list short. "Nothing as bold. The Nulls themselves were only a name until you heard one. We've been able to spot their ship landings, some anyway—damaged vegetation and disturbed earth. If we're lucky, there's slime."

Mac wondered how anyone could say that with a straight face, but didn't interrupt.

Trojanowski went on: "Neither the Ministry nor the IU is ready to make a direct connection between these beings and what's been happening along the Naralax Transect—the disappearances—"

"But you—you personally—think there is," Mac stated, shading her eyes to make out more of his face.

His shoulders lifted and fell. "Anyone who goes to this much trouble to hide themselves has a reason. And there have been landing sites in systems along the Naralax, on worlds where and when such events have taken place."

"'Events.'" Mac shook her head in disgust. "'Missing person reports.' 'Disappearances.' Why don't you say what really happened? The eradication of all life, of every living molecule, as if it had never existed—just like the worlds in the Chasm. A minor detail I had to learn from an alien! Why wasn't it in the report?"

"I'm sure the Ministry would have briefed you more completely had there seemed a need from the start." Almost by rote.

"You mean if they'd taken Brymn seriously."

"Yes, but it was more than that." He shook his head. "The decision to keep a lid on this was made in order to prevent panic. We didn't want to alarm you or anyone else, unnecessarily."

The wind, previously soft and steady from the west, chose that moment to send a spray-laden gust over the end of the walkway. Mac had already tucked the portion of her braid escaping its knot into her collar, but sufficient drops landed on her face and head to steal the sun's warmth. She licked salty lips. "I'll tell you what's alarming me, Mr. Trojanowski, the idea of my people being stalked by these creatures. I think that's more than enough reason to close this facility immediately and send everyone home."

A sliver of steel entered his voice. "And I say that would be premature. They've only shown interest in you, Dr. Mamani, and possibly Brymn. There's every indication they've attempted to prevent inadvertent contact with anyone else. The power failures, the late night intrusions. If we change the routine at this facility, we might spook them into disappearing for good—or into more direct action."

"Not good enough," Mac snapped. "A pile of conjecture that does nothing but serve your interest in finding these Nulls."

"They are after you," he repeated, as if she hadn't spoken. "The obvious conclusion is that, despite all our security, somehow they've found out you and Brymn are looking into the—eradications. But why Emily? You know something, don't you?" His voice softened. "I've seen it in your eyes, Mac. You're blaming yourself. Why?"

Mac walked around Trojanowski so he had to turn to the sun in order to keep her in view. As if sensing what she wanted, he took off his glasses, put them in a pocket, and waited, a patient, if determined, compassion on his face. *Each time they had stood like this, face-to-face,* Mac realized with a small shock, *something fundamental between them had changed.* Was it only the circumstances? Was it him?

Was it her?

This time, it felt natural to say to him what she could hardly bear to think. "Emily was trying to tell me something, the last—the last time I saw her. She wasn't angry at me. I know it sounded like it, when we were together on the stairs, but she wasn't. She said I needed to understand that we—she meant Humans—weren't the only people investigating the disappearances. She said we had our parts to play, but they were small and we'd be back to normal soon. She said all this as if to reassure me." Mac paused to firm up her voice. "But I think it was to reassure herself." Tears spilled over her eyelids; she let them fall. "She was afraid, Nik. I didn't see it until too late."

"What was she afraid of?"

"Something that hadn't happened yet. Something—maybe something she was going to do. Emily asked me to promise to forgive her, but wouldn't tell me why."

Nikolai Trojanowski put his hands on either side of her face, then brushed his thumbs over her cheeks, once, ever so lightly, to wipe away her tears. "Did you promise?" he asked gently.

"I didn't need to promise that," Mac sniffed. "I told her friends always forgive friends. What could she have meant? What was she talking about?"

"I don't know. To figure this out, I need you to tell me everything you can, Mac." Nik lowered his hands. "It's your choice."

A gull complained about ravens. A fish jumped in the distance, visiting an alien realm. Mac weighed promise against reality, and knew there was no choice left.

"I understand. Brymn. He called me his *lamisah*," she told him. "Do you know the word? He said it meant that we were allies."

"I haven't heard it before. But please. Go on."

"Emily was his *lamisah*, too." Mac turned and gripped the rail in both hands, staring out at the simplicity of the inlet's life, and then told Nikolai Trojanowski everything she knew, from sharing the Ministry's message with Emily, to Brymn's desire to speak to her privately and what he'd said, ending with the meeting between the three of them in her office. The only time she sensed a reaction from the silent form beside her was his stiffening when she mentioned the figure watching the three of them from the terrace.

"Emily thought it was you," Mac told him.

"Hardly. I was waiting for ghosts on the mountain."

Mac's hands tightened on the rail until she felt twinges of pain up both wrists. "You should have been here protecting us! Protecting Emily!" The fury of her own sudden outburst shocked her. She put one hand over her mouth, then drew it down slowly. "It wasn't your fault. You couldn't have known. I'm sorry. . . ."

"Don't be. You aren't wrong, Mac." His tone brought her eyes around to look at him. A muscle jumped along his jaw and his mouth was a thin, stark line. "I wish I'd been here," he said grimly. "I wish I hadn't completely underestimated Brymn and the situation I placed you in. I thought he was a joke. I thought having to come here with him was a waste of my time and my superiors were fools to let him convince them otherwise. Oh, I did all the right prep—made all the right motions. Backgrounds on you and your people. Checked, what I could, on the Dhryn." Twin spots of color appeared on his cheeks and his voice lowered. "Getting that call to watch for a Null ship felt like a reprieve—until I found out what had happened while I was gone. It's I who owe you an apology, Mackenzie Connor. As if words matter now."

Emily assessed people in an instant and was rarely wrong, an ability Mac now envied. Her own way was to avoid such judgments, to wait and watch while time spent working together revealed the quality of a person, or its lack. *A luxury she no longer had.* There was only the seeming sincerity of this man's voice and expression, his actions over the past two and a half days, and a supposedly counterfeit-proof message, carefully transferred to her pant pocket because nowhere in her home was safe.

Like rolling a kayak, Mac decided. You had to believe your first drive of the paddle would bring you up again. Without that confidence, the timing never worked and you stayed head down and flailing underwater. Embarrassing at best. Deadly at worst.

"Words matter, Nik," she disagreed. "I've one for you. *Lamisah.* Allies." Mac poked him in the chest with two fingers. He feigned a grab for the railing and she almost smiled. *Almost.* "Taking your advice, *lamisah,* I won't shut down Base unless there is another incident. But if there's so much as a hint of a Null around, I'll empty this place and raise the pods so fast your head will spin."

He looked relieved. "More than fair, Mac. Meanwhile, I'll deploy more officers. For what it's worth."

"Appreciated. Now. Where do we go from here? How do we find Emily?"

An eyebrow lifted. "We?"

Mac shoved her hands in her pockets and stood braced against the now-gusting wind.

Nik considered her for an instant; *perhaps,* Mac thought, *forced into his own quick judgment.* Then he nodded. "We." His hazel eyes picked up some of the ocean's chill blue. "We start searching for your invisible intruder," he told her. "But first, I think it's time we woke our sleeping beauty."

Nik hadn't exactly lied to her, Mac thought ruefully. He'd merely neglected to tell her they'd be making a brief stop on the way to see Brymn.

Would a warning have made this moment easier?

She stepped inside Emily's quarters, hearing the police barrier hum back into place behind her, and seriously doubted anything would have helped.

"What are—what do you think I'll see that you haven't?" she asked Nik, who was moving carefully through the remains of Emily's glass table toward her desk. Focusing on him, a person who didn't belong with her memories of this room, was better than remembering how it used to look. *How it* should *look.*

Emily defined her space, Mac thought, picking her way among pieces of brilliant fabric her eye refused to recognize as a wardrobe. *The delay Emily had coaxed from her on arriving?* In part so she could, as every year, disappear into her new assigned quarters to "scent mark the place" as she'd call it. One or more of her travel cases would contain oddments from home: a new ceramic sculpture, a rug, a watercolor, a colorful woven throw. Once it had been a set of stuffed llamas, in striking white and black, adorned with magenta sunglasses. The only common-alities from year to year were the confusion of cosmetics in the bathroom and satin sheets on the bed. The end result, regardless of scheme, was a space that had nothing in common with those of the other scientists in the pod, something that suited Emily Mamani very well.

Mac didn't look up again. She didn't dare. Looking at the floor was bad enough, littered with treasures become debris, glistening with hardened slime. Her first involuntary glance around the room had been trapped by the marks on one wall, a combination of deep gouges and a single, blood-red handprint. The marks had been linked within an irregular black outline, as if a child had thought to frame them.

There were other signs of the forensics team at work: labels and code numbers stuck seemingly at random around the room, vidbots hovering in every corner to record any evidence tampering, accidental or deliberate.

Mac fought the urge to show her empty hands to the nearest lens.

Nik was looking through what was left of Emily's desk. "See anything that doesn't belong?" he prompted.

She considered several replies to this, settling for: "You're joking."

He glanced over at her, his face inscrutable. "I mean it. Look around. If some-thing isn't right, you'll notice. Trust your instincts."

"How can you be—" Mac stopped what she was going to say and gave a nod. "I'll do my best," she said, wondering where or when he'd had occasion to prove that for himself. *She probably didn't want to know,* Mac told herself, raising her eyes at last.

It helped that the marks were behind her now. She pushed the emotions crowding her behind as well. Time later to worry about Emily, to be angry at the defilement of her things, to be afraid.

Fear was the hardest to dismiss. Slowly, insidiously, it sucked the moisture from her mouth and disrupted the rhythm of her heart. There could be another of the creatures clinging to the ceiling above her head, or in the shower stall. The walls could be crowded with Nulls, silent and waiting.

Let them wait, Mac told herself fiercely.

Nothing in the living room drew her attention. Mac made herself walk into Emily's bedroom. She felt Nik's presence at her back, as if he offered support but wouldn't interfere. *Scant comfort,* she thought. He couldn't shoot what he couldn't find.

Even prepared by the state of the outer room, Mac gasped. The bedroom, half the size of the living room, had been the site of battle. Streaks of slime criss-crossed others of rust-red. Numb, Mac bent and picked up a fragment of blue and yellow, all she could see that looked familiar. It was from a lamp Emily had "borrowed" from her office. A lamp that had been shattered against a wall—or a body.

"They left through the window."

Mac ignored the words as she ignored any attempt by her mind to reconstruct what had happened here. She edged around the mattress, sliced as had been the one in her quarters, hurrying her inspection over every surface. *Almost done . . .*

"What are you doing here?" she muttered in surprise, tugging at a piece of brown plastic that peeked from beneath a fragment of chair leg. The piece tore free and she brought it to her nose. The soufflé had smelled much better two days ago.

"What is it?"

Mac frowned in puzzlement as she held out the scrap to Nik. "Dessert."

"I beg your pardon?"

She dropped to her knees, digging after more pieces. "Leftovers," Mac clarified as she searched. "Brymn brought this bag of soufflé to my office that night. He didn't know I'd eaten . . . said he picked this to bring me because others praised it. I don't think he eats what we do."

Nik squatted beside her, helping to move aside the rest of the broken chair. "Dhryn diet aside, why does it matter that the soufflé ended up here?"

Impatiently, Mac pushed her hair behind one ear. She had a small pile of bag pieces now, several attached to dried clots of egg, chocolate, and cream. "It matters because the soufflé wasn't edible anymore. Em must have taken the bag to recycle it for me. I've had some—well, sometimes old food hangs around in my office." She coughed. "That's not important. Nik, what if whoever was spying on us through the window stayed nearby and saw her take the bag from my office. Maybe he—it—assumed it held something important, something secret. That could be why Emily . . ." She didn't finish the statement. The room around them did it for her.

"Not an unreasonable assumption," Nik replied approvingly, then made a clucking sound. "It doesn't explain why Dr. Mamani would bring a bag of dead soufflé all the way back to her quarters. I saw recycle chutes in every hallway."

"I don't know." Mac rocked back on her heels. "We were both tired. We'd said things, argued. I didn't even notice her taking it. She must have gathered it up with her sweater." Mac started to look around for the garment, but stopped herself with a shudder.

Nik produced a clear sheet from a pocket, unfolded it, then laid it over a fairly clean section of carpet. "Put all the pieces here," he ordered. "I'll have the forensics team reconstruct what they can."

Mac stared at him. He looked serious. "The soufflé?"

"And whatever else might have been in the bag."

She shook her head. "I looked inside—"

"Can you swear there was nothing else in it?" he interrupted. "Did you take it out?"

"Of course not, but—"

"That's why we'll have this analyzed."

Mac shook her head. "You aren't seriously suggesting that Brymn actually put something else in the bag? I was only speculating—"

Nik lifted the end of a drawer and exclaimed with satisfaction as he found another, larger mass of bag bits stuck to one another and to the floor. Rather than try to remove it, he drew out a knife and began cutting the carpet around the mass. "Speculating is part of good detective work, Mac," he informed her as he worked. "As a scientist, you should know that."

She knew she didn't like where this particular speculation was leading. Mac put her fingers on Nik's arm. "Wait." When he looked at her quizzically, she bit her lip, then went on: "What aren't you telling me about Emily, Nik? What's going on? Tell me what you know—what you think you know. Please."

The knife blade drove deep into the carpet to stand between them. "I know she's your colleague and closest friend, Mac," he said evenly, meeting her eyes. His were troubled. "But that's not all she is. I can't explain here—" a deliberate glance at the hovering vidbot, "—but I believe she might have taken the bag from your office because she suspected Brymn of trying to pass you a secret message—"

"Whoa! Stop right there, Mr. Trojanowski." Mac snatched her fingers back as though his skin burned them. "Why would *Emily* want to intercept a message from Brymn? She didn't even know he existed until you brought him to the field station! I involved her in all this. She knows nothing about his species, or—" His stillness penetrated her fury. He was waiting for her, for something from her. *What?*

Mac took a steadying breath, then another before asking as calmly as if after the weather: "Why would you believe such a thing?"

He bent his head, lifting only his eyes to hers. The regret in them made her pulse hammer in her throat, an ominous drumbeat underlying his next words. "Because Emily Mamani has lied to you, Mac. By omission if not more. She visited at least two Dhryn colonies in the past year; three the year before. I'm quite sure she knows more about Brymn and his species than either of us."

A pause, and his regretful expression turned into something more akin to warning. "And, Mac? It's never just one lie. Not once you start digging."

"No change, Mac."

"Thanks, Tie." Mac curbed her impatience. After Nik had passed the wrapped bundle of dried soufflé and bag bits to the officer who'd been waiting outside Emily's door, they'd come straight here, to her quarters. *No time to process what Nik had told her. No time to do anything more than shove all thoughts of Emily Mamani out of her mind.* "We'll watch him for a while, Tie. I'll let you know when we need to be spelled."

While she talked with Tie, Nik was heads-together with the police officer who'd been guarding Brymn. *If that's what she was,* Mac wondered abruptly. She'd never asked for any identification. She was reasonably certain Kammie wouldn't have bothered either. You had an emergency, you called for help, real police came. Who doubted that?

Suddenly, she did. *If the police at Base weren't real, and the Wilderness Trust no longer ruled the landscape around the inlet, and Emily had lied . . .*

"Mac?"

"Sorry, Tie," Mac said quickly, quite sure her expression had been a study in itself. "Distracting day, as you can imagine. What were you saying?"

His rough, round face puckered in distress. Tie was at his best with engines, not people, but he'd done an admirable job keeping cool and focused through this crisis. An unconscious alien on the floor of her quarters was about the only thing he couldn't handle. Mac knew how he felt all too well. "I'm saying, Mac, we should've moved our 'guest' yesterday. This isn't right, you not having your own quarters."

"Don't worry about me, Tie." Mac put her arm around his shoulders and gave him an affectionate squeeze before letting go. "The last place I want to stay right now is in here. It's going to take weeks to clean this up—let alone put everything together again." She didn't bother adding that her office was worse. He knew. "Did you get all our gear packed up?"

"Done by noon." He found a smile for her. "Only problem I had was convincing McGregor and Beiz to stop sunbathing so we could get back to Base. If it wasn't for the situation—" Here his voice finally faltered.

"It's okay, Tie," Mac said softly. From the corner of her eye, she saw that Nik and the "officer" were finished with their private chat. "I'm heading to the mainland this evening anyway. They're putting me up in a fancy hotel, with room service. What do you think of that?"

He brightened. "I think it's a great idea, Mac. You make sure you take full advantage. Just don't be gone long."

Something she couldn't promise. "Kammie has the reins," Mac assured him instead. "You keep things working for her until I'm back. Deal?"

This didn't sit well at all. She could see it in the unhappy look in his eyes. But Tie wouldn't argue, not with Outside Authority in the form of the bureaucrat and police officer now moving their way. He ducked his head to her in mute agreement, then started to leave, only to turn back. "Mac. I'm sorry. I don't know where my head's been. Your dad called again."

Mac blinked, then remembered. She'd promised to call him back—what was it now, last night? Something so normal and sane as talking to her father seemed improbable. *She'd have to do it, though.* "Thanks, Tie. You didn't say anything about what's been going on, did you?"

He looked offended. "'Course not, Mac. You know me better than that. I told him you were resting."

Mac hid a wince. Now she'd really have to call, and soon. *Resting?* Her Dad wouldn't believe that even without the bonus of an alien guest during her field season. *She'd be lucky if he didn't show up on the next t-lev out of Vancouver.* "Perfect," she told Tie, forcing a smile.

"Everything all right?" Nik asked, coming up as Tie made his exit.

"Perfect," Mac echoed, but gave the word a more appropriate intonation. When Nik looked interested, she gave a noncommittal shrug. "Nothing to do with this."

The officer, a stocky woman whose dark eyes, coppered skin, and straight black hair spoke of a heritage along this coast almost as old as the salmon themselves, gave Mac a look that likely memorized everything from braid to shoe size before saying to Nik: "If that's all, sir, I'd like to check on Simeon's progress."

"Yes. Thank you." Dismissed, the officer nodded and left without another word.

"So," Mac said as soon the door closed and they were alone. "What did your friend have to say?"

"Friend? Officer LaFontaine? There's been no change in Brymn's condition."

A shade too innocent, Mac thought, but didn't press the issue. "Tie said that, too." They both looked at the unconscious alien.

The Dhryn wasn't moaning anymore. Mac hoped that was an improvement. Otherwise, he lay exactly as she and Nik had left him, his arms curled over his torso, his thick legs bent back at their main joint and splayed. The sheet over him had soaked through with dark blue exudate in several spots. More liquid of that color puddled down Brymn's left side, the one closest to where they stood, flowing off the mattress onto the floor. It hadn't dried or congealed, suggesting it continued to flow. On the other hand, there wasn't enough of it to suggest the alien had lost a significant amount of a vital fluid.

Or maybe he had. Mac thought wistfully of the xeno course in her imp and promised herself time to read it before much more took place.

Unlike Emily's quarters, some effort had been made to push the remains of furniture and torn bedding aside. Mac assumed this had been to accommodate the various doctors and other Human experts trying to puzzle out the Dhryn's comatose state. There was only one vidbot, aimed at Brymn.

"However," Nik continued, "The officer did pass along one bit of news. The police think they've found your eavesdropper."

Mac looked at him, eyes wide. "And?"

"Human. Career thief. Several recent names. Born Otto Rkeia. He didn't come in with the media crush, but I imagine all the unfamiliar faces let him move around pretty much as he pleased. Probably swam in under cover of darkness."

"If he did," Mac said confidently, "we'll have a recording. We may not have much in the way of security from intruders, but we pay a great deal of attention to what moves in the water under the pods."

"Good. I'll have it checked. The more we can find out about Rkeia's movements, the better."

"You can't ask—" Mac stopped at his thumbs-down gesture. "Oh. Where did they find the body?" she asked, momentarily aghast at the calmness of her own voice. *Maybe she was learning to deal with repeated shocks. Maybe this is how the police—how Nikolai himself—dealt with such things as violence.*

"Your eager rescuers found it under Pod Six."

Yuck. Mac flinched. "I don't suppose it was an accident."

Nik snorted. "Not unless you can accidentally glue yourself to a support strut, thirty meters down. They're estimating time of death now." He shot a look upward, to where the remains of the adhesive netting still starred the ceiling. "Not too much of a stretch to believe our invisible friends were responsible."

"So they kill people."

"They *took* Emily, Mac," he responded, understanding her fear. "If they'd wanted her dead, there was no need for that."

As comfort, it was as cold and dark as thirty meters below the pod, but Mac made herself accept it. "Jirair—Dr. Grebbian—can help you determine when the body went in the water, if that helps." At Nik's interrogative look, she added: "He studies zooplankton, particularly those with a sessile component to their life cycle. Mr. Rkeia's body will have been colonized by several species. Jirair can tell how long each has been growing."

"That could be useful." Nik went to the com on the wall and passed a message to the forensics team to contact Grebbian. "Done," he said, coming back a moment later. "Thanks, Mac." He gave her a searching look. "How are you doing?"

She licked dry lips and gave a curt nod. "Better than he is. What can we do?"

He joined her in staring down at Brymn. "We have next to no data on Dhryn. Any thoughts?"

"I study—"

"—salmon," Nik finished for her. He smiled slightly. "Think of it as having no preconceptions in your way."

"I don't know," she replied slowly, but obediently walked around the alien on her floor. The first thing Mac noticed was a modest, regular expansion and contraction of his upper torso. *Great,* she mocked. *I can tell he's breathing.* There was a monitor on the floor connected to a sensor affixed to what corresponded to a chest. Its display was a confusion of peaks and valleys that bore no resemblance to any electrical rhythms Mac had ever seen in a vertebrate.

As she walked around a second time, she undid the knot of braid on her neck, then the braid itself. The third time, she started braiding her hair again, then stopped, fingers paused in mid-twist. "Play Jabulani's recording," she suggested.

Nik, who'd stood by watching her pace, obediently pulled out his imp, but didn't activate it. "Do you have a scientific basis for this experiment, Dr. Connor?"

Mac finished her braid and dropped it down her back. "Not really."

His mouth quirked. "Stand back, then. In case it works."

Scurry . . . scurry . . . skittle!

No reaction from Brymn that Mac could see, although her heart jumped. From the look on Nik's face, he wasn't too happy with the sound either.

Thrummmm . . .

Nothing.

"Here comes the last one," he warned her.

Spit! Pop!

A quiver raced along those of Brymn's arms Mac could see, starting from each shoulder and ending with a spasmodic opening of his fingers. Then nothing.

Spit! Pop!

An identical quiver. Nothing more.

Before Nik could play the sound again, Mac raised her hand. "That's it!" she exclaimed. "The missing part. I knew there was something between the 'spit' and the 'pop.' It wasn't something our ears could detect—but his should. It might make the difference." She hurried to the com. "Dr. Connor. Put me through to the Pred lab."

As she waited, she explained to Nik: "The Preds listen to infrasound all the time—from whales. They'll have something we can try."

"Predator Research, Seung here. What can we do for you, Mac?"

"I need you to play a single pulse, ten Hz, through the com for me. Fifty dB will do." She waved her companion over to the com. He understood, holding up his imp to catch the sound.

"Just a minute." A muttering of voices, some incredulous, then something bounced along the floor. Likely a basketball—the Pred lab wasn't the most formal. Mac shrugged at Nik's look. After "just a minute" stretched into three, Mac was about to signal again when Seung said: "Ready. Pulse in three, two, one . . ." The following silence made Nik look at her in question. She nodded confidently as the com came alive again. "There you go, Mac. Glad to help. Any word on Em?"

Mac met Nik's eyes. "Not yet," she said into the com. "Thanks, guys. Dr. Connor out."

"Now what?"

"I'm convinced Brymn's speech includes infrasound—sounds below the frequency detected by the Human ear. If he utters it, he should be able to hear it. When Jabulani was trying to recreate the 'spit/pop' sound I'd heard, that's what was missing."

"A sound you couldn't hear. How can you know?" he asked with a slight frown.

Mac stroked the hairs on her forearm. "If you're close enough to the source of infrasound, you feel it," she said, remembering. She pulled out her imp. "Send me your 'screen," she ordered, walking closer to Brymn. "I'll key the sounds through mine."

When nothing appeared in front of her eyes, Mac turned to frown at him. "I know what I'm doing," she argued.

"I'm sure you do," Nik countered, "but our devices aren't compatible. Tell me what you want and I'll do it." He approached, the 'screen from his imp disconcertingly afloat to the left of his face.

It looked like an ordinary enough imp to her, and he'd used it with Denise's equipment, but Mac didn't waste time arguing—although she did think dark thoughts about spies and their toys. "Play just the 'spit' of sound number three followed by Seung's pulse. We'll add the 'pop' later if necessary."

He nodded, drawing the fingers of his left hand through the display. "Now."

Spit! . . .

They might not hear a difference, but the Dhryn certainly did. As Nik played the sounds, the body on the floor convulsed upward, arching from neck to foot. Mac stepped back as the wire to the monitor ripped clear. Brymn's six arms stretched out as if grabbing for holds. His seventh arm shot straight up through the sheet, ripping it as if it were paper. An instant later, he went limp.

"I'd say that had an effect," Nik said dryly.

Mac walked over to the Dhryn and pulled the remains of her sheet from his body and arm, avoiding contact with any of the blue stains. "Insufficient. Didn't wake him," she said, shaking her head. "Add the final component of the sound."

"We don't know—"

She shot a look at Nik any of her students would have recognized in an instant. "That's the reason we're here, isn't it? Play the sequence."

"Move away first."

Mac obeyed.

Nik raised his hand to the 'screen in midair, then jabbed one finger into its heart.

Spit . . . pop!

For a terrifying moment, Mac thought they weren't alone.

She wasn't the only one.

Brymn let out a roar and surged to his feet. Nik leaped back, having come close to underestimating the reach of the Dhryn's wildly moving upper arms. For a moment, all Mac could tell was that the alien was alive and awake; she wasn't convinced he was sane or safe.

Then, like the branches of a great tree swaying in a storm, the six paired arms began to move in unison, from side to side, lower and lower, gradually coming to a rest at Brymn's sides. The seventh, always moving in opposition to the rest, tucked itself under an upper armpit. Then, finally, his eyes snapped open—along with his mouth.

Mac grinned at Nik as they both covered their ears. "I never thought I'd be happy to hear that again!" she shouted at him over the din.

As if her voice had been a switch, Brymn stopped keening. His eyes came to rest on her. "Mac—?" Then he folded at the knee joints, dropping into his tripod sit with a suddenness that probably hurt.

"*Lamisah,*" she said quickly, hurrying up to him but stopping short of touching any body part. "Are you all right? Can you talk to us?"

"Us?" He appeared to notice Nik for the first time.

That worthy turned off his 'screen and gave a quick bow. "Honorable Delegate. Is there anything you need?" Mac had no trouble interpreting the look he sent her: *let's be sure he's stable first.*

"A drink, maybe?" she added helpfully, looking in vain around her ruined quarters for an intact cup.

Brymn's eyes followed hers. Mac felt the floor vibrate. He must have made one of his low frequency sounds. "What has happened to your room . . . ?" his voice rumbled into silence as he looked up at the ceiling and saw the remnants of the adhesive webbing overhead. "Aieeee!" His shriek rattled everything loose in the room. "The Ro are here! We must run for our lives!" Even as he attempted to stand, he lapsed from English to what sounded to Mac like more of the Dhryn's own language, only so rapid that none of the words were remotely familiar.

They were going to get some answers at last. Satisfied, Mac leaned against the wall that had once held a set of shelves, the shelves in turn once holding a shell collection now shattered at her feet, and waited with some interest to see how Nikolai Trojanowski handled a bear-sized case of alien hysterics.

- Portent -

A STORM WITHOUT cloud brought the rain, sudden and hard. Its drops pockmarked the smooth rise of swells bringing the new tide, drops that tinted the ocean a deeper green.

Thrice daily, the tide brought life to life. Its return woke those who bided their time within airtight casings or hidden in moist crevices, so they might feast on the flood of organics. It drew to the shallows those from the depths who would, in turn, feed on the feasters. Yet they would leave their eggs behind in the protected pools, to begin a new cycle of life that would wash out with another tide.

Until this tide came in, storm-wracked and bringing only death.

First to succumb were those who opened their casings and extended fragile arms in anticipation, those arms dissolving with the ocean's tainted kiss.

Next were those who had risen in their multitudes to feed and breed in the shallows. Even as they tasted the layer of death above and would have fled, their flesh rotted from their bones, their bones washing into the tide.

The tide paused at its zenith, having filled the pools with quiet green.

Only those waiting onshore for the tide's departure were spared. They peered, bright-eyed and bold, from their holes in the rock face above. Some leaned farther out, into the daylight, tiny feet holding firm to the edge of the stone.

Shadows cut the sun.

In reflex, those leaning winked inside their shelters. Those who felt safe kept watch, chittering among themselves, then grew utterly quiet as the shadows surrounded what had been a tidal pool.

And began to drink.

11

INTERROGATION AND INVASION

IN THE END, it was the ruined mattress, not any particular heroics from Nik, that saved the day.

As Brymn prepared to run for his life, the man calmly reached down and pulled one end of the mattress. *Hard.* The mattress, already shredded, gave way entirely—taking one of the Dhryn's pillarlike feet with it. The alien toppled on his side like a crab tossed by a gull.

Before he could wriggle himself up again, Mac cupped her hands around her mouth and bellowed over his piteous—and loud—exclamations: "It was only a recording! You're safe. Brymn! Calm—" She found herself yelling into a quiet room and shut up.

Mac walked to where the Dhryn could see her. His small mouth was working, as if he couldn't help trying to speak. The vivid blue membrane flickered across his yellow-irised eyes with almost strobelike speed. She found it disconcerting and was glad when Nik joined her, going to one knee so he was face-to-face with the alien. "It's been two days since you were attacked," he informed Brymn, talking slowly and distinctly. "Do you require any care, Honorable Delegate?"

The flickering slowed. "Mackenzie . . . Winifred . . . Elizabeth . . . Wright . . . Connor . . . ?" the words came out punctuated by faint gasps. His eyes seemed to be searching for her without success; she wondered if the moving eyelids impaired his sight. "Mac?"

"I'm here," Mac assured him. *How remarkably tempting,* she thought, *to take his question for a Humanlike concern.*

Nik leaned forward, in range of those still-restless arms. Without the suit coat to disguise it, he was built like a swimmer, with that distinctively rounded cap of muscle on each shoulder and strong curves along both back and upper chest. Emily would approve, Mac knew. For a Human, his was not a small or insignificant form, yet he was dwarfed by the more massive Dhryn.

Mac restrained the urge to pull Nik back a safe distance. *Trained spy or whatever,* she told herself inanely, *while poor Brymn was, after all, an archaeologist.*

A very large, very anxious archaeologist. The eyelids slowed to a mere nervous-looking twitch. "Nikolai Piotr Trojanowski," Brymn said earnestly, his voice softer but prone to tremble. "We are not safe here. None of us. The Ro . . ." The violent shudder that accompanied the word seemed a reflex. "They are dangerous, evil creatures."

"Don't worry. These rooms were swept and sealed, with guards and a repeller field at every access."

He could have told her *that,* Mac grumbled to herself, feeling a knot of tension easing between her shoulders she hadn't noticed until now.

"Help me sit up, please."

It took both of them to steady the Dhryn as he rose, then settled back down more comfortably, two hands searching for and finding a bare patch of floor on which to balance his body. Touching his torso and arm was like taking his hand, Mac found. The skin was like sun-warmed rubber, dry and with an underlying musculature. This close, he had a delicate, floral scent. Mac recognized it. Her bottle of lily of the valley must have been a casualty of the attack.

"What happened?" she blurted. "After you left my office, I mean. And why did you leave?" she added, earning a slight frown from Nik, doubtless about to conduct his own, more professional interrogation.

Brymn folded his arms in an intricate pattern. Sitting, his face wasn't much higher than Mac's own. Right now, she couldn't read any expression on it that made sense to her. At least his eyelids had stopped flashing that blue blankness across his eyes. "I left because you did, Mackenzie Winifred Elizabeth Wright Connor."

"I did?" Mac considered this and felt herself blush. "Well, yes, I suppose we did. But we were only on the terrace for a moment—you thought we'd left you?"

"I did not think you had left. You did leave. Was I not to assume this meant our meeting had ended?"

Nik spoke before Mac could attempt an explanation. "Where did you go after you left, Brymn?"

"Here. I had a great deal of reading to do. The opportunity to access—" his voice faded, then strengthened, "—my apologies for my condition. I will require a few more hours to recuperate fully." A look of surprise. "You must have disturbed my *hathis,* healing sleep."

"Sorry," Nik said tersely. "As you were saying?"

"Ah. I was saying, I came here to read the Human journals I'd requested. When attempting to reconstruct the development of theories, I prefer to study the research in the original language of the author."

Implying he read more than English and Instella, Mac decided. Her species might appear—and act—united to those from other worlds, but there had never been a homogenization of cultures or tongues at dirt level. Part stubborn habit and part a celebration of distinctiveness. She'd read somewhere that humanity's extra-Sol settlements were pretty much the same: Instella with company and tradition at home.

The biologist in her approved. Just as a population's survival improved with a variety of inheritable traits, Mac suspected a civilization's ability to cope with change was enhanced by having a choice of approach. She'd lost the debate to Emily when she'd admitted to not comparing data on humanity with that of other sentient species. As usual, her friend had scoffed at what she called Mac's parochial attitude. There was more to the universe than opposable thumbs and nose hair, she'd insist.

What had Emily been trying to tell her?

Where did she break her arm . . . where had she been . . . ?

Why would she lie?

Mac snapped her attention back to the moment. Nik had continued his questioning. "What happened after you arrived in these rooms?"

"I do not wish to think of it." This with a tone of complete finality.

Nik sent her a warning look before Mac could say a word, then crossed his arms over his chest. *Meaningful mimicry of the Dhryn or thoughtless gesture?* Mac felt like tossing dice.

"We respect your wish, Honorable Delegate," the man told the Dhryn.

Brymn blinked and Mac thought he looked startled. *So was she.* She narrowed her eyes and studied Nik. He looked solemn, almost grave, but she thought there was a bit of smugness in his expression as well.

"Thank you," the Dhryn boomed, his voice closer to normal. "I—"

"It is, however," Nik interrupted without missing a beat, "my duty to inform you that your visitor's visa has been revoked—effective immediately. You will be escorted from Earth and Sol System within the hour."

"You can't do that. Mac?"

Mac nodded. "He can do that," she told the shocked alien.

Rather than distress, Brymn's face assumed a look of great dignity. He unfolded four arms and spread them widely. "You see, Mac? I told you your government considered my mission of great importance. They have assigned an *erumisah*—a decision maker of power—as my companion and guide." He proffered Nik one of his rising bows. "I am most gratified."

Mac wasn't surprised to see Nik take this in stride. *He must be used to dealing with cultures as varied as their biologies.* "Then you will understand, Honorable Delegate," he said, "why I cannot permit you to remain here, potentially drawing more dangerous attention from these 'Ro,' unless you are willing to provide whatever information you can to help us."

The arms wrapped back around the torso and Brymn looked at her, then at Nik, then at her again. "It is not permitted to speak of them," he began. Mac felt the vibration through the floor as he uttered something more in the infrasound and held up her hand to silence the Dhryn.

"We can't hear that," she advised him, then remembered what Brymn had told her about the lack of Dhryn biologists. "Our ears are not adapted to respond to the same range of sound frequencies as yours, Brymn."

He looked startled and glanced at Nikolai as if seeking confirmation. The man nodded. "We feel vibrations that tell us you are making certain sounds, but not what you are saying. If we need to hear them to understand you, Honorable Delegate, we'll have to bring in the appropriate audio equipment."

"This is fascinating. Let us find out—" The Dhryn uttered a series of hoots, each lower in pitch than the preceding. He hit some lovely bass notes Mac was reasonably sure no Human voice could reach unassisted, then went deeper still. Suddenly, though his mouth appeared to be making a sound, she couldn't hear it. Mac raised her hand at the same instant Nik lifted his. Brymn closed his mouth, his eyes wide with what appeared to be astonishment. "You're deaf!" he exclaimed.

Mac dredged up memories of choral practice, took a deep breath, and did her best to nail a high C. From Nik's pained expression, she mangled it nicely, but Brymn's brow ridges wrinkled at the edges. "And I must also be deaf," he admitted. "This is most—awkward. You have never heard my full voice. Or the foul tongue of the Ro. Then how—?"

She understood. "For the recording you heard, we re-created the sounds I remembered hearing," Mac explained, "then added a very low frequency pulse."

Another shudder ran through his arms. "It was realistic enough. But do not worry about our conversations, my *lamisah*. From this moment, I speak to you as if you were an *oomling*. It isn't respectful, but you need not worry about being deaf."

Nik's mouth quirked, but he bowed slightly. "You are most kind. For our part, we'll avoid shrill." Mac might have blushed, but the man went on immediately. "Am I right to say one or more of these Ro were waiting here when you arrived?"

"I was ambushed," Brymn agreed, fingers spasming open and closed. "With no time to call for help, nowhere to flee. I regret the damage to your quarters, Mackenzie Winifred Eliz—"

None of this mattered. "Why did they take Emily?" Mac interrupted, well past impatient. "Where would they take her?" The redundant *Will they hurt her?* died on her lips. Nik had said the blood on the walls had been Emily's alone.

"Emily Ma—" Perhaps the Dhryn had learned to read Human expressions. "She's gone? This is dreadful!" Despite his promise to keep his voice within human hearing, Mac felt the hairs on her arms rising and the floor vibrate. *Emotional distress,* she guessed, feeling sufficient of her own.

Mac suspected Nik would have preferred to have other answers from the Dhryn first, but he gave no outward sign of it. "Dr. Mamani's quarters were left in a similar state," he told Brymn, indicating the ruin of Mac's living room. "We've evidence she was involved in a struggle with the same type of beings as left you bound here, possibly at the same time. We're very concerned about her well-being. Anything you could tell us to help direct our search . . ." He let his voice trail away hopefully.

"I am so sorry," Brymn said to Mac, his lips drawn down at the corners. Moisture glistened in his nostrils. More briskly: "You said this happened two days ago?

Standard or Terran days? Wait, no matter. They differ by mere minutes. So." He lifted his supporting hands from the floor and rose to a stand. "I know little beyond rumor and legend, my *lamisah,* but we believe the atmosphere the Ro require can sustain our species. I presume this means yours as well."

There was a worry that hadn't crossed her mind. Until now. "Good to know," Mac said weakly.

"We also believe these dreadful creatures consume the flesh of other sentients."

A new nightmare. Mac looked desperately at Nik, who did his best to look reassuring. "It seems unlikely they'd take such risks if their goal was supper, Brymn," he pointed out.

"You said you needed information," the Dhryn said stiffly.

"And we appreciate everything you can tell us," Nik assured him. "What about our search for Dr. Mamani? Can you give us the location of the Ro system?"

Mac held her breath.

But the Dhryn rocked his big head from side to side, a passable imitation of the Human gesture. "My people have searched for it, but to no avail. They are as much a mystery to us now as when they first began to harass our worlds."

"'Harass?'" Nik repeated. "In what way?"

"They frighten our *oomlings.*"

Mac had the rare privilege of seeing Nikolai Trojanowski completely flabbergasted. Before he could recover, she stepped in: "Where would you look for Emily, Brymn?"

Six hands pointed up. "They will have a dreadnought behind one of your moons. You have moons?"

"One," Mac said automatically.

Nik pulled out a portable com and spoke into it in a quiet but urgent voice. He waved to Mac to continue.

"What did you mean when you said these creatures frighten your *oomlings?*"

Brymn brought his arms down again. "We are both scientists, Mac. But I must tell you, there are things which defy logical analysis. Such is the terrible malady the Ro inflict on my species. They use their stealth technology to slip through our defenses, but not to steal valuables or attack our cities. No, they come to terrorize our *oomlings,* touching them as they sleep . . . waking them with their hideous voices . . . taking those they wish and leaving the others bound as I was." Mac couldn't help looking up to where the remnants of the painful webbing scarred her ceiling. "Only the most rigorous protections now keep the Ro at bay." A heavy sigh. "Beyond the vanishing of *oomlings* and those left to suffer, we know nothing more."

Nik had finished his call and was listening intently. When Brymn stopped, his passion spent, he asked: "Why haven't the Dhryn reported any of this to the Interspecies Union?"

A blink. "We do not wish to think of it."

Mac caught the phrasing. He'd said almost those exact words when first asked about the attack. In a Human, it would be a statement of emotional preference, a plea to avoid a difficult or upsetting memory. From an alien, might it mean something else—perhaps be literally true? Could Dhryn deliberately pick and choose what they would deal with in life, and refuse to think about the rest? A willing blindness?

They did it with biology, she thought, suddenly overwhelmed by the unhuman. *Why not with abducted children?*

And Emily.

Waiting didn't get any easier. While Brymn had packed and Nik made his "arrangements" for their move to the IU Consulate, Mac had sat here in the gallery. She'd managed to force down a tasteless supper, reading in fits and starts. She hadn't managed to ignore her fear of what was sending them away.

The Ro.

Over an hour. *She could have brought in a t-lev from Japan by now.*

Mac was struggling to focus on the next image when Nik returned. Without preamble, he said: "Nothing. No mysterious ship in orbit, behind the Moon or otherwise."

"That you could detect," she corrected, shutting down her 'screen. He didn't appear surprised. Neither was she. Brymn hadn't been able to tell them much more about the Ro or the Null or whatever she was to call them now. The Dhryn, as a species, apparently felt the taking of precautions to protect their *oomlings* was sufficient and the entire existence of the invaders should now be ignored unless annoying Humans insisted on discussing it. But one thing was clear. The technology that had hidden her intruder from her eyes worked very well indeed to evade any other form of looking tried so far.

"Where have you been?" Mac asked, glancing at her watch. "Was there a problem?"

Nik dropped into the seat opposite her, looking decidedly rumpled. It wasn't his clothing, back to its bureaucratic perfection, she thought, so much as the strain around his eyes. *Had he slept at all since arriving at Field Station Six?* "Where have I been, my dear Dr. Connor?" Nik echoed, just short of a growl. He leaned the chair back, holding the table with both hands. "I've been doing my utmost to convince several levels of idiots that there could be such a thing as a starship able to fool our sensors. Then came the interesting part of convincing them that, even if they couldn't see it—which they wouldn't—it was still most likely in orbit around our Moon and did they not find it reasonable to tighten security at every possible point? Which they wouldn't without seeing the invisible ship! Do you want me to go on?"

Mac grinned and shoved her bottle of iced guava in his direction. "Not really. I'm familiar with the rock and a hard place syndrome. Don't forget, I deal with the Wilderness Trust to find ways to do research without breaking rules designed to prevent any such thing."

Nik put the bottle to his lips and drank half in one long gulp. Mac guessed he would have preferred something other than juice. "Thanks. How do you manage?" he asked, handing it back.

"I find a way around. Or more than one. Conflict isn't my nature."

"You could have fooled me."

"Part of my charm," Mac replied, then froze, aghast.

She was flirting.

Emily was fighting for her life on an invisible alien ship, a mysterious threat was facing the Human, as well as other, species, at any second she'd be leaving her home and responsibilities for who knew what—and here she was, trading bottle and banter with this—this . . .

Mac took another, deeper look. With this close-to-exhaustion, rather decent public servant who was in all likelihood also trying to find a moment without worrying about all of the above. *And likely more.* Mac was very glad not to have the secrets that rode Nikolai Trojanowski's back. So she eased her smile into something more normal and added: "In case you haven't noticed, Nik. My charm, that is."

But he undid all the good of her analysis and intentions by offering her no smile at all in return. Behind his lenses, his eyes, a paler hazel in the gallery lights, were unreadable. "It doesn't matter what I notice, Dr. Connor. You can't afford to get close to *anyone* right now," he told her. "There's too much at stake. I warned you before, for your own good. I'll keep doing it." He stood. "I'd better see what's keeping Brymn."

Before she could do more than flush, he walked away.

What did you expect? Mac scolded herself. She was the first to admit she didn't do meaningless babble well, although she didn't think she'd said anything to send Nik bolting from her company. Mac's social conversations normally slowed to a cautious crawl the moment they meant something to her. Emily? She was a different story. Em had the gift of gab, as Mac's father called it, able to send any conversation into pleasant, freewheeling innuendo.

The gift of gab. Mac brought up her 'screen again, but couldn't concentrate on the list hovering before her. Don't get close to anyone? He hadn't meant himself, not entirely. He'd meant Emily.

Mac could understand her friend not bothering to tell her about offworld trips. Heaven knows, Mac had made her lack of interest in anything extraterrestrial abundantly clear on too many occasions. But not once Brymn arrived. It would have been natural—more than natural, unavoidable—for Em to offer whatever she knew abut the Dhryn to help Mac work this all out.

Unless, Mac blinked ferociously to clear her sight, *unless Emily Mamani had wanted to keep her in ignorance.*

If she'd asked where Emily had been these past weeks—why she'd been late—would Emily have told her, or would there have been more *lies?*

Mac shuddered. She'd been flirting with someone who thought such terrible things for a living. "Don't get close." Had Nik been warning her, or merely revealing his own survival strategy?

Whichever it was, Mac didn't like it. Any of it. She planned to give Emily Mamani a piece of her mind the next time she saw her. After they hugged to be sure each was whole.

A tear hit the back of her hand. Mac wiped it off hastily.

A pair of hands gripped her shoulders from behind, thumbs digging gently into exactly the right spots. "Hey, Mac. You okay?" a familiar voice asked anxiously.

She sniffed, detecting the distinct odor of old salmon and new soap, then found a smile, reaching up to pat Seung's hand on her shoulder. "I will be. Tired. Waiting for answers. Just like everyone else here."

Seung gave her a final squeeze, then slid into the chair beside Mac. He moved like the animals he loved so much, the great orcas and sharks, possessing a rare combination of grace and impulsive speed. His worshipful students regularly arranged athletic competitions with other research groups, counting on Seung to win the prize, whether pizza, beer, or mainland transport on a weekend. Unfortunately for their hopes, as often as not he'd be called away seconds before the finish, leaving the Preds to gaze wistfully after their defaulted winnings before following their professor back to work.

Years outdoors and both on and in the water had mottled Seung's naturally tan skin with mahogany. Against its rich color, his eyes were a startling blue. The eyes of a hawk, Mac had always thought, full of bold curiosity and challenge. Even now, when he was obviously concerned for her, she recognized both and smiled again. "You want to know why I asked for the pulse," she guessed.

His grin crinkled the skin around eyes, mouth, and nose. "It wasn't your everyday request, Mac. Sooo?"

"So. I was testing an idea. Could our non-Human guest hear infrasound?"

"Ah," a pleased sound. "I thought it might be something like that. And can he?"

It was hardly a secret. "Yes. Perhaps well below ten Hz."

"The AudioCell would love to get their mikes on him—he must emit in that range too, right? Wonder if he'd like to listen to some of our buddies out there." "Out there" for Seung being the white-capped Pacific showing through the gallery windows.

Mac warmed to the enthusiasm in his voice. *This was why they were here, to ask questions and puzzle out answers.* "He might. We've no time now—scheduled to head for the mainland tonight—but if you could send me a recording, I'd be happy to play it to him and let you know what he says about it."

"That'd be great. I'll get on it—" He got up. "By the way, Kammie sent this down. Probably already complaining about me." His face wrinkled in another grin as he passed Mac a curled slip of mem-paper. "You take care and we'll try not to burn the place down while you're gone."

"Thanks," Mac said, sticking out her tongue. She hoped he didn't notice her hand shaking as she took the slip.

She'd forgotten about the soil assay. Kammie must have started it immediately to have finished by now. Mac burned with curiosity, but tucked the slip away in a pocket that she buttoned closed. *Later.*

The weather had remained generous, bright, and warm—all of which promised heavier rains tomorrow. For now, long rays of afternoon sunlight streamed across the tables and floors, warming backs and gatherings. One ray crossed in front of Mac; she laid her hand within its cheerful glow. Through the window, she could see the light frosting the tops of waves as far as the horizon. The water might be rough for anyone skimming its surface, but the effect was breathtaking. Not a cloud in sight.

The ray of light across the back of her hand dimmed.

Another time, Mac wouldn't have noticed, but almost the first thing she'd read while waiting was the essay concerning invisibility technology. The refraction of light around an object was one technique. Not perfected, not by Humans at any rate. The student author hadn't been impressed.

But Mac now found her attention caught by anything about light that wasn't normal or easily explained. She kept her hand in the sunbeam, staring at it. The light brightened, then dimmed a second time. It dimmed slightly more. Her skin felt chilled.

Mac glanced up. The window, really a transparent wall, arched overhead to form part of the ceiling. The sky was that achingly blue color that looked ridiculous in paintings. No clouds. No haze.

Her shoulders hunched in reflex, her imagination painting a regrettably vivid image of the outer skin of Pod Three being coated by Ro. Ro about to find their way in . . .

"There you are, Mackenzie Winifred Elizabeth Wright Connor!" The bass bellow turned every head, including Mac's, to the doorway where Brymn stood resplendent in yellow and black silk. With his slanted body posture and multiple limbs, this choice cemented an uncanny resemblance to an overweight honeybee and Mac could hear several amused comments, albeit tactfully quiet ones, being shared around the room.

Hand bathed in a beam of varying light, Mac was in no mood to laugh. *Was she going crazy, or the only one to see it?* It took her less than a split second to decide that being wrong wouldn't matter—but being right? She lunged to her feet, making sure her imp was safe in another buttoned pocket, and ran for the alarm on the near wall. Ignoring the questions flying at her, she punched the control, then pressed her back against the wall, wondering what on Earth to do next.

The alarm had visual and audio components, both designed to rouse the most groggy student and penetrate every corner of Base. Yellow framed doorways and emergency exits. Strobes of red flashed across the floor. A modulated hum grated—against Human senses at least—pitched high and annoying, but changing rhythmically in volume so people could shout commands and be heard.

Not that commands were necessary. The gallery erupted in motion. Although there were false alarms every so often, usually after a bar run, the events of the last few days had left everyone on edge. No one hesitated now. The pounding of feet shook the pod floor as staff and students ran for the exits.

Not their feet, Mac realized in horror. She could feel a throbbing in the wall behind her back and jerked away. *The pod!*

The entire room was *moving.* Out the window, the horizon tilted to an impossible ten degrees and kept going . . . twenty . . . Mac wrapped her arms around a support pillar as tables, chairs, cutlery, dishes, and people began sliding toward the kitchen.

Impossible! Pod Three was permanently anchored to the ocean floor. Even a collision wouldn't lift it like this, and they would have heard one—felt it. Mac let go of the pillar and, ignoring the shouts of protest from those at the door, ran diagonally across the sloping floor toward the far end of the window wall. *She had to see what was happening to the rest of Base.*

Mac pressed her face against the transparency and cursed. Only Pod Two was visible from here, and it was . . . it was *rising!* The walkways, normally detached and stored before the pods were raised for the winter, were being pulled up as well, people clinging to railings for dear life. As she watched, unable to do more than pound her fists on the wall, the walkways twisted and split, spilling their Human contents into the Pacific. She could see heads bobbing in the water . . . water that was starting to lip at the wall in front of her.

"Mac!" It was the Dhryn beside her. "We must flee!"

She could hardly breathe, let alone move. Her hands felt glued to the window, as if she could somehow pass through it to help, if only she could press hard enough.

Then she was in the air . . .

Clutched by a giant bee . . .

A bee who *spat* at the window, then somehow charged right through it into the ocean.

Mac had barely time to take and hold a deep breath before she was plunged underwater.

She had even less time to worry if a Dhryn could float without a repeller suit.

- 12 -

DEPARTURE AND DECEIT

"PUT ME DOWN," Mac croaked for at least the hundredth time. Her rescuer paid no attention. It was as if she didn't exist.

It turned out a Dhryn couldn't float unassisted, but it hadn't mattered. He'd lain on his back, holding her wrapped in that almost boneless seventh arm, while the rest of his limbs churned the water in furious strokes, their sheer power driving them through the waves when anything Mac knew of anatomy said they should capsize and drown. Once she'd realized what was happening, she'd tried to convince him to turn back to Base. But to no avail. He was taking them to shore.

She'd protested and struggled until common sense took over. Whether the Dhryn was hysterical or sane didn't matter, as long as he could keep swimming. The water was choppy and rough; the Dhryn wisely riding the swell of the waves in, but they'd been chased by the rest of the Pacific. Mac had held her breath each time she saw a crest about to catch up and douse them, gasping for air as her head broke the water again. Each splash stole body heat and she'd soon been shivering uncontrollably. Thankfully, the Dhryn's body had insulated her back.

What was happening to Base? Mac had tried to see past the waves, but it had been impossible—the Dhryn almost submerged at best and the water too wild around them. She'd grown sick with fear. For her friends, for her colleagues, for what they'd built.

For herself.

It wasn't much better now, on land. The Dhryn had brought them to shore by virtue of crashing into the rocks with a higher wave than most. Before the water washed them out again, he'd taken hold of a skeletal log jutting overhead. Mac had seen the wood compress and splinter under his three fingers. With that one arm, he'd pulled them both clear of the waterline.

The part of her mind still capable of analysis had put a check mark beside the idea of the original Dhryn home being a heavier gravity planet.

Without a word, he'd shifted her to two of his common arms, tucked away the seventh, and started to run.

He was still running, quite a bit later. *After almost three hundred and fifty years of complete exclusion, the Wilderness Trust might as well open the inlet's forest to the general public,* Mac decided, wincing at the trail of ruined vegetation in the Dhryn's wake. His method of locomotion had a great deal in common with a crashing skim, straight through what could be broken and rebounding from anything more solid.

Despite what had to be hysteria, he seemed aware that he was carrying some-one more fragile. *More or less.* Mac yelped as a branch snagged some of her hair and won the tug-of-war. She blinked away tears of pain, thinking of Emily. *Had she felt like this? Been imprisoned by alien hands and arms? Dragged to a destination she couldn't know? Unable to communicate with her captor?*

Mac pulled her mind back to the present—her present—assessing herself as best she could. They'd probably been running no more than a half an hour, though it felt longer. Any exposed skin was scratched. Her clothes had suffered, torn along the right leg and arm by exposed, reaching roots. She'd learned to keep her arms tight to her body after that. She'd lost a shoe. There would be bruises, perhaps a cracked rib, where his arms folded around her. But nothing worse—so far. It was almost miraculous, given the pace the Dhryn was main-taining as he raced through the rain forest.

He did slow to climb, although not as much as she would have. Two pairs of powerful arms and semiadhesive feet were distinct advantages, even if another pair of arms had to balance and protect her.

The next time he slowed, she tried again. "Put me down," Mac pleaded, doing her best to kick. "Stop. Please. We have to go back . . . I . . ." The words buried themselves in heavy, painful sobs as her frustration and rage took over.

He stopped.

Mac's hiccup echoed in the sudden silence. She tried to find her voice again. "Brymn?"

With a thrill of fear, she realized he hadn't stopped for her.

The forest around them swallowed the sun, disgorging dark shadows of every size and shape. *You wouldn't need invisibility to hide here,* Mac thought. Sound was smothered as well: birds waiting for twilight, insects too cool to buzz, no rain pattering cheerfully through the leaves.

The Dhryn's body was canted at its usual angle, and she was underneath, her head near his neck. From that position, it was impossible for Mac to look up when she thought she heard a familiar sound. Not the Ro; a lev, with a power-ful, unusually quiet engine.

Trojanowski!

"Nik!" she shouted. "Down here—"

The rest was muffled by one of Brymn's free hands. The Dhryn finally spoke, a whispered, anxious: "You don't know who it is!"

He lifted his hand away and Mac spat out the taste of bark and salt. "Put me down!"

The relief when she landed on the mossy ground was so great, Mac fought back another sob. She rolled quickly, partly to get away from Brymn before he could change his mind and partly so she could look up.

There! A shadow in the canopy, moving in a reassuringly unnatural straight line.

"It is Nik! Brymn, call him. Your voice will carry. Hurry!"

The Dhryn stared at her, hands hanging limply as if, having stopped running, he'd finally succumbed to exhaustion. His blue skin was marked with scrapes and gouges, each a darker blue as if they cut into another layer; his fine silks were in tatters. *"Lamisah . . .* are you sure?" he whispered.

"Now!" She didn't wait for the Dhryn, cupping her hands and shouting: "Down here! Here we are!"

Her voice disappeared under a startling bellow: "NIKOLAI PIOTR TRO-JANOWSKI!"

Mac dropped back on the moss to catch her breath. If Nik hadn't heard *that,* nothing short of an explosive charge would catch his attention.

He'd heard. She watched as the machine resolved itself from shadow and branch, sinking down more cautiously than she remembered. Mac climbed to her feet, wincing at bruises she hadn't felt until now. Brymn backed away, but not to run as she first feared. He was leaving the most level patch of ground for the lev to land. Together, they waited until it touched down.

Somehow, Mac couldn't believe until the black helmet rose and she could see his face, pale and grim. "How—is everyone all right?" she asked him, hands out as if the answer was something she could hold.

"Help's arrived," Nik said cryptically, climbing down. A quick assessing look at Brymn, then back to her. His voice gentled and he went on without her needing to ask. "The alarm gave everyone a fighting chance. Best thing you could have done, Mac. So was vanishing into the sea—although that did upset your friends in the gallery. I assured them you'd be all right. And you are." *Did she hear relief?* "My only doubt was if I'd find you two before nightfall. The bioscanner works fine, but there's the issue of navigating in these trees."

Mac shook her head to dismiss what was irrelevant. "Was anyone . . . hurt?"

"We cannot stay here!" This from Brymn. The Dhryn lifted his head and shoulders, then lowered them, rocking his body up and down the way a Human would rock from one foot to another.

She ignored him, walking toward Nik until she could put both hands against his chest and stare up into his face. "Please. Tell me."

He hesitated, then took her shoulders in his hands. There was a darkness in his eyes that had nothing to do with twilight. "There were casualties, Mac. Not many," he added, tightening his grip as she flinched involuntarily, "but I won't lie to you. There may be more. I don't know how many injuries were life threatening and—" he took a long breath and Mac held hers, afraid. "—and they've sent divers into Pod Six. It was totally submerged."

"It heard us play the recording," Mac said, lips numb. "It knew I was responsible."

His nod was almost imperceptible, as if he wanted to spare her, but knew she expected the truth. "They were after you, Mac. Once you were gone, there was no sign of them. As I said, leaving was the best thing you could have done."

Brymn burst out: "We must go!"

Without taking his eyes from hers, Nik replied with unexpected heat. "Where? Where will she be safe from them? Not here!" Only now did he turn his head and glare at the alien. "This is where they landed the first time! What were you thinking, Brymn? Were you saving Mac—or bringing her straight to them?"

"They were here?" Brymn shuddered. "I didn't know. I was trying to reach the nearest spaceport." He flailed two arms over his head at the forest. "Is there no civilization on this planet?"

"A spaceport? You wanted—you were going to take me to a Dhryn world," Mac said faintly, understanding at last. She leaned forward until her cheek rested on the cold hardness covering Nik's chest. She wasn't surprised. *Armor for a black knight.* His arms went around her, a welcome Human comfort, despite the flash of pain it sent through her damaged rib. She fought to focus on what mattered, fought to overcome a terror greater than anything she'd faced before.

Leave Earth?

"The Dhryn protect their—their *oomlings*," she reminded Nik—and herself— in a hoarse whisper. "They can protect me."

"Yes. Yes. Yes. Now," Brymn insisted anxiously. "Without the gift of more time to our enemies. They hunt Mac because of the importance of her work to mine. They will never stop! We must keep Mac safe!"

"I study salmon," Mac muttered out of habit.

A hand, five-fingered and Human, stroked the back of her head. Words, hushed on warm breath, stirred her hair: "Mac. You don't have to do this. We'll find another way."

"Before the Ro attack again?" she asked. "Before something worse happens to anyone in the way?" Mac pushed gently and Nik let her go. She offered him a smile. From his worried expression, it wasn't a very good one. "Emily is always telling me to travel more. Here's my chance."

He understood what she wanted him to—Mac could see it in the way his gaze sharpened on her face. Emily had visited Dhryn worlds. Here was an opportunity to find out why, perhaps find a clue to why the Ro had taken her and where.

And if leaving home protected her friends, her family? Mac straightened to her full height: "Get us tickets. Or a ship. Or whatever one does to go—thaddaway." She blithely pointed up to the canopy.

And beyond.

GOODBYES AND GENEROSITY

THE ADVICE of a blue-skinned archaeologist had brought Mac to the one place on Earth she'd never planned to be. The orders of a hazel-eyed spy had locked her in a box and so prevented her from seeing any of it. The fabled Arctic Spaceport, one of fifteen on Earth, was reputed to be an impressive spectacle, blending the awe-inspiring tundra landscape with the world's longest slingshot track, capable of heaving freight directly into orbit.

Of course orbit was the other place Mac had never planned to be, and one she also doubted she'd get to admire through a window.

"Are we there yet?" Mac asked after a novel series of bumps announced something different from the steady vibration of the t-lev.

The woman, older but fit-looking, dressed in a suit twin to Nikolai Trojanowski's usual disguise, had been reasonable company, if you liked your company silent and preoccupied with reading what appeared to be streams of mathematical data. At the question, she looked through her 'screen, blinking her dark brown eyes as if surprised Mac had a voice. "They'll let us know, ma'am."

Ma'am. Mac didn't have a name. Nik had been clear on that. She wasn't to give information about herself to anyone. She wasn't to bring out her imp where it could be scanned. She was, as he'd so tactfully put it, luggage on a conveyor belt.

Filthy, damp luggage, with scratches and scrapes that itched furiously. *Probably getting infected.* "Will there be a place where I can clean up?" Mac asked, drawing the woman's attention again.

"I'm sure I don't know, ma'am. Would you like a drink?"

Not without a bathroom in the offing, Mac grumbled to herself. Mind you, this place might be one of the armored cubicles in a city transit station, for all there was to look at or do. The box held only two chairs with straps, bolted to the floor; a small table, also bolted; and a bag tied to the table, from which her nameless companion would produce bottles of water. And, of course, the two of them, locked in for however long the journey from Hecate Strait to Baffin Island to orbit would take.

If he hadn't lied about where she was going.

Mac squirmed, the thought as uncomfortable as the chair. Like all uncomfortable thoughts—and the damned chair—it refused to be ignored, cycling back and back through her consciousness until she paid attention to it.

The last hours had been a blur in which the world moved past her. Mac had followed Nik's instructions, without question or argument, grateful not to think, clinging to the anchor of his calm voice. She'd waited for the two-person levs to appear in the forest, then sat behind a stranger. She'd flown between trees whose girths made her feel like an insect, then been swept out over the ocean as if in pursuit of the setting sun. They'd met a t-lev larger than any that came close to shore, towing a dozen barges laden with crates and boxes.

There, still lacking a shoe for her right foot, she'd climbed into one of those boxes with this tall, dark stranger. The box, Nik had told her, would join a procession of identical boxes, only the others would contain refined biologicals for shipment offworld. The boxes would be lifted to orbit—here he'd cautioned her about the sometimes rough treatment the slingshot provided cargo—then scooped up and brought to a way station. There, she'd enter the transport taking them along the Naralax Transect, bound for the supposed safety of a Dhryn world. Once safely "loaded," Mac would be free to move around like any other passenger. Brymn would meet her there.

What if he'd lied, Mac's thoughts whimpered. *What if this box was taking her straight to the Ro? What if it opened to vacuum? What if . . . ?* She looked at her companion and gave herself a mental kick in the pants. They'd hardly bother with someone to keep her company if this was anything but what it was: the way to move her that risked the fewest lives.

"Thank you."

The woman looked up, frowning slightly. "For what, ma'am?"

Mac gestured to their surroundings. "Good to have some company in here."

Her companion's sudden smile was magical, transforming her face from grim to gamin. "I know you wouldn't catch me in one of these alone," she confided with a wink. "Bad enough as it is."

"Could use a little decorating," Mac smiled back. "A cushion or two wouldn't hurt. Not to mention a mirror or—" she felt the tangled lump where her hair should be "—or maybe not."

The other woman gave another wink, then reached into her suit pocket and produced a thick-toothed comb. "If it works on my mop," she said, giving her tight black curls a tug, "it will work on yours."

"If you say so . . ." Mac yanked the rest of her hair from its hiding place down the back of her shirt, holding her hand out for the comb. The other woman tsked and, leaving her chair, came to stand behind Mac.

"Lean back and close your eyes, ma'am," she ordered softly, her voice low and rich, spiced by some accent Mac couldn't place. "Relax a while. Excuse a personal comment, but you look like you could use the rest."

Mac wriggled as deeply into the chair as she could, careful of the rib she'd decided was more likely bruised than cracked, and closed her eyes with a sigh. "There's likely bark," she warned, *though hopefully none of the blue that had oozed from the Dhryn's scratches.* "Sap's a distinct possibility. Insects." This last a mumble.

The comb slipped into the hair at the top of her forehead and worked back, firm yet gentle, making slow progress. "If I find something interesting, I'll start a collection."

Mac felt some of the tension leaving her shoulders and neck. Whoever this woman was, fellow passenger, spy, or guard, she'd combed out tangles before, for someone she cared about. *Or for a horse in from the range,* Mac told herself, laughing inwardly.

As each crackling lock came free, her "groom" carefully twisted it into a min-iature braid, then laid it over Mac's right shoulder. Lock after lock, braid after braid, until the mass rippled down Mac's chest and lap, and wisps tickled her ear.

Although there wasn't much but hair in the tangles, the process took time. Mac found herself drifting in and out of sleep, too uncomfortable in the chair to truly rest, but too exhausted to be anything more than a boneless lump. When she was finished combing, the woman gathered the tiny braids by the handful and began twisting those together, humming to herself all the while.

"You've lovely hair, ma'am."

Mac didn't open her eyes but snorted. "Has a mind of its own. As you can tell."

She felt the larger braids being pulled up into one long rope. *Interesting.* The woman gave it a gentle tug. "Yet you haven't cut it."

Because I promised. Mac remembered when. It was like yesterday.

Behind her closed eyelids, she could see the party lights strung along the Jacksons' dock as if she stood there again, admiring how they reflected in the tiny ripples across the lake. She could hear the band playing back at the cottage, something loud to get everyone dancing.

To help everyone forget what was happening tomorrow.

As if the memory had to replay itself to the smallest detail, Mac remembered how she'd smacked her neck to dislodge a mosquito from her bare shoulder, her new, daringly low-cut dress an invitation insects accepted, if not him. She'd gone down to the dock to escape both the effort and the reason for it.

Sam hadn't noticed she was a girl before, in all those years they'd been best friends and classmates—why would he now, the night before he left Earth?

She'd glared at the stars until they blurred. Why was he going? What was out there in the cold and dark that could match the splendor right here? They'd been accepted to the same universities. Were those schools not good enough? Not challenging enough?

Was the Earth not big enough?

"There you are, Mac. Seneal said you'd gone home."

Mac had stiffened at Sam's voice, as mortified as if he'd somehow guessed her thoughts. "Wanted some air," she'd managed to say.

"Know what you mean." He'd come to stand beside her, gazing out over the lake. The night air had carried the scent of him, brought his warmth to her skin. "I'm going to miss this place."

Then why go? had trembled on her lips. But before she'd dared speak, Sam had playfully tugged her hair loose from the mem-shape she'd paid a week's salary from her summer job to have installed for the party, hoping its uplifted complexity would make her seem different, older, so he'd notice at last.

Then: "There. It looks happier."

"My hair?" She'd felt stupid.

Then, wonder of wonders, Sam had run his hand through her hair, from forehead to shoulder, leaving his fingers there to burn her skin with their touch. "Always loved it. Don't cut it while I'm gone, okay?" Before she could speak, he'd kissed her, so quickly she might have imagined it but for the tang of salsa on her lips. "C'mon back to the party, Mac. We're supposed to be celebrating, remember? I can't do that without you."

She'd kept her part of the promise.

Wearily, Mac shook free of the past. "Never seem to get time for a cut," she told her companion in the box stealing her from Earth. "As long as it's out of my face I'm happy."

She'd be even happier once she was home again, for good.

When a light jostling marked their box being lifted into position, Mac hurriedly strapped herself into her chair, mimicking the actions of her companion. For an interminable length of time, she waited, hands locked on the chair arms and doing her best to emulate the outward calm of her companion as well. *She wasn't,* Mac thought ruefully, *fooling either of them.*

The slingshot itself was an anticlimax after Nik's caution of a rough ride. No warning sound, no sensation of movement, just a feeling of increasing pressure against her entire body, the pressure smooth and building to a point that was certainly no worse than she'd experienced in a dive. Perhaps the interior of the box was protected somehow from the worst effects of fleeing Earth's grip.

Mac thought of her salmon, leaping from pool to pool, defying gravity with only their strength and determination. They couldn't see what awaited them until making that final commitment.

She wished she had their courage.

The pressure lessened abruptly, signaling launch—the moment their box joined the line of containers curving upward through the Arctic sky, another ball tossed at space.

Courage or not, she'd made her leap, Mac told herself, determined to hope for the best. She began to unbuckle her straps.

"Don't do that yet, ma'am. The snatch can be bumpy. Should happen the moment we break atmosphere."

Snatch? Mac didn't like the sound of that. Of course, she wasn't very happy about the idea of breaking atmosphere either, so it was probably just as well someone was waiting to "snatch" them. Mac's ever-helpful imagination stuck on the image of a ball reaching the top of its arc then plummeting back to the ground. Fortunately, she was soon startled from that less-than-helpful thought by sounds from "outside" the box, a sullen series of thuds, as though a frustrated bear was trying to break open a waste container.

"They've got us, ma'am."

On the surface, the explanation was reassuring, but Mac had to ask: "How do we know who has us?"

"That's my job, ma'am." Her companion turned over her hands, which had been resting lightly on the arms of her chair. A weapon like Nik's nestled in each, colored to match the paler skin of her palms. "Welcoming committee," she announced with an easy smile, flipping her hands to lie innocently again.

Odd how one's view of the ordinary could spin on an instant. The woman in front of Mac was no longer companion, but warrior. The arrangement of chairs was no longer haphazard, but deliberate, to give her protector line of sight to the only entrance.

And Nikolai Trojanowski obviously didn't trust to subterfuge alone.

"Is there anything I should do?" Mac asked, her voice sounding normal to her own ears.

Perhaps not to others. The other woman's smile broadened. "Nothing would be safest, ma'am. Don't even worry. I'm sure— There." This reassuringly as the thuds were replaced by a staccato series of high-pitched tones and Mac jumped as far as the straps allowed, jarring her rib. "See? On schedule and with the right code. In a few minutes, you'll be on your way."

Mac made herself relax, made herself focus on the next steps. *One at a time,* she told herself, the way she would when climbing a rock face to check its ledges as potential field stations. Normally she wasn't much for heights, but necessity was admirable motivation. That attitude helped now. "The shuttle takes us to the ship?" *She didn't know what to call the damned thing,* Mac realized. Starship? Transport? Prison?

"Not directly, ma'am. Too many variations in freight handling in the Union, despite standards. We're being taken to a way station. You'll transfer to the—to where you're going." A smooth slip past what she was probably not supposed to say.

Mac didn't press the point. She'd be wherever it was all too soon anyway. "What about you?"

The other woman hesitated an instant too long, her cheerfulness too forced as she answered: "Paid leave, ma'am. Nice gig if you can get it."

"Is everyone who helps me getting a similar—vacation?" Mac asked. *Was Nik?*

A sharp look. "I wouldn't know, ma'am."

A warning she'd trespassed? Mac disliked games and secrets. Now it seemed she was to be surrounded by them. It left a foul taste in her mouth as she waited through the next half hour; she kept swallowing to rid herself of it.

But when another round of bear-thuds marked arrival at the way station— whatever that was—and the other woman unbuckled herself, then came over to help her, Mac patted her crown of tidy, if slightly sticky, braids. "Thank you," she said, for the protection as well as the hair.

Another of those brilliant smiles. "All part of the first-class service on Box Airlines, ma'am."

Mac's laugh twanged her rib, so she rather breathlessly reached for help standing up. "I'll be sure to recommend you," she said, as the other woman hauled her to her feet. "Although I can't say I plan to do this again soon."

A shrug. "If you need us, we're here." It wasn't as casual as it sounded. Mac looked up into a pair of somber, worried dark eyes and could only nod.

Then, the side of the box fell away.

Revealing total darkness beyond. *Vacuum!* But when her guardian reacted by standing at ease, as if this had been expected, Mac could hardly do otherwise. But she moved ever so slightly closer to the other woman and tried not to hold her breath.

"Clear!" The darkness had a voice, male, loud, and authoritative. "Lifting shroud on three. One, two, three."

The darkness was gone, replaced by a whole new world.

"Go ahead, ma'am. It's safe."

Mac's first impression was of being outdoors again. She stepped forward, blinking in what seemed full spectrum sunlight. When she was out of the box, however, and could squint upward, she could see, far above, that the "sunlight" was coming from myriad sources. *A lie,* she thought, aware of the irony.

Scale was hard to grasp. The box she'd traveled in might be a child's toy, left lying on the floor near towering piles of others. Skims of a style she'd never seen passed overhead in multiple lanes, sending their shadows to the floor. The floor itself, drawn with broad lines of yellow, black, and green, wasn't of metal or any substance Mac could identify. A heap of what appeared to be fabric lay nearby, black yet with a sheen to it. *The "shroud?"*

Dismayed, she searched for anything familiar. Surely this was a Human station. Emily had traveled like this. Millions did every week. But the figures waiting for her were Dhryn.

Not all, Mac realized with relief, as two men—Human men—came toward her. *Odd, she'd never needed to make that distinction before now.* They were both wearing an alarming amount of protective gear and each cradled an item of weaponry Mac concluded had been designed to intimidate an enemy into surrendering without a fight, given the number of wicked protrusions and glaring red lights on each bulky device.

"Welcome to Way Station 80N-C, ma'am." His had been the voice in the darkness. Shorter of the pair by a hand's breadth, older by several years, with a face sporting implants on almost every possible surface of his caramel-toned skin. *Career military was a safe guess,* Mac concluded, swallowing hard. "Sorry for the delay opening your—" his eyes slid by her to the box as if seeking a helpful label, "—transport."

"We must leave this place at once!" An urgent boom that startled them all.

Mac didn't catch which of the five Dhryn spoke, but the volume and bass tones were familiar. She'd glanced at them once, quickly, expecting Brymn, but these were unfamiliar. Now she looked more closely.

Instead of colored silks, these Dhryn wore bands of woven fiber, either naturally the same cobalt blue as their thick skin, or dyed to match. No jewelry, but the upper portion of their middle arms bore what looked to Mac like black holsters, each holding a stubby cylinder. She had the impression they were smaller than Brymn, though that could have been their surroundings. Mac had never been inside anything so large.

Sam had loved to talk about way stations, she remembered, from how they were numbered for the Earth latitude above which they orbited, later given a letter to designate their sequence among the others in that orbit, to how they were the next logical outgrowth of Human cities. He'd set his family 'screen to receive live feed from the construction of 15S-C, the newest 'station of the time. Now Mac dredged her memories for those images, wishing too late she'd paid more than token attention.

The way stations were like the mining towns that had grown, or been planted, around points of access to treasures from Earth's crust, designed to process ore and house miners. Rather than ore, however, the modern incarnation processed materials being exported from or imported to the planet. They contained the refining and other industries no longer permitted within an atmosphere, as well as manufacturers who assembled products before shipment, or who specialized in repackaging for a varied species' marketplace. And they housed the teeming thousands required to run these operations, not to mention service the diverse shipping fleets that ferried both goods and people.

Mac had only the vaguest conception of the way station's ring shape, more a flattened doughnut than a circle, bristling with docking ports. She did know much of the structure was hollow, with buildings and industrial plants erected inside as required.

She hadn't known the reality would be sheer bedlam. She wanted to cover her ears. It was like standing beside a malfunctioning skim engine while Tie tuned it, only multiplied a hundredfold and with random explosions added. The larger skims roared around lumbering t-levs overhead, small skims passed both, all apparently lacking the mufflers required on Earth. Below them, teethlike racks stretched into the center from ports in the upcurved wall, ferrying boxes of various sizes from air locks to the receiving floor, the machinery complaining every step of the way. Shipping boxes were literally raining down atop the building-sized piles on every side of where Mac and the others stood, a cavalier treatment Mac was grateful their box had been spared.

There were automated shuttle trucks spinning among the piles like so many whirligig beetles on a pond, quiet enough on their multiple tires, but making their presence heard with a sharp *BANG . . . Clang!* as each rammed the box of its choice in order to slide it up on its flat back.

It was a wonder any cargo survived intact, Mac thought, staring around in astonishment. There were no other people in sight. A pair of skims sat nearby, one larger than the other, explaining the arrival of her welcoming committee. Was everything in this section automated? *It would,* she decided with a wince at a shrill grind of metal to metal, *explain the racket.*

"We must leave!" The Dhryn were visibly agitated, limbs shuddering. *Not all,* Mac corrected, leaning to one side to get a better look at the Dhryn standing behind the rest.

He—she kept assuming male for simplicity—was maimed, his left lowermost limb a mere stub, jutting at an acute angle from his shoulder, his right lowermost missing below the elbow joint. *How did he sit?* There were nicks along both ear ridges, too irregular to be decorative. More proof, if she needed it, of the Dhryn disdain for medical care.

"Our friend's right, ma'am," the Human said, though he looked none too pleased about agreeing. "Follow me—"

"We must leave NOW!" Two of the Dhryn jumped at Mac, arms out. Even as she opened her mouth to protest, she was grabbed and spun around so that her guardian could put herself between Mac and the oncoming aliens. The other Humans moved just as quickly to stand in front, aiming their weapons. The frontmost Dhryn stopped and, obviously not loath to escalate the encounter, used their uppermost hands to draw their weapons from their holsters and aim them at the Humans.

Cursing under her breath about trigger-happy fools of any biology, Mac shoved the other woman aside and stepped forward. She made eye contact with the maimed Dhryn and announced as firmly as she could, given the ominously nervous beings surrounding her: "Mackenzie Winifred Elizabeth Wright Connor is all my name. I thought we were cooperating."

The Dhryn, weapons still out, shifted aside so Mac and the maimed individual faced each other. She sent what she hoped was an "I know what I'm doing" look to her fellow Humans. At least they didn't budge. Unfortunately, neither did their weapons.

"I take the name Mackenzie Winifred Elizabeth Wright Connor into my keeping," that Dhryn said finally, giving one of those lifting bows. "Dyn Rymn Nasai Ne is all my name."

Four names. That would mean something to a Dhryn, but for all of Mac's research into the species, she'd yet to find anything to explain what that might be. *Best err on the side of being impressed,* she told herself. Mac remembered Brymn's reaction to her names and clapped her hands once. "I am honored to take the name Dyn Rymn Nasai Ne into my keeping." Courtesy having served its function and started them talking rather than shooting, she dropped it like a three-days' dead salmon. "What's going on? Why do you have weapons aimed at my companions?"

"We must leave," another Dhryn boomed.

"Fine. I don't want to stay here either. Put away those things!" This to all of them.

Mac wasn't sure who deserved the award for moving most slowly, but after everything stubby, pointy, or stealthy was off its target, she heaved a sigh of relief. "Thank you."

Dyn replied with a firm: "You must come with us, Mackenzie Winifred Elizabeth Wright Connor."

Tit for tat, Mac thought. She was spending far too much time lately arguing while filthy and tired. It made her inclined to be difficult, but in this case, being difficult might be safer. *Where was Nik? Where was Brymn?* were questions she couldn't ask strangers. "I cannot go with you. I require—" she stopped herself just in time. *No point saying "medical treatment" to a Dhryn.*

She was scrambling for something plausible the aliens couldn't provide when the other woman, who'd been silent until now, filled in with a perfectly straight face: "—the Rite of Manumission. It's required before she may venture farther from her home."

The Dhryn's tiny mouth flattened into a thin line of disapproval. "I have never heard of such a thing. Humans travel from this place constantly."

"Not one as important as Mackenzie Winifred Elizabeth Wright Connor."

Well done! Mac tried to keep a straight face. If the Dhryn didn't concede, it would diminish her importance after he'd just acknowledged it before witnesses.

And if there was one trait their species seemed to share, it was pride.

Someone had called ahead, Mac decided. *Ask no questions,* seemed the likeliest command given. Politeness was one thing; this bland acceptance of her torn clothing and barely scabbed scrapes by everyone they passed in the halls of this nondescript building was quite another. It was disturbing, as though in a way their inattention made her as invisible as the Ro.

"In here, ma'am."

"Mac," she said, entering the door the woman held open. "It's hardly a secret now, is it? Please."

That infectious smile. "Mac. You can call me Persephone."

Mac gave her a suspicious look, but there was nothing but good humor on the other's ebony face. They'd all been relieved to squeeze together, Human to Human, in the small skim. Once the weapons were stowed beneath the seats, that is. The Dhryn had followed their rise into the traffic lanes, then kept pace around the rim of the way station to the inhabited area. For all Mac knew, the five aliens were still parked outside this building, whatever it was, waiting for her to finish the "Rite of Manumission."

"That was quick thinking, Persephone," Mac complimented as they walked into what appeared to be a deserted med-clinic.

"Part of the job description," came the offhand response, but she seemed pleased. "There should be a gown in the cubicle over there, Mac. I'll call the doc in to dress those cuts."

"Don't call anyone." Mac's smile and greeting died on her lips as Nikolai

Trojanowski stormed into the clinic, his face dark with anger. "What the hell are you doing here?"

"Sir, the situation—" His look was nothing short of lethal. Persephone closed her mouth and, with a sympathetic glance at Mac, turned and left the room, shutting the door behind her.

Mac frowned. "I was *supposed* to let them take me away?"

"Shh!" From his suit pocket, Nik pulled a thin silver rod, giving it a shake to extend it to a length of over two meters. With his weapon ready in his right hand, rod in his left, he proceeded around the room, swinging the rod so that it brushed ceiling and walls, moving so quickly Mac found it hard to keep safely out of his way. She watched the anger fade from his face as he worked, replaced by concentration.

When Nik was satisfied, he shook the rod one more time to shrink it to pocket-size. His eyes found and fixed on her. Behind the glasses, they were smudged with exhaustion, but fiercely alert. *Probably stimmed to the gills,* she thought uncharitably. "Low-tech," he said, "but effective in an enclosed area."

"Whatever works." Mac couldn't believe she'd forgotten, even for an instant, that their foe could be hiding anywhere in plain sight. "You shouldn't blame your staff."

"You're right," he surprised her by saying. He leaned against the examination platform like a man conserving the last of his resources by any means possible. "I was trying to keep info splatter to an absolute minimum—which meant 'Sephe didn't know better than to back your decision."

"Info splatter?" Was no Human activity safe from jargon? "Have you heard anything more from Base?" she demanded, her voice feathering at the edges. "Any—names? Do they know I'm okay? What's . . . ?" Mac stopped herself. "I'm sorry. I'm anxious for news."

His expression softened. "I know. I've asked for the—for a list. I wish I could tell you more." When she kept looking at him, he continued, perhaps to comfort her. "Your people look to be good in emergencies: coolheaded, smart. I'm sure they did all the right things even before the rescue teams arrived."

"Real ones, or more of yours?" Mac asked. "I did figure out those police were nothing of the kind, you know."

A raised eyebrow. "Here we thought they were flawless. But yes, the rescuers were local."

Mac realized with a sinking feeling he'd avoided one of her questions. "You did tell them I'm okay, didn't you? And my dad . . . You'd promised to call him." Mac put a hand to her throat, something she'd thought only melodramatic movie heroines did until now, when it felt impossible to catch a full breath through the painful tightness of her throat. "Oh, god. You didn't tell him I was dead."

"Of course not!"

He could be lying and she'd have no way to know. Her father could be mourning her and she'd have no way to tell him the truth.

All her doubt and fear must have shown on her face, because Nik spread his hands out and said with unexpected honesty: "I would have, Mac, if faking your death would have thrown the Ro off your trail. Enough people saw you launched into the ocean with Brymn to make it credible that you drowned." When she began to sputter indignantly, he gave a faint smile. "Don't worry. Morality aside, it wouldn't have worked. Imagine the media uproar if the first and only Dhryn to visit Earth was killed. No, the Honorable Delegate had to make a very visible, very routine departure. When your friends catch the news and see Brymn escaped the attack at Base, and they know he took you with him, how could you be anything but well?"

Mac couldn't decide if she was more confused than relieved. "So what did you tell them? You had to explain my disappearance from the face of the Earth—" *literally!* "—somehow."

He looked insufferably smug. "*You*, Dr. Mackenzie Connor, have sent reassuring vid messages to Base and to your father."

Of course. As she'd spent years working with people capable of that type of forgery and more, if they hadn't been busier using their skills to investigate the natural world, Mac felt herself blush. "What did you—did I—say?"

"Oh, you explained how you'd been picked up by a police boat. Confirmed, naturally, by the 'police.' You related how Brymn was so unnerved by his brush with death—and you, so grateful for his help in escaping—that you accompanied him to the Consulate."

"And?" Mac prompted when Nik paused, as fascinated by this skewing of events as she would have been watching a skim about to crash. There was the same sense of inevitable disaster. *Her friends and family would never believe this.*

"And? As a parting gift," Nik told her, "Brymn arranged for you to access files he'd stored at the Consulate in hopes of finding something to assist the search for Emily and identify those who'd attacked Base. Because of understandably tight security there, you can only access those files within the compound and they will not let you leave, then return. So you are staying as long as it takes. There was more—your confidence in Kammie, condolences and wishes to be kept informed, reassurances to your father. I can arrange for you to view the recordings, if you like."

Mac gulped. "That's just—that's just—"

"Amazing?" he offered helpfully. "Brilliant?"

"Uncanny," Mac said, staring at Nik. "I *would* do that." They'd all believe it, too. Even her father, though he'd voice his opinion. She fought a wave of homesickness. "How could you know?"

His lips quirked. "You study salmon. I study people. Don't worry, Mac. We'll keep up 'your' messages and cover your absence as long as necessary. Right now, we'd better get you to the Dhryn. They aren't the most patient beings and, with the Ro as adversaries, I can't argue."

"Where's Brymn now?"

"He's aboard the *Pasunah,* waiting for you." An unnecessary stress on the last word.

"He can wait." Mac went to cross her arms, then decided against it when her rib protested. "I'm not leaving to go anywhere—especially a Dhryn ship—until I've cleaned up and had a Human doctor seal these cuts."

He'd either anticipated her reaction or knew better than to argue. "Shower's that way," Nik pointed with his chin. "It's got a sterile field. Thirty seconds ought to do it." He swung the office pouch from under his shoulder to the platform. "Here. This is for you."

"Supper? Is there time?" Mac said, trying to smile at her own joke.

"Sorry." He patted the pouch. "Clothes, hopefully your size. The rest of your luggage is already on the *Pasunah*." At her highly doubtful look, he smiled. "We had staff do some discreet shopping in the way station's stores while you were en route. Nothing fancy—don't worry. I did my homework."

For some reason, Mac immediately resented his assumption she preferred plain. *Not that Nik had any reason to assume otherwise,* she admitted.

The idea of being clean made every scratch and bite on Mac's body itch. She looked at the shower longingly. *But first* . . . "This is going to take time to undo," she waggled the end of the intricate braid at him.

"It's quite—thorough."

That surprised a laugh out of her. "That bad?"

"I confess I'm curious what you did to annoy 'Sephe."

Despite everything, Mac found herself grinning at him. "Let this be a warning to you. Never leave two bored women alone in a box."

"Warning taken," Nik said. "Here. Let me."

Mac turned to offer him her back, standing close enough that his knee brushed her leg. "Just get it started, thanks. I can work out the rest in the shower."

She felt him pick up the thick braid and run its length through his hands before his fingers began to puzzle at the knot at the end. "I had time to talk with Brymn on the way here," Nik told her. With each word, his breath tickled her neck in a way that made Mac suddenly aware of a problem.

She liked the way his breath tickled her neck.

She liked it in a way that sent waves of shivering warmth into places that should have been politely noncommittal, thank you very much, given where she was and who he was. *Not to mention the why of it all.*

Worse, she couldn't edge out of range of his breath without being obvious; by the movements of his hands, he'd found his way into the braid by now and was busy undoing it.

Mac gritted her teeth. *A cold shower.* "Did Brymn tell you anything more about the Ro?" she asked.

"Nothing to help us find or contact them. We'll probably learn more from the shroud the Dhryn used over your box."

The pile of dark fabric. "What was it?"

"Apparently the Ro can limpet themselves—more accurately, some kind of travel pod or suit—to other vehicles in either an atmosphere or in space. The Dhryn claim their shroud emits an energy pulse of some kind on contact that interferes with the attachment mechanism, shaking loose any such hitchhikers. It forms the basis of their defense for *oomlings*. They also told us they believe it stuns or kills any Ro inside, but that's never been confirmed. They haven't been able to retrieve any of these devices or their passengers."

Mac stiffened, fear rinsing away thoughts of warmth, in water or otherwise. "Then one or more could have come with us—could be on the 'station now."

"Given their capabilities?" She felt Nik spread apart the braids which had been twisted together, then begin to untwist the tiny braids of the one over her left shoulder. *No denying he was undoing the mass more quickly than she could.* "If not with you, then on any ship. All we can do is make sure we keep what secrets we can from them. It might be for the best that you refused to go with the Dhryn. That may have confused the issue, forced any Ro who were watching to decide which of you to follow."

Mac squeezed her eyes closed. Squeezed her hands into fists. Squeezed her thoughts into the tightest possible focus. Amazingly, her voice came out sounding almost calm. "I said my name. Outside the box. In the open. Anyone—anything—could have heard."

"Irrelevant." A tug. "They already know who you are."

"You could at least try to be reassuring," she protested, eyes flashing open.

"Could I?" a chuckle. Dozens of tiny braids tumbled free over her shoulder, a few spontaneously unwinding, and he went to work on the next twisted strand. "What's reassuring, Mackenzie Winifred Elizabeth Wright Connor, is that the Dhryn, particularly our busy Brymn, but also the captain of the *Pasunah* and apparently what passes for their government, also know who you are. And for reasons of their own, they are offering you what they never grant aliens—access to the heart of established Dhryn society, on a Dhryn-only world. Even your Emily didn't manage that, as far as we know." He sounded like a proud parent.

The lie had been larger than she could have imagined. Mac saw it with the stunning clarity of a lightning flash in a darkened room, her mind reeling with the afterimage of truth. Licking her lips, groping for calm, she said it out loud: "Which is exactly what you and the Ministry of Extra-Sol Human Affairs were hoping for all along."

His hands paused the barest instant, then kept unbraiding. "What do you mean?" Casual, but she didn't need to see Nik's face to know its expression. *Wary.*

"You—those who sent you—could have cared less about Brymn's reason for seeking me out. You never thought I'd be of any help either. It was the Nulls—the Ro—you've been after. You've known they were preying on the Dhryn. You let Brymn come to Earth and contact me to bring him where you could watch what happened! You were hoping he'd reveal something about the Nulls. You're probably glad they attacked us!" With that, Mac jerked away and whirled to face him, loose hair and unraveling braids flying in slow motion over her shoulders, breathing heavily with rage that finally had a target. She fumbled at the fastening of the pocket that had kept her envelope safe, drove her hand inside, then pulled it out and threw it at him.

It struck his chest and fell to the floor.

Nik held up the desiccated remains of a banana slug he must have found in her hair, then tossed it after the envelope. "You could be right," he said, each word slow and distinct. "I wouldn't know. I wouldn't have to know. And I wouldn't ask." His eyes became chips of stone in a face turned to ice. "A threat to the *species,* Dr. Connor. What part of that didn't you grasp? Where on the scale of that do you and I fall?"

"You put my people at risk—"

"They were at risk already. What's happening out here—" his violent gesture swept in an arc to encompass everything but the planet below, "—is destroying all life in its path. All life! If the Ro are responsible, yes, we'll do anything to stop them. I'll do anything. And from what I know of you, you would, too."

"I wouldn't put innocent people in danger without at least telling them why! Without giving them a chance to protect themselves!"

Nik surged to his feet. "Haven't you noticed? We don't know how to protect anyone! I can't—I can't even protect you!"

The words rang in the room as they stood, eyes locked. Mac inhaled air warm and moist from his lungs and didn't know which of them moved first to remove any distance between them, didn't know whose lips were more desperate, whose arms held tighter.

She did know Nik was the first to break away.

He thrust her from him so quickly she staggered a step to regain her balance. His face—she might have imagined that flash of vulnerability—became cold and still once more. "It's time to go, Dr. Connor," he said harshly. "We can't risk the Dhryn leaving without you. I'll let them know you're coming; don't take long getting ready. There's a field med kit in your luggage. You'll have to treat yourself."

Treat herself? Mac pressed one hand over the thrill of pain from her rib, brought the other to her throbbing lips. When she pulled it away, there was blood on her fingers. She stared at it, her eyes wide.

His hand appeared in her sight, pressed the envelope into her bloodied one. Her name rippled across the surface in mindless mauve. "Keep that safe and with you at all times," she heard him say. "No matter what you think of how you got involved, this message authorizes you to claim help and equipment from any Human you encounter."

Mac lifted her eyes to his face, seeing a smear of blood on his mouth too. Heat flushed her cheeks, but she held her voice as steady as his. "I won't encounter any Humans, will I?"

Instead of answering, Nik went on with a rapid-fire briefing. Mac struggled to pay attention, to quiet the pounding in her ears and chest. "There's a beacon in the handle of the smaller piece of luggage," he told her. "When the *Pasunah* sets her transect exit, it will send us those coordinates. There's also an imp—use it instead of yours. It has an automated transmitter and whenever you enter a transect, it will squeal a burst containing your latest log entries, coded so only we can translate."

"How will you find me if I'm not entering a transect?" Mac asked, all too familiar with the unreliability of beacons and transmitters once out of the lab and in the field. *Not to mention some unique problems.* "The Ro can wipe out stored power," she reminded him. *At least in civilian equipment, like that at Norcoast.* "And what if the Dhryn take these things away from me? What will happen then?"

"There is a backup." Nik reached into an inner pocket of his jacket. He drew out what looked like a pen.

"I take it—this time—that's not a pen," Mac ventured, eyeing the thing suspiciously.

"No, it's not." He held out his empty hand. When she gave him hers, thinking that was what he wanted, he grasped her upper arm instead. "Don't move," Nik warned as he pressed the tip of the pen to her skin, taking advantage of the tear in her shirt.

Mac yelped as her arm went on fire from shoulder to wrist. *"What are you—?"* But the pain was gone before she could complete the protest.

Nik released her and Mac ran her fingers over intact skin. "Bioamplifier. The nans will replicate your DNA signature, then concentrate in your liver and bone marrow."

"So you can still find me if I'm in pieces."

He paid her the compliment of not disputing the point. "Yes. Potentially even a century from now, under the right conditions."

"Good to know." *But not the happiest thought,* Mac decided, rubbing her arm, although the technology had interesting potential for her work. She wondered if she could get the specs.

If she ever worked again.

"There are some important limitations," Nik continued. "The one of concern to you is that it only works reliably if you're on a planet surface. The artificial gravity of ship or station tends to blur sigs together."

She appreciated his candor, especially when it answered questions she'd been ready to ask. "So, my orders are to stay on the ground. You don't mind if that's in one piece, do you?" *God, she was getting punchy,* Mac thought. There'd better not be any important decisions in her immediate future.

He frowned. "We are doing everything to minimize any risk—"

"So you can retrieve whatever I learn from the Dhryn about the Ro. I know my value." The moment the words were out, a gauntlet between them, Mac flushed again. "Nik, I didn't mean . . . I know you . . . This is . . . I'm not . . ." He was looking at her in a way that made it impossible to finish any of it. Mac knew her face had to show everything she was feeling: the bewilderment, the longing, the fear, all served with a hearty dose of pine sap, scratches, healing flash burn, and dirt.

Awkward didn't begin to cover it.

"You can do this, Mac."

"If you say so, Mr. Trojanowski," she replied, fighting to stay calm.

It didn't help Mac's equilibrium when Nik traced her swollen lower lip with a fingertip, his eyes following his finger as if mesmerized. "Just don't get close," he whispered, as if to himself, then leaned forward and kissed her again, so lightly it might have been a dream.

But all he said next was: "Locating the Ro home system is the priority, Mac. If it helps to keep it personal, remember that's your best chance of finding Emily. We'll stay in touch through regular, open channels, but be aware none of those can be trusted. Don't initiate any contact."

This wasn't happening, Mac told herself. Knowing it was, she struggled to be practical. "I don't suppose you put a Dhryn dictionary in that luggage? Anything to let me know what to expect?"

"Hopefully, most can speak Instella. I wish we had a sub-teach ready for Dhryn to send with you, but outside of a few entries in an encyclopedia, no one's bothered to compile one. We're working on it now, believe me. Mac—" This with a glance at his watch.

This was it, then. The last chance she had to drop to the floor, kicking and screaming that they couldn't make her leave everything she knew, to go to where her only expertise was forbidden and her very species, the alien.

Emily had done it. *She couldn't imagine why.*

Mac, at least, had Emily for a reason. Keep it personal, Nik had said. *Good advice.*

"Let's not keep them waiting more than necessary," Mac said calmly. "Give me five minutes. Clothes, please?" She took the bundle he produced from his pouch then, without another word or look, without another touch, headed for the shower.

Nik's footsteps echoed hers, one for one. She didn't dare turn around to see if he was following her, but when Mac reached the door to the stall, she heard the door to the corridor open and close.

She pressed her forehead against the cool metal.

"Emily," she whispered, listening to the hammering of her heart. "What the hell just happened?"

- Portent -

THE CAVES WERE ancient, hallowed, and worn. Ancient, as measured in cycles of mineral and water; hallowed, as sites praised in prayer and storied memory; worn, as befitted the only practical shelter in these hills prone to violent wind. Throughout recorded time, the noblest and humblest cowered and wailed here together while nature unleashed her worst on the mountainside. It was said the caves refused no one.

Had such things mattered to him, Eah, night shepherd and litter runt, would have considered himself one of the humblest to ever set footpads within this, the nearest of the fabled caves to his pasture, the Cave of Serenity. But his was a simple soul, content to have a useful place within his kin-group, and, within that place, he felt all the pride of any Primelord.

No matter the fear raising the bones along his spine, no matter the nervous bleating of his flock, no matter the ominous strength of wind in the valley—that pride made Eah stop inside the entrance to light his torch and show proper respect. The ritual three spits into the dust at his footpads, a gift from his body. The ritual claw scrape along the tall stone godstooth, a gift of his might. The ritual howl—

Before Eah could properly prepare himself to howl, the great depth and resonance of his voice something which had always given him profound satisfaction, his flock, which had never appreciated his voice, bolted for the inside of the cave, running between his legs and past him on either side. They almost knocked him down in their haste. He would have chastened them, but they were mindless beasts, always finding ways to challenge his authority. Surely the gods understood such things and would not take offense. To be safe, Eah sprinkled three handfuls of sweetened grain from the bag at his side on the dust, clawed the stalagmite once more, then drew breath to howl.

A runnel of liquid green trickled toward him in the dust, like a finger reaching out of the darkness. Eah leaped sideways and away, clinging to the rock wall. His ability to jump was another that pleased him, if not his mothers, but this time he trembled. Did he now offend the gods by marking their soft glittering stone with his claws?

Before he could decide whether to drop down or remain, one of his flock staggered into the light of the torch, still burning where he'd dropped it in the dust. It was the Old One, whose ability to find water in the dry season was more valuable than her age-bleached hair or tough flesh.

Hair that had disappeared along with the skin beneath . . . flesh that was oozing away from the bones beneath. Her next and final step landed in the runnel of green, her sharp little toes melting so she fell forward.

And fell apart.

Eah trilled like a kit for its mothers, his claws digging deeper into the stone, hearts falling out of synchrony when he didn't leap away and run, as instinct screamed he should.

But the runnel, having washed away the Old One as Eah might wash dirt from his hands, stretched out its fingers across the entrance. There wasn't room for his footpads.

Eah was not one skilled with tool or words, but things he put his hands to usually moved. Now, he used that strength, holding himself with one hand as he stretched the other as far as he could reach along the wall in the direction of the cave opening. The coming windstorm would drive sand through clothing and skin, blind and deafen those without shelter, but it was a threat he knew, a threat sent by the gods themselves. He'd rather die there, where his kin-group would find his body and carry it home again so his mothers could wash him one last time.

He drove in his claws, released the other hand, then pulled himself closer to escape. Again. Again. One claw snapped, and he almost fell into the spreading pool of green.

Drive and pull. *Again!* This time, his arm was bathed in light. He was almost outside!

Even as Eah gasped with hope, he realized something was terribly wrong.

The storm winds had a new, strange sound.

As if they carried rain.

- 14 -

FAREWELLS AND FLIGHT

PERSEPHONE—'Sephe—was waiting for Mac when she stepped out of the shower stall, dressed though damp. "I don't think I've seen anyone quite that shade of pink before," she said with a grin.

As every portion of Mac's skin, scraped or whole, felt as though it had lost three layers then been soaked in salt, she considered several scathing replies, but restrained herself. "I take it my time's up?"

"Skim's waiting. Put this on," the other woman ordered, "this" being a huge and hideous mottled brown cloak with a hood. "It's Derelan," she added, then, at Mac's blank look, finished with: "—feels better than it looks."

"That's a relief." Mac whipped her damp, slug-free hair into its normal braid before 'Sephe could offer, tying a loose knot with the result. Feeling that much closer to normal, she walked over and accepted the cloak, surprised by its light suppleness. 'Sephe helped arrange the unusual garment over her new clothes.

They'd fit, not that Mac had expected anything less. And they weren't quite as plain as Nik's description had suggested either. A blouse, white with a gathered bodice and hem, long sleeves with actual buttons, not mem-fabric, to hold them snug to her wrists. A skirt, shimmering blue and sleek, falling to her ankles with thigh-high slits on either side giving her legs freedom to move. A slim waist pouch that could lock relieved her mind on the issue of pockets, holding, with a bit of squeezing, both her imp and the abused, but not yet studied, piece of mem-paper with the results from Kammie.

There was even new footwear, shoes with a soft, studded sole of a type Mac had never seen before that molded comfortably to her feet. *A relief after the boots.*

She hadn't expected to find frankly luxurious undergarments in the bundle, of the sort she'd never bothered buying for herself, though Emily would certainly know the labels. An intimate thoughtfulness Mac found somewhat distracting, given her last encounter with their source, but they'd provided a choice of secure locations in which to tuck her envelope.

The cloak rested on her shoulders and fell almost to the floor, the folds adding bas relief to the brown, so Mac felt disguised as a tree trunk. *Derelan*. The species was hopefully in her xeno text; it wasn't in her brain. *She'd look it up when the universe granted her time for things like breathing.* 'Sephe was already at the door, her stance just short of foot tapping.

Wrapping the Derelan cloak around herself, like hiding in a cocoon, Mac didn't try to fool herself that it was only the Ro's eyes she'd like to avoid.

"Put the hood up."

Mac complied, only to find the hood drooped over her forehead and face to her mouth. "Don't you think this is a little—obvious?" she asked, pushing up the hood so she could see Persephone.

The other woman looked serious. "Maybe to a Human. Hopefully not to our sneaky friends. We don't know if they use scanners, but the cloak's fabric is impregnated with a jigsaw puzzle of DNA fragments, which even our toys can't sort into anything more sensible than a platypus crossed with a clam."

Mac gathered the folds more tightly around herself. "I'm convinced. Now what."

"Your chariot awaits, Mac. We just have to retrace our way in: three corridors and a lift, all guarded. Nik—Mr. Trojanowski's in a mood, all right. We had to sweep them twice before he was satisfied."

Aware that the other was giving her a more than curious look, Mac pulled down the hood. "Then we'd better go."

It should have been easy—the walk through the corridors, the brief trip on the lift, all with 'Sephe's tall, strong presence at her side, in sight of two or more armed guards at any time. Mac did feel safe.

But every few steps, a tear would sting her cheeks, the skin scalded twice now. She was grateful for the hood's shadow.

These steps would be her last among Humans for the foreseeable future. Already the world she knew—of rocks, growing things, and water—seemed a dream, a vision of a paradise she'd lost. Here, nothing was irregular. Nothing struggled to survive. Nothing was alive but the people themselves—and they were encased in armor and caution.

Mac indulged in one final sniff, then stiffened her spine. She was, after all, a scientist. Here was a chance to add to a woefully neglected data set—the Dhryn. She had Brymn, if not a friend, then an ally, by his own words. And, as 'Sephe and another figure preceded her out the door of the building, she added to her list the backing, however many light-years removed, of the Ministry of Extra-Sol Human Affairs, in the person of Nikolai Trojanowski.

He was waiting for her, standing with feet spread and apparently relaxed between another Human guard and a Dhryn, with his suit, cravat, and glasses looking as bizarrely out of place in this gathering as she likely did in her ungainly cloak. Despite that, or perhaps because he hadn't bothered with armor, Mac didn't doubt he was the most dangerous one of them all.

As if rehearsed, the Dhryn stepped to the side of their skim and gave some signal that opened its side door. It was a bigger model than most, so a ramp slid out, clanging to a stop against the flooring.

Flooring. Mac peered up from under her hood, wanting another quick look at this amazing place. What she called a door in the building they'd just left could be an air lock, if the need arose. What she called a building was a portable stack of preconstructed forms, reassembled as needs changed. What she called a sky— Mac lifted her face to sunlight that wasn't, imagining the far-off lines of traffic were clouds.

A touch on her elbow. Mac nodded in acknowledgment and began walking toward the skim, her eyes on Nik. He gave her a look he probably thought was encouraging. It was a little too haunted for that.

The touch on her elbow pushed harder, as if to say *no, that way.* Confused, Mac turned her head.

There was no one close enough to touch her.

Mac didn't stop to think. She threw off the useless cloak and broke into a run, arbitrarily picking the direction opposite to the one the touch wanted. "They're here!" she shouted to Nik, hoping he'd understand she hadn't lost her mind.

He began to shout orders, was already in motion.

Spit! Pop!

The sound electrified the Dhryn. The skim roared into the air, ramp still extended and hanging loose. The one left abandoned unsheathed his weapons and stood ready.

Mac caught all this in quick glimpses over her shoulder as she ran, arms pumping and grateful for a skirt that got out of the way of her legs. The twanging rib she ignored. She dodged around a pillar displaying notices to find herself face-to-face with a tall yellow barricade marked "under construction" in black.

Cursing the predictability of Human cities, Mac turned to run along the fence, hoping for a way around it.

Her skin crawled at the thought of another *touch;* her ears strained for any sound. *They must have cleared the area of passersby,* Mac fumed, slowing to a jog as she hunted in vain for a crowd or even an open door. *Nothing.* The place was locked up tight. Given a choice between a shadowed gap between two buildings and a wide, plazalike space, she ran into the open, hoping to be spotted.

"Mac!"

Well, that worked, she congratulated herself, panting as she stopped to hunt the source of that reassuring shout. Her rib throbbed in reminder and she pressed her elbow into her side to shut it up.

Scurry . . . skittle . . . scurry!

Mac launched back into a full-out run, dodging from side to side as though trying to make her way through a crowded soccer field.

Or like a salmon, trying to work upstream through rocks—only to find the flash and power of grizzly claws waiting.

She was halfway across the deserted plaza, still hunting the voice, when a figure appeared in the shadow of a building in front of her, frantically beckoning to her. Mac sobbed with relief and found an extra burst of speed.

"No, Mac! Stop!"

That voice she knew. *Nik, but from behind?* Mac stared ahead. *Then who was that?* The figure began walking toward her.

"Mac! Stop! Wait for us!" Now she could hear the thud of footsteps, his and others.

Who—was that?

Mac slowed to a walk, the better to see.

That shape, its easy grace? It couldn't be—

"Em . . . ?" The whisper tore its way up her throat as Mac started to believe her own eyes.

She was grabbed roughly from behind, held. "Mac, wait, dammit!" Nik shouted hoarsely.

She struck at him. "Let me go! That's Emily!"

Spit! Pop!

A sudden *whoompf* of sound, like a punch in the air. Mac felt Nik's body stiffen against hers, then go limp, slipping through her hands as she tried to support his weight. His eyes stared at hers, a terrible urgency in them. His lips moved. Nothing came out.

"He's hurt!" Mac cried, looking up desperately for help as she eased Nik to the floor.

She saw something else. Emily, dressed from neck to toe in skintight black, walking toward them while continuing to aim what had to be some sort of weapon at Nik.

This had to be a dream, Mac told herself. *A nightmare.*

"I am helping you," Emily insisted. "I told you I would. This isn't going to work, Mac. You have to come with me. Now. We won't hurt you."

We?

Scurry . . . skittle . . .

"Hang on, Mac!" More voices. Closer, with pounding feet as an underscore.

Beyond terror, past despair was a kind of numbness, erasing urgency and muting self-preservation. Mac sank to her knees, doing her best to keep Nik's head and shoulders off the floor. He'd lost consciousness. *Or worse,* that safe and detached part of her said. "What have you done?" she asked, as calmly as if she and Emily were still on that granite ledge, waiting for the first run.

"I'm trying to— *Ai!*" Emily dodged back as a huge shape descended on the plaza.

"Em!" A flash filled the air, bright enough to make Mac cry out in pain and close her eyes. She hunched over Nik's body, hoping 'Sephe and the others were responsible.

But the hands that tore her away were both irresistibly strong and very familiar.

Dhryn.

- 15 -

BOXED AND BOTHERED

SOMEONE had flung jewels at the night, the largest sapphire Earth, with her diamond Moon. There were others, smaller yet brighter, as if handfuls of cut gemstones had spilled over that black silk to catch sunlight and return it as fire to the eye.

Mac's fingers traced the cold metal outline of the vision. Her breath fogged the viewport and she wiped it clear. The Dhryn had given her this, a chance to watch as the *Pasunah* maneuvered from orbit into the appropriate orientation for the Naralax Transect.

She found a sharp burr on the metal and worried it with a fingernail.

They'd given her nothing more.

No comlink. No message.

No answers.

Mac drew her lower lip between her teeth, involuntarily remembering his taste, her tongue exploring the tiny cut along the inside of her mouth. Here she was, off on a mission whose primary goal—to her—was apparently safe, sound, and on the wrong side, not to mention back at the way station. And the Dhryn wouldn't or couldn't tell her if Nik was alive.

Well, Mac, she said to herself, bitterly amused, *here you are*. Same situation. Different box.

The transition from normal space into a transect might be worth watching, but they hadn't told her when it would occur. From what she'd seen through the viewport, Mac guessed the *Pasunah* was being guided into the required orientation by tugs. Once aligned with the desired transect, her engines would fire, sending the ship curving toward the Sun.

Not suicide, Mac assured herself. *Part of the journey.* Every schoolchild learned that the transects were anchored a few million kilometers outside the orbit of Venus and why. Inward and far enough from system shipping lanes—and the teeming populations of Earth, Mars, and the moons of the gas giants—to satisfy the most paranoid; close enough to make the trip to and from any transect itself economical. That this orientation also put outgoing freight from the Human system at the top of Sol's gravity well was a factor they didn't teach in school, but travelers foolish enough to buy round-trip tickets soon became acquainted with that reality. Mac had endured Tie's diatribe on that matter quite a few times following his first, and last, outsystem vacation.

Economics couldn't change where time was consumed in an intersystem trip. Travel through the transects was outside space-time itself. Mac couldn't quite imagine it, but she did know they'd leave this system and arrive in another with no perceptible passing of subjective time. The captain would enter the desired exit into the ship's autopilot just before they entered the transect—a crucial step since, in some manner fathomable only to cosmologists and charlatans, the act of specifying a particular exit created that exit.

Mac had read a popular article on the transects that compared their initial construction to training a worm to burrow outside space itself, leaving holes through which ships could slide. By that way of thinking, the Interspecies Union wasn't so much a political entity as it was a worm trainer, the result being the greatest collaboration of technology and effort ever conceived by any, or all, of its member species.

Conceived might be too strong a word. The transects owed their beginning to a discovery made hundreds of years ago, and millions of light-years away. The details tended to blur between various species' historical records—every species having members ready to claim they'd been about to make the crucial break-through themselves—but no one disputed that finding a key portion of the re-quired technology, buried in the ancient rubble of a once-inhabited moon in the Hift System, had moved that breakthrough ahead by lifetimes.

Academics would probably always argue what might have happened if any species other than the Sinzi had made the initial discovery. But the coolheaded, cooperative, and highly practical Sinzi had been the ones to shape the Interspe-cies Union into its present form, perhaps due to their having multiple brains per adult body. The Sinzi had set the initial criteria for any species to receive a per-manent transect exit, which was still in use today: desire for contact with other species, an independently developed space-faring technology, a demonstrated absence—or, at minimum, reliable control—of aggressive tendencies which might impact other species, and the willingness to adopt a mutual language and technical standards for interspecies' interactions outside their own systems.

All so most alive today in this region of space, including Mac, could take the ability to slip from system to system for granted.

Slip—through a nonexistent tunnel dug by unreal worms burrowing outside normal space?

On second thought, Mac decided, *maybe she should miss that highly unnatural por-tion of the trip entirely with a well-timed cough.*

Meanwhile, Mac had to endure the trip to the transect. No one had told her where the exit to the Naralax Transect was in relation to Earth but, being one of the less traveled and her luck staying its stellar self, it might be on the far side of the Sun right now. At minimum, they had about forty million kilometers to cover to reach Venus' orbit, and, to her knowledge, ships still obeyed the physics that involved staying below the speed of light. Maybe a week at sublight?

She had to read more, Mac decided. But it was like knowing the inner workings of a skim engine. You needed the knowledge most when the damn thing broke down, leaving you stuck where you couldn't possibly gain the knowledge you needed. And you had to walk home as a result.

Face it, Mac, she scolded herself. *You have no good idea how long you'll be in this box.*

Though calling her accommodations on the *Pasunah* a "box" was a trifle unfair, Mac admitted, finally relaxed enough to explore her new quarters. Her first observation proved she wasn't on a Human-built ship, had there been any doubt. There wasn't a truly square corner in sight, the Dhryn, or their ship designers, having built everything at what appeared closer to seventy degrees. Considering how the aliens themselves stood at an angle, this seemed a reasonable consequence. The lack of perpendicular didn't bother Mac. When she wasn't in a tent, she was in her office at Base, where the pod walls curved down one side.

Where there had been casualties. Plural. Pod Six had sunk. Who had been trapped inside?

Not Emily. She was alive.

Emily had shot Nik.

Was he a casualty, too?

As if it could quiet her thoughts, Mac pressed the heels of both hands against her closed eyes. The damn Dhryn could have told her. They could have let her contact those who did know. They could have told her where they were taking her.

But no. They'd brought her to their ship without a single word, either in answer to her frantic questions or to give her orders. They hadn't needed the latter. A Dhryn had picked her up as if she'd been a bag of whatever Dhryn carried home in bags, and only put her down here. While Mac had been sorely tempted, she'd kept her mouth closed over her objections and did her best to cling to the Dhryn, rather than struggle to be free. She'd preferred not to test her ability to splint her own limbs—or truly crack that bruised rib.

The skim ride had been fast and, from the frequent and violent changes of direction experienced by those within, probably broke every traffic regulation on the way station. *If they had such things.* Instead of stopping to argue with any authorities, the Dhryn must have flown right into their ship, because when the door of the skim had dropped open, Mac had found herself carried through a cavernous hold. The Dhryn had continued to carry her, reasonably gently yet with that ominously silent urgency, through tunnel-like ship corridors to this room.

While such treatment alone might be construed as a rescue, there was the troubling aspect of the door the Dhryn had closed behind her—a door with no control on this side that Mac had been able to find.

That door, Mac corrected herself, slowing her breathing, consciously easing the muscles of her shoulders and neck. There were two others. She picked the door on the wall to her left, relieved to spot a palm-plate, similar to the Human version but set much lower. It was colored to match the rest of the room, a marbled beige. *Inconspicuous to a fault.*

The plate accepted her palm, the door opening inward in response. Mac looked into what was patently a space for biological necessities. She'd assumed that much physiological congruence, since Brymn had stayed in her quarters without requesting modifications. Still, she took it as a positive note that the Dhryn had made provision for her comfort.

The remaining door was on the opposite wall. Mac found herself taking a convoluted path to reach it, forced to detour around the main room's furnishings. She did a tally as she went: one table, six assorted chairs, ten lamps of varying size and color, and other, less likely items, such as a footbath and a stand made from some preserved footlike body part holding an already dying fern. Judging by the combination and haphazard arrangement, someone had shopped in a hurry. The Dhryn might as well have posted a sign outside the *Pasunah* saying: "Human passenger expected."

Not her problem.

It occurred to Mac that unsecured furniture meant the *Pasunah* maintained internal gravity throughout her run, not common practice on economy-class liners if she was to believe Tie's vacation story. That, or the Dhryn had a peculiar sense of humor. She tugged a chair closer to the table as she passed. While she was curious about Dhryn furniture, Mac was grateful for something suited to her anatomy. At least it looked more suited than the one in Mudge's waiting room.

The door opened into what the Dhryn must intend her to use as a bedroom, judging by the irregular pile of mattresses occupying its center. Spotting luggage on top, Mac wasted no time climbing up to see what had been provided for her.

Trying to climb up. She wedged her foot between two mattresses, but the ones above slid sideways each time she tried to pull herself up. Taking a step back, Mac frowned at the stack.

Five high, each mattress about thirty centimeters thick and soft enough to lose the proverbial princess and her pea, the sum between Mac and her luggage.

"Bring the mountain," she muttered, then grabbed the nearest corner of the topmost, and yanked. The result owed more to pent-up frustration than power. She dodged out of the way as both mattress and luggage joined her on the floor.

The two cases bounced to a rest, a mismatched pair of the type so common on Earth that frequent travelers on transcontinental t-levs knew to pack short-range ident beacons.

Mac kicked off her slippers, flipped up the ends of her long skirt, and sat cross-legged on the mattress, pulling the smaller case toward her. Her hands lingered on its so-ordinary handle. She had to take on faith that it contained the very long-range beacon Nik had promised, believe that beacon could identify the destination the *Pasunah* chose, and trust that identification would reach only those who—

Cared?

Such a dangerous, seductive word, fraught with risk even among Humans. Even between friends.

What had Nik said? "A threat to the *species,* Dr. Connor . . . Where on the scale of that do you and I fall?"

Mac drew an imaginary line along the handle, then circled her finger in the air above it. "We're not even on it, Mr. Trojanowski."

Oddly, the image steadied her. She may not have paid sufficient attention to astrophysics, but Mac understood the nuts and bolts of biological extinction, in all likelihood better than Nik—or most of humanity, for that matter. She was accustomed to attacking problems at the species' level, not dealing with betrayal and violent death among those close to her.

Nik had warned her not to let anyone close. *A little late.*

The luggage's lock was set to her thumbprint—easy enough to obtain from Base. Once she had it open, Mac gaped at the contents. Someone was obsessed with neatness. Each article was individually wrapped in a clear plastic zip, varying in size from the dimensions of her closed fist to the length of the luggage's interior. Picking a smaller one at random, Mac unzipped it, hearing a tiny *poof.* Almost instantly the contents expanded to several times its original size, startling her into dropping what turned out to be a yellow shirt.

Not neatness. Saving space to give her the most they could.

Maybe she shouldn't unzip too many items until safely off the ship, Mac decided, wondering how to get the shirt back into the case.

She took out each small packet, turning it over in her hands as she puzzled at what might be inside. Some, clothes, were easy enough. Lightweight, soft. Those Mac tossed behind her on the mattress.

A narrow hard packet claimed her attention. She unzipped it cautiously, giving it room to grow, but it stayed the same size.

"So there you are." The imp Nik had told her about. Mac wasn't the least surprised when it accepted her supposedly private code and a small workscreen indistinguishable in format from her own appeared in the air over her lap. "Snoop."

Well, it was his business.

She waved up a list of most recent files—nothing newer than her last link to her desk workstation—then shut it down.

So. Emily's private logs were still hers alone.

As if it mattered now, Mac thought. The Ministry staff had seen Emily shoot their leader, likely had her in custody within moments. They'd use whatever drugs it would take to obtain an explanation; somehow Mac doubted 'Sephe and her colleagues required warrants or permission.

Mac tucked a wisp of hair behind one ear. "Or did you elude them, Dr. Mamani?" she asked aloud.

Another question no one would answer. *Not that she was in a hurry to know,* Mac decided, given the lack of any good outcome.

She took her own imp from the waist pouch beneath her blouse and compared the two. Identical to anyone else's, at least on casual inspection. Her fingers unerringly found the dimpling along one edge of hers where she'd used a knife to pry off hardened drops of pine resin. *Fair enough.*

Mac put hers safely away again, then activated the other. Nik had said any recordings she made would be transmitted whenever the *Pasunah* entered a transect. If this was true—*when had she begun to doubt everything she was told?*—she had a chance to communicate that mustn't be wasted.

Mac sat a little straighter, a few plastic-packed clothes sliding off her lap as a result, then poked the 'screen to accept dictation.

"This is Mackenzie Connor," she began self-consciously, stifling the urge to cough. "The Dhryn have taken me on their ship, the *Pasunah,* and we're heading for the Naralax Transect. Well, I don't know it's the *Pasunah*—or the Naralax— but I'll assume so until I have evidence to the contrary." Her voice slipped automatically into lecture mode as she went on to describe her quarters and give what details she could see.

Then, data recorded, Mac hesitated. *Who would hear this?* She had no way of knowing.

She had no choice.

"Please tell my father I'm okay. Lie about where I am if you have to, but don't let him worry. That's Norman Connor. Base—Norcoast Salmon Research Facility—will have his contact information.

"Please tell Nik—Nikolai Trojanowski—that I have my luggage." Blindingly obvious, since she was using their imp to send this, but it was easy to say. "And tell him . . ." Having reached the hard part, Mac paused the recording. *Tell him what?*

That he should have protected her from the Ro? From the Dhryn? Mac shook her head. *He'd never said he could.*

That he shouldn't have kissed her? She frowned at the display. As kisses went, it had been spontaneous and as much her doing as his. An impulse brought on by stress or something more? Probably best forgotten.

Easier said than done.

Mac restarted the recording. ". . . tell him I wish him well."

"Now this is a problem."

Mac lined her water bottles—one half empty since she'd decided to drink first from a source she knew and two full—in front of her small pyramid of yellow-wrapped nutrient bars, then rested her chin on the table to check the result. She'd found the supplies in the larger luggage, along with boots, outerwear, and a daunting medical kit. Oh, there were self-help instructions on her new imp. They didn't make owning needles and sutures any less intimidating.

That wasn't the problem.

Mac rolled her head onto her left cheek, the better to see her predicament.

Beside her attempts at reconstructing an Egyptian tomb, the table held what Mac presumed was either supper, breakfast, or lunch. She'd lost physiological track of time hours past. It had been waiting here when Mac came out of her bedroom. She'd immediately looked for the provider, but the door to the corridor was closed and still apparently locked.

She studied the six upright, gleaming black cylinders. Brymn had said they ate cultivated fungus, but these looked like no fungus—or food, for that matter—she'd ever seen. They were arranged on a tray of polished green metal, each sitting within a small indentation—presumably so they wouldn't topple while being carried. Thin, hairlike strands erupted from the tops. At the right angle of light, the cylinders exhibited traces of iridescence, as if oil coated the outer surface. When she poked one with a cautious finger, it jiggled.

Mac squinted. It didn't make the cylinders any more appetizing.

She sat up, grabbing a nutrient bar from the top of her pyramid. Unwrapping it, she broke it into three pieces, popping one in her mouth with a grimace. *Oversweet, overfat, over everything.* Emily always carried a dozen in her pack. Mac couldn't stand the things. But they could keep you alive if you were lost in the bush.

Or worse, she thought, with an uneasy glance at the cylinders.

She started to wash down the crumbs of the bar with a drink but stopped with the bottle at her lips. *How much worse?*

Mac put the bottle down, capping it with deliberate care, and lined it up with the other two. A moment later, she stood in the Dhryn bathroom, her mouth already feeling dry. The "biological accommodation," as the Instella term generically put it, was of the suck and incinerate variety. The sink, lower and much wider than Mac was used to, presumably to fit all seven Dhryn hands at once, had no drain or faucet. She lowered her left hand into it cautiously, feeling a vibration that warmed her skin. Sonics. The shower stall, sized for a Dhryn with a friend, looked to be the same.

No water.

Maybe this was something done on ships, she assured herself. After all, water would take up precious cargo space, so minimizing its use might be a priority. Then Mac thought back to the dinner at Base. Brymn had toasted her with a glass of water. She hadn't seen him drink any.

Off the top of her head, she could name fifteen Earth species who obtained all the water their bodies required from their food. *What if the Dhryn were the same?*

"Great," Mac said aloud. Humans weren't. Worse, the nutrient bars were concentrated by removing water from their components. Digesting them would only add to her thirst. The three bottles from her luggage contained barely a day's worth of water.

There were mirrors on two walls, sloping toward the middle of the room. Mac licked her lips and watched her elongated reflections do the same. "Our friends will be in for an unpleasant surprise if they leave me here too long," she informed them.

Not to mention Mac, herself.

After a quick search of her quarters to see if she'd missed a water outlet or container, studiously avoiding the hairy, black sticks, Mac spent a few minutes reminding the Dhryn they had a guest. When shouting and knocking on the door to the corridor failed to elicit a response, she chose likely objects and began pelting the door with them.

Smash! Lamp with a ceramic base.

Crunch! Chair.

Shatter! Statue of three entwined bodies created by an artist with outstanding optimism concerning Human anatomy. Mac blushed as she threw it.

Clang! Footbath. Which wasn't going to do her much good without water to fill it.

Mac stopped, having run out of disposable objects and temper. She waited, listening to her blood pounding in her ears, her breathing, a low hum that might be the ship, and hearing nothing more.

The Dhryn weren't deaf—particularly to the lower frequencies caused by objects hitting a metal door. They were ignoring her.

Or the Ro had killed or bound all the Dhryn and they *were ignoring her.*

Or she was alone on the ship, heading toward the Sun.

There were times Mac really hated having a good imagination.

Without opening her eyes, Mac yawned and stretched. At the halfway point of her stretch, her rib reminded her yesterday hadn't been a nightmare and her eyes shot open.

And half closed. The lights were bright again. She'd discovered the hard way that the Dhryn ship observed a diurnal cycle, having been caught in the midst of compulsive furniture arranging when the lights went out. Not quite out. She'd remained still, letting her eyes adjust, and discovered a faint glow coming from the viewport. Moving with hands outstretched and a step at a time, Mac had managed to reach it and look out. Sunlight was reflecting from some protrusions along the hull. She'd decided to find the safety of her bed before the ship turned and the room was completely dark, given the shards of ceramic, glass, and splintered wood product now littering the floor.

Falling asleep had been as difficult as falling on the nearest mattress.

Now thoroughly awake, Mac rubbed her eyes and groped for her imp—the Ministry one, which she planned to use most. According to its display, she'd slept for eleven hours. According to the stiffness of her spine, most of that had been in one position. *Likely fetal,* she grinned to herself, even though her lips were dry enough to protest.

Amazing what a good sleep could do. Mac stretched again, with more care to the rib, then rolled to put her feet on the floor. *Deck.* She should start using ship words or Kammie would never forgive her.

Kammie. *The soil analysis!*

Mac muttered to herself as she hurriedly unfastened the waist pouch—doubtless another reason her back was sore—and pulled out the crumpled sheet. *Her brain must have been turned off yesterday.* Remembering Nik, she blushed furiously. *No excuse* . . . she started to read line by line.

Ordinary composition . . . expected nutrient levels . . . high moisture content, which Mac found ironic under the circumstances . . . pollen levels reflective of last year's poor conditions . . . and unfamiliar biological material from which had been extracted strands of DNA.

Nonterrestrial DNA.

Kammie had provided the nucleotide sequence without further comment, but Mac could well imagine what the soil chemist would say if she were here. For the first time, Mac was glad she was alone. She had to trust Kammie's discretion would keep her safe. "Sorry, Kammie," she whispered as she studied the results. If the Ro had started chasing her, destroying Base in the process, simply because she might have received information from Brymn, how would they react to Kammie having some or all of their genetic footprint?

Mac didn't want to know. She did want to get this information into the right hands—ones with five fingers—as quickly as possible.

"Regular channels aren't safe," she mused, turning the imp over in her hands. "Not that they're giving me one to use."

After some thought, and a carefully small swallow of water she held in her mouth as long as possible, Mac resorted to a trick so old it probably dated back to stone frescos on buildings. She activated the 'screen and went through her personal image files until she found the one she'd remembered: Emily, all smiles and arms wide, wrapped in some man's oversized T-shirt, the shirt itself peppered with risqué sayings Mac didn't bother to read. She avoided looking at Emily's face as well, enlarging the image so she could concentrate on replacing the letters of the sayings with the letters of the sequence Kammie had found.

It was long, long enough that Mac didn't try to make the substitution letter-by-letter. Instead, she had the imp transfer blocks. There were breaks in several areas. *Incomplete,* Mac realized as she worked, but perhaps sufficient to be the basis of a recognizable reconstruction. She had never worked with alien DNA but was aware that some, like this, contained unique nucleotides. Those alone might suffice to identify a home world.

If they examined the T-shirt closely. Returned to its normal size, even she could hardly tell the words had been replaced by tiny, seemingly random strings of letters. "Let's see how smart you people are," Mac said grimly. Setting her imp to record, she spoke as clearly as her coffeeless throat allowed: "I found a picture of Emily that might help you find her. As you can see, she likes unusual clothing."

Feeling slightly foolish, Mac tapped off the imp and tossed the device on the mattress. For all she knew, Nik had obtained the same results during his scans of the landing site. It wasn't as if they would brief her on their findings. Still, as Mac told her students every field season, better found twice than ever overlooked.

Time to see what was new in the world of the Dhryn. Mac wriggled off the mattress, a process complicated by the fact that her skirt had done its utmost to tie itself in knots as she slept. Mac extricated herself, salvaging the precious message in the process, and unzipped clothing packets until she found a pair of pants to accompany the shirt she'd opened earlier. Both pale yellow, unless the Dhryn lighting was off spectrum from what Mac was used to, but she didn't care about the color. The style was loose enough for comfort and snug enough to move properly. *Good enough.*

Shower, then another mouthful of water. She'd gain the maximum benefit from frequent, small drinks. Until the third, and last, bottle was empty. *Which would happen sometime today,* Mac reminded herself unnecessarily.

As Mac padded through the main room, new clothes under one arm, she paused by the table. She'd had visitors again. A second tray of cylinders had joined the first, identical in every way. On the principle that if she was ever to eat them, it should be the freshest, she took the older offering—the tray closest to her pyramid—with her to the bathroom to dump it. *Emily would be impressed,* Mac assured herself.

Memory flooded her in darkness: the anguish of finding Emily gone, the horror of feeling Nik's body sliding through her hands, disbelief at hearing Emily urging her to leave him and come away.

There was never just one *lie—wasn't that what he'd said?*

Mac scowled at her reflections as she walked into the smaller room. "There has to be a sensible explanation," she told them.

Of course, any explanation that justified Emily shooting Nikolai Trojanowski in the back could very well condemn Nik himself, and, through him, all of those who'd put Mac on this ship. The same people she had to trust would get her home again.

"There's a choice for you," Mac growled with frustration. There was that other possibility, one she cared for least of all. *She shouldn't have trusted either of them.* "At this rate," she muttered, "I'll set a record as the worst judge of my own species."

A species who washed in water, whenever possible. Mac ran her tongue over chapped lips and glared at the shower.

Then, she stared at the shower.

Finally, she walked up to the opening and studied the shower.

The interior of the enclosure resembled the sink, coated in a rather attractive geometric pattern of finger-sized—Human fingers—tiles in beige and orange. But the shower had additional tiles, metallic and angled as if to focus something on whoever stood within. Mac had never seen such a thing in a sonic shower.

Crouching down, Mac shoved the tray with its jiggling, hairy cylinders along the floor into the shower and stood back to see what, if anything, would happen.

She wasn't disappointed.

The metallic tiles glowed fiercely, then what appeared to be shafts of blue-tinged light bathed the tray. The tiny hairs crisped and fell away; the cylinders themselves became limp and bent over. Before their tops hit the tray, they'd melted into puddles, producing tendrils of dark smoke.

Mac's first thought was one of calm analysis. The Dhryn had a thick, cuticle-like skin covered in glands. A brief burst of radiant energy could well be a pleasant way to sear off old skin cells and exudate, dirt and germs being efficiently removed at the same time.

Her second, less coherent thought involved imagining herself crisping and melting, all in the cause of cleanliness, and she couldn't help her outburst:

"Damn aliens! Can't you people even make a shower?"

Hours and ten sips later, Mac leaned her head against the door to the corridor, resting her eyes. Waiting was always the hardest part. She'd taken care of herself. Fresh clothing, although she herself was becoming somewhat ripe between anxiety and an ambient temperature above what her body preferred. A nibble of nutrient bar, those careful sips of water, no unnecessary physical activity beyond rearranging the furniture once more. Aesthetics hadn't been the issue; this time she was after clear passage between bathroom, window, and this door, along with a barrier of sorts in front of the table.

They were still on approach to the transect; she was still being ignored.

Mac's luggage was packed, locked, and beside her on the mattress she'd dragged from the bedroom, positioning it across the door's opening for her own comfort. She hoped it would also slow whomever might enter long enough for her to be heard—or for her to run out the door.

An ambush might not be subtle, but it was a plan. Mac was much happier having one.

The waiting? She opened her eyes, her attention reactivating the workscreen, and blinked patiently at the appendix to Seung's xenobiology text: "Common Misconceptions About Dining with Alien Sentients."

The material was fascinating, something Mac hadn't expected. In fact, under other circumstances, she would have tracked down the cited references to obtain the original sources for herself. It might be an introductory course, but Seung always challenged his students. She now knew enough about humanity's immediate neighbors and important trading partners to have questions whirling in her head. Sentience, it seemed, was a palette biology loaded with tantalizing variety. Let alone the consequences to culture and technology.

As for Emily's riddle?

"Why shouldn't you put a Nerban and a Frow in the same taxi?" Mac whispered. "Because the former sweats alcohol and the latter sparks when upset. Kaboom!" It would be funnier over a pitcher of beer.

She caught herself giving serious consideration to a sabbatical at one of the prominent xenobiology institutions, like UBC, and brought herself back to the "research" at hand.

Predictably, the Dhryn had been mentioned in passing as "a rare visitor, largely unknown in this area of space," part of a lengthy list. The text claimed there would be over two thousand species added to the Interspecies Union before the end of the school term and recommended students sign up for Xenobiology 201 as soon as possible.

Reading the appendix on Dining proved amusing, especially the anecdotal accounts of what shouldn't have been offered certain alien visitors, but Mac was disappointed to find no clues to her present situation.

The fungus.

Putting away her imp, Mac snared the tray with her toes and dragged it closer, the cylinders jiggling gracefully as they came along for the ride. The kit at her side contained treatments for allergic reactions and food poisoning. The medical info in her imp hadn't said anything about their effectiveness on a Human who'd eaten Dhryn food.

Arguing with herself was pointless. Her natural desire to postpone the inevitable experiment couldn't override the simple fact that she'd be better able to survive an adverse reaction sooner rather than later. Another day and she'd be dangerously dehydrated. As it was, her persistent thirst showed she was close. And the last bottle was down to one quarter full.

No, Mac told herself, eyes fixed on the tray, *she might as well get it done.* She'd made a brief recording about the lack of water, to warn anyone else who might land in a similar situation. *And so they'd know what had happened if her recordings stopped in a couple of days,* Mac added with a twisted smile.

As for the food? If this was all the Dhryn would have for her to eat, she had to know if her body could tolerate it. If not, recording a call for help might be her only chance of survival—and that recording would only be sent when they entered the transect.

It wasn't every day you faced the point of no return.

Step one. After her experiment with the Dhryn shower, Mac wasn't going to risk herself without due care. She chose the outside of her left arm as most expendable and pressed it against one of the cylinders.

It felt cold, which didn't mean it was chilled. *Room temperature,* Mac concluded. She examined the skin that had touched the food. No reddening or swelling. She brought her forearm close to her nostrils and sniffed.

Blah! Mac wrinkled her nose. She wasn't sure if it smelled more like hot tar or sulfur. It certainly didn't smell edible.

Step two. She picked up one of the cylinders, doing her best not to react to its slimy feel or rubbery consistency, and brought it to her mouth. Slowly, fighting the urge to vomit—a potentially disastrous loss of fluid—she stuck out her tongue and touched it to the side of the cylinder.

Nothing.

Her tongue might be too dry. Mac brought her tongue back inside her mouth, letting its tip contact what saliva she had left, then, cautiously, she moved that saliva around so it contacted all the taste buds on her tongue.

BLAH! Mac barely succeeded in keeping her gorge in her throat. *God, it was bitter.* Putting down the cylinder, she crushed a bit of nutrient bar in her hand

and licked up the crumbs. The sweetness helped, barely. She resisted the urge to take another sip. Thirty minutes until her next.

Step three. Mac breathed in through her nose, out through her mouth, centering herself, slowing her heart rate from frantic to tolerably terrified. Then she picked up a cylinder and took a bite.

BITTER! Before she could spit it out, moist sweetness flooded her senses as her teeth fully closed. Startled, she poked the jellylike mass around in her mouth. A tang of bitterness remained, but the overall impression was of having bitten off a piece of . . .

. . . overripe banana. Not that flavor, but the same consistency and texture. This taste was complex, more spicy than bland, and seemed to change as the material sat in her mouth. *A good sign,* Mac thought, chewing cautiously. The enzyme in her saliva was acting on what had to be carbohydrate. The moisture in the mouthful was more than welcome.

She swallowed. When nothing worse happened than the impact of a mouthful thudding into her empty stomach, Mac examined the cylinder. Where she'd bitten it, glistening material was slowly oozing onto her hand, as if through a hole.

Mac laughed. If the sound had a tinge of hysteria to it, she felt entitled. "I ate the damn wrapper," she said, wiping her eyes.

Choosing a fresh cylinder, Mac grasped the hairs coming from the top and pulled. Sure enough, they came up freely, the glistening interior remaining attached and rising too. What was left behind was a clear tube, with that oily sheen. She found she could pull the food completely from the tube, but it only held its shape for an instant before falling from the hairs.

"When visiting Dhryn, bring bowl and spoon," Mac told herself for the future. She experimented, finding the tidiest approach was to nibble the food from one side, while attempting not to eat right through the portion held by the hairs. The most effective was to dig in with her finger and lick it clean.

Step four would be the final test, but she'd have to wait a few hours to see how her digestive tract reacted to the alien . . . *what should she call it?* Mac concentrated on the taste and failed to find any one distinguishing flavor. The overall effect was pleasant, if strange.

A group of Harvs had tinkered with the supper menu at Base a few weeks ago. Mac hadn't believed it possible to make mashed potatoes one couldn't identify by taste or appearance, but the students had managed it. "You're officially 'spuds,'" she told the last three cylinders, using the silliness to control her relief at finding she could safely ingest the Dhryn food.

"Digest—that we'll find out." Mac wasn't looking forward to that part of the process.

Despite the moisture in the Dhryn food, water remained the issue, and Mac stuck to her post, back against the door. They'd bring her more spuds eventually. She'd be waiting.

She brought up the next in her list of reading and raised one brow at the title: "Chasm Ghouls—They Exist and Speak to Me."

"Oh, this should be good."

She'd finished "Ghouls," unsure if it was intended as fiction or advertising for the country inn near Sebright where apparently such visitations took place, but only on summer weekends, and had started scanning through more of Brymn's articles when the door to the corridor abruptly opened. It did so by retracting upward, a fact Mac rediscovered when the support behind her back slid away. Before she could fully catch herself, she was falling, but only as far as the Dhryn standing there.

Mac, her shoulders grasped by the being's lowermost hands and her forehead brushing the woven bands covering his abdomen, looked up and gave her best smile. "Hello."

The being shifted his tray into two right hands and contorted his head so one eye looked down at her. *"Slityhni coth nai!"*

Mac's heart sank. *Not Instella.* What had been the name of the captain? "Take me to Dyn Rymn Nasai Ne!" she said, as forcefully as she could from such an undignified and uncomfortable position.

The Dhryn reacted by pushing Mac up and forward out of his way. She landed on her hands and knees, mostly on the mattress which bounced as the Dhryn stoically climbed on and over it to carry his tray of spuds to the table.

"Wait!" She grabbed her remaining bottle of water and scrambled to her feet. "I need more of this!" Mac shook it, the water within gurgling loudly.

Job done, he was ignoring her, walking back toward the door. Mac launched herself in his way. The much larger being stopped, staring down at her. She couldn't read much on his face, which possessed sharper brow and ear ridges than Brymn's. His mouth was in a thin line. *Disapproval? Dislike? Impatience?*

Bad spuds? Mac thought wildly. She held up the bottle, pantomimed putting it to her lips to drink. "Water."

No response, although he gave a look to the door that was, "I'm leaving as soon as I can" in any language.

She pretended the bottle was empty, then grasped her throat and made gagging noises, sinking down and rolling her eyes.

That seemed to get through. The Dhryn blinked, then said, very clearly, the only phrase in his language Mac actually knew: *"Nie rugorath sa nie a nai."*

With that, he walked around her and left. Mac didn't bother to turn to watch him climb over the mattress and go out the door, locking it behind him.

"'A Dhryn is robust or a Dhryn is not,'" she translated to herself, clutching the bottle and feeling fear seep into every bone. "Guess that means I've been adopted."

It was easier than admitting their ignorance of Humans might have just condemned her to death.

- 16 -

TRANSIT AND TRIBULATION

MAC KNEW she was stubborn. It wasn't her most pleasant characteristic, admittedly, though it had served her well in the past. She'd break nails before cutting a perfectly good rope to free a water-tightened knot. She'd wear out boots before wasting time to shop for new ones. And she'd exhausted the entire funding review committee at Norcoast with her seventeen-hours long personal plea to get Pod Six built and running the year she wanted it, not in a decade.

Since then, they'd been remarkably prompt with approvals.

Now, she might be dying. *But it would be on her terms,* Mac told herself again. It had become a mantra of sorts. *Her terms. Her way. If she died, it would because she decided to die.*

The lights had gone off again; she'd slept, fitfully this time and on the floor by the bathroom, having pulled the mattress there. The spuds had gone through her system, all right—and had continued to do so at distressingly regular intervals for much of the ship's night.

Moisture she couldn't spare. Making the Dhryn's food a source she couldn't afford.

To avoid the temptation to eat the moist things regardless of the consequences, Mac had thrown the last of them in the shower. She hoped she'd have the strength to do the same when the next offering arrived.

It would be nice to have the strength to kick a Dhryn where it hurt, too, but she couldn't guarantee that.

When the lights came back on, Mac took her precious bottle and wove her way to the bedroom the Dhryn had given her. The dizziness wasn't a good sign, but she was healthy. Had been healthy. She was good for hours yet.

Then . . . there were drugs in the medical kit—enough for perhaps another day's grace. *After that?* Mac rubbed her arm over the spot where Nik had implanted the bioamplifier.

They'd find whatever was left of her—eventually.

There was a comforting thought.

Mac eyed the stack of mattresses and settled on the floor rather than climb up. She pulled out her imp, intending to make another recording. What she'd say she didn't know, but it was something to do. The workscreen brightened in all its cheerful, Human colors over her knees, showing her the list of what she'd left to read.

Emily's personal logs.

Wrong imp. Her brain must be addled. But instead of switching to the other, Mac watched her fingers lift and slide through the 'screen, keying the logs to open.

Password required.

A puzzle. Mac grew more alert. She keyed in Emily's code from Base.

Denied.

She tried a variety of old passwords Emily had used for other equipment.

All *Denied.*

On a whim, she keyed in, "there's no sex in this book."

Denied.

Then, for no reason beyond hope, Mac entered her own Base code.

Accepted.

So Emily had expected her to get these logs, if anything happened. *She'd wanted Mac to access them.*

"What's going on, Em?" Mac whispered, fighting back the tears her body couldn't spare. She stared at the new display forming on her 'screen, at first making no sense of it.

These weren't personal logs. They were sub-teach data sets.

Labeled "Dhryn."

Mac surveyed her preparations, one hand on the wall for stability. Her head tended to spin if she challenged it with quick movement. She'd blocked the bedroom door of her quarters on the *Pasunah* as best she could, using the mattresses and some crooked metal poles that had been standing in a corner. She'd found what she needed in the medical kit: *Subrecor.* Its tiny blue and white capsules were familiar to students of every age, allowing access to the subconscious learning centers. Those in the kit were larger than any Mac had seen before. *Perhaps spies had to learn more quickly.*

In this instance, she agreed, uneasy about making herself helpless while on the Dhryn ship. Even if it might be her only chance to be understood.

Mac took her imp, feeling for the dimples that said it was hers, and switched the 'screen to teachmode. In that setting, the display went from two dimensions to three, hovering over the mattress like a featureless, pink egg. She'd already queued Emily's data sets—all of them. She might not have this opportunity again.

For more reasons than the obvious, Mac assured herself.

One sip of water left in the bottle. One capsule. Mac swallowed both without hesitation, then lay down on the floor with her head within the "egg" of the display. She closed her eyelids, still seeing pink. The input would be delivered as EM wave fronts stimulating the optic nerves, shunted to the portions of the brain responsible for memory as well as those of language and comprehension.

All she had to do was relax and let the drug turn off cognition and will until the data sets had been dumped into her brain.

. . . not unconscious, but at peace . . . not paralyzed, but detached . . . Mac had never enjoyed being sub-taught, though many she knew did. Her father had told her teachers that she'd never liked taking a nap either.

The kaleidoscope began, flashes of light and color representing the data being transmitted. Normal *. . . familiar . . .*

. . . Wrong . . .

. . . Pain! . . . Whips of fire . . .

Mac writhed without movement; screamed without sound.

. . . Knives of ice . . .

Numbness spread from their tips, as though whole sections of her mind were being sliced and rebuilt.

As Mac plunged helplessly into an inner darkness, a cry built up until it finally burst, sending her into oblivion.

Emily!

How perverse, to be drowning when dying of thirst.

"Mac! Mac!"

She gasped and found air through the liquid spilling over her cheeks and neck. Her eyelids were too heavy to lift; Mac rolled her head toward her name. ". . . argle . . ." she said intelligently.

More liquid splashed against her face, filling her nose and mouth at the same time. Some landed on her eyes, making them easier to open as Mac sputtered, caught between swallowing and breathing. *Water?*

A gold-rimmed darkness filled her view, easing back at her startled cry to reveal a face that cleared to familiar when she blinked her eyes. *Brymn?*

"Ah, Mackenzie Winifred Elizabeth Wright Connor. You had me worried. You are such fragile beings."

"Brymn?" she managed to croak. Mac blinked again and focused beyond the anxious and silk-bedecked Dhryn. Same room. The door looked like it was in the wrong place.

He noticed her attention and gave a low hoot. *Amusement?* "You'd blocked the entrance, so I had to push a little harder. The *Pasunah* is a flimsy ship."

"Flimsy . . . not good word . . . about our transport," she managed to reply, starting to sit up. Four strong hands made it easier. "Thank you," Mac said, resting her shoulders against the mattress stack. She licked her lips.

"Do you require more?" Brymn lifted a bucket with one of his free hands, water sloshing over the top.

Famine or feast, Mac told herself, finding herself thoroughly damp from head to toe. Sure enough, a second, empty bucket stood nearby. He must have poured it over her. The tissues of her mouth were absorbing the moisture as gratefully as cracked soil soaked up rain. Mac licked her lips. "That's enough for the moment. Much better. Thank you. How did you know?"

Brymn sat, his mouth downturned. "I gave those in authority a list of Human requirements, Mac. They didn't understand these were essential for your survival. Instead, they regarded them as mere preferences, an imposition at a time when all aboard worry that your presence attracts the Ro. There was talk of leaving you behind."

Mac studied his face. "You don't mean at the way station, do you?"

"No, Mac."

Somehow, she found a smile. "If it wasn't for you, Brymn, I might have been dead soon anyway." Mac winced.

"Are you damaged?"

She shook her head, once and gently, then rubbed her temples. "No. Well, a few bruises. I seem to have a whale of a headache, though."

"I deactivated it for you." He held up her still dripping imp. "I trust it isn't damaged by water."

"Not and survive my line of work," she said absently, busy looking for the duplicate device. *Good, it was out of sight in the luggage—one less thing to explain.* Mac wondered when she'd become quite this paranoid.

She also wondered what could have been in that capsule instead of, or with, the Subrecor. Sub-teach might be boring and restrictive; it certainly wasn't painful. Her head felt swollen as well as sore. With all the flexibility and speed of someone five times her age, Mac rose to her feet, tugging her soaking wet clothes into some order. Her hair, as always, was hopeless. "How long until we reach the transect?"

Brymn blinked, one two. "Tomorrow. And may I compliment you on your word use? It is unexpectedly sophisticated this soon."

It was Mac's turn to blink. "It is?" She repeated the two words without sound, holding her fingers to her lips. Her mouth wasn't moving as it should be. "I'm speaking another language—I'm speaking Dhryn?" Then, the words "this soon" penetrated and her eyes shot to him. "You knew I would be. How?"

"You were using the subliminal teacher," he said matter-of-factly. "For what other purpose could it be than to accept Emily Mamani Sarmiento's gift?"

For a moment, Mac believed she was hallucinating under the drug, that she still lay on the floor, dehydrated and dying, only dreaming Brymn had stormed through the door to her rescue with buckets of odd-tasting water marked . . . she stared at them, reading "sanitation room" with no problem at all.

The words weren't in Instella or English. They were in some convoluted, narrow script that made perfect sense to her.

"Where did this water come from?" she heard someone ask.

Brymn waved four of his arms, two more helping him sit and the seventh, as always, tucked away. "Don't worry. No one will miss it. It is a regular product of our bodies. Most Dhryn don't care to know how it is removed from the ship."

She was drinking Dhryn urine. And was covered in it.

Somehow, that wasn't the shock it might have been.

"You knew Emily left me a sub-teach of the Dhryn language." *Possibly explaining the headache,* Mac told herself, given her brain had been forcibly retooled to think in—whatever this was. She couldn't tell if she was thinking in English, Instella, or blue marshmallow bits. Her temper started rising. "How did you know?"

"I helped her build it." Brymn paused. "It's the *oomling* tongue, so you do not have to worry about your disability with sound. All who hear you speak will adjust. It will be useful everywhere you find Dhryn. We thought you'd be pleased." He seemed a trifle offended. There was the hint of a pout to his mouth, which was almost cute in a giant seven-armed alien wearing sequined eyeliner.

Who had probably just saved her life, Mac reminded herself, although why was a question for later.

"You—" Mac found herself wanting to say "lied," but failed to find a word to utter that conveyed her meaning. Closest was "delayed information." She tried another tack. "Emily visited Dhryn colony worlds. Was she visiting you?"

"Yes, yes. Although my research keeps me moving about." His brow ridges lowered. "Why, Mac, do you ask what you already know?"

"Because I didn't. Not until now. Not about Emily. Not about you knowing her. Not about the sub-teach."

A silence that could only be described as stunned. Mac used her elbows to support herself against the mattresses, feeling a certain sympathy for the big alien. "You didn't?" Brymn echoed finally.

Mac thought back to their conversations as a threesome. She'd been the one leading the conversations with Brymn; Emily had volunteered very little. Why would Brymn have thought to mention what he supposed she knew? As for any Humanlike show of familiarity, for all Mac knew it wasn't polite for a Dhryn to rush up and greet an old "friend" in front of others.

Emily had only needed to keep quiet while Mac blundered on, never guessing, never suspecting.

Lies scabbed over lies.

She'd blamed herself for drawing Emily into danger. *Had it been the other way around?*

Emily had asked for forgiveness. Why became clearer every day.

"My humble apologies for any misunderstanding—"

"Don't worry, Brymn," Mac heard a new edge to her voice. "There are many things about my friend I'm learning as I go."

"I'll answer any questions, of course, Mackenzie Winifred Elizabeth Wright Connor, but if you will excuse a personal comment, you are beginning to sway from side to side in a most alarming manner."

He had a point. Mac steadied herself with an effort. "Pass me that piece of luggage, please." When the Dhryn put the larger case on the mattress within her reach, Mac opened it and pulled out the medical kit.

He crowded close, eyes dilated. "This is how you correct damage to the body?"

Mac tried to find better language equivalents for illness and injury, but failed. "There are some—chemicals with specific effects on the body. I'm looking for a . . . here it is." She ran her fingers over what she'd intended to use as a last recourse, then made her decision. Having Brymn here, and cooperative, was not a chance to waste by passing out. "This is what the students call Fastfix: a high concentration of nutrients and electrolytes—whatever's necessary to bring a depleted Human body chemistry closer to normal—plus a powerful stimulant of some sort. I should feel more energetic." *As opposed to about to fall on her face.* She held up the loaded syringe. "The needle is a way to deposit the chemicals under my skin, where they will do their work."

"Isn't that causing more damage?"

"Skin—Human skin—closes after the needle is removed." It was hard enough steeling herself to shove the thing in her arm, without Brymn looming overhead, hands twitching as if he longed to dig into the medical kit for himself. Mac gritted her teeth and pressed the point into herself as hard as she could. The syringe was intended for novices, set to puncture only as deeply as required by the type of medicine loaded in its tube, and sterilizing on insertion and withdrawal, so she could use it again if necessary.

"Ow!" *Practice must help,* Mac thought ruefully, rubbing her arm. Mandy's boosters didn't hurt like this. Of course, the syringe in a field kit need not be as patient-friendly as those in a clinic. "See? Easy as can be." She put the syringe away, counting the number she had left. Two.

Everyone knew Fastfix was addictive with repeated use, the body adjusting its base level requirements upward and upward until a user became essentially nonfunctional without a fresh dose. Mac assumed the kit contained a safe number, then wondered why she'd believe that.

As she waited for the drug to work its magic, she noticed Brymn's nostrils had constricted to slits while he continued to examine the medical kit. *Well,* Mac thought, *she was soaked in Dhryn urine, or its equivalent.* "Why don't you take that in the other room while I change out of these clothes?" she offered.

"May I?"

"Sure. Just don't sample anything. I've no idea what the effect on your physiology would be." *Not to mention her supplies were finite.*

He picked up the kit as tenderly as if lifting an infant—*assuming the Dhryn had that type of parent/offspring interaction,* Mac reminded herself. "Are you sure you will not require my assistance?" he asked, looking torn between his fascination and a desire to help.

Mac smiled and touched his near arm. "I'll be fine, my friend. Thanks to you."

With Brymn safely preoccupied, Mac worked as quickly as she could. Although warm, the air in the *Pasunah* was so dry the dampness of her clothes evaporated rapidly, chilling her skin. She stripped, keeping only the waist pouch into which she put her imp, Kammie's note, and the Ministry envelope. She felt warmer immediately, though she couldn't be sure how much of that was an effect of the 'fix.

Mac tried not to think of the chemicals circulating in her blood. There was nothing she could do but hope she'd done the right thing. Abused by the spuds, dehydration, and Subrecor, her body systems were doubtless plotting their revenge. The 'fix was only postponing the inevitable crash.

Until then, Mac reminded herself, *she had things to learn and do.*

First. Despite its origin, and now perceptibly musty smell, Mac went to the bucket of mostly water and, cupping her hands, made herself drink slowly. *She'd had worse from a stream,* she judged, although part of her mind was already busy thinking of how best to distill any future contributions. As a precaution, she filled her water bottles and put them aside. Finally, she soaked her shirt and used it to scrub herself clean as best she could.

Better than the 'fix, Mac decided, feeling herself becoming more alert by the moment. She didn't bother trying to bring order to her hair, beyond wringing out the braid and tying it up again as tightly as she could. Dressing was quick, the luggage again providing a yellow shirt and pants. Mac began to wonder if the color had significance to the Dhryn.

Or, her hands paused on a fastener, *was it much simpler?* To Human eyes, the color would stand out, making her easier to find.

A concerned boom. "Are you all right, Mac?"

"Yes. I'm almost finished." Fearing the Dhryn's active curiosity, Mac grabbed the other imp from the small case and crouched on the far side of the mattress stack from the now permanently open door.

Just as she was about to record what had happened, Mac closed her mouth and stared at the 'screen. She presumed she was thinking in English, because she could conceptualize terms for which there were no Dhryn equivalents. But, unlike her experience in switching from English to Instella, for all she knew, she was speaking English as well. Only the novel movements of her lips and tongue proved Dhryn, not English, was coming from her mouth.

How didn't matter—though the question was fascinating—what mattered was the consequence. What would Nik—or any Human—think of her voice suddenly switching to fluent Dhryn? Mac swallowed, feeling her pulse race. *Could they even understand her?* She had to believe so. The Dhryn had been members of the Interspecies Union long enough for actual translators to exist, although given how it had rewired her language center, Mac didn't recommend Dhryn for sub-teaching.

Brymn had told her they'd enter the Naralax Transect tomorrow. Mac checked the chronometer. Ship's night was only two hours away. Was tomorrow at midnight? How long did she have?

Mac started recording:

"This is Mackenzie Connor. I've been taught—" *how was that for skirting the issue?* "—to speak Dhryn, specifically what I'm told is the *'oomling'* language. I—can't speak anything else at the moment.

"We'll enter the transect tomorrow. I don't have an exact time. I've met Brymn at last. He brought me water, possibly saving my life."

Mac paused, then described, in clinical detail, her experiment with the cylinder food. She couldn't call it spuds, not in Dhryn.

"In case I am unable to add to this recording before it is sent," she went on, keeping her voice calm and even, "please tell my father I'm all right. Please tell Nik, if he—" *lives* stuck in Mac's throat, "—if he is available, that he was right. It wasn't just one." She hoped he'd understand she meant lies. *And Emily.*

Voices, low and angry, erupted from the other room. Mac ended the recording and secured the imp in her waist pouch under her clothes, on the principle that while the aliens would be unlikely to note a new lump around her middle, they could very well separate her from her luggage, or confiscate it altogether. She glanced longingly at the handle with the beacon, but had no way to remove it.

Mac walked into a dispute. "What's going on?" she asked, eyeing three new Dhryn, dressed in the woven blue she'd come to associate with crew of the *Pasunah*, and Brymn, resplendent in his red and gold silks. They were gathered around the table, on which Brymn had placed her medical kit. Two of Brymn's right arms were protectively covering the flat box, his left set gesticulating wildly.

"There you are, Mackenzie Winifred Elizabeth Wright Connor," her ally/ *lamisah* exclaimed. "Tell these Ones of No Useful Function they have no right to search your quarters!"

The "Ones of No Useful Function" didn't look at all pleased by this announcement. They were armed, as the Dhryn on the way station had been. One was missing a lower hand and he—she really did need to check on the appropriate pronoun—was the one who spoke. "Our apologies, Esteemed Passenger, but Dyn Rymn Nasai Ne has ordered that we confirm before transect to Dhryn space that you have brought nothing forbidden on board."

Mac guessed they'd already tried to check her belongings, only to find her luggage locked. "What is forbidden?" she asked.

He looked pointedly at her medical kit. Before Mac could even form a protest, Brymn hooted loudly and said: "Have you no education? These are Human cosmetics."

"Cosmetics," the other Dhryn repeated, eyes on Mac.

Cosmetics? Mac tried to keep a straight face. True, all the Dhryn were wearing some sort of artificial coloring on their faces, although compared to Brymn's bold use of adhesive sequins and chartreuse to outline his ridges, the crew's subtle mauves were next to invisible. Mac, on the other hand, was wearing healing scratches, a bruise or two, and that lovely pink of healing skin.

Still, this was the group who hadn't grasped that another species might have differing dietary requirements. "Don't all civilized beings take care of their appearance?"

Mac demanded, swooping up the kit and closing the lid. She tucked it under one arm, gearing herself to defend it.

"Our mistake, Esteemed Passenger."

Something in Brymn's posture suggested the other was somehow insulting her. *By not using her name?* "What is your name?" Mac asked, making her voice as low and stern as she could.

"Tisle Ne is all of my name."

"Adequate," she sniffed. "I take the name Tisle Ne into my keeping. You have, I believe, mine? Mackenzie Winifred Elizabeth Wright Connor is all my name." Mac couldn't help emphasizing the *all*.

A rising bow, tall and seemingly sincere, from all three. "A prodigious name. I am most honored," said Tisle Ne. "I take the name Mackenzie Winifred Elizabeth Wright Connor into my keeping."

"Would you care to examine the rest of my belongings, Tisle Ne?" Mac asked, waving expansively at her bedroom. "Please. Be my guest."

Their noses constricted and the other two crew Dhryn wrapped their arms around their torsos. *A better-than-Human olfactory sense,* Mac decided, grinning inwardly. The mattress on the bedroom floor had soaked up most of the first bucket.

"If you would vouch that there is no forbidden technology in your luggage, Mackenzie Winifred Elizabeth Wright Connor, these Ones of No Useful Function can trouble someone else."

Mac had a feeling Brymn was pushing his luck with Tisle Ne, and hoped "her" Dhryn knew what he was doing. It seemed he did. "That would suffice," Tisle Ne said, his tiny lips pressed together after the words.

"You are most kind," Mac told him, doing her best to imitate their bow without tipping over backward. Then she considered the possibility of months with these beings and took what seemed the safest possible course. "Remind me what is forbidden, please. Then I can truthfully vouch I don't have such things."

"That which is not Dhryn." Flatly, and in every way a challenge.

Brymn bristled, arms rising and hands opening and closing. He put himself slightly in front of Mac, torso lowered so she could see right over his head. *Physical threat,* she judged it, clear and simple. *An unlikely knight.* "Then there can be nothing forbidden here," Brymn rumbled, "for the Progenitors have declared Mackenzie Winifred Elizabeth Wright Connor welcome."

Tisle Ne's body tipped forward to the same angle. "You overstep yourself, Academic."

The crystals of a lamp tinkled. Infrasound, Mac realized, feeling the rumble through the floor as well. Presumably they were growling at each other. It seemed she was to be inflicted with territorial posturing even here.

However, in this instance, Mac felt no desire to interfere. Instead, she took a discrete step back, then another, wishing her huge protector luck.

Chime!

Mac took a discreet step back, then another, wishing— She stopped dead, bewildered. She'd done this before.

What had just happened?

The Dhryn knew. Tisle Ne straightened. "It is too late for arguments now, Academic. We are home." With that, he turned and left the room, the other two Dhryn following behind.

Brymn clapped his hands together joyfully. "We are safe from the Ro, Mac!"

"That was—was—" Mac tried again. "The transect?"

"Yes, yes. From Human space, to no-space, to Dhryn space. It always amazes me. Does it not you?"

"You can get used to anything." *He didn't need to know it was her first time.* Mac headed for the viewport. "Which Dhryn space is this?" she threw over her shoulder. Nik had implied she was being taken to a world of only Dhryn. Her guidebook to the Naralax Transect had listed the Dhryn as having one home system, unnamed and closed to aliens. That might be it. But there was also a relatively modest colonization of forty-eight others whose exits were open to traffic from members of the Union. Some of those might also be only Dhryn. None had been identified in the guide as the Dhryn birthplace; Seung's text had emphasized that not every species shared such information willingly.

She couldn't tell from here. The view was disappointing. If Mac hadn't experienced that odd déjà vu, she would have assumed that fingernail-sized spot of yellow was the sun she'd always known.

Just as well. A different view might have taken what her mind knew and transferred it to a gut certainty. Light from that sun wouldn't reach Earth for millions of years—an impossible, unfathomable distance. There was only one way home—the Naralax Transect.

Of course, if the transects ever failed, her problem would be trivial on the grand scale. That failure would end the Interspecies Union. Every species would be separated by an impassable gulf; each isolated and alone, as they'd been before the Sinzi had made their discovery and shared it.

Mac had no doubt Earth would continue, as it had before the transects. She was equally sure every species would work to rebuild the system and eventually succeed—but would reach out to their own lost colonies first.

So, if the transects failed, Mackenzie Winifred Elizabeth Wright Connor would be trapped on the wrong side of this one until the end of her days, an alien curiosity for the Dhryn. Their token Human.

When she died, would they have her stuffed for a museum?

Mac's stomach, though empty, expressed sincere interest in emptying further. Brymn came up beside her. "This system is called—" A vibration.

"A little deaf," she reminded him.

"Ah. My apologies." He paused, then his eyes brightened. "You may call the system: Haven. Any Dhryn would agree."

Haven? Mac shifted the medical kit from under her arm to in front of her chest and wrapped both arms around it. When she noticed, she shook her head at her own defensive reaction. It was only a name, like "Earth."

"What's it like, Haven?"

"There is one world—our destination. You may call it Haven as well."

She might not find her way around a star chart the way she could a salmon scale, but Mac knew enough to feel a shiver. "No other planets? Asteroids? Moons?"

"There were, but they were unsuitable for Dhryn," Brymn told her, his tone implying surprise at her question. "Such are hiding places for the Ro. The Progenitors do not tolerate them in our home system. We must protect our *oomlings*."

The home system. *Well, now she knew where she was,* Mac told herself. *Not in the guidebook.* But . . . *one sun, one world.* Feeling somewhat faint, a not surprising reaction to technology capable of sweeping an entire system clear of unwanted rock—and a species that would use it—Mac put the kit on the table and sank into a chair. "The Progenitors. Tell me about them."

Brymn sat as well, after checking the floor for debris. *She really should tidy the place.* "They are the future," he said.

Cryptic. *Or was it?* How much of what the Dhryn said should she take literally? "The Progenitors produce new generations of Dhryn?" Mac hazarded, too curious to worry about offense. *"Oomlings?"*

Brymn clapped his hands and smiled at her. "You see, Mackenzie Winifred Elizabeth Wright Connor? This is why I value your insights into living things. You understand us already."

"I wouldn't go that far," she said under her breath. Louder: "Are they your leaders as well?"

"Of course. The Progenitors are the future. Who else could guide us there?"

There had been an entire unit on alien reproduction in the xeno text, sure to titillate the most jaded students. All Mac recalled was having the familiar reaction that nature found the most ridiculous ways to propagate. Adding intelligence and culture to biology seemed only to compound the issue, not simplify it. "I don't know anything about Dhryn biology," Mac reminded him. Before he could be too helpful, she continued: "And now isn't the time, Brymn. It's Human biology—mine—that concerns me at this moment. I need a constant supply of water. Here, on the *Pasunah,* and on . . . Haven. Can you provide it?"

A debonair wave of three hands. "Water I can guarantee."

"Wonderful. How about distillation equipment?" At his puzzled frown, Mac shrugged. *Archaeologists.* "I'll manage that myself. Let me talk to a chemist. But food's another matter." She went to the table and picked up one of the remaining spuds. "Is this all you have available?"

Brymn took it from her. Bringing the cylinder almost to his lips, he deftly plucked the contents from the cylinder by the hairs, then sucked them into his mouth before they could ooze free with a slurp that could only be described as gleeful. "Ah. They listened to me about this one thing. I remembered your delight in the soufflé and thought you'd enjoy another sweet."

Dessert? Mac didn't know whether to laugh or pull her hair. "So there are other types of—wait." *That damned soufflé.* She had to know. "Did you put a message—anything—in the bag with the soufflé? Something for me?" Mac hesitated, then went on: "Or for Emily?"

Brymn startled her by tilting his head on its side; combined with his golden eyes, it gave him a striking resemblance to a perplexed owl, albeit a giant blue one. She had no idea that thick neck was so flexible. "Was I supposed to?" he asked.

"No. No, you weren't." She couldn't help a sigh of relief. *So much for Nik's suspicion.* Mac wasn't sure how real investigators went about their business, but her own research typically involved eliminating the obvious before the truth began to appear. *As now.*

More and more, she was coming to believe the truth was that Brymn had been used, by the Ministry, by Nik, and by Emily. He'd traveled far from his kind, alone, in search of answers—and been betrayed by those who were supposed to help him.

For two aliens, they had a remarkable amount in common.

"Are you sure, Mac?"

"Forget the soufflé. It isn't important. Brymn," she said, choosing her words with care, despite an urgency to *know* that had her hands clenched into fists. "What were you told happened on the way station?"

"Only that you were found without difficulty and brought to the *Pasunah* ahead of schedule." He pursed his lips and looked troubled. "Was there a problem? I admit to having felt some concern. There was unusual urgency about our departure and I wasn't to visit you until permission came from the Progenitors."

"Before I could leave with your people, the Ro found me," Mac told him. "I—" She stopped to let the big alien compose himself. The word "Ro" had started his limbs shaking.

"I—I—" Mucus trembled at the corners of Brymn's nostrils. "We wanted to keep you safe from them, Mac, as we would our *oomlings.* Were you—damaged?"

"No," Mac assured him. "I ran. Your people found me and brought me to safety. But . . ." She hesitated a heartbeat, unable to control her own trembling. *Great pair of brave adventurers they were.* Mac struggled to remain calm and detached. "Emily was there, Brymn."

"What? You saved her? You found her? Is she here?" He looked around wildly, as though Mac might have tucked Emily into a corner.

"Em didn't need saving. She wasn't a captive. On the way station, the Ro chased me to her. She asked me to come with her, with *them.* Nik—Nikolai Trojanowski, he was there. He tried to stop me. Then she—then Emily—shot him."

Her voice failed her. Vision went next, blurred behind tears. Mac waved her hands helplessly.

Then she was almost smothered in a six-armed hug. His uppermost shoulder was almost nonexistent, his skin was the wrong temperature and felt like rubber, and his ear ridge dug painfully into her head. None of this mattered.

She wasn't alone.

Mac let go and sobbed until she would have sunk to the floor without those arms for support.

- Portent -

THE DROP WIGGLED and slipped its way down the shaft, leaving a faint green stain behind, its reflection in the gleaming metal leading the way. New, the shaft, as was all the equipment collected here.

Another drop. Another. They drummed and chimed against every surface, mirrored as they struck and stuck.

As they wiggled and slipped downward.

Until there was no surface without its trails of green.

The drops met each other in antenna couplings and on access covers, at joints and along ductwork. They grew together in pools and spread until they tumbled over new edges. Wiggling and slipping downward again.

Seals began to bubble and ooze.

More drops fell, tracing the paths of the first.

A hatch cracked. The drops poured through, a hungry flood.

Giving those inside no time to scream.

- 17 -

APPROACH AND ANTICIPATION

"WHAT ARE YOU doing, Mackenzie Winifred Elizabeth Wright Connor?" boomed the voice from the doorway.

Mac, her nose touching her left knee, thought this should be obvious even to a Dhryn, but as she uncurled, she wheezed: "Exercising."

Brymn walked around her as she continued to lift her head and shoulders from the floor and lower them again. He leaned up and down with her, as if keeping her face in focus, arms carefully folded. "Is this pleasant?"

Surprised into a laugh, Mac gave up. She tucked her chest to her bent knees and wrapped her arms tightly around her legs, feeling the stretch in her lower back as she squeezed. "It's better than the alternative," she informed the alien. "Don't your muscles atrophy without regular use?"

"Muscles?"

Ah. "Don't you feel stiff if you remain still for prolonged amounts of time?"

A one/two blink. "Stiff? No. Bored, yes."

This was a hint, Mac knew. Now that Brymn was allowed to visit her on the *Pasunah*, he preferred to stay with her. She'd had to insist on privacy while she slept—or rather crashed—yesterday, a blissful oblivion that lasted about three and a half hours before he'd walked in to find out how much sleep a Human required and was she finished?

Not that she'd minded the company, but she'd been groggy enough to keep the conversation to safe, neutral topics like the difference between Coho and King salmon, Brymn countering with an enthused lecture on ways to detect technological remains, such as electronics, under layers of soil and rock.

At least he'd left once the lights went out.

With the perversity of an exhausted body granted peace, Mac hadn't been able to fall asleep right away. The 'fix had raced along her nerves for restless hours. Then, when she had dozed off . . .

She flushed, remembering she'd dreamed hazel eyes and a kiss . . . dreamed warm breath along her neck . . . dreamed more and more until the heat of her body had awakened her to lie gasping and alone. Staring at the ceiling, bright with the *Pasunah*'s version of morning instead of any hope of home, Mac had judged herself a pathetic fool. It hadn't been passion. It had been a release of tension between virtual strangers, perhaps attracted to one another, nothing more.

She'd known herself vulnerable at the same time. She hadn't been caught in such intense fantasy about anyone since Sam. *What did it say about a woman whose fantasy lovers died after a kiss?*

Not that she knew Nik was dead. *And he'd kissed her three times, all told.*

Which had occasioned more thoughts, waking ones, about a fantasy lover. *Which had led to exercise.* Given the lack of cold showers.

Mac focused on Brymn. *Exercise surprised him?* She'd assumed the Dhryn had evolved under heavier gravity, but that in the *Pasunah* was set to what felt Earth normal. Through that thick skin, it was impossible to tell which was a lump of muscle and which was of fat. "How often do you need to eat?" she asked, getting to her feet while ignoring the immediate growling of her stomach. She'd manage on nutrient bars until Haven. The *Pasunah*'s crew was unwilling or unable to understand her request for analytical equipment. After their dessert, Mac had no intention of further personal experimentation.

"As often as I am served food." Brymn had sat, looking content.

Semantics or biology? "Don't you get hungry?"

"Adults do not become hungry until food is within reach. To feel otherwise would be impractical. *Oomlings* are preoccupied with the seeking of food—but they have little else to do."

Mac chuckled. "Reminds me of students." Which reminded her of less happy things, wiping the smile from her lips. *What was happening back home?*

Today, before they reached Haven—*who knew what access she'd have to Brymn there?*—it was time to discuss what they hadn't yesterday. Things less safe and definitely not neutral. "Did you get an answer about the com packet?" Mac asked, dropping into a chair. Intersystem communications traveled the transects as packets, signals collected at an entry, then cued to a particular exit. Regular and reliable. *If you had access to the result.*

"There have been several since we entered Haven," he told her, but his expression turned sober. *Not a good sign.* "I'm told they go directly to Haven for distribution and only those affecting the operation of this ship within the system would be shunted to us." Some of her disappointment must have shown, for he offered: "I can ask again."

Mac took a long drink of water—imagining it tasted better after being filtered through several layers of fabric—and shook her head. "Getting them faster won't change what's happened. And there's no guarantee a packet to Haven would carry news from Earth anyway."

No guarantee, although Mac couldn't help but hope. Maybe Nik or the Ministry would find a way to send her a message. Maybe they'd plant something in the news for her benefit, something broadcast so widely it offered no clues to the Ro, but might reassure her.

The more pragmatic part of her, the part that relied on Mac first and the universe second, disagreed. *Maybe they wouldn't bother.* After all, she was here now, where they'd wanted her to be. Mac wasn't naïve enough to imagine her peace of mind was important in the larger scheme of things, although being informed about other attacks by the Ro could be useful.

Or terrifying.

"Where is Haven in relation to the attacks?" she asked Brymn, very aware of the Ministry envelope in the waist pouch she now wore waking or sleeping. Then Mac realized her mistake and blushed. Distance was irrelevant, given the attacks were along the same transect.

But the Dhryn, perhaps as little attuned to the rigors of space travel as she, didn't think it a foolish question. "The reports coming from the Consulate were of locations farther and farther from here. More importantly, Mac, the Progenitors of Haven have recorded no attempt against Dhryn for several years. Here you are as safe as any *oomling*. It is why we came to this place, over all others. For you."

Farther from the recent attacks meant closer to the Chasm. Mac took another, more deliberate swallow. In a way, it helped that the invisible Ro were more frightening than any imagined ghouls could be. Nik—perhaps others at the Ministry— saw a connection. She didn't attempt to make one, not yet, not on so little evidence. Finding the Ro homeworld, learning how the Dhryn successfully resisted them, those were her goals. Fortunately, she had Brymn for help. "What's Haven like?"

"I have no idea." Her sequined, brightly garbed archaeologist actually beamed. "I haven't been to the Dhryn home as an adult, Mac. I was sent to a colony shortly after Freshening."

"'Freshening?'" Mac echoed, her heart sinking. *Fine time to learn her local guide wasn't local.*

"My attempt at the real word." He boomed something that went lower and lower, then became silent. "Freshening is like your Human passage from child to functioning adult. Emily Mamani was kind enough to explain how this affects Human behavior. If you forgive me, it's quite bizarre, *Lamisah.* What is your word?"

"Puberty," Mac supplied. She fought back a rush of questions about Emily to focus on the more pressing issue. "Are you familiar at all with Haven or its Progenitors?"

"I've seen images, but I'm sure they fail to reveal the true beauty of the place. This is as much an adventure for me as for you, Mac! We will be tourists together and explore this magnificent world."

Had Brymn's distinctiveness misled her? To a Human, individual style was a mark of self-confidence. Was it to a Dhryn? To a Human, being the first Dhryn to set foot on Earth imbued Brymn with importance. Did it to other Dhryn?

He published in non-Dhryn academic journals. He associated with Humans. *Was he even sane, by Dhryn standards?*

Mac sank back in her chair. At least Brymn hadn't coauthored "Chasm Ghouls—They Exist and Speak to Me." *As far as she knew.*

He might be an alien crackpot, but he'd learned to read Human expressions. "Something's wrong, Mac. What did I say?"

There was no way to be tactful about it—and lives, including his, might be at stake. Mac straightened and looked Brymn in the eyes. "I don't mean to insult you, Brymn, and I'm grateful—more than I can say—for the help you've given me. But I need to know. What's your status among other Dhryn?"

He didn't appear offended, answering mildly: "I have not yet served in *grathnu*, Mac. But this is obvious."

Mac heard *grathnu* as a Dhryn word, as she did *oomling,* implying her mind held no equivalents for it in English or Instella. "Let's not assume anything between us is obvious," she cautioned. "What's *grathnu?*"

Two pairs of hands danced in the air, making a convoluted pattern ending in a paired clap. "The creation of life. One must earn the honor. I have not yet accomplished enough in my life so Brymn is all my name. But you. Surely you have served in *grathnu* abundantly, to become Mackenzie Winifred Elizabeth Wright Connor."

In Dhryn terms, she'd been listing her sexual exploits? Mac didn't simply blush. Her face burned. *Who else knew about this?*

Beyond doubt, Emily. Given five minutes alone with a new species, she'd ferret out such a thing and more.

Nik? He'd known about the importance of naming, back at the Field Station. "Oh, dear," Mac said aloud.

"Is there a misunderstanding?" Before Mac could possibly form a reply to that, Brymn went on anxiously: "I hope not. Your accomplishments require other Dhryn to treat you with respect and do their best to accommodate your needs. Our time on Haven will be much less comfortable and productive if I have been mistaken."

"I'm not Dhryn—" Mac started, then paused, unsure what to say next that wouldn't land her in more trouble.

"Of course you are," Brymn said, eyes wide. *Surprise?* "Otherwise, you would not be here. Only that which is Dhryn may enter the home system."

Mac had prided herself on avoiding any major pitfalls during her conversations with Brymn. In fact, she'd begun to think herself rather talented at this interspecies' communication stuff.

She changed her mind.

"Define," Mac said carefully, "if you would, 'that which is Dhryn.'"

Brymn's eyeridges scowled exceedingly well. "Everyone knows that."

"Humor me, *Lamisah.*"

He looked uneasy, but obliged. "When it is necessary for the survival of *oomlings* to think about the Ro, it is clear that all which opposes the Ro is Dhryn. I reported your deeds and your bravery—which were far beyond my own. I gave them all of your names. The Progenitors named you *lamisah,* ally, to all Dhryn. You, Mackenzie

Winifred Elizabeth Wright Connor, are Dhryn!" He became passionate through-out this little speech, rising to his feet, his eyes almost flashing with enthusiasm. Then, a little doubt crept into Brymn's expression. "Did I misunderstand?"

Mac crossed her fingers, a childhood habit. "No, no," she said briskly. "You were quite right. I was only checking that the Dhryn properly appreciated my—accomplishments. Thank you. You've set my mind at ease."

"I am most gratified." Brymn settled himself, then went on in a very matter-of-fact voice: "Of course, being Dhryn, you must adhere to Dhryn ways while on Haven." He shrugged all his shoulders as if admitting an impossibility, add-ing: "Or appear to do so. It's fortunate you learned to speak fluently before our arrival. Home system Dhryn would find it alarming to meet anyone who could not communicate properly." His little mouth assumed a grim line. "We don't want to alarm them."

Mac folded her hands on her lap and studied how the fingers laced together. Ten fingers, not six, twelve, or twenty-one. *How wide a gulf in comprehension did those numbers represent?* "You told Emily this, didn't you." It wasn't a question. It couldn't be, not when it answered too many. Why the sub-teach disguised as personal logs . . . why the logs cued to Mac's password . . . why Emily Mamani chose to work with her and salmon instead of studying manatees . . .

Why they'd become friends.

Mac watched her knuckles turn white.

Promise to forgive me, Mac.

As much as the Ministry and Nikolai Trojanowski had taken advantage of events to get Mac here, where no Human had been, Emily Mamani and her "allies" had wanted her here even more, and planned for years to achieve it.

Why?

"It's time you told me everything, Brymn," Mac said in a tone that expected complete and total compliance. "Starting with where you met Emily. And how."

It had been a classic Emily pickup: transit station, spots a likely guy waiting and looking bored, asks directions to somewhere very close by, a place that turns out to be a cozy bar with Emily's favorite music filling the dance floor. A playful night ensues. Mac found it eerie, hearing about something—someone—so fa-miliar through the interpretation of a stranger.

Oh, there was a modification or two. Brymn had already been in a cozy bar, waiting for a skim ride out to an archaeological dig on Renold 20. He'd been pleasantly surprised to be approached by a Human of culture and education, even more surprised when she'd asked directions to the same dig. Another scholar, he'd thought. A common interest.

Interest? With a sour taste in her mouth, Mac thought of Emily falling asleep in her office. Exhaustion? More likely the boredom of hours pretending to read what she'd already read.

Their first meeting had taken place two years *before* Emily applied to Norcoast.

Brymn, used to being alone, had been easy to charm. He'd seen it as a mutual regard and growing friendship. Mac, hearing the steps Emily took to win his confidence, gain access to his work, saw it as something else.

Premeditation.

Emily had chosen Brymn as her target—a Dhryn crazy enough to work on his own, far from his kind. Mac wondered if any Dhryn would have done, but it didn't matter. Here was one ripe for the taking.

Not that Mac let her thoughts interrupt Brymn's recital. She let him keep talking, taking sips from her water bottle, eventually pulling up her knees so she could watch him over the top of that barrier. He needed no encouragement to continue; a natural storyteller who must rarely have an audience. Emily's rapt attention must have been intoxicating.

Brymn and Emily made plans to meet in a few months and work together. She would help Brymn with his work and teach him English so he could directly access the material of those Human researchers who didn't publish in Instella. Meanwhile she was building a dictionary of Dhryn and wished to test terms and grammar on him.

His work. Mac knew it from her readings, but it was clearer described this way, filled with the fervor academic writing leached away. The Dhryn was hunting through the past of space-faring species, looking for evidence of the so-called Moment—the date of the destruction of the worlds within the Chasm. His hypothesis? That there had been transects connecting these worlds, and these had failed during the same catastrophe, stranding species where they hadn't evolved.

No one doubted there had been transects—or the technology to develop them—before. The discovery by the Sinzi proved at least the beginnings had been around for over three thousand standard years. But had such a network existed within the Chasm and beyond? Could all of those transects have failed at a single point in time? If so, was that the cause of the disaster that had befallen all of those worlds?

Even "Chasm Ghouls—They Exist and Speak to Me" devoted less than a footnote to the idea. Despite his years of searching, Brymn had yet to find a single shred of evidence.

That didn't mean he was wrong, Mac thought.

Her project. Emily had been coy, but eventually Brymn had convinced her—*hah!*—to admit they shared a related goal. She hoped to prove the existence of the Survivors, an entire species rumored to have escaped the Chasm. Legend painted the Survivors with everything from advanced technology to a godlike beauty no matter your physical preference. Emily's expectations were simpler. If such existed, they might be able to explain the mystery of the Chasm once and for all.

Were the Survivors the Ro? Had Emily found them, or they her? Regardless, Mac had a question of her own. *Had they escaped the annihilation of life on those hundreds of worlds—or been its cause?*

Were they starting again?

Perhaps Emily would have chosen to work with manatees and travel to the Dhryn home system herself—*they might never have met*—but for a single consequence of teaching Brymn English. Among the obscure publications in that language, he discovered a series by that curiosity to Dhryn, a biologist. Not any biologist, but one working on how species survived catastrophic events. He expressed the desire to meet this scientist.

It took Mac a moment to realize he was talking about her work. *About her.*

She could only imagine what had gone through Emily's mind then. Why was the Dhryn interested in an obscure salmon researcher's work? Was this a problem, or an opportunity?

Brymn went on, blithely unaware of the impact of his retelling of events on his audience, liberally adding mentions of the weather at each dig and other non-essentials. Mac lowered her chin to one knee, her arms wrapped again around her legs, but this time to hold herself in, not to stretch.

Not surprisingly to anyone who knew her, Emily had chosen to consider Brymn's interest an opportunity. She confessed to being a biologist and more. She claimed to be already working with the esteemed Dr. Connor. What a happy coincidence! Brymn had been delighted, especially when Emily promised to forward any new work from Dr. Connor directly to him, so he could keep up with her—their—findings.

Mac's head lifted, nostrils widening like those of a startled doe searching for a hidden predator. She couldn't help but remember her joy at finding Dr. Mamani's application on her 'screen, how she'd rushed to complete the year's budget in order to clear funds to bring the highly reputed scientist to Norcoast, even how they'd all pitched in to give the place a quick cleaning, in case appearances would make a difference.

It's never one lie.

Forgive me.

Brymn remained oblivious, words flooding out of him now to tell her how anxiously he'd waited to receive each transmission, how honored he'd been to hold raw data and see her analysis taking shape, how enthralled by each leap to a new experiment . . . then, finally, the opportunity of a lifetime. The Interspecies Union had quietly alerted the authorities of member species along the Naralax Transect to what it called "a mysterious threat," asking for investigators with knowledge of the Chasm to cooperate. When the Progenitors searched for such a Dhryn, there was only one choice: Brymn.

And Brymn chose to work with Humans, so he could finally meet . . .

"You, Mackenzie Winifred Elizabeth Wright Connor!" he finished, holding four arms toward her. "Despite all that has happened, meeting you has been the most joyous and significant moment in my life. For this reason, I had the name of Emily Mamani Sarmiento recorded within the vault of my Progenitors, in gratitude for having made our meeting possible." When Mac didn't immediately reply, the Dhryn wrapped his arms around his middle and looked worried. "Are you not pleased we met?"

"I could wish for better circumstances," she said honestly. "But not a better companion," this with a depth of emotion that surprised her. *She was,* Mac scolded herself, *anthropomorphizing.*

Still, his sudden smile implied the Dhryn could understand and reciprocate what was, to Mac, a Human feeling. "We are *lamisah,* Mac, and friends. As is Emily. Do not let yourself worry. I am sure she will be able to explain what happened on the way station. She will be well—we will find her."

Perilous thing, friendship. Mac rubbed her chin on her knee, debating which of Brymn's illusions to shatter first. "I don't believe Emily needs our help, Brymn."

"What? How can you, her friend, say this?" Outrage, in a Dhryn, appeared to involve standing, lowering the torso angle, and arm waving. Brymn did all three before blurting out: "She was taken by violence from her sleep! I saw the reports, the images. There was fluid over the walls—her fluid! The Ro—" His limbs trembled. "The Ro—"

"Oh, I believe they took her," Mac agreed miserably, hugging her legs. "But the signs of a struggle can be faked. Humans can lose a fair amount of fluid—blood—without permanent damage. Broken furniture?" She nodded at the pile in one corner, where she'd collected the remnants of her assault on the door. "Nothing easier."

"But why make it look—? I don't understand."

"I don't have answers, Brymn. For what good a guess will do? Emily knew I'd never willingly leave Earth. For some reason, she—and others—wanted me to do just that. Badly enough to fake her own kidnapping. Badly enough that the dictionary she built with your help was to make a sub-teach of your language—for me. Badly enough that they made it seem impossible for me to be safe anywhere but here. In the Dhryn home system."

"A Human working with the Ro? Impossible!"

Mac raised a brow. "I'm working with a Dhryn."

"Even if it could be—why? With apologies, Mac, you make no sense. Why would they do all this to force you here, the one place you're safe from them?"

"That's the question, isn't it?" Mac tucked her chin back on her knee.

Brymn sat in front of her, one three-fingered hand covering hers. "What if you're wrong about Emily?"

"Then I'll owe her a beer. More likely ten," Mac promised. "But there's too much at stake, Brymn, for us to ignore the evidence. Emily wasn't working with me before you told her of your interest in my research. She lied to you. Emily knew you—she'd prepared the sub-teach in your language before arriving at Base this year, before the Union knew there was an emergency. She lied to me."

"She must have had good reason."

The alien's staunch defense of Emily—*so like her own, to Nik and to herself*—wasn't making this any easier. "At this point," Mac decided, "I don't care about her reasons. We need to be careful. Why am I here? Why does it suit Emily, and perhaps the Ro, to have me on Haven? Something's going on, Brymn."

He took his hand away. "We must not trouble the Progenitors with this—supposition, Mac. They would not react well. Not well at all."

Mac studied Brymn's face, seeing the fear there. Reluctantly, she nodded. "When it comes to Dhryn, I must rely on your judgment."

As he nodded, seeming more relaxed, Mac caught her reflection wavering within figure eight pupils, surrounded by gold. What did he see, when he looked at her? What did he think, feel? How could she begin to fathom what had no connection to her flesh?

How could she know if he lied?

- 18 -

REGULATIONS AND ROUTINE

MAC HAD HAD her preconceptions of other worlds. They'd all be Earths, of a sort, perhaps with different shapes to their treetops or unusual birds in their skies. She'd even imagined some sort of alien marketplace, filled with otherworldly scents and sounds. But there would be treetops, birds, and skies.

Until she was brought to Haven, home of the Dhryn, enclave of Progenitors, and home to only three forms of life: cultured fungi, the Dhryn . . .

And one *Homo sapiens*.

As for a sky?

She'd never complain about the rain at Base again, Mac vowed, staring out her window. It hadn't stopped pouring since their arrival. Four days without variation, without thunder, lightning, or wind, just this heavy, monsoonlike drenching. Handy for distilling, but she'd filled every container Brymn had obtained for her by the end of day one.

Be grateful, she reminded herself.

Water and food. On her second day, Mac had received a portable analytical scanner to rival any at Base. In fact, it had been exactly the same model Kammie had ordered last year for her lab. Mac couldn't recall the species of manufacture, just the price tag. Seemed the Dhryn, like many Humans, obtained technology "off the shelf." They'd even adopted the habit of having tiny vidbots along their streets and hallways, in such numbers that they seemed more like swarms of small round insects than machines. Useless against the Ro, but perhaps it reassured the average Dhryn to know there were watchers on their streets. Mac did her best to ignore them.

After testing various Dhryn offerings other than spuds, while arguing with her stomach that it could exist empty a while longer, Mac had succeeded in finding several preparations that contained nutrients her body needed, without toxins to cause less happy results. Although the food ranged from bland to eye-watering heat in taste, and lack of texture was definitely a Dhryn issue, she had the start of a diet to live by.

For which she was also grateful, Mac thought, watching rain wall the world. *For however long it took.*

Day, night, weeks. Like most sentient species in the IU, the Dhryn divided and tracked time. Mac had entertained herself by working out Earth equivalents. A twenty-seven hour rotation, with eight of that being night—summer, perhaps? A more northern latitude?

What did it matter on a one-species world?

Not that the Dhryn allowed the dark outside their rooms. From what Mac could see from her window and terrace, the city was illuminated throughout the night, buildings and concourses aglow to extend the dull light of Haven's day. A city that extended from pole-to-pole, she'd been told. *Perhaps the light did as well.*

Brymn had professed himself in awe of this place. While Mac had tested tray after tray of sculptured, vividly colored fungal concoctions—most with hair— he'd explained how the rain was deliberate, part of an ongoing program to remove an ocean from the other hemisphere by filling artificial underground reservoirs here. The lighting? A convenience for a species that needed very little sleep and prided itself on productivity. He'd assured her Dhryn colonies were also highly developed and civilized, with full weather control, of course. Then he'd looked wistful. Very few colonies could approach the population and energy of the home system. All had to rely on the home system for *oomlings.*

None had Progenitors of their own.

Because of the Ro.

She might be safe from them here. At the thought, Mac closed the shutter, a process that took two hands and force. Doors were hinged as well, as if Dhryn didn't waste power on what could be slammed by six strong arms. Quaint, until the second day of struggling with what could have been controlled by civilized wall plates.

Where was Brymn? He'd come faithfully the first three days, though his visits were shorter each time. Mac presumed his duties elsewhere were increasing. But he hadn't come or sent word since. All she knew was that he'd warned her not to leave her apartment, that she had to wait for the Progenitors' permission.

Mac adjusted a lamp, then fussed the bright gold and red tablecloth into a straighter alignment, wondering why she bothered. Her hosts had provided generous accommodations for her, but the furnishings from the *Pasunah* looked lost and out of place in rooms designed for Dhryn, the perpendicular angles of chairs and tables at war with walls that tilted in—or out—and asymmetrical window frames placed at differing heights. Lining up the tablecloth only fueled the discord.

The furniture was fine, Mac told herself. *She was fine.*

There wasn't much choice in attitude for either.

The Dhryn, at least in this area, lived in apartments which appeared to be built on top of preexisting ones. Mac's was the highest on an elongated pyramid, with access to one of a spiral of round private terraces that stuck out like so many tongues. She'd braved the rain out there more than once to try and make out the details of her surroundings. At best, she'd gained a vague impression of rounded rooftops and irregular shapes, punctuated by straight towers. A great deal of traffic flew overhead, at all hours; not skims, but vehicles at once longer and sleeker. Silent and grouped, they were like so many schools of fish passing through the gray ocean of cloud.

Entertaining as it was to stare at the undersides of rapidly moving fliers, Mac wasn't on the terrace often. Constant and straight down, Haven's rain was— different—from the one she'd grumble happily about back home. This rain was sharper, harder, as if falling from a greater height. Drops stung any exposed Human skin, though they probably felt fine to a Dhryn.

Not that Dhryn liked being wet, but they appeared capable of cheerful endurance when necessary. On the way from the spaceport, Mac had glimpsed walkways filled with pedestrians, each clutching two, four, or six brilliantly colored umbrellas. The effect, despite the dim light, was as if giant blue-stemmed bouquets with rain-bent petals paraded between every building. *Not that there were living flowers here.*

Mac tugged the tablecloth askew again, knowing exactly what was the matter with her. She was so far beyond homesick, so offended by this place, it amazed her she still bothered to breathe.

The rain. *It didn't matter.* There was no soil to turn to fragrant mud, no vegetation to grow lush and wild, no overflowing rivers to tempt fish into flooded meadows. Here, the rain bounced against stone, metal, umbrellas, and other lifeless things, collecting in downspouts and gutterways to be carried underground before it could disturb the tidy Dhryn.

She couldn't bear to think of the ocean about to disappear, being literally flushed away. *It didn't matter.*

There was no struggle here, no change, no surging, inconvenient mess of living things competing for a future. Everything Mac knew, everything she loved. *Didn't matter.*

Mac refused to judge, knowing other species lived on worlds like this, where technology took the place of ecosystem. Even within Sol System, Humans had colonized sterile moons, many professing to prefer such a life.

She didn't judge. But, as each waking hour passed, she felt a little of herself slip away.

Did it matter?

"Maudlin Mac. Melancholy Mac. Oh, hell, let's go straight to the Mighty Melodramatic Mac, why don't we?" In sudden fury, Mac swept up the tablecloth and draped it over her head. She spun around and around, the fabric a maelstrom of red and gold, her hands slapping furniture to keep herself upright. "The Famous Dr. Mac—" *slap,* "—taking full advantage of her unprecedented access to a unique species and culture—" *slap, slap,* "—discovers her true calling! Self-pity!" The final *slap* sent a chair tumbling backward and Mac lost her balance, falling after it. The tablecloth drifted to the floor.

"Is this typical Human behavior, or are you mad?"

Mac scrambled to her feet. "You aren't Brymn," she blurted at the Dhryn standing in front of her.

"Are Humans incapable of recognizing individuals?" the being asked reasonably.

"Sorry." Mac blinked, belatedly taking in details. This Dhryn was smaller than others she'd met, intact, and had adorned his face with chubby lime and pink curlicues that matched the bands of cloth wrapped around his middle. His hands were burdened with several boxes and his expression was frankly curious. "Are those for me?" she ventured.

"Do Humans make assumptions?"

For some reason, Mac found herself grinning. "All the time. We can recognize individuals. And yes, all Humans probably spin at some point. Mackenzie Winifred Elizabeth Wright Connor is all my name."

"Oh! Truly magnificent!" A bow that faltered as the Dhryn realized he couldn't clap with his hands full. He settled for tapping four of his boxes together. Mac hoped there was nothing fragile inside. "I take the name Mackenzie Winifred Elizabeth Wright Connor into my keeping. Ceth is all my name."

"I take the name Ceth into my keeping. A privilege," Mac said, tipping back her head and offering her own clap. "May I ask why you are in my apartment, if those aren't my packages?"

"You invited me. These are for the esteemed Academic."

"Brymn?"

Ceth shuffled impatiently from foot to foot. "He is waiting."

Mac opened her mouth to say she hadn't seen Brymn for over a day, when a clatter announced her kitchen was occupied. Wordlessly, she pointed in that direction, then followed the small Dhryn.

Her apartment had four rooms, designated in Dhryn-fashion by function. The one with a desk, other furnishings, and a door to the terrace, her place of work. *Where she spun with tablecloths.* The one with luggage, bed, and shower—which had thoughtfully been replaced with a sonic variety safe for Human skin—her place of recuperation. *Where she longed for water and dreams that didn't include fantasies about a man who was probably dead.* An entranceway, with display screens she'd yet to figure out. Her place of greetings. *Obviously not locked.*

And a kitchen, as well as, oddly to a Human, the biological accommodation, called the place of refreshment. *Where she practiced her chemistry.*

It seemed she wasn't the only one. "You aren't Brymn either," Mac informed the Dhryn busy emptying the storage unit where she kept her Human-suited foods. This one wore bands of white and gold, not silk but something woven. He looked up as they entered, a packet Mac recognized in one hand. His gold-irised eyes blinked one/two beneath ridges painted silver. "And that," Mac said, "is my supper."

"Ah!" Looking at the packet as if it was now more interesting, the new Dhryn punctured it with a sharp, hooklike object carried in a left hand. "And why is this your supper?" he demanded as he read some type of display on the object. A scanner, she presumed. "Why not—" and he rattled off a list of food names that meant nothing to Mac.

"Because— What are you doing in my kitchen?"

"Have you found anything peculiar yet?" A third Dhryn, also in gold and white, squeezed into the narrow space—just missing Mac's toes. "I made a wager with Inemyn Te."

"I have the items you requested, Esteemed Academics," Ceth announced, adding to the confusion as he put his boxes on top of Mac's precious analyzer.

"STOP!"

The three Dhryn paused to look at Mac. She coughed and said more politely. "Who are you and why are you here?"

"I am Ceth—"

"I know who you are. These others?"

Despite the facial dissimilarities, all three gave her a look of thoroughly offended dignity as plain as any Mac had seen displayed by Charles Mudge III. She drew herself as tall as possible—unwilling to risk leaning forward in threat display to beings three times her mass and of unknown motive—and glared. "I am Mackenzie Winifred Elizabeth Wright Connor and these are the quarters I was provided by your Progenitors. I demand an explanation for this—this intrusion!"

"But you invited us, Mackenzie Winifred Elizabeth Wright Connor," the one with her supper dangling from a hook said quizzically. "We are researchers interested in developing new presentations of—" he lifted the hook, "—food. You requested equipment and samples from us."

"And I brought more," Ceth volunteered.

The other Dhryn spoke up, shaking the room before uttering what Mac could hear. "—curiosity is not welcome? If so, your entry misled us."

It seemed she had an interspecies incident brewing in her own kitchen. Had to be some kind of record—not that Mac was happy about it. "I am honored by your presence," she said cautiously, on the assumption it was a safe enough phrase.

"Ah! You have met the Esteemed Academics!" This voice she knew. Mac turned with relief to see Brymn's smiling face. He couldn't fit into the kitchen unless she climbed on the lid of the accommodation, something Mac didn't want to attempt in a room filled with so many swinging arms. Mind you, both Academics were missing at least one hand. *Grathnu,* she reminded herself. *Great. Rank.* Even more like dealing with an Oversight Committee.

"These are the individuals who made sure you had what you requested, Mackenzie Winifred Elizabeth Wright Connor," Brymn continued glibly. "Did I not tell you they would want to examine the results of your investigation?"

Mac scowled at Brymn to let him know he most certainly hadn't, then smiled at the scientists stuffed into her kitchen. "A moment of confusion," she said graciously. "How may I assist your esteemed selves?"

She only hoped they didn't want to examine her as well as her diet.

Much later, Mac dropped into the most comfortable of her chairs and looked at Brymn. "Well, that was fun."

"Sarcasm or truth?"

She put her feet up on another chair and grinned. "A bit of both." The two scientists had been charmingly fascinated by her food requirements, if a little inclined to doubt her analyses until they'd repeated each and every one for themselves. *Some things,* Mac had concluded with satisfaction, *crossed species barriers with no trouble at all.* They'd left intrigued with the challenge of finding more fungal preparations she would prefer.

The notion of Mac having a functionally distinct digestive system was carefully avoided by all parties.

"I am gratified. You look more as you did, *Lamisah.* If you don't mind a personal observation."

Mac eyed the Dhryn. She did feel unexpectedly at peace. "And you, my dear Brymn, are becoming much too good at reading Humans."

He didn't look worried. "It is not as difficult as I once thought."

"I could say the same."

Two more Dhryn wandered into the room, exchanged the briefest of bows with Brymn, then wandered out again. Mac watched them leave and sighed. "I guess this is going to happen all the time."

"Of course not. You keep inviting them."

"I—I do not."

"You do, you know." Brymn hooted.

Mac narrowed her eyes. "I'll bite. What aren't you telling me?"

He seemed overcome with laughter, rocking back and forth, hooting softly to himself all the while.

She pretended to throw something at him. "What's going on?"

"Ah. I see there remains a gap in your excellent knowledge of Dhryn." Another hoot. "Come with me, *Lamisah.*"

Brymn wouldn't explain until they stood in her place of greetings, nothing more than an almost square room forming the entrance to her apartment. It was marked by a door to the large common hallway that faced an inner wall decorated with a painting; the remaining walls opened into arches that led into her place of work and her kitchen. Mac waited, more or less patiently, for the big alien to get to the point.

"This is your problem." Brymn lifted his three left arms to the display in her hall, a rendering of a selection of fungal food items.

"It's a painting," Mac said dubiously. "I found the display controls yesterday." She didn't bother mentioning that she'd gone through about fifty choices before finally settling on what looked recognizable and hopefully harmless.

"Of course it's a painting. It is also an invitation. By exhibiting food in your entry, you elicit the reaction of hunger and the expectation of a social gathering. There is a pronounced subtext of professional discourse which doubtless excited the Esteemed Academics beyond restraint. Let us hope your dispute with them over the analysis did not leave a bad taste." He hooted at his own joke.

Mac looked at the painting, then at Brymn, then back at the painting. "You're saying that this is why I have strange Dhryn roaming through my apartment? Because I changed the display?"

He smiled. "Insightful as always, my *lamisah*."

"Then why didn't any walk in before today?"

"Ah." Brymn tapped the wall below the painting and a tiny door opened to reveal a now-familiar control. "This is the catalog that controls your greeting display," he explained, holding up the silver oval to activate a shimmering screen on the wall, similar to that displayed on a Dhryn reading tablet. "There. This is what I left when I was here." Now a plain green cube slowly rotated in the air before the wall. As it spun, one side flashed blue.

Mac made a face. "I know. That's why I changed it."

"Leading to your visitors. This is a request for privacy. No Dhryn would enter. The Human equivalent—" Brymn gave it thought, then looked smug. "An agenda posted on a door. Home system Dhryn expect you to display a meaningful work of art."

"Then you'd better leave me an all-purpose 'ignorant Human' piece," Mac said. "I don't know anything about art beyond my own reaction to it. And that goes for Human as well as Dhryn."

A quieter but no less amused *hoot*. "Neither do most Dhryn. Don't worry, Mac. The catalog is organized by conversational topic. Once I show you how to search it, you will have no trouble conveying your meaning to potential visitors." Brymn paused, then made another selection. "However, knowing you are deaf, I'm switching off the audio art option just in case."

Brymn had brought his company—and put an end to the invasion of Mac's apartment—but no real news. The situation remained unchanged. The Progenitors had granted Mac sanctuary; they had yet to decide if they'd grant her access to anything outside of it. The Dhryn delivered this with a wary look, as if Mac was likely to explode. Another day, she might have. Today, she simply nodded and questioned her *lamisah* on protocol and manners, in case any more home system Dhryn came to visit.

Whether her earlier mood had been caused by coming off the Fastfix, the change in food, or real homesickness—or all three—Mac found herself finally jolted back into the mind-set that kept her happily busy at the most inhospitable field stations. *The work.* She made Brymn promise to bring more information the next day.

Not that she needed to wait, Mac thought triumphantly. *Had the Dhryn realized what a tool they'd left her?*

She almost pushed Brymn out the door. The moment he was gone, she dragged a chair into the place of greetings and pulled out her imp. *The one that would transmit her data.*

Focus, Mac, she told herself. The choice of art was determined by the topic about to be discussed between host and visitor, or visitors. Brymn claimed it inspired and focused the conversation, something Mac thought could be very useful at Norcoast before funding meetings. Here, Mac deemed it a stratagem to cope with a very dense population. Brymn had told her that his kind liked being close together. "A Dhryn is with other Dhryn or he is not," had been the phrase of the moment. But even if they enjoyed close proximity, Mac thought, it must help to have a mutually understood protocol.

Brymn had shown her how to use the catalog. Many pieces were abstract, listed by mood as well as topic. *Perfect.* She didn't have to know what a Dhryn thought of what he saw for her purpose.

Mac began flipping through the cataloged pieces at random, recording her emotional response to each on her imp. After a while, the place of greetings filled with semiconscious whistling as she became more and more absorbed. The chair was abandoned for the floor, then the floor for the chair.

Biological necessity interrupted, so while Mac was in the kitchen she grabbed a packet and water bottle. Back to work. Supper was a blue stick that reminded Mac of chalk, washed down with tepid water. The Dhryn didn't refrigerate.

Globes, bubbles, spheres of all sorts. Lines and shadow plays. Harsh geometrics. Mac gave each equal consideration, sometimes wincing at the colors, sometimes struck by beauty that perhaps crossed species lines. Or her pleasure misunderstood the artist.

That was the point.

She stopped when her eyes could no longer focus. After rinsing her head with water, Mac returned. This time, she recorded the expected Dhryn response to each abstract as claimed by the catalog. The entries were filled with florid and extravagant language—*what was it about describing the impact of art?*—so Mac was careful to only use those that referred specifically to reactions. There were colors listed by the catalog for which her mind had no English equivalents, implying the Dhryn saw into the ultraviolet end of the spectrum. Mac avoided those works of art as well.

Mac carried her results to her workplace, noting absently that it was night. Leaning her elbows on the desk, she watched the flickering display as her imp took her responses and compared them to the Dhryn's.

Ah. Reasonable congruence over which shapes, colors, and tones induced feelings of peace, contentment, or harmony in both Dhryn and herself.

Mac's fingers drew through the display, bringing up a troubling divergence when the emotions involved alarm, discomfort, or rage.

Turquoise, for instance, was the dominant shade in images the catalog listed as eliciting anxiety and anger. Black was not an option before civil conversation, sure to incite violence. And yellow?

"Well, well." Mac tilted her chair back, shaking her head in disbelief. Apparently, the brighter hues were guaranteed to set one's limbs trembling with fear. The catalog recommended its use only for hazardous material storage.

So naturally, her entire wardrobe was yellow.

No wonder the poor Dhryn tended to be agitated around her. Mac couldn't begin to guess what *Pasunah*'s captain and crew must have thought.

"Another great first impression, Em." Mac's chuckle came out tired, but real. "Drenching myself and my quarters in their urine couldn't have helped."

A fine way to introduce humanity to the home system.

Mac took the time to make a recording for the folks back home, viewing this as the least she could do for Haven's future Human visitors.

Mind you, she'd love to see the faces of those who'd done her shopping.

The next day, Mac enlisted the aid of the Esteemed Academics to make her wardrobe more suitable, envisioned panicked crowds should she walk about clad in yellow. They'd accepted the challenge with alacrity, fascinated by the various fabrics of her clothes.

She then spent two long and anxious days wrapped in a tablecloth, reading reports and hoping for the best. Eventually, Mac found herself nursing the increasingly faint hope the Dhryn had understood she expected her clothing back.

She needn't have feared. The Dhryn managed the improbable. Even her raincoat, a thoughtful inclusion in her luggage, was returned a different, more Dhryn-friendly color.

Colors.

Mac had put on the quietest of her improved wardrobe and been unsure whether to laugh or tear at her hair. Bold stripes of purple, red, blue, white, and lime-green had raced around her middle, lined both arms, and plunged to her feet. *She'd just needed a pair of oversized shoes and a red nose.*

"*Lamisah.* You look wonderful." Brymn had applauded her new look, but Mac held dire suspicions that her Dhryn's taste didn't match that of anyone else on this world. She tried not to believe the Esteemed Academics had done their best to turn her into either a laughingstock or a target.

Clothing issues aside, over the following week, Mac discovered that Brymn hadn't exaggerated the importance of her greeting hall. Her *lamisah* might be exceedingly casual in his approach to such matters, as Dhryn went, but home system individuals were only truly comfortable with her after the ritual exchange of names. Better still were greetings that included a lengthy admiration of whatever art was on display—a decided inconvenience, since Mac hardly knew what to admire. Fortunately the same works were available to all Dhryn, so her visitors came equipped with compliments no matter what she'd picked.

Mac wasn't at all surprised when her increasing grasp of things Dhryn was matched by a decrease in the number of her visitors. The novelty factor she provided by simply existing must have worn off. Even the Esteemed Academics had realized she had no startling Human insights into their subject. Food, tablets, and other supplies were delivered without requiring a formal greeting. Of course, Mac, not realizing this for the first while, had done her utmost to prove she knew the protocol and insisted on bringing the delivery beings into her place of greetings to admire art. As a result, those bringing deliveries now left them outside her door, preferring to knock, then run.

Brymn found it amusing, though he still didn't bother with any ceremony with her. As the days passed, however, her constant companion had become less so. Soon, he was coming only once each morning to deliver more reading material. Not even offers to discuss his own research would tempt the Dhryn into delay. He claimed to be busy "making arrangements" and "consulting with colleagues." Mac, in response, busied herself as well. She was here, after all, to learn about the Dhryn.

Who knew she'd miss the company of a big blue alien?

ADVENTURE AND ANXIETY

MAC CHECKED the time display on her desk. *He should be here in a few minutes.* She'd breakfasted and dressed in record time, anticipating a welcome change in routine. Brymn had promised her a tour of the city today. *Maybe,* Mac thought, *the rain would actually let up a bit.*

Eleven days. She was ready for a break. *To be honest, she was ready for anything that took her out of this apartment.* Already her desk was cluttered with the digital tablets the Dhryn used in place of mem-paper. More lay on chairs around the room. The Progenitors had allowed a Human on their world—they hadn't, until today, been ready to let her walk around on it. It was being deliberated, Brymn had promised day after day, asking her for patience.

In return, Mac had asked for information.

Her collection had grown rapidly: Brymn's work, abstracts from other fields, the Dhryn version of local news reports, and even samples of fiction, though these were presented in verse and difficult to follow, since the rhyming conventions were based on tones below her hearing. It didn't help that fiction presupposed the reader was at least familiar with the author's culture.

Mac was doing her best to learn the Dhryn's. She'd reached the point of being able to tell which public announcements were from the Progenitors, on topics ranging from finance to the proper education of *oomlings*. There was a distinctive formality, almost an aloofness—as though they considered themselves removed from the rest of Dhryn society, yet at its core.

Although she dutifully and unsuccessfully hunted references to the Ro, Mac found the Dhryn themselves becoming something of an obsession. The air of respect and mystery surrounding the Progenitors tantalized her. There were no images in any of the materials she'd assembled with Brymn's help. He'd expressed belief such didn't exist. So Mac had asked to meet one.

Apparently that request was being deliberated as well.

Their persecution by the Ro was another reason she'd begun to focus more of her attention on the Dhryn themselves. Apparently no adult Dhryn had ever been harmed by the Ro. The invisible beings stole or abused *oomlings* whenever they could; the heinous crimes stretching back almost two hundred standard years.

No wonder Brymn trembled at the name.

No wonder the Progenitors guarded the home system. Under the circumstances, Mac was amazed any Dhryn dared leave that protection, let alone continuing the practice of sending almost mature *oomlings* to the colonies. It was a stiff price to pay for interstellar travel, since the transects were obviously how the Ro were able to come and go. But the Dhryn had come to a sort of peace, having developed technology to keep the Ro at bay, at least here, and chose to exist that way, always on guard.

The average Dhryn didn't think about it.

They appeared to lack interest in other things as well. Selective ignorance was a blindness Mac was beginning to deplore in herself, let alone in an entire species. She ran into it again when trying to determine if the Dhryn had evolved here or elsewhere. There were no living clues left, no animals strutting about with bilateral symmetry and three pairs of arms. A fossil record would have been helpful, but Brymn had confessed such a thing would not have been valued or saved, if found. The study of life, he reminded her regularly, was forbidden. If she was to live here, she would have to be careful no one suspected her of such interests.

Mac shuddered. Over time, a place like this, ideas like this, would kill her. She knew it. Brymn was keeping her sane as well as safe, a combination of amusingly eccentric uncle, friend, and comrade-in-arms, bundled in a package surely unusual even for Dhryn.

And rarely on time, Mac thought fondly, gazing at the clock. She pulled on her raincoat, but left it open. The Dhryn had turned down the heat in her apartment after numerous requests, although Mac still found it too warm. In their way, they were good hosts. Not xenophobic in any way she could detect—though there was that issue of her being deaf, as Brymn called it. Careful that she not be bored or neglected. Curious, where her interests crossed theirs.

Speaking their language had proved essential, as well as safer. Brymn had checked and found that only a few official translators on Haven spoke Instella. That skill was reserved for the colonies, where one might reasonably expect to need it.

Not on Haven, where Mac was the only alien—other than attacking Ro—to ever set foot.

Some mornings, that was inspiring. In a "just don't look down" kind of way. *Where* was *he?*

Mac went to her place of greeting and began flipping through the art catalog to keep herself occupied.

Where was he? Before Mac could do more than form the question again, a knock on the door answered it. *Finally.*

Brymn didn't wait for her to open the door, bursting through with a cheerful: "Ah, Mackenzie Winifred Elizabeth Wright Connor! Good morning!"

Mac stepped out of the way. As she closed the door, he paused in front of her art display, which her random shuffling had left at an abstract of silver reflections of globes within globes, gave an inexplicable *hoot hoot!,* then kept marching into her workroom. "I have good news!"

She hurried after him. "What?"

Brymn held out a tablet with his middle left arm, his small mouth stretched into the largest smile she'd seen him produce. "Those of No Useful Function at the communications center finally admitted I was entitled to receive non-Dhryn news reports. I have collected all those from the past two weeks for you. Here."

Mac took the tablet, her hands shaking. These would be summaries, of course. There was far too much interstellar information for every system to receive news from every other. Interests were more focused. But there could be something from the Interspecies Union. *There could be . . .* she fumbled at the display control.

"I haven't read them myself," Brymn told her. "I came straight to you. What's wrong? Isn't it working?"

"I—" Dumbfounded, Mac could only stare at the tablet. "I can't read it." The symbols were twisted and completely unfamiliar. "What language is this?"

"Instella." Brymn took the tablet and raised it to his eyes. "The display is clear enough, Mac," he said. "Are your eyes damaged?"

No, Mac realized with horror, *but her mind might be.* The sub-teach Emily had made for her—the pain she'd felt using it. Had the input crippled her ability to communicate in other languages?

If so, had it been accidental, or deliberate?

Mac forced herself to calm down. "Read it out loud to me, please. Instella, not Dhryn."

The floor vibrated once, as if Brymn muttered some comment about this, but he obeyed her request. "'Bulletins from the Interspecies Union are intended for the widest possible audience. Failure to disseminate such bulletins in every applicable language will result in fines, censure, and potential restriction of transect access . . .'"

"That's enough." Mac heaved a sigh of relief. "I understood you. How about English? A few phrases."

Brymn nodded. "'Humans consider it impolite to disgorge or otherwise release body fluids in public places. When eating in a Human restaurant, please notify your waiter if you will require a private room.'"

"That was English?" It sounded the same in Mac's ears as the Instella—and the Dhryn, for that matter.

"A quote from my *Guide to Earth Etiquette.* A most useful resource, Mac."

Mac reached inside her shirt and dug into her waist pouch for her imp. Her original, with Emily's sub-teach, lay at the bottom of her largest water tank for safekeeping, wrapped in plastic. She carried the one from Nik, but hadn't used the device other than to record new entries in her personal log. Now that she thought about it, Mac couldn't recall paying attention to the 'screen, just hitting the right spots to control the function.

She cued the 'screen, in Instella first, then found herself staring into the incomprehensible mass that floated in front of her. A slide of her hand through the display changed it to English.

She sagged with relief. Some words looked odd, as if her mind was trying to reorganize the letters, but it was legible. Mac concentrated on one line, trying to read out loud in English. It sounded right to her, but Brymn, guessing what she'd been attempting, was already tilting his head from side to side in negation. "That was Dhryn."

Mac requested an input pad and the almost transparent keys formed under her hands. She typed carefully in English. She could read the words. But when she auto-translated to Instella, they were so much gibberish floating in air.

"It appears I have some new gaps in my education," Mac said, replacing the imp in her pouch. Her voice sounded remarkably calm under the circumstances. *Why hadn't she checked this before?*

Easy. She'd been too busy using her knowledge of Dhryn to investigate her novel surroundings, too enchanted by her new power to understand something so utterly foreign. Mac thought dourly that she'd probably never have noticed, if Brymn hadn't brought the tablet.

"In sum, I can write and read English, but not Instella. I can understand English, Instella, and Dhryn, though they sound exactly the same in my head. I speak only in Dhryn. Which also sounds the same in my head as any of the others." She sighed. "I'll lay odds there'll be some researchers itching to take apart my head when I get back."

Brymn blinked. "A figure of speech, I hope?"

Mac smiled faintly. "We both hope. Now, can the tablet translate to English?"

"No, Mac. And home system technology will not match yours. I can translate for you myself, but it will take some time." He brightened. "Or I can read to you—our tour will include several hours of traveling the tubes."

The tablet was still in his hand. Mac looked at it hungrily. If there was any message or information for her from Earth, it would be there. Whether she trusted Brymn to read it accurately or not, she had no other choice. She nodded.

"Let the tour begin."

A world without vegetation, yet with individual works of art given their own plazas and viewing stands. A city wrapped around the equator that shot itself upward in magnificent towers and rooted itself with a labyrinth of spacious tunnels. Buildings whose design could be breathtakingly strange—the Dhryn no fonder of the perpendicular outside their rooms. An endless rain gathered into waterfalls and used to animate statues before plunging below the surface. And a people as varied in dress and manner as any gathering of Humans Mac had seen.

"It's not what I thought," Mac confessed to Brymn as they walked toward the tube entrance along a concourse shielded from the rain. She suspected Dhryn kidneys worked hard enough to remove excess water from their bodies, so it wasn't surprising they'd avoid unnecessary exposure to more. Not slavishly. Some ventured out under umbrellas but she'd witnessed several at work in the downpour, bodies protected only by the decorative bands around their torsos. Their waxy skin was probably better protection than her raincoat.

Not evolved under such conditions, Mac pondered.

"In what way, Mackenzie Winifred Elizabeth Wright Connor?" In public, where they might be overheard, Brymn was careful to use her full name. Under the circumstances, Mac wasn't about to argue.

"It seemed—bleak from my apartment," she explained, gazing about in wonder. Here, the tiles of the walkway extended up the slope of a neighboring wall, their colors forming a mosaic. The mosaic in turn formed an illusion of other walkways and other buildings, stretching into the distance. Mac imagined at least some Dhryn walked right into it. They had a pronounced sense of humor, much of it able to tickle Mac's funny bone as well.

There were a great number of Dhryn walking everywhere she looked. As they passed one another, they'd briefly and seemingly automatically raise up their bodies and heads, then dip again, turning any dense crowd into a blue sea with waves that passed along in remarkable synchrony.

Unlike the media madhouse that had ambushed Brymn at Base—or the rapt curiosity of Base's own inhabitants—Mac found herself treated like any other Dhryn. Those passing her only bowed, as they did to Brymn. She couldn't copy the full movement without losing her step, but Mac lifted her chin each time in acknowledgment. For her neck's sake, she hoped there'd be less bowing in the portion of their tour through the tube system.

Brymn excitedly brandished a map of the system at every opportunity, as if they didn't look sufficiently like tourists. *Another behavior that apparently crossed species' boundaries.* Mac had taken a peek at it before they'd started, trying for a sense of how long they'd be traveling, but Brymn had refused to spoil what he referred to as her anticipation by providing a destination. Given she'd no idea what Brymn would consider a reasonable amount of time for a "tour," and knowing her hosts by now, Mac had hurriedly stuffed a bag with her three sealable water bottles and some of what she'd christened "cereal bars." They weren't bars or cereal, being more like flat, wrapped sticks of purple gelatin with thicker lumps of white along one side. But they were the most completely nutritious, to a Human, food item she'd discovered on the Dhryn menu thus far, and, well, pleasantly peppery.

On the principle that her life had become highly unpredictable, Mac had also retrieved her original imp from its bath, tucking it into the waist pouch with the envelope, the imp from Nik, and the letter from Kammie. *No one could say she didn't know how to travel light.*

The tube system, according to the map, dove under the planet's surface in a maze of crisscrossing angles. If the scale was accurate, some penetrated the crust to a depth of 50 kilometers, while others skimmed barely beneath the footings of the buildings above. Mac hoped the Dhryn grasp of seismology was on a par with their chemistry, because the overall effect was that Haven consisted of more tunnel than rock.

Not to mention souterrains of every size, from small artificial chambers budding from tube junctions to what appeared to be cavities extensive enough to hold a midsized Human city. Altogether, the interior of Haven could well offer the Dhryn more living space than its surface.

Space for how many Dhryn? Mac ignored the temptation to guess. Salmon were amazingly prolific, but only if you knew where—and when—to do your counting.

"There it is!" Brymn's exclamation was hardly necessary. As they turned the corner at the end of the plaza, the entrance itself loomed in front of them, easily five stories high and wide enough to accommodate several walkways. The clusters of vidbots kept to the sides as aerial traffic zipped in and out without changing speed, implying either reckless abandon or a great deal of space inside.

It made even Brymn seem small.

"Is there a fee?" Mac asked, endeavoring to be the practical one of their twosome. She hadn't seen any evidence of money or credit among Dhryn; her deliveries and supplies were apparently the responsibility of the Progenitors. That didn't mean there wasn't commerce at the service level.

"Fee? For something required by Dhryn?" Brymn was almost light on his feet. "What a Human notion, *Lamisah*."

"Only kind I have, Brymn."

He hooted, the volume attracting the first overt attention Mac had noticed. "Shhhh," she urged, waving her hands at him.

"There is nothing impolite about expressing pleasure in a companion's wit," he countered, but his voice dropped to something closer to a whisper. Brymn saw her look at the nearest hovering 'bot. "They watch for signs of trouble, not humor, Mac. Visual only."

Mac slipped her arm around the arm nearest her, his lower right, and chuckled. "Just don't get us arrested—or whatever the Dhryn version is."

The tube Brymn had selected for the start of their tour was immense. Mac could feel the pulses of warm, humid air climbing upward before they reached the station complex itself and she took off her raincoat, tucking it into her shoulder bag. Ahead, pedestrians boarded disappointingly normal, Human-looking trains, albeit with doors twice as wide. Fliers zoomed by overhead, disappearing beyond the first great downward dip in the distance. Mac presumed they navigated the tube under their own power and resolutely ignored the potential for disaster, in light of the nonchalant way every other being was moving toward their trains.

Mac was standing beside Brymn on one of the long, tiled platforms, waiting their turn to board, when a movement along the wall caught her eye. As the Dhryn ahead in line were now sitting where they'd been standing, she judged there was time to indulge her curiosity before the train left.

There couldn't, in Mac's estimation, *be an entire world without its version of a rat.*

She turned to ask Brymn, but he was deep in conversation with their next-in-line neighbor, again waving his map and generally making sure everyone in earshot knew he was from a colony. The vibrations of what they were saying came up through her feet.

A step to the side gave Mac line of sight. There was a slice of shadow, beginning where the end of a pushcart full of packages waited against the wall.

Mac let her gaze rest on the edge of the darkness, as patiently as she'd ever waited for a fin to reappear by a rock, keeping herself peaceful and still.

There!

But what slipped across the line of darkness and back again wasn't a fin. It was a three-fingered hand, wizened and strange.

No one else appeared to have noticed. Mac eased closer. One step . . . then another . . . keeping her eyes on the boundary of shadow rather than challenge the privacy of the one hiding within.

An odor, thick and foul on the humid air. The breeze of beings passing, distant trains, the breathing of the tube itself carried it to her, then past. Again. Mac wrinkled her nose, knowing that smell.

Rotting flesh.

"Are you all right?" For some reason, she whispered, as if only the being in the shadows and herself should hear. Reaching the limit of light, she slowed, then crouched lower, trying not to seem a threat. "Do you need help?"

The darkness roared at her, followed by a nightmare form that fell against her, knocking her flat. Panic-stricken, Mac fought to free herself, only to realize the weight pressing on her was completely limp, as if lifeless.

Hands tugged at her arms, shoulders, and bag, plucking her from underneath . . . *what?*

Even as Brymn half carried her to the train, Mac looked back at the form collapsed on the platform, trying to glimpse what she could of it between the Dhryn walking by; the only attention they paid to the unconscious form being to avoid stepping on it.

It? Suddenly, Mac had a clear look. A Dhryn lay there, facedown, all its limbs splayed on the pavement. The body—something about it wasn't right. Mac gasped as she saw it was shriveled, the blue skin split everywhere along thin, irregular lines, those lines dark as if oozing some fluid. The arms were no better, mere sticks with the twisted remnants of hands at each end.

One of the hands *moved,* turning so the fingers grasped at empty air.

"Brymn." Mac resisted, a futile effort against the determined alien. "We have to help him."

"Hush. You must not see—there is nothing there." He heaved her in front of him and through the door. Other Dhryn were coming in behind them, blocking Mac's view.

There were windows, if no seats. Mac hurried to the nearest, muttering apologies as she bumped into already seated Dhryn.

But when she looked out to the shadow, the pathetic form was gone.

"We do not think of it."

"What kind of answer is that?" Mac braced one foot on the luggage rack, the closest thing to a seat on the Dhryn train, and glared at Brymn. Despite the number waiting on the platform, it seemed there was more than enough room.

The crowd had spread itself through the various cars. Theirs was almost deserted, shared by the usual handful of 'bots near the ceiling and a group of three Dhryn busy in their own conversation at the far end. They wore the woven blue that reminded Mac of the *Pasunah* crew.

The privacy should have made Brymn more communicative, but so far, he'd refused to admit there'd been a 'damaged' Dhryn on the platform at all.

"I'm a trained observer, Brymn," she said, not for the first time. "I know what I saw. What I don't understand is why you won't tell me what was wrong with that Dhryn."

"A Dhryn is robust—"

Mac held up her hand to stop him. "I know the rest. Are you trying to tell me damaged Dhryn are left to die in the streets? I don't accept that. You may not have—" *even a* word *for medical care,* she realized with frustration, "—but you have sanitation. That being was rotting away!"

Brymn looked as miserable as she'd ever seen him, arms tightly folded, brow ridges lowered, mouth downturned. After meeting her eyes for a long moment, he said very quietly: "It is the Wasting."

"'Wasting,'" Mac repeated, leaning forward. "What is it?"

"We do not think of it." He shivered, looking around as if to see who might overhear.

She had an answer for that. "Speak in English."

"English?" The Dhryn pulled out the tablet, an almost pathetic eagerness on his face. "Then shall I read the news reports, Mackenzie Winifred Eliza—"

As the Ro had been the other Dhryn reality they preferred "not to think about," Mac had no intention letting Brymn slide past this without an answer. She pushed aside the tablet, though gently, and shook her head. "Later. Tell me about the Wasting. Please."

"Why do you want to know?"

"Asking questions is what I do." For some reason, she thought of Nik, of how aggrieved he'd looked whenever puzzled. "I don't like mysteries—or secrets."

"What if the answer is something you do not like?"

Mac's lips twisted. "I seek the truth. It has nothing to do with likes or dislikes."

"Ah." A sigh, barely audible over the soft whoosh of the train through the tube. They were moving at a pace that made Mac queasy each time she glanced at the lights flashing by the windows. "The Wasting is a truth, Mac, which we Dhryn do not like. This is why we do not think of it." Mac held her breath as he paused, willing him to continue. After a moment, he did.

"I do not know how it is for other species, Mac, but we Dhryn have stages in our lives—moments of great change. The Freshening is the one that turns us from *oomling* to adult." For some reason, Brymn stroked his eye ridge with one hand. "After the Freshening, next comes the—the nearest word in English is 'Flowering.' Its timing is less predictable. We can Flower at almost any age and, for most Dhryn, Flowering is a peaceful, almost unnoticed event that marks maturation." His expression turned suddenly wistful. "A privileged few are transformed and set on the path to becoming Progenitors."

When he stopped, Mac could almost hear the word he didn't want to add. "But—" she offered.

"But if the Flowering goes wrong, instead of change, there is—degradation. It is the Wasting. The body loses its flesh and proper shape. The mind goes mad. Some—linger. In the colonies, they may wander into the wild areas. Here, it seems they haunt the tunnels." Brymn's nostrils oozed yellow. Distress. *At the topic, or a memory?* Mac wondered. "None live more than a week or two."

"And you don't do anything? Aren't there—" Mac bit her lip, then said carefully: "You could ask other species. Some must have knowledge that could help."

Brymn gave another, deeper sigh. "It is not something one helps, Mac. The Wasted are just that—Dhryn who have failed to be Dhryn. We give them the grace of ignoring their fate."

"That's not good enough," Mac objected. "Any such metamorphosis has a biochemical basis. You have chemists—surely some could find ways to monitor the change, control it, help those who are in difficulty—"

Brymn looked horrified. "You'd ask us to tamper with the very process that defines our future, that determines the rightful Progenitors of our species! Are you mad?"

A rebuttal trembling on her lips, Mac made herself stop and think. *Who was the alien here?* she asked herself. *How dare she impose her values on their biology, their culture?* Chastened, she subsided, settling farther back on the luggage rack. An arm around the upright support kept her from slipping, but the rack itself was making serious efforts to reshape her posterior. "I withdraw the suggestion, Brymn," she said quietly. "I never meant to offend you. It's my nature, part of being Human, to be affected by such suffering. I feel a need to act . . . to help."

He held out an empty hand and she willingly put hers into it. "I could never be offended by you, Mackenzie Winifred Elizabeth Wright Connor. Confused, yes," this with the tiniest of smiles. "But that is the beauty of our differences, that you see possibilities I do not. Perhaps I shall surprise you, one day."

"Oh, you've already done that, Brymn." Mac gave his hand a squeeze, then let go, along with her questions. *She'd find the answers herself.* "Do we still have time for the tablet?"

A broad smile now. "But of course! I have taken the liberty of reorganizing the reports by system of origin. Excuse me," he said, while he relocated himself with a bustle of moving limbs and shuffling bags—he'd slung two around his torso. Eventually he sat so his right side was against the rack and she could look over his shoulder—thoughtful, even if the words on the tablet in his hand were no more legible now than they'd been in her apartment. "There. I shall start with reports from Sol."

As he began to read aloud, something about sports scores, Mac stretched out on her side as best she could, finding it more comfortable if she laid one arm over his warm, rubbery shoulders.

Even as she listened to his deep bass rumble, she couldn't help but wonder. *How close was Brymn to "Flowering?"*

- Portent -

IN HER DREAMS, the world was hinged and could swing open like a door. She struggled with bar and latch, with lock and bolt, until only her hands held the world closed. Held the world safe.

In her dreams, green liquid, like pus from a wound, seeped under the door that was the world, leaked along its sides, dripped from its top until it burned her from toe to hand to face, until it ate from her skin and flesh and bone.

In her dreams, she had the choice. To turn away and run, letting the world take care of itself . . .

Or to hold the door against death as long as she had life . . .

". . . We're losing her."

"There's nothing left to lose—"

"Tell that to her family! Forget the legs—get more gel on her midsection. Damn it—I said more . . ."

"No use. It's over."

In her dreams, the world was hinged and could close softly, like the lid of night, shutting out pain and fear, letting her rest.

"Next."

- 20 -

CAVERNS AND CURIOSITIES

MAC PRESSED her nose against the window. Another stop identical to the five before. "You could at least tell me where we're going," she complained, pulling back.

"No, no. I know Humans enjoy surprises."

Mac nudged Brymn with her toe. "Some Humans. Others are happier knowing where they are going."

"That is coaxing. I am able to resist."

She grinned. "I'm impressed."

Of course. He'd had Emily to teach him about humanity.

Mac pushed aside the thought, shunting it deep inside with the bitter disappointment of no message from Earth. *Or none she could find.* The reports from Sol System had consisted of racing results from Neptune's rings and the announcement of discounts to species who brought their own ship engineers when accessing Earth's repair and refit facilities. Brymn had reread them until they'd both memorized every word. Nothing sounded like code. Nothing hinted at a hidden meaning.

So there was nothing she could do, about Emily or Nik or Base. Mac had decided she owed herself—and Brymn—a few hours without the troubles of the universe.

Brymn seemed to have less difficulty immersing himself in the moment. "It is the very next stop," he proclaimed cheerfully, waving four arms about. One clutched the ever-present map; the other three, assorted bags. She assumed he'd brought snacks as well.

Mac had saved her cereal bars, but gave herself a carefully small drink of water. Given the rainfall, she hadn't expected a shortage. Then again, she hadn't expected Brymn would be taking her what felt like halfway across—or, more accurately, through—the planet. *Rationing seemed prudent.*

"Next stop, is it?" Mac tried to snatch the map, but his arm bent at an impossible angle to keep it out of her reach.

"You will see, *Lamisah*. Soon enough."

"Soon enough" translated into the longest distance between two stops yet on their journey through the tube. Mac loosened and rebraided her hair uncounted times. Brymn's bright blue eyelids closed and he let out tiny, quiet hoots, as though dreaming something amusing. Eventually, Mac found a way to scrunch herself into the luggage rack so she could almost nod off, if not quite. The train was making too many turns for her to trust any one position.

They were alone in the car. Fellow travelers—in three instances—had chosen to move elsewhere at their first opportunity. *Nothing to do with her,* Mac decided, though the presence of a Human must seem bizarre to home system Dhryn. It was Brymn the Tourist, who missed no opportunity to praise Haven and explain he was from the colonies, making his first trip back since Freshening and wasn't the tube system a magnificent achievement involving a full century of effort and did they appreciate how many . . .

Mac could recite the spiel verbatim—in fact, it was hard to get the facts and figures to stop dancing around in her head hours later. She gave up and twisted upright again. *Time for another walk.*

On straightaways, like this, the train might have been standing at a station. There was no vibration underfoot she could detect. *To avoid interfering with infra-sound conversation?* Intriguing concept. As Mac paced down the middle of the empty car, her fingers automatically tugged her braid from its knot and undid it, combing through the hip-length stuff.

Seung was always looking for quieter tech, quieter in terms of whale acoustics. She should arrange for a Dhryn engineer to work with the Preds at Base next season. *You never knew where you'd get a breakthrough,* Mac hummed to herself, splitting her hair into three and rebraiding as she paced. *Or from whom.*

Take the Dhryn technology to defend against the Ro. Judging from the tube system and the removal—Mac still found that incredible—of whatever else had orbited Haven's sun, part of that defense relied on physical barriers. *For a reason?* Was the attack on the pods typical Ro behavior, when stealth failed them?

An idea—no, less than that—*a combination of possibilities* paused Mac's busy hands, slowed her feet to a standstill. She adjusted to the slight tilt of the flooring without thinking, accustomed to more unstable surfaces than a polite train.

The Ro hadn't made a single mistake in their attack on Base.

Minimum action for maximum result. The anatomy of a salmon modeled the concept. Power applied where the least amount of effort would push the stream-lined body through the water—or air—with the greatest force.

No mistakes, minimal action implied advance planning. Advance planning meant a source of knowledge.

Mac tied her braid in a tight knot and shoved it inside the back of her shirt. *Base wasn't that sophisticated,* she argued with herself, *not to beings who could knock out power and evade sensors.* The Ro didn't need any help.

But she'd told Brymn: *"I seek the truth. It has nothing to do with what I want."*

She'd better damn well mean it. Mac stared ahead and saw nothing but a face with its trademark smile, a touch lopsided for perfection, which made it so perfectly friendly.

Emily could have given the Ro the plans to Base. She could have told them how best to knock out the power. She could have . . .

. . . been responsible for the injury and death of how many innocents?

Forgive me.

Mac ground the heels of her fists into her eyes.

"*Lamisah?* Is something wrong?"

She dropped her hands to meet Brymn's anxious gaze. "Too much thinking, my friend. That's all."

"Ah. Soon you will have new things to think about. Are you ready?"

Feeling the train slowing beneath her feet, Mac knew what he meant. "I don't suppose you'll tell me now where we're going?" she asked one final time, going to the rack to pick up her bag.

"Where we will stand between one beginning and another."

"Riddles, now?" She made the effort to smile as she turned to face him. No need to spoil Brymn's pleasure.

He wasn't smiling. She noticed the map was no longer in sight. His body was canted down, not as far as threat, but certainly lower than it had been for the role of Brymn the casual tourist.

This was Brymn with a mission.

Mac nodded to herself; somehow, she'd known. "This isn't a tour, is it?"

"I wish it could be, *Lamisah,*" the Dhryn said. "But I have something to tell you, something I couldn't mention above, where the air could have ears."

"You're so sure we're safe here?" The train slowed to a stop. All Mac could see out the windows were walls on both sides, lit only by the lights from the train. It made her feel trapped behind bars.

"If this place isn't safe, Mackenzie Winifred Elizabeth Wright Connor, then it is too late for anything we might do to save ourselves."

Not the most reassuring reason she'd heard lately.

Brymn led the way off the train. Once on the platform, Mac understood why he'd sounded so confident.

The walls were dark because they were lined with the same glistening black material as the shroud the Dhryn had tossed over her box on the way station, supposedly able to disrupt the Ro's technology. She followed it with her eyes up to the ceiling, where it became part of the shadows stretching overhead and to either side. There was more underfoot. She wanted to lift her feet from it. *Afraid of a carpet?* Mac scolded herself.

The train pulled away—backward, not ahead as she'd expected.

So this was the end of the line.

"This way." Brymn didn't give her any choice, almost running down the platform in the opposite direction from the train. Mac swore under her breath but hurried after him.

The platform narrowed and became a ramp leading down to the tracks. There was a dim illumination in the distance. Mac squinted, trying to make out details of what looked like a large opening. She guessed the tracks continued into a cavern.

It wasn't their destination. Before they reached the tracks, Brymn halted in front of a section of wall. After studying what appeared to Mac to be more of the same glistening fabric, he spat onto one hand, then pressed it against the wall above and to the right of his head.

Smoke began to appear between his three fingers as the fabric shrank away to reveal an illuminated plate. *Finally,* Mac thought, *a civilized door control.* She wrinkled her nose at an acrid smell. *A being of unexpected resources, her Brymn.*

Her mind flashed back to Pod Three and the Ro attack. She'd only a fuzzy recollection of their actual escape—being dumped into the ocean along with the gallery and kitchen tended to overshadow fine details. Not to mention fear, horror, and utter screaming confusion. Still, Mac had no trouble remembering one very unusual aspect.

Brymn had *pushed* them through a solid window.

Seeing how he'd cleared the fabric from the control, she also remembered how. He'd *spat* at the window wall; it had shattered when he rammed it.

Not typical behavior for the transparent, strong, yet flexible material. The Preds had been caught testing the ability of the pod window walls with harpoons. Needless to say the students had suffered more than the window.

Mac eyed the smoking, ruined edge of the shroud fabric wistfully. *Never,* she told herself, *ever, travel without sample vials.*

Meanwhile, in plain view of the dozen or more tiny vidbots stationed along the ceiling, Brymn was tapping what had to be an access code into the plate. "This is going to get us in trouble, isn't it?" Mac asked with what she considered remarkable aplomb, considering she stood in the bowels of an alien world, a world she was visiting on the sufferance of its leaders.

With an individual whose sanity hadn't been confirmed.

"Ah." The fabric split along two lines that met overhead, the triangle thus formed moving away from them and to the side so Mac stared into a very unappealing and dark cavity. A cavity out of which rushed cooler, damper air.

She covered her nose with one hand. "What's that smell?"

Brymn was already half inside, his stooped body posture fitting perfectly within the available space, although he had no room to spread out his arms. "Hurry, Mac."

Couldn't a Dhryn smell that? Mac swallowed hard and obeyed, breathing as little as possible through her fingers. It wasn't so much sulfur, she decided, as rancid cream. With sulfur. And maybe the stomach contents of a five-days-dead seal.

Whatever it was, it diminished to a background misery after her first few steps. Either her sense of smell had overloaded and quit, or opening the door had released a pocket of collected fumes, rapidly diffusing into the tunnel.

Mac only hoped to avoid finding the source.

The cavity proved to be part of some kind of accessway, with a maze of branches to the left and right. They were free of 'bots, at least. There were lights, but they were little more than glows on the walls. Brymn moved confidently enough, so perhaps the lights were brighter in the nonvisible, to a Human, part of the spectrum.

Mac let her mind worry at Dhryn senses and experiments to test their differences. It was better than letting her mind think about the mass of planet mere centimeters above her head, or the way her imagination raced back to all the old horror films she'd watched with Emily, in which the heroes were inevitably lured into a dark, deadly basement.

She'd complained how unrealistic the scenario was. *Who would do such a thing?* Emily had argued that each basement was a test of courage. Until the heroes faced such a test, the audience couldn't believe in their ability to ultimately defeat the monster.

Mac didn't feel courageous. She felt trapped. And she didn't feel capable of arguing with one exasperating Dhryn, let alone defeating a monster.

If this was a trap, and she never left here again, what was the range of the bioamplifiers accumulating in her liver and bones? Even if the rock overhead didn't matter, what of the shroud lining every cavity down here? Was she as hidden from Human sensors as the Dhryn's *oomlings* were from the Ro?

If so, she'd become a mystery that should annoy Nikolai Trojanowski for some time.

Thinking of another Human was the last straw. Mac stopped, hands carefully away from the walls leaning together over her head. "Brymn! Wait!"

If anything, her shouts spurred him to move faster. His voice trailed back to her, low and anxious. "No, no. This is no place for us, *Lamisah.* The Wasted could come to die here. Hurry."

"Wonderful." At the thought of rotting, mad Dhryn waiting to grab her from the more-than-abundant shadows—yet another horror staple Mac could do without—she scampered after the Dhryn, almost running into him from behind. "I hope you know the way out of here."

"As do I."

Luckily for Human-Dhryn relations, Mac had no time to formulate a suitable response. The very next bend in the accessway brought them to where it almost doubled in width and height. A welcoming brightness streamed across the floor from an entrance larger than those they'd been passing. As her eyes adjusted, Mac sniffed cautiously. The breeze lifting the wisps from her forehead was warm and sweet. She took a step toward that beckoning light.

"We aren't going that way," Brymn said. "Come, Mac."

She paused. "Why? What's there?"

"A crèche. Come. It's only a bit farther." He pointed down another of the dark, forbidding accessways.

"*Oomlings?*"

Mac was already moving, Brymn's plaintive, "we've no time!" echoing in her ears.

The sight greeting her eyes made her forget the Ro, forget Emily, forget herself.

She wasn't standing in an entrance. This must be the opening of a ventilation shaft of some kind, for beneath her feet the wall dropped at least thirty meters to the floor of the cavern in front of her.

Cavern? As well call Castle Inlet a rock cut, missing the glorious play of light, water, and life. This hidden place was nowhere as large, but it gave the same feeling of wonder. The far end of the crèche was so distant Mac couldn't make out its shape, but its tiled, colorful side walls swung out and open like the arms of a mother. Golden rays of light from suspended clusters on the ceiling bathed the floor below, crisscrossing so even the shadows were faint and welcoming.

The light was only the beginning.

The floor, which rose and fell in wide steps, was covered with what Mac could only think of as immense playpens, each carpeted in some kind of soft green and bounded by woven silk panels in rainbow shades. Each held one or more adult Dhryn surrounded by a mass of miniature ones. Her first impression was of ceaseless movement and Mac eagerly searched for patterns. Sure enough, within a 'pen directly below her, the *oomlings*—for the tiny copies of Brymn could be nothing else—were sitting carefully on their rears, heads oriented toward an adult who was gesturing with four arms, the way Brymn would do whenever enthused about a topic. In the adjacent 'pens, *oomlings* were milling around their adults, every so often hopping into the air with a random exuberance that brought a smile to Mac's lips.

And the sounds. Low booming voices almost disappeared under what could only be called cooing. *The oomlings?* The hairs on her arms and neck reacted to something—more infrasound. *From the adults,* oomlings, *or both?* Mac wondered. In such a large space, the lower frequencies could be heard by all. Perhaps something being taught to all at once? Or was it as simple as a communal lullaby, for many of the 'pens held jumbles of smaller *oomlings,* arms and bodies wrapped around one another in peaceful confusion as they slept.

As if all this wasn't enough, Mac thought, thoroughly enchanted, *the* oomlings *weren't blue or rubbery.* From the tiniest to the ones almost the size of adults, they were white from head to footpad, and either wearing clothing like feathers, or their torsos were covered in down.

They might have six arms—she couldn't see any with a seventh—but they called forth parental instincts even from a distance and even from an alien.

Brymn had come to sit beside her, his arms folded. "Our future," he said warmly.

"Are those the Progenitors?" Mac nodded into the crèche to indicate the adult Dhryn.

"Of course not." A subdued hoot. "Why would you think such a thing?"

Mac was tempted to retort: *because you Dhryn keep your biology as secret from others as you to do from yourselves,* but settled for: "If these were Humans, the parents—Progenitors—would be responsible for caring for their offspring—*oomlings.*" She couldn't help but think of her dad.

And hope she'd be able to describe all this to him in person.

"Ah. Our Progenitors are responsible for the Dhryn. What you see below are—" he paused as if searching for the right word. "These are caregivers. They remain with the *oomlings* at all times. Just as the *oomlings* must remain here until they Freshen."

"To keep them safe from the—" Brymn touched her mouth to stop what she would have said.

"Please do not speak that name here, *Lamisah*," he said as he took his hand away.

Mac nodded, seeing the crèche from a new perspective—that of a vault protecting a living treasure. She tried to estimate how many such vaults would be required to house the new generations of an entire planet, the organization to feed and care for them, and gave up. But her imagination could encompass the desperation of a species that had to bury its helpless young to protect them.

The Ro had a great deal more to answer for than the destruction of Base.

"A sight to warm the hearts," Brymn said softly, "but we haven't time to waste, Mac. Come. It's not far."

Mac turned to follow her guide, resisting the temptation to look back.

"It is here. The answer to everything."

Given the conviction in Brymn's voice, Mac sat on the nearest cratelike tube, pulled out a water bottle, and studiously broke off a piece of cereal bar to chew. They were, barring any more secret doors and chambers the Dhryn hadn't revealed, sitting in a storeroom.

A storeroom packed to its ceiling with tubes marked: Textile Archives. Some were dusty enough to have been down here since the Dhryn began burrowing.

She watched Brymn dump his bags, then rush to one particular stack, running his hands greedily along the outside of the bottommost tubes as if they were treasure. "Help me, *Lamisah*," he ordered, busy peering at labels. "We must find the oldest specimen. It will be marked the 'year of beginning' or some such thing." He gave a dismissive gesture to the packed corridor they'd walked through to come here. "Anything outside this area is too recent. The curator was adamant."

"Why?" But she was already packing away her snack and coming to join him. "What are you looking for, Brymn?"

"Proof. I know it's here."

That was all the explanation he'd give her, perhaps assuming, correctly, that Mac was ready to desert him if she had the slightest idea how to get herself back to civilization. The labyrinth they'd traversed to reach the crèche had been nothing compared to what Brymn had taken her through to reach this . . . this . . . storeroom. Twists, turns, another small access door to break through . . .

Implying, Mac suddenly realized, looking at the large storage tubes, *that there must be another, more normal way in—something she could find and use herself.*

She set to work with greater will, part of her attention on the labels, and the rest looking for any sign of a door. It wasn't going to be obvious, of course. Who'd worry about the inside of a storeroom, for one, plus shroud fabric lined these walls as well as those of all the accessways. The time and labor to shield nonessential areas had to have been staggering, a convincing display of the belief of the Dhryn in its effectiveness.

Mac hoped they were right.

The labels were straightforward enough, date of preservation—Mac thought it likely the tubes contained a controlled climate—and a code number that she came to realize was the order of preservation. The process had begun not that long ago, hence the relatively uniform nature of the tubes, and it appeared the curators had elected to preserve the older specimens first. Perhaps they valued the antiquities most.

Or they'd been deteriorating fastest in the nearly constant rain on the surface. Mac chided herself as she climbed over a low stack to see what was behind it. She was growing too familiar with them, with Brymn, with the Dhryn as a whole. Drawing conclusions as if they were Earth-born and she understood what drove them, as if they were Human and foreign, not alien.

"I've found it! Mac! Mac!"

Obeying the summons and her own curiosity, Mac climbed back into the main area in time to see Brymn staggering into the middle of the open space, a tube taller than he was clutched in all three pairs of arms. Before he teetered forward again and dropped it, she added her arms to his and helped him put the heavy thing down.

Mac read the label and blinked in awe. Without doing the conversion to standard union years, she didn't know how long ago it had been preserved. But the code was a single digit. *Dhryn for one.* She had no idea how old the specimens inside might be, but they were doubtless the irreplaceable gems of the archives. Mac couldn't believe Brymn, an archaeologist, had almost dropped the tube.

"Quickly, quickly! We must open it. No. Wait!" Almost panting, Brymn bounced away to get one of his bags, then bounced back, ripping the bag open. "I must be ready to take the readings. Now open it."

"What? You can't open it—there have to be preservatives inside. You know better than I do what could happen to the contents if they contact the air." *She was guarding the cultural heritage of a species from a mad being.* "What readings? Brymn, what's going on?"

For a wonder, he stopped waving his arms and gave her his full attention, his expression both sad and solemn. "We both seek the truth, Mackenzie Winifred Elizabeth Wright Connor. Trust me. Help me. I know what I'm doing."

"Then will we go home? Up there? Out of here?"

"I promise, *Lamisah.*"

Mac threw up her hands in surrender. "Fine. What do you want me to do?"

Her job, it turned out, was to crack the seal of the tube while Brymn stood ready. The hooklike device in his hand resembled that used by the Esteemed Academic on Mac's food supplies. It didn't look like any scanning tech Mac knew, but then these storage tubes were odd enough themselves. He had to show her how to unlock them first, a matter of sliding four sections of metal past one another in a specific order. Not a lock, but protection against doing accidentally what they were doing deliberately.

Mac held her breath as she slid the final section and broke the seal.

A cool mist formed along the edge within seconds, condensing along the tube itself. Brymn avoided it as he pushed his device inside the tube, the hook slipping in as if designed for that purpose.

He read the display in silence. *Not quite,* Mac thought, feeling vibrations along the tube.

"What is it?"

His eyes didn't leave the device. "Pull the lid wide open, Mac."

In for a penny . . . Mac didn't bother with the rest of her dad's saying, too busy struggling with hinges meant for Dhryn musculature. The lid lifted, then toppled over so she had to dodge smartly out of its way or risk her toes. It fell to the floor with a clang.

As the metallic echoes died away, Mac came around to Brymn, peering over his shoulder. Three of his hands were busy inside the tube, pulling free pieces of fabric so fragile they crumpled in his fingers as he brought them close to his device, their bright dust sparkling as it drifted back into the tube.

"Brymn." Mac tugged one arm. "Stop it. You're ruining the specimens!"

He stopped, but not, Mac decided, at her urging. The Dhryn sank to a sitting position of his own accord, staring into the tiny display of his device as if trying to burn the image into his brain.

"So it's true," he boomed slowly. "I believed. Yet at the same time, I couldn't. But here is the proof."

"Of what?" Mac did her best to sound patient.

"That what is Dhryn, on this world, in our history, began no more than three thousand standard years ago. We began, when so much else ended forever."

She sank down herself, using the end of the tube as a bench, despite its damp chill. "The Moment. This is why you've been trying to fix a date," Mac said wonderingly. "You believe the Dhryn survived the devastation of the Chasm and came here, before the transects failed." Mac paused, feeling the irony. "So Emily was working with one of the mythical 'Survivors' all along and didn't realize it." She frowned at Brymn. "Why didn't you tell her?"

A halfhearted hoot. "I'm thought crazy enough by my own kind—do you think I'd spread that to other species?"

Mac patted the tube. "But you weren't. You were right. But why? Why was this a secret?"

"The Progenitors must have decided it was for our own good."

"Why? Surely it was a great triumph for your kind?"

"Or so great a fear, so intense a trauma, that our ancestors chose not to think of it, in case thinking made it stay real. Without that fear, the Dhryn could rebuild, move outward, accept the gift of the transects when it was offered us."

"For the second time," Mac mused.

"What do you mean?"

"You must have had the ability to travel between systems to arrive here, Brymn. The question becomes, did your species develop the transect technology in the first place, only to somehow lose it?"

The Dhryn was embarrassed. *She could read that by now.* There was a shifting of his eyes from hers, a rising slant to his posture. "We Dhryn do not value innovation or change—the Progenitors prefer we adapt the technology we have, or use that of others, wherever possible. Having been to the worlds of other species, to Human worlds, I can say without any doubt, Mac, the Dhryn are fundamentally incapable of such a thing."

"Well, we didn't invent it either," she soothed. "So your entire species, as far as you know, abandoned its past when it fled here, to this world. Quite a feat."

"And one we must keep to ourselves, Mac," with a worried look at her, "until I can prepare a full argument to present to the Progenitors. It is not our place to release such inflammatory information. Others, wiser than we, will know what to do with it."

"I won't say that's been my experience," Mac warned him, but she nodded. "I promise, of course."

Brymn stood, scanner in hand. "Thank you, *Lamisah*. When the time is right, we'll tell everyone. You do realize, this is more than confirmation the Dhryn came from the Chasm—it also provides the first clear dating of the Moment. It was at least three thousand five hundred and seven years ago, using the system of the Interspecies Union."

Since life was stripped from hundreds of worlds, leaving only ghosts, ghouls, and ruin. Mac didn't need the shiver running down her spine to remind her. "I don't care about the dating, Brymn. Do you realize this world might contain the truth about the Chasm? We could find out what happened—what's starting to happen again!"

"The Ro." He wrapped his arms around his middle, tightly enough to crush the blue silks wrapping his torso. His nostrils oozed yellow mucus. *Distress or anxiety?* "Ah, Mac. I may be a fool, but you're a dreamer. My ancestors must have decreed that everything from before our arrival here be destroyed. I've questioned other historians and archaeologists. They have no interest in anything earlier—because nothing earlier exists."

"There's a way," Mac pressed. "We need to find your place of origin. The world within the Chasm where the Dhryn began."

He looked puzzled. "Dhryn have always been."

Archaeologist, not biologist, Mac reminded herself. *Fine.* "Where the Dhryn lived before they came to Haven. That place could tell us what we need to know."

"Ah! Yes, I concur." Then his little mouth formed an unhappy pout. "Even if we could find it, Mac, how would we get there?"

"You're asking me?" Mac snorted. " I don't know how to get to my apartment from here."

A definite hoot. "That I can do," Brymn reassured her. "Through the main entrance will be a commuter tube. It will take us almost into your place of greeting!"

Thinking of the past hours spent tunnel-skulking, Mac felt entitled to some exasperation: "We couldn't have come that way?"

Brymn spread six arms. "If we had, you would not have seen the *oomlings.*"

And you would have been seen breaking in here, Mac added to herself, but didn't question the Dhryn. She was all in favor of a more direct route home. Perhaps his culture was one in which you could be stopped from committing a crime, but weren't punished once it was a *fait accompli.*

Home. Wondering at how comfortably the word wrapped itself around a cockeyed apartment on an alien planet, Mac helped Brymn close the tube, hopefully protecting what he hadn't irreparably damaged, then push it behind some others. *Did she feel at home here?* Or was this more evidence of the adaptability of the Human psyche, that she could satisfy her need for shelter and territory using whatever was offered?

Even her? The self-proclaimed "Earth is quite enough" Mackenzie Connor?

As she pondered, Brymn went to a section of seemingly ordinary wall, spreading his arms so all six hands could touch certain points at once. As it obediently revealed itself as a wide, slanted door, Mac realized why she hadn't found the exit. *Damn Dhryn don't know how to make anything convenient for humanoids,* she told herself, rather fondly.

They did know how to intimidate humanoids.

The door flashed open to reveal a bristling fence of weapons aimed in their direction. Mac lost count after thirty-six, implying more than half a dozen guards waited behind those ominous bores.

To make matters worse, the floor began vibrating underfoot. Brymn wrapped himself into a silent knot, responding to what Mac couldn't hear.

Swallowing hard, and doing her best to imagine a staff meeting, Mac stamped her foot. "I am Mackenzie Winifred Elizabeth Wright Connor," she informed the host of round black muzzle tips, attempting to stretch a little taller.

"We know."

21

VISIT AND VIOLATION

"THIS IS so exciting, *Lamisah!*"

Mac, busy trying to maintain some dignity while walking quickly enough to keep her heels from being trampled by their escort, rolled her eyes at Brymn. He was beaming, insofar as his small mouth allowed. Those hands nearest her—the Dhryn was on her left—kept patting her shoulder or arm at random intervals. It was as if he had to reassure himself she was with him, a friend to witness this "so exciting" moment.

They weren't being arrested, or the Dhryn equivalent. Mac had figured that much out when none of the twenty-two Dhryn waiting in the wide corridor had bothered entering the Textile Archives nor waited to close the door. Instead, she and Brymn had been informed they were late.

They were expected below.

Below, Brymn had whispered to her, were the Progenitors.

Their escort had ended further conversation by raising their weapons again. It hadn't quelled Brymn, who'd almost danced beside her. She'd only hoped the big alien didn't burst into ecstatic song and land them both in deeper trouble.

"Below" was accurate enough. Within their cluster of armed Dhryn, each wearing individual colors but similar in that all had lost one or more limbs and so were of higher accomplishment than Brymn, they'd been taken into the heart of Haven. First had been a series of sloping ramps, each barred by a massive door better suited to being an air lock under the ocean in Mac's estimation. Following the ramps had been a lift, which had carried all of them, in very tight proximity, down for a remarkably long time. Mac had leaned on Brymn after a while, grateful she'd never suffered from claustrophobia.

Yet.

Now they walked very quickly down another, much wider ramp. The soft-soled Dhryn feet were almost silent on any surface, but here lush carpeting underfoot muffled Mac's boots as well. Without voices, they walked to their breathing alone, Brymn's the loudest and most rapid.

Well aware hers were the first Human eyes to see the Dhryn's inner sanctum, Mac did her best to memorize everything she saw. The shroud material was everywhere, of course, but here spirals of silver began to overlay the black, illuminated so they appeared to be in motion. There were words picked out in silver as well, as if the spirals were the breath carrying the sound. Between the bodies of her escort, and Brymn, Mac couldn't make out more than snatches of what was written. It seemed a combination of historical record, exhortations to enjoy life, and the occasional complaint about building standards.

Then Mac remembered. Brymn had told her he'd recorded Emily's name in the hall of his Progenitors. At the time, she'd taken it as metaphor. Obviously, she'd been wrong.

Was her *name here?* If so, what did the other Dhryn think of it?

Not that she'd have a chance to find out on this trip. Mac didn't understand the urgency of their escort, but there was no slowing the pace. When she'd attempted to do so, they'd grabbed her as if to carry her along. Only a loud protest—and a well-aimed kick—had put her back on her feet.

The spirals and their utterances grew denser and denser until the silver was almost blinding. The air grew as fresh as a summer's day, though the scent of growing things was replaced by an unknown but pleasant spice. Mac belatedly thought to look for more mundane aspects such as lighting fixtures, ventilation grates, and doorways, but unsurprisingly the Dhryn technology eluded her. *Well, security wasn't hidden.* Since leaving the archive, tiny round vidbots had hovered in every corner. Several had followed overhead, as if accompanying them. Mac had expected no less on the route leading to the Progenitors.

She would have liked to ask questions, prime among them: why was she, an alien, being brought here? *On the other hand, this way she couldn't get into trouble by saying the wrong thing—until she stood in front of the leaders of the Dhryn.*

There, Mac would let Brymn do the talking.

As if their escort had heard her thoughts, one came close to her on the opposite side from Brymn. "Mackenzie Winifred Elizabeth Wright Connor. I am Parymn Ne Sa."

Two hands missing, two extra names. *Hopefully coincidence,* Mac thought. "Accomplished," she said politely, doing her utmost not to pant. They hadn't slowed during this consultation. "I take the name Parymn Ne Sa into my keeping."

"Gratified." Parymn seemed older than the rest, grimmer somehow, although, like Brymn, he favored lime-green eye ridge paint with paired sequins. He was frowning. *Not at her,* Mac guessed, but as if worried by some task she represented. Sure enough, "There is a strict protocol which must be followed when intruding on the space of a Progenitor. Failure to do so will have—extreme consequences."

Given their entire escort carried weapons in all six hands, Mac had little doubt about the nature of such consequences. "I trust your guidance," she said, determined to put the onus on her escort instead of Brymn. That worthy was still bouncing along, seeming oblivious to the importance of the occasion, or the armament surrounding them. *Great.* Mac thought. *Stuck with a famished student sniffing pizza.*

Parymn sheathed the weapons in four of his six hands, using those in a gesture Mac recognized from Brymn's fits of anxiety. "Your ability to speak is remarkable, Mackenzie Winifred Elizabeth Wright Connor, and there is no doubt you are Dhryn, but—but—you lack the physical equipment required to—" Words seemed to fail him, then: "I fear you will offend simply by being what you are."

At some point, the ridiculousness of the universe rendered all other things moot. Smiling, Mac shook her head and patted Parymn on one arm, as familiarly as she would Brymn. "Don't worry. You said the Progenitors invited me—they must know what I am."

"Knowing isn't the same as believing."

A philosopher? Mac raised a brow, impressed. "Should I wait outside, then? I have no wish to offend them."

"It is too late. Your presence is expected."

Brymn, who'd seemed oblivious, suddenly jumped into the conversation. "Gloom and doom," he challenged. "That's all you *erumisah* ever say. If I'd listened to you, I'd never have studied the past, never have traveled, never learned—" Somehow, Mac managed to transform an artful stumble into a firm kick at what would have been an ankle on a Human leg. Brymn gave her a look, then closed his mouth.

Parymn didn't appear to notice. "It is our role to consider the consequences, Academic, and guide the growing generations of Dhryn along the safest path. In this case—ah. We have arrived."

Mac's eyes widened. The shroud-and-silver walls and ceiling continued through the entranceway ahead, but the passage itself was blocked by a mammoth vaultlike door of gleaming metal. Curiously, it was arched by gaps wide enough for Mac to squeeze through on either side and at the top. As she puzzled at the point of a door surrounded by holes, an inset within the door opened, nicely Dhryn-sized and shaped.

"Follow me," Parymn said, moving to the head of what now became a single file column of two Dhryn guards, Brymn, Mac herself, then two more guards. The rest of their escort took up stations on either side, apparently remaining behind. The 'bots rose to the ceiling as if ordered to wait as well.

They walked through the door, itself fifteen of Mac's steps deep, which opened into a passage both metal-scented and cold. She tried to see past Brymn, but could only make out a brightening ahead. Their escort moved too slowly now, as if there was some barrier ahead to be passed. Mac would remember the rhythmic movement of warm air past her face and neck, then back again, for the rest of her life.

Between one footfall and the next, she left what she understood or imagined, to enter a place nothing could have prepared her to meet.

Her eyes lied, frantic to make sense of what they saw. Mac was several paces into the Chamber of the Progenitors before she appreciated that what she thought was the ceiling was a shoulder, that what she thought a floor was a *hand.*

Believing and knowing weren't the same at all.

You've swum with whales, Mac reminded herself, even as the hand drew them away from the door, as steady and level as any machine. *At least they weren't underwater.*

Though they might have been. She wrenched her eyes from a vista of hills and valleys cloaked in dark blue skin, mottled with ponds of shining black liquid, and stared at what else lived here.

Her first impression was of rather silly-looking pufferfish, her mind fighting for equivalents. Her second was that the creatures looked nothing like fish at all. They were similar in size to herself, a relief after the shock of the Progenitor, but their oblong bodies were inflated, as if filled with gas. Indeed, many were drifting overhead like lumpy balloons. Fins lining the back and sides stroked at the air, guiding them in all three directions. Boneless arms hung below those drifting, as if they'd lost their function.

Most were crowded around the ponds, their bodies flaccid and low to the "ground," arms in the liquid. Mac couldn't tell if they were somehow taking it up or replenishing the Progenitor's supply. They had heads, but smoothed, so only the mouth and nostril openings remained. They varied in color, but all were pastel, like so many faded flower petals strewn about by the wind.

Air moved through Mac's hair, and back again. Over and over. The Progenitor's *breathing.*

These, too, were Dhryn?

From a world of only technology, she'd been transported to a wonderland of only biology. Mac crouched to brush her fingertips over the palm of the hand supporting them. Warm, rubbery, muscular. Like Brymn's.

"That is not permitted!" This urgent whisper from Parymn.

Mac looked up from her crouch. *He had to be kidding.* However, she stood. "My apologies, Parymn Ne Sa," she said absently, looking around.

Two pufferfish Dhryn intercepted them and hovered, close enough for Mac to touch, their arms—no, they were more like tentacles—groping the air toward her as if hunting for something lost. Disconcerted by the eyeless, silent beings, Mac eased back as much as she could. Parymn made a shooing motion with his upper arms and the two veered away with unexpected speed.

"Who are they?" she whispered to Brymn.

He blinked. "Who are who?"

Mac pointed to the flying forms now on all sides. "Them! Who are they? Those two seemed interested in me."

Brymn gave a low hoot. "Not who, what. Those are the Hands and Mouths of the Progenitor. They cannot be 'interested' in you, Mackenzie Winifred Elizabeth Wright Connor, or in anything else. They no longer think for themselves."

"Then they weren't always like this," she said, fighting back horror.

"It is an honor to become one of those who tends Her," Parymn broke in, his stern look at Mac intended to quell more questions.

Her. They were passing over what had to be the torso, as if the Progenitor brought them up and along her body. Mac moved as close to the edge of the palm as she dared, in order to see over the edge.

The blue skin below was smudged with white, as though every ripple was frosted with sugar. Mac fought the imagery to understand what was below. Not sugar crystals. *Oomlings!* They were erupting through the Progenitor's skin— thousands upon thousands upon thousands. As they appeared, they were being swept up in the arms of the pufferfish Dhryn, to be taken away into the distance. *To the nurseries?*

But their own destination almost shattered Mac's trained observer's calm. She glanced up and saw it coming. All she could do was grip Brymn for comfort and try to breathe without screaming.

Beneath nostrils the size of train tunnels whose breath filled this chamber, the Dhryn-who-had-been smiled at Mac with its normal mouth, blinked its normal eyes one/two below their sequined ridges, and said in its quiet, normal voice: "Welcome, Mackenzie Winifred Elizabeth Wright Connor."

The remnants of the face were embedded in a wall of blue flesh. The hand came to rest with its fingertips pressed against that wall, a platform as solid beneath Mac's feet as the deck of the *Pasunah,* and as much a lie. She spared an instant to long for a piece of honest granite, then deliberately let go of both Brymn and her fear. "Thank you—" She glanced at Parymn for the right honorific, but it was Brymn who answered.

"Progenitor! It is I, Brymn."

As Brymn was bouncing up and down, much as he'd done on the walkway to the shore, Mac waited to see the reaction. Their escort, predictably, looked highly aggrieved, bodies lowering in threat. The Progenitor, however, hooted. "Yes, I can see that. Welcome, Brymn," she/it said in a soft voice, higher-pitched and with a slower cadence than that of other Dhryn Mac had heard. "You have done well."

"I—have?" Brymn turned to Mac and picked her up with three arms. The rest were busy flailing about. "Did you hear that, *Lamisah?*" he bellowed in her face, squeezing tightly enough to threaten her ribs again. "I've done well!"

Mac fought for air and considered a timely kick. Fortunately, Brymn put her down before either became an issue. "Congratulations," she gasped, keeping an eye on the weapons all too nearby.

"Does this mean . . ." Brymn's voice faded into a whisper, ". . . dare I hope?" Mucus trailed from his nostrils and one hand groped blindly for Mac. Not understanding, but assuming it was an improvement over being grabbed, she took and held it. Then, in a heart-wrenching tone, he asked: *"Grathnu?"*

The Progenitor's eyes were identical to Brymn's. As they moved to pin Mac in their gaze, she was struck by the warmth that could be conveyed by yellow and black. *"Grathnu,"* she agreed, then shocked them all. "To be served by Mackenzie Winifred Elizabeth Wright Connor."

Brymn's hand left hers.

Mac coughed into the ensuing silence. "If I may, Progenitor, Brymn is much more deserving of such an honor," she said cautiously, making every effort to focus on that disembodied face and ignore the city-sized body that supported it.

A whine of weapons being activated. "You mustn't argue with the Progenitor!" Parymn shouted furiously.

"I'll argue with anyone I please!" Mac shouted back, then closed her mouth.

With a minor shake, the floor space doubled. Another hand rested beside this one. "Leave us, Parymn Ne Sa."

The older Dhryn bowed without a word, then glared at Mac as he and the remaining guards obeyed, climbing on the Progenitor's other hand. They were whisked away, *hopefully,* Mac thought, *to the door.*

She had to smile.

"What amuses you, Mackenzie Winifred Elizabeth Wright Connor?"

Something about the Progenitor's gentle tone made Mac grin even more broadly and admit: "I was wondering if you ever clap your hands, Progenitor."

The laugh was only on the face—likely wise, given that otherwise it would shake the world of all those Dhryn below and startle the *oomlings* during their first breath of life. Mac imagined there must be a small respiratory shunt formed, to allow the mouth to form sound so the Progenitor could continue to communicate with other Dhryn. *Quite the metamorphosis.*

"A habit I left behind," the Progenitor assured her with a smile of her own.

Along with mobility, independence, and the sky, Mac thought, feeling the weight of that choice—or was it a choice? Brymn had said they only knew the next Progenitors when those individuals Flowered into their final state.

As if following Mac's line of thought, the Progenitor continued: "As you can see, I have gained far more than I left, Mackenzie Winifred Elizabeth Wright Connor."

"How long does it take to grow this big?" Mac asked, leaning her head back as she estimated the bulk of shoulders and what had been head looming over them. Brymn made a strangled noise; Mac ignored him.

"Five hundred or so of your years," the Progenitor answered. "I am the most recent to begin producing *oomlings.* My name—no longer matters. Few endure the change; fewer still the growth." A tinge of pride. "Those who do, are the Dhryn. What else would you like to know?"

At this, Mac looked straight into the face in front of her. "As Brymn can testify, Progenitor, I have a great many questions."

"Once *grathnu* has been served, you may ask until I tire."

Mac had no idea what *grathnu* involved, but she was sure she wanted it to happen to someone else no matter how curious she was about the Dhryn. But as Mac opened her mouth, the Progenitor smiled. "Yes, Brymn may serve first."

Brymn stammered his thanks until the Progenitor frowned slightly. Then he gave a bow so deep he almost tipped over backward, which would have sent him over the palm and tumbling onto the torso far below. Mac breathed a sigh of relief when he straightened again. "My life's work has been for the Dhryn," he announced, coming to stand before the face. "I am Dhryn." He spread his six arms outward, fingers outstretched.

The seventh arm burst into the open, its edged fingers stretched as well. As if it had eyes, it swayed and turned, boneless as the hanging arms of the pufferfish Dhryn. Mac took a step closer, fascinated. The fingers stopped and oriented toward her.

"Not so close," warned the Progenitor quietly. Mac backed a step. The fingers turned to Brymn.

"I return to my Progenitor that which I am." He brought his lower left arm to his chest. Like a striking snake, the fingers of the seventh lunged forward to seize the limb at the wrist. Before Mac's horrified eyes, the sharp fingers sliced through the arm.

Brymn's left lowermost hand dropped to the palm of the Progenitor, followed by a few splashes of blue-black. *The wound must be self-sealing,* Mac realized numbly. The Dhryn's face bore an expression of rapture and his seventh arm, task complete, hung limp down his chest.

"I am Brymn Las," he said with so much joy in his voice Mac hurriedly reassembled her face into something less horrified.

She hoped.

"I take the name Brymn Las into my keeping," the Progenitor acknowledged. "And his gift of self, which shall enrich that which is Dhryn through my flesh."

Mac flinched to one side as a pufferfish Dhryn swooped down, battling its way through the streams of air leaving the gigantic nostrils above to hover beside her. This close, it looked even less like a Dhryn. Instead of thick blue skin, it appeared made of membrane and air, its organs tantalizingly visible. Before she could study it further, the pufferfish Dhryn collected Brymn's hand in its tentacles and lifted away again.

If she hadn't known, Mac wouldn't have believed.

Brymn was looking at her expectantly. *How could he be thrilled to have been maimed?* Mac, feeling more Human than she had for days, licked her lips and said, "I take the name Brymn Las into my keeping. A fine name."

"Now it is your turn, Mackenzie Winifred Elizabeth Wright Connor."

Mac's pants had pockets. She rammed both hands into their protection, as if that could possibly help. "I'm not worthy," she said weakly.

"You saved Brymn Las, you forced our ancestral enemy into flight, you left your home and risked yourself in order to protect what is Dhryn. You are Dhryn. You are more than worthy. Come," the Progenitor insisted gently. "Serve."

Of the predicaments Mac had ever imagined for herself, or dreamed in her worst nightmares, being trapped on the hand of a giant alien who expected her to cut off her own hand wasn't remotely one of them. It likely would be from now on.

They don't know biology.

Mac stiffened her shoulders and tried to remember Brymn's phrasing. *Ah, yes.*

"My work has been for the Dhryn." She tugged her braid from the back of her shirt, letting it fall down her chest. "I am Dhryn." She stretched out her arms, then brought both to her chest. "I give to the Progenitor that which I am." She'd palmed the small knife from her pocket in her right hand. Now, she grasped the braid in her left hand and sliced it off with her right.

The hair twisted as it fell to the palm of the Progenitor. What remained on Mac's head tumbled asymmetrically over her cheeks and down her neck, a lock dropping into her eyes. Without brushing it aside, Mac said firmly: "I am Mackenzie Winifred Elizabeth Wright Connor Sol." It hadn't been as hard as she'd feared to find one syllable to add to her name, something she could stand to hear repeated every time a Dhryn spoke to her. The name of Earth's Sun would be a promise to herself.

She would get home.

"I take the name Mackenzie Winifred Elizabeth Wright Connor Sol into my keeping," the Progenitor said gravely, "and her gift of self, which shall enrich that which is Dhryn through my flesh."

The pufferfish Dhryn who arrived to pick up Mac's braid appeared slightly confused, dipping up and down several times before finally grasping its find and heading away with it.

Brymn wasn't the least confused. He swept Mac into a hug, thoughtfully not using the arm still dripping fluid. "I knew you would serve *grathnu* with us as well as your own Progenitors, Mackenzie Winifred Elizabeth Wright Connor Sol!"

Mac's hand strayed to the jagged remains of her hair, a fair amount just past shoulder length and nodded, unable to smile. She'd broken her promise to Sam. *He wasn't coming back.*

How odd that letting him go had taken this.

The Progenitor was as good as her word, willingly answering Mac's questions. Unfortunately, despite Mac's care to avoid forbidden topics such as biology, every one of those answers was the standard Dhryn "we do not think of it," complete with a warm smile. After a dozen such responses, having learned nothing useful about the Ro or the Dhryn, Mac decided she'd tire before the Progenitor.

Now, she sat cross-legged beside Brymn on the palm of a giant. Amazing how easily the mind could put aside considerations like incredible size and inconceivable power when it came to a war of wills. Mac eyed the face on the blue wall of flesh and knew there were real answers behind it. *Good thing,* she told herself, *she herself was stubborn to a fault.*

"What should I ask you, Progenitor, that I haven't?" she inquired innocently.

The eyes blinked, one/two, as if she'd surprised the other. "I—"

Mac took advantage of the Progenitor's slight hesitation. "You must have expected me to ask you something in particular, or you wouldn't have invited my questions." She kept her voice set to sweetly courteous when it tried to slip into sarcasm. "I'd hate to disappoint you."

Brymn gave her a look that, from a Human companion, would have been asking, "What the hell do you think you're doing?" Mac ignored it, on the basis that from a Dhryn, for all she knew, it meant approval.

"I admit, Mackenzie Winifred Elizabeth Wright Connor Sol, that I have waited for you to ask why the Progenitors who preceded me chose to destroy our past, why we allow our system to remain at risk through the transects, and why I permitted you to be the first alien to meet a Dhryn Progenitor face-to-face."

"Good questions." So good, Mac hadn't dared ask them. "Would you answer them?"

They stared at one another, Brymn shifting unhappily as if he wished to say something but didn't dare. In this instance, Mac realized, she had an advantage over her friend. He was too used to revering the Progenitors, handicapping his ability to challenge different viewpoints.

Mac, on the other hand, was well past caring about protocol, and her only feeling about the Progenitor was a familiar awe for the way biology managed to work around civilization.

"Very well." The Progenitor pursed her small lips. "Our past has not been destroyed, although it has been made inaccessible to most Dhryn, including curious academics such as Brymn Las. Progenitors live a very long time. The three who survived the attacks of the Ro to settle this world lived long enough to share their knowledge with the next generation of successful Progenitors. That knowledge has been passed to those of my generation. Thus, we know what has been, what is, and what may be the consequence. Other Dhryn do not need to think of it."

"So the Ro are responsible for the destruction in the Chasm?"

"We barely escaped them," the Progenitor acknowledged, her eyes closing. "Had we not discovered technology to defend against theirs, we would have been destroyed again."

"Then why the transects?"

Her eyes opened in a flash of yellow-gold. "Before the Ro found us again, we had reached a point at which our *oomlings* must have new homes or suffer the consequences of overcrowding this one. We cannot change what it is to be Dhryn, Mackenzie Winifred Elizabeth Wright Connor Sol. Our colonies are essential to our survival."

Population pressure. Mac had to give the Dhryn credit—from what she'd seen, they'd made thorough use of this planet before venturing outward to others. If the Progenitors were physically incapable of slowing the birth rate—and culturally unwilling to find a biological way out—new worlds were the only answer.

The last of the three. Mac tilted her head as she asked: "Why did you permit me, a Human, to meet you?"

The Progenitor's eyes, though embedded forever in this mountain of flesh, could still sparkle. "Young Brymn Las is not the only curious Dhryn, Mackenzie Winifred Elizabeth Wright Connor Sol. I wished to see an alien with my own eyes, not through sensors and vids. At the same time, only one who is deemed Dhryn may be allowed in this chamber. You are both."

Mac pressed her hand against the palm supporting them. She doubted its thickened surface could feel something so small, but the Progenitor could see and hopefully understand the gesture. "I hope I haven't been a disappointment, Progenitor."

"In no sense, Mackenzie Winifred Elizabeth Wright Connor Sol, though I fear I must now disappoint you. One final question, if you please. I tire easily."

One? Mac almost panicked. *What if she asked a question that received only the stock answer? What if she missed the most important one?*

For no reason, Mac thought of the envelope in the pouch around her waist. She settled herself, abruptly sure what Nik would want her to ask. "If the Ro are beginning to attack other species as they did yours in the Chasm, what can we do to protect ourselves? Will the Dhryn share their effective defense?"

Two questions, but they would be one if the only answer was the Dhryn technology. Mac chewed her lower lip as the Progenitor deliberated. At least, Mac thought, the delay meant it wasn't going to be another "we don't think of it."

It wasn't. The palm shifted beneath them, sending both Mac and Brymn to their feet, staggering to keep their balance. "We remember!" the Progenitor cried out in a pain-filled voice, eyes wild. Mac heard cries from below as the torso landscape shook with emotion, churning the pools, spilling *oomlings*. "There is no protection! No safety! There is only emptiness and regret!" The wall in front of them became stained with yellow as mucus boiled from the huge nostrils above. Quieter, but no less intense: "The gates between worlds will close again and the only hope is to run before they do. Tell your species to run, Human! Run while you still can!"

The hand swept them away from the grief-stricken face before Mac could open her mouth to reply.

Mac had worried the distraught Progenitor would mean equally upset guards. But the Dhryn escort waiting at the doorway might not have noticed, Parymn nodding a greeting and beckoning them forward. *Perhaps,* Mac thought, eyeing their impassive faces, *the emotional turmoil of a buried Progenitor was another aspect of Dhryn life they chose not to think about.*

She could think of little else, silent and self-contained throughout their journey back to the tube trains, offering no more than a nod of farewell to Parymn and his guards at the station, curling up in a luggage rack without a word to Brymn.

The Progenitor knew what life had been like for the first of her kind on this world. The three survivors must have arrived on ships, but then? Mac tried to imagine such huge, fragile creatures lying out in the open, desperate to repopulate their species, utterly vulnerable until they had established themselves. The fear of the Ro following and finding them, despite the closed transect, must have been horrific.

No wonder they had spared their children that nightmare. *No wonder,* Mac thought as they passed from the area protected by shroud and rock, *they had reacted as they had to the Ro's return.* Hiding here, sending only the newly adult outside the system. The Progenitors must have been nearly hysterical at the news that the Ro had begun attacking other species again—that the nightmare from their past was coming to life, exactly as they'd been told.

No wonder they'd sent Brymn to Earth. *They must be trying everything.*

"Mac. Are you in pain? Should we hurry? Do you need your case of special supplies?" The concerned whisper from a being cradling a mutilated arm shook Mac from her preoccupation.

"I'm fine, Brymn. How about you?" The wound itself was covered in a pale blue membrane, but Mac couldn't imagine the underlying damage had already healed.

Brymn looked tired but found a smile. "A Dhryn is robust or a Dhryn is not. I have been honored beyond my dreams, Mac. What we gave the Progenitor will inspire the coming generation of *oomlings*." At her puzzled look, he explained. "*Grathnu* is required for a Progenitor to perform her function. Only adult Dhryn such as ourselves can provide what is needed."

Mac studied Brymn's chubby three-fingered hands with new interest. Sexual reproduction in many Earth species involved the female receiving a packet of sperm contained in a male body part. It offered the convenience of allowing the sperm to be stored for later use, not to mention dispensed with several potentially unsuccessful methods of exchange. "Will it grow back? Your hand, I mean."

He looked shocked and tucked all his hands under the silk banding his torso. "Certainly not!"

"Sorry. Just curious." Mac combed her fingers through the remains of her hair and hoped the pufferfish Dhryn could detect that her gift didn't have quite the same potential. "Was that your Progenitor?"

"Of course. All Progenitors are mine—as they are for all Dhryn."

She'd definitely disturb him if she pursued this, Mac realized, longing for a good DNA scanner. She changed the subject. "We need to take another look at all the reports, *Lamisah,* now that we've confirmed your theory about the Chasm and the survival of the Dhryn. I don't understand why the Ro have suddenly stepped up their attacks—against others as well as your people. Perhaps there's a clue we've missed."

"We shouldn't talk of private matters here, Mackenzie Winifred Elizabeth Wright Connor Sol." Brymn freed one of his hands to wave at the lone 'bot still hovering at the other end of the train car. "This one has come with us from the Chamber. It could have more capabilities than the others."

Startled, Mac stared up at the thing. It looked like all the rest, a featureless globe, but then again, she'd stopped noticing them. *Parymn probably set it to follow them after he and his guards put them on this car.* She restrained the impulse to stick out her tongue.

"When we get home, I'm going to trim this," Mac said instead, flipping back the hair that seemed intent on falling into her left eye.

She was as good as her word. A pair of Dhryn scissors—which took two hands to use—and an underlying anger at a universe out of control had proved a potent combination. Mac dug her fingers into her scalp and ruffled its minimal covering, unexpectedly pleased. *Who knew there was still curl?* The stuff was out of control, of course, twisting in any direction it chose, but it couldn't get into her eyes now. She pulled a few pieces down over her forehead, unsurprised to find some were gray.

Mac studied her reflection, comforted by a stronger resemblance to her Mom than ever. There had been a lady who could cope with the strange and alien.

She sighed. *Coping.* That was a word to live by. Mac pulled out Nik's imp and entered as complete a description of the past few hours as she could. She had to believe such things mattered, that what she was learning would make its way to others.

Done, she headed for the "place of refreshment." Mac tossed the last of her shorn locks into the biological accommodation and watched them flash into nothing, thinking of Emily's story about the Sythian living with Humans, who'd cremated her mandible trimmings every night. Sitting in a tent on her own world, Mac had judged the behavior amusing and more than a little pathetic. Now the shoe was firmly on the other foot. Mac didn't want any Dhryn to find samples of what she'd given in *grathnu.* Although she hadn't really served, as Brymn, she appreciated the significance of the Progenitor's request. It seemed— impolite—to leave extras lying around.

Mac discovered Brymn had been busy while she'd tamed her hair. Having learned which foods suited her, he'd prepared a meal for them both. As usual, however, while waiting, he'd nibbled his way through most of his portion. Mac imagined the stress he'd endured was taking some toll, even if he'd never admit it.

"Ah!" he exclaimed, staring at her. "A healing process?"

The hair? "Of a sort," Mac answered, her stomach growling. Her head felt strangely light, something she chose to attribute more to hunger than haircut. "Let's get started."

Shoving a piece of what she'd come to call "bread" into her mouth, Mac made room on the table—Human and thus not slanted—for an assortment of items. Prime among them was the shimmering envelope that had drawn her into all of this. Brymn added the tablet of news reports. "I don't hold much hope for more information from these sources, Mac," he rumbled. "We've gone over them all."

Mac chewed and swallowed, managing not to make a face at the bitter aftertaste. "Interpretation is affected by other knowledge," she reminded him. "I analyzed these without knowing the connection between the Chasm, the Ro, and the Dhryn—or the time frame involved. Information about your biology might also influence what we find in here."

"How?"

She gulped something yellow and lunged for water, having forgotten the heat the innocent jellylike substance contained. Eyes watering, Mac gasped: "If I knew how, I wouldn't need to look through this again."

"You are not savoring your meal, *Lamisah.* These can wait until you are done."

Mac shook her head, then tried to explain the driving anxiety she'd felt since leaving the Progenitor. *Had it been the utter vulnerability of the creature and her offspring?* "We can't assume we have time to spare. We don't know for sure what's happening outside this system. I—" She stopped, staring at the water in her glass.

Ripples stirred its surface.

Within the same heartbeat, Brymn surged to his feet, turning toward the window.

"What is it?" Mac asked quietly, standing as well.

"I'm not sure." He headed for the door to her terrace. Mac started to follow, then, muttering a curse at her own paranoia, changed her mind. She grabbed what she'd brought to the table, returning the imp and envelope to the waist pouch, tucking Brymn's tablet into her shirt. She even took a bottle of water with her, feeling like a fool.

Better a fool now than sorry later, she told herself.

Mac caught up to Brymn at the door. It was raining outside, of course, and he hesitated to step out in it. She patted his shoulder as she went by, starting to offer: "I'll take a look—" Suddenly, the vibration intensified, shaking loose objects inside the apartment, making Mac clutch at the doorframe for safety.

"Quake?" she shouted.

Brymn was holding on to the door with all five hands. "Alarm!"

The shaking stopped and Mac stared at Brymn. "That," she said in the eerie silence, "was an alarm? For what?"

The flash and concussion swept away his answer—*was the answer,* Mac knew with despair as she whirled to look out.

A fireball had plunged into the midst of the Dhryn city, sending gouts of flame and debris—whole buildings—into the air. No—not a fireball—the tip of an unseen torch that continued to burn its way down, down, as if seeking the core of the world.

Not the core of the world. Mac *knew* the area under assault. They'd come out of the tube tunnel right there. *The core of the Dhryn!*

"The Progenitors!" Mac gasped. "The Ro are attacking the Chamber." She found herself at the railing of the terrace, staring out at a violence all the more terrifying because she knew its target.

"How could they?" Brymn was beside her, his entire body vibrating with distress. "How could they know where to dig?"

It was as if horror had heightened Mac's senses. She spotted the gleam from the shadow of the leaning wall. "Brymn. Brymn!" He answered to her tug on his arm, followed her pointing finger to the vidbot hovering harmlessly above.

"What—? Those are Dhryn."

"Not that one! We have to get it," Mac said desperately. She threw her water bottle at the thing, but it only dipped aside. "Brymn!"

Whether the Dhryn's outrage at the attack helped or if he was always this accurate, Mac couldn't guess, but he *spat* at the 'bot, striking it dead center. Metal hissing to vapor, the device plummeted from the air, landed on the terrace, and rolled to Mac's feet.

Wincing at the sounds of destruction from behind her, guided by a red, glowing light that wasn't from the sun, Mac bent to study the half-melted device and saw what she'd feared. She tried to speak, to tell Brymn, but her voice trapped itself in a sob. She tried again.

"I led them!" She had to scream to be heard over the rain of bricks and girders, tile and rock. The words tore from her throat like vomit, scalding as they came. "It's one of Emily's Tracers! She used it to track me into the Chamber. I led them there, Brymn!"

Emily and the Ro had wanted Mac on the Dhryn home world for only one reason. To get them past the Dhryn shrouds and protections. To guide them to their helpless quarry.

To help them kill the Progenitors as they'd failed to do three thousand years ago.

Another vibration, deep enough to shudder through Mac's heart.

"Mac! Mac! Hurry. We must get below."

Still crouched, Mac blinked through the ash now filling the air. The torch tip had sunk below the surface now, the sky darkening. The world hissed in pain as the true rain fought the fires clawing toward them. "Below?" she echoed. "What can we do? We can't fight—that—" a wave at the crater growing before their eyes.

"The alarm has been given. The Progenitors want all from the surface below. There isn't much time."

When she simply stared in confusion, he gave a deep thrum and picked her up. "Below, Mac!"

Another shake—sharper, shorter.

It meant they were already too late. Mac knew by the way Brymn's movements abruptly stopped. He put her down again, steadying her with his hands. "I am sorry, *Lamisah*."

Mac looked outward, expecting—what? What did you see when attacked by an invisible foe?

You saw death, she told herself numbly, holding onto her friend.

- Portent -

"OVER HERE! Quick! We have a survivor!"
The sounds had no meaning. *The world had ended; how could there be a survivor?*
"Take it easy. Help's here."
The words had no truth. *There could be no ease, no help. All was over; all was lost.*
"There's the transport. Careful. Don't hurt him."
The voice had no future. *Had they thought it was safe? Had they thought the mouths gone?*
The wordless screams made more sense.

22

RESCUE AND REDEMPTION

LIKE HER aunt's terrier, the Ro were single-minded in their violence, expending all their force against a hole in the ground. Mac and Brymn huddled together on the terrace, feeling that force through the ground beneath their building. Mac tried not to imagine the carnage and destruction deeper still, in the tunnel system, but her breath caught in her throat at the thought of the helpless *oomlings* and their caregivers, the Progenitors and their pufferfish, even the Wasted hiding in their tunnels.

She wasn't proud to hope she might not die, too.

Brymn had his own opinion, expressed in a doleful bass. "The end is near, Mackenzie Winifred Elizabeth Wright Connor Sol. I am grateful to spend my last moments with you."

Mac used the hand not trapped against the Dhryn to thump him gently. "I won't admit to last moments just yet, Brymn Las. They seem to be confining their attack to one area. We may be safe here—"

"It is not the Ro which will end our lives, but the Progenitors."

"The Progenitors? How?" Mac rubbed soot from her eyes, already stinging from the acrid Haven rain, and tried to see anything through the low clouds of smoke. At least the constant downpour was washing the lighter particulates from the air, making it possible to keep breathing and watch for falling objects. She'd dared to relax, very slightly—until now. "What do you mean?"

"It will be a spectacle, *Lamisah,* worth dying to see."

"I prefer living, thank you."

His arms tightened. "As do I. But I see no—ah. It begins."

It? Mac didn't see anything happening, beyond the Ro's assault. Brymn's more sensitive hearing must have given him advance warning, for the terrace abruptly began to tremble in earnest, the vibrations continuing until portions of the rail began to spring loose and drop away, landing with a clatter on the terrace below.

Brymn might have sounded fatalistic, but he moved as quickly as Mac could wish to pull them both close to the shelter of the wall.

The trembling went on and on, enough to put Mac's teeth on edge and drive her heart to pounding so hard she thought it could be heard outside her chest. Except that Haven was making noise of its own.

The planet was screaming.

Mac covered her ears, but the sound drove past flesh and bone, threatening her sanity. Just when she started screaming herself, it changed to a dull grinding from every direction at once. She closed her mouth and dropped her hands, looking out on the unbelievable.

Lines drew themselves in the city below, some crossing the angry sore that was the Ro attack. The lines deepened as Mac watched, ripping wider and wider. All of them at once.

The destruction caused by the Ro was nothing to this. Buildings toppled into newly formed valleys, roadways were torn apart, and still the lines widened as far as Mac could see.

"What's happening?"

Brymn didn't hear, or he didn't know.

Then, Mac no longer needed to be told. She could see for herself. The planet was breaking apart. Her mind's eye flashed to the tunnels, the massive doors she'd compared to air locks. *What if they had been exactly that?* What if the Progenitors had rebuilt this world so it couldn't be a trap for them?

Being on the surface was a very bad idea, Mac decided.

"We have to get below," Mac shouted at Brymn. "Maybe there's a door still open!" Standing was like riding a skim through a gale. Mac braced herself and pulled at the Dhryn. "We have to try!"

"We do not matter. That which is Dhryn will survive," he said, lowering his big head. "The Progenitors have always been ready."

"To run again?" Mac found herself trying to shake him, as if her muscles could shift Dhryn immobility when the entire planet couldn't. "The Ro will follow. We can't let—"

The universe *winked.*

"The Ro will follow. We can't—" Mac stopped. "I've said that before . . . I just said that—"

"Mac. Mac. Look!" She turned as Brymn stared past her, two arms pointing.

The fire-rimmed hole caused by the Ro was no longer empty. Now, it contained a towering splinter of bronze and light, shaped like no ship or machine Mac had ever seen before. More splinters, smaller yet identical, hung in the air above it. More, smaller still, above those.

And breaking through the clouds were ships Mac did recognize. "Those are Human!" she yelled at Brymn, jumping up and down. "Human!"

The Human ships headed straight for the Ro, weapons firing. Mac was no expert, but the combination of percussions and lightninglike arcs looked deadly as they landed among the motionless Ro. She waited for the splinter-ships to fall from the sky, or blow up, or . . . do anything but what they did do . . .

. . . which was to rise into the sky, large and small combining into one blinding mass, then disappear.

"The Ro—in retreat?" Brymn sounded astonished.

Mac was almost tossed to her knees by another, more powerful tremor. The Human ships hunting the Ro were flying over a landscape being torn apart along multiple fault lines. "Is there any way for the Progenitors to stop splitting the planet?" she demanded. "Is this reversible?"

"I do not know such things, Mac."

"Next time—" she staggered and grabbed Brymn for support, "—next time I'm stuck on a dying alien world, remind me to make sure it's with an engineer, not a damn archaeologist!"

A faint but courageous hoot. "I'll do my best, Mac."

Settling down together, side by side, Mac and Brymn looked out over the end of a world. In the distance, entire portions of the planet were already lifting free, shedding their thin cover of civilization to reveal the thickened forms of the ships beneath before vanishing into the clouds. Wind was howling around the remains. Mac wondered what the Humans thought of it all. They'd come to vanquish the Ro and, instead of triumph, were watching the planet they'd successfully defended destroy itself, its inhabitants so many refugees fleeing what should have been victory.

"Someone's coming for us, Mac. There."

Had too many hopes failed? Mac wondered when she could feel nothing but numb at this news. She glanced up anyway. Brymn wasn't wrong. One of the Human ships had released a handful of skims, now heading in their direction through the rain.

Self-preservation took over from hope. Mac rose to her feet on the cracking terrace, pulling Brymn with her. She started to wave, then dropped her arm. *They'd never see her.*

It didn't seem to matter. The skims continued straight on course toward them. How? *The bioamplifier!* "Nik?" she whispered, tasting the rain and soot on her lips, feeling life surging through her entire being. "Nik!"

Mac drew in a deeper breath, when from behind and above she heard:

Scurry . . . spit! Pop!

- 23 -

DESTINATION AND DISCLOSURE

TIME SAT on a shelf.
Rolled off.
Landed at her feet.
Turned into a shiny salmon and wriggled its way *into* the floor.
"Okay, now I know I'm crazy."
She heard the words but stretched so thin she could *see* eternity between each syllable.
When was she?

Breathing. That was the sound. Deep breathing, so deep it was more a moan than exhalation. A moan so full of pain she hurt to listen.
It wasn't her.
Who was she?

"Don't open your eyes."
Mac opened her eyes on light, fractured and moving, filled with shapes formed in impossible dimensions. She promptly threw up.
"I warned you." A pressure on her now closed eyes, hot then cold, wet then dry. Hot/wet, cold/dry. Mac rolled her head, trying to be rid of the confusion.
"Give it time, Mac. You've got sensory overload on top of the sub-teach."
Mac? The voice thinned and thickened, deepened and raised, but the name caught her attention. *She* was Mac. If she was Mac, where was . . . "Brymn?"
"He's here. Don't ask me why."
Mac grappled with consciousness, feeling it slipping away again, knowing herself close to an answer.
Where was she?

Brymn. The moaning had to be Brymn. Mac groped in the dark, fingers catching on cloth—a blanket?—then on a hard coldness—rock? Her eyes fought the dark even as she remembered legs, feet, and a body, even as she somehow contorted all of those to rise to her . . . knees. Hands and knees.

Good enough.

The moaning had direction, if no consistency of volume or tone. Mac stayed as she was to follow it, moving her left hand forward on the hard, rough coldness, then the right, bringing forward her left knee, then her right, all motions small and cautious. *Just because she was blind, didn't mean others were.*

Time remained slippery and unpredictable. Mac couldn't tell if she'd crawled for seconds or hours before her outstretched fingers touched *something.* Warm, rubbery. She sagged with relief. "Brymn," she whispered. A moan answered. She sat, freeing both hands to explore what she'd found.

One touched flame!

With a cry, Mac fell back, but her hand stayed in the fire. No matter how hard she pulled, it wouldn't come free. The flesh was searing off—the bone would be next—it would take her arm—

"I should have known you wouldn't stay in bed, Mac."

Light blinded her as the fire went out in her hand. Whimpering, Mac cradled her injured fingers to her chest, only to find they were no longer burning. She touched them with her other hand, amazed to find them whole, as if nothing had happened.

The light was more normal this time. Mac blinked over and over again, trying to make sense of the images moving in her field of view.

"You'll see soon enough. Go back to bed and stay there." The voice was as distorted as the images; as distorted as time itself. Mac let herself be guided to an area of rock that felt the same as the rest, then lay down while the blanket was replaced.

Under it all, the moaning.

Time found its teeth at last, ripping apart illusion.

"Emily!" Mac shouted, sitting bolt upright as she *knew* the voice.

"Here."

Here . . . ? Mac squinted against what still seemed too bright a light. She brought her legs underneath, but didn't try to stand. "I can't see you."

"How's this?" The light dimmed, cut by a piece of familiar fabric held as an umbrella. A Dhryn shroud.

Mac focused first on the figure blocking the light. The stylish black jumpsuit was coated in pale dust and cut down the left sleeve, the edges of the cut ragged and frayed as if the damage had occurred weeks ago. The face was older, worn to the bone.

But the raised eyebrow and challenging look was pure Emily Mamani.

Mac had her priorities. "Where's Brymn?"

"Behind you."

They were outside, in some rough sort of camp on bare rock. That much Mac gathered as she looked around for Brymn. When she saw him, she scrambled to her feet with outrage. "Take those off! Take those off now!"

The Dhryn had been wrapped, once more, in the painful threads of the Ro. Mac curled the fingers of her hand, reliving the burning pain. No wonder Brymn moaned with every breath.

"Not my call, Mac."

Mac took a step closer to Emily, moving so the sunlight wasn't in her eyes. "Then whose is it?"

"The Survivors." Emily tossed the shroud material to one side.

"The Dhryn are your damned Survivors!"

That challenging look. "Are they?"

It was so—*normal*—of Emily to force Mac to rethink her position on a subject that she actually paused. Then Mac shook her head in disgust. "If you have something to say, say it. Otherwise, either give me what you used to free my hand from that stuff, or get out of my way while I look for it."

Not that there were very many hiding places. The camp, such as it was, consisted of two large dirty-white bags, some sheets of shroud material—one of which had been Mac's blanket—and a fist-sized portable heating unit. Their surroundings were even less hospitable: an overbright sun, dry air with a bite of morning chill to it, and dull gray rock that formed a cuplike shelter around three sides.

Except it wasn't rock, not all of it. Mac's eyes narrowed as they traced what might be the line of a wall, the remains of a doorway, perhaps a window. Farther away, what appeared to be the ruins of other buildings rose in the distance, giving the horizon a jagged edge. *She'd seen that lack of perpendicular before.*

"I take it this is somewhere in the Chasm," Mac said, refusing to be impressed—or terrified. A lower moan than the rest brought her attention back to Brymn. "I'll ask why here later. Right now?" She made her hands into fists. "Help him."

"And have this two against one? Do you take me for a fool?"

"I took you for a friend."

The word hung between them until Emily's lips tightened. Without grace, she reached into a pouch on her belt and drew out a tiny vial she tossed to Mac. "Use this on the nodes—where the threads cross." She brought out a weapon. "If he makes one move I don't like, he dies."

Vial in hand, Mac paused to look back at Emily. "Like Nik?"

"The bureaucrat?" Emily frowned. "He's dead?"

"You should know!" Mac snapped. "You were the one who shot him!" She believed she'd seen every expression possible on that face. Now she watched puzzlement flash across it, followed by stunned comprehension.

"I remember now. You'd think you'd never forget something like that,"

Emily said in a strange voice. "But the trans-ships mess with the brain—the humanoid brain, at any rate. I'm sure you noticed. Takes days, sometimes, to sort it all out. Some stuff is just . . . gone. Takes getting used to, Mac, believe me." A pause. Emily opened her mouth, inhaled a sharp, deep breath then let it out slowly. "I do remember. Shooting our Nikolai, that is. Didn't know who he was at first, but it didn't matter. I was making the wrong move, Mac. I knew it even as I called out to you. I thought I should get you out of it—I couldn't handle it anymore. But everything was in motion, the players onstage. It was too late to stop. Wrong. I shouldn't have tried."

"You aren't making any sense!" Mac cried.

"The idea was to make everyone believe you were in danger, convince everyone you were important to the Dhryn. That way, they'd offer you their very best protection. The protection they only give their own. But you've figured that out."

Mac pushed the words aside with an angry gesture. "You killed him, Emily."

Emily raised her eyebrows, something closer to sanity in her eyes. "Didn't. He wasn't dead—not from that, anyway. Sore, maybe. Mad as hell, likely. Not that you'd care, right?"

Emily knew her face, too. Before it could betray her, Mac turned back to Brymn, blinking fiercely in order to see what she was doing. Bad enough her relief was making the ground as unsteady as the death throes of the Dhryn world. *All this, including shooting Nik, so she could blithely lead the way to the hiding place of the Progenitors?*

Forgive me, Mac . . .

Mac had never experienced anger like this, anger that waited deep inside her like a mountain lion ready to leap from ambush, nerves aquiver and muscles locked.

The vial had a closed slit along its length. Mac took a guess and aimed the slit at the nearest "node," squeezing the vial from both ends. It didn't spray out a substance, as she'd anticipated, but instead released a narrow beam of greenish light. The thread reacted to this as it had to Nik's weapon, shriveling away from that contact in both directions. It was the work of seconds to free Brymn.

He stopped moaning, but remained still, eyes closed. "How long was he bound?" Mac asked, running her hands over his skin and relieved to find no areas of oozing or obvious damage.

"Two hours," Emily answered. "Maybe three. We came straight here, but you didn't take the trip well."

Straight here? What did that imply about the Ro? Mac shook her head to dismiss what didn't matter at the moment. She eased the positions of two of the Dhryn's arms, then sat beside him on the rock. Or rather dust. The dullness of their surroundings was due to it, a fine powder that filled in crevices and pillowed corners. She glanced down at herself. Her brilliant Dhryn colors had picked up a layer already, especially on the knees. "Why did you bring us here?" she asked coldly, finally looking at Emily. "Wasn't my work for you done?"

Emily did contrite better than anyone. She tried it only as long as it took for

Mac to stare her down. "Two reasons," she said then, sitting on the bags and stretching out her long legs. Despite this show of relaxation, Mac noticed her dark eyes flicked constantly to Brymn and her hand rested on the weapon she'd put back in her belt. "We need to—share—certain facts with you. And I'd made them promise you wouldn't be harmed. I told you I'd help you."

Mac ignored the wistful look on Emily's face. "You're helping the Ro," she accused.

Emily shook her head. "The Myrokynay," she corrected. "'Ro' is a Dhryn corruption of the name."

Myrokynay? Mac dug her fingers into the dust. "The transects—"

"Were their invention, yes. Their—gift." Emily's mouth twisted over the word. "The Myrokynay are masters of no-space. Their entire technology is based on it. You've experienced some of it. Their ships create their own temporary transects. They wear suits that allow an individual to be here and not here, at the same time. It would drive most other sentients quite mad. Sometimes I wonder if it's why communicating with them is so difficult."

"But you can."

"To a point. The effort to understand us originated with them; first contact, if you can call it that, was made by their choice. Me. Others. I don't know who or how many, so don't bother asking."

"Why?" Mac breathed. "Emily, what could they possibly want that's worth any of this?"

Her friend's face had never looked this old and tired. "What *we* wanted, Mac, was to stop this—" her toe kicked the dust, "—from ever happening again. But we've failed." Emily lifted the corner of a piece of shroud fabric with one finger. "Did you give this to Nik and his misguided cronies?" At Mac's puzzled frown, she shrugged and let the fabric fall. "Irrelevant. We're a clever species, Mac. Too clever for our own good, sometimes. Show a monkey a new approach to a problem and *caramba!* A new problem."

"What do you mean?"

"You were there, Mac. On the Dhryn world. Where we so-clever Humans took the Dhryn's method of nullifying the Ro's devices and adapted it into something that could yank their ships right out of no-space. Quite a shock, believe me. I thought the Ro were going to abandon us there and then."

Mac held up her hands. "Whoa, Em. Yes, I was there. And the Ro weren't helping anyone—they were attempting genocide. For the second time!"

Another flick of the eyes to Brymn, then a somber gaze at Mac.

"Yes."

- Portent -

THE RAIN continued to fall, obedient to gravity and dew point. It cratered dust and puddles, it slipped through abyssal cracks to become steam and rise again.

It tracked like tears over the great ships as they pulled free of the earth below, froze as they passed beyond cloud into the fierce glow of the sun, outgassed to randomly drifting molecules as those ships left air and world behind.

The great ships, silent and swifter now, ran for the Naralax Transect. The Others, witness to grief and flight, gave way. Well wishes followed the survivors of a world as they fled its system forever.

Back on that world, the rain continued to fall, driven by new winds, controlled and re-marked by no life at all.

24

EDUCATION AND ENDINGS

"'YES?' THAT'S all you have to say?" Mac kept her hand on Brymn. Emily leaned forward. "No. That's not all." Her eyes flashed with fury. "We had a chance to end it for good. You gave us that chance, Mac. You and my Tracer, with some modifications. The Dhryn had learned to shield themselves from the Myrokynay's scanners, to keep out their scouts. We couldn't sample the population anymore. All we could do was wait for the signs—"

Mac cut in, her own voice hoarse with passion. "Signs? Of what? Did traveling with them scramble what's between your ears, Emily? Or have you somehow failed to notice it's your damn Ro killing people—not the Dhryn!"

"Some casualties—"

"You helped them sink Pod Six. It was midday, Emily. You know how many students were in it. You know who they were." They both rose to their feet, but Mac didn't let Emily speak. She flung her hand toward Brymn. "I lived with them, Em. Thanks to you and your 'friends,' I know the Dhryn better than most of my own relatives. They're alien, I'll grant you, but they're a lot closer to us than your murderers."

"Don't you think I wanted them to be wrong?" Just as hot; just as sure. "Don't you think I went over the data—searched for another answer—did everything I could *not* to believe them? Gods, Mac, you should trust me by now!"

Dry-eyed and utterly still, Mac let the words drop between them, listening to the sigh of air over the ruins and the slither of dust that followed.

Emily spat out a string of Quechua epithets and went to the bags, digging through them with a violence that promised to leave little intact. She pulled out a too-familiar waist pouch. "Here." The pouch landed at Mac's feet, stirring a knee-high cloud. "My personal logs are in there, too. The real ones."

Mac bent down and picked up the pouch. She opened it and looked inside. Both links and the envelope. "So you aren't a thief," she said coldly. "Yet." The words were to give her time to think. *The imp from Nik—had it sent its record? Could it tell them where to find her? Could a Human ship reach this system at all?*

"I know what's in there, Mac. I know you respected my privacy enough to keep what you thought were my logs in your own imp, away from our Nikolai and his cronies."

The logs? ". . . sensory overload on top of the sub-teach." *Had she dreamed hearing that?* Mac worked her mouth around the words without speaking them, finding the movement of her lips and tongue suddenly unfamiliar. "What language—?" she fumbled.

Emily's expression was grim. "Some of the Myrokynay defense systems are cued to the sound of Dhryn. You were muttering it. For all our sakes, I retaught you English and Instella. I don't know what Dhryn you'll recall, but I advise you not to use it."

"No 'is this okay with you, Mac?' Or 'do you mind if I meddle with your brain again, Mac?'" Mac growled. "Why am I not surprised?"

"Hey, I left your imps alone—with the exception of adding my logs to both."

"Both?" Mac tried to look puzzled.

Emily's laugh was forced. "Don't bother. We knew all along, between the tech we have and knowing the Ministry's standard operating procedure. Which included that beacon they stuck in you. Boosted the gain for our needs nicely. Don't worry," she said, misinterpreting Mac's look of dismay. "I've sent your location. We want you found."

"So you can kill Nik when he comes for us?" Mac accused. "That is your next move, isn't it? To kill anyone and everyone who knows about the Ro and their tech?"

"Mackenzie Connor!"

"What?" Mac countered icily. "Can you be shocked at any level? Is that still possible, Dr. Mamani?"

Emily ducked her head then looked up, the ghost of the old smile on her lips. "Well, the hair was a surprise. What did you use? A filleting knife? And those clothes . . ."

They were enemies. *How could they still feel like friends?*

"Damn you, Em," Mac said, feeling the rage draining from her, leaving something harder to name behind.

"That's what my dear mama always said."

"Wise woman."

"Stubborn, too."

"And you aren't?"

"I've known worse. A certain salmon researcher comes to mind."

"Salmon." Mac squeezed her eyes shut, then opened them again. "I don't begin to understand how we got here," she waved one hand at the desolation, "from Field Station Six. I don't want to know, to be honest. But wanting—it's not something you and I can put first, is it?"

Emily shook her head, once, her dark eyes suspiciously bright.

"Where do we go from here, Em?" Mac asked wearily.

"You? You go over that hill." Emily's long fingers traced the low rise before the next cluster of ruins. "You'll find some people there, including Humans. They'll take care of you until the cavalry charges into orbit. Archaeologists, treasure seekers, ghoul hunters. I doubt they know what this place is. He will." She nodded at Brymn, still unconscious on the dusty rock. "You do," with a challenging look.

"The Chasm—and the Dhryn Homeworld."

"The start of it all, Mac. You'll find some of the answers here. Don't take too long. Time isn't on your side."

"And you?"

Emily drew herself up, her face assuming an expression Mac hadn't seen before. Regal, determined, and unutterably grim. "The Interspecies Union picked the wrong enemy, Mac, and won. Now you'll face the real one and lose—unless I can convince the Myrokynay not to abandon our sector of space."

"You're going with them."

"It's the only way."

Mac took a step closer, held out her hands. "It isn't. If there's something dangerous about the Dhryn, you can warn us. If there's something about the Ro— the Myrokynay—we need to know, you can help us communicate with them. You don't have to leave."

Emily took Mac's hands in hers. "It's not that easy, Mac," she said, turning their clasped hands so the tear in her left sleeve was uppermost.

Mac gasped. The cast that should have been there was gone. *It had only been a disguise.*

The skin that should have been there was gone, too—replaced by what looked like a slice of space, dark as pitch and dusted with stars. Mac gripped the fingers within hers as tightly as she could, as if Emily might drift away at any moment. "What is that?" she breathed.

"It's what it appears to be," Emily said gently. "The Myrokynay use space and no-space the way we use electronics or sound. This—diversion—of my body is part of what allows me to communicate with them, helps me endure travel on the trans-ships. It—I think the closest description is that it enfolds me as required."

"Can it be removed?" Mac released Emily's right hand, so hers could ease open the tear. The slice of space continued up the other woman's arm, but didn't encompass it. Tanned, olive-toned skin edged the depths. *Life guarded the emptiness.*

"Some changes are for the better," Emily said evasively, using her free hand to ruffle Mac's new curls.

"Em—" Before Mac could finish, Emily let go and took a step back.

"As I said, time's not a friend. My ride's waiting and they've been unusually patient while you recovered."

Mac sent a despairing look at Brymn. "Brymn has saved my life. He's as dear to me as—as you are. At least tell me why I'm supposed to fear his kind."

"I—" Emily shook her head. "Mac, I don't know all the details. I've put everything I could beg or steal from the Myrokynay in the imps. I hope you can work it out. I do know one thing. It involves the metamorphosis. That's why the Myrokynay wanted to check the Dhryn offspring before they became adults. They were watching for a particular change in the species. Something that's happened before."

"Before—before when?"

"Before this." It was Emily's turn to wave at their surroundings. "Before the Myrokynay understood that not every species should be given the ability to leave their systems. Before the Dhryn—" She winced, drawing her left arm to her side. "They're calling me. Mac, I have to go—now."

"Be sure you're back before the next field season, okay?" Mac warned, her voice unsteady. "And don't be late. We've work—work to do."

"I will. I'll try." With each word, Emily backed a step, as if it was important to put space between them. "Look after the old rock for me."

Mac lifted a hand in acknowledgment, no longer trusting her voice. Dust began to whirl between them. *A Ro version of a skim*, she assumed. Yet she could see Emily through it, see the tears scoring the dust on her face.

"Mac!" The urgent words sounded oddly distant. "The Ro never took adult Dhryn because of the risk. Injury can trigger the next metamorphosis. Be careful!"

This from the woman leaving in an invisible ship? Mac found herself smiling through her own tears. "You, too!"

The dust grew to a column taller than Mac and she moved away, covering her mouth and nose with one hand.

The dust blew past her in a single, violent gust, then the air grew still again.

Emily was gone.

Mac smeared away dust and tears with the back of her hand. "A camp over the hill—possibly with real food," she reminded herself in a thick voice. "Human ships on their way—possibly containing someone I—well, someone. Life could be worse." She glanced at the very still, very large Dhryn decorating the rock. "Okay, so maybe there's still a problem."

But it was a Mac-sized problem, as opposed to an end-of-life-as-we-know-it-sized problem. She busied herself at the bags, presuming Emily had left them for her use.

The first contained more strips of the shroud fabric. Toxic-to-Ro waste being dumped on her? Discards from Ro experiments? Trophies? It didn't matter. The stuff was soft and strong, so Mac stretched out each strip, organizing them by size. None were quite as large as Brymn, but together she had enough for either a shelter or a sled.

The second bag proved more interesting. That was the one where Emily had stashed Mac's waist pouch. Sure enough, Mac pulled out several long boxes. Two contained stiff brushes of varying sizes, an assortment of drills, sieves, and hand scanners—all well-used. The tools of an archaeologist. Emily's own, perhaps.

Well, Mac thought, putting them aside, *they were probably of more use on this planet than those of a biologist.*

The next box contained a tent, sleeping bag, and other outdoor equipment, definitely not new. Mac hoped not to be out here long enough to need them, especially after she opened the last box.

No food or water. No signaling device. The box was full of bright scarves and baskets, dresses and shoes. A folded jewelry case. Emily's notion of traveling equipped, back when she traveled with Humans.

Mac closed the lid carefully, her hands shaking.

"No clouds. It's going to be cold at night." The dryness of the air didn't promise much in the way of condensation, but Mac knew, in principle, how to make a dew-catcher. Dhryn physiology gave her another source of water, but she'd have to be very thirsty before she'd go that route again.

However, her priority was Brymn himself, so she went to sit beside the big alien. "We've three—make that four—choices," she told him, stroking the handless arm. "I find a way to wake you up and we walk to the camp. I drag you to the camp. I go to the camp and bring back help. Or we both wait here for the ships Emily said will be coming."

Mac sighed. "I agree. There's only one choice," she said, as if the unconscious Brymn had expressed an opinion. "Who knows how far the permanent transect is from this planet? They could take days getting here from there. I don't want to leave you—and I doubt I could roll you onto a sled, let alone pull it. We'll try the waking up."

She'd been thinking about this. The composition of the ruins, here at least, appeared mostly ceramic, with some natural rock beneath. Perhaps the original building had been tucked against a cliff. Brymn was lying on what might have been a floor. Or a collapsed roof.

It took Mac a few moments to find the implement she wanted, a rounded, solid piece of stone. She pushed Brymn's head so one ear was against the floor, then took a few steps away. Lifting the rock over her head, Mac let it fall.

Definitely a vibration beneath her feet, as well as the sound of the rock smacking into the ground. The Dhryn didn't so much as twitch.

She retrieved the rock, lifted, and dropped it again.

And again.

And again. *Had an eyelid moved?*

Her arms began shaking as she lifted the stone yet again. "C'mon, Brymn," Mac urged, keeping her voice as low-pitched as possible. Down went the rock.

His eyes shot open. Mac rubbed her sore arms as she hurried to his side, falling to her knees. "Brymn. Brymn!" She hesitated, belatedly remembering the violence of his last awakening, and prepared to scramble away if it was repeated. "Brymn?"

Fortunately, this time all the Dhryn did was open his eyes and turn his big head in the direction of her voice. "Mac," he said weakly, his mouth working as though struggling to find words. "What——? Where——?"

"What was Emily. She'd arranged for us to be scooped up from Haven during the Ro attack. Where?" Mac found a smile. "Where you've wanted to go since you first believed it existed, *Lamisah*. Home."

"I really think we should find that camp before nightfall," Mac observed, not for the first time. She had to grant Brymn was enthusiastic about his subject. Once he'd fully comprehended where they were, he had to explore everything, consumed by the wonder of Dhryn artifacts older than any he'd seen before. Mac had made the mistake of mentioning Emily's toolboxes, so now he was waist-deep, in Human reckoning, in a hole whose location Mac suspected was pretty much a matter of chance, humming to himself. She had to admit, multiple arms made for quick digging.

However, the sun was closing in on the far horizon, stretching long fingerlike shadows in the direction they should be heading. *Now.*

"Brymn. We can come back tomorrow. For all you know, there's a better site over the hill."

"I'm almost through to the next level. The floors collapsed on one another, Mac. It's quite fascinating."

Mac stood up and brushed futilely at the dust coating her arms and legs. "What's going to be fascinating is seeing if you can keep up with me."

Two giant yellow-irised eyes appeared at the top of the hole. "You wouldn't leave me, Mac?" He'd turned from blue to gray with dust. "I don't feel safe without you."

The Dhryn outmassed her two to one, not to mention his extra appendages. He was also a touch superstitious. Mac sighed and assured him again: "There are no such things as Chasm Ghouls, Brymn."

"How do we know for sure?"

She shook her head. *Archaeologists.* "Nothing could live here." Mac had used one of the hand scanners to test the dust and air. No organics. Almost no water.

"Something did," Brymn pronounced, as if this was proof.

"Yes, something did." Mac looked into the distance. The shadows teased images of the original buildings from the ruins, their odd angles joining into a growing darkness.

The Dhryn used his upper arms to pull himself from the hole, like a sea lion climbing on shore. "You don't believe what Emily said, do you?" he asked in a low rumble after standing. "About the Dhryn and the Ro—the Myrokynay? You don't believe we could harm other species, that we caused this ourselves?" He didn't bother to indicate the ruins.

"I—I know that we don't know," Mac said with frustration. "All we have is finger-pointing, like two kids standing beside a broken skim, each blaming the other. Who to believe? Your Progenitors? The one who spoke to us admitted to hiding your past. The Ro? I'm hardly sympathetic to a culture that either hides or kills, but that could be Human prejudice. I'm a salmon researcher, Brymn, not a diplomat." Mac controlled herself. "What matters is that people are dying and this place . . . this place could hold some answers. That's what Emily said."

"So I should keep digging," Brymn offered hopefully.

"So we should walk over that hill and learn what's already been found."

"Are all Humans this stubborn?" he asked.

Mac began piling the boxes under the shroud fabric, using stones to hold the material in place. "There's worse things to be," she said.

There wasn't a roadway or tracks to guide them, but Mac had memorized the most distinctively shaped ruins as landmarks. She was hoping those at their destination would have lights up and running. Despite finally budging Brymn from his hole, they'd be lucky not to be walking in full darkness before reaching Emily's promised camp.

The one thing Mac didn't doubt was that the camp existed. Emily would have left her rations and water if there had been any doubt she could find those on her own. While Mac was unhappily sure Emily could commit murder if she had to, it wouldn't be like this, by marooning her friend on a desert planet.

She and Brymn carried only what they wore. As for weapons—or proof of identity? Mac was counting on the envelope in the pouch, now safely under her clothes and around her waist.

The terrain rose in low upward swells, but the footing was better than Mac had expected. The dust had been blown into firm curls and dunes, often exposing the tiles of what might have been courtyards and walkways. Her boots created echoes. They rarely had to walk around the remains of walls, although there were tall piles of debris. Mac was uncomfortably aware that this meant the buildings had been destroyed, not left to time and the elements. She was even more uneasy about the lack of life. It was one thing to read about the Chasm and its stripped worlds—quite another to be the only living things on one.

Brymn, on the other hand, was thrilled to his core, keeping up an unceasing commentary on their surroundings. "Do you see that . . ." indicating a partial archway that looked like all the rest. "Could we stop and measure . . ." this, concerning a raised basin, filled with dust. "This could be a good place to stop and rest . . ." at almost every new ruin they passed.

Finally, her feet starting to hurt and far too thirsty for patience, Mac snapped at him: "Must you talk the entire way?"

Brymn was silent for several more footfalls, then said in a small voice: "Dhryn worlds are never this quiet."

"Oh." Mac ran the fingers of one hand through her hair. "I could hum."

He tilted his head to look down at her. "You mock me?"

Mac kept any hint of a smile from her face. "Never. Humming makes it easier to hike."

"Ah. Then we shall hum together."

And they did.

"Who's out there?"

The faceless challenge in Instella was reassuring. Mac put her hand on Brymn's nearest arm to hold him beside her. They'd just crested the top of the hill and, as Emily'd promised, there was a collection of tents and a solar array below, all the markings of a field camp. Mac felt a certain sense of homecoming. The tents were illuminated from within—everyone settling in for the night.

They likely hadn't expected humming from the darkness. Discordant humming at that.

"Drs. Mackenzie Connor and Brymn Las," she called down. "We're looking for shelter."

The subsequent rush of bodies from the tents was even more familiar. *Grad students,* Mac thought fondly.

A very short while later, she and Brymn were seated in the largest tent, surrounded by curious faces. Well, she assumed the look on the faces of the four Cey was curiosity and not indigestion, and it was anyone's guess what was under the writhing mass of tentacles that served the five Sthlynii for mouths, but the Humans, in the majority here, were unabashedly bright eyed and intrigued.

Mac smiled at them all before taking another sip from the glass of juice they'd provided, her taste buds sparking with joy.

"Yes. We have Ministry ships insystem, Dr. Connor, and on approach. They're about two days from here. Yours?" Lyle Kanaci was the group's spokesperson—a short, chubby Human with pigmentless hair and skin. Mac found this living evidence of diversity within her own species fascinating and had to remind herself not to stare.

"My ships? Unless you were expecting visitors, they should be," Mac said.

"Weeee dooon't aaaallooow viiisiiitooors." The Sthlynii who hissed this leaned over the table, saliva dripping from its tentacles.

Mac felt Brymn's annoyed rumble and nudged him. "Good, good. That's essential to our work, isn't it, Dr. Brymn Las?"

Either his new name or her nudge conveyed the desired message. "Essential. As is the availability of . . ." Brymn began to rattle off technical questions about the camp's equipment, excavations, findings, and other minutiae understood only by archaeologists. Mac settled into her chair, trying to decide between cookies and soup.

It hadn't hurt their reputations one bit that the text of choice in the camp was Brymn's collected works, a discovery that meant Mac didn't have to produce her envelope, nor explain her clothing.

Much better to be accepted as one of the group.

Mac nibbled and watched, finding herself less comforted by the Human faces than she'd expected. *Probably instinct,* she told herself. Several should have had "crackpot" stenciled on their foreheads before being allowed out, just to save time. She knew the type. They probably slept with "Chasm Ghouls—They Exist and Speak to Me" and hoped desperately for an encounter with the undead.

They should meet the Ro.

On the way here, she and Brymn had discussed whether or not to reveal that this world had been home to the Dhryn. In the end, it was a moot point. Despite the presence of several nonscientists, the rest were doing significant work here. They'd already determined the former inhabitants had been Dhryn. In fact, they'd sent their findings to the Progenitors but had received no acknowledgment. *No surprise,* Mac thought. They'd been worrying about the protocols involved in releasing such information elsewhere without permission.

Yet another reason they were overjoyed to see Brymn.

Mac's first opportunity to ask her own questions came when the majority of the camp researchers headed off to rearrange the sleeping quarters to accommodate the new arrivals. *First things first.* "Brymn," she whispered. "Can you eat any of this?"

"It is not permitted to eat that which is not made by Dhryn."

Great. "Preference or physiology?"

"Are they not the same?"

Mac snorted. "One you can bend; the other bites back."

"Ah." He considered. "My preference, then, would be to wait until the ships arrive with your fine medical supplies, in case of bites."

She grinned. "Converted you, have I?"

He looked smug. "I have always been open to new ideas, Mac."

"I'll remind you of that," she warned, then spotted Lyle deep in conversation with someone who'd just entered the tent. From the way those nearby stopped talking and turned to listen, the news was either very good or very bad. Mac stood. "Excuse me a moment."

Lyle saw her coming and waved her over. "Dr. Connor. This is Nicli, our meteorologist."

Another Human, female, in a coat buttoned against the growing chill outside. She gave the newcomer a distracted glance before turning her attention back to Lyle. "We have to lock everything down. It's the biggest event we've had yet."

Of course it would be bad *news.* Mac was learning to expect it. "Dust storm?" At Lyle's nod, she asked: "Where do you want us?"

"Here," Lyle told her, looking grateful. Perhaps he'd expected a list of demands; Mac, having lived through her share of storms, planned nothing of the kind. "We get pretty wild ones—kick up out of nowhere and can last days. This tent is the sturdiest. We'll set up the kitchen here as well."

"We'll stay put and out of the way," Mac assured him.

After the violence of the Ro assault on Haven, and the dismantling of the planet right under their feet, Mac had been confident a simple dust storm would seem an anticlimax. She'd been through pounding surf and rain, floods and landslides, lightning and hail. This was only a bit of wind and a bit of dust. She'd planned to curl up with a blanket and snooze.

She should have known better.

"Remind me again why I let you and Trojanowski talk me into this!" she shouted into Brymn's ear at the top of her lungs.

Snoozing in a blanket? After the rousing excitement of losing the tent and most of what was inside it, they were now huddled under the only remaining structure, a massive transport vehicle that rocked with every new gust of wind. The Cey on her left side had talked about some taking shelter in the excavation itself. Mac hoped so. She'd lost count of the others with her almost immediately. She thought there were six of them here, out of nineteen, but Brymn's extra arms made it tricky to tally by feel.

The dust made it hard to breathe, as well. Mac had wrapped her head in the filter hood they'd provided. They'd had a bag large enough for Brymn, though Mac presumed the Dhryn would close his blue inner lids to protect his eyes. The mask helped her, but she had to keep her eyes closed and continually spat dust from her mouth.

Meanwhile, why had Mac thought this a lifeless world? Surely the dust storm argued with itself. A low roar shook the ground and a shrill voice shrieked and gibbered. Competing with both was the dust hammering into whatever it could hit.

The noise must be worse for Brymn, Mac thought, with his sensitivity to the lower ranges. She held one of his hands. Or he held hers. She was sure he worried as much about her reaction to all this as she did his.

Emily had warned her about the Dhryn, about Brymn himself.

The Myrokynay, so advanced and powerful, had tried to extinguish the entire species.

Did Brymn know about the storm raging inside *her head?*

Mac squeezed the three thick fingers holding hers. Of course he did. This was more his nightmare than hers. Either his species was being persecuted to extinction or his species threatened all others.

She couldn't imagine living with that choice.

"Dr. Connor. Dr. Connor."

"Mmphfle." Mac spat out what tasted like half a dune's worth of dust in order to answer that anxious call. "Here."

"Storm's over, Dr. Connor. You can take off the filter." Someone began helping her. *Two someones,* Mac decided, feeling herself being pulled bodily from a pile of dust and the filter coming unwrapped. The first thing she saw was a bottle of water. "Here. Rinse and spit. Then drink."

Mac took the bottle from the nameless Human and obeyed, making her mouthfuls as small as possible. There couldn't be a limitless supply here, especially in the wake of the storm. "Everyone all right?" she managed, handing back the bottle and peering around.

The storm had aged the camp into another ruin, broken walls and sticks jutting through smooth mounds of gray dust, an overturned table now one side of a small dune. Figures of dust moved through the setting, salvaging what they could find to add to the growing heap in the middle: a jumble of broken equipment and still intact boxes. A few more were winching the transport upright. It must have flipped sometime in the night. Mac hadn't noticed. Then again, she wouldn't have noticed an attack by the Ro at the height of the storm.

Had she fallen asleep or unconscious?

"We haven't found Nicli," her caretaker said, enunciating each word with the exaggerated care of someone running on nerves alone. "She went to clear the com tower. But she knows the digs. We'll find her yet."

"Go." Mac passed the bottle back to him. "I'll get my partner and we'll help look."

"Your partner?" Human faces were too transparent. Mac felt the blood draining from her own face.

"Where?"

The man pointed to where some rescued tent material had been used to form a makeshift shelter.

Mac broke into a run.

25

CATASTROPHE AND CRISIS

THEY FOUND Nicli, suffocated at the base of the tower she'd gone to check.

Mac found Brymn, being cared for as best the camp medic knew how. The Dhryn's shoulder and three left arms had been pinned under the transport when it was lifted and dropped by the storm. He was conscious and smiled at her. She took one look at the dark blue seeping through the bandages and smiled back.

"That bad?" Brymn gave a weak hoot.

The medic shrugged, safely out of Brymn's line of sight. Mac nodded as imperceptibly as she could. "*Nie rugorath sa nie a nai,*" she reminded Brymn. "A Dhryn is robust, or a Dhryn is not."

"Your accent remains impeccable, *Lamisah*. If only we could do something about your squeaky voice."

Mac fussed with the blanket covering his torso. They'd put two others in here, both seriously injured from the look of the transfusion gear. Sedated and free of pain. *Naturally.* Both were Human. Male and female. She should ask their names.

Brymn first. "Is there anything I can do to make you more comfortable?"

"It will be all right, Mac. My body knows what to do." Brymn's eyes were unusually bright. *Fever?*

Emily had known. *Injury can trigger the next metamorphosis.* "You're changing," Mac guessed uneasily. "Is it the 'Flowering'?"

Brymn nodded. "I can feel it, as I did when I was but an *oomling,* waiting to become adult. The damage I've sustained will be repaired. I enter the next, more worthy stage of my life." A pause and the corners of his mouth turned down. "You must stay with me, Mac, in case something goes wrong. Promise."

She glanced around. There was no one within earshot—no one awake, at least. She remembered the terrible figure at the train station and said: "The 'Wasting.'"

"I—" a tremor racked his body and the blue stain spread. "It would not be a kindness to let me live through that."

Mac took one of Brymn's good hands in her own, then nodded. *She'd decide if and when the time came.* "You'll have to tell me how."

His smile was a beautiful thing, lighting his eyes. "Spoken like a biologist. I will, *Lamisah,* and trust me, you will know if it is necessary. But—" his smile disappeared. The Dhryn seemed to struggle for breath, then recover. "But there is something worse I fear."

Worse than failing to change and having his only friend on this world kill him out of mercy? Mac stared at Brymn and thought she knew. "You could change into a Progenitor, couldn't you? Is there something I have to do then? The Dhryn ships should be in contact with the Union."

Brymn rolled his heavy head from side to side, leaving impressions in the bag they'd made into a pillow for him. "An honor, but so rare as to be most unlikely, Mac."

Finally, she understood and shook her head vehemently. "No, Brymn. No. Emily was wrong."

"We don't know for sure. You said so yourself."

"Guesses. Assumptions. Incomplete data. The Ro can't be trusted—"

"Mac. What if she's right? What if I change into something uncontrollable, something dangerous. I might hurt these people—I might hurt you. You must promise me you won't hesitate if that happens. A Dhryn is vulnerable to a puncture or projectile here." He threw off the blanket and stabbed his torso along the midline, just below the bulge marking where his seventh arm began. "If that fails, insert a sharp object here or here." Throat. Eyes. "Do not bother with blunt force. A Dhryn is robust, after all."

"Or a Dhryn is not," Mac finished for him, sick at heart.

She made herself comfortable beside Brymn and began to wait. *Not that she knew what she was waiting for,* Mac told herself.

Obviously, the Dhryn didn't wrap themselves in cocoons for this act of self-reconstruction. She would see the transformation. Mac's curiosity warred with her concern for Brymn. He was weak—surely a factor. He was away from his kind, not that they provided care. *Survival of the survivors.*

And he was afraid. For himself, for his species. She could see it in how he lay, arms wrapped as if to hold himself together, eyes rarely closed. "Mac," he said during a period of restlessness. "I have studied the Chasm. I know how much was lost—the life, the culture, the potential. I can't believe my kind were responsible."

"I know."

"We aren't violent—we couldn't even hunt the Ro, despite what they did to us. We didn't fight back. We'd rather laugh than be serious. How could we be something so terrible?"

She understood he would accept nothing but honesty. "If it's true," Mac said slowly, "then there's an answer, a way to understand how it could be. I'll find it. I promise."

"If it is true, what will become of the Dhryn? Must we be destroyed, for the safety of all?"

"I can't—" Mac stopped, unsure if she meant she couldn't answer the question, or she couldn't bear the answer. "Please, Brymn. Rest. The Ministry ships will here tomorrow. That's all you have to do. Rest until tomorrow."

"They're here!"

Mac rubbed her eyes, still half asleep, and blinked at the flapping curtain. Whoever had brought the news was already gone, but she could hear excited voices outside in the dark. From the snores closer at hand, the other two patients hadn't noticed.

"Go."

She glanced down at Brymn. "Are you—?" What she saw took the words from her lips. "How do you feel?" Mac asked instead, pleased her voice was steady.

The lanterns hanging in the shelter were enough for her to see that the metamorphosis had begun while she'd dozed. His eyes were *smaller,* though no less warm; the bony ridges that had surrounded them and defined his ears were now smoothed back into the skull. The intense blue of his skin seemed to have washed away, leaving it light and almost translucent. His arms lay flaccid on the blanket, thinner, so that their bandages, soaked in drying blue, had come loose and slipped around. She couldn't be sure without moving the blanket, but she had the impression his torso was wider, flatter.

His voice had changed, too. No longer a bass, with that hint of infrasound, it came out sounding almost Human. "Feel? Glorious, Mackenzie Winifred Elizabeth Wright Connor Sol. I feel glorious." A pause. "And hungry."

She reached out her hand but drew it back, fearing the consequences of touching a body in the midst of re-forming itself so quickly. "The ships arriving will have synthesizers, Brymn Las. I know the makeup of your food. Hold on a little longer, okay."

"I do not know this self. What am I to be, *Lamisah?*" Brymn asked her, giving a one/two blink. He lifted an arm and stared at it. So did Mac, fascinated. The bone was distinctly pliable between joints that had shrunk to one third their former size. The musculature was less rounded beneath the skin, as if what had been distinct bundles were lengthening and connecting. Brymn tried to open his hand but couldn't. The fingers were fusing together at their base, forming a hollow where there had been a palm.

"Not one of the Wasted," Mac assured him, for lack of a better answer. He nodded as if satisfied, then used a free hand to poke at the coverings on his shoulder. "Do you want the bandages off?"

"Please. They—itch."

Mac looked around. There wasn't much in the shelter besides the three cots, the other two still occupied by slumbering Humans, and the ration boxes she'd arranged as a seat. "I'll have to get scissors. Will you be all right?"

Another blink/blink, and a smile. "In your care, Mackenzie Winifred Eliza-beth Wright Connor Sol, how could I be otherwise? But you should greet the arrivals."

Mac brushed her fingertips over the blanket. "They'll find us," she assured him. "I'll be as fast as I can." She stood to leave.

"Mac."

"Yes, Brymn Las?"

"We've come a long way together, you and I."

Mac smiled down at the Dhryn. "There's an understatement. I don't even know where this planet is."

"I meant—"

"I know what you meant." *There were no words.* Instead, Mac put her fingers to her lips and blew Brymn a kiss. "I'll be right back with those scissors."

The camp was alive with lights, bobbing in hands, hung from poles. And people, dozens more than Mac remembered, busy transferring gear to and from a bank of skims parked in the dust. She kept to the shadows, not deliberately, but from a sudden shyness. She wanted to see him first.

No, she wanted scissors.

Mac spotted the medic standing with two others and walked over to him. "Excuse me," she said brightly, having to look up. "I need a pair of scissors. For bandages."

The other two were in uniform, beneath sensible coats. Seeing those, Mac felt the bite of the night air for the first time and wrapped her arms around her middle.

The medic, presumably in the midst of arranging transport for his patients, spared her hardly a glance as he produced a microscalpel from a pocket. "This do?"

"Yes, thanks."

They resumed their discussion. As Mac headed back to the shelter, she flipped on the 'scalpel to check its power supply. The tiny blade formed in the air with a reassuring gleam.

"Mac!"

The shout gave her barely time to turn the 'scalpel off again before she was being crushed while a voice said desperate, incoherent things into her hair.

Rather nice things.

The universe could stop right here, Mac decided, putting her arms as far around Nikolai Trojanowski as their length, and his gear, permitted.

It didn't, of course. A shaky breath later and they were apart, Nik doing his best to look official and not flustered; Mac grinning like a fool. After a second, he relaxed and smiled down at her, his hazel eyes taking green sparks from the lights.

"You're alive," she said, finding it necessary to say the words.

"So are you. And it's over, Mac. We did it," he told her. "Drove away the Ro."

The name sent a shock through her body. Mac managed to ask: "What about the Dhryn?"

"Don't worry. The IU made sure all of their colonies received the equipment to disrupt the no-space fields. The Ro's advantage is gone. It should be a case of alerting Union members what to look for—what's wrong?"

"Maybe nothing." Mac looked up at Nik, drinking in the sight of him, wanting to believe in safety, then had to say it. "Maybe everything. Emily told me—"

The first scream hit the air.

- Portent -

THE FIRST drop fell.
It was the purpose for being.
Green and glistening, it landed on the blanket, etching through the woven fibers as fire would consume kindling.
Another followed. Another.
That which is Dhryn must survive.
Another, reaching the bandages beneath, eating through those to find flesh.
Another. Another.
The flesh responded, instinct fighting drug. The scream should have had meaning.
That which is Dhryn must find the path for the future.
More drops, until they began to collect in the dust.
And the mouths could drink.

- 26 -

REVELATION AND REGRET

BECAUSE she didn't need to understand, grab weapons, or bark orders, Mac was first to the shelter. She tore back the flap that protected the occupants from the dust and staggered inside.

The screaming had stopped.

The lights were gone.

"Brymn?"

Air stirred wisps of her hair. "Goooooo," it said. "Gooooo."

Gooseflesh rose along Mac's skin. She felt the flap open behind her and reached to stop Nik, knowing beyond doubt it would be him.

"Brymn. It's Mac."

"Goooo—ooo."

That voice alone could give nightmares. *No wonder they'd inherited legends of ghouls and monsters from the Chasm.* Mac wrinkled her nose, smelling rot. "There are two people here," she whispered to the man waiting by her shoulder. "We need light to find them." When Nik hesitated, she pushed. "He won't hurt me."

He won't want to hurt me, Mac told herself, trying to keep very still. She heard Nik ordering people away, calling for a light. Closer, she heard rain and pictured Brymn curled in agony, bleeding from his wounds. She could picture it, but something kept her at the entry.

A hand touched her arm, followed it down to put a light in her hand. Mac aimed it at the dust, then switched it on.

On Brymn. *What had been Brymn.* He—it—was lying on the floor, arms ending in a pool of bright green, a pool disturbed by drips from . . . Mac let the light trace the drips upward . . .

. . . from what had been a woman. Now, ribs dissolved as she stared, the mass turning into droplets as Mac tried to breathe, the droplets collecting in the pool, the pool where Brymn—*drank.*

The light had followed her gaze. The metamorphosis was complete. His hands had become mouths. His shoulders and sides had grown membranes that shimmered. His organs shone through his skin, including the stomach where green gathered with each sucking sound. *A pufferfish Dhryn*, Mac thought inanely, too terrified to move, unable to believe she'd seen this form before without screaming.

She had to help Nik. He'd yanked the other casualty from his bed, and was now dragging him to the door flap without care for anything but speed.

But Mac couldn't move. She watched as yellow mucus trailed from Brymn's nostrils. *Grief?* His eyes, lidless, their orbs sinking below the skin as she watched, looked at her. *Knew her*—even as the light of intelligence flickered and died. Still, his real mouth trembled around a word: *"Promisssse."*

"I know, *Lamisah*," Mac said, activating the 'scalpel even as she threw it into one sinking eye.

What had been Brymn filled its body with a single breath and launched itself toward the ceiling, green drops spraying outward from the mouths. One hit Mac's hand as she covered her face. She screamed. Another. Somehow she remained conscious as Nik grabbed her around the waist to carry her outside.

Behind them, she could hear weapons fire and closed her eyes, sobbing with more than pain.

REUNION AND RENEWAL

THE LAST salmon run was over, the harvesting fleets were docked, the students had gone home. Mac leaned her shoulders against the damp outer wall of Pod Three and took in the unusual neatness of cleared walkways and laundry-free terraces. "Looks like the start of winter," she told Kammie.

"That it does. Same old thing, every year."

Mac glanced at the chemist. "You don't have to do that."

"Do what?" A look of innocence in the almond-shaped eyes.

"Treat me like I'll break."

Kammie tried to look outraged and failed. "That obvious?" she relented, then smiled. "Must be the hair. Not used to it yet."

"Or this?" Mac held up her left hand and wriggled the fingers. The prosthesis was excellent work. *The Ministry looked after its own,* Nik had told her. Mind you, she'd upset the warship's surgeon by insisting on a ceramic finish rather than re-grown skin. The resulting pseudo-flesh tone had a faintly blue tint in sunlight.

She could stir acid with the fingers.

"The new hand?" Kammie shook her head. She stared out at the ocean for a long moment, then said softly: "If you must know, it's your eyes, Mac. Since you got back, you always seem to be looking somewhere else."

The Ministry had maintained the fiction that she'd been staying at the Interspecies Union Consulate, learning Dhryn, hunting for Emily. The loss of her hand and wrist? A skim accident on the way home, adding to the delay. Mac was reasonably sure Kammie and some of the others—not to mention Charles Mudge III—suspected this wasn't the whole story. She hoped they'd never need to know it.

She almost wished she didn't. *Almost.*

"Elsewhere?" Mac managed to keep it light. "Let's say I've discovered an interest in extraterrestrial biology. I may do a sabbatical offworld, one of these years."

That earned a laugh from Kammie. "You? This I have to see. Seung—" She faltered, then went on: "He'd have liked to hear you say that."

Mac nodded. The casualty list had been hard reading. Nik had given it to her while she was receiving her new hand, since everyone at home believed she knew and had grieved. Five dead, including Dr. Seung and the irascible Denise Pillsworthy. Her grieving had only begun. Still, the alarm had saved far more than she'd dared hope, even in Pod Six.

Mac tossed her head. "Let's go over the reconstruction estimates. I want to be sure you didn't grow an extra lab while I was gone."

"Well, I didn't. But that's not a bad idea. You do realize this is the optimal time in which to rethink some of the space allocations within the pods . . ."

Mac let Kammie's peaceful voice wash over her, the way the waves were washing over the bleached logs and stone of the shore. She drew in the rich, moist air and held it inside her lungs, filling her eyes with ocean, forest, cloud, and mountain.

The Dhryn had vanished as effectively as the Ro, their colonies as empty as the rocky remnant of their former home world, a mystery on every level. How had they reached the planets they'd attacked without being seen? Why? The Ministry had Emily's logs, experts presumably going over every entry. She might have a turn—but only if they ran into messages that could make better sense to a friend. *Need-to-know*, they'd told her, before sending her home. They did reveal that the IU had sent urgent messages to all its members about the Dhryn "feeder form," as they now called the pufferfish transformation.

And that the foremost archaeologists from fifty species had been rushed to the Chasm. *Brymn would have been pleased,* she thought, cautious around what felt like an open wound.

Nik? Mac could close her eyes here and now and see his face. He'd been there, when she'd awakened to find her arm gone; he'd stayed until ordered away. Had looked at her in a way that still warmed her, before going where he had to go.

It might have been respect and sympathy. It might have been something more. She'd have to ask Emily's advice.

When, not if, she found her again.

"Forgiven," Mac whispered.

"Pardon? Mac, you haven't heard a word I said. Are you sure you're all right?"

Mac focused on Kammie's concerned face and smiled. "Fine. I'm fine. You go ahead and I'll meet you in your office."

"And where will you be?"

Where? Everything and everyone Mackenzie Connor cared about, on Earth and off, was at terrible risk, including the Dhryn. But, abruptly, Mac could let it all go for now, leave the worry to others. *For now.*

Salt spray kissed her lips. A gull complained overhead, then tipped its wings to slip straight down to the water, snapping level above the waves at the last possible instant with what could only be called a laugh. In the distance, a whale breached, conquering the boundary of ocean and air with a casual toss of its mammoth head.

She was home.

"I think I'll call my dad."

MIGRATION

By what measure

should we

condemn ourselves?

Survival is

a moral choice.

(Recent corridor inscription,
Progenitor's Hold, Ship.)

- Encounter -

THE GREAT JOURNEY has been renewed. That which is Dhryn has remembered. All that is Dhryn must move.

That which is Dhryn . . . *hungers*.

That which is Dhryn remembers this place, knows its *Taste*.

All that is Dhryn must move.

It is the way of the journey, that all follow the Taste.

It is survival.

The language of the Eelings didn't lend itself to emotion. There was no need; the bioluminescent beings were able to flash patterns of excitement, joy, or strife.

Or fear.

"We have incoming ships," the transect technician reported. His voice didn't change, but his lithe body was suddenly ablaze. "Sir."

There should have been no reason for such a display. There were always incoming ships. The Naralax Transect was like an artery to Ascendis, the Eeling home world, anchored between the orbits of her two moons, constantly pumping trade goods to and from the lush planet, bringing ships to her famed refit stations on the nether moon, sending them away again faster and more powerful. And in debt.

"Multiple collisions. Sir."

"On my station." Sometimes a freighter strayed from its assigned path; dealing with aliens and their differing perceptions made that inevitable. The supervisor, as suited One Responsible, covered his feelings beneath an opaque cloak. Despite that caution, as he took in what his own screen now showed, alarm ringed each wrist with light and spilled past his collar, catching fire on the spikes of chin and frill.

The screen showed mayhem. Over fifteen ships were reporting hull impacts, several careening into other ships in turn. But there was no time to think about those lives, lost or at risk. For the legal traffic had virtually disappeared among a cloud of new arrivals. This was no confused freighter captain. It wasn't a convoy of audacious *iily* poachers, orbiting Ascendis herself while their servo scoops netted blossoms, relying on surprise and speed to evade the rangers who protected the rich forests of the north.

This was . . .

The supervisor drew himself up. "Send a planet-wide alarm. Do it now."

The cloud wasn't assuming orbit; it was heading for the upper atmosphere. It expanded at the same time, sensors translating the splitting of each new arrival into multiple targets, those into more, then more, all on the same trajectory. To the surface.

So many ships were breaking through the atmosphere at once, they set off weather control alarms as they shattered programmed winds and burned through clouds. Thousands, perhaps millions.

"What should I say? What are they?" The technician glowed so frantically the supervisor wondered he could see his own screen past that light.

Not that any of them needed to. Not now.

Now was too late.

The supervisor pulled his cloak closed, dousing the flickering light of his despair.

"The Dhryn."

RECOVERY AND RESUMPTION

"**Y**OU ASK HER."

"You."

"Not me. Don't you know who she is?"

"Doc Connor."

"*The* Dr. Connor, Mackenzie Connor. The one who lost her arm in that terrible accident last fall. You know. When the moorings collapsed under the pods and dozens of students were killed—"

"Five, not dozens."

"Whatever. Well, I heard it wasn't completely an accident."

"What do you mean?"

"Sabotage. I'm not joking. And when Dr. Connor tried to stop it, the ones responsible took her best friend, a scientist on contract here. They've never found the body." A meaningful pause. "What kind of person could come back and run this place after something like that?"

"Oh."

"Yes. 'Oh!'"

"Weellll . . . Someone has to ask her. He can't stay out there all day. Go on. You do it."

"Not me . . ."

Mac, who could hear the whispered argument quite well through the half-open door to her office, ran her fingers through her hair and gave those short curls an impatient tug. *A reputation for solid science and fair, if tough, marking was one thing,* she thought. *But these ridiculous rumors spreading through Base were becoming a royal pain*—not that she had any hope of setting that record straight. The Ministry of Extra-Sol Human Affairs had been succinct, if highly unhelpful. Mac's role was over. The rest of humanity had been informed. Measures were being taken by the Interspecies Union. There was, with perverse predictability, no hysteria and barely any press.

After all, any threat was out there, to others.

If anything, humanity's reaction had been rather smug, as if reassured to learn that, like themselves, another species had its share of troublemakers. *Somehow,* Mac thought with a sour taste in her mouth, *her kind seemed to view the entire business as over, now that the "unpleasant neighbors" had been found out and—oh so conveniently—left "town."*

Meanwhile, there was the small, inconvenient issue of what had happened here, on Earth. Now that friend was foe, and foe possibly friend, the politics were, to put it mildly, mud.

So Mac was to say nothing, accept whatever lies they'd planted in her absence, and get on with her life as if nothing had happened.

Some days, she almost could.

Others?

"I'm not deaf!" she snapped.

The ensuing silence could only be described as terrified.

Eyeing the door to the hall, Mac poked her forefinger into the workscreen hovering over her desk, the gesture sending the files she'd been updating back into the Norcoast main system. Those waiting for them would doubtless notice she hadn't finished and complain vigorously over lunch. She stretched and gave a rueful smile. *At least some things never changed.* The salmon would migrate, come what may. And those at Norcoast Salmon Research Facility would be ready, watching, learning, and . . .

Two heads appeared in the door opening, one above the other. "Dr. Connor?" hazarded the topmost.

Mac crooked the same finger, blue-tinged through its pseudoskin glove.

The students sidled into her office, each doing his or her utmost to stay behind the other without trying to be obvious. *Ah.* Lee Fyock's newest arrivals, shortly to be sent up the coast to sample intertidal zones. *Interesting pair.* The young woman so worried about disturbing her, Uthami Dhaniram, was already published, having spent three years studying sea grass dynamics in the Gulf of Mannar for Bharathiyar University. She'd arrived eager for her first winter, an ambition that would have to wait a few months.

In every way a contrast, tall, fair, and freckled Cassidy T. Wilson would likely consider Norcoast's mild, damp winters a joke, given he came from a family-run North Sea trawler. No academic credentials on his application, but experience enough to have drawn fine creases around his washed blue eyes and leave permanent ruddy patches on his cheeks. A deep-water fisher. Mac looked forward to his insights.

If Lee could keep him. Case, as the young man preferred to be called, had originally applied to work with the Harvs, the research teams investigating the Human lines of the salmon equation. A logical choice.

Until Dr. Kammie Noyo, Mac's coadministrator of the facility, decided otherwise. As Mac had been an unfathomable number of light-years distant at the time—on a world without oceans, let alone salmon cruising their depths—she could hardly protest after the fact.

Not that she would. Kammie's instincts were often on target. This wouldn't be the first time she'd deliberately cross-fertilized a lagging area of research by dumping an unwitting and typically unwilling student into the mix. If the student lasted and had talent, the results could be spectacular.

Of course, since Lee's research moved young Mr. Wilson into the so-called "Wet" half of Norcoast's projects—an arbitrary division based on the likelihood of wet socks at any given time—and Kammie administrated only the "Dry" now that she was no longer in sole charge, making sure this student lasted became, naturally, another of Mac's responsibilities.

"Sorry to bother you, Dr. Connor," Case began, ducking behind the hint of an awkward bow. His voice, higher-pitched than one would expect from his frame, tended to squeak. There were beads of sweat, not rain, on his forehead.

Mac raised one eyebrow in challenge. " 'Mac,' " she corrected. Uthami's dark eyes widened into shocked circles. Before she could argue, Mac continued, lifting a finger for each point: "We're doing the same work. We live in the same place. And I can guarantee you, we'll smell the same in a very short time."

A broad grin slowly spread over Case's face. "Mac, it is." He looked suddenly younger.

What was it like, to be so young, to know so little yet be so sure?

Mac shrugged off the feeling. "Now. Who can't stay out—and where's out— all day? And why?" The hammering of rain on the curved ceiling underscored every word, but the weather was hardly noteworthy. Castle Inlet, where the pods, walkways, and docks of Norcoast's Base nestled, was surrounded by coastal rain forest for good reason.

"There's a man who came with some Preds this morning, Dr. —Mac," Uthami explained, gamely stumbling past the name. "Security won't let him in because he doesn't have a pass, but he won't leave. He's been waiting outside the pod since before our last class, a couple of hours at least. Tie—Mr. McCauley— said just leave him there, but we—we thought—you should be told." Uthami stopped and looked to Case, patently out of her depth.

Mac felt a little that way herself. Security. Locked doors. Things hadn't all stayed the same; most of the new changes hadn't been for the better. *Even these youngsters could see it.*

"Did you talk to him? Get his name?" she asked, venturing over the abyss of a startling hope. *Could it be?* Then common sense took over. Nikolai Piotr Trojanowski would hardly be stopped by the very security he'd put in place before leaving.

To go where?

Someplace she couldn't.

"No. We just saw him, standing in the rain."

From the fresh worry on both faces, she was scowling again. Mac forced a smile. "Then I'd better go see for myself. Thank you, both."

Norcoast Salmon Research Facility, or Base, as those with even the slightest acquaintance with it learned to call the place, was made up of six large pods pretending to be islands, connected by a maze of mem-wood walkways from spring
through fall, with equally temporary docks and landing pads for its fleet of
mostly operational skims and levs. Base was staffed, again from spring through
fall, by a varying number of research teams who followed their equally varied
interests along the coastline and into the waters of not only this inlet, but from
Hecate Strait and the Pacific to the smallest glacier-fed lake that fed a stream that
completed the circuit traveled by salmon. For that was Base's unifying purpose:
to learn about these fish whose daily existence mattered to other life throughout
this part of the world.

It was a part of the world Mac loved with a passion, from the rain-drenched
forests to the wave-tossed ocean, from the wood-strewn beaches to the gravel beds
high in the mountains that edged the coast. She loved Base as well, with its tidal
flow of activity and eager minds. It didn't matter if they struggled for funds, like
any research institute. They were experts when it came to getting the most done
with the least. There was pride here, a feeling that creative solutions were the best
kind, and self-sufficiency mattered. In a sense, they worked the way their subjects
lived: finding a way around any barrier, fixed on goals beyond themselves.

Goals kept you sane. Mac listened to the echo of her own footsteps, no longer
muted by carpeting. Pod Three had been lucky: no major structural damage
above the first floor, only one anchor pylon ruined beyond repair. A mess inside,
mind you, having been tipped on its side by the Ro, but most of that cleanup had
been finished before Mac's return. The only lingering change was on the floor.
It had been more economical to remove the seawater-soaked carpet than replace
it. The cleaning staff were happy.

And these days, Mac preferred to hear footsteps.

Goals were better than waiting. Repairs to the rest of Base had taken all winter,
and everything they'd had. Like an echo from the past, when Mac herself had
been a student helping to repair storm damage to the original Base, winter staff
and students had put aside their own projects to work alongside the construction
crews. The months had sped by in a frenzied blur of activity, indoors when
forced by wind and ice, outdoors whenever the elements cooperated, however
slightly. The salmon would come again in spring—their goal was to be ready to
greet them, intact.

And they were, Mac told herself proudly. Aside from minor cosmetic work that
could be done over the summer, Base was back in business.

And if Mac had thrown herself into the reconstruction more than anyone
else, if she'd lost more weight, gained more calluses, suffered more frostbite and
cuts, no one had appeared to notice. It was just her being Mac.

And if she'd needed drugs to sleep without nightmares, if she'd dared not
think beyond mem-wood rails and skim repairs, if she'd clung fast to what she
could do, to escape what she couldn't—well, that wasn't anyone else's business
but hers.

What was happening, all those light-years away? What had already happened? When would the other shoe drop?

Pushing such thoughts away, deep into that cold, distant place she'd learned to keep them, Mac trailed the fingers of her right hand along one wall, lifting them to avoid a fresh cluster of hand-drawn posters. The corner of her mouth twitched. A little early in the season for a challenge between Preds and Harvs, but then again, the rivalry served to get the new students' feet wet. Literally. Today's posters were inciting an improbable combination of sponges, bats, and beer.

Pod Three—being administration and thus blessed by "official guests," usually without notice—wasn't supposed to have posters, particularly this type. Someone more concerned with official appearances would take these down later. Later still, they'd go back up. Mac grinned.

A pound of feet from behind. She glanced over her shoulder for the source, ready to leap out of the way if it were Preds heading for their skims. Whale song of any type tended to get them moving, in a hurry. *Not Preds.* Mac raised an eyebrow in surprise at the lanky man hastening toward her, his hands grabbing at the air as if to hold her in place. "John?"

"Mac! Wait!" John Ward, her postdoc student for several years, wasn't a person to raise his voice indoors. Come to think of it, she'd never seen him run indoors either. *An alarming combination.*

"What's wrong?" Hearing the edge in her voice, Mac took a deep, calming breath as John panted to a stop in front of her. *They couldn't be under attack.* Things were back to normal. Earth had defenses and, as Mac had been told in no uncertain terms, there were People In Charge. What had happened here last year would never happen again.

She'd never let it.

Somehow, Mac pushed her dread aside, realizing there was a likelier scenario. "Did the new Harvs burn lunch?"

John's scowl turned puzzled, then he shook his head and scowled again. "Maybe. Probably. But that's not what's wrong, Mac. You have to do something. Dr. 'My Way or No Way' Noyo has gone too far this time. Too far!"

This, from someone who wouldn't criticize the weather, let alone a colleague? Mac leaned her shoulders against the wall to gaze up at the distraught man. The corridor was a bit public for a discussion of staff politics; on the other hand, it offered a choice of escape routes. *Bonus.* "What's Kammie done now?" she asked, resigned. In Base, getting from A to B typically involved the entire alphabet.

"Only hired my new statistician without so much as asking me first. Honestly, Mac, one minute I'm so qualified you two make me overwinter here to help run the place—the next, I'm not consulted on what impacts my own department."

"Your department?" Mac narrowed her eyes at him. Postdocs didn't, in her experience, morph into administrators without notice. "And what department would that be?"

John turned pink from collar to hairline. "Oh. It's not really a full depart-ment—not yet. You're right, I shouldn't call it that, but—"

"What are you talking about?" Mac interrupted.

"You know," he insisted, then looked perplexed at the slow shake of Mac's head. "You don't. Oh, dear."

"Enlighten me."

"But . . ."

"Now would be good."

John took a deep breath. "While you were—gone—and since I was stuck here over the winter anyway—I sent a proposal to Norcoast to offer a couple of new courses in stats, some higher level stuff, you know." He warmed to his topic. "Filled the classes through to next fall with the first mailout. It was amaz-ing! Which led to this little extra team of us, an office in Pod One, the need for a new theoretical statistician . . . of course someone who can add to ongoing research . . ." John's voice trailed away as Mac continued to stare blankly at him. "It was in Kammie's report," he offered, then the pink drained from his cheeks so quickly he might have had chromatophores under the skin, like the octopi he loved. "I'm sorry, Mac. I didn't mean—I know—it hasn't been easy for you—"

Whatever showed on her face by this point stopped him in his tracks. "Sorry," he finished lamely.

Would it ever end? Mac made the effort and shrugged off the apology. It hadn't been possible to arrive back at Base and pretend she was the same person. There was the new hair, for one thing. The new hand and wrist, for another. *Not that her postdoc, her friend, was agonizing over those changes.* He meant the brain damage they'd been told Mac had suffered in the supposed skim accident that had taken her hand.

That the damage was nothing of the sort, but rather the consequence of a se-ries of high-handed and ruthless reconstructions of the language center of her brain to suit the needs of others? That when she was tired, words on a screen or page turned to gibberish and she'd resort to audio?

That when she dreamed, it was in no language spoken on Earth?

Not things she cared to admit to herself, Mac decided, let alone explain. But it wasn't John's fault.

She shrugged again, conscious that her silence wasn't reassuring. "No need to apologize, John. You know what Kammie's reports are like."

He nodded his understanding. Kammie Noyo might be one of the foremost soil chemists on this or any planet, but her administrative reports were the driest possible combination of numbers and lists imaginable. *Not to mention the woman's compulsive use of footnotes.* Even before Mac's 'accident,' she'd read Kammie's re-ports under bright light, with loud music and a cold ocean wind blowing through the room. *And still nodded off.*

After receiving Kammie's mammoth accounting of what had happened at Base during her absence—and after one too many frustrating nights trying to puzzle through it—Mac had cut to the "Work Needed" list and filed the rest for later. Much later. If ever.

It seemed she'd been a bit hasty.

"Tell me now," Mac scowled. "Starting with where you two found funds to expand teaching programs when a third of this place needed repairs." The insurers had, with uncommon, if unknowing, accuracy, declared the destruction due to an act of war and refused to pay. Base might have been left crippled in the water, if it hadn't been for Denise Pillsworthy, who, it turned out, had bequeathed everything she'd owned in life to Norcoast, including her patents.

They shouldn't have been surprised, Mac reminded herself. Denise had only been happy when locked into her claustrophobic lab in Pod Six for days at a time, wearing thirty-year-old clothes, wrapping wire and her considerable brilliance around inventions she'd blithely toss at the world so it would leave her in peace. She'd had no family, only colleagues she alternately ignored or badgered. A couple of closer ties, perhaps, but none she'd let interfere with her work. "Don't tell me you tapped Denise's legacy—"

"Mac! No. I'd never use the repair funds. Kammie helped me apply for a grant. I thought—" He achieved a striking likeness to a puppy caught with a well-slobbered slipper. "I thought you'd be pleased."

Mac remembered seeing the budget, albeit vaguely. Those hadn't been numbers to her. They'd been faces. She'd blinked fiercely and skipped to the next section, having shed her tears for those lost in the attack last summer, when Pod Six had been sent to the bottom of the inlet by the Ro. Drowning the acoustics lab. Drowning friends and colleagues. *Denise . . . Seung . . .*

She stopped herself before the roll call kept going. Some nights, it ran an endless loop . . . a list of loss.

Which mustn't tarnish the future. "Of course I'm pleased," Mac said, her firm nod for both man and concept. "More stats up front? Just what we need around here. I've been hoping to find a way to boost students' analytical skills—get them to the level we expect. My apologies for any misunderstanding, John. My fault."

John still wore that anxious look, as if she hadn't finished grading his latest paper. "I never meant to surprise you with this, Mac."

Mac rolled her eyes theatrically. "I'm getting used to it. Just don't assume I know everything, okay?" She tapped him lightly on the chest with two fingers. "So, what's the problem with your new staff member? Not qualified?"

One of John's virtues, both as a scientist and a person, was his transparent honesty. Mac watched the war between offended dignity and the truth play out on his face, and carefully didn't smile. "She's more qualified than I'd hoped," he admitted glumly. "It's just . . ."

". . . you expected to be involved in such an important decision," Mac finished for him. "Nothing wrong with that, John. Look at it this way. If the new prof doesn't work out, you can fire her." His look of dismay was almost comical. "Hadn't thought of that?" she asked innocently.

"Mac—!" he sputtered.

Mac chuckled deep in her throat. "I suppose congratulations are in order. It isn't every day I lose a postdoc and gain a department head."

"You're worse than Kammie."

Her smile broadened.

"Fine," John surrendered, hands in the air, relief brightening his expression. "You on the way to lunch or Box Hunting?" *Valid question.* This time of year, preparing gear for shipment to the varied field stations assumed the proportions of an emergency evacuation. Tie was already in his protective huddle over Base's stockpile of tape, rope, bags, and crates. No matter. Students and staff were resourceful scroungers, not to mention creative. The only rule, unspoken but upheld—mostly—was packed boxes were off limits. If taped and labeled. And someone was sitting on them.

"I'll have you know I finished my packing last week," Mac informed her new department head serenely. The move to the field was something felt in her bones; she grew as impatient for it as her salmon for their natal streams. *This year,* she told herself, *more than ever.* To get away from everything and everyone. To lose herself in work. To escape the temptation to obsessively scan every available news release, looking for any signs of . . . "Lunch," Mac blurted. "I'll meet you there." Turning to leave, she paused and smiled at him. "Don't worry, John. The day will come when you get to trample over other people."

"Thanks. I think."

With a chuckle, Mac headed for the lift. She squeezed in with a group of damp, noisy Misses, short for "miscellaneous," the catchall phrase for those researchers looking at areas other than predator/prey interactions or harvesting issues. On the way down two floors, to the surface level and walkway, she listened with half an ear to their discussions, a jargon-rich blend of technical chatter and shameless gossip. Not to mention an impassioned debate on the aerodynamics of flying monkeys.

At moments like these, if she hadn't seen the Ro come close to destroying this pod for herself, she could forget it had ever happened. She could forget the sinking of Pod Six, the rooms ransacked by one or more of the invisible beings, Emily being abducted—or rather recruited—by them. She could believe the story planted by the Ministry of Extra-Sol Human Affairs: that a fringe group of xenophobic Humans had used violence to protest the first visit of a Dhryn to Earth.

Above all, she could forget the Dhryn.

"You coming, Mac?"

A student was holding the lift door open for her. The rest had already walked out. Mac managed a smile and nod. "Thanks."

The main floor was jammed shoulder to shoulder with people bustling to or from lunch in the large common gallery. This early in spring, with teams waiting to head to field stations or out to sea, Base bulged with its maximum population. Late fall saw the return influx, but most went back to their respective universities or institutes for the winter, to write papers and take other courses. Mac and Kammie stayed year 'round, with those few whose work continued despite the ice, or because of it.

In normal years.

Mac made her way against the flow of foot traffic, nipping between those intent on their companions, their stomachs, or both, and managing, for once, not to sacrifice her toes. Mac wasn't short, but it seemed each new crop of students arrived larger and more oblivious than the last. She could use warning lights and stilts at this rate.

The noisy, moving crowd thinned, then was gone by the time Mac reached the main entrance. She nodded a greeting to the two in body armor standing to either side, receiving an unusually wary look from both in return. Today's pair was Sing-li Jones and Ballantine Selkirk. Quiet, reserved men who, being lousy poker players, had already "donated" most of their free time to Tie's pod repairs. *Knew why she was here, did they?*

They were part of the team of four security personnel assigned by the Ministry to Norcoast, initially ordered to remain discreetly anonymous. This silly notion had immediately inspired the curious denizens of Base to a series of escapades aimed at filching underwear as well as identification.

Moreover, the notion had annoyed Mac. She expected names and personalities from everyone around her, even those whose job was to overdress, stand in one place, and loom. She got them.

Not that she'd needed them, she reminded herself. Selkirk was the tallest, Norlen shortest, Zimmerman had virtually no neck, and Jones tapped his left forefinger against his holster when thinking. *Anonymous? Hardly.*

Nothing against the men themselves, but on any given day, Mac's feelings about guards of the looming variety ranged from still-annoyed to resigned. The suits of black gleaming armor made them easy to spot, if about as useful as coded door controls. At times less useful, given last week they'd let in three tourists and a census taker for the upcoming local election who'd insisted on interviewing everyone despite Mac's repeated assurance only five people on Base qualified as residents, of whom only two ever voted.

If anything, the blinding obviousness of the guards at their post made Mac suspect other, more subtle precautions in place, not that any of the four had yet to admit it. All to protect this one pod against the return of a nonexistent group of fanatics.

Mac wouldn't mind being guarded against the return of the real culprits, the Ro. After all, according to all experts and the Ro themselves, their previous attack had been aimed at her alone.

Not the flavor of the day, she reminded herself.

No mistake, anywhere the Ro had been, anyone they'd touched, was being watched. But the Ro—the powerful and mysterious Myrokynay—were now sought-after allies, popular with everyone. *Everyone else,* Mac corrected to herself. Apparently they'd been aware of the dangers of the Dhryn all along; supposedly they'd tried to communicate that peril without success; the assumption was, they'd been on guard.

There was no doubt the Ro *knew* about the Dhryn and the Chasm worlds.

And that knowledge was now the most important commodity in the Interspecies Union.

For regardless of anyone's guesses as to their actions or motivations, one thing seemed clear: the Ro had been about to destroy the Dhryn Progenitors once and for all. But in a classic case of misunderstanding, the IU, with abundant and clever help from humanity, had managed to grant the Dhryn the means to expose their ancient enemy by defeating the Ro's stealth technology.

The Dhryn? They'd vanished into the unimaginable depths of space encompassed by the transects and the planetary systems those pathways connected.

The Ro? They hadn't been heard from since, despite what Mac was sure were frantic efforts by any culture with communications technology to reach them.

Aliens should come with labels, she grumbled to herself. "Friend / Useless / Planning to Eat You" would cover the current possibilities nicely.

Were the Ro friends? Not by any standard Mac accepted. The enemy of my enemy? She knew the logic. She didn't believe it for an instant.

Actions mattered.

As now. Mac didn't bother asking questions. The entrance was transparent— from inside, anyway—and she could see the reason for Jones' and Selkirk's "she's not going to like this" looks for herself. *Though why they'd chosen* this *poor soul to lock outside was anyone's guess.*

The rain was striking so hard that each drop bounced back up from the memwood walkway, as if simply falling from the sky wasn't insult enough to the solitary figure standing in its midst. Miniature waterfalls poured from every crease of his yellow coat and hood, giving him something of the look of a statue abandoned in a fountain. A hunched, thoroughly miserable statue, staring at the shelter so near and yet so unattainable.

"For the— Let him in," Mac snapped. Instead of waiting for her order to be obeyed—or debated—she headed for the entrance control herself.

Jones and Selkirk scowled in unison. "He's not authorized—" the latter began.

"And you started caring about this when?" Mac asked in disbelief. "Need I remind you about certain tourists? Or Ms. Ringles, the Census Queen?"

The two managed to look abashed and determined at the same time. "We have our orders, Dr. Connor."

"Here's your new one. Authorize him once he's out of the rain." Knowing full well neither would stop her, although both shifted automatically to loom in the appropriate direction, hands closer to weapons, Mac keyed open the door.

Without hesitation, the figure stomped inside, ignoring the looming guards and instantly creating his own small pond as water from rainsuit and hood puddled around his boots. Then he yanked back that hood to glare at her.

"About bloody time, Norcoast."

Should have listened to Selkirk, Mac sighed to herself. Aloud, and before either guard could do more than look interested, she said quickly: "It's all right. I know this man." Then Mac frowned. "Since when do you make house calls, Oversight?"

Charles Mudge III, the man who was the Oversight Committee for the Castle Inlet Wilderness Trust, which made him her—and Norcoast's—personal demon, stood shivering with cold and damp. His eyes were no less fierce than his voice. "When I revoke a license to enter the Trust. Your license."

Fresh-caught and grilled salmon, geoduck chowder, fiddleheads, new potatoes bursting their skins, wild rhubarb pies—a promising menu, though tasting would be the proof. Spring meals tended to alternate between triumph and disaster. This year they'd added a brand new kitchen to the equally new cooks. Mac was fond of the irony that by the time any given set of student cooks gained enough experience to be reliable in the kitchen, everyone, including those cooks, would be too busy to make or eat anything but cold pizza and oatmeal.

Despite today's tantalizing aromas, Mac found herself with no more appetite than her "guest," who'd brusquely refused her offer of lunch. Nevertheless, she'd brought Mudge to the gallery, hoping the sheer volume of voices and clattering utensils would keep him from shouting at her immediately. At least until she knew what was going on and could justifiably shout back.

She hoped his threat was simply to get her attention. Surely revoking their license would require hearings, presentations, proof. *Not that proof would be hard to obtain,* Mac thought glumly, staring uneasily at her visitor. It might not have been her fault, or Norcoast's, that the Wilderness Trust lands had been disturbed so profoundly on the ridge overlooking Base. That didn't matter. They'd joined in the lie that nothing had happened, agreed to a silence that sat on Mac's stomach as an uneasy weight, on her conscience as a stain.

She'd hoped not to face Mudge. Not this soon. Kammie had handled the applications for the spring/summer research before Mac's return, saying the approvals had been given. Everything was routine.

Nothing in the haggard face watching her warily from the other side of the table agreed with that assessment.

"What's this about, Oversight?" Mac asked, bringing her imp on top of the table, ready to call up the active research proposals. The imp, or Interactive Mobile Platform, could use its own data or access that held within Norcoast's main system. In use, it projected a workscreen almost as powerful as her desk's. Given the number of people currently eating lunch through hovering workscreens of their own, imps were likely the most common portable technology in the gallery after forks.

"Can we talk here?" he whispered. "Talk freely, I mean."

Was everyone around her going to act like a damn spy? Mac glowered at him. "We don't have vidbots hovering everywhere, if that's what you mean. No budget and no point." Not to mention it was illegal to put surveillance on private individuals inside their homes, which Mac considered Base to be. She'd threatened her new security force on that issue until their eyes glazed.

"If that's so . . ." Mudge paused and leaned forward, eyes intent. "Where have you been, Norcoast?" Quiet and quick, like a knife in the dark.

"Didn't Dr. Noyo tell you? In New Zealand—at the IU's consulate."

Quieter still. "Why are you lying?"

Mac tapped her imp against the table, then put it away in its pocket. She knew what she was supposed to say; she'd said it often enough. To her father and brothers. Her friends. Total strangers. Somehow, this time, the words stuck in her throat. Maybe it was the innocent din from all sides, people in her care as much as the land nearest them was in this man's care. *Their care.* When neither she nor Mudge had any real power to protect them.

"You didn't come here and stand in the rain to ask about my trip," she said instead. "What did you mean, revoke our license?"

Mudge hadn't removed his rainsuit. Not camouflage, since the only other person at Base who knew him on sight would be Kammie. The students and staff likely thought he was another insurance adjuster. No, Mac decided, he stayed rain-ready in case she had him tossed back outside. *Tempting, that.*

As he laid his arms on the table, the fabric made a wet rubber protest. His face, usually flushed, was mottled and pale. *Gave up the beard,* she noticed, with that distressingly familiar jolt of missed time. "Please." Again, a whisper. "No one will tell me what's been going on. No one. I waited for you, Norcoast, but they wouldn't let me talk to you. I still can't believe I made it this far."

"What are you talking about?" Mac resisted the urge to look over her shoulder, but couldn't help lowering her voice to match. "I've been right here. You haven't called me. You've been dealing with Kammie—Dr. Noyo—"

"Pshaw! I've dealt with no one. And yes, Norcoast, I called *you.* They'd connect me with some nameless fool who'd prattle on about how busy you were. So I came in person. Twice." He stabbed at the tabletop with a thick finger. "The first time, I made the mistake of using the trans-lev from Vancouver like a normal visitor. They stopped me at the dock and sent me back. This time, I didn't tell anyone where I was going. I bribed some of your students to bring me here with them. I wouldn't give a name or ident until you showed up at the door. Wouldn't let them have a chance to send me away again." He stopped to catch his breath, managing to look outraged and smug at the same time.

They. Them. Mac didn't doubt who'd been keeping Mudge away from her. The Ministry. The arm of Human government that dealt with offworld issues of interest to humanity, now patently interfering on Earth.

Answering the question of how much they relied on her willing silence, Mac told herself, feeling cold. If they could impede the movement of a government official, however annoying, who knew what other powers they'd been granted since declaring the Dhryn a threat to the Human species? *Obviously no paralysis of jurisdictions in the way.* Given the circumstances, Mac supposed such streamlining was reasonable, probably even commendable.

She just preferred her bureaucracy a little more on the cumbersome side, with things like forms, delays, and names attached.

Mudge was distracted by students with trays crowding past him, forced to lean sideways to avoid a close encounter with chowder; distracted by her own thoughts, Mac was grateful for the reprieve.

She'd drawn too much comfort in the lack of news, believed it impossible to keep something as noteworthy as attacks on entire worlds a secret, assured herself she'd be among those to know. *Had she been naïve?*

What might be happening?

Enough, Mac scolded herself, reining in her imagination. It wasn't as if knowing would make any difference in her life. She was packed for the field; she had experiments to run. So what if the Ministry had reserved to itself, and presumably key leaders of Earthgov, the right to decide how much truth to release about the Dhryn? That was their job. The press releases had been masterworks of reassurance. "The Dhryn posed an unspecified hazard." Late-night comics joked about explosive alien flatulence. "The Dhryn had gone missing." Enterprising, if unscrupulous, individuals advertised colonization rights on their abandoned worlds. "System approach controls were to report any sightings." Shipping schedules and security hadn't changed.

Avoiding panic, keeping order in space-bound traffic, concealing needful preparations for defense or attack. Those were valid reasons.

Weren't they?

The truth might come out in years, never, or this afternoon. Mac feared the timing would depend more on how soon the crisis grew out of control than on anything more sensible. But she wasn't a politician.

She was someone who understood the need to protect others. Maybe secrecy was the best way. It wasn't hers, mind you. *But they hadn't asked her opinion.*

"Pardon? What did you say?" Mudge demanded. His rainsuit squeaked as he turned to face her.

"Nothing." Mac pressed her fingertips, real and artificial, against the tabletop. It resisted without effort, being as hard as the truth. *Truth.* She licked her lips, trying to think of the best approach. "It was a mistake to come here, Oversight," she told him at last. "You have to leave. Now."

He settled deeper into his chair.

Oh, she knew that look. Growing roots and planning to be as stubborn as one of his damned trees.

As easily cut down.

Mac closed her eyes briefly, then gave in. "Let's continue this in my office."

She'd picked one of the smaller tables, off to the side. It didn't share the ocean view afforded by the rest of the room, though it made a decent spot for watching hockey or vids when those were playing. It was, however, close to an exit. Mac had grown convinced of the value of such things. Now, spotting the intent pair approaching them as Mudge stood up, she was even more grateful. "Don't talk to anyone," she hissed. "Out this door, left to the end of the hall. Take the lift to the third floor, last office on the right. Wait for me there. And don't touch anything," she added hastily, suddenly beset by the image of Mudge rampaging through her drawers. "Go!"

He walked away as John Ward came up to introduce his companion, a companion who not only gave the departing Mudge a curious look, but was also someone Mac hadn't expected to meet again—and certainly not here.

"Mac. This is Dr. Persephone Stewart, my—our new theoretical statistician. She arrived ahead of schedule." To say John was beaming was an understatement. He practically radiated joy. His companion smiled at him, then at Mac.

Emily would say this Dr. Stewart had done her homework, Mac decided. An older, but athletic figure, their new statistician was dressed to blend in a casual, not-too-trendy shirt and skirt. An interesting personality was hinted at by intricate rows of red, bronze, and turquoise beads braided scalp-tight over the top of her head like a tapestry cap, dense black hair below framing her ears and neck like ebony mist. Slung casually over one shoulder was a well-used portable keyboard. No wonder the students in the gallery were tracking Dr. Stewart's every move. John, hovering at her side, was patently smitten.

So much for his complaint about Kammie's high-handed decision-making.

"Call me 'Sephe," invited the tall dark woman, her smile as magic and mischievous as Mac remembered. "Everyone does."

Oh, she remembered the smile. And the name. And more. Mac remembered the weapons, ready in each hand, as this woman guarded her against the Ro. 'Sephe might well be a statistician.

She also worked for the Ministry, not Norcoast. *Why was she here? Why now?* Mac's mouth dried. *Something had changed.*

"Everyone calls me Mac. Nice to meet you," she said calmly, offering her hand.

But Mac wasn't sure if it was in welcome or self-defense.

SECRETS AND STEALTH

THE OUTER RIDGE of Castle Inlet curled its arm against the Pacific, hoarding an expanse of coastline virtually untouched by Human intervention for over three hundred years. It was a steep, tree-encrusted coast, where eagles perched at the bottom of clouds and rivers gnawed the growing bones of mountains.

The land might trap the eye, but water defined it. Waves alternately slapped aside cliffs or gently lipped fallen logs to shore; mist, rain, or snow filled the air more often than sunlight. Water, locked in glaciers and snowcap, even set the distant peaks agleam by moon or star.

Today's downpour had eased to the point where Mac, looking out her window, could see the toss of waves and the mauve-gray of cliffs, if not the trees above and beyond. She didn't need to—those trees were the heritage of the man standing beside her. In a sense, Charles Mudge III was the Wilderness Trust.

In all the years they'd tussled, spat, and outright battled over scientific access to this Anthropogenic Perturbation Free Zone, she'd always respected that. *Now?* "They've promised me privacy here," Mac said finally, turning to look at Mudge. "If that's a lie, I've no way to know. I can only warn you."

"The same 'they' who wouldn't let me talk to you."

Mac nodded.

The Ministry of Extra-Sol Human Affairs. An office on each Human settlement, station or colony, two or three local staff. Census-takers. Bureaucrats who arranged travel visas and sent inoffensive messages of congratulations or condolences as necessary, keeping somewhat neglectful track of humanity's widespread offspring. Mediators, when Human expectation collided with alien reality. There was a central office on Mars, ostensibly to be close to the transects anchored outside Venus orbit, but also because matters within Sol's system, or on Earth herself, hadn't been part of the Ministry's jurisdiction.

Until aliens came to live and work here as well, and that jurisdiction began to blur. For who better to forestall any interspecies' confusion, than the component of Human government accustomed to dealing with it daily?

Mac had been brought home on a Ministry ship. On the journey, as her arm
had healed, as she'd grieved, as she'd answered their interminable questions and
received few answers to her own, she'd made a pact with herself. She'd think the
best of those who'd taken control of things, do her utmost to believe they meant
her well and could do their jobs—at least until there was clear evidence to the
contrary.

On those terms, Mac tolerated guards on her door and accepted 'Sephe as
staff—assuming the woman's work as a scientist measured up to Norcoast standards—even though that acceptance meant ignoring the other aspect of their
new statistician.

Mudge's complaint, however, was another matter.

He appeared uneasy. Perhaps he hadn't believed her assurance of privacy. Mac
wasn't sure she believed it either. She watched Mudge pace around her office,
pausing beside her rebuilt garden—presently receiving an overdose of chill mist
which made the floor nearby somewhat treacherous. Its weather mirrored that
of Field Station One: last to feel summer, first to freeze again. Of course, since
the floor near the garden consisted of fist-sized hunks of gravel embedded as if
the bottom of a river, walking with care was a given. Her staff had worked hard
to restore what the Ro—and, to be honest, the Ministry's investigators—had
torn apart. The reconstruction had been a pleasant but unsettling surprise upon
her return, Mac remembered. Unsettling, because she could look over there and
believe nothing had changed.

Almost. Mudge didn't glance up at her collection of wooden salmon, swaying
on their threads below the rain-opaqued curved ceiling. If he had, he would
have seen that not all were carvings. Between the stylized Haida renderings, the
realistic humps of pinks and the dramatic hooked jaws of coho and chum, hung
slimmer, more nondescript fish, fish with hollow bodies filled with motion sensors and alarms.

It was likely Mudge also missed the significance of the reed curtains beside
both doors into Mac's office. At night, she pulled them across. Not for privacy:
the walls themselves could be opaqued at will. No, like the false carvings, the
reeds were hollow and contained metal chimes. When touched they made, as
Tie bluntly put it, "enough noise to wake the dead." Low-tech security, perhaps,
but comforting nonetheless.

Everyone else might want a visit from the Ro. *Never again,* vowed Mac, with
a restrained shudder.

Did her staff and friends consider her obsessed by her midnight visitor? Maybe. For
Mac's part, she was appalled by how completely everyone else had accepted the
Ministry's version of events: that she and Emily had surprised vandals planning
to sabotage the pods; that Emily had seen too much, and been taken to keep her
silent, that Otto Rkeia, career thief and presumed ringleader, had met his death
by misadventure during that sabotage.

*As if "death by misadventure" could somehow encompass being glued to an anchor of Pod
Six, thirty meters below the surface of the Pacific.*

Not only had everyone at Base let Emily Mamani slip from their lives, they actually believed they themselves were safe. That anything was safe.

What was she thinking, Mac chastised herself, *bringing Mudge here, hinting she'd reveal secrets others had died, were likely dying, to protect?* "A threat to the species . . . where on that scale . . ." She refused to remember the rest of that voice.

Heedless of her inner turmoil, her unwelcome visitor stopped to point at a shoulder-high folding screen of black lacquered wood, presently perch to three gray socks, a large lumpy brown sweater, and a pair of faded blue coveralls twin to those Mac wore. "Don't they give you living quarters?"

Mac waved at the lab end of her office. "I like to stay with my work." He gave the worktables loaded ceiling-high with boxes and storage bags a doubtful look. "Incoming postdocs," she lied, unwilling to admit she'd had no students apply to work with her this season. Why would they? She'd abandoned Base last year, produced no results, attended no conferences, ignored messages, missed interviews. *Unreliable. Unproductive. Unworthy.* Mac was counting on the coming season and its results to set things right.

The boxes and bags were Emily's. Her belongings kept being sent here, without warning, from wherever they were found. Thoroughly searched and documented before Mac saw them, with no explanation or advice on what to do with them; she let them pile up. Archaeologist's tools and flamboyant jewelry from the dead home world of the Dhryn. Slashed silk and broken furniture from guest quarters on Base. Sleeping bag and tent from Field Station Six. A collection of erotic novels and exotic kitchen gear from the Sargasso Sea. Mail-order llama statues.

Flotsam from a woman's life. *How far could you drift before being lost?* Mac wondered.

The Ro had taken part of Emily's flesh and somehow traded it for no-space, so she could travel with them, talk to them. *How long could a body endure that connection? How long could a mind?*

Well aware of that connection, the IU and the Ministry desperately wanted to find Emily Mamani and any like her, to reestablish communication with the Ro. The real reason for their attention to Base. To Mac. *Emily's things?*

More bait.

Forgive me, Emily had asked, the night she'd left.

She was a hero now, of sorts. To those who knew. A Human who'd given up everything to try and stop the Dhryn. She'd known the truth; tried in vain to tell Mac.

Forgive me, Mac thought, then tensed as Mudge laid his hand on a nearby crate, one of several forming a lopsided pyramid in the center of the large room. The stack, Emily's equipment from Field Station Six, looked regrettably like a shrine. No guarantees any of it still worked. The Ministry had left it in pieces. Mac had reassembled the console as best she could, but Emily would have to rebuild the tracers, test everything first.

It had been Mac's decision to keep Emily's field equipment at hand and ready, a decision those who'd been here last year acknowledged with silent, dismayed looks whenever entering her office. Especially Lee, once hopelessly smitten with Emily's lush looks and boldness, who'd found the love of his life in quiet, shy Lara Robertson-Herrera from biochem a mere month after Emily's disappearance. When he saw the crates, he'd actually flinch.

Did they think she didn't notice? She was stubborn, not blind.

The waterproofed gear she'd use this field season was stacked outside on the terrace, ready for pickup by t-lev. Mac was simply ready for Emily's return.

Whenever that might be.

Mudge tapped one crate with a stubby forefinger, as if he'd guessed its contents from her reaction. "Haven't you found a replacement for Dr. Mamani yet? Surely she had collaborators."

Oh, yes. Invisible aliens, able to sidestep space, utterly ruthless and bent on genocide. Mac shook her head. "No. No one available, that is," she qualified. His skeptical look made her fumble for an explanation. "The tracer technology we were using was imported." The present euphemism for anything alien, although eager innovation rapidly blurred whatever was in Human hands for more than a week. Patent law was a booming business. "Em— Dr. Mamani was working with it on her own."

As far as Mac knew. From scuttlebutt through academic channels, she'd heard how "officials" had swept through the Sargasso Sea Research Outpost, Emily's other home, with such fierce thoroughness that lawsuits had been filed and lost, five doctoral students had attempted to transfer elsewhere, an effort that resulted only in attracting further scrutiny (Mac had heard the phrase "scoured to their toenails" used and didn't doubt it), and the reputation of the scientists left rocked by Emily Mamani's wake best described as "tenuous."

The "officials" had claimed to be hunting clues to Emily's disappearance. Mac wondered how long anyone would continue to buy either the excuse—or its truth. Emily's younger sister, Maria, wouldn't take Mac's calls anymore. *Not that she had news to give her.*

Mac's troubled thoughts must have shown on her face. Mudge came back and sat in one of the two chairs in front of her desk, eyes fixed on her. "This place is what I expected, Norcoast. Not you." His eyebrows drew together. "You've changed."

Somehow, Mac knew he didn't mean her new hairstyle or lack of The Suit. "People do," she said noncommittally.

"It's more than that." His frown deepened, acquiring puckers beside his eyes. "But I didn't come here to pity you."

Ouch. Mac almost smiled. "You came to revoke my license," she reminded him.

His eyes gleamed. "I would if I could, believe me."

"What do you mean?"

"They've taken the Trust away. Surely you knew?"

Mac was grateful her desk was close enough she could put her hip to it for support. "There was," she ventured, "some talk of emergency measures during the—incident—last year."

"Some talk?" Mudge slammed his palm against the arm of the chair. "The government—don't ask me what branch, because I get a different set of names every week—took control then and kept it. I get no reports. Your Dr. Noyo's applications went over my head . . . approved without my so much as seeing them. I spent months waiting for the one person I could expect to tell me the truth about the Trust, only to find I wasn't permitted to talk to her. In all but name, Norcoast, there is no more Trust."

Her heart fluttered in her chest, as if looking for a way out. *If this was some favor from Nik, it was no favor at all.* "I didn't know," Mac said. "I—I'd assumed Kammie was a better negotiator than I'd been. Or that, under the circumstances, you'd been unusually—" she changed *kind* to "—amenable to this year's projects."

"Convenient, your being away."

Provoked, Mac lunged to her feet. "I was looking for my friend—"

Mudge waved his hand placatingly. "Sit down, Norcoast. You might be pigheaded and narrow-minded, but I never believed you were a willing part of this."

Sorting a compliment from that could cause a headache. Mac settled for a testy: "Thanks. Given you can't revoke my license, for which I won't deny I'm grateful, why did you come?"

"I want to see for myself."

"See what?" Mac asked, dreading the answer. Sure enough, Mudge thrust a thick finger in the direction of shore. "No. Absolutely not. I can't possibly—"

"Why? If there's nothing wrong, what will it hurt?"

"With you," Mac pointed out, "there's always something wrong."

He leaned back in the chair and didn't quite smile, although Mac sensed Mudge felt close to victory. "I'm willing to overlook your people's usual transgressions," he said generously. "The footprints, the broken limbs, the misplaced sample vials. Picnics."

How about the massive scar from a Ro landing site—the tracks from teams of investigators—the doubtless intact passage left by a panic-stricken Dhryn carrying her up the slope? Aliens where they didn't belong. Not part of Mudge's worldview.

Or, until recently, her own.

Mac swore under her breath.

"Pardon?"

"I said it's not possible." As his face clouded, she temporized, "Yet. The webbing lines to the shore haven't been set up. No way to get there. You'll have to come back in—" Mac gauged the limit of Mudge's patience and doubled it for negotiating room, "—say, two weeks."

He pursed his lips, then shook his head. "Too long. The undergrowth will be up, obscuring details. You have skims, levs. I'd settle for a kayak."

Feigning shock, Mac widened her eyes. "I can't believe you said that, Oversight.

After all the precautions, the truly extraordinary care Norcoast insists on using to protect the Trust lands—"

"Where *were* you?" With a quickness as surprising as his change in tactic, Mudge lunged forward to try and capture her left hand. *Her new hand.* "How did that happen?"

Mac stepped back, putting her fingers out of reach. "A skim accident."

"You don't lie well, Norcoast. Not to me."

"I've never lied to you," Mac protested.

"Until today."

Was this some bizarre test of her obedience? Had Oversight been part of what happened last year? Was his arrival within the same hour as one of the few of the Ministry's agents she knew on sight, 'Sephe, a coincidence or by plan?

Her head hurt. *Spies and lies.* If it weren't for the stakes involved, she'd gladly forget both. "You've missed the last transport, Oversight," Mac informed him. "I'll have someone set you up with quarters for the night."

Mudge stood, looking as dignified as possible considering he was still dripping wet despite his rainsuit and patently frustrated. And angry. Possibly even betrayed. *Oh, she knew that mix.* "We'll find you dry clothes," Mac offered. With an inward shudder at the thought of Mudge in conversation with anyone else at Base, she continued: "But I'll have to ask you to stay in your room. Supper will be sent up. There'll be a t-lev at dawn to take you back to Vancouver."

"Don't bother. I'm not leaving."

Mac blinked at him. *This was her tactic, not his.* Salmon tipped and touched overhead, music on the damp sea breeze coming through the partially open door. "There's a time to be stubborn, Oversight," she began, "and a time—"

"Would you?"

She didn't dare hesitate. "Yes. In your place, I'd go home."

"Lying. I told you that you aren't good at it, Norcoast."

They glared at one another. Mudge's usually florid face was pale and set. His thick fingers fussed at the fasteners of the raincoat he'd kept on, as if confident they'd be leaving at any minute now to head out in the rain. That she'd give in.

The worst of it? Mudge only asked for what was right and due. Mac thought of the interminable arguments they'd had through the years. Those she'd lost had been exactly like this one, where the moral high ground hadn't been under her feet, but his.

She steeled herself. The landscape had changed. The stakes weren't research proposals or summer funding. She owed loyalty to more than a single stretch of glorious wilderness.

"Go home, Oversight," Mac said very gently.

These days, Mac's office boasted a couch that could reassemble itself into a bed. A handy place to dump her coat in the daytime; convenient at night, for the long hours she'd been keeping in order to catch up with her work. Comfortable enough, given sleep had become a duty she'd rather avoid. It went without saying that the security team applauded her decision to stay in one location, instead of reopening her separate living quarters upstairs. Equally obviously, her friends and colleagues trusted this wasn't a lifestyle choice she planned to foist on them, too. As far as Mac could tell, they'd at last abandoned hope she'd return to normal herself.

Tonight, as usual, Mac didn't bother changing the couch to a bed. She shrugged off her coveralls and left them on the floor. Turning off the interior lighting, she padded barefoot to the door to the terrace. She pushed it wide open with one hand, stepping around the half-drawn curtains, and stood gazing out.

No stars in sight, but the rain had taken a rest, leaving drops to line the undersides of every surface. The drops sparkled, refracting light from the dimmed glows marking step and rail, catching on spiderwebs. The ocean was dimmed as well, its ceaseless movement damped to a complex murmur rather than a roar. That would change with the tides and the wind.

Mac absorbed the calm of the world, breathed in its peace.

It was only the chill dampness that raised gooseflesh on her arms, belly, and legs. It was only her supper, sitting uneasily on a day that put Charles Mudge III in guest quarters and a Ministry spy on her staff, that made her flinch at a splash in the distance.

Mac refused to admit otherwise, for the same reason she came outside every night, to stand in the dark until it was clearly her choice to go inside and turn on lights.

She would not be changed by *them*.

The near shore of Castle Inlet was out of sight from here, even in daylight. "I should talk to Kammie," she whispered aloud. *And say what?* That this year, approval for Norcoast's research would have been granted for anything? That this year, they wouldn't have to confess their missteps to Charles Mudge III? "And I'm sorry about it?" Mac asked the empty sky.

Maybe that was why she was still awake, well past midnight.

Patter patter patter. Thud.

Heart pounding, Mac rushed to the railing and peered downward, trying to find the source of the sounds. *There!* A hunched silhouette passed in front of the lights on the walkway below, then ducked under the railing.

A *splash*—followed by the rhythmic sound of someone beginning to swim, badly.

"I don't believe it," Mac muttered, wheeling to run into her office. *Give the security team some real work?* After all, Mudge was hardly an athlete; he could drown. "Solving a few problems," she spat, but ignored her imp, instead grabbing her coveralls from the floor. She didn't bother trying to find shoes.

A moment later, Mac was in the lift tapping the clearance code for the lowermost level of Pod Three. She paced back and forth during the seconds it took to reach her destination, then squeezed shoulder first through the opening doors.

The smell of the ocean was intensified here, seasoned with the tang of protective oils and machinery. Like the others, this pod was open to the ocean underneath. Unlike the others, a third of that access was at wave height, through a gate wide enough to accommodate their largest t–lev, though with some admitted risk to paint and toes. Pod One held the fabrication and maintenance shops for the equipment and submersibles. This area was reserved for the repair and storage of Base's well-used surface fleet—Tie McCauley's domain, his meticulous nature clear in the gleaming order of tools and parts lining the curved wall. Woe betide the student—or staff—who disturbed a single item without permission. It was astonishing how unlikely timely repairs could become.

Tie had been elsewhere during the partial sinking of the pod. *How guilt had stained that joy, to have an old friend safe when so many others . . .*

An assortment of craft bobbed at anchor or hung from cabling. Mac headed for the gate itself, running along the dock that floated down the center of the expanse. Without a wasted move, she keyed open the inset access port within the gate, then dropped into the antique but always-ready skim Tie kept berthed next to it. The combination of grad students, fickle ocean, and Saturday parties made a quick retrieval craft an essential resource.

Mac ducked as she sent the skim beneath the half raised port, swinging it in a tight turn toward shore the instant she cleared the pod wall. Her hair somehow found its way into her eyes, despite its shorter length, and she shook her head impatiently. The skim, true to its name, paralleled the water's surface once in motion. She kept it low, needing to slip under the walkways between the pods to find Mudge. It meant a teeth-jarring ride as the repellers—at this intimate distance—faithfully copied every tiny rise, shudder, and fall of the waves beneath.

He would pick the middle of the damned night, Mac growled to herself. There was barely enough glow from the walkways to pick out the pods on either side. That wasn't a problem; Mac could have piloted through any part of Base with her eyes closed. But she wouldn't find Mudge that way. Fortunately, Tie had rigged this skim with searchlights. Mac aimed two over the bow as she slowed, sparing an instant to hope everyone else was in bed sleeping.

The fool should be right there.

And he was. Mac let out the breath she'd unconsciously held as the light passed over the sweep of an arm against the black water. She brought the skim down in front of the swimming figure and leaned over the side, steadying herself as the craft rocked from end to end with each swell. "What the hell do you think you're doing?" she demanded as quietly as she could given her mood and the water.

Goggled eyes aimed up at her. Mudge had come prepared; she gave him that, noting the wet suit and hand flippers. One of those flippers waved at her. "Get— out of my—way." Gasping, but not out of breath. Mac was impressed. Not always behind a desk, then.

It didn't change anything. She glanced over her shoulder, checking for any sign they'd been noticed. All quiet, but Mac knew it couldn't last. "Get in the skim, Oversight."

His answer was to put his head down and start swimming around her.

Mac muttered a few choice words and restarted her engine.

It was worse than arguing with him face-to-face. They played a game in the dark, under the dips of walkways and around the massive curves of pods. Mac would circle ahead; Mudge would have to stop. Then he'd duck beneath the night-black water, swimming under or past the skim, and Mac would have to circle again to get ahead of him.

After her third try, sorely tempted to use the boat hook to knock some sense into the man, Mac admitted defeat, along with a grudging respect. "Get in," she told him, "and I'll take you to shore tomorrow."

Mudge bobbed in the water like a dubious cod from some myth. "Your—word—Nor—coast."

The boat hook had such potential. Mac sighed. "Yes, yes. I promise. Just get in. Please?"

With an effort that had them out of breath by its end, Mac managed to get Mudge onto the skim's bench. For all of his bravado and wet suit, he was shaking and alarmingly cold to the touch. She wrapped a self-warming blanket from the skim's emergency chest around his shoulders, laying another over his lap. "Damn you, Oversight, you could have drowned," she accused, rubbing his back as hard as she could.

"Ther–rre—ther–re's worse—things," he sputtered.

Mac's hands stilled for an instant on the blanket.

"Yes," she agreed numbly. "There are."

Either Mudge had believed her, or he'd swallowed enough ocean for one night. Mac didn't particularly care which, so long as he stayed in his room. She yawned her way down the night-dimmed corridor to her office. With luck, she'd get a few hours' sleep before having to deal with what she'd promised.

It wasn't going to be easy. They'd somehow avoided being noticed tonight, but tomorrow, with all of Base awake and moving, it would be a different story. Not to mention the tiggers, the automated pseudo-gulls which reacted to any unauthorized intruder with an arsenal ranging from ear-piercing alarms to adhesive droppings containing any of a variety of unpleasant and increasingly debilitating substances. Mac didn't put faith in Mudge's assurance the tiggers should still be programmed to let him pass into the Trust lands. She'd have to find some way to circumvent them.

But how?

"I study salmon," Mac protested out loud as she let herself into her office. She didn't bother with lights, aiming straight for her couch after closing and locking the door behind her. The night was going to be short enough.

The lights came on anyway.

Somehow beyond surprise, Mac squinted at the figure seated all too comfortably behind her desk, chin resting on her hands, brown eyes fixed on her: 'Sephe.

Was no one going to let her sleep?

"It is the middle of the night," Mac observed.

"So it is. Where have you been, Dr. Connor?"

Mac straightened from her tired slouch, enjoying a welcome surge of adrenaline-rich anger. "Is that why you're here?" she snapped. "To check on where and when I sleep? There's no—"

"Answer the question, please."

"I took a walk." Mac marched to the couch, where she thumped her pillow into submission and threw it to one end. "Now about that sleep."

Rapier-sharp. "This isn't a game, Dr. Connor."

Mac yanked her oversized sweater from the screen and laid it on the couch, adequate blanket for a warm spring evening. "If you say so."

"You can't take Mudge ashore tomorrow."

Her back to 'Sephe, Mac squeezed her eyes shut, her heart giving a heavy, hopeless thud, anger draining away. *They'd promised her privacy, at least here, where she lived.* Like a fool, she'd believed.

Had they made charts of her sleepless nights? Recorded her cries when she did sleep and the nightmares woke her? Counted the times she'd called out their names? Emily. Nik.

Brymn.

Mac unfolded the fists she'd unconsciously made and turned. "If you heard that much, you know I gave him my word."

Dark fingers flicked the air. *Dismissal.* "Tell him you lied again."

At the somber look in the other woman's eyes, Mac choked down what she wanted to say, settling for the blunt truth: "That won't stop him. He's determined to check on the Trust lands. He'll do it by himself if he has to."

"Unfortunate."

A pronouncement of doom? With the bizarre feeling of having switched places with one of her students called to task, Mac went and stood before her own desk. "Oversight isn't part of this, 'Sephe," she insisted. "Leave him alone."

The Ministry agent stood as well, her full lips thinned with disapproval. "That's not your—"

"Leave him alone," Mac repeated, forced to look up. *Had she shrunk since this morning?* "We'll go onshore tomorrow. I'll show him the bare minimum, trust me. Oversight will go home and write a scathing report about our mistreatment of his hillside that your people can bury however deep they want."

"Inadequate." 'Sephe's expression didn't change. "Stick to your fish, Dr. Connor. On-site risk assessment and management are my responsibility, not yours."

"At least use what I know!" Mac retorted. She shook her head, then leveled her tone to something if not completely civil, then hopefully persuasive. "I've handled Oversight for fourteen years. Believe me—the best way to deal with him, the only way, is to let him see what's there with his own eyes and file his own report. Anything else will simply raise more and louder questions than your Ministry is willing to answer." She hesitated, worrying she'd gone too far—*or not far enough?* "Don't underestimate him," Mac continued. "He has connections at every level of Earthgov." She spared a moment to be grateful Mudge wasn't one of those eavesdropping. *Pleading his case was something she'd never live down.*

A long, more considering look. Mac kept quiet under it. Whatever orders 'Sephe had to follow, surely she had some discretion in how.

"Fine," 'Sephe said abruptly. "Take him. Give him the tour. But not first thing in the morning. I'll need time to manage the ramifications."

Mac guessed those "ramifications" would include briefing those who watched over Base. *Sensible.* "That works," she replied, relieved and willing to show it. "It'll probably take me till noon to find a way to get Mudge past the tiggers anyway."

The magic smile, the one that pretended they were old, dear friends. "Leave that to me." The smile disappeared. "But keep your friend away from the Ro landing site."

Mac's nod was heartfelt. She'd no desire to return there herself. "Thanks," she said.

Another dismissive gesture. "Next time, don't make promises you shouldn't." Her face softened. "It's good to see you again, Mac. Even if you have tamed your hair."

"Easier to keep bugs out," Mac said, giving the curls a deprecating yank.

'Sephe chuckled. "I'll take your word for it. Good night, Mac." The Ministry agent walked to the door.

She knew better. Mac couldn't stop herself. "Wait. Please."

'Sephe paused, eyes never blinking. She had a way of becoming still that went deeper than not moving, as if she disengaged everything but her attention. *Her students,* Mac decided, *were going to find that ability disconcerting.*

"Have you—is there—" *She sounded like a blithering idiot.* Mac took a steadying breath. "It's been over four months. I'm not asking you to breach protocols or orders," she hastened before the other could say a word. "I—it hasn't been easy, not knowing what's happened, who might be . . ." her voice failed and Mac coughed to cover it. "If there's anything you can tell me, anything at all, I'd be grateful."

Maybe 'Sephe had listened to her nightmares. For the briefest of instants, Mac saw sympathy in the other's eyes and felt a rush of hope. Then 'Sephe shook her head. "Mac, I can't. News is locked up tight, these days. Even if I had any myself, it would be classified by the Interspecies Union. It's not just the Ministry, or Earth, in this. You, of all people, know that. We aren't alone—or even the ones most at risk right now. We can't think in terms of one species, let alone one person."

Aliens. Had there really been a time, Mac wondered, when they didn't matter to her? When she'd truly believed that what took place outside this one world's thin coat of atmosphere was insignificant, without meaning to her life? She wouldn't go back to that ignorance, would never again accept so small and inaccurate a view of reality. No matter the cost.

As well think salmon didn't need trees.

"I understand." She lifted and dropped one shoulder. "I'm sorry I—"

"Don't apologize," 'Sephe told her, shaking her head in emphasis. "You didn't ask to be involved. Hell, none of us did."

Mac surprised herself by smiling at this.

'Sephe took a step closer and lowered her voice. "I can tell you one thing, for what good it does. He checks on you, Mac. As often as he can. There's a breach of protocol for you." A flicker of a grin. "Drives the deputy minister bats."

He? Nikolai Trojanowski. *If it were true . . .* Mac locked her reaction away so quickly even she wasn't sure how she felt. It didn't matter. 'Sephe was trying to distract her, deflect her curiosity in a safer direction.

You need lessons from Emily.

Mac had learned the hard way to ignore outrageous claims about men. She'd have never lasted one Saturday night out with Em otherwise. "I appreciate everyone's efforts, whether security or on staff," she said blandly, refusing to ask anything else. *It revealed too much, at no gain.* "Speaking of staff, 'Sephe, I hope you enjoy being busy. At Norcoast, we keep our people on the run."

Chuckling at the in-joke, poor as it was, 'Sephe's eyes brightened. "I'm looking forward to it. In case you had doubts, I am an excellent statistician."

She hadn't, actually. No matter what references or threats backed an applicant's claim, to get past Kammie in an interview, 'Sephe would have to be exceptional and prove it. "A skill useful at the Ministry, no doubt."

"Extra-Sol Human Affairs. That wretched hive of bookkeepers and actuaries." Mac must have looked skeptical, for 'Sephe gave a short laugh. "I'm not joking. When the alert came from the IU, the Ministry had to scour the ranks to find anyone with the right clearances who qualified for fieldwork."

Like a certain someone who'd looked more at home skulking around in camouflage and armor than in suit and cravat. "Nik," Mac suggested. "And you, of course."

"Me, qualified?" 'Sephe's eyes turned bleak. "You could say that. Lasted three years in an orbital colony where revolution was the polite name for anarchy. Made me the logical choice to accompany you to the way station." Her full lips twisted. "Make that the only choice, given the other three in the Earthside office at the time couldn't find the arming mechanism of a hair dryer on a good day."

Which implied too much about 'Sephe's current assignment, Mac realized, her mouth suddenly dry. "Is there going to be trouble here?" she demanded. "Is that why you've been sent?"

"Gods, I hope not."

Mac blinked at the vehemence in the other woman's voice. 'Sephe hesitated then lifted her hands in the air as if in surrender. "They didn't exactly send me."

"Pardon?"

"They didn't send me. I asked to apply for the job."

There had to be something wrong with her hearing. "Job? What job?"

"I found out you, I mean Dr. Ward, was looking for a new staff member. I took a peek at the listing, just out of curiosity, and—" *Was that a blush warming 'Sephe's ebony skin?* "—it was perfect. I did my doctoral thesis on topographical analysis of multidimensional systems. Assessing failures in glassy metal moldings. My work has obvious application to the analysis of dissolved substance variances in tidal currents."

"Obvious . . ." Mac's eyebrows rose as she stared at 'Sephe, becoming convinced despite herself. "You're really here to work with John and his crew." Her lips twitched, then curved up. "Don't tell me. Let me guess. You had no trouble getting approval from your superiors at the Ministry, who have a vested interest in this place and in me. All so you can do topographical analysis." She couldn't help laughing. "Some spy you are. Anyone else know?"

'Sephe looked offended. "I keep secrets for a living."

Mac could picture Emily rolling her eyes at this.

"It's not that I don't take my work for the Ministry seriously—"

"But if you can serve and do what you love at the same time, why not?" Mac offered as the other woman appeared to hunt for words.

Another smile. "Exactly. I knew you'd understand."

So now she had a reluctant spy—or was it an enthusiastic statistician—on staff? Mac sighed to herself. Still, it had to be an improvement to work with a spy who valued their research. She cheered. Maybe, with luck, 'Sephe would become so engrossed in her own work she'd ignore minor details such as who was swimming among the pods in the middle of the night. *Or was it morning?* Mac stifled a yawn.

'Sephe noticed. "I'll let you get some sleep, Mac." She paused, having almost made it to the door again. Mac, almost to the couch again, waited politely, if impatiently. "I'm glad you know," the erstwhile agent confessed. "I'll do my best for Dr. Ward and his team. But I'll have to follow orders from—you know who—over his or yours."

"Just hope Kammie never finds out," Mac said. At the other's puzzled look, she smiled: "You'll learn. Good night, 'Sephe. And thanks for your help with Oversight."

"It's Nik I hope never finds out," the other echoed back to her.

"Mr. Career Spy," Mac quipped before she could stop herself, then waited, curious how 'Sephe would react. *It was late enough for them both to have lost a little mutual caution.*

Sure enough, 'Sephe actually winked at her. "I'd take that bet. Scuttlebutt says Nik's posting Earthside was an early retirement, but no one knows from what. He must have traveled outsystem a fair amount, though."

Mac fluffed her pillow. "What makes you say that?"

"From the day Nik arrived, he was the one the consulate would call to nursemaid the, well, call them 'less familiar' aliens visiting Earth. The weirder the better. Some of the stories he'd tell? Let's leave it that if they weren't in filed reports, I'd say he made them up."

Mac had no wish for 'Sephe to give an example of "weirder." Her own studies into alien life-forms and their cultures had progressed sufficiently to realize her wildest imaginings probably brewed beer or its equivalent, gambled on a pre-planned vacation at least once in a lifetime, and contemplated their existence in terms of joy, tedium, or despair, depending on the moment and substance involved. It didn't help her feel capable of understanding an alien mind. It did help explain why the IU had picked Nikolai Trojanowski as Brymn's guide while on Earth.

Nik's motivation? *Nothing so simple.* The Ministry had had its own agenda, which included maneuvering Mac herself offworld to learn more about the Dhryn.

She'd learned too much.

And not nearly enough.

'Sephe mistook her thoughtful silence. "Mac. He wants you safe. We all do. Don't resent the precautions we're taking, our presence here. But—"

"What we want can't always come first," Mac finished calmly. "You don't need to tell me, 'Sephe. Nik and I have had this conversation."

"Watch yourself. Okay? He can be a ruthless bastard."

Mac blinked. She considered taking the bait for no more than a heartbeat. *Trust was earned,* she told herself. And she'd prefer to learn about Nikolai Trojanowski on her own terms. "Isn't that part of the job description?" she replied.

"It's recently been added."

Lines drawn and acknowledged. The two women shared a moment of perfect understanding, then Mac yawned so widely her jaw cracked. "We've all summer," she concluded. "You are planning to work the full season." It wasn't a question.

"Unless the world ends."

"Not funny."

"No."

"Where on that scale . . ." Odd, how the reminder was a comfort. Exhaustion from chasing Mudge through the dark, Mac decided. Or maybe it was finally having someone else who *knew,* so she could believe she wasn't the only one facing the truth.

"Good night, Dr. Stewart. Welcome to Base."

"Good night, Dr. Connor. And thanks."

Later, as Mac lay sleepless in the clarity of the dark, she clutched the sweater covering her upper body with hands real and synthetic, and considered the truth.

Had Nik, who doubtless knew 'Sephe very well indeed, made sure she heard about the opening in John Ward's fledgling department, so suited to her true interests?

Mac nodded to herself. *Likely,* she decided. Why? How better to get 'Sephe here, close to Mac, than to have the woman think it was her own idea? More importantly, how better to convince Mac herself that in 'Sephe she had a potential new friend, someone to let close?

It would have worked, Em, before you.

Mac shook her head. Too much left to chance. *Nik* made *opportunities. He didn't wait for them.*

So. Easy enough to orchestrate that opening on staff. Mac could have done it herself. Simply arrange a flood of applications for John's proposed new courses. Applications weren't students nodding in their seats Monday morning.

Still too much chance.

What if the request for a new staffer had been tailored to match 'Sephe's own passions?

An image of John Ward in Trojanowski's trademark suit and cravat floated up behind Mac's eyelids.

Where had that come from? If there was one thing Mac could be sure of, it was that her transparent postdoc was incapable of anything more clandestine than his biweekly beer run for the Misses, a trip John somehow continued to believe was his deep, dark secret. No one had the heart to tell him his routine was so well known that Mac herself put in orders on occasion.

Perception was everything, Mac mused.

Or was it nothing? However Persephone Stewart had been brought to Base, Mac could only be sure of one thing: it wasn't to follow the dream of applying her training and knowledge to the statistical analysis of dissolved substances in tidal currents. Or any other research.

"Poor 'Sephe," Mac whispered into her sweater.

Which brought her inevitably back to one question: why was the Ministry's only other "field-ready" Earth agent in Pod Three?

She nodded to herself. *Because something terrible had happened. Or was happening, even now.*

Mac got up to find a real blanket.

- Encounter -

THERE were tales told of ships that appeared in the right place at just the right time. Heroes were made of such tales. Legends were born.

It was yet to be determined if the anticipated arrival of the dreadnaught *Guan Yu* into the definitely unanticipated chaos that was the Eeling System qualified.

"Report!"

On that command, displays winked into life in the air in front of Captain Frank Wu: feeds from navigation, sensors, ship status. The first two pulsed with warnings in red, vivid yellow, and mauve—matched to the circulatory fluids of the *Guan Yu's* trispecies' crew. Threat should be personal.

"What in the—" Wu leaned forward and stabbed a finger into the sensor display to send its image of the planet they were approaching to the center of the bridge, enlarged to its maximum size. "The Dhryn!"

"Mesu crawlik *sa!*"

No need to understand gutter-Norwelliian to grasp the essence of that outburst from the mouth cavity of his first officer, Naseet Melosh. Wu shifted back in his chair, instinctively farther from the image, fingers seeking the elegant goatee on his chin out of habit. *Nice if swearing would help.*

The bridge of the *Guan Yu* grew unnervingly silent as everyone, Human, Norwellii, and Scassian alike, stared at the sight now hovering in front of them all.

None of them had seen a planet being *digested* before.

Two of Ascendis' land masses were visible from their approach lane. Both had been verdant green, dappled with the blue of waterways and the golden bronze of the Eelings' compact, tidy cities. Now, huge swathes of pale dirty brown cut along perfect lines, as though the world was being skinned by invisible knives. The lines grew even as they watched in horror, crisscrossing one another, growing in width as well as length, taking everything.

The cities? They were obscured by dark clouds, as if set ablaze.

Perversely, the sky itself sparkled, as if its day was filled with stars. *The number of attacking ships that implied . . .* Wu swallowed. "Tea, please," he ordered quietly, then "Amsu, are there any more in the system?"

His scan-tech started at her name and bent over her console. "No. No, sir. No other Dhryn. There's scattered Eeling traffic heading—there's no consistent direction, sir."

"Yes, there is consistency," Melosh disagreed. "They go away." His voice, a soft, well-modulated soprano, was always something of a shock, coming as it did from deep within that gaping triangular pit lined with writhing orange fibroids. "They flee in any direction left to them. These are not transect-capable vessels; the Eelings have no refuge within this system. I must postulate hysteria."

"Understandable. Communications, I want every scrap of sensor data transmitted to Earthgov. Start sending relay drones back through the transect. Two-minute intervals. Keep sending until I tell you to stop or you run out." Wu didn't wait for the curt affirmative. "Anyone come through the transect after us?" He accepted the fine china cup from the ensign. Out of habit, he sniffed the steam rising from the dark liquid. Odd. He couldn't smell anything. Still, the small habit comforted.

"No, sir. Not yet. But I can't raise the Eeling's transect station to confirm and—" the scan tech waved her display to replace the planet, "—it's a mess out here. Damaged ships is the least of it. There's no organized defense."

"There's us," Wu corrected.

"Us? We came here for an engine refit," Melosh reminded his commander. "We off-loaded our live armaments. We cannot close the transect from only one end. We cannot save whatever remains of this world. We can run, but the Dhryn could follow."

Wu turned and met his own reflections in each of the Norwelliian's immense emerald pupils. Not surprisingly, he looked grim in all three.

Timing, Wu knew full well, didn't make heroes. Resolve did.

"You're right, Melosh. There's only one way we can hope to stop the Dhryn and that's to catch them on the planet surface. Get the crew to the escape pods." Putting his tea aside, Wu stood, straightening his uniform jacket with a brisk tug. "But first, find me the weakest spot on this planet's crust."

The mighty *Guan Yu* spat out her children, all nestled in their tiny ships, then sprang in silence toward the twitching corpse of a world. Her captain sat quietly at the pilot's console, tea back in hand, ready to do what had to be done.

No hero. Not he.

A chance, nothing more.

He'd take it.

Then, the scope of the nightmare made itself known as the Dhryn's Progenitor Ship came into view from around the far side of the planet, catching the sunlight like a rising crescent moon. Glitter rained down from her to the surface, still more returned, until it seemed to any watching that the mammoth Dhryn vessel didn't orbit on her own but instead floated atop a silver fountain of inconceivable size.

Then specks from that fountain swerved, heading straight toward the *Guan Yu*. Hundreds. Thousands.

He had no means to destroy her.

Wu's lips pulled back from his teeth and he punched a control. The *Guan Yu* hurtled downward even faster than before, seeking the heart of what had been the home of the Eelings.

He could only make the Dhryn pay.

The escape pods went first, each disappearing within a cloud of smaller, faster ships. Swarmed. Consumed.

Clang. Clang. Clang.

Wu tossed aside his teacup and secured the neck fastenings of his helmet. Lights flashed and dimmed, flashed and dimmed. The *Guan Yu* lost atmospheric integrity. One or more seals had failed.

Dissolved.

"Don't worry. I'll take you with me," Wu promised his unwanted guests.

As the first feeder, clothed in silver, drifted down her corridors, the *Guan Yu* screamed her way through the atmosphere and stabbed into the weakest part of Ascendis' crust. Shock waves rippled across the continent, setting off quakes and volcanoes.

The air itself burned.

The Great Journey must continue until home is attained. That which is Dhryn has remembered. All that is Dhryn shares that goal.

There will be danger.

There will be hardship.

It is the way of the Journey, that most will not reach its end.

So long as that which is Dhryn achieves safe haven, all sacrifice is joy.

- 3 -

TOUR AND TROUBLE

"**I**TOLD YOU to go, *Lamisah*. Why didn't you listen?" A soft, reasonable voice. The voice of friendship, of trust.

The words. It hadn't been those words. Those—were wrong.

She'd go, but she couldn't see.

Mac shoved her hands outward, pushing at the darkness.

The darkness *burned*.

She screamed as her fingers dissolved, as the backs of her hands caught fire, as the bones within her palms curled like putty and dripped away. *Drip. Drip.*

She screamed as the drips were sucked into mouths—into mouths that insisted, in their soft, reasonable voices, voices of friendship, of trust:

"We told you to go, *Lamisah*. We warned you. Didn't we?"

Her arms went next . . .

Mac rubbed her hands up and down her arms, shudders coursing through her body until it was all she could do to sit still, to stay on the couch, to fight for calm.

"That was—" she began, then pressed her lips together. *A familiar nightmare, although it usually started at an earlier moment.* If she had to dream it, Mac preferred this version. She'd rather face a floating bag of organic acids than look into those familiar yellow-irised eyes and see their warm glow dim, see them sink, watch him become . . .

"No!"

She leaped to her feet and went to her desk, gripping it with both hands. *One hand and one substitute,* Mac corrected herself, always aware of the difference, though she couldn't feel one. *Illogical.* Both delivered the same sensory information. One simply used nonbiological circuitry.

One wasn't hers.

No chance of more sleep, not with her body wringing wet with sweat and her heart jumping in sickening thuds within her chest. Mac unopaqued the wall and ceiling, hoping for dawn.

Close. No stars, but the distant peaks snarled against a paling sky. *Time to be up and moving,* she assured herself. Not that she felt like either.

A shower, short and cold, a fresh set of coveralls, and a barefoot prowl after coffee made the coming day seem slightly less impossible. Merely onerous. Before it had to really start, Mac took her steaming mug outside, finding a perch on the stairs leading up and around the wall of Pod Three where she could watch the rest of Base wake up.

The muted, directionless light of predawn made mysteries of pods and walkways, turned them into pale-rimmed shadows curved one into the other. The walkways were still damp from yesterday's rain, evaporative drying rarely a factor around here. *Something a few new students hadn't learned yet,* Mac decided with amusement, eyeing a series of towels hanging heavy and soaked from the terrace of Pod Two. *Probably wetter now than last night.*

The moisture played tricks with hearing, too. The lapping of ocean against pod and rocky shore was as intimate as breathing; footsteps and yawns loud and clear well before Mac spotted the first group of students making their way to Pod Three for breakfast.

The sun leered over the mountains at her, a reminder time wasn't patient. She cradled her mug between her hands, lifted it to savor the rich aroma of coffee on sea air, impatient for it to cool. Habit. Mac tended to ignore minor details such as how long her cup had sat on desk or workbench, so she'd grown used to what she gulped being cold, eventually liking it that way. Unfortunately, grad students were prone to random helpful acts, and she'd scalded her mouth more than once since coming to Base when someone reheated her coffee without warning.

What first: Mudge or breakfast? She was not combining the two.

"Mind if I join you?"

Mac turned her head with a smile. "Morning, Case." She gestured to the stair beside her and the student sat down. He was dressed for diving, though his wet suit was open at the neck and sleeves, the hood hanging down his back. His bare feet were porcelain pale and his toes, like his fingers, boasted reddish hairs at their joints. Like Mac, he carried a steaming mug in one hand. In the other was a promisingly plump bag.

Case grinned at her interest. "Muffin?"

"Thanks." Mac pulled one from the proffered bag. Warm, yes. Also lopsided and unexpectedly green. *New cooks.* She took a generous bite, chewed, and swallowed. "Mint," she said, raising her eyebrows. "Now that's original."

"But is it edible?" Case examined his own muffin dubiously.

"You'll have worse," Mac assured him. She was pleased he'd sought her out; it took some students a tedious amount of time to realize research staff were people, too. They ate in companionable silence for a moment, watching a raft of bufflehead ducks bobbing on the swells. "Where are you diving today?" she asked.

"We *were* heading for the reefs—down to the glass sponge observation station." He didn't try to hide his disappointment. "I've seen remote images of the deep corals off the coast of Norway, but nothing as up close as you have here."

"Were?" Mac had learned long ago how to instill a wealth of interested neutrality into both voice and expression. Lee's plans weren't hers to question—in front of his still-shiny student, anyway. "What changed?"

Case looked taken aback by her question. "That's what I was going to ask you. A memo came through everyone's imp, just when we were suiting up. No diving. No skim traffic. Nothing on-water today. Even the t-lev from Vancouver's been delayed until tonight." A sideways, very wise look from those sea-faded eyes. "That's not usual stuff here, is it, Mac?"

"No, Case. No, it's not." Mug in one hand, Mac dusted crumbs from her thighs with the other as she rose to her feet. "Then again," she smiled, "what is? Someone's probably forgotten to post they're running a sensitive assay in the inlet this morning. I'll look into it. Thanks for breakfast."

His "You're welcome," hardly registered. Mac's thoughts were racing ahead even as she climbed the stairs to her office at her normal pace.

Seeing the tactic for what it was, knowing she had no reason to feel any special bond to 'Sephe, any friendship, didn't help. Mac still felt betrayed. *What was 'Sephe up to?* Whatever it was, if she'd interfered with Base operations . . .

She'd be leaving on the next t-lev.

"We're leaving. Now."

As if accustomed to having his breakfast interrupted by an infuriated woman in hiking gear, Mudge put down his coffee, calmly wiped his mouth with a napkin, and left the table to find his rainsuit. He pulled on the garment, still without a word.

Just as well. Mac doubted she could engage in reasonable conversation at the moment.

She hadn't found 'Sephe. She had found, however, the source of the stay-put, stay-dry order.

Dr. Mackenzie Connor.

Not by name, but 'Sephe—or someone—had used Mac's codes to essentially shut down operations for the day, on a day when a good third of Base should be heading out to the field. The day before Mac herself planned to go, meaning she'd be delayed at least that long herself. She wasn't the only one upset. Her incoming mail this morning ranged from polite protest to profanity, although Mac had taken a certain satisfaction from replying "wasn't me" each time.

If the Ministry agent thought this would keep her from taking Mudge to the ridge, Mac fumed to herself, *'Sephe hadn't read the right files.*

Meanwhile, Mudge had fastened his last boot and now looked at her interrogatively, his small eyes bright with anticipation. Mac jerked her head at the door, then led the way.

A shame security didn't try to stop them. Mac had prepared several versions of a scathing protest at such misuse of her codes, her people, and her facility. But no one appeared to notice another two figures in rainsuits wandering the corridors, so she filed her protest for later.

Mac waited for an empty lift to take them to the pod roof. Stepping out first, she reached back and punched in the command for the lowermost level, sending the lift where it would wait until someone from administration could be found to input the retrieval sequence. This early in the season, when students were having trouble finding their own boots, let alone responsible staff? Her lip curled with satisfaction. *Why make 'Sephe's life easier?*

"This way," she told Mudge, walking through puddles. The rain hadn't started again, but yesterday's deluge had filled every depression and dimple on the roof. Not that the roof was large. In point of fact, it wasn't supposed to exist at all, being another of those "handy, that" modifications. The original pod design had called for an irregular upper surface, transparent from within and appearing as mauve-and-gray stone from without. No one and nothing else was to be on it. Ideal camouflage, sure to appease those who wanted no sign of Human presence in Castle Inlet.

Which had lasted as long as it had taken the first grad student to find a hammer. Tell imaginative and curious scientists they couldn't use the top of their own building? *Who'd thought that would work?* All but Pod Six eventually grew a small roof consisting of a labyrinth of narrow bands and bulges made of memwood, often, but not always, flat. Each new bout of construction had been justified with a scientific purpose: to secure an antenna or collector, to house a weather assembly, and so forth. Over the years, as the roofs became more useful and used, those purposes had expanded somewhat.

Mac led Mudge past planters filled with mud—the planters had withstood the Ro attack but last year's vegetable gardens hadn't fared well, around the jumbled heap of newly replaced lawn chairs belonging to the Norcoast Astronomy Club—though the frequent cloud cover made precious little difference to attendance at "meetings" and almost none of the members could tell a star from a planet—and, finally, to a small, sturdy shed that had, alone among all the structures perched on Pod Three, been constructed to look as much like a natural rock formation as mem-wood, plaster, and imagination could allow.

It had been a nice gesture. It might even have worked, had it not been for the giant parrot adorning one side of the shed. *Appeared five summers ago,* Mac recalled, patting the bird's technicolor wing fondly. Preposterous thing, but with a cheerful, jaunty look. There was a pirate flag firmly in its beak; the traditional skull and crossbones replaced by a salmon skeleton. Barnacle Bill, they called it, and students learned to sing the parrot's exploits in bawdy detail. *Emily knew every verse.* Mac had once accused her friend of making up the worst of them to shock her new students.

Emily had only smiled.

The memory might have been a floodgate. Mac tried to concentrate on stepping over real puddles, even as her mind swam with questions. *Had Emily left with the Ro? Had the aliens truly left? And what did "leaving" mean to beings who could make their own transects through space at will?*

Or had Emily been taken? But by whom? The grim, black-garbed defenders of Earth? Their counterparts from any other threatened world?

Or was Emily on Earth, sipping margaritas in a bar decorated with parrots, teaching bawdy verse to handsome tourists . . .

Swearing under her breath, hiding the trembling of her hands, Mac yanked aside the weather screen covering the end of the shed.

Was Emily dead? Had it happened months ago?

Or had she waited for rescue, for friends, only to die alone?

"It's nothing fancy," she warned Mudge, her voice less steady than would have been reassuring under the circumstances, "but it'll get us to shore."

"In one piece?" he asked, eyes dropping from the parrot to stare in dismay at the personal lev cowering inside the shed. It was, as Tie referred to it, at that delicate age between junk and vintage. To survive long enough to be vintage, it shouldn't have belonged to Mac.

She wiped cobwebs from the yellowed canopy. "It's this or nothing. Help me push it out."

Together they wrestled the old lev out of its shelter. The gentle light of early morning wasn't kind. There were more patches than paint on its sides, the upholstery had endured too many buckets of overripe salmon, and a regrettable, although essentially harmless encounter with a barge had permanently resculptured its prow. Remarkably, last year's tip and righting of the pod didn't seem to have added any more dents. *As far as she could tell.*

Mac gave the lev a surreptitious kick for luck. She'd bought the thing well and truly used her first year of tenure at Norcoast. Granted, it had been shiny, clean, and intact back then. Even better, dirt cheap. It was only later that Mac learned why few people bothered with levs for anything smaller than freight transport. Compact antigrav units were, to be generous, finicky beasts prone to suicide.

Levs, boots. Same thing. Mac was satisfied when either got her where she wanted to go with dry feet, although she had noticed footwear was more reliable. Little wonder everyone at Base conspired with Tie to arrange to ferry their co-administrator from place to place, keeping her lev in this shed and out of his workshop.

Which kept it out of inventory, too. *More problems for 'Sephe and crew,* Mac rejoiced.

Much to Mac's surprise, the engine started on the first try. No death rattle or strange clanking marred the steady hum. That slightly strangled wheezing? *Hardly noticeable.*

"You get in first," Mudge said after a moment's thoughtful consideration.

"Brave man," Mac quipped, not entirely sure herself. Then she looked out at their destination, the outstretched arm of Castle Inlet, where mist hung like dust-gray garlands around the deep green trees. "Let's go."

Besides, she told herself optimistically, *it wasn't far.*

Mac shut down the lev's engine, which continued to wheeze and gasp noisily as if to prove its rise into the air, plunge to a handbreadth above the ocean, and subsequent erratic hobble over the boulders and logs of the shore to land here had been a fluke.

"WE COULD—" the last wheeze died and Mudge stopped shouting to be heard over the racket, "—swim back," he finished.

Mac patted the lev. "It just needs a rest." *Not a bad landing,* she congratulated herself, hands sore from holding the controls perhaps a little tighter than useful. The tendency of levs to simply drop if their antigrav failed had crossed her mind on the way here. Several times. Over a combination of height, wave, and rock that didn't make such a drop appealing in the least, given the high probability of deer mice in the safety chutes. *This was much better.*

Much. Mindful of the Trust, and her companion, Mac had brought them down on a bare outcropping on the ocean side of the ridge, close to one of the pathways leading up the ridge. The minimal damage caused by landing here would be easy to record. Mudge couldn't fault her on this. *Could he?*

Rather than ask, Mac looked out over Hecate Strait, the cool, salt-fresh wind playing with her hair and teasing the hood on her shoulders. Clouds were getting organized for the day, small puffs scudding above the waves as if on parade, longer wisps holding court above, a tumultuous line forming in the distance. There would be salmon beneath it all, driving through the depths. The young smolts preoccupied with filling their own stomachs while avoiding being food themselves; the mature, powerful adults who would never eat again, guided by the tastes and scents of home, answering that one final call, to spawn—

"Ahhh."

The soft exclamation drew her around. Mudge had his back to the ocean. His arms were outstretched, his head tilted, his body dwarfed before the rising ranks of trees that began mere footsteps away. *To someone else,* Mac thought, *he might look foolish.* A man past middle age, wearing a faded yellow rainsuit that had doubtless fit better several kilos earlier, what hair he had tossed by the wind like stray grass. Standing in what could only be called worship.

Mac felt a tightness in her throat. She didn't interrupt. Instead, she looked where he did, tracing the underlying ridge in the arrogant skyward thrust of pine, cedar, and redwood with her eyes, understanding one thing at least.

She'd been right to bring Mudge here.

"I should never have brought you here," Mac snapped, catching the branch whipping toward her face in the nick of time.

They were walking three meters above the forest floor, using the suspended walkway set up by last year's researchers. That forest floor was visible beneath their feet, the walkway of a transparent material which allowed the passage of not only light, but rain and small objects. *Minimal presence.* It conveniently glowed a faint green with each footfall, so they knew where to step next. Repellers kept the surface clear of spiderwebs and other nests.

Repellers didn't stop branches from growing or leaning across their path. Mac fended another from her face. Mudge either didn't realize that what he pushed out of his way would spring into hers, or didn't care.

His voice floated back to her. "Why? Do you have something to hide, Norcoast?"

Should she count on her fingers or pull out her imp to do the calculation? Mac snorted. Aloud, she said: "No. I don't have anything to hide. But you're—OW!" The tip of a branch snapped against her cheek despite a last second duck. "Will you stop!" she shouted.

Mudge, for a wonder, did just that. Mac fingered her cheek and glared at him, breathing heavily. Ever since she'd showed him the path, he'd hurried along it as if possessed by demons. *If she didn't know better,* Mac thought darkly, *she'd believe he had a destination in mind.*

As this particular path swung all too close to the Ro landing site at the top of the ridge, she sincerely hoped not. *There were some things she needed to believe,* Mac admitted to herself as she studied his sweating face. Among them, that Oversight was here for his trees, nothing more.

He was fumbling in a pocket. Before Mac could do more than tense—*when had she developed that appalling reflex?* —he pulled out a wad of white and pressed it into her hand. "Here. You're bleeding."

Mac lifted the tissue to her cheek. "What's the rush, Oversight?" she asked, holding his gaze with hers. His face was flushed with effort. *No surprise.* They were both too warm in their rainsuits and had their hoods down, even with the light drizzle falling. Drops collected in the creases beside his eyes and erased what hair he had.

"Was I rushing?" All innocence.

Mac waited.

"Oh," Mudge gave an embarrassed-sounding harrumph. "I—Sorry about that, Norcoast. It's all a bit—much, you know. Being here." He looked up and around, eyes wide, then back to her, his expression somehow desperate. "I must make as complete an inspection in the time we have—" he raised the hand holding the recorder, "—but there's no way to see it all. No time."

"Beautiful, isn't it?" Mac commented.

"Beautiful?" Mudge blinked raindrops from his eyes. "Of course it is." She merely gazed at him, letting silence speak. Finally, he heaved a sigh and lowered the recorder. "Of course, it is," he repeated, more slowly and with emphasis. "Thank you, Norcoast." He looked past her again. "It's worth everything we do, isn't it," he said softly.

Mac nodded, drinking in the sights, sounds, and smells for herself.

Spring. Regrowth, renewal, reproduction. They stood encompassed by living things answering those imperatives, urgently, impatiently. Birdsong, from hoarse to heartbreakingly rich, filled the air. Pollen powdered highlights of yellow on the bark of trees. Green shoots burst through the dark soil below like fireworks exploding in a night sky, their color so vivid, so intense, it seemed to leave a taste. Anywhere sheltered from the tiny raindrops, the air was filled with motes, some in flight, some adrift, all intent.

Mac drew a deep breath through her nose, savoring the rush of molds and damp wood, of distant flowers and brand-new leaves. *Regeneration.* She could feel it, just being here. She would know it, when she was at the field station, waiting for the first migrating salmon of the season. Her life would regain its purpose, its balance—

"It's stopped working."

"What's stopped working?" she echoed.

"This thing." Mudge banged his recorder against the palm of his other hand. "It's gone dead on me."

Mac couldn't pull air into her lungs. Her eyes searched the surrounding maze of crisscrossing branches and shadow. Not that those she feared would trouble to hide. *The Ro.* Masters of stealth, when they wished.

And their favorite tactic? To interfere with power supplies, broadcast or stored.

Their strange allies. Who could be close enough to touch, and neither she nor Mudge would know.

The Dhryn?

Mac didn't dare look up. If there were any above them, it was already too late.

Mudge's annoyed "Well, Norcoast? Where's your imp?" made her jump.

"My—" Her voice caught.

"What's the matter with you?" he demanded, but went on without waiting for an answer, hoarse with frustration. "You did bring it? Oh, I know it's not ideal. This—" a wave of the recorder, "—would be better, much better, more complete and reliable." He shoved it into a pocket, the rubber protesting. "Piece of junk. I assume your imp has at least basic data recording capabilities, ambient conditions, that sort of thing? I have to collect as much as I can . . . make notes."

Nodding, Mac took out the small device and laid it on her palm, unable to help stealing glances in every direction. She tapped in her code with a finger, lower lip between her teeth.

The workscreen formed before her face, its display so bland and normal she gasped with relief.

"Good," Mudge said, either oblivious or assuming Mac's emotions reflected his own. "Let me use it."

Without warning, the current display, a checklist of her field supplies, disappeared. In its place, a string of incomprehensible symbols tumbled among the raindrops in the air, flaring yellow, then red. *A message?* Mac jabbed a finger through the 'screen to save it.

As she did, the symbols were replaced by a flicker of light that, so briefly it could have been her imagination, formed a face.

Then the display winked back to its list of equipment, tents, and rations.

Mac closed her fingers over her imp. Rain washed her cheeks, conveniently hiding the tears she couldn't control. Of joy or terror? *Interesting question,* she told herself. But whatever she was feeling, Mac knew she hadn't imagined what she'd seen. Or rather who.

Emily.

"Well? Are you going to let me use it or not, Norcoast?"

"What? Oh. Not. Sorry." Mac opened her rainsuit and secured the now-precious gadget in the upper zipped pocket of her coveralls. "Old model," she said smoothly. "Forgot it doesn't have direct data recording. Try yours again."

His expression was the familiar "are you nuts?" one she'd grown accustomed to ignoring over the years. Presumably hers was the equally familiar "willing to wait forever" one, because Mudge didn't bother arguing. Instead, he grabbed out his recorder and activated it one more time, grumbling under his breath all the while. Then his eyes widened. He gave her a shocked look. "It's working!"

Why wasn't *that reassuring?* As Mac suspected the answer involved the Ro, or at least their technology, neither far enough away, she was proud of her calm: "Oh, good. Shall we proceed?"

"I expect you to show me what's been happening here, Norcoast," Mudge scowled fiercely. "No tricks." He started moving without waiting for an answer, the walkway edges flashing green with each impatient step.

So much for sharing the beauty of the place, Mac sighed to herself. "I don't know what you think you'll find, Oversight," she informed his back as she followed behind. "There's been no one here since the last field season and you've seen those reports."

The walkway climbed with the mountain, each step etched in light. Mac forced herself to stop looking for Emily at every turn. She'd been given a message, that's all. 'Sephe and company would help her find out what it meant. At least now, there was hope.

If only Emily's face hadn't looked so . . . strange.

Mac and Mudge soon reached the section where the walkway spiraled both up and around a series of mammoth tree trunks, each wider than a transport lev, rising vertically as if they were columns supporting the unseen sky. *An otherworldly place,* Mac thought, trying to shake free of the aftermath of Emily's message. There had been a time when being here gave her a sense of permanence, of safety, of life that needed nothing but itself to continue.

Having walked on one of the lifeless worlds of the Chasm, she knew better. *The trees were something else at risk. Something else to lose.*

The rain collected in the dense canopy of leaves, branches, and moss far above their heads, so drops continued to fall long after cloudbursts ended for the day, an absentminded deluge that skewed time the way the scale of the trees skewed perceptions of self and importance. Mac could see it affecting Mudge. His pace gradually slowed from impatient to reverent, the recorder in his hand lifting until he held it like a torch.

They were still some distance from the Ro landing site, and well away from the trampling done by, well, several individuals including herself last year, which was why Mac didn't pay attention when Mudge disappeared from view around the next trunk. He was only footsteps ahead. Besides, the bark on that tree trunk was festooned with a string of amorous slugs, so Mac paused to do a quick count, admiring their glistening yellow and brown. *Quite dapper beasts.* Five . . . six . . .

Snap. It was such an ordinary sound, Mac didn't bother glancing up. Branches cracked all the time. Eight . . . nine . . . There was a red velvet mite, vivid and soft, climbing up the back of the tenth slug. Mac peered closer, curious as to how it was managing to find traction in the slime.

Crash, snap, CLANG!

"What the . . . ?" Abandoning her slugs and muttering under her breath, Mac hurried around the tree trunk, light flashing underfoot with each step. A bell-like metal-to-metal clang wasn't ordinary. *What was Mudge doing?*

She stopped in her tracks.

Mudge was standing in the middle of the next rise of the walkway. His arms were being held by two large figures encased in the Ministry's black armor from head to toe. Even their faces were hidden behind gleaming visors. A scuff mark on one of those visors, and the sad condition of the recorder lying at Mudge's feet explained the *clang.*

The rip through the forest ahead explained everything else.

Another new Ro landing site. This time, they'd knocked over giants, flattened centuries' old growth, scraped soil to expose the mountain's very bones. Not a large area, as if they'd lost control and crashed, but of a certain size, a certain shape, as if they'd come down and shoved aside whatever was in their way.

Levs, the silent, expensive, probably-always-work type, hovered between the standing trees. More figures, twin to those confining Mudge, moved through the debris on the forest floor. Mac sniffed. There was a faint charred smell to the air. *Gone,* she reasoned.

After Emily sent her message.

Had the Ro ship been waiting for her? Had they spied and known she was coming? Or had they been here all along and only now been chased away, the message a last minute attempt—at what?

Mac shook her head free of questions. They only served to make her more anxious, not less. "Let him go," she told the guards holding Mudge. "I'll take him to Base."

"You know about this, Norcoast?" Mudge struggled, futilely, against his captors. "I demand an explanation! Do you see what's—what's—" words appeared to fail him as he looked out at the destruction. Then, eyes brimming with tears, he turned to her. "What have you done?"

Mac winced. She wasn't sure what was worse: the horror on his face, the ravaging of the forest, the return of the Ro . . .

Or the way every visored head in view was now aimed right at her, as if waiting for something.

"Tomorrow," Mac said loudly and clearly, so there could be no possible misunderstanding by anyone or anything in earshot, "I am leaving for Field Station Six. To study my salmon."

How many times and in how many ways had the Ministry told her they didn't want her involved any longer?

Fine. She'd give them Emily's message. As a bonus, she'd also let them explain a major Anthropogenic Perturbation of a Class Three Wilderness Trust to its Oversight Committee.

Who would never talk to her again, anyway.

"Your Mudge is not a happy man."

Something she had no authority or ability to change, Mac thought sadly. She tilted her office chair back so she could rest her bare feet on her desk. Her toes complained about their time in wet socks and she wiggled them slowly. "What will happen to him?"

'Sephe shrugged, her loose-fitting yellow shirt bright enough to use as a signal flare. If she'd been one of the black, visored entities on the ridge, there was no sign of it. *Unless,* Mac told herself dourly, *you counted snug black jeans.* She'd come quickly enough when Mac sent for her.

Which had been after Mac had had the dubious thrill of hiking all the way down the ridge walkways to her lev, finally getting it started during the worsening rain, and somehow keeping it running until it squatted safely on the roof of Pod Three. Where the machine had given every indication of coughing out its last breath. *One day,* Mac vowed, *she'd get a ride home.*

Oh, they'd have taken her in one of their levs had she mentioned the message in her imp, Mac knew, spinning the device in circles with pokes of her big toe. *But likely not back to Base.* She'd learned a few things about the spy mind-set by now.

"I can't speak for my superiors, Mac, but Mudge was in the wrong place at the wrong time—and so far he's refusing to keep quiet about it. He's been taken home, but with a security blackout on his communications."

"That can't last."

"Maybe he'll give in—see how important it is to cooperate with us."

Mac snorted.

"It's to everyone's advantage," 'Sephe insisted. "The consulate's satisfied with our reports, but if news of a Ro landing here gets out to the public, we'll have to allow who knows how many IU representatives to come and inspect the site. Then there's the media. Think they'll respect the Trust? You know the stakes—"

"Oversight won't care." *You are such clever little toes,* Mac congratulated her feet as they managed to roll her imp back and forth.

"You do."

Mac couldn't stop the look she gave 'Sephe.

"Sorry," the other woman said quietly. "If I'd known about the new site, Mac, I'd never have let you go with him."

"You tried hard enough to stop us as it was."

"The travel ban?" 'Sephe raised her hands. "Don't blame me. That came straight from the head office when the sensors detected Ro activity. We didn't want to spook them."

"To not 'spook' them, you disrupted normal routine here and sent in storm troopers?" Mac shook her head. "Excuse me for missing the logic."

"Our people only moved in after the Ro launched, to preserve the site and look for clues or messages." 'Sephe made an exasperated noise. "Which they had to do, because you and your friend chased the Ro away! Thanks for nothing."

"Ah." Mac stretched forward to snag her imp with one hand, then brought her feet flat on the floor with a triumphant thump. "Thanks for everything, you mean."

'Sephe's eyes narrowed. "What haven't you told me, Mac?"

Ignoring the slot on her desk, where she'd normally insert her imp in order to use the desk, Mac activated her imp's workscreen. With a flick of her fingers through the display, she brought up the Ro's message.

The glyphs scrolled to the end.

Emily's face flickered in and out of view.

"Dr. Mamani's alive," 'Sephe whispered.

"It's only an image," Mac said, resisting the temptation to replay the message, stare at that face, hope . . . *Hope was reckless.* "The message—that should tell us more. You can decipher it, can't you?"

"We've resources," the other said noncommittally. "I've certainly never seen anything like it before." 'Sephe drew out her own imp, identical to Mac's but doubtless more sophisticated.

Probably comes with a stunner, bomb, and ropes as well as self-destruct, Mac told herself, only half kidding.

'Sephe set her display beside Mac's. Without needing to be told, Mac stroked through the control portion of her display and pointed to its neighbor, sending the message to 'Sephe's device.

"Thanks. Did you copy it?" 'Sephe asked.

Mac gave another snort. "I'm not about to dump Ro coding into Norcoast's vital systems."

"Good." 'Sephe touched one end of her imp to Mac's where it lay on the desk. Mac's workscreen winked out of existence.

With a wordless cry, Mac picked up her imp and tried to reactivate it. Nothing. "You've wiped it," she accused, leaping to her feet.

"Just the message." 'Sephe put away her imp. "What did you expect?"

She'd hoped otherwise. Mac didn't bother to scowl. "I expect to be told what that says."

"I'll relay your request. That's all I can do."

Not enough. "Promise you'll tell me if it's really from Emily. If she's asking for help."

'Sephe frowned. "Why would she need help?" she demanded, her tone sharp. "The Ro aren't the enemy."

"Easy for you to say. You didn't see her," Mac countered. "You didn't see what they'd done—how it was affecting her—"

She might have struck a nerve. "Your Emily isn't the only one making sacrifices for the good of all," 'Sephe interrupted passionately. "At least she might be alive. At least she hasn't been sucked into one of their—" The full lips pressed into a thin line, but it was too late.

"So," Mac dropped the word into the ringing silence their shouts had left. She felt numb, having the truth arrive like this. "What happened in the Chasm— it's begun again. The Dhryn have attacked a world, haven't they? Which one?"

'Sephe sat on the couch as if she'd lost the strength to stand, her hands cupping her imp and Emily's message. "Ascendis." Just the name.

It was enough. "They went back for more," Mac said tonelessly.

"I don't know what you mean."

"Yes, you do. The letter I received from the Secretary General of the Ministry—" *The one that had started it all,* Mac thought, remembering her name in mauve crawling over the envelope's blue and green. The colors of a threat to the Human species itself. "It listed a series of mysterious disappearances. One of them concerned an eco-patrol that went missing on Ascendis." She glared at 'Sephe. "Why isn't this on the news? People need to know the threat is real— and that there's evidence the Dhryn have been—" Mac paused to think of a word and rejected *tasting,* "—scouting."

"We're aware. So is the IU. So are the worlds who may have suffered previous Dhryn attacks. What would a more public news release say, Mac? That the Dhryn were able to enter a populated system without warning, pass any defense, consume what they wanted, and leave? No one wants panic." 'Sephe hesitated, then went on: "The IU wouldn't have informed us about Ascendis—not yet— but a Human ship was there. Her captain sent home every bit of information he could before—"

"Before what?"

'Sephe's dark eyes were haunted. "Before his crew was consumed—and he crashed his ship into the planet in a futile attempt to stop the Dhryn. Would you like to know his name, Dr. Connor? It was Captain Frank Wu." Her voice rose, became husky with emotion. "Would you like the crew list? Would you like population stats for the Eelings? Biomass data? A complete list of the devastation?"

"Yes." Mac held up her imp, her voice sounding cold and set to her own ears. "I want all of it."

'Sephe blinked. "What did you say?"

"I said yes. If we are going to understand the Dhryn, we need to know what they do, the impact they have, every scrap of data. Thanks to this Captain Wu's quick thinking, there's finally something other than rumor and legend. Can you get it for me?"

"To do what? You study salmon—isn't that what you're always saying? What good could you do?"

The words were like a slap. Mac gritted her teeth. "Can you get me the data from Ascendis or do I have to ask someone else?"

'Sephe's laugh wasn't amused. "You want to be locked up with Mudge?"

"No," Mac snapped back. "No. And I don't want him locked up either." She held her breath, then said more calmly: "I want to help."

"Then listen to me, Mac. Keep doing what you've been doing. Run this place. Study your fish. Forget last year and let us do our job. The message from Dr. Mamani? That's crucial. Thank you. But even that—" a dark look, "—you shouldn't have waited to give it to me, Mac. You can't make decisions like that."

Em, she's definitely not read the right files. Mac sat down in her chair and propped her bare feet on her desk, wiggling her toes thoughtfully. "I understand. But what about Oversight?"

"The Ministry is putting together an explanation for him, something to cover what he's seen. It may not satisfy him, but it should keep him from convincing anyone else."

"You're good at that."

"I—" whatever 'Sephe started to say, she decided against it. She got to her feet, the movement awkward. "I have to go—get the message to those who can make sense out of it. Mac, I promise to ask if you can know what it says. That's all I can do."

"Help Oversight. He can be too stubborn for his own good."

'Sephe's dry: "So can you," made Mac smile.

Almost.

"We're on the same side," she reminded 'Sephe. "You, me, even Mudge."

The Ministry agent's lips twisted. "It's never that simple, Mac."

After she left, and the door closed, Mac leaned as far back as she could, pressing the heels of her hands against her eyelids. "It is for me," she said, not caring who overheard.

- 4 -

CALAMITY AND CONSEQUENCE

THE MINISTRY'S NEED to explain anything to Charles Mudge III expired at 6:01:34, Pacific Time. The earthquake lasted one minute and twenty-three seconds, with a recorded epicenter 2.34 kilometers below sea level, directly under Castle Inlet's protecting arm.

The coast knew earthquakes. After all, something had to give—and often did—when three immense tectonic plates met to argue about who'd reshape the ocean floor and resculpt the edge of the continent on any given day. Seismic warnings from the network of waiting sensors set off alarms. Signals sped up and down the coastline, out to sea and inland, sent via every means of transmission available. The birds, of course, hadn't required one. They'd launched themselves from trees and rocky shoreline as the first tremors began deep underground. But people needed time, time to shut down systems at risk, time to seek shelter, time—

They had barely moments. As the tremors intensified, the sharp shifts of the ocean floor moved up Pod Three's anchoring pylons to jiggle its infrastructure. Mac's hanging salmon clashed against one another, setting off the independent motion sensors. Adding to the cacophony, the curtain reeds on the door clanged in warning.

Base's internal alarm system, a varying shriek of light and sound penetrating every nook and cranny, was something of an anticlimax.

Mac couldn't tell what woke her, too torn by the dual assault of sensation and memory to think straight. Haven, the Dhryn home world, had shaken like this under attack by the Ro. It had split in every direction as the great buried ships of the Progenitors tore themselves free of the planet, seeking the safety of space. *Brymn had held her in his arms to keep her safe—*

Brymn? Mind suddenly, terribly clear, Mac pressed her hands over her ears as she ran outside. "Damn you, Emily!" she cursed, unable to hear herself past the din. "Don't do this again!"

The outside terraces on each pod were filling with staff and students. Mac sagged with relief at shouts of "earthquake!" among steadier voices, hearing those taking charge, giving orders. *When had a natural disaster become less threatening?* she wondered inanely, gripping the rail with numb hands even as the world stopped trying to shrug them loose.

Then she roused herself to follow the procedures she'd practiced with the rest. The gates would have opened to release anything captive in Pod Six. What remained was to make sure everyone was safe and inside, ready for what would follow.

For the mere heave of earth and stone wasn't what threatened Base.

It was water.

Imagine lying in a bathtub, legs out before you. Imagine lifting and dropping your legs, not too high but very quickly, to make your own small quake. Watch the water as it hurries to fill the void, then is pushed aside again as your legs settle. The quake is over.

Now watch how the water surges to crash over your knees and threatens to spill over the sides of the tub.

The bathtubs used by the designers of Norcoast Salmon Research Facility were larger, and featured immense paddles instead of legs, but the principle was the same. They knew there would be earthquakes. And when there were earthquakes near water, that water would move. *Tsunami.* The giant waves that raced away from the disturbance faster than a skim, traveling entire oceans as a line of shadow, a mere ruffling of the surface, until cresting to a hideous destructive height against any shoreline, a threat to all who lived in sight of the sea.

Enclosed areas, like bathtubs, like Castle Inlet, faced their own maelstrom. Here, confined by cliffs, the water shoved aside would surge back, racing from side to side, tumbling up slopes and down again, over and over until it built into huge tortured piles that would slam against anything in their way with inescapable force.

The designers knew this and planned for it, as much as technology could plan for nature. If an earthquake of sufficient force was detected by the pod anchors, they would loosen their grip and become tethers. Walkways would disconnect. Shielding meant for ice and storm would wrap around the walls of the pods and doors to the ocean would close. The pods would rise and fall with the water. A bumpy ride at best, but survivable. Hopefully.

While inside . . .

"I'm just saying—I hate this part."

Mac leaned shoulder to shoulder with Kammie Noyo, and couldn't disagree.

Leaned wasn't exactly the word. Like everyone else in this pod and all the others, she was pinned where she'd last stood in the corridor by the protective foam hardening around them. It had erupted from orifices throughout the interior of the structure the moment the pod's sensors had detected the terraces were clear of people and the storm shields were in place, filling labs and rooms, holding objects in place as well as people.

"And I don't see why it has to be the color of bile."

Mac had remembered to keep her arms up as the foam rose up their legs and bodies, stopping chest high on her. During a test of the system, years ago, she'd left them down and spent three hours unable to deal with a maddening itch on the side of her nose. The foam was harmless, if you didn't mind the paralysis aspect. You could lie down on the floor and be completely covered. *Not her first choice.* The foam arched overhead as well, following the wall and ceiling material to effectively seal anything that might otherwise shake loose and fall on their heads. Its join was, presumably, also waterproof. Even if the pods were flipped right over, they should be safe.

The Ro had known. They'd known to disable the pods' protections before sabotaging their anchors. They'd been told how by Emily Mamani, their spy. Emily, who had come to Base to find out why Mackenzie Connor and her obscure work so interested a Dhryn. Emily, who had come to use that interest to hunt the Dhryn's weakness, their Progenitors. Emily, who with the Ro had used Mac to befriend a Dhryn and betray his kind, for the good of all others.

"Forgive me."

"Mac? How can you sleep through this?"

"Thinking, not sleeping." Mac looked down at Kammie. The other woman's pupils were dilated. Otherwise, she looked calm enough. Mac glanced along the corridor. Everyone in sight looked reasonably comfortable, if a bit nervous. Understandable—the floor was tilting beneath them and, from the feel of her stomach, the pod was dropping at the same time. Mac raised her voice. "Hope you like roller coasters, folks. At least none of us has had breakfast yet."

A few laughs at that.

"There'll be a few more tremors—aftershocks. And probably a few wave events—" The pod gave a sharp roll back and left, its pinned occupants gasping in reaction. Mac waited until everything settled, then continued. "Like that. The foam will be dispersed once the sensors—" This time the swing of the pod was to the right and up, putting Mac and those with her temporarily where the ceiling should be. Several students now below her hooted and waved as the pod rocked back to level, trying their best to intercept someone's hat as it tumbled along the foam's surface. Beside Mac, Kammie shook her head in disgust.

"—once the sensors say everything's settling down," Mac finished. "Meanwhile," she grinned at Kammie. "You might as well enjoy the ride."

"Three skims are still missing, but I 'spect those will turn up on shore someplace. You can see for yourself the condition of the walkways. They're a total loss. Otherwise— Mac, are you listening?"

Skims. Walkways. *As if those mattered.* Mac rested her chin on her fists, elbows on the cowling of the lev, and tried to pay attention to Tie's briefing. They were circling the pods, assessing damage, and it was all she could do not to cry.

Base had survived. The pods had bobbed like so many corks, and several people had to be treated for nausea, but the foam had vanished under the mist of dispersal agent and very little had been shifted, let alone broken.

She couldn't say the same about the landscape.

The ridge that stretched between Castle Inlet and the strait beyond had been scraped clean, as if the coating of forest and soil had been a frosting licked away. Close enough. The quake had momentarily liquefied the sandy substrate beneath, creating a downward sag and flow rather than a landslide's bump and tumble. Now only rock showed in a swatch stretching from the highest point to the shoreline, the fresh dark line of a fault plain to see. The shore? It was a confusion of mud and debris, leaves and branches sticking out at random as though a child had decorated a mud pie. Scale was impossible. What appeared twigs from this distance were giant tree trunks, snapped and torn. What appeared lines of gravel and sand were boulders. Mac spotted an eagles' nest, half covered by the remnants of a mem-wood dock. Streams and river mouths would be choked, some completely dammed.

The air stank of ruined trees and rotting kelp.

The sea hadn't been spared. It was brown and clouded as far as she could see, dotted with drowning bits of land-adapted life, sediment quietly smothering what aquatic life couldn't swim away.

At least it had been a minor earthquake, 4.3 on the revised Barr-Richter scale, barely rattling cups in Prince Rupert, unnoticed in Vancouver or Anchorage. A local event. Hadn't brought down anything more than this slope. Hadn't seriously affected rivers beyond this side of the inlet.

Hah, thought Mac.

One of her first priorities would be to assemble a team of researchers to record the state of land and water, to monitor the successional stages as the ecosystems rebuilt. Some of the scientists were, very quietly, overjoyed by the opportunity. It was rare to have such access to the destruction of a well-studied area, to be the first to see life restore itself. Their work would have immense value.

Mac watched as a gull settled on a root now aimed skyward, perhaps attracted by the line of silent, unmoving tiggers perched on a nearby scar of rock. The servos were still on guard, protecting what was to come.

"Mac. Stuff happens."

She looked at Tie. His weary face was streaked with drying mud and a line of grease. A bit of pink foam was stuck in his hair above his left ear. "That it does," she agreed. "Let's head back. I've seen enough."

And if she believed this earthquake "happened," Mac told herself, so far beyond mere fury she felt nothing but cold, *she should invest in that fabled bridge across the Bering Strait.*

A few meetings were actually fun—those rare events involved pizza, a tub of ice-cold beer, and the joyous task of celebrating a colleague's latest success, whether publication or offspring.

Most, like this one, were thinly disguised battles, usually with the outcome predetermined and of no joy to anyone.

Mac planned to make it quick. Speed didn't help when pulling off bandages, but she hoped in this case it would limit the fallout. With any luck, everyone would leave mad at her instead of each other.

She hated meetings.

"Let's get started," she ordered quietly, surveying the gallery from the center-most seat at the head table. That table was raised on a small dais, allowing the entire roomful of people a clear view of Mac, Kammie, and the other five senior scientists. Or guest speakers, hired bands, talent shows, and the like.

No one expected entertainment today, not with Pod Three reverberating each time a floating, dying tree bumped and scraped against its supports, not with the view out the transparent walls showing an ocean stained with the blood of a mountain.

"We've conferred with—" *everyone possible,* Mac almost said, then changed it to "—experts. The bottom beneath the pods is stable, but seriously disturbed. You've seen for yourselves the state of the shoreline. Rather than reinstall the permanent anchors and resume our work here—" The shock traveled across the room, mirrored in all of their faces. *Did they think nothing would change?* Mac raged—but kept it to herself. They didn't need her pain as well as their own. "—Pods One, Three, Four, Five, and Six will be towed to a new site."

From any other group, there might have been pandemonium or some protest. Not here, not now. Three hundred and fifteen faces looked back at her, many of them familiar, some new, very few she didn't know on sight yet. Her eyes couldn't find Persephone, but she took that as a positive. *Someone better be investigating what had happened.* Just as likely, 'Sephe hadn't dared face her. Mac spotted Case, sitting with Uthami and John Ward. Everyone was silent, waiting.

They knew there was more to come.

"The process, barring storms or more rumblings from beneath, will take three weeks. Norcoast is sending haulers to tow the pods. We'll have to secure all gear—move out what's going to be needed during that time. Check your imps for details. The sooner we're ready, the sooner we can get moving."

"Where?" came a voice from the back.

Mac glanced at Kammie. That worthy stood, having learned long ago her soft, high-pitched voice needed all the help it could get to project past the first line of tables. She smoothed the front of her immaculate lab coat with both hands. A nervous habit. *Who wasn't on edge?* Mac thought with sympathy. "We're returning Base to its original home, beside the mouth of the Tannu River itself," Kammie informed them. "It's an ideal location. And was ideal, until the natural disaster before this one. I assume that when history repeats itself, Base will be towed back here again." Her comment drew a laugh and Kammie smiled faintly as she sat down.

Mac resumed her part of the briefing. "Pod Two is being refitted as a self-contained research unit, to accommodate what will be an ongoing, multiyear, and very well-funded exploration of the successional recovery of the life in this area. Congratulations to those who will be staying. We look forward to your findings." Martin Svehla, freshly minted head of the new unit, beamed beatifically at the world at large. Mac was reasonably sure he wasn't hearing much else.

A hand rose.

"Yes, Case."

He stood, glancing once around the room before looking up at her. "Dr. Connor. What does this mean for those of us packed and ready to head to the field?"

"It means—" Mac began answering.

Kammie stood so quickly her glass of water rocked on the table. "It means a temporary postponement," she interrupted, steadying the tumbler. "You'll have the choice of going home for three weeks, travel costs covered by Norcoast, or joining some of us on the University of British Columbia's campus for course credit. I believe there will be four topics offered."

So this was how it felt to be ambushed by a puma, Mac told herself. Only the cat had good reason for pouncing on you from behind and driving its fangs into your skull.

"Dr. Noyo is talking about some individual circumstances," Mac said harshly. *If you didn't want to be lunch, you fought with whatever you had.* "Each case will be decided on its own needs and merits—"

Unfortunately, tiny Kammie Noyo was more dangerous than a hungry puma. "Now, Dr. Connor," she interrupted again. "We mustn't confuse the issue. Norcoast will not be broadcasting power during the tow. The main system will not be operating. There will be no backup of data, no supplies, no—"

Mac leaped to her feet. "So bloody what? I don't need all this—" she waved her hand around furiously, "—to do my work. I'll use a pencil if I have to!"

But the others at the head table didn't meet her eyes when she looked to them for support.

"Norcoast has been very clear, Dr. Connor," Kammie said into the painful pause. "They won't send anyone into the field until Base is up and running to support those efforts. It's only three weeks—a month at most."

"A month—" The first runs would be over. The first salmon would be dead, their legacy mere specks of eyeball and yolk left in the redds, the nests their mothers dug in the gravel upstream.

Mac closed her mouth, afraid of what might come out next, afraid she was wrong, that she was overreacting for reasons incomprehensible to both mystified students and troubled colleagues.

Most of all, she was afraid of staying here one more instant. *What else would she lose if she did?*

She sat, slowly. With an effort that left her dizzy, she nodded at Kammie, gesturing graciously that the other was to continue.

Mac didn't hear another word that was said.

The foam wasn't supposed to leave a residue. Maybe it was her imagination that everything she touched in her office was faintly sticky. Mac ignored the sensation as she ignored everything but the task at hand. She was packing. Quietly, quickly. One small bag. They'd been told to take only personal valuables, to leave everything else behind. For three weeks.

It wasn't Kammie's fault.

Kammie had anticipated Mac's reaction to the "take a hike" order from Norcoast perfectly. She'd known better than to bring it up in private, giving Mac a chance to launch herself at those responsible, fly to the head office, make a pointless nuisance of herself and possibly lose her post here altogether. It wasn't only potential students who were wondering about the qualifications and commitment of a particular salmon researcher.

It wasn't Kammie's fault.

If she'd anger to spare, Mac thought as she zipped up her bag, she'd save it for those lackwits who'd forgotten how real scientists worked. Hands-on, with nets and serum syringes, scales and insta-freeze pouches. A zapper to discourage bears who preferred her fishing techniques to theirs. She'd done it before.

Not that they'd listened.

There was temporary power throughout the pods, enough for lights and to run whatever systems needed to go through an off cycle before storage. *Enough for coms to work,* Mac noticed morosely, as hers gave a fainter-than-usual chime.

Listen to them? She grabbed her sweater instead.

A second chime. A third.

Fine. "Mac," she said, thumping the control with the side of her fist. About as satisfying as slamming a door when no one else was there to appreciate the gesture.

"Hi, Princess. Going that well, is it?"

Oops. Mac sank down on the corner of her desk, shaking her head at herself. "Sorry, Dad. I should have called you back." They'd all contacted family and friends after the earthquake, taking the time to give reassurances if no details. *She'd really meant to call again.* "Did an inspection. Held a meeting. Packed. It's been hectic."

There wasn't power to waste on the vid screen—not that Dr. Norman Connor had ever needed to see her face to know. *Sure enough.* "What's wrong?"

"Norcoast is shutting us down for three weeks." *Shutting me down,* Mac told herself, penning in her now-familiar frustration. *It wasn't his fault.* "They're moving the pods back to the Tannu."

"While you're away in the field. Sounds like good timing."

"You'd think so." Mac sighed and stared out the window at the fittingly sullen sky. "But they won't authorize any work until Base is up and running again."

"That's bloody ridiculous," he exploded. She could picture him pacing angrily around his apartment, dodging the table he insisted belonged in the middle of the floor. "Since when do you need all that? This ridiculous nonsense of interactive data-feed. Voyeur-scientists, that's what they are! Never get their feet wet or dirty, but oh, they want their input, oh, yes."

Dr. Connor Sr. had spent most of a century doing fieldwork on owls, from an era when that meant disappearing for weeks at a time. His indignation, right on target, eased some of Mac's own. "Trust me, Dad, I argued the point. But it's a done deal. I—" A plan crystallized Mac hadn't been aware of forming until now. "Is that guest room of yours ready? I haven't been to your place since, well, since I came back." When he didn't answer immediately, she went on, feeling suddenly desperate: "We could take a trip, maybe even visit William. You could play granddad while I play aunt."

"I'd love to have you here, Mac, you know that, but—" her father's voice trailed away, then returned. "Now might not be a good time."

"Why?" she asked, surprised into worry. "Is something wrong there?"

His "No. Nothing's wrong," came out too fast, too definite. Mac stared down at the com control, as if it could transform into his face.

"What is it, Dad?"

A pause, then, slowly: "There are vidbots hanging outside my building, Mac. Outside your brothers' homes as well. All authorized and legal—we checked. Our guess is some nosy reporter hopes to catch you away from Base. I really don't think you feel like giving interviews."

Attract media attention? Oh, the Ministry would love that. Mac shuddered at the thought of black-armored Ministry agents trying to loom discreetly among her father's geraniums. *Bad enough she'd had to lie to her family already. How to explain that?* She rubbed her hands over her face, as if to scrub away the image. "You're right, Dad," she agreed. "It was just a thought. I need a break from all this." Mac realized how wistful that sounded and went on more firmly: "Don't worry. I'm sure Kammie could use help with her courses."

"That's hardly taking a break," he protested.

Mac shrugged, even though he couldn't see. "Best I can do."

"The ice is off the lake, Mac."

The family cabin? She snorted. "I haven't been there in—in a very long time. And neither have you."

"Blake went up last month. He said the place was in great shape."

"Have you seen Blake's house lately?" Mac retorted. "His idea of great shape is knowing where the leaks are so he can avoid the puddles."

Her father laughed, but went on, a warm, coaxing note to his voice. "Think about it, Mac. May at the lake. Peace and quiet."

"I don't need to think about it. I remember. Black flies. With occasional flurries. No thanks."

"The birds will be coming back."

Mac closed her eyes, tilting her head back, her hands tight around one knee for balance. "You know why I don't like it there anymore, Dad."

"Maybe it's time. Things change. People."

"I don't."

Mac imagined her dad shaking his head ruefully, that half proud, half exasperated look on his face she usually managed to elicit at least once a visit. "Fine. But it's yours if you want it."

"Kammie will need me—" Mac began.

"No, I won't," an unexpected voice interrupted, startling Mac's eyes open. Kammie Noyo met her scowl with a wink. "Hi, Dr. Connor," she added, approaching the desk. "It's Kammie. How're you?"

"Frustrated," her father answered. "You ever try explaining the concept of a vacation to my daughter?"

"You're a brave man."

Was she invisible? "I don't need a vacation," Mac growled at them both. "I don't want a vacation. I want to get to work."

"Well, if you change your mind, Mac, the door's open. Let me know what you decide."

"I will. Bye, Dad."

"Bye. Nice talking to you, Kammie."

"You, too, Dr. Connor." Mac turned off the com.

"Go."

She glared at Kammie. "Pardon?" she said at last.

The chemist put her hands on her hips, a posture which combined with her oversize white lab coat to make her resemble a small bird ready to take flight. *A whirlwind temporarily touching down was more accurate,* Mac thought warily. "You heard me," Kammie stated. "I want twenty-one days without you. Go."

"That's harsh."

"The truth."

Mac swung her leg back and forth, then gave the other scientist a thoughtful look. "I've been that bad?"

"You got a few hours?" Kammie's stern expression faded into something worried, a little frightened. She touched Mac's shoulder, let her hand drop. "Mac. You're the strongest person I know. But even you can break. You've—it's been hardest on you, these last months. We've all seen it. Listen to your father. Listen to me. You need some time. To look after yourself first for once."

Mac stood and took a step away, stopping to study her garden, with its sprouts of growth through the melting snow. *Plants had such optimism.* She felt stiff and cold inside. "What I need is my work," she said. *It wasn't Kammie's fault.*

"That's not what Em—" The other's voice broke.

Mac turned, catching the pain in Kammie's eyes, meeting it with her own. *Not forgotten after all.*

"I know exactly what she'd say." Mac shook her head, her lips twitching involuntarily. "But loud music and sex aren't the answer to everything."

"She'd argue it," Kammie chuckled, her dark eyes sparkling with mischief now, instead of tears. *Something had eased,* Mac decided, *but she wasn't sure what.* "So. You going to take that vacation?"

Mac grimaced. "Let me fight the concept a while longer."

"And then you'll go," the tiny chemist nodded with satisfaction. "See you in three weeks, Mac." With that, she sailed out of the room, lab coat snapping as if finding the perfect wind.

"If not sooner," Mac muttered under her breath. She bent to pick up her bag, wondering who'd won that little encounter.

"Mac . . . Dr. Connor? Do you have a minute?"

She straightened to find Case standing in the doorway to the terrace. *Bother.* Her own fault. She'd left the door ajar, open invitation to the sea breeze as well as anyone passing by.

Mac smiled a welcome. "Always. Come in, Case. I thought you were off to the family trawler."

"I'm on my way. Getting a ride to Kitimat with some of the Preds," he told her, stepping into the room, carefully avoiding the gravel section of the floor and giving her garden a bemused look as wet snowflakes began plopping down from its weather grid. May was a chancy month at Field Station One. "I wanted to say good-bye."

"Good-bye? That sounds rather final. It's only three weeks—so everyone keeps telling me," Mac added darkly.

"I—well, that's what I need to talk to you about, Mac. Unless you're in a hurry." He looked pointedly at her hand.

"Oh, this?" Mac dropped the bag, nudging it aside with her foot. "No rush. The haulers won't connect until the wee hours of tomorrow morning. Besides, I haven't made up my mind yet where I'm going. Have a seat." While Case folded himself into one of her chairs, she took the other. The unhappy set of his mouth, the shadows under his eyes? Something was up. *Though students,* Mac reminded herself, *could escalate a minor problem to a full-fledged life crisis if they worried hard enough.* Which didn't make the problem less real or painful.

She deliberately settled deeper, stretching out her legs. "So. Looking forward to some time at home?"

"Looking forward to it? Not really." Case gave a strangled laugh. "But I need the open sea. I can't hear myself think in a place like this." This last, hurried and thoroughly miserable. His shoulders hunched.

"You don't like it here," she suggested, disappointed but not showing it. *Hadn't picked him as one of the terminally homesick.*

His glance up at her was shocked, followed by a quick blush Mac didn't try to interpret. "Of course I like it here. I love it. Base is great. Everyone's—everyone's great. That's not it. I need time alone. I've a decision to make. I don't want to make the wrong one."

So that was it. Mac nodded triumphantly. "A decision about coming back. You're not sure about working with Lee."

"How did you know?" He gave her such a soulful look, Mac had to stop herself from smiling.

"Educated guess. Why?"

"I'm a deep-sea fisher." Case held out his hands. They were crisscrossed with a maze of white scars. Filleting knives, hooks. Even with gloves and the latest tech, harvesting wasn't for the thin of skin. "Tidal ecosystems are interesting, I grant you, but not what I came here for."

Mac pursed her lips. Then asked: "Are you good at it? Harvesting, that is."

His pale eyes gleamed. "Wilsons have been heading out to the North Sea for thirteen generations. I've more family drowned than buried." A hard shrug. "Why won't Dr. Noyo just let me work with the Harvs? That's where I belong, Mac. Isn't it?"

Ah. Not homesick. Intimidated. Mac put her hands behind her head and considered Lee's troubled student. *Just as well this had come to a head now,* she decided. She had a feeling about this one; she didn't want Base to lose him. "In your opinion, Case," she said carefully, "from what you've seen so far, nothing else, does Lee's line of research have any relevance whatsoever to harvesting?"

Another shocked look. "Of course it does. He's examining nutrient cycling within estuaries. Those are key feeding grounds for fish in transit, not to mention habitat and spawning nurseries. The list of species affected? Everything we'd want to haul aboard, as well as their primary food source and predators. You should see the prelims he's done on the impact of mitigation upstream on the yield of . . ." Case's passionate voice trailed away as he took in Mac's rather smug smile. "You know all of this."

"I should," she agreed calmly. "And you find his work interesting?"

Case actually squirmed. "Yes, but that's not the point, Mac. Lee, Uthami, the rest in the team—they're experts at this stuff. Me? I don't know anything."

"Yet."

"Sure, I could learn it. But in the meantime, I'm dead weight," he protested. "What can I contribute? With the Harvs, at least I'd understand the terms— know what I was doing. I'm useless as a Misses."

Mac brought her arms down and leaned forward on her elbows, holding his eyes with hers. "Listen to me, Case. You know what a catalyst is, right?" At his nod, she continued: "Kammie and I share a fondness for them. Mind you, to her, being a chemist, catalysts are what make a reaction more likely to occur—in many instances, make it possible in the first place—without being consumed themselves. But here? In a place like this? Catalysts are those individuals who can connect different lines of research. They bring together ideas which wouldn't meet otherwise. That's crucial to what we do here."

He rolled his eyes. "And I felt inadequate before? You aren't helping, Mac."

She sat up. "Yes, I am. Think about it, Case. You bring the perspective of a Harv, the knowledge of your deepwater fishing heritage, to the work in tidal systems. Every question you ask will have the unique value of coming from that knowledge. Bottom line? Lee and his team don't know what you know, and they'll benefit from your insights." Mac grinned. "I admit there's the chance you'll drive Lee nuts—but I think his new lady love is already doing that."

There was something immensely satisfying about the stupefied look on the young man's face. "You're saying Kammie assigned me to Lee's research team be-cause I don't have a clue about his work and he doesn't have a clue about mine."

Mac nodded cheerfully. "Couldn't have said it better myself."

"That's not—I'm really—Mac?" He gave her a desperate look. "What do I do now?"

"You go home," she advised. "Spend some time on that open sea. Think to your heart's content. Just be back here in three weeks, 'cause we have work to do this season, despite earthquakes and Norcoast."

Case stood when she did, then offered his hand. Mac took it, enjoying the feel of warm calluses, noticing the strength. "You believe I can do this," he told her. Almost a question, as though he had to be sure.

"I believe neither of us will know that until you try," she said honestly. "I hope you will, Case."

His grip tightened before letting go, his freckles prominent on his very seri-ous face. "I promise. Thank you."

The ensuing pause had the potential to become awkward, but Case relaxed and smiled before it did. An unexpectedly mischievous smile. "So if I'm to try what Kammie says, will you do the same? Take a vacation?"

Mac raised one eyebrow. "Eavesdropping?"

"The door was open," he said, appearing completely unrepentant.

Grad students, she sighed to herself. "I'm considering it."

"You're welcome to come home with me." The young man blushed and added hastily: "Don't worry. My parents and sister will be on the trawler, too."

One of the few times to be grateful Emily wasn't *around.*

Mac coughed. "I appreciate the offer, Case, but I'll probably help Kammie with the courses she's running. Or there's a taxonomy conference in Brussels—"

"When was the last time you took a vacation?"

Mac found herself at a loss.

"Aha!" Case crowed. "I bet you've never taken one. I bet you don't even know how!"

"Of course I do," Mac huffed. "I haven't bothered."

He gestured at her cluttered office. "So it's true!"

"What's true?" she asked cautiously.

"What they say. You really do live here all the time. Year in, year out. You don't even bother with sleeping quarters."

"There's nothing wrong with a passion for one's work," she said primly, then winced. *No doubt about Emily's response to that line.* "Don't you have a ride to catch, Mr. Wilson?"

Unfortunately, grad students loved nothing more than a mission. Case, Mac realized glumly, happily relieved of his own conundrum, had his teeth firmly in this one.

Which would have been fine, if it wasn't her.

"I promise to think about it, Case. Oh, no," Mac forestalled his next out-burst. "This is where I get to pull rank. End of argument."

He chewed on his lower lip, then nodded. "You promise, though."

"Go chop fish heads," Mac suggested with a grin, making a shooing motion with her hands.

She closed and, as an afterthought, locked the door to the terrace, before making one last walk-through of her office and lab. She opened cupboards. Counted Emily's boxes of belongings. Found a hose clamp in the wrong drawer and put it with the rest.

Strange, how final it felt.

Mac shook off the foreboding. She was tired. Tired and thoroughly offended by the current state of things. Neither led to peace of mind.

Of course, it didn't help her mood to return to her office to find two black-garbed monoliths guarding her desk.

They'd left their visors down for some unfathomable reason. *It had to be hot in there,* Mac thought, not for the first time. She scowled until, one after the other, they flipped them up on their helmets. The revealed faces shared a sheepish look. "Jones. Zimmerman," she acknowledged, feeling uneasy. *Nice guys; but they never came to her office like this.* "What can I do for you?"

"Hi, Mac," Jones said. "We're here to help you pack."

Mac reached down and grabbed her bag, holding it up for inspection. "Done."

Zimmerman, dark-skinned, dark-haired, and perpetually dark of mood, so far as Mac could tell, heaved a sigh, rattling something loose among the weapons clipped to various parts of his armor. "Told you we didn't have time for supper, Sing-li."

"I thought you'd left by now," Mac commented.

"We're waiting to take you to join the others at the university," Jones informed her.

Were they, now.

Mac tightened her grip on the bag handle. "Why?"

The two exchanged looks, likely reflecting on other situations involving that question in that tone from Mac. "It's a nice campus. Great facilities—"

She lifted an eyebrow. "I do know the place. The point, gentlemen?"

Jones managed to shrug his encased shoulders. "It's a secure option, Mac," he told her. "'Sephe's already there, doing the prep work. After what's happened—well, we all felt some extra precautions might be necessary. I know you won't be happy about this, but—"

"Why wouldn't I be? Sounds perfectly reasonable," Mac said blandly. "Just give me half an hour to locate the samples I'm taking from storage. One of the courses we're teaching has an anatomy component. Where shall I meet you? Front entrance? Back here?"

They probably should leave their visors down more often, Mac decided, amused by the war between suspicion and relief on their faces.

Suspicion won. "We'll come with you," Zimmerman said. "Help you pack."

Mac smiled. "Perfect." She slipped her arms into the shoulder straps of her bag, and waved her "helpers" onward.

Mac had no idea what Kammie and the University of British Columbia would make of five preserved orca heads, two bottles of giant squid eyes, and fifty-three huge, "too good to discard but on the way to rancid" clumps of mutually cemented rock barnacles. If they got there.

As expected, however, her "samples" made admirably awkward burdens for two overly helpful Ministry guards.

By the second load, they'd begun working together, leaving her to pull out the next load from the stas-unit in Pod Four.

By the third, Mac was no longer at the stas-unit, but on her way to Kitimat, having squeezed herself and her bag in with a bunch of homebound and very happy Preds students, much to the delight of Case Wilson.

"Vacation, here I come," she told him, dropping into the tiny space they'd cleared her for a seat.

She hoped the universe would behave itself while she was away.

- Encounter -

*O*EISHT WALKED restlessly up the hillside, each step bringing front legs forward, brace, then drawing the hind set through. The rhythm was soothing and efficient. *Oeisht* covered ground rapidly, each step a surge of muscle and bone.

Behind *oeisht,* on the lower third of the slope, *aisht* huddled in the homes of the settlement, *isht* of every life stage safe in their pouches.

Safe. Was there meaning to the word? This far from kin, *oeisht* panted with despair. *Oeisht* had seen for *oeishtself* the desecration of the farmland in the next valley to this. A single *isht* had survived, jammed inside a hollow roof pipe, the only living thing between the hills of scoured rock. Too young to grieve; too young to have concepts for what had happened.

But Others knew. Others had sent urgent messages. Travelers, the infertile *aisht,* restless, always seeking, ever curious, had interpreted their meaning for those who dwelt within the Pouch of their kind.

Oeisht let the latest swing forward of his hinds stop, easing to his haunches. By the new thinking, the Pouch was far larger than this one place. *Oeisht, aisht,* and *isht* lived on a world within its star system, that star within a cluster of stars, that cluster, within others. *Oeisht* wasn't a theologian, but this new concept, that the dark sky of night was itself the inner folds encompassing the universe, had a good feel, a comfort to it.

Oeisht had come to the hilltop for comfort. Now, *oeisht* gazed upward, elongating and thinning *oeisht's* eyestalks to sharpen the focus of the stars winking above. Each, if *aisht* were to be believed, might have worlds, worlds with those who had eyes looking toward *oeisht. Oeisht,* out of sight of *aisht,* who might think *oeisht* foolish, flared ears in greeting. Then, *oeisht* crouched, retracting ears and eyestalks.

The stars were wrong.

The stars were coming closer.

Oeisht leaped to all fours, surging downslope in prodigious leaps, moaning *oeisht's* despair.

The stars were faster.

And they brought the Dhryn.

It is the way of the Great Journey that what can be gathered cannot satisfy. That which is Dhryn cannot be filled.

That which is Dhryn . . . *hungers.*
Only at Haven, will there be enough.
All that is Dhryn must move.
Or all that is Dhryn will end.

- 5 -

REST AND RECRIMINATION

MAC COULD SEE them all now. Case, triumphant. Kammie, openly smug. The Ministry's finest probably still explaining the presence of orca heads and the absence of hers on campus. Her father, who'd let her pretend this trip had been her idea all along.

"Vacation, hah!" Mac grumbled to herself, staring out the window of the public lev. "Bet I last two days before I'm bored sick or resorting to chocolate."

Since she'd been one of the last to leave, there hadn't been an onerous round of good-byes. Suited her mood. *They wanted her gone for three weeks? Fine. She'd go.*

From Kitimat, Mac had caught a public lev to Whitehorse, another to Ottawa—in which having two seats to herself meant room to nap—and this last to North Bay, where she'd stood for the final leg to let a family with young twins and even younger kitten sit, or rather squirm.

Par for the course. *Weren't vacations supposed to be relaxing?* So far, Mac hadn't seen any evidence of it. Other things, yes. Vidbots hovered everywhere, in the doorways and passages of transit lounges and hotels, even hung from the ceilings of stores and restaurants. Governments swore those in public areas were reactive and nonrecording, keyed to switch on only if a disturbance was detected or during special events to provide news feeds. Rights groups kept testing that claim; the average person hardly noticed the things anymore.

Mac did. They weren't allowed in Castle Inlet. Away from that refuge, she resented their little shadows, felt their presence like weights on her shoulders, knew a steady anger that they kept watch on her family.

She liked the devices even less, having been tracked by one on the Dhryn world. *Emily's trick.*

Then there was the pace. Mac was used to taking transit off-hours and to odd locations. Now, she was forced to join the brunt of the Human stampede. *Worse than students heading to supper on Pizza Tuesdays.* Her initial curiosity over why all of these people had somehow picked her route to follow soon changed to a frantic hope they'd all go somewhere else entirely.

Fortunately for her sanity—and peace aboard public transit—by the time she reached North Bay everything eased to a civil crawl. The station received only one lev an hour, so she disembarked to welcome, open space. *No more elbows and backpacks threatening her nose.* Even better, the ever present vidbots became scarce, then nonexistent. Not much to watch in the northern woods, and fewer places where being watched was permitted. *Part of the charm.*

From the station, Mac shared a ride with a group of cottagers just in from Toronto to the Misty River Cottage Association docks. The courtesy ferry was, as always, nowhere to be seen, so the cottagers shared their picnic with Mac while they waited, along with their eagerness to check on their respective properties after the long winter. Ice breakup north of Algonquin had been two weeks later than predicted; relying on such predictions, Mac agreed with the cottagers, was about as smart as feeding bears from your porch.

They were pleasant, cheerful people, intent on leaving their mundane lives behind while "up at the lake." Much as she hated to admit it, Mac began to warm to the concept. Maybe this enforced vacation wasn't such a bad idea. Each stage of her journey had seemed to lift a layer of dread from Mac's shoulders. Each took her farther from what might be, back to a time when her biggest concern had been getting Sam to notice she was a girl. That, and making it into the school of her choice.

She had a new definition of life crisis now.

The ferry arrived midafternoon, an actual float-on-water boat with an equally quaint waterjet engine that purred quietly to itself as its operator brought it to dock. Wide and low to allow room for cottagers and whatever paraphernalia was going up with them this year, the ferry's only protection from the elements was an awning over its stern half. The awning and seat cushions had once boasted vivid red, purple, and yellow stripes, now mellowed to pastel by sun and time.

The sun, as suited mid-May, was set to brilliant, as if it had forgotten all about spring and gone straight to summer. Mac drank in the intense blue of the sky, marked only by a few puffy white clouds stuck behind the low rolling hills to every side. The ferry headed upriver, loaded with carryalls of food and other supplies, bits of cottage-ready furniture, and a stack of mem-wood for a tree house that would be a surprise for a trio of lucky great-grandchildren.

They chugged peacefully alongside tilting cedars, reflections mingled with the lichen-stained boulders of the shoreline. The forest had a manicured look, branches starting a tidy two meters or so up every leaning trunk. Not the work of a gardener, just the heavy snow pack pressing lower branches down until they snapped. There were still patches of dirty white snow here and there in the shadows, the remnants of deeper drifts that grudgingly melted away.

Mac sat on the bow, bare feet dangling to either side despite the occasional splash of still-cold water, elbows on the gunnel so she could lean forward with her chin in her hands. The sun was warm on her back; the ferry slow enough she could see the river bottom clearly. Mac watched for turtle scrapes and schools of darting minnows, counted mussel beds and spied the tail of a pike, lurking beneath a sunken log. A beaver nosed by, bubbles streaming from its fur, staring up at Mac before ducking below the surface.

She smiled.

The river took a wide bend, then they were at the lock to Little Misty Lake. Rapids tumbled white and busy beside the structure which lifted water and shipping more peacefully between levels. Like much in this part of the world, the lock was revered as an antique worth saving and considered a hopeless and expensive bottleneck to progress. Usually at the same time, by the same people.

Once inside the lock, Mac helped slip the rope from the ferry's prow around the cable running from the top of the lock wall to below the water. She ran her real fingers along the corded steel. It was cold and wet, slimed with algae, utterly practical and simple. She experimented with her new fingers, trying to detect any differences in sensation. None. The cable and its predecessors had been here, doing their job, since before humanity achieved orbit. *Her new hand would probably outlast her, too,* Mac decided, amused.

The gates closed behind them and the lock began to fill. Mac and one of the cottagers at the stern guided their respective ropes up the cables as the ferry rose. The operator, meanwhile, was lying back in his seat, hat over his eyes. After a few moments, a gentle snore began to compete with the gurgling of water around the hull. *A little early in the season for the novelty to have worn off,* Mac thought, then yawned herself.

Little Misty, despite its name, wasn't small. It was one of those long and convoluted northern lakes, deep and cold, filled with rocky, tree-bearded islands. Its shoreline was a sequence of points and hidden tiny coves, making it possible to surprise a moose or otter every few minutes.

The ferry operator paid attention here. May meant deadheads in plenty— floating logs, often marked by little more than a twig dimpling the water's surface. There were rocks below as well. Mac could see them from her perch on the bow. Great jigsaw pieces of basalt loomed from the depths like the broken pavement of a giant's road or the ruins of a vast city. Fish cruised every edge, hovering over drops so deep the bright rays of sunlight faded to black. Other times, the ferry slid past uplifted stone whose eroded surfaces kept a painted score of past collisions at low water.

They put the cottagers ashore first. All were on Heron Island, the second largest on the lake. Someone's son had come a week earlier to set out the floating docks. Mac helped carry belongings and construction materials from the ferry to land, amid numerous, earnest pleas to visit sometime. Having seen the amount and quality of food these particular cottagers were laying in, she didn't say no.

Mac's destination was at the far end of the lake. She was as eager to reach it as the ferry operator, who reminded her, several times, that he'd have to be back through the lock by twilight or sleep over.

Around a final string of islands, ranging from bare rocks with the requisite possessive gull on each, to a stunning tower crowned by gnarled white pine. An osprey watched them from the skeletal tip of the tallest tree. Then, another cove, so much like the others the operator gave Mac a doubtful look.

"That's it," she assured him, tying her boots to her bag and making sure that was secure on her back.

No dock here. The operator brought his boat in until the keel kissed the sandy bottom. "Thanks," Mac told him. She hopped over the side, sucking air through her teeth at the bite of chill water on her warm feet and ankles, and waded to shore. She waved good-bye as the ferry headed home, not that the operator turned to look.

Mac dropped her bag on a flat stretch of rock and let out a sigh.

"Been a while," she whispered.

Behind her, forested hills, deep lakes, and flat marshes marched north until the tundra began, an expanse of wilderness punctuated only by small quiet towns and isolated camps. To live here year-round was to accept seasons, value solitude, leave doors open for strangers and, above all, depend on oneself. Preparation and habits mattered here, helping you survive when civilization wasn't around to help.

Cottagers—those summer migrants—who wanted only to play, party, and unwind didn't come this far, and certainly not to lakes like Little Misty where you couldn't zoom around on skims or have every modern convenience delivered to your door. *To come here . . . to stay here,* Mac thought, perching comfortably on that piece of driftwood the size and shape of a dragon's head, the one which had waited for her here as long as she could remember, *you had to let yourself assume another shape.*

She lay back along the wood, soaking in sun and silence, and let her tears flow.

Before the shadows lengthened too much more, Mac put on her boots, grabbed her bag, and headed up the hill. It was a steep slope, slippery with last autumn's leaves, but there was a stair of a sort. Where the winding path didn't take advantage of natural rises in the rock—themselves treacherous when wet, short pieces of wood had been set sideways in the slope to provide a foothold. Surprisingly, most were still intact, though Mac stepped carefully and, near the top, had to avoid eroded sections where the path had become steeper than the hillside.

She climbed past the cedars, through arrow-straight white pines, until a glint of reflection ahead marked her goal. A red squirrel, tail flailing back and forth, scolded her from a branch overhead. "Is that any way to welcome someone?" Mac told it. Unimpressed, the squirrel cussed louder.

The cabin sat within a circle of pines whose tops met far above. For a wonder, nothing seemed to have fallen on the roof besides pine needles and cones. It was a rambling structure built to take the weather, nothing fancy or pretty about it except the aging logs of its construction, and more bunkhouse than home. The senior Dr. Connor had routinely brought up students and visiting peers as well as family. Family, particularly Mac's brothers, had used it for the occasional party, inviting numerous friends. As far as Mac could recall, they'd found room for everyone. Somewhere.

The long building was T-shaped due to an addition tucked on the back, and had a second floor that was mostly slope and tiny, web-coated windows. It did boast that essential northern convenience, a covered porch which circled the front and sides. Visitors were usually taken aback to learn there was a separate outhouse farther into the forest. Not that there wasn't indoor plumbing, but it saved having to power up the cabin in winter.

Otherwise, the landscape was as it had been, a hush of moss and pine.

Mac climbed the five steps to the porch and unlatched the outer screen door, ready to jump to the side if any recent occupants made a run for the woods.

Nothing large, anyway. She opened the door to the cabin proper and could hear a rustle or two that likely meant squirrels in the rafters or mice under the floor. Stepping inside, she gazed around, admiring the abundance of right angles. Pod Three was home, but she'd developed a positive hunger for the perpendicular.

The first floor was divided in thirds, with sleeping quarters to the left and right. In the center was the common room, an expanse of dark wood and scattered couches, shelves and tables, with braided rugs tossed here and there on the floor. The massive fireplace on the back wall had been cobbled together from loose stone from the lake itself, glints from embedded crystals of pink, white, and amethyst now catching the low rays of sun entering through the porch and windows. Two narrow doors stood open on either side of the fireplace, one to the kitchen and the other to stairs leading up.

Other than the scurrying of four-footed houseguests, the cobwebs curtaining the windows and hanging from rafters, and the truly remarkable paper wasp nest hanging from the eaves outside, the place did look in "great shape," as Blake had stated. Not bad, considering Mac's father hadn't been up for at least ten years and Mac herself—

She hadn't set foot on the shores of Little Misty Lake or in this cabin since Sam had left for space and died there.

"On the bright side, Em," Mac said aloud, "I finally cut my hair."

While finding someone new to obsess over. Mac put her bag on one of the tables. She'd come for peace and quiet. It wasn't going to happen if her heart gave a peculiar lurch at the mere thought of Nikolai Trojanowski being here with her. Of being alone, just the two of them. Of what it would be like, to discover each other. To . . .

"He probably prefers cities, Em. And blondes. Curvy blondes who giggle and wear sequined nail polish." Mac giggled herself at this. *Though the idea of being here had merit.* Physical attraction, however intense, was one thing—cheerfully sharing an outhouse quite another.

Though, maybe, being a spy, Nikolai liked his women dangerous and full of secrets. Maybe . . .

Mac snorted. "And maybe I should get to know the man better before letting him in my head, let alone through the door. There's the difference between us when it comes to relationships, Emily Mamani," she said as she went to the kitchen. "I don't want any surprises in mine."

Not that getting to know Mr. Spy better was likely to happen.

There were, as Mac had expected, a few nests scattered through the cabin, the most palatial where a chipmunk had hollowed out a down pillow in the upstairs bedroom. All were abandoned, their occupants awake from hibernation and scattered to greener—and mate-filled—pastures. The pantry cupboards had kept out any non-Human guests, though many of the supplies were newer than the rest, implying others had used the cabin and courteously replaced what they used. Others who weren't Blake, Mac chuckled to herself.

Mac made a quick supper of self-heating stew and then took a cup of cocoa out to the covered porch, making room for herself among the cobwebs on the swing. She sat down with care; the old chains and wood held.

A loon called urgently in the distance, a spring arrival eager for company.

"Better you than me," Mac told him peacefully.

Compared to the vastness of mountains, ocean, and rain forest offered by Castle Inlet, or the glaciers, canyons, and powerful rivers of the inner ranges, the view from the porch wasn't much. A small sweep of dark blue lake, a couple of rocky islands, the approach to the cove below, all framed by pine branches, several bare of needles. If Mac went upstairs and bothered to clean a window, she could see a bit farther. Catch the osprey on its perch during the day, spot the Milky Way at night.

Yes, there were more dramatic vistas, but this one offered an intimacy she'd experienced nowhere else. With the exception of the stars, she could be part of everything she saw. She could climb the trees and smell sap on her fingers; lie on the rocks and be warmed by the sun; swim to the islands and hear her heart in the waves. She could cup lake water in her hands and drink, feel it trace the inside of her throat to become part of her.

And having been to the stars, Mac decided, *she'd take this anytime.*

Her father had picked this spot for its owls, several species calling this forest home year-round, the rest visitors in season. Tiny, opinionated screech owls, hopping through the bush at night. Curious great horned owls, who'd stare down from their perches, heads pivoting almost full circle to follow what Humans were doing. Busy barred owls. Arctic owls, alien and elusive. More. Mac planned to hike to some of the old nest sites while she was here. There had been three within a few hours' walk, ten more if they camped out at night. Some would likely still be occupied and Mac would record what she could. Her father'd be pleased to catch up with his "old friends."

Recording. Mac frowned. She'd left her imp on her desk at Base. Partly by accident during the rush to elude her keepers, partly consciously. She'd seen no reason to stay connected to the world or to her work while she was away on this forced rest. *Okay, maybe some petulance in there,* she admitted to herself. The Ministry hadn't wanted her input when she was accessible.*Why make it easy for them to contact her now?*

It wasn't as if she was hiding. Or could hide if she wanted to. Thanks to the nans injected into her bloodstream by Nikolai Trojanowski, her DNA signature had been replicated and concentrated in her liver and bone marrow. As a result, finding Mackenzie Connor—or her remains—anywhere on Earth took only the right equipment and motivation.

Mac shrugged. *Old news.*

Of course, right before the injection, which had hurt like hell, there had been that kiss. She traced her lower lip with a finger, imagined a tiny scar. There had been anger. Blood. Perhaps passion. Certainly, regret.

More old news.

She focused. *Owls.* There might be a recorder stored somewhere in the cabin. Or she could buy one when she went for supplies. Fresh-baked bread would be nice.

Mac pushed the swing into motion with one foot, having made enough plans for one night.

May in the great boreal forest shared one thing with the same month in Castle Inlet. *Life, getting on with life.* Mac shut the screen door on a horde of disappointed black flies and shook the remaining hitchhikers from her hair. It never failed to amaze her how the insects all seemed to emerge, ready to feed, on the same day. At least it meant hummingbirds and swallows wouldn't be far behind.

"Mackenzie? Mac? It can't be! *Bienvenue, ma petite!!!!* I can't believe it."

Mac was swept into a tight hug every bit as warm as the voice. *"Bonjour,* Cat." For an instant, she let herself indulge in feeling safe, of being known and loved without question, then pushed gently to free herself. There was no safety, even here.

But there was Cat Palmer.

The proprietor of Little Misty Lake General Store stepped back to study her with those bright blue eyes. Joke was that Cat could not only see in the dark, she could see a kid "thinking" how easy it would be to tuck that chocolate bar or fishing lure into a pocket. Kind eyes, with the puckered corners that sun, snow, and frequent smiles left behind.

Kind eyes that began to frown at what they saw.

"Place hasn't changed a bit," Mac said, looking away.

Cat shook her head, its tight curls barely up to Mac's shoulder, and grinned. "Who wants it to?"

The General Store sat where a point divided two coves. Sand and pine needles competed to cover the real wood of its porch and steps, while a gentle shoulder of granite sat companionably close to the east end of the one-story building, so those inclined could clamber up and eat fresh-baked pie while watching for loons. From the doorstep, a zigzag of uneven boards led to the water's edge in either direction. Going west brought explorers to where a small river entered the lake, sandbars and isolated clumps of reed grass framing its mouth. Moose wandered out at dusk, leaving plate-sized footprints in the sand below the water. Going east, a rickety dock floating on barrels stretched out in welcome to where the water was dark and deep enough for diving. It was presently owned by a pelican and several mergansers.

In deference to the waterfowl, dozing in the morning sun, Mac hadn't used the dock. Instead, she'd run her canoe on shore, then lifted it out to lean against the logs set along the beach for that purpose. Accommodating birdlife was tradition here. Any day now, swallows would start colonizing the roof overhang. Cat would fuss and pretend to chase them away, all the while keeping track of how many returned and how well they built their nests.

Inside, the store was a maze of too-close shelves, some filled until they appeared ready to fall, others half empty, as if they'd forgotten what they were to hold. Tourists dropping in to buy bug repellers, ice cream, or tent mem-tape invariably stayed longer. Their children found treasures. Maps to the best fishing holes, eyeballs painted on stones, balls and archery sets in brilliant colors, those card games no one bothered to play at home that kept everyone up at night here, gadgets that must be useful, if only you knew what they were. Cat would offer homemade cider and conversation while the children—and, truth be told, most adults—explored in fascination.

There were local crafts as well, fruits of those who spent the long, short-dayed winters here. Russell Lister, Cat's husband, couldn't say no to any budding artist. Some of those mercifully one-of-a-kind items had been on the shelves as long as Mac could remember.

She picked up a dusty ceramic pig, the eye that wasn't winking aimed at the ceiling, and grinned. "Still here?"

"I don't think Russ could bear to sell her after so long," Cat chuckled. "Now come. Millie sent over a batch of her Chelsea buns. They're still warm."

"Extra walnuts and cranberries?"

"Mais oui!"

Mac followed Cat to the end of the store where three handmade tables competed for window space with a stuffed black bear. The bear was so old its fur had started falling out; years ago someone had taken pity on the beast and applied a sticker to a bald spot. The whimsy became tradition and now the bear's glass eyes peered wistfully from a coating of funny slogans, comic book characters, beer ads, and sparkly place names from all over the world.

And beyond. As Cat grabbed mugs of cider to add to her tray, Mac squinted at the bear's left ear, now covered in a pale yellow sticker inscribed with lettering that looked faintly hieroglyphic.

"Imported," Cat confirmed proudly, taking a seat. "We've started to get a fair amount of traffic from 'out there.' Good spenders. Some of them, anyway."

Aliens. How small they'd made the world. Mac traced the sticker with a finger. "Ferry brings them?" she asked curiously, trying to wrap her head around the non-Human making the trip through the locks in that little boat. Once the ice broke up, Little Misty Lake, and the other rivers and lakes associated with this watershed in the heart of Ontario could only be accessed by canoe or on foot. An essential part of its allure.

"No. We take them tripping from here." Cat pushed over a plate barely wide enough to contain the bun, let alone the syrup and melting icing that oozed down its sides. The confection smelled even better than it looked.

Mac's mouth watered, but her fork paused in mid-assault. There had been only one kind of trip leaving the General Store when she'd last been on the lake. "As in canoeing and camping?"

A brisk nod. Cat was already into her first bite. Around it, she continued: "Russ worked out a deal a few years back with the IU, letting us advertise. He and Wendy—that would be Wendy Carlson, you haven't met her yet. Wonderful girl. Comes up each season. We let the consulate make sure whoever's coming can physically sit in a canoe, walk up paths, be out in full spectrum sunlight, breathe the air—the basics. Russ and Wendy pack whatever odd things have to be in the diet, but that's all the fussing we do. Portage with their own packs, paddle with the rest, sleep on the ground."

Mac blew nutmeg-scented steam from her mug and narrowed her eyes. "So how do the aliens get here in the first place?"

Cat winked. "At night, using one of those pricey stealth levs—the kind that no one notices." A sip of cider. "No complaints yet." She laughed at Mac's expression. "Don't look so scandalized, Mac. As if it's never been done before!"

Only in a bloody emergency! Mac thought, then her own lips twitched. "Sam used his skim more often than not," she relented. "He couldn't stand how long the ferry took." She'd tease him about being impatient; he'd counter about wasting time. The memory was like pulling on old slippers found in a closet, comforting and warm. Startled, Mac took too big a bite of her bun, syrup running down her chin, eyes smarting. Her only worry coming here had been facing the pain of such memories.

Not that the pain would be gone.

"He had plans," Cat said matter-of-factly. "Places to go." Her fingers touched Mac's, once, with understanding. "And he got there. That's more than many can say."

Swallowing, Mac wiped her mouth with a cloth napkin embroidered with mosquitoes, another craft success, then blinked hard to clear her eyes. "You take aliens canoe-tripping," she pointed out. "I doubt anyone else can say that."

If her voice showed any strain, Cat kindly pretended not to notice. "Probably not," she smiled. "You should come on the next trip. Be fun. We could use you."

"Thanks anyway," Mac said firmly. "But I'm up for some peace and quiet, not looking to shepherd novices through the bush—any kind of novice."

"C'mon," coaxed Cat. "You get along with aliens."

"I do?"

"Didn't you get pretty close to that—what was he called—Dhryn? We heard how he helped you during that attack, the one at that place you work. Everyone was so worried."

Mac's blood turned to ice. *Here,* she thought desperately. *Even here. Like a contamination spreading through her life.*

Cat misunderstood Mac's silence. *"Ma pauvre petite,"* she breathed, eyes wide. "What was I thinking, to mention that terrible time, to upset you? I'm so sorry. Here, have more cider. Let us talk of other things, happier things. The bears are awake. I saw a sow with three fat cubs just yesterday. Mac? Mac, don't go."

Mac had stood. "I'll be back for my supplies," she managed to say. "Thank you for—for the cider and dessert."

Cat stood also. She nodded, lips together in an unhappy line, but didn't speak. Another of her gifts, to know when silence was the only answer.

Mac went out the door, pulling it closed behind her. She ignored the clouds of hungry black flies competing to land on her face and ears.

She went straight to her canoe, launched it.

And paddled as if the Ro were behind her.

Three days passed. Mac aired the bedding on lines strung between the pines, keeping an eye on the squirrels to be sure none decided to snatch pillowcases for themselves. She flipped the mattresses in all nine bedrooms, twelve in total, and found only one more nest, this of mice and most certainly occupied, thank you. After relocating the litter and aggrieved mom to a new home in a box of rags, Mac swept the floors.

She tackled the shelves and rafters next, tying together some fishing rods and more rags to reach as high as possible. The windows had to be washed three times on both sides before recovering any sparkle. Cleaning the eaves troughs required a shovel and snips, since they'd acquired not only debris but healthy clumps of goldenrod and several optimistic tree seedlings. She caulked the gap under the doorsill leading into the kitchen, likely the entry for most of her current roommates.

The kitchen and indoor washrooms were in the best shape, likely because both had been used more recently than the rest. Still, Mac spent a morning scrubbing until every surface gleamed.

By the afternoon of the third day, she'd run out of chores. The powered systems had functioned normally from the moment she'd arrived, receiving a feed from North Bay Generation as well as solar backups contained in a pine that wasn't anything of the sort, the device so well camouflaged it hosted a raven's nest every year. Not that much in the cabin required power: a few lights, a boxed furnace which could sit in the fireplace and heat the main room if necessary, water pumps for the washrooms and kitchen, a huge walk-in chiller—presently empty—and a stove, though old, that would have been the envy of the cooks at Base. Dr. Connor Sr. liked to cook.

Not something she'd inherited, Mac grinned as she sat on the swing, now made cozy with clean cushions, and popped the top of a self-heating chili.

There was also a receiver. With an effort of will, Mac had left it wrapped and in its cupboard. The weather station on the outhouse roof would give ample warning of natural and programmed storms. Out here, anything else she'd need to know would be announced by shout from a passing canoe—eventually. She'd spent too many hours trying to eavesdrop on the universe. *It could function without her attention for three weeks.*

Besides, how could she trust the news? Ascendis had been attacked without a ripple of attention. *Better,* she decided, *not to try and sort lie from truth.*

As Mac ate, she admired the porch, brightened by rugs, its screens now free of years of pollen and dust so the breeze from the lake moved lightly through. Black flies and their ilk beat helplessly against those screens, attracted by her warmth and breath but unable to enter. No matter. They could afford to wait. She'd be going out again.

Mac curled her spine deeper into the cushions, feeling the pleasant burn of well-used muscles along with the occasional twinge. *A swim before bed would be just the thing,* she decided.

Tomorrow? Back to the store to apologize and get her supplies. She'd overreacted. "Hard to find peace in a place if you don't bring some with you," Mac informed the black flies.

She'd found a measure of it, tidying the place. Dirt and grime put things into perspective. They didn't belong; effort removed them. The final result was comfort for herself and pride of accomplishment. *Not to mention sheets free of eight-legged friends.*

The sun, about to dip below the southwest shore of the lake, touched fire to water and turned tree trunks to gold.

"Nice one," Mac approved.

Then, while the light lasted, as she'd done every quiet moment alone, Mac pulled a folded sheet of mem-paper from her pocket. Technically, she wasn't supposed to have a copy of Emily's message, if it was from Emily at all and not the Ro using her friend's face as some sort of signature. Or extortion.

Technically, the message had been erased the moment 'Sephe had wiped Mac's imp. Who hadn't been able to promise she could tell Mac its meaning, or if it could be understood by anyone at the Ministry.

Mac opened the sheet, holding it to the remaining light. The red symbols, aligned in columns, each intricate and no two obviously alike, meant nothing to her. From the onset, it had dashed that faintest of hopes, that the damage to the language center of her brain might actually be useful. She had no other resources or knowledge to even try to decipher whatever it said.

But making a clandestine copy for herself the moment she'd returned to Base? *Nothing easier.* "The Ministry should have enlisted students, Em," Mac said aloud.

No to mention have more respect for print.

Mac refolded the sheet and tucked it away. *Silly, to feel better having it.* "Probably a grocery list gone astray."

Or, finally, word from the lost.

The lake breeze was starting to carry a chill. Mac picked up her empty container of chili and went inside.

The moon was below the horizon when Mac walked down the hill to the cove. She didn't need its light anyway. The stars were enough to pick out the familiar path and her bare feet quite adequately informed her of the difference between moss, wood, and stone.

And they found sand.

Dropping her towel, Mac brushed away the solitary mosquito singing in her ear. Early for them. She'd waited until the black flies settled for the night, the chill air of May more than they'd tolerate, but there was always something hungry out here.

She walked into the water, blood-warm at the very edge from the day's sun. Her first few steps were through fine floating debris, the black sawdust and old leaves that drifted up against the narrow beach. Her next steps, the water cooling as it rose to her calves, were over small, sharp pebbles and the occasional larger, smooth stone that she avoided, knowing how slippery each would be.

Thigh-high and out of the shadow of the trees. Bitter here. Her skin tightened in reflex, hairs rising, and Mac's feet began to numb, though the upper water remained warm to the touch. She stretched out her arms, dappling the still water with her fingertips, real and otherwise, watching the ripples stir the stars laying in the lake.

For the water was more than calm. Except for where she touched it, the lake might have vanished, replaced by perfect reflection. Mac stood in the center of a sphere of stardust, divided only by the utter black silhouette of forested hills.

There'd be mist in the morning. She could taste it starting to curl into the air.

In a single swift motion, Mac drew her hands over her head and dove.

She kept it shallow, wary of rocks below. And no more than an arm's length below the surface, the lake was winter-cold. The lightless chill of it drove the air from her lungs and set her heart hammering. It was like some potent liquor, heat following the shock of taste. The water became satin to her skin, slipping between her fingers, catching on her palms, sliding along her sides and legs.

Mac rose with a sputtering gasp. *Awake now,* she grinned and rolled over to catch her breath, leaning her head back in the water so more of its heat escaped, taking tension with it. It was just possible to float with most of her in the relatively warmer layer. She relaxed and looked up at the stars . . .

. . . only to see them blotted out by the hull of a rapidly descending and very silent lev.

- 6 -

CANOES AND CONVICTIONS

"SHE'S OOZING red liquid. Is that normal?"

"Idiot. It's internal fluid. Blood."

"What about the oozing? Is that normal?"

Mac lifted her head to glare at her new guests. "Yes. No thanks to you." She went back to picking gravel from her right knee, thoroughly scraped when she'd swum frantically toward shore to evade the landing lev and managed to beach herself like a deafened whale. *There was,* she shifted uncomfortably, *gravel elsewhere,* but she wasn't removing her towel to find it.

Not in front of the three sitting in the common room, staring at her.

Well, Russell Lister wasn't staring. He was doing his utmost to demonstrate that not only wasn't he staring at Mac now, he most certainly hadn't been staring at Mac when the lev's floodlights had pinned her as she climbed out of the water.

At least the lights had helped her find her towel.

The lev, a monstrous self-important beast too large to land anywhere on the sloping land around the cabin, presently floated in the cove, its driver staying with it. Mac, wrapped in towel and dignity, had tried to ignore it as she limped up the path. But the others had followed her up here anyway, without invitation. Or warning about the eroded section. There'd been a fall or two.

Shame the porch door didn't lock.

"A light was on, Mac," Russell began. "I didn't think you'd be—" He blushed crimson, something that appeared to fascinate his companions.

So much for not *looking.*

North woods protocol: a light meant an open door and willing host. Mac couldn't very well argue the point, having left a small lamp aglow in a window in case she'd needed a guide on her return through the trees. "I'm here now," she said, taking pity on the man's obvious distress.

Like his wife, Cat, Russell was a fixture on Little Misty. The couple had operated their store and guided canoe trips into the various connected waterways for over seventy years. A little weathered by time, like cedar grayed by the sun, but Mac had no doubt both could still outpaddle, outhike, and outlast any in-coming camper, including herself.

Gracious, gentle people. Friendly, with a quiet reserve.

Mac finished cleaning her knee and glanced at Russell suspiciously. *Not to mention insatiable gossips with a wicked sense of humor.* It wouldn't be long before the man's embarrassment faded and the night's little exposé was thoroughly embel-lished—and shared all over the lake.

"It's okay, Russ," Mac gave in. "What can I do for you?" Her eyes slid to the two sitting together on the biggest couch and she automatically switched from English to Instella, the common language of the IU. "What can I do for all of you? My name is—" she hesitated, well aware cultural norms varied. *Then again, this was her family's cabin.* "—Mac."

The alien to the right gave a deep bow, its trisegmented torso letting it fold a disturbing amount while seated. It wore a beautifully embroidered caftanlike garment in shades of browns and golds, large and billowy enough to reupholster the couch. *It did a great job of concealing anatomy,* Mac thought curiously. Shorter of the two, the fabric-covered alien possessed a broad face, wider than it was high—Mac supposed she could call it a face, though there were no features showing through the mass of shaggy gray hair that covered head, neck, and shoulders. A pair of jointed eyestalks protruded from the hair on either side of the head, a purple beadlike eye at each tip. The upper eyes on both sides were looking at Mac. The lower "eyes" were lidded and to all appearances taking a nap.

Its voice was a smooth, immaculate tenor. "We are pleased to make your ac-quaintance. We are Mr. Kay and Mr. Arslithissiangee Yip, respectively. And how are you today, Mr. Mac?"

Before Mac could do more than blink, the other alien belched and announced loudly: "Fourteenth. You never introduce me properly. It's Arslithissiangee Yip the Fourteenth." This alien was close enough to humanoid norm to be wearing a Little Misty Lake General Store cap and sweatshirt, extra large, complete with leering moose on the chest. Close, but not that close. The alien's eyes were side by side, but too small, almost embedded in folds of sallow skin. The nose stuck out a little too far, and had a hard shiny surface. The mouth, however, had full lips, shaped like a Human ideal of sensual beauty. *Well,* thought Mac, *they would have been the Human ideal except for their color.* They were either naturally beige or the alien had made an unfortunate choice in cosmetics, given they parted over four yellowed teeth and a forked white tongue.

Mr. Kay produced a pair of gloved hands from within the voluminous caftan outfit he wore and proceed to groom the hair down the front of his "face" in an agitated manner. "Having a number as part of your name is ridiculous. Mr. Mac does not. I do not. Mr. Lister does not. Mr. Carlson does not. Mr.—"

"Irrelevant. Irrelevant! IRRELEVANT!"

Mac and Russell exchanged looks as the aliens bickered. He shook his head and shrugged. She sniffed as a pungent odor that had nothing to do with pine trees, chili, or cleaning fluids began filling the room, then glared at the aliens. One of them, Mac decided, had released something.

Hopefully, it wouldn't stain the couch.

"Excuse me."

The two ignored her. "Fourteen!" "Do you require I give out your ident number too?" "Idiot!" "You're the idiot!"

Mac tightened the towel across her chest and stood up. "QUIET!"

The one who'd called itself Kay managed to look smug despite the hair.

"My name is Mac, with no 'mister,'" Mac told them. "I've got your names, including the number," she added quickly when Arslithissiangee Yip the Fourteenth opened its mouth. "Now, I'd like to know why you're here." Her look of inquiry included Russell Lister, whose fault this most likely was.

Sure enough, he was the one who answered. "These gentlemen booked a trip with us."

"Gentlemen" either answered the gender question, Mac thought, *or Russell was guessing.*

"So?"

"Five days and four nights. We're portaging into Crow Lake then taking the Sagani River over to that fabulous stand of—" Russell stopped as Mac frowned at him. "It was a last minute booking. They've arrived too early. We can't head in until Friday morning, so—"

"Oh, no," Mac interrupted, aghast. "Don't you even—"

"It's only two nights, Mac. We don't have room at the store and you have all these beds. Cat sent you supplies . . ." This last was delivered with a pleading look.

Two purple eyeballs on stalks and two beady ones did their best to copy it.

Mac gripped her towel and eased her weight off the leg with the throbbing and skinned kneecap.

"The place looks great," Russell added. "You've really cleaned it up."

A hairy head and a becapped one nodded.

If only there wasn't a standing tradition on Little Misty of sending overflow guests to the bunkhouse-style cabin of the Connor family. If only locals like Russell, lonesome after the winter, comprehended that not everyone wanted company.

If only she didn't owe Cat a few dozen favors, including an apology for her abrupt departure . . .

She was going to regret this.

"Fine," Mac growled. "Two days."

"Our thanks, Mac." Mr. Kay reached into his caftan and pulled out a small box, holding it up triumphantly. "And look! I obtained a game of cards from the store in anticipation of our time together."

The second alien gave a hum that sounded downright blissful. "There are numbers."

Okay, Mac thought, scowling at Russell, who was trying—and failing—to keep a straight face.

Already regretting it.

Mac threw her pillow into the air. She'd tried putting it over her head. Hadn't helped. Was it some kind of rule that aliens had to snore? Loudly, arrhythmically, and with alarming pauses as if one or the other had suddenly died? She should have known better than to put them at opposite ends of the cabin. The two front corners might be the largest, best rooms. It didn't matter an iota when she was the one inflicted with stereo snoring.

Mac lay on her back and studied the beams meeting overhead. The moon was up and full, bright enough to pull color from the old quilts on the walls. The racket had probably cleared the nearby woods of anything that could run, including moose and bear. The idea had its appeal.

Then a particularly piercing whistle, followed by a moist sputter and rising moan, made her giggle.

Mac covered her mouth with her hands, hoping their hearing wasn't as good as hers. But it was no use. She gave in, laughing so hard at each new improbable snore that tears poured from her eyes and her heels drummed the mattress.

Finally able to stop, though she still snickered helplessly every so often, Mac got up and sat on the bench under the small window.

What were they? She'd done her best to learn more nonterrestrial biology, but the number of intelligent species, let alone their spread beyond their original planets, made it impossible to know them all. If only she'd brought her imp, she could have accessed the considerable library she'd amassed.

And if wishes were horses, Mac nodded to herself. "I'll ask," she said aloud, wiping a last tear from one eye. "If it offends them, Em, they can leave. If not . . ." *Oh, she knew that itch—her curiosity was fully engaged.* Mac could no more ignore it than stop aliens snoring.

Then another thought widened her eyes. Mac hugged her knees to her chest and considered it.

She kept her promises. But was it her fault that no one, Ministry agent or otherwise, had ever asked her to not question a couple of alien campers about what was happening beyond this system? Casual questions, of course.

Seen any Dhryn lately?

There was no humor left in Mac's smile.

For some reason, falling asleep took no more than a return to bed and snuggling under the covers.

When Mac next awoke, it was to the drumming of rain on the roof. A reprieve, of sorts. She knew perfectly well Russell hoped she'd show Kay and Fourteen, as she'd come to think of the other alien, how to paddle a canoe. It wouldn't be this morning, unless the sky cleared.

She listened as she dressed. No snores, but a promising clatter from the kitchen.

Mac pulled an old sweater over her head and fluffed her hair into a semblance of order—as much as the short, curly stuff ever had these days. Times like these she missed her obedient braid, sacrificed in *grathnu* to a Dhryn Progenitor. She'd been so proud of herself that day. Mackenzie Winifred Elizabeth Wright Connor *Sol*.

She'd believed she was close to understanding the Dhryn.

Fool.

And now, when she least expected it—and hadn't asked for it—she had a new batch of aliens to attempt to understand. *When was the universe going to remember her field was* salmon?

"They'd better not want any hair," Mac grumbled as she went downstairs in search of her guests.

The aliens were, as she'd surmised, busy producing breakfast. The long table, with its top of scarred maple, was set for three at the near end. Fourteen was pouring coffee while Kay stood in front of the stove, stirring something. Mac sniffed cautiously. Despite the condition of the path to the cabin, they'd brought up a considerable amount of baggage, including a crate of 'their' food packed in unidentifiable round packages, most of which had gone in the chiller. She'd learned to be wary of extraterrestrial diets.

Another, bolder sniff. *Bacon?*

An upper eyestalk bent backward, aiming its purple eye her way. "Good morning, Mac!" Kay greeted without leaving his task. "How are you?" He might not have a visible face, but his voice conveyed friendliness. *Always assuming,* Mac thought as she entered the kitchen, *a concept like friendliness meant the same to them both.*

"Fine, thanks. I hope you both slept well?" If there was a certain irony in the question, Mac felt it was deserved.

Fourteen looked up, his small eyes bright. "I hate sleep." Without his Little Misty River cap, she could see he possessed a fine down of reddish hair in a ring on the top of his head. It made him look more Human, one of those who chose to go bald with maturity. Yesterday, Mac had assumed these were young beings, perhaps adventurous students or wealthy offspring after an Earthly thrill. Now, she wasn't sure. "Sleep wastes time," Fourteen informed her. "Coffee?" As Mac nodded, bemused, he snapped at the other alien. "This cooking of yours wastes time, too. I told you to use something ready-to-eat if there wasn't any *poodle* to be had."

Mac blinked, then realized it must be a word without an equivalent in Instella. Still, good thing her Great Aunt Roxy, whose house swarmed with dog-type poodles, wasn't in earshot.

Kay seemed unperturbed by Fourteen's complaints. He turned with a large skillet in one hand, a spatula in the other. "It's ready."

Mac was about to protest she'd make her own, thank you, "poodle" or otherwise, when she saw what was in the pan. Scrambled eggs, fried tomatoes, golden-brown potato slices, strips of bacon. They'd all been in the supplies Cat had sent for her, the store owner foolishly optimistic in thinking Mac had finally learned to cook for herself. "Wonderful," she said weakly, sinking into a chair.

Fourteen finished pouring her coffee, then grabbed a basket of toast from the counter and placed it on the table between them. "Eating wastes time," he announced firmly, but sat as well.

Mac's mouth watered as Kay filled her plate. If it wasn't for the elongated, many-knuckled fingers gripping the spatula, light pink out of their gloves, and the faint, not-unpleasant dried hay smell of the being leaning to serve her, she might have been sitting down to one of her father's meals. That and the hair, which at this range proved to have fine strands like very tightly wound springs, more metallic than gray in color. It moved more stiffly than Human hair, too, and Mac wondered how it felt.

Without thinking, she lifted her hand to find out, then realized that might not be particularly tactful and reached for toast instead. "Looks great," she said truthfully.

Dividing the rest between himself and Fourteen, Kay joined them at the table, sitting to Mac's right. "Please, Mac. Enjoy your breakfast. We don't wait on ceremony," he assured her.

"I'd guessed that," she replied, glancing across the table at Fourteen, who was using a fork in each hand to deliver huge mouthfuls one after the other. Despite having front teeth, he wasn't, Mac concluded, chewing. Just shoveling and swallowing.

Kay's lower two eyes remained closed. Now the lids wrapping his upper ones did the same for a brief second, as if in exasperation. "You must forgive my companion, Mac," he said. "He does know table manners, I assure you." This last forceful and directed at Fourteen.

"Waste of time," came the reply, between rapid forkfuls of potato and egg. "Irrelevant."

Kay, on the other hand, waited courteously for her to start, so Mac took a bite of the egg. It was hot, fluffy, and flavorful. Perfect, in fact. She smiled and nodded at him. "Great," she repeated, having no problem being emphatic.

"Just wait until you taste supper," he assured her, seeming pleased by her reaction.

Trying not to be obvious, Mac kept glancing at him. *How would Kay deal with the hair in front of his face?*

He didn't have to, she discovered. The alien drew open the front of the caftan he wore, the same or identical to last night's garment. The fabric draped as though heavy and stiff but moved as easily as silk. His chest, below the hair hanging down from his head, was hairless and smooth, cream-colored except for a blue-tinged tattoo of what appeared to be a pair of eyestalks staring longingly at one another with lettering between, and a horizontal crease of skin marking a second waist, halfway up his torso from the first.

The crease opened by itself, like the mouth of a recycle bin. Mac's fork, with its delectable morsel of fried tomato, paused in the air a few centimeters from her mouth.

Kay picked up his plate and, using his knife, scraped its contents into the cavity in one tidy swoop. Next, he poured in his mug of coffee. Almost like an after-thought, he took a spoonful of honey from the jar on the table, and carefully dripped the sweet after the coffee.

The crease closed, Kay retied his caftan, then sat back. "Tasty. I do enjoy Human food."

"Just don't forget your supplements," Fourteen reminded the other. His own plate was empty, exhausted forks lying across the middle. "Ready? Let's not waste time."

Both aliens looked at Mac.

She finished putting her fork into her mouth, drew the now-cold piece of tomato from it with her lips, and chewed very deliberately, enjoying the flexibil-ity of her tongue. She swallowed.

"You might want to play some cards," Mac suggested.

"Go fish."

"You 'go fish' yourself."

"You are withholding information."

"Never said I had the—" pause, "—purple spotted fat one with a hat. Go fish."

"I will not. I have counted the numbers! You have the card I need!"

"Do not!"

"CHEAT!!"

Mac shook her head and dried her hands. The argument in the next room was growing louder by the minute. She was sorry she'd even suggested they play. *Aliens.* Hadn't even helped with dishes.

"Is there a problem?" she asked, standing in the door of the kitchen. "Oh."

There were cards everywhere, including two stuck in Kay's hair.

And that smell again. Mac wrinkled her nose.

"Trisulians always cheat," Fourteen informed her in a tone of vastly offended dignity. "It is their nature." Since he was the one balancing on a table, hands paused in midair, Mac didn't have to guess who'd flung the deck.

"We pride ourselves on flexible strategy," Kay rebutted, feeling for the cards stuck to his face. "That is not cheating. You, on the other hand, are a fine exam-ple of Myg predictability. I could tell your every move from the beginning. Boring. Boring."

"CHEAT!"

"BORE!"

"The rain's stopped," Mac announced, walking between the two glowering beings to open the door to the porch. "We could—" she winced inwardly, "—canoe."

The ensuing silence could only be described as shocked.

Mac turned back around. "You did come here to go tripping," she com-mented. "A little practice now will help."

Fourteen scrambled from the table. His center of gravity appeared more to the rear than a Human's, Mac observed. "But there was a storm!"

She glanced outside again. Beams of sunlight were beginning to slice down-hill through the trees. The trees were dripping, but beyond that, she could see the water of the lake. Sparkling and peaceful. "Weather's fine now."

"We're not ready." This from Kay, who moved to stand beside Fourteen al-most protectively. Almost, since the top of Kay's upstretched eyestalks barely reached the height of Fourteen's humanish ears. "And there must be preparations to make first. Many preparations."

"All taken care of," Mac assured him, starting to enjoy herself. "You two can easily fit into a regular canoe and we've several under the porch. Russell left personal repellers, on the off chance you end up in the lake. Just be in clothing you don't mind getting wet—"

They spoke in unison. "Have none." "Left mine in the lev."

Mac's eyebrow rose. Any of her former students would have recognized the look, the one that meant they'd better formulate a new approach now, or she'd do it for them.

"Then strip," she said firmly.

Stripping hadn't been necessary after all. In the face of Mac's determination, Kay had admitted his garment could withstand immersion if necessary. Fourteen had rummaged through the spare clothes Mac's father kept in a trunk until he found some that fit. They were a little musty, but the alien didn't seem to mind—or perhaps couldn't tell.

Oh, for a recorder, Mac wished. Between Kay's mane of overgrown hair and brown-bronze flowing caftan, and Fourteen's proud donning of a faded orange Ti-cats' football jersey and paisley shorts—which revealed rather too much of his lumpy calves—her eyes hurt.

But finally the two stood, albeit with obvious reluctance, beside their canoe. Mac's was nearby. She planned to go out with them, neither having been very reassuring about their ability to swim.

If she didn't know better, Mac wondered, having shown each how to hold and use a paddle, *she'd think canoeing was the last thing they wanted to do.* But they'd paid to go wilderness tripping with Russell. He wasn't going to give them time to adjust to life on the water. It would be heigh-ho, a full day of paddling to go. The least she could do was provide a few pointers.

"Fourteen, you get in the stern—that end," Mac told him after floating the canoe into the cove. She stood in water over her knees and held the craft in the middle, bow just touching the beach. The rain had eliminated the warm surface layer, so the sunshine was very welcome. "Climb down, keep yourself low, hold the sides. That's it. Easy. One step at a time."

Once the alien was turned and seated, he gripped the gunnels of the canoe as if it would tip any second. "Did you call me 'Fourteen'?"

Oops. "Sorry—" Mac tried to remember all the syllables of his name.

"Efficient. I shall be 'Fourteen,' on your world."

"Glad you like it," she said, relieved, and handed him a paddle. "Hold this across the canoe. Don't move till I say so. Kay, your turn."

The second alien, the Trisulian, took a quick step back. "The boat appears unsteady. It is dangerous."

"Idiot." Fourteen gave a loud belch and brandished his paddle in the air. Mac grabbed the canoe just in time. "I—the boring one—am already in position. What danger is there? Are you not 'flexible'?"

"Kay, you have to eventually," Mac coaxed, trying not to shiver as her blood lost heat to the water's chill. *Think hot, humid July,* she told herself sternly. "It's the only way to travel these lakes. You came a long way to do this. C'mon. I'm here. Take it slow. You'll enjoy it. Trust me."

Kay kept shaking his head. Hard to say if that meant no, or if he was trying to dislodge the black flies that clung to his every hair. Knowing the morning would involve passing through clouds of the wee things, Mac had hung a camouflage disk around her neck, and clipped one on the repeller belts each alien wore. The small devices emitted a compound that confused the sense organs of the insects so they couldn't decide where to land. The disks worked almost as well as Cat Palmer's legendary ability to sit outside all day without a bite.

Well, except on poor Kay. He'd continued to attract black flies as if exuding sex pheromones. The insects were particularly enamored of his eyestalks. All four were coated in tiny black specks, as if dipped in mobile pepper. *No sign they impaired his vision, but that had to be annoying.*

"No black flies out on the lake," she offered. "They prefer land."

Ah, Mac thought triumphantly. *That did it.* Kay went toward the canoe. He moved like a timid deer, arms up and back as if to keep as far as possible from the craft until the last possible moment, each footstep a painfully slow edge forward.

Fourteen began bouncing up and down with impatience, almost dumping himself and splashing Mac up to her chin.

"Stop that!" she snapped, teeth chattering in earnest now. Calming her voice, she continued: "Hold the sides and step into the middle, Kay."

For a wonder, both aliens did as they were told. Mac made sure Kay was turned and securely seated, with a paddle in his hands, before she pulled the canoe around to point out into the cove. She gave it a gentle push into deeper water. "Remember what I showed you about paddling. Try it now. Gently. At the same time, if you can."

Their first strokes weren't bad for amateurs, Mac decided. No flailing about or splashing. Not too much power. Reasonably straight. "Very good," she complimented, then added: "Just don't argue."

Mac hurried to shore to launch her own, smaller canoe. She didn't bother to dry off before jumping in to follow. The sun would do that.

As they left the cove, a curious loon took one look at the canoeful of nonterrestrials and submerged.

They may have hesitated and fussed, but the two of them worked together well. Their canoe left a zigzag wake, but was heading in a more-or-less consistent direction. Mac studied the movement of their arms and shoulders, comparing them with her own. Similar body parts, able to perform similar functions. Perhaps there was more muscle layering Fourteen's shoulders, but Kay, though shorter in height, had reach on him, and what appeared to be a more flexible elbow.

Mac called out some instructions; they listened and began moving in a straighter line. *Quick learners.* She had to dig into her paddling to keep up.

She was sure Kay and Fourteen had never canoed before, Mac mused as she eased into the soothing rhythm of reach, pull, twist, and hold, but judging by their ability and the way they carried themselves in general? She might not know the norm for their respective species, but she'd bet both were active individuals among their kind, able to use their bodies well—perhaps exceptionally so. Hardly unexpected in anyone who would travel light-years to camp in an alien wilderness.

Why make such a trip? she wondered. *Didn't their worlds have wilderness?*

Mac had only experienced two alien planets, both Dhryn. The first had been Haven itself, the world where the Dhryn Progenitors, mothers of their species, lay deep underground. Haven's surface had been totally urbanized, every square centimeter containing only the Dhryn and their buildings. The second? She had no name for it. The planet had been the Dhryn home world, before a cataclysm stripped it of all life, leaving wind to carve its haunted, dust-coated ruins. A cataclysm repeated throughout the hundreds of worlds of the Chasm.

The Ro claimed the Chasm had been caused by the Dhryn. That they'd destroyed their own world. That unless found and destroyed first, the Dhryn would wreak the same havoc throughout known space.

Green drops dissolving flesh. Mouths that drank . . .

Mac shuddered. She had sufficient nightmares—she didn't need them in broad daylight, too. "Keep to the shoreline," she told her pupils. No need to shout; sound carried admirably over the calm water. Fourteen lifted his paddle in acknowledgment and almost tipped their canoe. Mac winced, but they righted again. "And watch for logs and rocks," she advised.

She'd given them the novice craft, glad to have found it under the porch instead of borrowed yet again. It looked like hers, though a bit larger and heavier, being cream-colored with mem-wood seats and gunnels. Novice craft, however, had certain additional features. There was a keel that expanded downward if a strong broadside wind was detected, giving more control. If they struck anything, the canoe's bow would absorb the impact and, if they tipped too far to one side suddenly, the canoe would release a stabilizer bar to recover itself. *Not that she'd told them.* Russell's canoes were like hers, the classic dance-with-me-or-swim type. Kay and Fourteen might as well start thinking that way.

So far, the two were doing fine. As they entered the next and wider cove, Mac let her mind drift again. *Alien wilderness.* Until now, she'd focused on learning about various aliens and their cultures. There had to be so much more.

There had to be worlds different from the Dhryn's, worlds like this one, with life everywhere you looked. She rested her paddle on her lap and gazed over the side of her canoe. Streams of tiny light-touched bubbles rose from the silt as bacteria digested debris. A twisted thumb-wide furrow led to a mollusk where it sat, pretending to be a rock. Fish fry—barely more than eyeballs and tail—skittered through the bubbles; their shadows flying over the shell.

What would she find in a lake on another world, under another sun? Mac shivered, not because she was still cold, but with the sheer delight of it.

Mac dipped her paddle again, shattering the view. The Dhryn. They were the puzzle. *How could such beings even exist?* She could comprehend, if not envy, those who lived apart from other living things. The Dhryn she'd met had fed themselves with cultivated fungi, simple organisms refined into an industrial process. There were Human colonies on inhospitable worlds who lived much the same way.

For that matter, she knew a few individuals on Earth who managed to live as though they were the only life on the planet.

"But we didn't start that way, Em," Mac whispered. "We can't survive that way. Not without technology to replace all this—" She gazed over the lake, up at the sky with its fading wisps of gray clouds, down again to the tree-fringed shore.

The IU had sent archaeologists to the Dhryn home world. Good as far as it went, but Mac had urged them to send those who would look much farther back, to when the first Dhryn had floated toward its prey. "There's an answer, Em." She nodded to herself, once, firmly. "There's a way being a Dhryn, how they live, all of it, makes sense."

Not that she had the faintest notion what that could be.

"Yet," Mac promised herself.

While distracted, she'd temporarily lost sight of her charges. Like all beginners, they'd learned to pick up speed before developing skill at maneuvering. Unworried, Mac sent her canoe around the next point, only to frown. No luck. She was about to activate the finder beacon—another handy aspect of a novice-level canoe—when she spotted a familiar brown and orange well past the next island, bobbing in the now-choppy water of the middle of the lake.

More speed, but less sense of direction.

Mac shook her head and paddled after them.

"Kay complains the world continues to move up and down, side to side. Along with his *douscent*."

"His what?"

Fourteen pursed his generous lips in thought, then gave a nod. "His pouch-storage-assimilation organ."

Mac didn't know how well Fourteen could read Human expressions. To be on the safe side, she arranged her face into something sympathetic. "Sounds as though he's seasick—a sensory conflict due to the motion of the canoe over the waves. If that's it, Kay should be better shortly." *A Human would be, anyway.*

Her compassion was wasted. "Irrelevant. He's a coward," Fourteen declared, "even for a Trisulian. Afraid of being hungry. Afraid of high places. Afraid of moving water."

Why the little . . . "You took him out there on purpose," Mac accused.

A sly tilt of his head. *Not quite a yes. Not quite a no.*

"Flat water is boring. Waves are fun." Fourteen settled deeper into the couch, stretching his arms along the back. His expression could only be called smug. "Kay ate too much Human food this morning and refused to take medication before our paddling. He has only himself to blame. Idiot."

Mac hoped this meant the Trisulian would be able to manage rough water during their trip with Russell. Otherwise, it was going to be a very long and unpleasant five days for all concerned. Except perhaps for Fourteen, apparently vastly entertained by his companion's discomfort.

At least she had her chance to talk to one of the aliens alone. She would have preferred Kay, simply because he had better manners. *And there was that smell.* Mac was reasonably certain it came from Fourteen when he was agitated. *So don't get him upset,* she warned herself, resigned to whatever happened.

Mac draped a leg over one of the fat arms of her chair and made herself comfortable. It wasn't easy, when she felt anything but relaxed. "While we wait for Kay's *douscent* to recover its equilibrium, Fourteen," she said casually, trailing her fingers along a line of mending in the fabric of the other chair arm, "mind if I ask you a few questions?"

"You may ask, but there will be none of this—" Fourteen thrust his pelvis up from the couch with great vigor. Three times. It was quite a display, given the oversized paisley shorts. "Impossible. I don't have external genitalia," he explained.

Emily, Mac knew, *would be convulsing with laughter.* She, on the other hand, could feel her face flame with embarrassment. "I didn't—"

"I'm well aware of the Human preoccupation with copulation with aliens, Mac. Do not seek to deceive me. There was a brochure."

"A brochure," she echoed.

"At the consulate. It strongly recommended informing any Human making advances that I state an appreciation of the implied compliment but explain I am physically unable to participate and would prefer to be left alone." Fourteen paused. "I didn't waste time with the appreciation part. I don't feel complimented by your lust."

Mac blinked. "My lust."

Fourteen threw up his arms in what appeared to be exasperation, then clambered to his feet. "If you are so desperate for the act, I believe Trisulians have some capability. We will go to Kay and obtain his service for you."

"That won't be necessary," Mac assured him. "I—I've taken a drug to subdue my carnal urges," she said matter-of-factly. "Being here alone?" Mac gave a theatrical shudder. "It would be so very—difficult—otherwise. I'm sure you understand. It must have been in the brochure."

It was his turn to blink at her.

Fourteen's mouth suddenly stretched in a huge grin, revealing that his teeth consisted solely of four squared incisors on top and a chitinous ridge along the bottom, with that disturbing white tongue lashing between. His inset eyes opened as much as they could as he gave a harsh barking sound Mac had no trouble translating at all.

When Fourteen finally stopped laughing, he claimed: "I had you! I had you!"

As if she'd admit that. Mac raised one eyebrow. "Not for a millisecond."

The alien pointed to the door to the west bedrooms. "We can try it on Kay. C'mon. C'mon." He was bouncing on the couch, his splay-toed bare feet slapping the wood flooring.

"No." Mac threw her other leg over the chair arm and slouched deeper. "And no. Just how immature are you?"

"As immature as I want to be," Fourteen asserted, sounding slightly offended. "I'm on vacation."

Mac grinned. "I can't argue with that. Though I confess I'm wondering why you've come all the way here. To Earth, I mean."

Fourteen dropped back down on the couch, looking pleased by her question. *His knees,* Mac noticed, *were another almost Human feature.* If you ignored those extra lumps on the insides. They sunburned like Human knees, too. He'd come prepared, she'd give him that, slathering an ointment over his reddened skin when they'd arrived back at the cabin. A bright green ointment with what appeared to be flecks of sand in it. *Positively alluring,* Mac chuckled to herself, *with the paisley shorts.*

Fourteen held up his five-fingered hand, folding a digit with each item. "Earth has exotic landscapes . . . varied cultures, hardly touched by those of other species . . . the legendary politeness of Humans . . . a most favorable exchange rate within the IU. And—" Fourteen paused, one finger still straight, and looked at her as if trying to read her face.

"And?" Mac prompted, fascinated by this view of her world. *Exotic? Polite?*

Another voice answered—Kay, from where he leaned one shoulder against the doorframe.

"And Earth has you, Dr. Mackenzie Connor."

Without realizing she'd moved, Mac found herself behind her chair, her hands gripping its back for support. Common sense had her eyes flicker to the door to the porch, estimate her chances of getting there first.

Curiosity held her still.

"Not on vacation," she stated.

"Unfortunately, no." Fourteen sat up, his posture subtly different. *The hand-me-down Human clothes,* Mac thought, *no longer looked quite so silly.* He reached into a pocket of his shorts and brought out an envelope that looked remarkably familiar, except that its blue and green was barred with gold. "The Interspecies Union is hosting a gathering of experts on our common problem, the Dhryn. We wish you to attend, Dr. Connor."

"Mac," she corrected automatically, while such fierce joy burned through every part of her, she had to struggle to keep it contained, to hold her expression to something resembling curious interest.

At last, a chance for answers.

"Mac," the Myg smiled. "Efficient as always. Please excuse our small deception. Mr. Lister will be paid in full, but we never intended to take his trip. We had to come in person. Our invitation was not reaching you through, shall we say, regular channels."

Why was she not surprised? The taste was bitter, as was the certainty others would have known about this—and how desperately she'd want to be part of it. "Then how did you find me?" Mac answered her own question: "You're spies."

Kay, weaving slightly, made his way to the opposite chair, sitting with a groan. "We are not spies," he denied stiffly. He reached for a cushion and pressed it to his abdomen. "*Usish.* The room keeps moving."

"Irrelevant," Fourteen snapped. "Do not withhold meaningful information. Mac should know how we found her."

Did she really want to know? A faint mental alarm went off. Ignoring it, Mac eased around her chair and rested a hip on the arm nearest the door. "It would be a nice gesture of mutual trust," she suggested. "Something I could use about now."

The two looked at one another. Kay's eyestalks dipped and rose. As if this signaled permission, Fourteen began. "Since your government would not let us contact you directly, nor pass along our invitation, we arranged for an individual in your facility to notify us when you left for your research in the mountains, somewhere we could contact you discretely, privately. We thought we'd lost that opportunity when the quake struck, then you came here. Everything was perfect!"

"*Perfect?*" Mac could argue the word choice, considering it encompassed an IU spy among her colleagues and students at Base. *Not to mention if these two had walked in on her at the field station, she'd have sent them packing so fast eyestalks would have spun.*

Fourteen offered the envelope. Sure enough, her name crawled across the surface in mauve. *Just like last time.* Then, it had contained a letter from the Ministry, proclaiming a threat to the species and requesting her help—the sort of request no Human would refuse, or could, without the most severe penalty.

Mac eyed the latest incarnation, but made no move to touch the thing. Yet. *Learned my lesson, Em.* No matter how badly she wanted to be part of what was happening, *to know,* she wasn't going to jump blind again. "Where is this gathering taking place?" she asked.

"Irrelevant," came the reply. "Even if we knew, it would be kept from you until reaching our destination. For security reasons."

"Do you object to travel offworld?" This from Kay.

Mac's fingers dug into the upholstery, the fabric a little worn and dusty. Worn by Human use. Dusty from the processes of life on this planet. Familiar. *Home*.

"No," she said calmly. "I'll go wherever I must." She didn't bother asking for a guarantee they'd bring her back again. In Fourteen's terms, it was irrelevant.

Instead, Mac took the envelope in her hands, feeling its familiar metallic texture between her fingers. She drew a breath, then prepared to rip it in half.

"What are you doing?" With that cry, Fourteen tried to snatch it back.

Mac hung on, startled. "I'm opening it."

"Violence is not necessary. Apply any body fluid." Kay then pressed the cushion tighter to his abdomen as if the idea offended his *douscent*.

"Ah." With a doubtful look at each alien, and doing her best to forget the envelope had come out of those paisley shorts, Mac touched the moistened tip of her tongue to one edge.

It unfolded in her hands like a flower, the envelope itself becoming a flat sheet of multisided mem-paper. Its now-white surface was coated in black text beneath the seal of the IU. But as she adjusted her grip to angle it toward the light from the nearest window, the words winked in and out of meaning, sentences fragmented. The more she tried to make sense of it, the less she could understand. It was Instella, the interspecies' language. Mac was sure of it. She should be able to read this with a little work.

Should and could were different things.

Rather than shout her frustration—*and reveal her ongoing issue with print* —Mac casually folded the sheet, which reformed into a sealed envelope in her palm. "Fine," she said. "When do we leave?"

"As soon as I inform the IU you are ready and willing—"

"Not so fast," Kay groaned from his seat, eyestalks tilting in different directions. "Some of us aren't up to moving vehicles."

Fourteen pursed his lips and made a ruder noise than usual. "Idiot. I told you to take your medication. Your discomfort is irrelevant. As soon as I inform the IU, arrangements will be made—including notifying your government, Mac, and the helpful Mr. Lister. Tomorrow would be the earliest for all to be in place. More likely the day after that." He made an expansive gesture at their surroundings, then bounced where he sat. "But is this not an excellent place to wait? We have Mac. And we have *poodle!*"

Kay muttered *"Usish"* again and turned his eyestalks from the exuberant Myg.

Mac tucked the envelope from the IU into a pocket, fastening it closed with a press of the mem-fabric. *One thing to be swept up in the moment, Em. Another to have time to think things through*. She hoped her courage would last two more days.

She slipped her leg over the arm of the chair and sat down. "What else can you tell me about this gathering?"

"It is unprecedented—if you are familiar with the politics of the IU . . . ?" Kay let those words trail into a question. Mac shook her head. "Ah."

"Idiot," Fourteen said promptly. Mac wasn't sure if he meant his companion or her. "All you need to know is that everything about the IU, everything it does, has a shape." His hands described a series of circles, each larger than its predecessor. "At its center are the oldest species, the ones first to the group. The Sinzi, of course, are at the core. Together, these are the decision-makers. Outside of this lie those species who are well trusted by the oldest and are wealthy, or wield some other power. These are asked to carry out those decisions and to communicate them to others. Beyond are all those species come recently to the transects, who haven't proved either economic worth or stability. Informed, but rarely consulted."

"This is the political position our two species share with yours, Mac," Kay broke in. "It would normally remain so, but our systems lie along the Naralax Transect. The IU realizes we must be all included—perhaps even in the innermost councils. This is what is unprecedented." He sounded more exasperated than grateful. Mac could understand that reaction.

Fourteen laced his fingers together, as if in prayer. "You see, the Dhryn are not some nebulous threat to us. They wait on our doorsteps, ready to strike either of our worlds next. Indeed, our closest trading partner, the Eelings, recently succumbed."

"I'd heard Ascendis was attacked. A Human ship was there—it sent a report." *Before it crashed and everyone died or was consumed by Dhryn,* Mac reminded herself, breath catching in her throat. "I don't have the details. What happened?"

"The Eeling light has been extinguished forever," Fourteen's lips trembled and he put his hands over his eyes.

"By the Dhryn?" Mac demanded sharply.

"The Human ship finished the job of destroying Ascendis," said Kay, his voice growing cold and harsh. "To their credit, many of the—feeders—were caught on the surface. But the planet can no longer support the life it knew."

Feeders on the surface . . . Mac shook off the horrific image, focusing on the puzzle. "I was told the Dhryn left the system."

"There was no one to stop them."

Mac leaned back and stared at the ceiling rafters, seeing something completely different, a world made of flesh. "Dhryn wouldn't leave without their Progenitor," she mused out loud. "So she wasn't on the planet when Captain Wu sent his ship into it. But why?"

"Isn't it obvious? They wanted to be able to leave quickly. As they did."

Mac looked at Kay. "Nothing," she warned him, "is obvious about the Dhryn."

"Except the destruction they leave behind," he countered, upper eyestalks rigid. "The only Eelings to escape had crowded into sublight ships and scattered through their system to hide. They are delicate beings, Mac, too delicate for such stress. Most died before they could be found and rescued. Those we did save were taken to our systems, Trisulian and Myg, but a pitiful few are of breeding age, even if they have the will. The Eelings didn't colonize other worlds."

Fourteen dropped his hands, his eyelids glistening with moisture. "It is the end of a vibrant species."

How could the mind comprehend a loss on that scale? Mac didn't even try.

"Worse than that," added Kay. His fingers were busy combing the hair down the front of his head. *A nervous habit,* Mac decided. "We fear—" he made a sharp quelling gesture when Fourteen opened his mouth as if to protest, "—we fear our systems will be next. We'll either feed the Dhryn, or become the chosen battleground where they are fought by the IU. That we will lose, no matter the outcome."

Bureaucracy. Hierarchies. When survival was at stake, Mac thought sadly, *how soon they could become a threat instead of protection. How little the parts could seem to matter, when the whole was in peril.*

She studied the two of them. Whatever else, she had no problem reading the anxiety in their body language—no matter how alien, they shared that peculiar tension of limbs needing to move but forced to wait. "Then we'll have to trust this gathering will think of safer alternatives." Mac tapped her head with a knuckle. "It might just be a case of digging out the right idea."

Fourteen lunged from the couch to grab Kay's arm. "Hurry!" he urged. "There are knives and a spatula in the kitchen!" He peered at Mac. "Perhaps a spoon."

Kay's left eyestalk twisted to glare at him and he shook his arm free. "Mygs have the most inappropriate sense of humor," he said to Mac.

Mac didn't quite smile. "It helps, sometimes."

"Exactly." Fourteen rubbed his palms together, then slapped them on his knees. He cried out and lifted his hands again. From the shocked look on his face, he'd forgotten both sunburn and ointment.

"Now that's funny," Kay announced, eyestalks waving.

Mac sniffed. *Sure enough.*

"Why don't we continue this on the porch?" she suggested. *Where there was fresh air.* "You go ahead. I'll make some coffee and bring it out."

Without waiting for an answer, Mac stood and went to the kitchen. Her hands were trembling as she lifted them to push open the door. She frowned at them. *This was no time to be thinking about a devastated world and its survivors.*

Yet she couldn't help remembering . . . Brymn had come to Earth, sought her out for one reason. Mac's work with salmon considered populations in terms of genetic diversity; she calculated evolutionary units, the minimum amount of diversity required for a group to respond to evolutionary stress without going extinct. The Dhryn . . . he'd asked her about determining the evolutionary unit for an entire species. For a world.

Without knowing what was to come, what he'd become, Brymn had desperately wanted to know it was possible, that she could produce a number, reveal some formula to show how many must survive, in order for some to continue.

Mac pressed her forehead to the door and closed her eyes.

They'd both been so dangerously ignorant. He'd asked for the sake of his kind, fearing their persecution by the Ro, sensing an approaching doom. She'd become his friend, begun to work on the problem, only to learn, too late, it wasn't the Dhryn who were threatened.

But what if Brymn had asked the right question, after all? Mac thought. Not about any one species. About the Interspecies Union. That population. That diversity.

How few species could it contain, and survive? At what minimum would the transects between systems fail, if they weren't first destroyed to keep out the Dhryn?

What if Earth was alone, again?

Mac shoved the door open with all her strength.

The resulting bang didn't startle the man sitting at the kitchen table, who merely leaned back in his chair.

"You do keep interesting company, Dr. Connor," Nikolai Trojanowski remarked.

- Encounter -

THE IMRYA fleet waited with the patience of their kind, settled into position where the Naralax Transect was locked into their system's space, orbiting Mother Sun with the other transects' mouths like one pearl among many. A perilous black-hearted pearl.

Such disturbing analogies were produced each day and posted throughout the fleet, from engine rooms deep in the bowels of every ship, to the suites of the battle cruisers where officers maintained households, from navigation arrays to the galleys. For the Imrya were a lyrical folk, renowned for their poetry as well as the interminable amount of time it took for them to get to any point in conversation.

Trade negotiations with non-Imrya were best accomplished by remote.

Months ago, an Imrya outpost had been decimated by Dhryn. Not that they'd had a name for the attackers back then. Imrya newscasters had spent weeks composing anguished rhapsodies about an unseen terror, an unimaginable power able to eat through safety seals and make entire crews simply vanish as if they'd never existed.

But now the IU had named this fear, that name and warning sent to all. The Imrya, as befitted a species who had contributed to the IU for generations, one of the strong arms upon which all depended, had received even more. Details of ship structure. Potential weaknesses. Unconfirmed rumors of attack strategy.

Warning that where the Dhryn had been, they would come again.

If the Dhryn dared return, the Imrya fleet would be ready.

Watching the poisoned fruit in their orchard.

That which is Dhryn feels fear, knows dread, but not of others.

There is only that which is Dhryn.

All else . . . *sustains*.

That which is Dhryn fears time, dreads distance.

Being too slow? Losing the Taste?

Either ends the Great Journey.

PRODIGAL AND PROBLEMS

MAC QUIETLY CLOSED the kitchen door behind her and latched it. *What did it say about her that her first thought on seeing Nik again, here and now, no matter what else was on her mind, was "yummy?"*

Emily would agree, of course. The Ministry's favorite spy was dressed camper-casual: a faded brown shirt with long sleeves rolled to his elbows and open at the neck, shorts, and sandals. The clothes revealed a pleasing expanse of tanned skin and the working of lean muscle. His brown hair had grown out its office trim, reaching his collar at the back, and was now more waves than curl. No glasses hid his hazel eyes, but a charmingly scruffy beard framed what was almost a smile.

Yummy.

Mac coughed. Her second thought: *keep it safe.* "Is this an official visit?" Cool, a little formal.

She thought he'd been about to rise and come to her, only to check the impulse as she spoke. *She was probably mistaken.*

For her part, Mac concentrated on the spot of floor beneath her bare feet, a spot she had no intention of leaving without answers. "Well?"

"No," Nik said, putting his arm on the table and rubbing the tabletop with his fingers. *If it made any sense,* Mac thought, *she'd swear he looked shy.* "I had some personal time coming."

As if she believed that . . . Mac focused. "Which doesn't explain why you're here."

"No?" The word invited fantasy. Mac felt herself blush. *Wood floor. Toes. Wood floor. Toes.*

"No," she echoed.

"I got a report about the quake. I wanted to see for myself if you were okay. Are you?" This last with concern.

How odd, Em, Mac said to herself, *to be almost more afraid of an answer than of asking the question.* She steeled herself. "Did you cause it, Nik? Did you destroy the ridge?"

"Oh." A wealth of comprehension in one syllable. "No, Mac," Nik said finally. "It wasn't me."

She hadn't been sure. It might have been a wild guess, a slip toward the paranoia she feared as much or more than anything else. To counter the tendency of the floor to betray her and tilt, Mac laid her hand on the side of the nearest cupboard. "So it wasn't natural. Those—" She launched into a lengthy description involving several unlikely acts and more than a few unprintable adverbs.

"Feel better?" Nik asked when she paused for breath.

"I knew it! An earthquake? How bloody convenient—for everyone but us."

"And our people on the mountain."

"What? Oh, no." Remembering those visored heads looking up at her on the mountainside, Mac stumbled to the chair next to Nik's. *There had been over a dozen.* "How—how many were trapped?"

"Luckily, only two. Robillard and Masu were guarding the Ro site. When the quake hit and the slide followed . . . they didn't have a chance."

"No, they wouldn't." Without thinking, Mac reached for his hand where it rested on the table and laid hers on top. "I'm sorry, Nik."

His hand turned, fingers wrapping around hers. Mac met his eyes as they searched her face, felt herself drowning.

Time stopped.

"Mac!" from the other side of the door. "Are you coming? Where's the coffee?" A rattle. "Why won't this idiot door open?"

"A spill. I'm washing the floor behind it," Mac explained, pitching her voice to make it through the hefty door. "I'll be right out, Fourteen." She stood. "Have to go," she told Nik, starting to pull her hand free.

His resisted.

That and his smile did disturbing things to her sense of priorities. "Careful or I'll introduce you," Mac said.

"Later." Nik rose, still holding her hand, then brought it to his lips, pressing them to the inside of her palm.

"Will you—" His beard tickled her wrist, the sensation rushing up her arm. Mac blamed it for the quite remarkable difficulty she was experiencing putting words together. "Aren't you staying—" she heard herself say and flushed crimson. "I didn't mean—"

"Kay needs something for his *douscent,* Mac," the alien bellowed. "He says any bovine secretion will do, but he prefers ice cream. Idiot should have taken his medication when I said so." The voice faded, as if Fourteen muttered to himself as he walked away. "What's a vanilla, anyway?"

"Trisulian, I take it," Nik said.

"And a Myg," Mac sighed. "If I leave them alone too long, they'll get into an argument, there'll be shouting, the place will start to reek—you probably know who'll do that—and then stuff will be thrown around . . . it'll be worse than the last day of class, trust me."

"Always." Nik's eyes laughed down at her. Her lips twitched in response.

"It's good to see you," she confessed. *And it was. No matter why he'd come.* Emily would doubtless have something to say about that.

Nik traced her jaw with a light finger. "I promise I'll be back tonight. Probably late."

"Good thing we don't lock doors up here."

His teeth gleamed. "Think that would stop me?"

Mac put her hands on his chest and pushed gently. "What I think is that any minute now two aliens are going to break down that door in search of vanilla ice cream and coffee. Go. From the sound of it, we're here until tomorrow at least."

As easily push a cliff. "You're leaving with them?" Nik glanced at the closed door then down at her with a darkening frown. "What the hell's going on here? What do they want? Who are they?" He started to walk past her and she grabbed his arm. It was like iron.

"I don't have to tell you," Mac said quietly, "what you already know." Without letting go, since he seemed as tightly wound as a spring—*posturing or real?*—she used her free hand to open her pocket and pull out the envelope. "You came to stop me from accepting their invitation. You're too late. I'm going." She offered it to him.

He took it, all the while staring at her in obvious dismay. "Oh, Mac."

She swallowed her pride. "When you come back tonight—if—I need you to read that to me. Please. I can't."

"And you still agreed to go." Harsh.

"You knew I would. You—" She bit off the accusation that wanted to tumble after; there was no gain to it now. "Even if I'd wanted to say no—how could I? You know what's at stake, Nik. We all do."

"All I know is that you have a limitless capacity to worry me, Mackenzie Connor."

"That's never been my intention." Her hand, her real one, lingered on his arm, trapped by the heat of his skin, the texture of fine hairs, the corded strength beneath her fingertips. "I'd rather—" Mac stopped herself just in time, snatching her hand away. *Emily was the bold one; she wasn't.* "—I'd rather make coffee," she finished breathlessly, heading for the pot. "And you, Mr. Spy, should get going before you're seen."

Looking over her shoulder, Mac found herself alone in the kitchen, the back door sighing as it closed. She put both hands on the counter and leaned forward, shaking her head ruefully. "And how brilliantly smooth was that, Em?" she asked.

Did he guess what she'd almost said? What she'd wanted to say?

Did she even know?

"Seasick alien on the porch," Mac reminded herself. "Serious questions to answer and ask. Saving the universe tomorrow."

She hadn't believed in the coincidence of Nikolai's arrival—less than a day after her new guests—any more than she'd believed in the earthquake. *Right on both counts, Em.*

But if she occasionally thought "yummy," Mac decided, *that was nobody's business but her own.*

The first interspecies' problem of the afternoon was, predictably, Emily.

The second, less predictably, involved poodles.

Mac took a long swallow of her beer and kicked the swing in motion. While she'd been inside, making conversation and coffee, the aliens had rearranged her porch. Kay, understandably not fond of swings at the moment, had brought out one of the overstuffed comfy chairs from inside. Fourteen, who probably did like swings, was not to be outdone, and had somehow maneuvered one of the couches through the door.

As befitted a proper porch gathering, they'd all switched to beer when the sun was low enough to hit the back wall, and were now too warm and comfortable to budge.

The two had listened eagerly to her synopsis of her experience with the Dhryn, asking few questions, seeming impressed—and occasionally dismayed. Now, however, both were firmly stuck trying to comprehend one aspect: Emily—or rather, Mac's continued loyalty.

"Dr. Mamani remains my friend," Mac insisted, trying to find the right phrasing. "Emily—" *lied and betrayed,* "—acted on behalf of the Ro in order to try and stop the Dhryn. I—we—hope she's still safe and with them. It's perfectly normal Human behavior."

Fourteen chugged his third bottle in one long swallow, then belched for an impressive five seconds. "Perhaps 'friend' in Instella does not convey the Human meaning of the word, Mac."

Back to that again. "Perhaps," Mac said, doing her best not to sound testy, "you could convey to me why finding a word to define my relationship to Emily matters, Fourteen. I keep telling you, we have shared experiences, we feel affection. We look out for one another. We get angry; we forgive mistakes. Call that combination whatever word you like and let's move on."

"The clarification is important, Mac." Kay, who'd been alternating scoops of melted ice cream with dollops of beer into his *douscent—which must be about to explode by now,* Mac judged—paused to wave ineffectually at the halo of black flies that had somehow passed the screens to find him. "We need any clue to help identify those of our respective species who might be, like your Emily, affiliated with the Myrokynay—the Ro."

"You believe they've recruited individuals from other species in the IU?" Mac considered this, then shrugged. "Maybe. But there's the issue of the Ro technology—I explained how Emily required an implant in order to communicate with them, to help her tolerate how they travel." *Her fine olive skin, rent along one arm to reveal the depths of space and wheeling stars where flesh belonged.* Mac blinked away the memory. "That's your best way to identify their representatives. But it's likely something not every species could integrate into their bodies."

"We neither believe, nor disbelieve, such recruits exist," Kay replied. "We can't discount the possibility. Such individuals could help us talk to the Ro, convince them to protect us. If the Ro prefer to find those who already claim loyalty and trust like yours, it is somewhere to start."

Mac stared into the forest for a moment. She had to squint to see past the tree trunks to the glitter marking the lake. "That won't help you," she said heavily, turning back to her companions. "Emily was working with the Ro long before we became friends. I didn't tell you—I didn't think it was important." *And still hurt.*

She kept it simple. How Emily had cultivated a rapport with Brymn, how she'd learned of his interest in Mac's work, how she'd managed to be hired at Norcoast, how she'd cultivated Mac as a colleague and as a friend—

Her voice faltered.

"That's enough, Mac," Kay said quietly. "We've no wish to cause you pain. At least, now we know you were right. The word 'friend' in Instella will not bring us any closer to those who work with the Ro."

Fourteen had pressed his hands over his eyes as Mac told her story. Now he dropped them down to gaze at her. "Your Emily did not have to become your 'friend,' Mac," he said. "She could have arranged what she did and still kept her distance from you, safe from exposure or compromise. Perhaps you were what she couldn't resist."

This, from a being who set speed records eating or drinking, and belched or released noxious fumes without warning? "Thank you, Fourteen. You are very kind."

The alien looked embarrassed. At least, that was how Mac interpreted the irregular pink blotches along his cheekbones. *One never knew,* she reminded herself. "Irrelevant," he barked. "It's time to take a break. Have supper. You ready to make some *poodle,* Kay?" To Mac, "This will be such a treat."

Kay's upper eyestalks had developed a droop. *The beers or time of night,* Mac judged. Now they shot erect. "Is this the right time? I thought we were going to save it."

"Idiot! Save it for what? What better time than now? With what our new friend, Mac, will share at the Gathering about our enemy—not to mention your success with the canoe? Tomorrow will be soon enough for more words, words, words, words!" Fourteen bounced on the couch with each repetition. Mac, listening to the creaks of protest, hoped the old furniture survived the alien's gusto. "Tonight, we party! We must have *poodle!*"

Kay patted his middle, having tucked away his *douscent.* "I am a little hungry," he admitted. "And I promised Mac a memorable supper."

So much for Human/alien relations, Mac decided, stopping her swing. "You really don't have to go to any trouble for me," she said cautiously. "Save your supplies."

"Idiot!" Mac supposed it was a positive sign that Fourteen now freely applied the term to her. "It is our duty to share with you the best of what we have brought." His beady eyes narrowed to tiny slits. "Or are you not familiar with *poodle?*"

Kay stood, smoothing his caftan and straightening the mass of hair tumbling over his face. "You insult our host, Fourteen. Mac is an intelligent, cultured being. Of course she's had *poodle* before—no doubt prepared by the finest Human chefs. I will have to make an extraordinary effort to compare. Extraordinary." With that, he strode into the cabin and Mac could hear his determined footsteps heading for the kitchen, presumably to be "extraordinary."

Mac glanced at Fourteen, who was looking insufferably pleased with himself. *They ate her food. How bad could theirs be?*

Given her past experience with non-Human sustenance?

Good thing there was a med kit in the cabin.

"Humans didn't invent outdoor cooking, you know."

Plomp. Mac's stone hit a ripple and sank. "We were searing our meat on grills long before the first transect," she countered.

Fourteen took aim and launched his own pebble into the cove. *Tic . . . tic . . . tic . . . plop.* "Five!"

"You can't count the initial toss as a skip. Four."

They were sitting on the small stretch of sand that Mac's father proudly called a beach, having been banished from both the kitchen and the brick barbeque in the clearing behind the cabin.

It seemed "extraordinary cooking" required privacy and concentration.

"Irrelevant."

Mac found a nice flat stone and tried again. "What's irrelevant?" *Tic . . . tic . . . plop.* "Three."

"That your species has a long record of outdoor cooking. You originally obtained that technology from us, the Myg. Your own history tells of our visits." *Plomp.* "Doesn't count. That was a defective rock."

Mac snorted. "Let me guess. There was a brochure at the consulate."

Another of those sly looks. "Don't you believe your own mythos? That aliens have been here before?"

"Oh, those guys. They were looking for virgins in cornfields." *Tic . . . tic . . . tic . . . tic . . .* Mac lost count and whooped triumphantly. "Beat that, Fourteen!"

The alien made a show of shading his eyes and looking outward. "Beat what? I was watching this small creature dig in the sand. What do you call it?"

Mac gently bumped her shoulder into the alien's. "A beetle, and I win."

"Are there virgins in your fields?"

"All the time. We call them heifers."

Laughing, Fourteen wiggled his bare toes. They were wider at base than tip, so they looked more like miniature fingers than the Human version. Mac noticed he used them quite readily to sift the sand for skipping stones. "You are joking with me again, Mac."

"Maybe so," she said peacefully, resting back on her hands. "Tell me, Fourteen. What do you think of Earth? Of this place?"

He joined her in gazing out at the lake. The sun was about to set, its last rays seeming to calm every ripple. Near the shore, the dark water was already glass-smooth, except where water striders—and skipping stones—briefly disturbed it. A series of expanding rings marked the rising of a fish. Black flies skimmed the beach; midges danced in self-obsessed clouds.

As if on cue, the loon gave its throbbing cry. It echoed from the trees on the opposite shore, then faded to a waiting hush.

"You don't want to know what I think of it," Fourteen said in a strange, low voice.

Mac turned to look at him. There was moisture along his thick eyelids. Noticing her attention, he brought up his hands, as if to hide it.

Not so alien, after all.

"There's an answer to the Dhryn," she promised him. "I believe we will find it. I believe we'll save our worlds—yours, mine, all of them." Hesitantly, unsure if the gesture would be welcomed by a Myg, Mac put her arm around his broad shoulders.

Fourteen's hands didn't budge, but she heard a muffled: "No external genitalia."

"No one's perfect," she laughed, then squeezed his shoulders lightly before letting go. "Shall we go and see if the *poodle* is ready?"

The hands came down as Fourteen shook his head. "Waste of time. Wait until Kay calls us. If we go too soon, he'll have us skinning the creature." A sniff. "Trisulians don't mind that sort of thing, but I certainly do." He seemed to perk up. "At least he bought it already dead. If you don't, they make so much noise—well, puts me off the meal, Mac, let me tell you. Then there's all the jumping around you get with live *poodles*. It's a mystery to me why Humans didn't properly domesticate this food beast."

Aha! Mac hid her smile by reaching forward to collect a handful of stones. *A game was afoot.* She had to admit, these two had come prepared to do their part enhancing Human/alien relations.

"First to seven wins," she challenged.

"So. This is *poodle*." Mac swallowed. "Sorry to refute your lovely compliments, Kay, but I can't say I've ever had it."

Two purple eyeballs, atop their stalks, and two beady eyes, within their fleshy lids, were locked on Mac.

The table was beautifully spread. Kay must have gone through every cupboard to find serving platters, fluted glasses, and a wide, if inexplicable, array of cutlery. There had even been a candle, although tying twenty birthday-cake candles in a bundle had produced more momentary conflagration than light for dining. Once the fire was put out, leaving only a minor and hardly unique scorch mark on the tabletop, they'd settled to enjoy their repast.

Repast was the word, Mac decided, admiring Kay's ingenuity. Her mammalian anatomy might be a tad rusty, but even she conceded a resemblance between the mass of meat and bone in the center of the table and a small dog. *If you pressed the animal flat and took other severe liberties with its skeletal structure.* Four legs, similar in size but not quite, jutted proudly into the air at forty-five degree angles. Where there logically would be paws, Kay had affixed ones of foil. *A nice decorative touch,* Mac thought.

There was no head. Perhaps that had been too tricky to reproduce. But there was a distinct tail, with a white pompom of what looked suspiciously like cushion stuffing at its tip. Complete with pink ribbon.

Other dishes held an array of vegetables and fruits. Some, Mac recognized, some she didn't—marking the latter down as to-be-avoided, tactfully, of course.

It was a work of, if not art, then artistic determination. Mac did her best to look dismayed instead of about to laugh. Personally, she had no problem eating anything if hungry enough—being a biologist studying a carnivore who ate the same way tended to instill a certain "fits in my mouth" mentality.

Her great-aunt, though, would have needed her new heart immediately, not next year.

"Let me carve you the first piece."

"That's not really necessary, Kay," Mac said, her voice sounding appropriately strained even to her. *If she didn't laugh soon, she'd choke.* "You go ahead."

Fourteen leaned over the table. "No, no, Mac. This is our thanks to you. Our treat. You must go first."

"Oh."

Kay took the sound as a "yes" and began sawing away at the carcass with the largest knife the kitchen boasted. He was careful to keep his facial hair away from the food.

The "poodle" had a crispy skin that parted with a puff of steam and clear fluid. Mac sniffed surreptitiously but couldn't smell anything over the nearby plate of yellow-spotted pickle-things.

Kay carefully freed a large piece of meat, laying it on a plate with great ceremony. He passed it to Fourteen, who placed it in front of her.

They waited, staring at her again.

Mac gazed at the offering and pressed her lips tightly together. *It was that or grin.* "I didn't realize poodle meat was white," she managed to say.

"It is 'the other white meat,'" Fourteen quoted proudly. "As proclaimed by one of your famous twentieth century authors."

Before she lost all self-control, Mac took her knife and fork in hand. Moving very slowly, conscious of her rapt audience, she pushed the tines of the fork into the meat at one end and even more slowly cut a morsel free with her knife.

Mac lifted the morsel to her lips and paused, looking at her guests.

Kay's eyestalks were bent forward as if that helped him see her better.

Fourteen was quivering, as if he wanted to bounce but knew that might be hard to explain at supper.

Mac smiled to herself and plopped the meat into her mouth, chewing vigorously. As she cut a second piece, she commented: "Tastes like chicken."

Absolute silence.

"Mind?" Mac reached over and violently yanked one of the legs free. She tore off a bite with her teeth, chewed and swallowed, then glanced up at the others. "That would be because it is chicken," she told them. "Or rather several. Nicely done, Kay."

"What do you mean, Mac?" that worthy blustered. "I bought this before we came. From a certified poodle dealer recommended by the consular staff!"

Mac gestured a denial with her drumstick. "Chicken."

"Idiot!" shouted Fourteen. "You should have checked before telling me you had obtained this rare delicacy. Mac, I am mortified."

"Because it didn't work?" she grinned.

Both managed to look crestfallen, Kay by drooping eyestalks, Fourteen by sagging in his chair.

"Don't worry," Mac assured them. "You would have fooled quite a few Humans with this—and any non-Human you wished. I have some expertise, you know."

Fourteen's sigh was heart-wrenching. "'Aliens Eat Poodles' was number three on the Human-Alien Mythos list. I knew we should have picked something else."

"There's a list?" she asked dubiously. "You aren't still trying to trick me, are you?"

"There's a list, Mac." Kay began carving meat for himself and Fourteen. "The consulate maintains an impressive collection of anecdotal and verified instances of Human presumptions about the non-Human. The funnier and more preposterous of those is put into a list. Any visitor to your system gets a copy. It's partly for humor's sake—"

"And partly to improve understanding," Fourteen finished, taking his plate. "How better to learn to tolerate an unfamiliar culture than by knowing its intolerance about yours?"

Mac did her best to wrap her mind around the logic or its lack, then shook her head. "That list can't flatter humanity," she said.

"Trust me, you aren't alone. There are lists like this on most worlds," Kay told her. "But I will admit an obsession with alien sex ranks uniquely higher on yours. Care to explain why that is?" His eyestalks gave a suggestive waggle.

Fourteen belched. "She didn't fall for that one either. Don't waste your effort, Kay. Or your poultry-poodle."

The serious, albeit momentary, business of eating "poodle" began. As Mac expected, Kay was finished in the time it took him to fill and scrape his plate into his waiting *douscent,* with Fourteen a close second. As they stood, she pointed her fork at each in turn. "No cards. Dishes."

"But you aren't finished yet, Mac," Fourteen protested, his tone implying this was some adorable silliness on her part.

"Don't worry about me. I'll keep eating while you tidy up." As they looked to one another, then back at her, Mac firmed her voice. "Cabin rule. No one leaves this kitchen until it's clean."

Efficient when they want to be, Mac thought moments later, helping herself to more mushrooms after checking them carefully for otherworldly origin. Kay and Fourteen were making quick work of their task, despite the quantity of dishes and implements Kay had used. The subject of almost constant complaint from Fourteen, of course. Whatever Mac hadn't wanted to eat had gone in the chiller. The grill outside had been sprayed with enzymes to digest any attractive poodle bits before a bear came to explore.

Mac yawned and realized she was not only full, but tired. Standing, she collected her things and added them to the pile beside Kay. "This is the last of it. Thanks," she said, grabbing another towel from the drawer to help Fourteen dry.

The three of them doing dishes might almost be Mac, her father, and Sam. She smiled at the memory. Sam would be talking about space; her father, his owls; and she—she'd listen to both and dream her own dreams.

"This is a waste. You should install a recycler," Fourteen commented.

Kay nodded, shaking both head and hair. "Not that this isn't charmingly archaic, Mac."

"A recycler requires power," Mac explained serenely, taking the next dish. "We enjoy sharing a task. Sometimes, anyway." She nudged Fourteen. "On vacation—a different pace and way of doing routine things." *Although this wasn't what Kammie et al had had in mind,* she thought happily.

"Idiot. Better things than dishes."

Mac smiled and took a stack of dried plates to the cupboard. "We'll need them tomorrow morning at least." Fourteen had sent his signal; the answer about the lev's arrival to pick them up had been the predicted "as soon as we know, you'll know." "Probably for lunch."

"You are more than kind, Mac, to keep us in your home," Kay replied, his voice warm.

"Least I can do," she said. "If it's going to be another day, are you sure you have everything you need? If not, we can canoe over to the store."

Kay shuddered, his mass of hair adding to the effect. Fourteen laughed. "A most excellent notion, Mac," the Myg proclaimed. "We shall obtain more card games! Numbers! Numbers!"

Mac didn't ask her guests how much sleep they needed, sure that if they roamed around the cabin in the wee hours, it could hardly be any noisier than their snoring. They seemed content to bid her good night when she was ready for bed, both going to their respective rooms. Perhaps fresh forest air made aliens groggy, too.

After checking that lights were off and window screens were secure, Mac walked through the darkened main room to the stairs, knowing the way. She put her foot on the lowermost step and stopped cold.

"I'll be back tonight."

She'd done so well, managing not to think of Nik until now.

Of course, now was the worst possible time, when there was no one and nothing else to distract her.

Mac considered knocking on one of her guest's doors, then could almost hear Emily's voice in her ear: *Coward.*

Be that as it may, she wasn't doing much good standing paralyzed at the base of the stairs, her heart pounding in her ears so loudly she'd never hear a door opening anyway.

With a sigh, Mac brought her foot down. With this much adrenaline in her system, she'd never fall asleep. She tiptoed across the common room floor and out to the porch. There, she snatched her towel from the line by the swing and headed for the lake. *A cold swim should solve this.*

The walk didn't. A *rustle rustle* seemed to follow her all the way down. Mac knew it was most likely a raccoon hoping she'd brought a midnight snack, but it made the hairs on her neck stand on end.

When she reached the cove, she breathed a sigh of relief. The lake seemed waiting for her, its water calm, dark, and inviting. Mac checked the stars, although she was reasonably sure there wasn't another stealth t-lev full of aliens about to land. And for a wonder, the mosquitoes were cooperating, showing a distinct lack of interest in her skin—which would likely change by tomorrow, given the way the evening air was growing warmer.

She stripped and headed for the water, then froze. *Rustle. Rustle.* Without a second's hesitation, she grabbed her towel and wrapped it around her middle, tight as a corset, then sat on the cold sand.

What was she thinking!

Mac picked up and threw a stone. *Plop.* The water even sounded welcoming. *Not tonight,* she told it. *Not with Sir Nikolai possibly wandering the woods.*

"Never liked those movies, Em," she muttered aloud. The ones where the heroine, regardless of anything else happening around her, would plunge naked into the first pond she could find and stay put until her prince arrived. Usually to plunge as well, given the seemingly irresistible allure of soaking wet heroine. Pushy, presumptuous, desperate heroines. Wet, pushy, presumptuous, desperate . . .

Not that Mac didn't fully appreciate the underlying rationale. *Gods, her breath caught at the mere thought . . .*

"Official business." She threw another rock and managed to miss the entire lake with it, hearing it thud against a log. "Stopping me from finding answers, from doing what I can. Keeping me locked away at Base while the universe moves on. He's here to do his job. That's it."

All of which was true, Mac thought. *So why not take advantage . . . why not enjoy the night?*

"Because I don't want just one," she whispered to the rising moon. "I don't know how to want that. I always want tomorrow. Nights without end. Endless tomorrows." Emily had understood. She'd given up trying to talk Mac out of her grief for Sam. The dates she'd arranged, when Mac couldn't avoid them, had been with men who were fun and forgettable. Her type, not Mac's.

Emily had teased her about having a heart with two settings: don't care and forever.

Which would be more helpful, Mac sighed, *if hearts came with a switch.*

Without another look at the cove, she climbed to her feet and trudged back uphill to the cabin.

"Mac. Mac. Wake up!"

She'd slept through the alien snore-a-thon? Mac rubbed her eyes and fought to pay attention. *Who?*

"C'mon. Wake up!"

That voice—it was like a plunge in the cold lake. Mac found herself on her knees, staring at the figure sitting at the end of her bed. "Emily! What? How?"

"I can't stay, Mac. They're calling me back already." Was it the moonlight that made Emily's face thinner, sharper, turned her eyes into black gulfs?

Choking on a sob, Mac scrambled to reach her friend, but Emily stood and moved away. "I can't stay, Mac. Not until you read my message. Why haven't you read it yet?"

The mem-sheet under her mattress. Mac froze. "I've tried, Em. We've all tried. Just tell me what it says! Let me help you!"

Emily pointed to the window. "See what you've done?"

Mac swiveled to put her bare feet on the floor. "What is it?" she whispered.

"See?" Emily pointed again.

Humor her, something in Mac said. The woman's been living with the Ro for most of a year now, or however time passed for them. Another part of her whimpered in protest even as Mac pulled a sheet around herself and walked to the window.

And looked outside.

Whisper: "You should have read it, Mac."

She should have seen the forest, the moon. Instead, Mac found herself standing on a rocky path, under a morning sky. The wind was sharp and she clutched the sheet to her body. *Where—?*

The air splintered.

At first, Mac couldn't make sense of it. Overhead, on both sides, silver objects were flashing by. They were part of the wind, or its cause, a mass moving together until, in the distance, so many met they obscured what should have been skyline. Lines of smoke curled up, there were explosions . . .

Mac squinted then gasped. She knew that shape. Those buildings. That curve of shoreline. This wasn't some alien landscape. This was Vancouver. The university was right there—Kammie and the students—

Then the rain began to fall. Green and hungry rain. It fell in great sheets and torrents that would have hidden what was happening from her . . .

Except that it fell here, too.

The flower buds on the scrubs beside her dissolved and washed away, leaves following, branches bending then gone.

Something slowed above her; it cast a shadow. Mac lifted her head and saw the arms dangling, coated in silver except for their mouths.

Whisper: "Why have you failed me, Mac?"

Then green rain struck her face and washed away her screams . . .

"Mac! Mac, wake up!"

"No," Mac begged, "not again! I'm sorry, so sorry. Emily, please not again—"

"Mac!"

That *voice?*

Mac opened her eyes, finding herself soaked with sweat and supported half sitting by a grip on each of her arms. "Nik," she greeted the latest apparition on her bed. "I've dreamed you before, too. It never ends well."

She couldn't remember a dream where he stroked the side of her face, or pushed her hair back from one ear with a shaking hand. "I can't understand what you're saying, Mac," Nik said. "It's Dhryn, isn't it?" He swore under his breath as he released her arms, only to wrap his around her and hold her tight. *That was new, too.*

Emily paying her a visit wasn't.

The Dhryn consuming her city wasn't.

The burning of her flesh wasn't . . .

Shuddering, Mac burrowed against a chest she hoped was real and not illusion, listened to a heartbeat she hoped could drown out the screaming. As both stayed strong and steady, her shudders stopped and she began to cry. No mere tears, but deep, heaving sobs that burst from her lungs and tore her throat.

The arms stayed around her, held her close. "They told me you still had nightmares," a low, uneven murmur into her hair. "Shhh. It's okay, Mac. You're awake. I'm here. Really here." He rocked her back and forth, very gently. "Shhh." She felt a blanket adding its warmth to his. "I won't leave, Mac. Rest. Shhh. Just rest, now."

The voice faded into darkness.

- 8 -

MEANINGS AND MISGIVINGS

MAC OPENED her eyes and winced. *It hadn't all been a dream, then.*
So much for worrying about Nik finding her skinny-dipping in the cove. *Let's try that other cliché, Em,* Mac told herself furiously as she tried to extricate herself from his arms. Woman screams herself hoarse in her sleep until Prince Charming visits her bed.

If this was a vid, she would have waked prettily to his call, hair and skin perfect. She wouldn't have sobbed herself into a stupor, said sobbing likely including both mucus and horrible noises. And now a pounding headache.

His arm lifted, letting her scramble out. "You okay?" Nik said sleepily.

Mac clutched something—a blanket—to her and scowled down at him. He was still in yesterday's shirt, with long pants instead of the shorts. Bare feet. The hint of morning light through the window stroked shadows along the planes of his cheekbones and neck.

Even rumpled—still yummy, she thought, and had to smile. He smiled back.

"I'm—fine. Thank you. It's not usually that bad." *No, usually it was worse,* she told herself honestly.

Nik raised himself on an elbow, resting the side of his head on two knuckles and a thumb to consider her. "Want to talk about it?"

Mac hesitated, then asked: "Would it help?"

"I can't see how."

She was surprised into a laugh.

Nik winked. "See? Now that helped," he boasted, sitting with a smooth, quick motion that brought his feet to the floor. For some reason, she clutched her blanket and tensed. As if it had been his intention all along, he eased back against the wall, arms folded. *Deliberately neutral,* Mac judged his positioning. Training or sensitivity to her mood?

They didn't, she realized suddenly, *preclude one another.* "I need to know why you're here."

"Officially here?" An eyebrow rose and dared her. "Or here—" he patted the bed.

Mac refused to blush or dwell on the intriguing dimple starting to show in the light beard beside his mouth. "I know why you're—there." *In her bed.* "You heard me having a—a nightmare. You heard me and came—" she stopped as Nik shook his head. "You didn't?"

"Here already, Mac," he confessed, that dimple growing deeper. "I was watching you sleep."

She blinked. "Why on Earth would you do that?"

"Spy. It's a lifestyle." Flippant and quick.

Trying to distract her. Mac frowned at him. "Then let me clarify my question for you, Mr. Spy. Fourteen and Kay said the Ministry wouldn't let the IU contact me. When they finally found a way, *poof,* you show up. It's no stretch to know you're here to try and stop me from going with them. Going there." Making sure one hand could hold the blanket securely, she lifted the other to point to the ceiling. "What I want to know is why."

Nik pushed himself off the bed in one lithe motion. Between the sloped ceiling and small room, Mac would have had to press against the window to let him pass and reach the door. She had no intention of budging.

But he wasn't trying to leave. Instead, he came close and gazed down at her. "I can't stop you," said Nik soberly. "You've accepted this from IU representatives, who will bear witness, believe me, if you try to deny it." A flick of the wrist, and the IU envelope was in his hand, held at his shoulder.

Mac's eyes locked on it. "What does it say?"

He folded it between his fingers. "I made a recording for you." His other hand tugged his imp from his pocket.

"I didn't bring mine," Mac confessed, feeling like a student caught without homework.

Nik didn't comment, simply tucked the device away again. "I'll get you one. Meanwhile, most of this is fairly harmless. Statements of common goals, common good, a mutual desire not to be consumed by the Dhryn. That sort of thing. There's a lengthy list of regulations and protocols regarding deportment at the Gathering, how to share information et cetera."

She could hear the *"but"* coming. "What is it?"

"You're expected to put the needs of member species of the IU ahead of your own. That goes both ways. This—" Nik passed Mac the envelope; it was warm from his hand. "—lets you demand help from any IU member. But not for yourself as a Human. Not from other Humans. Once you took and opened this, you were, to all intents and purposes, no longer a citizen of Sol System. Or of Earth."

"It's an invitation to a conference," Mac protested. *She'd been to dozens, probably more, ranging from fascinating to how-soon-could-they-hit-the-bar boring.*

"It's an invitation, Mac, to join an elite group drawn from all over the IU, whose sole function is to stop the Dhryn. However long that takes. Whatever it takes."

It was as if she heard trumpets, the call was so loud and sure. "If you think I regret this, Nikolai Trojanowski," Mac proclaimed, glaring up at him, "you're wrong. I want to find Emily. I want answers. If this piece of illegible text gives me access to the resources of the entire Interspecies Union, so be it."

His lip twitched. *A grin?* "And far be it from me to argue your flawless logic, Dr. Connor. Not when I'd do the same in your place."

Aha! "You disagreed with keeping me away from the IU, didn't you?" It was as though a weight had dropped from her shoulders. "You never intended to stop me accepting this. You—Nikolai Trojanowski—you disobeyed orders."

Nik made a show of looking offended. "Me? Never."

Mac snorted. "Just like you're never late."

"It took longer than I expected," he said serenely, "to find one old cabin in the woods." Then, his own expression serious: "I wanted this to be your choice, Mac, whatever you decided. If you'd said no, I would have taken the aliens with me last night and left you alone."

"Alone is overrated," Mac told him unsteadily.

He seemed closer without moving. "Yes, it is." Softly, searching her face: "Gods, do you have any idea—of course you don't—how dangerous your eyes are? A man could forget anything in them. Forget to breathe."

For some reason, Mac found herself intensely conscious of both breathing and wearing only a blanket. *What if she—*

A clatter from downstairs shattered the moment, restoring Mac's badly skewed equilibrium. "I've aliens in my kitchen," she explained. *Damn, he was too good at distracting her.*

And knew it.

"Worried they'll burn the place down?" That dimple again.

"No. Kay's a great cook. He— Stop changing the subject," she snapped.

Nik held up his hands in surrender. "Whatever you say."

Mac took a deep breath. She tapped the floor with a bare foot. "What I say is that the Dhryn, the Ro, Emily, even traffic reports on Little Misty Lake are higher on your list right now than—" *She hadn't meant to go quite that far.*

"You," Nik finished, his face now inscrutable.

"Yes." Mac stood perfectly straight and still, daring him to deny it, knowing that if he did, she'd never believe him again. "So why were you watching me sleep?"

Nik lifted his hands, then let them drop at his sides. "We don't—" he had the grace to look uncomfortable, "—have this place rigged. You took us by surprise, coming here."

"It's our family cabin," Mac said tightly. "Last time I checked, my movements weren't restricted, even if my privacy is."

He shook his head. "You dream about the Dhryn, Mac." As if that was sufficient excuse.

"You didn't need to climb into my bed to find that out."

The corner of his mouth twitched. "No, I didn't." That dimple. "I'm here under orders, Mac. Allow that I can also be glad to be here. With you." This last in that low, quiet voice, the one Mac found disturbed things, things she didn't need disturbed while trying to think clearly.

She marshaled her thoughts. "If you're planning to stay until we leave, unless you want to introduce yourself as a Ministry agent . . . ?" He made a face. "Thought so. Then we'll need to explain your being here with me. In the cabin—not here," she added quickly, gesturing at her bed.

"'Here' would keep it simple," Nik proposed, smiling down at her, eyes warm.

Mac couldn't smile back. Her hands tightened on the blanket until her knuckles turned white. *Coward,* she railed at herself. Fun was fun. She'd accepted offers before now, had a pleasant dalliance, forgotten names the next day.

It wouldn't be that way, Em. Not with him.

Nik lost his smile. "I see," he said, his voice grown thick. "It wouldn't."

Mac made an effort. "You could be my cousin, visiting for the week."

"Better if I could come and go without questions asked," he said, the sound reassuringly normal again. *Spy training,* Mac thought enviously. *Her voice still had a wobble to it.* "A neighbor?"

"You'd need a reason to hang around." Then Mac began to smile. "I have an idea."

Nik gave her a suspicious look. "Why does that make me nervous?"

"Depends. Are you any good with a shovel?"

"Good morning, Mac! I have made potcakes!"

"Idiot. Pancakes. It's not hard to remember," Fourteen grumbled. He busied himself pouring coffee, but gave Mac a quick wink.

Mac winked back. "Good morning. And thank you. It smells amazing." She took her seat in the kitchen, heart pounding. *Great spy she was.*

"We are serving you first, Mac," Kay announced, stepping to her side with a plate stacked five high with fluffy pancakes. Fourteen passed her the container of syrup. Both waited, watching her. "And will wait for you to eat."

"If this is so I can help with the dishes," she grinned, "it's a deal."

"Irrelevant," Fourteen claimed. "It is so I can tell if Kay has poisoned us with this concoction."

Kay's eyestalks, the two alert ones, bent to glare at Fourteen. "I refuse to serve cold poodle for breakfast. If you have to eat it, go outside."

Mac used her first mouthful of pancake to hide her smile. Their bickering, to her Human ears anyway, had an affectionate undertone, much like her brothers. It was odd how homey it was, sitting to a meal with them, despite the twisted gray locks that served Kay for a head, and Fourteen's dubious color sense. He must have raided the clothing trunk for that red plaid shirt. *If only he'd changed the paisley shorts.* It didn't help that his knees were again coated in bright green ointment.

Knock, knock. "Hey, Mac? You home?"

Kay and Fourteen froze at the sounds coming from the porch. Despite expecting Nik's imminent "arrival"—he'd slipped from her room and gone outside—Mac jumped in surprise. "Door's open," she called, recovering. The two aliens stared at her, then at the kitchen door, as if expecting the worst. "It's okay," Mac reassured them. "It's only—" *Oops. Nik went to the consulate regularly, his name would be on records.* "—Sam," she continued, taking a deliberately casual sip of her coffee. "Sam the landscaper." *Emily,* Mac sighed to herself, *would have quite a bit to say about that slip of the tongue.* "He's local," she finished lamely.

Nik/Sam popped his head around the frame of the kitchen door. "Sorry to intrude on your breakfast—"

"This is Sam Beckett," Mac said hastily, before Nik could introduce himself. He shot her a look she didn't dare read.

"How are you, Mr. Beckett?" Kay said, rising to the occasion like a born host. "Have you eaten yourself? We have plenty. Please join us."

"Call me Sam. And thanks. If that's okay with you, Mac?" a respectful salute of fingers to brow in her direction.

Nik must have taken the time to rummage through the workshop portion of the outhouse building. Her father's old leather tool belt hung around his lean middle, complete with ax-hammer and pliers. He'd put on a slouch as well, a subtle drop of shoulders and hips that stripped away his usual grace.

Mac narrowed her eyes. *He was enjoying this.* "Of course. Sam, this is Kay and Aslith—"

"Fourteen," that worthy interrupted. "Don't waste more time. Sit. Eat. Coffee? Potcakes?"

Kay, putting out another setting, stopped and pointed his eyestalks at Fourteen. "I thought you said they were pancakes."

"Idiot."

Mac giggled and everything seemed to settle, including her stomach. Nik took a mug of coffee as he sat, with every appearance of needing it. The aliens continued to chatter between themselves. *Checking out the new arrival,* she decided.

The new arrival was doing the same. Playing the role of "Sam the landscaper" with consummate skill, Nik somehow ate his breakfast while gawking at everything the two aliens did, up to and including a small gasp when Kay upended the last of the syrup into his *douscent.*

Being more familiar with her guests, or rather their skewed sense of humor, Mac had her doubts about this strategy. Sure enough, when Fourteen and Kay finished their meal—predictably before either Human—the Myg stood and scowled quite fiercely at Nik. "I have no external genitalia."

Fourteen's timing was impeccable. Nik sputtered and almost choked on the mouthful he'd been about to swallow.

"My companion has no tact," Kay said, his tone contrite. "What he means to say, with sincere regret and no disrespect to your species, is that neither of us are physically capable of satisfying your overwhelming urge to copulate. You'll have to use Mac."

Oh, she should have seen that coming. Mac shook her head with appreciation. Nik, meanwhile, had an alarming gleam in his eye. "Sam's too old," she informed them calmly, before he had a chance to say anything. *And make it worse.* "He doesn't have those urges anymore."

Fourteen blinked, then broke into his barking laugh. Kay drummed the palms of his hands on the table—presumably his version.

Nik?

The look he sent Mac wasn't official at all. In fact, it was the next best thing to ominous.

Mac grinned. "Hadn't you better get to work, Sam?"

After the dishes were done, and Kay had gone to his bedroom for, as Fourteen put it, time to commune with his overstuffed *douscent,* Mac left the Myg rearranging porch furniture for some obscure reason and went to check on Nik.

Black flies lifted from every leaf as she left the porch steps, hovering in confusion an arm's length away—aware she was close, but not knowing where. Mac waved at them cheerfully. *Technology wasn't cheating.* "Go chew a moose," she advised.

The top third of the path from the cabin was the most seriously eroded, convenient for Nik—since she assumed he'd want to overhear anything said on the porch. Mac edged her way alongside the deep crevices of exposed gravel and sand, keeping to root-tight soil. Unlike the coastal rain forest, here the dimly lit forest floor was a brown carpet of decaying needles, punctuated only by absurd balls of moss, vivid and vulnerable, and clumps of blushing mushrooms. If a tree fell, letting in the sun, the ground exploded with grasses, blueberry bushes, and eager saplings. If sun touched stone, the smallest cracks became lined with stubborn willow shrubs and packed with moss, its surface crusted with lichens.

The path bent sharply before the next drop; Mac heard the thud of his ax before she spotted him working just below.

Mac stopped, her real hand resting on the cool moist bark of the nearest tree. It wasn't hot yet, but Nik had already stripped off shirt and tool belt. More confused black flies circled his head, hunting a landing. He was chopping back a huge, upthrust root to make room for a wider stair. The new timbers were stacked behind him—they'd been stored under the porch for years, waiting for someone with time and inclination.

For once, Mac didn't wonder about Emily's reaction to the easy play of muscles over his shoulders and back with each confident rise of the ax, or the sweat plastering hair to his forehead and neck, glowing on his skin in the morning light.

She felt her own.

How complicated brains made the basics, she mused, putting her back against the tree, content to enjoy the moment before he noticed her. *Which biological drives remained untouched once you added intelligence and tossed in civilization? Breathing. Leaping away from flame.* Past that, even something so central to being Human as caring for a child evolved regulations and customs, habits and judgments.

Now, interaction with non-Human intelligence. What effect did it have, blending biology so three species could share breakfast, and thousands could share space?

What were they missing about the Dhryn? Mac frowned.

Nik chose that instant to look up and see her. "What's wrong?" he asked immediately, shifting his grip on the ax.

Mac found a smile. "Just thinking. You're doing a great job."

He used his forearm to wipe his brow. "It's a wonder you didn't break your necks climbing this," he commented, gesturing at the ground. This section did look worse in daylight, more dry gully than path.

"It keeps casual visitors down. Usually."

Nik glanced up the slope, then lowered his voice slightly. "There's nothing casual about those two. Fourteen's been at the Gathering for several weeks. I've asked for background information, his area of expertise, but nothing's come through yet. As for Kay—he's a more recent arrival, for all they seem pals. Does he only have four eyestalks?"

"That's all I've seen so far. Why? Do they come and go?" *Within that hair, it was possible.* Mac was quite taken with the notion. "How many should he have?"

"Four is normal," Nik said disappointedly. "But your Kay is no ordinary messenger, judging from the clout he had in arranging this little ambush in the woods. I'd have thought he'd have more by now."

"Care to explain that?"

"I—"

"Mac-ac-ac-ac!" They both looked downslope as the hail echoed across the lake and back. They could hear the rub of paddle against a canoe. "Mac-ac!!!"

"What? I don't believe it. That's Russell," Mac said, recognizing the bellow. "Fourteen told me he'd called to cancel their trip last night," she growled. "Should have done it myself. You'd better stay here," she said as she clambered past Nik and jumped the timbers, heading for the cove. He started to follow her anyway, and she paused to look back at him. "He'll know you aren't local," she warned.

"And not Sam Beckett."

He knew? Then she understood. *Damn Ministry dossiers.* "I had to pick a name," Mac defended, grabbing a handful of cedar for balance. "There wasn't time to consult."

"You don't let go of people, do you?"

"No." Mac's lips twisted. "Not first," she admitted, beyond caring what that revealed about her. "Just keep busy and out of the way. Trust me. Russell won't stay long."

Another of those offhand salutes, but his hazel eyes were troubled. She felt them watching her as she went down to meet the canoe.

"Wendy Carlson," Russell Lister introduced. The tall woman slogging through water to her ankles waved at Mac, then kept pushing her canoe up the beach. They'd brought the store's two largest, Russell fully aware how much gear Kay and Fourteen had brought.

"Nice to meet you," Mac said, taking the paddle Russell shoved at her. "But you've made the trip for nothing. They canceled their trip. I thought Fourteen—the Myg—called you last night about it."

"He did," Wendy said, then nodded at Russell. "Made us come anyway."

Mac turned to him. "Why?"

His face went bright red. "No reason. You're fine. I can see that. Plain as day. We'll just head back now. Sorry to trouble you, Mac." He reached for his paddle and Mac returned it with a puzzled frown.

Wendy, a friendly-faced young woman with a glorious mane of red hair blowing free in the wind, broke out laughing as she pulled the front of her canoe onto the sand. "Honestly, Russ, you're hopeless. Don't mind him, Mac. He expected to find you hanging from a tree in some alien bondage ritual. It was all Cat and I could do to stop him calling in the police last night to storm the place."

"Bondage . . . ?" Mac repeated incredulously. "You're kidding." *But from Russell's embarrassment, Wendy wasn't.*

Mac couldn't decide if she should laugh or tear out her hair. On second thought, maybe she should put Fourteen and Russell in the same room for a while. *Or maybe not.* "Russell? What on Earth put that in your head? You were the one who dumped them on me in the first place."

He rested the blade of his paddle on top of his boot, crossing his hands on the handle. "I know. Just made it worse, Mac. Worrying you'd come to harm because of me. Glad you're okay." He heaved a sigh, then shook his head. "I feel like such an idiot."

"You should," she agreed. "Alien bondage? You and Cat watch too many vids over the winter. I should send you some comparative anatomy texts." She put her hand on top of his, pushing gently. "Thanks for checking." Mac paused, then the light dawned. *Aliens,* she sighed to herself. "What exactly did Fourteen say to you?"

"That's the thing." Russell lowered his voice conspiratorially, although the three of them were the only beings in sight who'd conceivably hear. Wendy sent Mac a look of sympathy. "We weren't in, so he'd left a message."

Mac waited a long moment, swatting at an inquisitive—and precocious—deerfly. When Russell still didn't speak, she burst out: "Well? What did the message say?"

Russell gave her a hurt look. "Give me a minute, Mac. I'm making sure I get it right."

A spy on her path, aliens on her porch, and Russell taking his time. Mac pinched the bridge of her nose to make sure she was awake. "The gist," she suggested acidly, "will do."

"I heard it," Wendy volunteered. Ignoring Russell's *humphf,* she shifted into a credible imitation of the Myg's gruff voice. " 'The canoe trip is now irrelevant. The female Human meets our needs. Charge Kay triple and stay away. And send four more of your fine shirts to the address I left. Add them to Kay's bill.' "

Mac winced. *Damn Myg sense of humor.* "Okay, I can see how you might take that the wrong way. My apologies, Russell."

He rolled his eyes and didn't move, doing his own credible impression of Man Terribly Wronged. *The one that never worked,* Mac remembered, *but always made Cat laugh and give him a hug.*

She grinned. "Why don't you and Wendy come up to the cabin for a drink?" she invited. "We can get your bill settled there."

"Great!" Wendy smiled cheerfully and gave the older man a light push. "C'mon, Russ."

Nik had taken her suggestion and made himself scarce, Mac noticed as they negotiated the path to the cabin, although she suspected he was capable of hiding behind the thinnest tree. She led the way up the steps and opened the porch door.

The two aliens had arranged three armchairs around a trio of mismatched tables this time, and were busy playing another card game. So far, the cards were safely in their hands or on a table. *The IU's finest,* Mac grinned to herself.

"Mr. Russell! Mr. Wendy!" Kay greeted them warmly. "How are you this morning?"

"Fine, fine," Russell got the words out somehow, though Mac could tell he was still trying to regroup. Admittedly, aliens playing cards was a far cry from what Russell had imagined he'd find here. She was sorely tempted to knock his and Fourteen's heads together. Interspecies communication was difficult enough, without throwing in erotic and anatomically unsound vid dramas—*not to mention,* Mac fumed to herself, *brochures on human sexual behavior.*

"Are you sure you don't want to take the trip?" Russell had continued. Not being privy to Mac's thoughts, his voice was closer to normal. "It's an amazing opportunity—"

"Irrelevant," Fourteen interrupted. "You were told not to come. We have other plans. Be amazed without us."

Kay's upper two eyestalks—four in total, Mac confirmed involuntarily—bent to aim at Russell. "Ignore the rude creature," Kay told him. "Please, make yourselves comfortable. We will, of course, pay the full price for our trip regardless. Send my companion here the bill."

"But he said to send it to you," Russell protested, giving Mac an anxious look. Fourteen seemed oblivious, busy rearranging cards.

"You don't need to send anything, Russell," Mac said firmly, glowering at her guests. "They will each pay you double the cost of the original trips before you leave here. And you—" she pointed at Fourteen, who froze with a handful of cards in midair to stare up at her, "—will pay for your own shirts before they are shipped."

"Sounds fair to me, Mac," Russell said with a huge smile.

Since no one from another world seemed inclined to comment, Mac went on: "Coffee anyone?"

"Something cold, please, if you have it," Wendy answered. She'd been studying the card game. "What are you playing?" she asked Kay.

"Something he made up," the Trisulian answered morosely.

Fourteen grinned. "Involving more numbers and less cheating!"

Wendy looked entranced. "Would you show me? Please?"

"Be my guest," Kay stood, offering her his seat.

Russell dropped into the swing and put his head back on the cushions, closing his eyes. "Take your time, Wendy. We're in no rush. Oh, I take three sugars these days, Mac. Thanks."

Kay accompanied Mac to the kitchen, holding the doors for her courteously each time. "Should we prepare a beverage for Sam?" he asked.

"Got my own, thanks." Back in his shirt, sawdust frosting his hair, Nik leaned against the kitchen counter, sipping a glass of water. His eyes laughed at her.

She was going to put a tracer on him, Mac thought, exasperated. She went to a cupboard and snooped through Cat's gifts until she found a bag of cookies. "So Fourteen invented his own card game—just like that?"

"He lives for numbers," Kay said, putting on the coffee. One eyestalk watched what his hands were doing, its partner swiveled between her and Nik, while the remaining two stayed asleep. Mac was fascinated.

"What does he do with them—when he isn't playing games?" Nik asked, stealing a cookie as Mac put them on a plate.

"Do? I've no idea." The aroma of coffee began filling the kitchen. "He is paid ridiculous sums for whatever it is and considers himself very clever. Numbers," Kay put out mugs, "bore me."

"What do you do?" Mac asked. "When not vacationing on Earth, that is," she added quickly. Remembering who was supposed to know what about whom was the worst of it. *Or was that who knew which who knew what?*

Mac's head threatened to throb. *Salmon,* she promised it, *were much simpler than spies.*

"I'm a—I believe the Human equivalent is civil servant. I obtain information, prepare meeting summaries, that sort of thing."

How—normal. Mac spooned sugar into Russell's mug, at a loss for what to ask next. *This,* she said to herself, *from the woman with a spy in her kitchen.*

Said spy was presently using his skills to sneak another cookie. Mac passed him the bag with the rest. "Help yourself."

"Thanks. By the way, I'll be gone a couple of hours. Need to get some setting posts from my shop."

Gone? She gave him a sharp look, but the Ministry agent seemed more interested in eating than clandestine signals.

"We have ample poodle. I will save you a sandwich," Kay promised.

Nik looked startled, then worried. *Was either expression real?* "It's okay, Sam," she said, playing along. "I had some last night. Delicious."

"If you say so, Mac. Till later, then." Nik gave her that half salute, then ducked out the back door.

"You're sure he's too old," Kay ventured. "Seems fit."

"Appearances can be deceiving." She hesitated. *How did one casually ask about eyestalks? Was there etiquette?*

"True for all species, Mac. Shall we serve our guests?"

Opportunity lost, for now, Mac followed Kay back to the porch.

Leftover "poodle" did make excellent sandwiches. Mac had Kay leave a plateful in the kitchen for "Sam," so he wouldn't mention the name during lunch on the porch. Wendy and Russell helped finish off the rest, both operating on what Mac's father had called "cottage time." In other words, lingering whenever politely possible until the next meal showed up.

Mac went down to the cove to help launch their canoes, just to be sure it didn't occur to Russell or Wendy to linger for supper.

Russell still had his doubts. "You're sure you want to stay alone with these guys, Mac?" he asked, standing beside his canoe. Wendy was pushing hers out. "They seem nice enough, but you never know."

"If I detect the slightest hint of evil intentions, you'll be the first one I call," Mac promised, then grinned. "I plan to wear them out anyway. A good long hike, probably a few days' worth into the bush," she improvised, "then I'll get a ride back with them to Base. Time for me to return to work by then. Tell Cat I appreciate the supplies and I'll visit more next trip." Then she beckoned Russell close to whisper: "We paddled a bit yesterday. Kay gets terribly seasick. Don't tell anyone—I think it's a pride thing with his species."

Russell drew back with a knowing look. "Ah. Thanks, Mac. Good to know."

And if their supposed itinerary wasn't all over the lake by midday tomorrow, Mac thought with satisfaction as she watched the twin canoes head out into the lake, *nothing would be.*

Just then, a v-shaped flock of seven huge birds appeared over the trees on the far shore, their powerful wings beating in synchrony, flying toward her and north. Swans. Mac smiled as she hooded her eyes to watch them pass overhead. The pelicans would arrive next, with their unwelcome nesting companions, the gulls. Cormorants were here already, competing for space with early arriving geese. Herons would push them both out soon, reclaiming their colonies.

It was like welcoming old friends home.

There was no sign of Nik as she walked through his construction site to the cabin. Mac didn't bother wondering where he'd gone—or how, since there'd been no sign of an additional canoe along the cove. The sun was blazing down now, bringing that heady scent out of the pines and adding a pulsing heat even in the shade. Late May.

Some years, that meant snow, Mac thought with a grin.

Kay and Fourteen were waiting for her, the latter curled into a ball on his chair, lumpy knees in front of his nose. Mac resolutely avoided looking at the expanse of strained paisley this offered. "We have been discussing the Dhryn life cycle and wish your thoughts, Mac," Kay informed her as she joined them.

"I'm not a xenobiologist," she cautioned. "I told you yesterday. My field is salmon."

"Nonsense. You are a trained observer, with a relevant background. Your insights would be most valuable."

No one at the Ministry had wanted them. Mac couldn't help but feel a little glow of satisfaction. Then she quelled it. "Valuable? Not without more data."

"At the Gathering, you should find the data you lack," Fourteen said. He seemed strangely subdued.

Mac took a closer look at him. "Are you feeling all right?"

"He received a message while you were saying your farewells. The news wasn't good."

"About the Dhryn," Mac guessed, sitting down. *The air wasn't this close,* she told herself, making herself breathe more slowly. "Tell me."

"You tell her," Fourteen said, covering his eyes.

Kay combed his facial hair with one hand. "We called them the Pouch People. They lived on a moon in the Osye System. Prespace technology, a peaceful, pleasant culture. The Osye were letting them develop with minimal cultural interference. Some trade. Farmers, for the most part."

"Harmless!" the Myg wailed softly.

Mac swallowed bile. "Go on," she said.

"There is nothing more to say. The Dhryn had come before. The Pouch People were warned of the signs but had no defense, no ships. The Dhryn came again and consumed every molecule of organic matter. Their world is lifeless. They are gone."

Mac leaned forward, her elbows on her knees. "And the Dhryn. Did they stay?"

"No."

"Again," she whispered, chin in hand, tapping the side of her nose with one finger, deep in thought.

"What is it?"

Mac's finger stopped tapping. "After complete victory, they abandon a world suitable for their species. Why?"

Fourteen lowered his hands, wiping his eyelids as he did so. "They were afraid of being caught by the Osye."

"They had what they came for," Kay added.

Mac pursed her lips. "Or is it that they couldn't stop there? Not yet, anyway."

"What do you mean?"

She rested her artificial fingers on one end of the nearest table, then drew a line with her other hand from that point to the far side. "What if the Dhryn are on a journey," Mac mused slowly. "A journey with a purpose—a destination. They don't stay, because they can't stay. They haven't reached their final goal."

"Disturbing."

Mac sat up and gazed at Fourteen. "Yes, it is."

"If we knew that goal," Kay ventured, "we could predict where they will strike next."

She shook her head. "We already have evidence that the Dhryn are returning where they've been before, as if following a trail set by advance scouts. But from what you told me, there was only one Progenitor ship seen at Ascendis. That's a problem."

"Why?"

"Previous attacks—our only reports are of a few, scattered incidents. We don't know which of those were Dhryn for sure. And we can't know where else the Dhryn have been. Add to that? We don't know how many Dhryn there are. When I was on Haven, I saw the Progenitors leaving. It looked like dozens—but the Human ships reported more, at least three hundred."

"Why would only one attack at a time?" this from Kay.

Fourteen: "Where are the rest?"

Mac nodded at each question. "That's why we can't predict the attacks. If they are on a journey, a migration of sorts, all Dhryn should be making it. If only some are actively feeding—" she was proud of how the word came out without cracking, "—that implies the rest don't need to feed themselves yet, or are being supplied by others, for all we know by ships going off the main path. There's no pattern established."

"Our military strategists are plotting the Dhryn's most likely moves based on time-honored space tactics. Trisulians," Kay said almost smugly, "were once highly respected combatants."

"Ruthless invaders," Fourteen corrected. "Good thing you civilized yourselves or you'd have lost your transects."

Irrelevant, Mac caught herself thinking. "Nothing the Dhryn have done suggests they have some plan for conquest," she objected. "They don't occupy territory. They don't communicate or negotiate. They just—are."

The other two were silenced by this. Mac didn't blame them. She wasn't too happy about the idea of a space-faring aggressive species that wasn't behaving like one either.

In the hush, she could hear a shovel and gravel being poured. Mac turned to look out the screen.

Nik was back, working at the top of the path, making a great show of moving gravel from side to side. *An excuse to stay in earshot,* Mac decided. He was working in the full sun at the moment, his shirt tied on his head to shade his neck.

"What about the Myrokynay, the Ro, Mac? Can they predict where the Dhryn will strike next?"

Mac swiveled back to face her anxious companions. *Almost time for beer,* she thought. "I've seen no indication they can. They needed help to find the Dhryn Progenitors." *But not the Dhryn world,* she thought suddenly. They'd known where Haven was. They'd attacked it before. *The Ro were after the oomlings,* Brymn had said.

Why?

"If only we could talk to them . . . ask what they know . . . maybe we could have protected those already lost . . ." Fourteen covered his eyes, making a quiet clicking sound Mac hadn't heard from him before, like a cricket lost in the kitchen at night.

She sniffed, trying not to be obvious, then held her breath as long as she could, hoping the faint breeze through the screens would help. *He was definitely upset.*

Kay's eyestalks drooped. "The Ro ignore us."

Mac unzipped her upper pocket and pulled out the sheet of mem-paper. "Not always," she said very quietly, hoping her voice wouldn't carry. She tapped Fourteen on his knee to get his attention, then spread the page out so they all could see it.

"What is it?" Kay whispered, eyestalks bent down.

Fourteen bounced on his chair. "It's a message from the Ro, isn't it, Mac?" he said, with regrettable volume. Mac winced.

"We can't understand it," she whispered, doubting he'd take the hint. "Kay said you were good with numbers. Maybe it will make sense to—" Before the words left her mouth, Fourteen snatched up the mem-sheet and ran into the cabin. "—you," Mac finished.

Kay gave her shoulder a quick pat. "He may be annoying, but he isn't just good with numbers. He's one of the best cryptologists of any species. If anyone can make some sense of it, Fourteen can. If he can't, then someone at the Gathering surely will. Thank you, Mac. Thank you."

"Ah, Mac?" The air might be stifling warm, but that voice through the porch screen was only a fraction above absolute zero. "May I have a word with you, please? Now."

She closed her eyes for a second, then somehow smiled at Kay. "Why don't you grab us some beers, Kay, and make sure Fourteen has what he needs? I'll just go—" *see how angry Nik is,* "—see what Sam needs."

Feet crunching through gravel, then scuffing pine needles, Nik marched around the cabin to the outhouse. He opened the door and walked inside, leaving her to follow.

That angry, Mac told herself, and squared her shoulders. *Fine.* She was a member of the IU, now. Not that it seemed likely to help at this instant.

The outhouse, despite its name and practical function in wintertime, was primarily a workshop and storeroom. Stuffed owls stared down from their shelves, surveying the irregular stone floor crowded with barrels and boxes. One wall held a rack of tools, most older than Mac. The back wall had the door to the privy, within a forest of skis, poles, ice drills, hockey sticks, and snow shovels, while the remaining wall was taken up by the requisite wood stove. The only light, at the moment, came through the skylight Mac hadn't bothered to clean of pine needles and cobwebs. Its beams sloped down in a cascade of pale yellow dust, to cast four bright squares on the floor.

Nik stationed himself beside the stove, stiff and straight, eyes hooded in the relative gloom. His arms were folded across his chest, like armor.

"Before you spout 'threat to the species' at me, Mr. Trojanowski," Mac told him, standing straight herself, "consider who was given that message in the first place. Me. I'm the one Emily expects to figure it out—not you, not 'Sephe, not your experts. Me. And this is how I'm going to try. With Fourteen's help. With Kay's help. I'm a member of the IU now."

He gave a curt nod. "Getting Fourteen on it was brilliant, Mac. Couldn't have done better myself."

Brilliant? Mac, all set to defend her decision, with colorful language and a brandished hockey stick if necessary, was thrown off-balance. "Why drag me out here then?"

"I'm leaving. Now." Flat, neutral. "I won't be coming back."

It was like that first moment of her swim, skin hitting ice cold water, the shock driving the breath from her body. Mac fought to see anything of Nik's expression in the shadows; she couldn't. *Hiding, Mr. Spy?*

That, more than anything, convinced her.

Her heart started hammering. "You haven't finished the path."

It wasn't what she wanted to say. Should say. Couldn't.

"I know. I'm sorry."

Did he mean he knew what she hadn't *said, Em?* Mac refused to follow that path into complete incoherence.

"Mac, I don't have much time." She thought she heard a hint of regret. *Or imagined it.* "We have to talk before I go."

Go where? Why? Mac longed to demand answers, to protest . . . *And how,* she asked herself, *could that be fair to either of them?*

"I'm listening," she said quietly, surrounded by memories and dust.

The words came out staccato sharp, like some battlefield briefing. *There really wasn't time,* she thought, beginning to worry why. "A name you need to know. Bernd Hollans. Career Ministry. Spent the last two years seconded to Earthgov as adviser on Human-IU trade. He's the one who persuaded the Secretary General to take the investigation into the disappearances, the Chasm, seriously. Just been appointed our voice in IU policy regarding the Dhryn and the Ro."

"Making him your new boss?" she guessed. *Was Nik's sudden departure this Hollans' doing?* Better that, than any of the other options she'd imagined.

Nik took a step forward; a beam of light struck his leg. The contrast turned the rest of him darker, deepened shadows. "He knows my value," he said just as obscurely. "I know his. He'll make the tough decisions. You won't like him, Mac, but don't let that fool you. Hollans—he can be trusted."

Politicians. Something she usually avoided. *As for trust?* Mac wrapped her arms around her middle. "What else?"

"The Trisulian rescue mission to Ascendis turned out to be something else."

"What?" Mac frowned. "Kay told me they'd sent more ships to retrieve Eeling refugees than any other species."

"Oh, they sent more ships, all right." Sharp and edged. "Settler convoys. Ascendis may be ruined for the foreseeable future, but her moons and their very lucrative refitting stations remain intact. As do her transect connections. The Trisulian Ruling Council has petitioned for official recognition of the system as part of their holdings and it's unlikely any will argue. Certainly not the few Eelings left alive."

Mac's eyes widened with understanding. "Ravens."

"I don't see what—"

"Ravens survive winter by scavenging deer and elk carcasses, Nik. They follow predators in order to find their kills."

"The Trisulians as ravens to the Dhryn?" Nik was silent for an instant, then said slowly, as if thinking out loud: "I want to say it's unlikely, but they've a history of snatching new territory by force. It almost cost them their transects. With the prospect of conveniently uninhabited worlds, complete with atmosphere, water, even most buildings and roads intact? All they'd need are some climate regulators to keep the first miners happy, long-term reclamation projects for agriculture. It would be tempting."

"If," Mac emphasized, "they learn to predict Dhryn movements. They'd have to know, in order to arrive in time to feed on the corpse first."

"Remind me not to use your phrasing in the discussions of the issue."

She didn't quite smile. "Is Kay involved in this? Is that why he's here?" *Really tired of betrayal, Em.*

"No reason to think so." Nik's voice lost some of its edge. "He's a minor official, good record if undistinguished, presently serving his species' contingent at the Gathering. Handles catering, runs errands, that sort of thing. I can't see an underling being privy to the Ruling Council's actions. He volunteered to approach you for the IU and was someone who could be spared, that's all."

She could feel his doubt. "That's not all, is it? You suspect Kay of something."

He hesitated, then shrugged, a shadow shifting its shape. She still couldn't see his face clearly. "It's my nature. Trisulians are fond of secrets. They like collecting information; knowing things—even trivia—before everyone else. Didn't surprise me to find Kay had offered to meet you. For someone like him, chances to learn or do something first must be rare. But I was puzzled why he'd invite Fourteen. They barely knew one another before coming here. Then you, Mac, showed me the reason."

For some reason her mind stuck on poodle. "I did?"

"The Ro message. If Fourteen translates it while still at the cabin—" He waited.

"Kay could learn what it said before anyone else," Mac finished. She began to pace, real hand rubbing at the false. "But how would he know I had such a message?" She stopped and whirled. *How could she have forgotten to tell him?* "Nik, the IU—"

"Has someone working for them at Base. We know."

Of course they knew, Mac told herself, feeling foolish. "It's 'Sephe, isn't it? She knew about Emily's message. You put her there in the first place—to help the IU reach me. Right?"

She could see him shake his head, barely make out the gleam of reflected light that marked his eyes. "I put her there, yes. But she's not the IU's informant—and before you ask, you don't want to know who it is."

Mac bristled. "I most certainly do."

"How many secrets do you want to carry around, Mac? Besides, you'll meet this person again. Think you can act normally if you know?"

"What's 'normally'?" Mac exclaimed in disbelief. "If you don't tell me, I'll have to suspect everyone I know."

He laughed. "Welcome to my world."

"You can keep it," Mac growled. In the ensuing silence, she listened to a trio of white-throated sparrows outside, contesting territory with song instead of subterfuge. *Lucky birds.* Finally she grumbled: "Okay. Don't tell me. If I knew, I'd probably chuck whoever it is in the ocean and be done."

"We'll be watching," Nik promised.

"You'd better." *When had leaving an unknown informant among her friends become a lesser evil?* The eyes of dead owls gazed at her. *Not helping,* she told them. "If it wasn't 'Sephe, how could Kay know about Em's message?"

"He didn't have to. We aren't the only ones who've been waiting for Emily to contact you, Mac. You wouldn't have had a moment's privacy on Earth if the Ministry hadn't stepped in and insisted you be left in peace. The Trisulians wouldn't be the only ones to believe you've been receiving such messages all along, keeping them to yourself."

"I have not!"

From his tone, he was amused by her protest, but all he said was: "To Kay, Mac, such secrecy would make perfect sense. And be an opportunity. Tell me. When I wasn't here, did Kay ask about Emily?"

In how many ways was she a fool? "Yes," Mac said, the word bitter in her mouth. "About our friendship, how close we are—were. It didn't make much sense at the time, but I went along. Tell me, Nik. Is there a memo about me at the consulate that says 'totally gullible,' or is it just obvious to any being who meets me?"

Nik took a step closer, the light playing over his face. *Regret. Something less definable.* "The only thing obvious about you, Mackenzie Connor," he informed her, "is your heart."

There was a conversation stopper. Mac could feel her cheeks flaming.

He had to notice, but went on as if he didn't. "Kay's only worry would be his ability to understand a message from the Ro. So he finds a cryptologist interested in a jaunt to Little Misty Lake. It's all a gamble, but one that could pay off. Looks like it has."

"And I thought funding committees were cutthroat," Mac muttered darkly.

"Don't take it personally, Mac." Nik took another step, and the light finally reached his eyes, their hazel dark with emotion. "Species advantage. Kay probably doesn't know about the Eeling System yet—but be prepared for him to approve when he does find out. And this is only the beginning. The Gathering—you'll have to tread very carefully. I don't have to warn you about alien motives, how easy it is to believe you understand those around you, how suddenly everything can change."

"I remember an earthquake," she said tightly.

"We've people going over every bit of that data, Mac. When I have an answer, I'll make sure you get it." Nik paused and studied her face, a frown starting to form between his brows. "This doesn't feel right."

"What?"

"Leaving."

It wasn't about leaving her, Mac thought. She knew him well enough by now to understand the source of his hesitation. It wasn't about what warmed his eyes when he really looked at her. *It was about trust.*

"Am I safe alone with them or not?" she asked bluntly. "I mean, other than the ever present risk of snoring, Fourteen's warped sense of humor, and alien bondage rituals."

Nik ached to say no. Mac could see it; part of her wanted to agree. *For reasons,* she admitted to herself, *that had nothing to do with aliens.* Then he pressed his lips together and gave her a reluctant nod. "Kay and Fourteen are accredited members of the IU, sent as your escorts. It's no crime to be interested in what the Ro have to say—we all are. You seem to be enjoying each other's company." He waited for Mac to say something. She didn't speak. "It still doesn't feel right," he finished, for the first time since they'd entered the outhouse showing a clear emotion—frustration.

On impulse, Mac tugged the shirt from Nik's head. Conscious of him watching her, she untied the knot turning it into a hat, then gave the garment a hard shake. Dust and a few dead flies joined the motes in the sunbeams. The beams flickered and brightened as if a cloud had gone by. "Here." She handed it back. "You'll want this on in the woods."

"Thanks." He pulled it over his shoulders. "Your ride should be here tomorrow, probably after the weather goes through. You're sure you'll be okay, Mac? I could arrange for someone to stop in tonight."

"Worry about the aliens," she told him. "I've hosted fund-raisers."

"There's that," he acknowledged solemnly, that dimple showing as he finished fastening his shirt. A truly serious look. "I hope Fourteen can do something with the message. We've had no luck."

Mac took a deep breath, that nightmare image of Emily—her voice, her face, her desperation—swelling up behind her eyes. "If he does find out what it says, what do I do about Kay?"

Nik shook his head. "Nothing. He has as much right to the information as any of us, Mac, and the immunity to do with it as he sees fit. Representatives of the IU, including Kay and Fourteen—and now you—are outside Ministry jurisdiction. We can—and will—follow him if he leaves, monitor any transmissions, delay him with bureaucracy to a point. But that's it. We can't stop him sending anything he wants to his government." A gleam of teeth that could only be described as wolfish. "Though the IU may smack his eyestalks afterward."

Nik's smile faded. "Just don't lose either of them in the bush. Or yourself. Okay? And, Mac?" He cupped one hand, then tipped it over, as if proving it was empty. "The message might not be from Emily at all. Don't get your hopes up."

Mac gave a helpless shrug. "I have to hope."

"I know." Nik opened his arms, very slightly, as if in invitation.

It was good-bye. Mac didn't move. She studied his face instead, compelled to memorize details: the patchy beard and tired lines of dust and sweat, the dark sweep of lashes and that unruly lock of hair over the forehead, the strength along jaw and throat.

"I watched you this morning," she confessed. "When you were chopping the root."

"Why do you think I was working so hard?" At her shocked look, he gave a quick, shameless grin. "Spy, remember?"

"Oh."

"Makes us even. I watched you sleep."

"There's that."

Another of those abruptly strained pauses. Mac had no idea what to do with it and concentrated on digging her toe into a crack in the stone floor.

Nik finally gave a quick nod. "I'd better go." He started for the door.

How do I say good-bye, Em? Mac tried to think of something, but he slowed and stopped before she could. *Maybe,* she told herself, *he was having the same problem.*

Which didn't bode well for their ability to converse.

"Mac. One last thing. In case I don't see you for a while."

Promising.

"What?" she prompted.

"I heard you tell Fourteen that the Ministry doesn't value your insights. I wanted to tell you. You were wrong," he said, gazing down at her, his eyes clouded. "Everything you know, everything you've postulated about the Dhryn? We take it very seriously, Mac. You have unique ideas—they may be important ones. That's why your office was monitored, your privacy violated. As much— more—as we were waiting for Emily or the Ro, we wanted to hear you."

It hurt, even more than him leaving. "You could have asked, the way the IU did," Mac snapped. "We're on the same side."

"Yes." Nik's lips pressed together in an unhappy line, then he shrugged. "But we're not the same. Not anymore."

The owls appeared to lean closer. *Illusion,* Mac decided, just like the way there seemed no air left in the small room, despite the open door. "What do you mean?" she whispered.

"You still dream in Dhryn."

Another ambush. Mac stared at him. "That's why you were in my room last night. You were hoping I'd have a nightmare so you could—" her voice cracked. "So you could hear me."

"Yes. We had to know."

"Why?" Mac balled her hands into fists, but kept them still. *Not anger; despair.* "Why, Nik? Does it make me some kind of traitor to my kind? Is that it?"

"No one questions your loyalty." As she watched, he seemed to wrestle with some decision, then make it. "We've tried using the self-teach Emily made you for the Dhryn language on others—I've tried it myself. It doesn't work for anyone else, Mac. Worse, we can't make one that does, not for a Human brain. Yours doesn't copy. Existing vocabularies for the adult language lack syntax for the infrasound component and there are none for the *oomling* version. That self-teach was specific to you; what it did seems unique. We can't even predict what its full impact will be on you."

Damn you, Emily, Mac thought wearily. "What you're saying is that the Ministry, anyone in authority, doesn't trust me because they can't translate what I say in my sleep."

"It's not a matter of trust. The psych experts were clear that none of your personality, nothing of you, Mac, has been affected. It's only—well, some view anything you say about the Dhryn as potentially tainted. That doesn't mean it isn't valuable, but, to be frank, my superiors aren't confident having you as the source."

"Are you?"

He hesitated an instant too long.

Mac shook her head. "I see," she said.

"No, you don't 'see,'" Nik snapped, eyes flashing. "I fought to have you brought in as an analyst. I argued for weeks, went over the heads of my superiors, and came close to losing my job. Even though I knew about your nightmares, Mac; knew you were hurt and grieving, how much you wanted your life back, your fish, to get to work. I wouldn't let any of it matter more than learning about the Dhryn. But all I could get was the authorization to arrange surveillance, to send 'Sephe to stay near you, so we wouldn't lose anything you could tell us. Why do you think I helped the IU reach you? They can do what I couldn't. Get you working."

He rubbed his face, smearing dust, and wound up with a charmingly chagrined expression. "I still can't tell if I felt more frustrated or vindicated when I listened to you, sitting on a porch swing with a beer, make more sense than any 'expert' I've heard yet. We're all fools."

"No argument from me," Mac said. She licked her thumb and used it to repair a smear on his cheek, paying attention only to his skin and the dust. "That's better."

Nik caught her hand before she pulled it away. "Don't." Harsh and low. "Don't forgive me."

"For what?" Mac tried not to smile. "For being right? Spying on me all this time was a waste; I should have been working with you. Do you think there's been a day I haven't picked at the puzzle, tried to comprehend what's happening, make sense of it? You asked me if I ever let go, Nikolai. Well, here's the thing." She turned her hand in his so their fingers intertwined, and gripped as hard as she could. "I really don't. Not of Emily. Not of Brymn. Not of the questions we have to answer to find her and understand him." Mac searched his face then nodded to herself. "Not of you."

His fingers tightened in response. "I thought I warned you about getting close to anyone in this business."

Now she did smile. "I wasn't paying attention."

A perilous glitter in his eyes. "I thought you told Fourteen I was too old, Mackenzie Connor."

"Something to discuss when I don't have an alien in my kitchen," Mac said primly, pulling free. "Go. You have spy stuff to do." *Keep it light,* she warned herself. *Make it simple.*

But in answer, Nik cupped her face in his hands before she could step out of reach. "We're the worst fools of all," he told her, leaning so close the warm breath of each word was like a kiss against her mouth, his eyes burning into hers. "I can't promise not to hurt you, Mac, or those you care about. Not with what's at stake. Not with the Dhryn out there. I'll spend us both—use anyone I can. I must. You can't bind me."

"Do you really think I would?" Mac put her hands over his and gently loosened his hold, with a reluctance every cell in her body felt. Pretending to smooth his shirt gave her a safer reason to touch him. "The way I look at it, Nik," Mac explained, her voice husky but firm, "fools are the ones who wait for the universe to rearrange itself, then wonder why nothing ever happens." She lifted her eyes to his. "The wise give it a shove."

"Explaining why I ended up in the ocean," Nik recalled, then gave a crooked smile. "Okay. I'll leave. I don't suppose you'd promise to leave the universe alone until we see each other again."

She stuck out her tongue.

"I thought not." Nik leaned forward to touch his lips to her forehead. "Take care, Mac." Then he spun on his heel and left.

At the same instant, one of the sunbeams hitting the floor flickered again.

Startled, Mac glanced up at the skylight. Then stared. *Nothing.*

Suddenly afraid, she rushed to the door, but Nik was already out of sight among the trees. *Damn, he moved fast.*

She froze in place to listen, hearing only the pounding of her heart at first. Gradually, the distant scolding of a squirrel overlaid the faint buzz of uncounted hungry black flies, the drone of a passing beetle. Mac turned her head sharply at a rustling, most likely a sparrow, through a drift of pine needles beside the cabin.

Everything normal.

She shuddered, not reassured in the least.

- Encounter -

THERE IS NO advance warning of a ship about to arrive through a transect. In the bizarre universe of no-space physics, only the act of arriving can create the passage along a transect itself. You arrive at B, because you left A with the intention of arriving at B. Before and after this intention, there is no passage at all. Poets are frequently more at ease with the process than the astrophysicists responsible for it; the few who combine these skills can name their price in any system of the Interspecies Union.

There being no advance warning, management of a transect consists of controlling the approach path of all departing traffic, keeping it to the exterior of a cone of space funneling into each gate probability area—and charging the applicable tariffs and duties. Arriving traffic is granted the interior of that cone and each starship is expected to vacate that privileged space as quickly and expediently as its sublight drive permits, heading immediately, of course, to be assessed for the required arrival tax or fee.

This is the way transects are managed by every species of the IU, as set out in the agreements put in place by the Sinzi, who'd rediscovered the transect technology and made it their quest to share it with any species peaceful or at least law-abiding enough, to maintain their end. After all, when it came to instantaneous intersystem travel, the more destinations, the merrier.

However, the Sinzi being peaceful, practical, and fundamentally prone to cooperation—having several brains per adult body—it wasn't surprising they hadn't appreciated the full range of opportunities that would be presented by having doors to thousand of systems which couldn't be shut. Or even effectively watched.

Like the wide expanse of a river mouth which carries its assortment of vessels to ports on either side as well as out to sea, each transect gate area is large enough to accommodate vast numbers of ships at a time. Unlike boats on a river, who share the level plane of the water's surface, starships don't have to be aligned in any way to one another. There is only intention: coming in or going out.

While by treaty members of the IU shared responsibility for improper use of the transects, in reality warfare among systems belonging to the same species was typically overlooked, so long as it didn't impede the passage of other species' shipping. Moreover, the monitoring of smugglers, tax evaders, and other scoundrels was viewed as a system responsibility. This was not only practical considering the transects themselves, but also necessary given the variety of attitudes among species. As the saying went: one Sythian's pimp was another Frow's grocer.

The Imrya version was, naturally, more elegant, much longer, and constantly evolving through language forms to be trendy. But the gist remained the same. Species who wished to control certain elements within their space maintained patrols or a military fleet, or locked up their precious thirdborns. Whatever worked.

Until now, when the Imrya inserted their entire battle fleet, from mighty cruisers to slaved clusters of solitary fighters, within the whirling spiral of normal traffic moving to enter the Naralax Transect. Several enterprising merchants abandoned their original plans to exit the system altogether, choosing to sell their luxury wares directly to the hulking ships. Others dropped bribes to hurry themselves through the application process, hoping to avoid being too closely checked by a bored deck officer.

Every morning, a new analogy for the potential danger of this particular transect was shared. Today it was "Abyss in the Darkness."

Later, the poet responsible for those fateful words—a minor talent who'd had an admirer sneak three and a half dozen entries on her behalf into the command sequence—committed public suicide. It was considered a prideful gesture among Imrya, with its implication of having reached the pinnacle of success in one's field. The debate would rage for decades whether "Abyss in the Darkness" had been powerful enough in its syntax and subtlety to cause the disastrous events of that day. Regardless, the carapace of the poet, her fateful words inscribed along one edge, would sway in the wind with the thousands of others hung for posterity along the Immortals' Bridge. That those immortals' words couldn't actually be read from this honorable location was never mentioned.

The Imrya always had more words.

Perhaps the new analogy was more alarming than its predecessors. Perhaps the day itself was inauspicious, given the discontent throughout the Imrya fleet over missing the opening of the Playwright's Festival on the home world, an event that only took place every thirteen solar cycles and was claimed to usher in the next great phase of Imrya literary masterworks.

Or, perhaps, it was the startling clang of metal against the hull of an isolated, lonely scoutship, bits of debris dumped from a passing ship that seemed, for the merest instant, to be the silver-clad tentacles of a grappling Dhryn.

An instant is time enough for an alarm to be sent, but not for it to be rescinded. An instant is more than time enough for the wink of a ship to appear from the "Abyss in the Darkness." And it is exactly long enough for a well-trained, terrified fleet to open fire.

If the arrival had been a Dhryn Progenitor, with her cloud of horrific feeders, the carapaces of heroes would have hung alongside poets on the Immortals' Bridge.

But it was the vast Sinzi starliner, *Wonder's Progress II,* filled to capacity with twenty-five thousand, three hundred and fourteen souls, a mix of tourists, actors, and drama critics, members of the founding species of the Interspecies Union plus diplomats from a hundred worlds, en route to the Imrya's famed Festival.

To die with no more advance warning than they gave.

That which is Dhryn must pause the Journey.

Feeders, replete and heavy, return to cling to their carriers. The carriers rise from the empty husk of a world to link together, then rejoin the Progenitor. The Progenitor accepts what is brought, gracious as dawn to the day it brings.

Done with care; done with haste. Any pause is delay. Any delay is threat.

The Journey continues, to the relief of all that is Dhryn.

BETRAYAL AND BRAVERY

"HOW ABOUT FROM here?" Mac tilted her head back to admire the distant pile of sticks. "What do you think?"

Kay came to where she stood and brought his recorder up to his upper left eyestalk, peering through it in the direction she recommended. "So long as you are sure it won't fall on us, Mac," he fussed.

She laughed. "That nest's been up there since I was little, and likely before that. So long as the pine lasts, it will."

"Remarkable." The Trisulian took a few more images, using one hand to hold his small round device and his other arm held perpendicular to his body, as though having an eyestalk preoccupied affected his balance slightly.

Or maybe he thought the posture made him look artistic, Mac thought to herself, as always careful not to jump to conclusions about aliens. "Are you game to find the next?" she asked when he was satisfied.

"Lead on, O Guide."

"This way."

Mac followed faint memory and a fainter trail deeper into the woods north of the cabin. It had been easier than she'd hoped to keep both aliens occupied. When she'd returned to the cabin, she'd found Fourteen in the common room and Kay banished to the porch, where he was watching the other alien through the window. Meanwhile, Fourteen, having pushed the furniture and carpets against the walls, had begun arranging everything small and portable he could find in patterns on the floor. Completely oblivious to her or Kay, he scurried among the items on all fours like some demented carrion beetle, pushing and pulling each into new locations. The floor was already littered with utensils, plates, food containers, and Mac's childhood collection of porcelain frogs, all casting tiny distorted shadows in the sunlight coming through the porch.

Kay had agreed wholeheartedly—or whatever would be the corresponding body part for his kind—to Mac's suggestion they leave genius at work and hike out to the owls' nests to make the recordings she wanted.

Mac was satisfied. Fourteen was—presumably—working on Emily's message, her father would get his nest images after all, and, as per Nik's instructions, she was keeping the aliens out of trouble.

So long as she didn't get them both lost.

A trifling worry. Worst case, the bioamplifier in her bone marrow would locate them for anyone looking. *Not,* Mac told herself firmly, *that she would get lost.* A few years weren't going to change her forest beyond recognition.

Mac halted when the trail, a generous word for a slot of mud last used by a moose with a healthy digestive tract, took a steep drop. Steeper than she remembered. So steep, in fact, she could hold out her hand and almost touch the tops of the trees below. She stretched out to try.

"Is this the way, Mac?" In spite of his anxiety over plummeting nests, Kay didn't appear worried about a plummeting trail. Then again, he was a much better hiker than Mac had expected. His caftan, its variegated colors almost perfect camouflage in the shade-dappled forest, didn't snag on branches. *Certainly better on foot than paddling a canoe,* she grinned to herself. A little too good at times. Although because of Mac's height, Kay took two steps for each of hers and regularly bumped into her from behind.

"I don't think so," Mac said, backing away from what would be a challenging descent with ropes, let alone with a Trisulian on her heels. "Let's go around. That way."

Hiking—without getting lost—took a respectable amount of concentration. Mac had gradually relaxed, able to push the rest of the universe—from vanishing spies to Dhryn—aside, for the moment at least. Besides, the maples and birch of the upper slopes were still unfurling flowers, not leaves. Their branches let through warmth and sunlight, sufficient to trigger a blaze of early blooming lilies and other wildflowers underfoot.

The black flies had even taken the afternoon off, much to Kay's relief. Mac didn't have the heart to warn him such reprieves were temporary until summer. Whenever they approached a meadow, Mac checked for bears, groggy from hibernation and likely to be with young, but the largest mammal they encountered was a porcupine, dozing in the crotch of an ancient apple tree.

They'd found two nests so far, both high, wide, and messy platforms originally built by eagles or ravens and preempted by pairs of great gray owls. No one was home. If owls still used them, the young would have fledged by now and be perching in neighboring trees.

The next nest wasn't the one Mac had been looking for, not that they were lost, but she was delighted to find it. A promising cavity beckoned in a towering stump, riven by lightning years ago. The rest of the tree lay in pieces at their feet. "Ah," she exclaimed triumphantly. "Pellets!" Sure enough, neat finger-length cylinders of compressed fur and tiny white bones lay tumbled among the logs beneath the cavity.

"Look." Mac picked a nice fresh one to show Kay.

"What is it?" he asked, an eyestalk bending closer. *Curiosity or a way to change focal length?* she wondered.

"A pellet. The indigestible remains of the owl's prey," explained Mac. "Likely from a Boreal Owl. Handy for research." She regarded the pellet fondly. "The bird just coughs it up." She began teasing the fur apart. "Yup. See? Vole bones."

"*Usish!*" Kay scrambled backward. "Get that away from me! Disgusting Human!"

It took Mac a fair amount of convincing, and a couple of threats, to get the Trisulian anywhere near the tree again. Once there, he stood like a statue, eye-stalks riveted on the cavity as if on guard against falling pellets.

"C'mon," Mac coaxed. "The owls aren't active in the daytime. Besides, regurgitation is a normal function. You can't tell me you've never needed to remove something from your *douscent*. Same idea."

"I most certainly can," he huffed. "It's disgusting. Scandalous! I insist we return to the cabin this instant!"

She planted her feet. "After you've recorded it."

Kay whipped up his device, clicked it in the general direction of the tree, and started walking away as quickly as the terrain permitted. Following behind, Mac grinned and tucked the pellet into her pocket to examine later. *Not so much raven,* she judged, *as fussy old bachelor.*

It didn't take long for Mac to regret her glib reference to Kay's digestive pouch. He remained offended and silent. The trip back to the cabin took on the rigor of an endurance race. It helped that they were going mainly downhill, with their return path clearly marked by footprints—especially those in moose droppings. The race aspect was purely Kay, who not only appeared to know exactly where he was going, but couldn't get there—or perhaps it was away from her vomiting owls—fast enough.

Mac finally let him scurry off into the distance, dropping her pace back to a more reasonable amble. It was too hot to rush and she was too annoyed with his reaction to be particularly gracious. "By the time I'm back, Emily," she promised aloud, grabbing a sapling to help her clamber past a puddle, "I'll be civil. But honestly. Even sea cucumbers barf." She amused herself with visions of the dignified Trisulian attempting to deal with having dropped a knife or coffee cup into his precious *douscent*.

By the time Mac reached the last stretch of trail, the sun was low on the horizon. It would be bright out on the lake for a while yet, but under the pines the lighting was already growing dim. She didn't mind. This portion of the forest contained fond memories. There were a few more deadfalls, the closest of which she earmarked to raid for wood for a nice campfire if they stayed long enough. *And if the aliens liked fires.* The rest could shelter varying hares and ptarmigan. Her father's "owl feeding stations." The thought made her laugh.

A laugh that died on her lips as Mac entered the clearing behind the cabin and saw the kitchen door was open.

Not just open, but hanging at an angle from one hinge. The screen was shredded, as if by a bear's claws.

It wouldn't be the first time a famished spring bear took a walk through the kitchen. *It would be the first time it found aliens there.*

Mac broke into a run, feet soundless on the pine needles and soil, but making plenty of noise herself as she took the stairs two at a time. "Big Scary Human Coming!" she shouted as she rushed into the kitchen. "Fourteen! Kay!"

The kitchen was fine.

No mess.

No bear.

Mac looked back at the ruined screen and frowned. *How much of a temper did Kay have?* "You're going to pay for that," she vowed, walking into the common room. "The door wasn't locked. Oh . . ." Mac stopped with her hands on either side of the doorframe.

The Ro! Her first thought. But they left glistening slime with their destruction. No slime here. *Not the Ro, then.*

But there was destruction, of a sort. Mac picked her way into the room, eyes surveying everything, careful to touch nothing. One of the couches—two small tables. They'd been tipped over. *A struggle?* The organized, if bizarre, arrangements Fourteen had been creating were gone; the items he'd used swept into piles. Mac picked up a yellow piece of porcelain. A frog's leg. Not much broken otherwise. It was more as if the Myg's arrangements had been tidied, but in a rush. *Why?*

She searched the rest of the cabin, unsure why she stopped calling out the aliens' names. Fourteen's room first. The door was open. Mac peered in and snorted. No destruction; the Myg was about as tidy as a second-year Pred in June. Bedding was in a lump, there were clothes strewn all over the floor, and— Mac sniffed, then hurriedly closed the door. *She'd air the room out later.*

Kay's room was a pleasant surprise. The bed was immaculate; he might not have slept in it. *Well,* Mac thought reasonably, *for all she knew he slept on his hairy head.* No sign of clothing or baggage, not that she was sure he'd brought any personal belongings. He'd worn the same or identical garments every day.

Quickly, Mac checked the remaining rooms, then went out on the porch. Nothing. No note, no sign of either of them. She began to feel a sick certainty they'd left her behind, but why? *An emergency?* She checked the sky with an involuntary shudder. It couldn't have looked more normal, evening blue, curled wisps of high cloud harbingers of the rain scheduled to move through tomorrow.

Or had Nik been wrong about the two aliens? Like some bad spy vid, were Fourteen and Kay somehow traitors on a cosmic scale, their credentials fake, the envelope itself a forgery capable of fooling the Ministry's finest? Had their promise to take her to the Gathering, to work on the Dhryn, been nothing more than a ruse? Had they'd taken what they'd come to get? *Emily's message?*

Mac gave herself a shake. *She could be fooled, Em, but not Nik.* "Then there's the whole poodle plot," she told the forest, her lips twitching. "Quite the masterminds, those two."

Unfortunately, that brought her back to some emergency that had taken the two away—without her.

As for Nik? "Asks me to do one thing," she muttered darkly as she went down the steps to the path, intent on checking the cove. "Watch two aliens. How hard can that be?"

The sun was touching treetops on the far shore. Mac shaded her eyes to scan the lake. All of her canoes were either under the porch or leaning against the rocks behind her. The only movement she could see on the lake was a delirious pair of courting grebes running along the water, necks curled forward. *At least someone was having a good time,* Mac grumbled to herself.

She climbed back to the cabin. Nik had found time to repair the worst spot and Mac delayed to admire his work. Then she looked uphill and sighed. "If I don't fix that door, Em, I really will have four-footed guests for supper."

As for aliens? They could have been scared off by a bear. Or suddenly recalled by the IU, unable to wait for a slow Human.

Or were laughing at how easy it had been to fool them all.

Morose, Mac kicked at a root, missed, and sent a spray of fine grit off the path.

Rustle, rustle.

"Sorry," she called to whatever wildlife she'd offended.

One leg of the couch had snapped off. "Finally have a use for you," Mac told the truly dreadful ornamental box her brothers had kept trying to lose outside and her father had somehow kept retrieving. She righted the couch and shoved the box where the leg had been, turning it so the sneering clowns were out of view. "Perfect."

Mac tossed a cushion back in place, then dusted her hands, deciding to leave the piles for tomorrow. Everything would need to be washed—what wasn't chipped or broken. To be honest, she wasn't in the mood to discover how much remained of her collection.

They'd trashed her home. Left her behind.

Interstellar incidents had begun with less motivation.

She'd rehung the kitchen door as her first task, wiring the bottom hinge in place. It would do for now. The screen was ruined, but Mac found a board to tack over the opening for the night. No point making it easier on the black flies, who'd come out in droves once the air began to still.

What she wanted was for a certain spy to make an appearance.

"What I want, Em," Mac said with a firm nod, "is a beer. And supper. But the beer first." She went into the kitchen and pulled open the chiller. Small items were arranged on narrow shelves along the inside of the door. At first, she *tsked* with disappointment. "None left. Damn aliens." Then she spotted something promising on the lowermost shelf and bent to check. "Aha," Mac crowed. "Even cold." She began to close the door, then stopped, leaning her head to one side.

She'd heard something.

There.

A series of soft clicks, hardly louder than the snap of dragonfly wings.

It had come from the back of the chiller, behind the stacked boxes of alien provisions Russell had brought. *Which they hadn't bothered to take with them.*

Mac switched her grip on the beer bottle to turn it into a club, noticing her fingers were numb. *Cold wasn't the word.* She exhaled a plume of condensation. *Odd. She hadn't set the chiller to freezing.*

Bottle raised and ready, she peered over the boxes.

The Myg lay on the floor in a very Human fetal curl, eyes closed, his skin patched with frost. Dropping the bottle, Mac hurried to kneel beside him. He was cold to the touch, but not frozen solid. She started to give him a gentle shake, then saw the damage to the back of his head. "Oh, no," she whispered.

It had been a terrible blow. The skull itself was indented knuckle-deep along two parallel lines, the surrounding wisps of hair covered in pale green blood, already congealed. She couldn't tell if he was alive or dead.

Someone had tried very hard to make sure.

Forcing down her grief and anger, Mac concentrated on the task at hand. First, get him out of the chiller.

After a moment's consideration, she took hold of Fourteen's ankles and pulled. His body was rigid and stayed curled, but it slid along the floor. At least until the chiller door, where his hip stuck on the rim. She tried lifting him over it, but the alien was unexpectedly massive.

Think. How had Seung moved that shark by himself? "Wait here," Mac told the comatose—and probably dead—alien, feeling foolish. She ran to a bedroom for a blanket. It took a bit of effort to roll him over and slip the blanket underneath, but she managed. Then it was one strong pull to ease him over the rim and into the warmth of the kitchen.

Which was far enough, Mac realized grimly. If Fourteen was dead, she'd have to move his body back into the chiller for safekeeping. Nik or someone would want an autopsy. *Had there ever been an alien murdered on Earth before?* The paperwork alone boggled.

What sunlight was left sent beams along the floor of the common room, barely reaching into the kitchen. Mac turned on the lights and gathered her courage.

"You'd think," she told Fourteen as she examined him, "you people would learn not to visit me." The only other injuries she could find without disturbing his clothes were to his hands. Both were bruised and bloody. She couldn't rule out cracked bones. His left was clenched into a tight fist, as if holding something. Being as gentle as she could, Mac took his fist in her hands and turned it to see.

An eyestalk?

Kay.

"So," she said quietly, lowering Fourteen's fist. "While I took my sweet time coming back, you were fighting for your life." *In how many ways had she been a fool?* The Trisulian's headlong rush to the cabin had had nothing to do with alien squeamishness—he'd known he could outpace her on the trail, had doubtless calculated how far they'd have to hike to give him sufficient time to return and attack Fourteen before Mac could catch up. He'd planned this. Planned it all.

Wasn't that what murderers did?

"Here's hoping he failed," she told Fourteen softly. "But how do I know?"

Mac licked the back of her real hand and placed it in front of Fourteen's nose and mouth. The generous lips were slack and the tips of his white tongue protruded. She waited, but felt no moving air. "Not good." His thick eyelids wouldn't budge short of using pliers, so Mac pressed her ear to his chest instead. *Silence.*

She rocked back on her heels. "If you were me, and I were you, I'd be dead," she informed him, proud of her calm tone. Hearing it gave her more confidence anyway. "But you're not. Me, that is." Mac gave him a gentle poke. "You stopped bleeding, which isn't necessarily a good sign. But why would Kay waste time to put your corpse—not that I'm saying you're a corpse, Fourteen—in the chiller? I wasn't that far behind."

Mac stood and opened the chiller door. Her beer bottle had smashed open on the floor, the liquid already slush at the edges. She ignored the mess, going to the climate control. Not only was it set to minimum, but a bloody green handprint smeared the wall beside it. *Fourteen. But to try and turn it up, or had he turned it down?*

Hopefully, she'd be able to ask him. Mac cranked the temperature back to normal, then pulled the door closed again. Now that she looked for them, there were green smears on the kitchen floor leading from the common room. Not many. The number that might have been left by bleeding hands if Fourteen had dragged himself along.

Rustle . . . scritch, scritch.

A little early for a raccoon or skunk to be checking the kitchen door, but Mac didn't bother shooing the creature away. "Good thing I fixed it," she commented, going back to Fourteen. "Imagine what they'd think of you."

The flutter of dragonfly wings.

Much too early in the season for you, Mac thought with rising hope. "Fourteen. Can you hear me?"

Another series of those faint clicks. *She wasn't imagining it.* The sounds were coming from the Myg.

Mac wrinkled her nose and grinned with relief.

So was that smell.

She made Fourteen as comfortable as possible on the floor, pushing the table out of the way and slipping cushions from the common room under his head and feet. Rolled blankets supported the curl of his back. *Now to get help.*

Seconds later, Mac stared into the box where the cabin's receiver/transmitter had been. *Well,* she thought pragmatically, *it was still there, just in pieces.*

Fourteen had carried a standard-looking imp; Mac had watched him use it to send various messages yesterday. A quick search of Fourteen's clothes—he was back in the Little Misty Lake General Store sweatshirt but still in the paisley shorts—turned up nothing that didn't seem permanently attached.

In the interests of being thorough, and an irrepressible curiosity, Mac did confirm his claim to no external genitalia.

She could canoe for help. That meant leaving Fourteen helpless for several hours. The novice canoe had a distress signal she could activate, if willing to paddle out and capsize it in deep water or run it into a rock. Again, leaving Fourteen alone too long.

The one time privacy wasn't a bonus. "If anyone's listening," Mac announced in a loud, clear voice as she walked to the door to the porch and looked out in the fading light, "I've a seriously injured Myg on my kitchen floor. Could be dead," she said honestly. "The Trisulian, Kay, tried to murder him. We need help. Anyone?"

Nik might have planted one of his toys in the cabin after all. *For once,* Mac decided, *she wouldn't mind.* "Where's a spy when you need one, Emily?"

Louder clicking.

Mac hurried back to the kitchen. Fourteen was still in his distressed curl, but she could swear an arm had moved from where she'd placed it. The warmth of the room might be helping—

Or she was imagining a dead alien was clicking and moving in her kitchen. "And the night's young, Em," Mac sighed.

Optimism was more useful. Acting on her hunch, Mac tossed a handful of towels in the sink, running hot water over them until they were soaked and steaming. After cooling them from scalding to hot, she began to apply the towels to Fourteen's shoulders and chest. She didn't attempt to wipe the blood from his head or hands. The clots were holding the wounds together. She placed the last towel around his neck.

Three soft clicks.

His fist eased open and the eyestalk rolled free with a clatter.

Clatter? Mac caught the thing before it went too far, holding it gingerly. "Well, I'll be . . ."

Up close, the eyestalk was clearly artificial, an elaborate hollow fake complete with pincerlike clamp at one end. The clamp presently contained a twisted gray lock of Trisulian hair. Fourteen must have yanked it free.

Mac touched the hair. It didn't feel real either.

Nik had commented on Kay's eyestalks, told her four were normal. "Now would be a good time to know why," she mused uneasily.

She added it to her growing list of questions and focused on her patient, replacing towels before they cooled too much. In between, she went through the first-aid kit she'd brought to the table. Nothing seemed worth trying.

A few minutes later, Fourteen suddenly and unmistakably moved again, straightening out with a ragged sigh. Mac held her breath and listened for his. Sure enough, as if the sigh had been the first, the Myg began taking shallow, labored breaths. She stripped off the last of the wet towels and tucked a thick quilt over him.

"See, Em? I wasn't wrong," Mac said rather smugly, sitting cross-legged on the floor. She kept one hand resting lightly on the Myg's chest, gratified to feel it continue to rise and fall, ever so slightly. "Not dead."

She'd sat like this with Brymn. Only instead of recovering, she'd witnessed the change in his body, felt it alter beneath her fingers, seen the horror in his fading eyes mirror her own as they both realized what he'd become—

And what it meant.

A pufferfish Dhryn, the feeder form. Green drops consuming a helpless woman, digesting her arm . . .

A tear splashed the back of her hand. Mac jerked in reaction, then gave an unsteady laugh at herself.

"Mumphfle . . ."

"Fourteen?" Mac kept her voice soft and low. He had to have an intense headache. Her eyes flicked to the ugly wound and she winced. *If any brains were left intact in his skull to feel it.* "It's Mac. You're . . ." *All right* seemed premature, given she'd thought him likely dead minutes ago. ". . . you're safe. He's gone."

His lips moved. She leaned down to listen. "Pardon?"

"IDIOT!"

Mac fell back in surprise.

"Idiot! Idiot. Id . . ." the word weakened with each repetition. Just as Mac was sure she was dealing with serious brain damage, Fourteen's eyes cracked open. "Not safe," he whispered in a thick but clearer voice. "It's still here. It will kill us both."

It? "What? The Ro?" Mac looked around her kitchen, seeing nothing out of the ordinary and certainly no slime. "There's nothing here but us, Fourteen."

"That Trisulian. THAT DEVIANT!" The shout brought on a spasm of painful coughs. Mac hurried to get Fourteen water, holding the cup to his lips and helping him drink.

"I've checked the cabin," she assured him. "Every room. We're alone. Tell me how to treat your injuries—"

"Then it's . . ." His damaged hand lifted toward the boarded-up kitchen door, gave a weak gesture.

"Outside?" Mac took a steadying breath. "Then whatever it is can stay there. Right now, I'm concerned with you. Kay tried to crush your skull, in case you haven't noticed."

"Not Kay."

That wasn't good news. "Someone else was here?"

"No."

He struggled to sit; Mac forced him down again. "You're not making sense, Fourteen. Stay still. Please."

The effort had cost him. Fourteen's already pale skin looked more green than beige. "Mac?" His small eyes fixed on her and she thought they showed surprise. "I thought you were dead."

"I thought you were." Mac's hands paused on the quilt she was settling around the alien's shoulders. "I see. You thought Kay had attacked me, too?"

"He came back alone." As if it was obvious.

She supposed it was and flushed. "I'm very sorry, Fourteen. This is my fault. I'd been warned about him—but not that he was dangerous. I didn't see any harm in letting him come back first. I thought you were—" She hesitated.

"Friends?" He coughed and raised a hand to his head. "Irrelevant. We remain in terrible danger, Mac. Listen to me."

Mac swallowed. "Kay's still here?"

"No. Yes. Irrelevant. This structure will not keep us safe. We must—" Fourteen's voice faded again. He waved urgently at the chiller. "In there."

"You were hiding," Mac realized.

"Like this." He touched the black fly disk on her belt. "It hunts by heat. My species enters torpor—sleeps—in the cold." A spasm of pain. "It couldn't find me."

"What hunts by—"

Rustle, rustle.

Bleeding hands grabbed Mac, pushed her toward the chiller door with unexpected strength. "Hurry!"

"That?" She resisted, careful not to hurt him. "Calm down, Fourteen. What you're hearing is local wildlife. A raccoon or squirrels in the rafters. They're just a nuisance."

He didn't look convinced. "We must hide until daylight. Then take a canoe—"

"Yes, tomorrow I'll paddle to the store and get some help. Meanwhile, let's work on getting you into a bed."

"No!" He pressed his lips together, then said: "If you won't go in the chiller, then close the door and we'll stay here. Leave on the lights. It doesn't see well in light."

Mac sighed. "What 'it'?"

"Kay."

"I thought you said he'd left."

"Yes. Deviant!" Fourteen coughed again and closed his eyes. "Please, Mac."

"Fine. We'll stay here tonight." By this point, she'd have done anything to calm him down. The head wound had reopened at one end of the gash. His breathing, never even, was more shallow than before. Mac closed the door to the common room. It didn't lock, but a chair wedged under the knob did the trick. The windows were already closed, but she checked the back door, feeling self-conscious. Her patch job was holding up.

Fourteen had watched her. He appeared more at ease now that she was taking precautions against "it." *Whatever "it" was, beyond his imagination.*

"Can I make you more comfortable?" she asked. "Is there anything I should do for your injuries?

"Irrelevant." Somehow the word was both tired and kind. "I have a thick skull."

Mac brought him a fresh cup of water anyway, and put it within reach. She went to a cupboard and pulled out the first self-heating meal she could find.

Scritch.

The sound of tiny claws on the outside of the kitchen door turned Mac's head, but sent Fourteen into an arm-waving, heel-drumming frenzy as he tried to get up and couldn't. Hurrying to him, Mac held him down until he stopped, then sniffed and sighed. "I'll go see what it is," she said, standing.

"No! No! Mac! No!"

She opened the door anyway.

Only to jump in fright as a lean raccoon scampered off the porch, equally startled.

"Damn aliens," Mac muttered under her breath. Furious at herself for taking Fourteen's babbling to heart, and quite thoroughly shaken, she stepped out on the landing.

Something heavy landed on the back of her head, grabbing her shoulders with what felt like teeth. Mac cried out and staggered, trying to pull it off. She felt hair come lose between her fingers. It wasn't hers.

A muscular writhing, then a blow against the top of her skull like a branch falling from a tree. Through tears of pain and blood, driven to her knees and half falling down the steps, Mac fought for a hold, some way to pull the thing from her. She felt it convulse again, as if coiling to strike. Remembering the parallel wounds on Fourteen's skull, Mac rolled and threw her head backward against the wood rail as hard as she could, trapping whatever it was.

One set of claws released her shoulder. Mac fumbled with her left hand, trying to grab the thing, and felt something bite and tear at her fingers. She only pushed harder, shoving those fingers deeper and deeper into what she devoutly hoped was a mouth. "Choke on that," she yelled. It spat her hand out and Mac threw herself against the wood again.

The weight on her head was gone as abruptly as it had arrived.

Rustle, rustle.

Hot blood poured down her face. Holding the railing with both hands, Mac searched the darkness beyond the light spilling down from the kitchen door. When nothing moved, she slowly rose to her feet, backing into that light step by cautious step.

A gleaming spot of red, a reflection from a solitary eye no taller than a raccoon, stared back at her from the shadow, as if in promise.

Then was gone.

"What was that thing?" Mac balanced the pack of no-longer-quite-frozen vegetables on her head and popped another painkiller. There were advantages to being besieged in a kitchen.

Fourteen sat at the table across from her, elbows on a cushion. He'd tried to come to her aid, but had barely managed to stand before Mac had bled her way into the cabin, shutting the door behind her and ramming a chair beneath its handle.

Now she understood his hands. The surface of her prosthetic hand was deeply scored; the ring finger had been snapped off at the joint. If she'd made a mistake and used her flesh and bone to fight off the creature, Mac was quite sure she'd be lying outside.

As it was, she had a probable concussion—hopefully nothing worse. Its first blow had glanced, tearing loose an appalling amount of scalp, but sparing her the full force, a force which would likely have crushed her skull.

She'd used skin patches from the first-aid kit to hold the gash together and stop the bleeding, more on the pinprick-sized holes in her shoulders—at least the ones she could reach. Her shirt was still damp but now with mostly water; she hadn't tried to get the blood out of her shorts.

"What was it? Kay." Fourteen smiled faintly at her scowl. He'd taken a couple of Human painkillers over her caution and was certainly looking better than she'd expected. *In all likelihood,* Mac thought, *better than she did.* "Trisulians keep their sex with them—their sex partners, to be precise. Each mature female accepts as many males as she can afford. They attach themselves to her body for the rest of their lives. She feeds them, they mate with her as she requires it. You have organisms with similar biologies on this world, as do we. Symbiosis?"

"Symbiosis." Mac used her damaged hand to pick up the artificial eyestalk. "They attach under the hair on his—her head," she guessed.

"'His' head. Once a Trisulian possesses at least one male, the pronoun changes. Unless both are gone. Then he is a she again."

Meaning she should avoid pronoun issues. "So the eyestalks belong to the males?"

"Two are the females. One more for each male. Theirs are the eyes closed in daylight. Male Trisulians see only heat—infrared." Fourteen made a rude noise. "Kay was a deviant—removing an attached male to do his bidding, replacing him with that thing so no one would notice. It is something desperate criminals do, not civilized beings."

Mac did the math. "So there could be two of them out there?"

"No. Despite his greed, Kay was not willing to sacrifice both his symbionts." He indicated his own head wound. "But even one unattached male is dangerous. They hunt for receptive females in the dark and use their external genitalia, a formidable armored club, to strike and kill rivals, defending the virtue of their prize. Males mature on Trisul Primus. Interested females let themselves be hunted through its jungles." Fourteen gave her that sly look. "It's all terribly romantic—if you're Trisulian."

He must be on the mend. "I was clobbered by genitalia?" Mac almost wished she'd had a look at the thing. "You're kidding."

He laughed, though weakly. "You are safe with me, Mac. Remember, I have none!"

Rustle, scritch.

They both fell silent at the sounds from the closed back door. Sounds that had earlier tried the windows; once the door from the common room.

Mac cleared her throat and adjusted the cold pack on her head. "How intelligent are the males?"

"Idiots. Barely sentient. I believe a valid comparison to your Earth fauna would be a weasel. Something violent and persistent. And stupid. Luckily for me. Otherwise, it would have stayed to be sure I was dead, and not merely unconscious. But all it wants is to kill other males, attach, have sex forever."

"Yet controllable, at least to the extent that Kay could make it leave—him—and attack us."

He shrugged. "So it seems. Or maybe rejection has driven it mad and it blames us. All we can assume is that Kay knew his abandoned paramour would do its utmost to kill us both."

Wonderful. Oversexed and overwrought. Mac tried to think through the pain and the cloud of post-adrenaline fatigue. "But why? Why would Kay want us dead?"

The Myg covered his eyes with his hands. "Because I'd finished the translation, Mac. When he learned what it said, Kay grew agitated, insisted his government had to have it before any other. I told him he was an idiot and we struggled. Here. The other room. It was a great battle. When he realized he couldn't win, he turned out the lights to allow his genitalia to find and kill me." He lowered his hands to peer at her. "But I was too smart for it."

"Yes, you were," Mac said soothingly, mind racing. *Emily's message.* Her own pain forgotten, she put down the cold pack and leaned forward eagerly, but carefully. "What was the translation?"

Fourteen rested his head in his hands. "Kay took my notes as well as your original," he said miserably. "I would show my work but I'd already swept up my cipher."

"You broke my frogs for nothing!" Mac punctuated this highly irrational statement by slamming her good hand on the table, an impulse she immediately regretted as the jolt made its way up her arm to pound between her ears.

Fourteen peered at her. "I could tell you what the message said," he offered.

Oh, for patience with the alien.

Mac composed herself. "Thank you, Fourteen. I'd very much like to hear Emily's message."

He began reciting a list of numbers in a monotone. Mac listened. The numbers kept coming. He paused for a drink of water. More numbers.

Finally, she had to interrupt. "Wasn't there a message? Some words?" Mac asked. *Something she could imagine was Emily's voice. "Hi Mac. Wish you were here. How're the salmon."*

"There is no need for words."

"I need words," she begged.

"But . . . there are none."

Mac dropped her face into her hands. *Gods, Emily,* she thought. *Couldn't you have done this one thing for me?*

"I understand, Mac. You want words from your friend. We are both idiots, are we not?"

Rustle, scritch.

She mumbled: "I can't believe you tried to talk me into sex with that."

"Good. Your sense of the absurd returns."

Mac laid her cheek along her arm and peered at Fourteen. "What do the numbers mean?"

"To me? Very little." His wide mouth stretched in a tired smile. "But to those who know how to build signaling devices they will mean a great deal. They are communication settings. Adjustments. How to call for help against the Dhryn."

She lifted her head. "What are you saying?"

"Using this information, Mac, we can finally contact the Ro. The IU will be very pleased."

Scritch, scritch, THUD, *scritch, rustle.*

"Still after our heads, Fourteen," Mac commented after the noise subsided. *Going to need a new door at this rate.* "But why would Kay want this information for his species first?" Mac closed her eyes. "I know. Idiot. The Trisulians want to make some kind of deal with the Ro to protect themselves. Then they'll be safe to follow the Dhryn, like salvagers who follow a plague ship until its crew is safely dead. Adding planet after planet to a new Trisulian empire." *Kay didn't have to be a mastermind. Just ruthless enough to seize an opportunity.* She took the bag of nearly-thawed vegetables and threw them across the room, hard enough to break open and spatter mixed greens on the wall, kernels of corn bouncing on the floor. "How dare they!"

"We forestall them, Mac, if the IU contacts the Ro first. So that is what we must do."

You don't know the Ro, Mac almost said, then stopped herself in time. She didn't either, not really. And this wasn't the time to air her private grievances with their new allies.

If one ever came.

- 10 -

FLIGHT AND FRIENDSHIP

THE FLIGHT PATH TO THE COVE would be the worst part. Mac and Fourteen both knew it, without need to discuss his weakness or hers. As for leaving the safety of the kitchen? They'd hoped for strong sunlight to blind the lurking Trisulian, but dawn had lost itself in the gathering storm, right on cue.

Beneath the trees it might as well be dusk.

Mac had spent the night torn between wishing Nik had changed his mind and would soar up on a white lev and a more rational hope he had someone following Kay. Besides, how would even Nik suspect one of the little weasels, as she'd come to think of the male Trisulian, would be roaming the woods?

And how could you guard yourself against a sex-starved weasel with night vision and a hammer?

This being the unanswerable question of the moment, Mac resolutely ignored it.

"You ready?" she asked Fourteen, inspecting him carefully.

They both looked like death warmed over, she thought. Blood where it shouldn't be—neither having energy to spare for a change of clothes—and precious little of it in their cheeks. They tended to lean until they'd tip, overcorrect, then stumble into one another. But the best part, Mac decided, would be the look on Cat's face when they arrived at the store.

Given they arrived at the lake to start with.

"I'm ready," Fourteen said, making that faint click of distress as Mac checked the tightness of his repeller belt for the third time. "I don't plan to swim to across the lake," he protested.

Time to share her final worry. "This isn't going to be like your last paddle, Fourteen," explained Mac, pushing hair from one eye. "The wind's gusty; waves are already white-capped. We could very well tip and that water is cold enough to put you back to sleep. This—" she patted the belt, "—will be all that stops you sinking like a rock."

"If I will be a hazard, Mac, you should leave me here."

They'd talked about this before, too. But the dawn had made its way into the kitchen through a ruined portion of the back door. While they'd slept—or more accurately passed out—sitting at the table, the little weasel had almost made its way inside. It wouldn't take much for it to succeed.

She wouldn't have risked Fourteen before. Now, she couldn't, not with the meaning of Emily's message in his head.

"I need you for ballast," Mac said. *Not altogether untrue.* "Let's go."

Pride had nothing to do with their progress from the cabin. More dizzy than not, Mac sat to skid down the steep sections, waiting for Fourteen to do the same. It had the added advantage of speed; *although,* she sighed inwardly when they reached level ground, *there'd definitely be gravel to remove.*

Even the cove had turned ugly, slapping at the beach with crisscrossing waves. The sky was the next best thing to sullen. Mac could see a dark band of rain on the other side of the lake. Spring had an edge in the north the weather regulators left alone.

"Wait here," she shouted over the wind and splash. Fourteen leaned on his paddle in answer.

The novice canoe—where they'd left it, but not how. Mac glared at the burned-edged holes along the hull. Doubtless the "rescue me" signal device was in need of more help than they were. Kay was thorough, she gave him that. *Probably all the catering.*

Her canoe rested beside it, untouched. It didn't have the toys of the novice, but she knew and trusted it. Mac reached down and flipped it over.

The Trisulian came with it, a grimy mop of snapping claws that just missed catching hold of her face, but snagged in her shirt.

So much for getting a good look at the thing. Eyestalk up and closed against the light, it curled like a scorpion over her chest, aiming an immense hornlike structure at her eyes. Mac couldn't move, couldn't raise her hands in time.

Smack!

The swing of a paddle blade in front of her nose freed Mac from the paralysis. She staggered back into someone's arms, knocking him down as well. She landed in a smelly heap of upset Myg and Human, squirming around to try and see.

Where was the damned weasel?

Then she saw it, a pile of broken claws and hair, like so much storm wrack washed ashore. It gave a last twitch and was still.

"What was that?" a horrified woman's voice. *How odd,* Mac thought, clinging to Fourteen, *that it wasn't hers.*

"Rabid skunk," a man replied in no uncertain terms. "First things first, Wendy. Help me get them up to the cabin."

It couldn't be.

Brain damage, Emily. That's what it is. Mac thought this very clever.

Until Oversight, in his familiar ill-fitting yellow rainsuit, leaned down and offered her his hand. "Hurry up, Norcoast. It's going to rain."

"How's that?"

"Better. Thank you."

Mac cradled a mug of hot cocoa in her hands, her feet and legs tucked up beneath her in the big chair, and watched Charles Mudge III deftly apply a field dressing to a Myg. In her father's cabin. On Little Misty Lake. Earth.

And in case she doubted the veracity of her senses, she had only to look in a mirror to see the Trisulian blood drying on her face, splattered there when Oversight had—

—*had saved her life.*

"May I help you wash up, Mac?"

She turned her eyes to Wendy's anxious ones and lifted her cocoa a few millimeters. "Let me get this down first." *And have a chance of standing without falling over,* Mac promised herself.

Wendy nodded and sat in a neighboring chair. "Charlie's amazing, isn't he?" she said very quietly. "You should have seen him leap from the canoe, straight after that—" she hesitated.

"Skunk," Mac supplied helpfully. *Charlie?*

"Right. Skunk. I didn't know old guys could move like that."

By the slight stiffening of Oversight's shoulders, he'd overheard Wendy's comment. Mac smiled. "He's not old," she explained. "He just dresses that way."

This drew an indignant look. Mac lifted her mug again, this time in salute. "Welcome to Little Misty Lake, Oversight."

He made a noncommittal noise and went back to bandaging Fourteen's hands.

"We've contacted the authorities, Mac," Wendy went on. She'd half carried Mac up the slope, then gone back to help Oversight with Fourteen, who'd been near collapse. Quietly competent, making no comment about the state of the cabin—or its occupants—she'd sent a call for help, found her way around the kitchen to make hot drinks and sandwiches, and located the first aid gear for Oversight. The kind of person who radiated comfort and competence. Mac was mutely grateful.

Oversight, of course, was nothing of the sort. He finished with Fourteen, making sure the Myg was settled comfortably on the couch, then came over to glare down at Mac. "Authorities?" he barked. "Which ones will show up? Real police or your friends? You do realize it took every connection I had to get out of that ridiculous house arrest—"

"They aren't my—well, maybe some are," Mac corrected herself. "Let's hope it's them, Oversight. Sit." When he didn't, she sighed. "Please. We have to talk before they arrive. Wendy—I'm sorry to ask, but would you go out on the porch and watch for the lev? That path will be a minor river by now. Whoever comes might need help finding their way up."

"Sure, Mac." Wendy stood and shrugged on her coat. The wind was whipping rain against each wall of the cabin in turn from the sounds of it. The porch screens wouldn't be much protection. There was a deep rumble of thunder as well.

Oversight scowled and bent over Mac. "Hold still." She did, scowling back at him. He gently tilted her face toward one of the lights in the room, thumbs easing open her eyelids. Mac winced. "You know you have a concussion," this in a tone that implied she'd probably earned it.

Diagnosis complete, he sat where Wendy had been, pulling the chair toward Mac's until their knees almost touched. "At least we had the sense to beat the storm here. What were you thinking, trying to canoe in your condition?"

Mac took a sip of cocoa, feeling it warm her throat. "As I remember, I was thinking I was about to die."

He harrumphed, as if she'd embarrassed him. "I admit, Norcoast, I wasn't expecting to see a Trisulian male going for your head."

"You know what it was?" Mac was astonished.

"Of course." His round face creased in disapproval. "Didn't you? I took my share of xeno at university. Jokes about those walking gonads have been a standby of frosh parties for years."

Was she the only Human who hadn't studied aliens? Mac could hear Emily's answer to that. "Yes, I knew what it was." Then, because she hadn't said it yet, she did. "Wendy's right. You are fast for an old guy. Thank you, Oversight."

That look, the one saying he was set to be stubborn. "If you want to thank me, tell me what the hell's going on. I was flying over the Trust, cataloging earthquake damage, and see the pods being towed. I try to find out where, and lo, your staff's dispersed. You? Gone again without a word. Why?"

"I had no reason to stay," Mac ground out. "Norcoast's suspended all research until the pods are reanchored at the mouth of the Tannu River and the main systems are running."

"And you let them get away with that?"

Mac shrugged, her head instantly making her pay. "What should I have done, Oversight?" she asked wearily. "Chain myself to a pod?"

From his expression, Oversight thought this a perfectly reasonable notion, but he didn't pursue it. "At least your father had a good idea where you were this time," he said with considerable satisfaction. *Enjoying being a detective,* Mac judged. *There, Em, was a scary thought.* "What are you doing here, Norcoast? With him?" a nod to Fourteen. "Like this?"

"You deserve to know," Mac agreed. She gazed at the man she'd fought with most of her professional career, over what they both loved. *Funny, how clear that could make a relationship.* "But be warned, Oversight. If I tell you—you'll be caught in it too."

"I am already. You're wasting time." He steepled his pudgy fingers and leaned back in the chair, regarding her with a placid, already-bored look Mac didn't believe for a second. "Get to the point, Norcoast."

Typical. Her lips twitched. "Fine. I've never been to the IU consulate, Oversight. Or New Zealand, for that matter. You were right. They were lies. I didn't make them up, but I was ordered to live with them."

"By your friends in black."

"Who work for the Ministry of Extra-Sol Human Affairs. The Secretary General himself enlisted me. You've heard of the Dhryn."

Fingers waved dismissively, then returned to their positioning. "Implausible hysterics."

"The Dhryn are deadly," Fourteen interjected, his eyes staying closed. "Everything you've heard about them in your news is true—and more. Idiot. The Chasm will be only the beginning of the devastation, unless they are stopped."

"He's right." Mac continued. "Last fall, a Dhryn—Brymn Las was his name—came to me at Norcoast. At that time, none of us—not even Brymn— knew the truth about his species."

"The media covered that—the first of his kind on Earth. I couldn't believe you'd let him interrupt your work."

Mac smiled into her cocoa. "You know me pretty well, Oversight." Her smile faded. "The Ministry asked me to help Brymn investigate some mysterious disappearances that seemed related." Her hands shook and she took a moment to cover it by drinking from her mug. "They were. That's when the trouble began."

"The incident at Base," Mudge frowned. "More lies, I take it."

"Yes. It wasn't sabotage or any 'Earth-First' protest. We were attacked by the Myrokynay, the Ro." Mac shifted into lecture mode. *Easier that way.* "No one alive knew they still existed except the Dhryn, who feared them. We—experts believe the Ro invented the transects in the first place, thousands of years before the Sinzi found the remnants of their technology in the Hift System."

"I know all that."

"What you don't know is that the Ro watched the Dhryn destroy the Chasm worlds. They've been hiding ever since, waiting for the Dhryn to stir again. To stop them."

"So they're the good guys."

Mac raised her eyes to his. Whatever he read there made him add: "Or not."

"The Ro's methods," Fourteen said for Mac, "are repugnant by the standards of cultures like yours and mine. They wanted Mac and her Dhryn companion to flee Earth, so they attacked the salmon research station with no regard for life. They used Mac to locate the Dhryn Progenitors, in order to attack them without warning. Even now, they use members of other species as their agents, altering their bodies with no-space technology."

"Including Em—Emily Mamani," Mac continued, finding her voice again. "She went with the Ro, to help them stop the Dhryn. To—to push me in the direction they wanted. She hasn't come back. Not yet. The rest—" she reached out with her mug blindly, trying to find a place for it. Mudge took it from her hand. "—Brymn thought I was in danger from the Ro, so he took me with him to his home world. Yes," Mac said, fully understanding the stunned look on Mudge's face, "I abandoned my research and went offworld. Amazing what a little carnage and kidnapping can do to a person.

"As a result," she finished, "I now speak and read Dhryn better than any Human language—and, I'm told, better than any other Human. So far as I know, I've spent more time with Dhryn than any other non-Dhryn being. I've even been semiadopted, I guess you could call it, as a Dhryn. All in time for the Dhryn, for my dear friend Brymn Las, to be revealed as the greatest threat civilization has ever faced." She showed him the remaining fingers of her new arm. "Did I mention surviving a Dhryn attack? And helping kill my friend?"

Mudge didn't say a word, staring at her as if she'd changed into something he couldn't recognize anymore.

She knew the feeling. Mac patted Oversight's knee. "Oh, it gets better. Our walk in the Trust the other day? A chance for Emily and the Ro to slip me a message that only Fourteen here has been able to translate. That earthquake? Deliberate. Someone, and I don't know who yet, making sure the Ro landing site wasn't explored by you, or I, or anyone else. And this?" Mac waved at Fourteen and gestured to her own cap of dried blood and first-aid patches. "One of the side effects of a threat to members of the Interspecies Union. Which does, you see, include us."

"You'll come with us, now, Dr. Connor."

Mac turned her head slowly, completely unsurprised to see the cabin porch filled with rain slicked black-visored troops, three more coming in the door, all with weapons not quite not aimed their way.

"Welcome to my world, Oversight," she told him.

"A sight to warm the hearts, *Lamisah* . . ."

Mac nodded. She didn't move, letting puppy-sized *oomlings* explore her lap and arms. Their white down quivered as they cooed to her, the sound itself low and soothing. Tiny hands, six from each, stroked her clothing, patted her cheeks, investigated her eyelashes. Each touch was feather soft.

They hadn't touched her.

"Our future . . ."

The cooing grew louder, gained an undersound that raised hairs on her skin, intensified her emotion. It came from everywhere around her, though there was nothing but precious, vulnerable *oomlings* as far as she could see, all reaching their tiny hands to her over the low walls of their pens.

But she'd only glimpsed the crèche from above.

"We haven't time to waste . . ."

Shadows passed overhead. The first green drops fell at a distance. The *oomlings* beneath cried out and crowded together, but there was no escape.

No. They weren't trying to escape. They were raising their faces, opening their rosebud mouths, calling eagerly for their share.

It hadn't been like this.

All but the ones in Mac's lap. They were changing—their down falling away from pulsating transparent flesh, their shape lost, eyes vanishing. They were rising from her hands into the air . . .

She screamed as drops fell from mouths that insisted, in their sweet cooing voices: "We told you to go, *Lamisah*. We warned you. Didn't we?"

The ground beneath shook as the Progenitor laughed . . .

"Promise to let me know the next time you feel so much as drowsy," Oversight warned Mac in no uncertain terms. "I'll sit with someone else."

"There isn't anyone else," she pointed out.

He couldn't argue, since they were alone in the rear compartment of a large transport lev. There had been three crowding the storm-tossed cove. Another had taken Fourteen. Mac presumed the third had been courteous enough to return Wendy Carlson to the Little Misty Lake General Store, where she'd have an interesting, if mysterious, tale to relate to Cat and Russell. A tale doubtless provided by one of their companions in black.

One day, Mac swore to herself, *she was going to park herself on the dock, shoo away the pelican, and tell the truth to everyone who stopped or paddled by.* Her head dropped back against the seat. *Maybe she should tell the pelican, too.* She wished she'd washed her face. The dried blood was itchy.

Mudge's movements disturbed her. "Can't you sit still for two minutes?" Mac complained.

He finished unbuckling his safety harness and turned to face her. Without asking, he grabbed her chin and tilted her face upward, checking her eyes again. "We've been in this thing over an hour. You need medical help."

Mac pushed his hand away. "I need sleep," she muttered irritably. "You keep waking me up."

"You keep screaming," he countered. "What do you expect?" Mudge stood, presumably to storm the door to the pilot's compartment where the large persons in black armor traveled—persons who'd refused to say anything more than "hurry" and "now." Mac caught his arm.

"Don't bother, Oversight. I'll be fine." He didn't look convinced. She was touched by his concern, but tugged a little harder. "Sit. I promise to do my best to stay awake until we get there. No more screaming."

He gave the sealed door another look, then sighed and sat down. *Probably remembering the "large" and "armored" part of their hosts.* "Get where?"

"Where?" Stealth vehicle with the latest tech or not, the lev vibrated in a way that didn't help her head. "Last time, Oversight," she managed to say, "I ended up in orbit."

Rather than alarmed, Mudge looked intrigued. "Really?"

It didn't help her stomach either. "Really." Mac leaned back and closed her eyes, pressing her lips together and breathing lightly through her nose.

He didn't take the hint. "I've a pilot's license, you know."

Ye gods. Oversight doing small talk. "Really."

"Really." Definite smugness to his tone. "My brother, Jeremy, designs golf courses. Travels more than a diplomat. Before I joined the Oversight Committee, I'd copilot his jumper. Racked up enough transect passages to go commercial, if I'd wanted."

Mac cracked open one eye to stare at Mudge. "You?" Realizing how this sounded about the same instant she drew an offended breath, she opened both eyes and added: "You seem so focused on Earth."

He seemed mollified. "I can understand why you'd get that impression, Norcoast. Certainly, the Trust has been my mission in life these past years. But I was first and foremost an explorer in my early days. Quite miss it, at times."

"I've never wanted to travel."

"Oh."

Could she be any less tactful? "Last time," Mac offered, "they brought me to a way station and we—Brymn and I—took a Dhryn ship from there."

"What was it like? Their ship?"

He was so interested, she felt guilty. *As well as nauseous.* Hopefully, Fourteen was faring better. "I didn't see more than my quarters and one corridor. A bit of the hold, I think. Sorry. The doors and walls weren't perpendicular. There was gravity and—" Mac paused, then finished reluctantly, "—not a drop of water." She fell silent. *Brymn had saved her then, too.*

"That was a brave thing to do."

"What? Oh, my going with the Dhryn?" Mac would have laughed if she could. "I'm not sure how brave it was. There didn't seem any other choice. Everything happened so quickly and he—they—" she fumbled "—the Ministry wanted me to go."

Too late. Over the years, Mudge had developed radar for exactly what she tried to avoid. "He? He who?"

Mac pinched the bridge of her nose between thumb and forefinger. It didn't stop the ache, but provided a welcome distraction. "The Ministry's liaison for Brymn, during his visit to Earth. He made the arrangements to get us offworld." *Now there was a distraction,* she thought. *Was Nik on this lev? Had he been one of the anonymous figures in black?*

"Doesn't 'he' have a name?"

Not if he hasn't shown himself, Mac decided. Not with this compartment undoubtedly monitored. Aloud: "Something complicated, eastern Europe-ish. Annoying civil servant type. You'd like him."

The lev picked that moment to swoop downward. "Someone's in a hurry to land," Mudge observed, refastening his harness and giving hers a test pull.

"Suits me," Mac said.

"What can we expect, Norcoast? One call and a small cell? Or just the cell."

He deserved to know, she decided, hearing the feather of understandable anxiety in Mudge's voice. *Not everything.* The IU's invitation was still in her pocket, but Mac had no idea what her status was anymore. She concentrated on picking the right words, annoyed with how difficult it seemed. "The Ministry has unusual powers right now, Oversight. 'Threat to the species,' that sort of thing. Odds are good this is about information. They'll have questions for us. Order us to keep silent or not bother. Send us home."

"Or?"

"Or we disappear, for as long as that threat exists and we're an added risk." Mac studied his face as the lev leveled out again. "I guess you're sorry you followed me."

His expression was set and pale. There were drops of sweat on his forehead, more beading his nose and upper lip. But he shook his head emphatically. "I'm sorry you didn't come to me with this—tell me what was happening."

"I couldn't tell my own father," Mac reminded him. "Besides," she added lightly, swaying with him as the lev did some more maneuvering, "I didn't think you'd—" *care,* "—be interested."

He might have heard the word she didn't use. "I care about what affects the Wilderness Trust," his voice was as cold and hard as she'd ever heard it. "Because of you—because of what you brought to Castle Inlet—an entire ridge has been artificially stripped. Grant you, it's an opportunity to regenerate some of the rarer successional species—but we have sufficient natural disasters without your help. This is your fault, Norcoast. You were selfish. Thoughtless. You should have stayed away! You should never have come back!"

The last were shouts that echoed in the compartment, pounding inside her wounded head, every word horrid and familiar. Mac could hardly see past the tears welling up in her eyes. She turned and struck wildly at him. "Don't you tell me what I should have done!" she shouted back. "I know! I know!" Her face grew wet with more than tears. Warm blood ran down her left cheek. Some or all of the patches holding her torn scalp had ripped free. Blood entered her mouth, making her choke on the words: "I know!"

He had hold of her. "Stop," she heard him say in a shattered voice. "Stop, Norcoast. I didn't mean any of it. It isn't true. I'm sorry. I'm scared. I'm angry. I don't blame you. Of course I don't. The trees will grow back. You have to survive, too. Who—" she felt him press his hand against her head, trying to stem the bleeding, "—who else will I argue with?"

This last sounded so plaintive Mac laughed, though the sound was more gurgle than anything else. She swallowed the blood in her mouth and worked on steadying her breathing.

Later, for some reason she couldn't be sure how much later, other hands intruded. Other voices. "We've got her, sir." "This way, please." "Watch her head." Mac blinked and tried to focus, then gave up as the effort sent her stomach lurching toward her throat again. She was picked up—*must have missed the landing, Em*—and carried a short distance. Someone, or someones—*lost count of the hands, Em, wouldn't do on the dance floor*—put her on a firm flat surface that spun in slow, sickening circles—*or we're crashing, Em*—and it began to move as well.

The last thing Mac remembered clearly was Oversight's familiar voice. But it wasn't complaining about clumsy grad students or research proposals, or berating her about the fine print of a report.

It was shouting furiously: "Who's in charge here?" Then: "Stop! Where are you taking her? I demand to speak to someone in authority!"

She wished she could tell him what a bad idea that was.

11

ARRIVAL AND ADJUSTMENT

O NCE CONVINCED she was awake and not dreaming—*an uncomfortably full bladder always added that firm dose of reality*—Mac listened before she opened her eyes, trying to gain a sense of where she was before admitting to being there. *It worked in novels.* But this? Waves against rocks. A shorebird?

She couldn't be home again. Could she?

Mac peeked through her eyelashes. Bright enough for sunlight, or someone wanted her awake. Nothing for it. She had to open her eyes. *So much, Em, for peace.*

All that happened was being able to see the room around her. No sudden assault of words or people poking at her. *No pain or nausea either.* Mac sighed with relief and took a better look, turning her head cautiously on what felt like heated jelly.

The ocean sounds were coming through a pair of French doors, trimmed in white and ajar to frame a picture-perfect view of water, sky, and tumbled cloud. There was a terrace just outside the doors, complete with a table set with sun-touched flowers and chairs cushioned to match.

Mac investigated the strange pillow with one hand. Not fabric but something almost organic. Soft and soothing, it caressed the skin of her cheek as she rolled her head to look the other way, yet fully supported her shoulders and neck.

On the opposite wall, the room had a second pair of French doors, these closed and their windows frosted in intricate patterns as if to grant privacy. To the left was an arch into another, wider room, also, from what Mac could see, white. Between arch and doors stood a pedestal topped by a vase filled with pale, nodding roses.

On the other side of the arch, however, was a large lump of what appeared the same white jellylike substance as Mac's pillow, shaped something like a chair. In its midst, curled into a ball of yellow rainsuit, slept Charles Mudge III.

Now there was an unexpected development.

Careful to move quietly, Mac sat up and put her legs over the side of what was an elegant, if unusual bed. Her pillow was part of the mattress, the mattress itself having a pouch on top she'd mistaken for being between satin sheets. She stroked the surface, admiring the lustrous feel.

Her artificial hand still lacked a ring finger, but the rest of her, Mac discovered, had been washed and dressed in a long, sleeveless gown, again white, which might have been made from the same stuff as the bed. Light and incredibly comfortable, the fabric was generating warmth along her shoulders and upper back, as if detecting the small ache she felt there.

Speaking of aches. Mac decided against exploring her head wound by feel, and stood, cautiously, in search of the washroom.

The floor was another delight. She glanced down, startled to find cool sand— or its counterpart—oozing between her toes. She didn't need to tiptoe to move silently past Mudge.

The area beyond the arch resembled a sitting room from a Human home, in that it held four more of the large lump-chairs, gathered in the center around a low, rectangular table. *But the table?* Mac walked over to it, going to her knees in the sand to have a better look. It was as if a slice of the undersea world had been transported here. The effect was so real, with no signs of a boundary between water and air, that she hesitated to touch it. Finally, she did, feeling a hard slickness under her fingertips her eyes insisted wasn't there.

It didn't fool the school of bright coral fish who swam to investigate her fingers. They stopped just short, then flashed as one in a tight turn, swimming into the protecting fronds of an anemone. The depth—she could see an improbable three, perhaps four meters down, as if the table went through the floor and sunlight followed, yet her hands told her the table ended above the sand, sitting on six round feet.

"You're coming home with me," Mac promised the table.

One wall of the sitting room was window, looking to sea. The rest were unornamented, finished in plain white, as if designed to urge the eye outward. She dug her toes in the sand, seeing no footprints but hers. *Designed by whom?*

The washroom itself was through a door on the far wall. It featured reassuringly Human plumbing, with water, as well as a tall s-shaped curl of perfectly reflective material surrounding a similarly shaped podium. The function was obvious, but Mac felt painfully self-conscious climbing into the elaborate thing just to check her head.

"Could have been worse, Em," she decided. A wide swathe of hair above her left ear had been replaced by a kind of bandaging she'd never seen before. Similar to her skin, but with a bubbled texture. She could touch it, even put pressure on it, without pain.

Mac tried to coax a couple of curls to lie over the gap. They sprang back to their original position as if insulted. *Hair could be so opinionated.*

She considered the rest, looking over her shoulder. The gown, simple as it was, was more elegant than anything she'd worn in years, clinging, as the expression went, in all the right places. To Emily's despair, Mac usually went for functional and clean. Or The Suit.

That didn't mean she was unaware of the potential of other types of clothing. Or that she didn't approve of what she saw at the moment.

Would he?

Interesting if totally unhelpful question. Mac grinned at the serious look she caught on her own face. "It's only a nightgown," she reminded herself.

Her eyes followed the exposed line of shoulder and upper arm to where flesh ended in pale blue, like the porcelain of a doll.

If she'd wanted to hide it, she'd have gone for the cosmetic skin, not this strong and useful material. *It had saved her life.* Mac traced the marks gouged into the wrist and back of the hand with her fingers, grateful and troubled at the same time.

"Does it cause pain?"

It was quicker to glance in the mirror than whirl to find the source of the soft-voiced question. Mac found herself looking into a face beside her own, a face that was a study in bone and angle, as aesthetic as the rooms. She had no doubt she was looking at their creator—or rightful inhabitant. "No," she answered and turned. "Hello. I'm Mackenzie Connor."

Sinzi. There could be no mistaking a member of the first sentient alien species to make contact with humanity. Any child would recognize those upswept shoulders, rising higher than the top of the head; every history book held images of their tall, straight forms, standing like sapling trees among smaller, rounder Humans. And every biology text rapturously described those two great complex eyes, comprised of a pair for each individual consciousness within the body, and speculated on the psychology of being many in one. For the Sinzi were the only group mind yet encountered.

Mac stepped down from the podium. The Sinzi courteously bent her long neck, for the graceful shape of the shoulders was feminine, to keep their eyes at the same level. Mac could see herself in a dozen topaz reflections. *Six minds.* Not unusual, but as far as she knew more than average. "We know who you are, Dr. Connor, and are enriched by your presence."

She couldn't remember if a Sinzi referred to him or herself in the plural, or if "we" meant more nearby. *Must read more,* Mac promised herself. "Thank you. I appreciate the care . . ." she hesitated. *What was Sinzi protocol?* All Mac could remember at the moment was that they were polite. *But one species' "polite" was another's "insult."* And among the species of the IU, the Sinzi were the next best thing to royalty.

The Sinzi made a gracious gesture with her fingertips. Humans had originally mistaken the fingers for tentacles, apparently amusing the Sinzi representative. The aliens had true hands anatomically more similar to those of whales or bats, than primates. Their arms had been reduced to a series of joints within the upper shoulder complex, fingers beginning at that point and extending below the waist. Each of the three fingers per "hand" was the diameter of a human thumb, with such strong bones and joints that they appeared skeletal rather than flesh. The nail at the fingertip was thick and functional.

Far from elongated bony claws, the fingers were sleek and flexible, capable of subtle moments of extraordinary precision. This Sinzi had coated the upper third of her fingers with delicate rings of silver metal, sparking light each time a joint flexed. She wore a shift identical to Mac's, simple and as white as her skin. On her curveless body, it fell in straight pleats to the floor, brushing the sand and the tops of her long toes, four of which pointed forward and two behind, to act as heels.

"You may call me Anchen, Dr. Connor," the Sinzi said. *"Me" answered the pronoun question,* Mac thought, fascinated as Anchen turned her head as though to bring particular eyes into closer focus on her. "While your injuries are not serious, I would recommend you spend the next period of time resting and regaining your strength. There was significant blood loss. Please stay here until you feel able to join your fellows. No one expects otherwise."

"Mac, please. My fellows? I don't understand."

"The Gathering, Mac."

The Gathering? They'd been transported by agents from the Ministry of Extra-Sol Human Affairs; she'd swear to it. The same people who hadn't wanted her to receive that invitation, but . . . Nik had implied accepting would put her under IU jurisdiction, not Human.

Yet Humans had brought her here. *Okay. Where,* thought Mac a little desperately, *was here?*

"Anchen, where am I? What is this place? Am I on Earth?"

The thin-lipped Sinzi mouth was triangular, but quite flexible. Anchen demonstrated that by forming a pleasant, albeit it toothless, smile. "My apologies, Mac. I realize the Gathering is being held secretly, for security, but I thought you knew. These are part of my apartments within the residence wing of the Interspecies Union Consular Complex. Definitely on Earth. New Zealand, southern hemisphere, to be precise. It is the consulate's honor to host the delegates who gather to share their knowledge of the Dhryn."

Mac frowned. "Humans brought me here. Didn't they?"

"Yes, of course. The consulate has always relied upon your government for transportation. Any movement of non-Humans on Earth continues to attract attention, Mac, and your species has a limitless curiosity under normal circumstances. I'm sure any unpredicted traffic over your world would be noticed, given the tensions of the times." *An understatement.*

Well, she was into it now. Feeling her way around the concept, Mac said, "What do I do in this Gathering? Has it started? Where do I go?"

"The Gathering has been underway for some time, Mac, but we continue to add new delegates such as yourself. Please, rest. You will have full access to all information and sessions which have taken place over the past weeks, and meet the others as soon as you are fit."

"I'm fit now, Anchen." Beyond eager, Mac came within a breath of asking for access to reading material, then changed her mind. *Learned the hard way, Em. Check the fine print.* "Anchen, I'll need my things, from Norcoast. And to contact my family and friends—let them know I'm all right." *Even if she couldn't tell the whole truth.* In Mac's firm opinion, one mysterious disappearance was enough for a lifetime.

"I will look into appropriate arrangements." It wasn't a resounding yes, but it wasn't no either. *And no one would miss her for a couple of weeks, anyway,* Mac reminded herself. "In the meantime, I advise you to more fully recuperate," the Sinzi bowed, a complex and graceful movement Mac didn't even attempt to emulate. "You and the other delegates face a daunting task."

Mac nodded. *Daunting covered it.*

She'd been ready to go into space, to work on some alien world.

Instead, she was in the one place in Human-settled space where Humans held no power at all. Where they were only permitted on business for the IU.

Where she was the alien.

After showing Mac how to contact consular staff with any needs, which involved nothing more difficult than pressing her hand anywhere on a wall and asking out loud, Anchen left as swiftly and silently as she'd arrived. Mac watched the sea life for a while—an admirable selection of local fauna she would have believed no more than images suspended inside the table, except for the convincing way those animals with eyes reacted to her presence. It begged the question: could they see her because they really were in the room or were they able to see her because she was an image sent to where they really were?

There was headache potential, she decided, *if it wasn't enough a weasel had tried to split hers open with his gonads.* Mac grinned to herself. Which would make one of those stories to tell Emily. One day.

Time to deal with Oversight.

Back in the bedroom, Mac found Mudge, to all outward signs, still asleep in his raincoat. *And if she believed that?* She sat on the bed, briefly startled by its ability to immediately form to her body. "That can't be comfortable, Oversight," she observed.

Silence. Then, a faint hoarse whisper: "You'd be surprised." He didn't move. She might be talking to a stuffed yellow ball. Wearing boots. "Are we alone now?"

"I doubt it."

More silence, then a slightly mortified: "I didn't see any 'bots."

The innocence of those used to legal surveillance, obvious and familiar. "I was going to order lunch." Mac glanced at the long rays of sunlight on the terrace. "Breakfast," she amended.

"You're sure? Bother." Mudge unfolded with a groan, pulling off his raincoat. Beneath, his shirt was wrinkled and sweat-stained. He glared at the room as if its crisp surfaces were to blame for his condition. "And it's supper. New Zealand. We arrived around midnight local time and you've been out of it for almost fifteen hours. It's now four in the afternoon. Fall, by the way, not spring. Nippy." He rubbed his eyes and peered at her. "And tomorrow, not today."

Mac snorted. "I can do the conversions, Oversight. Don't tell me you've been in that chair the entire time."

"No." His tone did not encourage curiosity. Nor did his expression, with its classic Mudge-stubborn clench to the jaw.

She ignored both. "What happened?"

"It's not important. Order the food. I haven't eaten since getting here."

Mac smoothed the fabric over her knees. "I can wait."

"You can—" he started to bluster, then grimaced. "And you would, too. Very well." He slid lower in the jelly-chair, heels digging lines into the sand of the floor. "After they carried you out of the lev, they tried to leave me in it." Mudge stretched his hands over his head. "I didn't agree," he said simply.

Which doubtless meant numerous threats to contact authorities of every ilk, all delivered at significant volume. She had heard some of it. Mac shook her head in wonder. "And that worked?"

"No. They locked me in the hold and ignored me for quite some time. Luckily, someone already at the consulate who knew me heard I was being forced to leave against my will. He straightened your friends out in a hurry, found out where you'd been taken, brought me along. So here I am."

Leaving Mac with two pressing questions. One Mudge couldn't answer. *Why had that someone helped him stay where the IU was hosting a very secret meeting?* One he could. "Why didn't you go?" she asked.

His round face reddened. "How can you ask me that, Norcoast?" Mudge objected gruffly. He got to his feet and shook his finger at the light fixture hanging from the ceiling. "Think I'd let you carry her off to who knows where, hurt and unconscious?" he told it. "Think I'd take a chance you meant to finish the job the Trisulian started?" He looked back to Mac, his eyes round with distress. "What kind of old friend would do that?"

Old friend? There was a novel interpretation of fourteen years of conflict. *It had led to a certain depth of mutual understanding,* Mac conceded. But not to expect Mudge to stand up for her as though she was part of his Wilderness Trust. *Proving him a better friend than some,* her inner voice whispered.

It didn't matter. Couldn't matter. Mac fought the warmth of having someone think of her first, aware above all else that Mudge didn't belong here. It wasn't just the IU. She could hear Nik's warning: *"Don't let anyone close."* It wasn't meant for her protection alone. Mudge could have been safely, if angrily, on his way back to house arrest by now.

Of course, then she'd be without a friend.

"I suppose hugging is out of the question," Mac said, smiling at his alarmed look. "Thought so. Supper do?"

Despite her good intentions, which included regaining her strength as quickly as possible, supper was wasted on Mac. Her stomach rebelled the instant the steaming platters arrived—brought by courteous staff of some humanoid-type species she didn't know, clad in pale yellow uniforms. They set it out on the table on the terrace, where Mac spent the meal watching enviously as Mudge ate his portion, then accepted most of hers.

"Splendid," he informed her when done, wiping his lips and sipping the last of his wine. "You're sure you don't want anything else?"

Mac assessed the status of the few spoonfuls of soup she'd forced down. *Uncertain.* "Quite sure." She gazed into the distance, estimating there wasn't much time until full sunset. The view was of water, with perhaps the hint of islands on the horizon. She'd taken a quick dizzying look over the rail to confirm they were on land. A great granite cliff, to be exact, sheer enough that incoming waves struck and rose in gouts of foam. *She'd have to check the tides.* This building was a white curved tower, four stories high as Humans measured, the curve another s-bend like the mirror, following the edge of the cliff. These rooms were on what Mac estimated was the third floor, though she assumed the building extended below ground, into the rock itself.

She was no closer to knowing what to do about Mudge, Mac admitted to herself. Nik might help, but she'd have to wait for him to contact her. His people had brought them here, presumably willingly, so he either knew where she was, or would find out. *Didn't mean she'd hear from him anytime soon.*

Or at all.

"What do you know about the consulate—this place?" Mac asked Mudge, not hopeful.

He surprised her. "I applied for a job here once, so I made sure I was pretty familiar with it."

"Let me guess," she smiled. "Shuttle pilot."

"I was young, Norcoast. Alien worlds sounded more interesting. What I know isn't up-to-date, though."

"Tell me about it. Anything," Mac pressed. She'd learned to value knowing her surroundings.

According to Mudge, who tended to describe things with as many numbers as possible, the consulate occupied a stretch of coast five kilometers long and three wide, along the southwestern edge of New Zealand's South Island, occupying the tip of one of many fjords that fingered the Tasman Sea. No roads or walking trails led here. The only docking facilities were for consular traffic, and those only by air. The complex itself had grown over time into a sprawl of connected buildings, a few Human-built, most contributed by those handful of species interested in a more substantial presence on Earth, the rest being the original constructions of the Sinzi themselves.

The nearest Human habitation was the town of Te Anau, the hub for those seeking the vast wilderness preserved along the coast, the Te Wāhipounamu. Accustomed to tourists tramping through in all seasons, few residents took much notice of the consulate or its visitors. In fact, local New Zealanders were so accustomed to aliens wandering their streets that most shop signs were in both English and Instella.

There had been many obvious reasons for setting the consulate here: a temperate climate, if you didn't mind meters of rain per year; nearby mountain ranges offering microclimates from lush forest to desert to snowpack; even the lease arrangement between New Zealand and the Ministry of Extra-Sol Human Affairs, who acted as titular landlord to the IU. Less obviously, the area was off the beaten track and sparsely populated, making it easier to isolate alien from Human and vice versa. And, though no one said it out loud, if anything nonterrestrial was released and spread, it wouldn't be the first time New Zealand had had to deal with foreign biologies.

Mudge stopped, rubbing his face self-consciously. "You let me talk too much, Norcoast."

Mac gestured to her head. "With this? I'm more than happy to listen to someone else. Interesting stuff. Thanks, Oversight."

He harrumphed, managing to sound pleased. "Did I mention the trout fishing? It's quite famous here. I'd assume at least some visitors to the consulate indulge."

Mac contemplated a fast-flowing stream filled with aliens in paisley shorts and fly-fishing hats. "It wouldn't surprise me," she chuckled, "but it might the trout."

"Norcoast. I know you should rest, but . . ." She recognized that anxious wrinkle between his eyes. Mudge was preparing to fuss over something.

Warily. "But what?"

"Why did they bring us here? Why the consulate?"

Right to the heart of it. Again, typical. Not that Mac had ever had reason to doubt Mudge's intelligence. He probably knew as much about the research underway at Base as she did.

Lie or evade, Em?

Evade, Mac decided. It wasn't a moral choice—her head was too fuzzy to attempt anything as profoundly complicated as falsehood. "The IU must have questions about Emily's message—and the Trisulian, Kay." Or not-Kay. *Once-Kay?* Mac wasn't sure how one referred to an abandoned symbiont.

"But they didn't bring you here for questioning after the Chasm."

"No," Mac answered, wondering where Mudge was going with this. "The IU had people on the ship that brought me back. I answered their questions—" *for days on end, hazed with grief and pain, repeating the same details over and over and over,* "—and they have copies of everything I know. I'm sure the Ministry kept them informed since." Easy to picture Nikolai Trojanowski in this place, delivering the latest recordings of her dreams into Anchen's long fingers. Mac shivered.

She hadn't intended it as a distraction, but it worked. "You're getting cold," Mudge noted with a scowl. "Let's go inside."

"I'm warm enough," said Mac truthfully. The terrace floor was warm underfoot; she suspected it generated heat to combat the chill of evening. As for herself, the Sinzi's gown was either insulating or warming; regardless, it kept the skin it sheltered at a comfortable temperature. "I like it out here." *It was home,* she thought, the familiar scent of salt and seaweed, the tireless argument of wave against stone so normal she felt as though her bones had melted into the chair. *Probably couldn't stand if I wanted to, Em.*

Mudge muttered under his breath and then went inside for a moment, returning with his raincoat. "The blanket's part of the bed," he explained, putting the coat over Mac's shoulders despite her protest.

It was heavy and somewhat redolent, but it did feel good on her bare arms. *Almost as good as the gesture itself.* Mac looked up at Mudge. "Thank you."

He harrumphed again, but a fleeting smile escaped before he sat again himself. "There's something going on here, Norcoast," he insisted, earnest and determined. "Something other than normal consulate business. When we came in, you probably didn't notice, the pilot hovered for some time—my guess is there was traffic landing ahead of us. I've kept watch most of the day and there was a steady flow of incoming levs with very few departures this morning."

After their arrival? Not good, Em. "They entertain," Mac said, aware how flimsy it sounded. "Really big supper parties. Famous for it." He didn't need to respond; Mudge's face, she'd often thought, might have been set on skeptical at birth. *Or else she brought that out in him.* "What else have you seen?"

Mudge's expression went from skeptical to grim. "The security here. I'm no expert, but it's as though they expect to be attacked at any minute. They even searched me. I will spare you the details, Norcoast, but I have," this with the gusto of one truly offended, "written a memo."

She didn't doubt it. Mac tucked herself more snugly in his raincoat. "It might have been better if you'd left when they gave you the chance. You still can." *Maybe,* Mac added, honest with herself at least.

"Not without you." *Stubborn as his trees.*

Don't make promises. Mac made herself smile. "You make it sound as though I'm in some kind of danger here." Light, confident. "Nothing could be farther from the truth. They've taken care of me, offered their hospitality. As for being here, meeting the Sinzi? What an amazing opportunity! I intend to take full advantage of it. It's that, or fix the cabin door and wait for Base to be running again. I think there's no—what?"

He'd puffed out his cheeks, now adding a frown just shy of thunderous. "Tell me it's the concussion."

"Too much?" Mac pulled a face herself. "The bit about the door, wasn't it? A little over the top, I know."

"This is no joking matter, Norcoast! They wouldn't let me contact anyone outside the consulate. I'm sure they won't let you either. That's hardly benign."

"No," Mac sighed. "But since the Dhryn, it's become business-as-usual, Oversight."

He put both elbows on the table and leaned forward, eyes harder than Mac had ever seen before. "I'll tell you what I think is going on, Norcoast. I think there's some kind of secret meeting being held here, something the IU doesn't want the rest of Earth to know about. I think those incoming levs are bringing others like you, who've had some experience with the Dhryn. You've been coerced—kidnapped—and you're trying to protect me by not telling me the truth."

Now he'd done it.

Mac closed her eyes, unable to decide if she'd let anything slip or if Mudge had put his foot in it all alone, estimating how long it was going to take for someone in authority to show up on the terrace. *Not long.*

"Well?" he demanded hoarsely.

She looked at him. "What do you want me to say, Oversight? That your usual blend of mistrust and cleverness just cost you the chance to leave here anytime soon? That you should have stayed in Vancouver? That you should have repotted that damned aloe plant by now?"

Sure enough, over his shoulder Mac saw the doors to the bedroom open, helmeted figures in all-black uniforms following those in yellow. "I wasn't kidnapped. I was invited," she told Mudge in an urgent, low voice as the others approached. "Don't you understand? Working with these people is the only way I can do anything, the only hope I have. It could be the only hope any of us have. Yes, I've tried to keep you out of it—for your own good—"

Too late.

They'd lined up behind Mudge, four who appeared identical to the Ministry agents she'd seen before, visors down, plus three consular staff. Only now realizing he was essentially surrounded, Mudge lunged to his feet, his eyes wide.

"Would you come with us please, Mr. Mudge?" Respectful, proper. *Somehow looming over the poor man spoiled the effect,* Mac thought resentfully. "Dr. Connor needs her rest."

"Dr. Connor," she informed the one who'd spoken, "wants to know where you are taking her friend and colleague. And how to reach him there."

One of the yellow-clad humanoids, consular staff, bowed so deeply Mac had an excellent view of how her short bristly hair was trimmed in tidy brown spirals from crown to the base of her neck. *Not that she cared at the moment.* "To his quarters, Dr. Connor. You will have ample opportunity to visit tomorrow, I assure you. But Noad, your physician, left firm instructions as to rest. Please. We must insist."

"Noad?" Mac didn't recall the name. Then again, she didn't recall being seen by a physician either.

"It's okay, Norcoast," said Mudge, making a valiant effort to take this in stride.

"It is not okay." Mac rose to her feet, taking off Mudge's raincoat and folding it carefully as she spoke. Her voice was the one she reserved for negligent students and unreliable skim salespersons. Mudge probably recognized it too, given their history. "I will not let these—these people—push you around. You came to help me." She put the raincoat on the table, her hands flat on top. The gesture nicely covered the need to hold on to the table in order to stay on her feet. "Oversight can stay right here. There's plenty of room."

The consular staff began whispering among themselves in another language, as if she'd proposed something scandalous. Three of the four in black turned their visor-covered faces toward the one who'd spoken to her. Their leader? *Good to know.* Mac kept her eyes on that one, standing as straight as she could. The cool sea breeze tugged at her hair and gown, but she ignored it. The pounding above her eye was another matter. *Any minute now, Em, she was going to throw something or throw up.*

"Well?"

"Such an arrangement would not be acceptable to our hosts." Before Mac could protest, the Ministry agent continued: "But there's an apartment across the hall. Will that be close enough, Dr. Connor?"

She caught Mudge's look of relief out the corner of her eye. She shared it, but waited for the rest. Concessions from such people always involved something in return. Sure enough, the agent held out his hand for Mudge's raincoat. To pass it to him—or perhaps her, given the armor—Mac would have to lift her hands from the table.

Something she couldn't do without falling on her face.

Mr. Ministry Agent could wait forever before she'd ask for help on those terms.

He appeared prepared to do so.

Stalemate. *At least until she passed out.*

Then Mac noticed his left forefinger tapping the side of his holster.

"Across the hall would be perfect. It's good night, then, Oversight," she said cheerfully, sitting down and shoving the raincoat across the table. "Talk to you in the morning."

Mudge took his coat, giving her a puzzled look. "In the morning, Norcoast."

"But I'll talk to you now," Mac said, pointing at the agent who'd tapped.

The cant of his helmet shifted and he gave a signal to the others. Without a word, the remaining agents and three consular staff escorted Mudge through her bedroom and out the door, although Mudge looked back at the last minute as if about to object. Mac waved reassuringly.

They were alone. Mac could see her reflection in his helmet. She looked rather smug. "'Sephe told me you were short-staffed, but this?" said Mac, shaking her head. "You can take that thing off, Sing-li Jones. I know it's you."

"Hi, Mac." Jones tucked the now-pointless headgear under one arm, then took a seat, shifting to accommodate his weaponry. His expression was more rueful than embarrassed. "How are you doing? That's—" he looked at her scalp, "nasty."

"What I'm doing is wondering why all the hardware, the secrecy, here. I thought you cooperated with the consulate."

He tipped his head toward the now-empty bedroom. "Your friend."

"Oversight?" Mac said in disbelief. "Don't tell me you suspect him of anything other than being difficult."

"You know I can't tell you things like that, Mac."

She waited.

Jones' caramel skin blushed nicely. "I don't know," he qualified. "Our orders were to keep him under surveillance and intercede before he found out more than he should about the present situation. Which, by the way, he seems to have done without any help."

"He's annoying that way," Mac agreed. "But the gear?"

"Just staying anonymous." He grinned. "It works with most people, Mac. Trust me."

"Trust him?" The words were like cold water on her skin, but Mac made herself smile. "It's nice to see a familiar face. Although I suppose I can't ask you any questions."

Jones' forefinger tapped the table, then stopped. "Everything back at Base is as you left it," he offered. "Including, by the way, your fish heads and barnacles. Pretty slick, Mac. Zimmerman still can't believe we fell for it."

She tilted her head. "That's okay. Neither can I."

He smiled comfortably, but didn't admit a thing. *She hadn't expected he would.* "Last I heard, they were on schedule for the move. There hasn't been much media attention."

"You need bodies for that," Mac said. She gathered herself with an effort Jones noticed.

"You look about to fall on your face, Mac."

"Oh, not quite yet. First, help me out here." She smiled at the sudden caution in his eyes. "Don't worry, it's nothing compromising. I'm under the IU now, remember? Not your responsibility."

"Maybe not the Ministry's. We still watch your back."

"We" implying she would recognize others without their helmets, Mac realized, but didn't press him. She acknowledged the words with a grateful nod, then said frankly: "I need my things."

Jones' eyes narrowed in suspicion. "What things this time?"

"My imp, clothes, records from my office. Anything else would be appreciated. No one knows how long this Gathering will take. I asked Anchen, about my stuff, but . . ." She gave an expressive shrug. "It didn't sound promising."

"Because Pod Three's sealed and being towed," he pointed out.

"I know. Not to forget security systems . . ." Mac let her voice trail off.

"Oh, let's not forget those."

She held his eyes with hers. "Sing-li, you know I wouldn't be asking if it wasn't important. I've files on my imp that aren't in Norcoast's main system: my research on the Dhryn, on what we're here to accomplish. There are references, notes in my office I want here. I can't wait weeks or more until Base is set up and running again."

"I'll have to consult, Mac."

"Consult all you want," she told him, then added with abrupt ferocity: "You asked me to trust you, Sing-li. I trust you to know if I find out Pod Three was capsized and ruined so your people could fetch my underwear—"

"Mac. Mercy. Please." He held up both hands. "It won't come to that, believe me. We've been keeping watch on the pods; we've people on the hauler. Give me a day."

Mac drew a breath that shuddered and caught in her throat. She nodded, mute.

He put on his helmet, the man she knew disappearing behind the visor. But his voice was the same, warm with concern. "Now. Bed for you. And no arguments."

She accepted his help, a strong arm, but when they were standing beside the bed, she squeezed it once and let go. "Good night, Sing-li. And thanks."

Mac stayed standing until the door closed. Only then did she collapse on the most comfortable bed on the planet, not bothering to do more than close her eyes.

For once, she didn't dream.

- Encounter -

The sacred caves were, as they had always been, ancient, hallowed, and worn. They were, as they had always been, shelter to all who sought protection from the elements or war; source of gods' comfort for those in need or grief.

Now, for the first time in recorded history, disaster had struck and the sacred caves were empty. Oh, they had sheltered the people. They had taken in the terrified flocks and food-stuffs, accommodated what belongings could be carried. They had even accepted the wild things, driven from the fields.

But shelter did not mean safety.

The green flood had greedily followed them inside, chased them deeper underground. It surged through every water-carved channel, licked away the life that dug its hopeless claws into wall and ledge, that clung to the stones called godstooth and howled for the pity of gods.

Had he, Oah, Primelord, not howled loudest for his people? Had he not sought the highest point in the cave, the secret shelf where gods would endure only those who ruled? Had his mighty voice not been loud enough to drown out the screaming and be heard at last?

But the gods did not mean to save them.

Instead, they'd sent ghouls to drift through the silent caves, unmindful of the darkness. Oah, Primelord, had cowered like any milk-thieving runt at their coming, had panted like a mother in birth pain as one after the other brushed against the stone below his hiding place, had felt the bones along his spine rise in horror at their—drinking.

When all was still, Oah, Primelord, waited in the dark, nostrils burning with acrid remnants of what he didn't know.

When all was still and his body weakening from hunger and thirst, Oah, Primelord, waited in the dark, pressed against the stone that should have saved them.

When all was still and his body failed him, Oah died in the dark, Primelord and last of his kind.

It does not matter if it this is the wrong place or the wrong time.

That which is Dhryn hunts for the Taste, but cannot find it.

Perhaps others have come before. Perhaps the scouts mistook the path. Perhaps technology failed.

None of this matters.

The Progenitor must survive to continue the Great Journey.

That which is Dhryn turns to the *oomlings*.

There is no future but now.

12

WONDERS AND WOUNDS

HOLDING ON TIGHT, Mac bent as far as she could over the delicately wrought, but strong—*hopefully*—railing, trying to see past the outer wall of the white building. *There.* To the north, the building ended where the cliff continued its upward climb, a climb staggered by hanging valleys filled with green forest and braided with waterfalls that plunged to the sea. The sea itself was unusually deep here. She longed for a chance to dive it. However, first things first. Mac hunted for anything that didn't belong. *Ah. Might be a landing field,* she told herself, squinting at a flat patch of lighter green within the nearest indentation in the rock.

Or cricket pitch. It was New Zealand.

"Careful!"

The warning startled Mac into losing her grip and she had an unpleasantly intense perspective on the sheer drop to rock and froth before grabbing hold again. With a heave, she pulled herself back on the terrace and whirled to glare at the new arrival. "I was being careful—"

She stopped and grinned. "Fourteen!"

"You did not appear careful. Idiot. It would be a waste to fall from this height so soon after breakfast."

Mac laughed. "Glad to see you, too. How are the head and hands?"

"Mygs heal quickly." He held up his hands and she was astonished to see only fine green lines where there had been scrapes and gashes. "My head? All better. Unless I bump it. Which I attempt not to do."

He looked better. *In fact,* her eyes narrowed, *the Myg looked very different.* Gone were the ill-fitting Human clothes, replaced by a set of finely tooled leather plates made into pants and vest. Beneath the vest was a tailored red shirt, generous sleeves widest at the elbows and caught at the cuffs. There was a red gemstone at his throat and another hanging from one ear. Three small black imp cases hung from a strap across his chest. Black polished boots and a wig of immaculately groomed silver-gray hair completed the transformation from clumsy tourist to—

—to someone important, Mac decided, pinning down the change. *Maybe a touch reminiscent of a pirate from old vids, Em, but a classy one.* Not that she'd point that out.

It was, of course, not the clothes alone or the posture that went with them. His eyes were still mere glints within those fleshy lids, but Mac thought the lines of his face had altered, as if he acknowledged a weight of responsibility.

Given why they were here, she wasn't surprised. "I didn't think of a wig," Mac told him lightly, taking one of the chairs at the little table and waving him to the other. "Looks good."

"Irrelevant," he grumbled as he sat. "It's been the fashion since my grandsires' day. You'd think the transects would have freed us from tradition—instead, we now export it as part of our identity. Bah."

She brushed her fingers across her patch of bare scalp. "There are advantages."

Opening one of the cases on his strap, Fourteen brought out what indeed looked like an imp and put it on the table between them, after first scowling at the vase of flowers as though they took up valuable space. "Irrelevant. You do not need a wig and your head is intact. The Sinzi-ra has done us a great service with her care." He busied himself with a second imp.

"'Sinzi-ra,'" Mac repeated. "Is that Anchen's title?"

Fourteen didn't look up from the confusion of overlapping workscreens he'd set hovering parallel to the tabletop. "No. It's what she is. She is the Sinzi contingent to this consulate."

"So she's a physician."

"Noad is a physician, yes. A fine one."

"Another Sinzi."

That sly look. "You Humans are a pleasant species, but hardly important or annoying enough to require the attention of more than one." Fourteen grinned at Mac's expression. "Yes, Mac, I will explain. The name any Sinzi gives to a member of another species is a composite of the initials of the names of the consciousnesses within that body. It saves confusion for those less familiar with their ways. Noad is one of these consciousnesses—an expert in xeno-medicine." He plucked a bright orange flower petal and laid it in front of Mac. "The others are Atcho, Casmii, Hone, Econa, and Nifa. Atcho is the consulate administrator. Efficient and very thorough. Don't break anything." Another petal, beside the first. "Casmii is a member of the IU's judicial council. A powerful voice. Econa and Nifa are both scientists whose specialties have to deal with this planet of yours in some way. If you let them ask you questions, they'll never give you a moment's peace. Hone is a transect engineer. A bit young, if you ask me, for such responsibility." A petal joined the group for each name, until there was a tight circle of six, their bases touching. "Sinzi-ra Anchen."

Talking to one alien was fraught with interspecies' confusion. *This?* The potential for disaster made Mac gulp. "How do I know which one's speaking to me?"

A tall shadow crossed their table. "If it is necessary to identify an individual mind," Anchen said, "for clarity or proof of intent, that identification is provided. Otherwise, all who are awake and participatory speak as one."

Fourteen scrambled to his feet. "I meant no disrespect, Sinzi-ra."

"The effort to understand one another is never disrespectful. Quite the contrary, Arslithissiangee Yip the Fourteenth." Anchen's head lowered in what seemed a bow. "I am honored."

Mac had remained seated, regarding the Sinzi with a mix of awe and regret. Few Humans met this species face-to-face; she hadn't been wrong to tell Mudge it was the opportunity of a lifetime. But regret won. She wasn't here to explore their differences. She was here concerning another species altogether. "If you've come to see if I'm fit to join the others this morning, Anchen, I am."

"Are you?" The alien's fingers swayed as if the light, but growing sea breeze had the power to move them. *Indecision,* Mac guessed, then wasn't sure why she thought so. "I find it unlikely you are free of pain so soon."

"It's nothing—I mean, there isn't enough pain to impair my ability to work," qualified Mac. If ever she needed to express herself clearly and accurately, it was now, in this place, where the shortcuts of Human conversation were likely to be pitfalls.

"The in-depth sessions are in the afternoon. Every morning, there is a greeting arena. It would be appropriate for you to attend. Several others arrived yesterday as well, so you will not be the only newcomers." Anchen gestured expansively. "Although you and Arslithissiangee Yip the Fourteenth are the only ones who join us courtesy of the Myrokynay."

Mac's blood ran cold. "The Ro are here?" she asked, schooling her voice.

Anchen didn't laugh, but something about her posture suggested amusement to Mac. "No. And we do not yet have the ability to invite them, much as we wish." A more sober note to her voice, a gesture toward Fourteen. "The message you brought us only proves the difficulty. Its coding was so complex few could have deciphered it. An achievement of note. And yes, the results suggest its purpose—all agree—but the requirements to implement this signal? A puzzle we are not close to solving." Her fingers bent upward at their lowermost joint. *A shrug?* Mac wondered. "If this is the Myrokynay attempting clarity, it could take years to attain true conversation."

A pause. "Thus we start with basics," Anchen continued. "Their presence has been confirmed on this world before; it was Human ingenuity which disabled the Myrokynay's stealth technology during the attack on the Dhryn home world. It is our assumption they will continue their interest in Earth—our hope they will acknowledge this gathering and its purpose although to us, so far, the Myrokynay have been silent. But you, they contacted. And you," a lift of a white-clawed fingertip at Fourteen, "were able to decipher the meaning of this contact. There is deep significance within your combination."

Which meant . . . ? Mac filed the Sinzi's cryptic statement to mull over later. "Then it's time to get to work," she said hopefully, then paused. Today, Anchen's upper fingers shone with golden rings, but she wore another of the simple white gowns, twin to Mac's. Perhaps the garment was "significant," too.

The problem was, Mac's own belongings had yet to appear. *There were worse things than walking around in a nightgown, Em.* Mac grimaced inwardly. *Like meeting a roomful of strangers while walking around in a nightgown.*

Rings caught and shattered light as Anchen gestured to the doors and beyond to Mac's rooms. "In that case, I trust you will find suitable attire among the selection of Human clothing we've provided, while you await your own things. If not, please contact the staff or myself."

"Thank you." Mac let out a sigh of relief, adding before she thought: "Mind reading must be a Sinzi trait."

"Mac!" This exclamation, plus Fourteen's shocked look, drew Mac to her feet, fumbling to apologize, not that she knew why or how. "Just kidding," probably didn't cut it. *Or was there something about being multiple minds in one body that made the very concept of shared thoughts repugnant to Sinzi?*

Fortunately for interspecies' relations, Anchen merely smiled. "We take great pride in anticipating the needs of our guests. I am gratified to have 'guessed' yours so well."

"You are a superb host. My thanks," Mac said sincerely. "I'm grateful to have other clothes for the Gathering."

"You do mean to attend today, then." At Mac's confident nod, the Sinzi's shoulders shuddered, the motion traveling down every finger so her rings flashed in sequence. *Acceptance?* Mac guessed. It could as easily be just a random shudder, and Mac could almost hear her great-aunt, who was fond of strange old rhymes, saying: "Cat walked over your grave." "You do not have the thick skull of a Myg," noted Anchen, luckily not telepathic. "I request you return to your quarters at once if you experience any significant pain or dizziness."

"I will."

Anchen bowed and turned to leave. Mac slipped around the table to intercept her. The Sinzi's head twisted to bring her lower sets of eyes directly to bear. "I see there is something further," she acknowledged before Mac could utter a word. "Let me 'guess' again. You wish to know the status of your companion, Charles Mudge III."

"Yes, please."

"He's here?" Fourteen stood and joined them. "How did that happen?"

Mac snorted. "Very quickly, as you may remember."

"He saved Mac's life, Sinzi-ra Anchen," the Myg told her. "I, for one, place a high value on that."

"As do we all, Arslithissiangee Yip the Fourteenth. What is your wish for him, Mac?"

She glanced at Fourteen, who nodded encouragingly as if they'd discussed the issue beforehand. *That obvious, was she?* "My wish, Anchen, is that Oversight—Mudge—be offered the chance to stay and contribute to the Gathering. He's—" *a minor stretch here,* "—been essential to my work over the years. I believe he'd be an asset." And she did. *In his annoying, pinpoint-every-flaw, way.*

"And if he chooses not to stay?"

Mac imagined Mudge working at his desk, completely oblivious to the row of black-visored guards behind him. *That wasn't the problem.* "He would be at risk," she admitted. "There could be others, like Kay, interested in any information about the Dhryn and the Ro. He'd need protection. He wouldn't like it." *Any more than she had.*

"Among those gathered is a Human-ra of diverse and as yet unproductive individuals," said Anchen, no readable expression on the sculpted contours of her long face. "It is my understanding you are accustomed to coordinating such a research group. If you wish to undertake that responsibility, I will look into ways Charles Mudge III can be included."

Blackmail—very civil and reasonable—blackmail. *Was Mudge worth it?* Mac didn't hesitate. "I agree, of course. I'll let him know." Then, more as a test than anything else: "If I think of anyone else who might be of help, what should I do?"

"By all means, let me know at once, Mac. I will consider every suggestion." If there was a hint of irony in the voice, Mac was willing to ignore it. "If there is nothing else? Then I will leave you to your preparations, Mac. Arslithissiangee Yip the Fourteenth." Her long-toed feet made virtually no sound on the tiled terrace, less on the sand.

Fourteen went back to the table. "Idiot."

"Me?" Mac joined him, eyeing the complex of workscreens still displayed over the pair of imps he'd laid out. "Why?"

He gave his vest a proud tug. "You didn't check the clothing before she left. What if it doesn't fit?"

She grinned. "Irrelevant. I'll walk beside you and no one will notice me." Fourteen barked his laugh. "So what's all this?" asked Mac, waving at the displays but careful to keep her fingers out of them.

"This," he slid one of the imps closer to her, "is for you. I accessed your messages—oh, don't rumple your face. I didn't read them."

"I didn't rumple—" Mac began.

Another laugh. "I've loaded it with schematics for the consulate—at least those areas for which the Sinzi provide schematics. You will find the latest list of attendees—again, those the Sinzi wish known to all, as well as some information about each. Our number is presently four hundred and thirteen beings. I counted Anchen as one. Hmm. Four hundred and twenty-three, if you count the Nerban translators who travel with each of the Umlar delegates. Their mouthparts can't handle Instella. Idiots refuse to use appliances."

Never put a Nerban and a Frow in the same taxi . . . Mac shook off the memory of Emily's voice. "Any external genitalia I should know about?"

That sly look. "Didn't you bring your drugs?"

She grinned. "I see you're back to normal. Thanks for this." Mac picked up the imp. She turned it over in her hands. Not much to see on the outside. A palm-length dark cylinder, stubbier than the Human version, but otherwise plain. She spotted what should be the activation pad and looked inquiringly at Fourteen.

"Your first entry locks in your code," he assured her. "Do it once, then repeat."

Automatically, Mac tapped in the code from her imp at Base. She almost changed her mind, then shrugged and repeated it. *Odds were good she'd forget a new one anyway.*

The workscreen was crisper than hers, but either the Myg used the Human interface or he'd preset this one to suit her vision. *And hers,* Mac admitted to herself, *had been in the water more than a few times, let alone its trips with her through no-space to the Dhryn worlds.* Mac put the device on the table, then drew a finger through its display to lift it to vertical from horizontal. No problem accessing the data Fourteen had provided. Mac held her breath.

The consulate schematics were visual representations of rooms and corridors. Furniture was absent—reasonable enough, furniture was often moved—but there were symbols showing each room's function floating within it. Mac was entranced. Someone, more likely several someones, had gone to a great deal of trouble to design symbolic representations of functions not necessarily shared— or done the same way—by different species. The washroom symbol alone was a masterpiece of tactful suggestion.

The rest?

Text. Text. Text. None of it more legible than the IU's letter. Mac poked through the 'screen until she found the audio option. A selection began reading itself to her. *In Fourteen's distinctive, somewhat gravelly voice.* Stopping it, she looked through the display at him. The Myg appeared remarkably smug. "My entire family adores my reading voice," he proclaimed.

"No offense, but since I'm neither a relative nor a Myg, how do I change it?"

His generous lips actually pouted. *As likely mimicry as a shared expression,* Mac decided. "We'd need a recording of another voice. Does it matter? Who uses audio anyway?"

She hadn't told him about having trouble reading. Or Kay. Or Mudge. Or anyone who didn't already know or have to know, for that matter.

It had been possible to hide it at Base, where Mac knew everything and everyone.

Here?

She needed help.

Might as well start asking now.

"I suffered more damage than losing an arm and hand, last fall." As she spoke, Mac focused on the display, finding a visual list of delegates and starting to scroll through their faces—or what corresponded to a face. "My language center was affected. You heard me telling Oversight that I can speak and read Dhryn. That's true. What I didn't tell him—" Mac considered the possibility others were listening and nodded to herself. *They'd have to take her as she was. Bent. A bit scuffed. But capable.* "—I didn't tell him it's now very difficult for me to read anything else. I can muddle through English and Instella. Sometimes. Others, the words fragment in front of my eyes." She was startled by her own face in the list and closed the display. "So you see, it does matter. I find it less—frustrating—if it's my voice reading to me."

"Who have you consulted about this? Other than Humans."

Mac blinked at Fourteen. He seemed serious. "Who else would I consult?" *The Ro?* "Besides, with all that happened—is happening—my own government wasn't about to let me wander too far."

"They no longer have jurisdiction over you. Discuss this problem with Noad. The Sinzi, as you might gather, are exceptional neurologists."

There was an idea that qualified as terrifying, Em. "I'll think about it." Mac stood. "First things first. I need to get ready to meet the masses, Fourteen, not to mention talk to Oversight." *A conversation she wasn't looking forward to.*

"I will help you choose appropriate clothing."

Mr. Paisley Shorts? Mac shook her head. "Out. I can manage. I need you to check in with Oversight—make sure he's ready for this. Please."

"Of course." Fourteen stood, then gave a bow from the waist, deep and prolonged. When he straightened, Mac was surprised to see moisture beading his thick eyelids, and his mouth working with some emotion. "What's wrong?" she asked.

"Noad has assured me that, with my wounds, I would not have survived that night alone. I'd set the temperature too low in my panic; I was too weak to voluntarily awake from torpor. By warming me, you saved my life."

"Lucky guess, believe me."

"It was not a guess when you continued to protect my life with yours, even when injured yourself. You could have left immediately. You could have left in the morning and sought safety for yourself. You didn't." He stopped and placed both hands over his eyes. "I, Arslithissiangee Yip the Fourteenth, cannot thank you, Mackenzie Connor of Little Misty Lake, for saving my valued life," he said formally, lowering his hands again to look at her. "Twice."

"I don't need—"

He frowned at her and she closed her mouth. *Not done.*

Hands over his eyes. "I, Arslithissiangee Yip the Fourteenth, can only offer my firstborn offspring to you, Mackenzie Connor of Little Misty Lake, in return for saving my valued life."

Mac's eyes widened in shock. "No, I—"

Hands down. Another, sterner look. She closed her mouth again.

Hands up. "But since I, Arslithissiangee Yip the Fourteenth, have not yet produced an offspring and do not, in fact, ever intend to do so unless forced by my grandsires or in a weak moment under the influence of illicit drugs, I can only offer you my allegiance, flesh, mind, and spirit, so long as I may live, in return for saving my valued life."

Mac waited.

Hands down. "That's all of it," advised Fourteen, sounding normal again. "Tradition. Sorry about that."

She lifted one eyebrow. "A simple 'thank you' would have sufficed."

The Myg tucked his imp back in its case. "Idiot," he commented fondly. "Of course not. Within my sect, only ethical acts can move a lineage into the highest possible *strobis*. You do know the word?" Mac shook her head. "The closest Instella equivalent is 'class.' Irrelevant. To all Myg, *strobis* is the measure of a life's value to the whole. Actions determine that value. We act according to the allegiances we hold, to ideals, to others of our kind, very rarely to an alien. Allegiance must flow toward greater value; it is thus not given lightly." That sly look. "Though there is a recent trend, much deplored by my grandsires, to offer allegiance to favorite sports teams."

In a Human, thought Mac, *she'd assume he was trying to lighten the moment.* For her sake or his? Regardless of species, this was obviously a significant commitment for the Myg.

She just wasn't sure what to do about it.

Fourteen reached out and tapped her nose. "It was a joke."

"I got that," Mac said dryly. "I'm honored, Fourteen, by your allegiance. I don't see how I deserve it."

"Irrelevant. It's for me to give, not you to deserve. Enough. Traditions waste time. I try to tell my grandsires, but they never listen to me. You, Mac, must dress. I will go and see if the valued Mudge has done the same."

"Tell him I'll be right over."

After Mac closed the doors behind Fourteen, she ran her fingers along what felt to be painted wood and frosted glass. No guarantees about the materials, but the style was vintage Human. Nice to be reminded the transfer of culture and knowledge went both ways.

She took out her new imp and sank into the jelly-chair. *Messages.* Setting her 'screen hovering above her, Mac hunted until she found the very short list. Three—she squinted—likely meeting announcements. One that seemed intended for someone named Recko San. Mac deleted that, having enough to struggle with as it was. And one more.

The source was marked 'personal,' with no return. A recording, not text. Her hand trembled slightly as she activated it.

"Hello, Mac." Nik's voice.

She stopped it immediately.

Coward.

Emily's judgment or her own?

Mac restarted the recording. "Hello, Mac. The complete text of your letter from the IU follows. I've indicated the clauses I feel you need to pay particular attention to, but the overall gist is that you've accepted citizenship within the IU for the purposes and duration of the Gathering. Within that framework, you are protected and governed by intersystem law . . ."

Eyes closed, Mac lay back in the chair to listen, feet tucked up. His voice flowed over her, as intimate a caress as the warm waves that kissed her toes in summer. The words didn't matter, not right now. She'd pay attention to meanings later. For now, she relaxed and let herself own this, own the sounds that had left his mouth, come from his throat, sounds meant for her.

All too soon, it was done. Mac resisted the temptation to listen again. Instead, she put away her imp and went to stand where she could see the distant horizon, a line of deepest blue against the sky, a hint of cloud marring its edge. She wrapped her arms around herself. It could be land. She'd have to see a map to know for sure.

As for Fourteen?

Here we go again, Em, she thought.

If she'd understood Fourteen correctly, an alien she'd come to view as a friend had just sworn to be her ally for life. It was a promise that didn't always work out well.

Her lips moved silently. *"Lamisah."*

As daunting settings went, Mac decided, the consulate's "greeting arena" wasn't as bad as say, the busy loading docks of an orbiting way station.

The noise level and utter confusion to the unfamiliar was, however, even worse.

"Where do we go from here?" Mudge shouted in her ear.

Mac pointed helplessly at Fourteen, who was pushing his way though the throng clogging the ramp. "Follow him."

"I still haven't agreed to all this, Norcoast," another shout.

She nodded. Mudge had been predictably reluctant to commit himself. This was, after all, the man who routinely took six long months to renew a research proposal he'd approved for the previous three years' running. Accepting an invitation to leave his work and join an alien conference? She'd allow him a little time for that decision, even if the outcome was, as far as she was concerned, never in doubt. With Oversight, a push always produced the opposite reaction.

That he was willing to come along this morning without being dragged was, Mac judged, a significant accomplishment for their first day. Given the Ministry somehow had him under surveillance, probably a device in his clothing, she only hoped Mudge would watch his tongue.

Suggesting he do so? She shuddered at the likely consequences.

The consulate's greeting arena wasn't a room or hall. They'd followed Fourteen outside to where a sequence of gardens connected the protected east side of the complex to the true wilderness of the mountains behind, manicured slopes merging into the massive upward steps of the rising hills. The plantings had the tired, proud look of fall, more seed heads than buds, those leaves intending to drop rattling and loose on the trees. The air was warmer than crisp, but not by much. The building itself protected them from the rising wind, but if the sun hadn't been shining, they'd all need coats.

Those without a natural version, anyway. "This," Mac decided after her first incredulous look at the host of beings spread over the patio below them, "is a caterer's nightmare."

There were so many different aliens milling in front of them, and so many different types of the same aliens, Mac didn't attempt to dredge up the names of any she might have studied. *It's a masquerade ball, Em.* With her and Mudge the only ones not in costume, from their viewpoint anyway.

Although she was well-dressed. Mac smoothed the front of the jacket that had been one of the choices hanging on the rack she'd found in the sitting room. Midnight blue, knee-length, tailored to perfection. With, she was delighted to discover, pockets. There'd been pants to match, flat shoes, and everything else, including a comb, to make her comfortable—and ready for inspection.

Her clothes from the cabin lay clean and folded on a counter in the washroom itself. She'd found the invitation from the IU in her shirt where she'd stuffed it, no worse for whatever laundry technique the consulate staff used. Or they'd taken the envelope out and replaced it. The owl pellet was gone. *Just as well.*

Mac patted her left jacket pocket. Both envelope and the imp from Fourteen were there.

An elbow dug into her back. "He's getting ahead of us," Mudge fussed. Mac barely avoided stepping on someone's flipper but stayed in place.

"Don't worry. I still see him. Hang on," she ordered.

The central consular building, itself a mammoth warren of halls and varied internal environments, sprawled behind them. Where they stood, at the top of the ramp leading to the gardens, was high enough to afford a good view of the grounds.

Although it had seemed a kaleidoscope of moving, fragmented colors, Mac gradually made sense of what she was seeing. The main arena was a sunken patio, irregular in shape and bordered by stately trees to the left and right. Several shaded paths led off to either side. Farthest from them was a set of broad terraces cut from the granite, rising like giant stairs to another garden above this one. The result was a bowllike space, capable of holding, barely, what appeared to be far more than four hundred and something delegates.

Within that space were three main clusters of activity. The first, to the left, focused around a series of clear bubblelike structures. *Ah,* Mac decided, intrigued. *Non-oxy-breathers.* Clever.

The next was in the center, around a series of curved, elaborate fountains. Mac took a closer look. The fountains themselves overflowed with delegates.

Made sense. There were several aquatic species in the IU. *First group she wanted to meet,* Mac decided.

Last and the most popular area, judging by the sea of heads, was near the first terrace, to the right. Mac didn't need to glimpse the long tables in the shade of the trees to know this was where food and beverages were being provided. She smiled. *Never met an academic who couldn't find the bar, Em.*

The noise—and the smell—at close range? Mac began to suspect at least one reason the Sinzi held these mass meetings outside.

"There he is, Norcoast. He's waving to us. Can we go now?"

Looking ahead at the crowd, Mac put her arm through Mudge's. "Lead on."

After making their way through a bewildering mixture of body forms, they reached Fourteen, who was standing under the first of the great trees. Mac noticed Mudge sneaking looks into its branches, despite the truly fascinating aliens to every side, muttering to himself: "Silver beech. Southern species . . . bigger than the ones I saw in Argentina. More podocarps—rimu, I'd say—aha!" Mudge tugged at her arm and exclaimed. "Tui!"

Mac guessed this wasn't a sneeze. "Pardon?"

"Look, up there."

Obediently, she craned her neck back. The lowermost branch, just above a group of intensely debating delegates, contained a fairly large, albeit nondescript bird, with white feathers at its throat. "Tui?" she guessed.

"Shhh. Listen."

As that seemed improbable, given the volume from all sides, Mac shook her head, but tried anyway. Nothing. Then, she noticed delegates under the bird suddenly looking up as well, which in their case, being Frow, meant unfolding their neck ridges and leaning left.

Then she heard it and grinned. The bird was mimicking Frow laughter, something like rattling coins in a bucket. The delegates were not impressed.

Welcome to Earth.

"Trees. Birds. Idiots. Wasting time," Fourteen said impatiently. "Come. The first of those you should meet is over there."

At that moment, a large group of brown-cloaked furry somethings stampeded by everyone else, as if it had been announced the bar was about to close for the day. Doing her best not to be swept along, trampled, or pushed into the already testy Frow, Mac dodged to one side.

When she looked for her companions, both Mudge and Fourteen had managed to get themselves lost in the crowd.

When opportunity walks in the door, Em, Mac grinned. It wasn't that far to the fountains, which were roughly in the direction the Myg had indicated anyway. Winding her way between beings whose reaction to her varied from polite acknowledgment to oblivious, she moved as quickly as seemed inoffensive. With luck, she'd meet some of the aquatics.

As if to thwart her, the crowd thickened until Mac had to slow down to avoid stepping on anything attached to someone who'd be offended. Finally forced to stop, she stretched to her full height, trying to see a better way. Hats, fleece, antennae, feathers, lumps. The few Human heads looked out of place.

One of those heads turned with familiar grace.

For an instant, a heartbeat, it was as if the world went silent, the pushing of others against her meant nothing, and Mac saw only dark eyes set against smooth olive skin.

It couldn't be.

"Emily?"

A tall, shaggy Sthlynii stepped in front of Mac, blocking her view. She tried to move around him, but he grabbed her arm. "Sooooo," the vowels extended in emphasis. "Yooouuu aaaareeee heeereeee!"

"Excuse me," Mac said, twisting frantically, but somehow resisting the urge to kick a fellow delegate. "Please. Let go. I have to see someone! I have to go!"

"Aaaas beeffoorreee yoooouuuu weeent, leeaaaviiiing ooonlyy thee deeaad."

"I don't know what you're talking about. Let go of me!" This time, Mac did kick, with force enough to hurt her toes, if not to impress the larger alien. Around them, the crowd suddenly fell still. *Not the first impression she'd hoped to make.* Somehow, she composed herself. "Do I know you, sir?"

"You should, Connor."

Mac turned to face a short, no longer chubby Human, his skin and hair pigment-free. The name and context snapped into place. "Lyle. Lyle Kanaci." The ruined Dhryn home world. The archaeological team who had sheltered her—and Brymn—during the sandstorm. *Of course, they'd be here.* She had so many questions for them—but first, Emily! She pulled at her arm. "Tell him to let go!"

"Therin. Be civil. Remember our host."

Rubbing her arm, Mac realized she recognized every face, or equivalent, surrounding her. Two Cey, their expressions impossible to read. Therin, now flanked by three more of his kind, their tentacled mouths disturbing to watch. The rest of the circle, Humans, including Lyle.

In contrast to the aliens, the Human faces expressed their feelings a little too well. Mac had never seen such disgust and anger, never had loathing directed at her before. Her mouth went dry.

This was what it felt like, to be the target of a mob. She knew better than to move. She couldn't imagine what to say that wouldn't ignite the violence in their eyes.

Why was the one thing Mac did understand.

For she had brought a Dhryn into their camp and he had killed one of their own, digesting her alive as she'd lain helpless and injured. They'd all heard her screams.

She still dreamed them.

"Mac. There you are." Those around her fell back, giving way to the tall, graceful form of the Sinzi. "I see you've found the Human-ra I told you about, including these, their research companions," Anchen said, fingers rising to encompass them all. "Excellent. I know your group will produce fine results."

She was wrong.

It couldn't have been Emily.

Mac sipped the drink she'd been handed without tasting it, eyes hunting through the crowd, seeing only what wasn't there.

There were dozens of other Humans, not to mention humanoidlike aliens. Consular staff, diplomats, other delegates. Tall women with dark eyes and olive skin weren't uncommon.

These morning outdoor gatherings were designed to attract the Ro. There'd been no sign of them.

Every security guard and staff member, likely most of the delegates, would know Emily Mamani's face.

It couldn't have been her. Yet . . .

"Had enough?"

"Of what, Oversight?" she answered wearily. "This—" a lift of her water glass, "—or them?" The archaeologists had remained in their tight defensive huddle since Anchen's poorly timed announcement. Mac had only to look their way to be seared by glares from everyone capable of glaring.

"Of pretending your head doesn't hurt."

She didn't bother lying to him. "It doesn't matter. I can't leave." *Not when there was any chance Emily really had been here, had looked at her, was waiting.*

Fourteen poured two glasses of wine into his mouth simultaneously, then belched. *Apparently,* Mac thought, *clothes weren't everything.* "You will have to— all delegates are to report to their assigned research areas this afternoon. Charlie is right, you need a rest. And they—" the Myg deliberately didn't look around, "—promise to be a challenge."

"Charlie?" Mac glanced at Oversight.

"Please don't," that worthy said with a shudder. "It wouldn't sound right coming from you, Norcoast." An expert in glaring himself, Mudge had been trading a few with the archaeologists. "As far as I'm concerned," indignantly and not for the first time, "you can't work with those people."

"I can," Mac disagreed, quietly, but firmly. "And I will. If they know any-thing of use to me, I want it. If they have anything to offer, I want it. Everything else—anything else—I'll deal with my own way."

He harrumphed, giving her that look. "Well, I'm staying to help you. Some-one has to—you can't expect Fourteen here to know the depths of academic depravity our kind is capable of."

A second bright spot on a very dark morning, Mac thought. She raised her glass in a toast to both of her supporters. "I appreciate that."

A low hum vibrated through the air and underfoot. Fourteen caught Mac's eye before she could ask. "A request for attention. The Sinzi-ra is going to make an announcement."

The sounds of conversation and movement dropped away like magic, leaving only the wind in the treetops. "Thank you, Delegates." Anchen's voice came from everywhere, not loud, but impossible to miss. "As we have done each day since the Gathering began, let us give the Myrokynay the chance to join us and share their knowledge of our common peril that all may survive it. A moment of silence, please."

Every being Mac could see aimed its head, eyes, or whatevers at the sky, as if that was the most likely place to find Ro. She could tell them otherwise. *But it was an impressive display.* Hundreds of such diverse life-forms, all intent on one result. Would the Ro pay attention?

The Tui decided to practice its Frow laughter again. *Entirely too appropriate,* Mac thought grimly.

The voice began again, drowning out the bird. "Our new arrivals have been assigned to existing research teams. Provide requests for additional equipment and other needs to any member of the consular staff at the earliest opportunities. Record all findings and results for review and assessment.

"As of this moment, the IU confirms three worlds lost to the Dhryn. We fear more have been consumed. It is up to you to end this."

The semi-party atmosphere of the greeting arena vanished as if it had never existed, replaced by subdued tones and purposeful movement. Everyone seemed to know where to go. Consular staff appeared and began to remove tables. The bubble tents for the non-oxy-breathers rolled away, presumably self-propelled. Some of the aquatics from the fountains donned helmets, walking or slithering away. Others, to Mac's frustration, slipped away down large drains before she had a good look.

Maybe tomorrow, she thought wistfully.

"Where to now, Norcoast?"

"Where?" Mac eyed the huge building presently being restocked with aliens. *Not there.* Not yet. "Why don't you both go ahead—see what you can find out about our research colleagues and facilities?" she suggested.

Fourteen didn't look happy. Mudge, on the other hand, positively glowed. *Definitely had the detective bug, Em.* "What about you?" the Myg asked her.

"Don't worry. I'll meet you there." Mac drew out her imp. "Got a map." She made a gentle shooing motion with her hands. "I'm fine. I need a few minutes alone, that's all. Here." Here being the garden around them.

As more and more left, the place was revealing its true self, an outdoor palace of magnificent proportions, shaped by growing things and stone, bordered by widely spaced trees whose dappled shade enticed the explorer. Birds who couldn't compete with the crowds like the Tuis had begun to flit about, adding their song and chatter to the restored babble of fountains. Fat pigeons waddled the patio, cooing as they hunted dropped olives and bits of pastry amid the litter of leaf and seed case.

One wandered by them, making its methodical, unhurried way down the path of shredded bark and moss that led under the trees, away from the patio. That was enough for Mac. "See you in a while," she announced.

She half expected one or the other of her companions to follow. She'd been reasonably certain one of the many yellow-garbed consular staff would object to pigeon pursuit, or at least send her off with the rest.

But no one followed or objected. The pigeon left the path on its own business. And after those initial dozen or so steps, Mac slowed her pace, answering both her mood and the thumping of her skull.

Had it been Emily?

Should she have called out—told someone?

"More likely the little weasel knocked something loose, Em," Mac only half joked as she walked.

Not a wild forest, she decided, but designed for the peace and contemplation one could provide. Mac grew absorbed in the patterns and textures, admired the skills of those who coaxed living things to remain tame, while showing off their natural beauty. Ferns swept alongside the path like still-life rivers. In openings, groves of miniature conifers guarded pale roses. And everywhere birds. High above, in the canopies. In the shrubs, busy at their business. Perched and watching her with bright, distracted eyes.

The path was lined with white benches, some designed for anatomies Mac couldn't imagine. She found one that suited hers and sat.

But not to rest.

After looking around to be sure she was alone, and not daring to hope, Mac folded her hands on her lap. "Here I am, Em."

Nothing stirred that didn't belong.

"Short of stealing a lev and heading out to sea, this is the best I can do."

Nothing.

"Your mother said you always were difficult," Mac said, her voice thick. She coughed to clear it. "In case you don't know everything, Em, I'm here to work with other Dhryn experts for the IU. I tell you though, what they really want is to talk to your—to the Ro. If you can arrange that, first beer's on me. And the next ten. Mind you, after that I'm probably broke. No one's talked about paying me here. I suppose I'm out of a job at Base. I know. I could have asked. You're the practical one. You should have reminded me."

The sunbeams cutting across the straight, tall trunks were the only answer.

Mac drew up one leg and put her chin on her knee, watching what appeared to be an extraordinarily large cricket, disturbed by her arrival, as it pushed its way through a pile of twigs. If she picked it up, it would almost fill her hands, real and artificial. "You probably aren't here, Em," she went on. "But I've been talking to you when I knew you weren't, so talking to you when you 'probably' aren't is a step closer to sane, don't you think?" She paused. "Sane's overrated, in my opinion. But still. There's perception."

The insect, free of the twigs, stroked its long antennae through the air at her before marching under a nearby bush.

"Would it be so hard to answer me back, Em?" Mac turned her face so her cheek rested on her knee, let her eyes trace the textures of chipped bark and fallen leaf. "Won't they let you? You, who can charm grant funding from a stone? You know what to say. Tell the Ro we're on the same side. Tell them we're sorry about that misunderstanding at Haven—we're only Human, right? Make a joke. Beg. Bribe. Whatever it takes. Whatever they understand. Spout prime numbers."

Mac closed her eyes, seeing the familiar, graceful turn of a head. "Don't worry, Em," she whispered. "I won't let go. I'll wait."

ACCUSATION AND ANSWER

THERE WASN'T SAND on the floor, but the expansive curved room assigned to her research group had all the other hallmarks Mac had come to expect of Sinzi design: clean lines, light, unornamented walls, and abundant windows overlooking the patio—presently revealing the shadows of gathering clouds. Not to mention comfortable chairs—although these were better suited to being moved from conference table to console than the giant jelly-chairs in her room.

The room also possessed all the hallmarks of a bad start to a field season: too-quiet staff; resentful looks; everyone sitting as far apart as possible. Worst of all, no one already at work. They'd waited for her. Even Fourteen and Mudge greeted her with somber looks.

Not a good sign.

Assessment completed with that one glance, Mac strode through the door. "Good afternoon." Without waiting for a response, she went straight to the table in the center and leaned on her knuckles, gazing around the room from face to sullen face, or reasonable facsimile, as she spoke.

"Yes," Mac said, her voice ringing out. "I brought Brymn Las to your camp. No, I did not kill your friend. Yes, Brymn changed into the deadly form of his kind. No, we didn't know that would happen or we wouldn't have come to you in the first place. And yes, for his sake as well as for the sake of the friend you lost, and for the millions dying as we waste time with what can't be changed," she drew a deep breath and gave them all her most intense "get on with it" glare, "I will have every single thing you've learned, suspected, or outright guessed about the Dhryn from you. In return, I promise you not a moment's peace. But I will give you everything I know. Together, we may have a chance to stop them. Do we understand one another?"

Fourteen put up his hand. "The waste of time is this group. Studying the past is irrelevant."

Mac hid a smile as the archaeologists leaped to their feet, at least four shouting at once. She did enjoy the passion.

But not the way Lyle Kanaci was looking at her. He was ignoring the others. His eyes burned and his jaw was clenched tight enough to hurt.

"I see." She propped a hip on the table edge and stared right back at him. "We don't understand one another."

The silence following those words had an ugly quality to it. Those who'd stood, sat. No one moved otherwise.

"Oh, we understand you have 'special' knowledge about the Dhryn," Kanaci spat. "What we don't understand, Connor, is why you aren't still in jail and why we have to put up with having you here."

"In jail?" If Mac's eyebrows rose any higher, her forehead would hurt. *Too late.* "Pardon?"

Therin, if she'd identified the Sthlynii correctly, spoke up. His voice surprised her, the words as crisp and clear as anyone's. Mac was distracted by the thought that the elongated vowels he'd hissed at her earlier had been some kind of vocal threat display, an intimidation. *Which only worked if the one being intimidated knows the rules.*

"We saw them take you away under guard after helping your *friend* kill Myriam—before you could attack the rest of uuuus! Saaaaaaw yooooouuu!"

So. Mac nodded, gesturing to a flustered Mudge to keep seated and quiet. She pulled up her left sleeve and flexed her hand. The ceramic pseudo-flesh caught the light, returning its strange hue, more blue-pink than flesh. "This is why they rushed me away," she corrected, keeping her voice matter-of-fact. *They had a long way to go here, and no time for mistakes.* "I'd been injured as well. There are people at the consulate who can testify to that—you don't need to take my word for it."

"As if we would!" Surly, then louder. "Liar! Murderer!"

"Anchen will make sure you get the facts." Her calm invocation of the Sinzira's name seemed to startle them. *Good,* Mac thought grimly. *About time they realized she had support from higher up.* She hoped it was true. "Brymn couldn't help but attack me," she continued. "He'd lost all reason by that point in his metamorphosis. As for my being under arrest?" She didn't have to force a laugh. "I don't know where you got that idea. I went straight back to work until being invited here."

"What work? We tried to find you." This from another of the Humans, a dour-faced individual Mac remembered only as one of the non-scientists in the original group. "We couldn't."

"What were you using? Only my name?" He gave a reluctant nod. Mac felt sympathetic. Mackenzie Connor, in Sol System and throughout the colonies, must turn up hundreds of times. *Hundreds of thousands.* "Remember something under Norcoast Salmon Research Facility?"

Lyle frowned. "Yes, but . . ." his eyes widened. "That's you? The Earth-based fish biologist?"

There was a moment of bedlam, most shocked and none flattering. Mac waited it out, tapping the table with one finger. Therin's voice won; not by volume, the others deferred when he spoke. *Good to know, Em.* "Lies!" the alien exclaimed. "You're a criminal working with the Dhryn—a murderer! They'd have us believe—these twooo, theee staaaff here—you're an experienced science administrator?" He made a rude noise that fluttered his mouth tentacles.

"Oh, that I am," Mac replied coldly. "I've helped run Base—the Norcoast facility—for fourteen years. Ask Oversight here. Check government records. My life isn't a secret. You just didn't see it."

Before Mudge could make his contribution—something he seemed adamantly determined to do, being on his feet with a fist in the air—Lyle leaned forward and shouted. "Then what the hell were you doing on the Dhryn home world, Dr. Connor?"

"Mac." She waved Mudge down a second time before he obeyed, and finally took a chair herself. The ordinary act stopped some of the background muttering, but not all. Mac ignored it, concentrating on Lyle. He led them as much now, in this room, as he had during the sandstorm. She chose her words with care, aware the moment was fragile, and said quietly. "I was looking for the truth."

"What truth? The Dhryn's? Yours? I doubt it's ours." Murmurs of agreement.

"There's only one truth." Mac's eyes traveled from person to person as she spoke, making sure she had the attention of all twenty-seven. "The problem is finding all of it. If anyone understands the danger of extrapolating from partial evidence, it's you. Everything we think we know so far? Fragments. Pieces. We can't use them; we can't even see where they belong. We must find the connections to put those fragments together. Into one truth. The truth."

"First time I've heard the word since we've been here." This from a gray-haired woman sitting between the two Cey. "No one at this Gathering of the Sinzi's is talking about truth. We're supposed to build a weapon or dream up some strategy to destroy the Dhryn. Not exactly what our lot's qualified to do."

There was a smattering of laughter at this. Mac felt some of the tension leave her spine. *Not all.* She raised her prosthetic arm again. "No one," she emphasized, "wants to be eaten alive. Or see the life of a world stripped bare. But we, all of us here, know some new weapon, even if it does wipe out an entire species and end the threat, isn't an answer. We need to understand how something like the Dhryn came to exist, learn where they came from, what might happen in the future. We need the truth."

"We've been singing that song to deaf ears since arriving." Another voice. More nods.

"Then don't waste your breath. Let's get to work." She looked at Lyle Kanaci. He gave her the barest of nods, his eyes guarded. *Good enough.* Mac rose to her feet. "I'll need to talk to you individually to find out your fields and areas of strength. Yes," to those exchanging puzzled looks, "I have the conference list, but I'd rather hear what you want me to know. While I'm doing that, give Oversight here, Charles Mudge III," she introduced quickly, hoping his glower didn't scare anyone off, "a list of whatever you need. It can be data, people, equipment. Anything relevant; I don't need to approve it. For once in our lives, budget is not the issue. Time is." This induced another, happier round of murmuring. Mac raised her voice to be heard over it. "Last, but not least. While all this is going on, I'd like you to turn your attention to a particular aspect of salmon biology."

Silence again, but this time incredulous. Mudge and Fourteen looked as dumbfounded as the rest.

Mac didn't smile. "Most species of salmon live out their lives around a single imperative, folks. A hardwired need to leave where they are and go somewhere else, no matter what's in their way, in order to survive as a species. Migration."

She could identify the bright lights in the room by the way they took the word and absorbed it like a blow. Some turned immediately to colleagues. A few sat without moving. There were the inevitable individuals who still looked as though they thought she was certifiable.

They could be right, Em.

But most were giving off that indefinable energy that, among scientists at least, meant a new paradigm had begun to take hold, a new framework was shifting conclusions and inferences. These were researchers who dealt in vast stretches of time, in cycles. Mac had thought they might be the ones to appreciate the significance.

If the Dhryn had ever been a migratory species, there should be evidence from their planet of origin.

If the Dhryn still answered that call, these researchers might already possess clues as to where and why.

Mac met Fourteen's eyes across the table, quite sure he'd told Anchen her supposition about the Dhryn being on a journey. This group who had been studying the Dhryn home world were the best choice to investigate that possibility. So her working with them now had nothing to do with her qualifications as an administrator or even her history with them. With a deftness Kammie Noyo would appreciate, the Sinzi had put Mac where she had to be.

Refreshing, that.

"I will personally check your story and credentials before doing anything else, Dr. Connor," Therin said loudly, cutting through the chatter.

"Great idea," Mac beamed at the Sthlynii. "And it's Mac. Don't take too long. Meanwhile . . ." she pointed to someone at random and crooked her finger. "You. Let's grab a couple of chairs and that corner, shall we?" Without looking to see if she was being obeyed, Mac left the table and began pushing her own chair closer to the window.

Hands took over the job. Mudge. "I hope you know what you're doing, Norcoast," he whispered over his shoulder to her. "They aren't convinced—not by a long shot."

"Got you to stay, didn't I?" she whispered back, lips twitching. "Give them time. They made a mistake. At least they're listening."

He harrumphed, then was pulled away by a boisterous Cey eager to know how soon she could receive a . . . Mac didn't bother trying to make sense of the name of the device or whatever, but it sounded expensive. *She'd thought the lure of a wide-open budget would help get things moving.*

"Mac."

She positioned her chair and turned, not surprised to see it was Lyle, not the person she'd indicated, pulling his chair up beside hers.

They faced each other, with their respective pieces of furniture in hand like jousting knights waiting mounts, for a ridiculous length of time. Just as Mac was about to give in and sit anyway, he said very quietly, as if each word had to be forced out: "Myriam Myers. The woman who died. She was my wife, Connor. I've been hunting you, as best I could from the Chasm, ever since. Now, I . . ." His pale eyes glistened.

Mac gestured to the other chair and dropped into her own as he sat, pulling out her imp as though they were about to exchange data. Her hands trembled. "Now," she finished for him, equally softly, "you don't know what to do or think. You feel empty. Cheated. Lost."

"Yes." He looked up at her, having slumped to rest his elbows on his knees. "How did you—"

"It's a three-pint story."

A hint of a smile. "Haven't heard that in a while."

Mac shrugged. "I'm an anachronism. Either that, or I don't get out much. But I will tell you everything that's happened, Lyle. If we're going to work together, you'll need that."

He sat a little straighter. "I needed this as well." A nod to the rest of the large room, where everyone was now standing in small groups to talk. Except for the line that had formed behind where Mudge had taken a seat at the table, his workscreen already up. "We've been here two days, Mac. No one's felt necessary until now. Oh, the IU promised to quarantine the Dhryn home world while we're here, preserve our excavations. But they have their own people there and no one's said when we go back. No one's given us any direction what to do here."

"Not to mention you heard a Dr. Connor was taking charge. No wonder you were ready to hang me from the nearest tree this morning."

"Not quite." His pigmentless skin blushed, beginning as rosy dots on either cheek and a band low on neck, the colors rushing together. "But that wasn't our best moment. Now it looks like we jumped to conclusions, maybe ignored data that led elsewhere. It's a shameful thing. I'm sorry."

"Keep your doubts about me until you've checked my side of things for yourself. All I expect now is that you listen with an open mind."

"Fair enough." Lyle's eyes flicked to Mac's head. "That a three-pint story, too?"

"A misadventure with external genitalia!" supplied Fourteen helpfully, coming to stand beside Mac. "So Human." He squinted at Lyle. "Oh. You're Human, too. Couldn't tell. No offense."

"None taken." The archaeologist almost smiled. "Sounds like a story worth hearing."

Mac glared at Fourteen, who took advantage of his thick eyelids to pretend not to see her. "It had its moments," she said to Lyle. "But first—"

"But irrelevant. First, Mac," Fourteen interrupted, "you are wanted." Mac followed his gesture to the doorway, where a pair of consular staff stood waiting.

"Is it an emergency? The Dhryn attacking? Any sign of the Ro?" *Of Emily?*

"They say Sinzi-ra wishes you to return to your quarters and rest."

"Then please advise her I'll do so in—" Mac did a quick calculation. Five minutes an interview—if no one was long-winded, which was unlikely, so half would go ten—twenty-four researchers left to meet. "Three hours. Plus. Make it four."

"But, Mac—"

She finally caught and held Fourteen's small eyes. "I could take five if you keep delaying me."

"Very well." From his tone, Mac might have asked him to do more dishes.

As he walked away, Lyle half smiled. "If I needed more proof you run a research station in the middle of nowhere, there it is."

"What's that?"

"You're used to doing things yourself."

"You know what they say, Lyle," Mac said primly, smoothing the fabric of her lovely blue jacket over her thighs, "about doing something right. Now, who should I speak with next?"

As he stood to call someone over, Mac looked past and saw Fourteen arguing with the staff, who were not looking at all happy.

And sometimes, Em, she smiled to herself, *it wasn't about doing it right. It was about setting rules.*

Either this room and all it represented was hers, or it wasn't.

She intended it to be hers.

There was nothing quite as soothing as sand to tired Human feet, Mac decided as she kicked off her shoes that night. She lay back in the jelly-chair and dug in her toes, head back and eyes closed. Her scalp throbbed, her stomach was beyond empty, and she thought it likely she'd fall asleep before being able to stand again.

Haven't felt this good in months, Em.

Every member of the group—she'd dubbed them the Origins Team—was exceptional. No surprise, given they'd organized, funded, and established an independent research camp on one of the lifeless Chasm worlds. *Not bad.* Mind you, a significant proportion of those funds came from private donors they preferred not to name, but Mac had no problem with generosity, so long as there weren't strings attached.

Lyle Kanaci? She put her teeth together and whistled tunelessly. Brilliant, determined, responsible, obsessed. An asset she'd invite to Norcoast in an instant, if only he was as interested in living things as he was in what they built and left behind. He'd expressed the doubts Mac found many of the Origins Team shared—what could they contribute here? Even more frustrating, they'd been forced to suspend much of their work to help set up the influx of new researchers to the Dhryn world.

The new arrivals, all sponsored by the IU, hadn't been asked to attend the Gathering in person; their findings and data were being fed here. Mac was well aware her group considered their invitation a sign their independent research was in jeopardy.

It probably was.

"Are you in pain?"

Mac opened her eyes and sat up as quickly as the amorous chair allowed. "Anchen. I'm sorry. I didn't hear you come in." *She never did.*

The room was dimly lit. The Sinzi was little more than a pale, slender silhouette against the dark night sky that showed through the terrace doors. "It is I who must remember not to startle my guests, Mac. May I examine your wound, please." It wasn't a question.

Mac stood and let the Sinzi explore her bandaged scalp. The alien used her fingertips, gently pressing in various spots until Mac winced cooperatively. "Very good," Anchen assured her. "The regeneration of your skin should be complete soon. We'll be able to remove the covering shortly." A pause, her touch lingering on Mac's forehead. "Do you wish treatment for pain?"

"I just need some supper and a night's sleep, thank you."

Anchen spoke one word: "Attend." The lights brightened and Mac stifled a yawn as a trolley of food floated through the open doors into her room, guided by another of the staff. She didn't think she'd seen the same one twice.

"Once more, you anticipate my every need," Mac said gratefully.

"As is always my intent. Now I wish you to anticipate mine."

Mac, who'd found the energy to follow her supper into the sitting room, stopped and looked over her shoulder at the taller alien. "I'm afraid I don't have your skill at anticipation, Anchen," she said, stalling. What did the Sinzi want? *Hopefully nothing that involved a body part.* "What can I do for you?"

The Sinzi produced an imp, white and more disk-shaped than Mac's or Fourteen's. "I visit the team leaders each night to record their impressions and insights for the IU. I need yours, if you please."

Mac was afraid her relief was obvious. *Still . . . there were over thirty separate research teams.* "How do you get any sleep?" she asked involuntarily.

Anchen looked amused. "At this moment, four of my 'selves' are asleep, Mac."

"Oh. Of course." *Handy.* "Why the imp?" she asked, thinking of the light fixture Mudge had suspected. "Isn't the room monitored?"

Anchen's head snapped up to an impressive height. "It is not. We could not host honored delegates from the IU here if they had the slightest reason to doubt their privacy."

Her vehemence was convincing. Mac felt a twinge of guilt. Sing-li must have hidden some Ministry snooper of his own on Oversight—an abuse of consular protocol Mac doubted the Sinzi would tolerate. *If she found out.*

So, how close together did Humans stick?

Mac's stomach chose that moment to gurgle. Loudly.

Being in charge of a consulate on Earth led to certain understandings. Anchen lowered her head and lifted three fingers in the direction of Mac's supper. "You can provide this information while you eat."

Refusing didn't seem an option, but Mac went for a gracious, "Then please join me, Anchen."

"I would be honored."

They each took one of the jelly-chairs, the attendant arranging the floating trolley at Mac's side. Before Mac could offer to share, Anchen reached to the table between them, aglow with fish, sponges, and anemones. Her fingertip pointed at a bristling shrimp, marching delicately over a coral.

"I saw that one earlier—" Mac began, then closed her mouth as the attendant extended a small rod into a long silver implement which he deftly stabbed into the table. The tip instantly adhered to the small animal and the attendant smoothly withdrew both implement and now motionless shrimp, proffering both to Anchen.

Without a drop of water hitting the sand.

"I'm impressed," Mac said as Anchen delicately but efficiently used her nails to peel shell and pluck appendages, putting these in a small bowl provided by the attendant before consuming the remaining morsel of flesh in one tidy mouthful.

Mac looked at the table, where the sea life seemed completely unconcerned, and scratched her own fingernail along the top. Hard and solid. A parrot fish tried to nibble her finger before diving deeper. "Okay. I have to know how you did that."

Anchen beckoned to the attendant. He bowed to Mac and said: "The table is both menu and larder for the Sinzi-ra, who consumes only fresh marine life."

Mac raised an eyebrow. "Preference or physiology? If you don't mind the question."

The Sinzi smiled, cleaning her fingertips on a cloth the attendant had exchanged for the bowl. "Assuredly I do not. It is both, Mac. On Earth, these delicious organisms are also the most easily digested by my species. In addition, I find the movements of these beautiful creatures to be soothing as well as appetizing, so there are tables like this in several locations in the consulate. Do you enjoy them as well?"

"Very much. Soothing always. And several are very tasty." Still perplexed, Mac studied the table. "But—the water appears deeper than it can be. And how did you catch the shrimp and pull it through the table?" This to the attendant. "Trust me, I know what it's like trying to net something in water."

The attendant looked to Anchen, who lifted two fingers. *Granting permission,* Mac decided. "The table is more than a convenience for the Sinzi-ra," he explained. "It is a demonstration of a brand new technology the Sinzi is offering to qualified members of the Interspecies Union. This—" he indicated the table, "—is not a tank filled with water and living things. It is an access gate, permanently opened to another, much larger tank." He showed Mac the slim featureless rod, collapsing it. "This device acts much the way the navigation array on a starship does when it stipulates a destination through a transect, creating a pathway. In this case, the destination is an object in the tank. The connection is instantaneous and the object, the shrimp Anchen favored, can be retrieved."

She'd been tapping the outside of a transect through no-space.

Mac lifted her fingers from the table.

"It is an accomplishment in which we take great pride," noted Anchen. "However, there remain serious constraints. It takes a constant input of power to maintain—we have been permitted to draw directly upon the geothermal energy beneath this building. More significantly, there is an impact on the living things within the tank. They appear normal and thriving, do they not? So far as we can determine, they come to no harm entering or existing in what is essentially a fixed bubble of no-space. Once inside, however, they cannot be removed alive."

Emily.

Perhaps the Sinzi interpreted Mac's look of horror as one of awe. *Or understood all too well.* "How to survive upon exit is among the most important of the many questions we have for the Myrokynay," she said. "We Sinzi have but built on the fragments they left thousands of years ago." Fingers cascaded, rings flashed light. "We do our best—yet how pitiful our efforts must seem to them. From your own account and those of others, now the Myrokynay can form transects at need, live themselves within no-space, pass freely into this reality. While we achieve shrimp snacks, using as much power as this entire complex."

Pitiful? Mac stared at the table, with its imprisoned life. She wasn't so sure. Many living things staked out territories, defended what they viewed as theirs; Humans could do it with a look. *What would the Ro think of the Sinzi's shrimp, Em?* Would they have the proud attitude of parents who see their children strive to exceed them? Or might they see trespass—a challenge to their supremacy over no-space itself from those who still walked planets?

Mac shivered. "You want a great deal more than help with the Dhryn."

"Of course," with that lift of the head indicating surprise. "In our wildest imaginings, we never expected to find the creators of the transects still lived. To work with them? To learn from them? The Sinzi aspire only to be worthy."

"If I were you," Mac said dryly, "I'd aspire to find out what they'll want in return and be sure you can afford it."

Anchen's head tilted to bring another set of eyes closer to Mac. *Whose attention did she have now?* "First contact is by its very nature doomed to misunderstandings, Mac." Her voice was gentle but firm. "We can only proceed in this by stepping from known to known. The Dhryn feared the Myrokynay. For good reason, since the Myrokynay tried to destroy their Progenitors before they could launch their ships. All we know about the Dhryn is that they pose a devastating and terrifying threat to life. Surely the Myrokynay, who possess knowledge and technology far beyond any other species within the Interspecies Union, know more. We need them as allies. We will pay their price, if one is asked."

This was the being who represented the IU on Earth. *Nothing she says, Em,* Mac told herself uneasily, *would be less than policy for all.*

Still, she couldn't keep completely silent. "I urge caution in every dealing with the Ro, Anchen. We know even less about them than about the Dhryn."

"An insight of value, Mac, which is why you are here." Anchen brought out her imp and put it on the table. "Please, if you are ready, eat your meal and share any thoughts you have from your first day." She made motions with her fingers, implying a workscreen in existence over the device, but Mac couldn't see one— unless that shimmer when she tilted her head marked a portion. *Differing visual range? Interesting.*

If things hadn't gone so well today—*after that appalling start,* Mac admitted— she might have been stuck with nothing to tell the Sinzi, but as it was, her food grew cold as she described the potential of her group of researchers. "I wouldn't be surprised," she finished, waving her fork in emphasis, "to have interesting results as early as tomorrow."

The Sinzi had listened without comment until now. "Why do you expect this, Mac? They had nothing to contribute yesterday, beyond what was recorded about the death of their fellow scientists. Today, they have requested data on you, not on the Dhryn."

"The information about me will restore trust. As for my expectations?" Mac tilted her head, trying to decide which of Anchen's paired eyes were most intent on her. "They don't know what they know," she said at last. "It's about context, Anchen. I've given them a new one. I think it will shake some things loose."

"Ah, yes. Migration. You believe the Dhryn are on such a journey. That their motive may be biological. That they act, at least in part, out of instinct rather than conscious plan. A novel approach."

Fourteen had made a full report, Mac smiled to herself. Aloud: "Believe? No. Not yet. I simply see value to assessing what we know about the Dhryn in those terms. That could be the prejudice of my own specialization. I admit that. But consider this, Anchen. At least since the Chasm, Dhryn Progenitors have out-lawed the study of living things, including their own physiology. Why?"

"Is this an important question?"

"Any question we can't answer about the Dhryn is an important question."

The Sinzi lifted her fingers, touching them tip to tip to form a hollow ball before her complex eyes. "I concur, Mac. I will share your insights with the other delegates in hopes of granting them a new 'context.'" She lowered her fingers and smiled. "I am personally gratified by your behavior with the Human-ra since this morning. You exceeded the expectations of some of myselves for you, and those were already high."

Given the time of night, and a mind this side of putty, Mac wisely avoided try-ing to understand that, accepting the implied compliment. "The Human-ra—" *the term must be loose enough,* she decided, *to include Kanaci's non-Human colleagues,* "—lacked the information it required about me. I've begun to rectify that. Call it a misunderstanding during first contact. We have a common purpose, after all."

"We do. Ah. I am reminded." *By what,* Mac wondered. *One of the group minds?* A deft finger stroke through empty air, away from where Mac had assumed the invisible-to-her workscreen hung. *Separate 'screens for each mind?* "There is a query for you. It comes from the team correlating our data on the Myrokynay."

"Me? I don't have anything new to add to my original statements," Mac reminded the Sinzi. "And I made those when things were fresher in my mind."

"We have your very useful information, Mac. This query concerns a more esoteric interpretation of your experience. Yes. I see it is posed in mathematical terms which, while elegant and succinct, do not translate into Instella. If you will permit me to approximate?" At Mac's nod, she continued: "Did you observe anything about Emily Mamani implying the passage of biological time in no-space?"

"Biological time." While several possibilities came to mind, Mac chose not to guess. "I don't understand."

"The state of being alive is postulated to require time that at least appears to move linearly, from what was to what is, thus permitting growth and metabolism to take place in sequenced steps. There are other modes of time which do not support this state. Within our tank," a gesture to the glittering fish, "there is movement and thus the impression of biological time, is there not? We are divided in interpretation. Is this true biological time or its echo, since what passes for life here is, in real space, already dead?"

Mac gamely attempted to wrap her brain around the philosophical connections between linear time and death, other than the one being at the end of the line. After a moment, she gave a helpless shrug. "I'm sorry, Anchen. Salmon researcher, not physicist. What's the point to this?"

"If we accept that the Myrokynay truly live within no-space, the answers to questions of time have significance to our hope for mutual understanding."

"If they live in time as we do," Mac narrowed her eyes, "they're like us. I get that part. But as opposed to what?"

"Some other state of being." The Sinzi brought two fingertips closer and closer together as if to touch, only to have them miss each other at the last instant. "An alarming possibility, Mac. You and your fellow Humans experience misunderstandings, as does any species within itself, despite shared biology and history. Negotiations between IU species involves more effort to sort through unintended confusion than all other deterrents to agreement combined. This, despite a shared language and technology." Anchen shuddered, her hundreds of tiny rings tinkling. "Imagine the difficulty communicating with beings who don't share the very experience of life itself with us."

They'd have a better chance explaining Trisulian sex to a salmon through a straw. Mac became acutely conscious of her heart beating, the air passing in and out of her nostrils, the way her head ached. A body plan reasonably similar to the Sinzi's.

The same ability to exchange complex ideas. "Puts my problems with the Origins Team into perspective," she said at last. "I wouldn't worry too much yet. After all, Emily's managed to deal with the Ro."

Anchen's small mouth formed a smile. "A comforting observation to end the day." Putting away her imp, the Sinzi rose from the jelly-chair without a wasted motion. Mac stood up as well, feeling as though she flopped in every direction possible before finding level ground. "Good night, Mac, and thank you for your insights. I will return tomorrow evening—late again, I assume."

Mac smiled. "Good thing you sleep in shifts, Anchen."

By early the next morning, the now officially named Origins Team was well underway. They skipped the mill and swill, as Mac called it, in the garden in favor of getting to work. Not to mention being set out as mass enticement for the Ro was the last thing she felt like doing, no matter how determined the Sinzi. Fourteen showed his approval by showing up sans wig and in those paisley shorts, clean at least. As for the others, it hadn't hurt that she'd arranged for breakfast to be served here, then refused to let the staff clean up, knowing perfectly well they'd be grazing the leftovers before lunch.

The room itself had a completely different look from yesterday. The research consoles had been moved into five clusters, Lyle suggesting those to be included in each. The big conference table had been shoved against one wall to provide the expanse of empty floor space archaeologists apparently required. Mac didn't ask.

Fourteen had brought in three large tables of his own, setting these up in a u-shape so he had his back to the window—Mac presumed so he could see what everyone else was doing, curiosity being one of the Myg's traits. Each time she looked at what he himself was doing, there were more small objects scattered over the tables, each new acquisition placed with the rapt concentration of a chess master. Objects like other people's writing implements, combs, and buttons. And a shoe.

She'd better send around a memo, Mac decided.

Mudge had taken a corner for himself, adding a desk. He'd stayed up most of the night, by the bags under his eyes, managing to send their initial supply requests through in time for the first arrivals to accompany the catering staff.

It had been a toss-up which had been more warmly received, coffee or image extrapolation wands. *Whatever they were.*

Mac wandered over to Mudge, leaning on the wall behind him to survey the bustle, mug in hand.

"Do you," he asked acerbically, "have the slightest idea what they're doing?"

"Not a clue." She took a sip and sighed contentedly. *Cold already.* "How about you?"

"I've placed requisitions for equipment I didn't even know existed, let alone how it could possibly be used by—by archaeologists!"

Mac smiled down at him. "They aren't all archaeologists."

"Don't," he growled, "get me started."

There was now a curtained-off section of the room, behind which the author of the ever-popular "Chasm Ghouls: They Exist and Talk to Me" and his trio of followers were apparently conducting chats with the departed. "Here I shared a sandstorm with the famous man and didn't even know it," Mac mused.

"I wish I didn't."

"We're all talking to the dead here," she pointed out, taking another sip. "I don't care who gives me the answers."

"You've never settled for other people's before, Norcoast."

Mac half smiled. "I've never asked these questions before."

Mudge fussed with his workscreen. "Kirby and To'o are qualified climatologists, but according to your list, we need a xenopaleoecologist."

"I know. Fourteen's working on it. Says he knows one."

"There's another thing. Why is a cryptologist working with us? We have translators." He consulted his workscreen. "An even dozen. There must be other groups who could use him."

She could see the Myg from here; he'd abandoned his object arranging and was deep in conversation with Lyle. "Probably. But he's attached himself to—" *me,* she almost said, "—us for now and no one's objected. He may come in handy."

Especially if Emily tried to send her another message. Something Mac was quite sure had occurred to the Sinzi, and whomever else was in charge.

"Mac, do you have a minute?"

The question, asked in that hesitant "don't know you yet" tone, was so familiar, Mac was smiling before she turned to answer it. "Of course."

It was To'o, the Cey climatologist. Or Da'a, the other Cey. They dressed like twins, and Mac hadn't seen enough of their species to pick out the physical features that distinguished individuals. *Or,* she told herself honestly, *she couldn't get past the heavy wrinkles of their faces.* The dark brown, pebble-textured skin hung in great, limp folds, starting with small ones at the top of the head to free-swinging cascades by the elbows. It was as if each Cey wore another organism like a veil.

For all she knew, they did. Mac shuddered, thinking of the Trisulian symbionts. She'd been very happy not to have to converse with another of that species quite yet.

The problem wasn't that the folds were ugly—*okay,* Mac confessed, *grotesque came to mind*—but the ones on the face itself gave each Cey a perpetually miserable look, as if nauseous. It might have helped if they'd had less Human-like features between the folds.

"If you'll come?"

Quite sure she'd been staring, Mac waved the Cey to proceed her.

Moments later, Mac seriously considered finding a wrinkle to kiss. "This is—this is splendid work, To'o, Kirby. I hadn't expected anything so soon."

Kirby, Human male and probably no older than most of Mac's first-year grad students, grinned up at her from his seat at the console. "It wasn't soon. We'd looked into longer cyclic events with respect to climate for over two Earth years. The research didn't point us anywhere, so we moved on to another topic. Till you. I have to admit, yesterday I thought you were nuts, Mac."

"I get that," she replied absently, leaning over the display with one hand on the console for support. "Why were you looking at cyclic events in the first place?"

To'o replied, "My home world experiences long-term climatic shifts, though none so dramatic as this world's. When you mentioned migration, Kirby and I began to reexamine our old data, looking specifically at the livability of the northern hemisphere relative to the south. We had some more recent data as well from the IU's team back on Myriam."

"'Myriam?'"

The two exchanged guilty looks. "Sorry. Slipped out," To'o said quickly. "We're not supposed to call it that here."

Mac had no idea of the protocol involved in naming planets—especially planets doubtless named by those who'd evolved there. *Still.* She shot a troubled glance at Lyle, preoccupied with his work, then looked back to the climatologists.

Who were, just like her grad students, holding their breath.

"You named the Dhryn home world after his wife?" she asked, keeping her voice steady but low. "She died there."

"We all agreed." Kirby shrugged. "Lyle's—well, he felt she'd have liked it. And we renamed our research station after Nicli Lee. She died in the storm."

"We keep saying their names, that way," To'o volunteered. "It's important to speak of those we've lost—not to forget them."

She could hardly disagree. "It's shorter than 'Dhryn Home World'," she commented, tacit approval. "Now, what did you want to show me?"

Kirby took over. "We'd collected data on the Dhryn System, including planetary orbits, solar intensity, and so forth. You have to keep in mind we went to—" he seemed at a loss for the name.

"Myriam," Mac helped without thinking. *Damn. She knew better than to encourage this.*

But his smile was so heartfelt and sincere Mac knew she'd committed herself for good. *Another memo,* she sighed inwardly, *so the Sinzi-ra isn't perplexed by reports on planet 'Myriam.'* Kirby had continued, meanwhile. "We went to Myriam to answer questions about the destruction occurring throughout the Chasm. Our initial results showed climate change wasn't implicated, although plenty took place following. Last few months, To'o and I were pretty much left to predicting sandstorms." He surveyed their display with possessive pride. "Wobbly little orbit, isn't it?"

"One way to put it." Mac traced the line without letting her finger invade the active portion of the image. "It doesn't take much," she murmured. "How would this affect the planet?"

"We'll have to do more detailed models," explained To'o, "but my preliminary estimate is that before whatever happened to cause the Chasm-effect, Myriam cycled through polar desertification every five hundred plus orbits."

"At the same time as one pole baked dry, the opposite pole may have experienced near ice age conditions," Kirby offered. "We're not sure. It's a tight orbit. Might have been enough solar radiation transmitted throughout the atmosphere to keep the entire planet above freezing. If so, it would likely have been very wet in temperate zones, ocean currents would have shifted, upper air movements be affected." His voice conveyed awe. "Frankly, an Earth-type seasonal change would have been trivial compared to this. I don't know how a culture would cope."

"More to the point," Mac said, straightening, "how would life?"

"You said migration—but can this fit the bill?" Kirby sounded doubtful suddenly. "I'm no biologist, but aren't migrations annual? Running from winter, that sort of thing. Five hundred year cycles?" He shook his head. "I dunno, Mac."

Mac didn't quite smile. "Nothing is that simple. There are species on Earth, like my salmon, who only migrate when their bodies are ready to reproduce, however many years that takes. There are others whose individuals never complete a migration, having generations born, reproduce, then die as steps along that journey. Look at us," Mac put a hand on Kirby and To'o's shoulder, feeling the differences in the joints beneath her fingers. "If there's anything biologists have learned, it's that life offers a variety of ways to get the job done. Survival first."

"We'll get on a model for you," To'o offered. "Should let us infer what conditions existed over evolutionary time lines."

"I look forward to it. Good work, you two."

Mac left the climatologists and began wandering the large room, listening to conversations and the hum of equipment. There were no looks of condemnation today. If anything, there were a few more sympathetic smiles than she liked, each of which she had to acknowledge with a polite nod.

Anchen's doing. During breakfast, Mac learned that last night the Sinzi had sent everyone a copy of the report the consulate had received on her experiences with the Dhryn. She'd held a faint hope not all had taken the time to read it, but, from the looks now—and given their original attitude toward her—it seemed everyone had.

Personally, while Mac had planned to give her colleagues any information that might trigger a connection or produce an idea, she hadn't planned to share every detail of the events themselves. *Not going to guess, Em, what these people think now.*

She supposed she should relax and be grateful her team no longer believed she'd been imprisoned as a murderous traitor to her kind.

"Someone die?"

At the sound of Fourteen's voice, Mac started, then smiled and shook her head. "Sorry. Just thinking."

"Idiot."

"Probably. Did you want something? I was going to talk to Lyle."

"Talk to me first. Outside."

He wasn't happy about something. Mac gave a discreet sniff, detecting nothing but mint. Without argument, she followed Fourteen from the Origins room out to the Sinzi version of a corridor, which consisted of a broad ramplike balcony that wound around a central opening, eventually reaching every floor of the building. A few pigeons perched on the edges, taking full advantage of the practice of wide-open doors every morning. Mac presumed they'd find their way out again or be fed. *Then again,* she thought, amused, *maybe they'd be fed to some of the delegates.*

"Well?" asked Mac when they were out of earshot of the room. "Quickly, please, Fourteen. I'd like to get back."

"Your Dhryn, Brymn Las. You said he'd published work on the Chasm, correct?"

"Yes, of course." She frowned. "What's this about?"

"Significant work?"

"Yes," Mac said again. "I believe some are considered definitive on the subject. Core texts. Why?"

The Myg's answer sent her marching straight back into the research room, straight to Lyle Kanaci. He looked up as Mac approached, then stood with alarm as her expression registered.

Good, Mac thought. Despite an overwhelming urge to shout and tear hair, not necessarily hers, she toned her voice to quiet fury. "How dare you refuse to use the work of the foremost expert on Chasm archaeology?"

Lyle's face settled into stubborn lines. Silence spread in ripples from them. *So much for subtle, Em.* "You lost your wife," she snapped. "Are you willing to lose everyone in this room—everyone and everything alive on this planet—the same way?"

He opened his mouth, face ashen. Mac quelled whatever he was about to say with a sharp upward gesture of her hand. "Use your grief and rage however you want," she continued just as angrily, meaning them all to hear. "But don't let it blind you. Don't ever let it *think* for you."

She took a ragged breath. "Brymn spent his life seeking the truth about what destroyed the worlds of the Chasm. I hope none of us ever feels how he must have felt, to learn it was his own kind, to have his own body betray everything he believed." Mac's eyes never left Lyle's. "I will not permit his life's work to be lost or ignored. How dare you . . ." She lost her voice somewhere in fury, then regained it. "I will supply complete sets of Brymn's work to everyone on the Origins Team. If you or anyone is unwilling to use it, find somewhere else to be. I won't work with you."

Without waiting for an answer, Mac spun on her heel and left.

"No one left."

Mac's fingers tightened their grip on the terrace railing, but she gave no other indication she'd doubted the outcome. "Lyle?"

"Staying, Norcoast, but not happy." Mudge leaned on his elbows beside her, shaking his head. He reached out to touch the invisible barrier protecting them both from the blustery northwest wind and the driving rain it carried. "He'll be looking for flaws in the Dhryn's research, questioning every piece of data, suspecting hidden motives. Could be difficult."

She turned her head to grin at him. "Sounds familiar."

Mudge pretended to be shocked. "If you are implying a comparison to my annual reviews, the word you want is 'thorough.'"

"Not 'obsessive'?" she chuckled, then relented. "Thanks for bringing me the news. I knew the consulate had everything I needed. It's already been sent to their imps and consoles. Now all I have to do is unpack."

"Your belongings arrived?"

In a manner of speaking. Mac straightened. "Let me show you."

She led Mudge back through her bedroom and the sitting room, to where a new door had appeared—or rather been revealed, since Mac didn't doubt it had always been there—since she'd left this morning. She pushed it open and waved Mudge to precede her. "Watch your head," she cautioned as she followed.

Behind the door was, for lack of a better term, the Sinzi version of a closet. It was more like a warehouse. Larger than the sitting room, but with a floor constructed of the same weatherproof material as the terrace, the closet had no window on the outer wall. Instead, that wall was sectioned and fitted with a mechanism to both open and extend its panels into what Mac assumed was a landing pad for a t-lev. A rope of bright light ran along the junction of walls and ceiling.

The three inner walls, other than the entranceway, were studded with hooks, as was the ceiling. From each hook hung a large bag, roughly the length of a Human being, but varying in width. There were dozens, the ones from the ceiling swaying gently.

"When I first saw this, I thought it was a Sinzi nursery," Mac said. Mudge, who'd gone to the center of the closet and was poking at a bag above his head, quickly withdrew his hand. "It isn't," Mac laughed. She grabbed a strap attached to a bag hanging near the door, using it to pull down both bag and hook. The assembly paused where she stopped it, and Mac tugged open the bag, stepping to one side as she did.

Boxes and boots tumbled out on the floor. Her boots, still caked with mud from the pod roof. Mac regarded them fondly. *Such a homey touch in an alien closet.*

"You mentioned the word 'thorough,' Oversight?" Mac flung her arm at the bags on every side. "This would appear to be an example. They must have—" she paused to grunt with the effort of pulling down two more bags at once, "—brought everything that wasn't attached."

Mudge helped her free the bags' contents. Sure enough, they were shortly surrounded by a mix of sweaters, wooden salmon, and an eclectic variety of lab equipment. "Wrong—some things were attached," he offered, holding up the end support of Mac's desk for inspection.

She shook her head in astonishment. Sing-li, or whoever he'd sent, was a literal sort.

The floor was soon littered with the contents of Mac's office and lab. Nothing was in order, but it was all intact. They began taking turns moving items to the other room to leave space for more. On one such trip, Mac returned to find Mudge hurriedly closing the bag he'd just brought down from the ceiling. "What is it?" she asked, curious. He hadn't flinched when her underwear had come flying out past his head.

"Stuffed llama. With sunglasses." Mudge gave her a wide-eyed look. "Is that yours?"

Emily's things. "Of course. I don't need it now. Please close it up, Oversight." Mac looked up at the rest of the bags hanging from the ceiling.

They had *brought everything.*

He looked, too. "Let's stop here," he suggested reasonably, arms limp at his sides. Sweat beaded his forehead and cheeks. The bags had held heavy equipment as well as pressed leaves. "You can't need all of this immediately. You probably don't need any," this opinion with a scowl at her curtain beads, piled around his feet. "We should get back to the team."

"I want to give them some time to go over Brymn's material without me breathing down their necks. Or whatevers." Mac kept digging through a stack of promising reference works. They'd been near her desk. Her desk had had her imp. *Mind you, dismantling her desk hadn't helped in using it as a locator.* The parts were spread among fifteen bags so far. "Have to find my imp," she insisted.

"You have one."

"That?" Mac shook her head, burrowing deeper. Inside a bag she'd thought empty was a small assortment of objects, difficult to see and too deep to reach. She half climbed inside. "One of Fourteen's," she said, voice muffled by fabric. "I want mine."

It wasn't just her voice that was muffled. She could barely make out Mudge saying something. "Can't hear you," she muttered, feeling the end of a promising cylinder. "Aha!" *Sample bottle.* Mac put it down and leaned in farther.

Another voice answered Mudge's, deeper and familiar.

Mac squirmed out of the bag, hands clutching whatever they'd last grabbed, and half staggered to her feet. A guest?

In her closet?

"Norcoast, meet my friend at the consulate, Stefan Young, the one who helped arrange for me to stay. We've known each other for years." Mudge beamed, his hand on the shoulder of the man he was introducing. "Stefan stopped by to see how I was doing. Stefan, this is Dr. Mackenzie Connor."

The suit and cravat were immaculate. The glasses gleamed. The brown hair was neatly trimmed above the collar, the skin of cheek and chin free of beard. Perhaps the smile was a bit forced, the eyes caught by her bandaged scalp.

But otherwise, Mac decided, *Nikolai Trojanowski appeared in fine form.*

"Hello, Dr. Connor."

- Encounter -

THE GREAT JOURNEY must continue. That which is Dhryn cannot falter. All that is Dhryn must move.

That which is Dhryn . . . *starves.*

That which is Dhryn remembers this place, knows its *Taste,* rushes forward.

Then stops. There is not enough here to sustain the Journey. That which is Dhryn cannot afford waste of effort.

But it is the way of the Great Journey, that all must follow the Taste.

That which is Dhryn . . . moves.

"Did you check the L-array, David? It's been acting up."

"Yes, Mom, I checked the L-array."

The woman alone in the operations booth winced at the patience in his tone. "Asked already, have I?"

"Twice, but who's counting?"

"Obviously you. A little respect for your commander, young man, if you please, or I'll make you wait to park your shuttle until Maggie's brought the freighter up."

"Fine by me. Sooner I park, the sooner I'm back cleaning tubes." A pause. "Just kidding, Mom."

"I know. C'mon in. You should be in time for supper. Thanks for the check, David."

"Shuttle coming in, Commander Mom."

His laugh lingered, warming ops. Even so, her eyes wandering ceaselessly over the remote feeds, Anita Brukman lost her smile.

She couldn't ask often enough. They couldn't be careful enough.

They'd survived once—if surviving was blowing clear of the station as her seals dissolved and hatches breached to vacuum—if surviving was listening to the desperate, futile struggles of those too late to escape pods or shuttles—if surviving was returning to make repairs and go back to the work and ship out ore as if everyone else who should be there, be part of your life forever . . . wasn't gone.

Anita drew a deep breath and relaxed her shoulders. They'd survived and they were careful. Fact was, the station was close to shipping at sixty percent capacity again, or would be once Maggie's freighter was filled and on her way. A tribute to Human determination, the company rep called it. Bonuses all around by tour's end.

As if fate heard her, two-thirds of the remote feeds flared red at once.

The com crackled with overlapping shouts: "Incoming!" "Dhryn everywhere." "They're heading for the station!"

Then, one voice, with a calmness that made her proud: "Mom, get to the shuttle bay. I'm coming for you."

"It's too late, David," Anita said gently. "Go. Everyone in a ship. Go."

Seals began to breach. A claxon would sound as long as air carried it.

"Mom."

"David." Anita put her hand on the cold metal of the station wall and closed her eyes.

"I love you," she told him.

One last time.

ACQUAINTANCE AND ANGUISH

"THIS ISN'T A SOCIAL call, Charles," Stefan/Nik informed them both. He'd acquired a faint accent Mac couldn't place; it changed his voice significantly. *More annoying spy stuff, Em.* She frowned, mind racing with questions, none pleasant, about 'Stefan's' connection to Mudge. But he didn't give her time to say anything at all. "Dr. Connor, I'm to escort you to reception. There's someone to see you. Please come with me."

Mac's hands lost their grip, the objects in them falling to the floor with a clatter. She couldn't help the hope.

She couldn't utter it.

Mudge harrumphed. "Dr. Mamani?" he asked, for her sake. *A kindness.* "Is she here?"

Even through the glasses, Mac could read the flash of pity in those hazel eyes. "No," she answered, for him.

To recover, she bent to pick up what she'd dropped. Another sample bottle, this filled with salmon otoliths from three years ago, a hairbrush she didn't use anymore, and . . . her imp. *Well, Em,* Mac told herself, feeling hollow, *something positive.* She clutched it in her hand and tossed the other items back in the bag.

"Dr. Connor. If you'd come with me, please? We're pressed for time."

"Yes, of course," she said quietly. Mudge puffed out his cheeks and Mac shook her head at him. "You should get back to the group."

A disapproving look. "What about all this?"

Mac held up her imp. "Now it can wait. Thanks for your help, Oversight. I'll check in later."

Mudge patted Stefan/Nik on the shoulder. "You're in good hands, Norcoast." To Nik, "Make sure she gets lunch, Stefan. Something nourishing."

This, Mac decided, *was too bizarre for words.* Both Nik and Mudge had some explaining to do.

It wasn't going to be now. Nik was already out of the closet and through the sitting room, walking so quickly Mac was reasonably sure he'd have sand in his shoes. With a last look and an apologetic shrug at Mudge, who was stepping his way free of her beads, Mac followed.

She caught up with Nik as he led the way down the corridor ramp to the nearest lift. The suit disguised any tension in his shoulders or posture—*convenient, that*—but she felt it coming in waves from him anyway. *Something wasn't right.*

Mac grimaced. *Nothing new there, Em.*

Once in the lift, Nik waited for the door to close. The Sinzi-built device responded to voice or an input pad with five choices, corresponding to the four aboveground floors and the roof. He didn't use any of these, instead placing his hand flat on the wall beside the pad and pressing it there. "This will work for you as well, Dr. Connor," he said, still with the accent. The lift began to drop. There was no sensation, but lights coursed down the sides to indicate movement, a brief ring of green announcing every floor. Three. Two. One.

" 'Stefan?' " she commented, watching the lights.

"Long story."

"I'll bet."

They kept going. The flashes reflected from Nik's glasses as he looked at her, hiding his expression.

She'd been sure there was a basement. *Just never planned to go there, Em.*

They kept going, floors blinking by so rapidly Mac lost count at seven below ground.

They kept going.

Finally, Nik removed his hand and the lift stopped.

"Reception?" Mac asked dubiously as the doors opened on a white, featureless corridor, flat and long.

"In a sense. Please hurry."

Hurry? Mac swallowed and kept up with Nik, giving a little hop every three steps to match his longer ones.

The corridor ended at another, perpendicular to the first. A figure stepped out from the left in front of them. With astonishing quickness, Nik pushed her to that wall and down, using the effort to dodge right and to the floor himself, his hand swinging up to aim before Mac knew he'd drawn his palm-sized weapon.

And before she had time to be more than shocked, Nik was putting his weapon away again. "What happened to patience?" he asked, accent gone.

It was a Trisulian. Mac automatically counted eyestalks—*two upper, no lower*—as the being answered: "Patience, my good Nikolai, is a virtue without value at this time. Dr. Connor. Forgive my partner's deplorable reflexes. Are you all right?"

Partner? One hand on the wall, Mac rose to her feet. By the feel, she'd have a bruise on her shoulder, another on her hip. As for her head? *Bah.* "Mac. And yes, I'm fine, thanks." She couldn't help herself. "Partner?"

Nik gestured to the alien. "Meet Cinder. Who usually knows better than to surprise me." This with a glare.

An eyestalk coyly bent in his direction. "You haven't shot me yet."

"Day's young."

"I thought we were in a hurry," Mac commented dryly.

Nik gave her the strangest look before he nodded brusquely, motioning her to follow the Trisulian.

Recognizing the look, Mac felt a chill as she obeyed. *Why sympathy, Em? Who or what was waiting for her?*

Whatever it was, it was well-protected. They took the left corridor as it gradually bent to the right. *Following the cliff and coastline, not the building,* Mac deduced. Along the way, Nik and Cinder escorted her through three checkpoints, set equidistant along the plain white hall, the last two within sight of each other.

The checkpoints appeared an afterthought. At each, a member of the consular staff waited at a table set to block half the width of the corridor. The remaining gap was guarded by an assortment of aliens, also in the yellow consular uniform, but with armor showing beneath—those who didn't have their own natural version. After the second of these pauses, during which the staff courteously inquired after their needs and clearances, questions Nik answered for her, Mac decided the choice of guards wasn't completely random. No two of the same species were present at one checkpoint. *IU policy?* she wondered as they passed the third. *To prevent collusion—or share some risk?*

Beyond the third checkpoint, the corridor took a sharper bend, widened into a bulb, and came to an end. They stood in front of a choice of three ordinary-looking doors. Mac was a little disappointed, having geared herself for a more spectacular destination.

"Wait here, Mac," Nik ordered. He gave her another of those disconcerting looks, seemed to hesitate, then went with Cinder through the first door to the right. Mac peered past them, seeing nothing but more white walls. *Another corridor?* They closed the door before she could be sure.

Well, Em, this is an anticlimax. Mac put her shoulders against the nearest wall, tipping her head back to rest it on something solid. It was, to put it mildly, throbbing. Somehow she didn't think Anchen—*or would it be the physician mind, Noad?*—would consider being violently slammed to the floor as proper care of a concussion. *Spies.*

Mac closed her eyes. Odd. The throbbing had a second component, out of sync with her heartbeat, *elevated,* or breathing, *steady.* She concentrated, turning her head slightly. The bare part of her scalp happened to touch the wall. Through that contact, the throbbing developed a fascinating, singsong pattern. It wasn't sound, Mac decided, not as she could hear.

But it had meaning.

Mac straightened, her eyes wide. Without hesitation, she went to the middle door, the one closest to her, and shoved it open.

The smell caught her first. She covered her nose, staring at the shape huddled at the far end of the cage. For that was the only feature of the rectangular, white room: a floor-to-ceiling enclosure of vertical white bars each the width of her hand, set her shoulder-width apart. The cage filled half of the floor space, away from any wall by several meters. Within was nothing but the shape, motionless, naked, and blue.

It was as if her blood congealed within her veins, leaving nothing but a lump of flesh incapable of movement, of feeling. *Oh, not incapable of feeling,* Mac realized. Emotions surged through her, battering at her senses. Blinding rage. Betrayal, deep and sour. Fear like a chorus that sang along every nerve. *How had she dared lecture Lyle?*

Suddenly. Unexpectedly. A whisper of hope.

Shaking, Mac clung to it, desperate to clear her mind, to think. *No time for gut reactions,* she pleaded with herself.

She began to hear her own breathing again, deep and ragged, feel her hands, clenched into aching fists. There was sweat running down her sides.

Hope. Opportunity. She focused on those.

Mac reached down and took off her shoes. Barefoot, she could feel the vibrations through the floor. The hairs on her arm and neck rose. *Distress.*

She walked around the cage until she was as close as possible to the shape, then sank to the floor herself, balancing on the balls of her feet, and nodded.

Dhryn.

Even huddled in its misery, she couldn't mistake that rubbery blue skin, dotted with weeping pits of darker blue. No mistaking the three pairs of shoulders either, or the massive, podlike feet. There were wounds, marked by more dark blue liquid. It was smeared over much of the cage floor, as were other stains.

Mac hugged herself.

The *oomling* tongue, the Dhryn language spoken by those too young—or unable—to produce and hear the deeper infrasound—came to her with sickening ease, as if more natural than her own. "Who are you?"

A once-powerful arm pushed against the floor, then another. One after the other, each slipped and lay flaccid.

Conscious, then.

Mac stood and walked around to the other side of the cage.

She hadn't expected to be relieved his eyes were closed behind their marble-like lids, that she'd unconsciously stiffened in anticipation. *Fool,* she told herself.

"I am Mackenzie Wini—" her voice failed and Mac coughed to free it, starting again. "Mackenzie Winifred Elizabeth Wright Connor—" after a hesitation, she finished, "—Sol is all my name."

His hands scrabbled at the floor, as if the Dhryn tried to rise and couldn't.

She understood. Manners dictated he rise and accept her name with a clap of all six hands. *Three hands,* Mac realized, as the last arm, middle left, moved into view. Its wrist ended in a fresh scar. *Grathnu.* Dhryn sought all their lives to sacrifice their hands to their Progenitor. It was a mark of Her greatest favor. Mac suspected it was also a contribution to the gene pool, allowed only the most worthy.

But three? This was no ordinary Dhryn.

Emily had warned her—the Ro claimed a wounded Dhryn was dangerous. Brymn had transformed only after being injured in the sandstorm, but not after giving up his hand. *Does it matter how severe the damage, Em, or did the Ro lie to you?*

It wasn't the first time she'd asked herself that troubling question. An answer this living Dhryn could provide. *It would be the last one.*

Mac shuddered. "Don't try to move," she said. "Who are you?" The face shifted on the floor, shadows changing beneath the thick ridges that overhung the closed eyes, where they played over the curved rises of skin-covered bone sculpting nose and ears. The small mouth was tight and fixed. *Pain.* Mac felt the vibration of complaint through her feet.

The eyes snapped open, their huge pupils black and lustrous, like figure eights on their sides. The oval iris of yellow filled the rest. She'd seen it warm. Now it was a cold, accusing gold.

With the eyes and changing light, despite the scars and sunken appearance, Mac suddenly knew who this was. "Parymn Ne Sa," she whispered.

"—Las."

So it had been *grathnu* and not more violence from his keepers. Numb, Mac repeated his full name. "Parymn Ne Sa Las. Honored. I take the name Parymn Ne Sa Las into my keeping." She clapped her hands together. His eye coverings winked blue. *Acknowledgment.*

This was not a Dhryn who traveled, before his entire species had taken flight. This had been the Progenitor's officer and gatekeeper, the same Progenitor with whom Brymn—and Mac herself, though with hair not hand—had committed *grathnu.* More, Brymn had called Parymn Ne Sa an *erumisah,* one who is able to make decisions.

Not an ordinary Dhryn at all, Em.

Mac knelt, not daring to touch the bars. "What are you doing here?"

"I was sent to talk to you."

"Me?" She rocked back on her haunches and began shaking her head. "No. No. There are people in authority—important people. I—" *study salmon.*

Parymn managed to raise his head and first shoulders to better look at her. She could see his flexible seventh limb now, curled out of the way, its scissorlike fingers tucked under an elbow. "They are not-Dhryn," he gasped out, then sank to the floor again. "You are Dhryn," more quietly but with as much effort. "Unlikely . . . as that appears . . . to me."

"Oh, dear," Mac said in Instella.

A touch on her shoulder. She startled from under it, rising and turning to put her back to the bars.

Nik let his arm fall to his side. Mac searched his face, but it was like a mask, fixed and expressionless.

And he wasn't alone. Others walked around the cage to array themselves on either side of him, all confronting her: the Trisulian, Cinder, hands combing the mane over her face; another Human, older, male, and in a brown suit almost twin to Nik's; a scaled humanoid Mac couldn't identify, with a dainty beaked mouth and feathered crest; and a stout Imrya, carapace dark with age spots, her hands clutching what looked like an unusually ornate recording device. Two of the consular staff remained by the door.

Last, but not least by any measure, the Sinzi-ra herself, regal in her white gown and long silvered fingers. "You were right, Nikolai," Anchen said. "I see you can communicate with our visitor, Mac. Most gratifying."

"Visitor," she echoed incredulously. Mac felt vibration through the soles of her feet as the Dhryn subvocalized. She couldn't understand it. *Perhaps it wasn't words at all, Em, but a moan.* "Well, you haven't taken very good care of him."

Anchen lifted two fingers. One of the staff members stepped forward. "What have I done wrong, Dr. Connor? I cared satisfactorily for the Honorable Delegate from Haven during his stay with us. This individual has proved more, forgive any impertinence, challenging a guest, but I have followed every established protocol for his species."

She'd forgotten Brymn had been here. Mac blinked. Finally, she managed to ask: "Do you want him to live or not?"

Nik shifted involuntarily, but said in a noncommittal voice. "It's preferable."

"To start with, they—" Mac pointed at the yellow-clad staff, "—shouldn't wear that color near him. Why doesn't he have furniture and clothes? He looks to be starving."

His wounds? *That was territory she didn't dare tread, Em.*

"Your concern is admirable but misplaced, Mac," responded Anchen, making a calming gesture with her long fingers. "Our guest was originally provided with civilized accommodations. He tore them to shreds, along with his clothing. He refuses food." Again, as if able to read Mac's thoughts, *or,* Mac judged, *with the awareness of a superb negotiator,* the Sinzi went on: "The wounds you see? Self-inflicted. We've done our utmost to keep him healthy and comfortable. It is our in own interest as well as his. But he has rejected all of our efforts. We feared he was attempting to die."

The floor vibrated more intensely. "*Oomling* language," Mac hissed in Dhryn.

Sure enough. "Mackenzie Winifred Elizabeth Wright Connor Sol," Parymn almost bellowed. "These are not-Dhryn! You must not interact with them!"

"What did he say?" Nik, quietly.

"He's not happy," Mac summarized, then frowned. "You said the teach-sets weren't working, but surely you've servo translators."

"They function without adequate success, thus your cooperation is most essential," said the beaked alien, in precise, feather-edged Instella. He/she/it lifted his/her/its elbows, the other Human moving to avoid those sharp ends. "We predict our current technology capable of reliable translation of no better than twenty percent—"

The other Human broke in: "He hasn't said a word to translate until now—"

"Mackenzie Winifred Elizabeth Wright Connor Sol! You must desist!" Parymn's bellow faded into a desperate whisper.

Mac shot Nik a look and he nodded reassuringly. She turned to the Dhryn. "It's all right, Parymn Ne Sa Las. It is—" she tried to think how to calm him, "—it is my task among Dhryn, to speak with those who come to you like this."

Faint. "I do not understand. How can it be so? They can talk?" It was almost plaintive.

Save her from cloistered Dhryn, Em, Mac sighed to herself, the problem yawning like a pit before her feet. Brymn had warned her that the Haven Dhryn, those who stayed on their world, avoided contact or information about other places or other life. Why should they care about what would never matter to them? She'd seen it for herself. "That which is Dhryn" was enough.

Not anymore. Not for Parymn, if he was to survive. No doubt the others here were anxious for the answers to a long list of questions. No doubt everyone from physiologists to weapons designers would be eager for the answers his living body could provide.

Em, why did it have to be a Dhryn she knew?

Mac planned to sit down and have a talk with herself, a long one, later. Likely with something stronger than beer.

In the meantime, how to solve this? "Think of them as Dhryn," she ventured.

He closed his eyes. *Rejection.* "Only the Progenitor decides what is Dhryn."

There was the rub, Em. The Progenitor—any of them—wasn't here. *She hoped.* Things wouldn't be this calm if a Progenitor's ship, with its millions of feeder Dhryn, were in Sol System, or orbiting Earth. She'd dreamed it often enough. There'd be alarms, news, panic, running for shelters, for ships . . .

Nik had urged her to hurry.

Mac licked her lips. "Are they here?" she asked without turning from the Dhryn, proud she sounded so matter-of-fact about nightmare.

"Just him," Nik answered.

She shuddered with relief, closing her eyes for an instant.

"Do not . . ." Parymn began weakly, ending with a handless arm flailing.

Mac looked over her shoulder. *A mistake*—they were all staring at her, waiting for something worthwhile. "He's upset," she stated the obvious, then went back to Parymn. "You said the Progenitor sent you to talk to me. Why? What about?"

"You must not . . . interact with the not-Dhryn. I forbid it." Weaker. She wasn't sure how conscious he was—or perhaps he wouldn't tell her anything more while not-Dhryn were present.

This particular Dhryn, his upbringing, was the problem. The Progenitor Mac had met on Haven had been fully aware of other species, curious, in fact, to meet Mac, an alien, in person. The Dhryn had accepted membership within the IU, had their gate to the Naralax Transect, although not-Dhryn traffic was forbidden to their home system and Haven. They'd maintained colonies in other systems to take overflow population, those colonies freely conducting trade with other species. Brymn himself had been fluent in Human languages as well as Instella, although he'd been, she'd freely admit, unusual for any species.

"The Progenitor values the abilities of all Dhryn," Mac began cautiously. *Interspecies communication, Em, is carpeted quicksand. With hair-trigger wasps on top.* "Is this not so?"

The eye coverings opened again. "All that is Dhryn must serve." Stronger, with that familiar sarcastic note. *Good.*

"So the Progenitor must value my ability to talk to the not-Dhryn." She re-phrased hastily: "She sees that ability as having use to Her, to all that is Dhryn. Thus I must use my ability. For all that is Dhryn." *Stop now,* she told herself.

His tiny lips pursed, then moved in and out a few times as if hunting teeth no longer there.

Just when Mac was about to try another tack, Parymn's lips formed a tight smile. "Your reasoning would have more impact if you weren't talking like an *oomling.*" Mac felt a thrumming in the floor as the Dhryn added what he knew she couldn't hear. By her estimate, adults used infrasound for more than a third of their vocabulary and most of its emotional overtone.

Even Brymn had had difficulty with the concept of their differing auditory ranges. He'd been willing to try, at least.

Parymn Ne Sa Las, Mac knew without any doubt, *would not.*

"You understand me well enough, Parymn Ne Sa Las. Do you understand them?" she gestured to the others, still silent and waiting. When he gave her a baleful look, she nodded. "I do. So you are to talk to me and the Progenitor needs me to talk to them. All that is Dhryn needs me to talk to them. Will you permit it or not?"

A final vibration through the floor. Another unhappy look. "I somehow doubt, Mackenzie Winifred Elizabeth Wright Connor Sol, that you require my permission."

She crouched lower. "I ask your cooperation, Parymn Ne Sa Las."

He considered so long, eyes almost closed, that Mac feared this time he was unconscious. Then: "You have it. For now."

"Thank you." She stood, giving her sweater a tug to straighten it. "First order of business—to look after you, Parymn Ne Sa Las. Why did you—" Mac stopped there. *On second thought, she probably didn't want to know why Parymn had attacked the furniture.* Doubtless something alien and complicated about not-Dhryn up-holstery. "To serve the Progenitor," she said instead, "you must look and behave with pride, as an *erumisah.* Even among the not-Dhryn."

"That is so." His hands fluttered along his skin, explored patches of congeal-ing fluids. "Bathe. I must bathe."

"I'll make arrangements. What else?"

"Clothing." Fingers trailed along his eye ridges and his mouth turned down. Mac added cosmetics to her mental list.

"What else? Food?"

His eyes closed again. *Rejection.*

It was a beginning, Mac decided. She turned back to her observers and made herself smile.

Anchen's fingers rose and fell, the silver rings making a waterfall of light down her sides. *Approval? Or aggravation at the delay.* Mac wasn't about to guess. "What was said?" the Sinzi asked her.

"Every word?"

The beaked alien leaned forward, her body quivering. *Eagerness? Or a chill,*

Mac thought. "Yes, we will need every word, every nuance." The Imrya, still silent, lifted her recorder in agreement.

"In-depth analysis can be done later," the other Human snapped. "We don't have time to waste. The gist, Dr. Connor. Summarize."

"Summarize." *Mr. Brown Suit had something up his . . .* Mac raised her eyebrow and caught Nik's cautionary look. *Fine.* "To start with, this isn't just any Dhryn. I can't imagine how he got here, but this is Parymn Ne Sa Las. I met him on Haven. He's a decision-maker, someone who speaks for his Progenitor. He's the closest thing to an ambassador the Dhryn could have sent us."

This raised eyebrows and elbows, as well as promoted an almost frantic moment of facial grooming by the Trisulian. Only Anchen seemed unaffected by the news. And Nik, who Mac doubted would show his reaction to an explosion unintentionally.

"How he came to be here, I can tell you, Dr. Connor," the beaked alien offered. "Our patrol stopped a starship, no larger than one of our single-pilot vessels. It contained him alone and was operating on a preprogrammed path to our world, N'not'k. He wore no clothes, was already damaged, and would not communicate with us. He grew increasingly agitated by our attempts to do so. We brought him to the IU consulate, where our Sinzi-ra had no better luck with him, but understood the significance of the artifact within his ship, that it was a message indicating he should be brought here, to the Gathering."

"To Earth," Anchen corrected gently. "I would show Mac the artifact, if you please."

One of the staff went over to a wall and pressed on a particular spot. A drawer opened from the wall and he reached in, pulling out a bag identical to those in Mac's closet, but a fraction of the size.

Mac's eyes widened as she saw the black velvetlike lining of the drawer before it closed again, then gave the rest of the white wall a suspicious look. *Had that lining been of the fabric the Dhryn used to hide from the Ro?* She wouldn't be surprised.

The Sinzi opened the bag, passing its contents to Mac.

Mac took what at first glance seemed a plain disk of some gray metallic substance, cool at first, then warming to the touch. She lifted it within the curve of her thumb and forefinger. Held in better light, there was a dense spiral marking one side. No, Mac realized, rubbing her thumb over it lightly, the spiral was formed by something inlaid into the metal. At what could be compass points were small raised areas, three intact, the fourth hollowed as if something had been removed from it.

As "artifacts" went, this one was neither old nor beautiful. Mac looked at Nik, who gave a tiny shrug, then back to the Sinzi. "What is it?"

"A biological sample, Dr. Connor. A sample of you, in fact." A finger reached over Mac's shoulder, the pointed tip of its nail tracing the spiral. Another feathered one of Mac's curls. "If removed, you would recognize this part by its pigmentation, perhaps. Or its length might be sufficient."

"A hair," Mac breathed, eyes wide. "Mine." From the braid she'd given in *grathnu* to the Progenitor on Haven. She'd thought it would have been digested or discarded long before now.

The nail tip touched one of the raised dots. "Beneath each of these, a single intact epithelial cell. One was removed for analysis. Your genetic code was, of course, in the report sent to all IU consulates and officials."

"Of course," Mac said faintly. The cells would have come from the skin of her scalp or hands; probably thousands had been lodged in the braid, given how she'd habitually fussed with it.

"Make no mistake. This was prepared by someone who not only knew exactly which biological materials would bring you and this Parymn Ne Sa Las into contact, but that we would be capable of interpreting and acting on this— message. Succinct, practical. It speaks the language of science rather than species, yet acknowledges shared individual experience." The Sinzi took the disk from Mac. "I remain impressed."

"You promised we wouldn't waste time, Anchen, time we don't have." This, predictably, from the man Mac had now dubbed "Mr. Brown Suit." "It doesn't matter how he came here! What we need to know is why! What does he want?"

As the latter part of this appeared directed at Mac, she chose to answer. "Access to a sonic shower," she informed him, "though we'll have to take off the safeties and set it to cook pie. Several bands of silk this wide." She held out her arms. "About four meters long. Any solid color but yellow. Jellied mushrooms. Lipstick and eye liner. Assorted shades." She fastened her best "don't mess with me" glare on him. "He can barely talk in this condition, let alone think to answer questions."

Mr. Brown Suit took an abrupt step toward Mac, his face red and mouth working. The consular staff followed, as if alarmed, but Nik put himself in front of Mac first. "Sir. This is why Dr. Connor is here," he told the other in a low urgent voice that nonetheless carried perfectly. *I'm right here!* Mac frowned at Nik's back, quite willing to scrap on her own behalf. "She's our only chance to make use of this resource; the IU has graciously granted us access to her expertise. Let her work."

The other shoved Nik aside—that Nik allowed it told Mac a great deal about who Mr. Brown Suit probably was—but didn't come any closer to where Mac stood, barefoot and still. "Do it," he told her, pale eyes drilling into hers. "But do it knowing Humans joined the list of confirmed Dhryn targets last night. A helpless refining station. Families—" His voice broke on the word. "Do it knowing the Secretary General of the Ministry has declared humanity under imminent threat. From them." He didn't need to raise his voice. He didn't need to point to the Dhryn.

Threat to the species, Mac said to herself, ashamed she'd taken offense. *Where on that scale do any of us fall, Em?*

"Whatever Parymn Ne Sa Las requires will be arranged immediately," Anchen promised; Mac didn't doubt her in the least. She gestured to the ceiling and Mac paid attention to the clusters of vidbots for the first time. *Too used to them everywhere else on Earth,* she realized with some irony, *to notice.* "There are monitoring devices throughout this room; staff will await your needs. Simply

ask. We will prepare our questions." She began to leave, her long fingers sweeping the other Human, Imrya, and beaked alien with her, leaving Nik and the
two staff.

"Oh, no. Wait! Anchen, please." Mac stopped short of lunging for one of
those fingers. "I can't stay here. I've work to do with my team." She glanced at
the huddled Dhryn. "Now more than ever."

"Now, this is your work."

"Yes. No. Not all of it. The Dhryn don't understand themselves. Don't you
see—no matter what he can tell us, we'll have to learn more." Mac took a deep
breath and said firmly: "Your word I'll be allowed to spend part of every day
working on the origins problem."

"Nonsense." Mr. Brown Suit again. "Questioning him is the only priority."

And she thought a righteous Mudge could set her blood boiling. "I'll be free to come
and go," Mac added, forcing the words between her teeth. "Four hours a day
with my research team, when I choose."

"Absolutely not!" "Three and you sleep here."

The words overlapped, but it was Anchen's counteroffer that silenced the Human's protest.

Outranked and knows it. Mac ignored him, sure she was right, that what she
wanted was important. "Three, I sleep in my own room, and I can consult with
my people at any time no matter where I am." She took a gamble and quoted the
alien's own words about her work with the Myg. "There is deep significance
within our combination."

"How so?"

How? Mac hadn't actually expected to explain. *Note to self, Em. Never gamble
with alien terminology.* Her lack of answer stretched toward awkward.

"Clearly, Anchen, there has developed an interwoven circularity of purpose,"
Nik stated.

There has? Mac wisely kept her mouth shut. If anyone knew the Sinzi-ra, it
should be the liaison she'd requested most often. She hoped.

"Elaborate."

"Between Kanaci, Mac's team, and Mac herself, their work weaves into the
goals of the IU and their member species, while involving an additional circularity of accomplishment from the present with that of the past, in order to resolve mutual debts, a resolution, I might add, which may well produce future
gain for all." *Nik sounded confident,* Mac acknowledged, even if what he said made
no sense to her at all.

What mattered was that it made sense to the Sinzi, whose shoulders rose as
she pointed a white-clawed fingertip at Mac. "I am corrected. My thanks, Nikolai. You may begin on the basis you wish, Mac, to fully take advantage of these
opportunities afforded us by your combinations. Be aware," she added, "failure
to produce meaningful insights swiftly will require modifications."

Mac nodded, then caught the eyes of Mr. Brown Suit with her own. "We're
here to prevent more tragedies," she said quietly, the words for him. "That's all
that matters. You'll have your answers as soon as possible. I give you my word."

His scowl faded, replaced by something akin to respect. "Dr. Connor," he said, then turned to leave with Anchen and the other aliens.

Their departure roused Parymn. "Mackenzie Winifred Elizabeth Wright Connor Sol . . . what has happened?"

She'd wait till he was better to stop that full-name business. Try to, anyway. This wasn't amiable Brymn . . .

. . . who'd consumed Lyle's wife and her arm. Mac shivered, just slightly.

Nik noticed. "Concussions are nothing to fool with," he said, frowning down at her. His eyes explored the wound. "If you need to rest—"

Mac raised her hand to stop him, answering Parymn first. "They've gone to bring what we need to help you recover your strength."

"*Nie rugorath sa nie a nai.*" A Dhryn is robust or a Dhryn is not.

"You don't have the luxury of that belief here, Parymn Ne Sa Las," Mac snapped. "The Progenitor has given you a task and you must not fail. You will accept care."

He lay back. *She'd take that as agreement.*

"He's not in good shape," she told the others—*who knew how many others, Em,* Mac corrected, remembering the room was monitored.

"We're here to help, Mac," Nik assured her.

"You'll stay?" She closed her mouth too late, hearing the relief in her voice. *So what?* Anyone listening would assume she was pleased to have a familiar face—and species—to help. Nik?

Oh, he knew. A flash of warmth from those hazel eyes, the hint of a dimple. Nothing more, but that was enough. *It wasn't as though a weight had lifted,* Mac decided, *but more as though someone else had taken a share from her shoulders.*

"What do we do first?" This from Cinder.

Mac felt herself coming back to normal, as normal as possible under the circumstances, but she'd take it. She swept the Trisulian with a critical look, seeing what she hadn't before. He—*she,* Mac corrected, *since no male symbionts were present*—was taller than Kay by a considerable amount, closer to Mac's own height, though shorter than Nik. Instead of Kay's caftan, a clothing choice perhaps for his work when not concealing unattached weasels, Cinder's limbs were wrapped in tight ribbons of black, while her stocky torso was covered by a brown-red shift, belted at both waists. The lower belt was festooned with gadgets, some of which were probably weapons, if she was in Nik's line of work. The upper belt simply held the fabric together over the opening to her *douscent.* The hair cascading over Cinder's entire head was a fine shiny brown, almost Human, and matched the skin showing on her hands.

Nik's partner. *She'd like to know about that.*

First things first. "We do something about his living conditions, starting with this cage," Mac decided. "Where's the door?"

Cinder pointed to the ceiling.

Mac snorted. "That's ridiculous—how am I supposed to get in?"

"You don't." Nik's voice had such an edge that Cinder bent an eyestalk his way.

"Not until it's clean, I'm not," Mac agreed. She didn't give him time to argue the point. "What are the options? For this room," she added quickly.

"We can make any modifications you require, Dr. Connor," said one of the staff.

Mac considered the two of them. One male, one female. *Maybe.* With some discreet padding, they could pass as Human on a dark night, doubtless the reason they were the species chosen to work at the IU's Earth consulate.

She spared an instant to wonder about that. Were they chosen to provide "familiar" faces to visiting Humans? Hands suited to the local technology? Or were they to help acclimate other, less humanoid species to the body plan before leaving the consulate to visit Earth. *Probably all three.* She respected the Sinzi's thorough dedication to hospitality.

Meanwhile, those faces looking back at her bore identical expressions of what would be bright, willing attention, if they'd really been Human faces. "What are your names?" Mac asked.

Bright and willing changed to guarded and stubborn. "We are consular staff," one said, as if Mac were confused. The male.

"I know that. I want to know what to call you."

They exchanged quick looks. "Staff," the female said.

Nik made a muffled sound. Mac didn't bother glaring at him. "I have no wish to offend, but I need to be able to refer to you as individuals."

Another exchange of looks. "Call me One," said the male.

"Two," said the female. Then both gave her pleased smiles.

Whatever worked, Em . . . Mac nodded. "Thank you. Now, please change into something that isn't yellow. It alarms Dhryn."

"Yellow?" Two repeated, sounding puzzled.

Cinder volunteered: "Xiphodians are polychromatic. They do not see color as Humans do. Or Trisulians, for that matter."

So they likely saw ultraviolet. *Made sense.* Mac was entranced by the notion of the all-white Sinzi decor covered in staff memos. *Or rude comments about guests with fewer visual receptors.* She focused on business. "Cinder, would you look after this please?"

"Of course, Mac. Staff?" The three left the room.

A room empty but for the Dhryn in his misery, herself, and Nik.

Watching Parymn, Mac stole a look at the spy, and caught him watching her, by his expression finding something amusing in all this. "What is it?" she asked.

"You do realize this is the second time I've brought you a Dhryn?"

Mac grinned. "Some guys bring pizza." That drew a smile. She savored it for a moment, then nodded at Parymn, who had opened his eyes to study them. "I had to persuade him it was all right for me to talk to you—to any of you. Home world Dhryn like Parymn don't view other species as civilized. No. Nik, that's not the right word. I'm not sure what is," she finished, frustrated.

"It's a starting point." To Nik's credit, he didn't appear to take offense at Parymn's opinion—a reminder she was in the presence of someone with far more experience comprehending the non-Human.

Not just a comfort—an asset. One Mac suddenly appreciated. "He's here be-cause the Progenitor sent him to talk to me," she explained. "That's exactly how he put it: to talk to me. I've convinced him that She would also want me to talk to you, to not-Dhryn."

"About what?"

"We hadn't got to that part yet." She tightened her lips, then nodded. In Dhryn: "Parymn Ne Sa Las, what does the Progenitor want you to say to me?"

"We . . . are to talk, Mackenzie Winifred . . . Elizabeth Wright Connor Sol."

She crouched down, pitched her voice lower in hopes it made it easier for him to hear. "I know. But about what?"

"The Progenitor . . . searches for . . ." His voice disappeared into vibration.

"Searches for what?" Mac urged. "Please try, Parymn Ne Sa Las."

With abrupt clarity:

"The truth—the truth about ourselves."

As if that last effort had been too much, Parymn's eyes closed.

"The Honored Delegate Brymn did not ask for such treatment."

"Brymn Las," Mac corrected automatically. "And he was trying to fit in, so of course he didn't ask for special treatment. Trust me. A sonic shower. Will that clean the floor as well?" There were dried and drying smears of Dhryn blood everywhere.

"At the requested setting, yes. But Brymn Las did not—"

"You can do it, can't you?" she challenged the pair. Nik, watching the ex-change, rubbed a hand over his chin as if to hide a smile.

One and Two traded offended looks. They stood side by side, a matched set in Dhryn-neutral pink. *Not the time to ask if they liked whatever color that appeared to their eyes.* "We will make all of the arrangements you've requested, Mac," an-swered Two stiffly. "We suggest you occupy yourselves elsewhere for an hour."

"Or be crisped," Mac said jovially. She reassured herself with a last look at Parymn's thick, rubbery hide and a memory of the hazards of Dhryn "bathing." "Good. Then I'm off to check on my team."

Nik nodded at the door. "There's fresh coffee—and a com link. You'll want to be here when he's ready for questioning." She scowled and he gave her that too-innocent look. "Or not."

Coffee and a few moments' peace and quiet, versus retracing her steps and plunging—for too brief a time—back into the turmoil she'd deliberately stirred behind her.

Coffee with Nik *and a few moments' peace and quiet,* versus confronting a host of testy archaeologists who'd doubtless noticed Fourteen's predilection for acquir-ing small objects by now. She winced. *Forgot the memo.*

Mac noticed the dimple deepening in Nik's cheek and scowled again. *Just enough to let him know it was her idea.*

"Coffee works."

- 15 -

DISCLOSURES AND DILEMMA

"**I** ADMIT I WAS EXPECTING something—smaller. And damp." Mac gave the subject of basements another moment's serious consideration. "Maybe a troll," she said finally.

To be truthful, while she'd assumed there was something beneath the consular complex, Mac had leaned toward wine cellars and seasonal storage, with perhaps accommodations suited to those aliens who liked it small, damp, and dark. A vault or two seemed reasonable to protect whatever precious goods might be moving on or off Earth with guests.

Basements were good for such things.

There was, she acknowledged with an inward shudder, *a dungeon of sorts.*

But the reality, behind door number three, was—*like walking into one of Emily's favorite thriller vids.*

Having been in the Progenitor's vast cavern, Mac would have scoffed at the suggestion she'd ever again be impressed by a large room in a basement, even a very large room in a very odd basement.

Until Nik opened the third and final door at the corridor's end, the one beside Parymn's cell, the one she blithely assumed would simply lead to another corridor or room, and, as promised, coffee.

It didn't. *And she was.*

"Impressive, isn't it?" Nik said into her ear.

Mac grunted, too busy struggling to grasp it all.

Straight ahead was easy, almost ordinary: a floor, although it widened to the right like a great fan until ending at the far curve of a wall. It was bounded by one other wall, this Mac touched with her right hand. She looked up, captivated by how this wall rose not to a ceiling, but to meet another floor, set back from the first; above it, another, and another, stretching up and away like a staircase.

To her left, the floor dropped away. Mac walked to the unprotected edge and looked down. *Another floor below this one, and another.*

It was as if they stood on the steps of a giant pyramid buried underground, only revealed here.

There was more. The pyramid's partner, mirror image, rose across a gulf between the two. Mac could see figures moving about on a floor at the same height as this one—but so distant she couldn't have shouted and been heard. There was, she realized belatedly, a third series of steps ahead. She turned. The tiny door they'd used came through a wall that was itself part of a step.

The pyramids re-formed in her imagination to a well, sunk deep underground, she and Nik mere droplets on bricks near the bottom. Like the building aboveground, she realized, hollow within, floors linked by a central spiral ramp as well as lifts. *As if the Sinzi valued open space above all.*

Space filled with light. The white walls and floors almost glowed. Mac craned back her head to see the distant ceiling, squinting to make out a familiar pattern edged in brightness. *The patio!* The tiles were allowing sunlight through. She couldn't find any tree roots hanging down. *Neat trick.*

This space was filled with life. Everywhere she looked, Mac saw purposeful movement. Raftlike platforms laden with passengers and cargo sedately crossed the space between the steps, as many moving vertically as horizontally. Some hung in midair, overhead or below, grouped into workspaces or forming bridges from side to side.

The steps themselves, each forming immense "rooms" of their own filled with labyrinths of equipment, were connected by lifts along their walls. The nearest sighed to a stop beside Mac, as if in invitation. Along the wall itself were doors, implying a maze of rooms beyond all this.

And the space sang. Granted it was the drone of voices and machines, rising and falling, punctuated by the occasional metallic clang or whoop. But song nonetheless. There had to be hundreds of beings working here. *Answering one question, Em.* Mac drew a quick breath. "So this is where they've been hiding."

"Who?"

"The other researchers from the Gathering. Mudge and I went over the consulate schematics Fourteen gave me. We couldn't figure out where the Sinzi had put everyone."

"Yes, but hardly hiding." Nik chuckled. "Several teams are down here to make use of the equipment."

"What equipment?" Mac gave him an uneasy look. "Why is all this here, Nik? What are these beings doing?"

He smiled. "Coffee first."

"'The truth.'" Nik handed Mac her coffee and took one himself, shaking his head. "I didn't expect that from our visitor."

They'd taken the lift to the next step up, Nik leading the way to what was, if not a lounge, a reasonable facsimile. Like the eye of a storm, benches made a circle of calm around a tall water-touched sculpture of—*well, she wasn't sure, but if three Sinzi finger-wrestled, this could be the result.* The sculpture's base provided unobtrusive storage for beverages and snacks, watched over by another of the ubiquitous consular staff, only too eager to provide whatever they'd like.

The rest of the area was a bustle of activity. Doors opening and closing. Consoles and other equipment communing with their operators. Platforms docking and undocking all along the edge, so the floor space and those on it constantly morphed around her. *Like a termite mound,* Mac decided, *where everyone else knew what to do.*

For her part, she'd asked for coffee, hoping to gather her thoughts.

The coffee, Em, she'd got.

Mac's thoughts were another matter entirely. She had enough questions about this place and what was done here to set her head spinning. *But she did know one thing.* The Ministry of Extra-Sol Human Affairs was well aware of what the Sinzi-ra kept in her basement.

Nik knew this place.

More. He was at home here, the way she felt among the pods of Base and the rivers of Castle Inlet. His body posture had subtly altered, losing that tiny "ignore me" slouch, regaining his true height. His movements lost none of their suppleness, but gained confidence, as if here he finally shed a camouflage intended to make outsiders underestimate his abilities, misjudge his strength. This was the real Nikolai Trojanowski, the version she'd only caught in glimpses.

Albeit yummy ones.

Scowling at her seemingly infinite ability to focus on the trivial, Mac raised her hand to their surroundings. "Speaking of truth—this is where you really work, isn't it."

He didn't bother denying it. She was pleased—unless that meant she was so deeply into all this now it couldn't matter what else she learned. *Not the most comforting thought.*

"This is the Atrium. The IU shares its facilities with us," Nik informed her, one arm outstretched along the back of the bench. His eyes darted about, rarely still. *Checking on things,* Mac guessed, the same compulsion she always felt when walking into a lab or waking up at a field station. "There's one in every consulate, with a Sinzi administrator. Some of what's done here is to monitor the transects—the Sinzi are devoted to maintaining the flow of traffic. The upper levels are where any technology proposed for import or export is given a final assessment by their people and ours."

Mac looked up with some alarm. "Is that safe?"

"Safety tests are done in orbit or on the Moon," he assured her, the corner of his mouth twitching as if he tried not to smile at her reaction. *Wise man, Em.* "Here they look at other factors. Economics, appeal. As often as not what's a good idea for one species simply won't interact as hoped with the technology base or culture of another. You don't know until you tinker with it."

"But you," Mac persisted, "do something else. When not escorting tourists or pestering innocent biologists, that is."

"True enough. Most of my time is spent right there." Nik pointed to the opposite side, indicating an area up a step from their level. Mac couldn't see anything distinct about it, unless she counted the three platforms presently attached, and more lined up to do so. "Telematics center," he explained. "Sends and receives information over long distances."

Mac was quite sure the 'long' in this instance referred to very long distances indeed. She also guessed moving information was only one step. Every iota of data must be translated as necessary, then analyzed, compiled, and stored. Within the Interspecies Union, information would be the currency of value to all.

"Looks busy," she observed.

"It is."

Something in his voice caught her attention. "That's where they're working on Emily's message, isn't it? Doing whatever it is the Ro want them to do." A chill fingered her spine.

Nik didn't deny it. "Off-limits, Mac." Clear warning.

She didn't argue, busy looking for Fourteen.

"Mac."

A few possibilities—none in paisley. "Is it off-limits to you, too?" she wondered aloud.

"Why?"

Surprised, Mac glanced at Nik. "I like to know things."

"That I've noticed." Nik lowered his head, but she could see the curve of his lips as he lifted his mug and sipped. "Hollans and I have access," he said finally. "I can't take you there; he could. Want me to ask?"

"No, thanks." *She could imagine* that *conversation.* Mac shifted around on the bench. "You work there—doing what?"

"Whatever needs to be done." She frowned at him and Nik smiled. "It's the truth. There's no job description for what I do, Mac. I'm one of the links between the Sinzi-ra and the Ministry, between the IU and Human interests both on and off Earth. Most of my time I spend analyzing the information flow, what matters to whom, basically observing the workings of the IU for us. Every so often," a chuckle, "I have to interpret us for the IU. Or escort aliens around the home planet." A shadow crossed his face. "I'd retired from anything more intense until the Dhryn."

A reminder of the topic at hand, Em. "You said the Sinzi monitor the transects—watch traffic through the gates—" Mac swallowed, then went on. "They must have data on the Dhryn attacks."

Nik's face sobered. "Some. But system-to-system communication obeys real space physics. Even where there's a facility like this, information has to be transmitted to a ship before it enters a transect gate—or someone has to have the presence of mind to prepare and launch a self-guiding com packet. When the Dhryn swarm through a gate, the result has been utter chaos. People trying to escape, defend themselves. They aren't making observations. While on Ascendis?" He paused, eyes darkening. "The Dhryn penetrated and destroyed that consulate as easily as everything else."

The Atrium wasn't a refuge for scholars—it was a cup from which the feeders would drink.

Mac hunched her shoulders. "You must have something," she insisted.

"Data's coming in—late and in pieces. Whatever we have is put together for the experts. So far, though, it looks as though the Dhryn attack at random, then leave the moment their target is devastated. What is it?" this as Mac began shaking her head.

"I don't understand what the Dhryn are doing," she said fiercely. "It makes no sense."

"To us," Nik corrected.

Mac shook her head again. "No. Not just to us. It doesn't make sense for the Dhryn. I realize I don't know as much as everyone here about aliens—okay, anyone here or most people on this planet," she rushed to say before he could. "But grant me that I know a fair bit about living things and how they evolve. There's something here we're not seeing. Something besides the Ro."

The hair rose on her arm and neck at the thought of them. She couldn't help it.

Nik didn't dismiss her. He didn't agree either; Mac could see it in his slight frown. "Your old friend should be able to explain," he suggested, pointing over her shoulder.

Mac turned. She hadn't paid particular attention to any one area yet, too busy comprehending the overall scale of the place. Even so, there was no excuse not to have noticed they'd sat within meters of where One and Two were busy working on— "That's the ceiling of Parymn's cell," she concluded, quickly estimating the distance from the small door they'd entered on the step below this.

The staff were directing the transfer of crates from a platform docked beside them through a pair of larger, open doors. Through those doors . . . more crates blocked Mac's view of the section of floor where she presumed the access to Parymn's cell was located. *A secret in plain sight,* she thought with wonder. *Why not? Everyone here was focused on their work, their problem to be solved.* She'd have missed it, and she knew.

The area Mac could see was two, possibly three times larger than that of the cell beneath it, bounded by a complex of what she presumed was monitoring equipment. An assortment of beings in lab coats paid rapt attention to their devices or each other.

While the two standing on either side of the open doors paid attention to everything else. Familiar black armor, engaged in very familiar looming. "Who's here?" Mac asked, waving a greeting at them. Sure enough, one nodded back. By his height, she guessed Selkirk. She swung herself back around on the bench to face Nik. "Or is that a secret?"

Nik took a slow sip of his coffee, eyeing her over the rim of his cup. "I suppose if I don't tell you, you'll find out for yourself anyway."

Mac grinned. "Exactly."

"We've six in gear within the consulate itself. Four you know from Base. One, Tucker Cavendish, you met—briefly—at the way station. And Judy Rozzell. She was at the Ro landing site. I believe," he added pensively, "Charlie dented her visor."

"What about 'Sephe?"

"Busy teaching a course, I'm told. Corrupted by evil statisticians."

"Which would be your fault," Mac pointed out. *A relief, to know the capable agent was with Kammie, John, and the rest who'd gone to the university.*

She curled one leg under her, leaning back. The noise was loud but constant, reminding her of waves babbling their way through beach pebbles. Just as easy, after a while, to push to the background. Mac rolled her head, stretching the kinks from her neck, then sniffed at her coffee. *Still too hot.* The Sinzi mug must be self-warming.

"Want some ice?"

He surprised her into a laugh. "And here I'd hoped you'd missed something in my dossier." *Which really wasn't funny,* Mac decided, losing her smile.

"There's a great deal about you that's not in any record, Mac." Nik's raised brow and dimple dared her to ask.

Emily would.

Mac deliberately turned back to the subject at hand. "We can't assume," she cautioned, "that Parymn knows about the attacks committed by other Dhryn."

"Agreed. But I believe his Progenitor knows. Why else contact you?"

Mac nodded as she blew steam from her coffee. She thought out loud: "Nik, the N'not'k were on the Ministry's list of previous Dhryn attacks—a balloon ship lost, wasn't it? But instead of a second, more devastating attack, the pattern everywhere else, the Progenitor sends in one ship—Parymn's. Why?" Mac answered her own question. "She somehow knew they wouldn't shoot first—and that they'd understand the message. Or realize it was a message. Which leads to another why. Bah."

"That one I can guess." Nik's smile was crooked. "Unlike the rest of us," he lifted his mug and used it to indicate the varied species working around them, "the N'not'k are obligate pacifists. To travel their space, incoming ships have to disarm—even Sinzi. So if there's one species in the IU who wouldn't destroy a Dhryn ship on sight, who couldn't, it's the N'not'k."

Implying the Progenitor, this one at least, knows a great deal about the IU. Aloud, Mac settled for an acknowledging: "Oh."

"Leading us back to other whys. Why him? Why you?"

"What 'truth?'" Mac got to her feet, and Nik followed suit, looking his question. "I should go back upstairs while I can," she answered.

"Don't worry. Anchen will keep her word." Mac's turn to raise her eyebrow. Nik smiled and motioned her to sit. "Circular combinations, remember?"

"I admit, that was slick," Mac commented. *Truth, Em? She wasn't ready to leave.* Parymn, the bench, or him.

Nik mimed a small bow as they both sat again. "Part of the job, Dr. Connor."

As if sitting was a signal, the attendant hurried to refill their coffees. Mac protected hers, studying Nik. When the attendant moved away, she asked: "Is this a good time to add to my dossier on you?"

"It's never a good time."

Which wasn't outright refusal. "Oversight and 'Stefan.' What's their story?"

"That?" Nik took off his suit coat and laid it on the bench, easing back on the seat as though preparing to rest awhile. "Nothing for you to bristle about."

"I never bristle," Mac protested. He raised an eyebrow. *Fine.* "Okay. Much. So explain."

"Regular procedure, Mac. We had to do background checks on Norcoast—and you, Dr. Connor—before the IU would allow Brymn to visit. First Dhryn on Earth, unlikely mission, that sort of thing. The Sinzi-ra, as you may have noticed, believes in anticipation." At Mac's nod, he went on: "Some at the Ministry are content to go through channels in order to—"

"Snoop," she finished when he paused for a word.

"Precisely. I prefer to make contact, engage in conversation, ask a few casual questions of acquaintances. That sort of thing. But in your case, I ran into a small problem."

"Base," Mac grinned. "Not the easiest place to drop in and visit."

"Not without gaining your immediate attention." He made it a compliment.

"But—Oversight?" Mac made a face. "He's the most meticulous, stubborn, paranoid . . . to start with, I can't see him letting a stranger waltz into his office." *Though the thought of Mr. Spy stuck with the aloe for a few hours had a certain justice, Em.*

Nik stretched like a cat. "My dear Dr. Connor," he said in his "Stefan" accent. "A member of the Wilderness Trust Awards Committee is always, always welcome, especially when what that member really wants is to hear the down and dirty about that scandalous salmon researcher Mackenzie Connor and her appalling treatment of the Castle Inlet Trust. Over supper at his favorite restaurant, of course."

Meaning Mudge gossiped about her over beer and pierogies. "You are a sneaky and dangerous individual, completely without conscience," Mac told him. "I'll have to warn Oversight about you—or 'Stefan.'"

"Want to know what he said about you?"

"Spare me."

"You sure?" His eyes glittered behind their lenses. "There were juicy bits."

"I'm quite sure. What I want to know is how you explained being here—that had to be a shock."

A smug look. "Not really. Mudge is well aware of ongoing talks between the awards committee and the consulate regarding the allocation of a substantial portion of its leased and unused coastline to the Te Wāhipounamu Wilderness Trust lands. He's been writing in support of it for years. When he saw me, I didn't have to say a thing—he immediately assumed I was working on that negotiation. Wished me luck, in fact. It's always best," Nik grinned, "to let others make the lie for you."

Which left only one question, Mac thought, loath to ask it and risk ending his honesty, see the return of the spy. As she hesitated, his eyes narrowed. *Damn, he was observant.* "Oversight should have gone home," she said, resigning herself to whatever happened. "Why did you help him stay?"

"Why?" Nik reached out to gently touch the side of her head, below the swathe of bandage. "He was there. When I wasn't." Suddenly, there was nothing gentle in his look; nothing calm in the lines around his mouth.

Just like that, even here in this busy room, he could make her believe no one else existed, scatter her thoughts into this strangely urgent confusion, a confusion that wanted to spread elsewhere.

The man had the worst *timing, Em.*

For some reason, the notion made Mac duck her head and smile. "Fourteen did warn me about external genitalia," she said lightly, looking up. "Guess I should have paid attention."

The hazel eyes were still dark, the lips pressed together. Mac wanted to say other things: how she'd spent half that night glad he was safe; how she'd spent the other half equally convinced he'd changed his mind and come back, that she'd find him in the morning, lying within reach of her steps, his head shattered among last year's pine needles.

"He must have been desperate—or insane," Nik said grimly. "I know the species, Mac. It never occurred to me any Trisulian would risk their symbiont. It would be like you or I ripping off an arm to use as a club. Worse." He collected himself. "I didn't get the tracking report until morning. Kay was picked up by a lev and taken to the Baffin spaceport. A Trisulian courier ship with diplomatic clearance was sitting at a way station—another stood ready to enter the Naralax immediately, which it did after receiving his transmission." Nik nodded, more to himself than her. "With what he's delivered to his government, our Kay will get his moment of glory. Mind you, he'll also be arrested for deviance."

Nik continued, saying again: "I didn't realize Kay would go to such extremes just for a head start with the Ro message. I shouldn't have left you alone with him."

"If I'd realized what that furry excuse for a gonad could do," vowed Mac, "I'd have taken the cast iron skillet with me down to the lake."

"No, thanks." Nik's lips curved into something easier. "Hard enough to explain a paddle to the Trisulian ambassador. I'd rather not involve cooking utensils."

"I see your point." Mac smiled at him. "It worked out well," she offered. "Oversight seems willing to stay. He'll be—" she almost said 'a comfort' and stopped herself in time, "—useful."

"Useful." That dimple beside Nik's mouth.

This time, Mac let herself bristle. "We're not friends," she insisted, wondering who she was trying to convince. "He's—annoying."

"As long as he's useful. And stays quick with a paddle." This last wasn't amused. "You're the only one who can talk to Parymn. That puts you at risk."

"Oh, no," Mac objected, sitting back and cradling her coffee. "I'm not going to start looking over my shoulder, here of all places. This is an academic conference. A secret academic conference. With—" she freed one hand to wave wildly at the atrium, "—this! Our guys in black. You!"

She regretted the last when Nik's face darkened with shame. "Me. Where was I when you were attacked in your own cabin? When an earthquake almost drowned you?"

"We'll concede the weasel," Mac quipped, trying to ease the moment. "But you couldn't have predicted the earthquake. Right?"

"No." His lenses caught the light, hiding his eyes. "They gave us no warning."

"They? You found out who caused it?" she breathed, leaning forward. "Wait. If it wasn't the Ministry . . ." Mac narrowed her eyes. "I knew it. The damn R—"

Nik's finger was across her lips before the word could come out. "Not here," he said very quietly. His fingertip stroked her lower lip before leaving it, as if he used the intimacy to add weight to the warning.

A warning the Ro could well be here, with them, and they'd never know.

Mac shivered. Maybe someone here, a level above, on one of the hovering platforms, behind a wall, was close to penetrating the Ro's stealth technology, would make it possible to detect the thinning of reality when the aliens used no-space to defeat the senses and devices of other species, make it possible to yank them into real space. Surely the IU would be fools not to work on at least a defensive weapon. *Surely the Sinzi-ra was not a fool.*

Unfortunately, Mac was equally sure they'd see the Ro only when the Ro wanted them to, and not before.

She thought of the ruined hillside and coast, the lives lost, and began to shake with rage as much as fear. *Couldn't you have picked—safer—allies, Em?*

"Mac."

Nik's voice drew her back into herself and this room, made her remember the mug in her hands, the bench beneath her. "How can we work with them?" Mac demanded, keeping her voice to a harsh whisper. "If they'd do this? If they'd do what they did before? How can we dare?"

If she'd wanted reassurance, there was none in his grim face. "I'm no happier than you are," he said, again very quietly. "But it was an impressive demonstration of power—listen, Mac—" when she would have objected to that description, probably loudly. "I'm just letting you know that's the way the earthquake damage's being seen—by Human eyes as well as others." He paused, as if waiting for her comment.

There were no words, Em, Mac thought with disgust, waving him to continue.

Nik pressed his lips together, then went on. "With no success against the Dhryn, the strain is showing on the IU itself," he told her. "The Sinzi have their fingers full. A coalition of newer species has petitioned to have their transects cut off from the rest. Then there's nonsense like the Trisulians taking advantage of utter misery." His voice deepened. "It's going to get worse. More transect connections are being made all the time, Mac, at every edge of the IU. That can't be stopped without threatening the entire system, even though it adds new, unknowing systems to the reach of the Dhryn. The Sinzi—we all need the hope of a strong ally, Mac, even a ruthless one, to hold everyone together." A curt nod drew Mac's attention to the telematics center, with its knot of researchers huddled around. "Unfortunately, it's a hope waiting on a miracle. Transmit a signal into no-space?" His lips twisted as if over a bad taste. "No one's convinced it can be done. I'm told the Myrokynay's instructions, if not interpreted correctly, are as likely to ruin the entire communications array as retune it."

Mac jerked her thumb toward Parymn's cell. "If you want the Ro that badly, put him on the roof."

"It's been proposed," Nik said matter-of-factly. "So has putting him in a suit and dragging him through transects like a worm on a hook. Both risk the most potentially valuable resource we've got at the moment. Some of us have prevailed otherwise—for now."

She wrinkled her nose. "I take it 'us' includes you, Anchen, Elbows, and Mr. Obnoxious in the Brown Suit. Bernd Hollans," she added.

Nik leaned back and hooked both hands around one knee. "Oh, I knew you two would hit it off."

"With sparks," Mac confessed, half apologizing. "But he wasn't hearing me."

"He's everything you think he is, Mac, but cut him some slack." Nik half shrugged. "Hollans' job is to provide humanity's help to the IU, while making sure nothing puts Earth and humanity in special danger. Thankless from all sides. Having the Dhryn brought to this consulate was over his protest. He wanted you taken from Sol System instead."

Mac said quietly: "I would have gone."

"I know." His eyes glowed with warmth. "But the Sinzi-ra wasn't budging. Neither was 'Elbows,' better known as Dr. Genny P'tool, the N'not'k. Genny is—" Nik hesitated.

"Is what?" Mac prompted.

"Her people enjoy a special closeness to the Sinzi. Genny herself is not only of high rank within her government, but has been mentor to Hone for many years, one of Anchen's selves. She's considered one of the IU's leading no-space theorists. And . . . there is one other thing you should know, Mac. Since it might come up." Nik let go of his knee, sitting straighter. "It's a little personal."

"Personal?" Mac grinned at him. "Let me guess. This important, brainy alien has a crush on you."

He actually blushed.

She'd been kidding. "Oh. Well. Any chance of you two . . . ?" Mac waggled her fingers suggestively.

That earned her one of those warm and dangerous looks.

"Guess not." Mac tilted her head at him. *Fun was fun, but . . .* "I can't argue with her taste," she admitted, smiling.

"What about taste?" Cinder asked, wandering into their oasis at exactly the wrong moment.

Or exactly right one, Em. They weren't alone. They had vital tasks to perform. Mac told herself the sensible things, sure Nik was doing the same.

It would help, she thought wryly, *if he'd stop looking at her like that.*

Cinder sat on the opposite bench, eyestalks forward with obvious interest. "Lunch? Or something else?"

Mac turned and forced a bright smile. "Nik was about to tell me how you two came to be partners," she improvised.

"Now there's a story worth telling." The Trisulian waved away the staff who'd hurried up, pot in hand. "Where shall I begin?"

"Don't," Nik said flatly.

"Nik . . ." Mac stopped. He'd tensed, from the fingers around his knee to the muscle jumping along his jaw. *New topic,* she decided, filing the first for another time. "What about Trisulian males?"

Nik's tension disappeared in a burst of surprised laughter. Cinder, on the other hand, began combing her front hair furiously, apparently struggling for composure.

Oh, dear. "I take it that was inappropriate," Mac concluded, looking from one to the other. "Sorry."

Cinder relaxed, her hands dropping to her lap. "The Unbonded—females—may only discuss such things in private. Girl talk—isn't that the Human expression, Nik? Maybe later, Mac, you and I can compare notes about our opposite sexes?"

The biologist in Mac rose to the bait. "I'd be delighted." Nik's expression turned to one of comical dismay. *Not buying it, Em,* Mac thought. Both of them were trying to distract her.

Not likely.

Not when her guts were churning just sitting this close to a Trisulian.

Mac took an appreciative swallow of now-cold coffee, weighing the chances of offending both Nik and his partner. It didn't matter. *She was who she was, Em. Honest, yes. Subtle?*

Not so much.

So. "If we can't trust your species, Cinder, why should I trust you?"

Nik merely tilted his head, the light hitting his glasses and hiding his eyes. Cinder's hands stayed calm and quiet in her lap. "Good question. All I can say is that—like you, Mac—I'm here as a member of the IU. I'm not bound by the policies of my kind, which I believe lack *nimscent.* Nik—the word?"

"Nimscent," Nik told Mac, "is an expression meaning 'future thinking.' Its lack implies going after a short-term gain in a way that may jeopardize ultimate success. Risk-taking." He reached over the low table and smacked the Trisulian affectionately on one leather-wrapped knee. "Don't worry, Mac. Cinder's okay."

Friendship? Trust. Nik should know better.

Abruptly weary, Mac wondered if she'd ever see them as a source of strength again, and not a trap.

Dismayed by her own reaction, she did her best to smile cheerfully at both of them. It must have been a miserable effort because a worried crease appeared between Nik's eyebrows and even the Trisulian bent a concerned eyestalk her way.

"Excuse me, Dr. Connor."

It was One, wearing a long white coat over his yellow uniform. Mac looked at him with relief. "Yes?"

"The Dhryn is ready."

Nik and Cinder stood to accompany her, the former giving her a small nod of encouragement, still with that worried frown.

Well, Em, Mac told herself as she stood, *there'd been coffee.*

"Parymn Ne Sa Las."

"This was your doing, Mackenzie Winifred Elizabeth Wright Connor Sol?"

Mac walked around the two sides of the cage left with bars, astonished. "Not alone," she said. The other two sides of what had been the cage were now walls, one with a door leading into a biological accommodation, complete with smaller sonic shower, and the other featuring a pulldown cot, Dhryn-sized. The nearer barred side had developed a door, her size.

Not bad for an hour.

The Dhryn hadn't recovered. She could see it in the way he listed as he sat. It likely didn't help that he had no hands on his lowermost arms, so had to balance himself on the stubs of his wrists.

But, like his accommodations, he'd improved immeasurably in that short time, even without *hathis,* the comalike Dhryn healing sleep. The floor was clean, and so was his skin, glowing its rich blue. With the ooze removed, Mac could see his wounds were regular, as though he'd used the sharpened fingers of his seventh arm to carve thin stripes along his midriff and over one shoulder. None of the wounds looked dangerous. Most were days old and healing.

None, her eyes narrowed, *appeared older than the severed wrist, his latest act of* grathnu.

Completing the picture, Parymn's body was wrapped in bands of white silk. He'd had trouble doing it; the layers weren't perfectly aligned. It didn't matter. When you were used to clothing, wearing it went a long way toward restoring confidence.

That was the real difference, Em, Mac cautioned herself. He might be weak, but Parymn was again every bit the stern, formal *erumisah* she remembered from Haven, the one who'd warned her about the impossibility of her succeeding as a Dhryn.

"I wish to be returned to my own chambers."

"Your chambers?" Mac echoed, with a puzzled frown. "These are your chambers, Parymn Ne Sa Las—"

"Of course not." His great black pupils dilated further. *Stress?* "My chambers adjoin the Progenitor's. I do not know where this place might be or how I got here. Nor—" a scowl, "—why not-Dhryn have been permitted on Haven, but I rely upon the Progenitors to have good reason."

He wasn't aware of leaving his world, Em, Mac told herself, amazed. *Or he chose not to believe it.*

An attitude she fully understood.

"You must stay here," she said.

Parymn Ne Sa Las pursed his small lips and stared at Mac for a moment. But he didn't press the point, saying instead: "Then you will express my desire for warmer air to the not-Dhryn."

Definitely back in form, decided Mac. "So now you believe they can talk."

He'd folded his arms just so. "Now I believe they can hear you," he qualified. "Have you come to talk to me, Mackenzie Winifred Elizabeth Wright Connor Sol?"

Mac gestured to Two, who brought forward a tray of jiggling black tubes. They'd had her data on the Dhryn diet and no trouble reproducing something comparable—only in stopping Parymn from throwing it.

"If you eat."

"If you do."

Oh, in fine form—Mac smiled. "Of course." At her signal, Two brought the tray to her, a finger discreetly indicating the nearer cylinder. Mac deftly pulled it free, tipping its contents into her mouth. "Delicious." Which was true, considering what she'd consumed was a fruit jelly.

The Dhryn's turn. Mac didn't look at Nik as she took the tray from Two and walked to the new door in the side of the cage. Mr. Trojanowski had made his objections to the door known, strenuously, and now stood close by it. His hand was in his pocket, doubtless with a weapon already in his palm.

She didn't, Mac shivered inwardly, *really mind.* Not that she needed to fear Parymn. Not in this incarnation, anyway. Memories were what chilled her blood as she stepped inside his enclosure, door snicking locked behind, then walked close enough to bend down and place the tray on the floor within his reach, sitting, despite Nik's hiss of displeasure, on the floor herself.

"Eat," she said. The rest of the tubes contained a fungal concoction that should, the dietitians said, help alleviate the nutritional cost of days spent fasting.

One arm unfolded, but instead of reaching for the tray, Parymn's hand shot toward her head. Mac forced herself to remain still as his fingers, three in number and arranged much like petals on a flower, roughly explored her scalp. "What is this?"

Dhryn didn't have a word for bandage. " 'A Dhryn is robust or a Dhryn is not,' " she quoted, amazed her voice didn't shake. Behind, she heard the door close for a second time. Nik must have started through, then backed off as he realized the Dhryn meant no harm.

"True." His hand left her and found one of the cylinders. Mac concealed her relief as he sucked it empty, then went for a second. "These are adequate. Ask the not-Dhryn for—" and he rattled off a series of dishes.

"I'll see what they can do, *Erumisah*," she said doubtfully, having recognized only the first.

He was on his third tube. Adult Dhryn didn't experience hunger until they were shown food, Mac remembered. That being the case, Parymn's new appetite had at least days, possibly more, of starvation to overcome.

"You said the Progenitor seeks the truth," Mac began carefully. "The truth about what?"

Parymn put down his fourth empty; his hand was markedly slower going after the fifth and last. "Where is Brymn Las?"

Mac pressed her real hand against the floor, keeping her voice steady. "Brymn Las Flowered into his final form, then—"

"Stop." Parymn's eyes could be very cold. "This is nonsense. He would not have done so. What are you talking about?"

"His body underwent its final transformation," Mac explained, searching for the right words. "It wasn't the Wasting."

Parymn flinched at this—no Dhryn willingly acknowledged that type of death, where the body failed its change and withered. Sufferers were shunned and left to die alone, preferably in the dark.

"Brymn Las," Mac continued with difficulty, "became one of those who serve the Progenitor." She lifted both hands, fluttering them as if in flight.

"That is not possible."

"I assure you it is. I was there. He was—damaged—in a storm. Then he began to change." She fought to control her voice, to be careful what she revealed. "He didn't survive very long after that. I was there—at the end."

"No!" Parymn threw the final cylinder across the room as he staggered to his feet. "None of this is possible!" He towered over her.

"It's okay," Mac called in Instella, knowing Nik would react. Then, in Dhryn, as steadily as she could: "Sit, Parymn Ne Sa Las. Perhaps this is part of the truth the Progenitor seeks. Please. Calm yourself and sit."

He obeyed—*probably*, Mac thought, *more because he was about to collapse than due to her urging.* "Talk to me," she suggested. "Tell me why you say what I saw with my own eyes is impossible."

Parymn wrapped his free arms around his middle and rocked gently. Mac could feel thrums of distress through the floor. "He could not have changed yet. Even if he had . . . our final form is known to Her," he whispered. "During *grathnu*, she tastes what we will be. I carry that knowledge. Brymn Las . . ." His eyes winked open and closed repeatedly, their blue covers flashing like strobes. "I had to learn his fate. Brymn Las was to be one of the glorious ones. Not—not mere hands and mouths—a mindless, servile beast. He was to be one of our lights, our guides to the Return. Our future." He rocked harder. "It is impossible. Impossible. Impossible."

"Brymn . . . a Progenitor?" Involuntarily, Mac's hand rose to her mouth, as if to hold in the word. "What—what could have gone wrong?" She grabbed the Dhryn's nearest elbow, gave it a sharp tug. "Parymn Ne Sa Las. Please. That's not what happened. I swear it to you. Is there anything that can change the final form? Could the Progenitor have been wrong?"

"IMPOSSIBLE!" His arm flung outward, sending Mac skidding across the floor.

She rolled to her hands and knees, reassuring Nik and the others with a look, then stood, rubbing one hip. *Not good for the head either,* she told herself, shaking off a wave of dizziness. *Should have seen that coming, Em.*

Parymn was huddled on the floor again. Stepping over the remains of the tray and its contents, Mac knelt by his head. She rested her hand on his shoulder. His skin was warm and dry; it quivered at her touch as if to shake her off. "I will find this truth for the Progenitor," she promised. "I will learn what happened to Brymn Las. Rest, Parymn Ne Sa Las."

Mac collected the tubes and tray, then went to the cage door. Nik opened it for her, his face pale and set. *He'd trusted her judgment.* Grateful, she held out her hand and Nik took it in his, using that hold to draw her from the cage. Someone else, One, took the tray.

"Are you injured, Mac?" Cinder asked, eyestalks bent forward at her.

"From that?" she forced a chuckle, but didn't let go of Nik. "Parymn wasn't trying to hurt me—just get rid of me. He's a little shaky at the moment. I went a bit farther than I should."

"What did you find out?"

For a fleeting moment, Mac had the unsettling impression that worlds upon worlds of beings suddenly hushed, waiting for her answer to Nik's question. *Foolish, Em?*

Still, for all she knew, the Sinzi were *broadcasting what was viewed from this room.*

"Mac?"

Brymn. She couldn't talk about him, not yet, not here, not to all those listening.

Not when she didn't understand.

"Are you sure you're all right?" Quieter, with an undertone of concern.

If Brymn Las should have Flowered into a Progenitor—how was it possible that he'd changed into the feeder form instead?

"Mac," sharper.

Mac gave Nik a smile. "Sorry. I was trying to remember the names of the foods Parymn wanted. He's on the mend. We should have a good session once he's rested a bit more." She looked at those she could see, One, Two, and Cinder, and thought of those she couldn't, then deliberately put weight on her hand in Nik's, as if needing his support.

"Time for you to rest as well," he said immediately. "I'll take you upstairs."

"Mr. Hollans awaits your report, Nik," Two disagreed.

One added: "We will escort Mac to her rooms."

Two continued: "And discuss with her the importance of absolute discretion."

Mac snorted and Nik smiled. "No need for that," he informed both staff before she could make an acid comment.

She squeezed Nik's hand once, then released it, letting her eyes say what she couldn't. "Then I'll see you later, Mr. Trojanowski."

But it was the huddled Dhryn she glanced back to see before the door closed between them.

And the question he'd given her was what kept her silent during the trip back to the surface.

Why had Brymn transformed at all?

- Encounter -

THAT WHICH IS DHRYN has followed the Taste, followed the path.
   There is harmony. Concordance. The Great Journey must be completed.
That which is Dhryn resists change.
That which is Dhryn resists . . . resists . . . resists . . .
. . . succumbs. Obedience to the Call is the Way as well.
Change.
That which is Dhryn follows the new path.

At night, even without moonlight, jungles aren't quiet. This one was no exception, although the babble of voices was an addition that startled most inhabitants into hiding.

It attracted others.

Movement began, high in the canopy. Stealthy, cautious movement. The kind that let one watch for rivals as well as predators.

Not that predators were allowed here. This was, after all, a civilized jungle, with wide paths to prevent the snagging of fine cloth on a rough branch; paved, to protect expensive shoes. It even boasted landing fields, so visitors needn't exhaust themselves reaching . . . here.

The voices were closer. There was laughter. The sort of nervous laughter that meant some weren't sure being here was such a good idea. Maybe some weren't as ready as others. It wouldn't matter.

Movement reached the tree trunks, became a climb downward. Always careful. Always ready.

Always . . . hungry.

A rival came too close. The battle joined, loud and urgent. The voices were silenced by it; footsteps ceased.

Movement continued.

As if only now realizing the nature of this place and their purpose in it, the voices began again, but lower, more . . . eager. The need to be here, in the dark, had supplanted any other.

The voices drifted apart, not to seek, but to be found.

The movement became quicker, came from every direction. Battle raged at each trespass, but more kept coming. The hunger was upon them all.

The jungle night rang with startled cries of ecstasy.

Until the rain began to fall.

And the cries became screams.

Then silence.

CONUNDRUM AND CHANGE

MAC SHOOED One and Two from her bedroom, feeling as if she was back at Base and dealing with overly helpful grad students. Despite Nik's assurance, they'd been unable to resist "briefing" her on the Sinzi's requirements for secrecy all the way to her quarters. Only those approved by the Sinzi-ra could know about the Dhryn. Only information assessed by the Sinzi-ra could be passed along to those who knew about the Dhryn. And so on.

Rubbing her throbbing temples, Mac avoided so much as a look at the extraordinary bed, walking through to the sitting room with the intention of splashing water on her face, then heading down to meet her team. *New questions to ask; hard ones.*

But two steps into what had been the sitting room, Mac stopped. "Oh my," she whispered.

The Sinzi's fish table was still there, its improbable contents moving in and out of rays of sunlight that didn't match those shining through the windows. The jelly-chairs remained, and the sand on the floor.

Everything else was hers.

Her desk, reassembled complete with clutter, was in front of the rain-streaked window, her chair where she liked it. There were new shelves on one wall, white, but filled with her things. The silly screen stood guard by the curved Sinzi mirror, complete with an old sweater tossed over it, while salmon . . .

Salmon hung everywhere. Wood glowed where light caught an edge. Potent lines of black and red outlined fins, eyes, and gave meaning. Their shadows schooled across the white walls and ceilings, oblivious to gravity, intent on life.

Her salmon.

"You're early!" Mudge gasped as he came out of the closet and saw her. He was carrying an armload of beads which he promptly dropped on his feet. As he bent to retrieve his burden, he muttered something she couldn't hear over the rattle and clank of the beads.

"You did this?" Mac asked incredulously.

Feet rescued, Mudge fumbled the beads into a mass against his chest and stood looking at her with charming despair. His hair, what there was, was sweat-soaked to his scalp, and he was out of breath. "Ah. Norcoast. Back so soon. How was your meeting?"

"You did this?" she repeated.

He gave an offended-sounding *harrumph* and actually scowled at her. "You'd left a mess in there." A jerk of his head to the closet behind him came close to freeing the beads again. "And we have to do something with these," he said anxiously, struggling to contain the noisy things.

Mac didn't know whether to laugh or burst into tears. As either reaction would no doubt embarrass her benefactor, she merely blinked a couple of times and asked: "What did you have in mind?"

It turned out that he wanted them on the terrace. Mac followed Mudge outside, and helped hold the mass of beads while he climbed on chairs and affixed the end of each strand above the French doors. She was impressed. He'd obtained some type of glue from the staff that was delivered by spray. It seemed to hold well. *Probably need a chisel to get them off again,* Mac judged.

Her hair danced against her face in the light breeze allowed through the Sinzi's screen. The air was cool enough Mac was glad of her jacket. *Better than the basement,* she thought. "Why outside?" she asked him, passing up the next strand.

Mudge glanced down at her, one hand pressed against the door for support. He'd already left a series of sweaty palm prints on the glass—or whatever the transparent material was. The staff would not be pleased. They obsessed about her footprints in the sand, raking them away every time she left. *As if a person could float to the washroom.* "Outside?" he repeated. "Where else do you expect the Ro to come from—the basement?"

As this was far too close to her own notions for comfort, Mac wisely shut up and kept helping.

"That's the last of them," Mudge said with distinct pride as he stepped down from the chair a few moments later. Mac managed to save both from tipping over. The chair was more grateful, Mudge shaking her hand free with an annoyed *harrumph.*

The strands weren't evenly spaced. They didn't even all hang straight down, a couple having a decided list. They did, however, thoroughly fill the space left when the doors opened. The noisemakers within the beads were heavy enough they wouldn't sound at the harmless touch of a sea breeze.

It would take a body trying to push past them, or a hand trying to move them aside, to sound the alarm.

When they finished, instead of "Thank you," Mac merely asked: "You hungry, Oversight?"

But she wouldn't forget. What Mudge had done was an act of friendship as pure and real as anything she'd have expected from Emily.

Nik had known, when she had not.

"You're late."

"Lunch meeting. Anything come up?" As she waited for Lyle to open his imp—*implying something had*—Mac let her eyes wander the Origins' room, noticing nothing unusual, unless she counted a second Myg. "Who's that?" she asked.

Lyle glanced up. "Who? Oh. Ueen-something. Nope, Uneen-something. Unensela, that's it. I have an awful memory for Myg names. All the vowels. She's your xenopaleoecologist."

"Just Unensela . . .no number?" Mac asked.

"Number?" His pale eyes crinkled at the corners with amusement. "You were expecting a number? She's female."

Would every single Human she'd meet here know more about aliens than she did? Mac asked herself with exasperation. "Any good?"

"Your friend thinks so. Hasn't been more than three steps away since she arrived."

Sure enough, Fourteen was hovering behind his fellow Myg like Lee used to hover around Emily—until that worthy would send him on an errand or four. "This Unensela better know her stuff," Mac muttered under her breath.

She brought her attention back to the archaeologist, who was, rightly, wondering why she wasn't looking at the display hovering between them over the conference table. He'd commandeered it as a very large desk, shoving what appeared the remains of the communal lunch to one end. "Sorry. What am I looking at, Lyle?"

"This is from Sergio's most recent assays of Dhryn ceramics from the ruins on their home world. I've correlated them against the references you gave us yesterday—Brymn Las' work—and the results are, well, you can see it's quite remarkable."

Mac dutifully examined the complex three-dimensional chart, then turned back to Lyle. "Salmon," she reminded him. "I know ceramics are in tiles and mugs, that's it. Tell me what this means."

"Biologist." He had the gall to grin at her, then put his hand inside the chart, pulling at a serpentine mass until it expanded to reveal more, to Mac, incomprehensible detail. "Ceramics is an entire field of engineering. You can build a civilization around it. Several in the IU have. Dhryn were very good ceramic engineers. Were," he emphasized. "A long time ago, over a relatively short period of time, ceramics virtually disappear from their technology. There's a massive switch to other materials. Plastics. Metals. Spun glass. Microgravity crystals. Now your friend didn't have access to our fieldwork. All he had to go on were artifacts from within the Chasm purported to be Dhryn. From before the event. None were ceramic, Mac. None."

"Imports," Mac guessed. "You're thinking the change in the Dhryn materials came when the Dhryn home system was first opened to others by a transect. New technology arrives, better than the old. We see it here."

Lyle bit his lip and closed the display with a quick gesture. "No, we don't. Here we take alien technology and blend it with the best or most popular of our own. Half the time, no one remembers what came first, but you can find the roots if you look. This? The Dhryn abandoned everything they had and replaced it. That's not a natural pattern, Mac."

"The Haven Dhryn had tile mosaics on their buildings." *Lovely ones,* she remembered, *as well as outright jokes on passersby.*

"Alien technology, Mac. Sergio's already determined the Dhryn imported their ceramics from other species after joining the IU."

"Give me a time line." A moment later, Mac stared at the resulting display. "That's . . . old."

Lyle leaned so close to the display that millennia played over his pale cheekbones. "We estimate the Chasm was home to a thriving interspecies culture like the IU when our particular ancestors had pointed noses and hunted bugs."

"Connected by transects made by the Ro."

A few more had come up to listen. One volunteered: "We don't know that."

Another: "Of course they were. The Chasm transects were reactivated when the Sinzi re-initialized the Naralax Transect from the Hift System."

"All of them?" Mac asked, curious. "What if some were destroyed—or connected in other ways?"

"The Sinzi sent probes designed to generate random destinations into every transect they encountered, Mac, probes that could multiply and send copies of themselves through any additional gates. All returned to their starting point in the Hift. The Chasm transects form a closed network. Everyone knows that."

Everyone? Mac didn't protest.

"Why?" She frowned at the now larger half circle of researchers.

"That's how many systems were ready for the technology," someone offered.

Mac held her hands up, palms together, fingertips touching. "I meant, why a bottle?"

Mutters of "Bottle?" "What bottle?" "What's she talking about?" went around the group.

With a look to get Lyle's permission, Mac replaced his imp with hers and set the screen high enough so that all could see it. She pulled up a map of the Tannu River watershed. "If I wanted to count all of the salmon born and ready to migrate from every one of these lakes and streams, I could wait here." She pointed to the mouth of the Tannu, where it opened into the Castle Inlet. "It's like a bottle, with only one opening. So is the Chasm, if I understand you correctly. Why build something with only one opening? Control over what moves in or out."

"But the Dhryn were already inside," Lyle protested.

"Yes," Mac agreed. "They were."

A buzz of conversation started around the edges of the now-complete group, much of it involving jargon that didn't translate in Instella or any language Mac knew. A pair sat at one end of the table to argue with each other. She waited.

The Sthlynii, Therin, had sat beside her. Sure enough, he found an inconsistency. "If there was only one 'opening' to the Chasm, and it led only to the Hift System, how did the Dhryn escape? You said they claimed to be pursued by the Myrokynay until they found a hiding place in the Haven System. But how did they get there?"

"I'm not sure even the Progenitors know," Mac said.

"Sublight?" this from one of the Chasm Ghoul followers.

"They'd still be in transit," from Therin, with disapproval. "We're talking no more than three thousand years."

"The IU connected the Naralax Transect to the Dhryn's new home," observed Lyle. No frowns or remarks followed, a testament, Mac judged, to the respect the Sinzi had earned with their care in choosing new species to invite into the union.

If any other species had let the Dhryn out of their system, there would have been blame enough to start wars.

"I don't know about you," one of the Humans looked around at the rest, "but I really don't like the idea that the Dhryn ships might have the capability to form their own passages."

"We haven't seen it," Therin said calmly.

"Yet."

"If they could do it, they wouldn't risk using transects."

"What if they do?"

The room filled with speculation. Mac let it go a while, finding and meeting Lyle's eyes. She waited until she saw them widen with comprehension, then she stood to get everyone's attention. When they were quiet, she asked: "What is a planetary system without a transect?"

Lyle didn't hesitate: "A sealed bottle."

"A sealed bottle that can sustain life," Mac elaborated. "The Dhryn didn't escape, folks. They were preserved."

All that could be heard was breathing, some of it rather odd to Human ears. That, and a shuffle of feet.

Followed by a cheerful bellow from the back row: "My colleague warned me you were full of surprises, Dr. Connor. Glad to see it's true." There was an abrupt parting of the line—Mac suspected a shove—and the new Myg made her way forward, Fourteen predictably behind. "Preserved, is it? By who? And why?"

"Who is obvious." This from one of the wrinkled Cey. "The only species with that level of no-space technology are the Myrokynay."

The female Myg, Unensela, seemed the only one not shocked by this bold statement. Unensela and her—Mac blinked—her family.

The Myg was built so much like Fourteen she'd have had trouble telling the two apart, if it weren't that Unensela's hair was short, sparse, and black, compared to his short, sparse, and red hair. Their features were a match as well, though Unensela was wearing color on cheeks, forehead, and lips. All the same shade of vivid fuchsia. She wore a crisp white lab coat, open at the front apparently to supply a view for her offspring.

There were six looking out at the moment, each about the size of a half grown kitten and, as far as Mac could tell, identical to one another and their mother. Naked, they clung with hands and feet to a harness Unensela wore under her coat. Their necks were flexible enough to allow them to stare over their shoulders with huge brown eyes that reminded Mac of Sam's irresistible beagle, who had successfully haunted so many supper tables.

Unensela, meanwhile, was peering under her thickened pink eyelids at the Cey. "Idiot," she proclaimed. "Why would the Myrokynay ferry the Dhryn to a new home and keep them there?"

"A prison," shouted someone else. There was a chorus of "yes, aye, has to be," and species-appropriate nods. "What else could you do with them?"

"What they'd do to us."

Everyone looked at Lyle after he spoke. He was standing now, too, his cheeks suffused with red. There were a few nods, some quick, some reluctant. With the exception of six Myg children, everyone listening understood what he meant.

Genocide.

Mac coughed. "Fortunately," she said, "we're not being asked to make that decision. We're being asked to provide answers to help those who must."

"We don't have the power of the Myrokynay." "We need to contact them." "Get their help!"

"In this room—" Mac stopped and raised her voice to be heard over the bedlam. "In this room, our job is to understand why the Dhryn are acting as they are." She lowered her voice back to normal as they began listening. "Where they came from. Origins. Focus on that, people. There are plenty of experts here working on other aspects of this problem—and its solution. Have you seen the daily reports from the Sinzi-ra?"

Mudge was the only one who nodded brusquely at this. Mac wasn't surprised. Of course he paid attention to everything going on, read every scrap of information. Even the deluge of information synthesized by Anchen for dispersal.

They'd have to talk, she decided. *Meanwhile . . .*

"If you have ideas how to contact the Ro, give them to any member of the consulate staff on your own time. My time, you are on my questions. Is that understood? Let's get back to work."

As they exchanged wary looks and sorted themselves out, grabbing lunch remains on the way, the Myg stepped up to Mac. "Well? What questions do you have for me?" Unensela demanded. "This is a bunch of irrelevant archaeologists." One of her children started to wail and she patted it absently. "And idiots."

At least she didn't point at the ghoul chasers, Mac thought. There was sufficient tension in the room as it was.

"I promised you a famous xenopaleoecologist, did I not, Mac?" Fourteen pushed himself forward. A sly tilt of his head. "Is she not thoroughly splendid?"

Unensela ignored him. "Well?"

"I want you to work with To'o and Kirby," Mac said, choosing to ignore Fourteen for the moment as well. *So long as he doesn't start drooling over her console, Emily.* "They'll provide you with what climatological information we have. I believe Oversight has obtained scans from cores into the planet itself."

Mudge, who'd stayed tucked behind his corner desk during all this, gave a start at the sound of his name. "Scans? Scans?" He realized he was repeating himself and shut up with a nod.

"From those," Mac continued, "I need you to tell me if there have been significant and predictable biome shifts. And why. As soon as you can. Tomorrow, if possible."

Unensela's hands patted offspring at random, her attention firmly on Mac. "A challenge, Dr. Connor. Interesting."

"Mac. And welcome to the team. All of you," she added, gazing into a dozen limpid eyes. "As for you, Fourteen?" Mac had every intention of assigning him a task at the other end of the room, if necessary.

"I have my task." The Myg held up his hands. "Yours are irrelevant," he said. "I continue to help the idiots downstairs interpret my perfectly clear translation. Helpless without my genius." This last directed at Unensela, who seemed to make a point of being preoccupied with her offspring.

Mac opened her mouth, not that she was sure what was about to come out of it beyond a question concerning the usefulness of a stolen shoe to a genius, when a shout drew everyone's attention, including hers, to the door. "Dr. Connor! Dr. Connor!"

She stared at—yes, it was Two, back in her yellow uniform. Consular staff, in her admittedly limited experience, never shouted, much less burst into rooms. "Dr. Connor. You must come with me immediately!" Two insisted loudly. Mac glanced at Lyle, then Mudge. Both men nodded back to her, Mudge with an anxious frown.

"I'll be back later," Mac promised the room at large, following the obviously impatient Two out the door.

Out in the hall, everything seemed normal enough. A few delegates walking about. A non-oxy breather hummed down the ramp in his/her/its/their bubble. *No sign of panic.* "What is it?" Mac demanded, controlling the impulse to check over her shoulder first. "Is he awake? Is there a crisis?"

"No, Mac." Two's voice had returned to its normal dignified calm. "Please excuse my abruptness, but we were briefed this was the most efficient way to extricate one Human from a group."

Mac stared at Two in disbelief. "In a life-or-death emergency, maybe. You startled everyone in that room! Including me!"

"My apologies." Somehow, the voice lacked sincerity. Mac harbored a sudden dark suspicion about what the staff on an alien planet did for fun.

"Where are we going?"

"The Sinzi-ra wishes to hear your daily insights."

Before they entered the lift, Mac checked the light streaming down from above. "It's not evening. Isn't this a bit early?"

"I was not given the Sinzi-ra's reason for the change in schedule, Mac." Two's hand paused at the control. "Would you like me to use the com system to inquire?"

Aliens. Mac leaned a shoulder against the wall of the lift. "No. Just take me up."

The Sinzi-ra was waiting in Mac's apartment, playing with salmon. Mac assumed it was play, although she was willing to believe there could be other motivation for Anchen to use her long fingers to poke a series of the statues into motion. *Distraction, perhaps.*

"I'm here," Mac announced. Two had left her at the doors.

"Ah, Mac. Thank you for coming." Anchen's fingers dropped gracefully to her sides. The salmon swayed back and forth, slower each time. Their shadows had elongated as the sun dropped lower, giving them an urgent look. "I see you've obtained your belongings."

"Yes, although I hadn't expected everything." Mac gestured to the room. "I hope you don't mind all this. I would have asked first, but . . ."

"But your friend wished you comfortable. It is understandable." The Sinzi took one of the jelly-chairs. She'd come alone this time. "I trust you don't feel you require these additional security measures."

"The beads?" Mac smiled without mirth. "They've become a habit."

"Ah." Anchen drew out her imp, waving it in the air like a wand before laying it on the table. A ragged tooth barracuda within the table targeted the device, then ignored it. "Shall we begin? First, please, come here. I wish to remove your bandage."

Mac sat cross-legged in the sand beside the Sinzi's chair, waiting patiently as the alien's fingertips feathered over her scalp. She felt a sudden coolness. "Excellent," Anchen pronounced. "See for yourself."

"It's healed remarkably well. Thank you," Mac told Anchen a moment later, trying not to grin as she ran her fingers over scalp that was now intact, instead of torn. No pain or tightness. *But there was—* "Excuse me, Anchen, but why is my hair growing in like this?" Mac felt the fine silky stuff. It looked as though she had a pale c-shaped stripe along the side of her head. *Not the fashion this decade, Em.*

"The regeneration process starts with biologically young cells," explained Anchen. "They will mature quite quickly. By the end of this week, you should see no difference. If you wish, a staff member can apply coloration to this portion immediately."

Baby hair? Mac wrapped some around a finger, forming a curl. "This is fine. I'd forgotten I started blonde." Her eyes met the Sinzi's in the mirror and she came to a decision. "There is—I have another injury."

"*Alexia.* Word blindness. Yes. I know."

"You know." *She shouldn't feel surprised,* Mac scolded herself. The Sinzi and the Ministry had shared their data about her. "Good. Then you're probably aware it's beyond our physicians. Can you help me?"

Anchen moved aside to let Mac step down to the sand. "Can our medical science repair the damage done to the areas of your brain involved in language? Of course." Then she shook her head. The gesture looked forced, unnatural, as if the Sinzi had learned it in order to communicate with Humans. "But the process would risk your ability to communicate with our guest, Mac. Until the situation changes, all we dare do is begin to retrain your reading centers—your greatest need at the moment, I assume. I will provide materials to help you. Practice when you are rested. Be patient."

As if she had a choice, Mac thought grimly. "I understand, Sinzi-ra. I won't say I like it."

"Nor I, Mac. It is a compromise—in this case one that burdens you most. You have my sympathy."

With a sigh, Mac nodded to the chairs. "Shall I give you my report? There's quite a bit."

"And I have much to tell you. There has been another attack."

"Who?"

The Sinzi didn't answer until she'd sat, Mac following suit. The alien activated her imp. Mac squinted, but again could see no more than a glimmer. "The Trisulians have suffered a terrible loss."

Mac closed her eyes briefly, then opened them again. "Their males?" she asked, sure of the answer.

"Yes. Word arrived within the hour. Trisul Primus was consumed by the Dhryn. How did you guess?"

"It's where the Trisulians are most vulnerable. But what I don't understand," Mac added aloud, but to herself, "is how that helps the Dhryn." Mac drew both feet up on the chair and hugged her knees.

"It did not. They paid dearly for the attack. The Progenitor's ship and all Dhryn in the system were destroyed—thankfully in time to save the remaining populated planets: Secondus and Tierce."

"So the Ro came to their aid?" Mac felt a surge of relief. "The message from Emily? It worked?" *This time, Em, she'd wanted to be wrong about so much.*

Anchen paired her fingertips. A cautious, slow movement. "It remains unclear whether the Myrokynay were involved and, if so, to what extent. The Trisulian Ruling Council has never been forthcoming in matters of strategy— understandable when you consider their unfortunate history with neighboring systems." She aimed her lower eyes at Mac. "If they received help from the Myrokynay, I admit being astonished the Trisulians were able to reconfigure their technology so quickly upon receipt of the instructions in the stolen message. It is a feat our experts have yet to accomplish."

"Perhaps they were already close to such a device themselves."

A graceful tilt of the head. "It could help explain Kay's willingness to commit violence—a last piece of the puzzle, an advantage within reach." Anchen's fingers rippled from shoulder to tip. "Perhaps they had reason to anticipate a Dhryn attack."

"Or provoked one."

"An insight, Mac?"

Mac shrugged. "I'm no strategist. But the Trisulians were resettling the Eeling System. They hoped to find a way to be first in line to take advantage—that word again—of the other devastated systems. Not every predator will tolerate a scavenger on its kill."

The Sinzi's fingers shot into the air as if avoiding something offensive, their rings, silver today, sliding toward her shoulders. *Like a melodramatic willow,* Mac thought. "You believe the Dhryn continue to watch their victims? How? Is this what our guest told you?"

"No, Anchen." The jelly-chair rewarded every posture but sitting up straight. Still, Mac made the effort. "I was only speculating why the Trisulians might have been a target for the Dhryn. I have no evidence, no reason for saying so. Forgive me if I distressed you."

"The search for truth is worth any distress," Anchen said feebly. One by one, her fingers gracefully slipped back down, each quivering as it moved, the whole process mesmerizing, as though the Sinzi hypnotized herself—and Mac—into a measure of peace. "But another subject would be easier at this moment. Perhaps insights about our guest? You've done wonders anticipating his needs."

Our guest. "Insights," Mac repeated, staring down at the Sinzi's imp. *On the record,* she reminded herself, unsure why she felt impelled to caution. *Same side, Em. Still . . .* "Anchen, should we speak freely here?" She gestured to the room.

The Sinzi aimed all of her eyes at Mac. "We have privacy here, Mac." She touched fingertip to her imp. "But no secrets from fellows within the IU," she said calmly. "Particularly this Gathering."

Other than a room lined with the Dhryn cloaking material, complete with Dhryn. Mac's lips twisted wryly. She understood the need for that discretion. There probably wasn't a single researcher here who wouldn't want to see the Dhryn—or, her blood chilled, *worse.*

The Sinzi read her expression with practiced ease. *Unsettling,* Mac decided, *when she couldn't do the same.* "I admit the inconsistency, Mac. The situation calls for some information to be—delayed. All will be recorded and shared. To those working on physiology, we have provided data; there was no need to specify its source. Nor do we see a need for experimentation or invasive tests at this time. Your interrogation of Parymn Ne Sa Las comes first. What results do you have?"

Mac gazed into multiple reflections of herself in alien eyes, feeling twisted inside, as though her lunch expressed an opinion. "Very little yet, Anchen. He's come to talk on behalf of his Progenitor. She wants to learn the truth."

"About what?" the other asked reasonably.

"We didn't get that far. Parymn's unaccustomed to alien life-forms. He's had trouble adjusting."

"A poor choice of ambassadors."

Was he? Mac frowned thoughtfully. "It would seem so," she agreed at last. "Parymn did have a question of his own for me. He wanted to know what happened to Brymn Las." Her voice held, steady and sure. *You'd be proud, Em.* "When I told him, he didn't believe me at first. He still might not."

"How is this significant?"

"I don't know," Mac admitted. "But the transformation to the—feeder form—is the point at which individual Dhryn become a threat. We should find out as much as we can about it."

"I concur. Is there anything more?"

Something went wrong. Brymn was to be a Progenitor. Mac, grateful she hadn't said the words aloud, gathered herself. "Yes. I think we should be careful how literally we take what Parymn tells us. I have doubts about his ability to—" she hunted for the right word, "—reconcile his worldview with ours. What he thinks he knows? Very little may be of use."

"Is he insane?"

Mac blinked. "I'm not qualified to say—"

"Give me an opinion, Mac," Anchen insisted. "We have already seen him be self-destructive. Is he sane for what you know of his kind?"

"He's angry. Frightened. Resentful. Who wouldn't be?" Mac paused to consider, watching fish swim inside the impossible table. "Otherwise? I honestly don't know, Anchen. I'll need to talk with him more first."

"You are a remarkable being, Dr. Mackenzie Connor."

Surprised, Mac looked up at the Sinzi. "I am?"

"There are few within this building I would trust near our guest, even if they had the courage to step within his cell. Fewer still I would trust to act as interpreter, under such dire and unhappy circumstances, even if they had the ability. Yet you, with what has happened, all you have endured, continue to act with clarity and compassion." The Sinzi bowed. "Remarkable and rare. I deeply cherish our connection."

"Thank you, Sinzi-ra. I cherish it as well." Mac sighed. "All I can I do is try my best. I hope that's going to be enough."

A shrug that set rings sparkling. "So do we all."

Mac made her way to Parymn's cell, having grabbed a bag of supplies before leaving her room. She'd also moved the information she wanted from the imp Fourteen had given her into her own—along with an astounding number of messages from other attendees of the Gathering, all collected within the last twenty-four hours. *Which was what being named head of anything really meant, Em.*

Needing only one hand to control the lift, Mac set her imp so the list hovered in front of her, the flashing lift lights a minor distraction. She pushed the device into the waistband of her pants to free her left hand. Now to attempt to organize the mess.

Sorting by priority didn't help, since almost all were marked "urgent!"

Trust academics, even alien ones. "Some things never change," Mac muttered out loud. By source, then. She found and pulled aside those from her group and the Sinzi. She looked at the rest rather helplessly, then forwarded them to Mudge with one sweep of her hand.

What were friends for? she grinned to herself.

The door whooshed open on the white corridor.

Mac took a deep breath and closed the display. As before, the corridor was empty and featureless, like the inside of a throat. She found herself reluctant to step from the lift, started to reach for the controls to close the doors. *As if she could stay here, Em,* she scolded herself. Settling the bag over her shoulders, and her imagination with it, Mac started walking.

At each of the three guard stations, she was stopped while beings of varied species examined her small bag. Mac wasn't sure what they were looking for—or in one instance, sniffing—considering she was one of the "assets" being protected by their presence. *Bored,* she decided.

Faced with the three doors again, Mac looked wistfully at the one which led to the vastness of the Atrium, then went toward Parymn's. She hesitated, looking over her shoulder. She was still alone. No obvious surveillance. Her eyes were drawn to the door Nik and Cinder had gone through first.

What was behind it?

"Probably nothing," she assured herself, again turning toward Parymn's.

Then again, Em, she'd never have guessed what was behind the other two.

That did it. Mac left her bag on the floor by the door she should go through and went briskly to the one she likely shouldn't.

It wasn't locked. No alarms sounded when she pushed it open. At first, Mac was disappointed. Another white corridor, this time offering only one large door before turning right and heading into a perspective-turning distance. It sloped downward at the same time, like the hallways above ground.

"'In for a penny,'" Mac whispered to herself, pushing against the large door.

Instead of swinging forward, this door reacted by sliding to one side, disappearing into the wall. Sunlight, dappled and moved by water, lay across Mac's toes. It was an invitation she took without hesitation.

"Oh," she breathed as she walked inside.

The impossible table in her room was a window here, to this place. A block of ocean, for it could be nothing less, stretched three times her height and wide enough to vanish into shadows on either side. Sunlight, either brought from the surface or feigned, cut through the water in great beams. Fish of every possible color and form slipped in and out of them, alone, in schools, flashes of life wheeling above the corals, oblivious to anything but themselves. Shrimp scurried everywhere, antennae flicking in the currents, too busy to hide despite being on everything's menu. Including the Sinzi's.

Mac laid her palms flat against the transparent hardness of the tank wall, stopping short of pressing her nose to it. The floor of this room wasn't the bottom. She could make out the edge of the coral shelf, slim dark shadows below that marking where barracuda and shark loitered.

No-space. Remembering, Mac took her hands away and swallowed uneasily. Remarkable, that she could see inside it from here. *If she was.* Now that she wasn't transfixed by the marine life in front of her, she noticed the steady throbbing of the floor and paid attention to the writhing mass of machinery overhead that started halfway up the wall behind her. The hairs rose on her arm and neck. She gave the imprisoned fish a sympathetic look. Trapped forever, like insects in amber. But trapped alive.

Was Emily?

"Mac?" Cinder walked out of the darkness to the right of the door. "What are you doing here?" She didn't appear pleased.

"Got lost," Mac said, not surprised her voice was higher-pitched than usual. Her heart was racing, too. *Was there some memo she'd missed about scaring her today?* "This is quite the setup," she added.

"The fish?" Caught in sunbeams, the Trisulian looked as agitated as she sounded, stroking her facial hair, her eyestalks shifting in jerky movements. "I suppose so."

Then Mac understood. "The Sinzi-ra told me about—about Trisul Primus."

As if she'd somehow used a weapon, Cinder folded at both waists, collapsing to the floor. Mac hurried to crouch beside her, unsure how to offer comfort. *If it was even possible.* "Cinder," she said gently. "I'm so sorry. Is there anything I can do?"

She hadn't expected an answer, but the other pressed something small, round, and cold into Mac's palm. "Take this." Muffled.

It was a weapon, identical to the one Nik produced at need.

Mac wanted to drop it. Instead, she put it into the pocket of her jacket.

"This, too." Cinder's hand shook as she pulled a sheathed blade from her boot.

"I—" Mac didn't know what to say.

"One of *them* so close. In reach. I can't think straight. Don't trust myself. Not yet. *Usish!* Take it! Please."

Mac obeyed, putting the knife with the weapon. "Should I get someone—Nik?" she offered.

"No!" Then, quieter but a hoarse undertone. "No, thank you, Mac. I must collect myself before I see a male. This is—I am—it's unseemly." Cinder's hands clenched in her hair, round knuckles white. "You are unmated, are you not?"

By Trisulian standards? "Yes."

A sigh, closer to a moan. "Yet you—you have that future. Thanks to his kind, the *usishishi* Dhryn—there are no mates for my generation, Mac. Can you understand? Oh, our kind will survive. There will be a new jungle. When all are satisfied it is safe to do so, those already bonded will impregnate themselves. They will give birth in its warmth, take their daughters home with them, leave their sons to grow. Sons who will be ready when those daughters are ripe. Our kind will survive," she repeated in a dull whisper. "But I . . . I will be forever alone and incomplete."

There had to be options. "Forgive my ignorance, Cinder," Mac began with care. "I only want to help. I've heard a female Trisulian can bond with more than one male. I've seen a male removed from his mate." *At close range.* "So wouldn't it be possible for your people to—redistribute—" *what a crude word* "—the males you have? To share?"

"Deviance." The word wasn't harsh, it was chill, matter-of-fact. "You could say waste. Or murder. All fit. You see, Mac, bonding is permanent. There is a—I don't know the word in Instella—a body part of the male which becomes part of the female's flesh. Insertion of it is—I'm told," Cinder corrected herself softly, wistfully, "a moment of the most exquisite rapture my kind can know. To remove a male severs him from this part. He can't mate again. He lives on, impotent." Eyestalks steadied as Cinder looked directly up at Mac, her rust-brown hair catching sunlight. "As must I."

Mac hesitated, then asked: "Must every female take a mate?"

"No. Some choose to remain alone, for control over their lives. I might have been one of them . . . now, I have no other choice." Cinder pressed her hands over her lower waist. "Fertility, for us, is a matter of mere minutes, its occurrence unpredictable." *Hence the value of symbiotic males,* Mac couldn't help thinking. "Three cycles in a life is exceptional. Most, only once. So it is expected that one allows pregnancy whenever possible, regardless of career or situation." She began rising to her feet, moving as if wounded. "You must think me lacking in *nimscent*—grieving for myself at a time like this. I am shamed."

"Nonsense." Mac offered her hand to help Cinder straighten. "We were going to have some girl talk," she said, but not lightly.

"Thank you." Cinder squeezed her hand then released it. "I feel able to be around others now—just not—would you—I—"

Mac patted her pocket. "I'll hang on to these for a while," she suggested.

The Trisulian shuddered, her hair quivering from forehead to chest, but didn't disagree. "I should return to my post," she said instead.

And would probably appreciate a little space from empathic Humans, Mac decided. "Would it be all right if I watch the fish for a while?" she asked. "A moment or two, not long. Thought I saw a sand shark."

One eyestalk regarded the tank at that angle suggesting anxiety. "Glad it's in there," Cinder said, her voice close to normal again. "Don't stay long, Mac." With that, she left.

Once the door closed, Mac walked to the right, looking for—there, a mass of wiring, looping down through some kind of clamp. Standing on tiptoe, she took Cinder's weapon and knife and pushed both as far back in the mass as her arm could reach.

Keeping the deadly things in her pocket hadn't been an option.

"Trained spy, target in a box, and me holding the hardware," Mac summed up for the fish. If the grief-stricken Trisulian doubted her self-restraint that much, what was to say she wouldn't lose it? Then what was she, Mac, supposed to do? Fight her off? Throw herself in front of the Dhryn?

"No winners, Em," Mac sighed. "Like all of this."

Time to get back to Parymn and hunt answers. But she couldn't help one last look at the Sinzi's living larder.

Odd. Mac walked along the tank, following the coral as it built up from the depths, then rose to her shoulder height and more. Anemones bent under what appeared natural wave motion, fingerlike extensions hoping for unwary swimmers.

She leaned closer, staring at what had caught her eye.

There. The play of light and shade over the irregular coral had disguised the damage from the doorway.

The living coral was colorful, each hollow containing its tiny organism, like so much shrimp-beaded concrete. Mac's fingers traced the lines where living coral had been dug out and pushed aside, or peeled back, as if someone had used the tines of a large fork to remove it.

Her hand dropped to her side as Mac took slow, careful steps back.

She'd seen such marks before.

They'd scarred the moss carpeting Mudge's mountainside. She'd followed them as if they were footprints. For all she or anyone knew, they could be, since their makers showed themselves to no one.

Mac felt the door at her back. The occupants of the tank looked completely normal. *If she didn't know—if she hadn't seen—*

She threw herself around, yanking open the door and running out as if chased.

"Whoa, Mac. What's wrong?" Nik's voice jumped from surprised to urgent.

"The Ro," she gasped, pointing behind her. "In there."

"And I'm telling you, Mr. Trojanowski, unless you want to order a diver to commit suicide over some broken coral, there's nothing more we can do."

Putting down her bottle of water, Mac glared at the speaker, an unnamed, overdressed, vaguely bovine alien. He/she/it had arrived with a small army of scan techs and their equipment. And, as far as she was concerned, a supremely unhelpful contempt for Human powers of observation. Particularly hers.

Granted, they'd aimed their devices at the marks she'd found, and everywhere else in the tank, for over an hour. An hour during which Mac had leaned against this wall to wait and watch. An hour during which Nik, who had taken her very seriously indeed, had arranged for guards—sans armor, in case the Ro took offense, but armed nonetheless.

One of those guards wandered over to Mac as Nik and the alien began a heated argument over monitoring equipment to leave in the room, the alien, predictably, opting for none. "Didn't you get your stuff, Mac?" he asked, taking up some wall space of his own.

"Hi, Sing-li." Mac looked up at the tall man. "Yes, thank you. More than I imagined, in fact. Nice work."

"Good. You had me worried."

She lifted a brow. "I did? Why?"

"Didn't think you'd willingly stay dressed like that."

Mac stood away from the wall to stare at him. "Why—" then she grinned. "I don't wear coveralls all the time, you know."

"Could have fooled us."

"Obviously not," she said, shaking her head. "Let's say this place is a little intimidating for my usual gear. Besides," she held out her arms to show off the well-tailored jacket, "this came with the room."

He grinned back. "Goes with the hair."

Self-consciously, Mac ran her fingers through the downlike stuff where her wound had been. "Thanks. I think." She put her back to the wall again, companionably close to Sing-li. "Nice to see a friend."

"Nice to see you, too, Mac. But here?" He lowered his voice. "This is pretty intense stuff. The Sinzi don't let many Humans see it."

"Trust me," Mac said fervently, "I didn't ask for the privilege." *Unless one counted sneaking in, but she didn't see any point going into detail.*

Battle of wills resolved, Nik approached them, leaving the alien to complain, loudly, but wisely in something other than Instella. "Jones?" he asked, giving the other man a searching look. "What are you doing here?"

"Just checking on our Mac," the guard said with a nod. "I'll get back to my post."

"'Our Mac,'" Nik repeated, raising an eyebrow at her.

"He's from Base," she explained.

That almost drew a smile. "You can't just adopt my field operatives, Mac."

She shrugged, then wrapped her arms around herself to stop the motion from becoming a shiver. "Nik, I know what I saw."

Nik's eyes grew shadowed. He looked over his shoulder at the tank, where the alien's staff were busy setting up their devices, then back to her. "The marks look the same to me, too, given the difference in material. But scratches in coral aren't enough—especially in there. It could be coincidence."

"'In there' they should be more than enough!" Trying to keep her voice down, Mac only succeeded in producing an impassioned growl. "The Ro live in no-space, Nik."

"And seem to move around in normal space just fine. Why hang out in a bowl of fish?"

"It's more than that—and you know it. The Sinzi built this thing. That means it could be new to the Ro. We've no idea what that might mean."

Nik held up his hands. It wasn't quite surrender. "I know I've done all I can, Mac. You need to go. He's awake." One of his hands gestured a summons. "Jones?"

"Still here."

"New orders. Please accompany 'our Mac' to her destination. Stay at the door until relieved by me personally, or she comes out." Nik considered the other man, then added so quietly Mac could barely hear. "She's in your care, Sing-li. Priority One."

"Priority One," Jones echoed, his lips tightening. The look he sent Mac was worried. "Something I should know, Nik?"

"Right now—only that there may be a threat. Full gear when you get the opportunity. Meanwhile, don't take chances. Any doubt—act first and I'll back you." Nik reached out and fluffed her newly grown hair. "Oh, and trust Mac."

"Thanks," she said dryly.

"Don't mention it. Are we clear, Sing-li?"

"Crystal, Nik."

With her new nursemaid looming at her side, Mac headed for Parymn's cell, Nik remaining behind to supervise. She wasn't sure if she felt frustrated they hadn't found incontrovertible evidence of the Ro, or relieved.

In either case, she was glad of Sing-li's substantial presence. The empty white corridors of the consulate were no impediment to creatures able to hide in plain sight.

Her bag still sat beside the door. Mac picked it up, then hesitated before entering. "Do you want me to have them bring you a chair?" she asked.

Sing-li, who'd already stationed himself to one side, shook his head. "I'm used to being on my feet," he assured her. "Worked way station customs before this." His finger tapped the large weapon he carried. "I'll be here if you need me."

"That's good to know," she told him, meaning it.

Then Mac went into the room, closing the door behind her.

To be immediately greeted by a bellowed: "Where have you been, Mackenzie Winifred Elizabeth Wright Connor Sol?"

Someone was definitely on the mend, she thought, hoping the door was soundproof. The floor wasn't. The Dhryn, on his feet, arms folded, was broadcasting in the lower ranges as well. *Probably something disparaging about her eating habits,* Mac decided.

There was no one else in the room, unless you counted those watching and recording. Mac preferred to ignore that aspect as much as possible. She dug into her bag, producing a handful of small rings she'd found among her belongings. They were for banding ravens and their golden shine was to help an observer spot them, but she trusted Parymn Ne Sa Las wouldn't know the difference. "I brought you something, *Erumisah,*" Mac told him, opening the cell door and walking inside. "Here."

He took the rings in his hand, eyes cold, then turned his palm downward so they dropped and danced on the floor. "I want to be released from this place. Now."

Mac didn't bother bringing out the "cosmetics" she'd found in the Sinzi washroom. "This is the only room protected from the Ro," she snapped.

Brymn had shrieked and tried to run at that name. *There had been,* Mac recalled quite vividly, *a moment of alien hysterics.* But Parymn was made of sterner stuff. He merely tightened his arms as if their folding was somehow a defense against his kind's greatest fear. "You are sure, Mackenzie Winifred Elizabeth Wright Connor Sol?"

"Yes."

Magnanimously, as if granting her a favor, "Then I will stay."

Someone had added a boldly striped carpet in every color but yellow to the cell's furnishings, along with a Human-suited stool. Mac made a mental note to ask for a proper chair, but perched on it anyway. Her feet didn't quite touch the floor—*of course*—but there was a rung to support them. Parymn sat as well.

Mac took a quick breath, then blew it out between pursed lips. *Where to start?* She hoped Nik would arrive soon. This "interrogation" business was well over her head. Emily would be better at it.

Her stool. Her alien. Mac settled herself. "What truth does the Progenitor seek, Parymn Ne Sa Las?"

"I do not wish to think of it." The pat Dhryn phrase for a forbidden topic.

A little soon for that. Mac frowned. "Where is the Progenitor?"

"I do not wish to think of it."

Was it because she'd invoked the Ro? Or was Parymn being honest with her? *In either case, Em, not helpful.*

"*Erumisah,* you were the one sent by the Progenitor to talk to me. You must answer my questions."

Parymn drew himself up, clearly offended. "I must do nothing."

Mac opened her mouth to argue. At that same instant, Parymn's seventh hand slipped out from the others, striking at his upper shoulder like a snake, leaving a blue gash behind. "Aieee!" he cried, rocking back and forth, his eyes wide and staring. "No! No!"

"What's wrong?" she demanded, dismayed. *Was he going mad?*

Another strike, another gash. Another cry of anguish.

Mac gripped the stool. "Parymn—stop it!" She almost called for help. *Almost.*

The blue-stained hand hovered before the Dhryn's eyes, as if controlled by something else. He spoke, the words monotonous and low, like a chant. "I am become . . . I am become . . . I am become . . ."

Become what? Mac leaned forward—afraid but fascinated. It was the way she felt whenever a grizzly came so close it crossed that line, the line beyond which she knew she had no chance to run and she had to wait on its motives, not hers, her life held by no more than skin. But to be there, to see such a creature, to be part of its world . . . "Become what?" she breathed.

"No! I am Parymn Ne Sa Las!" A strike, a gash. "I am Parymn Ne Sa!" Another. His white silk was soaking up fluid, growing streaked with blue. "I am Parymn Ne!" Drops flew everywhere as a slash opened one cheek, staining the carpet as the Dhryn chanted more quickly, urgently. "I am Parymn! No! I am become—" A pause. The seventh arm slipped back to its resting place. His entire body seemed to adjust itself, as if relaxing into a more comfortable fit.

Then, "I am the Vessel."

- 17 -

TRANSFORMATION AND TRIAL

MAYBE ANCHEN was right, and the Dhryn insane. Mac began calculating the distance to the cell door. "The Vessel?" she repeated.

"Yes." Parymn's voice—it had changed somehow, becoming higher-pitched, smoother, *familiar.*

Mac stared. "Who—who are you?"

"I am the Vessel," the Dhryn said again, gently. His small lips formed a smile. "Greetings, Mackenzie Winifred Elizabeth Wright Connor Sol. You have done well."

It couldn't be. But it was. "Thank you—Progenitor," Mac acknowledged. "It is you, isn't it?"

A graceful, somehow feminine gesture of three hands. "In a limited sense. I gifted Parymn Ne Sa Las with a minute portion of myself. This is our way, when one Progenitor must travel to another, to exchange information, to debate or discuss. Are you troubled by this?"

The Progenitor's body filled a cavern—it was a world unto itself, covered with a dust made of new life, enriched by blue ponds replenished by feeder-Dhryn. Yet her face had been like Parymn's, golden-eyed, expressive. Mac swallowed hard. "What of Parymn Ne Sa Las?"

The lips turned downward, the great eyes winked closed, then open. "*Grathnu.* He will be remembered as Parymn Ne Sa Las Marsu. These names will be inscribed in the corridor of my ship." The Dhryn clapped two hands together.

His protests, the tearing of his own flesh. She'd watched Parymn sacrifice himself, here and now, and done nothing. *Alien ways,* Mac chided herself. Who was she to denounce them? *Hard enough to follow without a game plan, Em.*

"It was an honor to know him," she said, at a loss for anything more.

The Dhryn—Mac couldn't think of another name yet—folded his arms again in that intricate pattern. "We have little time, *Lamisah.* What has happened since I was sent? Have you heard from others? Has the Great Journey begun?"

"Mac." From behind—with her. Human and anxious. "Are you all right? What's going on?"

"Your pardon," Mac told the Dhryn, then turned to look up at Nik. He was flushed, as though he'd run some distance and quickly—doubtless alerted by some watcher that the Dhryn was slicing himself, with her in range. "Not now," she urged. "Things have become—complicated." *There was an understatement, Em.*

Tense. Sharp. "You've his blood on your face."

Mac wiped her cheek, looked down at her blue-coated fingers in surprise. "I'll clean up later," she assured him. "We're fine."

"Fine!" Nik took her arm in a tight grip, as if preparing to pull her from the stool by force if necessary. "He's losing it again." Urgent and low. "You aren't safe in here!"

"I'm safer here than out there," she retorted, giving her arm an impatient tug to free it. "Let go of me, Nik. I know what I'm doing."

"You haven't proved that to me," fiercely. "The Dhryn's changed. Something's different about him. We need the med team in here—"

He was good, Em. To recognize the switch from Parymn to the Vessel from body language and tone? Mac was impressed.

Not that it was saving time.

She grimaced. "I don't suppose if I asked you to trust me, to just leave us alone, you'd do it."

"I trust you to be stubborn," he replied, eyes dark behind their lenses. "To take chances with your own safety. Not a good combination, Mac. You're too valuable to risk."

She made a rude noise. "I'm valuable only when I'm doing the job you're interfering with, Mr. Trojanowski."

"You know better than that."

Mac shrugged, her own temper keeping her from anything more gracious. "There's no need for concern—or a med team. This—" she nodded at the wounded Dhryn, who was waiting, if not patiently, then at least quietly, "—is normal." *Not the word she'd initially planned.*

"In what possible way is cutting your own flesh normal?"

She lifted one eyebrow, considering the question. Had the cuts been Parymn's futile protest against the coming death of his personality, or the Vessel's cue to emerge and take over? Or was the self-damage completely unconnected—the body's involuntary reaction to the very odd things happening in the Dhryn's mind? "I've no idea," Mac said at last, keeping it honest. "The psychologists can work out the details later, but essentially the person who came here, who spoke to me earlier today, has been—replaced—by another personality. Nik, I watched Parymn Ne Sa Las sacrifice himself. It's *grathnu,* but of the mind, not the flesh. He acquired the name 'Marsu.'"

It spoke volumes to his experience with the non-Human that Nik's first reaction wasn't the scorn or disbelief Mac half expected. "Then who is this?" he asked.

"I'm not sure 'who' is the right way to put it," she countered. "Because Dhryn

Progenitors can't physically visit one another, they imbue one of their *erumisah,* a decision-maker like Parymn, with something of themselves, their personality. I can't begin to guess the mechanism—for all I know, *erumisah* grow so used to their Progenitor's way of thinking, they somehow switch to it and abandon their own. It doesn't matter now. This Dhryn," Mac nodded to the silent alien, "is now such a Vessel. From what I've learned—which isn't much yet—I believe he is meant to convey information from his Progenitor. He's able to carry on a conversation that's consistent with what I remember of his Progenitor's nature and wishes. He's very much Her, in a way I can't explain, Nik."

"A living message," he said, a look of awe on his face. "A biological, preprogrammed, interactive message. Remarkable."

"And impatient," Mac nudged. "Can I get back to talking with him now?"

"Yes. Yes, of course." Nik studied the Dhryn, seeming distracted. *It was,* Mac judged, *a reasonable reaction.*

Then the Dhryn hooted softly. "I see he should know better than to argue with you, my *lamisah.*"

Feeling as if she moved in slow motion, Mac swiveled her head to meet a pair of golden eyes. "You understood what we said?" she asked in disbelief, careful to speak Dhryn. "The language of the not-Dhryn?"

A regal nod. "Of course. A Progenitor must not rely on translation, *Lamisah.*"

A rock and a hard place moment, Em, Mac told herself. Aloud, in Dhryn: "Do you trust me?"

"You are Dhryn. Of course I trust you, Mackenzie Winifred Elizabeth Wright Connor Sol."

More like a crossing the chasm on a swaying cable bridge moment, Mac thought, *an old, decrepit, untrustworthy bridge.*

Nik stood so close she could feel his body heat, a possibly insane Dhryn bled at her feet, and her backside was all but paralyzed from the uncomfortable stool. *She had to decide. Now.*

The Ro. They were here, or they were coming. Mac felt it in her bones. The situation wasn't stable or safe. And if Anchen or the Ministry learned anyone could talk to their guest, anyone at all, Mac would be back upstairs, waiting. On the outside.

No. Not again.

Mac gave herself a shake. *Decision made.* Until she had the answers she was after, *until she had Emily,* this Dhryn was hers alone. No one, not the Sinzi-ra, not even Nik, was going to get in the way.

"Vessel, give no sign that you understand anything but what I say in Dhryn. Please. They will take me away from you."

"I would not permit it."

Mac shook her head. "You wouldn't have a choice. Trust me. And—" she added, struck by a sudden, better thought. "Trust this Human, Nikolai Piotr Trojanowski. If ever he comes to you alone and says my name, speak to him in his language. Consider him as your *lamisah* as well. Will you do this for me?"

A clap. "I take the name Nikolai Piotr Trojanowski into my keeping. An honor. Of course, I will do what you say. This is, my *lamisah,* a strange and unsettling place."

"Yes," Mac agreed. "It is." She climbed down from the stool. "Stay if you wish, Nik," she told him calmly, in Instella, careful not to look at him. *Em always said she had the worst face for poker.* "You might want to grab a chair, though. I've a feeling this is going to take a while." She sat cross-legged on the carpet in front of the Dhryn, avoiding the spots of blood.

That neutral voice. "If you're staying, so am I." She felt, more than saw, Nik sit beside her on the floor.

The Dhryn towered over them both, his great yellow eyes warm and curious. *Amazing how like the Progenitor's his every expression had become,* Mac thought with awe. On impulse, she held out her hand. Immediately, the Vessel put his into it. The opposing fingers, three in total, were as warm, rubbery, and muscular as Mac remembered. Brymn's hand had been thus. The fingers gripped, very gently, then withdrew. "We have no time," the Dhryn reminded Mac.

She nodded, swallowing hard. "Yes. I'm sorry. Vessel. Is that what I should call you?"

"It is what I am."

"You want to know what happened since you were sent. There's no easy way to say it. Other Progenitors have destroyed inhabited worlds, taken all life from them."

The Dhryn frowned. "This cannot be."

"It is," Mac said earnestly. "You must believe me. Millions—billions of not-Dhryn have died already."

He reared up, giving her a suspicious look. "Why would we do such a thing?" Then, more kindly: "I see that you are confused, *Lamisah.* The not-Dhryn kill one another. Dhryn do not take life."

Confused covered it from all sides, she thought and turned to Nik. "He doesn't believe me, that other Dhryn have been attacking worlds. I'm trying to explain, but—"

His eyes were guarded as he looked to the Dhryn and back to her. "How specific do you want to be?"

"There's no time to waste."

"In that case—here." Nik pulled out his imp and activated its screen, setting a display to hover at eye level in front of the Dhryn.

Ships appearing at a transect. A confusion of attackers and defenders. Mac could barely make out which was which, except that the Dhryn seemed intent above all on reaching the planet, squandering tactical advantage in order to drop their smaller ships—that appalling number of smaller ships—ships that produced a green rain—

Mac wanted to close her eyes but couldn't. The images were fragmented, nightmarish. Most were brief, as if the ships doing the observing were under assault themselves.

"Aiieeeeee!" The Vessel's cry bounced around the room. He surged to his feet, backing away from the images, hands out as if to block them. "Aieeeeeee!"

Turning off his screen, Nik looked at Mac. "We can't assume it's shock—it could be his reaction to the Dhryn ships being destroyed."

She scowled back. "I know Her—him—better than that."

"Careful, Mac."

Rather than argue, Mac shrugged and switched back to the *oomling* tongue. "This is what has happened. It's still happening, in other systems. That's why we're all here, Vessel. Why you're here. To try and stop more loss of life."

"This not the Way." With an undertone of despair. "I don't understand."

She'd been afraid of that. "Neither do we," Mac admitted. "What should be the Way?"

"The Way?" A calmer, but puzzled look. "All that is Dhryn answers the Call. Then the Great Journey takes us Home. All that is Dhryn must move."

"Why?" Mac held her breath. "Why do you move now?"

"I do not," the Dhryn answered. *Was he being literal?* Mac worried. Then: "I believe—I hope—that others—do not. We must resist this Call if we are to survive."

"What Call?" Without thought, Mac reached for Nik's hand and found it. He didn't interrupt or ask why. "Whose?"

The question sent the Dhryn rocking back and forth, arms wrapped around his middle. Blue kept flowing from the gashes, and Mac worried how much he could spare. "We do not know," he said finally. "The oldest stories passed from Progenitor to Progenitor tell of a time when the Call came over generations of *oomlings,* that new Dhryn were born readied for it; able to grow stronger, larger in preparation. The urge to move would then spread through a lineage like breathing into a body. Inevitable, natural. The Great Journey would spend all but the Progenitors, who would await the future, remembering the Way home again. So the stories say."

"That's not what's happening now."

"No, *Lamisah.* I fear what is happening now is not only the deaths of others, but of all that is Dhryn."

"Is this why you told me to run?" Mac remembered that moment when she and Brymn had balanced on the palm of the Progenitor and heard Her horrified warning. "You said my species should run before the gates between worlds closed again."

"As we ran to Haven," the Vessel said, a reverberation in the floor attesting to some emotion. "Were it not for the great buried ships that awaited us, to shelter us from the rain, to feed us, all that is Dhryn would have perished as the rest."

The rest? Hundreds of other species. Entire worlds, scoured to dust. Mac swallowed. Suddenly, their differences overwhelmed her, the blue skin, the bony ridged face, the arms, maimed and moving restlessly. Even the smell. If it hadn't been for the solid, so-Human, presence at her side, she might not have dared go on: "You mean the other species in the Chasm. Did the Dhryn consume them, too?"

"Dhryn do not consume other life. It is not the Way."

Around to that again. Mac frowned. It wasn't that the Dhryn defined life as only including themselves. Brymn Las had certainly understood there were other living things, that other worlds than Haven were homes.

In the pause, the grip on her hand tightened a fraction. "Mac."

She glanced sideways at him. "It's still complicated."

"That was Dhryn, Mac."

Blushing, she took a moment to be sure what she was about to speak. "Sorry, Nik," in English. "It's still complicated."

"I understand that. But we need something tangible, a place to start. Ask if this Dhryn, the Vessel, can help us communicate with others. Arrange negotiations."

Doubtful, Mac nodded. "Vessel," she began, "we'd like to speak to the other Dhryn—"

"How?"

"That's what we'd like you to tell us."

A lift and fall of six arms. "Within a lineage, only *erumisah* may speak to their Progenitor without invitation. You have not yet committed sufficient *grathnu* to be so elevated, my *lamisah*. And only a Vessel may approach another Progenitor."

Mac repeated this, in English, to Nik. He nodded thoughtfully. "What about the colonial Dhryn, those who lived away from Haven and the Progenitors? They were accustomed to com systems—many traded freely within the systems of other IU species."

She hurried to translate. The Vessel gave a soft sigh. "The great ships launched without their return. They have no Progenitors to guide them. They are lost, Mackenzie Winifred Elizabeth Wright Connor Sol."

"Lost as in dead—or lost as in they've become a separate faction?" Nik responded when he heard this.

"Do you want me to ask?" Mac said, rubbing her temple.

He gave her a worried look. "English."

It had sounded right. "It's getting harder to keep it all straight," she confessed in that tongue, ashamed.

"You're doing fine, Mac. You aren't trained for this." Nik shook his head. "I'd like to give you a break, but . . ."

"I know." Mac stretched her arms and spine. "I'm okay. Do you want the question about factions?"

"No. We'll deal with that later. It's the Progenitor ships we need to stop. Try and get a time frame. How long do we have between attacks?"

Good question. Mac nodded. "Vessel—" she paused to be sure what language her tongue was shaping.

"The great ships were not prepared for the Great Journey," the Dhryn answered—too soon, Mac realized. *Nik didn't miss a thing; he wouldn't miss this.* Sure enough, he was sitting straighter, starting to frown.

Damn.

This time, she grabbed for his hand deliberately. "I know what I'm doing," she insisted, trying to convey the same message through look, words, and touch. *Trust me. Be patient.*

His fingers squeezed hers again, twice, before letting go. She'd have been more relieved if his face hadn't worn its patented "spy on the prowl" expression.

Later would be soon enough. Mac turned to the Vessel. "What does that mean—the ships weren't prepared?"

"Before my time, we broke with the tradition of keeping each ship ready to depart. We believed it a meaningless duplication to have food production in every ship, when there were new, more modern facilities above ground. So most was centralized in a few key locations. If the Progenitor is not producing *oomlings,* and adults fast, it is possible to go for a considerable time without a new source. But . . . that which is Dhryn must not starve."

"Nik," Mac translated quickly, her mouth dry, "the Dhryn can't grow their food, not on every ship. They'll need an outside source. Given their numbers—probably often."

His lips pressed into a grim line. "Noted. How many per ship? Weaponry? Insystem speed? We need details—as much as you can get."

Before the Vessel could open his mouth again—and confirm Nik's growing suspicions, Mac said quickly: "Don't answer his questions. Not yet. We need to talk about the Call, first. Was it the Ro?"

"The Ro? The Ro are the Enemy, Mackenzie Winifred Elizabeth Wright Connor Sol." A humoring tone, as if she were young and lost. "They do not Call the Dhryn. They steal and terrorize our *oomlings.* They wish us gone. As, I fear, do all not-Dhryn. Including this one." An arm ending in a stump pointed at Nik.

"What we wish is not to be food for Dhryn," Mac snapped back.

"I do not consume not-Dhryn," the Vessel replied. "Others do not."

"You saw for yourself. Dhryn are doing this."

"Aiieeeee! Yes, but I do not understand." More rocking. "Do not speak of it."

"For now. The *oomlings,*" Mac circled back. "Why would the Ro go to such effort to steal them? If they wanted to harm you, they could have destroyed Haven any time they wished."

"To threaten the *oomlings* is to threaten all that is Dhryn." The tone flat and with a hint of threat itself.

Nik heard it and reacted. "What's wrong, Mac?"

"Nothing," she snapped, then waved an apology. To the Vessel: "Why do some Dhryn consume other species and other Dhryn do not?"

"I do not know. In the Great Journey, all that is Dhryn must follow the Taste."

"Scouts," Mac crowed triumphantly. "I was right! The disappearances earlier—they were caused by Dhryn scouts, weren't they? They were collecting the Taste of what was on various worlds, bringing it back to the Progenitors. Those that digest and feed—" somehow, she didn't shudder.

"Impossible."

"What do you mean?"

"The mouths and hands of the Dhryn must stay with the Progenitor. They do not exist elsewhere. They have no purpose elsewhere."

"Then how do you find the Taste to follow?" Mac asked, thinking it a reasonable question.

The Dhryn's mouth turned downward at the edges. *Disapproval*. "The Taste is not found. It is that which the Progenitor requires on the Great Journey. All that is Dhryn then follows the Taste."

Mac sighed. Somewhere, she was convinced, buried in the mythic, convoluted language, there had to be a greater truth than she was hearing, some clue. "Vessel, I—"

She was interrupted by Nik, as he rose to his feet. "We need to talk. Now." He stood, looking down at her.

"I'm going to consult with my companion," Mac told the Dhryn as she stood, too. "Don't react to what we say to one another. It is important."

"As you wish, *Lamisah*."

Nik led her a few steps from the Dhryn, but didn't leave the cell, as she'd expected. "What's going on, Mac?" he demanded in a low, urgent voice.

"We're a little stuck on aspects that seemed to be fixed in Dhryn myth. I'm getting stuck," Mac corrected. "Maybe you can help me—"

"Forget that. What did he say about weapons, deployments, their ships?"

"The Vessel?" Flustered, Mac blurted: "He doesn't know things like that. I'm trying to find out what's controlling the Dhryn. Where they go. Why—"

"You didn't ask, did you?" Nik didn't let her finish, a new edge to every word. "Mac, that information's crucial. There are worlds filled with beings needing help now. All the rest—the whys, the past—we don't have time for your curiosity!" He took a deep breath, as if tamping down his temper. "From now on, I want you to translate for me. Word for word. Nothing more."

It hurt, seeing his anger, knowing she was the cause.

Couldn't be allowed to matter, Em.

"I can't do that," Mac told him levelly. "You aren't asking the right questions."

His eyes, now stone-cold, flicked up to the vidbots and down again. *As if she'd forget their audience.* "You study salmon, Dr. Connor. I'd like to hear how that makes you an expert in the gathering of strategic information."

"What strategic information?" she fumed, losing her own temper. "The Dhryn are being led around the universe like a hungry bear following a bait bucket. What would you ask the bear, Nik? How long his claws are? How sharp his teeth? His ultimate intentions toward fish heads?"

Mac watched as it hit him, gave the tiniest possible nod as Nik's eyes widened, felt a dizzying wave of relief when he didn't say it out loud, as he realized the consequences if the Ro could somehow hear. *He sees the real question,* she thought triumphantly.

Who's carrying the bait?

Then his eyes narrowed again. "It doesn't matter what theories you're investigating. We need that information. Either you ask what I want you to, now, or we'll find another way." From his grim expression, she knew exactly what he meant. *He'd tell others the Vessel understood Instella.*

"You can't!" Mac gasped. "Not now. I'm close. I know I am."

"Close to what? You can't make decisions for the IU, Mac." Trying another tactic, Nik put his hands on her shoulders, bent to look into her eyes. Quietly: "There'll be time later for your questions, Mac. Please."

Unfortunately, it wasn't a tactic all understood.

A bellow rattled the metal stool. "Release my *lamisah!*" The Dhryn rushed toward them, his head lowered in threat, three hands rising as if to reach for Nik.

Everything happened so fast Mac was never sure of the order. Nik shoved her aside, but she managed to twist from that force, using its momentum to half fall toward the angry alien. Nik was shouting something she didn't hear—likely frustrated and directed at her—but Mac was intent on only one thing.

Sure enough, the Dhryn coughed.

She slapped her hand over his mouth and pressed it there as hard as she could, shouting herself.

"Stop, *Lamisah!* He wasn't hurting me!"

The sideways figure-eight pupils of the Dhryn dilated, as if to encompass her so close. His three hands had automatically grabbed to stop her from colliding with him. She winced at their tight hold—*there'd be bruises*—but didn't release her own. She said more calmly: "It's okay, Vessel."

She could feel his muscles ease. The convulsive retch already underway subsided. Still, enough acid spurted between the Dhryn's lips to dissolve most of the pseudoskin from the palm of her hand. *So much for stirring acid,* Mac thought inanely. She was careful not to touch any of it with clothing or flesh as she let go and backed away.

"Careful!" Mac admonished as an equally powerful Human hand took hold of her and pulled. *More bruises,* she thought fatalistically. She held her acid-coated fingers as far from Nik as she could. Drips hit the carpet, sending up smoky plumes. "It would help," she snapped, as he released her, "if you both calmed down." For the benefit of watchers, she repeated it in the *oomling* tongue.

Almost casually, Nik dropped something from his palm into his pocket. His face was pale and set; a muscle jumped along his jaw. *He'd been about to kill the Vessel,* she realized numbly. *To save her.*

"Don't get close." His warning to Mac; he should have listened. She could see the bleak awareness in his eyes, the shame of letting his emotions make a choice. They both knew the Dhryn had to live, even if it killed her before his eyes.

He wouldn't make the same mistake again. She saw that, too, and acknowledged it with a half smile.

"*Lami-sah . . .*" The alien's voice was weak. Mac turned even as he stumbled. Nik reached out to support him before he fell. The Dhryn flinched, but couldn't avoid him, letting the Human guide him to a sitting posture.

"Nik meant no harm to me, Vessel. None to you. Please. Don't worry." Mac used her real hand to stroke the Vessel's forehead, feeling the shivers coursing through his body. A body, she realized, that had been through a great deal, especially for a Dhryn as old as Parymn must have been. She looked at Nik; "He needs rest."

Their eyes met over the Dhryn's blood-slicked back. "So do you," Nik agreed. "And to clean up that hand. I'll give you both as much as I can. Half an hour, hopefully more."

"'A Dhryn is robust, or a Dhryn is not,'" she quoted, giving Nik a nod of agreement.

But, as she listened to the Vessel's labored breathing, Mac hoped she was wrong.

- Encounter -

That which is Dhryn accepts the Great Journey.
    That which is Dhryn must *move*. It is the Way.
The path changes more often now. It is the Way as well.
As before, the Call is heard. Irresistible . . . dominant . . . *urgent*.
That which is Dhryn must obey.
It is survival.

18

MEETING AND MAYHEM

"**I** TOLD YOU to run, *Lamisah*. Why did you stay?" Kindly. As though fond. Those had been the words.

She'd answer, but her mouth was sealed.

She'd run, but her limbs were wrapped in a net. Mac struggled, feeling the bonds around her tightening, feeling them *burn*. Tears ran down her cheeks, tears of helpless rage.

"You never learn, do you, Mac?" *Emily*. "Trust. Friendship. Coin of the realm, dear girl. Nothing more. Survival's what counts."

Hard to breathe. Mac lunged out with her bound feet, trying to find a target.

"Getting late, Mac. You really should run. It's the only choice you have."

Light, sudden, blinding, from everywhere at once. Reflecting from the hard silver of tiny ships. Thousands upon thousands.

Mac fought for freedom even as the rain began to fall, even as her feet dissolved, her legs, her . . .

"I told you to run, *Lamisah*."

Jerking awake, Mac rested her forehead against the back of the Sinzi shower, letting the water from three jets pound her shoulder blades, letting the steam and roar keep the universe at bay for a few minutes more.

She hadn't meant to fall asleep.

Even less to dream.

Mac turned, letting the water hit her face. The Dhryn's blood and acid was gone; the nightmare wouldn't wash away. *Something she knew full well.*

"Time to get back, Em," she said, licking drops from her lips as she hit the control to start the dryer. "Wonder what time it is." Late, for sure.

Nik and Sing-li had brought her here, back to the Atrium. A swift, dizzying ride up three steps on a platform, a choice of rooms to suit any body plan. Staff, of course, ready to offer her whatever she might need. A jelly-chair, a table with sandwiches, juice. This shower. *She wasn't the only one who worked late down here,* Mac thought. She'd spend some time huddled over her workscreen, trying to catch up while the Dhryn rested, listening to notes from her team. When she'd begun to feel sleepy, she'd stopped trying to pull sense from fragments of disparate information, and went for a shower to wake up.

That hadn't worked.

Dry, she pulled on her clothes. The staff had performed their discreet magic again. There'd been blood on the beautiful jacket, acid damage to a sleeve, but while she'd showered, it had been replaced by another, this time red. What mattered was her imp was in its pocket. Mac dropped into the chair, pushing still-damp curls from her forehead, and checked for messages.

Nothing new. "I've been cut off, have I?" she muttered, closing her 'screen and pocketing the device. "We'll see about that—in the morning."

One more minute. Mac leaned her head back, careful to keep her eyes open and fixed on the ceiling, breathing slow and steady through her nostrils.

Not surprisingly, given her past experience with such things, that was when a quiet knock sounded on the door, followed by the door cracking open. "Mac?"

Sing-li. Doubtless looming outside since she'd arrived. "She's not here," she told him.

"You dressed?" he asked, coming in anyway. He'd changed into full armor, but left his visor open.

It let her see his face, now set in sober lines, so she swallowed what she'd intended to say. She sat up. "What is it?"

"The Sinzi-ra wants your report—now."

"Here?" Mac lifted her eyebrows.

"No. There's a meeting of the Admin council for the Gathering underway. The major players. She wants you to report to all of them."

"I hate meetings," Mac informed him. *Especially when she didn't know what to say.*

Sing-li's teeth flashed in a quick smile. "I remember. But I can't see you skipping out of this one, Mac. We'd better hurry. They're waiting for you."

"I'm sure they are."

"Oh, Mac? Nik sent you this." Sing-li held out a long supple glove. Mac took it with a nod, pulling it over the now-exposed workings of her left hand and wrist.

As gestures went, she thought with an inward smile, *it wasn't bad.*

Her guide led the way. Rather than a platform, he took her via three lifts to the level with the door they'd used, then through that door to the corridor. Once there, Mac hesitated outside the Dhryn's room. "I should check on—things."

Sing-li shook his head. "He's asleep—or unconscious. Nik said to tell you you'll be notified."

Answering the question of whether her companion was kept fully briefed, Mac told herself.

They took the door to the next corridor where two guards, neither Human, now stood watch on either side of the entrance to the tank room. Mac restrained a shudder as she passed it, moving closer to Sing-li. They turned right with the corridor.

Another series of plain doors. The place was a maze of featureless white. *Or was it?* "Just a minute," Mac said, stopping. "I want to try something." She reached into her bag and took out her imp.

"Mac, you don't want to be late. There's no time for this."

"There's always time for a quick experiment, Sing-li," she assured him absently, setting up her 'screen to show a chromatic display of the walls in front of them. With a slide of her fingers, Mac removed the filtering from the display.

Silvery ghosts, representing ultraviolet reflections, appeared over the normal image. The white walls were aglow with symbols and images. Portraits, schematics, a few rather nice landscapes. And each door in sight had a label. Not Instella, but definitely a script. "Thought so," Mac exclaimed with satisfaction. This was only an approximation. *One thing for sure.* The world of the Sinzi and her staff was neither plain nor white.

Sing-li stepped into the area she was imaging. His initials glowed on his chest and Mac nodded her understanding. "I take it the Sinzi-ra doesn't like faceless strangers."

"Bad as you, Mac," he agreed, grinning. "As for the walls? You could have asked for a look." He tapped his visor meaningfully with a finger.

Mac put away her imp. "I prefer to experiment," she informed him. "Which one?" She waved at the doors.

It was the third. Sing-li opened it for her, but remained outside as she stepped through, taking his post.

"Greetings, Mac," from Anchen, rising from her seat at the head of a long, well-populated table.

There was always, Mac thought glumly, *a long, well-populated table.*

The Sinzi's fingers indicated the position opposite her, at the far end. There was a second empty seat, halfway up one side. *Neutral turf.* Mac eyed it longingly, but obediently took her place at center stage.

She'd like a moment to take notes on who sat where. Hard enough to keep twenty-five Humans straight, let alone assorted sapients. Her eyes went to Nik, at Anchen's left. He gave her a comforting look. *One ally.* He faced the N'Not'k, Genny P'tool. Mac spared an instant to wonder if she'd try footsies with him under the table. *Probably not. The ambience was pretty far into stress range.* Bernd Hollans sat midway down the right side, facing the empty seat. An Imrya, likely the one who'd accompanied Anchen to Parymn's cell, was at his side, taking notes already. No other Humans, not that Mac expected more. Two beings in full environment suits. She'd love a closer look, but they were near Nik.

Cinder sat to Mac's left. *Perhaps another ally. Perhaps a complication.* Mac gave her a nod and received one in return.

The rest were strangers. She had to assume they represented the innermost circle of the Interspecies Union. Those who had set up this Gathering.

Those would decide the fate of the Dhryn.

She was so out of her depth, she might as well be in the Sinzi's tank, Mac thought despairingly.

The room itself was square, with four doors set opposite the ends of the table. No ornament visible to Mac's eyes. No other furnishings. The lack drew her eyes back to that last, empty seat.

Mac glanced at Nik. He'd followed her look and now gave an almost imperceptible shrug. *Didn't know either.*

"Are you ready to give us your latest report on the Dhryn, Mac?"

For once, Mac would have preferred "Dr. Connor," which at least sounded reputable. "Yes, Sinzi-ra."

Anchen gestured to the empty seat. "Our remaining participant will join us shortly. Implementation of the Myrokynay's instructions is going very well at last. I'm sure none of us wish to delay it."

Nods, a few grunts, and one of the suited figures pounded the table with a heavy fist. Mac hoped she'd remember how each indicated agreement. Not that she expected much to what she had to say.

"Mac?"

Automatically, she stood up again, resting her fingertips on the table. Real and artificial. The table felt the same to both. Mac pondered the significance of that as she collected herself. "Parymn Ne Sa Las is dead," she said. No one moved or spoke, waiting for her to clarify. This wasn't a group who startled easily. *Good.* "His personality has been replaced."

"By whose?" Anchen prompted, her head tilted to one side as if one of her minds was more keenly interested than the others. Noad the physician, Mac guessed.

Time to make her first choice, Mac told herself. If there were Ro hiding in this room, listening to what was said, dare she risk the truth? But would Nik contradict her if she lied? Had he already given his report? *She hated thinking like a spy even more than meetings.* "His personality has been superseded by another's, called the Vessel. The Vessel is a messenger from a Progenitor, in this case, the one I met on Haven. In practical terms, he is the Progenitor, as She was before Parymn Ne Sa Las Marsu accepted his—fate."

Even the IU's representatives had to mutter among themselves about this. Mac gave them a moment, glancing at Nik for his reaction. Nothing showed beyond the glint of his lenses.

"Continue," Anchen said, silencing the rest. "What does this 'biological message' say?"

"The Progenitor—this particular Progenitor—took damage to her ship during the Ro assault on Haven. She's in hiding. The Vessel doesn't know where—"

"As if it would tell us!"

Mac looked at who'd interrupted. "Dhryn has no word for lie, Mr. Hollans. The Vessel's sole function is to communicate as accurately and completely as possible. That information wasn't supplied for obvious reasons." She looked to the rest. "The Progenitor has a question for us, for the Interspecies Union. She wants to know what's happening to her species."

Someone on the left. "She doesn't know?"

Another moment of choice. Mac licked her lips and nodded to herself. "She knows they have begun what she calls the 'Great Journey.' As far as I could determine, this journey is something cyclic, a shared compulsion, but it hasn't occurred in living memory. The Dhryn weren't expecting it—they hadn't prepared. She doesn't know why they've embarked on it now, only that they have."

A shiver of gold-clad fingers. "Where are they going?"

"Home." Mac held up her hand to stop any questions. "Which doesn't help, I realize. I don't know where the Dhryn 'home' is, if it isn't their world of origin. The Vessel doesn't appear to have that information—maybe the Progenitor Herself doesn't know. However, my team has uncovered evidence supporting an hypothesis that the Dhryn might have been a migratory species. This Great Journey could be just that. In which case—"

"Migration, is it?" a low bass rumble from an alien to Mac's right. "We have beasts who migrate on our planet. They respect no boundary, no law. You cannot train them to avoid farmland. We build fences to protect our crops. When those do not work, we are forced to destroy any herd that trespasses."

Another delegate: "We could dismantle the transects, lock the Dhryn into one system. Trap them."

"Sacrificing the life in that system!" bellowed another. "Whose will you pick? Mine?"

Worse than Preds scrapping over pizza. Mac rapped on the table with her gloved knuckles. The strange sound got their attention. "I wasn't finished," she told them.

"Please continue, Mac." Anchen's eyes took in all those at the table. "There will be no more outbursts."

"If the Dhryn's Great Journey is impelled by a migratory drive," Mac proposed, "it is an adaptation that has helped them survive on a planet, one planet. There, they had a destination—a 'Home'—where they could take advantage of drastic changes in their environment. None of that applies to a space-faring civilization. There's no reason to believe the Dhryn have a real destination anymore, that there is a 'Home' for them to seek.

"If they are responding to an innate drive," she continued, "it may simply compel them to keep moving and moving until their ships fail or they run out of supplies. No matter which happens first, the Dhryn will starve and die." Mac paused. When no one offered comment, she continued: "As that will likely be after they've consumed as many worlds of the IU as they can reach, the Dhryn migration must be stopped as quickly as possible."

"By killing them all!"

"How?" Nik spoke for the first time, face impassive but his voice rising above the muttering. "We don't know where they are, let alone where they are going.

If I understand what you're saying, Mac, they could begin picking targets at random. How will we find them then?"

"The Dhryn didn't expect this," Mac reminded them. Another choice that wasn't. *She had to try.* "The Progenitor wants to know why it is happening. Migratory behavior is stimulated to begin by certain cues. And ends. If something outside the Dhryn started them moving—provided that Call—maybe something outside the Dhryn can stop them."

"The assault on their world set them off—that's what started it," offered Hollans. "What we need to do is reach the Myrokynay. They can find the Dhryn—end this."

Another chorus of agreement—from all but Nik, who was watching her.

Brymn hadn't been ready to transform. But he had. *He had.*

The Ro had lied.

Had they done more than that?

"We don't know if that was the stimulus," Mac countered, feeling sweat trickling down her shirt. "After all, there were Dhryn attacks, perhaps by scouts, before the assault on Haven. We need to look more closely."

"The Myrokynay will stop the Dhryn. You have their word."

That voice!

With a wordless cry, Mac was in motion before her eyes fully comprehended what they saw, rushing toward the tall, slim, *familiar* figure standing in the now open doorway behind the N'not'k. She was only dimly aware of Nik surging to his feet, of the excited rumble of voices . . . *None of it mattered.*

"Emily!"

But the face which turned in answer was the image from the Ro message: cheeks sunken, eyes like dark pits, skin cracked and shadowed. Her hair hung limp and dull with filth. Her body? A skeleton, barely filling its mockery of clothing. And the clothing? Torn and ragged, its rents going deeper than fabric, revealing tears in her flesh that held nothing but space and wheeling stars.

Mac didn't hesitate, arms out to gather in her friend.

But the face turned away.

The body walked to the final empty seat at the table, sitting as if nothing and no one else existed.

"The Myrokynay will be gratified you have completed the signaling device," Emily stated in that clear, dead voice. "They will respond to your messages through that medium, and through myself."

She couldn't breathe.

Anchen made a graceful gesture. "It was only with your assistance that we were successful, Dr. Mamani. You have our gratitude."

As if from a great distance, Mac heard her own voice, strange and broken. "Emily—Em? It's me. It's Mac."

Hollans said something; she couldn't hear it, didn't know if it was impatient or kind. Someone, it was Nik, took her arm, gently but firmly, and led her from the room.

Once outside, Mac came to her senses. She whirled and tried to go back. Nik stopped her. "Not now, Mac. Please," he pleaded.

Sing-li hovered. "What's wrong?"

"It's Emily! Didn't you see her?" Mac demanded, struggling wildly against Nik's grip. She freed one hand and struck at his face. He caught the blow, holding her wrist. "She needs a doctor—help me, Sing-li!"

"Nik?" Sing-li was frowning. "What's all this? Dr. Mamani?"

Mac threw her weight back, tried to break free. Nik held on. "Stop it, Mac. Stop! Gods, will you let it go a minute? I don't want to hurt you."

The desperate tone penetrated, when the words meant nothing. Mac shuddered and stood still. "It was Emily."

"I know. I saw. Something's terribly wrong with her. We'll get help—but we can't interrupt them. We can't force her. She's still connected to the Ro, to nospace. Do you understand me, Mac? We have to wait."

Mac stared up at Nik, eyes swimming with tears. "She didn't know me."

He gathered her in his arms like something inexpressibly fragile. "We'll get Emily back," he promised, lips against her hair. "She's alive, Mac. She's here. On Earth. It's a start."

"They've taken too much of her," Mac whispered.

Nik heard. "Let the medical team worry about that." He lifted her chin so Mac had to look at him. "You study salmon, remember?"

"Do I?"

"That's the rumor." Ignoring an interested Sing-li, Nik bent and kissed her on the mouth, once, very soundly. Mac's eyes widened until she felt like an owl. "Go to your quarters, Mac," he said gently.

It was all Mac could do not to look at that door, knowing who was behind it. "I'm in the IU now, not a citizen of Sol, of Earth. You told me I can't—I can't ask for help. But, Nik, I—"

He didn't let her finish. "You don't need to ask. I'll keep an eye on our Dr. Mamani and find out what I can." A flash of something dangerous in his eyes. "Including why her return was kept from the Ministry until now. I don't like surprises, especially from allies." Nik paused. "But, Mac, I'm asking you a favor in return. Please. Go."

She gave in. "You be careful."

"I will. Sing-li?"

"I've got her."

Feeling remarkably like an unwanted parcel—which was infinitely better than feeling like an unwanted friend—Mac let Sing-li escort her to the lift.

"No."

Mac narrowed her eyes. "'No,' as in you think you can stop me?"

"'No,' as in you aren't going anywhere without me."

She made an exasperated sound. "You can stand by the door. You like that."

Sing-li looked anything but willing to negotiate. He tapped his weapon. "No."

"Fine." Mac knocked on Mudge's door. "But he's not going to like having you wake him up, too."

"I'll take my chances, Mac."

The left hand door to Mudge's quarters opened a crack. Mac waved at a bleary eyeball.

"Norcoast? What—?" Mudge opened the door the rest of the way. He wore, Mac noted, managing not to smile, one of the Sinzi's elegant nightgowns.

"May we come in?" she asked.

"We?" Mudge glared at the Ministry guard. "Certainly not. It's three a.m!"

Ignoring his protest, Mac started walking inside. "I know. Hence the chaperon," she told him. "The Sinzi-ra doesn't approve of fraternization."

Blushing furiously, Mudge moved out of the way. Mac and Sing-li followed. "At least let me put something on," their host muttered, hurrying to the other room as fast as he could move through the sand. To his closet, to be exact, closing the door behind him.

Mac studied the place, curious. Sure enough, the room was the mirror-image of hers, right to its impossible table of fish. She noted the arrangement of anemone and corals—same view as hers as well. Feeling slightly foolish, she went to the washroom and grabbed the wrap and extra nightgown she expected would be there. *Not going to explain,* she vowed, aware of Sing-li's rapt attention as she used the garments to cover the table.

But his attention wasn't concerning her compulsion to redecorate. "So, Mac. How long have you and Nik been—?"

Mac's look dared him to continue. Sing-li wisely resumed his task of silent looming. *Something,* she realized, *being in black armor allowed a large Human to do rather well.*

Nik had wanted her back in her room. Mac herself wanted nothing more than her jelly-bed and some time to think—or blissful oblivion. But there wasn't time.

Besides, why should Mudge sleep when she was still awake?

"Now," Mudge blustered, "what's so important it can't wait till dawn at least?" As he said this walking out of a closet, it was less impressive than he'd likely hoped.

"Sit down, Oversight." Mac did the same, but perched close to the edge of the jelly-chair. If she sank into it, she'd likely spend what was left of the night here. "I wanted to be the one to tell you. Emily Mamani's back. She's here, at the consulate."

Mudge knew her face a little too well. "Something's wrong with her."

"Yes. She's been altered by the Ro again. Much more. Physically. Maybe mentally. I don't know the extent of it. She's—" Mac looked up and said in a shaky voice: "—I don't think she's Emily anymore, Oversight."

He harrumphed. Twice. Then: "She's been living with something stranger than any of us can imagine. Give her time to remember herself, her friends."

"That's the rub. There isn't time." Mac waved Sing-li to the other seat. He obeyed, lifting off his helmet. "Oversight, this is Sing-li Jones, from Base. Sing-li, who can hear us right now?" she asked him.

Sing-li raised an eyebrow, but didn't bother with denials. He pulled out his imp. "The transmitter on Mr. Mudge feeds directly to this—nowhere else. Unless something warrants an immediate report, I bundle the recordings and send them to main for analysis and file when I go off shift."

Before Oversight could do more than turn red and begin to sputter, Mac nodded. "Good. Stop recording, on my authority."

Sing-li didn't hesitate. He stood and went to Mudge, who twisted around in alarm. "Oh, hold still," Mac told him.

"This might sting a bit, sir." Sing-li peeled a fingernail-sized patch of what had seemed skin from the back of Mudge's neck. "There."

The look on Mudge's face promised an abundance of pithy memos, once the situation permitted such ordinary means of retribution.

Mac resisted the temptation to feel her own neck. "Do I have one?"

"Not to my knowledge. You're aware of the bioamplifier in your tissues." Mac nodded. "It's concentrated enough of your DNA signature to let us pinpoint your location with reasonable accuracy." Sing-li paused thoughtfully. "Unless you're in a null gravity field."

"Not planning on it," Mac assured him, waving him back to his seat. Then she leaned forward to put her elbows on her knees, studying both men. "I've reached certain conclusions about our situation here," she said. "If I'm wrong? At worst, I'll be sent home as a nuisance. If I'm right?" She pressed her lips together then continued. "If I'm right, and we do nothing about it, the next blow to strike the IU will fall here, at this Gathering, at Earth. And soon."

Sing-li tensed. "So that's why Nik wants me to stick like glue. In that case, you're the logical first target, Mac. We should get you out of here." He started to rise.

"Relax." She gave him a faint smile. "I appreciate your concern and his, Sing-li, but I'm not what's important. It's what I know and what I suspect. I have things to tell you both. I won't risk being the only one who knows outside the Sinzi-ra's inner circle. I can't, for all our sakes."

The two men exchanged grim looks. They understood what she was asking. "Get to it, Norcoast," Mudge grumbled.

"First. There's a Dhryn in the basement of this building, sent by the Progenitor I met on Haven to talk to me."

"About what?" asked Mudge.

"What's happened to their species. They don't understand any more than we do. Oh, there's no doubt the Dhryn are attacking planets. That they're a horrific threat to other living things. But what's the advantage to the Dhryn? I haven't found one—not to the Dhryn. Which made me ask my own question. Are the

Dhryn the hands or—" Mac indicated the weapon strapped to Sing-li's leg, "—the tools in someone else's hands?"

"You can't be serious," Mudge said, eyes wide. "An entire sentient species?"

Sing-li's lips thinned. "You think the Dhryn are being used as a weapon."

"I think they were made to be one. I think they've been used before, to annihilate the civilizations in the Chasm, then put away in a bottle until needed again."

"By the Ro?"

"By the Ro," Mac nodded. "And who shows up when we finally have our own source of information about the Dhryn? The Ro's puppet: Emily Mamani. Just like she did before, when Brymn came to us." She gave a short, bitter laugh. "You'd think I'd have figured it out sooner, having had practice."

"Guesswork, Norcoast," Mudge pointed out. "Even if you had hard evidence—which you don't, I might add—your feelings about the Ro are no secret. Who here will believe you? They're doing everything they can to welcome the Ro, not defend against them." He brought out his own imp. "I've gone over the messages and daily summaries. Teams are working feverishly on new weapons—mining the transect gates was thankfully abandoned. Dhryn detectors; predictions of where they'll attack next; three groups working on the Dhryn acids and how to create shields—none going well, by the way. Four others preparing defensive simulations. Ten spending their time on evacuation logistics and worst case scenarios—most productive of the lot, if you ask me. And a significant investment in Ro psychology—most of their work," he sighed, "makes the ravings of your ghoul chasers sound sane."

"The Origins Team, Oversight," Mac told him. "We're close. I can feel it. Unensela has findings about the vegetation and ecology that may prove a Dhryn migratory pattern. Others have discovered evidence of outside tampering with Dhryn technological development. All we need is the missing piece—what, if anything, happened to the Dhryn themselves, their physiology." Mac's enthusiasm faded. "And time. Emily helped get the Ro signaling device up and running ahead of schedule. It's on right now, begging for their help with the Dhryn." She paused to rub her eyes with the back of one hand, then was startled by the feel of glove instead of skin. "Believe me, I'd give anything to be wrong. I keep hoping I am. But the Dhryn—everything I know tells me they couldn't have come to exist on their own. And if that's true? The rest makes too much sense to dare ignore."

"What do you want us to do?" This from Sing-li.

Mac looked to Mudge. "You have the room assignments for the members of the team, right?" He nodded. "Wake everyone up. Start with Lyle Kanaci—he can help with the rest. We have work to do."

A familiar scowl. "And where will you be?"

"I'll join you as soon as I can," Mac promised. "We'll wake up Fourteen on the way—I want to talk to him first." She turned to Sing-li. "We should—"

"I don't think so," interrupted Mudge, giving the larger, younger man a disdainful look. "You need protection. I should go with you."

Snooping was one thing; risking himself was another. "You're a fearsome administrator, Oversight," she said gratefully but firmly. "Unusually deft with a paddle, I'll grant you. But I'd better stick with the professional with the large weapon, don't you think?"

He harrumphed. "A P917-multiphasic pulse pistol—pardon, P915, I'd thought it was the newer model—is no substitute for experience."

Sing-li raised his eyebrow again, but didn't say anything; Mac, less tactful, grinned. "Experience?" *He had to be kidding.*

Mudge put on outraged dignity the way anyone else put on a coat. "Experience with you, Norcoast. And your propensity for dashing off on a whim to find trouble."

"I do not—" Mac reconsidered. "I don't try to find trouble," she temporized.

"Don't worry, Mr. Mudge," Sing-li reassured him. "I lived with her at Base for six months. We all know the signs."

Mac's head snapped around. "What signs? Signs of wh—" She stopped, startled.

What was that?

Mac held up her hand for silence, listening, her mouth dry. *There.* She lunged forward and swept the covering from the table.

Clear water and fish exploded into a writhing mass of sediments and broken coral, as whatever had been closest to the glass fled into the depths.

Sing-li had surged to his feet with her and now stood, his pistol drawn and ready, although somewhat nonplussed to be aiming it at a piece of furniture. Mudge, who'd managed to jump right over his jelly-chair, peered over the top of its dubious shelter. "What—what was that?" he gasped.

Heart still hammering in her ears, Mac said fiercely: "That, my dear Oversight, is what happens when guesswork meets evidence. The Ro." *Were they aquatic?* she caught herself wondering for the first time. *Did they rejoice in the seawater tank, or was the liquid inimical to them? Did they prefer the same mixture of gases she breathed?*

What could you breathe in no-space?

You know, Emily, Mac thought grimly. She'd like to believe her friend would answer questions. *She'd also like to be standing beside the Tannu River right now.*

The probability of either was the same.

"There are tables like this everywhere," began Sing-li, worry creasing his forehead. "Can the Ro exit into rooms through them?"

Staring at the table, Mac resisted the impulse to duck behind her own chair. "Let's not wait and find out. Can you reach Nik, discreetly, without using the consulate's system?"

"Who's Nik? Mudge demanded. Mac silenced him with a look.

"Sure." Sing-li pulled out something like an imp. "What do you want me to tell him?"

"Have him meet us in the Origins Room as soon as he can." She looked from Mudge to Sing-li. "Let's move, gentlemen."

At this hour, the residential corridors of the IU consulate were deserted, lights dimmed to night levels, everyone asleep or at least quiet. Mac was reminded of the times Emily had talked her into staying out late, late enough they'd have to sneak back into the Pods to avoid waking other researchers. Of course, then, the consequence of discovery had been a continuation of festivities till dawn in someone's quarters, with Mac doing her best to excuse herself and Emily all for it.

Tonight, she was with Sing-li, who managed to turn walking into something ominous and silent. Tonight, Emily was the one person Mac didn't want to encounter, hard as that was to admit.

Tonight, dawn wasn't a sure thing.

Technically, Fourteen's quarters were the floor above hers, but the Sinzi's ramplike corridor wound its way from level to level steeply here, making it faster to walk than take the lift. Mac found herself moving quicker as well, stretching her strides to match Sing-li's longer legs, almost breaking into a run.

Running out of time, she fussed to herself and hoped Fourteen wasn't a sound sleeper.

"Here," Sing-li said quietly, stopping in front of the next set of double doors. "We shouldn't wake the neighbors."

"Wait a moment." Mac leaned her head against the door. "He snores," she explained. "Loudly." *Nothing.* She reached for the door handle. The consulate didn't lock doors, presumably to allow staff discreet access at any time. *Or to encourage clandestine activity?* Mac thought inanely. Who knew what went on after-hours here?

A large hand got to the handle first and the Ministry agent gave her a gentle nudge to one side with his shoulder. "My job," he informed her.

"Go ahead," she agreed, but stayed close by.

Sing-li opened the door. No lights, as expected. "Fourteen?" Mac called out as they stepped inside.

Nothing.

"Something's wrong," her companion said abruptly. At that instant Mac realized her feet weren't walking on sand, but through jelly. "Stay back."

Sing-li hit the lights.

The room before them was in ruins. The Sinzi's jelly furnishings, both bed and chair, were slashed apart, their contents—*light blue,* Mac observed numbly—staining the sand. Glistening trails of slime crisscrossed everywhere she looked: walls, ceiling, and floor. Where the slime touched sand, that material was already hardening into a crust.

"Fourteen!" Mac shouted, bolting for the other room.

Sing-li made a grab for her but missed. "Mac! Wait!" He pounded after her through the arch, cursing under his breath, only catching up when she staggered to a stop before a pile of ripped clothing.

"It isn't—him," she managed to say. *No body.* Just the pile beside the table, the only intact furnishing left in the Myg's quarters. Sing-li, weapon drawn, quickly checked the closet and washroom, then came back to her, shaking his head. "The terrace," she whispered, and he went into the other room, coming back a moment later.

"Clear," he told her. "No evidence of a struggle—no blood."

"That doesn't mean they didn't take him," she ground out. Just then, something about the pile of clothing caught Mac's eye. It seemed different, somehow.

"Sing-li," she hissed as she bent and teased the top layer free, wincing at the cold stickiness of slime on her fingers. Most of the material was Fourteen's fine leather, ripped to ribbons, every edge jagged as if the damage had been caused by serrated knives.

Or teeth.

The pile beneath *shifted*. Just a bit, but enough to make Mac drop to her knees and pull more urgently at the mass. Sing-li, muttering various dark things under his breath, loomed at her shoulder, weapon ready.

The last lump of slime-coated leather came free in her hands, as much because what was beneath was digging itself out of the sand as Mac's tugging. A faint muffled *coo,* then two limpid eyes stared up at her, blinking grains from their eyelashes.

A baby Myg? "Come here," Mac urged gently, carefully helping the tiny creature from its hiding place. "Shhhh. It's okay."

With a pounce that would have done a cat proud—or an aroused male Trisulian—the baby attached itself to the front of her jacket, doing its utmost to shiver its way through the warm skin of Mac's throat. She cradled it there with one hand as she got to her feet.

"I've a pretty good idea where Fourteen might be," Mac announced. "Let's go."

"We have to report this." At the shake of her head, he protested: "Mac!"

"Raising an alarm—likely too late, I might add—will only stop us from getting to the Origins Room. I have to get there, Sing-li. I have to work with my team." Mac looked at the too-familiar damage. "Ro don't tend to stick around."

He wasn't happy, but didn't argue.

They made their way to Unensela's quarters, Sing-li having contacted Mudge for the location within the building. He'd signed off the com link to frown worriedly at Mac. "Mr. Mudge says there was no answer from her room either. Do you think the Ro—?"

Mac, busy trying to convince a certain small and persistent Myg that a Human female was physically incapable of offering it a snack, merely grunted: "Doubt it." Unensela's quarters were on the uppermost residential floor. This time, they took the lift, Sing-li stepping out first to sweep the corridor with a glance. After a long second, he waved at her to follow. Mac didn't argue, too busy listening. She knew the sounds of the Ro, heard their *scurry . . . spit pop!* in her dreams.

"Clear," he said, then frowned. "What's that noise?"

"That noise" being a series of loud squeals that incited the Myg baby to squirm up to Mac's shoulder, chattering with excitement, Mac didn't feel particularly worried. "I think we've found out why Unensela isn't answering her com," she said.

A knock on the door did no better—the squealing having grown too loud anyway. The two Humans exchanged glances. "I don't know if we should just walk in, Mac."

"The Ro?" she reminded him.

"Good point." He pushed open the door . . .

. . . giving Mac perfect line of sight on a pair of madly vibrating paisley shorts, an unexpected alignment of body parts, and a wildly squealing female Myg who, upon spotting new arrivals, freed an arm to wave them inside with every appearance of sincerity.

Clandestine meetings indeed. At least his grandsires would be pleased.

As for that smell . . .

"Let's give them a moment," Mac suggested, stepping back into the corridor. Sing-li didn't argue with that either.

Fourteen had exchanged his formal wig for his Little Misty Lake General Store hat, jauntily dipped over one ear. Mac was fascinated to see that his forked tongue, white until now, was engorged and distinctly pink. *No external genitalia indeed,* she speculated.

A happy Myg. Or he would have been, if it hadn't been for her news. "Whaddyou mean, dey've sdarded sending da signal?" The tongue was causing him problems.

"Idiot," this from Unensela, who seemed unaffected by anything other than containing the offspring who kept trying to jump to Mac. *She didn't blame it.* Neither adult Myg had evinced concern about the child having narrowly escaped the Ro; after his initial trauma at missing the successful signal, Fourteen had worried more about his clothes.

Probably why he'd so glibly offered her his firstborn, had he had one, Mac recalled, struggling with this variation on parental behavior. "I suppose now you'll want to celebrate," Unensela continued. She leaned confidingly toward Mac, necessitating another grab at the offspring. "I was consoling him on his failure," she explained. "Males. Any excuse."

Sing-li made a choked noise; Mac didn't bother turning around. "Could we focus on the problem at hand, please?" she asked both Mygs. "And walk a little faster?"

Fourteen put a protective arm around his partner, avoiding the offspring climbing on her shoulders. "Of course she can't," he claimed, both expression and tone highly smug. "Not yet."

Unensela squealed; Sing-li smothered another laugh.

Was she the only one intent on saving the planet? Mac began to wonder about their collective sanity.

When they reached the lifts, she drew Fourteen aside, scowling at his somewhat theatrical sigh at leaving Unensela's side. "I need you to do something for me, Fourteen," she told him, keeping her voice low. *Not that she knew the auditory acuity of a Myg,* she realized belatedly.

Abruptly serious, his tiny eyes riveted on her. "You haf my allegiance, Mac. You know dat."

And she was about to test it—severely. Mac bit her lower lip, then took him by the arm and walked him a few more steps away from where the others waited. Probably an unnecessary caution. The offspring, having discovered Sing-li's armor made interesting noises, were keeping both Human and their mother preoccupied. *But she'd rather not share this.*

"I want you in the signal room in the Atrium—yes, I know what's in the basement," she said at his attempt to look surprised. "Where do you think I've been?" Mac firmed her voice. "They're monitoring for a response from the Ro. I need to know when they get it, Fourteen. What it says. This isn't something the Sinzi-ra would approve," she warned.

"I will be your eyes and ears, Mac," he promised, puffing out his chest. "If anything happens, I'll send a message to your imp. I can do it so none are the wiser, even our omniscient host." The tongue only tripped him on "omniscient," the word coming out more like "ombliffivy," but Mac understood.

She gave a grateful nod, trusting he could read the gesture. "There's one other thing, Fourteen. This won't be as easy to hide. I want you to find a way to disrupt the outgoing signal—to do it if I say so, without question."

His chest collapsed in a quiet moan and the Myg put his hands over his eyes. She grabbed his wrists and pulled his arms down again, quickly but gently, hoping Unensela hadn't noticed the despairing gesture. *The smell she couldn't help.* "The Ro are to save us, Mac," he protested, unhappy but quiet in her hold. "This is not an act of *strobis.* I cannot."

"And if they are not saviors, Fourteen? What then? They've been spying inside the consulate. Who knows what they intended to do with you!"

"Idiot. I'm the only one genius enough to make progress with their code. They could have been trying to communicate with me."

Save her from wishful academics, regardless of species. "For that same reason, Fourteen, they could have wanted you dead." She held his eyes with hers. "Just go there, please. Keep an eye on things. Keep me informed. And, for all our sakes, have a plan in mind. I've a feeling whatever choice you have to make will be clear—I only hope you have time to make it."

Fourteen nodded, then reached out and tapped her nose. "And I hope to embarrass you about this for many years to come, Mac."

So did she, Mac thought, watching the lift doors close behind Fourteen.

So did she.

Night elsewhere, but on the main floor the illumination was daylight normal. Knowing the ways of researchers, Mac had assumed they wouldn't be the only ones awake in the dead of morning. She'd counted on it, in fact.

Sure enough, each of the six consular staff they encountered was towing a cart of coffee and pastries, including one outside the Origins Room. "Good evening, Dr. Connor," he said without a blink. "We noticed activity in your room and anticipated your group would also require refreshments. Was this correct?"

"Perfect," she said a little too warmly. *Should pacify the ones who don't wake well,* she thought, following the staff through the door. Sing-li, on her signal, came with her.

A series of high-pitched squeals announced them as they entered. Unensela's offspring left her, bounding across the floor to intercept the cart, only the staff's quick move to lift the tray beyond their reach saving the pastries. *Just as well,* Mac thought. The female Myg hadn't been pleased to see Fourteen sent on a mission of his own—although it seemed her pique was more because she didn't have a secret mission, than any worry about risk to him. *Implying,* decided Mac, *a certain lack of personal commitment in more Myg relationships than parenting.*

Mudge hurried up, relief on his face. "Everyone's here, Norcoast."

Except Nik, she thought, having swept the crowd with a look, but didn't say it aloud. "Good work."

"Where's Fourteen?"

"He's busy elsewhere—"

"What's going on?" Like most here, Lyle hadn't wasted time to do more than throw on clothes. His sparse hair stood on end and his eyes were bloodshot.

Mac pitched her voice to his ears only. "We're going to prove the value of your work once and for all. Or look like blithering idiots. Game?"

His lips stretched in a bitter grin. "Game."

"Give us a moment first. Sing-li?"

He followed Mac to a quiet part of the room, not that there were many options. When they stopped, he gave her a troubled look. "Mac, I have to raise the alarm."

"I know. One last thing before you do." She put her hand on his armor-coated chest, irrelevantly noticing tiny Myg prints marring its gleam. "I want the rest of you here."

He took a look around the room, then frowned at her. "This room isn't defensible, Mac, if that's what you're thinking. Those windows? The door's a joke. And who knows what the Sinzi buried in the walls? Specs have this place capable of morphing into a fortress—from the outside, at least."

She shook her head impatiently through all of it. "I want them here—you, too—in case Nik needs you."

"For what?" Low and worried. "Mac, what are you planning now?"

"See the signs, do you?" she said, trying to keep it light.

"Mac." A growl.

"Nik might have to retrieve our guest from the basement. Fast."

That earned a grim look. "You might be sent home if you're wrong, Mac. Nik—the rest of us—we won't be that lucky. Not if we disobey the Sinzi-ra and the Ministry. That's treason."

What had Nik said? "I'll spend us both—"

If I have to, Em, Mac told herself, cold and calm, *I'll spend them all.*

"Let's hope it doesn't come to that," Mac said aloud.

"Let's." Sing-li pressed his lips together for a moment, then gave a curt nod. "No offense, Mac, but we're not the kind of assets you're used to—can't risk being penned in here, for starters. Leave it with me."

Gladly, Mac thought, feeling one of the knots in her spine ease. "Whatever you think best, Sing-li."

"Trust me, you don't want to know what I think." But he smiled. "Anything else?"

"The door may be a joke, but can you make sure we aren't interrupted?" His anticipatory grin matched Lyle's. "Good."

Leaving Sing-li to contact the others—*and make whatever plans such people made for treasonous activities*—Mac headed into the middle of the room. She grabbed the nearest stool and climbed up on it, finding her balance.

"Good morning, everyone!" she called out.

The answering chorus was ragged, spiced with some complaints about her time sense, though less than she'd expected. The faces Mac could read looked understandably tired and puzzled. "In this room," she told them, her voice clear and calm, "are two very important things. You. Experts on understanding the past. And your data. Everything collected to date about life on the planet that spawned the Dhryn.

"We can't answer every question we have tonight. But we must answer one," she said. "One I believe you'll find worth losing a little sleep over."

"It better be!" someone called from a back row. Sing-li, a dark presence now blocking the only door, gave the speaker a menacing look. There was a ripple of uneasiness as the rest noticed.

"You tell me," Mac challenged. "Here's my question. Were the Dhryn—their biology, their technology—deliberately modified into a weapon by the My-rokynay, the Ro?"

Only the patter of baby Myg feet broke the ensuing silence. Even the consular staff, who'd been preoccupied dispensing coffee to those nearest, stopped to stare at her, his hands in midair.

Mac raised her eyebrows. "We don't have much time. Tonight, this Gathering began transmitting the Ro's contact signal. I, for one, would like to know who we're inviting to the party—before we throw open the door."

"You heard the lady," Lyle said into the stunned hush. "Let's get to it."

19

HYPOTHESES AND HORRORS

MAC COULD FEEL it along her nerves. She walked quietly from group to group, listening, absorbing, not saying a word. The focus was there; the drive had taken hold. *If she tried to stop them now,* she thought with satisfaction, *they'd ignore her.*

Even the meditation chamber was humming. *Literally.* Mac stopped beside the gray curtain, but could tell nothing about what was happening on the other side beyond some nice harmonics.

If her route tended to circle back most often to where Unensela and the climatologists pored over data, no one noticed that either.

Mac shifted two Myg offspring to her shoulders, balancing a third on one hip. *Almost no one,* she sighed, taking the trio with her. She went to stare out the window, seeing the patio where the Gathering met each morning. No sign of dawn, but there were glows out now, as yellow-clad staff moved over rain-wet tiles to set up tents between the trees. A little morning drizzle wasn't going to stop the Sinzi-ra's efforts to coax the Ro.

And beneath it all, the Atrium, where a signal was even now being sent.

Mac's shudder made the Mygs grab where they shouldn't and she snarled in protest. "I'm not a horse," she muttered, heading back to their mother.

Not that she knew for a fact Unensela was the biological mother of the pack. Caretaker, at least, although absentminded.

Before Mac reached the climatologists, Lyle intercepted her. "I think we have something," he said, jerking his head back to the circle of tables and consoles they'd dubbed "the view" for no reason anyone had explained to her.

Before joining him, Mac glanced at the door. Sing-li's shrug was the same as his last dozen. *No word from Nik.* He'd sent his report about the Ro; nothing, as far as Mac could tell, had resulted. No klaxons or alarms, no rush of searchers through the room. She supposed she should be grateful not to be disturbed.

It felt more like a serious threat was being ignored.

Carrying her passengers, Mac joined Lyle, nodding a greeting to Therin and his compatriots. "What is it? Sorry, one minute." She restrained the little Myg who'd spotted the Sthlynii's oral tentacles, giving the nearest Human, Kirby, a pleading look. Once he'd pried the annoyed offspring from her shoulder, Mac continued: "Lyle says you have something for me."

"You are standing on it."

Mac backed out of the empty circle of floor. Therin gestured to another Human, who lifted a pair of image extrapolation wands. Like Mudge, she knew the name of the devices, if not how they were used.

Seemed she was about to find out.

Without warning, the floor and the space above it filled with an image of dust and ruins, so perfect Mac felt as though she could put her hands into it. The archaeologist did just that, only reaching with the wands instead of hands as Therin spoke. Each time, it modified what was being displayed. "We've gone through our surveys and those from the IU team still on the planet. This is the largest Dhryn building either group has found." Dust disappeared and the building was restored before Mac's eyes. She walked around it. Perfect on all sides. The walls had that characteristic nonperpendicular slope so dear to the Dhryn. Its walls were coated with mosaics. "Note the size." A Human figure, a duplicate of Mac herself, walked into the image to stand beside the building.

Mac frowned at her doppelganger. "I'm too big."

"No, Mac," Lyle said, a note of excitement in his voice. "The building's too small."

Therin concurred. "We haven't found a single structure large enough to contain one of the Progenitors. Including underground," he added, anticipating Mac's question.

"That's—" As Mac walked around the image, her little echo doing the same until she glared at the operator. "Tents? Could they have lived in the open?"

"I don't see how," said one of the others. "The climate was harsh before the vegetation was stripped from it. And you said the Dhryn offspring were born from a Progenitor's skin—that sounds vulnerable. You'd want protection."

"He said there were ships waiting for them," Mac whispered.

"Pardon? What ships? Who said?"

She blinked up at Lyle. "The Haven Dhryn," she covered quickly. "One talked about how the great ships were buried and ready for them when they arrived. Could the Progenitors have lived on similar ships, orbiting the planet?"

"They did not have these ships. They could not make them." Da'a, the other Cey, heaved a deep breath, sending a quiver through his hanging folds of skin. "I do not say the Dhryn are stupid. But we have no evidence from this world that they were space-faring at all. There are none of the precursors of such technology."

"You could say the same for most of the technology in this room," Mac pointed out. "Imports, with no history of development on Earth."

The archaeologists smiled and exchanged looks at this. Lyle gave a grim laugh. "You can see the pattern of evolution in living things, Mac. Trust us to know what to look for in what a culture can and cannot do. The Dhryn might have wound up in space. Someone else put them there."

"Before the Progenitors needed larger buildings." Mac frowned. "How sure can we be that the Dhryn are from this world?"

A voice from behind. Unensela, without offspring. "Idiot. The fossil record's solid. I've a progression of eight-limbed, primarily colonial animal forms stretching back to preflowering plants. DNA to match. The Dhryn started here, all right. Come and see what we have."

"Weeee're nooooot done, botanist." The Sthlynii's diction slipped momentarily.

Mac hid a smile and focused on Therin. "What else?"

The building image was replaced by a satellite view of the Dhryn home world. A few strokes of the wand pushed back time, until buildings sprang from ruins. Mac leaned closer and the image obligingly zoomed in. She fought vertigo as she inspected something that seemed unlikely. *Then again, she didn't want to be called a biologist,* Mac grinned to herself. "Did they have powered flight?"

"You noticed." From the triumphant look Lyle gave Therin and the others, Mac presumed there'd been a bet placed. She didn't bother reacting.

"No roads," she obliged.

"And no sign of flying machines either."

"The feeder form?"

"Irrelevant," Unensela snapped. "The prevailing winds would have blown them halfway around the continent. Only in there—" she stabbed her hand and arm into the image, distorting it and getting a protest from the operators, "—would they be able to float about without assistance."

"In there" was a series of deep rifts, running roughly north/south. They were immense and, in this presentation, filled with lush vegetation.

"Fantastic, aren't they?"

"They are more than that." Unensela made a rude noise. Mac prepared herself in case a smell was to follow. "The forest growth on this world was as cyclic as the climate. Seeds for the dominant species, large and filled with nutrients, were produced underground and stayed there, safe from extremes and foragers. The surface growth, even of trees, would die to the soil in each hemisphere in turn, starting at the pole, then germinate and regrow when conditions improved again. Food would have ebbed and flowed like a tide that took centuries to pass any one place." She disrupted the image again, jabbing at the rifts. "These—they would have been like roadways to anything following that tide. Your feeder Dhryn could use them."

Mac noticed a heated discussion underway to one side of the group. She caught the eye of one of the participants and gestured her closer. It was the gray-haired woman, Mirabelle Sangrea. "What is it, Mirabelle?" she asked.

"We've been mapping the Dhryn—well, you can't call them cities, Mac, not like you'd see on most IU worlds—we've started calling them havens." She smiled at Mac's raised eyebrow. "It seemed right. They built clusters of buildings, like beads, but, as you noted, unconnected. Therin? Could we display Sim 231 for Mac, please?"

The Sthlynii blew out his tentacles, but complied.

The view was again of the planetscape, but now dotted. Mac didn't need the Myg's triumphant "Hah!" to see how lines of dots, each representing a haven, paralleled a rift. Not every line of dots did so. Some were on their own. *But the overall pattern?* "Were these all inhabited at the same time?" she asked.

Mirabelle's smile widened. "There's evidence of sequential abandonment, then reuse."

"As if the Dhryn population moved down from one pole, going from haven to haven, then back again," Mac said.

"Yes. Well, until they stopped doing so—not long before the rest of the Chasm worlds were stripped bare of life. We're working on that interval. It definitely overlaps the time when the Dhryn abandoned ceramics."

Mac met Lyle's eyes, then looked around at the rest. They'd attracted another crowd, not everyone by any means, but a solid ring had formed, stood shoulder to shoulder in order to see. All appeared equally disturbed.

Da'a spoke first. "I see a piece missing, Mac."

"Only one?" Mac couldn't help but murmur. She nodded for him to continue.

"If the Ro took the Dhryn and modified them, produced these gigantic Progenitors as breeding machines, why doesn't Myriam—the Dhryn planet—show some early sign of it?"

"Because the entire planet was a trust," Mudge said loudly, pushing his way through to stand by Mac. "Protecting the diversity of the source material."

Mac grinned. "I knew I brought you for a reason, Oversight." Her grin faded as she studied the strange world now slowly turning in front of them all, showing its seasons. "That had to be what the Ro did. Until they had new Dhryn, the species exactly as they wanted—modifications tested, sure to reproduce in kind—they'd want the real thing healthy and close at hand. But once they were satisfied—any living members of the original genetic stock would be a threat, a potential for reversion. They'd have to be destroyed."

"None of this absolves the Dhryn of guilt."

Lyle. Mac understood the pain in his face. *No time,* she told herself. "Right now the issue is the signal going out to those who may have modified the Dhryn into a menace. My next question, folks. Was it the Ro or not? You have," she made a point of looking at the windows, "until they answer."

With that, Mac turned and walked away. It was that, or scream at all of them to hurry, to forget another coffee, stop chatting with friends. *Not reassuring behavior in a team leader.*

Automatically, she glanced at Sing-li, only to see him heads together with Nik, here at last, both men deep in conversation. Mac changed direction to join them, but she wasn't as quick as Mudge, whose glad shout of "Stefan!" was enough to turn several heads.

There were times, Mac growled to herself.

Fortunately for Mudge's continued existence, Nik was more than capable of dealing with distraction. After a brief handshake and a quiet word—accompanied by the pair of them looking at *her*—Mudge nodded and walked away.

He did, however, pause beside Mac long enough to say: "At least Human authorities are taking us seriously, Norcoast. Stefan wants to talk to you."

She muttered something under her breath.

"Pardon?"

"Nothing, Oversight."

Nik smiled as she approached. A smile for others that did nothing to warm his eyes. "Is it my imagination, Dr. Connor," he said cheerfully, "or are these the same people we spent the last months keeping away from your doorstep?"

She collected herself, reading the message. *Keep it calm; keep it normal.* "Pretty much," she said as lightly. "But I don't think you needed to try very hard. They're better at hunting the past than the present."

"Let's hope so. You certainly have them working late—or is that early?"

Her ability to stay calm and act normal was, Mac realized, *severely limited at this hour.* "We need to talk," she said bluntly.

Nik said: "No argument there." Then he looked past her and that carefree smile reappeared. "Is that—? I don't believe it—that's Wilson Kudla, isn't it? Author of 'Chasm Ghouls—They Exist and Speak to Me.' I'm such a fan."

Mac and Sing-li were left standing dumbfounded as Mr. Spy, Nik Trojanowski, dashed to where the sweaty author and his trio of equally perspiring supplicants were emerging from their curtained-off alcove.

She didn't, Mac decided, *want to know what they'd been doing.*

Or, for that matter, what Nik was doing.

Sing-li coughed once. "You're supposed to go with him, Mac."

"I am?"

"Trust me."

Fuming at the waste of time, Mac stormed up beside Nik just as he was greeting the Great Man himself. *The slight stammer while asking for an autograph was,* Mac decided, *a particularly nice touch.* Kudla, despite being one of the most nondescript Humans she'd ever met, was virtually preening.

"And, may I, could I?" Nik touched the curtain with one visibly trembling hand. "I've never had success before—but where you've been meditating? It must work!"

"Of course," the Great Man intoned. "May the Ghouls speak to you as well." *His smug look in her direction,* Mac told herself, returning that look with a scowl, *said more than the specters ever would.*

"You'll want to see this," Nik promised Mac as the ghoul hunters walked off—hopefully to shower. Ignoring her protest, he took her real hand and pulled her with him through the curtain.

The alcove was little more than a tent, its fabric opaque and—Mac sneezed—a bit dusty. Small lights, designed to look like candles, ringed the junction between ceiling and walls. Mac did her best not to step on anything. It wasn't easy, given the number of small ornate gongs lined up in rows around what was, without doubt, a very well-used mattress.

Not a place she wanted to stay. Mac turned to protest "What's—" but Nik's mouth smothered the rest, the unexpected kiss making her completely forget whatever she'd planned to say anyway.

Before she could decide whether or not to lose herself in it, his finger replaced his lips against hers. "Shhh." His eyes were hidden behind the reflections on his lenses.

Satisfied she understood, Nik climbed on the mattress and, shaking out the small telescoping wand he drew from a pocket, used it to sweep the space around them, poking into every corner, even along the ceiling. "Clear," he pronounced an instant later.

Of Ro. Lo-tech. Effective.

She wanted to hug him. Instead: "Is anyone else checking?" Mac asked, her arms wrapped tightly around her middle.

"I'm told the consular staff is aware of the situation." Low, with some frustration. "What that means, I don't know. The Sinzi have defenses within the building but . . . no one was hurt and the Ro certainly aren't the first aliens to trash a room here." A shake of his head. "I came as soon as I could, Mac."

"I know."

He ran his fingers down her arm to the glove, giving the fingers a gentle tug. "You okay? You haven't had any sleep, have you?"

"Better than you," Mac asserted. "I grabbed a nap." *It wasn't a lie.*

"We can't stay in here long," he said, hand dropping to his side. His nose wrinkled. "Just as well. Sing-li brought me up to speed. Now, Dr. Connor." A note of familiar exasperation. "Why aren't you sleeping? Why aren't all these people sleeping? Why is that Myg in the signal room instead of sleeping? And—"

Mac raised one eyebrow. "And?"

"What the hell are you doing giving orders to my people?"

"Hopefully making a fool of myself."

"Well, you've got company," he said, shaking his head. "Remind me not to station anyone on Base again. The place corrupts."

She couldn't smile. "Nik, we've found evidence the Dhryn were taken into space, that their present state isn't their natural one—implying they were modified. My team's now hunting anything that ties in the Ro. When we find that—"

"If."

"When," she countered defiantly. "It's them, Nik."

He lowered his head a moment, then looked up at her over his glasses. His eyes might have been chipped from ice. "You can't be wrong on this, Mac."

"I'm not."

"You know what's at stake."

Mac looked at him, but saw a raindrop pausing on a leaf, the surge of salmon against a current, the curious tilt of a duck's head. Heard the cry of an eagle hidden in cloud. Felt the silky coolness of a slug resting in her hand. *And that was just Field Station Six*. A mere speck on this world. This world a mere speck among the uncounted number like it.

"Everything is at stake," she said, her voice hard and sure. "That's why I won't let the Ro get away with this. Please, Nik. Come and see the evidence we have. Decide for yourself."

"I did," Nik snorted. "Come now, Mac. Surely you didn't believe Sing-li could redeploy the Ministry's assets within the consulate on his own? You had to know it would be my name on those orders—my head on the block." His grin took on that dangerous edge, dimple showing. "Though you were late. I'd moved them into position around the Dhryn and launch pad an hour before."

"Then why—" Mac flung her hand at their surroundings.

"Call it one chance for you to pull the plug. To tell me it had been a mistake; the Ro were going to save us after all; that you and I should head back to your cabin. It needs some work, you know. The cabin."

The last almost made her smile.

Almost.

"Were you similarly ahead in dealing with the signal?"

His lower lip went between his teeth for a second. "That's trickier. Anchen, Hollans, the rest? They're hovering around the consoles, to be there when the Ro answer back. Hardly a group to take kindly to our request they turn it off. What's Fourteen up to?"

"He's to let me know if there is a response. I don't imagine I'll be informed otherwise. And—if I ask him, he'll try to stop the signal going out, somehow."

"Somehow." Nik filled the word with doubt.

Mac blushed. "Neither of us are spies. I know that. But it was the best I could do. I couldn't very well call and ask you. No one else would listen."

"Don't count on that. The Sinzi-ra, Hollans? They heard my concerns—our concerns. Emily Mamani's arrival, her appearance, shook them badly. They aren't sure about the Ro, not anymore."

"Not sure as in stopping the signal?"

"Not sure as in waiting to see what comes of it."

Mac shook her head. "Risky."

"Present situation to the contrary, they aren't fools, Mac."

"Comforting." She found a smile. "We'd better get out of here before anyone starts to notice. Especially—" she added with a wince, "Sing-li."

"One more thing, Mac." He hesitated.

No need to guess what drew down the sides of his mouth like that. "Emily."

"I wasn't able to talk to her. She's—it's as if she's detached from those around her, paying attention only to certain words, certain tasks. The Sinzi-ra has promised every assistance. But until we know more of Emily's state—"

"I'm aware of the priorities!" Mac interrupted, her voice sharper than she'd intended. She closed her eyes, sighed once, then opened them again. More gently.

"Thank you, Nik. As you said. She's here. She's alive. That's infinitely better than yesterday."

He nodded, but Mac understood the pity in his eyes.

They left the tent, its closed-in warmth making Mac feel as sweaty as any ghoul seeker. The air of the open room felt like a reprieve. Nik, as usual, appeared able to wear a suit and remain immaculate under any circumstances.

From the activity everywhere, no one had paid attention to their sojourn communing with the departed. *Well, almost no one.* Sing-li, obviously waiting for them to emerge, gestured impatiently for Nik to join him. He looked upset.

That couldn't be good.

"I'll be right back," Nik told her, heading toward the door with long strides. "Check on your people."

Mac took only her first steps across the room before: "Mac? A moment?" She nodded automatically and turned toward the voice, only to have all six Myg offspring hurtle up her jacket, at least one finding its way inside the collar. "What the— Unensela!"

Then Mac paused, feeling how the tiny things were quivering. Putting a protective hand over as many as she could, she looked around for what had frightened them. Her heart hammered in her chest. Everything seemed as before, normal, busy. People moving in all directions or leaning over equipment. It wasn't enough to reassure her.

Not the Ro.

Please not the Ro.

It wasn't, Mac realized as Unensela came hurrying up to her, prying loose her now-hysterical little ones with a running commentary about the inconvenient unavailability of a certain male Myg and whose fault was that she'd like to point out.

It was Emily.

Where she stood opened like an eddy within a river: researchers gave her space, moving past with sidelong looks of dismay, none willing to risk curiosity.

"Hello, Em," Mac heard herself say, as if this was a normal day at the lab, and they were meeting over coffee.

The eyes. They were the worst. Flat, dull, the whites so bloodshot they made Mac's own eyes burn in sympathy.

Emily hadn't come alone. Two consular staff flanked her to either side, discreetly behind. They met Mac's inquiring look with that impassive, attentive expression. Watchers.

Not the only ones. They had Nik and Sing-li's attention as well—explaining Sing-li's urgent summons. Nik caught her eye.

Mac shook her head, very slightly.

"Need some help?" The words were Emily-normal; the voice anything but. It could have been a recording. *And what would Emily say to you, Mac? What sequence of syllables would make you believe she still existed within that frame?*

Play along, Mac thought, sick to her soul. "Always. You could help me with the—" *not near the Mygs,* "—cartographers. That group there."

The body turned in the direction Mac indicated, graceless yet with coordination and strength. *Not starved—emaciated from something else,* she judged, giving a frantic hand signal to Mirabelle as they headed her way. *How did you warn someone about your best friend?* Emily's bizarre appearance would likely do it for her.

Her being here, now, couldn't be coincidence, Mac decided.

It could be opportunity. *How much of you is left, Emily?*

"Welcome to the Origins Team, Em," Mac began. Her voice sounded strained even to her and she coughed to clear it. *She could do this. She* had *to do this.* "We're working on where the Dhryn came from—had some breakthroughs already this—morning." *The word was appropriate,* Mac told herself, even if dawn was still some hours away. "I think you'll be impressed by our findings."

Emily might have been a walking plague, the way silence spread ahead of their little procession and murmuring followed it. Mac scowled at everyone in general, to no avail, then her eyes found Mudge. She beckoned him with a curt nod.

He came, eyes filled with the horror Mac felt. "Dr. M-Mamani," he managed. "Good of you to join us."

"This is Oversight—Charles Mudge III—Emily. I'm sure you remember all my stories about him." Mac shot Mudge a warning look.

He gave a miserable excuse for an offended *harrumph,* but gamely offered his hand. *No lack of guts,* Mac thought gratefully.

Forced to stop walking or run over him, Emily looked down at his hand for a few seconds, then turned to stare at Mac.

She was frowning.

No, not frowning, Mac thought with sudden hope. She knew that thoughtful crease between Em's dark eyebrows, had seen it every time the other scientist focused on a problem. "What is it, Em?" she asked gently.

"Where is this place?"

Hadn't anyone told her? Mac felt a rush of sympathy. "On Earth," she offered. "You're home."

"Earth isn't safe." The crease eased away. "It will be, when the Myrokynay are made welcome."

Over my dead body, Mac said, but kept her expression as close to neutral as she could.

"Perhaps you could help us understand the Ro better, Em," she suggested, changing her mind about the cartography. "We've questions."

"Always glad to be of help, Mac." Cold. By rote.

Mac felt the sting of tears in her eyes and fought them back. "Great. Let's get a spot out of everyone's way, shall we? Oversight? Will you get Lyle and—Stefan—to join us please?"

She started walking, too abruptly, and bumped into one of Emily's shadows. The collision was startling enough, given how adept the consular staff were at avoiding contact, but even more was the feel of a small object being thrust into her hand. Mac didn't look down, she just pushed the thing into her pocket.

No telling what it was. From the feel, a cold metal cylinder of some kind. Perhaps the Sinzi-ra had sent her a message. Some kind of imp. *If it was a weapon*—Mac jerked her hand from her pocket. *New rule,* she told herself. *Don't fondle unknown alien objects.*

A moment later, the four of them sat at one end of the conference table, the staff standing their precise distance behind Emily. The rest of the room's inhabitants were too carefully uninterested. Unensela's offspring, now mute, had taken refuge under her lab coat. *Excellent survival response,* Mac thought. She avoided thinking against what.

Nik showed no expression beyond polite attention, although Mac had learned the signs. He wasn't pleased—whether because Emily was here at all, or because Mac was preparing to discuss their work with her, she couldn't tell.

So long as he was there. He'd warn her if the discussion went in dangerous directions. He'd act, along with Sing-li, and hopefully the two staff, if Emily herself became the threat.

Then why, Mac thought, dry-mouthed as she looked into her friend's eyes, *did she feel alone?*

"What are your questions about the Myrokynay?"

Lyle leaned forward eagerly. Mac presumed Mudge had given him some idea who Emily was, though she'd no idea what. *An expert on the Ro? Their spy?* "Do they live on planets now?" he demanded.

"This is—" Mac began.

"Dr. Lyle Emerson Kanaci," Emily interrupted. "Administrator for Chasm Studies Site 157, financed by Sencor Research Group, a company owned by a consortium of Sthlynii, Cey, and Human corporate and governmental interests."

Nik raised a brow at Mac. Lyle flushed in blotches of pink, but didn't deny any of it. "What about his question, Emily?" Mac prompted. "Are there Ro worlds?"

Emily's immaculately manicured hands, even in the field, had been a source of bewilderment to Mac, who couldn't keep a nail intact in her office, let alone on a granite ledge. Now, the fingers crawling restlessly over the tabletop, back and forth, were dirty, with split, fractured nails at their ends. "The Myrokynay moved beyond the limitations of a planetary biosphere before the Sinzi knew what one was."

"Harding was convinced they hadn't originated in the Hift System. Too young for one thing," the archaeologist muttered, as if to himself. Louder, "If they have no planets to risk, why do they fear the Dhryn?"

"The Myrokynay fear nothing." The fingers were drumming now, distracting all of them. "They wish to help those of us at risk."

"Did they help the Trisulians?" Mac asked. Nik shot her a look of caution she ignored. "Emily?"

The fingers stopped. "Where is this place?" An air of confusion.

"Home," Mac told her, wishing her voice wouldn't shake. "You're home, with me, Emily. The Trisulians. They had your instructions on how to signal the Ro. Did they use them? Did the Ro—the Myrokynay—come?"

"You read my message, Mac." Emily's smile exposed yellowed teeth and swollen gums. "I told the Myrokynay you would. You're stubborn that way."

"The Trisulians. Did they send the signal?"

Emily's gaze wandered to the ceiling, to the far wall where Sing-li stood watch, brooding and focused on them, to the alcove, to the windows.

Mac half stood. "Emily?"

"Mac," Nik said quietly.

Okay, new subject. Sinking back into her chair, Mac made herself take a couple of breaths. "Emily." The dead eyes shifted back to her. "You told me the Myrokynay had been watching for the Dhryn to reappear since the destruction of the Chasm. Once the Ro found Haven, they took some of the immature Dhryn from their Progenitors—you said it was to test them. For what, Emily?"

"For signs the Dhryn were producing another migratory generation. Your own work uncovered this. I told them you were clever."

"The *oomlings* who were taken," Mac pressed. "What happened to them?"

The fingers started to crawl again. "Where is this place?"

Oh, Em. Mac hardened her heart, rejected pity. "They underwent metamorphosis into the feeder form, didn't they, Emily? Even though they weren't supposed to—like Brymn! The Ro can somehow induce that change, can't they?"

"Where—is this place?"

Mac couldn't stop. *She didn't dare.* "Then the Ro took them to different worlds and set them loose. That's how they aim the Dhryn, isn't it? By taking advantage of their instinct to seek more of the tastes returned by scouts. They returned those feeders to Haven, so they'd give those tastes to the Progenitors. Bait."

Emily's body rose from the table as if tugged by competing strings, arms and legs out of proper sequence. The rest stood as well, everyone but Nik focused on Emily. Mac met his eyes, seeing the warning there. *Careful,* he all but said aloud. *Don't lose her.*

The signal was being sent. *There wasn't time for care.*

She'd spend them all if she had to. "Emily," Mac urged, going around the table to where her friend stood, eyes wide and staring. "You used to think for yourself. Please. Listen to me."

Emily hesitated. Something almost sane looked out at Mac. "Mac?"

"Yes. It's me."

A shudder. Every rip in Emily's clothing glowed for an instant, as if the space held within her flesh had tried to accommodate a sun. "Mac," more sure. Her hand wrapped itself around Mac's wrist, fingers strong as they were cold.

"That's right, Emily," Mac whispered, her voice husky. "I'm Mac, your friend. We need your help. I need it. We have proof—"

"I found you," Emily said as if she hadn't spoken. Her grip tightened until Mac couldn't help but wince. "I'm to bring you. Now."

It seemed fitting that Nik's shouted "Mac!" coincided perfectly with the universe turning itself inside out.

- Encounter -

"WE HAVE INCOMING ships, sir," the transect technician reported, calmly, professionally. Only someone standing close by could have seen her hands tremble. "Sending to your station."

"Got it." One look at the display and her supervisor smacked his hand on the emergency com control.

"To all of Sol System. This is Venus Orbital," he announced. "We've incoming Dhryn. Two ships through—three— My God, how many are there?"

The technician assumed she should answer. "Fifteen Progenitor ships have now arrived through the Naralax, sir. There are more coming behind." She turned to look at him. "Should I keep count, sir?"

He shook his head, reaching for the control again. "This is Venus Orbital. If you're going to do something . . . do it now."

- 20 -

DANGER AND DISMAY

T IME SAT on a shelf.
        Rolled off.

Dropped her on a hard surface, in the dark.

No, not dark. Light splintered over impossible shapes. She closed her eyes but couldn't escape it.

Not alone. Words. The sound was elongated, wrong. She tried to cover her ears, but couldn't find them.

"Here is Mac."

The disorientation, the pain, were all too familiar sensations. *No-space.*

Mac opened her eyes slowly. It didn't help. She turned her head and retched helplessly.

"The Myrokynay will be here soon, Mac."

Emily.

Explaining the how and the why, but not the where. Mac wiped her mouth and squinted at her surroundings.

A sand shark looked back at her, then curved its sinuous body in a disdainful arc to swim away.

Mac blinked and found herself staring at the scuffed toe of a boot, a once-expensive hand-tooled black leather boot. She rose on her elbow and looked up the leg. "This is the tank room," she said, unutterably relieved to be still within the consulate.

Where Nik could find her. Would *find her.*

"The Sinzi have been clever." Emily flattened her hand against the wall separating them from the night-lit water and its life. "It is disconcerting for the Myrokynay to perceive our world directly from theirs. They had to rely on allies such as myself to be observers. This novel interface?" She drew her fingers along the surface in a caress. "It permits the Myrokynay to witness our doings with new clarity, to be heard."

"So they're in the tank."

Emily started, as if she'd forgotten Mac was there. "In here? No more than they are in any one place," she said. "Only Tactiles ever limit themselves to our dimensions."

"'Tactiles,'" Mac repeated, managing to sit. *Sitting was enough for now,* she assured her unhappy stomach. "Are Tactiles a kind of Ro?"

The illumination was dim, a mottled glow reflected by the coral within the tank itself. It played tricks with the dark floor and walls, hid the ceiling. Still, by it Mac thought she saw a flash of fear cross Emily's face. If so, it was the first true emotion she'd seen.

Which didn't bode well.

"They are tools," Emily said at last.

"Like the Dhryn?"

"The Dhryn are the enemy of all. They will destroy life until none is left. They must be stopped."

Mac ignored what sounded like a mantra, concentrating on getting to her feet. *There.* Wobbly, but better by the minute. "Short trip," she commented. "Does it get easier with practice?"

"What?"

"Moving through no-space."

Emily's hand fell from the tank. "I cannot move," she said. "I cannot feel. I cannot breathe. I cannot move. I cannot feel. I can—"

Shuddering, Mac broke in: "It's all right, Emily. You're going to be all right."

"Where is this place?" Plaintive, in a small voice.

Mac eased back. The door was behind her. *With guards behind that.* She estimated her chances. Emily was taller, had always been faster. But her body had to be paying a price for the abuse it had suffered, the gaps in her flesh a terrible stress on her system.

As if guessing Mac's intention, Emily took three quick steps, but not to block Mac from the door. Instead, she went to a curl of pipe, hand reaching into the shadows. "You must not leave," she said calmly, pulling out the hidden weapon to aim it at Mac's stomach.

So much for physical advantage. Cinder's weapon. With their "new clarity," the Ro must have watched Mac hide it.

At the thought, Mac turned, careful to make it slow and easy, until she could see the tank.

"Why do they want me here?" she asked.

"You wish to stop the signal. You are an enemy of life."

Mac gave a harsh laugh. "Me? An enemy of life? You can't believe that, Emily Mamani. I don't care what they've stuffed into your head; you know that isn't true."

"You are Dhryn."

"Nonsense. Two arms," Mac held out her arms, dropping them again as the weapon rose in threat. "Two arms, five fingers, call an insect-eating primate ancestor. Human, Emily. Human like you." *Like you used to be,* she added to herself.

~~DHRYN ACCEPT YOU~~

~~DHYRN YOU ARE~~

Every word tore into Mac's skin, the sensation so real and agonizing she cried out even as she looked down at her body, expecting to see blood, even as she touched herself, unable to understand the pain.

Somehow, she raised her head, stared into the tank.

Illusion. It had to be.

The water, the coral, the fish—they couldn't have been replaced by this confusion of appendages and swollen dark mass, this shifting *emptiness* filled with disks that burned like stars, winking in and out of this reality with a distortion that threatened sanity.

Mac threw her arm in front of her face, looked frantically for Emily.

Emily had lowered the weapon, eyes on the tank, the lines of her face softened as if she gazed upon a lover.

~~YOU WILL NOT INTERFERE WITH US~~

Mac gasped and fought to stay on her feet. "Too late!" she shouted in fury. "We know about you! We'll stop you!"

~~YOU KNOW NOTHING~~

~~YOU ARE NOTHING~~

~~YOU WILL BE REMOVED~~

The words. *The pain was more than she could bear.* Mac felt herself drop to her knees, threw out her hands to save herself from falling flat.

"Why—why bring me here, then?" she forced herself to say. "What do you want from me?" When no answer dug its unseen claws into her flesh, Mac lifted her head to glare at the seething void that marked the Ro, her eyes weeping with the strain. "We can stop you. That's it, isn't it? I've learned about you. No one else has before. Well, get used to it," she shouted defiantly. "We'll find out the rest. You'll be nothing!"

~~YOU ARE HERE SO WE MAY WITNESS~~

Mac tried to cover her ears. It made no difference—the words came through her flesh, not the air.

~~YOUR ENDING~~

Agony!

~~WE SUMMON YOUR DOOM~~

Emily had fallen to the floor as well. Mac tried to crawl to her.

~~WE ARE WHAT WILL LIVE~~

"NO!" Mac surged up to her feet. Desperate for a weapon, a rock, anything, she snatched the Sinzi cylinder from her pocket. But as she raised it, it extended itself into a gleaming rod. A rod she'd seen used before.

A gift from Anchen, who'd believed her enough for this . . .

"No!" she screamed again, thrusting the rod at the tank. As before, it went through the wall as if nothing was in the way. Mac immediately threw herself back, holding on to the rod with all her strength. *Pulling something with it.*

She hadn't snared a shrimp; she'd hooked a whale.

A furious one.

Mac's hands couldn't hold it. She let go, fell in slow motion, saw the rod disappear into the tank.

Then, for an instant, everything *stopped.* Eternity ticktocked its way through her heart. She saw . . . she saw . . .

. . . reality snap back into focus. Mac had barely time before the wall gave way to grab Emily, hold her close as they were both swept by a torrent of now-dead fish and warm sea.

"Mac? Mac!"

"Mummph!" Mac spat out a mouthful of seawater. *Hopefully free of Ro bits,* she thought, spitting again in case. "Over here!"

The lights coming her way—their way, for she still held Emily—were flashing. Mac put up a hand to protect her sore eyes, then realized it wasn't just the hand lights. The door to the corridor was open, explaining why the floodwater had receded so quickly around her. But the light from that source was pulsating rhythmically. *An alarm?* About time. "What's going on?"

Nik, suit jacket replaced by an armored vest he hadn't bothered to fasten, splashed to her side. "I could ask you the same. Later. C'mon. We're under attack."

Mac flinched. "The Ro?"

"No." He helped her to her feet as someone else helped Emily. "The Dhryn. They're through the gate. They're coming here!"

"The Ro—"

"I told you—" Nik began, half carrying her toward the door.

"Listen to me!" she begged even as she found her feet and hurried with him. "The Ro are calling the Dhryn. That's what the damned signal's for, Nik! We have to shut it down. Now. It's calling them!"

He didn't hesitate. "Confine her," he snapped to the man carrying the unconscious Emily. "With the Dhryn—it's the only Ro-proof room I'm sure about. Let's go," to Mac.

They stepped over the flaccid body of a shark, wedged in the doorway, then Nik pulled her into a run, every urgent step splashing through the water puddled in the white corridor.

They ran through death as well as water. Large, small, brilliant, dull, it floated or lay abandoned, innocent eyes staring. It tripped her feet, made her even more clumsy. Mac tried to keep up, but at the second slip, she told him: "Go!"

Nik simply put one arm under hers and around her waist, taking most of her weight with ease. "You're the one who knows what's going on, Mac," he reminded her.

The floor shook under their feet. "Is that—are they here?"

"Not yet. The building's morphing. That's what took me so long to get here. Had to evacuate the outer rooms first."

He threw open the door to the other corridor, held it for her and the man carrying Emily like a sack over one armored shoulder. Fortunately—or more likely due to foresight by the Sinzi—the floor sloped up to this point, stopping the tank water and its cargo from spreading any farther.

Just as well, Mac told herself as they entered another kind of flood. Beings of every kind were moving in the corridor, the majority making their way through openings along the walls—doors, hidden until now. Like her closet, waiting for a purpose.

Emergency shelter. Did they know how it wouldn't be enough?

Some walked past the still-closed door to the Dhryn's cell, more were arriving down the corridor as far as Mac could see. A few had weapons out, but most were clutching other things. *Possessions,* Mac realized with a jolt. *Research.* Whatever could be snatched up; whatever couldn't be abandoned.

They'd evacuated the upper floors. To come here. She sought familiar faces. "Nik. My team. Oversight?"

"Safe as anyone else." Nik snapped orders over her head. Tall forms separated from the crowd, made a path for them. "Come on!"

No delay at the door to the Atrium. Those guarding it weren't Human, but they moved out of Nik's way. Given the look on his face at the moment, Mac thought that entirely wise.

Others pushed in behind them before the door closed again, so close Mac was shoved forward until a hand took her by an elbow. "Can't have you trampled, Mac," said a voice she knew very well.

Mac twisted her head around to make sure. "'Sephe!" she said with relief. "I thought you were in Vancouver."

"Got a call."

Behind her were other familiar faces, all equally grim. Mac blinked to clear her eyes. The Atrium seemed deserted. They must have been evacuated as well. *No,* Mac realized, *not entirely.* The next step up to the left hosted a cluster of floating platforms. Telematics.

Another platform was waiting for them. "Let's go," Nik ordered. Somehow, they all fit—*likely overcrowding the thing*—but Mac didn't argue. She only hoped no one would fall off the edge.

But they made the short trip to the next step without incident, connecting their platform to another. Both shifted underfoot like docks on water as they hurried across.

A mass of beings had gathered around a series of screens toward the back. Nik led the way. "What's going on upstairs?" Mac asked 'Sephe quickly.

A gleam of teeth as her lips parted in a tight grin. "The Sinzi-ra sent as many of the attendees offworld as could be moved in the time we have. The rest are waiting it out down here." Her thumb jerked upward. "Every out-facing room and hall has been filled with impact-resistant foam. Every vent, door, window has been sealed. Quite the feat. Reminds me of your pods."

"That won't stop the Dhryn."

A shrug. "Then let's hope you can," the other woman said quietly, but with an earnestness that silenced Mac.

Those ahead moved aside to let Nik through. Mac, not particularly willingly, followed behind, walking between aliens who stared down—or up—at her with expressions she didn't try to guess.

She smelled anxious Myg before spotting Fourteen. He stood in the inner circle, nodded a greeting.

Three techs, all consular staff, sat in front of what appeared an ordinary communications system, manipulating their 'screens as matter-of-factly as if this was an ordinary day and those representing the power of the IU in this system weren't an audience. But their display was twinned so another, larger version hung in the air where everyone could see it.

Mac studied it. She didn't know the specifics, but she understood the management of incoming threads of data. This had to be a simplification—a focus on what the decision-makers needed to know. She approved, in principle.

But seeing the Dhryn ships speeding toward Earth—

"I've dreamed this." Mac didn't realize she'd spoken aloud until Nik turned and beckoned her forward.

"Tell them."

She didn't need urging.

"You have to stop!" Mac pointed at the display, the splatter of pulses down one edge that gave transmission status. "Don't send the Ro signal," she ordered. "It's calling the Dhryn! They told me!"

Reaction came from all sides. "Ridiculous!" "Who let this Human in here?" "Get her out."

Anchen stepped into the open. "We will hear her. Tell us your concerns, Mac. Give us your evidence."

"There's not time. Trust me, Sinzi-ra—please. Turn it off now!"

"She's right." When no one moved, Nik did, heading for the console.

A figure blocked him just as quickly. Cinder. "What do you think you're doing, Nik?"

"Out of my way," clear threat, partner or no partner.

"This isn't necessary." Hollans came up beside the Sinzi, eyes going from Mac to Nik. Whatever he read there—*besides desperation,* Mac thought wildly—made him turn to the alien. "Shut it down. This is our world, Sinzi-ra."

More harsh words filled the room. "This is IU territory." "You have no authority here, Human!" "The Ro will save us!"

Hollans raised his voice: "I've a right to be heard. So do these two. Until we're sure about the Ro, I say shut it down!"

The display was growing complex. Mac assumed some of the moving specks were Human ships, on their way to intercept the invaders. Others had to be evacuating—trying to save what they could.

Grabbing what couldn't be lost, like the beings stuffed into the shelters behind her, waiting for . . . what?

Time's up, Mac told herself with despair.

"Fourteen!" she shouted. "Now!"

Her shout might have been a signal of its own. Nik used the distraction to launch himself at Cinder, the rest of the Ministry agents thundering past Mac to support him, an even greater number dressed in IU yellow leaping out to stop them. No weapons were fired, likely because of the proximity of so many prominent scientists and diplomats, but there were as many cries from those scampering out of the way of the conflict as there were from those now struggling hand to hand. Or hand to whatever.

Only two hadn't moved. Mac and Fourteen. He looked at her, then put his hands over his face, shaking his head. "Oh, no," she whispered.

Then Mac realized someone else hadn't moved either. Great complex eyes met hers as she stared up at the Sinzi-ra. *Not one individual,* Mac thought suddenly. *Six.* A species reliant on innate diversity; a culture that sought the same across space itself. "You gave me the means to save myself from the Ro," Mac told Anchen, her voice as calm and certain as if giving her own name. "You suspected them yourself."

"Noad convinced Hone and Econa there was risk. He is prone to intuition." Anchen made this sound a failing. "Still, all of us, I, are grateful you weren't harmed. We had no idea the Myrokynay could use our tank this way. Their attack against you was more than a serious breach of protocol. We are troubled."

If any single mind in that body would be—*not in charge, but feeling the greatest pressure of events*—Mac decided, it would be that of Atcho, the consulate administrator. Despite the battle raging around them, she took a step closer. "The Ro make no connections, Anchen. They intend to be the only life, to end ours. We mustn't help them. Please. Stop the signal. Now."

"I concur." Two long fingers lifted into the air. Their tips snapped by one another. A too-quiet sound, considering the grunts and scuffles on every side, but the techs must have been waiting for it. Hands stroked the display.

The transmission stopped. Mac staggered with relief.

"Hold!" Hollans bellowed, the word repeated by others.

Like that, it was over. Mac could hardly believe such intense fighting could end as suddenly as it began. She also found it incredible that the combatants of an instant before were helping each other stand, as if this had all been some kind of practice scrum.

Not all. There was something unfinished and deadly in the way Nik and Cinder remained facing one another. Mac saw it. So did Sing-li, who came up to both. She heard him say in an urgent voice: "Save it for the Dhryn."

"Look, Sinzi-ra!" cried one of the techs. "The ships!"

"What is it?"

"They've stopped forward motion. The Dhryn—they're just sitting there."

Mac thought this a very good time to sit herself and, spotting an unoccupied bench, headed for it with a single-minded concentration that would have suited one of her salmon.

- Encounter -

"REPEAT THAT!"

"All enemy vessels have ceased movement toward Earth, sir. They're maintaining a fixed position relative to the gate."

Captain Anya Lemnitov chewed her lower lip. An old habit. "Nav. Time to intercept."

"Thirty minutes at our present speed, sir. If they keep sitting there like ducks."

"Bloody big ducks."

Lemnitov grinned without humor at her Weapons officer. "Then I hope you've an appropriate solution planned, Mr. Morris."

"Of course, sir." But she wasn't surprised when her old friend came to stand beside her, dropping his voice for her ears only. "It'd be easier if they were our usual troublemakers. Smugglers. Insurance defrauders. Lost tourists."

"Sol's been lucky," she countered. "Boring. Peaceful. Maybe we were due for a shake-up. We'll do okay. *Tripoli* hasn't let us down before."

"What worries me are the claims that each of those ships can split into hundreds, maybe thousands more. If they do, well, we can't stop more than a fraction of them, Captain. And the Dhryn don't care about casualties—only their target."

Target? Home to most of those here. She was Mars-born, but had an apartment in Prague that two cats and a lover kept warm. "We do our part; others do theirs," she reminded him. "Confirm ready status to fleet command."

"Captain?" Uncertain, from the com tech.

Morris and the captain exchanged looks. "What is it?" she asked.

"Incoming message from command, sir. Orders—sir, we're ordered to hold position as well. No hostile moves."

Lemnitov stood up. "Do they say why? Belay that," she grunted. "They never say why."

"That's crazy! We can't just leave them there, Captain."

"Calm down."

"What if they split—getting moving before we can? Do you realize how many would slip past us? Reach Earth?"

The entire bridge hushed, everyone listening, every eye on the captain. Lemnitov deliberately took her seat. "Settle back, folks," she ordered, crossing her legs and getting comfortable. "We're parking."

She didn't dare show her fear.

But whoever had ordered Sol's defenses to stand down before the nightmare that was the Dhryn had better be right.

If not, none of them would live to complain.

- 21 -

STRAINS AND STRESS

"I WILL HAVE ORDER and attention."

How did she do it? Mac wasn't bad at harnessing a room, although it usually involved shouting or leaping on a tabletop. *Brandishing something unlikely helped.* The Sinzi-ra simply spoke those words, in her quiet voice, and everyone presently bickering, stopped.

It didn't mean they suddenly agreed with one another, Mac realized, surveying the room from her seat, this time to the left of Anchen herself. Promotion or protection? *Both likely applied.* From what she'd heard so far, more than a few of those here felt the Dhryn had stopped by coincidence and that they should continue all efforts to contact the Ro.

Others, now believing the Ro were as much a menace as the Dhryn, and one capable of breaching the walls at that, wanted the Sinzi-ra to abandon the consulate and run for safety.

That left, Mac counted in her head: herself, Nik, Hollans—who'd proved himself, as far as she was concerned—and the Sinzi-ra herself. Hollans, meanwhile, had upset the majority here by ordering Earth's defenses not to engage the Progenitors' ships, the situation, he'd insisted, being too volatile.

So the only thing they'd agreed on to this point was that the Dhryn wouldn't stay cooperatively still much longer.

Mac yawned, covering her mouth with her gloved hand. *Which,* she sniffed, *smelled like dead fish.* The staff had done wonders cleaning the corridor; they could give lessons to those students prone to fish tank disasters. *Always a few.*

She should have asked them to clean her as well.

"We are in crisis," Anchen continued. "The IU has sent urgent messages to all members warning them not to activate any signal or device provided by the Myrokynay. We have not—yet—extended this warning to avoiding the Myrokynay themselves," this with an elegant wave of her fingers that managed to convey informed caution.

Mac shifted unhappily in her seat, but didn't say anything. *One problem at a time,* Nik had told her on the way to this meeting. *One enemy.*

As far as she was concerned, there was only one. *But,* Mac thought thankfully, stifling another yawn, *she didn't have to make such decisions.*

"We have also made it clear that the transects must remain open, regardless of the risk of attack. Our connections to one another are not only defense, but lines of safety. We will resolve this problem as a group, for the good of all."

"What about the Dhryn?"

"Ah. For this we must turn to Mac."

Mac, well into a very pleasant "not asleep, really, resting my eyes" daze, snapped back to attention at her name. "We do?" she said blankly.

"While not all here agree, you have proved to me that your doubts about the Ro were well-founded. Their motives remain unclear and potentially antagonistic; their methods are not those of civil discourse." *Now there was an understatement.* "However, now I must call upon your other area of expertise, Mac."

Salmon?

"It is time to share with all of you that we have, in this building, a representative sent by the Dhryn." Even the Sinzi-ra had to wait out the round of outcries this created, finally holding up one finger for order. "He was unwell. There were doubts he would live. Thanks to Mac, who knew this individual and is fluent in his language, he is recovering. More to the point, he presents us with an opportunity to negotiate with the Dhryn Progenitors threatening this world."

That silenced everyone—who then turned to direct their appropriate visual sensory organ or organs at a certain weary salmon researcher.

Might as well paint a target on her forehead, Mac decided. Given the worried look Nik sent her, the same thought had occurred to him.

Everyone, including the Sinzi-ra, waited for her to speak. *She'd much rather join Emily in a drugged stupor—sleep for a day would be nice.*

Mac swallowed and said the only thing she could: "I'm not a negotiator, Sinzi-ra, but I'm willing to try."

Nik stopped her in front of the Dhryn's door, where they were shielded from sight by a rather reassuringly protective clump of Ministry agents. *Most of whom she knew by name.* "Here." He held out a loaded syringe.

"Why did I know you'd have that handy?" Mac asked, but took it. A field kit dose of Fastfix, a cocktail designed to let the Human body continue past its natural collapse point. She'd used one before and knew to quickly drive the tip into her real arm, ready for the sharp pinch. In minutes, her electrolyte balance would head for normal, and stimulants would convince her she'd slept like a baby. *If ever there was a time,* Mac thought, and returned the now-empty syringe with a faint smile.

"You do realize this negotiation idea is a long shot. At best."

He arched his eyebrows as if shocked. "This from the person who single-handedly destroyed the Sinzi's no-space tank system?"

"You don't know I destroyed it. The Ro probably did the damage. I—" Mac flushed, "—okay, maybe I poked it."

"Proving my point. Put some of that 'shove the universe' attitude of yours to work for us. You can do this, Mac, if anyone can," he said, low and sure.

"That's just it, Nik. It doesn't have to be me—" The rest of Mac's explanation was cut off by the opening of the door.

"Greetings, Mackenzie Winifred Elizabeth Wright Connor Sol!"

The booming greeting was the most cheerful thing she'd heard in a while. Mac walked up to the cell bars. "You look—you look great," she said with wonder.

While she'd been awake, at work, worried, jumped on by baby Mygs, transported through no-space, and tortured by an impossible-to-bear alien's voice—not to mention the flood of dying fish and a brawl in the signal room. *And,* Mac summed up dourly, *another meeting with a long table,* the Dhryn had been resting.

The result? One about-to-stagger Human and a robust, hearty alien. With, she noticed, every one of the little rings she'd brought adorning his ear ridges, and a bold, yet pleasing accent of burgundy at eyebrows, cheek ridges, and lips. Mac doubted she could have done as good a job with a mirror.

The golden irises of his eyes almost glowed. "While you, *Lamisah,* have neither rested nor bathed. What's wrong? And why does that one sleep without waking?" A gesture to the left.

Where Mac saw the new addition to the room. A smaller version of the jelly-bed, with Emily lying on it, unmoving. She resisted the impulse to run to her side. Two was already there, standing attentively.

"She's—" Dhryn had no words for illness or its treatment. *'A Dhryn is robust or a Dhryn is not.'* Mac sighed. "That's my friend Emily."

The Vessel, who'd been sitting, abruptly stood. "Emily Mamani Sarmiento?" he exclaimed. "*Lamisah* to my beloved Brymn Las? She is found?" He hurried to that side of his cell. "This is wonderful news, Mackenzie Winifred Elizabeth Wright Connor Sol!" But once there, he stopped and stared at the unconscious woman. "She is damaged."

Two, who'd stood impassively as the larger blue alien rushed toward her, gave Mac a look of inquiry. Mac walked along the cell bars to stand beside the Dhryn, careful not to look at Emily. "Brymn Las told you—the Progenitor—about Emily?"

"Of course. And that she was taken from your side by the monstrous Ro." Empty food containers in the cell shook as the Dhryn said something too low for Mac to hear. *Likely something she'd agree with,* she thought bitterly.

Unfortunately—or otherwise—Brymn's last chance to communicate with his Progenitor had been before they'd learned of Emily's betrayal. *Not the time to share,* Mac decided. Instead, she said quietly: "The Ro damaged her. We hope for the best. Vessel, we have to talk about something else—" Mac started walking toward the door to the cell.

But the Dhryn stayed where he was, leaning as close to the cell bars as he could without touching them, implying they were in some way dangerous to touch. *Not an experiment she'd been interested in trying.* "*Lamisah,* wait. Did they place their channels within her flesh?"

Mac nodded, startled by the question. "Yes. Links to no-space. But how—"

"Aieee! Then the Ro have not yet released their grip. If they do not steal her from you again, they will take what is theirs. You must be ready! Bring those among the not-Dhryn who understand the workings of a Human body, who can deal with extreme damage." The Dhryn gazed at Mac with distress. "You doubt me, *Lamisah?*"

"I have seen no awareness of—" Mac was forced to use the Instella words "medicine or biology" before continuing: "—among Dhryn. Brymn Las told me these subjects were forbidden. 'We do not think on it.'"

"Ah." The hint of a smile on those burgundy-tinged lips. "And why should Dhryn waste a moment's breath puzzling at that which is incarnate in every Progenitor? We are the study of life, *Lamisah.* The workings of living things, Dhryn or not, are our passion. Like yours! This is why I know," the smile disappeared, " that Emily Mamani Sarmiento must be in the care of those with such knowledge or she will end."

Mac didn't argue further. She turned to Nik, who'd stayed close behind her. "The Ro can still harm Emily," she told him. "The Vessel—I don't know how he knows, but he says she could need medical assistance at any minute. Please, Nik."

He gave her a dismayed look but nodded. "We can't risk moving her until we have another shielded location. I'll get someone on it, Mac, but you need to work on the problem at hand. The ships."

"I know." Mac took a deep breath, feeling a rush of energy that had more to do with the Fastfix taking hold than any remaining adrenaline in her system. As she did, she checked who else had come into the room with her.

Nik, of course. 'Sephe and Sing-li, now standing to either side of the door. The rest must have stayed outside to loom appropriately.

Under the circumstances, Mac highly approved.

One and Cinder stood on the other side of the cell, as if awaiting instructions. The Trisulian seemed calm enough, although one eyestalk was definitely bent in Nik's direction. *Still angry or wanting to apologize?* For all Mac knew of the species, it could have been neither.

Last and not least at all, the four who had come in that first time: Anchen, Brend Hollans, Genny P'tool, and the still-silent Imrya with her recording pad.

"What ships?" the Vessel echoed, in Dhryn.

They could yell at her later, Mac decided. She knew her strengths. Negotiation and diplomacy weren't among them.

She opened the door and walked into the cell. The Dhryn met her in the middle. "What ships?" he said again, almost impatiently. "What's happening, Mac?"

"How do you feel about crowds?" she asked, then patted the Dhryn's shoulder. "Dumb question."

"Indeed," the Vessel replied. "Even the presence of not-Dhryn is better than being alone."

"That's good. Because you're going to be meeting quite a few shortly. And you must speak to them so they can understand you. Their language. Please."

Real alarm tightened the muscle beneath Mac's fingers. "You said they would take you away from me, *Lamisah!*"

She nodded, swallowing hard. "That may happen. If it does, I want you to trust those you see here, in this room. And anyone Nik—Nikolai Piotr Trojanowski—brings to you. Will you do this for me? It is," she added sincerely, "what you need to do for all that which is Dhryn."

An arm draped itself heavily and awkwardly over her shoulders. "You are also that which is Dhryn. I will not permit you to come to harm, *Lamisah.*"

Despite their audience, in this room, beyond it, despite the contradiction between fear of this species and memories of friendship, Mac let her forehead rest against the Dhryn's cheekbone, managed to stretch her arms as far around his body as she could. The alien stood perfectly still. Brymn had done the same for her. Their species might not share the use of physical contact for comfort; both shared the need.

Mac stepped free, giving the Vessel a final pat, and swallowed to moisten her throat. "Nik?" she called.

He joined her in the cell. Hollans looked as though he wanted to say something. Mac shook her head once, receiving a tight-lipped nod in return.

Nothing like a demonstration, she decided. "Nik, the Vessel would like to know what ships you were talking about. Tell him."

The understandable outbursts from those outside the cell didn't matter. *Nothing mattered,* thought Mac, except the instant comprehension in his eyes, the determination that replaced it. "Twenty-three Dhryn ships—Progenitor Ships—have entered this solar system," Nik said, moving to stand where he could look straight into the Vessel's golden eyes.

A long silence, then: "Why have they come?" Instella, clear and unaccented, yet with an undertone that rattled the furnishings.

"A signal—a call—has drawn them from the Great Journey," said Mac, careful not to mention the Ro. "We've stopped it and they've stopped. But they haven't left."

Nik continued at her look. "We've tried to communicate with the ships, but there's been no response."

"Because you are not-Dhryn," the Vessel explained, as if this should be obvious.

The Ministry's top alien liaison merely nodded. "That's why we need your help—to open negotiations with them."

"Negotiate what?" It seemed honest puzzlement. "The Great Journey has begun. That which is Dhryn will not be distracted by other concerns."

Hollans had come close to the bars. "You're waging war for the Ro, aren't you?"

Mac winced. *That wasn't going to go over well.*

Sure enough, the Vessel immediately wrapped his arms around himself in that complex, defensive positioning. "Who is that being?" in Dhryn, flat and angry.

"*Erumisah* for Humans," Mac said in the same tongue, giving Hollans a warning glare. In Instella, *hopefully,* she continued: "Vessel, that which is Dhryn shouldn't be here. We," she put her hand on her chest, "—I—don't want to be food for Dhryn."

A shocked "o" of his mouth, but he replied in the same language. "Is that why you think they have come? To consume your world as others were consumed? Impossible!"

"The dead planets of the Chasm. You—your Progenitor—spoke to me of remembrance. Of regret. Do you want that legacy again?"

"I do not speak of it."

"You must!" A touch on her sleeve stopped her from more.

Nik's eyes were gleaming behind his glasses. "Vessel. What could turn that which is Dhryn from one path to another?"

She knew she'd been right to have him do this, Mac thought, relieved.

The Dhryn's torso tilted up slightly. *Threat,* she judged it, *but not at them.*

Yet, anyway.

"A risk to the Progenitor."

Mac looked at Nik in dismay. *If Earth's defenders, nose-to-nose with the Dhryn ships, weren't considered such a risk, what would be?*

He didn't seem flustered. *Or didn't show it,* she thought enviously. "How would such a risk be discovered by the Dhryn?"

"The Progenitor would reveal it."

Around again, she thought, frustrated, but kept silent.

"You are a Vessel," Nik said calmly. "You can speak to other Progenitors—tell them this world is dangerous, that they should avoid it."

A rapid series of blinks, like blue shutters covering those huge eyes. Then: "This world is not dangerous to a Progenitor," the Dhryn said in a reasoning tone. "You two are my *lamisah.* The rest," a gesture to the silent group outside the cell, "I am to trust."

What had she thought about rocks and hard places? Without thinking, Mac breathed: "Let me try again."

Nik studied her face, then nodded. "Go."

Mac sat cross-legged on the floor. To keep his eyes on her, the Vessel had to relax and lower his head. "Things are not as they should be, Vessel," she said carefully. "That which is Dhryn has been shown a wrong path. A path that risks all Progenitors. I believe this."

"I do not wish to speak of—"

"Stop!" Mac said sharply, looking up at the larger being. "You were sent to talk to me."

Miserable, with yellow liquid oozing from one nostril. Tears. "Yes, *Lamisah.*"

"Explain to me. How does a Progenitor reveal a risk to her Dhryn?"

His mouth closed tight. Mac was about to ask again when she felt the floor beneath her start to vibrate. The reverberations traveled up her spine, jarring her teeth. "Like that," she said with satisfaction. *Though at a much greater intensity, given the size of a real Progenitor.* It would be like an earthquake.

She'd felt it on Haven, before the planet split to release the ships, the Progenitors using their own bodies to warn their people. A warning that traveled through the ground and air, over vast distance, unstoppable.

A warning that this time might save more than Dhryn.

There was something about watching capable people getting things done, Mac decided happily, *that satisfied the soul.*

Either that, or she was experiencing Fastfix euphoria.

The distinction wasn't important. She stayed where Nik had essentially parked her, near Emily's bed, while he and others swarmed about to make and send a recording of what had been dubbed the Progenitor's alarm cry. *Which was more an alarm* throb, Mac corrected, not that the name mattered.

They'd circumvented the need to bring in additional equipment—or move the Dhryn—by simply sliding aside a good portion of the ceiling. It also removed a good portion of the Dhryn shielding, exposing them all to the Ro, but Mac doubted the secretive beings would bother entering a room packed to the rafters.

Not to mention the presence of armored beings of every sort, intent on anything that wasn't part of capable persons getting things done.

"You look pleased, *Lamisah.*"

Mac glanced through the bars at the Dhryn. "I do?" She considered the idea. "Relief," she said finally.

After all. Others knew. Others were taking action. She wasn't waiting to hear what was happening—she was in the midst of it all.

Okay, maybe that last wasn't such a great thing. Mac looked down at Emily. Even drugged unconscious, a state Anchen recommended for now, her face wasn't relaxed. Muscles spasmed in seemingly random order. Her arms shifted as much as the cover allowed. Mac hadn't guessed the bed could be adjusted into a restraint. It put a new light on climbing into her own later.

If there was a later.

She watched the lift they'd slung from the other side bring down its next load. The Vessel watched as well. He'd stayed as close to her as possible but didn't seem upset.

Which made sense. They were proposing to warn the Dhryn, not harm them.

A tactic that didn't satisfy everyone. Mac narrowed her eyes. The Imrya had spent most of her time with Cinder in the last half an hour, a conversation whose topic she could guess well enough.

"Let it go, Mac," easy and quiet.

She glowered at Nik. "Have you talked to her yet?"

His laugh wasn't amused. "In all this? We'll sit down over some beers when things calm down. Cinder and I—we've enough history to get past a difference of opinion."

"So you don't think the Dhryn should be exterminated as soon as possible?" The Vessel's only protest was a faint distressed sound.

"Gods, Mac," Nik shook his head at her. "Do you know any direction besides straight ahead?"

She was unrepentant. "Not when I know where I'm going. Nik—we need to—"

One came up to them. "We're ready to test the simulation, Mr. Trojanowski, Dr. Connor." A polite pause as he sorted out protocol. "Honorable Vessel."

"Go ahead."

The lights dimmed to request silence. The techs inhabiting the jumble of equipment now along the far wall gave a signal. Instantly, the walls and floor began to shake. Objects not secured fell and rolled.

While the Dhryn stood and ran as hard as he could in the opposite direction.

As that was the direction of the descending lift, the massive alien managed to knock most of the gear from it to the floor, sending himself rebounding to lie on his back.

Someone thought of shutting off the simulation.

"Well," said Mac brightly as the Dhryn picked himself up, apparently no worse for wear, "that worked."

Anchen touched fingertip to fingertip. "I had hoped we would be negotiating with the Dhryn, not shouting at them to run. You remain sure this is the only option?"

Nik shrugged. "Right now? Yes, Sinzi-ra. Given the time and situation, there's no choice."

Genny P'tool spoke up: "It will be a test. If it works, if the Dhryn are repelled, then we can provide this to other members of the IU."

"Even if it works," Mac cautioned, "it may only work once. The Dhryn are obeying instinct, but they obviously haven't lost their ability to function as intelligent beings. They can operate ships—navigate transects to find a specific target. They are making decisions. They'll soon realize they should ignore alarms that come from outside their ships."

"They don't learn to ignore the Ro's call."

"We can't know that," Mac insisted. "Some might be trying to. This Progenitor did—" a gesture to the Vessel. "And there's another difference. Organisms will seek food even if sometimes the clues are wrong. It's too essential a need. But they can't keep reacting to false alarms. It's better to risk ignoring a valid alarm, than to starve hiding from false ones."

"That which is Dhryn mustn't starve." The Vessel's comment, low and implacable, sent a shiver down Mac's spine.

Hollans turned pale as well. To his credit, his voice stayed calm. "Understood, Dr. Connor. But if it might save even one more world, it's worth a try, don't you think?"

Anchen's fingertips snapped past one another. "We will not test the patience of the Dhryn. Send the alarm."

- Encounter -

THE PROGENITOR'S warning is felt by all that is Dhryn.
   The Great Ships turn to flee.
The Progenitors must endure.
Conflict . . . confusion . . .
The Progenitors on each ship call for Vessels.
No time for consultation. In this, the will of all comes first.
The Call has been silenced.
The cry is paramount.
All that is Dhryn must *move*.

"Say again."
   "The Dhryn ships have come about, sir. Projected course—the gate to the Naralax Transect! They're running!"
   In the midst of cheers and whistles from her bridge crew, Lemnitov heard an astonished: "From us?"
   She gave her Weapons officer a sideways grin. "Don't think we're scary?"
   "Do you?"
   "There have been days . . ." Seeing the scan tech trying to get her attention, the captain raised her voice. "Quiet down, people. We can celebrate at the next way station. What is it?"
   "You need to see this, sir."
   "Main display."
   The center space of the bridge filled with the images of ships.
   Dying.

That which was Dhryn had lost the call.
   That which was Dhryn has turned to flee.
   ~~FAILURE~~
   It is not the Way to risk the Progenitors.
   ~~WITHDRAW~~

Holes appear down every seam of the Great Ships; their silver sides, like so many petals, fall open to vacuum. Gouts of air vent and freeze, icy splinters coat the figures that tumble into space.

Within, the Progenitors die even as they try to shield their newborn with their vast hands, *oomlings* floating free in every direction as gravity fails with all else.

As the last heartbeat sounds in silence, that which was Dhryn tumbles toward the Naralax Transect.

Nothing more than debris.

22

AGONY AND AFTERMATH

EMILY SCREAMED, a drawn-out shriek that choked on moisture. Mac hurled herself to her side, hearing other cries but understanding only this one.

"Emily!" Mac tried to free her from the blanketlike restraint, but the jelly-bed held firm. Emily's body spasmed in another scream, muted to a gurgle by the blood still pouring from her mouth.

"I need help here!" Mac shouted.

She was pulled aside, others pushed past. She didn't resist, trying only to see what was happening.

But when she could see, Mac screamed herself and turned away.

Someone held her.

No one could erase what burned behind her closed eyes, the bloody ruin of arms and legs, the wet gaping abdomen.

The Ro had taken back what they'd put in place of Emily's flesh.

Returning nothing.

"Dead." "It's confirmed. Dead." "Dead." Like a contagion, the word sped through the room. Mac choked back her tears, pushed away to free herself, heard clearly what at first made no sense: "All of them, you're sure?" "Yes, all dead."

All of them? All of who?

"AIEEEEEEEEEEEE! LAMISAH!"

Half blind, Mac fought to reach the new scream, struggling to get past what seemed an army intended to hold her in place as gently as possible. She flailed out, got ready to kick.

"Mac. Mac. They're helping Emily. Hang on. This way."

Nik. With the voice, movement in the right direction. No more screaming, although disquieting mutters of "dead" kept circulating around her, part of confused fragments of conversation.

Others were caring for Emily. Only she could help the Dhryn.

Emily.

Inside the Dhryn cell was peace of a sort. The area outside was crammed with people, the outer door opening and closing with a steady growl of permissions asked and given. Overhead, more noise, a heady buzz from the other side. *Cheering?*

Mac focused on the Vessel, a huddle of patent misery in the middle of the floor. Had he even stood again after running into the lift? She couldn't remember. Nik, faster than she, was already at his side. "We didn't do it," he was saying, confusingly if urgently. To her: "The Dhryn ships. They self-destructed. All of them. After they'd powered up on a heading to leave the system."

"Why would they do that?" she asked numbly.

"They didn't," Nik said between his teeth. "Their ships must have been rigged. Some kind of triggering pulse was sent from inside the consulate. We'd never have caught it, but we were set up to listen for a reply to the Ro signal. We're tracking the source." She'd never seen such naked rage on a face before. "It—Emily was affected at the same time."

The Ro.

Too cold for anger, Mac bent over the Dhryn, touched him gently. "Vessel. *Lamisah.* Do you understand now? The Ro are the enemy. They tried to use these Dhryn against us; when that failed, they destroyed them. We have to work together; find a way to stop the Ro before more die."

Low, in Dhryn, muffled by an arm. "I must go back."

Mac kept talking in Instella for Nik's sake. "What do you mean, 'you must go back'? Back where? Why?"

The arm shifted to reveal one golden eye. The Dhryn made the effort to reply in kind. "I was sent here to talk to you, Mackenzie Winifred Elizabeth Wright Connor Sol. To learn the truth. I have, to my unending sorrow, done so. Now, I must return to my Progenitor and tell her."

Mac sat back, giving Nik a startled look. "We can't—" she began cautiously. He put a finger to his lips, then leaned close to the Dhryn's ear.

"I'll make sure you get there, *Lamisah,*" she heard him whisper. "But please, don't speak of this to others until we've made the necessary arrangements."

As he spoke, Nik looked straight at her.

Oh, she knew that expression.

Full-scale plotting.

And no one had better get in his way.

"She's alive. I admit to being surprised. I had thought her body would give up the first night."

Mac pressed her lips together and stared out at the ocean. The Sinzi-ra had come in person to report on Emily's condition. She was grateful for that.

Once the Dhryn were gone, the consulate had morphed back to its normal state, giving them all back their beds and belongings, restoring access to the research rooms. She was grateful for that, too.

She wasn't grateful to have been sent to her bed the moment it was available. *Not,* Mac admitted, *that she'd been good for much by that time.* Fastfix made you pay. She had vague memories of a quiet, comfortable corner, some floor of her own, annoying people who claimed she was in the way and made her get up.

Mac shook herself. "Emily's always been strong," she said. "Thank you for your care of her. Strong or not, I'm not sure she would have survived what the— what the Ro did to her without Noad."

An elegant sweep of fingers to head, the meaning unmistakable. "It remains to be seen how much of her has survived, Mac. You should be prepared."

How could she do that? Mac asked herself. Aloud: "What else do I get to know, Anchen?"

"Whatever you wish. You have more than earned my confidence, Mac."

"Is the IU going to release the Vessel? Let him return to his Progenitor?"

They were sitting on the terrace. The storm front had passed, leaving a clear sky. The breeze lifting from the ocean played with Mac's hair and set the beads by the door in motion. It wasn't enough to move the Sinzi's fingers, yet she pretended it did, waving their tips before her great eyes like silver-coated reeds swaying in the wind.

Delay, Mac judged it. *Why?* She decided on patience, and was rewarded a moment later.

Anchen put down her fingers with what seemed reluctance. "Mac. The destruction of the Dhryn ships. How do you judge this act?"

"Murder. The slaughter of innocents."

"Innocents who may have been responsible for the deaths of billions. For the eradication of entire biospheres."

"I've seen eagles gather by the hundreds to feast on salmon as they spawn. If I could ask the salmon's opinion on that slaughter, I'm sure it would differ from the eagles'. I have none."

"So you see the Dhryn as part of nature."

Mac's lips twisted. "I see them as a perversion of nature. A perversion created and manipulated by the Ro. Who are, in my opinion, guilty of murder on all counts."

"To those who do not think as you—or I, Mac—the Ro's destruction of the Dhryn ships was an act of salvation."

Mac frowned. "How can that be? The evidence—"

"Is not definitive. Not yet. Not to all. Human ships are collecting debris, hunting clues. Meanwhile, you must continue your work, Mac." A lift of those tall shoulders. "But, as you do, be aware of this ambivalence among us. There will remain division, factions to be pacified and contained."

Too much to hope it would be simple, Mac told herself. *That all would see the same threat, interpret the same actions as she did.* She thought of how hard it was for her and Mudge to agree—and they started from the same information and had similar goals.

"For how long?"

"Until we know the Myrokynay's intentions beyond doubt."

"If they win," Mac grumbled, "we'll know, won't we?"

Anchen formed her triangular mouth into a smile. "Let us hope to gain this knowledge first. We must establish communications with both the Dhryn and the Ro, Mac. Since the Ro have proved—uninterested—in civil discourse, I will send our Dhryn back to his Progenitor, trusting to form a useful connection."

Mac's eyes sought the horizon again. Late afternoon. Some scudding cloud. That ridiculous blue sky hanging over a sea sparked with light. A sea with life spared for another day.

Good-bye.

"I'll go with him," she said.

A cool sharpness, light as the tip of a feather, stroked the back of her hand. For an instant, Mac couldn't remember if it was her real one or not. She looked at the Sinzi-ra. "I mean it."

"And I am grateful for your courage. But you cannot, Mac." Anchen stroked her hand once more. "We need you here, to continue leading your team. Even if they could manage without you," she said, anticipating Mac's protest before she did more than draw breath to make it, "Emily cannot. What hope she has to recover may depend in part on the presence of a—good—friend. I have a third reason—do you wish to hear it?"

Mac scowled but nodded.

"The Ro followed you once before, using the tracer signature within your body. It's true they had Emily's help and her device—also that they knew your destination and could stay close. But do you wish to take the chance that they could repeat this feat and, through you, find the Vessel?"

"The Ministry might have a way of masking it—changing it."

"Which brings me to my last reason, Mac. Although you accepted temporary citizenship within the IU in order to be part of the Gathering, your kind has claimed you back from us. The Ministry of Extra-Sol Human Affairs is unwilling to risk both of its experts on the Dhryn in such a venture. I find I concur."

"Both?" Mac nodded slowly. *Of course.* She'd heard Nik say it. *It just hadn't registered.* "Nik's going."

"Yes."

"When?"

Anchen gestured westward, sunlight glinting from her silver rings. "Today. I am sorry you did not have a chance to say good-bye in person, Mac, but the launch must be secret. We sought no agreement for this mission. We fear an act against the Vessel—followers on their trail. You can send a note to me. I will make sure Nik receives it."

A note, Mac repeated to herself, feeling as though the terrace had tilted toward the sharp rocks below.

And she'd wasted the last twenty-four hours asleep.

The knock at her door shortly after Anchen departed didn't surprise Mac. Who was knocking did.

"Come in, Mr. Hollans," she said, quite sure she was doing a lousy job of hiding her disappointment.

"Dr. Connor. If I might speak with you?"

If he made it quick. "Sure." He walked through the arch to the sitting room. *So much for quick.*

They took seats in opposing jelly-chairs. The fish tank table—every one, Mac had been told—had been replaced by a solid slab of local stone, polished and gray. She tucked her feet under the Sinzi gown. He was, predictably, in the brown suit. There were dark circles under his eyes, lines of strain around his mouth.

"Dr. Connor—"

"Mac."

He almost smiled. "Mac. I came to apologize."

"I've a temper," she admitted with a shrug. "Besides, you were right. Dhryn were killing Humans. I needed to know." Mac paused uncertainly. "Did you have family—at the refinery?"

He shook his head, then gave a strange laugh. "Yes. In a way."

"In a way?"

"My job—when I'm not working with Anchen—is to watch out for the ones who leave home. I don't know many of them as individuals; I don't need to. Those who go to space are different. They're travelers, restless, eager for something new and bigger. The seeds of our kind, in a way. Fragile, sometimes foolish. Sometimes with evil intent, often brave. They deserve to do better than survive out there. I want more for them than that. Sorry. I'm probably not making much sense." He rubbed his face with his hand. "Been a long few days."

Mac eyed him cautiously, then made up her mind. "I knew someone like that," she offered. "Just had to go to space. I didn't understand why he couldn't be satisfied with Earth. I argued with him, tried to keep him here." *With her.*

"Let me guess. He left anyway."

She nodded. "And didn't come back. It's taken me this long to understand, a little anyway. It wasn't that Earth was too small for Sam. He saw what I didn't, back then. Earth isn't isolated, complete in itself. This world is part of something else, larger, waiting to be known. He wanted that something, be it space or other worlds. Guess I'm not making sense either," she finished, frustrated.

A true smile this time, frayed with exhaustion, but offered as one friend to another. "Sounded all right to me," Hollans said, then stood. "Mac, I also came to make sure you understood why I asked the IU not to send you with the Dhryn. Nothing to do with your abilities." His smile turned rueful. "Believe me, Mac, I've become convinced. But—" he paused.

Mac stood, too. "Anchen told me. Nik Trojanowski is going and you can't risk us both." She was surprised when the words came out sounding normal.

"So you think he can do it?" A little too casual, given the anxiety she read in his eyes.

Mac didn't hesitate. "Nik doesn't speak the language," she admitted. "That's a disadvantage among Haven-raised Dhryn. But—he understands the Dhryn. And, to be honest, he understands this—" Her wave was meant to encompass not only Earth and the consulate, but all the IU. "—unlike me. You're better off with someone out there who won't shove the universe at the wrong time." She paused, then said: "And the Vessel does know where he's going, in case you were wondering."

"But I thought you said—"

Mac blushed, just a bit. "The Dhryn don't lie, Mr. Hollans. But I'm not a Dhryn."

A curt—and very relieved—nod. "Thank you, Mac. That helps."

She walked him to her door, scuffing her bare toes in the sand. About to leave, he stopped and turned to look at her. "We'll do our best for Dr. Mamani. Under the circumstances, I've arranged for the charges against her to be dropped."

"Charges?" Mac repeated, then stopped her automatic protest. *What hadn't Emily done?* "Thank you."

She closed the door.

As for the circumstances?

"He believes you're going to die, Emily," Mac said, her forehead against the doorframe. "Don't start being convenient now."

No messages. No more visitors. Mac's nerves stood the peace and quiet as long as they could, which was not at all, then she dressed and went out.

"Hi, Mac."

The voice from nowhere made her jump half out of her skin. "Don't do that!" Mac hissed.

'Sephe's lips stretched in that magical smile of hers. "Your feet left the floor."

Mac snorted, then shook her head. "I've things on my mind. Why exactly are you standing outside my door?"

"Even I pull guard detail." Not that 'Sephe was in full armor, although she wore one of the vests and had a weapon hanging at her hip. Underneath, she wore a bright red dress, complete with matching sandals.

"I thought the Sinzi had put up Ro detectors of some kind." Mac had heard the explanation given to another and tuned out all but the key, to her, part. *Safe, for now.* "Disrupts their ability to exit from no-space within the building."

"Untested technology to stop an unseen foe?" 'Sephe arched one eyebrow.

"And not everyone in this place is a friend of mine," Mac suggested.

A sober look. "Let's say we're going to stick a little close for a while. If you don't mind."

"Do I have a choice?" but Mac softened it with a smile of her own. "I don't mind the company, 'Sephe." In fact, she'd hoped for it.

"Where to?"

By way of answer, Mac held up a palm-sized salmon. It had been the smallest one hanging from her ceiling, and one of the nicest. A traditional Haida rendering, pale wood with dramatic lines in red and black, shaping eye and sweep of tail, offering meanings as well. *The cycle of life. The whole as a sum of its parts.* The dangling thread still attached caught on her finger and she wrapped the excess around the tail. "A token for a traveler," she said somewhat breathlessly.

"Mac, you know there's a security blackout. Clock's started—"

"Then why did you let me sleep so long?" she snapped, then, desperately: "'Sephe. Please."

Muttering something that wasn't Instella or English—or polite—under her breath, the Ministry agent turned and led the way down the corridor to the far lift. Mac stayed close behind, not daring to say another word.

Theirs didn't seem a particularly clandestine route—down a regular lift—main hall—outside along the patio, walking on top of the Atrium—but Mac knew better. They passed one too many faces she knew, faces that gave 'Sephe a look of disbelief and Mac one of pity.

This route was guarded.

She had to trust they were guarding against her as well, that 'Sephe wouldn't have given in this easily had Mac's impulse posed a risk.

That wasn't to say others might not. "There you are, Norcoast!"

'Sephe gave her a warning look. Mac just shrugged. *There were some people you couldn't lose.* "About time you woke up," Mudge went on as he caught up. "They wouldn't let me see you. Are you all right? I've had a briefing from the Sinzi-ra herself. Fine job you did. Risky, but—"

"Oversight," Mac interrupted, "we're in a bit of a hurry here. Do you mind if we talk about all this later?"

He harrumphed, his cheerful expression changing to suspicion as if she'd thrown a switch. "What's wrong? I thought we won. What's going on. Where are you going?"

Mac rolled her eyes, then grabbed Mudge by the front of his jacket, pulling him along in the direction 'Sephe had indicated until he scampered to keep up. 'Sephe, with a heavy, completely clear sigh, took a few longer strides to get ahead and lead. "We didn't win," Mac told him as they passed under the trees. "Not yet. And, thanks. I'm all right."

"This is the way to the landing pads." Mudge grabbed her arm, tried to slow her down. "What's going on? Are you leaving, Norcoast?"

Mac rested her fingers over his for an instant, smiling what she hoped was a reassuring smile. "No. But a friend is. I want to say good-bye, that's all. You can wait back at the consulate."

"And miss a chance to see the latest Sinzi machines?" he said. "Nonsense, Norcoast."

She'd tried. "Fine. But don't slow us down."

Much to Mudge's chagrin, the last part of their journey angled away from the landing field. Instead, 'Sephe paused on the path beside a bench like all the others, checked all around, then led them off the path into the forest. Behind a dense planting of shrubs with thorns Mac decided would make quite reasonable knives, they came to an access port built into the volcanic rock. "Through here," 'Sephe said quietly. "Watch your step."

The warning came suspiciously late, Mudge having gone first and a faint cry of pain coming from the open doorway.

'Sephe grinned at Mac. "I told him."

Mac followed 'Sephe, who, after closing the door, took her down three uneven steps, then up a fourth where a low rail required those passing it to duck underneath. Mudge was there, rubbing his head. "This doesn't seem very efficient," he complained.

"If you have to run through here," 'Sephe assured him, "you've other things to worry about."

The corridor wasn't Sinzi white, but crudely carved into rock, in some places so irregular that the ceiling protruded downward. 'Sephe activated the lights in each twisting segment as they approached, checking the way ahead but stopping short of making them wait while she did so.

Just when Mac felt they were probably under the ocean, the corridor widened into a disarmingly normal cargo loading space, complete with busy servos and workers moving crates to and from a series of rakish-looking surface-to-orbit craft lined up before immense closed doors.

Mudge made a happy sound.

'Sephe jerked her head toward what appeared to be a temporary shelter within the cargo bay. "In there, Mac. Don't be long."

Now that she was here, Mac's feet felt glued to the floor. She held out the salmon. "Take this for me—"

"Mac."

"Please." She shoved it into 'Sephe's hand and ran back into the tunnellike corridor.

She'd said good-bye to Sam.

She couldn't say good-bye to Nik.

"Stupid rail." Mac sat on the bench and rubbed her hip. She'd forgotten the trap and almost flipped right over the bar, saving herself in time.

Bruising her hip nicely.

She leaned back, grateful the bench had a back, although it wasn't quite meant for her particular body plan. *And those odd holes in the middle . . .* Mac bent over to look, trying to match their shape to the posteriors of the aliens she'd met here.

Rustle . . . rustle.

She froze in place. The sound was surely innocent in a tamed wood like this. Mac listened, but heard nothing further.

Suddenly, a wooden salmon appeared under her nose, peering up at her through one of the holes.

"Funny," she managed to say, sitting up with a jerk.

The salmon withdrew and Nik came around the bench to sit beside her. He didn't say a word, just held the carving on his lap, in both hands, apparently studying it for all he was worth.

Shy?

Mac looked at him. Gone were the glasses, the suit, the cravat. Now he wore a spacer's jumpsuit, faded enough to likely be his own, pockets everywhere. It might have been dark blue once. Maybe purple. The boots were newer.

"You didn't dream last night." Quietly, as if to the wooden fish.

She gave an exasperated snort. "If you were there, why didn't you wake me up?"

"I hadn't seen you sleep like that before." Mac watched the dimple suddenly deepen in his cheek. "You snore."

"I do not," she protested and was fascinated by the upcurve of the corner of his mouth.

"It's a cute snore."

"Oh, that helps."

They fell silent again, Nik watching the salmon, Mac watching him.

"I made some notes for you," she said abruptly. "I gave them to Anchen."

"Got them. Thanks. And this." He put the salmon in one hand, and drew out the amulet from around his neck, the one the Progenitor had sent with Parymn. Still not looking at her, Nik brought it to his lips, then put it back inside his coveralls. The salmon went in a pocket. He leaned back, his head tilted to stare up into the trees. "I left you some notes, too. Gave them to your friend, Oversight."

Mac memorized the strong lines of his throat, pleasantly tormented by the pulse along the side, the soft shadow below his jaw. "Aren't you supposed to be leaving? Soon."

"Now. They're holding the launch for me."

Time's up. Mac's hands felt strangely heavy. "Nik. Why didn't you wake me? We could—" She couldn't help the huskiness of her voice. "A night. At least that."

She watched his throat work as he swallowed. "I considered it." The voice was light. Then Nik lifted his head and her heart pounded at the heat in his eyes. "Then I realized I'd want tomorrow and the next night. That I couldn't imagine any amount of time with you being enough. That I had to leave then or I wouldn't leave at all."

"Oh."

He didn't smile at the single syllable she managed, gazing into her eyes as if he couldn't do anything else, motionless.

Sometimes, Mac told herself as she reached for him, *you had to give the universe a shove.*

The universe didn't seem to mind at all.

23

READING AND REUNION

MAC NUDGED the glasses on the table in a half circle, careful not to touch the lenses. They'd been with the notes Nik had left her. Mudge had thought them an odd sort of gift. Then again, he still thought Nik was Stefan.

They were an odd gift, she smiled to herself, *but useful.* Through Nik's lenses, the white walls and furnishings of the consulate showed their true Sinzi glory. Not a bad perk for being the Sinzi-ra's favorite Human.

There'd been no news. Not yet. The Ro were silent. The Dhryn might have all been killed—not that anyone believed it. Researchers were poring over every scrap of wreckage and space-chilled flesh. Nik hadn't reported in—that they'd told her. The two, Human and Dhryn, weren't traveling alone, although Mac hadn't been pleased to learn Cinder had been one of those selected. But Nik could handle it. She had her part of the puzzle. The Origins Team was busy and productive.

Although there had been, Mac scowled, *far too many meetings.*

"Where did I leave off?" she mumbled to herself, picking up the clumsy thing. The book wasn't a real antique, but a copy. A stack of others lay in the sand—gifts from her Dad. *The format was,* Anchen had assured her, *a welcome change for her eyes,* easily tired these days from practicing her reading skills.

"Ah. Here."

Mac had wrestled one of the jelly-chairs to where the afternoon sun would fall over her shoulder. Winter had already given them a frost or two, but also clearer skies. She curled herself up and looked over at Emily with a wistful smile.

Against the white pillow, her face was composed, at peace. As it had been for the last twenty-seven days. The skin had recovered some of its luster, though not all. The cheeks were still sunken, the arms above their prostheses too thin. Her bones, graceful yet ominous, pressed outward as if anxious to leave. The hair alone seemed right, shining black and thick.

Every third breath was that soft little snore Em had denied utterly when awake. Mac listened for it in the night, obscurely comforted.

"Any change?"

Two put a glass of water on Mac's desk, in reach of her hand. "No, Mac. Do you wish me to stay?"

"It's okay. Unless you want to hear the rest of this story?"

The staff came as close as ever to smiling, a crinkle at the corner of her eyes, a tilt to her head. "No, Mac. I heard sufficient of the last seven to know how it will end."

When Two had left, Mac took a drink, then found her page. True, the selection tended to a certain similarity in plot, but there were exciting bits. This part, for example. She cleared her voice and started to read aloud. " 'The trail through the bog had grown cold since midnight—' "

"There's no sex in that one either."

"There doesn't have to be sex in everything you read," Mac said automatically, turning the page.

Then, realizing what had just happened, she stopped. The book fell from her hands as she looked toward Emily.

Dark eyes, tired *sane* eyes, met hers. "I should have remembered," Emily said, voice weak but feathered at the edges with that familiar, amused warmth. "You never let go of anyone, do you, Mac?"

Grin or cry?

Instead, Mac took Emily's outstretched hand gently in hers. It didn't matter that neither were real.

"Welcome back, Em."

REGENERATION

- CONTACT -

THE PORTENTS WILL COME. And Change will follow, to take the landscape, to bring death. Those who can flee, will.

And still that which is Dhryn must wait—too frail to risk confrontation—too slow to race others from the doom.

Only in the lull time, when the emptied land has finished dying around them, will the Dhryn venture forth. Scouts first, to taste the land, seek routes to what the Progenitors will crave. They will find where the great forests rot, bring the feast to sustain.

That which is Dhryn shall cleanse the land, removing debris, clearing blocked rivers. All will sustain the Progenitors as they *move* behind the rest.

Most will not complete the Great Journey, spent by the effort, worn by toil. Lost. Left. Remembered.

All that matters is the Progenitors reach Haven, the place of safety and plenty. There They will rest, setting the Path in memory, bringing forth new generations who will not know Change in their lifetimes.

Until it begins again.

(Inscription found at southern hemisphere haven site 9903-ZA,
pre-alloy Dhryn ruin, Planet Myriam)

BEER AND BOTHER

"**A**RE YOU THINKING what I'm thinking?"

Dr. Mackenzie Connor, Mac to those she intended to talk to more than once, gave her closest friend a wary look. She'd learned the hard way where such conversational gambits could lead. *Especially when Dr. Emily Mamani was* this *bored.* "That," she ventured, "depends on what you're thinking."

That tilt of the elegant head, with that smile, spelled pure mischief. "Then you are!"

"Am not." As this didn't seem a particularly adult retort, Mac added primly, "I never think such things."

Emily's laugh, as rich and contagious as before, as always, warmed Mac's heart. She wished it could erase the shadows clinging to the other woman's cheekbones, haunting her eyes. *Time might do that.*

Or not.

"You're allowed, you know," Em continued, leaning closer. They were both sitting with their elbows propped on the dark, polished wood of the bar. The bar that stretched in a friendly manner right to the door.

The door Mac eyed wistfully. *She'd left so much work . . .*

"Oh, no, you don't," Emily protested. "You promised."

"So now you think you're thinking what I'm thinking?" Mac asked, dragging her attention back to her beer. "Hah!"

"Hah, yourself. We get a night away from that bunch of loons. You promised."

"They aren't—" Mac stopped as Emily raised a shapely, black, and highly expressive eyebrow. True, Wilson Kudla, author of *Chasm Ghouls: They Exist and Speak to Me,* was presently conducting the third night of what boded to be a prolonged—and already very sweaty—exorcism attempt, having, like the rest of the Origins Team, become convinced the Ro were not beings to welcome under one's roof. Or inside one's tent.

Not that the rest of the team had tents, Mac corrected hurriedly. Particularly tents full of perspiring Humans chanting themselves hoarse. "Not all of them are loons," she qualified. "Archaeologists simply have their own approach to the work. You'll get used to it." This last hope echoed inside her half empty glass as Mac lifted it to her mouth. She took a long swallow, thought about it, then took another. A local brew. By now too warm by her standards, but with an excellent aftertaste. She squinted into the foam. *Honey?*

Despite its colorful name, *The Takahe Nest* was little more than a long room, two thirds filled with wooden tables and assorted chairs. The floor was wood as well, rough and scarred by hiking boots—from the look of the trail leading past the bar, soaking wet and muddy hiking boots. The bartender, a big friendly man who'd introduced himself as "Kevin Maclean but not the actor," claimed it had rained every day of the first fifty years the *Nest* was open. The occasional sunny day since hadn't helped much. Mac and Emily had been directed here to experience firsthand a slice of the unique Fiordland atmosphere.

It had that. Mac surveyed the eclectic and dusty mix of objects suspended from every exposed beam and wall. Perplexed-looking stags' heads, antique hunting weapons, and odd-shaped drinking cups vied for space with what could only be bits and pieces of skims—most broken. The tip of a helicopter blade—Mac's curiosity had made her ask what it was—easily two hundred years older than the pub itself, held place of honor behind the bar. Nor'easters ripped down the mountain valleys without warning, Kevin had explained cheerfully. The wind took its tithe from anything that dared be in the sky.

The clientele matched the bar. *Well, except for themselves.* Emily—in her long black shawl and yellow top, with a full red skirt swirling around her calves—stood out like some exotic flower transplanted in the wrong place. Mac herself, in dark pants, blouse, and sweater, had attracted only slightly fewer stares when entering. She eased her toes in the dressy sandals Emily had insisted she wear, missing her boots. The few folks here looked to be straight off a hiking trail or farm—people who worked with their hands and weren't afraid of a little deluge.

Felt like home. Although she'd never had a beer as a namesake before. Mac tipped the rest of her bottle of "Mac's" into her glass and smiled.

"How long are we going to stay here?" Emily demanded in a low voice, with a gesture including more than *The Takahe Nest.*

Back to that again? Mac held back a sigh. "Your guess is as good as mine, Em," she said, truthfully enough.

The Gathering, the collaboration of every Dhryn expert the Sinzi could find within the Interspecies Union, had been—*disbanded wasn't the right word,* Mac decided. Sent packing was more like it. The synergy provided by their being in the same place, namely housed at the IU Consulate for Sol System, had been irrevocably outweighed by becoming a single, convenient target. The Dhryn assault could have eradicated not only life on Earth, but the best chance of coming up with a defense for the rest of the IU—those thousands of worlds linked by the transects that permitted instantaneous travel between star systems.

"The sum," Mac mused into her drink. "More than the parts, you know."

"Gods, Mac. Philosophy on the second beer? Way too early."

Mac's lips twitched. "Sorry." She ticked her glass against Emily's. "Bad habit."

"I'll say. Kev!" In answer to Emily's urgent summons, the bartender hurried over with two more bottles, lingering to trade smiles. *Mistake.* When Kevin turned away to serve other customers, Emily leaned well over the bar for a better look, lips pursed to whistle. Mac hauled her back to her seat. "Two beers are way too early for that," she muttered under her breath, hoping no one else had noticed. Luckily, few of the tables were inhabited this early in the evening. A couple held what had to be groups of regulars, engrossed in their own conversations; the rest of the patrons stood around tables at the far end, where each solid *thunk* of dart into cork was followed by a roar—frequently accompanied by jeering comments about coordination and the lack thereof.

Emily settled peacefully. Then she leaned closer, her shoulder against Mac's. "We don't need to be here, Mac," very quietly. "We shouldn't be here."

No chance she meant the pub this time either. For all of Em's insistence on a night out for the two of them, "just like any Saturday at Base," this was looking more and more like a night out to air grievances Emily didn't feel like discussing with anyone else. *One grievance in particular.*

Mac swallowed the dregs of beer number two before taking a healthy swig of beer number three straight from the bottle. Nice and cold. "I know," she admitted at last, pouring the rest slowly into her glass. "The Sinzi-ra—"

"The Sinzi-ra has already sent every other research team through the transects, each to a secret destination. Smart move. The right move, Mac. *They* know this place."

There was only one "they" to Emily, anymore. Her by now familiar stress on the pronoun sent a chill down Mac's spine.

In the six weeks and handful of days since Emily's reawakening, her scars had healed, flesh had reappeared over her bones, and her skin had regained its normal golden glow. The streaks of silver in her glossy black hair were new, but she'd never been one to avoid an attractive contrast. The repairs to the damage left by the Ro—the new arms, abdominal wall, portions of her back, one cheek, internal organs—had been made with an ability to match detail beyond current Human medicine.

Only the way Emily flinched from naming the Ro aloud showed what hadn't been fixed. So far, she'd remembered nothing of her time with the aliens. *It wasn't her memory that had failed,* Mac corrected, studying her friend. Noad, Anchen's physician-self, believed Emily's mind continued to struggle for some means to process those experiences, based as they were on stimuli from an environment no Human sense had evolved to understand. No-space. The chosen realm of the Myrokynay, the Ro.

Emily did recall, with devastating accuracy, everything else. How the Ro had used her to help destroy the very life she'd thought she was sacrificing herself to protect. How, through her actions, the Dhryn had been unleashed . . . to decimate worlds . . . to threaten Earth herself . . . and now, to wait like some hidden plague, ready to strike anywhere in the Interspecies Union.

They'd lied to her.

They'd discarded her.

That simmering rage deep in the eyes meeting hers, even here and now, above the cheerful smile Emily shaped with her lips? Mac knew what it meant.

They would pay.

Mac recognized Emily's fury because it matched her own. No matter what anyone else thought of the Ro, no matter that there was division in the IU, the same evidence maddeningly taken as proof by both sides, she knew the Ro were the true enemy. They'd turned a sentient species into a deadly weapon, one they'd used to scour the Chasm worlds of life, one they were using again.

Some night out. Mac looked away, letting her gaze travel the labels of the truly bewildering array of bottles lined up behind the bar. Single malt scotch, most with names as long and unpronounceable as those for local streets.

No luck. After a moment's struggle, she gave up. *Shouldn't drink and read,* Mac chided herself, refusing to blame her still-tenuous ability to sort meaning from the written word. *No wonder the devout kept lists.* "Here," she said at last, patting the bar. "Somewhere else. It doesn't matter where we are, Em. Whatever gets the job done. At least here we have resources—the backing of the Ministry as well as the IU. A little patience, okay?"

That drew a steady look, a nod, and finally a chuckle as Emily let go for the moment. "Patience? Oh, please, Mac. Not *that* word again." She wiggled her long fingers, gloved in textured black silk, in front of Mac's eyes. "If they made these things properly, it wouldn't take ridiculous, monotonous, 'patience, patience, Dr. Mamani' exercises! One dose of sub-teach, and I'd be performing solos on my cello."

"Cello?" Mac snorted. Emily's taste in music ran to a driving, heavy beat and flashing strobes, preferably delivered over a hot, crowded dance floor. She wrapped her own artificial hand around her glass and raised it, the faintly blue-tinged pseudoskin glistening as if with sweat. *Trick of the bar's light.* Mac glanced at her friend and stiffened.

Emily was staring at her own hands, as if suddenly transfixed by them, her eyes wide and unblinking. "They missed one," she mumbled in a strange, unsteady voice, bending then straightening each finger and thumb in slow motion, one after the other, again and again. "I told you, Mac. This isn't right. They missed—"

"Emily, no." Mac took Emily's nearest hand, gently pushing it down to rest on the polished wood of the bar. "Em. Em!"

She shivered, then gave Mac a thoroughly sane look of annoyance. "What's the matter with you?"

"Had a vision of you playing a cello, that's all," Mac lied.

She'd thought Emily had stopped this fuss over her fingers, the absentminded counting she'd continue until interrupted. *This quiet place was a mistake,* Mac decided. *Emily needed that hot dance floor, ideally crowded with young, athletic men. Distraction.*

Then again, her fellow biologist was once more making come-hither eyes at their dubious but willing bartender, who, to be honest, was a few years past young and looked to lately watch more athletics than he performed.

Dancing was one thing. *This could get complicated.* "Em," Mac warned.

"He's cute." Emily, perfectly capable of flirting and arguing at the same time, circled back to her subject like a shark circling blood spoor in the water. "Hollans. Ask him to get us out of the consulate."

A bubble fought free of the cream-tinged foam as Mac watched. She helped another burst with a fingertip.

"Well?" Em prompted.

"We aren't exactly on speaking terms at the moment."

"And whose fault is that, Dr. Tact?"

Mac pressed her lips together. Bernd Hollans, humanity's representative on the IU's council dealing with the Dhryn, was an important, capable individual of considerable influence who had, she gave credit where it was due, proved himself willing to listen and take action in a crisis. But with the immediate threat seemingly over, Hollans had reverted to the rule-following, overly cautious, pompous annoyance she'd initially judged him.

Who hovered *over her shoulder while she worked,* she grumbled to herself.

They didn't do well in meetings together. Not well at all. Mac winced. In fact, at the last one, she'd come close to throwing her imp at his head.

Hadn't let go. That had to count.

Out loud: "And I thought Oversight was bad."

"Old Charlie's all right," Emily asserted, taking a drink herself as if in toast.

While Mac agreed, she made a point of keeping any fondness for her former adversary to herself. They both preferred it that way. *But still . . .* She couldn't help herself: "He hates 'Charlie.' "

Emily grinned. "I know."

Mac's lips twitched. "No wonder you and Fourteen get along."

"Fish of a scale, my dear Dr.—" Emily began archly, then stopped, looking toward the door. "I see your friends have arrived."

"Who—?" Mac turned to answer her own question, then hurriedly looked away again. *Too late.*

She'd been spotted.

"Dr. Connor!"

"She's not here," that worthy muttered, glaring into her beer. "Not. Not. Not."

Emily's elbow dug into her ribs. "As if that's ever worked."

Stools and chairs complained as they acquired oversized passengers, the bar now filling up on either side of the two women. Kevin the bartender hesitated. Either he didn't know who to serve first, or he'd never been faced with so much gloom at one time in his entire career. Mac gave him a sympathetic look.

She wasn't entirely sure why the Sinzi-ra would choose Grimnoii to act as, well, she wasn't really certain what they did for the Sinzi either, other than wander about in groups of seeming misery from dusk till dawn. Intimidating groups of seeming misery, even without the ceremonial axes, knives, and spikes they were entitled to wear on consular grounds. Massive, furred, cloaked-in-brown misery.

Depressing giant teddy bears. Who'd have thought?

"Glad we found you, Dr. Connor," said several Grimnoii at once. Completing their doleful effect—on Humans, at least—they had low, melancholy voices, capable of instilling the most cheerful greeting with funereal undertones.

Mac lifted a suitably limp hand in acknowledgment.

The Human minority sent up another series of raucous jeers as a *clink/plunk* announced a significant failure of aim. Several Grimnoii rose to head in that direction, as if determined to possess the entire building. *Or,* for all Mac knew, *their apparent fixation on pointy things extended to darts.*

Mac caught Em's eye, gave the "last call" look honed through years of practice, and picked up her beer. She poured it down her throat with one easy motion, replacing the glass on the bar with a firm thump to cover a less-than-discreet belch. *Always, when she rushed.* "Just leaving, Rumnor," she informed the alien who'd taken the stool to her left. "Have fun."

"No." A thick, pawlike hand trapped her arm in its warmth as she stood. "You must stay and drink cider with us, Dr. Connor. Much cider."

"Cider," echoed the rest in their sad voices. "Dr. Connor." "Cider." "Stay with us."

The snicker was Emily's.

Keeping her face as straight as possible—*one never knew which being could read Human expressions*—Mac improvised. "Sorry. Gotta go and—go and give blood," she nodded briskly. "Late for our biweekly drain." That said, she used her free hand to remove Rumnor's. He didn't resist, though his pale brown eyes wept copiously. *Nothing to do with her or cider.* The tearing seemed a species' trait, producing crusty yellow tracks down the fur of both cheeks and dribbles over the mud-brown cloth that covered a Grimnoii's rounded chest. "You know Humans when we don't expel our erythrocytes on time," Mac continued glibly.

Which was #22 on the *Favorite Myths About Humanity* list published by the consulate, but she'd bet Rumnor wasn't the brochure-reading kind.

Sure enough, he grunted something inexpressibly sad, his attention drifting to the tray of cider the bartender was carrying past. One paw wavered out to engulf a mug, endangering the rest.

"Let's settle the—" Mac began, then realized Emily was halfway to the door. *Smart woman.* She stood to follow. "Put us on their tab, Kevin!" she called to the bartender, who raised a brow but nodded.

She caught up with Emily on the sidewalk, standing below the sign that read "Warning: Wreckers at Work" complete with an image of several large parrot-like birds in yellow construction helmets, each using a jackhammer to demolish a parked skim. *She'd forgotten to ask Kevin about that one.*

Mac and Emily crossed the street in companionable silence, sandals crunching through the remnants of late-winter leaves. This part of Te Anau had wide, quiet roadways lined with tidy buildings, each with a small patch of garden out front. Trees, most with no intention of dropping leaves despite the season, overhung the pole lamps. Their soft shadows blurred the circles of light beneath. Shivering at the difference from the too-warm indoor air to the evening's nip, Mac shrugged into the sweater she'd tied around her waist. Em had tossed her black shawl over her head as well as shoulders, the ends still brushing the backs of her ankles.

A skim passed in the distance, but otherwise the town appeared deserted. Lambing was starting, according to Kevin, an event guaranteed to keep a majority of the local population preoccupied for the next few weeks.

Emily didn't say a word until Mac paused to squint up at the road sign, trying to decide which lengthy assortment of vowels was which. Then, quietly but with conviction: "I told you we couldn't leave the consulate without being watched."

Of course not, Mac thought smugly. They had their protectors—out of sight, out of mind, until now. *Just not teddy bears on the town.* She shook her head. "You're reading too much into it, Em. There are only two bars within walking distance from the lev station. Rumnor's lot probably drank the other out of cider." *Making* The Feisty Weka *the place for us,* she promised herself. *Not to mention it boasted a dance floor.*

The third and hasty beer was trying to make itself felt, so Mac decided not to guess at the vowels lined up on the sign. She pulled out her imp to display directions in the air above her hands. The light from the map etched bone-thin lines back into Emily's face. Mac turned it off quickly. "Thaddaway," she announced, pointing.

"Wait. I see a shortcut."

Shortcut? Mac shook her head again, but willingly followed the taller woman as she picked a narrow lane overhung by vines, clearly not heading toward the *Weka.* She puffed as they passed through the glow from a back porch light, admiring the little cloud of condensed vapor her breath produced. Oh, yes. Winter. *Remarkable notion, winter in August.*

Mac gathered her thoughts. *She hadn't had* that *much beer, surely.* No, it had to be the deliciously familiar sensation of sneaking off making her giddy, of letting Emily lead her where she'd never—as a serious person with responsibilities she took, well, seriously—ever go on her own.

No point asking where they were going.

"I should have asked where you were taking me," Mac complained some time later. She was perched on the flattest of several large tumbled stones, trying to deal with the sodden mess that had been her new sandals. *Never,* she vowed, *go out in anything but sensible boots.* She finally managed to pull and twist the now-loose straps into some kind of knot, hopefully to stay on her feet until they got home.

"You know you like it here."

Mac grinned. "You had any doubt?" She leaned back, supported by her hands on the damp rock behind her, and admired the view.

Pasture climbed from the opposite side of the river in smooth waves of darkness that appeared to break against the distant silhouettes of trees marking the forest edge. All it would take were pale swirls of morning mist to complete the illusion of land become sea. For now, the moon, only a quarter full, picked out the rapids mere meters from their feet, split by long, fingerlike gravel bars: gray on black, the presence of driftwood and boulder suggested by faint, pale streaks of foam.

The pile of rock she was using for a seat must be the ruins of an old bridge support, a very small bridge, likely for four-footed traffic and trampers. New Zealanders, Mac had been told, loved nothing more than walking their countryside, carrying lunch. The support's abandoned partner huddled on the opposite bank, undercut and ready to fall into the water.

Mac drew a slow breath in through her nose, dismissing the honey-note of beer, the wet richness of grass, that pungent whiff of equally wet sheep. *There.* That smell. The river itself. *Its life.*

Mac doubted anyone but Emily appreciated how thoroughly she hated being stuck indoors. Then again, Lyle Kanaci could wax almost poetic about his research station on the lifeless Dhryn home world, now officially renamed Myriam after his late wife.

Amazing what Oversight could accomplish with a flood of officious memos on a topic, Mac thought fondly.

Emily stood to the right of Mac's stony perch, in this meager light as ephemeral as the rest of the landscape, as liable to shift or disappear as any shadow. Mac tasted the old dread. The damage left by the Ro had been extensive; the reconstruction of Emily's body a challenge to the Sinzi's skill. But it had worked. Emily lived. *She* was *here.*

"How did you know about this place?" Mac asked, pleased by the calm tone of her voice. *Mind you, she'd had practice there, too.* Calls to her father and brothers. Emily's sister. Kammie Noyo back at Base. Telling them what she could, without revealing what she couldn't: *yes, Emily's been found . . . she's been ill and needs time to recover . . . I'm staying with her . . . bit of vacation for both of us . . . you know me, catching up on some research, too . . . call anytime.*

She'd finally learned to lie, Mac thought with a mix of regret and grim pride. *Maybe not up to Emily or Nik's standards, but enough to forestall inconvenient questions.*

Emily gave a soft laugh. "I didn't." A pause. "You know me, Mac—always looking for the more interesting path."

As that path, from the end of the laneway, had involved several unseen but deep puddles—hence the ruined sandals—followed by a scramble up a rocky slope and down again until they could no longer see the lights from the town, "interesting" seemed a bit of an understatement. Mac stretched contentedly, giving the situation deep thought. "I don't suppose you brought beer."

A chuckle, then: "Tell me. Our Nikolai. Were you lovers before he left?"

Vintage Emily. Shocked sober, if she wasn't before, Mac was grateful for the darkness that hid her flaming cheeks. "I don't think that's any of your—"

"No, then." Another pause. "Trust me. It's just as well."

Not so vintage. Mac tried to avoid temptation but failed: "This," she asked, "from the woman whose motto is 'a night alone is a night wasted'?"

"Mac. You're such an honest fool," kindly. "Sex is the oldest excuse. Even low-class hotels keep vidbots out of their rooms."

Mac lost all interest in the river. She stared at the tall, slender shadow of her friend, trying not to think what she was thinking, trying not to let anything else *change.*

As usual, the universe was oblivious to the wishes of a certain salmon researcher. Emily spoke again, the words as calm and inevitable as the dew forming on the grass around them. "You alone, Mac, haven't asked me to explain what I did. Why I did it. Don't you think it's time?"

A night out like the old days? Hah!

Emily's invitation, this conversation with the two of them faceless and in the dark, snapped closed around Mac like a trap. They weren't supposed to have it. She'd gone out of her way to make sure they didn't. *Forgive and forget.* That was the way it should be.

She shook her head. Not to deny the ambush. *Oh, if anyone knew the risks of an Emily Mamani Patented Pub Crawl Shortcut, she did.* But at herself.

Emily had been debriefed by seemingly everyone else on the planet—and quite a few off. Mac had avoided those sessions. She'd chosen to accept Emily back without questions, give her what peace she could. *Forgive and forget.* She trusted the Sinzi, or the Ministry, would tell her any facts she'd need for their work.

For Emily's peace? Mac wondered with unexpected guilt. *Or her own?*

"You're back," she protested, knowing it was in vain. "That's all I care about."

"Don't be afraid, Mac," Emily replied ever so gently. "The truth—it's not going to change things. You won't lose me again."

Emily had asked for Mac's forgiveness. *She'd already given it.* Mac shook her head again. "I don't need to know."

"I need you to. Please, Mac. Don't be difficult."

She'd love to be difficult. Instead, Mac pulled one knee to her chest and rested her chin on it, staring into the dark. "Suit yourself."

CONVERSATION AND CONSEQUENCE

"IT BEGAN WITH FEAR," Emily told her. "I was only a child when I first heard about the Chasm, a place where all life had been mysteriously wiped from its planets. Only a child, but I understood too well. I had nightmares of everything around me disappearing. Over and over. Finally my mother gave me books about the Chasm. She insisted I read them; told me the only way to stop fear was to learn its cause. My fear turned to obsession." Her voice became rueful. "I grew up planning to save the rest of the universe."

Somehow, Mac wasn't surprised. Of course, she herself had grown up ignoring the universe, blithely confident it would return the favor. *Look where both attitudes had landed them,* she thought grimly.

"I continued to study everything I could find," Emily went on. "Until, one day, I stumbled on the key, Mac. Some believed a sentient species from the Chasm had escaped its destruction. Such a species would have my answers. All I had to do was find them."

"The Survivor Legend," Mac acknowledged. Brymn had told her Emily had been researching it when they'd met. *A scrap of truth within the lies.*

Emily's secret quest had succeeded. She'd found the Ro—or they'd found her. As far as Mac was concerned, the difference was academic.

Not a healthy topic of conversation. Not away from trained help, with Emily's mind fragile enough. There could be worse things than compulsive finger counting. "Good thing you went into fish biology instead," Mac offered, her voice strained to her own ears. "How did that happen?"

"I didn't. Not instead. Because."

Trust Emily to dangle the right bait. Worried or not, Mac couldn't help herself. " 'Because?' "

"I haven't lost it." Emily's laugh was too hollow to be reassuring. "Believe me, Mac, there's been good, legitimate science behind the search for a lost civilization from the Chasm, unlike your chanting friends. But . . . I felt it prudent to have a day job, to keep my private research exactly that. To this day, my sponsor—even my sources—don't know the full extent of my efforts. Just to be discreet around you."

Sponsor? Sources? Mac floundered after what confounded her most. "Around me? Who?"

"Who did you think I was with on Saturday nights?"

Anyone willing? Mac thought of the innumerable partners Emily had drawn from dance floors and bars during their times together. Was information for sale the common denominator she'd missed amid the loud shirts, lack of shirts, tattoos, suits, and the "only a mother could love" still-breathing? "There were quite a few," she concluded, feeling every bit the fool Emily'd named her.

A real laugh this time. "They weren't all sources, Mac."

Mac blushed in the dark. "Oh. Of course." *She was* not *going back through her mental list.* "I assume you had to pay them—the sources, I mean," she added quickly.

"Hence the sponsor. How do you think I knew about Kanaci's little group?"

She hadn't, Mac realized. *Given it thought, that is.* She'd gladly left the details of that grisly day to others, her attention divided between Emily's recovery and her research group. *Interspersed with daydreams about a certain absent and altogether yummy spy.*

Mac coughed. "Okay. How did you know?"

"Sencor Research funds us both. I had access to Kanaci's data, such as it was." Emily's voice grew amused. "Which reminds me. Bureaucrats have this lovely inertia—want to bet they've kept crediting my account?" The amusement faded. "Before you start on me, Mac, don't. The Ministry of Extra-Sol Human Affairs has everything I've done to date for Sencor—I gave your formidable Dr. Stewart my codes and contacts weeks ago. Surprised she didn't demand an impression of my teeth at the same time."

Mac refused to be distracted by Emily's opinion of 'Sephe, stuck on the improbably normal. "You had a sponsor," she echoed. "A real sponsor. To chase a—a myth!"

"Yes, Mac." Em's tone was the impatient but fond one she used fairly often during their discussions. *Usually when Mac was being willfully obtuse about some offworld topic.* "The Group very quietly supports a number of research projects into the Chasm. Their interest in the Survivors matched my own. They've funded my work for over fifteen years."

Mac snorted. The snort turned into a giggle. A giggle that multiplied until Emily interrupted, sounding rather offended: "I don't see what's so funny—"

"I know you're persuasive, Em, but how on Earth did you manage to talk these people into supporting you for years, pay for clandestine sources, send you offworld—" Mac stopped, considering what wasn't funny to her after all. "That's a great deal of funding." *Enough to finance every project at Base for a year, if not more.*

With trademark Mamani arrogance: "The goal was worth it. And so was I."

The goal had almost killed them both. Mac eased her bottom on the stone, stretching out her legs. *It still might.* "I don't get it," she said bluntly. "To start with, you're a fish biologist, like me."

"Haven't seen you studying salmon lately."

Not her idea. Aloud, and letting her exasperation through: "Putting aside the whole issue of searching for a species no one has ever proved existed in the first place, supposedly in hiding where no one can find them for the last three thousand years, why would Sencor sponsor you, of all people, to look for them? What could you possibly have had to offer? And, please, no innuendo."

"Spoilsport." Mac could hear the grin in Emily's voice.

The tone, the banter, was Emily at her most relaxed. Mac didn't buy it. Her friend hadn't moved since they'd arrived. She stood looking out over the river, a slip of darkness. The moonlight barely caught the fringes of her shawl, tugged by the light breeze. It didn't reveal her face.

The Emily Mac knew was restless and prone to pacing, said pacing typically accompanied by dramatic gestures liable to threaten both lab equipment and incautious vases. Her entire body could become an exclamation point. This new ability to remain still—it wasn't right. Mac curled up to hug both knees. *They should have stayed in the bar despite Rumnor and his pack.* "Well?" she prompted reluctantly.

"Weeellll," repeated Emily, stretching the word. "Tonight's supposed to be fun, Mac." That coaxing voice. *Emily the troublemaker voice.* More than anything, Mac wanted to be relieved by the sound of it. "C'mon, Mac. Take a guess."

Or maybe not. "Guess?" Mac repeated blankly.

"Guess. Don't worry. I'll give you a clue. Dr. Mackenzie Connor has left her salmon to follow aliens migrating across the stars, *si*? Dr. Emily Mamani did the opposite."

Gods. It struck too close to what hurt between them: that Emily came to work at Base, befriended Mac, only to lay the Ro's trap for Brymn.

Old, old news. Mac shook her head, impatient with herself and easily frustrated— as usual—by Emily's penchant for games. *It was that. Nothing more. Forgive me, Emily'd asked.*

She'd forgiven her.

What more did she want?

"You, Emily Mamani," Mac said through tight lips, "can be the most incredibly annoying—"

"Lazy, are you? Think! You haven't had that much beer."

Pity. "Fine," Mac surrendered for the second time. "That's the clue? You did the opposite to me, in terms of choice in research fields? I suppose that means you started with this obsession about Survivors and only later switched to fish biology, eventually developing technology to follow trophic movement in benthic-feeding fish species in the Sargasso Sea by identifying and tracing individuals. Promising topic," she added wistfully. "I don't suppose your sponsor was interested in that."

"Oh, yes, they were. Because I was interested. Think, Mac," Emily urged again, the hoarse emphasis in her voice abruptly making this anything but a game. "I need you to understand me."

Understand? Mac felt the hairs rise on the back of her neck, on her real forearm. Her stomach twisted to remind her it currently held an unfamiliar blend of sausage in thick pastry, plus three "Mac" beers. *She could almost feel Seung's hands on her shoulders . . . hear Denise complaining about the com system . . . see Norrey's . . .*

Understand *that level of betrayal?*

When Mac didn't—couldn't—speak, Emily pushed: "Why do you think I developed the Tracer device, Mac?"

Shivering free of ghosts, Mac found her voice, lips numb. "To record genetic information for individual fish in a moving group." *To find and track Mac's own DNA through the labyrinth of tunnels beneath the surface of Haven, to the Progenitor's Chamber, so the Ro could target their prey.*

Why? Mac puzzled, gladly distracted by the familiar problem. To set the great Dhryn ships in motion? They'd hardly needed to strike a specific portion of the planet for that. There had to be another purpose, some reason one Progenitor had been the target.

A question high on Nik's list to ask, for it was this same Progenitor he'd left to find. Mac looked up at what stars showed between the sheets of moon-grayed cloud. *Not that she'd the faintest idea where he was.* As few as possible knew where he'd gone and why. His mission with the Dhryn was a secret even from Emily. Though, given she'd already found out more about Nik than Mac had intended, it seemed only a matter of time till she learned the rest.

"Mac."

Emily's impatient voice dragged Mac's attention back, reluctantly, to the here-and-now. She scowled. "If you've something to tell me, Emily, I wish you'd do it. I hate games."

"I know. But this time, it's important to me. *Por favor?* I need you to feel something of what I felt, when I first recognized the potential of my approach. I want you to—"

"—understand," Mac snapped. "I heard."

"Is that so hard, my friend?"

"Yes!" The word was hard and sharp, like a weapon launched in the dark. Mac shuddered and hunched her shoulders. "Em—Emily, I'm sorry. I didn't mean . . ." *Forgive and* forget. *Why wasn't Emily cooperating?*

"Of course you did." Pure triumph. "About time, too."

"'About time,'" Mac repeated. *Something was wrong here.* "What are you talking about?"

"Poor Mac. You've held on to me, to our friendship, with that incomparable will of yours. It saved me; I love you for it. But it isn't real—"

"How can you say that?" Mac whispered, feeling the burn of tears. "Emily—"

"It's not—not if you can't bring yourself to admit the Emily you thought you knew was someone different. Mac, if you can't understand me, and still call me friend, you might as well give in to that anger you're holding just as tight."

"I'm not angry—"

"And I'm a cod. Honestly, Mac, you're the only one who doesn't see it. You're furious with me. You've every right to be! Look what I've done!"

"No," Mac exclaimed. "I know it wasn't your fault—"

Emily's voice turned cold: "No, Mac, you don't. You're hoping it wasn't my fault. You're doing your utmost to avoid any evidence that might prove you wrong. Damn poor science, if you ask me."

"I didn't ask you," Mac lashed out.

"Which is why we're here," Emily responded with equal passion. "I can't stand to have you like this, Mac. Clinging like grim death to an Emily you fear never existed. Refusing to find out if this Emily—" a low thud as Emily thumped her chest with a fist, "—is the friend you thought you had. Gods, Mac. Anyone else would have demanded answers the instant I was conscious. I waited. I wondered if it was that place—being among aliens, strangers. But even here, by water . . . ?" Emily stopped, then went on in a husky voice: "Must you always do things the hard way?"

Mac licked her lips, tasting salt. "I lost you once."

A heavy sigh from the dark. "You haven't found me yet."

The words were half accusation, half challenge. Mac rubbed her eyes with her real hand, feeling abruptly weary. *Hadn't found her?* Nonsense. Her friend was standing right there.

Or—was she? Wasn't that the root of Mac's reluctance to know more about Emily and her past?

That she didn't know this woman at all?

"Give me a minute," she pleaded. "I need to think."

"That would be a nice change."

"Shut up, Em," Mac muttered distractedly. She focused on one thing at a time, did her best to keep her thoughts free of emotion.

A brilliant, ambitious mind . . . a seemingly intractable puzzle. Emily and the mystery of the Chasm. A good fit, attracting the support of Sencor.

Perhaps good enough to attract the Ro as well. *There was irony for you.*

Mac flinched, circled back to Emily's obsession. Why switch to fish biology? Why that particular field . . . *unless* . . . She crowed: "You believed the Survivors were aquatic! You built the Tracer to find them!"

"Must you shout?" Emily complained.

"The sheep won't care," Mac observed dryly. "I thought you wanted me to react."

"React. Just no shouting." From her tone, Emily was making a face. "Humor me. It's not easy giving up my ace, even to you."

Ace? Mac shifted restlessly. *More old news.* The real Survivors had been found. "It's not easy sitting on this rock."

"I'm trying to unburden my soul here."

Wasn't her idea. Mac made her own face, but settled again. "What made you so sure the Survivors existed in the first place?"

"There was evidence from the Chasm itself, if you knew where to look. I did. You have to realize, Mac, at that time research was devoted to planets with ruins or potential for mining. Interest was sporadic at best; support, the same. It's not as if the IU lacks living worlds to explore, thanks to the Sinzi. And the Chasm—it's not a comfortable place."

Neither was a rock. "What evidence did you find?" Mac prodded, thinking wistfully of the warm, crowded pub. Not to mention barstools. *Easier to stop that hint of rain in the air than Emily on a roll.* Especially when that roll was for Mac's enlightenment.

"The anomaly," Emily said with relish. "The only system connected with the rest of no interest to archaeologists or miners. Chasm System 232. Oh, it had a world capable of supporting life. Once. It became so much orbiting rubble—by my dating, three thousand years ago, give or take a decade." She paused as if this was significant.

"One of us," Mac hinted, "didn't take astrophysics."

"Think about it, Mac. We know the Chasm worlds were destroyed by the Dhryn three thousand years ago; by your Brymn's estimate, that's the Moment, when the Ro locked his kind in the Haven System." Emily's voice held unusual patience. "Here we have a planet destroyed at the same time, in a completely different way."

"And no else one noticed?" Mac pursued. "C'mon, Emily."

"The team who originally mapped Chasm 232 pegged it as a natural disaster. There was no reason to look at it more closely—not with all those planets with ruins waiting to be explored. But we both know the Dhryn aren't *Their* only weapon."

Oh, they knew. The Ro had toppled a mountainside to cover their tracks. Sing-li Jones, chief among the Ministry personnel still assigned to her, admitted they didn't know how the aliens had done it. Mac shifted to another rock. She was no more at ease talking out loud about their invisible enemy than Emily was.

She always listened. The wind ruffling the grass. The scurry of something small and careful. The cheerful babble of water over stone. Nothing unusual.

Nothing unusual now. Mac didn't quite shiver.

What she didn't understand was where Emily was going with this. "Say I accept your dating," Mac suggested. "I don't follow what this has to do with aquatic aliens."

"Not so fast, Mac. This one world wasn't destroyed by the Dhryn. Think what that means."

"You think the inhabitants of Chasm 232 had some way to protect themselves. There's an easier explanation, Em," she frowned. "That world could have been home to—to *Them*—and discarded when they were finished with it."

"*They* abandoned orbiting rock before humanity stood up." As if uneasy, Emily moved at last, to pull her shawl tighter as the breeze lifted its edge. "It couldn't have been *Theirs*. But it was a world that somehow evaded the Chasm catastrophe. So I studied long-range scans of the rubble, looking for anything to set this place apart from the others. Insufficient. I had Sencor divert a salvage ship to collect samples for their experts to analyze. You should have been there when the first results came in, confirming my remote dating, showing refined materials. It was quite a thrill."

Given her intense lack of interest toward anything off-Earth in those days, Mac sincerely doubted that, but made a noncommittal noise to be polite.

Emily continued. "We found abundant evidence the world in Chasm 232 had supported a technologically advanced civilization during the same time span as the others. Perhaps they'd died with their world. But what if they hadn't? There was legend, other hints. So if these were the Survivors, the question became: how could they have escaped? *They* controlled the transects; the Dhryn attacked through the gates." Her hand lifted skyward. "Leaving sublight. Maybe they had ships from a time of exploration before the transects; maybe they were warned to build them. What matters, Mac, is where they could have gone. Chasm 232 doesn't have many neighbors. At one-tenth light, we're talking almost a thousand years to the nearest world suited to you or me. Multigeneration ship—or stasis."

A raindrop hit her nose. Mac looked up in reflex and another hit her in the eye. She pulled her sweater over her head, feeling nostalgic.

"Long trip," she commented.

"If you need our kind of planet. But there's something closer. Much closer. Within a couple of centuries. A system with a similar star, a planet of the right mass. But with no signs of civilization or technology. On land, that is. But it has oceans. Lovely, deep, wide oceans."

"You don't have to be aquatic to live underwater," Mac observed. "We do it."

"For three thousand years?"

"There's that." As hypotheses went, Mac had heard flimsier ones. *Not much flimsier.*

Meanwhile, she discovered she could tuck a remarkable amount of herself inside her sweater. *Human Becomes Sheep—had to be in some brochure.* "I take it your buddies at Sencor checked it out?"

"Mac, were you not listening to a—"

"Using a scan from their ship in the Chasm," Mac interrupted. "What did you think I meant?" she asked innocently. "That they'd closed their eyes and clicked their heels? 'Poof' go the light-years?"

"Nothing," Emily said with exasperation, "from you would surprise me."

The familiar complaint was oddly comforting. Mac grinned to herself. "I presume your next step is to ask Anchen for a transect-initiating probe."

"*Aie!* Mackenzie Connor. Okay, that surprised me. When did you start caring about transect technology?"

The night you disappeared from Base, Mac almost said. She settled for: "When I started using it."

"You're right. We need to send a probe. Assuming there's a civilization there, and it's still space-capable, they can use the probe's instructions to build a transect gate on their end. When they do, we'll be connected. They'll know what happened. Just think of the possibilities." The satisfied warmth in Emily's voice only made what Mac had to say harder.

"I know how I'd react to a transect opening in my system," she began cautiously. "Not well."

"Bah. The Sinzi have made successful first contact with thousands of species. They'll be able to reassure the Survivors."

So much for caution. Mac bristled. "Reassure them about what? It's not as if we can stop the Dhryn from using the transects."

"It's worth the risk. If there's a chance the Survivors can help us—"

"Then the Ro will destroy their new home, too. Do you want to find more victims for them to slaughter?" Mac regretted the words the moment they left her lips, but didn't apologize. *The truth didn't come in an easier format.* "The Ro don't need gates. If your Survivors exist and have been left in peace until now, it's only because the Ro haven't considered them a threat."

Unless they were discovered—by someone or something else first. "That's why the Ro noticed you in the first place, isn't it, Emily?" Mac breathed. "You were looking for what they didn't want found."

Instead of answering, Emily said, very quietly, "It began with fear. It became obsession."

The rain chose that moment to go from teasing random drops to a steady, if light downpour. "Emily—" Mac's fingers tightened their hold on her sweater, "—you said that already."

"I know. It's the truth, Mac. You see, the day came when I received data from a new, unnamed source. Out of the blue. Wonderful, fresh information. Different from anything I'd seen before—than anyone had seen—about the technologies of that world in Chasm 232, about the planet itself. And because of my obsession, I kept it to myself."

The trap the Ro had set for her. "Why, Em?" Mac asked, frustrated. "You must have realized something was wrong."

"It didn't matter. What mattered—" a swift, indrawn breath before Emily rushed on: "Mac, it wasn't enough to find the answer. I had to find it first. Do you understand? I'd worked on this all my adult life. To see the end—a discovery of such magnitude, just waiting? Oh, Mac, I could taste it. It was mine. My work, my life, my family—my friends? Nothing compared to being the one to do it—to solve the greatest riddle of our time."

Mac stood, stretched, and walked to the river's edge, cautious of the footing in her tied-together sandals, leaving Emily behind.

"Mac? Don't you understand?"

That word again.

She didn't turn, instead stooped to feel for a pebble to throw at the dark water, adding its sound to the faint drone of the rain. *Plonk.* "No," she said at last. "I don't. Discovery is a process, Emily. Looking for questions that can be answered; using those answers to choose new questions." Another pebble. She thought of Little Misty Lake and put muscle into the throw. *Plink PLONK.* "There's no end to it. There's no first. And certainly no 'mine.' You forgot that."

"And look what it got me?" Soft, bitter.

"I didn't say that—"

"You don't have to—I'm reminded every time I look in a mirror. Or at you. So is everyone else." Footsteps, then another rock followed hers into the dark. *Plonk.*

Was that what this was about? "No one doubts you, Em," Mac said firmly.

"You do. And we're staying here, rain or no rain, until you hear me."

"I've been listening," Mac pointed out. *Plonk* went her next toss. "You were hunting the Survivors, you received information from a mysterious source . . . then what?"

"Then a man—a Human—approached me. Gordon Stanislaus. He claimed to have sent me the data, to have more to offer. You know him as Otto Rkeia."

"The man killed under Pod Six," Mac breathed, turning to try and see Emily's face. But all she could discern was a darker shadow, taller and still. "Glued thirty meters down to a pod anchor. Ministry called it 'death by misadventure.'"

"They told me at the consulate," Emily said. "No surprise. *They* don't like to leave loose ends. Poor Gord—Otto. He was . . . within any field, Mac, there are those who warn of the consequences of success. You know the type. Whistle-blowers. Cassandras. That was Otto."

"Rkeia was a criminal," Mac objected. "Nik told me."

"Was he?" She could make out Emily's shrug. "We didn't talk about our day jobs."

"Emily Mamani!"

"It's raining, Mac. Can we move past your irrelevant morals?"

When Mac didn't bother to reply, Emily went on: "Otto told me he feared the Survivors were responsible for the Chasm. He wanted to find them, all right, but in order to prevent the same thing happening to us."

"Smart man," Mac muttered under her breath. *For a crook.* Louder, to be heard over rain and river: "But you didn't buy it."

"Not at first," Emily admitted. "The technology in Chasm 232 was no more advanced than the rest; there was no reason to assume they could have devastated the other worlds. Now we know it was the Dhryn. But then—what evidence Otto could offer was compelling. Details about the order in which the destruction had advanced across other systems, how quickly it had occurred. I checked everything I could—the data was solid, Mac. I still didn't believe the inhabitants of Chasm 232 were anything more than fugitives, but Otto did convince me whatever—or whoever—had destroyed the Chasm worlds so long ago might still exist."

Emily spoke more slowly, deliberately, as if this was something Mac had to hear, but hard to say. "That's when my obsession became—it became my mission. I was in a position to track down that threat; I would. Suddenly, secrecy wasn't about being first with a discovery, Mac. It was about staying out of sight of an enemy I couldn't be sure existed. About protecting those around me. And," a low humorless laugh, "there remained the very real possibility I was chasing my own imagination in steadily decreasing circles."

"But you weren't," Mac acknowledged, heart in her throat. "Emily, the Ro might have killed you then and there!"

"*They* prefer to manipulate." For a wonder, Emily sounded calm, as if they now discussed lab results. "And I made it easy, Mac. Once convinced I could be trusted, Otto revealed his secret. Far from fearing the Survivors, he claimed to be working with their descendants, that they'd been guarding against the true threat from their hiding place. Oh, I swallowed every word. After all, poor Otto believed it, too. I insisted on meeting them. He told me it was impossible—but they could communicate directly with me, if I was willing. The first . . . the first implant . . . Otto told me it was a translator. From the moment I let it be put under my sk–skin—" At the break in Emily's otherwise controlled voice, Mac's fingers clenched around the cold pebbles in her hand. "From that moment, I felt part of something important, something critical to the survival of every living thing I knew. I gave myself to *Them,* Mac, body and soul. There wasn't room for doubt. There wasn't room for anything but the mission. I was so . . . sure." A long pause.

Mac waited without moving. The rain softened to a mist she blinked from her eyelashes, tasted with her tongue. All the while, her heart hammered in her chest. *Gods, Emily . . .*

"Then," Emily said at last, "I found myself climbing rocks and sleeping in tents with the original woman of doubt. You questioned everything: yourself, your ideas, everyone else's ideas—everything, it seemed, but me. Me, you absorbed into your life as if I'd always been there. What were you thinking?"

"What was there to think about?" Mac shrugged and threw another pebble. *Plonk.* "You're good with salmon dynamics. A bit flighty, maybe, but I could put up with that."

"Flighty?" Emily choked on the word. "I was trying to save the universe and you made me count fish!"

Her outrage was so thoroughly "Emily," Mac had to smile. "You made me go dancing," she countered.

"You made me sleep on rocks."

"You got me thrown out of *Carly's Pig and Whistle.* Twice."

"Three times." Emily reached out and tugged Mac's hair. A pause that, for the first time in forever, felt comfortable. Then: "I didn't know *They'd* attack Base, Mac. I swear I didn't. *They* warned the disappearances along the Naralax Transect marked an imminent threat . . . *They* claimed the Dhryn had come from the Chasm, even as Kanaci's group confirmed finding the Dhryn home world. *They* kept insisting the Dhryn—who seemed harmless enough—were connected. There was growing pressure to spy on any Dhryn in reach. A desperate need to somehow penetrate the Dhryn home world. It was confused, unclear. Urgent. That, above all."

Words tumbled from Emily, more and more quickly. "When Brymn first mentioned your work, Otto and I, the others, we had to act. We knew it. *They*— always difficult to hold an idea—clearly Brymn's interest in your work was something *They* wanted to understand. We had to learn about you; I was the right choice. Brymn's coming to meet you couldn't have been better timed. Don't you see? I was already here. And once the IU and the Ministry forced your hand, Mac, everything fell into place. But—Mac, the plan was to lure you off-world in search of me, to draw you and Brymn to Haven, not chase you there." Emily faltered. "I'd never have done anything to hurt you or anyone else. It should have worked—"

"Should have?" Something inside Mac snapped. "You made me believe you'd been kidnapped!" she said fiercely. "I had to go through your room, see the blood on the walls. I sent divers looking for your body! I had to call your sister, Emily. Do you hear me?"

"I'm sorry—"

"Sorry?" Mac's harsh voice sounded strange to herself. "I had to find out from a stranger—a spy!—that you'd been—damn it, Emily, that you'd been lying to me from the start."

"Mac—"

Abruptly spent, she rubbed her hand over her eyes. "Shut up, Em."

Stiffly. "So that's it? You've made up your mind, and nothing I can—"

"I understand," Mac interrupted wearily.

A tiny gasp. *Just as well they couldn't see each other's faces.* "You . . . do?"

Mac nodded. "You got yourself into this by being who you are. And who you are . . . well, it's pretty much who I thought you were. I get it." *And she did, finally,* she thought with a relief that made her tremble. She'd been right to believe in Emily.

"You realize that made no sense whatsoever, Mackenzie Connor."

It would with more beer. Aloud: "Anyone else would have passed the mess to the authorities. Anyone else would have realized she couldn't save the universe by herself." Mac found herself close to smiling. *Odd, given the tears running down her cheeks.* "If you cared less and thought more, you wouldn't be Emily."

"Don't you dare make me into some damn hero," her friend snapped. "It was the worst mistake of my life."

Typical Emily, Mac thought. *Contrary.* "Your motives—"

"Motives mean nothing. *They* left me to die, so now I'm the noble victim to beings who fear *Them.*" *Plonk.* "But so far as others are concerned, I helped *Them* almost succeed in killing the Progenitors on Haven. You know who loves me for that." *Plonk.* "Both factions at me nonstop, trying to suck me into their scheme of things . . . I'm sick of being told I had the right motives, Mac. I was arrogant. There's no prize for that."

Mac understood Emily's frustration. There'd been no stopping the interrogations, the tests, the visits from anyone with clearance from the IU. How could there be? Emily Mamani was the only survivor. The rest of the Ro's informants?

They'd found their ruined bodies throughout Sol System—seven, so far. When the Ro had withdrawn their technology from the hulls of retreating Dhryn ships, opening them to vacuum, that same call had ripped the Ro's devices from the flesh of their—*what did you call someone who'd risked their lives to become eyes and ears for the alien?*

A hero, Mac decided. "Motives count with me," she assured Emily.

Plonk. "Stubborn. And a fool."

"I prefer to think of myself as internally consistent." Mac squatted to find more pebbles, using her nonflesh hand. The local spiders were opinionated.

"You're that," Emily said quietly, a hint of a quiver in her voice.

Mac stood with her handful and tossed the largest. *Pluuush.* "How's the ratio so far?" she asked. *In how much danger were they all?*

"I've lost track." A little too flippant.

Mac rolled the small, hard stones around in her palm. "You mean the idiot faction is growing."

Plonk. "You don't let me call them names," Emily protested mildly.

"That's because you'd do it to their faces—or whatever," Mac countered. "Things are tense enough."

"They aren't going to get better."

"They will, Em. We'll find evidence—proof that will convince even the idiots of the Ro's real intentions." *Evidence that couldn't be reinterpreted to suit species' self-interest,* Mac vowed to herself.

"It's not as though I've been any help." *SPLASH!* Emily must have tossed in a minor boulder.

"You could kill something that way," Mac chided gently. This land was full of odd birds wandering where an outsider wouldn't expect them.

"Haven't you noticed? Life's going cheap these days."

The despair in the faceless voice was too familiar. Mac let the rest of her pebbles fall to the ground. "We really need more beer," she concluded. Suiting action to words, she turned from the river and rolling pasture, squinting to pick out the path back to town from the shadows.

Emily took her arm, the grip tighter than natural. *Then again,* Mac thought, *the arm she gripped wasn't natural either.* "I've tried to remember, Mac," low, urgent. "I swear I have."

"I know." Mac covered the hand with her own. "We both heard Noad. Your mind may find a way. Or not. That's the way of it, Em. It's not your fault."

"It's not that I don't have any memories. I have too many. Being here, in the dark. This empty, open place. My pulse the loudest sound. It feels—" Emily fell silent. Mac held her breath, hoping for more, for anything, but Emily only sighed: "—familiar. A place I've never been before." She gave a short, hard laugh. "Little good that does."

"It's a start. Now, about that beer." Mac hesitated, squinting again. "Ah, Em?"

A tug on her hair. "This way."

"Whatever you do, don't use the washroom," Mac advised, slipping into her seat in the booth. "Trust me."

Emily grinned. "That bad?"

There was something terminally sticky on the soles of her sandals—clearly destined to be another set of footwear that would not survive a night out with Em. She abandoned them and tucked her bare feet underneath the curl of her legs on the bench. "Proves the Grimnoii were here first," she commented. Cider in, much worse out. *You'd think,* Mac sighed to herself, *they'd learn not to drink the stuff.*

Em wrinkled her nose. "Who'll foot the bill for cleanup?"

"The consulate, I'm sure. The bartender doesn't look worried."

"Probably has his own toilet. What say we find out where?"

Mac laughed at the eager look on Em's face. "Give him a couple of minutes first. You've got the poor man in a sweat."

The other woman nibbled the fingertip of her glove, eyes bright with mischief. "Like you make your poor Nikolai sweat, *si?*"

Mac arched one eyebrow. "For me to know, Dr. Mamani, and you to hypothesize."

"Bravo."

The Feisty Weka was larger and livelier than the *Nest,* although its tropical resort motif seemed a little embarrassed. The fake palms with their stuffed parrots were pushed into dark corners and the pineapple-printed tablecloths were covered with obscure local sayings in indelible ink Mac assumed were rude, given how much Emily had enjoyed them.

It was larger, livelier, and possessed not only these comfortable private booths, with soft benches, but an actual dance floor. Or Mac guessed that was the function of the area where people held their beer in their hands rather than sitting down at a table. Emily's face had lit up like one of the lanterns at the doorway. They'd finally found where all those not tending sheep were spending Saturday night.

Mac studied a cartoonish drawing of a small bird running off with a bag, wondering why it was considered funny.

"Can I interest you lovely ladies in a dance?" The voice was deep and smooth. *And male.* Mac looked up and scowled; Emily beamed. Mac's "No, thanks" was overruled by Em's warm: "And here I thought I'd sit here all night."

"Not in Southland. We take care of our guests."

There was a friendly smile to match the voice. A perfectly normal Human male body to match the smile. *Okay,* Mac admitted, a tall, blond, ruggedly handsome Human male, wearing, of course, some kind of ruggedly handsome clothing that emphasized all the right bits.

Mac scowled harder.

"Em," she hissed under her breath. "Don't you dare."

Tossing aside her shawl, Emily smiled as she stood, hips already finding the beat of the music Mac only now noticed coming from the dance floor. Her creamy bare shoulders tipped into the arm-covering black silk of her gloves, an exotic look for a New Zealand pub; Mr. Ruggedly's eyes were about to pop. "C'mon, Mac," Emily said, leaning over the table to smile at her. "You know you're thinking what I'm thinking. Someone this good-looking must have a friend."

Mac muttered something hopefully incomprehensible under her breath. "Broken sandals," she confessed brightly, trying for a rueful smile. *Technically also permanently stuck to the floor, but details weren't essential.* "You go. I'll order another round."

They abandoned her without argument, as she'd expected. Once Emily and Mr. Ruggedly were safely absorbed into the mass pretending to dance, Mac let her forehead drop to the table, hiding a yawn. *She usually caught a nap during their nights out.* She turned her head to press her cheek against her glass, one eye peering through amber at the couple. Emily was smiling. He must be a good dancer. Whoever he was.

The pattern of so many Saturday nights. *Why didn't it feel the same?*

Mac watched a bubble struggle toward the surface and knew why. It wasn't learning about Emily's sources, or her poor choice in obsessions.

This time, she was the one with a secret.

Why was the Origins Team still on Earth? Because she'd refused to let them leave with the rest. Those in charge wanted Emily close to medical treatment and protection. Then there was the ever-hopeful wait for Emily's brain to process anything useful about no-space and the Ro.

And if Emily had to stay, so would Mac.

Something plaid got in the way of the dance floor, and Mac waved impatiently until it was gone. She spotted Emily in the arms of Mr. Ruggedly and relaxed.

Mac yawned again and sat up, wondering if it was time to order coffee instead. She smiled at a familiar laugh, loud and abandoned. *Points to Mr. Ruggedly.*

It wasn't only the attractive stranger willing to tango to anything. As realization hit, Mac's smile faded. It was this thoroughly Human place bringing the old Emily back, from the stale air to the seats worn comfortable by the personal attention of generations of posteriors shaped like theirs. *Okay, some several sizes larger,* Mac corrected absently, shifting on the lumpy bench. Emily had needed—

"Watchit!"

The outcry was a signal for pandemonium to break loose. Mac snatched her beer glass to safety as a body, in plaid, landed on the table in front of her. She blinked as Mr. Plaid scrambled to his feet, teeth bared in a wild grin and shouting something highly improbable about someone else's mother. He vanished into the mêlée.

For that's what now filled the pub as far as Mac could see. Beer in hand, she climbed to stand on the bench, wrapping her other arm around the post behind it in case Mr. Plaid flew her way again. *Or someone else.* She tried to spot Emily in the press of bodies.

As barroom brawls went, this was starting out an orderly affair. Everyone seemed happily paired with a sparring partner of equal gusto, and the furniture was staying on the floor. Mind you, Mac hadn't bothered to check if the chairs and tables were bolted down as a precaution. No sign of what had started it. *There rarely was.*

As a precaution, she finished her beer in three quick gulps and, gently, rolled the empty glass under the table where it could keep her sandals company and not become a weapon if things turned nasty. She lurched over the table to grab Emily's shawl, a move involving a somewhat precarious dance with one foot on the table and the other planted firmly in sagging upholstery.

With a crow of success, Mac stood upright on the bench again, absently rolling her prize into a tube to tie snugly around her waist. She craned her neck.

There! Mac caught sight of glossy black hair and shouted: "Em! Over here!"

Somehow, Emily heard. She waved her arm, pointing at the door. Mac nodded and grinned. She considered the pair currently wrestling beside her table, albeit with little success and significant grunting, and chose to swing her legs over the back of the bench, dropping into the next booth.

Which wasn't empty.

"'Just a quiet evening out,'" Sing-li Jones quoted mildly.

Mac almost fell, keeping herself upright only by quickly sitting on the narrow rail dividing the booths. "This," she informed him with what dignity she had left, gesturing at the brawl, "is not our fault." The belch that punctuated the last word wasn't her fault either. *Chugging beer did it every time.*

The Ministry agent was slouched comfortably in the shadowed corner, for all the world like someone too drunk to care about the fight. He coughed a couple of times before saying: "I see."

"And I'm not drunk," she informed him. Mac eyed the half full glass in front of Sing-li. "Yet," she clarified. *A shame, that.* She could feel the weight of responsibility sliding back, as inevitable as the morning after. Despite being perched on the back of a bar bench, surrounded by the good-natured thump and crash of Humans being themselves, her mind helplessly began to ticktock through means to avoid tomorrow's meetings while setting priorities for the day's research.

"You've lost your shoes."

What else was new? Mac wiggled her bare toes, eyes searching the dark room for the door and Emily. Odd the bartender hadn't upped the lights to illuminate the fight. "Emily's heading for the exit," she said, abruptly uneasy. Sliding down to the bench, Mac scooted sideways to the edge of the table, preparing to launch herself into the crowd.

"Wait." Gone was the slouching, casual Sing-li, replaced by the version she knew better—tough, capable, and determined above all else that if he couldn't keep Mac out of trouble, he'd at least get there first.

On the scale of recent troubles, a bar fight barely registered so far as she was concerned, but Mac let the man do his job. Bare feet were a disadvantage. Not that sandals would have been much better. *Next trip out? Solid sensible boots,* she decided.

Sing-li was a good size by most Human standards, although Mac noticed *The Feisty Weka* was overly endowed with large men. Very large, annoyed men. *Maybe being annoyed only made them seem larger,* she thought hopefully, sticking close to Sing-li as he made his way after Emily. She winced as the Ministry agent took a low blow, then winced again as the person who'd struck him mysteriously faded to the floor with a shocked look on his face. "That's hardly fair," she hissed to his back.

Fair or not, her companion cleared their path. Mac stayed up on the balls of her feet as much as possible, grimacing as she stepped on, or in, who knew what. *Hopefully not glass,* she told herself, firmly banishing thoughts of Grimnoii and their reaction to cider.

Ugh. Slimy.

The wide door was open to the night, although stuffed with patrons enjoying the spectacle from its safer perspective. Sing-li lowered his shoulder as if to ram his way through, but the others parted amicably, pushing back into the doorway the instant Mac squeezed through.

"Well, that was fun—" she began cheerfully, looking around for Emily.

The road and sidewalk were deserted, except for a trio supporting each other as they stumbled away.

"Em?" Mac's eyes widened. "Sing-li!"

"You stay here. Right here." Sing-li's tone brooked no argument. He didn't wait for her nod as he strode off, his wrist to his mouth as he gave orders, doubtless bringing others into the hunt. Mac wrapped her arms around her waist and waited, standing within the overlapping circles of light at the entrance to the *Weka*. The sporadic bedlam from within made the outside world colder and too quiet.

No. No. No. Mac realized she was shaking her head repeatedly and stopped. She did her best not to think either, knowing she'd only blame herself for bringing Emily out too soon, which meant assuming the worst. And the worst meant . . .

No.

A few people passed her where she stood, on their way into the *Weka,* where the sounds of brawling had been replaced by music, loud and danceable. *Must be a typical Saturday night here,* Mac decided. An older woman hesitated, giving her a searching look. Mac did her best to look fascinated by the street.

"Are you all right?"

Mac the Transparent, Em called her.

"Waiting for a ride," she said, hoping to forestall any questions.

As if on cue, Sing-li was back. He took her elbow, offering the other woman a smile. "And the wait's over," he announced with just the right mix of chagrin and cheer. "I've found the skim. You were right, dear, I'd parked it down that alley. Good night." This to the woman, who hadn't left, still not convinced about Mac's situation.

Mac forced a smile. "Thank you," she said, meaning it. "But I'm really all right. Have a nice evening—just stay out of the washroom."

The woman rolled her eyes, relaxing. "Again? Appreciate the tip." She went into the bar.

Sing-li bent to put his lips to Mac's ear. "I found her. Steady—" This with concern as she sagged, his grip firm on her arm in support. "She's okay, Mac. C'mon."

He led Mac into the shadows along one side of the building, around a corner to where overgrown shrubbery formed an arborlike opening. Seeing two silhouettes within that shelter, Mac stopped. "Wait," she whispered. "It's Mr. Ruggedly."

"Who?"

Mac could feel the blush heating her cheeks and was once more grateful for the dark. "We should probably leave them be," she suggested. "For a while."

"You've got to be kidding," he protested.

She snorted, albeit quietly. "And you don't know Emily Mamani."

"No wonder she gets along with Fourteen."

Mac nodded. "Don't I—Wait." *Something was wrong.*

One of the figures had broken away, now coming toward them: the taller one, walking quickly as if about to break into a run. *Mr. Ruggedly?*

He didn't appear to see them, so Sing-li stepped in front of Mac at the last minute, preventing a collision. "Out of my way!" the man ordered, despite being startled. He tried to get past; the Ministry agent persuaded him otherwise. *Amazing,* Mac thought distractedly, *what an ability to loom intimidatingly could do, even in dim light.*

"We're Emily's friends," she said with haste. "We've been looking for her."

"Good. I was coming to find you." The relief in his voice sent an alarm through Mac. "Something's—something's wrong with her. It's nothing I did, I swear—"

Mac pushed by both men, hurrying to the unmoving form in the shadows. Sing-li's reassuring: "We'll take care of her," as he dealt with Mr. Ruggedly barely registered.

Emily was like a statue, staring at her gloved hands, their fingers outstretched and rigid before her face.

"—I tell them," she was saying. "They missed one. This isn't right."

Mac caught her friend's hands in hers. Emily resisted, making a fretful sound, but Mac held on until the other woman was still. "Time to go, Em," she said then, keeping her voice light with an effort, aware of Sing-li as a silent, distressed shadow at her side.

Making another of those lightning recoveries, Emily tugged her hands free and laughed. "We can't go home," she asserted, whirling in place. Her skirt brushed Mac's legs. "The dancing's started again. C'mon, Mac. Night's young!"

Suddenly, everything about this night and Emily crystallized in Mac's mind. She considered the result. *Could it really be that simple?* she asked herself with wonder.

First, to get Emily away from *The Feisty Weka.* "Mr. Jones insists," she claimed, knowing Sing-li would have already done so, if he'd thought it would work.

Next?

It remained to be seen if "simple" translated into Sinzi.

- CONTACT -

"**I**T'S A GHOST."

Meme spread his aural folds, a dismissive display to imply that no matter how much of his Human scan-tech's verbal utterances he collected to process, they would never make sense. His predecessor had failed to convince Meme such species-specific gestures were not comprehended by the aliens.

Meme was sure this lack of comprehension had more to do with his predecessor's unusually small aural folds. During the entire change of command ceremony, he'd needed all of his self-discipline not to stare.

Meme's own aural folds were magnificently broad, their skin kept well-oiled and supple. He had brought—

"Or maybe it's not."

The Human's strident voice intruded on Meme's pleasantly semidormant state. Worse, she—the matter of the creature's gender having been settled contrary to expectation, costing a fair sum in wagers—did not appear to have noticed Meme's display. *Nothing for it,* the Ar sighed, *but to actually pay attention.* "What are you mumbling about, Scan-tech?"

"Oh. You're awake?" The Human sat straighter and appeared confused. "Sorry, Captain. I've been following a tick in the aft sensor. Might be something."

"Define 'something.'"

"A ship, sir. Shadowing us."

"No. There is no 'something.' No ship." Meme closed his aural folds. *Annoying Human.* Their patrol area was days out from the transect gate—well beyond the orbit of what remained of the Dhryn world. Nice and safe and boring. No one and nothing came here. As if anything could get past the eager clusters of ships farther in.

Peaceful. Just the way he liked it.

"Captain?" Merciful silence. Then: "You can't just ignore this!"

He certainly could.

What Meme couldn't ignore was the shocking pain of his left aural fold being yanked open. "Captain! We must investigate any intrusion!"

Eyes watering, mouth working, Meme gestured helplessly at his tormentor.

She released his fold and Meme shuddered with relief. But the Human wasn't done. She leaned forward until her hideous eyeballs almost touched his. "Or should I contact the Trisulian?"

Meme shuddered. At last count, there were fifteen hundred and sixty-four ships orbiting

Haven's sun, courtesy of the anxious governments of systems along the Naralax. Most were like this, quick, sensor-laden scouts capable of squealing a near-light com signal to the packet ships waiting by the gate, crewed by those willing to sit in the darkness and wait.

The Trisulian warship was the exception, a bristling mass of threat that gave the Ar hives to even contemplate. *As for her grim captain?* "Let's not contact them unless we're sure," he pleaded, well versed in the reckless nature of females.

The Human gave him one final glare, then returned to her station. Meme took several calming breaths as he fingered his abused fold. Obviously Human females were no more stable than Trisulian. He could only hope she was capable. The Ar weren't a wealthy or adventurous race. When the call had come for ships to watch Haven, the Sinzi-ra of the IU consulate on Arer had thoughtfully hired this Human ship and its crew, asking only that the Ar provide a volunteer of their species to captain.

Meme was the fourth Ar to so serve, while the three Human crew remained unchanged. *It was as if they didn't need a captain at all.*

"Gotcha," the scan-tech announced. "Transferring to the bridge monitor. And yours, Captain."

Meme's aural folds clenched in dread at the sight of the large ship floating almost in his lap. He drew up his toes and began crooning to himself, the sound echoing inside his skull and nicely drowning out any Human voice.

He'd underestimated the decibels available in a Human's lungs. "IT'S DEAD!"

Meme paused in his croon, letting his folds unfurl slightly. "You're sure?"

"Scans read null," the scan-tech confirmed at a more reasonable volume. "Relax, Captain. Munesh is going to squeal a pulse about our claim while I collect as much data as possible."

"'Claim?'" Meme frowned.

"Sorry." The Human turned an interesting pink hue. "Old habit. We operated a salvage operation—before the Dhryn. I meant, Munesh is notifying the other ships."

Meme kept his toes close, away from the black hulk slowly spinning in front of him. "Is this—is it one of theirs?"

The Human pressed a control, studied the result, then stroked another. With that, a placid voice began to speak in Instella, the common tongue.

"This is an automated distress call from the freighter *Uosanah,* registered out of Cryssin Colony. Any ship receiving this message is required to render assistance under the provisions of the Interspecies Union. This is an automated distress call from the freighter *Uosanah,* registered out of Cryssin Colony. Any ship receiving this message is required to render assistance under the provisions of the Interspecies Union. This is—"

The Human lifted her hand from the control, silencing the voice, and turned to look at Meme. "Cryssin was a Dhryn colony. If this ship came to join the other Dhryn, why is it still here?"

"Ships break down all the time," Meme replied with the innocent conviction of someone who had no idea how his oil warmer worked. "Probably junk they left behind."

She shrugged. "The experts'll check the logs."

Feeling this settled matters nicely, Meme stretched out his toes and stood, edging around the display the Human had left wheeling in front of his chair. It wasn't easy. The bridge was cramped compared to where the navigator/pilot and com-tech worked. Meme often wondered why the captain's chair was here instead of there. *Likely a Human design flaw.* The nearby galley, however, was most ample and their success deserved a celebration.

"Another contact, Captain," the scan-tech said, interrupting Meme's happy consideration of appropriate treats.

"One of the others, come to see our prize," he guessed, flaring his folds triumphantly. "Who is it?" If it was Me'o, the Cey, there was a distinct possibility of young nerbly cheese. Its nip would go very well with—

"Not ours. Another drifter. Freighter. Dead like the first."

The Ar considered two an alarming number, fraught as it was with change. And unresolvable arguments. *Not that he'd lured a female into argument yet, but . . .* "Are you sure?" Meme demanded. "Two? Check again."

She did, then gave him a stranger look than usual. "You aren't going to believe this," she said. "I don't believe this."

Meme couldn't imagine what a Human would find unbelievable—he had to ask. "What don't you believe?"

"You're right. There aren't two."

His aural folds spread with pride. "You see—"

"Captain. There must be dozens, maybe more, along this vector." She put her hands flat on the console, then stood, turning to face him.

"We're in a Dhryn graveyard."

- 3 -

PROPOSAL AND PROMISE

THE INTERSPECIES CONSULATE for Sol System sat on a coast where mountains plunged into abyssal depths, part of a system of fjords that rivaled any on Earth for breathtaking beauty, in a country so remote from any other on Earth its residents were like a model for humanity within the IU itself: vaguely interested in what went on "outside," but believing themselves both isolated and self-contained.

None of them had a right to believe any such thing, Mac fumed to herself, for once oblivious to the view from her ocean-side terrace.

She laid her hand on the cool white roughness of the outer wall. "Request." The air might not hear, but a touch on any wall, plus the word in Instella, gained the attention of the hordes who serviced the consulate. "I need to see the Sinzi-ra. Immediately."

Mac strode through the doors to her quarters, into the bedroom, to be exact, unsurprised to find a member of the staff already waiting. She was beginning to suspect they had their own, equally discreet, doors and hallways. The staff, a female humanoid with the characteristic brush of red-brown hair shaved into elaborate whorls over her scalp, bowed slightly. Her uniform, like those of her fellows, was the same earthy tone as her hair, a change from the bright yellow they'd worn when Mac first arrived.

Sinzi seemed incapable of offering knowing offense to any visitor, even their common enemy, the Dhryn.

There had been other changes, less obvious. The consulate had swarmed with alien construction workers for a time after the Ro were found to be misusing the Sinzi-ra's fish tank. Guests were welcome. Uninvited ones were not. Mac didn't know the details; she accepted Sing-li's assurance she could sleep at night.

Most nights.

"The Sinzi-ra has been informed," staff announced calmly. "She will attend you later this afternoon, Dr. Connor."

By which time she'd have lost her nerve. Mac shook her head. "Is Anchen in her office?"

"The Sinzi-ra does not have an office, Dr. Connor."

Taken aback, Mac realized she should have known. The Sinzi had always come to her, or to where she worked. More formal meetings were in the Atrium or the larger room down the hall. "Then where is she? Right now."

"The Sinzi-ra is in her quarters, Dr. Connor."

Good. She knew where those were. "Thanks," said Mac, heading for the door.

The staff's eyes widened in an alarm response they shared. "Dr. Connor—where are you going? There are protocols."

Mac smiled over her shoulder. "I'm sure there are. Remind me on the way."

The consular staff knew Mac by now, well enough the other being didn't attempt to argue.

Her sigh, however, was almost Human.

The Sinzi-ra occupied a suite of rooms almost identical to Mac's. Glazed French doors from the hall opened into a large bedroom. There was a similar set of doors, clear this time, to a terrace overlooking the sound and ocean beyond. To the left, as Mac entered, was the archway leading into what she thought of as a sitting room. Mac's version was now distinctly her office, complete with anything that could be carried from Pod Three—her friends were literal sorts. The Sinzi's was white on white, simplicity itself, four jelly-chairs facing a white stone table, deep creamy sand on the floor, white walls windowed to the sky beyond.

The perfect frame for complexity. Mac stopped so quickly the unhappy staff behind her almost ran into her back.

The Sinzi-ra was busy.

Her left hand—or rather the trio of meter-long fingers that constituted the Sinzi equivalent—was adding blue and clear gems to a circular mosaic on an easel, the result scintillating like cold fire. Her right hand, meanwhile, worked some type of keypad. The faint outlines of three workscreens flickered in front of her face, each angled to favor a different segment of her eyes. Not that Mac's Human eyes could make out details. The Sinzi—and their servants—had a broader spectrum available to their sight.

To top it off, Anchen was humming in a minor key.

Normally, Mac would have been fascinated. The alien rarely gave any indication of the distinct individual minds, six in number, inhabiting her willowy form. Only the changing attention of her complex, compound eyes hinted at how many were participating in a conversation. Anchen: Atcho, the precise and careful administrator for the consulate; Noad, the curious physician, interested in all things alien, particularly the mind; Casmii, who preferred the background, not least on the IU Judicial Council; Hone, youngest or most recent, as such minds went, but already a notable transect engineer; Econa and Nifa, scientists who currently shared a passion for Earth, the former a gemologist, the latter a cultural historian, studying, to Mac's dismay when she'd heard, the incidence of familial homicide among Humans, with a side interest in cannibalism between neighbors.

You tidy the house for company, and they trip over the dirty laundry every time.

"The Sinzi-ra must compose her selves," said a quiet voice from behind. "Please do not speak, Dr. Connor, until she addresses you by name."

Mac nodded. She could use some composure. It was one thing to charge forward, sure she was right.

Quite another to be reminded who she had to convince.

"Feel free to enjoy the Sinzi-ra's collection while you wait, Dr. Connor." With this, the staff touched a portion of the plain white wall.

"What col—" Mac started to ask, then closed her mouth as every wall turned dark blue, honeycombed with small, bright openings. She stepped closer.

The openings were cubbyholes, each containing one object suspended in its midst, gently lit from every side. As Mac looked into the nearest cubby, the object inside seemed to jump at her. In reflex, she stumbled back a step, shoe filling with sand, then realized it was an illusion.

Entranced, Mac experimented. She found if she looked directly at any one object, it would become enlarged until she looked elsewhere. *A technology well-suited to the Sinzi's multipart eye,* she decided. Personally, she found it disconcerting to have item after item appear to launch itself toward her face.

It didn't help that the items were hardly art. A mug advertising a pastry shop. A crumpled snakeskin. A nondescript coin. A purple alligator with a snow globe stomach. A pebble. A pink kazoo. The entire room was walled in an eclectic array of Human trinkets, souvenirs, and odd devices. There was no apparent order. A studded cat collar was displayed beside a vial of sand. A ticket stub from a museum accompanied a package of candy.

Mac winced involuntarily as a miniature Human head in a bottle—hopefully a replica—invaded her personal space. She quickly stared at a section of harmless dark blue wall.

"My dear Mac," Anchen greeted her, coming to stand at Mac's side. "I apologize for being preoccupied." Her fingertips played with a sapphire and Mac spared an instant to wonder which personality might still be preoccupied. Her guess was Econa, the gemologist. "What do you think, Mac?"

She started. "About what?"

"About my collection."

"I've never seen junk treated so well," Mac admitted, then winced for the second time. *Tact. She needed lessons.*

"Junk?" Anchen's fingers rippled in a laugh, their coating of silver rings tinkling against one another like rain. "One species' junk, Mac, is another's treasure."

Really? Mac glanced into another cubby. Its contents, a tiny plastic fish bottle with a dark sauce inside and a bright red nose, obligingly enlarged itself to palm-sized for her inspection. "So long as no one charged you for them, Anchen," she said fervently. "I'd hate to see you cheated."

"Worry not, Mac. These—" Anchen spread her fingers out to their full length, as if to gather in her collection. "—were gifts. As for their value? To me, objects derived from a particular journey are beyond price."

Mac imagined the regal, distinctive alien wandering a beachfront souvenir shop and grinned. "I didn't think you left the consulate."

"Too rarely," Anchen told her. "These are from Nikolai. Whenever he travels on my behalf, he brings me a treasure. Thus." A languid fingertip indicated a cubby on the next wall. Mac walked over to look inside. A salmon leered back at her. A cross-eyed lime-green rubber salmon, to be precise, with the name of a restaurant glowing down one side.

Probably where he'd taken Mudge to find out more about a certain salmon researcher. Forgetting the illusion, Mac reached out her hand, only to curl her fingers around empty air.

She found herself utterly distracted by the knowledge that Nik had selected each of these things. He'd carried it here, in a pocket, in a pack. He'd explained its place in his past as he gave it to the curious Sinzi.

There was more of Nikolai Piotr Trojanowski in this alien's collection than Mac knew herself.

Not hard. Mac gave herself an inward shake. *Spy, remember? Mysterious past, tendency to consider anything a secret until proved otherwise. Annoying as hell.*

And she missed him, Mac realized with some astonishment, *the way she missed her salmon.*

The walls turned white again. "Forgive me, Mac," the Sinzi-ra said as Mac blinked at the change. "I should not waste your time with indulgences. Please, let us sit and you can tell me why you needed to see me right away." She led the way to the jelly-chairs.

Mac blushed at the polite reminder. "My fault," she explained, taking the chair indicated by the elegant tilt of the Sinzi's tall head. "I was in a hurry. Not that this is urgent."

Anchen settled herself, the pleats of her white gown falling perfectly over her long toes. Her eyes blinked. "A contradiction."

Score another for interspecies communication, Mac sighed inwardly. "Yes," she said, then corrected herself: "No. What I mean is—I need to speak with you. It couldn't wait. It's about Emily."

"You should feel no anxiety, Mac. Noad examined her last night following your return. She was tired, but otherwise fine. Overall, he believes your excursion was beneficial."

"I know." Mac wiggled so she could lean forward, wishing the alien chairs weren't so all-encompassingly comfortable. "Em's downstairs now, working with the others. That's why I'm here. Last night, Emily made me listen—" Mac couldn't subdue the twinge of guilt: *to what her best friend wouldn't listen to before . . .* "I understand now how the Ro involved her. The Survivor Legend. She was obsessed by it. I think she still is."

"The legend is speculation at best, Mac," Anchen said, her small triangular mouth tilted down in mimicry of Human disapproval. "I remain unconvinced this is a worthy line of inquiry, despite Dr. Mamani's persuasion."

Mac shrugged. "One thing I've learned. Living things are messy. They do the unexpected. In some ways, I find it more incredible that the Ro could completely eradicate life from the Chasm worlds than one species might escape them."

"This has become your obsession also?"

"No, Anchen. I've riddles of my own, starting with the Dhryn themselves." Mac took a deep breath. "I agree the Survivors could be wishful thinking—but they've been Emily's focus, her passion, for decades." *With a side interest in salmon,* Mac reminded herself. Kammie would approve of such cross-pollination of fields; poor Case Wilson, the deepwater fisher she'd plopped into a study of tidal ecosystems, would doubtless sympathize with Em.

Anchen's fingers rose to her shoulders, a positioning Mac had learned to read as mild distress. "She has asked for a probe. I have delayed a response. It has not been our way, to attempt to contact an unknown species by giving them the means to reach us in return. The risk is incalculable. And you, Mac, appreciate the moral obligation. Opening a transect gate may well doom any life there."

"You're opening new gates right now." Mac might not like meetings, but she valued the information they—rarely—provided. Such as the continuing expansion of the transect system to new worlds in every direction. The Sinzi might not approve, but they were involved. Every system connected by a transect became part of the Interspecies Union. To be part of it meant hosting an IU consulate—with a Sinzi-ra in residence to oversee the transect gates, because key parts of that crucial technology remained theirs alone.

Mac didn't concern herself with the details. Someone had to have a hand—or finger—on the switch. And the diplomatic, pragmatic, irreproachable Sinzi had the only fingers every other species trusted.

The Sinzi inclined her head in acknowledgment. "It has not been forbidden." The "yet" was implied. "Other species within the IU may expand the transect system from their gates, but they do so only where there is evidence of a thriving civilization capable of space travel."

And good manners. That Sinzi attitude permeated the IU: from the adoption of Instella, the common language used between species, to ships' hatches that matched regardless of origin, to the use of their consulates to indoctrinate visitors on local customs, before those customs could be violated. You could muddy your own backyard, but please wipe your feet before stepping inside the house.

The transects didn't carry war.

Until the Ro had unleashed the Dhryn.

"There is no such evidence from this world of Dr. Mamani's," Anchen finished. "I see no purpose to a probe without it."

"I'm not here to ask for one." Mac sensed confusion and pressed on: "Anchen, Emily's request—it means she wants to help. We couldn't stop her if we tried. I've had her working with my team, but what we're doing—what I'm doing—is a constant reminder of the Ro. Of what they put her through—of her mistake in trusting them. But what if she continued her work on the Survivors? Whether they exist or not—it doesn't matter. So long as she believes . . ." *Was any of this getting through?*

"I see." Two fingertips met, forming an arch. "I have been concerned how best to occupy Dr. Mamani's excellent mind during her recovery. Her Tracer device is part of her search, is it not?" At Mac's nod, she continued, "A novel application of life-form scanning techniques. Quite impressive. As is her incorporation of relevant principles from Myrokynay technology. While we have yet to discover any clues from that technology, the effort continues." The Sinzi dipped her head in a slight bow. "I applaud your wisdom in this matter, Mac. Dr. Mamani may have any resources she requires."

Mac swallowed and sat up straight. "Not here," she said. "At Norcoast."

"Why?"

That was the crux of it. Mac hesitated. It was the right answer for Emily. She knew it. But she couldn't explain why to herself—let alone to another Human. *How could she explain to the Sinzi?* She blurted out the first reason that came to mind: "She'll need an aquatic ecosystem to further develop her Tracer."

Brilliant.

Of course, Anchen lifted a long finger to indicate the view out her window. "Is this an insufficient body of water?"

"No," Mac sighed. "And before you say it, Sinzi-ra, I realize you can provide all the facilities Base has plus some. Emily's original equipment is already here, in my closet." In several pieces. *A minor point.*

"Then why risk moving her?" Anchen's head tilted so the eyes Mac had come to associate with Noad, the physician, were most directly aimed her way. "I have concerns. Both for her recovery, and what she may yet remember."

Mac nodded. "I know. I share them, believe me. But if you could have seen her . . . she was happy last night, Anchen. Her old self, mostly. For the first time since—since coming back. In that crowded, smelly bar—" She stopped, unable to read compassion or confusion in those sparkling amber eyes.

"Where everyone around her was Human," Anchen finished. Ever the consummate diplomat, the Sinzi formed a gentle, Human-looking smile. "What could be more natural, Mac? We can accommodate anyone you wish to invite here. A wonderful idea. I will arrange for an entire building to be Human-only, until Dr. Mamani is more comfortable. Is this acceptable?"

She should have expected nothing less; Anchen took particular pride in being a good host. Even so, it was an overwhelming offer.

Too bad.

Mac took a deep breath. "No, Anchen. I'm grateful, but what Emily needs isn't just to be around Humans—she has me and Oversight, Kanaci and his people, Sing-li, 'Sephe, and theirs. She needs a Human place. Base . . . it will be familiar, she'll have friends, distractions. Her sister could visit." Mac tried to keep the urgency from her voice. *This was right.* "Nik told me you have someone there," she went on. "'Sephe has a job waiting for her. It's protected from the media. It's—"

"This is where you wish to be, Mac, is it not?"

Irrelevant, Mac told herself and almost believed. "This isn't about me. Emily's been told what the Ro did to Base—the attack on the pods; the earthquake on shore. She knows she helped them do it. She might rationalize it wasn't her fault, realize people have gone on with their work and their lives, but that's not enough, Anchen. Humans—we have to be in a place, touch it, breathe its air, in order to know it." She firmed her voice. "That's why I have to go as well. But not to Base, Anchen. To the Chasm, to Myriam. With the Origins Team."

The Sinzi rose to her feet with a swiftness that suggested some strong emotion. "Mackenzie Connor," she started, her voice unusually high, then stopped, fingers lifting well above her shoulders. *Distress?* "You strike at the essence of my selves."

She'd done it now. "I didn't mean to offend—"

"Offend?" Anchen's triangular mouth shaped a tremulous smile, imitating the Human expression with devastating accuracy. "My dear Mac. I am overcome . . . the harmony of what you would achieve . . . I ask your patience while I compose my selves."

Mac's confusion must have been apparent even to the alien, for she waved her own comments aside with a long finger, sinking back to her seat. "This is what I have longed to propose to you and Dr. Mamani, but did not dare."

"You did." Mac closed her mouth, guessing she'd been gaping like a fish out of water. *So much for marshaling arguments.* "Why didn't you?"

"I had to assume you would resist this, as you have resisted every suggestion you be separated. Yet now, you offer to make a personal journey to achieve community." The Sinzi-ra gave an almost orgasmic shudder. "Can a Human possibly appreciate the significance of this to Sinzi?"

This Human? Mac resisted the urge to laugh. "Em at Base, me with the team—it just feels the right thing to do. I know it's not thoroughly logical or rational."

"Both admit limits," Anchen dismissed. "Limits are not useful in accommodating disparate ways of thought." She seemed calmer, though still intent. "Based on my studies of your species, I see your proposal as a Human need to put affairs in order. You plan a leave-taking, a change of magnitude and risk. Part of this plan deals with what you leave behind, so you are free to go. Is this accurate, Mac?"

Mac sat back in the jelly-chair, letting her shoulders sink into its soothing warmth. "I hadn't thought about it that way." She nodded slowly. "Yes."

"This is not how it 'feels' to me, Mac. In Sinzi terms, your proposal instills profound circularity by its plan to reattach sundered connections. The importance of any connection is demonstrated by the effort—the distance traveled—to accomplish it. Thus, this is a proposal I find aesthetically as well as fundamentally, worthy. 'Right,' in your terms. In our different ways, we seek the same result—to restore what was broken. To build harmony."

Mac held her breath, feeling close to grasping something innate about the Sinzi, about the transects and the IU itself. "The Atrium," she said finally. "The layout is inefficient by Human standards—researchers have to use a lev-platform or walk halfway around the consulate to meet face-to-face." More than inefficient, Lyle considered it a slight, as if they didn't belong with other scientists—*archaeologists were touchy that way.* Mac hadn't been sure. "But it isn't inefficient to you as a Sinzi, is it? Because the act of physically seeking each other matters." Perhaps explaining why the Sinzi-ra, despite being in charge of the consulate, constantly roamed its halls and rooms. *Intriguing.* Mac wriggled to sit straighter again.

Anchen tilted her head sharply left, as though Mac had drawn the profound attention of one of her personalities. "You are unusually perceptive today, Mac. Yes. To move to a common meeting point is the highest of courtesies. Effort reflects the significance of the desired meeting. Even symbolic travel, as done using the platforms, helps set the appropriate tone of connection."

"That's why you brought experts from all over the IU here, to the Gathering." Mac took the plunge. "Having them move through the transects was a message to all Sinzi. Or from the Sinzi. Or both. A demonstration of the significance of the Dhryn threat."

"We felt a profound need for congruence on this issue," Anchen replied, giving a gracious bow as her fingertips sought one another. Mac wasn't sure if it was agreement or explanation. *The danger with interspecies communication,* she cautioned herself, *wasn't when it went wrong, but when it seemed to make sense.* "We value the synergy of coming together. The Gathering proved insightful, as you know."

"But now you've had to send everyone away. What message does that give?" *Probably not the most tactful question,* Mac realized, too late.

"Message? It is the essential reflection, Mac. That which must take place after congruence. Circularity is movement. Congruence grants momentum. The farther we dare go from one another, while remaining always part, the stronger we—" The Sinzi tilted her head the other way and made a soothing gesture. "My apologies. I have lapsed into language inappropriate for discourse with an alien."

"If we stick to shrimp, we'll never understand one another," Mac assured her.

This drew a laugh, but when Anchen's fingers settled, she pursed her small mouth in a less happy expression. "I will miss our conversations."

The words took a moment to sink in. Then Mac struggled to her feet. "We can go?"

"Yes. However, there must be preparations."

Mac nodded and sank back into her chair, already thinking ahead to her own. Her heart was hammering. She'd wanted this outcome—it was another thing entirely to have it. Then, something in the alien's emphasis caught her attention. "What preparations, Sinzi-ra?"

"Although Dr. P'tool makes progress developing a teachable pattern for the Dhryn language, with the cooperation of the Vessel, it will not be ready for some time. We may need you." Two fingers lifted as Mac opened her mouth. She closed it. "For this reason," Anchen continued, "a transect-capable ship will remain in orbit while you are on Myriam. I trust it will not be required. There is considerable circularity in using that world for any negotiations, should we achieve that stage."

Mac swallowed. "You'd rather bring the Dhryn to me," she said, numbly contemplating the immense power and scope of the Interspecies Union, focused on one, out-of-water, salmon researcher.

It made sense beyond the Sinzi aesthetic. The Chasm worlds were already dead. Myriam was as close, through the Naralax Transect, as any other world connected along its reach, including Earth. *There was just one small problem.*

"I study salmon," Mac repeated aloud.

That tiny smile and a gentle correction, "You study life, Mackenzie Connor. But don't worry. In the event you are needed to translate, there will be senior diplomats to handle every aspect of the negotiations."

"Great. You'd better send someone to translate them for me," Mac muttered.

Anchen ignored the mutter, bringing her fingers together in a complex arch. *New topic*, Mac guessed. Sure enough. "You realize several here will protest losing their access to Dr. Mamani."

"The idiot faction," Mac identified without thinking. "I didn't mean that," she said hastily, then winced. *How confusing could she be?* "I do," she admitted. "I just didn't intend to say it. I apologize."

"There is no need." Anchen made a soothing gesture. "I envy your ability to speak what you mean."

Mac had to laugh. "Trust me, it's not a gift."

"You could start a war by yourself," the Sinzi agreed with remarkable complacency. "Hence the urgent need for diplomats." Before Mac could protest, the alien smiled at her. "A joke. You have shown gratifying restraint under difficult circumstances."

Well, she hadn't thrown anything, Mac thought. *Lately.* Despite temptation. She took advantage of the Sinzi's mood to ask what she hadn't dared before. "You agree with me, don't you? About the idiots."

"I agree that some of my colleagues on council have failed to overcome species' bias when interpreting the actions of others." The alien swayed to the left, then back. "It is more common than not, Mac."

"Interpretation?" Mac couldn't help herself: "The Ro are the threat, not potential allies! Their actions proved it!"

"Through your eyes." A lifted finger silenced Mac's response to that. The Sinzi went on: "Through other eyes, other minds, Mac, the same actions encourage differing conclusions. Actions alone, facts alone, are never enough. They must be considered within the species imperative. What matters to the Myrokynay? What is their nature? All of us must learn to see as they see before we can grasp their true motivations. That is why your exploration of the past is so important."

Mac scowled. "I deal in facts. The Ro are the enemy. Everything I've discovered supports that."

"Are the walls of the consulate featureless and white?" The Sinzi steepled all of her fingers, their rings cascading down with a sound like rain on ice. "Is this a fact?"

Checkmate.

If she said yes, the Sinzi would correctly inform her they were white only to her Human eyes. If she said no, she was admitting the Sinzi was right—that knowledge about an alien species was crucial to interpreting the actions of that species.

Mac shrugged it aside, not ready to surrender. "What if the imperative for the Ro is to destroy all other forms of life, starting with anyone who dares tamper with no-space?"

"Then our survival will depend on how quickly and well we answer that question, Mackenzie Connor." The Sinzi stood and two staff appeared in the doorway as if this had been a summons. "You know what to do, I trust."

Mac rose to her feet, but stayed where she was. "My team's ready to go," she stated. *More than ready.* Kanaci kept his clothes packed, according to Oversight. "But, Anchen. About Emily. I'd like to talk over the arrangements—"

Instead of responding, Anchen beckoned to her staff. One, a male, passed her a silver ring, just like any of the hundreds adorning her fingers from shoulder to final joint. Light reflected in a quick flash as her fingertip rolled to hold it. "Perfect," she said, her voice pleased. The finger, with its contents, reached toward Mac. "For you."

Mac took the smooth ring in her hand. Already warmed by the Sinzi's touch—*implying a higher body temperature*—it was a plain circle of precious metal. When she tried it on, it slipped over her right ring finger, fitting as if made for it. *A good-bye gift?* "Thank you, Sinzi-ra," she said, nonplussed.

The staff glanced at Anchen for permission. At her nod, he said: "It is a Sinzi *lamnas*—a private communications device, Dr. Connor. Each *lamnas* accepts only one message, intended for a sole recipient."

Which meant . . . Mac's eyes widened and she stared at Anchen's ring-coated fingers. She couldn't begin to imagine why a Sinzi would want to carry his or her mail this way, yet the small devices were obviously designed to be worn, perhaps at all times. And were the ones Anchen bore messages received or those waiting to be sent? She couldn't see any outward differences.

Before she could frame her curiosity into questions, the Sinzi gestured to the ring in Mac's hand. "This arrived today, in a transect com packet from the *Impeci.* You are the recipient."

The ship name wasn't familiar. *Which didn't mean anything.* "Why would you think it's for me?" Mac asked, proud of the evenness of her voice. Hope wasn't familiar, either; her heart began to pound with it.

With a left finger, Anchen stroked the rings on a right, setting up a faint cascading chime. "Each Sinzi-ra carries a supply of *lamnas,* uniquely marked, with which to send information," she explained. *Explaining those she wore.* "That is one of four Nikolai asked of me before he left."

Mac's fingers closed around the gift, her mouth forming a silent: *Oh.*

Anchen pulled free one of her rings. "It functions thus. To record." She brought the ring, encircled by her flexible fingertip, to touch her pursed triangular lips. She blew gently, then opened her mouth further to place the ring on her tongue. Her lips closed over it. After an instant in which Mac couldn't see anything happening, Anchen removed the ring and gave it to the waiting staff. "At first, Mac, I doubted. A Human, even one with so disciplined a mind as Nikolai, imprint a *lamnas*? But he insisted on making the attempt, and I could not refuse him. We share a deep and abiding connection." Fingertips touched. "The results were—interesting. Be aware, Mac, this is not a message which can be decoded and sent to another device. This is an imprint, affected by intent as much as event. I cannot say how your mind will interpret the result."

"So—it might not work at all," Mac ventured, her hope of an instant before fading.

"Oh, it will. But how? That only you can discover. To receive, act thus." The Sinzi chose another ring, identical to the rest as far as Mac could tell from a distance, and repeated the same initial movements, touch to the lips, a breath through the ring, but finished by holding the ring to one of her eyes, looking through its tiny circle. As if to avoid distraction, Anchen brought this ring down again quickly and replaced it on her finger, shaking it up to join the rest.

"Now, if you will excuse me, Mac, I am reminded of an appointment—"

Somehow, Mac wrenched her mind to the business at hand, preparing to stand her ground. *Emily.* If there was one thing she'd learned in dealing with bureaucracy—or aliens or most particularly alien bureaucracy—it was to never leave without a final answer. *Ideally signed and sealed.* "We need to talk about Emily."

Anchen turned so all of her eyes were directly on Mac, one finger sending her staff to other duties. "Be assured I have given this considerable thought. Dr. Stewart appears capable of monitoring Dr. Mamani's recovery, given instruction. I myself will be available to Dr. Mamani at any time via secure com to discuss her memories. What remains an issue . . . Mac, as you yourself said, there are many in the IU interested in your friend's relationship with the Myrokynay, 'idiots' and otherwise. I expect more delegates later this week. Sending her anywhere else on Earth ends their access except through your Ministry. I must consult with Mr. Hollans. There must be arrangements in advance, mutually agreed—"

"Or one lev, tonight," Mac interrupted, taking a step closer. "Discuss the details after she's gone. You can arrange vid meetings with Emily for those who want to talk to her. In the open, with you present. Whatever it takes."

Anchen bent until the tops of her eyes were aimed at Mac. It was so unusual a posture Mac guessed she'd attracted the particular attention of Casmii, the IU judge.

That wasn't, she decided, *necessarily good.*

"Relations between the Frow and Trisulian delegations have been strained over this issue," the Sinzi-ra mused. "There is merit in distancing the source of contention. It could serve to return attention to the problem at hand: developing a defense against the Dhryn."

Or, it could be good. Mac brightened. "We can be out of your way in no time."

"'We,' Mac?"

"I have to go with her," she explained, although surely it was obvious even to an alien with tentacle fingers. "I'll need to talk to Dr. Noyo and the other senior staff—make sure Emily's settled."

"How long would this process take?"

Mac pushed aside wistful thoughts of visiting field stations, inspecting the new anchors, and generally being a nuisance to Kammie and Tie, who were doubtless looking after all of the above and more. "Three days," she proposed and did her best to look regretful. "I realize I'll miss some meetings."

"I doubt that troubles you," the Sinzi commented shrewdly. "But, yes, so long an absence would be noticed." She paused—*consulting her selves?* Mac wondered—then tilted into her more usual posture. "It is not impossible. I should be able to schedule your team's departure for the Chasm to allow time for you to 'settle' Dr. Mamani and still meet them in orbit. The meetings—I will arrange a means of obtaining your input even while you are on Myriam." *Of course she would,* Mac sighed to herself. "You," Anchen finished, "face the more difficult task."

Mac, in the midst of congratulating herself for everything but the meetings, gave the Sinzi a suspicious look. "What might that be?"

"Convincing Dr. Mamani."

No problem.

Emily, Mac told herself, *would love the plan.*

Permission to free Emily from the consulate. Away from reminders and questions.

A private message from Nik.

And a return to Base!

If she'd been impatient before, Mac was nigh on to frantic now. Her mind whirling with plans, arguments, and the tendency to simply stall in possibilities, she somehow managed not to run down the ramplike hallway. Not quite, anyway. Her low-impact lope couldn't have been mistaken for a walk by any being. *Maybe it would stop anyone from pestering her on the way.*

"Ah! There you are, Norcoast."

Or not.

Mac growled under her breath but waited for Mudge to catch up to her. There wasn't a window, but diffuse light filled the hollow core of the building.

If she walked to the corridor's edge, she would see how its gentle slope spiraled to connect the main floors. *And probably startle a few pigeons.* "In a bit of a rush, Oversight—" she began.

As well talk to the walls. Charles Mudge III had successfully fought his end of their interminable arguments about Base's access to his Wilderness Trust for fourteen years. His recent career change to Mac's admittedly invaluable assistant, administering all the business and com traffic of the research team they ran— truth be told, together—hadn't softened his approach. *That she'd noticed.*

Now, predictably, he ignored her protest, instead shaking a crumpled mem-sheet under her nose. "Look at this!" Mudge fumed. "Dr. Kanaci knows how I feel about proper lines of communication. I've made it abundantly clear. Submissions must go through the main system. I'm telling you right now, Norcoast—"

Mac was acutely conscious of the *lamnas* around her finger. "Can't you tell me later?" she pleaded.

"Certainly not." For no apparent reason, he stopped at that, giving her the oddest look.

Maybe Mudge was *more annoying than Hollans.* "Oversight?" she prompted, shifting her weight from foot to foot. "What can't wait?"

He leaned forward and lowered his voice. "There's a message from Stefan."

"Nik," she corrected automatically. For all Mudge paid attention to Nikolai Trojanowski's real—or at least official—identity, she might not have bothered telling him at all. On the other hand, Mac assured herself, she no longer had to worry about using the right alias. They all seemed to work. *Spies.*

"You know who I mean." His eyebrows rose and fell suggestively.

While Mudge's attempt to be clandestine was entertaining, in a bizarre sort of way, Mac refused to be distracted. "Yes, I know who you mean. And I know about the message. The Sinzi-ra mentioned a com packet arrived today. It's being decoded."

"Done."

Mac stopped trying to escape and snatched at the mem-sheet in Mudge's hand.

He pulled it away. "Not this," he *harrumphed,* crumpling the mem-sheet into a ball. "I'll have you know I had to go in person to get a copy. Security reasons."

Mac nodded impatiently, barely restraining the impulse to search his pockets. "Where's the message?"

"I had to get it from that Myg." He waited.

Oh. Mac reined in her temper. "I trust he cooperated."

"I didn't take the chance." Stiffly. "I brought a Ministry agent with me. The one with no sense of humor. Selkirk."

She'd have to find a way to deal with this. Unfortunately, Fourteen's intellect either soared with brilliance or hung around bathrooms looking for entertainment. Which meant Mudge.

Give the alien credit, Mac thought with reluctant admiration. *He applied his genius.* The "mirror image" switch had involved not only every item on Mudge's desk but also each and every file accessed by his imp. Then there was the time Fourteen replaced the backside of Mudge's pants with a material that could be rendered transparent by remote.

The trick was to keep Fourteen busy, or the two of them apart. *Easier said than done.*

"You can't keep avoiding him," Mac insisted aloud, despite her utter lack of success on this point with Mudge to date. "It only makes him worse."

She couldn't very well explain that what made Mudge such an irresistible target for the Myg wasn't the Human's gullibility or his tendency to bluster. *Although they helped.* It was Mudge's constant, steady usefulness to her.

Not jealousy. She'd worried at the situation, observed their interaction long enough to believe she had it right. In their own species-specific and personally idiosyncratic ways, Fourteen and Mudge competed for the opportunity to serve her.

Mac frequently wanted to strangle them both.

Later. "Just give me the message, Oversight. Please."

His eyes widened dramatically. "Here?"

"Why not here?"

Mudge lowered his voice. "Someone could be listening."

On the verge of exasperation—*the man had vidbots on the brain*—Mac reconsidered. Mudge had a point. Given the open structure of this hall, and the variety of aural capabilities possessed by those roaming it, there was no way to know if someone could overhear them. *And there were idiots.*

"Fine. We'll go— What time is it anyway?"

"Don't tell me you've missed breakfast again."

"When I want someone fussing over my eating habits," Mac countered absently, "I'll call my dad." *That late?* She shoved the hand with its ring into a pocket. "Let's take a walk."

Mudge kept pace, even when Mac lengthened her stride. They were of a height, though he outmassed her by a few kilos. Less now—there wasn't much time behind a desk for either of them, especially with the Sinzi's predilection for distance between meeting places. Being needed had agreed with Mudge, put a sparkle in his eyes.

Being under threat of species annihilation had deepened the worry lines beside those eyes, and added gray to his already peppered hair.

Mac had some herself.

"What's Lyle after now?" she asked once they reached the lift and sent it heading down.

Mudge gave the ball of mem-sheet in his hand a surprised look, as if it should have filed itself, then scowled at her. "Same as always. He wants to know when they can get back to that rock of his—claims the IU station on Myriam isn't cooperating. This time he tried to go over your head to Director Hollans, whose secretary promptly sent everything back to me." He grew smug. "Protocol has its purpose."

Protocols. Politics. Mac was grateful to have someone who actually relished both on her side. "Use your power for good," she advised as the doors opened on the main floor.

Mac didn't say anything more until they stood outside on the terrace, over-looking the grounds of the consulate. Winter was losing the battle here, helped along by the eager efforts of a small army of gardeners. There were swathes of green beside the patio stones, color peeking shyly from the mulch. But in the distance, upslope, snow clung to ridge and treetop.

It wasn't raining, but the feel was in the air. The sky sported flags of cloud, torn loose by the westerlies that raced straight from the Antarctic to this shore. They were protected by the consular building and by the shoulders of ridges higher than this, but the wind tossed debris around below them—to the frustra-tion of the staff sweeping the stones.

The vast research complex called the Atrium lay deep beneath those same stones, quiescent now save for a cluster of irritable archaeologists and the usual groups studying the market impact of technology alien to Human and vice versa. The most active area was the Telematics section, where the Sinzi—and Earthgov—monitored comings and goings through the transects.

And watched for Dhryn.

Rooted above the bustle of science, giant graceful trees lined the sides of the patio, a tame forest laced with secluded paths and inviting entrances. Beyond them and the buildings, the cliff face plunged into the sound, where life usually found in mid-ocean depths came within reach of land.

No time left for exploring. Mac laid her hands on the cold, wide stone that topped the rail edging the terrace. "I'll be back," she vowed.

"Back from where?"

"The message, Oversight," she reminded him.

He unfastened the upper of the two pockets that bulged at his waist, fumbling inside. Before he pulled whatever it was out, Mudge gave her a wary look. She knew that expression, very well. He was bracing for her reaction.

"What is it?" *Nik had been discreet, hadn't he?*

Instead of answering, he finished the motion, passing her the result between two fingers. "Don't blame me," he said grimly. "It was that Myg."

Mac pressed her lips firmly together, determined not to smile, and took the folded piece of glittery pink paper. She sniffed appreciatively. *Lily of the Valley.* Her favorite.

Saying anything would only make it worse.

She opened the folds. It was real paper, not a mem-sheet, inscribed in block letters. Fourteen remained convinced she found large type easier to read. At the moment, Mac didn't care. She scanned the message three times to be sure, then stared at Mudge. "That's it?" she protested, her voice rising. "'Continuing as planned; situation nominal?' What kind of a message is that?"

He gave a faint *harrumph.* "Succinct?"

Unable to say another word, Mac crumpled the fragrant pink paper in her hand and glared at Mudge, seriously considering where to put it.

Mudge threw up his hands. "See? This is exactly why I didn't want to give it to you indoors. You do better with—space—to calm down. A great deal of space. I knew you'd be upset."

"Upset!" Realizing she'd shouted, Mac took a deep shuddering breath. Then another. *Fine.* She had the *lamnas* on her finger, with Anchen's promise it contained a private message from Nik. *This?* Mac straightened out the paper. "Why would I be upset?" she asked more calmly. "It does get the point across. But surely there was more than this in the com-packet."

"Nothing I thought you'd want. Language modules for the translation project. Private mail from the others." Mudge snorted. "Knowing Fourteen, he's tucked away a copy of anything embarrassing for later use."

Mac shocked herself by immediately wondering how she could gain access to any mail from Cinder, Nik's partner, and what it might reveal. *Not that she expected anything to have changed for the better.* Cinder had admitted she wanted nothing more than a chance to kill Dhryn. Any Dhryn. Including the Vessel, on whom everything depended.

When she hesitated, Mudge frowned. "Was I wrong, Norcoast? Did you want the rest?"

Mac noticed he didn't ask why she might. *Gods, the spy mentality was contagious.* She shook her head. "Let's leave snooping to the pros. We have enough to do."

Mudge gave her one of those too-keen looks. Mac thought her expression nicely neutral, but he *harrumphed* anyway. "Do? What's going on?"

Moving offworld? Mac found herself not quite ready to say the words. Instead, she began: "It's Emily—"

"I knew it!" Mudge pounced. "You shouldn't have gone out alone last night. What were you thinking?"

Are you thinking what I'm thinking? Mac's lips twisted, but aloud she said: "It's not about last night, Oversight." Once she told him, there'd be no turning back. Mudge with a mission was a force of nature. *So be it.* "We're leaving for Myriam. As soon as Anchen makes the arrangements."

"Who's 'we?'" he demanded, unwittingly echoing the Sinzi.

Mac reached out to tap the ball of mem-sheet clutched in his hand. "Everyone. The entire team. You, me, Fourteen, the archaeologists. We'll—"

"And when were you going to ask me, Norcoast?" Mudge drew himself up. "I don't recall agreeing to this."

She blinked. *Go without him?* The mere notion sat like a stone in her empty stomach. "You have to come," she blurted.

"I have to do no such thing." He wagged his pudgy finger at her. "And neither do you."

For a heartbeat, Mac believed she had that choice. She imagined returning to Base with Emily to stay, back to work, back to her life.

Home.

Then she imagined, all too easily, what the Dhryn could do.

Mac shook her head. "I'm not finished, Oversight. I've too many questions, questions only that planet can answer. But if you want to stay here," she added evenly, "that's fine."

"You wouldn't last a week without me," he huffed.

She wasn't sure if he meant her, or the Origins Team, or both. *Probably right on all counts,* Mac told herself. *Didn't matter.* She shrugged. "I'll manage. Fourteen can help me."

Mudge frowned at her. "Don't try to manipulate me, Norcoast."

"I know better," Mac assured him. She rested her elbows on the cool stone and turned her head to study him. "What do you want me to say, Oversight?" she asked quietly. "Admit I'm afraid? That returning to that world will be the hardest thing I've ever done? I'm still going." She considered his face, cheeks blotched with angry red. "It would be easier with someone I trust along. To watch my back."

A living friend when she faced the dead, she added to herself.

Brymn.

His *harrumph* sounded mollified, although his eyebrows still glowered at her. "Well, it doesn't have to be me. The Ministry will send its lunkheads with you."

"It's IU jurisdiction. I don't know if they can come."

"What about Dr. Mamani?"

Mac ran her artificial fingers over the stone, finding some moss to poke. "Emily," she said carefully, "will be returning to Base. To work on her Tracer device."

"What? You can't be serious. Whose stupid idea was that?" Mudge's voice rose to a regrettable volume. A gardener glanced up.

"Shhh," Mac hushed him, not bothering to be offended. *He could be right.* "Mine—and the Sinzi-ra's. And it's—Emily needs to be away from here, Oversight. It was the only way I could think of that would keep her safe."

"It's where you belong. You know it. You're out of your league here, Norcoast. Offworld? The Chasm? It's ridiculous. You can't go. I certainly won't."

Mac pressed her lips together and returned glare for glare, willing to wait all day if necessary.

It took three and a half minutes. Then Mudge *harrumphed.* Twice. "I'll have to round up some proper packing crates. The toss to orbit will wreak havoc with the equipment. You know who'll complain about that," he added, growing almost cheerful, a bundle of daunting efficiency about to be unleashed on his victims.

"Oversight—" Mac began, her voice unsteady. She straightened and turned to face him.

Mudge edged back, as if suspecting intent to hug. "I'll confer with Anchen's staff and book a meeting within the hour about the details—don't miss it," he warned. "We'll keep things close to the chest until the schedule's set."

She had to be sure. "You'll come with me?"

He feigned surprise. "Of course I'm coming, Norcoast. Who else could spot when you were about to fly off on some idiotic tangent? Or just wrong," he added magnanimously.

Mac grinned. "I'm so comforted."

"As you should be. Now. About the meeting. We should hold it—"

"Wait. Give me a chance to tell Emily before she hears the news from anyone else."

Mudge's mouth dropped open. "You mean—you went to the Sinzi—arranged this—without asking Dr. Mamani first?" He shook his head dolefully. "Norcoast. What were you thinking?"

"There was nothing to ask her about until I'd talked to Anchen," Mac snapped.

He stared at her, then heaved a distinctly theatrical sigh as if the entire matter was beyond him. "I'll go and get started with the rest, including Fourteen. It'll be easier than what you'll be doing."

As Mudge walked away, Mac threw up her hands. "Why does everyone keep saying that?"

Emily would love the plan.

- 4 -

OBSTACLE AND OBSCURITY

"ANCHEN LOVES THE PLAN."

Mac heard the pleading note in her own voice and winced. *Not the right approach.*

Sure enough, Emily spat out a frustrated string of Quechua Mac didn't want translated. "Of course she does," she finished in English, throwing her gloved arms skyward in emphasis. "Don't you see, Mac? It splits us up. Means you'll do whatever she wants."

"No!" Mac protested. Her friend would have to rediscover physical expression for this conversation, she sighed to herself, neck sore from following Emily's relentless pacing. Just as well they'd met in her quarters rather than outside. "That's not true. She—to Anchen your returning to Base would be—" *profoundly circular?* Somehow, she doubted spouting alien philosophy was going to help, even if Emily could be convinced that she, Mac, had any idea what she was spouting. *Not likely.* "She loves the plan," Mac repeated lamely.

"While I hate the plan. I'm not going. End of discussion."

Anchen and Mudge had been right, Mac realized with some disgust. The way it stood, if she had a month, she couldn't argue, cajole, or rationalize Emily into doing things her way. *That left . . .* Mac steeled herself. "You owe me, Em."

Emily stood still. "Owe you?" A shapely dark eyebrow rose—curiosity, not offense. *Yet.*

"Yes. And I'm collecting. You're going to Base. I need to know it's running." Mac didn't bother adding: *and you're safe.*

Here came the offense, right on cue—that proud flash of Emily's eyes, the passionate outrage. "I don't believe it. You—it's revenge, isn't it? Bizarre, twisted revenge! Aie! You're abandoning me. To—you want me to work on your damned fish for you! Well, I won't!"

"Good. Because I want you to work on your damned Survivors!"

They faced off, both furious. Then Emily's expression shifted to shock. "What did you say?"

"You'll have to rebuild your Tracer. But you'll have every resource." Mac considered this, then hastily qualified: "Short of interfering with the field season."

"Heavens forbid I do that." But Emily's slowly expanding smile took the sting out of the words. "You actually talked the Sinzi-ra into this. Supporting my research. Now that I don't believe."

"She owes me, too," Mac said succinctly.

"You always were dangerous in a corner, Mackenzie Connor." Emily shook her head, her hands spreading in a gesture of surrender. "Okay. I love the plan."

Mac tried not to sound smug. "I knew you would. Now. We don't have much time."

After sending Emily to prepare her "shopping list" for the Sinzi-ra—doubtless to be long and costly, judging by the other scientist's intense air of concentration when she'd left Mac—Mac sat behind her desk and began a list of her own.

She'd committed herself now, she thought, studying the 'screen hovering before her eyes, drawing a finger through a lower quadrant to retrieve her field station inventory. Emily at Base; Mac in space.

There was a switch.

She'd learned a few things about travel offworld. Mac didn't bother deleting any items, given she had no idea what she might face and now knew better than to believe anyone who said they did. Tools, dissection kits, syringes, specimen bottles, scales—anything might be useful. And they fit her hands. She'd become all too aware of the dearth of Human-oriented technology outside this system.

On that thought, she added a distillation kit and several collapsible jugs for water to her list.

Myriam was a desert. Never an overly moist world, lacking the large oceans cradling Earth's continents, what water remained on the Dhryn planet ran through underground rivers and lodged in aquifers. This was, in fact, another and troubling facet of the Chasm puzzle: the dust-dry ruins. What they now knew of the Dhryn feeding—Mac shuddered—did not include the removal of surface water. Oh, Dhryn didn't care for the stuff. For some reason they'd done their best to drain their new home, Haven, and chosen colonies that were arid and desolate by Human standards. But that didn't explain the rest of those worlds.

For a fleeting instant, Mac thought of Emily's Survivors. *What if they did exist? What if they were aquatic? Did the Ro remove any ocean that might have sheltered them?*

Did the Ro fear them?

She shook her head. *More likely the Ro had been their thorough selves and simply finished the sterilization of each world begun by the Dhryn.*

Because it was nothing short of deadly, that hope there was a species out there with the answers, more advanced than the Sinzi, ready to save everyone else out of the goodness of whatever passed for their hearts.

It had seduced Emily into believing the Ro.

It threatened their efforts even now.

Mac closed her 'screen and pushed herself to her feet, thoroughly unsettled. "The sooner we're away from here, the better," she told the empty room.

The *lamnas* glittered on her finger, as if in reassurance she hadn't lost it. Mac had a regrettable history with jewelry—something along the lines of her ability to keep dress shoes intact.

Was now the right time?

Mac glanced out the window. The sun was shining, doing its best to hurry spring along. Not quite as helpfully, the wind had picked up to a howl, and she didn't need to walk out on her terrace to know its protective membrane would be in place. *Where was the fun in that?*

Sing-li had refused to show Mac how to turn it off. He'd insisted a safety feature designed to keep guests of little mass—or sense—from being blown out to sea or worse, given the rocks below, was not to be treated lightly.

She'd only wanted to feel the rain. *Okay, and maybe toss her imp with the latest meeting notes into it.*

Spoilsport.

Mac tucked her imp into its pocket, and surveyed her room. Strange how putting a few personal belongings around had made this alien space hers. "Okay, more than a few," she admitted aloud, eyeing the salmon swinging overhead and the filled shelves on every wall. She hadn't asked for all of her belongings from Base. They'd just . . . arrived. Sing-li's doing. "It's going to take a while to pack all this."

If not now, when?

Mac heaved a sigh of resignation and went into her other room. The bed beckoned—too risky, given the struggle she'd had to leave it this morning. The jelly-chair by the door was promising, but it lacked a certain privacy.

Which was the problem, she abruptly realized, fingers wrapping around the tiny device.

A moment later, Mac sat on the floor of her closet, its door closed, content in the knowledge that, while undignified and likely silly, she was as alone as she could manage. She leaned against a storage bag, wiggling until its contents stopped digging into her spine. From the feel, tents.

Now.

She took the ring between forefinger and thumb, lifting it—

"Mac! What on Earth are you doing in here?"

Closing her fist over the ring, Mac glared up at the man in the doorway. "I'm meditating," she said stiffly.

"Meditating." Lyle Kanaci gave her a doubtful look. "In your closet?"

"I thought it would be peaceful," she grumbled, climbing to her feet. "What is it?"

"Not even you would call a meeting of this importance and not attend." His voice rose and he waved his hands. "Weren't you even planning to be there?"

Mac held back any number of retorts. While she'd known Lyle to be testy—and Fourteen knew he had a temper, *although the alien had deserved what he'd got, using Lyle's depilatory cream that way*—he'd never burst into her rooms before. Not to mention she usually heard about her attendance, or lack of it, from Mudge.

"I don't need to be there, but I was coming." *Eventually.* "What's wrong?" She waved him out of her closet and followed behind. "Besides, you're better at those things than I am," she added honestly. *And enjoyed being in charge.*

Like Mudge, Lyle Kanaci was Mac's height, but with an academic's tendency to slouch that made him appear the shorter of the two. It also made it easy to see the red mottling the pigmentless skin of his scalp and neck. *Something's definitely up,* Mac decided.

He whirled on her the moment they were through the door. "You could have at least warned me!"

"About what? Oh." Mac nodded. "The move offworld. Things fell into place—" she made a helpless gesture "—fast."

"I don't like it."

Déjà vu. She felt like grabbing Lyle by the shoulders and giving him a good shake. *While she was at it,* Mac decided grimly, *she'd shake the rest of the universe with him.* "You've been complaining for weeks about not returning to Myriam," she pointed out. "I'd have thought you'd be thanking me."

"Not when it's some trick by the Sinzi to make you cooperate."

Was he worried about her? Mac wondered. She scowled. "This was my idea. There's no trick, the Sinzi-*ra*—" the emphasis on the honorific a rebuke, "—and I are in complete agreement as to the benefits to everyone, especially Emily, and what made you walk into my closet anyway?" *Oh, for doors that locked,* she thought wistfully. *Just once.*

"You weren't anywhere else." He had the grace to look embarrassed. "Emily said you were still in your quarters."

She scowled a moment longer, just for effect. "I'd better have privacy on Myriam."

"You'll have your own tent," he promised, then half smiled. "Middle of a sandstorm, you'll be alone for days."

Mac rolled her eyes. "Don't remind me."

"Mac." Lyle lowered his voice. "Are you sure about this? Myriam, the Chasm. It's not what you're used to—we'd understand—"

Ouch. She decided to be equally blunt. "I do my best work in the field, Dr. Kanaci. As do you. A little—a great deal—" she amended, "—of sand doesn't change that. We can't learn what we must about the Dhryn here."

This drew a measuring look from his pale eyes, followed by a short, quick nod. "Then let's get going. Charles has the specs for the flight—if you're finished meditating?"

"All done," she assured him serenely, feeling a growing impatience herself.

Field season. Not to a river or her salmon, but the potential for discovery was there nonetheless. It quickened the heart, steadied priorities into one. *Move.*

"Let's go," she told Lyle.

If she replaced the ring around her finger, turning it twice with regret, that was no one's business but her own.

Familiarity couldn't breed apathy. Not here. As always, Mac slowed when she entered the Atrium, taking a good look at its remarkable space. The vast underground research facility beneath the IU consulate deserved it.

Aerial platforms filled the inverted cone that was the Atrium's core. Most were rooms without walls, linked in various temporary configurations to better serve the needs of the researchers using that space. Some were docked against the steplike levels that formed the outer walls, if you'd call a wall what resembled more the side of a giant pyramid under excavation, studded with entrances to still more rooms and facilities. Other platforms were in motion in every direction. Mac had yet to see a pattern to the traffic, although she had to admit she hadn't seen a collision either. *A few near misses.*

The ceiling, high enough to feel like sky, was the underside of the stones forming the patio, itself in the lee of the main consulate building. Tree roots formed wisps of brown cloud, the plants seemingly unharmed by finding air rather than rock beneath. Mac suspected extra care by the gardeners.

Space, bustle, changing shapes, but what Mac noticed most each time was the din. Her ears rang with voices from varied throats, machinery, and the incessant beeping of whatever felt obliged to beep. She'd only experienced silence here once, when they'd waited together for the Dhryn.

When they'd expected to die.

The Origins Team, as they styled themselves, had been granted space between the permanent researchers here, those who looked for the best fit between approved alien technologies and humanity. And vice versa. The trade in knowledge and invention went offworld as well. To reach their little pocket of xeno-archaeology, one had to take a platform into the center, then rise to the far back, uppermost level.

Mac reconsidered its location from her new understanding of Anchen's perspective. *If the farther you traveled to consult, the greater importance that consultation had . . . ?* "In that case," she mused aloud, trailing Lyle to the waiting platform, "she thinks pretty highly of our work."

"Who thinks highly of it?"

"Anchen." Mac shook her head at his incredulous expression. "Don't ask. I'm not sure I could explain."

One of the advantages to being the last remnant of the Gathering was, to Mac's not-so-secret delight, a reduction in ceremony and fuss. They weren't expected to hold their meetings at the Sinzi-ra's long table—although Mac herself continued to be called there far too often. For Origins, meetings had become practical affairs. Staff would bring food, she and her group would curl up in jelly-chairs, and they'd finish discussion and dessert at roughly the same moment. *Relaxing and effective.*

Except, obviously, for today. Mac and Lyle stepped from their platform to confront a maze of crates and bags, most stacked in piles reaching well over their heads. They exchanged a look. "Oversight," Mac guessed; Lyle nodded in complete understanding.

Consular staff were busy removing items from the maze to waiting platforms docked to either side, forcing the two of them to thread their way between. The entrance to the research area was equally cluttered. Its door had vanished, along with most of the wall to either side, to allow larger equipment to be rolled through.

"Is this a meeting or are we already packing?" Lyle shouted at her over the clang and clatter.

"Staff are packing," Mac observed, then lifted her hand to return a wave. "Looks like we're meeting."

The wave had been Fourteen's, whose head, shoulders, and wildly moving arm could be seen over the ranks of shifting crates. Mac used him as her guide, the room they'd worked in these past weeks being essentially gone.

Including the comfy chairs.

Luckily they still had a table, Mac discovered once she and Lyle passed the remaining obstructions. Fourteen was jumping on it, as if to be sure she'd seen him. "Idiots!!!!" the Myg shouted cheerfully. "Over here!"

"Do we have to take him with us?" Lyle whispered in her ear.

"Oversight would miss him," Mac whispered back. She'd already spotted Mudge, seething in the background. Given the alien's onslaught on the furniture, she was relieved he was only seething. "Fourteen," she called out before worse could happen. "Don't break the table. I need it."

"Bah!" the alien grinned down at her. "You are trying to stop Charlie from strangling me with his bare hands." But he obliged.

Like other Mygs of Mac's acquaintance—granted, a small number, including six tiny offspring, the xenopaleoecologist who might be their mother, and Fourteen's uncle, who'd visited last week—Fourteen was a stocky humanoid, similar enough in body plan to shop locally. Currently, he was challenging the optics of every other species in Origins by wearing fluorescent green, yellow, and mauve striped pants with an orange tank top emblazoned "Go Native!" in red across its stretched chest. He'd taken off the formal wig the moment his uncle had left; his brush of reddish-brown hair spiked wildly in all directions.

Mac was quite fond of him. *So long as he stayed away from her things.* Her family cabin on Little Misty Lake would never be the same after one of Fourteen's creative spells.

Lyle's words ran through her mind just then. Leave him? *Not an option.* Fourteen had declared some kind of Myg debt to her. He'd probably buy his own ship and follow anyway. Or hand her an offspring.

Who were cute—just not that cute.

Mac sighed. Ever since he'd failed to stop the Ro signal, for which she'd never blamed him, he'd been worse.

"About time you showed up, Norcoast," Mudge accused. He looked harassed, but in the "busy moving the world, coming through" way that meant he was enjoying himself thoroughly. *Not that he'd admit it,* Mac smiled to herself. "We had to start without you."

"Oh, I never mind that," she said calmly. "Hi, everyone."

The chorus of "Hi Macs" that ensued ranged from bass to soprano, with a "Hiiii Maaaaac" elongation in the tenor offerings. Extra vowels meant the Sthlynii were not enjoying themselves. *No surprise there.* She'd learned they didn't care for change, not at the pace Humans moved, anyway. The switch to the Atrium, even with better facilities, had twisted Therin's mouth tentacles into a foul knot for days.

You couldn't please everyone, Mac reminded herself, silently counting heads. *Speaking of which* . . . "Where's Kudla?" she sighed.

"Irrelevant!"

She sent Fourteen a quelling look. The Myg didn't play tricks on the author or his followers. *It wasn't a compliment.* "You can brief him later, then," Mac ordered, hopping up to sit on the near end of the table. When no one else moved, she made an impatient summoning gesture to gather them around her in a semicircle.

A semicircle Mudge immediately burst through in order to confront her, brandishing his imp like a miniature sword. "I protest, Norcoast. Even by your standards, this is no way to run a meeting!"

Mac brought a finger to her lips. He subsided, barely, and the others grew still, obviously expectant. "Oversight has the transport details," she informed them. "I dare say you've gone ahead without us to calculate the optimal allocations of effort and resources for everyone?" This directed at Mudge. He gave her his patented defiant scowl; Mac smiled peacefully back. "There," she exclaimed, rubbing her hands together. "Who needs a meeting? Oversight will give each of you your assignments, send any bills and additional requests to consular staff as usual, and then? We're out of here."

There was a verbal explosion as everyone tried to talk at once. Mac ignored them, swinging her legs back and forth. After a moment, the uproar sputtered, then died away. "You know we'd come around to his way by the end," she reasoned. "Think of all the time I just saved."

The easy victory clearly upset Mudge, doubtless armed with arguments for every point and particular. He *harrumphed* vigorously. "We should at least discuss sleeping quarters on board the transport. At least!"

"Really?" Mac raised an eyebrow at those assembled, collecting a few chuckles and one interesting hue change. "I think they can handle that. Now. If that's all?" She jumped down. "See you in orbit."

The wall of bodies didn't budge. Mac stood, confronted by anxious looks—or body tilts of the same meaning—and realized what was bothering them.

Emily.

She'd made quite an impact, even while recovering. Some here were smitten. Others, friends. And others . . .

Mac focused on Fourteen's small, flesh-enclosed eyes.

Others saw Emily as a tool.

They'd have their separate reasons for worrying about Emily being removed from the team.

Not one of which mattered now, Mac told herself grimly.

As if warned by some change in her expression, those blocking her path silently moved aside.

Mac stalked through the opening, thought, and turned abruptly. *For the friends and the smitten, and as a warning to everyone else.* "The Dhryn have been quiet. Do any of you think that's going to last?" She kept it calm, but some of them flinched. *Easy to forget fear, safe in the Sinzi-ra's snow-white palace.* "Dr. Mamani has work to do," Mac continued, letting them see her exasperation. "Work backed by the Ministry of Extra-Sol Human Affairs, as well as the full resources of the IU consulate on Earth. As do we."

With that, she left.

Or tried. Mudge caught up to her in the midst of the maze of crates. "Norcoast. Norcoast! Wait."

Mac stopped, narrowing her eyes at him. "You're ruining a great exit line, Oversight. I don't get many of those."

"Giving me carte blanche to make arrangements. Yes, yes. But what kind of an example do you set by not waiting for your own assignment? Hmm?"

She blinked. "Pardon?"

"Hold out your imp and I'll transfer your duty list."

Wordlessly, Mac did as asked. Mudge in this mood? *As well argue the arrival of spring.*

They shifted closer to a stack of bags to avoid being run down by a hand lev. Mudge leaned toward Mac as he fiddled with their small workscreens, presumably sending her the list. Presumably, because he seemed to be more interested in who was nearby, sending anxious looks in every direction. Then, as if satisfied, his hands stilled and he met her eyes. "I'm scheduled on the shuttle with the rest." A hoarse whisper. "I should be going with you, Norcoast."

Mac frowned. "Do any of the others know I'm taking Emily to Base myself?"

"No. They'll find out on the shuttle. But I must—"

"I'll meet you at the way station, Oversight," Mac assured him, resisting the urge to lay her hand on his arm. Such gestures made Mudge break out in a sweat, entertaining but hardly kind. *And he deserved kindness.* "I'll be fine. Don't worry. They aren't letting me stay more than a few hours. A day at the most. You can contact me anytime." *Unless she switched her com off,* but Mac didn't see any point in bringing up that habit. "Sing-li will be his annoyingly overprotective self."

He pursed his lips, eyes still troubled. "The defenses here, on the transport— I don't like you being outside them. Bad enough last night."

"Last night went quite well, all things considered," Mac asserted, pocketing her imp now that the transfer was complete. *If there'd been one at all, and all this wasn't a ploy to keep her listening to Mudge's protest.* The spy mentality was catching.

"The Ro won't have forgotten you. It was a foolhardy risk, Norcoast. Foolhardy!"

"No, it wasn't." She paused to let three staff pass, arms filled with empty bags. "A little secret, Oversight, between you and me. Last night? An experiment." She watched the color drain from his florid cheeks and gave a curt nod. "Everyone believes the Ro are waiting for something. No one knows what—yet. I needed to convince certain pigheaded committee members it wasn't for Emily or myself to be in easy reach. Or we'd wind up virtual prisoners here." *Or bait.*

"What if you'd been wrong?"

She shrugged. "Worth knowing."

"Norcoast!"

Mac gave a tight smile. "If it makes you feel better, I was sure nothing would happen. The Ro pulled out, remember, taking their technology with them." *Leaving twenty-three Progenitors and millions of their kin dead.* "I have no reason to think they'd bother with two Human scientists."

"One came to watch you die. I'd call that 'bothering.'"

There had been something personal, or its alien equivalent. *She wasn't a fool.* But Mac shook her head again, dismissing Mudge's concern. "The Ro have more on their minds," she said, to him and to herself, "however sane or insane those might be. Our little encounter could have been nothing more than an opportunity—a voyeur's chance handed to the Ro by the Sinzi's new no-space technology. We can't attribute Human reactions to the alien. Believe me, I've learned that lesson."

"You've learned a great deal more, Norcoast," Mudge agreed, surprising her, then predictably: "but not enough by a long shot."

She reached out and poked him in the chest with a forefinger. "Which is why I have you."

He *harrumphed,* color returning to his cheeks. "We'll have to work flat out to be ready by the Sinzi-ra's launch date."

"There's a date?" Mac demanded, startled. The trouble with making suggestions to Anchen was how quickly she acted on them. The floor suddenly felt like a river, rushing by underfoot. "When?"

Mudge held up his imp. "You've the details."

No doubt she did. On discovering Mac was to practice reading, retraining her mind to that skill, Mudge had taken to sending her daily message summaries with annotations. *Innumerable annotations.* To be honest, his comments were often perceptive and some outright funny, whether Mudge had intended them that way or not.

Time. "This week, next month?" Mac insisted. "When?"

He glanced around, again checking for listeners. *A reasonable precaution,* Mac fumed, *if they weren't by now almost shouting to be heard over the racket from all sides.* "You leave tonight, 21:00. The trip by lev takes about six hours; you can grab some sleep. That means you'll arrive at Base 8:00 am their time, but the day before—"

"I can do the conversion," Mac muttered. *Just after the second wave of breakfast through Pod Three.* She made a note to take some of the consulate's superb coffee in case Kammie hadn't finished her ritual: three cups to conscious, fourth to converse.

Mac's heart began to pound. Anticipation, dread, or a mix? She couldn't be sure.

Change. That at least.

"What about you and the team?"

"It's in—"

"Oversight, please?"

His *harrumph* was kinder. "The Sinzi-ra wants us out by tomorrow morning. We'll transport to the Antarctic station, hop to orbit from there, catch the shuttle to the way station, and meet you the next day."

She'd hoped to spend three days settling Emily, had been glumly sure she'd be lucky to get two. *One?* "Looks like we'll all be busy," Mac said, mind whirling. "Can you look after—?" She waved vaguely in the direction of the Origins Team.

"Don't worry. I'll get them to the way station. You get there, too."

Mac smiled at Mudge's anxious tone. "Just don't leave for Myriam without me."

Mac set her 'screen to hover beside her face as she strode briskly back to her quarters, preset at the angle permitting her to squint at it without walking into a wall, and the exact distance to stop her poking herself in the eye while manipulating the 'screen's display. She'd managed both wall-walk and poke-eye before now, when in a hurry to be somewhere while getting things done.

As now. She dictated in a steady whisper, ignoring any quizzical looks or neck flares from those she passed in the long white corridors. Instructions. Finishing lists. Those tripped off her tongue automatically. Moving to the field? *She could do that in her sleep.*

Harder were the private messages. On the lift ride up, Mac fumbled through, erasing more than she kept. Cautions to 'Sephe about Emily, when she wasn't sure what the Ministry agent already knew. Hints, suggestions—outright pleas for cooperation to Kammie, when there was no guarantee the other would do any of it. Kammie was being imposed upon here. Big time. In effect, Mac was asking the entire season, everything, be warped around Emily's needs. And she couldn't even predict what those might be.

Or that they were even real.

No matter friendship or professional courtesy, Kammie would have a fit. A quiet, professional, no-holds-barred-stubborn fit.

Mac wiped her latest recording. *Too needy.*

The lift opened, and she shifted well to one side to let Rumnor and four companions have the floor space the larger aliens required, particularly given the knife-encrusted bandoliers crisscrossing their torsos. "Good morning, Dr. Connor," the alien intoned sadly as the door closed. Thick yellow tears slipped down his facial hair, barely missing her feet. "I trust your bleeding went well."

Oh. That. Mac squirmed inwardly. *It had seemed brilliant at the time—could have been the beer.* "About that, Rumnor—" she began, intending to clear the confusion.

"You missed a fine cider," Rumnor interrupted, the others rumbling a doleful: "Wonderful." "Exquisite." "Never better." "Remarkable."

Then it was Mac's floor. She swallowed her explanation and patted his arm as she squeezed by to exit. "Next time," she promised.

"Is there cider on Myriam?"

Mac froze halfway through the lift door, turning to look up into those peppered brown eyes, rimmed in yellow crystals. "Why do you ask?"

"Dr. Connor. The lift cannot continue while you stand there."

Mac put one hand on the edge of the door. "What about Myriam?"

Five gloomy giant teddy bears stared down at her, none offering a word.

Seconds ticked by. Minutes. Mac made herself comfortable against the lift doorframe, crossing her arms across her chest, eyes never leaving Rumnor's.

A Grimnoii at the back made an uncomfortable sound.

"Myriam," she suggested.

Rumnor snicked his teeth together. *Threat or exasperation?* Mac wondered. It could just as well be a nervous habit. She smiled.

Low, almost a growl. "Our people have an interest."

In Myriam or her going there? Mac had thought the Grimnoii neutral to indifferent, here to serve the Sinzi-ra somehow.

She should know not to make assumptions by now.

"What kind of interest?"

More snicking. Then silence.

"Well, if you're planning a trip, bring your own cider," she said pleasantly, and stood back to let the door close between them.

Aliens.

She filed the question of Grimnoii on Myriam for another day, almost running to her quarters. Once there, she closed the door behind her, wished for a lock, then headed for the terrace.

Where there were chairs she could move. Stripping off their cushions, Mac wedged two under the handles of the doors after she closed them, considered the arrangement, then added the remaining two chairs on top. She threaded the beads hanging to either side—her own personal Ro detectors—around the legs and backs of the chairs, twisting the ends together.

It wasn't a lock. But it was a demand for privacy even the too-helpful consulate staff should be able to figure out.

The faint shimmer of the membrane kept out the wild sky, with its rain and now gale force wind. *She would,* Mac decided, *have preferred the weather.*

She took the chair cushions to the corner where the wall curved out to meet the railing, and sat on the pile. Then she pulled off the *lamnas* and held it between her fingers—fingers which trembled ever so slightly until she frowned at them.

"It's not as if you know what kind of message he'd send," Mac reminded herself. "'Feed my cat.' 'Tell Sing-li blah blah blah.' 'Forgot to mention . . .'" Here she stopped, unwilling to guess what Nikolai Trojanowski might have forgotten to say in their final, stolen minutes before he'd left.

Mac grinned. *Not that they said much.*

Whatever he wanted to tell her, using this strange method, she was willing to hear. More than willing. Mac brought the small ring to her lips, feeling foolish as she kissed it, then blew gently through the loop. *Nothing.*

Finally, slowly, she raised it to her right eye.

- CONTACT -

IS THIS EVEN WORKING? I feel . . .
      . . . like an idiot, staring at this thing . . . /determination/
   "Paging Dr. Mackenzie Connor."
   Where did . . . come from? No. Nothing formal . . . here . . . /warmth/ Never with Mac . . . safe with Mac . . .
   "Hi, Mac. Bear with me. Anchen . . . better with practice." */doubt/ Concentrate . . .* "Hardest part . . . time . . . busy." */anger/doubt/ . . . can't trust anyone here . . . except maybe the Vessel . . . /concern/ambivalence/ . . . doesn't lie . . . /belief/surprise/*
   Concentrate . . . "I'll . . . reports. Here . . . sharing . . . With you, I . . . pretending you're here." */heat/desire/need/ Calm it down, fool . . . she doesn't need . . . /need/longing/emptiness/ . . . even if I do . . . /effort/ . . . Concentrate . . .*
   ". . . Vessel . . . more . . . the programming . . . complex personality, hard to pin down. Misses you. We share that." *Concentrate . . .*

* layered over *

—She smells metal—
   The Vessel's voice was sad but resigned. "I wish Mackenzie Winifred Elizabeth Wright Connor Sol had come with us."
   "She had other duties."
   "Emily Mamani Sarmiento. Have you news? Is she recovering?"
   I wish I knew the truth. Mac . . . so worried . . . I wanted to stay, hold her, make it right . . . all I could do was walk away . . . /tired guilt/ . . . not my job.
   "The Sinzi-ra felt confident. It's going to take some time, Vessel. Our species doesn't recuperate as quickly as yours."
   "'A Dhryn is robust or a Dhryn is not.' We must be able to heal ourselves, Nikolai Piotr Trojanowski."
   /curiosity/ "Why?"
   "The Great Journey." As if humoring a child. "To stop for the lame or wounded would be to risk the Progenitor. She is the future."
   "The Progenitor. We haven't heard from Her ship. Our captain has a valid point: we should confirm the rendezvous coordinates. What if She's left?"
   "Then She's left." A hooting laugh. "What a strange face you make, *Lamisah.* Rest easy.

The Progenitor will be where She has said. That is why I was sent. To find and bring the truth to Her. She will not leave without it."

*   *layered over* *

—She tastes cinnamon and nutmeg—

"You shouldn't meet with that Dhryn alone." Cinder's voice was cold. "It's against procedure."

/sympathy/ *Hardest on her . . . losing so much to the Dhryn . . . resolve/* Need her eyes, use her hate . . . the Vessel only seems harmless . . .

"The vids were running. I knew you kept watch."

"I watch. As well I do—in all the years we've worked together, Nik," the Trisulian's tone turned to anger, "this is the first time I've seen you willfully blind."

"Blind to what?"

"This mission. The Dhryn with its so-convenient coordinates. We're being led into a trap. Can't you see it? I swear that female's turned your head inside out!"

rage/ How dare she . . . /caution/ *Not the only one on board who doubts the Vessel . . . who doubts Mac . . .* /effort/patience/icy calm/ "That's why I depend on you, Partner. What say we work up a few scenarios?"

/effort/ *Good little spy . . . lie to them all . . . lie to those closest . . . lead them where they must go despite their fear . . .* /pity/dread/patience/

*   *layered over* *

—She feels weight—

Concentrate . . . " . . . does this work, Mac? There's no one else I can talk to . . ."
/loneliness/
I never knew I'd miss you like this . . .
fear/vulnerability/anger/
I can't . . . Not and do my job . . .
What have you done to me? /despair/
" . . . go . . . doesn't . . . sense, Mac . . . better next . . ."
/emptiness/

PLOTS AND PERMUTATIONS

MAC SLIPPED THE RING back on her finger, turning it slowly around and around.

"That was—" She paused, considering. "Different."

Different. The Sinzi might refute any claims to telepathy, but what Mac had just experienced had to be the closest possible facsimile. Her mind hurt, as if pierced by shards of thought. On a more physical level, a headache brewed behind her eyes, promising worse to come.

In sub-teach, imposed images and impressions were organized; upon waking, they floated into the recipient's consciousness already part of memory and function. Useful.

This?

Emotion. Raw, uncensored. Nik's. That was the easiest to sort from the rest.

Mac wiped tears from her face, yawned to ease the knot of tension in her jaw. She'd clenched her free hand so tightly while looking through the *lamnas* the nails had left purple impressions in the palm. *Had to be the real one.* She rubbed it over her thigh, doing her best to stop reacting, to process instead.

As if that was easy. Mac blushed. *She'd felt what he'd felt.*

Which brought up an interesting question. Had Nik realized the Sinzi device would record his feelings as well as whatever words he tried to convey?

Probably not, Mac concluded. The man elevated privacy to a survival skill. This level of exposure couldn't have been what Nik intended.

It did promote a distinct realism . . . Mac closed her eyes, waiting for her treacherous body to settle to more reasonable expectations. *No time for a cold shower.*

The message—*what else could she call it?*—had been far more than Nik's words and emotion. It was as if she'd heard other voices as Nik must have heard them: the Dhryn's. The Trisulian's, Cinder. Overlapping and confused. Recollections. As if the *lamnas* had made a copy of specific memories. She focused, trying to sort out the babble. *Yes. Two different conversations.*

Not random choices. Nik must want her to understand or learn something from each. Or those conversations were important to him.

Or upsetting.

Mac chewed her lip in sympathy. *Still, nothing she didn't already know.* The Vessel was acting as its nature. So was Cinder. Her grief over the destruction of her species' males had been plain enough before they'd left Earth.

And Nik would use it.

Chilled, Mac opened her eyes. An insight she didn't want. *It wasn't the only one.*

There'd been fear to the point of dread mixed with his warmer feelings for her. Not fear for her sake; for his own. "Bet it was the salmon," Mac muttered. She clambered to her feet, then tossed the cushions on the table. "Give a guy a carving, next thing you know he's having nightmares about shared household bills and who drives the skim."

For a long moment, she stood staring out over the tumble of dark water and white caps.

Then Mac's lips softened into a smile.

"Cinder was right," she told the storm. "He's blind about one thing."

Caring for someone else might be inconvenient and damn distracting.

It wasn't a weakness.

"Where are my things?" Mac asked, doing her utmost not to sound aggravated or alarmed. Nursing a throbbing headache she blamed on the alien ring around her finger wasn't helping. Walking in from the terrace to find her quarters stripped of anything Human was distinctly not helping. "And who said you should take them?"

Two, the only individual among the consulate staff Mac could identify with any reliability, would, when they were alone together, show some emotion. *Usually disapproval of Mac's tendency to dig holes in the sand floor with her toes.* Now, she gave a small frown, one of several practiced Human expressions Mac suspected staff employed at will. "Your things, Dr. Connor, have been packed into a shipping container. Myriam is a restricted environment. All materials brought to the planet must be catalogued and sterilized according to IU protocols. Charles Mudge III sent a very clear memo."

No doubt. Mac absently scuffed one toe in the perfectly raked sand where her desk had been. She'd already looked into the closet. Its outer door had been opened—she could tell by the raindrops on the floor. The transport lev had probably docked alongside and loaded up while she'd been staring into the *lamnas*. Staff were efficient, she had to give them that.

Too efficient for their own good, this time. "Sorry, but you'll have to bring it all back," Mac informed the alien. "I have to sort out what goes with Dr. Mamani."

"Dr. Mamani earlier identified her belongings and equipment. They have been packed for shipping to Norcoast Salmon Research Facility."

"Base," Mac corrected automatically. There must have been a constant stream of traffic through her quarters while she was gone, every footprint carefully erased from the sand. *Emily could be too efficient as well.* She pulled out her imp and waved it in the air. "I'd made a list." Out loud, the protest was a little more petulant than she'd planned.

"Which we accessed and followed. The few items not on your list we included for your comfort, knowing your excellent care with budget. The IU will cover all transport costs." Two hesitated. "Was this incorrect, Dr. Connor?"

Picturing crates of wooden salmon now accompanying her to Myriam, Mac gave up. *Maybe they'd let her sort out what should be shipped back to Earth during the trip to the transect gate.* "Did you leave me any clothes?"

A hint of smug in Two's otherwise composed face. "We are informed as to your schedule, Dr. Connor. There is a bag packed for your trip to—Base. As well, we have set aside all of the personal items you most commonly access for use during your journey."

Efficient and thoughtful. Mac shook her head. Although, by that criterion, Two likely packed the hockey puck she liked to roll between her hands while thinking, instead of her comb. *As for clothes?* She refused to imagine. *Aliens.* "You win, Two."

"I wasn't aware of a competition, Dr. Connor."

Mac grinned. "I don't suppose you'd consider coming to Myriam? You know what a mess I'll make without you."

The other being shook her head just so, an accomplished mimic. "Our duty is to the Sinzi-ra and her guests, Dr. Connor." Two brought both hands to her throat and bowed, deep and low, to Mac. Rising, she lowered her hands and gave a short lilting whistle through her pursed lips.

This was something new. Mac wasn't sure whether to imitate or ignore the gesture. She compromised by ducking her head quickly and giving a self-conscious *chirp*.

"You have been reasonable," Two announced. "May your journey be a safe and successful one, Dr. Connor, so we may have the privilege of serving you once more."

With that, she turned and walked from the room.

A compliment, Mac decided. Though if that was Two's honest opinion of her, she assuredly did not want to meet any guests the staff considered unreasonable.

Left alone, Mac considered her options. She could slump in one of the Sinzi's jelly-chairs. She should be able to force her eyes to read Mudge's detailed notes. *That's what she should do.* Her stomach reminded her she'd missed another meal.

She caught herself turning the ring around and around on her finger. *Not going there again.* Not soon. Anchen hadn't really looked into her own *lamnas* while demonstrating its use, something Mac now thought she understood. That experience, if at all comparable to hers, was disturbing on every level.

Intimate didn't begin to cover it.

Perhaps explaining why the rings stayed on Anchen's long fingers?

She refused to speculate about what Anchen—or any of her disparate personalities—saw or felt.

"And I'm not sharing either," Mac decided aloud.

Problem was, this close to leaving? She couldn't sit still. Especially in an empty room. Mac grabbed the small round bag Two had left for her in the washroom. Time to go. Somewhere.

After one last peek.

She pulled Nik's glasses from her pocket—it had become a habit, carrying them with her—and held them in front of her eyes. They'd fall off her nose if she tried to wear them properly.

Through the innocuous-seeming lenses, the walls of her sitting room revealed themselves as anything but plain and white. Lines, varying in thickness, scrolled over their surface like intricately woven threads. Among those threads, some behind, some in front, gleamed creatures small and large. Mac knew many, or their Terran equivalents. Shrimp and hydra, corals and urchins, sea cucumbers and squirts, curly-shelled oysters. Others were hauntingly strange. Floating orbs with tentacles spiraled around their girth. Eyes that glittered in their threes and sixes. Ribbons and segments, differently proportioned from any on Earth. The artist who created this had loved sea life, and known more oceans than hers.

Mac had never thought to wonder why she'd been assigned this room, of all the rooms in the guest wing, until seeing it through Nik's glasses.

It hadn't been for her benefit—the Sinzi-ra knew Humans couldn't see this range of color unassisted. A recognition of her specialty, perhaps, or her interests. A visual signal to inform the staff of what might suit this particular Human best.

Regardless, her being housed here held a subtle rightness of the sort Mac was coming to believe Anchen enjoyed for its own sake, a generosity without the Human need for a recipient. *Important,* she decided, *to remember that.*

And unfair—having to leave when she was finally making some progress.

Mac tucked the glasses away and the room was white on white once more.

Since arriving, she'd kept a mental list of all the things she would do before leaving the Interspecies Consulate. With an impossibly few hours left, Mac sat under a dripping tree and tallied what she'd missed, which was most of it. "The aquatic delegates," she sighed, taking a bite of tart apple. Not that they'd cooperated. Their portion of the consulate had been out-of-bounds to air breathers, they'd left meeting attendance to representatives who did breathe air, and, to be frank, spent much their time sightseeing in the ocean itself. She'd hoped to casually bump into one of their groups doing just that. "Seen any groupers?" she grinned to herself, imagining herself trying to communicate underwater.

She pulled the hood of her raincoat farther over her head, strangely content despite her list. The storm had abated, but the leaves held sufficient drops to be a nuisance for a while yet. Moisture polished tile and stone; there were busy new brooks alongside the paths. With the settling wind, a chill mist rising under the trees added a nice touch of drama.

She couldn't imagine why staff had put up such a protest to her spending time out here. She grinned. In the end they'd provided both raincoat and picnic, almost shooing her into the garden.

Not that Mac had initially planned anything so restful while waiting for the lev to Base. No, she'd intended to be useful.

There'd been only one problem.

"No one needs me." She tossed the core into a shrub large enough to hide it from frantic gardeners, but not, she trusted, from anything hungry. "Imagine that."

Like old times, having Emily wave a distracted greeting from where she stood surrounded by crates and attentive staff, giving instructions in a staccato blur. Although at Base, Mac thought with amusement, those in attendance would have been worshipful students and a certain tidal researcher. The wave sent the same message. *Later, Mac. I'm busy.*

Mudge and Lyle had been much the same, and the Sthlynii downright stammering in their panic. She could have hung around to watch, but the harried looks of those still packing weren't as amusing as she'd hoped.

"You'd think they'd never expected to move from here," Mac told the chubby pigeon, or whatever, pecking near her feet. Another miss on her to-do list for this amazing place: learn the birds.

Picnic finished, she lay back on the bench, using her bag for a pillow. Most of her fit. She didn't mind leaving her feet on the ground. For now, at least.

The leaves overhead were tossing this way and that in the gusty wind, revealing glimpses of cloud doing the same. "That's me," Mac whispered, squinting upward. "Macthisaway, Macthaddaway, Macwhoknowswhichaway." Who'd have guessed the day would come when she'd be more anxious about a quick trip to Base than an indefinite stay on an alien world?

With Mudge. "Good old Oversight," she murmured, catching a cold drop on her tongue. That much of home, she'd have.

She'd wanted to say good-bye to Anchen. To thank her. Maybe dare ask questions about the *lamnas.* But no staff would say where the Sinzi-ra could be found, and Mac had to trust the gracious alien would find her before she boarded the lev.

"So now I'm relaxing," Mac reminded herself. "Everyone says I should. No one needs me right now. It's a gift."

She spent an eternity staring up at the leaves, determined to enjoy the peace and rustling quiet.

Then checked the time again.

"Gods. That was two minutes?"

She sat up and shrugged off her coat, tying it around her waist. The two bags, hers and the picnic remnants, she stuffed into the crook of a low branch. "Exploring this place," she explained to the pigeon, "was on my list, too."

Then Mac started walking.

She let her feet and the lay of the land dictate her choice of paths, which meant little more than avoiding the larger puddles. Two hadn't packed extra shoes in her bag. As for getting lost, Mac was sure if she did, staff would appear from behind a tree to tactfully suggest the correct direction of the consulate. This wasn't wilderness, despite the undergrowth and moss-coated trees. It was a politely dressed fortress, designed to protect those here as much as ensure their privacy.

Still, the illusion was pleasing, the footing deteriorating in a manner that promised something special to the intrepid hiker, be there two feet marching or more. Whistling happily under her breath, Mac came up with fourteen species she'd met who could manage this uneven ground without help, even if one didn't have feet so much as a slime-bedecked undercarriage she'd tried to examine without success. Multispecies social events, she'd discovered to her chagrin, brought out the same annoying proprieties as any Human affair. Crawling under a chair while in evening finery, though in the interest of scientific curiosity, still collected disapproving frowns.

She ducked a low branch. The minor obstacle reduced her list to twelve. Mac grinned, almost wishing the chance to test her newfound ability to predict who she might meet, eyeball to nasal orifice, while enjoying the less tidy path. Almost.

There was something to be said for tramping alone, she admitted, taking a deep breath.

And gagging on a smell.

"What the—"

Stopping where she was, at the base of a small rise in the path, Mac took a more restrained, scientific sniff. *Not one of her twelve.* She scowled, knowing what, or in this case who, was responsible for that cloying, expensive musk. And the only way *se* could be here, was if *se'd* flown.

Mac didn't mind Frow as a rule. *Except this one.*

"*Se* Lasserbee," she shouted. "I know you're here."

The forest continued to rustle and drip overhead and to the sides. A bird, unseen but loud, expressed a similar opinion of the intruders. Quieter, more distant, Mac caught the low snarl and thump of breakers against the cliffs. She'd gone east then, away from the landing field.

She continued to watch the path ahead.

Se's hat appeared first, a multipointed affair that marked, according to Mudge, both military rank and present dominance mind-set. *If that was the case,* Mac decided, seeing more points than usual, Se *Lasserbee was going to be a royal pain.*

The Frow were a stratocracy, their military forming the government as well as holding most civil service posts. This state had existed through so many generations of idyllic peace and prosperity that ranks were now inherited and uniforms were exaggerations of style totally without function in combat. The species itself was famed for its unique biochemistry and a certain unfortunate stress response, hence Emily's joke. "Why don't you put a Nerban and a Frow in the same taxi?" Mac mouthed the words. "Because the former sweats alcohol and the latter sparks when upset."

Despite paying very close attention, she hadn't seen any sparks fly yet. *The day was young.*

Under the unwieldy hat came the rest of *Se* Lasserbee, *se's* uniform a somber blue bedecked with thumb-sized silver springs, each marking the appropriate spot for one of *se's* family's honors—said honors being kept safely in the family vault at all times. Two other Frow appeared over the rise behind the first, their hats having a mere three points. *Lackeys,* Mac judged, but kept part of her attention on them. A little too easy, in her opinion, to don a misleading hat.

Se Lasserbee's cloud of musk proceeded *se* down the path and Mac sneezed before she could stop herself. Perfume, food choice, or medication, it had to interfere with more respiratory systems than hers. Just as well for interspecies' tact this was the only Frow who wore the stuff. Why, no one would explain.

Probably covering up something personal. Or some type of olfactory camouflage, however overdone to Human senses. *Or assault?*

"*Se* Lasserbee. To what do I owe this effort?" Mac felt constrained to acknowledge the obvious. The Frow body form was far from ideal for a narrow, irregular footpath like this. There had to be a large custom-equipped lev on the other side of the rise. They should have waited for her to come to them.

But no. The three continued toward her, each with eyes fixed on the path. Every step had to be premeditated and carefully taken. It was like watching a slow-motion accident.

She found herself flattered. *The Sinzi-ra must have rubbed off on her.*

Mac had seen vids of Frow scampering down the vertical cliffs of their home world, long arms outstretched to grab the tiniest holds. The membrane of leathery skin and fine bone from finger to ankle joint made them the closest to a flight-capable sentient encountered by the IU, other than the Dhryn feeder form. Close, but not close enough. A Frow who lost a fingerhold fell to *se, ne,* or *sene's* death as easily as the next being. She had noticed the membrane let Frow hide what they were eating from one another, presumably a critical need before they invented social dining or cooperative daycare.

Their heads sat on stiff necks that bore accordionlike ridges on either side. Those worked independently, in Mac's limited experience, to tilt the head an extraordinary distance one way or the other. There were two eyes with slit-pupils, four nostrils, and a fanged mouth without lips but still capable of forming understandable Instella courtesy of a thin flexible tongue. These features were tightly grouped in the lower left quadrant of the front of the head, giving a Frow the appearance of never really looking right at you, even when doing so. The rest of the face and the top of the head was kept beneath a hat, itself secured by a strap below the protruding chin.

The head and neck were set below the shoulders, but where Sinzi shoulders rose with delicate flare, those of a Frow were great lumps studded with spines that shot from the base of the fine bones supporting their membrane. Mac kept waiting to see the spines move in some display—they seemed flexible—but the Frow of her acquaintance hadn't done anything interesting with them. The fabric spikes on their hats mimicked the real thing. Already top-heavy in appearance, given their slender torsos, short legs, and long arms, the spikes made a Frow appear ready to tip over and impale the ground at any moment.

Which was the truth. On land, flat land, they moved on two widely splayed legs and only when forced to do so, greatly preferring to lurch into position when no one was looking to assume a dignified, upright posture as if they'd been there all along. It was only polite to let Frow arrive first to any meeting for this reason. As for chairs, they were pointless. The beings didn't sit; their torsos couldn't bend.

Or fit inside a taxi. *Ruining a perfectly good joke.*

Mac's visitors kept their arms wrapped tightly around themselves, as if protecting their uniforms from a possible fall was more important than using them for balance. She couldn't help putting her arms out in anticipation, though her chances of catching one if it toppled were remote. *Provide a softer landing, maybe.*

Se Lasserbee staggered to a halt, much to Mac's relief and *se's* own, then took a moment to compose *se-self*. As *se* wrapped *se's* arms proudly around *se-self*, *se's* membrane thus becoming a handsome mantle, the last of *se's* companions planted a foot on an upturned root and began to leave the vertical. From that moment, disaster was inevitable. All three collided and went down in a mass of silver-sparkled blue, membraned arms flailing and hands clutching whatever was closest.

There was a plaintive rattle as they settled.

Mac froze, not knowing if it would be a breach to try and help, or if she should look into the distance until they pulled themselves apart. She compromised, staying close enough to assist if they asked, but looking, mostly, away.

Between peeks to see how they were managing.

Not well. One of the lackeys had a grip on a tree. Another had *ne's* long, strong fingers wrapped over most of Se Lasserbee's face, while that worthy had *se's* hands firmly on the first lackey's leg. They didn't seem able to let go.

Great instinct for a cliff dweller, Mac thought with interest. "May I help?" she offered at last.

Se Lasserbee's mouth wasn't covered. "Ah. Dr. Connor," *se* said in *se's* metal in bucket voice, the words preceded by a breathless pant. "Ah. What a pleasant surprise. You might want to move away."

About to comply, Mac noticed wisps of smoke coming from beneath the motionless tangle of aliens. "You're sparking," she commented and then winced, having floundered yet again on the rocks of interspecies' protocol. *Never mention bodily functions.* "I don't mean you personally," she qualified. "But . . . there is something burning under—" an inclusive wave, "—you."

"Yes. Ah. Most observant. We aren't at risk, Dr. Connor. Please. A moment."

Although this close their skin looked more like flexible blubber than leather, their uniforms didn't appear flammable. *Sensible precaution,* Mac judged. Doing her best to keep a nonchalant expression, she tried to spot the source of the tiny sparks, clearly visible in the growing shadow of late afternoon. *Particularly,* she observed, *around the poor Frow on the bottom of the pile.*

The likeliest candidate appeared to be a narrow channel in the skin underneath the arms themselves, from which the tips of thick solitary hairs protruded like a comb's teeth. Might be some kind of spark-generating organ.

Or it could really be a comb, Mac chided herself. The spikes on the shoulders looked to require a bit of buffing. Who knew what lay under the uniforms themselves?

Let alone the hats.

With agonizing deliberation, the three Frow sorted themselves out. Mac found a flatter root than most for a perch and watched, fascinated. They acted as if a false move could plummet them all into some abyss. The simplest shift of a finger involved a great deal of discussion, some of it loud, in their own language. Several times, one grip was replaced in favor of shifting another.

It took, from Mac's surreptitious checks of the time, seventeen minutes and twenty seconds before *Se* Lasserbee stood free and proud in front of her once more.

Better safe than sorry had to be a Frow maxim, she decided, adding that to her knowledge of their kind.

The other two spent an alarming few moments lurching around to stamp out any smoldering spots where they'd lain on the path. Not that there were many, due to the storm's moisture. Mac held her breath until they were safely still again.

"Ah," began *Se* Lasserbee, dignity reclaimed. "Dr. Connor. What a surprise to encounter you in this—" *se* glanced around at the forest, as if lost for the word in Instella, the IU's common tongue, "—place."

"Forest." Mac stood, brushing shreds of bark from her pants. "What do you want, *Se?*" *Not that she couldn't guess.*

"Want? Ah. A moment of discourse with you would be pleasing, as always, Dr. Connor."

She did her best not to scowl. The beings were sadly out of their environment. The other two had unfolded their neck ridges to lean their heads left, in order to stare at the trees. *Maybe they hoped some would be climbable.* The occasional spark continued to flash.

"A private discourse," the Frow elaborated. "On a matter of great importance."

They might have watched for her to leave the consulate, or simply asked any staff where she was. Mac hadn't left instructions to be undisturbed. *Something to remember for next time.* She should have expected to be contacted by someone from the idiot faction before leaving. A pithy message she couldn't read, perhaps. An appointment she'd somehow miss.

Hardly this ambush by the woefully unable.

Clever, she acknowledged, and decided to oblige, curious despite good sense telling her it would be nothing she'd want to hear. "Of course, *Se* Lasserbee. Why don't we go back inside, find a meeting room—"

Se drew *se-self* up to full height. "What is wrong with this fine place, Dr. Connor?"

Fair enough. "Nothing," Mac said blandly. "Here it is. Now, what are we to discuss?"

Before *se* replied, the three Frow went through a great deal of neck ridge unfolding and looking about, which made them totter like broken twigs about to fall. Apparently satisfied they were alone with their quarry, they stopped and looked at Mac. "You are escorting Dr. Mamani to her new place, Dr. Connor," *se* said. "I must accompany her. Take me with you."

To Base? "You know I can't," Mac replied far more mildly than she felt. *Damn aliens.* At least here, this time, she had the rules firmly on her side. "The IU must petition the Ministry for Extra-Sol Affairs for any nonterrestrial to leave the consular grounds."

"We've filed such petition. Ah. But these things take time, Dr. Connor. We are aware you leave tonight. You can include me. I have a cloak."

Mac blinked. "A cloak," she repeated.

One of the lackeys volunteered: "A large one."

If the Frow thought a cloak, large or otherwise, could disguise their shape or movement for an instant, they'd been reading the wrong brochures. *Or a certain Myg was involved*—Mac stopped her train of thought right there. *This was serious.* "I might be willing to convey a message to Dr. Mamani on your behalf, if I judge its contents worth her time—and that's generous, *Se* Lasserbee. The Sinzira set strict protocols for future interviews. Emily's been through enough." This last with a ferocity Mac couldn't help.

Whether this particular species, or this individual, could detect the emotion in her voice was debatable. Not that she could detect any change beyond volume in *se's* tone either. Still, she had to believe those representatives sent to Earth were given some training in humanity.

"Ah," another of those breathless sounds, this time more pronounced. *A request for attention? New topic? Gas?* "Indeed generous, Dr. Connor," the Frow told her, "and we thank you. But we have no message. We do not wish to talk to Dr. Mamani. What recollections she has of the Myrokynay have been passed to our superiors by the Sinzi-ra. And, as you say, she's been through a significant ordeal. Ah. We would not wish to be responsible for causing her further stress in an effort to recall more."

Mac tilted her head to better line up *se's* angled eyes with hers. The pupils were black, slicing through an iris of pale green. Attractive eyes. In fact, without the black spiky hat, the Frow was quite a handsome being, in *se's* own gaunt way.

And a politician.

She couldn't afford to trade subtleties. "If you don't want to talk to her," Mac growled, "why do you want to come with us?"

"Ah." All three Frow repeated their look-around behavior before *se* continued. "Above all else, we desire contact with the Myrokynay. We believe they will take advantage when Dr. Mamani leaves the protection of the Sinzi—"

"Never!" The alien staggered back a step and almost fell. Se *obviously understood* that *Human tone.* Mac took a breath and calmed herself, though her hands shook. "You misunderstand," she said more quietly. "Dr. Mamani isn't bait. She remains under Anchen's protection—and ours—no matter where she is. More to the point, *Se* Lasserbee, the Ro aren't interested. She was a tool they used and discarded."

"In your opinion of events," *se* countered.

"My—" Mac's mouth fell open. Then she sputtered: "They did their best to murder her!"

"Ah. Conceivably a miscalculation. We Frow believe the Myrokynay could be beyond life and death as we experience such things. Ah. They could represent the next stage of all our futures." *Se* touched two points on *se's* hat. "How can we interpret their actions, using only our limited knowledge? How can we possibly guess their great plan?"

"The Ro's 'great plan' is to be the last ones breathing," Mac ground out. "Not interpretation. Not guesswork. That's what they told me, *Se* Lasserbee, while they waited for me and all of us to be killed by their Dhryn."

"Ah. The conversation not recorded by any means at the Sinzi's disposal."

"I heard it." Mac silently dared the alien to utter one more breathless 'ah.' That was all the excuse she'd ask to turn on her perfectly path-adapted heels and leave. Quickly.

The Frow did have a point. She'd wished for a corroborating recording every day since. But the Ro's terrible 'voice' had somehow been focused inside her body and Emily's.

And Emily didn't remember.

"I don't doubt you, Dr. Connor," *Se* Lasserbee said, unwittingly prolonging their conversation in the woods. "Don't take offense. I'm a soldier, not a mystic. I know protocols and procedures. Forms. Any form you like. I have a talent."

Mac's lips twitched at this.

"I have difficult—nay, impossible orders," the Frow went on. "I'm to go where I will have the best chance of encountering one of the Bless—one of the Myrokynay. Encounter invisible beings who live in no-space? That no one else can find? Yet my superiors expect me to succeed. You have been gracious to listen to me."

Se stretched out *se's* long arms and flapped the membranes from finger to hip, then dramatically wrapped *se's* arms to hide *se's* face. The others exchanged a look Mac couldn't interpret, but stayed as they were.

Se did appear miserable.

Mac frowned, aware she was extrapolating from Human. *Always a mistake.*

None of them moved or spoke. The minutes dragged. *Bad as relaxing,* Mac thought. "*Se* Lasserbee," she prompted finally. At this rate, they could be here past sunset. "*Se.* Please. There's nothing I can do. I've my own questions, believe me, but I don't know how to reach the Ro. No one does." The Atrium had an entire section devoted to analyzing the modification to their communications system provided by the Ro. Linguists from the original Gathering were working on the code used to convey the instructions for that modification.

Without success; so far, the Ro kept their secrets.

As for replaying the call that had brought the Dhryn to Sol System? Anchen had reassured Mac that the IU had sent a blunt warning to the Trisulians, the only ones outside the Gathering to possess that ability, not to employ it. They weren't ready to set a trap they couldn't, as yet, safely spring. The Trisulians had obeyed.

So far, Mac echoed, wishing again that Cinder had stayed behind. Nik was the alien expert, no doubts there. But he hadn't been the one Cinder had begged to take her weapons because she hadn't trusted herself not to commit murder.

In Mac's opinion, said weapons shouldn't have been given back, but Cinder had been as fully armed as her partner when they'd departed.

Not a topic for current company on any level. Mac knew better than to mention Trisulians to the Frow, both former military powers, both edgy where their historical spheres of influence now overlapped. Long memories. Their partnership within the IU rested on peace and prosperity, not friendship.

A little louder. "*Se* Lasserbee. Did you hear me?"

"Ah." A green eye peered over a fold of membrane. "Dr. Connor? Why are you still here?"

He'd dismissed her?

Mac didn't know whether to stamp her foot in frustration or laugh. She'd been given a polite exit and missed it. *Next time,* she vowed.

Now, however, she was stuck and hurriedly fumbled for something noncommittal. "What will you do now?" she ventured.

"Do? Ah. I do have an alternative in mind, but I hesitate to reveal it at this time."

Fine by her, Mac sighed with relief. Then she frowned, remembering a certain elevator full of cider-obsessed Grimnoii. "You do know Myriam is flat," this with a suggestive kick of her foot along the path.

Silence.

Mac's frown deepened as she tried to read anything but polite attentiveness on the part of the Frow. "With no trees," a gesture to their surroundings. "It's a desert. A flat desert."

"With the most magnificent rift valleys, Dr. Connor," one of the lackeys burst out enthusiastically. "Sheer, comfortable cliffs. We've seen stunning images—"

"Let me guess," Mac interrupted, eyes on the individual with the most points on his hat. "Your government has an interest."

Se Lasserbee answered. "Every government has an interest in the origin of the Dhryn plague."

Mac resisted the urge to pull at her hair. *Gods only knew what that gesture might mean to a Frow.* "Of course they do," she acknowledged. "But this is a scientific expedition."

"I'm sure, Dr. Connor, you don't mean to imply Frow lack qualified experts to contribute."

Definitely a politician, Mac decided. Given shouting was statistically unlikely to be diplomatic, and she had nothing worth saying that didn't involve volume, there was only one reasonable response.

Mac untied her coat from around her waist, took her time shaking it out, then draped it over her head.

And waited.

There was a hush she gleefully thought of as shocked.

A hush followed by rapid stumbling footsteps. Mac crossed her fingers. The way back to their transport was uphill. If they fell again, it could be messy. Sparks at the very least.

Not to mention she'd have to hide under her coat until they untangled.

She counted to a hundred after the last clear footstep, in case the Frow had stopped to see if she meant her dismissal.

At last, Mac pulled off the coat, taking a relieved breath of cooler air. A few sunbeams raked low through the trees, catching in the mist. No sign of the Frow. She was either getting the hang of this interspecies' communication thing . . .

Or the Frow had thought she was nuts and left.

"Whatever works," she muttered aloud.

First the Grimnoii and now the Frow implying they, too, were heading for Myriam. It was as if her decision to move to the field had been a signal to everyone else around here.

Mac started walking back to the consulate, deliberately admiring the plants she hadn't had time to name.

Let them come along.

If any of them thought they'd interfere with her team, they didn't know this Human very well at all.

- 6 -

FAREWELLS AND FINDINGS

THE REST WOULD LEAVE in the morning via the walkways outside, joining their equipment and supplies on the consulate's landing field. Emily was already in the more protected launch hangar, overseeing the stowage of her gear. Mac, after her walk under the trees, had decided on a different route.

"You could tell me why we're going this way," Sing-li protested half under his breath as they rode the lift to the basement. Mac, her hand on the wall control, grinned and shifted her bag to her shoulder. He gave that a glum look as well, having tried, unsuccessfully, to take it from her. "And why I have to wear this?"

Her grin widened. "Looks good on you."

He plucked the fabric. "There had to be something else."

"Blame Fourteen," Mac replied. "I just said cheerful." *And anything but black.* Everyone knew the Myg regularly shipped Human clothing back home—and not just any clothing.

"I'm a dessert tray."

"And a very cheerful one," she assured him, admiring the parade of dancing cake slices, happy-faced cookies, and improbable grapevines now stretching across the large man's ample chest and shoulders. True, the overall color scheme was painfully flamboyant and, to top it off, the artist had filled any gaps with dots of bright orange-red, making it appear from a distance that Sing-li had recently been splattered with overripe tomatoes. "At least you're inconspicuous."

"In what possible sense of the word?" he sighed, plucking at the offending shirt again.

The lift door opened. Mac paused before walking out, searching for a tactful answer to his question. Sing-li laughed ruefully before she could find it. "What am I worrying about?" he said. "We'll be at Base. I'll blend right in."

And can't possibly loom. Mac kept that satisfied thought to herself as she shot him a grateful smile. She had one day. Was it asking too much to try and make that time as normal as possible?

As for their destination, she wasn't sure herself why she'd had to come down here, only that she needed to walk this long white corridor once more. Not to the Atrium, with its preoccupied researchers and reconfigured spaces. She passed those access doors, Mac taking little hop-steps to keep ahead of Sing-li's longer strides, both of them nodding automatic greetings at the varied aliens stationed at security checks along the way. Fewer than there had been, she noticed. The consulate had other defenses now.

Here. Mac paused in front of another door. Sing-li didn't say anything as she reached for the control and pressed it.

The room was empty, an expanse of Sinzi white that might never have held a cage, might never have sheltered a Dhryn guest. Stepping inside, Mac glanced upward, seeing only an unremarkable ceiling that might never have opened into the Atrium itself, that might never have supported a mass of recording and transmitting equipment, so every move, every word could be seen and heard across the Interspecies Union, by more beings, and types of beings, than she could imagine.

There might never have been blood, Dhryn-blue, Human-red, on the floor.

She shivered, though the room was pleasantly warm. Parymn Ne Sa Las had been difficult and opinionated, but left all he knew to sacrifice himself in service to his Progenitor. The Vessel he'd become had harbored a new personality, Her personality, charming and strangely comforting.

Who was the Vessel now?

Mac sighed. She hadn't had much luck with Dhryn. She hoped Nik was doing better.

Sing-li had entered with her. He didn't say a word, but his fingertips brushed her elbow so lightly she might have imagined it.

He was right. No point lingering. Mac shook her head at herself and led the way back out to the corridor, heading for the next. The underground complex on this level twisted with the cliffs beyond, eventually connecting to the hangar.

She would have come here even if it hadn't, Mac realized, her feet slowing to a stop again in front of another door. It was closed.

Likely locked.

"Mac. You know we can't go in there."

She frowned, but not at her troubled companion.

"Mac."

She thrust her bag at him. "Here."

"Dr. Connor. The lev's waiting." More resigned comment than complaint. Sing-li had learned to read her by now.

"This won't take long," Mac promised absently, putting her hand on the door itself and giving a tiny push.

For some reason, she wasn't surprised when the large door swung noiselessly out of her path. She stepped inside and closed the door behind her, muffling Sing-li's unhappy protest.

Her eyes needed a few seconds to adjust from the brilliance of the corridor to this shadowed place. Impatient, Mac lifted her hands as she walked forward in case they'd rearranged the walls, something the consulate was prone to do. She'd rather not arrive at Base with a red nose or black eye to explain.

Although that would be easier than anything else from these past weeks.

This had been the tank room, a simple name for an extraordinary feat of engineering. Here, in this cavernous space, the Sinzi had built the first known permanent and accessible enclosure of no-space, a dimension beyond, behind, above, or after—whatever confusion you liked—normal reality. For no-space allowed certain liberties with time and distance, including winking a ship and its contents between connected star systems.

With Sinzi practicality, they'd used this marvel to house a block of shrimp-rich ocean, so their favorite delicacy could be instantly accessed from any room with a connected table tank. With Sinzi forethought, this not coincidentally provided an immediate demonstration of this breakthrough's potential for selected consulate guests.

The shrimp? Although tasty, they hadn't fared as well—direct exposure to no-space still meant what went in alive, came back dead. Albeit fresh.

The Sinzi were working on that.

No-space was at the core of everything Ro, who had no difficulties surviving it, or bringing along friends. The Ro hadn't, until encountering the Sinzi's little demonstration, found a way to directly observe areas of real space from inside their realm.

Small wonder the Ro had been drawn to the Sinzi's toy.

Mac's nose twitched. They'd cleaned up the flood of water and its dying life, released when she'd fought to save herself from the Ro. Destroying the main tank had been an inevitable side effect, but no one blamed her. To everyone's relief, the table tanks had been replaced overnight with burnished slabs of local stone, presumably spy-proof.

She hadn't been here since.

Her eyes caught a glimpse of light and Mac moved in that direction, hands still up.

They met something cool and slick and hard.

And familiar.

"Gods, no," she breathed as she stopped. Mac stared ahead until her eyes burned, gradually making out details.

She might have been looking through a porthole into abyssal depths. The lights she could see were indicators on shapeless panels, pulsating greens and blues and yellows. They were stacked in a pyramid arrangement, the other sides and top beyond her view. The dim flickers reflected from the waving arms of anemones, the lacy fronds of sea fan and tube worm, flashed from the back of a small white crab. They were residents of a rising mound of pale bone, stacked before the pyramid like an offering.

Whalebone, Mac identified, sagging with relief.

Some of the glow marked the edges of swaying spirals of kelp. The immense plants grew up into the darkness. Between, darker shadows teased, sending back glints of moving green or blue or yellow, as if the artificial lights caught knife blades slipping through the forest.

Salmon.

Mac pulled back, only now aware of the throb beneath her feet, and braced herself.

The Sinzi-ra had rebuilt her tank.

She'd counted on it.

"I'm here," she announced, proud of her clear, firm voice. "Mackenzie Winifred Elizabeth Wright Connor Sol." She wasn't talking to the trapped things. She was talking to what she couldn't see. *Yet.*

Silence. A curious octopus tiptoed toward her, its huge eyes unblinking. After a long moment of mutual scrutiny, the mollusk made its decision about the Human and suddenly jetted backward into the dark.

"You talked to me before. Here I am." *Talk?* Mac's hands became fists. She remembered all too well how the Ro's version of speech had seemed to rip through her skin and burn itself into the flesh beneath. "In case you're confused on the topic, I'm not dead." She replayed that last bit mentally. *Another gem of interspecies communication.*

The darkness developed chill fingers, pressing against her face, working their way down her throat. Mac wrapped her arms around her middle and cursed her imagination. "What do you want from us? Answer me!" she ordered, careful not to shout, but her voice echoed.

An echo complete with the tinkle of small silver rings.

Mac turned as far as she dared, unwilling to put her back to the tank and what might—she dreaded as much as hoped—might be hiding inside. "Anchen?"

A ball of translucent red ignited between them; Mac assumed it was some kind of portable light. It cast a warm pink glow over the Sinzi-ra's white gown and skin. The great topaz eyes remained in shadow. "Hello, Mac," Anchen greeted her.

"What are you doing here?"

"Waiting for you. I'd be a poor host indeed if I did not wish you well on your journey."

Mac swallowed, keeping a wary eye on the dark tank. "How did you know?" The consulate was clear of the vidbots annoyingly prominent in Human public places. Mac had grown rather fond of believing she could skulk at will. *Had that changed?*

The light was enough to see Anchen's half bow. "We are alike, Mac, in several respects. I felt confident you would revisit those places of meaning to you before you left, as would I. I confess, I hadn't expected to find you conversing with the past." A thoughtful pause. "Or do you truly believe the Myrokynay have slipped past our watch and returned? And, if so, that they will reveal themselves to you if you shout at them?"

Put that way . . . Mac winced and stopped there. "I thought it worth a try," she shrugged. "Everyone else thinks I matter to the Ro. And you did rebuild the tank," this last a half question. *Why?*

The Sinzi-ra moved to stand beside her, taller and more fragile, yet with an otherworldly grace even the shadows couldn't disguise. One fingertip, with its stiff useful nail, tapped the dark glass. "Like you, I thought it worth a try," answered the alien.

The *lamnas* slid along Anchen's long finger, sending glints of rose from the light she carried. Mac wondered what each might reveal. *If a Human brain could make any sense of it,* she added honestly, considering she wasn't sure how much sense she'd made of Nik's and they'd started with similar wetware.

Then she shook her head, more concerned with something else, something far more important. "Anchen. Don't make it easy for them. Don't invite the Ro back here."

"We cannot begin to understand one another if we do not converse, Mac."

"I'm all for conversation. Just let it be somewhere and someone else." Mac didn't bother being dismayed by her own bluntness. The Sinzi-ra was used to her by now. "I mean no insult, Anchen," she continued in a low voice. "I—" *Only the truth.* She took a deep breath and flattened her hand over the place on the tank where Anchen had tapped, feeling the cold. "I'm afraid. For you. For all Sinzi." *The whole truth.* "For us, if anything happens to you. You must be more cautious."

"I need not remind you, Mac, that all life is currently at risk from the Dhryn. It is inappropriate to fear for one species—or individual—over another."

"The rest of us don't stand in the Ro's way, Anchen. Your species maintains the Interspecies Union. Without you, the transects fail and we're each alone."

"If," the alien stressed the word, "the Ro are a threat."

"You can't take that chance!" Mac insisted, turning to face Anchen. The red glow danced back, as if courteously avoiding her face. She couldn't tell if it was somehow tethered to the Sinzi or floating free like a vidbot. In either case, its light enclosed them both in a bubble that might almost have been privacy, if not for the ominous tank and its instruments. *An audience to this was fine by her.* "You don't dare, for all our sakes. Please, Anchen. Tell me you'll be careful."

"Following your example?"

Mac snorted. "I'm not important."

Cool fingertips coated in dancing silver reached to her face, one tracing the line of Mac's jaw, another lifting a curl of regrown hair. It was the first time the Sinzi had touched her other than in Noad's role of physician; Mac's eyes widened in surprise, but she didn't move. "I—all of my selves—hold a different view of your worth."

Friendship as she understood it—or something more akin to the assessment of an experienced diplomat? Mac discovered she didn't care. The warmth inside her was enough. "Then listen to me, Anchen," she urged. "Don't expose yourself to the Ro. Let others do it. At least until we know more." Mac shot a suspicious look at the dark tank. "That includes not coming here by yourself again. Protect yourself. Promise me."

The Sinzi-ra didn't answer immediately. Her fingers wove themselves into something complex and troubled, hard to make out in the low light. *Answering,* Mac thought irrelevantly, *the question of whether the alien held the glowing globe.* "A promise is a connection between those involved," Anchen said at last. "Across any distance."

Mac grinned. "That it is."

"We do not make promises lightly."

"Neither do I," she assured the alien. *Never let go.*

Anchen gave an almost Human sigh. "I may have shown you too much of the Sinzi view of the universe."

"Fair's fair," Mac replied. "You know more about Humans than most Humans do."

That shivering laugh, then the other seemed to come to some decision, for her fingers unfolded with blinding rapidity. "Then we shall exchange promises, Mackenzie Connor, for such a connection must be forged both ways."

Uh-oh. "What would I have to promise, Sinzi-ra?" Mac asked, wary at last.

"To bring me something for my collection."

Somehow, Mac knew the wording was precise. *Bring.* Had Anchen elicited the same promise from Nik every time he'd ventured on her behalf? Complete the journey. Come back where you started.

The Sinzi ethic.

That to do so meant surviving whatever might intervene was in a sense incidental to Anchen. It was finishing the cycle that mattered.

The distinction, to quote Fourteen, was irrelevant. Mac didn't hesitate. "I promise."

Anchen leaned forward, tilting her head so the eye Mac associated with Casmii, the judge, faced her most directly. "What is promised will bind us both, Mackenzie Connor. Are you sure?"

"If you promise to protect yourself from the Ro, I promise to bring you something for your collection," Mac stated, content to finally encounter common sense when dealing with aliens. "I'm sure."

She could just make out Anchen's half bow. At no command Mac detected, the light from the floating globe increased until she had to narrow her eyes. The Sinzi-ra lowered her long neck so they were looking directly at one another before she raised her fingers, their tips curling inward to form a ring like *lamnas* in front of each pair of eyes. "I so promise," she said, holding that posture. "We are bound."

Then: "I promise." "And I." "Over my better judgment, I promise also." "You have my promise, Mac."

Finally: "Promise given and accepted. We are bound."

Every voice the same in tone, the words alone differed. The Sinzi-ra uncurled her long fingers then intertwined them, rings slipping back and forth like raindrops.

Mac realized she'd been addressed, for the first time, by each of Anchen's individual minds. *Not that she had a clue who was who.*

For a fleeting instant, Mac wondered if she'd somehow managed to commit herself to something far stranger than she could possibly imagine. *Again.*

Then she shrugged.

There had to be a tacky souvenir somewhere on Myriam.

"You're quiet."

Mac waved one hand, the other holding her bag. "Thinking," she explained. They were almost at the hangar; she could tell by the way the floor had become a down-turned ramp. The Sinzi-ra had left the tank room with her, bidding them both farewell in the corridor. Sing-li's eyes had been like saucers at the sight of the alien, but he'd asked no questions.

Until now. "Everything all right?"

She glanced up at Sing-li. Seeing the concern in his face, she decided against flippant. "More or less," she admitted. "It's suddenly real—the move offworld, going to Base. Leaving Emily—the rest of you. Didn't feel that way this morning."

He pressed his lips together in an unhappy line. "I should be going with you."

Pinching an errant grape between her fingers, Mac gave his shirt a tug. "If you aren't, you really should change."

"You know what I mean, Mac." The agent shook his head at her. "Some on the IU committee aren't pleased with Dr. Mamani leaving the consulate. They're resisting Hollans' efforts to negotiate clearance for more Humans on Myriam—doubt he'll get a straight answer before you clear the gate. Don't like it, Mac."

She wasn't thrilled either. "Don't worry," Mac told him. "The planet's going to be crowded enough as it is. And I'll have Oversight."

"Oh, that's reassuring," Sing-li said darkly.

"Be fair. He can be scary."

"You don't know what you might face."

"I'm minding a bunch of archaeologists on a lifeless world—what can happen?" Mac stopped and laughed without humor. "Don't answer that."

Before Sing-li could try, they rounded the last corner and saw who was waiting.

"Idiot!" Fourteen called cheerfully, his arm around Unensela, the Myg xenopaleoecologist.

Unensela's six offspring were seated at their feet, looking as angelic as hairless lumps with long necks and big brown eyes could. On seeing Mac, they immediately squealed and scampered at full speed to run up her legs before she could fend them away with her free hand.

Once they were firmly attached by clawholds on her chest and shoulders, a struggle since each had doubled in mass over the past few weeks, Mac recovered sufficient balance to glare at Sing-li. He gave a helpless shrug and appeared to be trying not to grin. "Wasn't me," he vowed, taking her bag.

She'd left orders with everyone imaginable that Fourteen was not to know about her little detour before Myriam. *It had been worth a try.* "He's not coming to Base," Mac muttered under her breath. Four of the Myg offspring excitedly demonstrated their recently acquired ability to mimic sounds, babbling "base-basebasebase" in their high-pitched voices. The remaining two merely howled along.

"You won't believe this, Mac," Fourteen announced as she staggered closer. "We almost missed the flight!"

Mac lurched to a stop by Unensela and waited. The female Myg gave her a sly look—an expression which came naturally, given the sunken Myg eyes and wide expressive lips. She was wearing one of Fourteen's shirts and apparently nothing else. Fortunately, the shirt went down to her knobby knees. Unfortunately, the shirt was a vile orange and turquoise patterned in juggling hamsters.

"Get them off me," Mac said as calmly as she could, given one offspring was gumming her left ear for all it was worth. "Now."

"You should be proud," the Myg insisted. "You're the only Human they like."

"I'm honored. Off."

Unensela pouted, another typical Myg expression in Mac's experience with the species.

Mac took a deep breath.

"Idiot!" Fourteen said hastily, pulling offspring from Mac with both hands and tossing them at his—*what,* Mac wondered, *did you call someone who appeared to dislike you but would have sex with you anywhere, anytime?* She settled for fellow alien. The offspring didn't mind the treatment, each making a "whee" sound as they flew through the air. Unensela didn't try to catch them, letting the small beings latch onto her shirt with their claws wherever they struck. They dropped to the floor at once, cooing contentedly by her feet.

Sing-li was making that strangled noise again. Mac rolled her eyes at him.

Once free of hitchhikers, she pulled her clothing back into some order, ignoring the myriad small holes left by affectionate Myg claws until her fingers found skin through a long tear in previously intact silk. At this, she growled something safely wordless in her throat.

"Hurry, Mac. We'll be late." Fourteen, she noted grimly, was bouncing in place, his favorite, and now-faded, paisley shorts threatening to slip loose.

"Late for—"

"Arslithissiangee Yip the Fourteenth!" A thunderous Mudge came striding up the corridor from the direction of the hangar. "What are you doing here?" He counted Mygs as he approached and amended, "What are all of you doing here?"

"Idiot," Fourteen proclaimed. "The glorious Unensela is here to warm me with her presence as long as possible. I am waiting to board the lev with Mac." The overlooked offspring, following all this intently, burbled "macmacmac."

Mac's "Oh, no you aren't," collided with Mudge's "I think not!" and Sing-li's alarmed "You don't have clearance." Unensela's "But you promised to take them with you!" came afterward, prompting everyone else to stare at her.

"Well, he did," she finished.

"Irrelevant," Mac told her, then looked at Fourteen. "You aren't coming."

The Myg covered his face with his hands. Distress, real or feigned. *Likely real.* She didn't doubt Fourteen's desire to accompany her, or his zeal to be of help. *Strobis*, the Myg version of obligation and promise. She seemed to be collecting a few of those lately.

Mac sighed and pulled his hands down. He peered at her, moisture dotting his fleshy eyelids. "I need you here," she said earnestly. "To find out who else is heading for Myriam—what they want there." She'd left him a message about the Frow and Grimnoii. If there was anything Fourteen relished, it was obliterating the secrecy of others.

"Irrelevant! Why must you go to Base?" he countered. "Charlie can take Emily. They can have sex." He stuck out his white forked tongue and Unensela giggled.

Mudge's face was a study in various hues of red. Mac silenced him with a look. Fourteen knew how to push his rival's buttons, not difficult at the best of times.

"He has abundant external genitalia," Fourteen persisted. "We all saw—"

"I'll see you in orbit," Mac interrupted. She let her tone imply she wasn't worried if Fourteen was inside a ship when she did or not. "Gentlemen?"

She grabbed her bag from Sing-li, who wisely surrendered it, and headed for the hangar doors, pausing only to make sure Mudge was coming, too.

"My apologies, Norcoast," that worthy panted. "He got past me."

Mac glanced at him without slowing. His face glistened with sweat and at least some of its ruddiness looked to be from exertion. The rest, she blamed on Fourteen. "Did you run the entire length of the consulate?"

"A bit more, actually." He wiped the sweat from his forehead with the back of his hand, then took a couple of deeper breaths. "Damn Myg cheated and took a skim."

"I should be the one to apologize," Sing-li offered glumly. "I told Selkirk to keep an eye on him—trickiest being I've ever met. I swear you could hide something at the bottom of the ocean and he'd have it copied and on display by noon."

Mac snorted. "Good thing he's on our side. More or less," this last to mollify Mudge.

"Of course I'm on your side," Fourteen said in her ear.

Mac jumped and swung her bag. Sing-li swore and Mudge simply stopped where he was, throwing up his arms.

Fourteen, having dodged Mac's swing, smiled unrepentantly as he rose from his crouch. "See? I sent Unensela away. It's me now. I was never bringing the offspring."

"Go away," Mac growled.

"You don't mean that."

"Oh, yes, I do."

"You won't win, Fourteen," Emily said lazily.

Mac turned to see her friend leaning against one side of the now-open door to the consulate hangar, arms folded across her chest. Beyond, through the opening, was a line of levs and other transports, beings of various species moving around them at their work. The wide doors to the outside were mere shadows in the distance. The Sinzi built on a generous scale. There were a couple of larger service corridors, as well as this one, leading into the hangar. Not to mention a small, hidden entrance from the surface, for those who preferred even more stealth.

Wouldn't have helped.

"Can you hurry it up, Mac? Pilot's getting antsy."

Mac raised an eyebrow. "I've no doubt." The outfit was remarkable, even for Emily. For her triumphant return, she'd donned a white dress of the Sinzi's favorite fabric that might have been painted over her curved torso, flaring in randomly transparent panels from thigh to ankle. Ropes of black pearls hung from her throat, almost reaching her waist; black satin gloves and sandals completed what was, to Mac, most definitely armor.

She gave her Myg-torn shirt a self-conscious tug and winced as she heard it rip further. *Hopefully she could change on the lev.*

"If he's going," Fourteen pointed at Mudge, "I'm going."

"Oversight's just seeing us off," Mac began. Which hadn't been part of the scheme of things, but she did appreciate Mudge's efforts to intercept the determined Myg—however futile. "Now you both can," she finished brightly. "Good-bye. See you on the transport to Myriam."

A *harrumph*. "Ah. Norcoast. I am coming with you."

At this, Mac's head whipped around so quickly she felt a strain in her neck. "Pardon?"

"Staff's done an excellent job," Mudge explained. "Stellar. No one needs me."

It was like some comedy routine, Mac thought with disgust, with her playing the the innocent victim from the audience. *Had everyone forgotten who was in charge here?* "No, Oversight." This firm and calm. "Emily and I are going. Sing-li is coming with us because I can't stop him without arcane paperwork or a sledgehammer. You are waiting for us in orbit, making sure everything is ready."

"Everything is ready."

So much for calm. "Then make up a bloody crisis!" Her shout echoed down the corridor and back again, drawing attention from those within the hangar. "I don't care!"

"It's okay, Mac," Emily said smoothly. "I invited Charlie along. Didn't think you'd mind."

Mac looked from one to the other and back again. Mudge's expression was an interesting blend of not-my-fault and uncertainty. *He didn't know why,* she judged. Emily's was pure mischief, her gleaming eyes and wide smile daring Mac to challenge her on this. She might have bought it, but Emily's gloved fingers were locked on her arms, as if to hide their trembling.

The look, like the dress, was designed to misdirect, to make everyone around Emily believe bringing Mudge was some playful whim.

To where the Ro had destroyed part of the Wilderness Trust?

This was no whim.

Mac gave a nod, more to herself than anyone else, but Mudge visibly relaxed—and Emily? Maybe no one else would notice the slight release of tension in the shoulders, the softening of the smile.

It wasn't, Mac knew, a favor she'd granted.

Meanwhile, someone else had watched this Human byplay with great impatience. "Idiots," Fourteen declared. "Charlie has no reason for going. While I–I–I've—there could be a threat. A risk! Yes. I'm sure of it! There's danger. You need me."

She might ignore Fourteen's protests—and the smell of distraught Myg now filling the corridor—but Sing-li felt otherwise. Mac sighed as the agent loomed over the smaller alien. Who, truth be told, didn't look the least intimidated.

Might be the shirt, Mac judged. "Sing-li," she said. "Sing-li!" sharper when he failed to acknowledge her. "He's making it up."

His voice was threatening despite the shirt. "If there's a potential problem, I need to know what it is."

Mac and Emily traded looks. "Stay here then," Mac suggested.

Sing-li's shocked "Mac!" gave her a twinge of guilt, but only a small one. She was almost dancing with impatience to be gone. By the glow in Emily's eyes, she felt it too.

Home.

If only for a day.

- CONTACT -

"**W**E SHOULDN'T BE HERE."

Inric didn't let his attention stray from the scanner readout. "No one will know."

His partner, an as yet unblooded Ehztif and thus certified for space travel with other life-forms, continued to pace. She'd taken the usename Bob for its supposed calming effect on Humans, obligate predators being uncomfortable company. Not that Bob was such a predator—not until that first ritual hunt, years in her future, when her digestive system would switch into its mature phase. For now, she drank packaged secretions like everyone else, and expressed a fondness for salted crackers.

Inric pursed his lips and tried to ignore the unsettling click of Bob's talons on the floor plate. It had seemed a good idea at the time to choose an Ehztif partner. No Human-centric games. Enough daring for any escapade but reliably steady.

He would have to find the one Ehztif with an imagination. "Relax," Inric said, leaning back to demonstrate. "Get the data. Get paid. There's nothing here."

Bob stalked—there was no other word for it—to the platform's edge and stared out over the waves. "Nothing. You don't know what that means, do you, Human. But I—I can taste it on the wind." The Ehztif released her prehensile tongue, flipping it through the air before she brought it back into her mouth. She appeared to chew for a few seconds, then sharply expanded her cheek pouches in disgust. "Nothing lives here."

As that was exactly what the Sencor Consortium hoped to confirm, Inric gave a tight smile. "If the scanners are as accurate as your taste buds, Bob, our clients will be pleased."

"Scavengers."

"An essential part of life," the Human replied.

The Ehztif sniffed. Her species shared their home system with the much-despised Sethilak, definitely closer to the scavenger scheme of things. That the two had managed to coexist after encountering one another in space was one of the marvels of the Interspecies Union.

Didn't mean they wouldn't eat one another when the occasion offered.

Inric sat up and leaned over the readout again. The platform's underside bristled with the latest in remote analysis gear, including two prototypes he'd obtained in return for initial field tests and favors to come. And that wasn't all they used to search this world. "Check the imagers again, will you, Bob? They should be close to finishing the latest flyover."

"They're coming," Bob answered, gazing at the horizon. Better vision was only one of the adaptations that made Ehztif useful companions. "Wait. What's that following them? *Ssshhh-hssahhsss!*" the Instella dissolved into an impassioned hiss.

Inric lunged to his feet and ran to the rail. "What's wrong?" He stared where Bob pointed, expecting the worst—an IU inspector, come to push them offworld. They had clearances. Just not real ones.

The worlds scoured by the Dhryn were restricted, even ones like this, where there hadn't been a sentient species to leave its accomplishments behind. In the present state of near panic, Inric doubted they'd be fined and sent on their way. Lately, there'd been rumors of entrepreneurs simply disappearing. "Can't be an inspection," he concluded as quickly. The ship they'd left in orbit was to send warning of any approach, as well as being nimble enough to elude almost anything transect-capable given that warning was received in time to retrieve her absent crew of two.

"It's gone. But for an instant, I could see—" Bob appeared to hesitate, cheeks puffing in and out. "Below the incoming 'bots," she said finally. "In the water. There was *sshssah*."

"Meaning?"

"The heat of life."

An Ehztif's ability to detect and react to infrared was the source of a thriving Sethilak industry in camouflage gear, but in this case? The Human exhaled his relief in a low whistle. "Impossible. We've been scanning this world for weeks. The Dhryn weren't interrupted here—they took every scrap of living matter." But Inric's eyes didn't leave the patch of unremarkable ocean.

The water was the only thing that moved on Riden IV. Water, he corrected, wind, and themselves.

"The Dhryn." Bob's head shrank into her shoulders. Her anxious shudders rattled the gleaming armor plates growing across her juvenile skin. When those met and fused, she'd be less flexible and thoroughly deadly to anything her instincts viewed as edible, basically that which generated body heat and wasn't Ehztif. It gave her species a unique perspective on the Dhryn, whose appetite seemed without limit.

They were terrified by a predator higher up the chain.

"We are not safe here," Bob continued, backing away from the rail.

Inric could see the incoming 'bots for himself now. There were a dozen; nothing fancy here, just the same off-the-alien-shelf design Earth had adopted for visual surveillance. They'd recorded mind-numbing images of rock, sand, and water. High ground on Riden IV consisted of chains of weathered islands, few of cloud height, their lee sides dressed in curls of unappealing brown sand. The poles had never, according to IU records, supported life.

The oceans had swarmed with it, fluorescing at the surface by starlight, submerging by day. The slow whorling currents of the tropics had spawned immense mats of jelly, themselves supporting landscapes of towering growth to rival the forests of the equatorial islands. It was said once you heard Riden's singing flowers, released to drift from mat to mat, you could never again enjoy the music of your own species, so intensely beautiful and complex was the sound of their petals on the wind.

The wind only howled now, when it didn't rattle their shelter or *skitter . . . scurry* like invisible mice around the consoles. Inric gave his companion a sour look and went back to his scanner. The consortium wanted assurance the world was lifeless before releasing development funds. Their surveys had cataloged sufficient mineral wealth to justify investment long ago, but Sencor had decided against proceeding. Ore was common; singing flowers, unique. Tourism was the new option.

The Dhryn had forever changed the equation, and the Trisulian hunger for expansion had made it economical for their competitors to take certain liberties with due process.

In other words, if Sencor delayed exercising its mining rights on Riden IV, it might find Trisulian colonists pretending to farm the barren islands and fish the empty seas.

Bringing them to the present situation, and his twitchy partner. "The Dhryn are gone, Bob," Inric stated. "They died in Sol System. Human space, my friend. Human space."

Scurry . . .

"Humans did nothing but cower in their ships. Everyone knows," the Ehztif countered. "And who said all the Dhryn were there? I heard it was only a fraction."

Before Inric could answer, there was a sudden *crack*, as if a whip had snapped across the cloudless sky. Human and Ehztif looked up in time to see the closest 'bot drop into the sea well short of the platform. The rest kept approaching.

"What the hell—"

CRACK!

Moments later, eleven 'bots arrived at their coordinates.

Obedient to their programming, they bobbed in the air precisely where the platform should have been.

Above where the empty sea boiled.

REUNIONS AND REVELATIONS

M AC HAD BROUGHT WORK, too excited to sleep a wink during the trip to Base. She was thus startled, some unmeasured time later, to have something warm grasp her wrist and give her a little shake. "Whaassa?" she asked intelligently.

"Landing in ten, Norcoast," Mudge informed her, moving back to his seat.

Shifting upright, Mac fumbled for her imp, its workscreen having turned itself off after her brain had apparently done the same, taking her closed eyes as its signal. Beside her, Emily's neck was bent at an unlikely angle, the pillows that had earlier propped her head and shoulders now scattered on the lev floor. Her friend snored contentedly, her body catlike in its ability to relax and pour into any shape necessary for rest.

Sunlight was streaming in through the overhead portal. A Human-built machine, but with alien tech and spy mentality. Mac hadn't been pleased to learn she wouldn't be able to gawk out the window like a tourist, nor hunt familiar landmarks as they neared their destination.

She shrugged and tucked her imp into a pocket. *Hadn't missed a thing,* she admitted, rubbing sleep from her eyes. She elbowed Emily. "We're here."

Instead of blinking sleepily at her, Emily sprang half to her feet, her eyes flashing open. "No!" she shouted, arms stretched to their fullest, fingers spread wide.

Mac pulled her back down. "Sorry, Em," she said hastily. She should know better than to startle her friend. "It's okay. We're about to land."

Sing-li had half-risen from his seat across from theirs. She shook her head at him. "We're fine."

"Fine? *Caramba,* Mac. Next time pour ice water down my neck." Emily fussed with her clothing, using the movements to cover how her hands shook. "It'd be less of a shock."

"I'll remember that."

"You do."

Mac wanted to see outside; she didn't need to. She put her head back and closed her eyes. Morning. Late August. Approaching Castle Inlet from the southwest. That meant coming up through Hecate Strait with its whales and long blue swells, closing on the coast where, on a clear day, the snowcapped peaks beyond stole the eye and played tricks of scale, until the forests between tumbling cliffs seemed nothing more than the thin verge along the base of some giant's fence.

When that same eye could make out the surf pounding at the exposed teeth of mountains, could slide up the rocky shore to where the rain forest began, catch a glimpse of a white-headed eagle that threw the trees into perspective . . . then it all became greater than one mind could hold.

A nip over treetops, a plunge down a slope, and the intense blue of Castle Inlet itself would be waiting, tied to the coastal mountains by ribboned rivers, edged in boulders that gleamed like so many pebbles in the hand. Rich with salmon.

Mac's lips turned up at the corners. And there would be Base, swarming with activity, skims and levs being loaded, students and staff trotting the walkways, half with breakfast muffins in their hands. *Possibly green ones.*

"Dreaming about our Nik?" Emily asked, nudging her shoulder.

Mac kept her eyes closed. "Get your own spy."

"Love to."

The ensuing pause was too much for Mac. She opened her eyes to see, as expected, Sing-li squirming beside Mudge, doing his best to ignore the beatific look Emily was bestowing upon him. Mudge, needless to say, wasn't helping, too busy interacting with whatever was displayed by the screen floating in front of his face.

"The man's working, Em," Mac said, getting up to stretch. "Save it."

Emily leaned to look past her. "Nice shirt, by the way."

"She made me," grumbled Sing-li.

"Camouflage," Mac explained, glancing at Mudge as she sat back down.

He didn't look happy. While she could imagine several reasons, starting with Emily's invitation and ending with proximity to Sing-li's shirt, something about his current focus made her gesture to the agent to switch places.

Dropping into the seat beside Mudge, Mac peered at his display. "Something wrong?" she asked, unable to make heads or tails of a tilted three-dimensional flowchart, with inset counters blinking red.

Especially when Mudge stuck his finger in the midst to close it.

"Oversight?"

"It's been a while," he said obtusely. "Sims aren't like the real thing anyway. Everyone knows that."

Ah. He'd been working on his piloting. Mac poked him gently in the shoulder. "Planning to take over the lev?" she joked, regretting it as the man flushed mottled red and *harrumphed* fiercely at her.

"I'll have you know the last time I left Sol System I was at the controls."

Twenty-some years ago. "Always good to refresh skills," she said, careful to keep it neutral.

The lev made a swooping turn felt by all aboard. Mac locked eyes with Emily. They were about to land.

Just enough time left to doubt everything she'd planned.

"Hang on, Mac. I go first."

"You've got to be kidding," Mac told Sing-li, trying without success to push by him. Somehow the wacky shirt hadn't diminished the large man's ability to become an immovable object. Frustrated, she tried glaring instead.

With perfect equanimity, he smiled down at her. "It's my job."

"C'mon, Mac," Emily said from behind. "Let him test that camouflage."

Mac threw up her hands. "Fine. But this is the last time while we're at Base you get in my way. Is that clear, Agent Jones?"

Sing-li's smile faded and he gave her the tiniest of nods. The nod that meant, in Mac's experience, that he promised to be discreet. Not that he promised to disappear.

Discreet she could live with. So long as they went through the door.

"You can get in my way anytime," Emily offered from behind.

"Em," Mac muttered in exasperation. "I'm serious."

"So am I." Emily tugged her hair. "It's not my fault you like your men unavailable."

Sing-li wisely chose that moment to open the lev door and step out.

The first thing Mac noticed was the smell rushing in. The consulate had been on a seacoast. This was *her* seacoast. She drew a deep breath of cedar, salt, and salmon through her nostrils, feeling as though she drew the air and its peace into her soul.

The second thing she noticed were voices. Many voices.

Too many voices.

Mac moved to the opening and cautiously looked outside.

Sing-li stood to one side of the ramp to the walkway, a big grin on his face. "Welcome home!"

Mac's fingers found and gripped the lev doorframe. She'd studied schematics and images of the pods in their new locale; they looked as she expected. Perhaps a little tidier than before, but then they'd had to take off anything loose, including the impromptu roofing, in order to tow the pods here. Some had been replaced; no guarantees they would last the first winter. There was laundry snapping in the breeze. That breeze could become a gale force wind with little notice here, in the more open portion of the inlet. She hoped someone had warned new staff. The surrounding water, tinted with sediment from the nearby Tannu River, was reflecting the sunbeams coming over the mountains. It was going to be a warm, bright morning.

All this she took in automatically, her attention caught by what, or rather who, was waiting on the walkways.

"What's going on, Mac? Hurry up!" Emily urged impatiently.

Because she couldn't see.

Sing-li reached for her hand. "It's okay, Dr. Connor."

It wasn't, she thought, staring at the sea of faces. There was a banner draped over the terrace of Pod Three. She couldn't make out the words. The voices—the shouts—died away as everyone gazed back at her. Some were smiling. Others were wiping their eyes.

Her father started walking forward. Her father? And—*gods, her brothers?*

Mac launched herself from the lev and ran for them, somehow noticing a knot of people nearby who suddenly cried out in what had to be Quechua and hurried past her.

Fortunately, she didn't have to try to hug them all at once. She reached her father, buried her face in his shoulder, and felt her brothers' arms go around them both. She sobbed for no reason but joy.

Mac didn't need to ask how or why. All those on Earth she cared about here, now? This was Anchen's parting gift.

Forget interspecies communication.

This, she understood.

"Emily's sister can't stay, but she plans to come back next month for a few days. We'll arrange quarters for her. Meanwhile, if you don't mind, we're thinking of putting Em into your old quarters and office."

Mac did her best to pay attention to Kammie's briefing, but it wasn't easy. Music and laughter permeated the entire pod, not to mention the aroma of grilled salmon. And pizza. Second breakfast or lunch. Her stomach was willing, given it would be early afternoon back at the consulate. Tomorrow. *Time zones weren't such an issue traveling to other worlds.*

"Mac. Does that cover it?"

"Oh. What? Yes, yes. Thanks, Kammie. I appreciate all this, more than I can say." To her surprise, Kammie Noyo had proved more than the Sinzi-ra's equal in grace. *If she'd been the one asked to accommodate changes in August,* Mac admitted, *she'd have dug in and resisted with all her might.* "But—"

"But?"

She couldn't help it. "Why is everyone here? Shouldn't someone be working? It's only August. Surely . . ." Mac stopped, mildly offended when the tiny chemist burst into laughter, clapping her hands together.

"Oh, Mac. Dear Mac," Kammie sputtered as she caught her breath. "If I needed any proof you were yourself again, that would be it. Honestly. People can take a day off. Even here. The world won't end."

Mac frowned doubtfully. "The salmon don't."

"There are monitors. Relax. This is your celebration. Enjoy it!"

"I am," Mac admitted. "But this interruption—"

"Stop, already. We needed it, too," the other told her, abruptly serious. "Seeing you. Seeing Emily. It's beyond wonderful. And after all that terrible business with the Dhryn, the earthquake—well, it's good to know things are back to normal. I can't tell you how much."

Normal? Mac stood and paced around Kammie's office. Hers—hers was gone. She'd peeked in, thinking to show her father and brothers the garden at least, but all that remained was the gravel bed along the floor, like the memory of a dried-up river.

This space was itself again. Piles of paper adorned every surface except for the benches in the attached lab. Even the soil samples Kammie had always insisted line her walls were back, so once more her view outside the pod had been replaced by ranks of silvered vials. Idly, Mac looked to where Kammie had first put the one she'd given her, the one from the Ro landing site.

It was there.

It couldn't just be sitting here, on a shelf, after all that had happened.

Mac had to know. She walked around Kammie's desk, and the curious chemist, to reach and take down the little thing.

It looked the same. Then again, they all did. Mac turned the vial to read the fine precise script on the label. The right date. Collected by Dr. M. W. Connor. Location unknown.

The location had been the outer arm of Castle Inlet, where an invisible Ro ship had touched down, and its passenger had paused before climbing the ramp, perhaps to look at the Human cowering behind a log. A mark in the disturbed moss and mud. A trace. Physical proof the unseen existed.

"Do you need it back?" Kammie asked.

The natural question.

Mac's lips were numb; she strained to hear the *scurry* . . . *Pop!* of a Ro walker amid the vintage rock and roll from outside. *Her brother Owen would be enjoying that.* "Yes, please," she said, as calmly as possible. "If you don't mind."

Her hand, the real one, wanted to clench around the vial. She'd never meant for this to stay at Base, to be a possible lure for the Ro. She'd believed Nik or his agents here had removed it, to bring to the Gathering and get it safely away.

Why hadn't they?

Mac's eyes strayed to the shelf with Kammie's deepwater sailing trophies. There was a new one taking pride of place. To buy time to think, she went close to puzzle out the print. The Millennium Cup. A regatta across Auckland's Hauraki Gulf.

Last year.

"You were in New Zealand," Mac heard herself say in a strangely normal voice.

"Don't you remember? I went for my holiday in February. Great sailing. I go as often as I can."

Where people went when they left Base had never mattered to Mac. It was how long until they returned to work that she noticed. *She should have paid attention.* "On second thought, you might as well keep this one with the rest. I know you prefer that. Here." She passed the vial back to Kammie. "I have your analysis."

Whatever was in that vial now, Mac had no doubt the soil she'd originally collected was at the IU consulate, where it had doubtless been examined by the experts of the Gathering. *Before she'd gone there herself.*

Kammie had wanted her to take a vacation—had known she was going to the cottage. The cottage where Fourteen and Kay, the Trisulian, had turned up almost immediately because, they'd said, the IU's informant at Base had told them where to find Mac.

How blind had she been? Mac asked herself. No wonder Kammie had accepted any and all changes to have Emily here with such uncharacteristic calm. *Anchen had made sure of it.*

Kammie stood very still, holding the vial. "Mac," she said slowly. "What's wrong? You look as though you've bitten a lemon."

There would be listeners. She knew it, even without a vidbot hovering quietly in a corner of the ceiling.

And what evidence did she have? Only that the vial was here, after Nik had assured her it had been removed.

Spies, Mac reminded herself, *told such flexible truths.*

Did it matter if Kammie Noyo watched Base for the IU? *She had,* Mac freely admitted, *superb and disciplined eyes.*

Nik had known who that watcher was. He hadn't told her, so she wouldn't have to pretend.

She was better at it now.

Mac grinned easily. "Just time creeping up on me, Kammie. The lack of, that is," she clarified. "I'd best get back to the party. My dad and brothers leave after lunch. If there's nothing else?" she looked around almost hungrily. "You can contact me by com. I'll leave the—"

"Go," Kammie smiled back. "We've managed fine without you—it's been tough, but I think another few weeks won't sink the place. Although I'm still not sure why they're insisting you go to this planet Myriam. And what kind of a name is that for an alien world?"

Mac made herself shrug. "Free trip. Chance to tie up some loose ends. Broaden my horizons."

The look Kammie gave at this was akin to the ones Mac had already collected from her family members; she met it without blinking. A twinge of embarrassment, however, she couldn't avoid.

She'd done such a thorough job of ignoring the universe until lately.

"Hallo, Princess."

Mac almost shook her head at the incongruity—not of her father and brothers sitting at a table in the gallery, since all three had visited her at Base before now—but of them sitting with Charles Mudge III.

Who looked, she thought, altogether too pleased to be surrounded by Connors.

"You haven't been spreading stories about me to Oversight," she warned her brothers as she sat.

Owen was eldest, the male incarnation of the mother they'd lost when Mac was a baby, complete with premature gray at his temples, a wonderful laugh, and sparkling green eyes. He'd responded to the production of his own family by somehow growing younger himself. Mac enjoyed his company when she could pry him away, which was seldom. Not that she didn't adore her nephew William, but her visits seemed to augment his boundless energy. Her eyes would glaze over by the second day. Nairee, William's mother, was one of those calm, utterly competent people; Mac kept trying to lure her away for a field season, but somehow Owen always caught wind of her attempts before they succeeded. "We'd never tell stories," he said.

"Not and admit it," corrected Blake, their middle sibling. He took after their father in his slight build, being more wire than muscle. He had yet to age or discover responsibility, having a blithe attitude toward life and his own genius that alternately exasperated and charmed the rest of the family. Mac, prone to stick at exasperation, refused to believe her father's frequent assertion they were alike.

She was the responsible one.

Though she'd never forget how Blake had stayed with her after the news came about Sam, not saying a word, not offering futile comfort, just there. As she knew they'd all be, any time she needed them.

On Earth, anyway.

"Oversight?"

Mudge spread his hands. "A gentleman never tells."

Mac dropped into her seat, laughing in surrender. "As long as you didn't mention that damn cat."

Norman Connor chuckled. "You returned just in time," he admitted. "Blake was working up to it."

"Blake!"

"Cat?" inquired Mudge.

"The food smells great," this from Owen, the peacemaker. "I can't imagine why you'd complain about it."

"I like cats," Mac said quickly, to forestall any ideas. Then she nodded at the kitchen, staffed by this year's crop of Harvs. "August. They've learned to cook by this point or given up."

"Mac." Her father lowered his voice. "How's Emily taking all this?"

From here, Mac could see where Emily sat, or rather perched, on a table edge, presiding over a noisy group she'd been told included not only Emily's younger sister Maria, but three aunts, a great-uncle on her father's side, and two cousins, all from Venezuela. They were speaking Quechua, a language perfectly suited to vivid gestures and dramatic expressions. She hadn't a clue what they were talking about.

"I haven't had time to find out," she admitted. Or the chance. Emily's sister, Maria, had turned her back when Mac had approached to say hello in person.

She didn't blame her. *Too many calls with bad news or evasion.* "Em's—I think she's lost her taste for surprises."

"Hopefully not for parties."

Mac smiled as she swung around to greet the newcomer. "John! How have you been?"

"Hi Mac, Dr. Connor. Owen, Blake. Nice to see you again. Mr. Mudge." Her former postdoc, now on staff with his own small department, returned her smile as he took the seat the senior Dr. Connor offered. Mac was impressed. When he'd first arrived, Emily's outspoken nature could send John Ward bolting from a room—her record was under five seconds. Mac didn't think that would happen now. He'd somehow grown into himself when she wasn't looking.

Or she was finally looking, Mac chided herself. "Keeping busy," she said. "And you? How's the new department?"

He shrugged. "I'll let you know once Dr. Stewart settles back in. Pretty disruptive, having her take off just when classes were starting at UBC. Kammie doesn't seem worried about a repeat, but I've let her know she's on probation with me."

John wouldn't have been told how his new statistics prof, Dr. Persephone Stewart, had been recalled from Norcoast to act in her other specialty at the consulate, nor would he know, with luck, that 'Sephe was back to help Emily. Luckily for both agent and budding department head, 'Sephe was delighted to return to academia. *Probation?* With luck, that would be the most danger 'Sephe would need to overcome.

How much of the Human side of things did Kammie know?

To avoid that labyrinth, Mac focused on John. "See?" she said, raising an eyebrow. "I knew you'd enjoy all that power over people."

"Mac!" John protested, and proved he could still blush.

She took pity and let her father proceed to ask interested questions about John's new program. She listened, but not only to the conversation at her table. Her eyes half-closed, Mac let herself bask in chatter, returning to a world where vying approaches to the remote assay of smolt stomach contents were as eagerly debated as the latest hockey trade. The inside of Base, its heart, hadn't changed.

Outside? She gazed through the transparent wall behind Blake's head. Base had been towed from this site, opposite the mouth of the Tannu, almost sixteen years ago. The layout of the pods was the same as before. Mac could believe no time had passed at all, that this was her first field season at Norcoast and her family here to check out the place.

Almost.

Blake's eyes met hers and locked, brimming with questions. Mac deliberately ran the fingers of her new hand over the tabletop. "Let's take a walk, guys."

"Surely we can eat first," Owen objected. His playful expression changed when he looked at her. He understood. She had things to tell them. *Difficult things.*

"Ah, Mac?" This from John. "After eating, there's some other—well—stuff. You know. You should stick around."

Her heart sank. Mac glanced over her shoulder and winced. Sure enough, the head table, usually empty unless there was a game on, was set for the senior staff. *And,* she sighed inwardly, *there were flowers.* Somewhat wilted and prone to lean, but definitely flowers.

She gave John a pleading look. "Tell me I don't have to make a speech."

"You don't have to . . ." John let his voice trail away.

Her brother chuckled deep in his throat. "Oh, this should be good," he predicted. "Remember that time up at the cottage, Mac, when you climbed on the table to lecture all of us about—"

"She's got that look, Blake," Owen warned. "You'd better watch it."

"They haven't served lunch yet." Blake smiled angelically. "She's got nothing to throw."

"Norcoast, no!" this from Mudge as Mac pulled her imp from its pocket. She merely smiled back at her brother as she tossed the device up and down in one hand. "Really, Norcoast."

"Don't worry, Charles," Norman Connor said serenely. "Well, unless shoes come off. Then you might want to duck."

Family, Mac thought, suddenly beyond content.

"Not bad."

Mac, mulling through what she needed to say, gave Blake a surprised look. The two of them were walking ahead, Owen and her father close behind. "The speech?" She'd thought it had gone as poorly as such things usually did. She'd said the expected as quickly as possible and hoped she hadn't sounded like an idiot.

The thank-yous, get-on-with-your-work part had been easy. The brief, supposedly safe announcement about her being temporarily seconded to an off-world research program, and not-quite-desperate plea to keep her updated from Base while she was gone, had brought a startling ovation, with no few tears and horrifyingly proud nods.

She was one of them, she'd thought in a panic. *She hadn't changed; she wouldn't change.*

As a consequence, she'd fumbled introducing Emily's new role as visiting scholar, but Emily herself had stood at the perfect moment to warm applause, thanking everyone here, and Mac, for the opportunity. *Em hadn't lost her touch with a crowd.*

Her brother rubbed her head. "The haircut. I like it. What's his name?"

The ocean was only a rope rail away. *Shame there wouldn't be time to dry him off,* Mac grumbled to herself. The lev taking the Connors back to Vancouver was already docked, doors open, at the end of the adjoining walkway. She scuffed the toe of her shoe into the mem-wood instead. "Think you're smart, don't you?"

Blake laughed. "I know I'm smart. So? Do we get to meet him?"

Mac slowed, trailing her hand along the rope. "I don't know," she admitted finally, looking up at her brother. "He's not in a safe place."

He lost the teasing smile. "I'm sorry, Mac."

She shrugged. "Nik's like you. Smart. He'll manage." She found the spot she wanted and stopped, putting her back to the rail.

Sing-li, whose idea of discreet had turned out to be staying politely out of earshot, stopped too, as inconspicuous as a bear on a beach. He shrugged off her glare, but sat down on the walkway, pretending to study a passing gull.

Her father didn't miss much. "Should I be grateful you have a watchdog or worried, Princess?"

"Both."

At this, the three exchanged looks. "What can we do?" Owen asked simply.

Anchen had given her this, too, Mac realized. No messages to be misunderstood or intercepted. No fake recordings to offer equally false reassurance. These few minutes to talk to her own.

The alien's predisposition with meeting face-to-face had its merits.

"Maybe nothing," she answered bluntly. "I can't see—not yet—how this is going to go. Forget the media release—most of the Dhryn Progenitor ships aren't accounted for. There could be over two hundred more hiding out there. They're still a threat—" She hesitated. *Honesty now, if ever.* "The Dhryn are capable of consuming all life on a planet."

Owen's face set into harsh lines she'd never seen before, likely thinking of William and Nairee. "Can we defend ourselves?"

Mac thought of them, too. Her real hand strayed to the artificial one. *Her wrist dissolving in fire . . .* If the Dhryn returned in numbers?

She shook her head, once, unable to speak.

"Can we stop them?" her father asked, after exchanging looks with her brothers.

"No," Mac found her voice. "Not alone. That's what's worse."

"Gods, Mac," Blake said. "What could be worse than the Dhryn?"

For an instant, she didn't see the faces of her family, or the surrounding landscape she loved almost as much. For an instant, all Mac could see was a seething darkness, reaching for her; all she could feel was that voice ripping through every nerve. She shuddered free of memory. "The Ro—the Myrokynay— you've seen some of the reports. They exist. It's true they killed the Dhryn who tried to attack Earth. What isn't being told is that the Ro called the Dhryn here in the first place. When the Dhryn failed to attack us, the Ro destroyed their ships. There's more." She took a deep breath. "I believe the Ro made the Dhryn into what they are. Made them to serve a purpose. More than a weapon—I'm sure of it. The Chasm worlds were sterilized for a reason. I don't know why. Not yet. I plan to."

Her brothers nodded, accepting what was, in truth, her promise.

Her father looked thoughtful. "Your trip to Myriam. You think the answer's there."

"It's the only place I have to look," Mac amended. "A start."

Blake's eyes narrowed. "You're more afraid of these Ro than the Dhryn. Why?"

"I'm afraid of them both." Mac paused, wondering how far to go. "This isn't about us," she said finally. "It's not about life on Earth or any one world. It's about the transects and all the living things they weave together. The IU. That's what the Ro threaten, because that's the only power we have to resist whatever they want. They'll attack the Sinzi if they must. They'll try to isolate us."

"Destroy the biospace," Blake said. At Mac's questioning look, he shook his head. "Something I read. Compared the species within the IU to a planetary biosphere, but on that unimaginable scale. The sum depends on the interaction of the parts. I thought it pretty simplistic at the time. Now?" He blew out his cheeks and glanced at Sing-li before gazing at her. "Geeze, Mac. What happened to studying salmon?"

"Don't get me started," she said unsteadily. The pilot was waving from the lev. *They were out of time.* "I'll stay in touch. There'll be com packets to and from Myriam. But . . . you should know the risk. The Ro don't need the transects; the Dhryn do. If the Dhryn attack again, there are species who'll lobby the IU to close their gates. If the Ro see our connection as too much of a threat, they could do it for us. In either case, I—" It didn't help that her brothers were looking hor-rified. "If I can't get home, I don't want you to worry," she fumbled. "I'm pretty good at getting along with aliens, these days. You'd be surprised. I'll be okay."

At that, she faltered and stopped, trying to memorize every detail of their dear faces. Her vision seemed to blur and she rubbed her eyes angrily.

"Solve this, Mackenzie," her father said. "Solve this and come home."

"You should have checked with me."

"Why?" Mac asked, looking up at Sing-li from her seat in the skim. "Don't you like boats?"

Emily laughed. Mudge squirmed. Tie grumbled something about tides and time under his breath, holding onto the stern rope as the little vessel bobbed up and down with the swells.

"I like boats. It's where you plan to go in this one that bothers me."

"You don't know where we're going," Mac pointed out.

Sing-li planted an oversized left boot on the gunnels of the skim. "Exactly."

Although tempted to see how long the agent could keep his balance and stay out of the water, given both skim and walkway were in motion, Mac relented and gave the seat next to hers a pat. "Bit of sightseeing. Hop in. This won't take long."

Tie expressed his opinion of their final passenger by letting go the rope and engaging the engine the instant most, but not all, of Sing-li was in the skim. The man was tossed into the seat, almost falling over it into Mudge's lap. His teeth showed in a wide grin as he righted. "I like boats," he assured Mac. "Better than Tie's driving."

The skim lifted to its cruising height, spending a few moments bouncing up and down as it echoed the choppy surface below. Emily let out a gleeful hoot. Tie sent the machine slewing about to follow the swells instead of crossing them and the ride smoothed immediately. Emily tried to persuade him to change back to the more exhilarating course, without success.

Mac envied Emily's ability to relish the moment. Her own eyes still burned and her chest felt tight and sore. Given the option, she'd have curled up in a fetal position with a large cushion and whimpered herself to sleep.

She'd completed her farewells without blubbering, thankfully. *In part due to Blake*, she smiled to herself. He'd whispered a most unbrotherly comment about her missing beau that would have made Emily proud. *Anything to break the tension.*

Mac missed them all. *At least she'd said good-bye this time, thanks to Anchen.*

She'd found time to change into shorts and shirt—her cottage leftovers, kindly included in her bag by consulate staff. Now, she watched the shore as it flew past. This part of the inlet was an estuarine lowland where the Tannu negotiated for entry into the inlet through a series of braided, changing outlets. The main channel, opposite Base, was a deep turmoil of fresh and salt water, the proportion of each varying with tide and season. The others were quiet, less determined flows, brown and slick between mudflats dotted with sandpipers and other birds already heading south for the winter. Farther in, the channels twisted out of sight behind expanses of reed grass and low trees. Debris from upstream testified that not all days were peaceful sunny ones. Immense logs, bleached soft gray by salt and sun, lay everywhere, as if strewn about by a giant's hand.

The first cliff rose up as if the river was of no consequence. The midday light was deceiving, smoothing out crags and jagged edges until the stone appeared dressed like some castle wall, revealing how the inlet had been named. The next cliff met it at angles, soaring higher, topped by trees and eagles.

Ahead?

"Aie."

The soft, unhappy sound drew Mac forward to her friend, sitting up by Tie. She put her hands on Emily's shoulders. "Bit of a mess," she acknowledged awkwardly.

The outstretched arm that defined the inlet from the Pacific curved westward in front of them, the sun striking harsh glints from exposed rock. The summer hadn't been kind: deep furrows eroded any patches where soil had escaped the tumbling rush into the ocean; any vegetation that had landed roots down and green was now either completely dead or sported bare branches.

Branches with eagles, fair enough. Those bare limbs lined by gulls who were nothing of the kind caught Mac's attention, especially when the tiggers, as one, turned their heads to inspect the approaching skim and its occupants. "You make sure we were cleared to approach," she shouted at Tie.

He grunted something annoyed. Reassured, Mac leaned against the gunnels near Emily. "There's the new station," she said, happy to take her eyes from the ruined slope.

Pod Two didn't quite sparkle in the sunlight. For one thing, it was colored, like the other pods now at the Tannu, to resemble the natural stone of the landscape. *For another,* Mac grinned, *someone had been very busy indeed.* The lead researcher, Martin Svehla, must have been overjoyed by his capital budget, given he loved nothing more than nailing things together.

Now, the roughly oval shape of Pod Two bristled in every direction with floating platforms, some enclosing large amounts of water. A myriad collection of levs, skims, and in-the-water barges were tied up on the lee side. There were cranes hanging from the terrace that spiraled up the outside of the pod. And, Mac squinted in disbelief, a slide dropped in a crazed swoop from the rooftop, ending a formidable height above the ocean surface.

That could hurt.

"I take it you let Marty play," Emily commented, making an obvious effort to keep her eyes from slipping west.

"He seemed the right choice." Mac, recipient of an impressive flow of data from Svehla and company courtesy of the Ministry, wasn't worried there'd been more fun—namely construction—than work, but now she shook her head in mock outrage. "I hope he's planned how to stow all this before winter."

While they talked, Tie brought the skim sweeping into Pod Two's new dock, an elaborate affair with steps as well as ramps. And, Mac noticed with mute admiration, a roof as well as a countertop for sorting gear. She sighed happily. About to climb out first, she paused and turned to Sing-li. "After you." *Only fair to let him do his job.*

The agent was busy whispering into his wrist com, eyes darting back and forth over the docking structure. Mac felt a chill. When Emily stood up beside her, ready to climb out, she lifted her hand to hold the other woman in place. "Something we should know?" she asked Sing-li, mouth dry.

"Do you see anyone here?" Sing-li demanded, getting to his feet. Like Nik, he moved differently when alarmed. *Like a barracuda, effortlessly keeping its jaws and muscular body aligned with the next doomed fish.*

"Why would there be?" An unconcerned Tie shut off the engine and tied off the skim. "Party tonight. Most're back at Base getting a head start. 'Spect we'll find Marty and his crew there." He pointed to the walkway linking the pod to land.

The one place Mac hadn't wanted Emily to go. *She should have called ahead, warned Kammie, done something to prevent this.*

But it was too late. Sing-li, with a nod, accepted Tie's explanation and climbed out. Tie followed suit, Emily going by Mac without a word.

She heard a gentle *harrumph*. "I could stop them," Mudge offered in a low voice, coming to stand beside her. His face was pale and beaded with more than ocean spray. "Make up something about new Trust regulations."

"Wouldn't work." Mac wasn't sure if she was touched or shocked he'd lie for Emily's sake. *Both,* she decided. She met his worried look and shrugged helplessly. "Maybe it's better to get it over with now, while I'm here. If Emily can't handle this . . ." She didn't need to finish. He knew as well as she did that if Emily Mamani broke, she'd be hospitalized again. This time, without Mac.

Worse, she could easily end up in a Human facility, where she'd be safe from pestering by the Frow and their ilk, but more vulnerable to the Ro. "Besides," sighed Mac, waving at Mudge to go first, "it's why she invited you."

He frowned and didn't budge. "She told you?" Almost outrage.

Mac hesitated. Tie had led Emily and Sing-li to the junction of walkway and deck, gesturing to something about its construction. *Likely complaining—he approved of change about as much as a Sthlynii.* "Not in so many words," she said carefully. "But it's obvious, isn't it?"

She'd never seen him smile like this before, a small, quiet smile that reached his eyes and made them twinkle. "I would have thought so, Norcoast, but you can be remarkably obtuse at times."

Obtuse? Interspecies communication suddenly seemed easier. "Oversight—" Mac swallowed, "—why do you think you're here?"

"Dr. Mamani's worried about you. It's going to be difficult—emotionally difficult—saying good-bye. To her. To your other friends. Base. She thought—" he actually blushed, "—she said you'd need a friendly shoulder on the trip to orbit and I'd be the best choice." He *harrumphed* and collected himself. "Not that I expect you'll do anything of the sort, Norcoast," this gruffly. "But I could tell my agreeing to come and offer my support eased her mind."

Mac tried to imagine weeping on Mudge's round shoulder and failed. What she could imagine, all too well, was Emily choosing to lie to him.

To postpone the inevitable.

"Emily's mind is a slippery thing," she said grimly. "Particularly when it comes to moving others in directions that suit her. I appreciate your kindness— really I do—but Emily?" A nod to the ruined slope. "She's brought you here as punishment, Oversight."

Mudge flinched. "Why?" he gasped. "What have I done to her? I—"

"Not yours," Mac interrupted gently. "Hers."

The blood drained from his face, but he gave a short nod before she could say anything more. "I see. We'd best not delay, Norcoast." He started moving.

"Wait." Mac stopped him with a touch on his lapel. *Only Mudge would wear an antique tweed jacket to visit Base in August.* "Damn Emily," she heard herself say. "You don't need to do this, Oversight. You don't need to go through it again. Stay here and wait for us."

"If I do," he countered with remarkable calm, "you know what will happen. Every time she looks at me, she'll blame herself again for what the Ro did here. There's enough guilt going around, Norcoast. None of us should carry more than our share. Especially Emily Mamani."

Each time she thought she knew the caliber of the man, he surprised her. "Probably not a good time for a hug," she decided out loud, her voice unsteady. At his look of horror, *likely feigned,* she patted him firmly on the lapel.

"Let's go."

The original walkway to land was gone, of course, along with the holdfast pillars and gate that had allowed access, if you had the right codes, to the system of suspended paths. It had been built with care so scientists could observe and record without leaving a record themselves. The new walkway was higher, to pass over the debris-crusted shore. If you could call trees larger than a transport lev debris in any sense.

The illusion of walking on air was disarming. Mac gave a tentative bounce, then another, stronger one. The membrane flexed like a giant trampoline.

"Norcoast!" Mudge protested. He looked inexpressibly silly with his fists clenched out from his sides, although Mac's own fingers were wrapped around the transparent rope rail. "What do you think you're doing? Stop that!"

"It's a fable," she explained but obeyed.

A Dhryn fable. Brymn's.

Finally, a memory that didn't sting.

Emily and the other two men were at the new gate, Tie keying in the code. Tiggers on top of each pillar watched him, as if eager for a mistake.

Gulls, Mac thought, *made vindictive watchdogs.*

Over land, the membrane lost its slight give, darkening as their feet approached steps to show the way in the bright sunlight.

At first, Mac noticed what was missing. Shade, for starters. The sun was hot as well as bright. Hot, bright, and unforgiving. The air smelled of dryness and dust. They were lucky, she judged, running her glance upslope to where the ridge overlooked the Pacific. When the westerlies were underway, it must be like a miniature dust storm here.

Life . . . as she looked closer, she realized it wasn't missing at all, simply changed. Every sheltered nook contained its blush of rich green moss, its feathers of fern. Fungi bracketed the lee sides of fallen wood and thrust its way through curls of dead bark. Exposed soil was peppered with sprigs of new grass and the coin-shaped seedpods of fireweed, except for a too-even scar where otters had made a slide to expedite their trip to shore. She smiled.

A squirrel scolded them from its perch on a half-buried tree, one tiny paw braced against an upturned twig, its tail swishing with outrage. Mac saluted before hurrying to catch up with the others.

"Told you," Tie announced. "There's Marty and his crew. Don't ask me what they're doing now."

As it was clear Svehla and his trio of students were ferrying mem-wood over the crest of the ridge, Mac could make a good guess. The observation deck on the opposite side had been one of his pet projects; she'd expect him to rebuild it as soon as possible. However, given the original construction had resulted in Mudge canceling a third of the proposals for that season—there being no way to remove the deck without more perturbations and him not being the sort to simply throw things at Mac and be satisfied—she also knew why Tie wasn't about to admit it to present company.

Not that Mudge would care today.

He was contained and too quiet, every step deliberate. Emily, on the other hand, flitted up the path ahead of them all like some frenetic butterfly, her long legs flashing through the panels of her improbable dress, waving to Svehla, who had put down his load and shaded his eyes to see who was paying them a visit.

Sing-li waited for Mac. "What are we doing here?" he demanded in a low voice.

She could see the strain on his face; a compliment to their relationship, that he didn't hide it. The Ministry had lost three of its own during the earthquake, men Sing-li knew, perhaps as friends, though she'd never dared ask. "Emily's penance," she replied, equally quietly.

As if the earthquake mattered—as if three lives mattered—against entire worlds lost and threatened.

Where on that scale are we?

Mac shook her head to clear it of Nik's implacable voice. Her companion misunderstood. "You don't approve." Sing-li stared at Emily, now hugging Svehla and talking so quickly her voice was like a bird's. "Then why did you agree?"

"Think I was asked?" Mac snorted. "Doesn't matter. I wanted to take a look myself. It's one thing to know succession will take place—another to see it happen. It's reassuring."

And it was, Mac realized, taking a deep breath and letting it out slowly. She'd held the image of wrack and destruction tight in her mind for too long, believed somehow it was her responsibility to be here and help fix it.

The reality of regrowth without her lifted a load she hadn't noticed she was carrying until now. *Complete with otters.*

While part of her wanted to stay and see more, Mac could feel time flying by. "This shouldn't take long," she promised, as much for Mudge's sake as anyone else's.

They lengthened their strides to reach the others. Mudge, Mac noticed, had stayed apart. The distancing hadn't reassured Svehla, who was standing somewhat futilely in front of his pile of unapproved mem-wood. "There you are, Mac," Emily sang out. "I told Marty he has to stop all this and get to our party."

The students, dust-coated and sweaty, looked hopeful.

"Hi, Mac." Svehla screwed up his grizzled face, apparently trying not to smile at the radiant woman in front of him. "Em, you know I'd like to, but there's only so many hours of daylight this time of year and we've a spore census to complete—"

Much as it pained her, Mac made herself say: "There's always tomorrow, Marty." His look of astonishment was almost worth it. The students' wide grins, however, made her worry about setting a trend.

His problem. Hers was fiddling with a rope of black pearls.

"Meet you back there, Marty. Em? Lead the way."

She'd guessed correctly. Emily turned with a flourish to take the walkway that now replaced the one she and Mudge had walked that fateful morning in May.

Mudge followed Emily, Mac followed Mudge, finding Sing-li's presence behind their little group no comfort at all, not when she could see the tension hunching Mudge's shoulders, not when she knew as well as he what should be here, and wasn't.

Mercifully, Emily slowed and stopped long before they reached the place where the Ro had last landed, their ship shattering the old growth like dried sticks. She looked confused, as if she'd expected a landmark. Mudge came up beside her. Obeying her instincts, not without pity for both, Mac kept back. Sing-li followed suit.

Emily was taller. The breeze lifted her gleaming black hair, with its streaks of white, and played with the panels of her dress so they brushed Mudge's legs. Her head tilted on her elegant neck to let the sun kiss her high cheekbones and bury her dark eyes in shadow. Her grace was paralyzed, as if she was as much stone as the mauve-gray rock around them.

She was taller, but Mudge, in his shapeless jacket, panting and wiping sweat from his rosy forehead, alive and real, seemed to tower over her.

Their voices carried easily over the desolation. "This was my fault," Emily began, matter-of-factly. "I don't ask you to forgive me."

"Of course not," Mudge panted. "You want to tell me why they did it."

Where had that *come from?* Mac closed her mouth and paid attention.

Emily hesitated, her hands lifting as if warding a blow.

"You want me to understand," Mudge continued, almost stern. "It's import-ant that I know why, isn't it, Emily."

"Y–yes," she faltered. "They were yours, these trees. Mac told me, Charlie. She said you put more value on the smallest twig here than her life's work."

Mac grimaced. *There were some things not worth repeating . . .* "Why did they do it?" Mudge's arm swept outward, but his eyes never left Emily's. "Why did they have to destroy it all?"

She swayed and Mac started forward in alarm, but stopped as Emily began to speak, her voice now reed-thin and gasping. "This world . . . would be cleansed. *They* . . . knew it would be. *They* don't have patience . . . but time . . . time . . . *They* own time. Make ready and wait, make ready and wait, make—"

Emily paused; none of them moved.

Then, *"They* had to destroy the signs . . . signs among the trees that would show what *They* left behind . . . what *They* sent into the ocean . . . destroy the signs . . . sweep it all away . . . those who walked for them . . . the signs . . . your trees, Charlie. Into the ocean. Forgive—" Emily sank to her knees, her arms reaching out to Mudge. "Forgive me."

He sank down with her, gathering her in, holding her tight.

Mac's eyes sought the cove, its dark blue water sparkling in the sun, its depths hiding . . . what? She was aware of Sing-li speaking urgently into his com, doubtless commandeering teams to rip up the recovering slope, to scour the ocean bed, to look for whatever the Ro had left behind for the moment the Dhryn wiped this world of life.

She stood on an empty mountainside, with nothing but open sky, familiar landscapes, and friends in sight, and had never felt so terrified.

And she'd brought Emily here for safety?

- 8 -

PARTINGS AND PERTURBATIONS

IT WAS A MEASURE OF HOW SERIOUSLY the Ministry of Extra-Sol Human Affairs, and Earthgov, took Sing-li's message that convoys of huge black levs whooshed over their heads toward the outer arm of Castle Inlet before Tie finished securing their skim to the dock at Base.

It was a measure of how little attention Base itself paid to the world that they were surrounded upon arrival not by aroused security but by staff and students wearing shirts that made Sing-li's downright conservative, several waving opened bottles, and all smiling.

Run away? Mac wondered numbly as she was hauled from the skim with a roar of welcome, *or grab the nearest beer?*

Sing-li vanished into the crowd, with Tie right behind. None of them had said a word during the ride back. Mac had pulled out her imp and worked. Emily had sat with Mudge, her head on his shoulder, her eyes closed. She'd looked exhausted, but at peace.

He'd looked thoroughly horrified—whether by Emily's revelation or her proximity, Mac couldn't be sure.

For her part, Mac was grateful. Intentionally or by luck, Mudge had asked the right question at the right time, accomplishing what no one else, including Emily, had managed in all the weeks of trying. She'd finally been able to express a memory of the Ro.

Something less disturbing would have been nice.

She burned inside. *What the Ro had done in the past was nothing to this, this violation!*

Hide a threat here? In her ocean?

Mac wasn't sure at what point her fury had turned into something cold and set, her determination into something implacable. She didn't care. All she knew was that she couldn't leave this to anyone else.

Here, she wasn't defenseless.

Of course, the party had begun without them and was now well underway.

Mac dodged and ducked her way between gleeful students, keeping an eye fixed on her target, the door to Pod Three and the administrator's office. She had to talk to Kammie Noyo. She wanted—if not answers, then reassurance. Reassurance that others knew, that the appropriate actions were being taken at all levels.

That this time, they'd listen.

It didn't help either her progress or her impatience when students started announcing her presence as loudly as possible. "Mac's back!" "Where?" "Over here!" "Hurry—hide the ribs!!!" "Why do we have to hide the ribs?"

Mac paused to wince.

A chorus bellowed the answer: "'Cause Mac's back!"

"You'd think they'd forget," she muttered under her breath. "But no." The story of how she'd eaten the last rib on the barbeque one night—quite by accident—had blossomed with retelling to each new crop of students until every rib night began with a chant of . . . she waited for it, resigned. *Easier to stop the tides.*

"No Ribs for Mac! No Ribs for Mac! No Ribs for Mac! Mac gets SALAD and BEER!"

Mac shook her head, an unbidden smile twitching her lips. *Their joy at her expense was irresistible.* "You realize it doesn't rhyme," she complained to those nearest, who only laughed and chanted louder. Someone handed her the beer in question. She waited for it, but this time no one had brought salad. Which usually landed on her head.

Emily put her hand on Mac's shoulder and leaned into her ear. "You should be staying here," she shouted over the din, "not me."

"Not if I want ribs," Mac tossed back. She stopped her futile fight against the human current before Emily could argue, letting herself be drawn with the surge to the line of smoking barbeques on the upper terrace.

It turned out to be the right choice. Mac spotted Kammie's immaculate white lab coat at the top of the first sweep of stairs and struggled, beer in hand, through well wishers to reach her.

When she did, Kammie nodded before Mac could open her mouth to speak, her face somber. "I've heard. Come with me."

"Just a minute." Mac looked around for Emily and Mudge. They were coming up the steps, making slower time than she had—in part because Emily was being accosted from every side. The attention made her sparkle, like a vidstar greeting fans.

"Mac!" Case Wilson had acquired more freckles over the summer, but otherwise the deep fisher looked exactly as he had when she'd left: lanky, muscular, and too young for his years. His wide grin faded as he approached. "What's up?"

Male, breathing, and new. *Perfect,* Mac decided. She grabbed his arm with her free hand and he flinched. "Sorry," she said quickly, relaxing her grip. The prosthesis could be overly firm. "Case, I need a favor. See that woman down there?"

"Dr. Mamani." His pale eyes flicked back to her. "Your friend who went missing. I wanted to say how happy I am she's okay—"

"She's not," Mac interrupted, lowering her voice. "Look after her for me, would you? Just for a little while. Get her a drink, something to eat, breathing space. I have to talk to Kammie. With Oversight," she added, catching Mudge's attention and beckoning him to follow. He detached from Emily's cluster with obvious relief.

"Who's looking after you?"

Mac, her mind already on Ro, ocean floors, and how to snag a savory rib or two on the way to Kammie's office, blinked at Case. "Pardon?"

"You heard me." He was frowning. Not, she decided, in anger, but with his own brand of thoughtful obstinacy. Case would latch on to what he viewed as a problem like a barnacle to stone.

And be about as difficult to dislodge.

Mac frowned back. "I don't need looking after. Emily does."

"Mac—"

"You heard me," she stressed as Mudge came panting to her side. He paused, giving Case an assessing look. "As I said," Mac continued smoothly, "don't eat all the ribs before we get back. Ah, Oversight. This way. Kammie's waiting for us."

Mac licked her fingers and looked around for a place to drop the small bone. Without a word, Kammie held out an empty petri dish and took her offering.

"The Ministry's expecting your full cooperation." From her tone, 'Sephe wasn't.

Mac hadn't been surprised to find the agent sitting in Kammie's office, although Kammie herself had had something to say about her new statistician invading her privacy—that is, until 'Sephe had pointed out they both represented interests beyond Base, so perhaps they could move on to the topic at hand.

Not a surprise either.

"Let me get this straight," Mac said quietly. She put her sticky fingertips together and studied 'Sephe. "You don't want Base evacuated. You want everything to continue as before." Music thumped through the pod walls and floors. The festivities outside were in full swing. A tiny light was flashing on Kammie's desk—incoming message. More than one. She ignored the display, intent on Mac.

The agent's generous lips thinned with distaste. "This isn't coming from me, Mac. You know that."

"Nor me," Kammie snapped. "The IU committee is not in favor of involving untrained civilians. Most of our people are students, Dr. Stewart. We must send them to safety!"

"Where?" Mac asked, receiving startled looks from both. "If the Dhryn come again," she elaborated in a cold voice, "if the Ro come again . . . where do you think they'll be safe?"

The music outside had stopped. *When would they notice?* she wondered.

Mudge stirred in his seat. 'Sephe leaned forward in hers, dark eyes now inscrutable. "Go on."

"The Ministry wants to keep Base operating as is," Mac elaborated. "Meaning everyone here remains ignorant while you bring in your experts to search for whatever the Ro dropped in the ocean. Base as camouflage. Everything outwardly normal."

"That's the gist of it. Sorry, Mac. I know you're—"

Mac raised her hand to stop her. "We'll cooperate—" and over Kammie's shocked "Mac!" she continued, "—but Base will conduct the search."

"Impossible." 'Sephe shook her head. "We must maintain secrecy—"

Mac's lips twisted. "Secrecy wastes time we don't have. No one knows these waters as well. Searching this ocean is what these people do for a living. Emily can retune her Tracer. You—" a nod to Kammie "—have sufficient genetic coding to differentiate a Ro walker from anything local." The little silver vial on the shelf seemed to wink at her. "It's a running start. Better than anything you have, 'Sephe."

Kammie's eyes were glowing. "We'd have to drop everything else," she warned. "Lose the field season."

Where on that scale . . . "There'll be another," Mac promised, aware she couldn't.

"I'll pass this along, Mac," 'Sephe said unhappily. "But you know Hollans. I can't see him approving."

"I wasn't asking." Mac rose to her feet, Mudge doing the same, his eyes fixed on her. She pulled out her imp and tapped it lightly against the side of her forehead. "On the way back I dumped all relevant information into Norcoast's main system, including a Base-wide message cued to announce itself in every way possible." She indicated the mass of flashing lights on Kammie's desk. "I'd say everyone's got it by now."

"I don't believe it," 'Sephe said flatly. "You're bluffing."

Kammie's mouth worked, her eyes swimming with tears. She made a helpless gesture, and Mac smiled. "Go outside and see for yourself," she told 'Sephe. "Me, I'm leaving the planet."

'Sephe pulled out her own imp and rushed out the door to the hallway. Mac watched her go, then glanced at the ceiling, transparent to the sky and clouds, doubtless filled with embedded eyes and ears. "Thank you," she said in Instella, putting her fingertips and thumbs together in a circle.

Anchen hadn't just sent her here to see her family.

She'd sent her to reconnect herself, and the whole truth, to her home.

The terraces, steps, and walkways were crowded with students and staff. Most sat with their backs to walls. All stared into flickering 'screens, fingers manipulating no-longer-secret data as they talked in urgent hushed tones to one another.

The barbeques with their loads of ribs had been turned off, the meat abandoned on the grills.

If it hadn't been for the lurid party shirts, *and the beers in hand,* Mac might have thought them cramming for finals.

She stood on the uppermost terrace, seeing the first impact of what she'd wrought, and trembled. To hide it, she gripped the rail and stared seaward. Two levs were coming into dock. Black ones. *Did they try to be conspicuous?*

"Your people are scientists," Mudge observed. "They'll manage." He leaned on the rail and gave a sad little *harrumph.* "Shame about the ribs, though."

Mac gave him a sharp look. "This isn't funny, Oversight."

"I know." He hesitated, then, in his firm, no-nonsense voice, "You did the right thing, Norcoast. Protocols be damned. In this instance."

She was touched. "You did pretty well yourself, Oversight. Oh, oh." Mac tensed as she saw who was debarking from the first Ministry lev. No mistaking Martin Svehla, although she'd never seen him this disheveled before a party, shirt half torn from one shoulder, hair mussed, missing a shoe. He saw her and began stalking toward Pod Three, shaking off the hands of his students with a rough gesture. "This can't be good," she murmured.

"He won't blame you."

"Trust me, Oversight," sighed Mac. "He will. It's a gift."

Svehla wasn't the only one noticing her presence. Others were starting to stand and migrate in her direction. "Time to go," she decided.

"What? No rousing speech?"

Emily.

Mac froze.

"Or good-bye? *Aie.* Coward."

The last word had bite to it. Mac turned with a sigh. Emily stood there, dark eyes smoldering with outrage. Case was with her, behind and to one side. He looked, Mac judged, equally upset. *Just less dramatic about it.*

" 'Time to go' was a figure of speech. I'm hardly running off, Em," she observed. "Our ride's not here yet." She checked on Svehla's progress. Luckily, he'd stopped to talk to Lee Fyock, who was now staring up at them, too.

Emily waved her pearls at him.

"Lara—from biochem?" Mac said testily. "Stop that."

"You're the one who's stopped everything. This was our party, Mac. There was to be—" Emily gave her hips a frustrated twitch, sending the transparent portion of her dress swirling across territory that made Mudge blush. "Dancing!"

"Dancing?" echoed Case in disbelief. "You're worried about dancing at a time like this? Are you nuts?"

"*Si, Senõr!* Ask our Mac."

Given the unlikelihood of explaining to the innocent Case that dancing, preferably sweaty hours of it, was a perfectly normal stress response for Emily Mamani under the circumstances, and equally unable to clarify, in under a thousand words, the state of her friend's sanity to herself or anyone else, Mac settled for a noncommittal grunt.

Charles Mudge III, however, had a definite opinion. *Not that she was surprised.* "You will apologize to Dr. Mamani this minute, young man," he ordered, in his most officious tone. "She's had a very trying day. Very trying."

"Why thanks, Charlie," Emily cooed, trailing her fingers up his sleeve and slipping one gloved arm around Mudge's neck. "We've always been close," she confided to Case. Mudge squirmed free with an incoherent squawk of protest. Emily laughed.

Mac shook her head at the three of them, simultaneously warning off a small group of approaching students. "Have you gone over your gear, Em? We should make sure everything's arrived."

She watched for the transformation. The Emily Mac had known could switch from audacious flirt to preoccupied scientist in the blink of an eye. Broke a new heart every Monday, Mac would tell her. Emily would shrug and reach for her work.

There. Emily abandoned Mudge, to his relief, and gave her a considering look. "I planned a quick assessment and initial power relay check after the party, Mac, but under the circumstances, I can get to it now—be done before you leave."

Mac opened her mouth to agree, then something in Case's face made her hesitate. She paused to take a good look around.

Everyone in sight was looking back at her, those nearest with expressions of confusion and dismay. Six mismatched barbeques stood nearby, stacked with cooling bones, while beer warmed in tubs of melting ice. The breeze caught the edge of the banner draped over the railing, flipping it up so Mac could make out the colorful curves of its lettering, "Welcome Home."

She'd really done it. "Bother."

Ignoring Emily's questioning eyebrow, Mac pulled out her imp, and activated its screen. She drew her finger through the audio control, took a deep breath, then said: "Hi."

The word boomed from every corner of Base and Mac made a face of her own. *She hated loudspeakers. Even more, her voice over loudspeakers.*

"You know how much I love talking like this," she continued, "so I'll make it brief."

She had their attention, no doubt about that.

"Despite what you might be thinking right now, the world hasn't come to an end. Trust me," she added dryly, "you'd know the difference.

"What has happened is that the Ro have made their first mistake. Hiding something here of all places . . . with you lot? What were they thinking?" Mac paused to let the concept trickle through and was gratified to see some half grins and nods. "If there's anything alien underwater, or ever was, who better to find it? You know what belongs—from inlet to strait, from deep reefs to tidal flats. Find what doesn't. And don't let anyone stop you." This last as Mac spotted 'Sephe and Sing-li stepping out on the terrace below.

"I know what I'm asking," she continued, hearing the huskiness in her own voice as it echoed. "It will take years to recover the data you'll lose by abandoning this season, if you even can. Some of your careers will suffer. And it might be for nothing. But, maybe, just maybe, what you do here might help save everything. All of—" she had to stop and settled for a sweeping gesture to include Base, ocean, shore, and sky.

The waves slapping the walkways was the loudest sound as Mac fought to calm herself.

Should have stuck with a memo.

"If ignorance protected you, I've taken that away," she went on. "If staying uninvolved was some kind of defense, I'm asking you to risk yourselves. Not because I don't want you safe—" The word broke. Mac clenched her hands into fists and forced herself to keep speaking. "But because I don't believe there is safety for anyone, or any world, until we resolve this.

"I know what you can do," she finished, "better than anyone. Will you?"

Her heart thudded in the hush. Just when Mac thought she'd have to keep talking, with nothing left to say, someone shouted from a walkway: "Can we have the ribs first?"

The irreverent demand was followed immediately by a distant warbling, "Hide them from Mac!"

As if they'd all been waiting for a signal, the chant began and grew. "No Ribs for Mac! No Ribs for Mac! Mac gets SALAD and BEER!!!"

Mac blinked away tears. An instant later, she was pulling salad out of her hair.

The Ro had waited this long, she reminded herself.

"What, exactly, was that?" Sing-li asked, leaning against a wall. He took a slug of his beer and regarded Mac thoughtfully.

Dusk had come and gone, laying its curtain of darkness everywhere but here. Base was lit from pod to dock, the guide lights along rail and stair upped for the occasion. Mac wondered what passing fish thought of the glow above. *If any approached given the volume of music.*

"Vintage Mac," Emily said, tugging Mac's hair. "Scary, isn't she? I did try to warn you."

He laughed. "Wasn't me who needed warning. Hollans was—well, let's say he was surprised."

"Will he interfere?" Mac asked.

"How? To move your people out of here by force, he'd have to declare an emergency—and prove one exists. Not a good time for false alarms. He certainly can't stop them doing what they normally do. Between us?" He tilted his head back for another slug. "Between us, Mac, I think Hollans and a few others are grateful for the help—not that they'll ever admit it. They aren't supposed to involve civilians, however qualified."

Mac snorted at this, but relaxed. She found another bit of wilted greenery in her shirt and pulled it out to nibble. The party had reached the friendly standing crush of people stage on the terraces, although some dared sit on the steps. There was dancing, but in the gallery—less chance of someone twirling into the ocean. "You'll keep an eye on the place."

It hadn't been a question, but he nodded. "Easier now that stealth isn't an option. Although," he indicated his flamboyant shirt, "there's something to be said for camouflage."

"Mac. You coming?" Emily was half dancing already, those around her clearing a small space and smiling. "There won't be any room left."

"Shame," Mac muttered, but she nodded. A promise was a promise, however onerous.

There was, however, one thing to do first. Before she could change her mind, she stepped up to Sing-li and kissed him firmly on the mouth.

And before he could say or do anything, Mac grabbed Emily's arm and hurried them both away.

"As good-byes go, not bad," her friend commented. "Quick. To the point. A tad public. I think you shocked poor Charlie."

"Shut up, Em," Mac suggested.

"Just giving my expert opinion."

"Didn't ask for it." Mac ran her tongue over her lips, tasting beer, and grinned.

Emily gave a throaty chuckle. "You never do."

Noticing they were about to pass her office, now Emily's, Mac slowed and gave the other a sidelong look. "I'm leaving in an hour. Did you want to check the gear now?"

"Do you?"

Mac lifted the beer she'd nursed since supper and tapped the one Emily carried. "Not really."

"Dr. Connor. You shock me."

A sudden buzz brought three Preds, who'd been sitting against the wall by Mac's door, scrambling to their feet. Mac stepped in front of the first before they could start running. "Turn them off," she said gently.

"What?" said one.

"Mac," protested another. "It's the transient pod off Field Station One. Gotta be. We've been waiting all summer—"

She heard the pain in their voices, saw the anguished curves of their shoulders as the full consequence of what they'd promised came home at last, and couldn't say another word.

"Turn'm off," ordered the third student, tearing free her own wrist alarm and stuffing it into a pocket. "It's okay, Mac. We forgot. Habit, you know."

"Look on the bright side," Emily told them. "You can go to the dance." This notion drew smiles and they trotted away—if not happy, then willing to be distracted.

Mac watched them go. "Thanks, Em," she said after a minute.

"You do realize I'd take all this as my fault—moan, beat my chest, and so forth—except you're doing such a great job of assuming the blame I can't be bothered."

Mac's lips twisted. "Anytime."

Emily tipped her bottle against Mac's. "Let's go visit your fish," she said. "I can dance later."

From the lowermost loading dock, at the end of Base closest to the Tannu River, the sounds of the party, the murmur of voices and music, blended into the restless slap of waves against mem-wood. Sitting on the stern of Norcoast's venerable barge, Mac stretched her bare feet downward and was rewarded by the occasional flip of chill water on her toes. She didn't need to see into the depths to know what swam there. *What the Ro had left was another matter.*

"One day you'll do that and something with teeth will think they're bait."

"Obviously, you've never tried fishing off the dock," Mac countered, wiggling her toes pensively. "I'd be lucky to get a nibble."

"What could *They* have left, Mac?" Emily didn't seem to expect an answer *which,* Mac thought, *was just as well.* "The memory of that day, of the earthquake . . . I know I was there. I know it. I remember being . . . feeling . . . insignificant. No. Small. That was it. I can't trust what I recall of dimensions, Mac. Time, space, they blur together. But this . . . I think I felt small because I was near something much bigger."

"Big could be good," Mac decided, leaning back against one of the huge coils of rope that lined the stern access. She studied the horizon. Black on black. A trace of mauve where clouds hovered over the mountains and caught starlight. Lines of fluorescence straggled across the dark water, rising and falling as if the sea itself was breathing.

"How?"

"Harder to hide."

"*They're* experts."

"So," Mac said firmly, "are we. And we have you." She looked at her companion, nothing more than a darker shadow. "We do, don't we, Em?"

"Looks that way," the other replied, the words spaced apart and thoughtful. "I admit it shook me, remembering . . . what I remembered. But being here, Mac?" Emily took a deep breath and let it out. "How did you know? I feel like myself, for the first time in too long. Oh, I'll be able to work, all right." A low, sparkling laugh. "And I still know the best pubs, for when I've had it with the peace and isolation."

Something for Sing-li to deal with, Mac thought, more amused than worried. "Try not to completely disappear on me again, okay?"

"You, too."

Mac couldn't help looking up, to where stars appeared between the clouds.

Some weren't stars at all, she realized, but way stations in orbit, shuttles moving to and fro, the endless traffic of a world whose markets and interests spanned thousands of solar systems beyond its own. *Such a long way from home.*

"I'll be back as soon as I can," she vowed, to herself as much as Emily. "And while I might not have a pub in reach if I get bored, well, there's the Fourteen and Oversight show."

"Poor Charlie," Emily chuckled, then her voice turned serious. "You take care of him, Mac."

"I'll do what I can, but that Myg . . ."

"You know what I mean."

Mac pressed her lips together, then let out a slow breath. "I won't promise, Em. I can't. You saw what I did today. I put Base, all these people, at risk without hesitation. You, too." She shuddered. "What's worse—I'd do it again."

"Don't take too much credit. You didn't put anyone at risk, Mac," Emily corrected. "*They* did. You simply cut some red tape. Although I hope you realize I'm going to continue my work on the Survivors, between helping the others search."

Tossed down like a gauntlet. Mac smiled to herself. "I couldn't imagine trying to stop you, Dr. Mamani."

Instead of the quip she expected, Emily said quietly: "You're the only one who could."

Mac let the words resonate between them, dismayed by Emily's trust. Who was she to judge the value of another's life's work? Who was she to be right—or terribly wrong—about the application of that work to the present crisis?

A salmon researcher, sans fish.

The image struck Mac as funny, for no particular reason, and she relaxed very slightly. "We'll stay in touch. Let me know if you need anything—at least while I'm still in Sol System. After that, it might be more efficient to have Sing-li steal it for you."

"I'll keep that in mind. Handy, having your own spy."

"Until he takes off on some doubt-I'll-return-intact mission," Mac said, then blushed. *Good thing they were sitting in the dark.* She coughed.

"You're blushing, Mackenzie Connor."

"How can you—?" she closed her mouth.

"Too easy." Emily chuckled. "Still, if you think Mr. Jones could disappear on me in similar fashion, I'd better have an assistant who'll stay put. Hmmmm. There were some firm and energetic specimens in the rib queue earlier."

"Now who's too easy?"

"Is it my fault I appreciate the finer things in life?"

"Yes."

They sat in companionable silence after that. Mac didn't need to check the time. Half an hour left. Part of her seethed with pointless advice and all the other things people say when they imagine never having the chance again. *Don't do what I'd do?*

When Emily Mamani never acted on another's impulses?

Stay off the ocean?

When that was where Emily's Tracer would be used?

None of it was worth saying, not now.

The rest of her wanted nothing more than to sit here in the dark as long as possible, cradled by ocean, and listen to Emily's breathing. No need to fill the air with words. They'd spent more time in such peace together than chatter; while working, hours could pass.

Although not working and staying quiet, for Emily, couldn't last seconds. "What was it like?" she began brightly.

Mac bumped her head gently against the rope, twice, before giving up. "What was what like?"

"Meeting the Dhryn female. A life-form the size of a small city—had to be incredible."

"The Progenitor?" Mac ran her fingers through her short hair. "Big."

"Mac."

"Okay," she relented. "My initial reaction? Glee. Those stuffy old biology texts were wrong again. She blew away any prediction on the maximum size of a living being. After that, I got busy trying to figure out how she could be that large: a colonial organism, perhaps a fluid body core with a living skin, a few wilder ideas. But once I saw her face . . ." Her foot was engulfed in a taller wave than most and Mac pulled it up, shaking off the drops. "Once we started talking, I forgot her size. The Progenitor's a remarkable person. I think you'd like each other."

Emily's reply was drowned out by a prolonged *whompf* of wind as a transport lev, a mammoth one, flew by overhead. It was towing sleds, each loaded with an orbit-capable shipping crate. *They'd better not be planning to put her into one of those again,* Mac told herself grimly, but the lev passed Base. They watched as it followed the coast, heading for what had been the Succession Documentation and Research Pod. *The Ministry was apparently done with subtle.*

"Poor Marty," she murmured. He'd avoided her altogether after her announcement. She'd last seen him curled in a corner, nursing a bottle of what hadn't been beer. "He'd built such a wonderful dock. And that slide?"

"Won't be wasted—the dock anyway. And they'll need his survey data and maps." Emily, apparently done with sitting, too, got to her feet. Mac, reluctantly, followed suit. "Hate to say it, but the next one will likely be yours, Mac. You'd better get ready. Unless you're wearing those on the trip."

Mac considered the notion of wearing her very comfortable cottage shorts to Myriam. *Fourteen would love it.*

"I'll change," she agreed.

They climbed up the short ladder and retrieved their respective footwear, Emily's glittering in the dock lights. Given it was August, Mac shook each shoe and, from the second, caught a spider in her hand. She released it on the dock.

"Mac, before you go—" Emily said. "About the Progenitor—"

"Oh. Right. Tell you what." Mac finished fastening her shoe and stood. "I'll record a better description and send it. There'll be plenty of time while we ship out to the gate. Right now, I—"

"Mac." Emily touched her arm. "Please. Listen to me."

She looked up and was warned by her friend's anxious expression. "This isn't another confession, is it?" *There had to be,* Mac sincerely hoped, *limits to even Emily's past.*

"No."

"Oh, good."

"No. It's not good, Mac. Don't you see? It's a pattern with you. This hanging on to the past—this loyalty to friends no matter what. You can't keep doing it. The Dhryn don't deserve it. Your friend Brymn transformed into a feeder and would have killed you. This Progenitor of yours, this remarkable person, could do the same, or worse. You can't trust any Dhryn."

Mac frowned. "We don't know enough about the species to make—"

"We know the Dhryn are a biological weapon, made and wielded by *Them.* Don't go out there believing you can save the ones you like." Emily took her arm, though she hadn't tried to leave. "The entire species has to be exterminated," she insisted. "*They* must be left helpless."

"It's hardly up to me, is it?" Mac said, freeing herself as gently as possible.

"Like it or not, you've become of interest to the people who will make that decision. A word at the wrong time, to the wrong ears? It could mean the wrong choice, Mac."

Mac felt her heart clench. "You're assuming there's a right one."

"There always is. The one that lets us survive."

Was survival a moral choice?

Mac shook her head, but not at Emily. "I'll try not to say anything to anyone. How's that?"

"Unlikely." Before Mac could say a word, Emily's arms went around and held her tight. "Less trust," she urged, her lips to Mac's ear. "I want you back. Hear me?"

"More air," wheezed Mac, doing her own holding. *Too thin,* she fussed to herself. *Her friend was skin over bone.* "No saving the universe without me."

"Deal."

They clung to each other a heartbeat longer, then Emily broke away. She pirouetted on the barge deck, pearls swinging. "Say hi to our Nik for me," she said. Three quick steps took her up to the dock where she dipped in a graceful curtsy, the Sinzi fabric flowing with the motion. "And don't be so serious all the time." Over her shoulder, as she tripped lightly along the walkway toward the music. *"Adios, hermana-muyo."* Sister-mine.

And Mac was alone.

"Just once," she complained, "I'd like to make the grand exit." The empty barge didn't comment.

She wrapped her arms around herself, holding Emily's fading warmth.

Mac made her way to Pod Four, where two first-floor student rooms had been upgraded to house visitors to Base. The upgrading, from what she could tell, consisted of temporarily moving out the students and most, though not all, of their gear. There was the charming addition of a clear vase filled with pebbles and a dead twig. Since she'd only wanted the room to change from her Myg-ripped blouse and store her bag, she hadn't bothered to ask for a live one.

Striding along the walkway, fingers trailing over the rope rail, she was aware of Sing-li following in the background. He'd more than kept his distance while she sat with Emily. Now, when she could have used the company, it didn't feel right to change the order of things.

Not to mention she'd said good-bye.

The party in and around Pod Three continued without her, a blaze of light and sound that made its own bubble within the surrounding night. *Just as well.* It had taken hours to say hello to everyone; doing farewells, especially after the shock of this afternoon, could take days. Not to mention the beer . . . and arguments . . . possibly maudlin behavior.

Better to slip away in the dark.

Zimmerman, his large head tucked deep into the collar of an orchid-print shirt, stood at the door of Pod Four. Shirt aside, he looked about as casual as the levs continuing to pass overhead. Mac smiled a greeting. "Hope my bag's been behaving itself."

"Hi, Mac." Almost a whisper—but that was Zimmerman's normal voice. "All quiet." He looked wistfully at Pod Three. "Here, anyway."

"Don't worry," she told him. "The students will be rolling home in a few hours and someone always falls in."

"I don't swim." As if fearing this sounded less than professional, he added: "Tie has his skim ready. I'll watch."

"Did you get any ribs?"

His teeth flashed. "Did you leave any?"

"Lies. All lies," she complained, but gestured back at Sing-li, standing in the shadows. "You can grab some while he's here, I'm sure."

"I'll survive. You—some of us should be going with you, Mac," he said glumly. "This isn't right."

Mac smiled. "I'm happier knowing you'll be here, looking after my people—and yourselves, okay? You know Sing-li. He's a troublemaker."

"Sure, Mac." Zimmerman heaved a melancholy sigh that strained the buttons of his shirt. *He'd make a good Grimnoii,* Mac thought. "You'd better get ready. The lev's docked." He opened the door for her.

The pod felt abandoned, as if ready to be lifted for winter storage. Only the posters lining the walls and a pile of rain boots, several large enough to be buckets, proved anyone currently lived here. Stepping around and over the boots, Mac pushed open the door to the guest quarters, so designated by a large "No Students" sign, and looked for the bag she'd dumped on the bed.

What she saw instead were large pale feet, with reddish hairs on their toes.

The feet were at the end of equally pale legs, also hairy, which disappeared into a pair of dark blue baggy shorts. Case Wilson's shorts, to be precise, Case himself snoring peacefully, using her bag as a pillow.

Mac walked to the head of the bed and tugged her bag free. Case's head thumped down on the mattress and his eyes popped open, horror on his face the instant he saw her grinning down at him.

She'd never seen anyone scuttle from a bed quite that fast.

Or turn quite that red.

To give him time to recover, Mac took her bag to the desk, pushing aside the vase of pebbles with twig to make room for it. She rummaged inside for something intact and travel-suited. "Never let an alien do your packing, Case," she advised, lifting out the hockey puck to show him. "Even the well-intentioned sort."

"Mac. Dr. Connor. I'm really sorry—"

She found a serviceable pair of Base coveralls and forgave Two immediately. "Turn around."

"I—what are you doing?" he blurted as she began undoing her shirt, then whirled to face the wall.

"Changing," she explained, thinking it was obvious. Dropping her shorts and stepping into the coveralls, Mac added: "What I want to know is what you're doing here instead of being at the party." *Or attending the briefings already underway.* Taking her mind off what she'd started, Mac ran her finger up the coverall seam to fasten the front, then ran a hand through her hair. "Well?" she prompted.

He kept his back to her. *Even his ears were glowing red,* she noted, fascinated. "I . . . I . . ."

"You wanted to say good-bye?" she suggested.

This turned Case to face her, his expression nothing short of desperate. "No. Mac. I want to go with you. To the Dhryn planet."

It had to be something in the air. Or a disease. She shook her head. "Impossible. You can't."

"Why? Sam's going."

She blinked. "Sam who?"

"Sam Schrant. Martin's postdoc."

"Oh." Mac gathered herself. "That Sam. The meteorologist." And more. Schrant was a storm chaser, presently a leader in the field of catastrophic event modeling. She'd asked Mudge to grab Schrant for their group weeks before; the request had been mired in bureaucracy ever since. "I didn't know his clearance had gone through. I'm surprised it has, really." She put back the puck, added shirt and shorts, and closed her bag. "Good for Oversight. Though between us, the man's a menace. In a good way."

Case took a step toward her, his scarred hands open at his sides. "Mac. Listen. I'm good with machines. You don't grow up on a trawler without being able to handle hard work and whatever nature throws at you. And you know I've a level head."

Mac's eyes narrowed thoughtfully. "All true."

"Then I can come?" He edged closer, like some overeager puppy.

Mac edged back, trying not to be obvious about it. He was too tall for her to see his expression from this range without bending her neck an uncomfortable amount. She hit the desk and made it seem on purpose by hopping up on it, which put them at a more even height. *Bonus.* "No."

"But . . ."

"Do you like dancing, Case?"

His sea-washed eyes stared down at her. "What?"

"Do you like dancing?" Mac repeated.

"No. Not really. Why?"

"Even better. I want you to be Dr. Mamani's research assistant."

She might have asked him to jump in the ocean. *With blood-aroused sharks.* "No!"

Mac frowned. "You don't know what her research is—"

He put his hands palm-down on either side of the desk and leaned forward until his nose almost touched hers. "And I don't care."

Barbeque sauce breath. She stifled a giggle, quite sure that reaction would thoroughly offend the earnest young man. Who was, she guessed, upset enough. This close, all she could see were freckles and some patchy stubble.

"What's going on here?"

Mac ducked her head to peer under Case's arm. He lunged back, all the color draining from his face this time. She didn't blame him. Sing-li on his own was intimidating, despite the shirt. Add Zimmerman, nostrils flared and those improbable shoulders jamming the doorway?

Poor Case probably thought he was about to be dropped into that ocean.

"Do you mind?" she said acidly. "I'm briefing Mr. Wilson. He's applied to be Dr. Mamani's assistant."

The expressions as her explanation registered—on all three—were vastly entertaining. *Had she time for it.*

"Briefing," echoed Sing-li, doubt in his voice and the searing look he gave Case.

"I don't want to be Dr. Mamani's assistant," Case insisted.

Zimmerman, not to be left out, relaxed in the doorway and added with a sly grin, "Well, I've never had a briefing like that."

"What are you implying?" The return of his fiery blush didn't help Case's outraged dignity one bit, but Mac gave him credit. He looked willing to take on both agents.

"I have a lev to catch," she reminded all of them. "You three can bond later. Right now, I need another minute alone with Mr. Wilson. If you don't mind?"

Zimmerman half bowed his way out, still smirking. Sing-li gave Mac his "I don't like this" look but followed, saying only, "We'll be outside."

Once the door closed, Mac put her hands on her knees. "Sorry about that," she told Case. "Where were we?"

"I was saying no to having anything to do with her."

"Ah, yes." She kept her face carefully neutral. "Not the best first impression?"

"I know you've worked together for years." His honesty got the better of him. "But I don't get how. She's a—a—" he stopped there, probably viewing it as wise, and threw up his hands. "She doesn't take anything seriously."

Mac chewed her lower lip for a moment. "Emily Mamani," she said at last, "is a brilliant scientist, an innovative engineer, and can drink someone twice her mass under the table, so don't ever try. She's also a fraud. Not take things seriously? She's so serious—about everything imaginable—it's almost killed her. Despite what I said to everyone today, it's her device, the Tracer, that offers the best chance of finding whatever the Ro sent into Castle Inlet in time to make a difference."

Case sat down on the bed and stared at her. "She's a pretty good actor, then."

"That, too."

"Why does she need me?"

Because firm and energetic is easy. Mac resolutely ignored that memory, focusing on the troubled young man in front of her. "Emily's protected by the Ministry— Sing-li and his lot. Her recovery is being monitored by Dr. Stewart, also Ministry. She's—"

"'Sephe the statistician? She jams with Sasha's band in Pod Six most nights." He looked incredulous, as if musicians couldn't be spies. "You're kidding—"

Although Mac sympathized, she raised her eyebrow and Case subsided. "Emily was authorized to spend what she must, to use any and all resources here short of disrupting the season. Now that I've done the disrupting, her work will take priority."

"Sounds like she has enough help."

"Help she has, Case," Mac agreed. "All of it complicated. All of it with strings attached. Obligations, expectations. Fear. What Emily needs is someone who won't lie to her, for any reason. Someone she can trust. Won't be you, not at first. It'll take work. And," she finished with equal honesty, "incredible patience."

His eyes held an odd expression. "You want me to take your place."

"You could say that." Mac slid from the desk, then straightened her coveralls. She absently patted the pocket where she'd put her imp, checking it was there. "Will you do it?"

Case had stood as well, more slowly, as if deep in thought. He gazed down at her and grimaced. "I'd rather go with you, Mac. But if this is what you want— I'll do my best."

Finally, something going her way.

Mac beamed at him. "There is a bright side, Case," she promised. "You'll be heading out to sea. Make sure Em knows your background on trawlers when you apply."

By his look, she'd dismayed him again. "Apply?"

Her lips quirked sideways. "Next lesson about Emily: if she makes a decision, she'll stand by the result. Just tell her the truth—I made you do it. She'll take a closer look. And she'll see what I do." *Integrity, inner strength, and a nice dose of stubborn pragmatism that will annoy her constantly—and keep her sane.* Mac was satisfied.

"What do you see, Mac?" Case asked in a low voice, eyes intent on hers. "I'd like to know."

She might not have Emily's experience with men, young or otherwise, but Mac was reasonably sure Case wouldn't appreciate the attributes she'd listed to herself as much as she did. Instead, she made a show of checking the time. "I see I'm going to be late." She glanced around the room once more, then gave him a nod. "Whatever happens, thank you, Case. I appreciate this more than I can say. Good luck."

"You're welcome," he replied. For an instant, she thought he meant to reach for her, and she braced for a hug, but instead he opened the door. "Good luck to you, too, Dr. Connor."

Relieved, Mac smiled at him and started through the door, already feeling the tug of impatience. *Time to move.* At the sight of her, Sing-li straightened from where he'd slouched against the wall in the corridor.

"Mac?"

She glanced back.

Case, who was much closer than she'd expected, ducked his head and kissed her on the mouth.

"'Bye," he added, then walked away.

Sing-li snickered. Mac gave him a look and he stopped, but the smirk looked permanent.

"Can we go now?" she asked dryly.

He gestured her ahead with a gallant bow that didn't quite work with the rows of happy-faced cookies on his shirt. "After you, Dr. Connor."

She went out, giving Zimmerman a smile, then strode down the walkway toward the dock, her feet making reassuringly normal sounds on the memwood. The music from the party was still thumping. The cool night air smelled of salt and fish and growing things.

The world was as it was.

She could just make out Case, his long bare legs pale against the dark water as he headed for Pod Three, and quickly looked away.

As kisses went, it had been quick and almost clumsy. His lips had been cold.

What it hadn't been, Mac decided with some misgiving, *was the kiss of a friend.*

A somber group awaited Mac at the dock's edge, consisting of Kammie, John, Tie, and, of course, Mudge. A slightly larger and noisier group of students surrounded their fellow who, thanks to Mudge, would accompany them. 'Screens hovered in the air as they hurriedly exchanged critical information at this final moment.

Likely games.

Mac's eyes widened when she saw Tie wearing what appeared to be an oversized flare pistol in a holster belted to his waist. "Where did you get that?" she demanded, keeping her voice down. *Not that the students appeared interested.* There was another sticking out of his pants pocket. "Those," she corrected.

Tie looked abashed but determined. "They're mine. A little old, but they work."

"You don't carry weapons," she objected. "That's their job." A nod to Sing-li

The agent wasn't smirking now, his face drawn in grim lines. "We can't be everywhere at once. We did thorough backgrounds, Mac. Tie, a few others, are qualified and we contacted them. What did you expect, when you made Base a target?"

"But—" Mac closed her mouth on what was, in truth, a meaningless objection. Instead, she gazed at Tie and tried to imagine Base's opinionated mechanic as a warrior. *Having seen him defend what he considered his fleet of vessels from neglectful students,* she decided, *it wasn't much of a stretch after all.*

Tie put two fingers to his forehead in a mock salute. "Did a stint in the military—before you were born, Mac," he told her. "Don't worry. My favorite discussion-closer is still a wrench."

At that moment, Sam Schrant, his friends having left—a couple in tears, walked up and offered Mac his hand. "Hi, Mac. I appreciate this."

His dark hair flopped over his high forehead, almost hitting the tops of his glasses. *She'd tucked Nik's in her bag.* Despite bruises of exhaustion lining his eyes—Sam was infamous for his all-nighters—he looked ready to go. A neon-orange backpack hung from his shoulders, its seams ready to burst.

"We'll see if you thank me once you've been to Myriam," she said, but smiled and took his hand. "Welcome to the Origins Team, Sam."

His eyes, tired or not, gleamed. "I've been doing some prelim work, Mac. That's one incredible orbit. I can't wait."

She could. Mac indicated the waiting lev. "Be my guest."

After Sam said his farewells to the rest and boarded, Mac faced Kammie and John, wondering what to say.

Find the Ro object and you can get back to work?

or . . .

Welcome to my life.

It didn't help that Kammie, always quick to tears, was quietly sobbing into a handkerchief, or that John Ward, for the first time since they'd met, had no expression on his face at all.

A quiet *harrumph* shook Mac from her paralysis. "Schedules, Norcoast, schedules. We can't keep the pilot waiting."

"Yes, of course." She looked toward the well-lit pod and waved. Several of the figures milling on the terrace waved back.

One, standing on the walkway below, didn't.

"Good-bye," Mac said, as much to Emily as Kammie and John, then walked up the ramp into the lev.

She didn't turn around again.

- CONTACT -

THE WINDS CURLED AROUND the standing ones, washing their feet with red sand. Their ranks were legion; their patience greater still.

If patience was felt by stone.

Beyond, where the landscape fractured into a maze of rock cuts and channels, dark eyes watched and measured from the shadows. When the winds paused, when the first rank could be seen through clearing air, then would begin the span of days in which the clicks of poet and penitent could be heard. Only then . . .

Only then, would the Loufta come forth to build.

Others waited, too.

"Remind me how rich we're going to be, *Se* Zali."

The Frow scampered headfirst down the sheer cliff face, fingers finding and releasing holds so quickly *se* appeared to be falling. "Stinking rich," *se* assured *se's* partner on reaching the bottom. Rather than stand, *se* hung like a crawling Myg *sketlik,* albeit with skinlike web stretched taut between *se's* limbs. *Se's* head twisted at an unlikely angle to show *se's* smug expression.

"I don't see why you can't stand up properly. Idiot. You realize you accomplish Numbers Two and Three on my list of why I should never have crewed with a Frow." Oonishalapeel's list was long and still growing, though since his encounter with a Human medic, he now had a word for Number Two, arachnophobia, and a drug to dull the symptoms.

Putting up with the smugness of any Frow came with the territory. "You're sure we're safe from the Dhryn?"

"My *mater's* fifteenth sib-cousin serves the home world station where all incoming data on attacks and sightings are processed, my anxious friend. You read Se Lasserbee's latest report. No attacks. No sightings. No Dhryn. The mighty Myrokynay have destroyed them. Calm your fears, 'Peel." *Se* Zali touched the solitary point on *se's* hat, the Frow equivalent of polite self-deprecation. "You would do well to remember I am a soldier, capable of ensuring our safety at all times."

"Irrelevant. And your irrelevant hat is Number Fifteen," 'Peel proclaimed. "Though I'll keep in mind you're willing to die first."

"Hush." The Frow swung about and scuttled up the cliff in a heave of membrane, uniform, and fingers. Grit rained down. "Do you hear that?" *se* asked, stopping a short distance up.

'Peel made a show of dusting himself. "Making false alarms is Number Ten."

"Forget your boring list, 'Peel. Attend. Is the wind quieting?" *Se* climbed a bit higher and leaned out, neck ridges unfolding. *Se's* eyes closed as *se* listened intently. "Yes . . . I think so."

'Peel opened his collapsible chair and sat down with a thump. "Idiot. You said the same thing yesterday." The Myg pulled out his imp, preparing to add to his list. "Let me see. I'm at two hundred and twenty-four, the smell of Frow breath in the tent. No, Two hundred and twenty-five, the way Frow leftovers always rot. This will be—"

"It's time!" *Se* Zali plummeted to the canyon floor, where he tilted upright cautiously, both hands reaching out in agonizingly slow motion for the support of nearby boulders. He kept shouting. "The winds are dying. The creatures will free themselves at any moment. Call the others!" he ordered. "We must set the nets. Get the processing units ready. They won't stay soft long!"

'Peel glared through his workscreen at the Frow. "Irrelevant. Irrelevant!" Their camp had been made in cooling shadows, but the constant wind-driven grit had made sleeping outdoors impossible. The other five, two more Frow and three blissfully quiet Dainaies, were still in bed. "Wait for the monitoring station to confirm it."

"If we delay, we could be too late. Any emerging Loufta will go through its ascension and be useless."

"Number two hundred and twenty-seven," the Myg crowed. "Making up ridiculous names for alien biology—geology. Whatever it is."

"The name fits."

" 'Ascension?' It's a word about climbing. You climb. Do they climb? No. Idiot!"

"Stop calling me that!"

"Calling you what?"

Neither noticed the wind settling around them, their argument loud in an ominous stillness. But both felt the rain.

The Loufta sensed the change in the wind as well.

They shuttered their ebony eyes and dug themselves deeper into stone. Perhaps in another thousand years conditions would be right. And they would pull themselves from the veins of the mountains, crawl across the hushed plain, and build the next rank of standing ones from their own hardening flesh in honor of their god.

Another time.

The desperate mouths drank what they could find.

It wasn't enough.

The Progenitor was starving.

The *oomlings* had been sacrificed. All that was Dhryn must follow.

Nothing mattered but that the Progenitor survive the Great Journey.

They hurried to fulfill their destiny.

- 9 -

DELAY AND DIVERSION

"**P**ERFECT TIMING, AS ALWAYS, MAC." Sebastian Jones, Earthgov wildlife liaison for this portion of the remote northwest, grabbed their bags and effortlessly tossed them into the back of his battered skim. He grinned at her. "Chinook've started up the Klondike. Looks to be a big run."

"I'd love to say that's why we're here," Mac answered, fastening her jacket against the evening's bite, "but we're just passing through." *Though why here, in Dawson City, was a question she'd like answered.* The public transit system connecting to the Arctic launch fields stopped in Whitehorse on the way, where there were year-round facilities.

The Ministry lev, for reasons not explained to its passengers, had touched down instead at the business end of the narrow paved strip that had first served Dawson City as an airport. It wasn't that anyone had intentionally preserved the entire strip, although it was handy for keeping levs, freight, and passengers out of the summer mud. It was more that the unassuming length of flat pavement was useful—a place to learn to ride a bike, land a glider, or race skims. What did get removed, regularly, were the signs prohibiting such activities due to the hazard of incoming lev traffic.

The Yukon was like that, Mac remembered fondly. *Regulations subject to reality. And who, or what, could survive on its own was entirely welcome to do so.*

What couldn't? "Thought you had a new skim, Sebastian."

He looked chagrined. "Locked up on me the first time it got chilly. Took it back to Edmonton for my mom. This one—" he gave the old machine a proud smack that shook something loose underneath, "—keeps going. Shouldn't have let them give me another."

Mudge had been talking to their lev pilot, *no doubt bonding.* After some mutual nodding, he came over to Mac, cautiously avoiding Sebastian's wheezing vehicle. "He's leaving. There's been some delay in our orbit connection," he said, sounding irritated. "We're to be picked up by another lev in the morning, rather than continue to the Baffin spaceport."

"Did he say why?" Mac shook her head to stop his answer. "Of course not." Not that it mattered whether they faced some bureaucracy or mechanical failure. Delay was delay. *Could have lingered at Base.* But the moment that thought crossed her mind, she dismissed it. Longer would only have made it more difficult.

What to do next was another question, Mac thought, looking around. They were standing in the overlapped pools of light that illuminated the landing area, the small building that, during office hours only, housed the ticket office and washrooms, and Sebastian's battered skim. The moisture from their breath fogged in front of their faces. *Not quite below freezing,* Mac judged. She didn't mind the temperature; it kept her awake. Mudge covered a yawn and she sympathized. Being in the dark might suit their body clocks, still on New Zealand time, but Mudge hadn't slept on the way to Castle Inlet and she had only slept a little. They were both down one night's sleep already.

"Where are you taking us, Sebastian?" she asked, stifling a yawn of her own. "Dawson?"

"Unless you prefer to stay here for the night." He made it sound a perfectly viable option, which to him it was, and Sam's eyes widened into saucers.

"Not this time, thanks," Mac said before the poor student thought she'd make them camp out on the tarmac. "We've a long trip ahead and I, for one," she yawned again, "could use a rest. In town would be great."

"But not in that, Norcoast, surely," Mudge protested, pointing to Sebastian's skim. "It's worse than yours."

The skim's engine had settled into an anxious mutter. The skim itself, however, was vibrating up and down—which, since it was floating atop a repeller field and the pavement beneath their feet wasn't moving, was, Mac admitted, somewhat alarming. "Few too many summers over gravel beds," Sebastian drawled. "Hop in. She'll smooth out."

"Don't worry, Oversight," Mac told him, climbing in first. "There are seat belts . . . oh, wait. Not anymore. Best hold on."

Sebastian kept the roof open during the ride and didn't use lights, relying on the feel of skim to keep them centered over the old road, made of coarse gravel dredged up during the heyday of mining. Such a road around Castle Inlet would have disappeared in a season without use. Here, regrowth took centuries and the stone remained exposed.

The vibrations, though teeth-chattering at first, vanished once the skim picked up speed. She knew the road followed the curved bank of the Klondike River, but the landscape was hidden in darkness. Mac leaned her seat back and watched the sky, picking out old friends. She'd missed the northern constellations.

She'd neglected to look at Myriam's stars, having been a bit preoccupied on the ground. *She'd have time now.*

She heard Dawson City before they got there, and smiled. The ghosts of the past were feverishly reliving their era before summer's end. Player pianos and other antique instruments hammered out tunes from the first, great gold rush; tourists and those who entertained them filled the dirt streets and danced along the wooden boardwalks, swelling the local population a thousandfold. Under a sun that spent most of summer in the sky, and surrounded by a sweeping landscape dominated by ice, water, and rock, it was a party setting like no other.

With one drawback.

"Are you sure there's room for us?" Mac asked doubtfully.

Sebastian gave his quiet laugh. "Not lying down. You'll stay at my place. I've turned out the dogs for the night."

"Thank you." Mac followed this with a gentle kick to Mudge's shin, having heard him take a deep breath as though planning to comment. Their host was a private person, despite his easy charm, more comfortable alone in the wilderness than with anyone else. Mac counted herself fortunate that Sebastian had taken her under his wing since she'd first come to sample Yukon salmon metapopulations a decade ago.

Then again, she thought, *we're both capable of going for days without a word. Not like some.*

At that, she poked her toe into Mudge's other shin for insurance.

Sebastian's home overlooked the Yukon River, downstream from its junction with the Klondike and Bonanza Creek at Dawson itself. Mac, having seen his place in daylight, knew it for a simple, sturdy wood building with a wraparound screened porch, nestled within a copse of twisted conifers. Smaller than her family's cabin, with only two rooms, but more like a home, with every centimeter crowded with personality. She remembered the rafters of the living room/kitchen had been laden with pale wood, waiting to be carved into paddles during the winter night. Two walls had been lined with shelves of physical books, like those she'd read for practice, while the third had boasted a mammoth wood stove, old enough for a museum. But it worked, so it was used. A small counter, with sink and cupboards; a big table, with one chair. For her previous visit, Sebastian had provided a folding stool.

Arriving now, in the dark, all that could be made out was a flickering glow in one window.

And barking. There had to be over two dozen huge huskies in the pack contributing to that enthusiastic part-welcome, part-warning.

"Back into trekking?" Mac shouted over the din. "Didn't think you had the time."

"My housemate's team."

Housemate? Mac shook her head in disbelief. *Leave the planet and look what happens.* "Anyone I know?"

"Not a salmon person." As if this settled it.

A little stung, she defended herself. "I do know people outside my field, Sebastian."

"Gloria McNeal? Polar bear endocrinology?"

"Maybe not that far outside my field," Mac conceded.

Sebastian kicked on the skim lights while they grabbed their bags, the wash of illumination passing over gray stone, swathes of sand, and low tufts of spent alpine flowers. The huskies, silenced as if by a signal, blinked their glowing eyes and yawned to show white gleaming teeth, before jumping back on the roofs of their doghouses. Sebastian had set wider, flat stones in a path leading into the house and they followed these to the porch. Sam's head twisted to look at the dogs. "Think we'll have time to see them run?" he asked her as they climbed the steps.

"Need I remind you, Dr. Schrant, that we're already behind schedule?" Mudge answered testily. "And what's wrong with your power?" This as Sebastian opened the door and the light within was revealed as coming from the stove's banked fire.

Their host lit the lantern on the table before answering. "We don't get broadcast here. Part of the charm."

"Charm?" Sam said faintly, hugging his backpack as if the devices inside were endangered.

Mac grinned. The lantern's rich warm light filled the room, revealing quite a bit of charm as far as she was concerned. Sebastian's housemate had added her touch in the presence of thick braided rugs on the floor, an artful mosaic of pelt samples hanging on the wall by the door, and a second chair at the table.

"Gloria's still in Tuktoyaktuk. You two can sleep there." Sebastian indicated the door to the bedroom. "Mac. Couch. I'll take the porch." He paused. "Anyone hungry? No? Then g'night." With that, he grabbed a blanket from a chest and went out.

Mudge looked at the couch, a sagging tapestried giant almost as old as the stove, then at Mac. She smiled at his expression. "It's more comfy than it looks," she promised, tossing her bag on one end. "Good night, you two."

Sam eyed the dark doorway and didn't move. "I didn't bring a light," he said, still clutching his bag.

Mudge *harrumphed,* pulling one from a pocket. "Come with me."

"Is there—?" Sam looked from one to the other. "Will we have to—"

Mac managed to keep a straight face. The meteorologist wasn't a camper—his data came from remotes and his idea of rough living likely included having to leave his desk to get a drink. *Probably imagined leaves and grizzly bears.* "There's a bathroom off the bedroom," she said, "with plumbing. And a very nice sauna. Sebastian lives independently. He doesn't do without." She didn't bother mentioning the solar panels he'd installed for his imp and skim battery.

A little northern mystique never hurt.

After the others disappeared into the bedroom, Mac turned the lantern down and sat in the new chair. She listened, chin on her hands, to the hushed but clear argument over who would have which side, the brief debate over the best way to light a lantern, and finally the exhausted muttering about trying to sleep and people who needed lights on and there was a schedule. The light under the door went off shortly after the voices stopped.

She smiled and blew out her light.

Outside, the view was forever. Mac sat on the bottom step, out from the porch roof so the stars made a dome overhead, and pulled the thick blanket around her shoulders.

Quietly, from the dark behind her. "Company?"

"Up to you," she replied.

Sebastian came and sat one step above her, easing his long frame back to rest on his elbows. His legs stretched past Mac, ending in white socks.

Without effort, she added him to her overwhelming awareness of the world around her, as intensely real as the long bare hills rolling like waves to the southeast, the black ribbon of water below in the canyon it carved, the crisp cedar-scented air she drew into her nostrils. A dog twitched in its sleep, its feet scratching furiously along the roof of its house. Closer, a scurry as something small dodged their feet to head under the step.

As if to remind her not all things were small or close or needing a roof, a howl sliced the night. The huskies gave low *woofs* of interest, then their heads thudded back down.

"Polar bears," Mac said finally. "How's that work?"

The man beside her gave a low chuckle. "Until pack ice, she helps with the grizzly census. Populations overlap near here."

"Handy." Mac pulled her knees up so she could wrap them in the blanket too, trying not to be envious. Here he was, in an area as remote and isolated as humanly possible in the modern world, and he'd found a fellow biologist to share his life.

While she had—what—an offworld spy who usually wore a suit.

As for sharing anything, that remained part of a future Mac wasn't interested in contemplating. Not now.

Not during her last hours on Earth.

"What's it like?" Sebastian asked unexpectedly. "Out there."

She considered the question. "Like here," she answered after a moment. "You watch your step. And everywhere else becomes—smaller."

He fell silent, as if she'd said enough.

Mac counted shooting stars for a while, then watched a pair of tiny lights trace out the river below. *Probably the ferry making its night run.* She followed the lights until they disappeared around the next sharp bend.

She looked up in time to see a luminescent sheet of green unfurl across the sky. With a gasp, Mac threw off the blanket and started to rise to her feet. She sank down again as pink joined the display, then purples. "Mouse," she lied, her teeth chattering with more than the chill. Ashamed, she fumbled to rewrap herself.

But it was the same color. The same . . .

"Admit it, Mac. You're cold." He sounded amused. "That'll teach you to live in the tropics and lose your conditioning."

Before she could protest she'd done nothing of the sort, Sebastian slipped down to the step she was on and gathered her up, blanket and all, so she could lean back against his shoulder and still see the stars.

Mac let herself relax into his so-Human warmth.

A shame it couldn't take away the fear.

"Dr. Connor."

The strange whisper woke her, but she froze, eyes shut, wondering why her name was the only sound she heard. *Why weren't the dogs barking?*

"Dr. Connor. We don't have much time." The voice became distant, as if speaking to someone else. "Why isn't she waking up? Is there something wrong with—"

She recognized that impatient snap, even muffled. *Hollans?*

Mac opened her eyes, finding herself nose to nose with a hulking silhouette.

"Good," she heard Hollans say. "Would you come with me, Dr. Connor?" The silhouette moved back.

As she sat up, the arm that had been around her fell away.

"Sebas—?" Mac lost the word, her mouth too dry. *What had Hollans done?* She moved her tongue around, found some moisture. "Sebastian!"

She reached out and found him. He was lying beside her on the steps, body flaccid, head back. Mac gave him a gentle prod but he didn't stir, snoring quietly. She glared at the silhouette and didn't bother to whisper. "What did you do to him?"

"Your friend will be fine." A hand appeared in her way, and Mac resisted the urge to slap it aside as she climbed to her feet on her own.

She felt normal. A little cramped and with a sore hip, but nothing that couldn't be explained by falling asleep on a cold rustic staircase. *Except she hadn't fallen asleep.*

No sign of dawn yet. A faint red glow illuminated the ground between their feet. *An invitation.* "This way, please, Dr. Connor."

"I'm certainly not leaving him like this."

"Someone will watch. Please, Dr. Connor."

Hard to argue with someone insistently polite. Giving in, Mac tarried to roll up her blanket and wedge it under Sebastian's head and shoulders, taking in as much of her dark surroundings as she could. No sign of Mudge or Schrant. Hollans must have come for her.

Wonderful.

Using the light to find the stony path, then to avoid larger stones once they'd left it, Hollans led Mac past too-quiet doghouses to the looming bulk of a waiting lev. Its door opened, the interior dimmed so she didn't have to squint to see there was no one waiting inside.

"You set this up," she accused, once they'd climbed in and taken seats.

"The delay?" He nodded and pulled off the goggles he'd worn. "Resume normal lighting." The increase was gradual, easy on her eyes. "Would you like a drink, Dr. Connor?"

Kid gloves were never a good sign, Mac decided, now more worried by this midnight meeting than irritated. "Sebastian didn't know," she said.

It wasn't a question, but he answered anyway. "We didn't need to involve anyone else. We can always find you, Dr. Connor."

At the reminder, she involuntarily rubbed her right arm, though the mark from the implant needle had faded months ago. Its result would outlast her bones. *Not a comfort.* "I'll take coffee, black," she said. "What's this about, Hollans? Why the secrecy?"

"Tea." He regarded her levelly. "Dr. Connor, we've had our differences. I'm aware you don't like me much."

"I wasn't aware I had to," she countered, then flashed a humorless grin. "You don't like me either. I'm too—" *what was the latest?* "—blunt."

"That part I like." His smile was barely warmer than hers. "If you're going to be wrong, you'll do it in the open. Saves all sorts of excuses and investigations."

Mac shot to her feet. "Is that why we're here?" she demanded hotly. "I wasn't wrong to bring my people into this, Hollans, and I'll defend that to—"

"Sit down. Please. You don't have to defend anything, Dr. Connor. Thank you." This to the black-armored agent, anonymous behind his or her visor, who arrived from the front of the lev with a steaming mug in each gloved hand. Mac took hers absently and nodded her thanks, eyes on Hollans. She sat and put the mug on the arm of her chair to cool.

Should have asked for ice.

Hollans waited until the agent had closed the door. "And thank you," he told her.

Mac narrowed her eyes, now more than worried.

Bernd Hollans, the Ministry's top official in matters of the Dhryn and Myrokynay, which meant representing all humanity in the current fight for survival, sat quietly, sipping tea, and let her study him.

A trim, tidy man, Hollans wore his usual suit, as if he'd come straight from a meeting at Earthgov or, more likely, the IU Consulate. He'd added a darker-than-usual shirt, with no cravat at its throat, and, she blinked, very sensible hiking boots. *Prepared, but in a hurry.*

His face gave her no clues. *No surprise.* From their first meeting, she'd thought his features well-suited his line of work: smooth enough to appear vigorous and friendly when he smiled, wrinkled enough to crease into imposing responsibility when he frowned. His eyes were the blue of old ice and missed nothing at all.

He'd been Nikolai Trojanowski's boss once before, and was again. What Mac had seen of that relationship didn't imply mutual liking either, but it held respect.

"You didn't come here to thank me for having common sense," she concluded out loud. Then, thinking over where they were, the way Hollans had drugged or otherwise incapacitated both dogs and people to approach her, the lack of guards, Mac nodded to herself, suddenly chilled. "No one else knows you're here, either. What's going on?" She heard the anxious edge to her voice and deliberately lightened it. "Don't tell me you want to come, too. We're crowded already and we haven't even left for Myriam."

He didn't bother smiling. "You aren't going to Myriam, Dr. Connor. Not the planet, anyway."

"I'm not?" Mac reached for her coffee, then decided against it. *Still too hot.* "Where am I going?" she asked numbly.

"Let me explain the situation, first. Like every species connected by the Naralax, we sent scout ships into the Dhryn System. Haven, not Myriam," he clarified.

Hot or not. She took the mug and a cautious sip. "I take it they found something."

"Several hundred somethings. Ships, empty and drifting. Freighters, transports, you name it. Some sending out automated distress calls—with Dhryn colony idents. We speculate—what is it?" This as Mac nodded.

"The Vessel," she recalled. "When I asked about the colonies, he said they were without Progenitors. That they were lost."

"Seems they found their way home. Looks as though they slipped through the gate in the initial chaos, then settled in a distant orbit to wait."

"No one saw them?" she protested.

"We're talking about spatial distances, not a puddle, Dr. Connor. Do you know how long it takes to sweep even a portion of a solar system for something the size of a Progenitor ship? Forget something a thousandth its size. The surprise isn't that they could hide—it's that we found them at all. The initial discovery was made by the Ar, also surprising—" at her blank look, he skipped what he was going to say. "The Trisulians in the system," his voice became flat, "initially did their utmost to contain the discovery, but the crew of the Ar ship was Human. They raised a fuss, our ships spread it, and details of the find were sent to the IU."

Mac realized she still held the hot mug and put it down, concentrating on keeping her hand and voice steady. "The Dhryn?"

"We don't know." She raised an eyebrow at this and he gave a tiny shrug. "I'm told the ships are nonfunctioning: some damaged, most with their doors open to space. Only three have been found so far intact and powered, but there's been no response from those to any signals. We'll know more when they're boarded. Which hasn't happened yet."

"Why?" She frowned. "What are they waiting for?"

"Reasonable caution, Dr. Connor. Some of the species in the recovery effort believe Dhryn sheathing can interfere with their scanners." He hesitated. "And there have been certain—jurisdictional—issues."

"Idiots." Mac snorted and picked up her mug again. "Let me guess," she told Hollans over its rim. "None of them wants the other to go first. Can they really believe we've time for this nonsense?"

"Some delays are useful," Hollans commented, the corner of his mouth twitching as if she'd amused him. "This 'nonsense' gave our Sinzi-ra time to consult with the IU inner council. As a result, the three intact ships—left that way—are being towed to the gates as we speak. To be brought to Myriam. And you, Dr. Connor."

Mac's mug dropped from her hands, tumbling to the floor. She lunged to retrieve it but missed. The arc of hot dark liquid ended on Hollans' sensible boots.

Bet he's glad he wore them. She made vague shooing gestures at the spill and looked in vain for something to wipe it.

"Leave it, Dr. Connor."

She'd been doing so well, too. "Sorry 'bout that," she muttered, sitting up.

"More coffee?"

"You've got to be kidding," Mac blurted.

Hollans' lips quirked again. "No coffee, then."

"It's bad enough you people have me working with archaeologists on a desert planet," she protested loudly, ignoring his comment. "I'm not a bloody starship engineer! I study—" Mac stopped there.

"Salmon," Hollans obliged, the quirk fading to something noncommittal. "We've engineers en route to Myriam, Dr. Connor. You know why we want you on those ships."

She glared.

He waited.

Games, even now. "To translate," she snapped.

"To translate," he repeated, giving a smug nod as if she'd pleased him by her startling grasp of essentials. "Until we can produce a full adult Dhryn lexicon, suited to Human sub-teach, we must make do with what we have. Or rather who. You, Dr. Connor."

She should have taken that second coffee, Mac thought grimly. *And aimed higher.*

"Earth orbit to the Naralax gate is a six-day trip," Hollans continued, as if unaware—or more likely unimpressed—by her simmering anger. "You'll be taking something a little faster and more discreet than your originally scheduled transport. I believe you're familiar with the *Annapolis Joy?* Her captain remembers you."

The ship's name was misleading. The *Annapolis Joy* was one of the Ministry of Extra-Sol Human Affairs' less-than-diplomatic dreadnaughts, bristling with armaments normally used to intimidate would-be smugglers before they entered or left orbit. She had been among those to engage the Ro at Haven.

And the *Joy* had brought Mac home from Myriam.

"He probably remembers the screaming," Mac said under her breath. She'd missed the instant, there on the cold sand, when they'd hurriedly removed most of what remained of her arm to stop the continuing digestion of her flesh. She'd made up for it by regaining consciousness on the way to orbit.

Fortunately, the *Annapolis Joy* had the sort of medical facility that specialized in battlefield trauma, right to replacement parts. Though she hadn't made a friend of the ship's surgeon. *He should have asked before preparing skin she didn't want.*

"Speed isn't the point, is it?" she countered. "If it were, we'd be at the space-port instead of here." Travel between systems might consume no time, but crawling along a planet's surface did.

Why else send a ship of war?

Because someone else was.

"Oh, no," Mac said as this crystallized. "Don't tell me those 'jurisdictional issues' are coming with the derelicts. Don't even think about dropping me in the middle of a squabble between alien governments. Hollans—you of all people should know better!"

"You won't be involved in any—"

"Wrong," she interrupted. "If everyone, Human or otherwise, is expecting me to translate whatever records, trash, labels, or vids the Dhryn left on those ships, how can I not be involved? Bah!" Mac tucked her knees against her chest and wrapped her arms around her legs. "I should pretend I can't read the stuff. I really should. Starting now."

Hollans appeared to hold back a smile. "You won't be on your own, Dr. Connor."

She rested her chin atop her knee to regard him. Hollans was still the image of calm civility, mug of tea in one hand, coffee-soaked boots neatly aligned.

Who'd waylaid her in the midst of the Yukon for this conversation.

"You could have told me all this by message, too," Mac accused. "It's not as if I've a choice." She lowered her voice. "Why are you here, Hollans? No more games."

His almost-smile faded. "I need your advice, Dr. Connor."

"My—" Mac's eyebrows rose. "Really." She tried, and failed, to imagine what possible advice she could offer Earth's Person-in-Charge other than to avoid Frow in parks. She tilted her head. "Was this Anchen's idea?"

"The Sinzi-ra respects your insight, Dr. Connor. As do I, in this instance."

"Our esteemed Sinzi-ra also collects rubber fish," Mac pointed out somewhat warily. "All this time at the consulate, you never once asked for my advice. Why now?"

"We're alone."

The implications of that sent a shiver running down her spine. Mac refused to take the bait, *if that's what it was.* This man had been Nik's boss. She was not in that league. *And didn't want to be.* So she simply nodded. "I'll do my best."

After a deliberate sip of tea, Hollans gazed into the liquid, as if considering how best to phrase his answer. A familiar habit. He'd sip and stare innumerable times per meeting. *Came close to getting her imp in his mug once.* Before she had to resort to that tactic, he looked up. "It concerns Trojanowski's latest report."

Mac lowered her feet to the deck and leaned forward, her impatience forgotten.

"The Dhryn—the Vessel—" he continued, "has directed them to enter a region which poses a significant natural hazard to several species on board, Humans included." He pursed his lips for an instant. "I can't identify that hazard without risking their security. I'm sure you understand, Dr. Connor."

As if it would help her *find them on a star chart.* Mac didn't bother saying that aloud. She burned to ask if there'd been a message for her, another ring, but knew better. The *lamnas* was the most private form of communication she could imagine.

Nik had chosen it for a reason.

Love letters, Mac thought wryly, *hardly needed alien tech.*

She twirled one finger in the air. "Can't they go around?"

"The Vessel claims his Progenitor is inside this region—that Dhryn can withstand it."

"A hiding place," Mac concluded and started to relax until she took in Hollans' bleak expression. "You think it's a trap?"

"It could be. The Vessel assured Trojanowski those on board can be protected in evacsuits long enough to reach the Progenitor's ship, where they'll be safe. What if he's lying?" He held up his hand to silence her instant objection. "Yes, Dr. Connor. According to you, Dhryn don't lie. Say I believe you." His tone made that improbable, but he didn't belabor the point. "Could the Vessel be wrong about Humans surviving this? Dhryn have made mistakes about alien biology before."

"I've noticed. What do you want me to say, Hollans?" Mac asked, abruptly weary. *Should have had that second coffee.* "Trap or Dhryn miscalculation. They can't stop now. There's too much at stake." *Where on that scale . . .* "I shouldn't have to remind you." The words left a bitter taste in her mouth.

"You don't." He put down his tea, then laid his hands palm down on his thighs. They were thick-fingered hands, with prominent knuckles and mottled skin. She'd asked Sing-li what Hollans had done before becoming a thorn in her side and been surprised to learn he'd grown up a miner, working first on Earth, then Saturn's moons. *He'd have appreciated the Progenitor's underground home,* she thought irrelevantly.

His blue eyes bored into hers. "I need to understand the risk I've asked my people to take. How far do you trust that Dhryn, Dr. Connor? How far can I?"

"Irrelevant." Mac shook her head. "The Vessel's a biological interface; a way for the Progenitor to disperse and collect information. As well trust your imp."

Hollans' face developed that look, the one he'd get at meetings when she went off on a technical tangent. *Usually,* Mac admitted, *when he'd been sipping and staring and she couldn't in good conscience throw anything physical.*

"What you can trust," she explained, emphasizing the word, "is this Progenitor's will to protect Herself and Her species. She's resisted the Ro. She sent Her Vessel to find us and learn the truth. To bring it back. And . . ." Mac shut her mouth.

"And what?" Now Hollans' eyebrows drew together, resulting in what Mac privately labeled as his don't-mess-with-me wrinkle set. "Dr. Connor," he prompted when she didn't immediately speak. "Please."

. . . *"Run while you still can!"* . . .

"She warned me," Mac said reluctantly. "She warned us all. At the time, I took it as the Dhryn fear of the Ro. They'd gone to such lengths to protect their *oomlings*. Since? I think She had some inkling of what might happen to the Dhryn themselves. Maybe something from their oral history. Maybe more."

"I—see." His stern expression eased into something closer to puzzlement. "Where are you going with this, Dr. Connor?"

Mac shrugged, uncomfortable speculating. "I'm not sure. This Progenitor's behaved differently from the beginning. She called Brymn and me to meet with Her, to commit *grathnu*—a bonding ritual, as much as a reward for service. When I was there . . . something about Her . . . a presence . . ." Mac let her voice trail away, her cheeks warm with embarrassment. "I doubt it matters."

Hollans sipped tea, his eyes locked on her. "Continue anyway, Dr. Connor."

"What about Sebastian and the rest? The shuttle to orbit?"

Hollans glanced at the closed door to the pilot's compartment. "Status of our sleepers?" he asked.

A disembodied voice answered. "Everyone's safe and comfortable, sir."

"Now, Dr. Connor. Indulge me."

It wasn't a request.

Mac thought of those vast underground spaces, home and safety for beings at the heart of their kind. *The breeze, a breath.* "Presence wasn't the half of it," she sighed, frustrated by mere words. *The landscape, a form.* She made herself focus on that small ship, heading into whatever additional hazard space had to offer— as if vacuum and radiation weren't enough. "The Progenitor wants Her Vessel back, with answers." *The warmth, a smile.* "Anyone who helps accomplish Her will? They'll be considered Dhryn. I'm not saying that guarantees their safety, but it has to be less risky than approaching Her ship uninvited. Best I can do, Hollans."

They'd called her Dhryn.

Mac touched her new arm, and made herself remember that, too. "None of us are safe anymore."

"No. But I'm encouraged. Thank you, Dr. Connor."

She gave him a searching look and, for an instant, saw only a man worried about others. *Someone should,* she thought, inclined to envy. "Mac."

Gods, a full smile. It threw his dignified wrinkles into disarray. "Mac."

"If you didn't trust the Dhryn before," she asked quietly, "why agree to go in the first place? Besides the chance to get close enough to destroy a Progenitor's ship." Her voice came out calm and level, as if it had become routine to talk about the annihilation of hundreds of thousands of beings, including the person currently inhabiting a large part of her heart.

Hollans lost his smile. "Remind me to stay on your good side."

A year ago, she'd have shocked herself. *Where had that Mac gone?* "If it comes to that," she said, flat and cold, "Nik will know."

"Not his call," countered Hollans. "IU mission. He'll have to get the other representatives on board to agree."

Mac frowned. Cinder, the Trisulian. Her reaction to the Dhryn should be predictable. Dr. Genny P'tool, the N'not'k. Despite the alien's advanced age, Anchen had asked her to go for her knowledge as a no-space theoretician as well as to continue her work on the Dhryn language. Apparently linguistics and eso-teric physics were a logical combination for the N'not'k, though Mac suspected this was Anchen's way of finding something useful for her friend to do. An obli-gate pacifist. The Imrya. A recorder of events, as well as a renowned designer of servo translations. She wouldn't have any problem making a decision. *Probably would take a while conveying it, though.*

Mac didn't know who else had scrambled aboard the shuttle with Nik and the Dhryn. Couldn't have been many.

Didn't matter.

"This isn't about the Dhryn at all," she said abruptly. "A Trisulian ship at Haven, causing trouble . . . you're worried about Cinder, aren't you?"

If she'd thought she'd seen Hollans' face wrinkled into grim lines before, she'd been mistaken. His eyes were like sparks set in pale, eroded stone. "This goes no farther, Mac."

She hated being right. "I've had the talk. What's going on?"

"What do you know about Cinder?"

Mac hadn't reported how an impassioned Cinder had begged her help to keep from murdering the Dhryn. She'd bet Cinder hadn't shared that moment either.

Some things weren't about saving the universe.

"She's Nik's partner," Mac hedged. "However that happened."

"Was," corrected Hollans. "The Ministry pairs field operatives with other species whenever possible. Experience for us, exposure to our ways for them. Trojanowski and Cinder were an exemplary team until his retirement."

She didn't think she imagined the slight hesitation before "retirement," but nothing in Hollans' expression or this situation encouraged her to ask about the past. "Things change," Mac observed cautiously. *Secrets went both ways.*

"Indeed. Cinder is, to all extents and purposes, now a widow, as is her species. Which is nothing new." At her startled look, Hollans nodded. "That's right. Floods, disease, war have decimated their male populations before now. Mated females respond by impregnating themselves, then seek out new, safer territory before their offspring are born. By whatever means necessary. Wherein lies our prob-lem. The Trisulians are looking outside their systems. And the means . . . ? They stole it from you."

She could be shocked after all. "You think—they'd use the Ro signal?" Mac sputtered. "Call the Dhryn?"

"Yes."

She licked dry lips. "Have they?"

"Not yet. Not that we know," he clarified soberly. "And the posturing by the Trisulians at Haven could be nothing more than heightened territoriality—to be expected."

He didn't look like a man who believed that.

"What does Nik say?"

"That, I need you to tell me, Mac."

She could almost feel the *lamnas* on her finger and resisted the urge to touch it in front of those keen eyes. "You read his message to me, I'm sure. 'Continuing as planned; situation nominal.' I could have used more." She managed a stiff shrug. "That's a spy for you."

"There was more."

Mac froze in place. "What do you mean?"

Hollans turned his hands palm up. "The Sinzi-ra didn't send me to see you, Mac. Trojanowski—Nik—did. Before he left orbit, he urged me not to trust even secured channels, concerned we don't have a handle on the Ro's capabilities. He said he'd arranged a safe way to reach you." He reached into a pocket and brought out a small wooden salmon, holding it out on his thick, callused palm. "I was to show you this."

Betrayal . . .

Or the most profound trust.

Mac found herself too tired to guess. She took the carving from Hollans and put it away in her pocket, then held up her right hand. The *lamnas* gleamed. "Did he send me another of these?"

"Yes." Hollans looked relieved as he took a gleaming circle from an official-looking envelope. He passed it to her. "I was hoping this was the message, but my people couldn't find anything on it."

The silver didn't show any damage, so Mac refrained from pointless comment about private gifts and privileged information. *After all, who had the coffee-soaked socks?* "You wouldn't. The *lamnas* is for me."

"What's a *lamnas*?"

Mac lifted an eyebrow. "You don't know?"

"Nik was consular liaison. He's been deeper in the Sinzi-ra's confidence than any other Human—until you, Mac." Hollans glanced at the ring she held up between two fingers. "It's some kind of communication device, isn't it?"

She considered him for a long moment, then snapped her hand closed over the ring. "It's more. And less. It gives me fragments of Nik's memories, layered one over the other. Hard to sort out; not random. Memories that matter to him. It's—" She took a deep breath and let it out, eyes roving the inside of the lev compartment. Their two seats, a door, curved blank walls. *And Hollans.* "I have to go outside." She stood.

"But—"

Mac headed for the lev door. "You do want me to try to read it now, don't you?"

"Yes." He rose to his feet as well, but seemed to change his mind as he met her eyes. "How long will it take?" he asked quietly.

"I don't know." Staff had packed her entire apartment while she'd peered through the first one. *Either they were incredibly efficient, or it had taken a while.* "It might depend on what's in here," she speculated, lifting the fist with the ring.

The door didn't open to her touch on the pad. *What did he think she'd do? Run?* Tight-lipped, Mac let Hollans reach past to key in a code. "You're sure?" he asked in a low voice, giving her a look she couldn't interpret.

"About going out, yes. I have to be alone. The rest?" She shrugged. "These days, I make it up as I go."

"That's hardly reassuring, Mac."

His aggrieved tone made her laugh. "I thought you liked it when I was blunt."

"I prefer my experts wallowing in self-confidence." Hollans gestured to the now-open door.

"So you," she rejoined, "can leave them stuck in it when they're wrong? Politics. No thanks. I'll stick with blunt and 'hardly reassuring.' "

Mac stepped down the short ramp to the mossy ground, doing her best not to shiver at reencountering the cool Yukon night. She paused to let her eyes adjust, a task made easier as the light from the compartment dimmed to a faint glow behind them. There'd been an old tipped stump not far from the lev. She spotted the dark mound that marked it and walked along until she found a more-or-less level spot within its dry exposed root mass. She sat on top, wiggling to settle herself between bristled sprouts of new growth, and took out the ring.

She was startled when Hollans, who'd followed, took off his suit coat and laid it over her shoulders. It was heavier than it looked, and warm. "Thanks," Mac said, pulling it close. "Now . . ."

"Alone," he acknowledged. "That much, okay?" A brief shaft of light from his hand slid over black armor: a guard stationed at the nose of the lev. *Doubtless,* Mac reminded herself, *equipped with night vision.*

"No." With regret, she took off his coat and passed it back. *Probably bugged.* "I get privacy for this, Hollans, or you can leave."

She couldn't see his face, but she heard his quiet order. "Expand the inner perimeter by fifty meters." And the result. An astonishing number of footsteps moved away in every direction, *doubtless snapping twigs and scuffing sand for her benefit.*

"You, too," Mac insisted, the ring warm in her hand.

"Of course." He took two steps away, then stopped. She could hear him breathe.

"What?"

From the dark. "I trust you saw the final report on the Ro attack on Haven."

"I saw it," Mac admitted. *Which was technically true.* She just hadn't read the thing, given it was jammed with jargon and offered footnotes on particle phys-ics. "The Ro fired some weapon at the planet. Your ships disrupted no-space around the Ro ships, exposed them, and they left. I was," she reminded him dryly, "there."

"Whatever else they accomplished, it's clear now the Ro wanted that one Progenitor dead. The targeting was precise. They almost succeeded."

"As I said. I was there." Despite the bite to her reply, Mac winced. If she closed her eyes, she'd see it. *The immense flame burning through buildings and pave-ment, penetrating deeper and deeper underground . . . the death cries of a world.* "She escaped."

"The point is that She attracted the Ro's attention, whether through Brymn's actions or yours. She has ours now. This being may be our only chance to nego-tiate with the Dhryn. This has to work, Mac. We must have a reliable source of information the Ro can't intercept."

A rustle from somewhere beneath the log made Mac hold her breath; only when frenzied squeaks added punctuation did she let it out again. "What if they're here, listening?"

"That," Hollans declared with surprising confidence, "we'd know. Trust me, Mac."

That word again. "Reliable, maybe," Mac said quietly. "Information? That I can't promise," she warned, running her fingers over the ring. "The last time— there wasn't much, Hollans. Things were the same. Everyone was the same." *Nik's despair at his own feelings was her business.* "Nik understands Cinder. He's— he's willing to use her anger at the Dhryn. I saw that."

She thought he nodded, but it was too dark to be sure. "Maybe this time," he said "there'll be something more. I'll wait in the lev. If you're sure about being out here alone?"

"I'm sure."

Mac waited while Hollans' red light traced his path back to the lev, the even fainter glow from inside the craft marking the opening and closing of the door.

She waited an instant longer, stroking her palm along the corded smoothness of the wood. It was like muscle, frozen beneath her hand.

Finally, she brought the *lamnas* to her lips, breathed once, and lifted it sky-ward until she saw three stars within its circle.

And then . . .

- CONTACT -

INDECISION/

"Mac . . . I have to believe this . . . working . . . I will believe it." /determination/ *Need you . . . /loss/ concern/*

Concentrate, fool. "Hollans . . . Hollans . . . he's got to know, Mac." /shame/ *Couldn't tell you . . . not then.* /heat/confusion/effort/ "Forgive . . ." *Doesn't matter. Nothing else matters.* ". . . tell him."

Concentrate. " . . . sabotage . . ." /rage/frustration/fear/ "Ship okay . . . casualties . . ." *friends, colleagues . . . part of me still slips away . . . what if it were you?* /despair/emptiness/

/effort/ "Vessel safe . . . systems okay . . . suits . . . most gone . . ." /irony/ ". . . same boat . . ."

* layered over *

—She smells soap—

The Vessel hooted. "Do not worry so, Nikolai Piotr Trojanowski. We shall soon be with the Progenitor and safe from harm."

I'll believe that when we head for home . . . but Mac believes . . . /wistful/ . . . wish she was here.

"You're sure about the protocols."

"Yes, yes. They are simplicity itself, my *lamisah*. Your ship will approach and dock, I will offer greeting, all will be well. You'll see."

/resignation/ *Those of us who live that long. Glad Mac isn't here. Radiation's not a grace-ful death.*

"Here. This is a recording of what I'd say to your Progenitor. I want you to keep it with you at all times."

A distressed *thrum*. "Do you fear more violence?"

I fear dying too soon. /determination/ "A precaution."

"All will be well. You'll see."

* layered over *

—She tastes blood—

"Hurry!" "This way!" "Aiiiiieee!!" "I'm hit!"

/agony/

The words merged with thudding footsteps, explosions, and anguished cries, a staccato sequence.

Followed by silence.

/calm/focus/ *Don't reply . . . don't reveal . . .* /flutters of pain/endure/

"Nik! Where are you?" Cinder's voice, anxious and sharp. "Anyone?"

/patience/

Footsteps. A sharp *ping*. Then another. And another.

/emptiness/ *It's come to this . . .* /dread/

"Stop!"

A roar, followed by a splatter. A crunch.

/pain/

* *layered over* *

—She feels blood, slippery and wet—

Concentrate . . . "Hollans has to know, Mac. Lost . . . Murs . . . Larrieri . . . dead." /urgent/ need/denial/ *Can't tell you, Mac . . . can't let you know what I did . . . had to do . . .* "Cinder . . . dead. Saboteur . . . dead."

A piece of me slips away . . . /anguish/grief/

"Ship okay . . . next stop . . . the Progenitor."

/guilt/ *She couldn't help herself . . . I should have known . . . stopped her somehow . . .* / failure/despair/ *It's only the beginning . . . will fall apart . . .*

Concentrate. "The Vessel misses you . . ." /need/loneliness/

/resolve/

- 10 -

JOURNEY AND JOLT

MAC SLIPPED THE RING on her finger, to join its mate. It was dark; the lev door was closed. When she eased to her feet, her left leg tried to fail, afire with pins and needles from hip to toe. *Answering the question of time,* she thought ruefully, rubbing her thigh.

Her cheeks were ice-cold. Drying tears, she discovered when she touched her face.

The message . . . "Gods, Nik," she whispered out loud as the horror of it surfaced. *What had he done?*

Fought a battle. Killed a friend. Made a decision to risk all their lives.

Day on the job, she told herself, and didn't believe it.

Again, the *lamnas* had revealed more than he'd intended. Far more. "He's hurt," she whispered to the dark. *Outside and in.* Mac didn't need to try and imagine what it had cost Nik. She could feel it, like a fever eating at every part of her body; taste it as ash in her mouth. " 'Part of me slips away,' " she repeated, without making a sound.

She stumbled toward the lev, hands out in case she fell. Before she'd taken more than a few steps, its door opened and Hollans came striding down the ramp. Before he reached her, forms materialized from the darkness on either side and swept her up between them. Mac wondered if these were people she knew.

Were they her friends?

Were they Nik's?

She rested her hands on their armored shoulders and silently wished them safe.

"I was hoping for information, Mac." Hollans' responsible wrinkles had settled into tired and old. "I didn't expect anything like this. Are you sure?"

Mac shrugged, feeling tired and old herself. "How can I be? Whatever words Nik wanted to pass along are mixed up with conversations he remembered. I could be mistaken about a great deal. What seems clearest? An unsuccessful attempt to sabotage their ship. Some of your people were killed." *She'd given him the names she had: Murs. Larrieri. Cinder.*

"The evacsuits." He circled back to that again. "Were all of them damaged?"

That was the crux of it. And she didn't know. "There was something about the suits. It—it wasn't good. Nik's sending the ship in anyway. He wanted me to tell you that."

"It'll reduce their safety margin. They won't all make it." He rubbed his face with one hand, then looked at her. "This is a disaster. Was the Trisulian responsible?"

Mac felt like one of her salmon. *Fish ladder or waterfall?* Without seeing the top, it was a leap into the unknown. The wrong guess meant failure and death.

She had the ear of a powerful individual. A wrong word in it now could precipitate a crisis—perhaps start a war. Emily'd warned her. *So,* Mac realized, *had Anchen.*

And what did she know? Only those fragments of Nik's memories and feelings. He'd done his utmost not to reveal more.

That should tell her something.

Mac held up her hand, the pair of *lamnas* sparkling around her ring finger. "From this? I can't say."

He gazed at her. Done talking, Mac slumped deeper in her seat and yawned so broadly her jaw cracked. *Exhausted biologist at your service,* she quipped to herself. *Just try getting me to make sense much longer.*

The last time Mac had left home, she'd been tossed into orbit in a box, caught by a freight shuttle, then ferried to a warehouse in one of the great way stations. Despite all this clever misdirection, the Ro—and Emily—had almost ambushed her there.

Which probably explained why there'd been no arguments made to an upgrade from box to proper passenger shuttle, complete with viewports and the in-flight vid of her choice.

Now, thanks to Hollans and some abandoned Dhryn ships, they were sealed in a compartment of a Ministry courier shuttle, with no view or entertainment.

Yup. Another box.

Schrant was curled in his seat, sound asleep. *Not a side effect of Hollans' little ploy,* Mac decided, since Mudge was anything but sleepy.

"This is most irregular, Norcoast," he announced. *Again.* With *harrumph.*

She closed her eyes and wiggled a little deeper into her seat.

"Norcoast!"

Mac cracked open one eye. "What?"

"I said, this is most irregular. We had prearranged transit. I don't understand why we aren't using it."

"Are you going to keep repeating that all the way there?" she asked wearily.

He gave her a strange look. "I fail to see why you don't find this all very ir-regular, too."

Much as she'd hated doing so, she'd agreed to Hollans' insistence that his visit be kept secret, even from Mudge. She'd gone back to the cabin, sat on the step beside Sebastian, who, true to Hollans' word, was sleeping soundly, and had waited while her visitors left. After a few minutes, to no signal Mac could detect, the dogs had stirred enough to stretch and roll over on their rooftops. Seconds later, Sebastian's left foot had dropped off the stair and his eyes had opened.

They'd gone to their respective beds as if nothing had happened.

She'd dreamed of interstellar war.

And now Mudge, who had every right to know and who knew her well enough to sense she was hiding something important from him, was pressing for answers.

Spy games. Mac was growing acutely aware of their cost.

"I'm sure something's come up," she said, as close to the truth as she dared. "Their budget, not ours. We should both try for some more sleep."

His eyes glittered. "I'm not tired. Amazing how quickly we all fell asleep last night. I was sure this young fellow's squirming about would keep us awake for hours."

"That Yukon air," Mac offered, but her own yawn spoiled it.

Mudge fell silent and she settled back into her seat, head back and eyes shut. Mac could feel his reproachful stare through her closed eyelids, but refused to do anything but pretend to sleep. After a while, pretense gave way to reality and she drifted off.

"Mac."

"Not here," Mac mumbled, curling into a defensive ball.

"Yes, you are," the voice insisted, "and so are we. We've docked with the transport ship. C'mon, Mac. Rise and shine."

While she had no intention of shining anytime soon, Mac peered at Sam Schrant's eager face, registered the flaming orange backpack already slung over his shoulder, and decided rising was likely inevitable. "Where's Oversight?" she asked, her mouth feeling as though she'd acquired a layer of barnacles. *Probably snored for the last hour.*

"It's not as if I could have left, Norcoast," came the caustic reply.

Man was consistent, she'd give him that.

Mac sat up, rubbed her eyes, and looked around. *They'd docked?* Nothing had changed within their tiny compartment, except for the stiffness of a certain salmon researcher. She rose to her feet and edged through their stack of luggage to reach the space between the pairs of inward-facing seats. Once there, she began stretching as best she could without hitting either of them on the head.

"How long was I out?" she asked, bending left. "And how do you know we've docked?" Right.

"Long enough. Mr. Mudge timed it." This with distinct admiration.

Mac stopped stretching to give Mudge a look that was anything but admiring. "Why would you do that?"

He *harrumphed* and crossed his arms over his chest, eyes narrowed with disapproval. From the bags under those eyes, he hadn't slept at all.

The meteorologist replied happily, "Mr. Mudge has a complete list of the capabilities of orbital shuttles. There's a grav unit on this one, so the only way to tell when we'd reached orbit was to figure out travel time. And he was right. We just heard the clang—Mr. Mudge told me it was the clamps locking on to our air lock."

By this point, "Mr." Mudge was doing his utmost not to look overtly pleased with this thorough description of his cleverness. Mac lifted one eyebrow, but refrained from saying anything. *After all, she'd slept through the "clang."*

She climbed back to her seat and made sure her own bag was close at hand. She wasn't sure how she felt about returning to the *Annapolis Joy.*

That wasn't exactly true. Her stomach was busy informing her.

As if nausea was helpful.

Mac swallowed hard, doing her best to push away the past at the same time. So what if the *Joy* had remained in orbit instead of rushing her home? They'd established a firm Human presence among the species scrambling to explore the Dhryn home world. So what if she'd spent those weeks in a haze of loss and pain, her questions buried under the urgent onslaught of everyone else's? She'd made it home eventually.

Where no one could know where she'd been.

Done was done, Mac told herself. She swallowed again, relieved to find it easier. *She'd take anything positive at the moment.*

"Will you hurry up?" This from Mudge, who was fuming as Sam repacked his belongings. Mac grinned. It looked as though the meteorologist had wanted something from the very bottom of his pack during their flight and had taken the easy route, dumping the contents over Mudge's neat stack. "Who knows how far we'll have to walk through the way station?" that worthy continued dolefully. "Our original plans took us into the same loading dock as our transport. Now? We could be facing a considerable journey. Perhaps requiring a skim."

Mac made a face. *Really should have told him before snoring.* "This isn't the way station." *Oh, she'd seen* that *look before.* Before Mudge could launch into full volume accusation, likely involving a litany of her past indiscretions at Castle Inlet and *how could she be trusted?* she said calmly, "You've heard of the *Annapolis Joy,* Oversight?"

"The *J*—" His mouth formed a perfect 'o' and his hands groped in midair, as if trying to grab the name to look at it for himself.

The side of their compartment chose that moment to slide aside to reveal a sunlight-bright hangar, the *Joy*'s half of the air lock equation. Complete with welcoming party.

"Mac!"

She froze with her hand about to close on the handle of her bag, then recovered, hoping no one had noticed. "Doug. Kaili," she greeted. "Nice to see you again."

In a sense it was. The two orderlies in light green coveralls had cared for her during her stay. They'd been kind, efficient, and friendly. *Not their fault her stay had been* . . . Mac found a smile. "Doug Court. Kaili Xai. Charles Mudge III and Sam Schrant."

The four exchanged hellos. Doug resembled a sturdy, younger version of Mudge, with an upright brush of red-blond hair and a neatly-trimmed mustache above his wide smile. Midnight-black Kaili was taller and willow-thin. Mac remembered her as the quieter of the pair, rarely expressive. Now she was beaming with pleasure.

"This is the *Annapolis Joy*, dreadnaught class," Mudge then informed them, seemingly oblivious to the name embroidered in gold on their uniforms. "The very latest. Top of the line. Twinned Ascendis-Theta in-system drives, multiplexed transect-capable sensor arrays. Why she's capable—"

"Oversight," Mac interrupted. "You're drooling."

He shot her a desperate look. "I simply must see her bridge, Norcoast. I must—"

While having Mudge reduced to this state had its plus side, Mac was too unsettled to enjoy it. "Later. Are we supposed to have a medical?" she asked the orderlies, curious why these two had been sent to meet them. She grimaced. "I do know the way."

"Nah. We're surplus at the moment, Mac," Kaili grinned. "Off shift."

"And we asked," Doug added. "Wanted to be the first to welcome you back. How are you?" His eyes flicked to her left hand.

Guessing what he wanted, Mac pulled up her sleeve and held out her prosthesis for inspection. "Been through a bit," she explained, although it was unlikely even these two could see any of the repairs without a scope. Noad, Anchen's physician self, had done a superb job of reinstalling the finger she'd broken fending off the Trisulian male. Then there was the touch-up to the burns where she'd caught spit from their visiting Dhryn.

Maybe she should have asked for souvenir scars.

She glimpsed Mudge's stunned expression as he realized which ship this had to be and kept her voice steady. "Doug and Kaili were my coaches." Mac wiggled her fingers. "See? Haven't lost my touch."

"Cayhill has some new—" She shook her head, just once, and Kaili stopped, finishing with, "If you want, I'm sure he'll take a look."

"We're here on other business."

"You're right." Doug snapped to attention. "Sorry, Mac. We'll catch up another time. This way."

For a ship whose external purpose was to intimidate, the interior of the *Joy* had surprised Mac with its attention to comfort—until she'd learned a typical patrol could keep the crew in space for months. The lighting resembled that received on Earth, from its spectrum to the length of a shipday. The air temperature varied accordingly. Doug had tried to convince her that on very long hauls the captain would occasionally drop it below freezing for a week or so, with everyone reporting to duty in mitts, but Mac hadn't swallowed that one. She had admired the lightly scented breezes that would randomly rush down certain corridors. What furnishings she'd seen were covered in a wide range of materials, having in common functionality as well as variety to the touch.

Sound was the only Human sense the ship's designers had seemingly neglected in their search for ways to stimulate the crew. Then again, the first and possibly only warning of a serious problem would be the shriek of an alarm or the cry of orders.

Mac, Mudge, and Sam followed the two orderlies from the hangar to a corridor, then to where a sequence of arched doors marked internal transit tubes. They were reserved for crew; in all her time aboard, Mac hadn't used them. Now, she shot a questioning look at Doug, who'd stopped by the first.

"Captain's in a hurry," he said in answer. "Wants you and the rest stowed as quickly as possible."

"The rest?" This from Mudge. "Do you mean to say all of our people and gear are aboard?" His eyebrows were on a collision course. "They were waiting for us at the way station. By whose authority—"

"I wouldn't know, sir," Doug replied politely.

Mudge turned to her. "Norcoast?"

Mac indicated the tube door. "We'll find out faster if we go, Oversight."

What she found out first was why the tubes were usually reserved for crew. Once they entered, a process requiring both a code and recognition of one of their escorts, Mac climbed into what felt like a stomach. The space had no straight lines, or rigid walls. Instead, her feet sank ankle-deep and her hands, as Mac groped for support, disappeared within whatever pale substance they'd used. There was something solid a few centimeters in, but it took an effort to reach and even more to free her hands.

She sniffed. *Clover.* "Nice touch."

The others climbed in with her, the crew adeptly bouncing their way to the far side where they leaned their backs against the wall. Mac copied their position, seeing her companions do the same. "What about our bags?" she asked, having dropped hers to the floor in her first startled step.

"Leave it there, Mac."

The door didn't so much close as the walls flowed together where it had been.

"How does—" Sam began to ask, eyes bright with curiosity, when the flexible wall beside him suddenly developed a pronounced curve, as if it were being sucked away.

The sensation of movement came at the same instant. Mac felt herself being pressed deeper into the yielding surface. The others were, too, as was her bag. Doug grinned. "It's called a bolus."

As in lump of food being digested? Mac laughed. "Perfect."

"Thought you'd appreciate it," he said. "They bud from each entrance to the tube system." Just then, the bolus turned sideways and dropped, but Mac felt only an instant of vertigo. Her body stayed firmly in place, as though the wall was now holding onto her. *Which it was,* she realized, after attempting to pry free her hands. Doug kept lecturing, presumably to keep the novice passengers distracted. "The tubes themselves are part of the recycling system within the ship. A constant stream of water, heat, wastes, you name it, travels through. Any freed bolus is whisked along with the rest until snatched from the flow at the next transit stop."

Mac grinned back. "Gotta love biology."

Doug chuckled. "The engineers will bend your ear about hydraulics and closed systems, but we know the truth."

"A flush a day," piped up Kaili.

"The bolus itself applies interior suction when in motion. The ride can get a little bumpy, but once you're used to it? Nice break from walking corridors, believe me."

"Fast and secure even if gravity fails," Mudge commented. "And practical, given the type of ship. A web strung with beads, Norcoast. Remarkably flexible design. How many pods is the *Joy* carrying now?"

The two spoke in unison. "You'll have to ask the exec, sir." "Really can't go into details, sir."

"You'll have four days. You can ask all the questions you want, Oversight," Mac said without thinking, then winced inwardly.

Mudge's face glowed with that familiar "gotcha" expression. "I wasn't aware you were privy to information about the capabilities of a Ministry dreadnought, Norcoast."

Before Mac had to cover her tracks, Doug spoke up. "Oh, Mac knows the *Joy.* We brought her home."

She'd counted every hour from the gate to orbit.

"Home from where, Mac?" Sam asked, eyes wide.

Mudge *harrumphed.* "This isn't the time for trading memoirs, Dr. Schrant. You'll meet your colleagues on the Origins Team shortly. I trust you were able to familiarize yourself with their work beforehand?"

Grateful for the distraction, if not for the questions Mudge was no doubt stockpiling to fire at her when they were next alone, Mac listened to Sam's animated listing of Kirby and To'o's work, all of which sounded more than familiar to him. *Enthusiasm was a refreshing switch from desperation,* she thought.

The bolus snapped to a full stop between one breath and the next, shuddering along its every surface. The shudders conveniently slid passengers and bags to what was now the floor. An arch formed a new door, the original having melded into the rest of the spongy wall surface sometime after they'd "budded" and joined the waste stream. She smiled to herself at the image.

"Status check?" Doug asked Kaili, who went to the arch and flipped open what was now a control panel.

"Other side's secure," she said after a second. "Clear and opening, now." With that, the door slid aside on an expanse of warm yellow.

Doug, moving nimbly, picked up her bag then offered his hand. Mac smiled and shook her head. She stepped out, pulling one foot at a time free of the tender grip the bolus still had on her feet, and managed not to stagger. "I can see it takes practice," she told him.

That wide, ready smile. *She'd seen it every time he'd arrived to check her new arm.*

It wasn't Doug's fault seeing him brought back such vivid memories. Mac made herself smile back. "Which way now?" she asked, glancing around.

"Idiots!!!" The bellow echoed from wall to ceiling. "I told you she would be coming!"

"Let me guess," Mudge said dryly.

The Origins Team was very glad to see them. The climatologists had swept away Sam Schrant, having arranged to share quarters so they could begin working on his model systems. They'd hurried off in a rosy glow of incomprehensible math. Mudge was accosted by all the Sthlynii at once, who over-voweled at him in anguish about the changes to the schedule they'd originally anguished about at the consulate. Not to mention the risk of lost equipment and did he notice they now had to change their quarter assignments? The *Annapolis Joy* was much larger than the transport the Sinzi-ra had promised, but their portion of it was smaller. It was all too much to bear.

If Mudge hadn't looked so thoroughly officious, Mac might have felt sorry for him.

The Origins Team had been put in an area of the ship unfamiliar to Mac. *Not hard, considering she'd spent most of her time in the medlab.* Meant for passengers, beyond doubt, though there was no evidence of who the *Joy* might normally carry. *Maybe they used her for conferences,* Mac decided, remembering that the ship hadn't seen combat until the attack on the Ro.

Their section was separated from the rest of the ship by a pair of heavy bulkheads that could be air locks at need. Once past this point, the long, gently curving corridor was lined with a series of identical doors, each leading into compact and efficient living quarters with their own biological accommodations. The walls between were removable, allowing some quarters to be larger than others. Mac counted fourteen doors on the left-hand side of the corridor, seven on the right, but was advised to knock first. The Sthlynii remained unsettled about their quarters and were turning up anywhere.

To the right, after the first two doors, the corridor bulged outward to provide a common space, itself split into dining and recreation areas with mem-wood tables. Someone well-versed in transporting scientists had further divided the recreation areas with sound and light screens, creating four workrooms, already in use. Past that point were the remaining five living quarters. The corridor ended in a closed bulkhead.

Feeling oriented, if not truly here yet, Mac munched on a sandwich, contents unknown. She'd joined Lyle Kanaci in the dining area, at a corner table. He wasn't happy about the change either.

"I tell you, Mac, I've been afraid to ask why we rated an upgrade." Always pale, he leaned so close Mac could see the delicate vessels pulsing beneath his skin. He pitched his voice to her ears only. "Can't be good news."

"It's not bad," she assured him, swallowing. "They've found ships from the Dhryn colonies."

He sat back, lips pursed in a silent whistle. "Haven?"

Her people weren't slow. Mac smiled and toasted him with a bottle of juice. "Haven. The ships are derelicts. Abandoned."

"We could use a look," he said eagerly. "We don't have much in the way of modern technology references—trade items, some catalogs. The modern Dhryn didn't export much of their own manufacture."

"Shouldn't be hard to arrange. They're bringing the best preserved to Myriam. Should arrive before we do."

Lyle looked startled, then frowned at her. "Why?"

Mac shrugged. "If I said it offers exquisite congruence to the Sinzi, would that help?" At his blank expression, she cupped her hands on the table, forming an enclosure. "The IU wants all valuable Dhryn artifacts in a place where they can't be claimed by any other species."

"Like that, is it?" Lyle pressed his lips together in a thin line, then nodded. "Explaining this ship. I had my doubts it was because the Ministry had suddenly realized the value of its crack team of archaeologists. Politics."

"We've done pretty well avoiding them so far," Mac shrugged. "Bound to happen. So long as it doesn't interfere with our work." She rubbed a spot on the tabletop with one finger, wondering how best to tell him the rest. "There will be a change, Lyle," she began.

"They'll take you off Origins. To work on these ships."

So much for how to tell him. She nodded, lowering her voice. No one was close by, but she'd noticed the Cey had superior hearing. *Probably the wrinkles.* "To start anyway," she admitted. "Ship controls and systems should be IU standard, Instella, but they're hoping for Dhryn records, vids. You should go ahead and take charge. I'm not sure how long this will all take."

Just then, the Sthlynii contingent went storming past, Mudge in their midst, tentacles and vowels flinging. There was the sound of doors whooshing open and a shout.

"You might want Oversight," Mac added thoughtfully.

"Definitely," Lyle agreed, whose eyes had followed the group out of sight. "Oh, here. You'll find one on yours." He pulled out his imp and activated his 'screen, setting it between them. It displayed their present location within the ship. Mac studied it, unsurprised to see most of what surrounded them left blank. *They were passengers, not crew.* Lyle ran his finger through the image, highlighting various areas in turn. "Down this corridor is the section entry station—where we can access additional stores, pick up an escort to the medlab, hangar etc."

Mac nodded. They'd passed the clear-walled room with its trio of crew sitting at consoles on the way here. Doug and Kaili had waved—likely so their group hadn't needed to stop and check in. *Escorts and guards.* She shook off a sense of being trapped. *Same side, remember.*

"Here we are. These are your quarters, Mac. We're all doubled up, so you'll be sharing with—" He consulted a text list Mac didn't bother to read. "Oh."

"Oh?"

The pink blotches deepened on his cheeks. "This has to be wrong. Someone's made a last minute change. I'll look into it."

Mac dismissed his concern. "Doesn't matter, Lyle. It's only four nights. I'll probably work through two anyway. Who is it, anyway?"

"We're too cramped," he fussed. "It's not just this ship. It's all the—" a sweep of his fingers illuminated the adjoining set of rooms "—others."

"Others? What others?" Then it dawned on her and her eyes widened. "Don't tell me the Grimnoii talked their way into coming with you."

He nodded, as glum-faced as one of the heavyset aliens. "Along with some Frow."

Mac wasn't sure if she should laugh or throw the rest of her sandwich at him. "Anyone else?"

"That's it."

"Should make for an interesting trip." She finished her drink.

"About your roommate, Mac—"

Before Lyle could finish, dozens of tiny claws fastened into Mac's back and shoulders. She yelped. Six Myg offspring cheerily yelped with her, then began gumming her neck, scalp, and ears with painful enthusiasm. *They'd missed her.*

"Er, that would be roommates."

Eyes watering, Mac glared at Lyle as she struggled with the Mygs. "You can't be serious."

He pointed at the text. "Says here Fourteen took a vow of celibacy when we boarded. He's sharing with Da'a. That leaves—"

"There you are, Mac!" Unensela swooped up to their table, completely disregarding her offspring or their current preoccupation. "I hope you aren't a noisy sleeper. I need peace and quiet at night. I must be able to concentrate on my important work."

What she needed, Mac decided then and there, *was to beg enough Fastfix from Doug and Kaili to keep her awake until Myriam.*

An offspring found her chin and began to chew.

The Fastfix hadn't been necessary, although Mac seriously considered the option that first night. She'd gone into her erstwhile quarters in search of her bags from the consulate and found both beds covered in Myg, the offspring curled together on one, purring like sinus-blocked kittens, Unensela sprawled over the other—snoring as only an adult Myg could snore.

What was it about her quarters being given to aliens?

With the ship's lighting dimmed to night levels, she'd hunted another option, prowling up and down the deserted corridor twice before spotting the glow from one of the workrooms. Sure enough, the climatologists—Kirby, To'o, and now Sam—had been huddled in front of their 'screens, talking in excited whispers. She'd poked thoughtfully at their stash of food, then asked when they planned to sleep. Their appalled looks had been most convincing.

Of course, they'd used their beds as equipment tables, but she'd cleared sufficient flat space on one for herself.

From all signs to the contrary, Mac thought with amusement when she woke the next morning and truly saw her surroundings, *the three intended to stay awake the entire journey.* Possibly fine for the Cey, but the two Human males would eventually crash somewhere.

They wouldn't be sleeping in their shower, she discovered moments later. *And didn't plan on washing either.* Their shower held their outdoor gear.

Something to mention before bodily odor became an interspecies' issue.

Mac made her way down the corridor to her assigned quarters, ignoring anyone awake and functioning—all of whom wisely ignored her as well. She was relieved to find the room Myg-free. Locking the door, she headed for the shower, then stopped.

Was she sure?

Five minutes later, having looked in every conceivable—and a few not so much—place where an offspring could wait to pounce, she headed for the shower again.

There was something essential about being saliva-free first thing in the morning.

Showered, in clothes she hadn't slept in at least once, and hungry, Mac whistled to herself as she followed the promising smell of coffee to the mutual dining room.

Her whistling stopped as she saw who filled the seats.

Grimnoii.

With mugs of—she sniffed and scowled—*cider.*

"Dr. Connor!" "Dr. Connor." "Glad we found you."

It was like walking into a funeral. Albeit a drunken funeral.

"Morning," she greeted, looking wildly for any escape.

There was a coffeepot. Mac focused on it, cautiously weaving her way between large humped backs and bandoliers studded with sharp objects. *Were they allowed to have such things on a starship?* Presumably so, unless the beings had smuggled them in to wear at breakfast.

With the cider.

"Going to be an interesting trip, don't you think?" This from the other non-Grimnoii in the room, Mirabelle Sangrea. Mac poured a mugful and weaved through more backs, feet, and sharp objects to squeeze in beside her.

"I had that feeling," Mac admitted.

Mirabelle pushed over a half-full bowl of fruit. "No use trying to reach the kitchen until they leave, Mac. Trust me, I've tried."

Mac scowled at the Grimnoii. The Grimnoii able to notice lifted their mugs to her and swayed from side to side, very slowly, altogether. "Dr. Connor." "Glad to see you."

"They're plastered," she observed.

"I'd say so. And exhausted. They've been working on their quarters nonstop since we arrived. You'd think, putting that much effort into modifications, they'd have stayed in them, but no. We get them." Mirabelle shrugged.

Mac grabbed an apple and took a ravenous series of bites, considering the situation as she chewed and swallowed. "Who gave them cider?"

"They brought their own."

Which would be her fault, Mac sighed to herself. Peeling a banana, she did her best to pretend it was toast. "Here's hoping they remember the way to their own bathrooms."

Mirabelle's eyes twinkled. "Bait them with a jug? Lock all the other doors? Install traps?"

"I've said it before," Mac grinned. "You are an evil yet brilliant woman."

They both sipped their coffee and munched fruit, watching the Grimnoii sip cider and, one by one, settle their huge heads on a forearm or tabletop. *A new spectator sport.* "How's Emily?" Mirabelle asked after the third passed out. "We got the report about the Ro—how they'd hidden something at the landing site." Always thoughtful, now she seemed to pick her words with extra care. "It must have been difficult for her."

"Em?" Mac thought of the fury in Emily's eyes, her defiant spin and exit on the walkway, and smiled. "She's back to work. She's good."

The other woman gave a self-conscious laugh. "I know what you mean. I can't wait to get back to my ruins. I've lost so much time."

If salmon are running the Klondike, they'll be passing Field Station Six.
With no one there.

Mac shook her head, but not at Mirabelle. "You'll make it up," she said firmly, as much to herself as to the archaeologist. "They've promised to set up full access to all the sites this time. That should help."

"Oh, it's going to be amazing. The data—I'll have to grab sleep now, I swear."

A Grimnoii slumped, then slowly fell off the table to the floor to form a boneless brown lump. The gleaming axes through his belt somehow missed puncturing either fur or cloth.

"Maybe that's their plan," Mac mused. "Sleep for four days."

"What's going on here?" The volume of the shout was almost as impressive as the level of outrage.

And before breakfast. "Oversight. Good morning." Mac waved.

Rumnor raised his mug before dropping nostrils first to the table.

After his shout, Mudge became speechless. He tugged at the nearest unconscious alien, succeeding only in spilling the contents of the mug the being wouldn't let go.

"We'll lock up their supply," Mac assured him. "Might as well let them sleep it off."

"This is unacceptable, Norcoast. Unacceptable!"

She surveyed the room. "It could be worse," she judged, having seen it first-hand. *Why the Grimnoii drank a substance that caused them such vile bodily reactions was beyond her.* "It will be worse," she amended. "You'd better contact the crew for a cleanup."

Mudge made unhappy noises every step of the way to their table. Mac was reasonably sure he could have missed treading on the alien at their feet with a little more effort, but she wasn't about to say anything. Sleep and a shower had done wonders toward restoring her sense of balance.

And drunken aliens first thing in the morning weren't a crisis, on the scale of things.

"Have my seat, Charles," Mirabelle offered, standing up to leave. "I'll stop by the station and pass the word about our friends."

"Thanks. There you go, Oversight." Mac grinned at him. "Apple?"

"You seem in a better mood this morning," he half accused. Rather than squeeze in beside Mac, he took the seat opposite, somehow wedging himself between the Grimnoii behind and the table. He shook his head at the fruit. "I had oatmeal and tea in my quarters."

"Foresight," she admired, smiling at her own wit, then proceeded to eat the apple herself, washing down the bites with her now-cool coffee.

"Experience, Norcoast." Almost a *harrumph.* "This hasty change was not part of my arrangements for our journey. I don't expect, nor have I seen, competence."

"Mmmfphlee," she said around a bite. *He was welcome to interpret that as he pleased.* Once her mouth was empty, Mac gestured with the apple. "All this looks pretty competent to me. It's not as if there was much notice." As far as she was concerned, drunken Grimnoii came under the heading "unforeseeable."

"It's the notice that troubles me, Norcoast." He put his hands together, just so, on the table and stared at her. Immobile and much too awake for comfort.

"How so?" She paused with the apple at her lips. *Oh, she knew that look.* She put down the apple. "I told you, Oversight. I received a message about the Dhryn derelicts being taken to Myriam and that the Ministry would help hurry us there."

"I'd like to see it."

So would she. "It was a read-once message," she said promptly, patting the pocket with her imp. "My guess is we'll get a briefing onboard. Maybe—" *she had no shame,* "—on the bridge."

Unfortunately, Mudge on a trail was as distractible as a wolverine. "For all we know, Norcoast, this is some ridiculous collusion between Earthgov and the Ministry. An ill-thought effort to put additional Humans on Myriam, flaunting the IU's per-species restriction. Who knows what problems could result?" A definitely troubled *harrumph.* "What assurances did you receive about the source of this message?"

"Enough, believe me." Mac's eyes rested on the silver rings around her finger. She'd hidden the carving deep in her luggage. "Were you always this suspicious, Oversight?"

"I could ask if you've always been this naive, but the answer would be obvious."

Mac opened her mouth to argue, when something caught her eye behind Mudge. Trying not to be obvious, she leaned to one side to better see it.

The kitchen proper was set aside from the dining area by a temporary wall, only chest high. *There.* Something small, and black, and pointy was hooked over the top, just above the table with the coffeepot and fruit bowls.

A claw?

She squinted. *Definitely.*

"I would have expected you to at least pay attention, Norcoast. This is a serious conversation."

"Oh, I am," Mac murmured, leaning the other way to follow as the claw slid sideways. It was abruptly joined by a second, slightly longer and bearing nail polish. Both pressed their tips deeply into the material of the wall, as if their owner hung on for its life.

"Norcoast?"

Mac focused on her companion. "Sorry. Insufficient coffee."

"I don't understand you," he complained, heaving a sigh so deep the nearest unconscious Grimnoii echoed it.

She chewed her lower lip for a moment, then made a decision. "How I found out isn't the point, Oversight." *Well, he'd disagree about the part where he was drugged unconscious for a good hour or more.* As Mac didn't intend to share that bit, she continued. "There's been—" she searched in vain for a euphemism remotely relevant and had to settle for, "—some difficulties on the ship with Nik and the Vessel. They're fine," *unless the radiation or whatever has killed them,* "but the—difficulty could also be related to some confusion over investigating the derelicts."

The claws, Mac noticed, were still in place.

Mudge pursed his lips and considered this for a moment. Mac took the last swallow of her coffee. Then he gave a brisk nod. "Sabotage to delay them; jurisdictional issues to slow crucial information; a rush to get us—or rather you—to Myriam. Someone's on a clock."

She forgot about the claws and gaped at him. "Pardon?"

"Really, Norcoast," Mudge pointed his forefinger at her. "It's the obvious conclusion. Do you have any idea who?"

None that she'd be willing to discuss here, surrounded by possibly conscious aliens and a set of interested claws.

"Isn't it time you were busy adding competence to something?" She said it half jokingly, but didn't smile. Instead, Mac deliberately glanced around the room and then back to Mudge.

"Ah. Yes. You have a point," he said, waggling his eyebrows with dramatic flare. "Understood."

They were, she judged fatalistically, *the worst spies ever enlisted.* Good thing there were professionals on the job.

He rose from the table as she did. Mac hefted her empty cup and nodded toward the kitchen. "I'm going to try my luck. Meet you later?"

"Later, Norcoast," with enough emphasis to make any eavesdropper pant and follow.

Once he was gone, Mac spent a moment planning her approach, walking back and forth to get different angles on her problem. As luck, or the social mores of aliens would have it, the opening to the kitchen area was behind a table with too many Grimnoii. They appeared to have started their binge facing outward. They'd ended it slumped shoulder to shoulder to shoulder, their abundant back ends lined up to form a complete barrier.

All of the aliens were comatose by this point; a few snoring, *if that's what the faint whistling sound was.* Mac put down her mug and gave the nearest a gentle poke. *Nothing happened.* A firmer one. When that drew no response, she looked at the group blocking the kitchen and assessed the slope.

Climbed worse.

It wouldn't be long before whomever Mirabelle sent to retrieve the Grimnoii showed up.

The claws hadn't budged. If anything, their hold on the wall appeared more desperate than before. Small flecks of paint were coming loose.

Mac took off her shoes, on the premise that climbing a fellow sentient while wearing them was somehow more rude. *She doubted the Grimnoii would notice.* Using a chair, she climbed gingerly onto the table in front of the kitchen, stepping through the maze of outstretched hairy arms and hands. Her right foot landed in a puddle of what she hoped was spilled cider and she wrinkled her nose in disgust.

Three of the Grimnoii were in her path, but only one had a pair of blunt wooden handles thrust through the bandolier that went around his torso. *Useful,* Mac decided.

Before she could reconsider, she grabbed the handles, one in each hand, then put her right foot on the most muscular part of the being's shoulder. When this didn't elicit a reaction, she slowly increased the weight on that foot until she was supporting herself on it.

She lifted her left foot and brought it forward, finding her balance.

Not bad.

The Grimnoii sneezed.

With a shriek, Mac went flying over its backside. Somehow she tucked herself into a ball as she landed and slid along the floor on her rump—until her rump hit something that rattled but didn't give way.

The back wall of the kitchen.

Fighting the urge to giggle, Mac stared up at her feet, then rolled her head to take a look at her surroundings. The first thing she saw was the owner of the claws.

"*Se* Lasserbee."

The Frow was clinging to a set of storage bins as well as the half wall. Like Mac, he was upside down. *A position,* Mac thought, *that looked better on him.*

She turned herself over, staying on the floor, and studied the situation. *No sparks at least. Se* appeared calm enough, though *se's* membranes were in a confused jumble concealing most of *se's* silver-sprung uniform. She decided *se'd* twisted while grabbing for handholds. The pointy hat was now under *se's* chin, exposing a plain, rounded head.

Se unfolded *se's* left neck ridge to turn that head to look at her, more or less directly. "Ah. Dr. Connor." A strained whisper. "Are they gone? Is it safe?"

Now a spark, luckily landing on the bin and not the carpeted floor. Mac hurriedly climbed to her feet, hissing as her rump expressed its opinion as to her means of arrival in the kitchen. "The Grimnoii?" she guessed, leaning over to see where the Frow's other limbs were. "They're sleeping it off."

"They were boisterous!" *Se's* pale green eyes looked almost humanly anguished.

"I'm sure they were."

"I sought refuge!"

Smart creature. "Well, you're safe now," Mac promised. "Let's get you out of here, okay?"

"Ahhh."

No more than the exhalation, but Mac thought she understood. "You're stuck?"

"I am not stuck!" This with considerable passion. Then *se* added more calmly, "The furnishings of this room are unstable and cannot be trusted."

Mac touched the nearest bin, which rocked slightly. The Frow's hand scrabbled for a better hold on it, further rocking the bin, and sparks began to fly in all directions. "Calm down," she soothed, doing her best to hold the bin steady against *se's* frantic movements. "Don't move!"

That, the Frow understood.

Once she was sure *se* wouldn't move—*likely ever*—and the sparks had subsided to a few forlorn glints, Mac slowly let go of the bin. She walked to the other end of the row and noticed all the bins were sitting on a wheeled trolley, presently locked.

She put her hand on the locking mechanism and stretched to look over the bins at the paralyzed Frow. "*Se* Lasserbee. I want you to trust me."

"What are you planning to do?"

"You told me you like protocols and procedures." Mac flipped open the cover on the lock.

"Ah. Yes." *Se's* voice lost some of its panicked edge. "I am expert in many formats."

She eased the lock a half-turn and braced her foot against the trolley. "So you know how important it is to be thorough. To follow steps in sequence."

"Yes, Dr. Connor. But what has this to do with the dreadful instability of this furniture?"

"I want you to count to three with me," Mac said. "One . . ."

"Dr. Connor!"

"Two . . ."

"What are you—" The bins shuddered wildly.

"Three." Mac unlocked the wheels and gave the trolley a shove with her foot. "Aiee!!!!!"

The bins and trolley parted company with a loud clatter. She jumped out of the way as the nearest bin lost its lid, spilling what looked like precooked spaghetti on the floor. The noodles writhed together for a few seconds before setting off across the floor, apparently drawn by the dark shadow under the half wall.

Not noodles.

Other bins deposited more sedentary masses, including puffs of white powder which drifted down to coat the now-collapsed Frow. Mac watched as *se's* clawed hands grabbed weakly at the smooth floor. "*Se* Lasserbee?" she called softly.

"Ah. Dr. Connor. Please. A moment."

Moving much more slowly than the freed spaghetti, *se* began to sort *se-self* out.

"No rush," she assured *se,* eyeing the cupboards thoughtfully.

Just then, a Human head, above a tan uniform, peered into the kitchen. "Is everything—what's going on here?"

Mac brushed powder from her hair and smiled cheerfully. "We're making breakfast."

"Where are the boisterous ones, Dr. Connor?" *Se's* neck tilted as if a Grimnoii might be hiding in the room that constituted the Frow allotment of the *Annapolis Joy.* "Are we safe?"

For a soldier, the being was remarkably timid. *Which made sense,* Mac reminded herself. *If she could be knocked over as easily as* Se Lasserbee, *she'd be timid around giant drunk teddy bears, too.*

Se'd explained *se'd* come to the dining area to wait for her, having been told every Human would appear in that room eventually. When the Grimnoii had arrived instead, *se* had prudently retreated to the kitchen to wait. Prudently yet quickly. That would be the kitchen with highly unstable furnishings, resulting in *se* being trapped.

Mac had had to help *se* file a formal complaint with the captain before *se'd* calm down enough to converse on any other topic. *In a Human,* she decided, *the being's outward reaction would mean humiliated pride.* Just as well *se* hadn't mentioned her rather crude assistance.

Of course, acknowledging help meant admitting the need for it.

She'd stayed in the kitchen, eating breakfast amid the mess, to let the Frow make *se's* way here in privacy. A very long, slow breakfast. And she'd stayed to help the crew clean up. *Still almost beat se back here.*

"We're safe. The Grimnoii are in their quarters." Without, Mac had checked, the remainder of their cider.

"Ah. Excellent. And are you comfortable, Dr. Connor?"

The Frow had managed to bring their own, more trustworthy furnishings with them. More impressively, as far as Mac was concerned, they'd managed to turn their combined rooms into an artificial forest.

Not that there were trees. Instead, everything Human had been removed, replaced by tall supports that filled the available floor space, leaving barely room for a Human to walk between, let alone a Grimnoii. The supports were identical in construction, each made of five burnished metal poles that approached but didn't quite touch the ceiling. The poles were held together by struts, again of metal. These mostly horizontal pieces were wrapped in padding at inexplicable, to Mac at least, intervals. Each support arose from a base that fit snugly against all others like a puzzle piece.

Someone had jammed rolled blankets along the edges next to the room walls, presumably to make up for a difference from expected dimensions. *Thoughtful.*

The supports were fixed, but their bronze poles had octagonal faces, catching and reflecting the ambient light depending on the angle of viewing. It gave the illusion of constant movement. The strung pads varied in color from yellow to deep red. *To Human eyes,* Mac reminded herself. The overall effect was of entering a landscape dominated by verticals and inhabited by perching lumps.

All three Frow were present, but the other two clutched poles as close to the ceiling as possible, their eyes closed. *Asleep or offering privacy?*

Se Lasserbee, hat in its proper place, had wrapped *se's* claws around a support at the room's center. Unlike *se's* lackeys, *se'd* climbed only as far as necessary to keep *se's* feet off the treacherously flat ground. *Courtesy to* se's *guest,* Mac judged it.

Arms resting on soft padding, she leaned her chin on a handy puff of bright red. She'd already discovered a convenient rail for one foot. *Not bad.* "I like what you've done with the place," she told the Frow.

"This?" *Se* Lasserbee tilted *se's* neck farther to the other side, as if there was something new to see in their surroundings. "These are portable *clocs,* convenient and secure, yes, but hardly admirable. I hope you have the opportunity to see one of our true homes, Dr. Connor."

"As do I, *Se* Lasserbee." Her lips twisted in a grin. "And my compliments. I'm impressed you managed to catch a ride on this ship."

"Ah." The metal to every side made it hard to see which glints were from *se's* eyes. "Unlike you, Dr. Connor, the other Human was gullible."

Poor Kanaci. Mac laughed. The lackeys overhead shifted positions with a click of claw to bar. One, she noticed, wound up upside down. *Didn't seem to matter.* "Why did you want to see me?" she asked.

"I have received most disturbing information, Dr. Connor. I didn't know how to handle it until you arrived."

Mac lost any inclination to laugh. "What do I have to do with it?" She lifted her chin from the pad and studied the Frow, whose offset eyes were apparently fixed on her left shoulder. "Couldn't you contact your superiors?"

Se drew *se's* left membrane half over *se's* face, allowing *se* to peek at her from its shelter. "I am a mere passenger. Those in charge of this ship permit me incoming messages only." *Se* revealed more of *se's* face. "Even if I could," this very quietly, as if trying not to be overheard by the sleepers, "I would not. This is my first field assignment, Dr. Connor. I am expected to act appropriately. And I have. I have found you. I will give you this information."

She was going to regret this. "What is it?"

"A report from our contingent at the Gathering. They were given an assignment by the Sol System Sinzi-ra, Anchen, to—are you aware of the condition of the Dhryn world, Haven, when the Sinzi first contacted them?"

"I—" Mac hesitated, thinking hard. *Was she?* "Beyond urbanized, with insystem space travel? Nothing specific. My team's been more concerned with the conditions on their planet of origin."

"Haven was stripped bare," the Frow revealed, *se's* left membrane flapping against the side of *se's* face in emphasis. *Or a nervous twitch.* "The probe found the Dhryn struggling to feed an exploding population, their resources almost gone. The building of the transect gate gave them trade as well as access to systems with worlds to colonize. We believe this saved their species."

"Good timing," Mac commented. "Hardly seems a coincidence, now, does it."

"No." *Se* clicked *se's* claws along a rail. *Approval?* "The Sinzi had received information concerning the existence of Haven and the Dhryn, information which led to their probe. Because of their dire situation and apparently peaceful society, the decision to offer the Dhryn a transect gate was hurried through the IU council. With hindsight, as you say, the significance of these events becomes painfully evident. Our researchers were asked to trace the original source of that information. It turned out to be a daunting task." He stopped.

Apparently their species shared a fondness for melodramatic pauses, Mac thought testily. "Did they find it?"

"They believe so." *Se* brought out an imp, wider but clearly kin to Mac's, and triggered a display.

Not words, was her first grateful thought. The display was a schematic of the worlds connected along the Naralax. Many were pulsing an angry red. As Mac puzzled over the now-familiar map, she began to see the pattern.

Oh, no, was her second thought.

"*Se* Lasserbee," she said, her voice unsteady. "Are those planets that have been attacked by the Dhryn?"

"Several, yes, including ravaged Ascendis. N'not'k. Regellus. Riden IV. Thitus Prime. Others have not suffered any recorded assaults."

"Yet." She clutched the bars on her *cloc*. "Multiple sources for the same message? Wasn't that unusual?"

"Ah. We thought so, too. The Sinzi of that time considered it congruent and thus somehow more credible. Between us, Dr. Connor, I don't think they are as smart as everyone thinks."

Mac didn't think *Se* Lasserbee was as smart as *se* seemed to believe, but refrained from comment. "Let me get this straight," she said, her heart starting to thud within her chest. "The location of Haven was sent to the Sinzi by all those different species. At the same time."

Se's claws tickled the metal struts, producing something remarkably like tinny fanfare. "Even from those worlds lacking the required technology. There can be only one conclusion, Dr. Connor." Another pause, but shorter, as if the being was too eager to wait for her prompting. "The Myrokynay!"

Mac heard the word and felt nothing. *It was as if she'd already known.* But a gut reaction wasn't enough. "Do you have any proof?"

"They have their agents, do they not? It's a pattern of behavior, to act behind others."

"So no proof. *Se* Lasserbee—" Mac shook her head.

"Who else could it be? Doubtless they were trying to warn the species of the Interstellar Union to avoid the Dhryn System, in hopes the Dhryn would die out on their own. The Sinzi misinterpreted. Interspecies communication," *se* announced firmly, "frequently involves such confusions."

"That it does," Mac agreed wholeheartedly, clenching her hands around the pipes until her knuckles ached. "What did Anchen say? Has she raised—" the alarm, she wanted to say, then remembered who she was talking to. *Idiot faction.* A waste of breath to argue; worse, he might stop talking to her. "Has she taken action to confirm all this?"

The Frow opened *se's* neck ridges to bend *se's* neck left, as if seeking another angle to view her. "Why would I tell Sol's Sinzi-ra before you, Dr. Connor? You are the ranking individual of our group. It has been confusing, I'll admit, but your promotion is now evident."

When interspecies communication fails, shut up. Having made this new rule, Mac followed it. She hung onto the Frow's idea of a chair and tried feverishly to piece together any sense from this.

If she believed *Se* Lasserbee's conclusion, the Ro had arranged for the Dhryn to join the Interspecies Union. *Which meant . . .* a shiver trailed down her spine . . . *the Ro had been on those red-marked worlds* before *Haven had been connected to the Naralax.*

Humanity hadn't joined the IU that much sooner than the Dhryn. The Ro had already been there, existing outside of normal time.

How old were they?

Mac deliberately pushed all such thoughts far to the side, for now. *Not helpful to reduce oneself to gibbering terror.*

"Ah. Dr. Connor? Have I said something incorrect?"

If se *only knew.* Aloud, "The Frow contingent from the Gathering reports solely to you," she ventured cautiously.

"I am the assigned nexus for all Frow reports on this subject. I handle the forms. There must be order." This last as though blindingly obvious.

It might be to someone in a pointy hat, Mac thought grimly. She plowed forward. "And you're part of my group, not Anchen's. Now."

"Yes. Yes."

"Reporting to me."

"Have I been confusing, Dr. Connor?"

Not the time for an honest answer. "Of course not, *Se* Lasserbee," Mac asserted, leaning forward as if relaxing. That every muscle in her body felt more rigid than the poles supporting her was beside the point. "I'm only—surprised—you didn't report this to Dr. Kanaci in my absence."

Or anyone else! The time se'd *wasted,* she thought with a mix of horror and disgust.

"Dr. Kanaci is subordinate," the Frow proclaimed. "All those immediate are subordinate. I am observant. You make decisions. You talk louder." A flutter of membrane. "And he was gullible." *Se's* dazzling list of evidence complete, *se* settled *se-self* more comfortably on the support and gazed at her.

Mac was beginning to suspect a certain inflexibility of thought in the Frow, or rather a channel *se's* thoughts preferred to travel. Find the individual of greatest authority. Give that individual the form. Congratulate oneself. The form's contents weren't as important as making sure it was handed up. *Probably saved time,* she mused, *but only if a reasonable chain of command was maintained.*

Abandoned on Earth, ordered to find the Ro by any means, and receiving information *se* had to know was crucial? Poor *Se* Lasserbee had made a truly stunning leap of faith to transfer *se's* upward obligation to the most likely alien.

Though se *should have picked Mudge.*

Someone more experienced in dealing with other cultures—or brighter— might have grasped the rudiments of Human hierarchies and told the ship's captain. Se *wasn't likely to get a second field assignment,* Mac judged.

She pulled out her imp and set its 'screen to intersect with *se's*. "Please transfer the relevant forms."

Se's claw tips scratched through the displays as if *se* couldn't wait to obey. Once finished, and their respective imps put away, *se* climbed partway up *se's* support and swung to hang upside down. "You will attempt to contact the Myrokynay at these locations?" *se* asked from that vantage point. "You will let me come, too?"

Mac stepped down to the floor, one hand on the nearest pole as she looked up. *Did one admit to having superiors or hold onto perceived power?* She compromised. "I must consult. You'll be informed. Thank you."

The Frow must have taken this as confirmation of all *se's* aspirations, because the next thing Mac knew, Se Lasserbee was scampering effortlessly from support to support, the close spacing of the furnishings now making perfect sense as *se's* hands and feet loosened and grasped one after the other. *Se* rushed up to the sleeping lackeys and yanked hard on each in turn. One almost fell, grabbing to save *se, ne,* or *sene's-self.*

Once awake, they immediately joined Se Lasserbee, all three flinging themselves up and down and around the room. Mac twisted her head to follow. It was like watching birds' flight, or fish darting through a clear stream. *No wonder they hate walking,* she thought, inclined to envy. Their claws made *tings* of varied pitch against the metal; their feet thumped against the pads; their membranes fluttered. The dance overlapped into melody.

To her ears anyway, Mac cautioned, smiling to herself.

She leaned on a pole, not daring to move until they stopped. A Frow at full speed took up a daunting amount of space.

Did explain the chin strap on the hats.

"Dr. Connor."

"Captain Gillis."

"Dr. Connor." With more weight, as if her name constituted some problem.

"I know who I am," Mac offered helpfully. "May I send the message?"

Captain Michael Gillis gazed back at her from his seat behind his tidy desk. He was a tidy man, his uniform impeccable, his silver hair trim and in place. He obviously ran a tidy ship; all she'd seen of the *Annapolis Joy* and her crew could be described as gleaming.

Mac, in their brief encounters together, had come away convinced he most likely folded his socks.

"To the Interspecies Consulate on Earth," he repeated her request, his tone making it clear this was as much a problem as her name. "Not the Ministry. A personal message to a Sinzi. From you, Dr. Connor."

She had no reason to believe he was hard of hearing or obtuse, so she restrained herself with considerable effort. "Yes, from me. Surely I was given authorization."

"That part was left out." Gillis' executive officer, Darcy Townee, stood to one side of her captain's desk. She was a small, round woman who might have been anyone's favorite grandmother, if you ignored the lines of muscle up her neck, the fingers missing from her left hand, and the parade-ground snap to her voice that made even Mac's shoulders itch. "We received orders to get you to the rendezvous in the Dhryn System, Dr. Connor, with all speed and stealth. Stealth, for your information, includes no outgoing signals from passengers we can't admit we have."

"Myriam."

Townee looked taken aback. "What?"

"The system and planet," Mac explained, feeling helpful. "They've been named. Myriam. It's official. You can look it up."

The exec declined to argue. "We will arrange to transfer any and all messages to a Ministry courier ship when we reach the gate."

"I'm surprised you didn't get along with *Se* Lasserbee," Mac said blandly.

"We're not in the habit of taking requests, Dr. Connor." The unspoken implication behind that being she should be grateful to be heard at all.

Mac, having argued her way past what seemed the entire complement of the *Joy* to reach this small antechamber—as close as they'd let her to the bridge—wasn't about to stop now. She leaned forward, eyes on Gillis. "We won't be at the gate for what—another two days? I assure you, Captain. This can't wait."

"You'd help your case, Dr. Connor, if you'd tell us what was so urgent." The captain raised his eyebrows. "An imminent threat to Human security? Some risk to the safety of this ship, perhaps?"

That the Sinzi themselves might have been manipulated by the Ro from the beginning? She owed Anchen the right to hear it first.

Mac pressed her lips together and glared. "Our leaving for Myriam was hardly a secret. You had to specify an approach path to move this thing safely through commercial traffic, so everyone knows you're heading to the Naralax, not another gate. What could possibly happen if anyone learns we're traveling together—a media scoop? Oh, I can see it now. 'Warship offers scientists free ride.' The demands will come pouring in—next will be physicists, mark my words. I know their kind."

Their expressions didn't change from polite attention. "Will two days alter the consequence of your message, Dr. Connor?" asked Townee.

That the Ro had been on those worlds long before the Dhryn?

That they could still be there?

Supposition. She had no proof—only the Frow's eager belief and her fear.

"Let's hope not," Mac told them pleasantly, giving up. *It was that, or a tantrum she couldn't explain.* She put her palms on the arms of the chair and pushed herself to her feet. "I appreciate your time, Captain."

Captain Gillis stood as well. "We're subject to orders, Dr. Connor." *Almost an apology.* "I trust you and your people are finding the accommodations satisfactory, the crew helpful?"

"As always," Mac acknowledged, involuntarily flexing the fingers of her left hand. "Thanks. About that message—" she looked to Townee.

"You'll want something more secure than the usual packet?" At Mac's nod, she added, "Then I'll stop by with the protocols, Dr. Connor. Is there a time you prefer?"

Mac opened her mouth to reply . . .

The alarm sounded.

11

PASSENGERS AND PROBLEMS

"**G**ET HER BELOW!" Gillis snapped, already on the move toward his bridge.

"I can—" Mac began, but Townee took her arm in a tight grip, urging her toward the door to the main corridor.

The ship's alarm cut off as suddenly as it had started.

A not-so-calm voice replaced it. "Standing down. Captain, we've a confirmed friendly on docking approach. A bloody fast approach. Permission to synchronize?"

Gillis and Townee exchanged looks. "Who is it, Ming?" she asked.

"You won't believe this, Exec." The voice developed a note of awe. "By the spec sheet, it's a Sinzi transect dart. I've never seen one before. No idea how it surprised us—Jim's looking into it. Could have been tucked behind a freighter we just passed. Sucker's bending the laws of physics—"

There was a sharp, short whistle.

"Ah, Captain—?"

Gillis shook his head. "I take it synchronization would be redundant."

"Yes, sir. They've docked themselves, sir. Hangar 1A."

With an unnecessary brush at his uniform and an uninterpretable look at Mac, Gillis headed for the bridge. When the connecting door opened, Mac could see nothing past him but stunned-looking faces.

Even after it closed, Townee remained where she was, eyes swimming with suspicion. "Impeccable timing, Dr. Connor," she said slowly. "Care to comment?"

Mac tugged her arm free, arranging her face in its best *how should I know?* expression. She'd practiced it often enough with Mudge. "Not really."

Townee's eyes hardened. "To my knowledge—and it's one of those things I would know, Dr. Connor—no Sinzi craft has ever approached and docked with one of ours. To my knowledge," she emphasized, "the Sinzi have only made appearances on planets, well-planned and prearranged appearances, with the right people in attendance. They don't sneak around other species' systems."

"*Sneak?*" The officer's choice of words made Mac snort. "I thought they were 'friendlies.'"

Townee gestured toward the door. "Everyone's friendly," she stated dryly, "until proved otherwise."

Word spread on board a ship even faster than on Base. *Due no doubt,* Mac decided, *to those on a ship not having to dry off and run up stairs first.* "Sinzi? That's what they said?"

"Would I make that up?" she said somewhat testily. "Can we get back to the business at hand, people?"

With the Grimnoii in their quarters and the Frow in theirs, Mac had hoped for some time with the seniormost members of Origins. *Gods knew, she had enough to tell them.* It didn't help that they were having difficulties concentrating, between the alarm itself and its cause. Therin kept puffing, the air setting his mouth tentacles in motion. The Cey, To'o and Da'a, poked fingers into their wrinkles as if searching for lost change, a nervous habit that made Mirabelle, sitting beside them, hold her hand beside her eyes to block the view. Busy writing his next novel, Wilson Kudla wouldn't leave the quarters he shared with his two acolytes, much to everyone's relief.

To make up for it, there was Fourteen, who shot up to pace around the table again, drawing yet another glare from Mudge.

"Would you please sit down?" she begged, rubbing her neck. "My head isn't built on a swivel."

"Irrelevant," he grumbled, but dropped back into his chair. They'd taken over the dining area, Mac and Mirabelle taking turns looking under the tables. All was gleaming, including the kitchen. *A tidy ship.* "We need answers!" the Myg declared, his eyes peering from their fleshy lids.

"For once, I agree with Fourteen," Mudge announced, his frown apparently set in place and now directed at her. "If you don't have them, Norcoast, we should call one of the ship's officers for a briefing."

Townee would just love that, Mac thought. She rested her fingertips on the table and looked at each of her colleagues, seeing trouble or concern on every face she could read, imagining it there on the ones she couldn't. "We've two days to prep for Myriam," she reminded them. "Whatever else is going on, you're heading for the planet surface, to continue our work. Important work. It's unfortunate there have been some—distractions."

"Distractions?" Lyle burst out in a laugh. "There's a Sinzi ship where it shouldn't be, the Ro have dropped something into the Pacific, and we're losing you."

"While gaining *Se* Lasserbee," she said, her lips curving in a wicked grin. "And friends."

Lyle made a negating gesture. "You can't blame me. They told me you authorized them to tag along."

"Explain to me again why you didn't request proof of any kind." This from

Mudge, who had yet to forgive the lead archaeologist for what he referred to as a logistical nightmare. Lyle turned a flaming pink and half rose in his seat.

"Let it go, Oversight," Mac ordered, sorry to have brought that up again. "Lyle. Lyle! Thank you," as the man sank back down, still scowling fiercely. *Academics and turf wars,* she sighed to herself. "The Sinzi are the captain's problem, whatever the Ro might have left is Earth's problem, and I'm hardly lost. For one thing, there could well be features on the derelict ships requiring your expertise, not just someone to read labels. If so, believe me, I'll be in touch. But before all that—I've a question for all of you. About Haven."

"We—ee are no—ot—" Therin shook from his head down and started over. "We are not experts on modern Dhryn, Mac."

"We're the other team, remember?" This from Lyle, obviously still smarting.

"You're here," she said. *Likely not making him feel any better.* "What was the state of the Dhryn world when the transect first connected them to the IU?"

By now, they'd learned her stranger questions had a purpose. They looked at one another, unease on the Human faces. Fourteen stirred first. "There are some numbers," he volunteered. "I will look at them, of course. But . . . Irrelevant? Important? Depends what you are looking for. Can you be more specific?"

"How close to extinction were they? How long—" Mac swallowed, "—how long would the Dhryn have lasted if the Sinzi probe hadn't arrived when it did? A rough estimate will do."

"A rough estimate?" Lyle looked flabbergasted. "Where's this coming from, Mac?"

"Perhaps from perception as much as reality."

Mac rose to her feet with all the others as they were joined by—her eyes widened and she heard Mirabelle gasp—not one, but two Sinzi.

Behind the tall aliens came Captain Gillis and Executive Officer Townee, both pointedly looking at Mac.

Not everything was her fault, she thought, rather resentful.

Please.

At first, Mac was struck by how much these Sinzi resembled Anchen. The same willowy form and grace, the same deceptively plain white gown, the same rapt attention to everything around them. Even Fourteen was silent.

Their differences gradually registered and she saw them as individuals. A lesser rise of shoulders, with more of an inward bend, made the one male. His fingers bore rings—*lamnas*—of red, their shimmer as he moved disturbingly like blood pouring from several unseen wounds. *Not that it likely looked that way to a Sinzi,* Mac scolded herself. His two great complex eyes were made up of five pairs. *Five minds.* He regarded her solemnly, offering a slight bow at her attention. "Dr. Connor. I am Ureif."

The second Sinzi bowed as well. Her rings were silver, set with flecks of green. Her eyes were two by two, and not quite aligned with one another. *Probably not the time to ask,* Mac decided, restraining her curiosity. "I am Fy," the female Sinzi said.

Mac hastily remembered her manners. "May I introduce—"

"You are known to us," Ureif said smoothly. "Greetings."

Now what? The Sinzi made the dining room seem cramped and overly— *Human,* sprang to Mac's mind, and she smiled involuntarily. "Are you from Anchen?" she asked.

Both raised their fingertips, forming a complex pattern, and gazed through them at Mac where she stood between chair and table.

"We participate," Fy said unhelpfully.

"Participate in what?" asked Gillis. "I'm still waiting for an explanation. Why are you on my ship?"

The Sinzi showed no sign of being offended. They lowered their long fingers, the sound of their rings an incongruous rain on water. "We participate in the promise," Ureif said, as if that should explain everything.

This couldn't be her fault, Mac told herself, despite the sinking feeling it most likely was. "So. You're here to—to help out," she said brightly. "How thoughtful."

Gillis and the rest looked perplexed. The Sinzi looked solemn.

The Frow who'd just clawed *se's* cautious way around the corner flung a membrane over *se's* face and moaned.

While the three massive Grimnoii who crowded in behind, forcing Townee and the captain to move or risk their toes, and sending the poor Frow tumbling out of sight with a squeal?

They gave a brisk salute and announced: "Sinzi-ra Myriam. Sinzi-ra *Annapolis Joy.* Your quarters for the voyage are prepared and ready."

There were times, Mac decided, *you just had to roll with it.*

She offered the beleaguered captain a cheery smile.

The *Annapolis Joy* did have a proper meeting room, Mac discovered sometime later. Like all meeting rooms of her experience, the victim was put at one end of a ridiculously large table, while all others took seats where they could stare at said victim. Although she'd never been able to prove it, she was also convinced such rooms tweaked environmental controls to create a zone of lower oxygen and temperature. *As for the sacrificial chair?* Mac thought grimly as she took her seat. *Its comfort wouldn't last.*

Mudge sank into the first seat to her right. "This is amazing, Norcoast," he whispered in a husky voice. "Simply amazing. What a privilege."

Mac glanced at the source of his ecstasy. The left wall of the meeting room was transparent, giving them a full view of the *Joy's* main bridge. Which could have been, so far as she could tell, any assortment of consoles, hovering 'screens, and intent operators from the Atrium.

Okay, there was the tree.

The tree, looking as embarrassed as foliage in that setting possibly could, stood guard beside the door to what Mac assumed was the captain's office. From here, she couldn't tell quite what kind it was. Healthy. Its upper branches had grown into the ceiling panels, leafy tips poking back out seemingly at random. Its irregular shape implied judicious trimming was all that kept it from blocking the door.

Was the tree a revelation about Gillis, she wondered, *or a legacy he's had to endure?* It might be helpful to know.

She could use any help possible. The captain hadn't been impressed to learn his visitors were now passengers. After the Sinzi left with the surprisingly alert Grimnoii, he'd scowled at her.

And all he'd said was, "Dr. Connor." *In that voice o'doom.*

Townee had jerked her head for Mac to accompany them as she'd walked out with Gillis.

Without being asked, Mudge and Fourteen had appointed themselves her escorts and tagged along. *Moral support or morbid curiosity.* A couple of crew had met them at the entry station, then all five had squeezed into a bolus for rapid transit here. The captain and his first officer had taken their own, apparently having another stop to make first.

Making their victim wait.

The Myg, uncharacteristically silent, now sat to Mac's left. He'd immediately busied himself with multiple imps, setting up palm-sized 'screens which he continued to study intently.

Out of habit, Mac felt her pocket for her own, making sure it was there. Fourteen hadn't changed his light-fingered ways. She'd asked him once why he continued to acquire the more portable belongings of others, especially since each would shortly turn up in a pile on whatever work surface he was using. *Where everyone learned to look first for missing socks.* The Myg had only smiled. The rest had grown resigned to him.

Except Mudge. Occasionally his outrage would overcome his better sense, and he'd dart in, sweep up the pile, and return the spoils to their rightful owners. Such recoveries held their unique risk, since the Myg, delighted by Mudge's fury, began hiding a noxious surprise in each pile and lurking nearby to watch. The results had been pretty entertaining, although she'd had to speak to Fourteen about permanent dyes.

Mac sighed. *Those were the days.*

"Sorry to keep you waiting." Captain Gillis and Townee entered with quick strides, as if to prove they'd hurried from wherever. Another Human came in behind the officers, not a member of the crew by his casual clothes and instant Mudge-like attention to the bridge.

Mac waited for them to take the opposite end of the table, to obtain maximum impact from glaring at her down its polished length, but the captain of the *Joy* sat beside Mudge instead. Townee took the seat beside Fourteen. Meanwhile, the stranger wandered to the transparent wall and stood gazing at the activity there, as if he wasn't part of the meeting at all.

That was an option? She wished she'd known.

"Our new passengers are making themselves at home," Captain Gillis began.

He now appeared more preoccupied than upset. *Something had changed,* Mac thought. "We've received some clarification," the captain confirmed. "Ureif— more specifically, his Iode-self—is a transect ship engineer of note and will assist Dr. Norris," a nod to the man still gazing out at the bridge, "in determining what happened to the Dhryn derelicts once we reach Myriam. We're told this Sinzi has particular expertise with their technology."

"Ureif is the Sinzi-ra for Myriam," Mac guessed.

Townee was frowning, but not at her. "Fy assumes that duty. She'll be assessing the state of the gate and monitoring all traffic. Ureif is apparently Sinzi-ra over . . ." she waved her hands to encompass their surroundings ". . . the *Joy.*"

"Not," Gillis said rather glumly, "that anyone in the Ministry can tell us precisely what that means."

Fourteen looked up, his pudgy hand slicing through all his 'screens to close them at once. "The presence of a Sinzi contingent establishes your ship as a place of significance, Captain Gillis. Ureif will not assert any control or interfere with you—but all Sinzi will pay very close attention to what happens here."

"He's a spy?" Townee pressed her palms flat on the table as she surged to her feet. "Captain, we can't permit any passenger to report on internal ship business, let alone how we carry out our orders!"

"Those orders include full cooperation with the IU and the joint investigation into the Dhryn," Gillis said mildly, tapping the table with his forefinger. He appeared thoughtful.

Although she sat back down, from her scowl Mac doubted Townee was finished. *Sure enough.* "Captain. At least let me make adjustments to our security—"

"Idiot!" Fourteen interrupted. "The Sinzi have never taken such a bold step before. That should tell you how high the stakes have become. These are beings of immense *strobis*! Your security is irrelevant. Bah! You are irrelevant!"

"Not helping," Mac whispered at him.

"Dr. Connor?"

She swung her head back to the captain, feeling like a student caught peeking at a fellow's exam. "Yes?"

"But, Captain . . ."

"Enough." Said quietly, but Townee subsided without another word. "Dr. Connor," the captain continued, "clearly Rumnor and his people knew the Sinzi were coming."

"I didn't," she said warily, guessing where this was going.

"I could tell." Gillis smiled. "No one's that good an actor." His smile faded. "Yet this is the second time today I'm faced with an unexplained connection between you, Dr. Connor, and arguably the most important species within the IU. No offense, but what's going on? Aren't you just a translator?"

"So I'm told," Mac agreed, beginning to see the poor captain's dilemma. Like the Frow, he was doing his best to find and navigate a rational chain of command. *Shame she couldn't offer one.* "Though most of the time I'm a biologist. This is only my second trip away from Earth."

Norris turned to face her. "Your first was aboard the Dhryn freighter *Pasunah*."

Part of the meeting after all.

"Yes. I provided a description."

He had a long face, the sort that finished puberty with middle-aged jowls and, in some personalities, laugh lines. *Didn't appear to have any of those.* His thick black hair was mussed, as if he hadn't noticed it yet this morning. His clothes were creased in odd places, implying they'd spent too much time packed.

"I've read your account, Dr. Connor," Norris said in a dismissive voice. He took a seat one away from Townee, as if needing space—*or a stage,* Mac grumbled to herself. He leaned back and steepled his fingers. "We'll have to see if you can recall anything useful."

Mac's lips twisted. "Have you been on a Dhryn ship, Dr. Norris?"

"I'm thoroughly conversant with the technical specifications of every transect-capable—"

"That would be 'no,'" she observed, her tone pleasant.

Mudge gave her a stern *not helping* look.

Mac ignored it. She recognized Norris' type. Academia let them flower in high-ceilinged rooms, with coffee machines down the hall. They published like clockwork and judged those around them accordingly. Fieldwork? That was for unproven grad students, who somehow never made it on the final author list.

Last conference, hip-checked one into an ornamental pond, she remembered fondly. *Landed knees up, covered with mud and lily pads.*

With frog.

"Is the *Pasunah* one of the derelicts?" she asked, fervently hoping not.

"You'll have ample time to discuss Dhryn ships later," Captain Gillis interposed. "What can you tell me about the Sinzi on my ship?" His eyes locked on Mac.

She quickly lifted both hands to show they were empty.

Gillis nodded and shifted his attention. "Arslithissiangee Yip the Fourteenth?"

"You may call me Fourteen, good captain," the Myg replied expansively, the forks of his white tongue showing briefly, as if savoring the sound of his full name. "Of course I know a great deal more. Ureif? By reputation. Don't insult him. Fy? Appalling youth for a post of importance; her selves—transect engineer Faras and student Yt—at their first accommodation. She must possess unusual gifts and/or experience to be so trusted. But Ureif?" His half buried eyes assumed their sly look, the one Mac knew meant he was anticipating their reaction. "You have on board, Captain Gillis, the former Sinzi-ra of Haven—and the Dhryn."

There had to be one, she thought numbly. The Sinzi not only maintained the gates, they acted as interspecies' oil, easing potential frictions, soothing conflicts before they escalated.

But on Haven? "I was there," she blurted. "There was no mention of a Sinzi-ra." She wasn't sure why she felt betrayed.

"Idiot," Fourteen said fondly. "Once the Dhryn had established a colony in another system, they applied to the Sinzi to exclude alien traffic from their home. Other species do the same . . . some to protect their biology, some because they realize their boring homes are not worth visiting and they wish to avoid embarrassment when tourists want their funds returned. Idiots! Never advertise a 'remarkable dining experience' when you can't cook—"

"Fourteen," Mac growled.

His pale lips formed a charming pout. "Always so serious."

She'd strangle him later. "Please."

"The Dhryn stayed within their systems, with only minor trade outside their territory. One consulate was more than sufficient. The office of Haven's Sinzi-ra was moved to the Dhryn's first and ultimately largest colony. A consulate Ureif closed when it became clear the Dhryn had abandoned their worlds for good."

Mac's lips formed the name she couldn't bring herself to say. *Cryssin.*

Brymn's home.

"Seems you're in luck, Dr. Norris," Townee observed. "Ureif will have first-hand knowledge of your derelicts."

Ureif must have known him, Mac thought feverishly. Brymn had been one of the very few Dhryn who regularly traveled to alien worlds; his research had been widely published in Instella. *There would have been discussions, arrangements, briefings on alien—on Human—behavior.* Brochures.

She had a brief, dizzying insight into how being with her, the last one to see Brymn before his transformation, might feel to Ureif. Add to that traveling with her to the site of Brymn's death, in the presence of ships from Haven?

How could a Sinzi resist?

Mac allowed herself a moment of smug. *It wasn't all her fault.*

Captain Gillis drummed his fingers lightly on the table, as if encouraging them back on topic. *It seemed his habit.* "Fourteen. What do you know of Ureif's selves?"

"Ulor, Rencho, Eta, Iode, and Filt," Fourteen listed promptly. "Ulor is the transect engineer. Rencho, consulate administrator and a sculptor of some renown, among Sinzi at least. Eta is a mathematician—not up to my brilliance, of course, but formidable. Iode, the ship engineer, you know. Filt?" Mac wondered if she were the only one to catch the slight hesitation before the Myg concluded, "The one to watch."

"Why?"

"Because, Captain, you host none other than the newly elected Speaker for the IU Inner Council."

If Gillis had wanted to establish a chain of command, he had one now. *Judging by the green hue to his cheeks,* Mac thought, *its links were a little bigger than he'd anticipated.*

Fourteen was doing his utmost to appear bored. Not believing that for an instant, Mac took a cautious sniff. *Ah, someone else wasn't too calm about this "Filt" on board.*

"And you just happen to know all this," said Townee, trading glances with her captain. "How?"

"Irrelevant," Fourteen answered, folding his arms over his chest.

"Captain," she continued, ignoring the Myg, "we're having more than enough security issues. I strongly recommend we wait for confirmation from a more—official—source before we act on any of this."

Mudge, beside Mac, rubbed his nose, but stopped short of covering it. "Confirm, of course," he said, "but, much as it pains me, I must vouch for our colleague's ability to find the most obscure or private information in minutes. I wouldn't delay necessary actions because he's obnoxious."

"Charlie!" Fourteen crowed with laughter and bounced in his chair, arms waving. " 'Obnoxious!' That's wonderful. As for you—" he snapped his fingers at Townee, a recent accomplishment of which he was very proud, "—and your security?" *Snap.* "Irrelevant! Irrelevant! I had your ship's logs and records open within five minutes of boarding. Idiots." He sat back with a smile that could only be called blissful.

Really not helping, Mac winced.

She glanced at the *Joy's* most senior officers and saw the stunned, then furious expressions she expected. Even Norris looked alarmed.

"Don't worry. He's with me," she said, before the uproar could start. *Or armed guards arrive to cause an interstellar incident.*

Or Fourteen release any more anxiety into the room.

"I was hoping not to need this," she added, almost to herself.

Mac took a blue-and-green envelope, barred in gold, from her pocket. She flicked it along the polished table.

Captain Gillis stopped it with a slap of his hand. She watched him stare at the words crawling over the face of the envelope. *Her name.* Giving her a very strange look indeed, he showed the envelope to Townee before sliding it back.

Mac put it away, along with any hesitation. "Whatever else you've been told about us—about me, Captain—we aren't subject to Human, or Myg, or even Sinzi authority. All on my team have agreed to work for the Interspecies Union. While Fourteen should have asked before dipping into your files—" she said with a glare at the being in question, who grinned back, thoroughly unrepentant, "—he did nothing outside our mandate. Earthgov and the Ministry have pledged full, unquestioned support of IU efforts to resolve the crisis, have they not?" She waited for and received Gillis' slow nod. "Those would be our efforts, Captain, among others. As for what that means to you and your ship?"

Her lips found the smile that gave grad students fits before a test. *She hated meetings anyway.*

"Thanks for the lift," Mac told the commander of the Ministry's newest dreadnought. "We'll let you know what else we may need. Now—I'm sure we all have to get back to work." She stood.

"Wait! Who do you think you are?" Norris blustered, rising to his feet as well. "You can't give us orders!" He looked from face to face, as if seeking support. Finding none, he glared at Mac. "You're just the translator, damn it!"

"Actually," Mac replied calmly, "I'm just the salmon researcher. But I'll do my best. I expect the same from you."

Townee appeared to hide a smile behind her hand. *Norris hadn't made any friends,* Mac observed without surprise.

Captain Gillis stood and offered a slight bow. "My apologies for any confusion, Dr. Connor. You will, of course, have our full cooperation."

After a thorough check on her claims.

"Tell the Ministry I'm behaving." She flashed a grin. "They worry."

"I'm beginning to see why," said Townee.

With nods to collect Fourteen and Mudge, Mac turned and left the room.

"Well, Norcoast," Mudge allowed once the door whooshed closed behind them. "That was impressive."

Mac sighed and shook her head. "I think I'm going to be sick."

"Idiot."

"And this would be your fault," she accused the happy Myg. "I was hoping for a nice, quiet, oh-who-cares-about-Mac, inconspicuous trip, but no." She poked him in the muscle of his arm with one finger. "Someone had to show off."

"Inconspicuous," he informed her, "is boring."

Boring was so much simpler, Mac thought wistfully as they followed their crew escort back to the transit system.

As well as holds full of gear, Lyle had brought himself, the original twenty-six from Myriam who'd come with him to the Gathering—Human except the five Sthlynii and two Cey—and two Mygs, Fourteen and Unensela (plus the offspring). He'd been flummoxed into adding the three Frow and five Grimnoii.

Mudge had provided Sam Schrant.

But even if the Sinzi were her fault, Mac decided, hands on her hips and glaring, *she wasn't responsible for—this.*

"How long has it been going on?" she asked finally.

Doug Court shrugged. "Since I got here, at least. You'll have to ask them."

"Them" being the Grimnoii, currently on all fours. From what she could see, their backsides tending to vast, they had their faces pressed to the base of the closed door to their—or rather the Sinzi's—quarters. As many as could. Since only two and a half Grimnoii could successfully press-face at a time, there was a slow-motion struggle underway involving far too much heaving and collision of weapon-based apparel for Mac's peace of mind.

"Might not be the best time for a question," she ventured.

The individual closest to her toes, and farthest from the desired door crack, chose that moment to burrow his way past the others. His huge padded feet worked frantically against the smooth floor until finding purchase against someone else. He disappeared beneath his fellows.

There was a great deal of moaning and one heavy thud, but, to Mac's fascination, he surfaced at the door, promptly plunging his face to the crack.

While it was all well and good for aliens to be, well, alien, this was the only corridor through the section allotted the Origins Team. Mac traded waves with those stranded on the far side of the scrum, and considered the problem.

"It's always about sex," Unensela offered, coming up beside her. She was dressed in a lab coat, open to let the offspring clinging to her chest see what was going on. They stretched their long necks and echoed, "Sexsexsexsexsex!"

Someone behind Mac snickered.

"That's not how—" Mac thought she'd best forgo the lecture and finished with, "that's not what they're doing."

"Irrelevant! The most glorious female ever to breathe must be right, Mac!" This from Fourteen as he joined them, while admiring Unensela from head-to-toe and back again. *Apparently his present celibacy was of the look, don't touch, variety.* The female Myg preened. "This is not the act," he continued, "which is highly improbable even for large mammals and must hurt—but its essential precursor. Romance!"

The Grimnoii happened to groan loudly at that moment. Mac was reasonably sure she smelled fresh vomit.

Well, they should all be hungover.

"Ship's corridors have to be kept clear, folks." Court backed a step as if to let her know he wasn't volunteering more than the regulation.

"Romance," Mac repeated. "You're kidding."

With a last longing look at Unensela, who stuck out her forked tongue, Fourteen took Mac's arm and led her a short distance from the mass of struggling fur. "The Grimnoii admire the Sinzi," he whispered.

"You don't mean—" Mac gave the pulsing mass against the door a shocked look. "They aren't trying to—With the Sinzi!"

"Idiot. You read too many brochures. Get a mate. The Grimnoii are a passionate, physical species. They suffer from—I believe the Human equivalent is an inferiority complex. A little too much passion. A little too physical. They break things," Fourteen summed up neatly. "They have come to admire the Sinzi above all other species. Since part of a Grimnoii's education is to observe the social behavior of accomplished adults, many Grimnoii instead send their unbred males to observe Sinzi." Fourteen shrugged and gave Mac his sly look. "Like Humans at this stage, they tend to be hopeless romantics."

More thudding, accompanied by cheers from the Humans on the other side. *At least one Grimnoii had acquired fans.*

"How is this romantic?" She held up her hand. "Wait. Wrong question. What do they accomplish by wallowing at the door?"

"They demonstrate their admiration for the Sinzi by doing their utmost to capture their scent." Fourteen smiled widely. "Stimulating display, isn't it? I've only seen discreet sniffing of footprints—pretend to drop something, quick nose to pavement, that sort of thing. Until now. Well, I've heard of attempts to bribe staff for used laundry, but they say that about any species."

She wasn't going to ask who "they" *were.* "Thanks. I'll take it from here."

"Idiot! They're quite fixated. And large. Wait, Mac. What could you do?"

Ignoring the sputtering Myg, Mac searched for and found their chemist on this side of the Grimnoii clot, just leaving the dining area. "Henri! A word please?" she called, walking over to him.

"Yes, Mac?"

After she told him what she wanted, his eyes gleamed. "I'll be right back," he promised and took off at a near run.

Court noticed his departure and raised his eyebrows in question. Mac grinned and gestured to him to follow the chemist. "He'll need your help."

"Idiots." Fourteen had watched all this. "Help with what? They cannot be distracted by tricks. Trust me. I know."

Mac merely smiled and went back to where she could see the Grimnoii. She found a convenient bit of wall and leaned on it.

All five appeared near exhaustion, still except for the occasional deep shuddering breath or hopeful wriggle of a shoulder. Some of the bandoliers had snapped; others were snagged together.

Reminded her of the fallen Frow, unsure how to sort themselves out.

The audience was getting bored. *Not to mention the air in the corridor was growing reminiscent of* The Feisty Weka's *bathroom.* The lucky ones on this side could go back to the workrooms or dining area. On the other, the choice was limited, since the Frow had the last two rooms to the left, the Mygs two of the five on the right.

Mac wondered what the Sinzi thought of the ruckus outside their quarters. Was it a familiar downside of working with Grimnoii—or did they put it down to something Human? Something to ask when she finally talked to them alone.

Among so much else.

She hadn't asked the captain to send her message to Anchen. Considering she'd made one miscalculation with the Sinzi-ra already, it didn't seem the right time to stick her neck out. *Atta girl,* she praised herself. *Retroactive caution.*

"Got just what you ordered, Mac." Henri and Doug Court looked inordinately proud of themselves as they returned. Henri held up a pressurized vial, about the size of his little finger. "Ethyl mercaptan. Our little low-tech trick to locate surface openings in ruins."

Mac considered the Grimnoii, still locked in their slow struggle to stick their fleshy nostrils into the door crack and sniff Sinzi. "It won't hurt them?"

"I checked. Cleared for all species presently on board. No one's going to like it," Court's wide grin was wicked, "but it's safe. Should dissipate almost immediately, but I've advised environmental to mop up the air through here."

She held out her hand. Henri looked crestfallen and Mac chuckled. "Do you want them to blame you?"

"Point taken." He put the vial in her hand. "It's potent, even dilute. One pump." He and Court covered their noses and mouths with medmasks. Unensela, who'd been hovering beside Fourteen, squealed something Myg and dashed down the corridor, the offspring squealing an octave higher. Fourteen followed at a more dignified pace.

"I thought you said it was safe," Mac protested. "And where's mine?"

Henri laughed, the mask muffling the sound.

Chemists, she muttered to herself.

This little byplay hadn't gone unnoticed. By the time she turned to face the clump of aliens on the floor, vial outstretched and ready, the corridor had emptied of all save Mac, the five Grimnoii, and the two men with masks. *Who could have brought her one.*

"One pump."

"I heard you the first time," she snapped, and pressed. *Once.*

The spray might have been next to invisible, but its result was immediate. Mac gagged as the world became one giant rotten egg. The odor lodged in her sinuses and coated the inside of her mouth. She thrust the vial back at Henri and blinked at the Grimnoii.

Who were peacefully blinking back at her. All five had sat up, their large noses—a couple scraped and bleeding—busy twitching in her direction.

"I thought Humans couldn't cook," said one mournfully.

"Someone can," sighed the next, as all began rising to their feet, loosened pointy objects clanging to the floor around them. Where they didn't land with a *splot.* As bodies uncovered the floor, it became clear there were a large number of deposits in which to *splot.*

Too much romance. Mac kept breathing through her mouth, hoping the Sinzi stayed in their rooms a while longer.

"Dr. Connor's here." "Dr. Connor."

To Mac's horror, the Grimnoii started walking toward her, arms out, nostrils working.

Feet *splotting.*

To limit the spread of the mess, she stepped to meet them, wishing she had a hose. As she got closer, she could smell the cider on their breath. Among other things.

There was something unavoidably familiar about all this.

Students on a binge.

"It isn't even Saturday," she began in disgust.

"Dr. Connor! You're here!" Before she could evade him, Rumnor grabbed her in a pungent, sticky hug.

Argh. Mac pushed free. "Glad to see you, too. Now, I want you back in your quarters."

A chorus of doleful voices: "Have supper with us first." "Come." "Smell that?" "Yum!"

"No!" she ordered firmly. "Wait! Stay where you are!"

Too late. The romantic five, apparently now famished, turned as one and shuffled into the dining area, their feet leaving prints no one would want to sniff.

Those already in the dining room rushed out, complaining noisily as they encountered deposits.

Mac sighed and turned to Court. "We'll need another cleanup in there, please."

Court and Henri kept their masks on, although the rotten egg smell had faded to a hint of decay. Henri, mute, pointed at her torso.

She didn't need to look. The damp was soaking through in several spots. "I'll be right back," Mac said. "Keep an eye on them. Please?"

A day into the trip, and she already felt sorry for Captain Gillis' tidy ship.

When it was time for a strategic retreat at Base, Mac would take out a skim and drift for a while, listening to the restless ocean. At a field station, she'd hike just far enough along the river to be out of earshot, should anyone decide to call her, and wade in the shallows to turn over rocks. Even the consulate had offered her a terrace, with its view of the deep sound and possibility of whale.

Water made everything simpler.

On the *Annapolis Joy*? Grateful to see Unensela back at work, Mac fled to their shared quarters, left the offspring pouting on the beds, and locked herself in the shower.

Good enough. With the bonus of removing Grimnoii bits.

There was only one problem with water, Mac discovered after a few moments spent relaxing in the sprays.

It coaxed unbidden thoughts to the surface.

Without asking her first.

Nik's memories intruded first, laced with pain and guilt and remorse. She wasn't surprised by the tears running down her cheeks, merely unsure whose they were.

If he were here, now, she thought with a betraying rush of heat, *they could both forget.*

But what might be happening now—what might have already happened— dissolved any warm fantasy. Mac dug her fingers into her scalp harder than necessary. Could you trust a being capable of consuming a world's life?

She should have gone.

Then who would have cared for Emily? Mac put her head under the sprays, holding her breath until her heart pounded.

Emily was in harm's way again, as much as any of them.

She should have stayed.

Fighting free of the past, Mac found herself facing her current dilemma.

"We participate in the promise."

She shivered despite the steamy water. "Only one Sinzi promise I know of," Mac whispered through the drops hitting her face. *What had Anchen promised?* "To protect herself from the Ro. While I'm to come back, with something for her collection."

Harmless enough.

Which it obviously wasn't, not if it meant other Sinzi—particularly very important Sinzi like Ureif—were "participating."

"Bother."

As a mutual language, Instella was showing some flaws.

"Norcoast?"

So much for her retreat. "Idiot!" she grumbled in a low voice, hoping he'd think she was Unensela and leave. A chipper chorus of "Macmacmacmacmac" demolished that notion.

She pressed her forehead against the shower door. "Go away, Oversight."

"We need to talk."

She'd expected him to track her down eventually, if not this fast. Mac sighed to herself and shut off the water by way of surrender.

She pressed moisture from her hair with her hands, slicking it from her skin out of long habit, although the *Joy* offered both air dry and large fluffy towels. She went for the towel option, wrapping one around her torso and securing it before opening the door to step out.

Mudge was sitting on the bed closest to the door, offspring cautiously investigating his back and arms. They had their feet and bottoms planted well back, in case he proved a hazard to young Mygs. At the sight of her, they swung up their long necks, huge eyes glowing. "MacMacMac!" they sang, with the exception of the one who couldn't yet articulate. He warbled along.

"Your cheering section," Mudge observed.

Mac sat beside him, absently collecting offspring in her lap. They'd finally grasped that she didn't enjoy having them climb on her head. *Most of the time.*

"I didn't know the Sinzi were coming, Oversight."

"But they are here because of you." An offspring charitably fell against Mudge's leg and stayed there, looking up hopefully. He offered it his fingers to gum. Another noticed and hopped over to the now-interesting Human.

"Keep them off your ears," Mac advised. She sighed, glancing at his somber face. "I think so," she agreed. "Anchen made me a promise. I had no idea—"

"What did you say?" he interrupted, twisting to stare at her. The new arrival, enjoying the game, fastened claws in his shirt and burbled. His face turned ashen. "A 'promise?'"

Not the most reassuring reaction she could imagine. "It seemed like nothing at the time," Mac defended. "We were saying good-bye. I asked her to be more careful of the Ro. She asked me to be careful, too. I promised; she promised. I thought that was it."

He blew out his cheeks, then shook his head, cradling the offspring in one arm. "Norcoast, if I didn't know you better, I'd swear you did this sort of thing to age me."

"What did I do?" Mac objected. *This time at least.* "Besides," she continued testily, "I assumed Anchen wouldn't let me do anything—complicated. She knows me pretty well." She subsided, rubbing small heads.

Mudge shook his head again, but sat back. The shock on his face gradually eased into something more fretful than alarmed. "True. The Sinzi-ra—our Sinzi-ra—is a courteous being. She understands us better than most. Not surprising she'd follow your lead—attempt to reassure you with a Human expression. Yes. I'm sure you're right." Fretful disappeared beneath a hint of chagrin. "My apologies, Norcoast."

"Don't be too sure, Oversight," warned Mac reluctantly. "There wasn't much Human about it. Her selves promised. Each in turn. By name."

"Oh, no." The shock was back in full force again.

When he didn't say anything else, only sat staring at her while hugging baby Mygs, Mac snorted. "Please don't leave it at that. If you know something, tell me so I can worry too."

"I know that Sinzi promises—the real thing—are infamous, Norcoast," he said, each word measured and careful as if to ensure she appreciated how much trouble she was now in. "They bind the individuals within a body, but it doesn't end there. To start with, any Sinzi who wishes to participate in an existing promise can arrange to do so."

"I was afraid of that," she said. "Ureif and Fy." *Did that mean extra souvenirs?* Mac wondered inanely. "Wait. You said . . . 'to start with'?"

Mudge nodded, his eyes wide as an owl's. Mac was sure hers matched. Not to be outdone, the offspring responded to the seriousness of their tones by sitting perfectly still, huge limpid eyes on whomever spoke. "Other Sinzi who share a—" he seemed to search for a word, finally saying "—who share a desire to accomplish a certain thing will also participate in a promise made by the originator of that desire."

"Anchen said they didn't make promises lightly," Mac recalled. "Now I see why."

Mudge *harrumphed.* "Excuse me, Norcoast, but you don't. Not yet. The Sinzi don't talk about promises either, but the Imrya keep excellent records. A Sinzi engineer once promised an anxious Imrya merchant his ships would always pass safely through the new transect system, a promise, I must add, made just before maintaining that system became the focus of the entire Sinzi species." He frowned. "I should mention Imrya ships were also given remarkable safety features, now standard throughout the IU."

"There are any number of perfectly reasonable explanations for the evolution of useful technology, let alone the Sinzi's focus on the transects," Mac insisted. "One promise? You can't seriously believe that, Oversight. The Imrya embellish grocery lists, let alone their own history."

Mudge *harrumphed,* his eyes sober and considering on hers. "What I believe, Norcoast, is that this promise of yours means a great deal more to the Sinzi than you appreciate."

"Maybe," Mac conceded morosely. "Aliens," she complained, "should come with manuals. Stop that!" An offspring had discovered the water drops on her back and was licking them vigorously.

Mudge took the Myg and put it on his lap with the other two. "And you should be more careful."

"That's easy to say now—" Mac stiffened.

"Norcoast?" After their years of scrapping, she wasn't surprised he could read her face as easily as she read his. "What is it?"

"Why would she do it in the first place?"

"Anchen."

"Yes. Why make me a promise, knowing it would draw in other Sinzi?"

An offspring was making its way, very slowly, up Mudge's chest, eyes fixed on his left ear. He pulled it down. "Tell me the wording. Exactly."

Belatedly, Mac thought of possible listeners and pointed to her own ear.

Mudge shook his head, the motion followed intently by the offspring. "Nothing we can do about it. What was the promise?"

"We each made one."

"No, you didn't," he said in that maddening *I'm always right* tone. "You exchanged them. Halves of a whole. The Imrya merchant promised to send ships through the transect, the Sinzi to keep those ships safe if he did. The words, Norcoast."

Mac shrugged. "I said to Anchen, 'If you promise to protect yourself from the Ro, I promise to bring you something for your collection.' She collects these tacky souvenirs," she explained, feeling foolish. "Anchen said, 'I so promise. We are bound.' She held her fingers like this." Mac mimicked the gesture, making rings in front of her eyes.

Always willing to participate in a new game, two offspring jumped for her hands. Mac hurriedly grabbed her towel.

Mudge didn't appear to notice. Putting aside his share of Mygs, he stood and began to pace, managing two and a half steps each way in the small room. Mac and the offspring sat on the bed, watching.

Finally, he stopped and gave a frustrated *harrumph*. "I've no idea what that could mean to other Sinzi, Norcoast. Are you sure you have it right? It's not like them to take such personal interest."

"Word for word," Mac confirmed. "Maybe we're reading too much into this."

"When the Sinzi-ra of the IU Gathering commits to viewing the Ro as a potential personal threat, despite there being no consensus from member species? And then the new Speaker to the IU Inner Council shows up and declares himself a participant?"

Put that way . . . Mac sighed and shifted. "I need to get dressed and talk to them. Straighten this out."

"Don't you dare!"

"I beg your pardon?"

Mudge did his impersonation of an immovable object. "You heard me, Norcoast," he said fiercely. "The last thing this situation needs is you trying to 'straighten it out.' You or any of us." He stressed the last word.

Not us? Mac tilted her head. "Then who—"

"Oh, there you are!" Unensela squeezed through the door before it fully opened. "Idiots! Starting without me!" She promptly dropped her lab coat, revealing far too much anatomy.

Literally, Mac observed, her eyebrows rising.

The Myg, or someone, had painstakingly drawn Human-ish body details on her torso. In hot pink. "I've wondered about external genitalia," she coaxed, stepping closer. "Show me yours, Charlie!"

The offspring, obviously familiar with the warning signs, dove under the bed.

Mudge, already crimson, gasped something unintelligible and fled out the door. As if part of the trap, the discarded lab coat caught him on the way and he almost stumbled, recovering to stagger out into the corridor and disappear.

"Get dressed and apologize to him," Mac said quietly, in the voice she re-served for certain students. *The ones who either straightened up or were gone.*

"Oh, come on, Mac," Unensela pouted. "Did you see Charlie turn color?" She collected her coat and pulled it over her "Human" paint job, leaving the buttons undone. "Besides, what else were you two doing, hmmm? It's a long trip and Fourteen's being tedious. You Humans must manage some fun despite your physical shortcomings. We are sharing quarters." This with that sly look.

Mac's lips pulled back from her teeth.

"Not anymore."

In the end, it was Mac who wound up with her bags in the hall. She didn't mind in the least, having discovered while hunting a shoe that the offspring had been going under the beds for more than shelter.

Never room with a procreating alien, Mac decided, making it her next new rule.

"Mac! There you are," Lyle exclaimed, jogging toward her. "I've been look-ing all over for you."

"Next time check the shower like everyone else," she said. "What is it?"

He pulled out a sheet of mem-paper. "I've been working on some projected needs, based on the data that came with the Sinzi. There've been some develop-ments on Myriam we should take advantage of before—"

Mac held up her hand to slow him down. "What data, Lyle? Did the Sinzi come from Myriam?"

"This?" He flexed the sheet. "No. The data was received at the consulate—the relay from the regular Myriam courier. Always takes a while for them to remember we exist and could use the latest reports." The bitter words were habit; Kanaci seemed as pleased as she'd ever seen him. "Good luck for us the Sinzi were coming. The courier wouldn't have caught the *Joy* before the gate and Gillis refuses to lift that ridiculous transmission blackout."

The Sinzi had traveled to Earth first. She wasn't sure what it signified, but tucked away the fact. "Did they bring anything else?"

He snorted. "Your student's boots. Seems he'd left them—Mac?" as she wheeled around to rush down the corridor.

He'd left his boots at Base.

"Where are you going? Don't you want to see the list?"

"Lists go to Mudge," Mac reminded him over her shoulder.

"Okay. Just don't forget to check your messages."

She stopped in her tracks and looked around. Lyle held up his imp and waved it back and forth, grinning.

Mac reached into her pocket for hers. "We're connected to the ship?"

"Fourteen doesn't waste time. Whatever's come in on the com squeal from the Sinzi dart's been routed per recipient. Although he's probably peeked. You know what he's like."

Mac nodded absently. *A message from Emily.* "I'll go take a look," she told him, walking backward with each word, then abruptly stopped, at a loss where to go. Privacy was nonexistent now that everyone was awake and working.

"This way," Lyle offered gently, no longer grinning at her. *She looked that desperate, did she?* "The Grimnoii did us a favor by annoying the captain—not to mention Charles has been sending memos every half hour since boarding. They've opened the level above this one for us—more quarters. Should be ready any time." He picked up most of her bags. "You've got your own, Mac. I'll take you."

Oversight comes through again.

Relieved, she grabbed the rest of her things and followed Lyle.

She wasn't the only one on the move. The end of the corridor was stacked with belongings, if not people. "We're taking advantage of the new space to re-organize," he explained. "Charles and my roommates are heading upstairs. And we've put the Grimnoii closest to the entry station. In case the crew has to clean. And—" Lyle opened the hatchlike door that had previously been sealed, reveal-ing a vertical shaft and ladder, "—they don't like climbing. So far, there's been only one glitch in the new assignments."

A flicker of shadow in the shaft and a pointy hat protruded from the top of the doorway. "Ah, Dr. Connor!" *Se* Lasserbee said happily. "Isn't this wonder-ful?" *Se* turned and disappeared upward, the click of claw on metal echoing in the shaft. Not echoes, Mac realized, so much as companions. *They must all be in there.*

"That would be the glitch," she guessed.

"The Frow won't leave the shaft," Lyle admitted. "But there's a bright side. Watch." He tossed one of her bags into the shaft.

Before Mac could do more than reach out in a futile reflex, her bag reap-peared in the firm grip of one of the lackeys, who swarmed up the ladder using three limbs. Another Frow appeared from below and hung in front of them, membranes fluttering as if eager.

She obliged, lobbing a bag into the shaft. The alien snatched it and was gone. Mac could swear *ne* chortled with glee. "Handy, that," she said.

"To a point. They'll bring everything back down again if you let them. And—they don't share well."

"Share what?"

Lyle gestured to the ladder itself.

"You've got to be—"

He shook his head. "Hold on tight. You'll be fine. It's only one level. Take one rung at a time."

The ladder ran through the center of the circular shaft, its rungs an easy step from the opening. Mac glanced down and swallowed hard. "It's more than one level," she told her companion, stepping back. *At least cliffs ended in rocks you could imagine hitting.* The shaft appeared to go on forever. For all she knew, it ran through the ship's interconnected arms.

"The rest are sealed to all but crew—unless there's an emergency." Lyle, apparently having no height or falling issues, leaned into the shaft. "If we need to evacuate, this is our closest exit. There's an evac drill scheduled before we enter the gate. Hey!"

A flurry of blue uniform and dark membrane swooped past, and Lyle dodged back into the corridor, the little hair on his head now mussed. There were whoops from inside the shaft. "They think it's a game," he said unnecessarily, running his hand over his head.

Did they? Mac wondered, but didn't bother to comment out loud. Far be it from her to disturb the archaeologist with things like territorial imperatives and the type of physical signals likely important to a species that clung to walls. *Sometimes, blissful ignorance went a long way in interspecies communication.*

Her own approach to the ladder was somewhat grim. Knowing she couldn't match the Frow in speed, she didn't bother letting them know she was coming by looking first. Instead, Mac stepped out and took hold. Firmly.

The *Joy* did have internal breezes, almost imperceptible but distinct. Mac quite liked them. But the wind that buffeted her seconds after she wrapped her arms around the ladder had nothing to do with any circulation system. All three Frow had plummeted by her, membranes expanded to move as much air as possible.

Cute.

Mac glanced up at the open door. *About twenty rungs,* she estimated.

The Frow had stopped some distance below, waiting, no doubt, for her to start climbing. That was what a Human would do.

Is that what a Frow leader would do?

Without stopping to consider the consequences if she were wrong, Mac closed her eyes and let go, spreading her arms out wide.

"Mac!" Lyle shouted as she began to tip backward and fall. "Mac!"

But even as her feet left the ladder, each of her arms was taken in a remarkably strong, but gentle clasp. Mac opened her eyes again to find herself rising, borne by the two lackeys. *Se* Lasserbee was climbing the ladder in front of her, *se's* limbs moving so quickly *se* was a blur.

Within a matter of heartbeats, they'd put her down on the next level up.

"Thank you," Mac said rather breathlessly to the aliens, now hanging upside down in a small cluster to look at her.

"Mac!"

"I'm fine, Lyle," she shouted, hearing him climbing below. One of the lackeys unfolded *ne's* neck ridges to look down and she added quickly, "He's with me."

The Frow subsided, although she thought *ne* appeared disappointed.

Maybe not a game, but certainly entertainment, she judged, and smiled to herself. "I hope you aren't tired," she told them, picking up her bags. "There's more luggage to come up."

"Your quarters are last on the right," Lyle said, stepping out beside her after a wary look at the Frow overhead. He wisely didn't ask any questions, but his eyes wondered at her.

Fair enough, Mac thought. *She wondered, too.*

"I'll go settle in," she said, impatient to check her messages. "I'll be fine," this when Lyle looked inclined to accompany her. "See you shortly."

The corridor was much shorter than the one below, with only four doors per side. Most were open, with crew from the *Joy* busy making beds. Mac assumed they used the sealed bulkhead at the corridor's end. She had no problem with being isolated from the rest of the ship. Not if it gave her privacy.

Her room was ready, almost identical to the one she'd briefly shared with the Mygs, but with a worktable instead of the second bed.

Mac dropped her luggage on the floor, closed the door behind her, and sat down at the table. She pulled out her imp, turning it around in her hands as she waited for her heart to calm down.

She'd made the right choice with the Frow. *A fifty/fifty shot.*

Now to find out if she'd made the right choice for Emily.

Taking a deep breath, Mac activated her imp and searched for messages. *There.* She touched the 'screen to open the first and found herself staring at her friend, as though they sat across from one another.

Then Emily spoke.

- CONTACT -

"**S**O THIS IS some Ministry *cabrón's* idea of keeping us in touch?" Dark eyes flashing, Emily made a rude gesture. "I hope they do better when you get to Myriam, Mac. This is ridiculous."

She ran a finger along her trim bangs. "*Ai*. All they'll give me right now. I'd better use it. But you know I hate making recordings. If I played this back, I'd erase it all. Then you'd be mad, wouldn't you? The things I do for friendship . . .

"First. Status check." She *tsked* with her tongue against her teeth, her tone growing businesslike. "I've rebuilt my Tracer. Bit of a trick. Whoever took it apart wasn't careful and I'm guessing you tried to put it back together. *Tsk*. But . . . gave me a chance to tweak things, make some improvements I'd come up with at the consulate, so no heads need roll." A flash of that wicked smile, then serious again. "Haven't tested it. Kammie's working with a few of the others to produce a better sample for the 'bots to sniff. We need to know what I'm looking for, right, Mac? Now that it isn't you."

One long finger began to tap.

"I'm giving your young friend a try. He knows his way around a deck, I'll grant you. We're installing the Tracer on one of the harvester levs this afternoon and, I admit, he's had some good ideas about that. Otherwise, he's a thorough pain and utterly, utterly boring. You did that on purpose, didn't you?" This without rancor. "I supposed I asked for it."

The finger kept tapping, a quiet, regular percussion.

Emily's lips stretched in a wide grin. "Zimmerman, though? He's been fun. Turns out to be quite the dancer. You know what they say about big feet—or maybe you don't. Poor Mac."

Tap tap.

"I hate making these. You're going to owe me, Dr. Mackenzie Connor. Where was I?" She nodded. "They're a third done with the sweep of the inlet floor—not that any of us believe we'll find anything that easily, but we have to start somewhere. The harvs and preds have a betting pool on the side. Who'll be the first to find it—whatever 'it' is. You'd think we were looking for sunken treasure. I'm the odds-on favorite, by the way."

Tap tap.

"Treasure." Emily's pupils dilated. "We know better, you and I. If we're exceptionally lucky, it'll be something we can destroy. They're outfitting the harvester with the latest and deadliest. If we aren't that lucky? Well, at least you're offworld." With a mercurial shift in mood, she laughed. "There's a switch, Mac. You gallivanting, me stuck here. Hope you're enjoying yourself. Met anyone interesting? Oh, that's right, you have. I don't have to worry about your sex life, or lack of, anymore. Whew. That's a load off my mind."

Tap tap.

"Otherwise, not much new. I haven't had time to do more than select a group to collate the latest info on the Survivors. 'Sephe's helped there—she's picked out the best statisticians among them. I'd like to bring in someone from Sencor, but that's a no. They're keeping the lid on pretty tight. I can't get onshore for lunch, let alone invite company." A pause. "That's okay. We're going to ship out as soon as the hookups are finalized. I've an idea or two for our search grid. It's a big ocean. I told you. *They* knew where to hide something, Mac. That can't be good for us."

The tapping stopped.

Emily lowered her head, showing her cap of shiny black hair, streaked with white, then looked up, a faint smile toying with her lips. "Don't worry so much. I'm fine. Recovery, scans, etcetera etcetera, better than expected, blah blah. That's what having a goal does, Mac. It keeps you moving in the right direction." Her face hardened. "You remember that, next time you look a Dhryn in the eyes.

" 'Bye for now. Stay tuned for your next exciting message from home. Whenever they let me send one. I'll expect some juicy details from you. *Adios.*"

"Hello, Dr. Connor." Hands behind his back, Case was standing on a walkway or deck, the horizon behind him delineated by the rise and fall of ocean swells. *Afternoon.* "They told me you wanted updates on everything here. From me that means news about Dr. Mamani." His cheeks reddened. "First, I want you to know I'm not going to apologize. When you get back, if you don't want to talk to me, that's fine. But you might not be back. So I did—well, what I had to do."

He coughed and moved his face away from the sun, his cheekbones growing shadows. It added years. "Dr. Mamani. Emily. You were right, Mac. She's not like anyone else. She's—" a frowning pause, "—she's like the ocean. Shows her surface to anyone. Calm one minute; stormy the next. But her depths? You'll only know those before you drown. Trust me. I'll stay clear. She scares me almost as much as she scares herself.

"Dunno if that made sense to you." A self-conscious shrug. "But I've seen the faces of people who want that one big catch so badly they'll gamble their lives—put out despite storm warnings. Emily has that look.

"Mind you," he continued, "she could be the one to do it. I doubt she's slept since you left and it doesn't show. I don't know where she gets her energy, but the rest of us catch naps when she's not looking.

"Anyway. I'll do what I can to help her. We'll put to sea tomorrow," this with transparent longing.

"You take care of yourself, Mac."

12

MESSAGES AND MEMORIES

Mac's fingers stroked through her 'screen, opening and then closing the remaining messages. Most were brief. A hello from Tie. A comment on the weather from John. A promise for more with the next courier from Kammie. The longest was a text list of indefinitely postponed projects, prepared by Marty Svehla.

Maybe it made him feel better, to share his loss.

She didn't bother reading it, past the venting stage herself.

Case's message was better than she'd hoped. She'd expected him to be perceptive, but to see Emily so clearly and still stay? "I did well by you, Em," Mac said out loud.

Emily's message?

With a sense of dread, Mac replayed it, muting the sound and enlarging the section of image that included Emily's fingertip on the desk. She slowed the replay and counted the rapid taps, recording each with the movement of her own finger within another field of the workscreen. When done, she closed the message, and brought up the results.

"Oh, Em," she whispered. "No."

Throughout her message, Emily had tapped eleven times, paused one beat, then tapped eleven times again. Over and over.

With the precision of a machine.

They'd tried—*all of them*—to find some significance to the number. Emily had been unaware. When finally shown recordings of her obsessive counting, she'd been disturbed but could offer no explanation. She'd listened with disbelief and considerable embarrassment to her own quiet complaints about the inadequate reconstruction of her fingers. Mac had stopped mentioning any occurrences. There seemed no point in upsetting her friend.

Yet the number persisted, as if from a wound that wept instead of healing.

Alluring as the idea of real privacy was, Mac didn't plan to waste time sitting in her new quarters. She had too much to do, starting with the Sinzi.

Too much to do, but she caught herself hesitating as she made to leave. Her lips curled to one side. "Why not?" she said, and dug into her pocket for what she'd carried since that night in the Yukon.

The little carving fit along the palm of her hand, its tail flexed to give the body a line of muscular tension. The pale blue of her pseudoskin might have been the waters of a river, the salmon surging upstream.

Her first gift, and he'd returned it. *Seemed her luck with men hadn't improved.*

There was a transparent shelf over the narrow desk, the desk itself beside the bed. Mac placed the carving so she would see it even when lying down.

He'd returned it because he needed her help, and knew she'd give it.

She'd never had patience for romance. *Her fault,* she admitted. But what was the point in not speaking your mind? Not to mention she failed to find pleasure taking forever over an elegant candlelit meal when there was data waiting.

To Emily's outspoken disgust, Mac usually found a way back to her data. Without her date.

Her eyes rested on the little carving. She pressed her lips to the rings on her finger.

Candles were irrelevant.

Promising herself a locked door and her own bed, Mac went in search of aliens.

The first she encountered was the Cey, Da'a, dragging a roll of fabric through the door nearest the shaft. "Hello, Mac," he greeted, both arms around the roll. She knew it was used as part of the Cey's mode of worship, although not how. The fabric was intricately woven and faintly aromatic, with more than enough in the roll to make a full-sized tent for the two Cey who'd come with Lyle. The other pair had stayed on Myriam, joining a Cey expedition. *Had enough of Humans or not invited by the IU to the Gathering?* she wondered, then thought it just as likely they'd simply preferred to stay with their work.

"Let me help with that," offered Mac.

As well she did, for the heavy roll was slightly longer than the room and it took both of them to finally wedge the thing inside so the door would close.

"Thank you," Da'a said when they were done. "My *au'us* fit in the other room. I didn't anticipate this problem."

"Why did you move?"

Impossible to read a face made of heavy, overlapping wrinkles, but Mac had come to some conclusions regarding a Cey's body language, when she had context. A slight hunch of the shoulders during a discussion signified agreement; the same posture while working alone, concentration. A gentle nodding while another spoke was the Cey equivalent of wild impatience; nodding while speaking himself, emphasis. And the ball of a thumb rolled just so against the other palm?

Amusement, at any time.

Although exactly what Cey found funny? She was still working on that.

"I changed rooms, Mac, because I was sharing with Arslithissiangee Yip the Fourteenth."

Aha. "Gotcha," Mac grinned widely. "I've heard Fourteen snore. He shook the rafters of our cottage."

"Snore?"

She hesitated. *Confusion about the word or the act itself?* "My mistake, Da'a," she said, which it likely was. *If anyone should know not to jump to assumptions . . .*

"Perhaps, Mac." His shoulders hunched agreeably. "Unless we both refer to our colleague's lovelorn poetry. Another stanza about Unensela's tongue, and I might have run shouting into the hallway like some well-nipped *sralic.*"

"Poetry."

"So he claimed. I myself judged it painful. The object of his obsession might disagree. I urged him to go recite to her, but he insisted on inflicting his verse on me. I spoke to Charles about new quarters, and took the first available."

Mac grinned. "You've made a wise choice, Da'a." She had to ask. "How did you find climbing the ladder?"

"I had no difficulties. But I believe Charles will be sending the Frow a very long and detailed memo on the subject."

She winced. "He tried to come up?"

Da'a hunched his shoulders. "Tried would be the operative word. He used uncharacteristic language. Loudly. It did not convince the Frow."

Mudge was going to blame her *for this.*

"Why would I blame you, Norcoast?" Mudge asked mildly.

Too mildly. Mac waited for the rest.

The Frow had snatched her from the ladder and carried her down faster than falling, then skittered out of sight before she could so much as open her mouth to chastise them. *They probably knew full well they were in trouble.* Lyle had only shaken his head and pointed down the corridor when she asked where Mudge might be.

She'd gone straight to his quarters—or rather his sanctum. Since losing his roommate, he'd managed to create a full office, complete with an intimidating desk facing the door, and chairs for supplicants. His bed was now a pull-down attached to the back wall. There were no personal belongings in sight. *Like Emily, he armored himself with his space.*

A *harrumph* as Mudge settled deeper into his chair, having greeted her at the door as if she was late for one of their 'discussions' about the Trust. "Just because you dragged me into this in the first place, made me spend a less-than-memorable night in a Yukon cabin, and have since failed to adequately explain even one of the events that have transpired since we left the consulate? Why would I blame you because the Frow tried to kill me?"

Mac raised a brow. "Don't exaggerate, Oversight."

He used his finger to describe a drop, then flattened his palm with a thud on the table. "Two levels before they deigned to stop my fall. Two! I could have died, Norcoast."

"You know perfectly well they were just—" Mac hesitated. *Fooling around?* wasn't quite the term for it. *Setting you beneath them?*

"Even when I insisted I was to meet with you, they refused to let me climb one rung. The only good to come of it all was that Da'a was able to use the ladder without torment. I have," he pronounced, "formally expressed my displeasure to the Frow representative."

Who'd been one of the beings tossing Mudge around. Mac frowned, afraid she understood too well why Mudge hadn't been allowed up. The Frow had established their chain of command, putting her at the top. It wasn't much of a stretch to imagine they'd given themselves a similar promotion by appointing themselves in charge of access to her.

Alien hierarchies were as abundantly awkward as Human ones.

"*Se* Lasserbee likes forms and protocols," she said at last, planning to have a private chat with the Frow concerning *her* chain of command. "As for explanations?" Mac leaned her chair back and stared at the ceiling, going through the list herself. The promise? The Sinzi on the ship? Mudge knew more than she did. What was happening with the Vessel and Nik? He knew as much.

Hollans?

One day, she cringed. *Maybe.*

"I wish I had some, Oversight," she said finally. "Back on Earth I could hunt my own answers. At least make the motions and feel useful. Right now? All I can do is worry about what might be happening."

"Which is out of our control, Norcoast." A pause. Then, quietly, "It doesn't help. Being here, on this ship."

Mac dropped her gaze to his too-knowing one. "It doesn't," she gave him, her hand, *that hand,* curled in her lap. "But we've enough real demons to keep us busy. What happened here . . . there was never ill will, Oversight. I was—" a rueful smile twitched her lips, "—just a fish out of water."

He didn't look convinced.

Time to change the subject, she decided. "Now, Oversight, what's so important you risked death by Frow to tell me yourself?"

Mudge sat straight, his face assuming a grimmer cast. "I believe there's been a discovery in Castle Inlet."

She tensed. "There was nothing in my messages." Then she remembered, like a bad dream, how Nikolai Trojanowski and the Ministry had produced vids purportedly from her to cover her absence from Earth—vids so realistic they'd fooled her family and friends. "They wouldn't dare," she snapped, ready to march straight to the bridge and demand to speak to Hollans himself.

"What, fake communiqués?" Mudge shook his head. "I see no point—we're supposed to work with Base on any data. But your people aren't the only ones looking, Norcoast, are they?"

The whoosh of giant levs overhead, the steady stream of equipment and personnel heading to Pod Two. "The Ministry?" she hazarded. "What makes you think they've found something? Not that they'd rush to tell us." *Perhaps for good reason,* she thought, remembering Nik's caution to Hollans.

"There are other channels," Mudge announced, a hint of smugness on his face. "I've maintained contact with staff at the consulate, of course, to ensure our group will receive full support on Myriam. To save time, I requested an updated inventory of materials of interest—on hand and in transit. Which I've received." He held up his imp. "It makes for informative reading, Norcoast."

Mac touched finger to forehead in salute. "I've always said you were a dangerous man, Oversight. Go on."

He didn't blush. *That serious,* she thought uneasily. "The consulate received an urgent request for equipment to be delivered to Castle Inlet. Specifically, Sinzi devices to inhibit the formation of a no-space transect, as well as their most advanced stasis chamber."

Mac leaned forward, her breath catching in her throat. For a wild moment, she imagined some pitched battle along the walkways of Base, with an intrepid Tie bringing down aliens with his trusty antique flare guns. Then she shuddered, knowing any such confrontation would be in the dark, with an enemy heard, not seen.

And involve blood.

"Do you think they've found the Ro?" she asked Mudge, unable to keep a tremor from her voice.

"The Ro seem to work through others wherever possible," he said soberly. "Dr. Mamani said they'd swept 'those who walked for them' into the ocean, along with whatever they were hiding there. My guess would be they've found one or more of those bodies. Or what's left of them. It's been months, Norcoast. You know as well as I do how efficient ocean scavengers can be."

The normalcy of crabs and bacteria steadied her nerves. "They may not be a factor," she pondered aloud. "The 'walkers' were swept down in the landslide." Sing-li had said they'd found the bodies of their agents within mud and stone. *The cold comfort of recovery beacons.* "They could have been buried." Mac's heart began to beat faster. *A look at what the Ro really were—or as close to it as possible?*

His face mirrored her own growing excitement. "And be virtually intact. If that's so—we might have gained our first advantage, Norcoast."

"I must contact Anchen. Hollans. Both of them." She rose to her feet. "I have to see the scans—get samples sent here."

He held up one hand. "Nothing can happen right away, Norcoast. The captain's right to maintain a com ban. It's just a day and a half till we meet the courier at the gate. You'll have to wait."

"Pointless waste of time," Mac muttered, but sank back down.

Mudge gave her his stern look. *The one where he planned to refuse a perfectly reasonable request on grounds that would make no sense to her.* "The point, Norcoast, would be to prevent anyone in this system confirming your presence on board until we've left for Myriam."

"Use codes. Do secret stuff." She gestured wildly. "It can't be that hard." *She wasn't that important.*

She didn't want to be.

"The risk isn't justified, not to satisfy our curiosity."

Mac scowled. "I don't see who would care."

"Do you want me to name all the species connected by the Naralax, or stop with the Ro?"

She pressed her lips together and glared at him as if this were all his fault.

Mudge *harrumphed.* "Whatever's going on, Norcoast," he mollified, "we'll learn more when we get the next batch of messages. Old-fashioned, but secure."

"I don't like waiting in the dark."

"Come now. You're capable of appalling patience, Norcoast. Use it."

Mac snorted. "Is that supposed to be a compliment?"

Mudge sat back, fingers laced together, and gazed at her.

She wasn't the only one, Mac realized with familiar frustration. "A day and a half." She made a face. "Fine. I'll start preparing my messages. Townee's going to show me their procedure for secure mail."

"Their procedures?" Mudge grimaced back at her. "That wretched Fourteen already broke those. Much as it pains me, Norcoast," he heaved a sigh in demonstration, "we'd better give everything private to him for encoding. I can't imagine anything more secure. Except for those." He nodded to her rings.

Mac shifted her hand below the table, then felt her cheeks warm. *Could she be more obvious?* "You know about *lamnas*?"

"*Lamnas,*" he repeated, as if, like Hollans, he fixed a new word in memory. "I didn't know, Norcoast. But I observe. You never wear jewelry, yet you leave the consulate wearing a ring identical to those on Anchen's fingers. It could be a token or gift. But before we leave Earth orbit, one ring has become two. Am I right to suppose you anticipate a third when we meet the courier?"

Only if Nik survived to send it.

Something of her despair must have shown, because Mudge grew very still. "These *lamnas* aren't from Anchen."

Mac gave the tiniest shake of her head.

"How dare he—?" The words were fierce and low. "It's unconscionable. Is there anyone who isn't using you in some way, Norcoast?"

"There's you, Oversight," she replied unsteadily.

"Totally unacceptable," he blustered. "Do you hear me? Unacceptable!"

"I'm not arguing," Mac said, comforted by his honest outrage. "But I'd rather know—be used—if that's what it will take to resolve all this and make sure everyone's safe."

Harrumph. "And at that time, I plan to tell a certain someone exactly what I think."

She wished Nik luck. "You do that."

Mudge *harrumphed* again, angrily, but calmed. "I suppose we must be satisfied that things are underway, Norcoast. The Dhryn ships, our going to Myriam, whatever the Ministry's uncovered . . . the other ship . . ."

That was what they called it between themselves, the "other ship," to be sure they weren't the ones to inadvertently discuss Nik's so-fragile mission.

If there was a ship the Ro would want to find, Mac knew beyond doubt, *it would be the one carrying the Vessel home to his Progenitor.*

Mac and Mudge spent the better part of an hour talking around what was to come. Neither could be sure what to expect in Myriam System, so they made contingency plans to the best of their ability. He didn't argue when she said he should go to the planet with the archaeologists; she didn't argue when he told her Fourteen should stay on the *Joy* with her. It was a measure, she thought, of how seriously Mudge took their present difficulties in communication that he wanted her to have the one being able—and fiendishly delighted—to circumvent ship's security.

When she left his quarters, she felt if not in control, at least prepared.

A feeling that lasted as long as it took for Mac to take two steps toward the dining room.

"Dr. Connor. Why haven't you reported to the simulation lab?"

Few people became this *annoying on second acquaintance,* she decided, wheeling to confront Norris.

"What are you talking about?"

He'd added a hovering 'screen to his attire, set to hang above his line of sight, so his eyes constantly flicked up to it.

Mac, considerably below, waited for him to look back down at her, mentally giving him a count of three.

At two, Norris returned his attention to her. *Disappointing.* "I sent you notification. Surely you read your mail."

"Not if I can help it," Mac said truthfully. "Is this something that can wait, Dr. Norris? I'm about to check on my team."

"Team?" His eyes lifted to the 'screen, as if seeking confirmation. "You've been reassigned to me. You have no team, Dr. Connor."

Before Mac could settle on what she would actually say in response to this, *it being early in their relationship for her to kick his skinny shin,* they were interrupted by the arrival of Sam and his new colleagues, To'o and Kirby.

"Mac! There you are. You have to come and see this."

She threw Norris a triumphant look. He didn't appear impressed. "Dr. Connor is busy," he said.

Mac wasn't sure which reaction was more telling: the sudden silence, or the way even the Cey's eyes opened wide as all three climatologists stared first at Norris, then her.

Too easy, she decided regretfully.

"Dr. Norris, why don't you grab a coffee and we'll continue this later," she advised, keeping it civil, then walked past them all, heading to the work area.

First to move wins.

But she'd underestimated Norris' ability to miss a cue. "Dr. Connor," he exclaimed. "Our time on the ship's simulator is not limitless. And Dr. Cayhill is waiting."

Mac's hand twitched. Despite her instinct to keep on walking, preferably until the entire bulk of the *Joy* was between them, she stopped and turned around. "What could Cayhill possibly have to do with some simulation you want to show me?"

Norris' show of surprise was a little too studied. "Aren't you aware of safety requirements when a subject is immersed? A physician must be present. Dr. Cayhill, being familiar with your physiology, kindly volunteered."

Familiar with what's left of my arm, she nearly said aloud, but knew too well how someone of Norris' type would respond. Instead, she gave him a withering glance before saying to the now-worried climatologists. "Oversight's in his quarters. Fourteen's somewhere in the work area. I want them both here, please. Now."

They hurried off, glancing back at her with questions in their eyes. Mac crossed her arms and stared up at Norris. "The *Pasunah,*" she said.

"A working facsimile, yes." He looked insufferably pleased. "I knew this class of ship carried a complete suite of training sims."

"Is this really necessary?"

"It wouldn't be if your 'firsthand' account had been at all adequate."

She felt her right leg tense and deliberately eased her posture.

"Mac?"

"Norcoast?"

From different directions—*and different-shaped windpipes*—came identical tones of disapproval.

"They'll be coming, too," Mac informed Norris.

Dr. Gordon Cayhill was a middle-aged man of average height, average mass, and—in Mac's estimation—above-average tenacity when it came to what he viewed as the most appropriate medical treatment for his patients. No doubt he'd performed miracles for those in his charge.

The only problem? He'd wanted to perform one for her as well. She'd said no. Loudly. Repeatedly. And with all the apparent impact of water rushing over a barnacle glued to stone. The only plus had been to leave the ship knowing they'd never have to deal with one another again.

Funny how things worked.

She didn't bother to smile. "Dr. Cayhill."

"Dr. Connor." He didn't smile either.

"Charles Mudge III," that worthy introduced himself, pressing forward into what was patently a conversation going no further without help. "I presume you are qualified to supervise such a procedure?" His voice implied anything but.

Now Mac almost smiled.

Fourteen wasn't to be left out. "Irrelevant. We presume nothing." He drew out an imp and set a 'screen up between them, muttering under his breath as he worked. Then, "Ah! Oh. You are." He closed the screen and gave Mac a shrug. "At least he hasn't let anyone die."

"There," Norris pronounced. "Can we get on with this?"

No? Mac swallowed, aware she'd gone as far as she could in terms of protest. More and Norris was capable of tossing Fourteen and Mudge from the room. *She didn't want to be alone here.*

Norris, with the inevitable escort of *Joy* crew, had brought them to this distant part of the ship. It was an area without the warm colors and natural light tones seen elsewhere; the corridors were lower, cramped, their walls curved in as if reinforced. Mac remembered it vaguely—she must have been carried through here when brought on board.

Screaming.

She made herself focus. The simulator lab was more of the same, function and form. The presence of life was mocked by sullen gauges and flickering displays. The center was taken up by a long, low box.

Great, Mac thought, licking dry lips. *It would have to look like a coffin.*

"Do you understand the procedure, Dr. Connor?" Cayhill asked.

She made herself walk to the box. "Incoming feeds supply the simulated environment I'm to experience. The firing of my nerves to move muscle will be translated into that environment seeming to move past me." She shrugged. "Everyone's played games on a sim."

"This is far beyond anything you've seen within a game platform," Cayhill stated dryly, opening the lid. Mac stared down into what appeared to be a nest of dark wire and somehow managed not to leap back. "We use a combination of sub-teach and other neural methodologies to induce a totally convincing experience. Your own memories will fill in any blanks. You'll believe you are again inside the Dhryn ship, Dr. Connor."

Wonderful.

She'd briefly explained what Norris wanted to Mudge and Fourteen on the way here. Neither had offered an opinion. *Not out loud.* She could read their disapproval; she knew they understood why she wanted them there. Now Mudge stepped up, his shoulders squared. "Given you will shortly have three Dhryn ships at your disposal to examine, Dr. Norris, I fail to see how this is anything but an imposition and a waste of Dr. Connor's valuable time."

"And who are you again?" Norris demanded, sneering at Mudge.

"Idiot!" bristled Fourteen. "To begin, he is someone immensely more important than you, and obviously of greater intelligence. Bah. This entire process is irrelevant. You are irrelevant!"

Mudge looked astonished; Mac hid a smile. Dr. Cayhill showed no expression whatsoever. "It's my understanding the captain requested this process, Dr. Connor," he said. "I'm aware you do not always follow regulations or recommended procedures. However in this instance I must warn you failure to oblige this request will not be taken—"

"Shut up, Cayhill," Mac suggested, turning back to the coffin. "I'm here." She poked at a wire. "Let's get this over with, shall we?"

"As you wish." He indicated one of the doors lining the near wall. "You'll find a jumpsuit through there. It contains the necessary receivers and contacts. Put it on while I get ready."

She nodded and took a few steps, only to be intercepted by Mudge. "Norcoast," he whispered, "are you sure about this?"

Fourteen was with him. "Idiot." His hands hovered near his face, as if he wanted to cover his eyes. "This procedure is intrusive. It could be dangerous. You should refuse."

Not helping, Mac thought, but reached out to touch both of them. "That's why you two are here," she said, not in a whisper. *Let Norris and Cayhill know she had brought not reinforcements but witnesses.*

Mudge understood—or else he read her determination in her face—because he stood aside and let her go.

Reality was a dream.

Mac ran her finger around the viewport, skin catching on the tiny burr of metal she'd found there once before. Her breath again fogged over stars and Earth and Moon. The air entering her nostrils was familiar, metal-tainted and dry.

The *Pasunah.*

Much as she hated to admit it, Cayhill had been right in this much. It wasn't like any vid game she'd tried.

The jumpsuit had clung to her skin, from fingertip to toe, the inside of the fabric prickly and uncomfortable, like shorts worn too long at a beach. That awareness had vanished the instant she'd lain in the coffin, swamped by overwhelming sensations of pressure and cold. She'd muttered something about improper calibration, only to have the words trapped as a mask was placed on her face. A moment of suffocation and utter darkness, then . . .

. . . she'd been here, in her quarters on the Dhryn freighter.

"Impressive."

Mac would have been more impressed if Cayhill had told her how to get out of this. But no, he'd insisted her vitals would be monitored and that waking her—*not that she felt asleep*—would be done automatically should it be necessary.

"Hopefully in time for lunch," she grumbled.

Her quarters looked exactly as they had when she'd first seen them. Walls met at angles closer to seventy degrees than ninety, well suited to the slant of an adult

Dhryn's body. The middle of the large room was filled with an assortment of Human furniture. She remembered breaking much of it.

Funny how she now saw it intact.

"Guilty conscience," Mac decided, heading for the door.

Starting her in this place, if there'd been a choice, could be Norris' first and last mistake. The Dhryn, frantic to escape the Ro who'd penetrated the way station, had rushed her on their ship and locked her in here for the duration. "Not going to explore much if that's still the case," she commented, hoping Norris could somehow hear her.

Then Mac spotted something new, a palm-plate beside the door. It hadn't been there before, at least not on the inside, where a passenger could reach it.

She studied it, oddly nauseated by the deviation from memory. *What else had Norris meddled with in the simulation?*

There was one way to find out. Mac stretched her left hand toward the plate, only to freeze in mid-reach.

Her hand was flesh.

"Of course it is," she scolded herself. She was experiencing the *Pasunah* as she'd seen it.

So much had been different then. She reached behind her head and touched the loose knot she'd half expected. It was still a shock to free the braid and bring it forward over one shoulder, to run the length of hair through her hands.

Mac shoved it back. "Move on," she warned herself. Her thumb rubbed the emptiness of her ring finger. She wasn't interested in reliving the past. *The present was sufficiently complicated, thank you.*

She touched palm to plate, determined to get this over with as quickly as possible. Norris wanted a Human perspective on the corridors and hangar deck, particularly where they would be entering the derelicts. It shouldn't take long, if she could get out of here.

To her pleased surprise, the door retracted upward to reveal the brightly lit corridor beyond. "Nice," she commented, stepping out. The corridor was more spacious than she remembered, which likely had to do with the Dhryn procliv- ity for carrying her from place to place like so much luggage.

Mac picked left and started walking, dutifully observing the occurrence of closed doors—*three*—and inset light strips—*continuous*. She counted her foot- steps, on the premise that the more data she gave Norris, however trivial, the less argument he'd have for a return trip.

Which she wasn't making.

The freighter wasn't the *Annapolis Joy*. Thirty-one steps took her to the end of the corridor and the large doors that led into the hangar.

Mac frowned. It had seemed farther. Of course, being clutched by a running Dhryn tended to distort one's sense of distance.

And she hadn't been feeling observant at the time. In fact, she'd been shout- ing at the top of her lungs. They hadn't answered her questions. They hadn't spoken to her at all.

She hadn't been Dhryn then.

Mac opened the hangar doors.

The space inside was empty except for a few cables along the floor and a large skim, crumpled nose-first against the near wall. Its front end wasn't badly damaged, but apparently whomever had piloted it hadn't bothered to slow down before entering. *Or they'd used the wall for brakes.*

Mac walked over to it, recognizing the skim. *There'd been a jolt,* she recalled. She'd put it down to alien driving, it being her first such experience. Norris must have made his own interpretation.

They'd been terrified. Mac ran her hand along the silent machine, walking toward its end. No matter what others thought now, the Dhryn she'd known had feared the Ro. "With good reason," she said aloud.

"What are you doing, *Lamisah?*"

"Just looking around," Mac said absently, reaching out to pat Brymn's warm, rubbery arm. "There's this annoying—"

She froze, whirling to look into those large golden eyes, their curious pupils like sideways eights. Violet sequins dotted the bony ridges above them, more traced the rise of cheek and curled above the ears. His lips, currently a rich fuchsia that matched the bands of silk wrapping his blue torso, shaped a cheerful smile as familiar as breathing. His hands were whole. *Brymn, not Brymn Las.*

"You're dead," she told him.

A hoot of amusement. "And why would I be dead, Mackenzie Winifred Elizabeth Wright Connor?"

He wouldn't be, she realized. "Damn Norris," she said. "He added you to the simulation."

"Why would 'Damn Norris' do that?"

"I—" she closed her mouth and thought about it. "You're right. He wants to know about the *Pasunah.*" Then, she knew. "Cayhill." The word came out like a curse. This had all the hallmarks of his well-intentioned interference.

When she'd become a "difficult" patient, he'd fixated on her inability to read and apparent lack of grief, believing her suffering from stress, if not outright brain damage. He'd declared her unable to make clear decisions and requested permission to take complete charge of her care.

She'd clearly decided to leave his care for good, Mac recalled. She'd stormed out of the medlab and refused to go back. *There might have been some broken glass.* Cayhill had been overruled not so much by Mac's own fury as by the needs of the IU investigators, who desperately wanted her full cooperation and weren't interested in inter-Human squabbles.

She had a great deal to thank aliens for . . . starting with this one.

Simulation or not, her eyes swam with tears as she looked at him, whole and blue and vibrant. "It's good to see you again, Brymn," she told him before she thought.

The golden eyes glistened, too. *They shared that response.*

"Have you missed me, *Lamisah?*"

The question caught her unprepared. *Did it come from the simulation program or her thoughts?* "We're both on this ship," she countered.

"Do you still grieve for me, Mackenzie Winifred Elizabeth Wright Connor?"

The form was perfect, from the curious tilt of his big head to his padlike feet. The words weren't.

Cayhill's Brymn, not hers. Mac edged away until her back hit the skim and she was pinned.

The Dhryn with his dear face loomed closer. "Why do you not answer, *Lamisah?* Is it because you are about to run? You know you should. You should run as far and as fast as you can."

Gods, no!

She covered her mouth with one hand, holding in a scream.

His eyes grew smaller and sank back. The intense blue of his skin faded, as if washing away with every pulse of his blood.

Mac lowered her hand, reached it out even though it trembled and her mind gibbered with fear. "Stop, Brymn," she begged. "This isn't what you were supposed to be. You were to be one of the glorious ones. A Progenitor. This—this is something the Ro did to you."

The bony ridges that defined his features smoothed back into his skull.

Mac couldn't get enough air. It was a *simulation.* She fought to see something else, *anything else.* She tried to imagine his arms growing larger instead of thinner; she tried to see his eyes as warm and gold and real.

She smelled rot.

His mouth opened, the only feature left to recognize. "Gooooooo."

His hands had become mouths, his shoulders and sides grown shimmering membranes. He inhaled and soared from the deck.

Green rain struck her face and upraised hands, dissolving flesh as she finally started to run, washing away her back as she fell.

Fell into a pool of liquid.

Then the mouths began to drink.

- 13 -

POMP AND PROMISE

MAC AWOKE, SURPRISED to find herself whole. She opened her eyes, not surprised to find herself in the medlab.

For a series of deep slow breaths, she considered Cayhill. Specifically, she considered the most practical way to dismember his body before feeding the bits to young salmon. *Who were,* she thought with satisfaction, *always hungry.*

Aware she'd never inflict such a fate on any fish, Mac regretfully abandoned her fantasy and sat up.

"Norcoast!"

"Morning, Mac." This from Doug Court, who gave a series of gauges by the cot a professional look before taking her wrist to check her pulse for himself. "How do you feel?"

Mudge hovered at the orderly's shoulder, his face paler than she'd ever seen it. "Rested," she said for his sake, looking around to see who else might be here. She relaxed when she saw the three of them were alone.

"Dr. Cayhill wants to be called when you wake up," Doug said carefully.

Meaning he hadn't made the call yet. Her hands found the sensors attached to her forehead and neck. She yanked them off. "Be my guest," she said, swinging her legs around and sliding from the cot in one more-or-less easy motion. The easy part was the swing; standing without obviously tilting was harder. Mac focused on Mudge. "I'm done here."

Without a word, he held out his arm.

"Your clothes." Doug went to a cupboard and brought out her things. Mac glanced down, only now realizing she wore one of the ill-fitting blue gowns Human medical practitioners felt obliged to inflict on the sick.

Maybe she would just feed his fingers to the fish.

"Ah, Norcoast?"

Mac looked at Mudge, whose face looked more pained than she felt. Immediately she eased the tight grip her artificial hand had fastened on his wrist. "Sorry about that." The *lamnas* were still on her other hand, she noticed with relief.

"What happened in the simulator?"

Cayhill kept recorders running in this room. She'd learned that lesson long ago. Mac arranged her face in its closest approximation to dazed confusion, *not hard,* and pretended to give Mudge's question some thought. "Not a clue," she said finally. "All I remember is falling asleep. Quite peaceful, really. Guess it didn't work."

Choke on that, she wished her listeners.

"There you are!" Fourteen came close to knocking Mac down when she arrived back at the Origin Team's section of the ship. He settled for bouncing up and down on his toes, shirttails flapping. "The idiots wouldn't let me stay while you were without clothes. I suppose one has to have external genitalia. Sexism. I left Charlie to enjoy the view."

Mac saw the moisture along his eyelids, and the way the Myg couldn't stand still. Beneath the foolery lay sincere concern. She was touched.

Mudge was insulted. "I did no such thing."

"Enjoy or view? That makes no sense. Idiot!"

Mac slipped her arms through both their elbows—Fourteen's being thicker and lower than Mudge's—and steered them away from their interested escort. She'd lost enough time. The corridors had brightened to daylight shortly after they'd left the medlab, meaning she'd been out of commission for over fourteen hours. Time she should have spent working, eating a couple of meals, followed by a night in her own new bed.

A strike against Norris and Cayhill.

"What's been going on?" she asked her companions, loath to let go. She didn't want to admit, even to herself, how good it felt to hold them, how much she needed to know she still had arms and it had been nothing but a simulation.

No nightmare had been as real. Strike two.

If she was kind to Cayhill—*unlikely*—she'd try to believe he couldn't have known how much memory she could bring to his little role-play, how accurate her sensory awareness of death by digestion would be. No physician would willingly put a patient through that, for whatever reason. *Would they?*

If she was paranoid—*getting there*—she'd believe he'd done it under orders to reinforce her fear of the Dhryn, to further taint her memories of Brymn so she'd view his kind as the prime threat instead of the Ro.

The idiot faction had Human members.

Unaware of her dark turn of thought, Fourteen rambled on, giving a typically personal answer to her question. "—I ate with the gorgeous Unensela, discovering that the most tasteless pap is exquisite if she is near me." He gave a huge smile. "After that, I returned to the task of encoding innumerable boring messages. You Humans spend too much time reciting your irrelevant daily routines to one another."

"And you don't?" Mudge snapped. He'd pressed the elbow wrapped by her fingers gently to his ribs, as if promising that support as long as she needed it. "Are you psychologically incapable of giving a simple status report?"

"Idiot!" Fourteen stuck out his tongue at Mudge, its forked tips flailing the air in front of Mac's nose. "Nothing. How's that? Everyone spent last night worrying about our Mac. There was no work done at all."

Strike three.

"Norcoast!" This as Mac tugged free her arms and started walking more quickly. The other two hurried to catch up.

"Find space and assemble everyone concerned—ten minutes," she said over one shoulder. "Including the captain."

It took forty-five minutes: sufficient time for a furious biologist to shower and change, albeit into an amber-and-blue silk suit the consulate staff must have deemed travel wear; abundant time for the vagueness of "everyone" when said to a certain Myg and a zealous memo-happy administrator to sink in.

So Mac was not completely surprised by the sea of faces that greeted her when she followed Lyle Kanaci into what must be one of the larger meeting rooms on the *Joy.*

New rule, she vowed, *be specific.*

However, their arrangement stopped her in her tracks.

The Sinzi had set up court.

It looked like nothing else. Grimnoii stood at slouching attention to one side. The Frow, desperately straight and balanced, stood to the other. Humans and other aliens formed an interested mass in front. While the two Sinzi, Ureif and Fy, were slender white pillars to either side of—

She was not *sitting in that chair.*

"Macmacmacburblemacmac!!!"

Any potential dignity afforded by the now-appropriate silk suit vanished under the onslaught of anxious offspring, who clambered up her as if she'd been a tree. She winced as fabric tore.

Mac carefully shifted the one nuzzling her neck to her shoulder. Again able to breathe, she gave a small, resigned sigh and took the few strides needed to bring her closer to the Sinzi, but not the chair. *At least there wasn't a table,* she told herself. "Hi, everyone."

"What's this all about, Dr. Connor?" Captain Gillis' face was set in neutral. She decided that wasn't because he didn't have a strong opinion about being hauled from his bridge to this—*whatever it was*—but rather was waiting for her to give him the opening to express it.

She was going to lock Fourteen and Mudge in a closet and . . .

"Hello, Captain," Mac said, setting her voice to confident. "Just a final strategy session. To—" There being no discreet way to stop an offspring from burrowing into an armpit, her smile became somewhat fixed. "To be sure we're all clear on what's going to happen post-transect. We are going through the gate this afternoon, are we not?"

"Eleven hundred hours shiptime." Executive Officer Townee's opinion was easy to read, her thinned lips and scowl cues to all Humans in the room. Mac appreciated that clarity. *There was something to be said about dealing with your own species.*

But Humans, in so many ways, weren't the issue. "We find congruence in Dr. Connor's desire to meet at this time," Ureif said, dipping his long head in Mac's direction. "This is a critical juncture, Captain. To all here, our thanks for coming."

Mac brightened. *Maybe the crowd in this room wasn't completely her fault.*

"Dr. Connor," Rumnor came forward and indicated The Chair.

She was being punished anyway. Seeing no way to avoid it, not without offending the Sinzi, Mac sat. With the offspring, who promptly started rearranging their holds on her clothing to better see what was happening.

Ureif leaned over and, without moving his lips, made a *chipchirrup* sound. The offspring swung their faces toward him and echoed it, eyes wider than usual. A second, more emphatic *chirrup* from the Sinzi, and the offspring climbed off Mac and scampered into the assembly, presumably seeking Unensela.

Despite being relieved her clothes would now stay intact, Mac found she missed their warm little bodies. *Probably because now she faced "everyone" without support.* She checked her posture and swallowed, hard.

There was a soft tinkling of ring to ring as each Sinzi rested the tip of one long finger on Mac's shoulder. Startled, she glanced up at them, but both were looking toward the captain.

Whatever its meaning, the gesture didn't go unnoticed. To'o's wheezing inhalations—the Cey being congested since morning—were the loudest sound in the room.

"We wish to hear your suggestions as to the deployment of personnel and resources, Captain Gillis," Ureif said, his voice soft and mellow. "I will, with your consent, establish a consulate within your vessel to service those involved with the Dhryn ships. I anticipate ongoing negotiations. I trust you can accommodate any who need to stay on board? Three staff—" a finger lifted to indicate the Grimnoii, who shuffled proudly, "—will be available to liaise with your crew."

"Two will travel with me." Fy's paired eyes caught the light as she nodded graciously to the remaining Grimnoii. "My dart will be insufficient. I trust you can provide additional small craft to convey us and our equipment to the transect station as well as to the planet surface."

Fingertips pressed gently into Mac's shoulders. *Her turn.* She coughed and gave the plainly astounded captain a sympathetic look. "The Origins Team will be divided during the investigation of the derelicts. I trust—" she deliberately echoed the Sinzi phrasing, "—you can provide those who remain on board full and independent communications with those on Myriam."

When someone opens the spillway, she thought smugly, *you swim.*

She saw the captain's hesitation, his quick glance to Townee and back to her, but couldn't guess which way he'd go. Her experience with Human government and bureaucracy had tended to be of the "maybe, if you shout long enough" variety—*no offense to Mudge.* Her experience with the military mind-set? Based on Emily's old thriller vids. *Likely unrealistic.* Her recent stint with the Ministry had been—*confusing.* Something of a blend of anxious bookkeepers and overprotective relatives.

The captain had the ability to stop the Sinzi from playing a role at Myriam. *He could,* Mac realized, dry-mouthed, *turn his ship around and take them back to Earth.* Or he could cooperate on every level. She didn't see any middle ground. Either he honored the intent of his orders, to assist the IU as it sought an end to whatever combination of Dhryn and Ro threatened life, or he retreated behind the doubtless innumerable regulations designed to keep a Human ship on Human business and under Human control.

Been there, Mac reminded herself. *"Where on that scale . . ."* The grim reality applied to individual species, as much as to individuals. *None of them were safe.*

As if he knew she understood, Gillis' eyes burned into hers. She dared a slight nod.

After twelve heartbeats, he returned it.

"Your trust honors us," Captain Gillis stated, his voice sure and strong. Townee's scowl vanished, as if she'd only needed a decision. "The *Joy* is at your disposal, Sinzi-ra. My exec will work directly with your staff. Dr. Connor, expect modifications to your working space. We'll have to install the equipment you need."

The fingertips lifted from her shoulders as the Sinzi performed one of their elaborate gestures. Framed by such grace, Mac stayed absolutely still. *The moment called for some dignity,* she decided.

Which again lasted only until the irrepressible Sam Schrant shouted "Hey, Mac! Ask for ribs!" from the safety of the crowd.

They might have stirred an ant nest, Mac decided two hours later. She dodged against a wall to avoid being run over as a pair of Grimnoii rushed past behind wheeled carts loaded with dark Sinzi bags.

The establishment of a formal consulate, or the best facsimile possible in the time before reaching Myriam, consumed the *Joy* crew as well. Ureif would remain in the quarters he now shared with Fy, but he'd provided an extensive list of requirements for the other space he would need. Mac heard bits and pieces, mostly from Mudge. Despite the bags under his eyes and her own guilt, she'd asked him to keep involved. Not only had he agreed without hesitation, he'd already managed to justify two trips to the bridge.

Among the more urgent Sinzi requests had been those for meeting rooms and accommodations with direct access to docking ports.

Expecting company.

The Grimnoii were a bustle of efficiency, when they weren't saying good-bye to one another. Mac spotted a couple rubbing noses outside Ureif's quarters. They seemed overcome by the urge to stand and sniff at regular intervals.

She assumed the Sinzi-ra were aware and had factored the trait into their schedule.

For a schedule it was. Sandwich in hand, Mac made her way to the work area, once split into four, now divided into three. The combined, larger space was being filled with consoles, displays, and chairs. Gillis was as good as his word. A shifting number of crew had taken up floor plates and were installing various feeds. Fourteen hovered excitedly, pocketing tools when no one was looking, producing one with an innocent smile whenever an irate Human shouted for it.

The waiting courier ship would dock with them within the approach funnel leading into the Naralax. A lesser gate, in terms of volume, but most of its traffic still required tugs to reach final approach positioning. The dreadnought was among the few permitted to enter on her own. Mac hoped that meant they went faster.

She didn't like waiting.

"Dr. Connor!"

She was pretty close to not liking Norris either.

"Over here." She sat on the nearest empty table and waited, taking the moment to finish her sandwich.

Norris wove his way through a confusion of bags and people to reach her side. "I sent you a—I've been looking for you."

"You've found me."

His imp was in his hand. "Have you had a chance to think more about your sim experience? Dr. Cayhill suggested some recollections might begin to surface."

Mac understood the almost pleading note to his voice. She'd been his hope for more data on the Dhryn ship; it wasn't his fault she'd explored so little of it. *Thirty-one steps, three doors, one friend.*

And death.

"Sorry, Norris," she said, surprised to mean it. She'd written her own memo to Gillis, copied to Hollans. It sat waiting with the rest of the messages Fourteen had, in his terms, "brilliantly convoluted." Cayhill, regardless of his motivations, would no longer be a factor in Mac's life.

Though dismemberment had its appeal.

She didn't believe Norris had anything to do with the perversion of the sim. He was too focused on his own work to care about anything else. *Something she could appreciate,* Mac admitted. "If I get a minute, I'll go back over my original statement. Might jog a memory," she offered. "Though the Dhryn didn't let me see much."

"You would?" His eyes widened. "I'd appreciate that, Dr. Connor."

She slid off the table. "Anything else? It's a little crazy at the moment."

"Yes. Please." Norris leaned over her, his free hand reaching as if to make sure she stayed.

Mac sidled to avoid the touch, trying not to be obvious. *Civil,* she reminded herself. "What?"

He lowered his voice. "I understood this was a Ministry operation, Dr. Connor. There was no mention of aliens being in charge."

Or biologists.

Nonetheless, she had a fair idea what troubled him. "You're worried they won't let you on the ships."

"Ureif knows more about Dhryn designs than I do."

Mac smiled at what seemed an honest complaint. "I can't see the Sinzi-ra exploring in person. You should be able to do all the crawling about you want. But if there's any problem, let me know."

"Why do they listen to you?" Norris looked perplexed, his voice plaintive. "Who are you?"

No one you'd know, she felt like saying, but settled for, "When we've time, I'll do my best to explain. Right now, I suggest you finish whatever prep you have to do. Once we're in Myriam, it's likely to be pretty hectic. First ready," her grin was the one that gave new students fits at the start of the field season, "first out the door."

From his expression, she'd presented him with a new concept. *Bet you've made plenty of others wait on your timing,* Mac thought less than charitably. But she'd done her best. Time to finish her own preparations. "See you on the other side," she told him, and walked away, aiming for the one work area where scientists were still actually working.

"Kirby, To'o," she greeted, stepping over piles that hadn't been there yesterday. *It was as if clutter found them.* "Dr. Schrant." She wasn't ready to let him off the hook—yet—for shouting her name in the meeting. *At least he hadn't done the entire chant,* she shuddered.

"Hey, Mac." The three looked up through their 'screens. "You got a minute now?"

She checked the time. "About that." The courier must dock soon. She planned to be first in line, not last. But these three had been at her heels since yesterday. "What is it?"

To'o grabbed a paper-laden chair and tipped its contents to the floor. "Have a seat, Mac."

"Corrupted by Humans," Mac observed. As she sat, Kirby hurried to reposition one 'screen in front of her face. She squinted at the now-familiar outlines of the planet Myriam. "What am I looking for?"

"Watch, Mac," Sam urged. "We've run this umpteen times. Here's the way this world should be."

"'Umpteen' is not a—" Mac closed her mouth. The world in front of her had transformed, the upper hemisphere blue-green, white at its pole, the southern brown and yellows. The image flickered, showing the world going through its annual seasons. Winter storms, dust clouds, cyclones. The pace of change increased, until a new pattern appeared. Over time, the seasonal changes shifted closer and closer toward one another, change coming now quickly until, like a flash, the moment came when greens appeared at the lower pole, while at the upper they faded to brown and dull yellow. *Triggering the Dhryn migration.* "I've seen this," she reminded them. "Myriam experiences a periodic shift in tilt, affecting the overall climate."

"Did you notice the oceans?"

Mac looked at the image, now flickering so rapidly the change from north to south was like a pulse. Myriam's oceans resembled narrow ribbons. Much of the planet's water had been underground; it had never been as moist as Earth. "What am I to notice? They look normal enough."

"Exactly." The three exchanged proud looks, then gazed happily at Mac. "Isn't it great?" Sam asked.

She'd utterly missed the point. Mac frowned at them. "Explain 'it.' "

"Oh." Kirby and Sam looked a bit too contrite. To'o, as if unaware the wrong Human might understand the gesture, rolled his thumb along his opposite palm.

They were laughing at her.

Mac sighed. *Students.* "Remind me to show you geniuses some comparative physiology one of these days. What's so great?"

Kirby poked his finger into one of the oceans hanging in midair in front of Mac. "This should still be here."

Sam took over. "Nothing we've done . . . no scenario we've input, no even more catastrophic climatic change or the loss of living matter . . . nothing removed the surface water in this way. And you know how good I am at catastrophe." He folded his arms, looking pleased with himself.

Mac nodded absently, staring at the image of a world that should be, and wasn't. "So it was a weapon of some kind. The Ro. We were assuming as much."

"Not so fast." Kirby leaned forward. "We checked with the other Cey group. They've been looking at the planet surface for signs of some kind of attack. Nothing."

She frowned. "Then where did it go?"

"Away." The three shrugged in unison, a gesture the Cey copied perfectly, then sneezed.

" 'Away,' " Mac repeated. "What kind of answer is that? Away where? How?"

"We need more data," To'o stated. The others nodded. "Further samples from the ocean floor could tell us if the water was destroyed on site."

"If not, maybe it was collected and carried off somehow." This from Kirby. "There are water miners—"

"Way too sudden for that," Sam objected. "I keep telling you . . ."

Mac stopped listening, her mind filled with a dark tank, boiling with life; she could feel that voice etched along nerve endings. "Or it was drained," she said very quietly.

"To where?"

"Anywhere. Through a no-space opening within the ocean. The Ro could be capable of that. Maybe they put some kind of device or gate underwater. In an abyss."

"Mac?" She hadn't realized Sam had freckles, but he'd grown so pale a smattering of them appeared on his cheekbones. "Do you think that's what they left in Castle Inlet?"

For an instant, it was as if she could see it happening . . . the low tide that didn't end, the drying continental plains and estuaries, the snap-crack of settling ice, the last-ever flows rushing down sea canyons, the belching of released gas as the floor itself was exposed . . . the tremulous few gasping in exiled pools, to die by sun instead . . . the rains that failed . . .

Mac tightened every muscle to hold in her shudder. "Good question," she said, making it brisk, rising to her feet. "Do you have all this ready to send to Base?" They nodded. *Your chance to save the world, Em.* "Give it to Fourteen. Tell him to mark it top priority. And Sam?"

His eyes were as haunted as hers must appear. "Yes, Mac."

" 'How' isn't as important as 'why.' There's a reason for all this," she promised, herself as much as the frightened climatologists. "It's our job to help discover it."

Mac left them to it, considering an addition to her own message for Emily. *Doomsday device. Have fun hunting.*

She shook her head. While she didn't doubt Emily would be exhilarated by the challenge, neither of them had believed the Ro would leave anything less.

And what she really wanted to ask, she couldn't. Not without undermining Emily's fragile self-confidence. Not without cueing those who'd doubtless scan all incoming messages that Emily might not have recovered enough to be trusted.

Mac intended to know, some day.

Why eleven?

Mac was halfway up the ladder to her quarters when the courier arrived, the Frow apparently otherwise engaged. *Maybe they preferred to spend transect in their quarters.* She wasn't quite sure who on board ignored passing through no-space and who fussed in a corner. Kudla, it turned out, was one of the latter. He and his disciples had locked their doors and asked not to be disturbed until safely through to Myriam.

She'd set her imp to an audible alarm, cued for that announcement from Mudge, waiting on the bridge. When it went off, she paused, hands tight on the rung. *Up or down.*

"Down."

Admit it. Her heart wasn't hammering in anticipation of a transmitted message.

Mac's feet and hands thudded against the rungs as quickly as she could move them, her left palm making a slightly crisper sound. *The one time she could use the Frow.* One rung . . . two . . . three . . . her right foot slipped on the fourth and she recovered. Five . . .

Chime!

One rung . . . two . . . three . . . her right foot slipped on the fourth and—

Mac stopped and held on, breathing more quickly. She knew what that moment of déjà vu signified.

They'd gone through the gate.

She resumed climbing down, trying not to estimate how long it took to dock a ship and cycle through an air lock, for someone from that ship and air lock to hand a small package over to the right authority, for that person to return through the air lock into that ship and for that ship to remove itself and move to a safe distance. Because if she did . . .

Mac stopped and rested her forehead on the cold metal.

She'd know it hadn't been long enough.

"As if I know anything about starships," she scolded herself, and started moving again. "Maybe they throw things at each other."

But Mac no longer hurried, afraid of what might not be waiting.

"You should have seen it, Norcoast." Mudge was practically aglow. "A splendid maneuver. Simply outstanding."

Executive Officer Darcy Townee preened. *The only word for it,* Mac thought, fascinated. "We work on our precision."

"And it shows." He seemed about to bow, but turned it into a more restrained duck of the head. "I was privileged to be on the bridge during the event."

"Anytime, Mr. Mudge," offered Townee.

"Charles, please."

"Darcy."

Gods. The woman was blushing.

Mac took a deep breath and let it out. She'd wandered up and down the section of the ship open to passengers in search of a courier package, trying not to appear too eager while asking anyone likely. Intercepting these two on their way back to the Origins area had been promising—until she'd realized neither was carrying any sort of pouch.

"I guess there's no mail," she said. *And Nik was dead.*

"Pardon?" asked Townee.

"She means messages," Mudge translated, remorse wiping the smile from his face as he took in Mac's expression, which mustn't have been the "don't care" one she'd attempted.

"We entered the gate too soon," she managed, looking only at Mudge. *What had it been—radiation, the Dhryn, his wound . . . some other danger no training or technology could avoid . . .* "There couldn't have been time."

"Now, Norcoast, there's no reason to—to think the worst," he told her, as if hearing her thoughts, not her words. "The *Joy* didn't rendezvous with a courier, she took one on board. It's sitting in the ship's hold now. The maneuver I praised was the *Joy* scooping up the waiting ship while launching another to stay in Sol. It will transmit our messages to Earth."

"While incoming messages were sent immediately to their recipients on board, Dr. Connor," Townee explained, looking puzzled. "Don't you have yours on your imp?"

Mudge *harrumphed* for her attention before Mac had to gather her wits to reply. "Darcy, there would be some delay releasing physical items, surely. Security and safety checks?"

"You're expecting freight?" She sounded mildly offended, as if the Ministry's fleet of couriers was being subverted to carry stuffed salmon.

Mac shot Mudge a look of pure gratitude, uncaring if the officer saw it. "Something like that," she said. "How soon—"

"Dr. Connor." "Dr. Connor." Rumnor and another of the Grimnoii came up behind, moaning her name.

Mac felt like moaning herself. *Aliens had the worst timing.* "Now's really not the best—"

"Now is when the Sinzi-ra must see you."

"Ureif?" Mac asked. "But—"

"Ureif's busy on the bridge, Dr. Connor." Townee's eyes narrowed. "We arrived into a situation. Com traffic's heavy and I'm sure he can't be—"

"Sinzi-ra Myriam." "Fy awaits. Hurry."

They might sound and look miserable, but Mac recognized determination when she saw it. *Along with significantly greater mass.* "I'd better go, then," she sighed, but gave Mudge a look she hoped he could read. "Oversight?"

He gave that brisk *man-on-a-mission* nod, and she felt a surge of relief.

To think, she used to find it annoying.

Mac resisted the urge to hug him.

The Grimnoii took up positions to either side on the way to the Sinzi's quarters. Given their bulk, and the variously jutting points that glinted menacingly with each ponderous step, their little procession effectively wiped the hall of other pedestrians. Mac grimaced an apology to those ducking into doorways or backing up. *It would take longer to argue with the Grimnoii than to get there.*

They stopped in front of the closed door, waiting. Mac waited, too, sneaking sidelong glances at her escort. Their eyes had stopped producing the congealing yellow tears, so obvious at the consulate. Without them, and the crust they produced, the hair on their faces and chests was a clean, shiny brown. *Much more appealing.* She couldn't resist. "Rumnor? Your eyes are much—" she sought a neutral term, "—drier."

"You noticed." He heaved a sigh that rattled knives. "They itch, too. We ran out of drops last night."

"Drops?"

The other Grimnoii lowered his voice to a confidential bass mutter, his breath vaguely floral. "We're allergic."

"To—" Mac realized both were looking at her, blinking, *now that she knew to pay attention,* their swollen and red-rimmed eyes. "Oh. To me?"

"Humans. Mygs. " Deep and sad. "Everyone we've met."

Feeling a quite extraordinary guilt, Mac tried not to breathe in their direction. *Nothing she could do about shed skin.* "I can ask the captain," she offered. "Maybe the medlab has something you can use."

"No need." "The Sinzi-ra knows and will care for us."

"Speaking of the Sinzi-ra," Mac ventured, eyeing the still-closed door. "Shouldn't we let her know we're here?'

The Grimnoii looked at one another, then at Mac. "There is a difficulty," Rumnor admitted.

"Faras wishes to see you," his companion whispered. "Yt is unsure."

"Hush!" Rumnor growled.

A Sinzi, with disagreeing selves? Whatever else, it didn't bode well for Fy as a Sinzi-ra. "When in doubt," Mac decided. She knocked firmly on the door.

The Grimnoii drew back in apparent horror.

The door opened on darkness. A long finger appeared in the light from the corridor. It stroked the air in a beckoning gesture, its rings of silver and gold tumbling up and down, before it disappeared again.

Mac stepped inside the room, unsurprised by either the white sand underfoot or the failure of her escort to follow.

The door closed, and she couldn't see a thing. From the restless tinkle of metal to metal, the Sinzi was to her left. *Somewhere.*

Mac considered the situation and hadn't a clue. *When in doubt,* she reminded herself again—as she had many students—*ask.* "Do you not want me to see you, Sinzi-ra?"

"You have eyes, do you not?" The calm gentle voice might have allayed concerns about being locked in the dark with a crazed alien; the underlying assumption gave Mac pause.

"Human eyes are adapted to use our sun's peak output, Sinzi-ra. I require light between four hundred and seven hundred nanometers."

"So narrow a range. Remarkable. How do you manage?"

A flashlight helps, Mac almost said, but restrained herself. She heard the Sinzi moving in the sand, her long-toed feet lifting and pressing down, the brush of her gown along the fine grains. Then she blinked in ship-normal light. "Thank you," she said at once.

Fy arched her neck and tilted back her head, a posture Mac had never seen Anchen perform. Her eyes glinted. She held this position for five seconds, then returned to normal, her mouth pursed as she studied Mac. *As if she'd been expecting something in return,* Mac decided. *What?*

"My apologies, Dr. Connor. I do not know about Humans. In fact, I do not know much about any non-Sinzi life-forms. My work has not involved you. Until now." A gesture with two fingers. "I feel woefully inadequate."

She *felt inadequate?* Mac wasn't sure whether to run from the room or not say another word. *She wasn't qualified for this conversation.* "Please, call me Mac. Anchen does," she added, waving her hand in a vaguely Earthward direction.

With startling speed, Fy rushed toward her. Mac held her ground and her breath, but the taller alien stopped short of contact. Instead, one finger lifted to indicate Mac's right hand. Or rather what she wore on that hand. The *lamnas.*

"These are not yours."

Was that a problem? Running became a serious option, but Mac kept still. "They're from Anchen," she agreed. "A gift."

"Yes. The other promise." The Sinzi leaned over as if to study her, head swiveling to bring one set of eyes after the other to bear.

"What other . . ." Mac's mouth snapped shut. *Of course.* "What promise did Nikolai Trojanowski make to Anchen?"

Fingers flashed to loop before her eyes and the Sinzi answered. "To find the truth about the Dhryn and bring it back to her."

Mac licked dry lips. "And—Anchen's?"

"To maintain his connection to you, regardless of distance. An interesting challenge."

"You were involved?"

The Sinzi dropped her fingers from her eyes. "Of course. A promise reliant on our system affects every transect engineer. In this case, we agreed to supply Nikolai's ship with six explorer probes, each capable of opening a temporary nospace passage to return home."

Handy, Mac thought numbly, aware it was far more than that. As far as she knew, no other species had been granted access to the Sinzi's cherished probes. They were used to contact and assess potential new members of the Interspecies Union.

When not carrying her mail.

"Home," she echoed. "To Earth."

Pursed lips. Then, "Was that an inappropriate word, Mac? I mean no disparagement to Human theological or historical beliefs but I refer to N, the system of Sinzi biological origin. From there, your *lamnas* and any other information are transferred to waiting Human courier vessels and sent to Sol System."

Human ships, in the famed Sinzi home system? *The Inner Council must have had polite fits.* The oldest friends of the Sinzi, the systems first connected by their transects. The powerful.

She could just imagine Hollans' glee when he'd learned of the plan Nik had arranged.

With more of that disconcerting speed, Fy went to sit in one of the room's four jelly-chairs. When Mac didn't move, the Sinzi again pursed her lips before speaking. *Confusion,* Mac judged it. "Don't Humans use chairs, Mac?"

A Sinzi with no experience with aliens, she reminded herself, missing Anchen. Mac sat in the jelly-chair nearest Fy, sinking in with an involuntary smile. "Oh, yes," she said.

"You must tell me at once if my behavior is offensive," the Sinzi urged. "Ureif believes I can manage, but—" Her left fingers trailed in the sand while the right formed a tense knot on her thigh. "Yt is disconcerted."

She knew that feeling. Empathy warmed her voice. "And you must ask me if you find anything about Humans confusing."

"I have been given brochures," confided Fy. "I plan to study them carefully when time permits."

Was no one safe from Fourteen? Mac shook her head. "You'll get more reliable answers from me, Sinzi-ra. Believe me."

"Anchen did state this. Which is why I asked staff to bring you to me, Mac. I will soon leave for the transect station and then the planet." The knotted fingers visibly tightened on one another. "I will be alone."

"I'll have access to communications—you can call me any time," Mac promised, bemused to be the one offering comfort and advice. "Before you go, Fy, I'll introduce you to Charles Mudge. He's going to Myriam as well. You can rely on him."

Fy's head went back, but only for an instant, as if she'd realized the gesture meant nothing to Mac. Meanwhile, her entwined fingers loosened, but kept moving with a slow fretfulness over the fabric of her gown. "I am grateful. But, while we remain congruent, I have questions, Mac."

"Please." Mac sat back and hoped for something easy. *Like external genitalia.*

"Why am I here?"

Okay, not easy. "What were you told?" she hedged.

"I participate in both promises Anchen has made with Humans. To fulfill my duty to yours, I was told I was needed here. That you would explain why."

"Me?" Mac said incredulously. "Anchen said I would?"

"Can't you?" The knot began to re-form, joined by the left fingers.

Mac tsked her tongue against her teeth. "You know about transect systems," she hazarded. "Myriam has one."

The fingers flew apart, dancing frantically in midair, rings tinkling like so many castanets. "I'm an archaeologist, not a traffic analyst! I should be back at my work!"

"But Fourteen said you were a transect engineer," Mac countered, then corrected herself: "Faras, that is. And Yt is your student. Oh. Sorry." *Don't identify the component personalities,* she scolded herself. "I didn't mean to be rude, Fy."

A lift of fingers that had to be surprised laughter, from what she knew of Anchen. "A transect engineer who studies the remains of alien technology discovered in the Hift System. And whose student is the inestimable Yt, a historian of promise. Our field is not one of wide interest. The Sinzi moved beyond the partial clues left by the Myrokynay long ago." Not pride, but certainty. "However, there remain interesting questions about the originators of the technology I hope to answer one day."

Mac could hardly breathe.

She'd asked Anchen to protect herself from the Ro.

And been sent the Sinzi's expert on Ro technology.

"You must have attended the IU's Gathering on Earth," she ventured.

Fy brought two fingers close, but not touching. "Anchen accessed potentially relevant data from all Sinzi, including mine. I study molecules of metal, Mac. I analyze dust for alien components. I interpolate design from pieces found in congruence. My work has nothing to do with the living."

"You'd be surprised," Mac said, feeling suddenly old. "Correct me if I'm wrong, but it's my understanding the transects within the Chasm don't use Sinzi technology, but were reactivated when the Naralax was—" *What did you call it when a nonexistent worm burrowed through no-space and left a hole that wasn't there?* "—made."

"Through the Hift System, yes. But it would be incorrect, Mac, to say the Chasm worlds continue to rely on alien technology. The first act of the Sinzi upon discovering the Chasm was to replace all existing transect stations. The originals were destroyed, of course."

"Why?" Mac asked, startled.

A look that in a Human would be astonishment. "They were less stable. We could not permit unsafe connections to our system."

The promise to the Imrya freighter? She wanted to ask, but thought better of it. *Really didn't want to know.* "So the remains at Hift are all you have to study."

"Yes. Which is why I am confused to be here." Distress. "How can I serve the promise?"

Fy's *lamnas* caught Mac's eye. The rings were bolder than Anchen's, their mix of metals reflecting unsteady white-and-yellow flecks that ran down the walls. *Like water.*

"There might be more remains," she told Fy. "We—the Origins Team—are exploring the hypothesis that the Ro—the Myrokynay—used no-space technology to somehow drain Myriam's oceans, very quickly. If they did, there should be some physical trace of their technology. Like Hift." She didn't let herself think about a working version. *Not yet.*

"Why would they do this?"

"We're looking into that as well," Mac said grimly.

With the swift grace of a pouncing cat, Fy lunged to her feet. She began to pace, the panels of her gown fluttering. "I must go down there. At once! I must have samples, scans." She lifted all six fingers before her eyes, as if searching for a *lamnas* to set it all in motion.

Though loath to leave its comfort, Mac extricated herself from the jelly-chair. "On that front, I have good news. Myriam's been a very busy corpse. I daresay every centimeter's been mapped and surveyed. Enough data for a start."

Fy stopped pacing to look right at Mac. "Even if your hypothesis is correct, Mac, there may be nothing to find. Much of the Hift site was left intact for us. There's no reason to assume any other Myrokynay site will be as cooperative."

"Left intact for you." *She didn't like where this was going.* "You think the Ro meant you to find it?"

"There is no proof." The Sinzi-ra spread out her fingers, then pulled them into her body. "However, our more recent history has become of concern. Anchen has brought forth the possibility that the timing of our discovery and its implementation as the transect system suited the purposes of the Myrokynay. The findings of how we were 'shown' Haven and the Dhryn only underscore this."

"You've heard." Some tension she'd carried until now released, and Mac smiled. "The Frow were so adamant about following their own chain of command." *To her.*

"Of course. We have arranged to hear everything of interest that travels the transects."

Mac blinked. "I don't understand," she said, fearing she did.

A graceful sway left, then right. "I do not know how it is for a Human in these times, Mac, but the current lack of consensus among the IU species on this situation deeply disturbs us. We do not easily comprehend such a state as sane. Though I am arguably closer to it during this difficult phase of my life, even I cannot imagine the ability of others to function while in disagreement." Fy ran the tip of one fingertip down the rings of another. "When disturbed, all Sinzi listen. Very carefully."

The Sinzi-ra in every system of the IU were eavesdropping? Mac had no problem imagining a unanimous reaction to that revelation from both sides of the Ro debate. "Please don't talk about this to anyone else, Fy," she warned uneasily. "It's important. You can ask Ureif, if you wish."

"I do not need to ask. I trust you, Mac. Do you require a promise?"

"No, no," Mac replied hurriedly. "I trust you as well. Focus on the problem— leave the politics to others." *Her own plan.* Fortunately, the problem was bigger than any politics. "Before we jump to any conclusions about Ro motives," she went on, "keep in mind their sense of time isn't like ours. I've a feeling they understand biological timelines, but there's no evidence they grasp how long it takes other species to change culturally." *Or care,* she added to herself. "Including the time it took you to develop no-space technology. I believe they were surprised by the Sinzi application at the consulate. The display tanks?"

"I will keep this in mind. Yet there is admirable congruence in their actions."

Mac hesitated, leery of misinterpretation. *Between her assumptions and Fy's Human-naïve enthusiasm, probably not much could be worse than the two of them talking.* "How so?" she asked finally.

"They return to you, do they not?" The pacing resumed, as if Fy were too excited to stand still. *Or she thought better moving.* "Demonstrably, Mac, you have come to occupy a rational nexus of attention, being of significance to both past and current Dhryn, and to the Gathering of the IU, while reestablishing your own connection to their former agent, Dr. Mamani. To be in your presence must be a powerful attraction for the Myrokynay."

Now there was a horrifying thought. Mac shook it off. "I appreciate the compliment," she told the Sinzi, turning in the sand to keep watching the alien as she paced around in a circle. "But it's a Sinzi perspective. Other species don't necessarily think in such terms."

Fingers swung from side to side. "What other terms are there?" Fy demanded, moving around the room faster and faster, her long legs flying.

Shoes full of sand, Mac began to get some idea of the effort Anchen had expended to learn to interact effortlessly with Humans. "Would you please stand still?"

Fy might have turned to stone. Sand drifted down around her hem.

"Thank you. And here's some advice about being around Humans. Fewer, slower movements. We get dizzy."

Fy's fingers twitched at their tips. "This is unnecessary with the Grimnoii."

"The Grimnoii," observed Mac, "shove their noses under your door. You could probably dance on their heads and they'd like it. Which reminds me," she continued, having a suspicion of what might constitute "necessary." "You do know about their eyedrops? They expect you to provide them."

Fy sat down again. Considerably more slowly, this time. "What are eyedrops, Mac?"

Interspecies communication fails again. Mac decided life was too short to keep score.

"We'll put Oversight on it," she said. "But first, let's take a walk. I've some colleagues you'll want to meet."

Prioritize.

Mac left the huddle of Sinzi, Human, and Sthlynii to its work. They'd plunged into the more esoteric realms of molecular archaeology, opening overlapping workscreens replete with jargon. She'd become unnecessary; Fy confident. *Leave it to a mutual passion to get past the little things.*

"Prioritize," she repeated under her breath, wondering what to do next. The hall and rooms were still buzzing with activity, but with an anxious underlay. Arrival in Myriam had revealed some complications.

Rumor, the fastest briefing, held that a Trisulian warship was on approach to the *Annapolis Joy,* demanding some kind of clearance from the Humans. Mind you, rumor also held that Dhryn Progenitor ships had been sighted in any of thirty systems, tonight's menu would include fresh N'not'k clams in mint, and Wilson Kudla had sold a new book which would detail his successful mystic battle with the Myrokynay.

Of that list, she'd go for the clams.

"Couriers can carry clams," Mac muttered, pausing to give a Grimnoii right of way. Yellow liberally stained his cheeks, chin, and clothing, and he looked as close to content as one of his kind could. *Mudge was a force.*

He'd been waiting for her outside the door to Fy's quarters. One look at his face, and Mac had known. There hadn't been a package for her.

Since, she'd gone through the motions. *Easy to be calm, when you don't dare think.* Mudge had wanted to talk; she'd sent him after eyedrops.

She felt enclosed in a bubble, detached from the conversations walking by with their preoccupied owners, their urgency. *She needed work.*

"Prioritize," she said again, forcing herself to examine the 'screen floating beside her face, using the effort of reading to stay focused.

Cayhill's entreaty for her to come to the medlab she deleted. The current set of complaints about Fourteen she grouped into one, forwarded to the Myg. *He'd enjoy that.* Mac frowned. Norris had sent her several messages, all marked, of course, urgent.

Spotting him coming down the busy hall, she deleted those, too.

"Dr. Connor!" He halted to let Da'a go past, then had to dodge around three intent Humans and their cart. *The man had a gift for finding traffic.* "Dr. Connor, a moment please."

Mac closed her 'screen. "Got your messages," she informed him. *Technically true.*

He came close and lowered his voice. "Can you be ready?"

Might have been a bit hasty on the delete, she realized. "Ready for what? When?"

"I've obtained clearance." He didn't appear to notice her admission of ignorance, perhaps used to her. *Or too intent on himself,* she judged. "The *Joy* is closing on the first derelict. We should be in range within the hour."

"They've settled the jurisdictional issues?" Mac felt a shiver of caution. *Nothing was this smooth with aliens.*

"We've permission for an external survey. A start. I want you to come. Please. I'll send someone from the crew to bring you to the hangar bay when it's time."

She was nodding before realizing she'd made a decision. *Fine, then.* "I'll be in my quarters."

Mac sat on her bed, knees and feet neatly together, hands in her lap. Her hands, palms up, cradled the carving she'd given Nik, and he'd sent back to her through Hollans.

"You've been around," she told it.

The wood took warmth from her skin, as the living version would from the water around it and the rays of sunlight penetrating the surface. She rubbed her thumb gently over the black lines representing the connections between life and world, aware she should find other things to do, unable to do them.

She closed her eyes briefly. They were dry and hot. Tears would have helped, but she wasn't ready to cry—not yet. *Not without proof.*

A knock on her door, too soon to be Norris' summons. Mac raised her voice. "Not now, Oversight."

"It is Ureif, Dr. Connor."

The one being on the ship she didn't dare refuse. *Had to be an alien conspiracy,* Mac told herself as she rose to unlock the door. *She couldn't always have this kind of luck.*

Unexpectedly, Ureif was alone in the hall. "Greetings, Dr. Connor." She glanced toward the ladderway. He gave a very Human smile and gestured in the opposite direction, to what had been a sealed bulkhead and was now an open door to another corridor. "The captain has granted me access throughout his ship."

Including a back door to her part. Mac somehow returned the smile, and stood aside to let the Sinzi-ra enter. "To what do I owe this honor, Sinzi-ra?" she asked, somewhat hysterically trying to gauge if her only chair or the bed would better suit the lower anatomy of the Speaker to the Inner Council of the Interspecies Union.

The chair. She pulled it out and offered it.

"Thank you, but I cannot stay, Dr. Connor. I've come to deliver this."

His finger uncurled, its coating of red rings ending in not one, but two of purest silver.

In slow motion, Mac reached out her hand. The Sinzi let the rings slip into her palm. She stared down at them, then up into his great complex eyes. "Forgive the delay," he asked, bowing his long head. "These came to me first, an unintentional error in procedure, and I was unable to leave the bridge until now."

He'd left the bridge—and whatever situation brewed among the species at Myriam—to bring her these himself. She closed her fingers around the rings. *A Sinzi could do nothing less,* she realized with some wonder. *Not even one as important as this.* "Thank you."

He produced a folded sheet of mem-paper from a pocket she hadn't noticed in his gown. *Nice trick.* "There have been more incidents, Dr. Connor, not as widely reported as we could wish. You should have this information."

Mac took the sheet with some trepidation. "What do you want me to do with it, Sinzi-ra?"

"Use it as you see fit. Although I would advise care discussing its contents with the Frow. They are a volatile species."

Great. Mac opened her mouth to ask for details, but Ureif gestured to the door. "Excuse my haste," he said. "But the good captain was not calm about my departure. I should return."

Tucking the sheet in her own pocket, the rings tight in her other fist, Mac went to open the door. As she stood close to the Sinzi, he lifted a curl from her forehead with one fingertip. "It was with this you committed *grathnu?*"

Hair or hand. Mac still blushed. "I didn't have much choice," she explained.

"The Dhryn." Ureif released the curl. His head tilted to focus his lowermost pair of eyes on Mac, his fingers meeting in a complex shape that reminded her of Anchen. *By far, more sophisticated than Fy.* "I found them pleasant. Industrious, courteous, with a playful humor able to cross many species' lines. Blind to the larger universe, yet the individuals I knew best sought nothing more than to be happy and contribute to the well-being of their kind."

Mac nodded. "You watched them leave for home, didn't you?" she dared ask. "The colony ships. You knew they were at Haven, all this time."

"They were devastated by news of the Ro attack," he answered without hesitation. "As the word spread, everyone put down what they were doing and went to the spaceports; nothing mattered but to return to their Progenitors as quickly as possible. They believed they were needed."

The Progenitors had already left—what had that been like, to arrive home to nothing? "What could they do but wait?" she observed sadly. "Until they died."

Ureif's fingertips twitched. "I am disturbed by their fate, Dr. Connor. By that of all Dhryn. I see no potential circularity. Do you understand this?"

"I think so," Mac said, leaning her shoulders against the wall. "You see no future for the Dhryn as they are now." She sighed. "I'd like to disagree. I valued them, too. But I don't see any hope either."

"'As they are now.'" Ureif straightened his head so all of his eyes looked at her. "What does this mean, Dr. Connor?"

"Mean?" Mac hesitated. "I suppose, being a biologist, I see the Dhryn as the culmination of two processes. We have ample evidence they evolved and were successful on their own world—and mounting evidence that those Dhryn, the original form, were acted upon in some way by the Ro to produce the Dhryn you and I know. A biological weapon."

"I see why Anchen spoke of your peculiar insights, Dr. Connor." While Mac puzzled at that, he went on, "Are you aware Sinzi regard no process as inherently linear? That there will always be circularity discovered, if the viewer is sufficiently discerning?"

"Not until now." *But it explained a few things.* "I don't feel at all discerning in the present situation."

"Nor do I, Dr. Connor."

"Mac."

Definitely a bow. *Ureif should teach that to Fy.* "Mac. Until our next meeting."

She locked the door behind him and leaned her ear against it. Once sure there wasn't another alien ready to knock, Mac opened her fist and gazed down at the rings. "An 'open me first' tag would have been useful," she told them. Her heart thudded in her chest. Now that she had news from Nik, she felt oddly reluctant.

Alive. That was the easy part. *The good to the soul part.*

What else he had to tell her remained to be seen. *Literally.*

Sitting in her chair, she stood the rings on the surface of the desk, holding them in place with the thumb and forefinger of each hand. She gave them a spin.

The left ring revolved twice, then fell with a faint clatter. Mac reached for it, then changed her mind, watching the still-spinning ring. "That eager, huh?" She took that ring to her bed, kicked off her shoes, and lay down.

She brought the metal to her lips.

Then looked through it.

- CONTACT -

/E/FFORT/

   "Mac . . . we made it . . ."/resolve/ . . . *so tired . . .* /doubt/

   Concentrate, getting easier. "All of us . . . left . . . safe. Can't go back . . ." /fear/ "Ship . . . damaged . . . contaminated." *The darkness almost claimed us. I could taste . . . death.* /determination/ "Made it this far . . . matters."

   Concentrate. ". . . Vessel introduced us . . . You were right . . . Progenitor . . . amazing sight . . ." *You did this alone, Mac . . . I have to be as strong as you were . . .* /awe/pride/

   Concentrate. "She listened . . . we must wait . . . Mac, she's weak . . . starving . . ." /pity/ fear/horror/ *She's consuming her own to stay alive . . . are we next?*

   Concentrate. ". . . She saw me alone . . . asked . . . you. How we . . . Where . . ." *Where are you . . .* /longing/ ". . . have a place . . . must convince Her . . ." /resolve/

* layered over *

—She smells mint—

   "Nikolai, I cannot endure—" Genny P'tool's beak closed, moist bubbles forming along the junction of top to bottom.

   How do you talk to someone already dead . . . . /anguish/ *. . . I would have spared you this, old one.*

   "Rest, Gorgeous. The Progenitor ship found us in time."

   Time for everyone else. /rage/frustration/

   "Take—take my work. Others can keep . . ."

   /despair/resignation/ *Be the last breath . . . I can't stay . . . do us that grace . . .* /pain/ *Die while I'm here.*

   "You'll do it yourself. Just stop making Mac jealous, okay?"

   The damned Dhryn have no doctors, no medicines . . . save us and let her die.

   "Hah. Saw you first. My pretty Nik."

   "You say that to all the . . ."

   /grief/relief/guilt/

   Good-bye, Genny.

* layered over *

—She tastes salt—

"Is She not magnificent, *Lamisah*?"

/disbelief/fear/ *I'm standing on a hand . . . a hand . . .*

"Magnificent is an understatement."

"I have told Her of your service to that which is Dhryn." A soft hoot. "And of your daring to argue with Mackenzie Winifred Elizabeth Wright Connor Sol."

/wry amusement/ *Even the Dhryn know . . . unfair . . . those eyes of yours could melt stone . . . only flesh, Mac . . . landed me in the drink . . . too busy daydreaming . . .* /despair/ resolve/ *. . . like now.*

"Will the Progenitor listen to me?"

"She will listen, but we must not tire Her. The Great Journey takes its toll on all that is Dhryn."

/hope/resolve/ *"You'll have to help me. She must learn the truth."*

Another hoot. "But of course, *Lamisah*. Is that not why we are here? Although," a sigh, "it is not a truth anyone would want."

/pity/determination/

"One step at a time, my friend."

* layered over *

—She feels silk—

Concentrate . . . "Let Anchen know . . . Genny P'tool . . . dead." *With Murs . . . Larrieri . . . Cinder . . . who next . . . doesn't matter.* "We couldn't save her." /anger/futility/

Vessel and I . . . only ones left who know . . . ./determination/ *. . . must survive . . .*

"Quarters fine . . . She remembered you . . . water in the shower." *You made an impression, Mac . . . not surprised . . .* /warmth/ "Wanted to know . . . everything. Searched . . . feeders touched me . . ." /horror/

Concentrate . . . ". . . tried to send more . . . didn't seem . . . work . . ." *We're underway as planned . . . easy part . . . tell Hollans . . ."*

/resolve/

- 14 -

TOUCH AND TEMPTATION

HER PILLOW WAS SOAKED. *Tears.* Her clothes were as well. *Sweat.* Mac slipped the new *lamnas* on her middle finger and ignored how both hands trembled. She looked up at the next ring, sitting like harmless jewelry beside the salmon carving, and fought for the courage to touch it.

Nik's messages, Nik's memories, were startlingly vivid now. *Practice makes perfect.* "His or mine or both." The information might be easier to sort through and understand—at least, she thought so.

But the emotional load was growing worse. Between his passions and her reactions to them, she felt as exhausted as if she'd somehow run a complete marathon in the last few minutes.

Her eyes swam with tears again; she let them run down her face and over her ears. *Poor Genny.* She'd been the most frail. Likely a factor.

Honest grief, honest joy. Nik was alive. The Vessel was alive.

And they were with the Progenitor.

The "easy part." Mac reached for the second *lamnas*. She had the impression Nik doubted it had worked. *Using a broken one couldn't be good.* "I'm not feeling braver," she warned it, "but you know what they say about curiosity and biologists."

She brought the ring to her lips, then looked.

- CONTACT -

—SHE HEARD THE OCEAN—
Waves crashed against cliff; seabirds screamed overhead; thunder rolled along the shore . . . under it all drummed a word.
"Lamisah!"

* layered over *

—She tasted bile—
Her teeth drove into her brother's flesh; her mouth flooded with heat; she swallowed life . . . within it all pulsed a word.
"Survival."

* layered over *

—She felt the cells of her body—
Stomach, ridged and acid; muscle tight with power; skin, the boundary line of who and what she was . . . through it all hammered a word.
"Truth."

- 15 -

REACTION AND RESOLVE

MAC FLUNG HERSELF to the side of her bed in time for the first uncontrolled spew to hit floor, not fabric.

By the fourth, she no longer cared where it went. She hung from one hand on the desk, her other having found purchase somewhere on the floor. The ship spun in huge looping circles and she was about to fall off. Her head pounded with a blinding white pain. Her gut persisted in its belief she had more to vomit.

Dying would be nice.

Between spasms, Mac counted each successful breath. When she reached five, she concluded she wasn't going to die after all. *More's the pity.* When she reached ten, she opened her eyes.

Big mistake.

A few arduous moments later, she managed five again. Ten. But this time she waited for twenty peaceful breaths before peering between almost closed eyelids.

No vomit.

That worked.

If she didn't count the stabbing sensation behind her eyes. *Sensitive to light.*

Working toward simple goals such as continuing to breathe, avoiding direct light, and hoping the ship would stop moving soon, Mac managed to sit up. Swaying in that position, she congratulated herself.

Then realized what had happened.

"She knew . . ." A whisper that hurt her poor head. *The Progenitor must have talked to Nik about the* lamnas, *what they were.*

Then used one.

The proof clawed its way through Mac's every pore. Dhryn thought and memory fought for space within her mind, as if she'd been turned inside out.

And the proof of that . . . ? She cracked open her eyes a smidge more to see the disaster she'd made of her new quarters. "Bother."

First things first. With one arm tight around her abused middle, and her hand shading her eyes, Mac staggered to the shower and stepped inside. Once there,

she pushed her head into the jets and kept the water and soap running—first
over her clothes, then over each subsequent layer as she stripped to skin. With
regret, she kicked the once-lovely suit to the side.

Offspring holes in it anyway.

Next, she turned the room lights to minimum and used her wet clothing to
mop most of the mess from the floor, slipping the sodden mass into disposal
sacks. Moving at the mindless task worked some of the knots from her neck and
abdomen. *Though she'd feel those muscles tomorrow.*

Mac set the air refresh to maximum, crossing her fingers the reek of almost-
dead biologist wouldn't simply be pumped to some other room and noticed.
Gooseflesh rose on her skin and she rooted through her bags to find something
that wasn't silk or suit.

At the bottom of one, plain coveralls—similar to those worn by the crew.
"I'll never complain about your packing again, Two," she promised the consular
staff as she pulled the garment on. Wanting to be quite sure to remember which
was which, she put the fourth ring on her left hand. *Quite the collection.* Mac considered putting the *lamnas* on a chain around her neck. But they weren't jewelry.
They weren't an imp or mem-sheet. They were pieces of Nik, intimate and hers.

Plus that other. She explored those memories with care, like probing a sore
tooth with her tongue. And found a question.

Had the Progenitor spoken Dhryn?

Being unable to tell scared her. Mac rested two fingers on her lips and
mouthed, "The rain at Base . . . two three four." First in English, then Instella.
Last, and with reluctance, Dhryn. *Oomling Dhryn.*

The oomlings. She sank into her chair, the words in Nik's voice blending with
that perverse mix of hunger and desperate remorse until she knew, beyond
doubt, one truth. The Progenitor, the future of her kind, was sacrificing the
existing generations in order to survive.

Even She would break, Mac realized. No matter this Progenitor's desire to
avoid killing others, instinct would rule before the end. And what of the other
Dhryn, hiding within the transect system? "That which is Dhryn must survive,"
she whispered.

They were all running out of time.

Their crew escort left them at the door. Norris continued to give her sidelong
looks as they walked through the *Annapolis Joy's* hangar deck. Finally, Mac
couldn't take it any longer. "What's the matter?"

"You look awful."

No surprise there. She felt awful. Having a Progenitor try to stuff meaning inside her head through a Sinzi device had produced a headache that continued to
mock the heavy-duty painkillers she'd gulped on the way to meet him.

Mac wanted to explain, but "Dhryn brain" was too dangerous and "simulator hangover" was petty under the circumstances. "Lunch didn't agree with me," she said, which was undeniably the case. *The mere thought of eating . . .*

She'd chosen to intercept Norris on his way to the Origins section. It had given her time to begin to sort through her new thoughts, and, more importantly to Mac, removed any possibility of him appearing at her quarters before they were cleaned.

Avoiding the person sent to clean her quarters had been a bonus.

After passing several large, promising craft, with uniformed crew bustling around them, Norris stopped by what looked to Mac like an ordinary transport lev, about the size used to ferry weekly supplies to Base. *With,* she noticed, *dents.*

Norris opened the door and climbed in. "C'mon," he said impatiently.

Without committing her feet to the ramp, Mac leaned forward to look inside. Other than mismatched seats for pilot and passenger, there was nothing but recording equipment—some mounted to the walls, some loose. There was also no other person, and Norris was climbing into the pilot's seat.

So not always behind a desk. "You're the pilot?"

"Of course." He busied himself with an alarming number of switches. Lights came on and a complex 'screen activated to hover in front of him. "It's my ship."

Mac pointed toward the hangar's launch bay. "It's space out there." She thought that came out nicely matter-of-fact, but he stopped what he was doing to gaze down his nose at her.

"We have a slim margin of opportunity, Dr. Connor. If you don't feel capable of accompanying me, stay here."

She rested her hand on the side of the lev in apology. "It seems a little small."

"To maneuver around obstacles." His hand caressed the console. "Are you coming or not?"

He didn't appear suicidal, she told herself. As reassurance, it did nothing to steady her nerves, but Mac climbed up the ramp and took her seat, tossing her pack underneath. "Of course."

Norris closed the door behind her. As he continued his final checks and preparations, Mac glanced around.

This "lev" was different from those that moved through air. For one thing, the roof wasn't retractable. *Brilliant,* she scoffed at herself. For another, there were no windows. It was really like being inside a box.

She could handle being in a moving box. She'd done it before.

She concentrated on relaxing in the passenger seat, leaning back with her eyes closed. The position—or the painkillers—began to make progress on her headache. After a few minutes, it faded into a sullen throb.

The craft lurched forward. *The tow to launch.*

She didn't bother watching Norris deal with that either. Her stomach gave a gentle gurgle, the kind that meant it was willing to try something when she was. *Progress.*

The lurching ended in sudden smoothness, then Norris gave a satisfied, "There we are. Take a look, Dr. Connor."

Mac opened her eyes. She didn't scream, but the sound that did come out of her mouth before she closed it had a good deal in common with that made by an offended mouse.

She was *in* space. *Without a ship!*

Hands tight on the armrests, Mac took a deep breath. *Something wasn't right. She was getting air.*

But the roof and walls she'd found so comforting had become transparent. Mac glanced down and looked up again quickly. *So had the floor.*

Norris' little craft had transformed into a bubble containing themselves, his packed equipment, and what bits of console he needed to consult. Interior lighting was reduced to that provided by his 'screen.

"Not a box," she said rather glibly.

"Warn me if you're going to be sick. I've bags."

She had nothing left.

Mac began to take in what was around them, twisting her head to see more. "I'm fine."

They weren't alone. Dwarfing the stars, Myriam's sun, and the world itself were ships. *A mixed school,* thought Mac, trying to find some frame of reference.

From their perspective, the *Annapolis Joy* lay below. The ship resembled a lacework coral, rounder buds held within a network of thick lines, but more random and three-dimensional than creatures bound by tropisms to sun and gravity and wave. If Mac hadn't known something of the *Joy's* inner dimensions, she'd have judged the ship fragile. Lights and reflections teased her complex shape from the darkness beyond and revealed other shapes—probably shuttles—moving over her surface like small crabs. Others moved farther away, difficult to follow at this range, but she spotted one set of lights that seemed to parallel their course. "Who's that?"

"Your escort," he stated. "The captain insisted."

She liked the captain.

To either side and—Mac looked up—above were other much larger ships. While she mentally tagged them as eel, octopus, grouper, sea cucumber, and so on, Norris abruptly noticed her interest and began to spout numbers and model years as if he'd checked a list before coming out. *Probably had,* she thought.

"Which is the Trisulian?" she interrupted.

He called up something on his 'screen, the changing glow doing unfortunate things to his long nose. "Nadir to the *Joy*—plus thirteen or thereabouts."

"Point," she suggested.

Norris got up and came to stand behind her right shoulder. He leaned down so their cheeks almost touched, then gave a *huff* of satisfaction that caught in Mac's hair. "That," he said, his arm reaching out, finger ending at a dim shape. "We'll get a better look when we're at the derelict."

He sat again. Mac stared into the darkness. "Do they see us?"

"I hope so. Otherwise, they'll believe we're violating our approved flight path to *Beta*."

"*Beta?*" She looked at him quizzically. "I thought we were doing a pass over the *Uosanah*."

Norris worked some controls before answering. When he did, his voice was subdued. "I prefer not to use real names for the dead."

Mac, who affectionately nicknamed turkeys before shoving them in the oven, decided not to comment. "How close is the Trisulian ship to *Beta?*"

"Close as it gets without being docked. They towed her here."

Lovely. "How—"

"Dr. Connor," Norris interrupted, sounding rather exasperated. "I've preparations to make that will take every minute before arriving at our destination. If you could please be quiet until then?"

Mac grinned. "Sure."

She leaned back and gazed out at a vista she'd never imagined seeing for herself. Dozens of ships, from as many or more species, hovering in space like a cloud of plankton. She'd have to coexist with Norris until Mudge could take a ride. Not to mention get the specs from the engineer. *Base could use something like this.*

"I need music," Norris muttered, jabbing his finger in the workscreen's upper quadrant.

Mac nodded, though he hadn't asked, ready to listen and relax.

Sound blared through the little ship and she winced. "What's that?"

"An accordion. From my personal collection. You don't hear music like this anymore." Norris began whistling along, slightly off-key. Whistling to . . . Mac closed her eyes and shook her head.

As she'd feared.

It was a polka.

Surrounded by vacuum, trapped in a bubble with an engineer who collected polkas. On cue, her headache throbbed anew.

A ride for Mudge in this thing was not, she vowed, *worth this.*

Specs for the bubble lev might be.

If it was a very short trip.

"Dr. Connor!"

"Wasn't asleep," Mac grumbled, opening her eyes. *Not for long, anyway.* The inside and outside of her head were blissfully quiet. Rubbing absently at the lingering ache at the back of her neck, she straightened and looked around. Beside her loomed not so much a shape but an absence of anything but darkness. "*Beta?*" she guessed.

"That's the Trisulian battle cruiser." Norris pointed downward. "There's our target." He stood and went into the back. "I'll show you."

Light flooded the floor, and Mac moved her feet to get a better look. The *Beta*—*Uosanah*—gleamed bronze against velvet where Norris had illuminated it.

Unlike the *Joy,* she appeared capable of entering an atmosphere, if sleek curves and a lack of external protrusions counted.

Norris resumed his seat. "We'll head for her belly."

The bubble rolled to reorient with the derelict overhead, then plunged toward it. Mac held her breath, but her stomach didn't react. At the instant a crash became inevitable, the bubble leveled out to travel forward along the Dhryn ship. She sent a searing look at Norris, but he was too intent on flashing displays to notice an irate passenger. *Probably never had one before.*

The belly of the *Uosanah* was studded with what looked like cranes and other handling equipment. *So much for her attempt to decipher ship design,* Mac thought, wondering if these were to take in orbital boxes, such as Earth exchanged with her way stations.

Her wonder turned to concern when Norris immediately took them into that maze of metal. Their lights flashed against girders and wires and giant hollowed plates. *Too close for comfort.* Mac held onto her armrests, planning exactly what to tell Norris when it was safe to distract him. From his look of concentration, he was hunting something.

He directed the bubble deeper and deeper until the irregular machinery closed around them like a trap. About to protest, *distraction or not,* Mac noticed their pace slowing and closed her mouth.

Just in time. The lights washed over what lay directly ahead. A series of large round doors. *Closed doors.*

Doors Norris continued to approach, although now with caution.

Enough was enough. "What are you doing?" Mac demanded.

"I have to concentrate." One particular door began to loom. Norris' fingers sped across the console.

The door filled the front view, reflecting so much light Mac squinted as she half rose from her seat. "Norris!"

"Hush."

Like a yawning mouth, the door slid open, the lights from their craft plunging within to reveal a launch bay almost identical to the one they'd left.

Of course. Standard technologies, Mac thought inanely. *Trust the IU.*

Trust Norris? *Only as far as the ride home.* "Nice trick, opening that," she said as calmly as possible.

He swung his head to look at her. The determination in it froze her in place. "Here's a better one, Dr. Connor." He did something to the controls.

And the bubble leaped forward to enter the bay.

Almost instantly, the great door closed behind it and the little ship lurched. Mac recognized the motion. They were being towed into the hangar.

Inside the dead Dhryn ship.

"This is why you brought me along," Mac said, furious with herself. *It beat being terrified at what now held them.* "You never intended to just fly by."

"You said it yourself, Dr. Connor." Norris seemed short of breath. "'First ready, first out the door.'"

"That didn't mean ignoring protocols! What about our escort? What about the Trisulians?" She lowered her voice from full shout; it didn't lose its hard edge. "You'll never be allowed on one of these ships again."

"There was no guarantee I'd be allowed at all. Don't you see? This is my one chance. To show I can contribute. That Humans should be involved." He surged from his seat and went to an instrument apparently suspended in midair near where the door should be. "Don't worry, Dr. Connor. Didn't you see the material lining the bay? It's the Dhryn stealth cloth. Can't see us here. Couldn't see us on approach either. I put us in on *Beta's* far side." Now he looked at her, pale yet defiant. "I've set a buoy to produce a false image of us crisscrossing the surface. Our flight plan gives us three hours' minimum before the *Joy* notices. More than enough time to discover what happened to this ship and the others. There."

Before Mac could do more than cry out in reflex, the lev regained its walls—and an open door.

The cold smell of death flooded in.

"Air's breathable," Norris promised, gathering up bags which he slung over both shoulders. "Bit dry."

Mac wrinkled her nose. "Bit rotten," she amended. Normally, she appreciated the smell for what it signified. *The annual carpet of dead and dying salmon, aswarm with feasting eagles, gulls, and bears. Waters enriched for the generation to come.* Here and now, on this ship?

"I'm guessing the Dhryn never left."

Norris had his back to her. "Ships don't die empty, Dr. Connor." Supremely nonchalant, except she could see his hands shaking as he snugged a belt around his waist, how they fumbled to clip tools to it, dropping one. "Are you ready?"

She couldn't let him go alone, Mac realized, though sorely tempted. For all his bold talk, he knew what he'd done. His career was over if this gamble didn't pay off. *If he didn't incite a war first.* "Remind me to introduce you to Emily Mamani, if we get out of this," she growled.

Mac pulled her pack from under her seat and fitted it on her back. "First I want your promise to get us out of here before the Trisulians—or anyone else—come looking."

"Of course. I do know what I'm doing, Dr. Connor. You read the labels; I'll do the rest. It shouldn't take long."

Save her from theorists loose in the field. "Three hours," Mac repeated, making a show of checking the time.

The hangar was improbably normal. Lights on standby raised to daytime levels as they left Norris' ship, a little brighter than Human norm, but Dhryn liked it that way. *Normal, but too quiet,* in Mac's opinion. The *Joy's* had been full of moving people and machines, rang with voices and mutters and vibrations. *Uosanah's* service shuttles sat silent and still.

Norris began taking scans of everything in sight, as if no one had ever seen a freighter's hangar deck before. She was no starship engineer, but Mac was reasonably sure this wasn't going to provide any answers as to what happened to the colony Dhryn in Haven. She walked ahead, hoping to lead by example, when she noticed the pool of congealed blue under the second shuttle in line.

"Norris!" she called, squatting to look underneath.

Three arms hung down, their ragged ends evidently the original source of the blood pool. Mac frowned and moved closer. *Grathnu* severed a limb cleanly. There'd been no massive blood loss when Brymn had given his to the Progenitor. These—She pulled out her imp and poked the nearest arm out of the shadows. "Wasn't *grathnu*," she pronounced, studying the dried shreds of skin, flesh, and bone. "What do you make of this, Norris?"

Careful to avoid the pool, Norris went on his knees, one hand over his nose. "I don't know what grath—whatever is. But he must have been desperate to squeeze in there. This—" he pointed to the underside of the shuttle, through which Mac glimpsed portions of blue skin and brown fabric, "—is part of the tow mechanism. If anyone had tried to launch her, he'd have been torn apart."

Mac straightened and glanced around. All quiet, all peaceful. *All empty.* "So he wasn't trying to leave the ship."

"Or he tried," the engineer disagreed, climbing to his feet, "but didn't have time to climb into the shuttle before having to hide."

Hide from what? "We could leave," she suggested, holding back a shudder. "We could leave right now and let a team come back." The look he gave her was very likely the one she'd given Kammie when told to abandon the field stations because of a mere earthquake. Mac sighed. "Fine. But this never ends well in vids."

"I don't watch them."

"I'm not surprised." She sniffed the air. "C'mon. There are more here."

More wasn't the right word, Mac decided a moment later, as she and Norris stared down at what had been Dhryn. "Three," she guessed, using a toe to shift what remained of a leg so she could see underneath. There was clothing. Bone. Little else. "They've been eaten," she added helpfully.

"I can see that." To his credit, Norris was stone-faced and calm. He raised his scanner, passing it over what was left. "Cannibalism," he concluded briskly. "There have been cases."

Mac raised her eyebrows. "There have?"

"Asteroid miners. Pre-transect deep space missions. Not uncommon."

"You're making that up."

He pulled out his imp with a challenging look. Mac shook her head, feeling again the Progenitor's remorse. *And appetite.* "You could be right," she admitted grudgingly. "Sure we can't leave now?"

"Of course not." Norris nodded to the hangar exit. "We've two and a half hours left. The only danger here is ignorance."

"I'll remind you you said that," she told him, but followed anyway.

The engineer knew the ship. *Knew the floor plan,* Mac corrected, watching Norris closely. He made the right turns. He announced, correctly, what would be be-hind doors before opening them. She was less impressed that he expected her to go first through those doors.

Sure, let the biologist find the icky bodies.

Although, to Mac's unspoken relief, they found no more corpses. The doors led to nothing more exciting than intersecting corridors and holds. Many holds, crammed to their ceilings. The *Uosanah* had been an active freighter, fully loaded with goods bound for Cryssin Colony, likely en route to Haven before the Ro attack had changed everything.

Norris was hunting for a link to the ship's data systems, which, he claimed, should be available within the holds. If they found one, they wouldn't have to go all the way to the *Uosanah's* bridge. On that basis, Mac was happy to tag along, but so far, they'd had no luck. *So much for floor plans.*

The latest hold was the largest yet. Norris cheered, convinced it must hold an access panel. While he checked his 'screen for details on this part of the ship, Mac pulled aside the wrapping on the nearest crate and picked apart packing material until she uncovered its contents. "Ah."

"You've found something?" Norris demanded, hurrying over.

She lifted out an umbrella and opened it for his inspection. Bold stripes of red, green, and orange ran around it. There was a second handhold, farther up the handle. Well-suited to Dhryn. "They don't like rain."

"Dr. Connor, we're looking for ship's data. There's no time for—"

"Speaking of which, it's suppertime on the *Joy.* I don't know about you, but I missed lunch." *Missed breakfast and lost lunch,* but the difference didn't matter to her empty stomach. Mac leaned the umbrella against the crate and pulled open her bag. From it, she drew two nutrient bars, one of which she passed to an aston-ished Norris. She found her bottle of water and took a slug. "I've learned to travel prepared," she said, biting into the bar. "Go ahead. I've more."

He sniffed it, then took a bite. He made a face. "This is awful."

"Stops you eating too many." Her stomach growled and Mac took another, bigger bite. She waved her stick at Norris. "We could use a ship like yours at Base—my research station. Any chance of getting the specs? When we get back," she qualified, handing him the water. "We have transparent membrane, of course, but to go to any depth we need something that can take pressure."

He gave her a strange look. "My ship? Oh. You mean the projector. It's just a fancy internal display, Dr. Connor. What—did you think my ship somehow turned transparent?"

Touché. Mac laughed. "Biologist," she quipped. "But the end result is extraor-dinary. I'd really like to have it."

"You're welcome to the schematics," he replied, tucking the rest of his bar into a pocket. "We should—"

"Get going. Yes." Mac finished hers and put away the water bottle, feeling almost normal again. *Amazing what a little sustenance could do.* "What now?"

"There should be a panel in here." Norris checked the time and shook his head. "It's taking too long. We'll have to split up to check along the walls. You know what to look for—"

"Not really."

"Any panel that has the outline of the ship on or beside it. Call me if you find one."

"No com." At least, none that he'd given her. *Fieldwork amateur.*

Norris grinned and shouted, "Hello!"

The echoes reverberated throughout the hold.

"Point taken," Mac said, grinning back. She looked around. In keeping with all Dhryn structures she'd seen, the hold walls were at angles less than perpendicular. Racks laden with crates lined both sides. Here, the left wall angled sharper than the right, its first rack barely above her head. Norris would have to duck. "I'll take this side," she offered.

On impulse, she grabbed the umbrella.

The center aisle of the hold had been bright and open. Along the wall, the light was lessened by the overhead rack. Worse, Mac found herself passing through the shadows cast by huge boxes. Each band of darkness was regular and sharp. Five quick steps took her back into light.

Two slow steps took her back into the dark.

It wasn't pitch. She could see well enough to know there weren't panels of any description, but to be sure, she trailed the fingers of her left hand over the cool metal. Her right clutched the umbrella. An unlikely weapon; uncertain comfort. She considered dropping it, but couldn't find the right spot. *Mustn't leave a mess.*

Within the next patch of shadow, her foot kicked something small and sent it skittering forward into the light. Mac bent to pick it up. "Well, I'll be . . ." she murmured. It was a Dhryn food cylinder. She held it up and peered inside. Not empty. Its contents had dried and shriveled into a lump.

There were more. The swathe of light at her feet was littered with them. "They weren't starving," she whispered uneasily. She followed the refuse into the aisle and found herself in front of an open door.

Mac stepped inside what could only be a storage unit. Its shelves were lined with tidy rows of food cylinders, thousands of them. Only near the door were any disturbed. There, a shelf was smashed and cylinders were scattered everywhere, as if . . .

She backed out of the unit, hand tight on the umbrella. "Norris!"

. . . as if someone or something had discovered they weren't edible.

"Norris!" Mac put her back to the hold wall.

Something *scurried* along the overhead rack.

Her breath caught. *It couldn't be.*

Scurry, scurry.

She could hear running footsteps and didn't dare call out again. Didn't dare do anything. Sweat trickled down her forehead, evaporating to chill in the dry air of the hold. She didn't dare shiver.

Skitter, scurry.

There. Above and to her right. The direction Norris would come.

An ambush?

Mac didn't think, she exploded into a run, weaving between crates, heading away from the Ro—*the walker*—and the man. As she ran, she found her voice and shouted. "The Ro are here. Go back, Norris! Call for help!" The words were punctuated by her thudding feet.

Spit! Pop!

Loud, but not as close. If the walker understood what she'd said—had chosen to chase Norris—they were in worse trouble.

There was worse? "Hurry, Norris!"

She'd run into the far wall of the hold soon. Mac began searching for a hiding place, cursing the tidy habits of Dhryn under her breath. Each crate was neatly aligned with its neighbor, offering nothing that would shelter a speck of dust, let alone a desperate Human.

Wait. Just ahead two crates overhung their pallet, as if pushed. Tearing off her backpack, Mac flung herself on her stomach and wiggled into the tight space beneath. She squeezed back as far she could, pulling the pack and umbrella under with her.

Then did her best to be invisible.

- 16 -

ENCOUNTER AND EFFECT

NOTHING TO SEE here. Mac did her best to believe it. *Maybe the Ro would, too*. Her legs were already cramping and her right arm, caught beneath her body, would shortly be asleep. These minor discomforts were welcome distractions. She wanted to avoid thinking about the corridors of the Dhryn ship—of Norris running back—of what it would be like to try and remember the way when something was chasing you, something you couldn't see . . . holding your breath so you could listen for any sound . . .

Stop that.

She hadn't heard anything more, from the Ro or Norris. She might have been wrong. Norris would have a comment or two about that.

For once, she'd love to take the blame. She took slow, light breaths.

Something stank. Mac took a deeper sniff and almost gagged. She knew that smell.

Dead Dhryn.

All her senses must have been shut down by fear to miss it. Mac only now appreciated that her shoulder and hip weren't pressed against another crate, but into something yielding.

She didn't panic. *Nothing wrong with sharing space with a corpse*, she assured herself.

Unless it was warm.

Mac held the air in her lungs, listening over the frantic thudding of her heart. No doubt about it.

Something else was breathing behind her.

She exhaled slowly and gently, resuming her own breathing. *After all,* she reasoned wildly, *she'd been fine so far. Why suffocate?*

She lay on her stomach, her right arm pinned beneath, her head turned so she could look out of her hiding place. *As if she'd see the Ro walker*. Now, gradually, Mac lifted her head and rolled it on her chin, eyes straining at the black shadows behind her.

A small piece of shadow moved closer, tentatively, slowly. She made herself stay still as a three-fingered hand formed in the light. It reached toward her face then withdrew, reached again and stopped in midair, trembling. Its skin was puckered and seamed, the digits twisted. Dark drops fell from the palm.

She'd seen a hand like that before.

Mac looked harder and made out the glint of an eye in the darkest shadow. *Just her luck.* She felt profoundly abused. *The only hiding place from the Ro, inhabited by the Dhryn version of insane.*

When adult Dhryn failed to Flower into their final metamorphosis, it was called the Wasting. Those trapped within their degrading bodies were shunned, and set aside to die. Brymn had feared that fate. Ordinary Dhryn "did not think of it." Mac had been . . . curious.

Really not curious at the moment, she decided. A Wasted was dangerous. Brymn had been emphatic in his warning. They were known to attack other Dhryn. Mac's heart began to race again.

The gnawed remains of the *Uosanah* crew . . . the available but ignored food within the storage unit . . . *yummy fresh Human.*

Just as she tensed to squirm away as quickly as possible, *Ro or not,* the hand fell to the deck, palm up. The fingers spasmed once, as if in entreaty, then were still.

Mac hesitated, remembering more of that conversation with Brymn, another lifetime ago. She'd told him she sought the truth. She'd claimed it was part of being Human to act . . . to help.

She'd watched him Flower into something far worse.

Her left hand was touching her pack. Moving very slowly, Mac reached inside until her fingers closed on a nutrient bar. She brought it out, bringing her left arm over her head until her hand was near the Wasted's. "This is our food," she whispered as quietly as she could. She laid the bar on its palm.

The fingers curled closed. The hand withdrew. She could see the glint of the eye, then it was gone; the head had changed position. *Trying her offering?*

The hand reappeared, empty and palm up. *Didn't bother to chew.* Mac reached into her pack and found another bar. It vanished in turn. When the hand came out a third time, she whispered, "I'm sorry. That's all I have."

A vibration she felt through the floor. Distress.

It understood?

"I'm Mac—" *Dhryn formalities seemed even more pointless than usual.* "Who are you?"

The voice was faint but clear. "I do not exist."

Aliens. Mac lifted her head until it touched the crate above, trying to see more of the Dhryn. "We can discuss that later," she told it. "Can you walk?"

Her first fear, that the Ro would be waiting for them, proved unfounded. Her second, that the Wasted was wedged under the crate for good, proved uncomfortably close to the truth. It was too weak to struggle free on its own. She'd finally had to lie down and pull at whatever emaciated limbs she could reach. She did so as gently as possible, gradually working the Dhryn free.

During this process, they'd been sitting ducks. *Proving the Ro was otherwise occupied.*

Doing her best not to think about how, Mac sat beside the Dhryn, letting it recover. In the light, the reason for calling this state the "Wasting" was apparent. The being was little more than fracturing skin over bone. She was astonished it still breathed. The arms were sticks, the legs not much better. *The hands . . .* she leaned closer. Three were missing, severed neatly. This had been a Dhryn of accomplishment, thrice honored by his Progenitor. No other clues. Its—*his,* she told herself—his body bore no bands of cloth. *They probably wouldn't have stayed up anyway.*

The rotting flesh smell came from the fissures in his skin. There was nothing she could do about those, not here, and the fluid they leaked was going to leave a trail.

"You need to stand," she said. *Where was Norris?* She saw the umbrella and offered it. "Use this."

"Why?" The Wasted lifted his face to hers. The yellow of his eyes was sallow and pale, the flesh pulled away from the bony ridges of his features to show her the precise shape of his skull. His lips barely moved. When they did, they bled. "I do not exist."

"The Ro do," she said deliberately. "There's one on your ship. We have to leave, now."

When his eyes half closed, as if in defeat, she sharpened her tone. "I am Mackenzie Winifred Elizabeth Wright Connor Sol. That which is Dhryn must survive. Do you understand me?"

"You are Human," he whispered in perfect Instella, "I do not exist. The Progenitors are gone. What is Dhryn now?"

Not a Haven Dhryn. *A more worldly creature.* Mac knelt beside him. "Not all the Progenitors are gone," she pleaded, using the *oomling* tongue. "Come with me. Don't let the Ro win."

His eyes closed and she thought he'd given up. Then, slowly, one hand reached for the umbrella. She hurried to put it in his grasp and help him stand.

If it hadn't been for his wheezing breath and halting, but steady steps, she might have walked with the dead. Certainly the smell was there. Mac ignored it. Normal Dhryn body posture, slanting forward at almost forty-five degrees, worked in her favor. Her right shoulder fit nicely under his left uppermost arm, which lacked a hand. He gripped the umbrella in his right upper and middle hands. As for his mass?

Right now, it was less than hers. She supported a body that shouldn't be alive.

And they made progress. The Wasted knew the ship and didn't hesitate as he led her back to the hangar. The trip was shorter than she remembered, without side trips to investigate every door.

Where was Norris?

Mac listened for the Ro, the skin at the back of her neck crawling with fear. No way to hide or outrun the creature now. Not with the Wasted; not in these open halls.

They turned a corner and Mac gave a sigh of relief, recognizing the final stretch of corridor. "Almost there," she said.

A voice in her ear, strained with effort. "Why are Humans at Haven?"

"Long story," she temporized. "Let's get out of here first."

She hadn't remembered the door to the hangar being open, but Norris could have left it that way, to help her get through quickly. *No choice.* Mac and the Wasted shuffled forward.

They passed the pile of cloth and rotting bone, neither glancing in its direction.

The lev came into view. *Nothing had ever looked so good,* Mac decided, trying not to hurry. Her blood pounded in her ears, making it hard to listen for what might be hiding between the shuttles as they passed.

"That is your ship?" said the Wasted.

"Yes—" Mac's voice broke as she saw the form crumpled in the lev's shadow. "Wait here," she said, disentangling herself from the being's hold as carefully as haste allowed.

Then she ran to Norris.

He'd almost made it, she realized in horror, dropping to her knees beside the body at the foot of the lev's blood-splattered ramp. Her hands didn't know where to touch. There was hardly anything of him not sliced apart, hardly anything but his face still recognizable. Red arched in all directions.

Slime glistened.

"Human!"

Mac whirled, unable to credit that deep bellow had come from the Wasted, amazed to see him rushing toward her, using his hands and stumps as well as feet. He reared up, drew in a deep breath, then retched. She flung herself away and back as acid spewed forth from his mouth, to coat a nightmare from thin air.

A nightmare that screamed!

Mac writhed on the floor, hands tight over her ears, but it made no difference. The sound penetrated her nerves until she could barely think. She tried to see what was happening.

The Wasted had dropped flat on the deck, limbs outstretched.

While some*thing* died.

The sound finally stopped. Mac took a shuddering breath, then two. She rose to her knees, her feet, and staggered forward. All the while her mind tried to deny what she saw.

This was a walker?

Mac didn't see how this thing in front of her could have walked at all. Its body, if there was one, was hidden beneath a convulsion of limbs, all distinct, drawn into fetallike curves. Tatters of material, glittering metal flakes, fibers—all drifted in the air above it, as though not ready to succumb to gravity and fall with the body they'd once wrapped. She saw no head.

There were the claws, though, long, straight, and needle sharp. *Scoring moss and soft wood like a fork; slashing through furniture, fabric—and flesh.* There were limbs like wings or fins within the mass, others thin and knotted on one another, fingertips and bony clubs and cable-thick hooks . . .

With utter calm, Mac turned her head to one side, threw up the nutrient bar and water, wiped her mouth with the back of her hand, then returned to examining the Ro's servant.

None of it made sense. It shouldn't function, not with this tangled, nonsensical structure. The strangest alien form—the weirdest Earthly ones—at least looked as though they could work. *This?*

"Human?"

How could she forget the Dhryn? Mac hurried to his side. He was trying to rise and she helped as best she could. "There could be more," he warned her, his voice barely audible.

"You're right. I know." She passed him the umbrella and they made their slow way around the two bodies.

The short ramp took the last of his strength. She managed to get him inside before he collapsed on the floor of the lev. Mac took the umbrella and used it to methodically sweep the air inside the craft. Once sure they were alone, she closed the door and threw the lock to keep it that way.

She rested her forehead against the door. "We won't leave you here, Norris," she whispered.

Could they leave at all? Taking the pilot's seat, Mac stared helplessly at the console. The console stared back, its dozens of winking machine eyes giving no clue as to their purpose, daring a mere biologist to guess and blow herself up.

"Are you a pilot?"

"No." She glanced at the Wasted in sudden hope. "Are you?"

"I do not—"

"Exist," she finished impatiently. "Yes, I know. Before that. Can you operate this ship?"

"Before . . ." The word was accompanied by a mournful vibration Mac felt through the floor. "I was, in your terms, captain of the *Uosanah*."

Finally, trapped with someone who had the right skills. "Then you can use this." She waved her hands over the incomprehensible console.

He pulled himself to a sit on his lowermost arms, his head beside hers. It drooped from his neck, as though too heavy for it. As he studied the console, she watched a new fracture open behind his ear and ooze blue. "No," he said at last. "Even if I could decipher these controls, they are locked."

"Oh."

"The ship is transmitting." A sticklike finger moved forward and pressed a button. A shaky voice filled the lev.

"This is Dr. Norris, on board the derelict *Uosanah*. Mayday. Mayday. We're in the central hangar. Dr. Connor has confirmed the presence of Myrokynay. Repeat, we have Ro on board. Mayday. Mayday. I'm setting this on auto and going back for her. Please hurry. This is Dr. Norris—"

The Wasted pressed the button again to silence the voice.

"He made it here," Mac said numbly. *And went back for her.*

"Was Norris all his name?"

She shook her head, trying to wrap her grief and guilt around an alien point of honor. "We hadn't been properly introduced. Not yet."

The Wasted lifted his head very slightly—*a bow.* "Then you must—" a gasping pause, "—learn all of his names, Mackenzie Winifred Elizabeth Wright Connor Sol."

"I will," she promised.

He sagged down where he was, between the seats, his face half under the console. Mac moved her feet to make more room for his left arms. She looked around, but couldn't see anything on the small ship to use to make him more comfortable. Norris had thrown his bags in the corner, but they were too small to be useful bedding.

Norris. Mac pulled up her knees and wrapped her arms tightly around them.

Had he hurried to his ship on her word, sent the signal, gone out only to be ambushed within reach of safety?

Or had he run all the way here, the Ro close behind . . . heard that horrible sound nearer and nearer . . . reached the shelter of his ship . . . yet gone back for her?

Mac looked at the locked door, thinking of what lay beyond. *How didn't matter.* "You saved our lives," she whispered. "Thank you."

She cocked her head, listening for any sign of life, hearing only the labored breaths of her companion.

Then dropped her head to her knees.

"Is anyone in there? Dr. Norris. Dr. Connor. Are you in there?"

Mac raised her head, looking to the door, but the voice was inside the lev. *The console.* Lights were flashing in various patterns, more lights than she imagined simply receiving a transmission would require. "This is Dr. Connor," she replied, hoping she didn't need to activate any control to be heard. "Who's this?"

"Your escort from the *Joy*." *Nothing could have sounded as good.* "Lieutenant Lee Halpern. Dr. Connor, is Dr. Norris with you?"

"No. He's been killed." Mac checked the Wasted. Given the proximity of the Trisulian ship, she wasn't about to announce his presence on an open com. He showed no signs of consciousness but was breathing.

"Are you in immediate danger?" Sharp and to the point.

"No. I don't think so," Mac qualified. "You can get me out of here, I hope?"

"Already on it. Intersystem craft have an auto retrieve function—safety feature. The captain asked Dr. Norris for his remote codes before you left. Ship's systems will reverse your course and head back to the *Joy*. Stand by."

Mac sat by, relieved beyond words. But as time continued to pass with only the same light patterns taunting her, that relief faded. *If she counted the number of times auto-anything had failed in the field . . .* She leaned over the console. "Halpern. I'm guessing there's a problem."

"We're working on options, Dr. Connor. The codes activated the retrieval of a probe, Dr. Connor, not your ship. Where are you exactly?"

Norris had made sure he wouldn't be stopped short of his goal, Mac realized, feeling more pity than anger.

"Inside the *Uosanah*. Parked in a hangar," she sighed, leaning back in the chair. "We entered through the middle of a row of round doors inside a mass of what looked to me like container-handling equipment. But I'm no engineer."

"Is there any way for you to determine the presence of hostile forces?"

The Ro? "The one I know of is dead. And," Mac took a steadying breath. "Dr. Norris is outside the ship, too."

"Is the area secure?"

"Of course it's not secure. That's why I'm locked inside!" Mac glared at the lights, then shook her head. *She wasn't at her best.* "I'm sorry, Halpern. It's been a little—I'm out of my depth here. I don't know if there are more of them. I'd really rather not go and look, if you don't mind."

"I don't want you to, Dr. Connor—may I call you Mac?"

The situation was that bad? "Yes."

"Mac, I don't want to alarm you—" *Didn't people realize how terrifying that statement was?* "—but things are a bit complicated out here as well. The captain launched tacticals at your distress call—they could get inside the derelict, deal with whatever—but the Trisulian commander won't let them approach. The Sinzi-ra is doing his best to change that." The tone was matter-of-fact. Mac winced, well able to imagine the furious negotiations. Everyone in the system probably heard Norris' distress call—including the part about Ro on board.

The idiot faction, trying to send diplomats; the rest preparing to blow up the Uosanah *and the other derelicts.*

And one trapped biologist.

She wasn't the only one at risk. Halpern's tiny shuttle was a provocation to all sides, simply by being near the Dhryn ship. "How about you?" she asked. "Can you stay?"

"Not going anywhere, Mac. Not without you." A pause. "I don't suppose you're a pilot."

"No. Why?"

"Oh." A pause. "If you were, and if you could find and access the protocols Dr. Norris used to enter the hangar, you could set the bay to auto. You'll drift out and I'd snag you and take you back to the *Joy*." Halpern grew enthused. "Maybe I can talk you through it."

And if she could breathe vacuum, she could walk. Mac sighed. "Norris locked the controls. Even if he hadn't, you should see this thing, Halpern. It's modified from standard. There's research gear, scanners . . ."

A hand brushed her foot and Mac stopped to glance down. The Wasted was still unconscious. *But breathing.*

"Wait." She bit her lower lip, then nodded to herself. "There's someone with me who might be able to make sense of it."

"Who?"

A dying Dhryn who'd survived this long on the bodies of his former crew? Mac thought fast. "Charlie. Charlie Mudge. He wanted to come along and we snuck him on board." Dead silence. Mac prodded the Wasted with her toe. "I know it was against regulations," she babbled on, "but he's flown starships."

"Regulations be damned. Let me speak to him."

"Give me a minute. He's—he's been hurt." She reached down and shook the Wasted, obtaining a low moan. "Charlie," she urged, careful to use Instella. Her hands slipped over fluid and flaccid skin. She gripped harder. "You have to get us out of the hangar. Do you understand? I need you."

"I—do not—exist."

"He's not himself," Mac said loudly. She got out of the pilot seat and crouched as close to the alien's head as she could. "Listen to me," she whispered. "This is your ship. You must know how to launch a shuttle—please, *Lamisah*."

An eye opened and regarded her, its yellow almost white. " '*Lamisah?*' " His bleeding lips twisted in what might have been scorn. "You are not-Dhryn."

"And you don't exist." Mac rested her hand on his chilled shoulder. "A great pair. Can you do it?"

"Mac? How's Charlie?"

"Oh, getting there." Halpern sounded anxious. *Good thing there wasn't a vid link.*

The Wasted sucked in air and held it. He rose, gripping the chairs and her knee for purchase, then almost fell again. She wrapped her arms around him, trying to avoid the larger fractures. As he leaned against her, she could barely make out his whisper. "Internal com. Command . . . I can command . . ."

She raised her face to the lev ceiling. "Charlie's accessing the codes." *He didn't need to know which ones.*

"Hurry," Halpern responded, distinct stress in his voice. "It's a little busy out here, if you get my drift."

"Can you do it from here?" Mac asked the Wasted. She took his slow reach for the console as yes.

A little busy?

Jurisdictional issues.

"I can't believe I'm doing this," she muttered and put her hand over the Wasted's to stop him. "Wait."

Halpern heard. "Doing what, Mac? There's no time—"

"Stand by."

Moving quickly, Mac dumped the tools and scanners from one of Norris'
bags, slinging it over her shoulder. She grasped the umbrella firmly and went to
the door. The Wasted turned his big head to watch her unlock it. "I'll be right
back," she promised, and threw open the door.

Once again, the odor of decay and death filled her nostrils. This time, instead
of being hidden, the bodies were steps away. Before she could hesitate—*as in
come to her senses*—Mac walked down the ramp. She took her time and poked the
air around and in front with the umbrella, feeling like a fool but unable to move
unless sure she wasn't walking into a Ro or its invisible servant.

The silence should have been reassuring. *It made it hard to breathe.*

"Way too much imagination," she panted.

She reached Norris, and gently laid the umbrella beside him. *He'd said "Ships
don't die empty."* She didn't think he'd mind resting in this one for a while longer.

Mac put the bag over her real hand and headed for the other corpse. Every
second counted. "Just another specimen," she told herself, hunting for something to grab that wouldn't cut through the fabric. One of the clubbed limbs
looked promising. Both her hands shook so badly she couldn't touch it on her
first try. "Call yourself a biologist," she muttered. "It's another dead specimen.
Doesn't even smell. Much."

A lunge and her fingers wrapped around what felt harder than ordinary flesh.
Without pause, she pulled back, her artificial hand clenching so tight she felt
something give. The body resisted, then moved, sliding along the deck, remaining limbs waving aimlessly.

scurryscurry

Mac froze, then realized the sound had come from the corpse, as if parts
rubbed together. "You're dead," she reminded it, and pulled. *scurryscurry* She
took a step and pulled, wishing for more slime. "Wait . . ." And again. "Till . . ."
She grunted a word with each effort, as much to keep herself company as to
cover the sounds from the corpse. "They . . ." The thing outmassed her, though
not by much. "See . . ." Keeping it moving was easier, though her arms were
already aching with strain.

"You!"

Her foot hit the end of the ramp. Stepping up, she blinked sweat from her
eyes and heaved. The corpse came partway, then stuck fast.

Was a little cooperation too much to ask?

Abandoning her prize was unthinkable. *They'd never be given a chance to examine it.*

Then Mac smiled. She'd loaded and unloaded levs in the middle of blizzards.
There were a few tricks. "Wait here," she told the corpse, and ran into the lev.

The Wasted hadn't died while she'd been gone. *One relief.* "Be ready, Charlie,"
she told him, then went to the ramp control, tossing the bag from her hands.
The air moving into the lev made her shiver despite the warmth of exertion. The
open door was like an invitation.

But, at long last, Mac-friendly technology. With a cry of triumph, she reversed the closing sequence, overrode the load safeties, and hit the emergency retract.

With a machine protest, the ramp snapped itself up against the ship before the door could shut.

And with a *skitter . . . scurry . . . POP!* the corpse answered momentum and rolled into the lev, Mac jumping out of its way.

"Always works," she said with satisfaction, turning to her companion.

The Wasted's eyes were huge and his limbs trembled so violently they clattered against the console.

"Don't worry," Mac soothed. "I can fix the door." She let the ramp back down, reset the controls, and let the door close properly.

"That—that—" The Instella stopped and the floor vibrated. Not that there was much floor left, the corpse having sprawled into a nasty mass of appendages, several either broken from her handling or with implausible joint structure. Or both.

Leaving no room for a panicked Dhryn.

"We do not think of it," she told the Wasted, slowly and clearly, making sure his eyes were on hers. "Do you understand me?"

"Mac!" Halpern's disembodied voice was close to a shout. "What's going on? Where did you go? Charlie didn't answer—has he passed out on you?"

"Lamisah," she whispered. "This one thing and you can rest. I promise."

Eyes blinked at her, then shifted to the console. "I am—here, Halpern," the Wasted said, the effort to speak at all plain to Mac. Her throat tightened in sympathy. Withered fingers touched a blue button among the dozens, slowly input numbers, methodically pressed a sequence of other controls. *How well could his mind function, given the wreck of his body?* Mac judged this an unproductive line of thought and dropped into the passenger seat.

The ship gave that characteristic lurch and she leaned with it, as if encouraging it to continue moving. *Last chance to stop us.*

"Sending us into the bay now," the Wasted said. "I've—I've set auto launch to put us—put us beyond the freight area."

"I'll be waiting for you." Halpern, quick and sure. "Good work, Charlie. Can't wait to shake your hand."

The Wasted gave Mac a look she had no problem interpreting at all.

- CONTACT -

THE FROW HUNG HEAD DOWN, the better to see the small black object lodged at the base of the crevice. Its surface was nonreflective. It might have been water-polished stone, heaved from a distant riverbed during the annual floods. *Se* Ferenlaa checked the signal detector once more to be sure. "Record this as number sixty-three and destroy it."

Se's lackey, *Ne* Liani, was perched on the opposite wall. *Ne* dutifully recorded the number. "Sixty-three. How many more are left?"

Ne was an individual of undeniable beauty in uniform, with the intelligence of drying moss. Why *ne* had been assigned to *se* when *ne* would have shone hanging at a ceremonial post or as a display model for a hat store, was beyond *se's* comprehension. *Mater* must be slipping. And now, when routine had become crisis, *ne's* blithe incompetence was a risk.

"I've told you before, sib-cousin, it doesn't matter how many remain. They must all be found. Now, be quick! Once this one is destroyed, I'll be able to tell if another lies near our position."

Quick movement was thankfully among *ne's* skills, along with—*se* was told—a finely developed moral sense. Both virtually guaranteed success as either a snatch-cross referee or pet retriever. After all, was not a family's highest goal to advance the next generation through the ranks? As *Ne* Liani fumbled with the acid pack attached to *ne's* chest, *se* mused on how best to broach the subject with *mater* when next home. If they had a home to return to, *se* corrected.

Ne struck a pose with the spray nozzle in one hand, membranes set to advantage. "Ready, sib-cousin."

"Just destroy it," ordered *Se* Ferenlaa. As the first blast bubbled its way through the object's outer casing, *se* monitored the signal detector. "Again. Good. It's silenced."

Se flipped *se-self* around and flowed up the crevice, pausing beneath the signs citing rates and regulations, ignoring the agitated flutters from the banished tourists clinging overhead. The Teinsmon Trickle was always busy, being one of the must-do wonders of this region. It wasn't *se's* fault that those waiting for the all-clear had paid a truly ridiculous sum for the privilege of hanging for an hour within its mineral-laden sprays.

Missing one of the transmitters would be.

Their Sinzi-ra had made that clear. The outgoing signal must be stopped.

The Trisulians—*may their offspring rot within their bodies*—had arranged for an unknown number of the devices to be strewn about the Frow homeworld. Most had been sold as landscaping ornaments, their black polished into a smooth hemisphere that could be affixed on a wall among rooted flowering climbers. Quite fetching, if cheap. Those had been easily traced and destroyed.

But the rest were of the type *se* hunted, dropped into shadows by Trisulian tourists. They'd known where to start looking—no Sinzi-ra let aliens wander a homeworld unremarked—but they hadn't found them all before the transmissions began.

Calling the Dhryn.

It had become a race against death. While ordinary citizens went about their business, unaware their world was at risk, those with the right training were given detectors and ordered to climb wherever a device might be hidden, to find and destroy it. *Se* Ferenlaa installed home com systems, with *se's* sib-cousin's dubious help. Close enough, they'd told him.

Se held out the detector, hoping they'd found the last here. *No. Another signal, nearby.* "Come!" Relieved *Ne* Liani hadn't noticed the admiration of the spectators—such things turned a young Frow's head—*se* led the way as rapidly as *se's* older limbs could move, leaving safer paths in favor of any shortcut that beckoned.

A planet-wide evacuation was impossible. Those of highest rank were told, but refused to leave. *Se* shared their pride. Frow clung fast and would not willingly fall.

When no handhold offered, *se* threw *se-self* forward and down in hopes of one, membranes out and humming, sulfur-stained rock flashing past. *Se's* claws snatched at one grip, then another, finally latching on to a barely perceptible crack. Making sure all four limbs were secure, *se* looked for *ne.*

"Right here, sib-cousin," came the reply. *Ne* Liani passed *se,* moving with easy grace.

Se checked the detector. "It's above us. There. Sixty-four."

The Trisulian had shoved the transmitter in a fissure near one of the larger trickles, the rocks to either side carved by the claws of the generations of Frow who'd sought miracles from the spring.

Ne recorded the number. "Sixty-four. Shall I destroy it now?"

Se wanted to grab the acid pack and do it *se-self.* "Yes, yes! But climb above it first, fool!"

"There's no need to be insulting, sib-cousin."

Ne even pouted beautifully. *Se* clung to the rock and swore to talk to *mater* if they survived this. "Just do it. Please. Quickly."

Ne Liani pumped the spray.

Se Ferenlaa stared at the detector. "Again."

Were they too late?

"Again. Hurry!"

It was silenced. *Se* climbed higher and checked. *Nothing.* Hardly daring to hope, *se* went to where cliff ended in the deadly flat land above and held out the detector.

Nothing.

They'd done it. Here at least.

Se put away the detector and climbed down to where *ne* waited. Without a word, *se* carefully stripped, hanging hat and uniform on the provided hooks. *Se* slipped into the nearest glistening trickle of water and relaxed.

"Sib-cousin. We haven't paid!"

Se Ferenlaa sighed. Maybe *ne* had a future in ticket sales.

At least now, ne *might have a future.*

Consternation . . .
    The Call ends. The path is lost. The Great Ships pause.
    All that is Dhryn is endangered. There is no life but that which is Dhryn.
    The Progenitors call for Vessels, seek accommodation.
    But that which is Dhryn understands the Truth.
    One must survive the Great Journey.
    Even at the cost of another.

PRESENTS AND POLICY

MAC WASN'T SURE if she was escorting one corpse or two to the *Annapolis Joy*. The Wasted, now curled at her feet, had grown quieter and more still throughout the journey. She hoped it was *hathis,* the Dhryn healing comalike sleep. She feared it was simply the end.

The lev continued, attached somehow to Halpern's shuttle. She couldn't switch to the surround view Norris had installed, which meant she sat in a box for the duration. *A very quiet box.* She'd told Halpern "Charlie" was sleeping. In turn, he'd expressed concern over who else might be able to listen. They'd agreed on silence.

Not even a polka.

The return didn't take as long as she'd remembered, despite having napped on the way out. Halpern's relieved, "about to dock, Mac," announcement startled her.

Mac sat straight. "And me without a shower," she muttered to herself, wrinkling her nose. Most of the stink came from her clothes. Sweat and vomit. *Lovely.* A brush of one hand did nothing for the overlapped stains of Human and Dhryn blood. *The hand was bloody, too.*

Her knees glistened with slime. The corpse didn't. She frowned at it thoughtfully. *Useful stuff, slime.* A healthy salmon wore a protective coat of it. Salamanders breathed through it. Slugs glided on a road of it. Nothing quite matched her observations. *Can't assume it's natural slime anyway,* she scolded herself, postponing any investigation until much later.

Moving around the lev was awkward, given the need to avoid contact with alien parts. Mac tiptoed and sidestepped to her backpack. Once there, she took out her water bottle and used what was left in it to wet her face and hands. She used the backpack itself as a makeshift towel, having to trust the end result wasn't worse.

Physically, she was in better shape than her clothing. Food was a distant concern; just looking at the corpse made her queasy. Emotionally, she was numb and content to remain so for a while longer.

Mentally, though, she'd reached the state Emily referred to as "crabby" and Mudge had frequently decried as "utterly unreasonable."

In other words, she'd had enough.

She'd ordered Halpern to bring them into the hangar set aside for Ureif and his consulate, using the premise the Sinzi would want to meet her anyway so it saved time and travel.

Hollans might have found a walker on Earth. He might even plan to share.

She'd make sure more than Humans would have a crack at this one.

Halpern, concerned about "Charlie," assured her he'd called ahead for a med team to meet them.

Mac's lips stretched in what wasn't a smile. *Weren't they going to be surprised?*

"Unlock the door, Dr. Connor."

Mac hugged her knees and didn't budge from the passenger seat. *All well and good to have a plan,* she thought ruefully. *Until no one listened.*

Halpern, either doubting the sanity of a certain biologist, or following the orders of someone whose sanity he did trust, had ignored her request and returned them to the same hangar from which Norris had left. The Human part of the ship. And now a very familiar voice shouted at her through the com system.

"Dr. Connor," Cayhill said, for the fourth time. "Open this door! Let me attend to Mr. Mudge!"

Funny how the best lie could come back to bite you, sighed Mac. She supposed he knew better than to pound his fists on metal, realizing she wouldn't hear it, but the image had its charm. "I've told you, Cayhill. I'm waiting for the Sinzi-ra," she said, for the fifth time. "It's not a hard concept."

A new voice. "Norcoast!"

Mac winced. "Oversight."

She waited for it.

Right on cue. "Charlie Mudge?" The words came out in a sputtering bullroar that had to hurt the man's throat.

The answering *harrumph* was that signature mix of dignified offense. "I am not 'Charlie.'"

"And you aren't on this ship with Dr. Connor, gravely injured."

"Idiot! Of course he's not."

Hearing the odds in the hangar shifting her way at last, Mac grinned. "Hi, Fourteen. Is Ureif there?"

"This is Captain Gillis, Dr. Connor."

Or not. Her grin faded. "Captain. I'd like to get out of here." She put aside her body's sudden agreement on that point. *There was a bottle handy.*

"Then unlock the door." Reasonable.

Mac put her hand on the Wasted. *Not dead yet.* She glanced at the corpse. *Still dead.* "Once Ureif is here."

Reason gave way to official outrage. "The Sinzi-ra is busy trying to keep the Interspecies Union together in this part of space, Dr. Connor!"

"So," she replied coolly, "am I."

She wasn't surprised by the ensuing silence, well able to imagine their faces as they tried to decide if she'd been through too much at last, or this was as serious as she claimed. Cayhill would be shaking his head sadly, but with a triumphant "I warned you about her" in the look he'd give his captain. Fourteen would have his hands over his eyes, worried about her and unable to do anything about it. The captain would appear thoughtful. While Mudge . . .

. . . *he'd know.* Maybe not what she had on board, but that she did have something—someone—with her she wouldn't risk being revealed without the Sinzi-ra's authority at hand.

There was, of course, a point beyond which she couldn't push Gillis, not on his own ship. If this had been one of the *Joy's* shuttle fleet, he'd have already ordered its door opened and have the codes to do it. Because this modified lev was Dr. Norris' pride and joy, a man he must believe was dead on his watch, she didn't think the captain was prepared, yet, to order his crew to cut their way inside.

Mac estimated she had no more than a half an hour left. She eyed the bottle.

"I am here, Dr. Connor."

Ureif's voice. Mac checked the time. Twenty-one minutes. *He'd cut it tight.* Something else had been occupying him; whatever it was, she was about to complicate it.

"Sinzi-ra." As she went to the door, she ran her fingers through her hair, finding a patch of something sticky. *So much for personal grooming.*

She opened the lev door.

Captain Gillis hadn't taken any chances. A semicircle of armored and armed guards posed threateningly, so close they had to shuffle back when Mac sent down the ramp. Both Sinzi, accompanied by Grimnoii, stood beyond that barrier with Gillis and Townee; Mudge and Fourteen beside them; Cayhill and a small knot of orderlies relegated to some distance away.

This well-thought out arrangement lasted only as long as it took her appearance to register, then Ureif and Mudge were on the move, Gillis only a step behind. The guards took the hint and lowered their weapons, stepping out of the way. Not fast enough for Fourteen, who shoved the nearest aside with both hands.

Mac lifted her hands to slow the stampede. "Nothing a shower won't cure," she said quickly. "I wasn't hurt."

Whether she convinced them or not, protocol paralyzed them at the base of the short ramp: the Humans unwilling to get in Ureif's way, the Sinzi-ra attempting to defer not to the captain, but to the ashen-faced Mudge. *Exceptional awareness,* she judged, relieved to be right. Not to diminish Fy, but this was a Sinzi of Anchen's caliber. *They all needed that.*

And while manners sorted themselves out, Fourteen ran past them all and thundered up the ramp, shouting, "Idiot! Idiot!" He stopped short of grabbing her in a full hug, perhaps realizing that would ruin his favorite paisley shorts, and settled for patting her shoulders. "There are others to take such risks," he scolded all the while. "Others of less value or interest. You should not have gone."

"Glad to see you, too," she said.

Then Mudge was in front of her. Fourteen stepped aside without a word.

Judging by his expression, she looked worse than she thought. If he'd offered concern or sympathy, she might have faltered, begun to react to the past few hours. Instead, a calm question. "What do you need, Norcoast?"

"A stretcher," Mac said immediately, having made her own plans. "Medical facilities within our portion of the ship. Guards and vids for that. And one of those bigger parts bins." Mac pointed down the hangar to where crew had stopped pretending to work on another shuttle while such interesting events were underway in their area.

Mudge nodded and, collecting Fourteen with a look, went back down the ramp. The two moved apart to allow Ureif to advance, the captain close behind. The captain spoke first, eyes wide. "You're sure you're all right, Dr. Connor?"

As she nodded, Ureif lifted one graceful finger to indicate her shoulder, his mouth turning down. "This is Dhryn blood."

Mac backed into the lev, mute invitation. There wasn't room for the other two to fully enter, but she doubted they'd want to anyway. Not once they saw what waited.

The captain's hand flew up to cover his mouth and nose, eyes staring. He managed not to retch, but beads of sweat formed on his forehead. For an instant, the Sinzi's fingers trembled, their blood-red rings sounding like the first hit of freezing rain on dry grass, then they stilled.

Both looked at her.

"Don't worry. The walker's dead," Mac assured them, well aware their reaction wasn't to the Wasted. She gestured to the unconscious being. "He killed it before it could attack me." *Learning how was high on her list.*

Gillis spoke through his hand. "Dr. Norris?"

"We were exploring the *Uosanah* when I heard the walker in one of the holds. While I hid, he went to call for help." Her voice came out flat and strange. *Just the facts.* "When he tried to come back for me, the Ro's thing ambushed and killed him." There was a rise in the sound levels outside. *Mudge and Fourteen.*

Gillis' hand dropped away. His mouth worked before he spoke. When he did, the words were harsh and accusing. "You left Norris there—"

"He's got company," Mac replied wearily. "The rest of the Dhryn are dead."

For an instant, she thought he meant to strike her. Then Gillis shook his head, the blind rage in his face subsiding into something more rational. His eyes flicked to the corpse, his throat working as he swallowed. "How the—never mind, I don't think I want to know. Good work, Dr. Connor. Good work." Real warmth. "What now?"

She wasn't surprised by his self-control. *This* was *the captain of the Ministry's latest and greatest.* "We need to preserve the body. And," she gazed up at the so-far silent Sinzi, "to invite IU scientists on board to learn everything they can from it. From both factions," she emphasized.

This was the key, Mac thought, hardly breathing. *Let those who still believed the Ro were the IU's saviors see this nightmare of flesh for themselves.*

Let them try to imagine its masters.

Gillis' eyes took on a gleam.

A cool finger's tip traced Mac's cheek. "I am overcome," Ureif said, and bowed his head, the white gown whispering with the movement. "What you propose . . . it offers profound congruence."

"I thought you'd like it," she grinned.

Mac didn't like where she had to spend the next hour. Instead of following either Wasted or corpse, or even providing a full briefing to someone, she was sent to decontamination and abandoned to the overzealous ministrations of orderlies with a hose.

Cayhill's revenge, she judged glumly, lifting her arms for yet another spray. She wore her rings, nothing more. Her imp and the little salmon carving sat in a bag, waiting where she could see them.

Humans hadn't been members of the IU long enough—by millennia—to be acceptable hosts for anything worse than Nerban shoe fungus. *And that only stuck to soles for a ride elsewhere.*

When they were done scouring every centimeter of her skin with pointless biocides, Mac thanked the orderlies for the cleanup. *No denying she'd been filthy.* She thanked them for providing clean crew coveralls and slippers. *Her latest clothing having been sent to disposal.* Though she hadn't much else anyway. Consular staff hadn't fully appreciated the rigors of life in space.

She didn't bother to thank them for the sandwich she pilfered on her way out.

Kaili Xai was waiting to escort her wherever. Mac smiled with relief, glad to see someone familiar. "Be honest," she said lightly. "Did they leave me a face?"

Kaili smiled back, then made a show of peering closely. "I think you've lost some freckles."

Mac shrugged. "More where they came from—and where are we going?"

"Where do you want to go?"

The calm question took her aback. *Returned with corpse and guest from a disastrous unauthorized mission, complete with loss of its leader?* "I thought," Mac ventured, "there'd be some yelling."

"Oh," Kaili's expression turned serious. "Enough of that going around. Half the ship is being turned into a consulate and the captain has his hands full fielding delegations to the Sinzi-ra already." A dimple. "I'm sure he'll yell at you eventually."

"No hurry," Mac said. "In that case, I know exactly where I want to go."

As she and Kaili walked to the Origins section, Mac wolfed down her sandwich and then began peppering her companion with questions. The orderly might not be an officer or have bridge access, but Mac doubted even Townee had as thorough a grasp on what was happening on board.

Kaili, who'd taken a certain homesick biologist under her gentle wing the year before, was happy to share the latest gossip. "Oh, no one minds," she replied, when Mac asked about the crew's reaction to the sudden changes. "Might be different if it weren't the Sinzi, but, gad—isn't it amazing, seeing them walking around? Everyone's sending mail home about it. I never thought I'd see one in person." She gave a shy smile. "I even spoke to Fy. She came with Charlie to the dispensary for eyedrops. Graceful. Polite. Quiet. She made me feel special."

"Charlie?" Mac's lips twitched. *Poor Mudge.* Aloud, "I tend to feel I'm wearing my work boots around them." They turned a corner and she waited until a couple of crew passed them before continuing. "What do you mean, everyone's sending mail? I thought there was a ban."

"Just while we were gatebound." Kaili made a rude noise. "You can bet that wasn't popular. The *Joy* may look like a warship, but we're more a glorified customs inspector. Sure we've all simmed on combat rigs, but the tightest we've had to play it was that business with the Ro. At that, the most we did was orbit Myriam and wait on the scientists. I'd expect a mutiny if the captain tried to shut us up here." She laughed. "Or my parents'll register a complaint."

"I'd like to call to my dad," Mac said before she thought.

"It's not quite talking," explained the orderly. "One stream of newspackets goes into the gate, addressed to Earth or wherever. Another set returns. They squeal at close to light when they hit the system. The bigwigs can arrange for sequencing, which is close. If both speakers are near a gate, the time delay can be seconds. But regular folks like us make do with a two- to three-hour swing. Still, keeps you in touch. Last I heard from . . ."

Mac let Kaili's voice drift by, nodding at the right places. *Plenty of time for some judicious editing,* she thought, almost appalled to feel reassured.

They didn't use intership transit, the medlab not being that far. Kaili made Mac laugh with tales of her newly retired parents' efforts to coax an Earth-type garden from their yard on Mars. For her part, Mac talked about her brothers, finding unexpected peace sharing Owen's fall from dignity upon fatherhood and skirting like an abyss how much she could use Blake's advice.

"Not taken, hmm?" Kaili's teeth gleamed in wide smile. "You should introduce us, next pass by Earth. He sounds yummy."

Blake? Mac considered her brother, trying to see it, and shook her head. "I'll introduce you, but then you're on your own. He's the type the family likes to call 'an individual.' Translates as royal pain, sometimes."

"But not always."

"No," Mac said softly.

The Origins part of the ship was deserted. Gillis had merely expedited the move to Myriam. *Probably like releasing a flood.* Everyone, she'd been told, had willingly packed and were now busy checking the transfer of their equipment to planet-bound shuttles. *Leaving her behind,* she sighed to herself, then wondered how she'd become so attached to archaeologists and their work. She'd see them before departure. *Doubtless the time to become maudlin.*

They stopped outside the door Kaili indicated as the Wasted's quarters, both nodding a greeting to the guard stationed beside it. "Thank you, Kaili."

"I'll be around. Stay out of trouble for a while, Mac. Hear me?" With that, Kaili left.

Mac steeled herself and entered the room.

For an instant, she was sure Kaili taken her to the wrong place, even though she'd been told they'd used a portion of the newly abandoned work areas.

There'd hardly be a guard at any other door.

Implying this was the right room. But there were candles burning beside the bed, albeit a bed with an unconscious Dhryn on it. And the last person on the ship she expected to find seated beside that bed looked up at her, dipping his head in acknowledgment, while Doug Court rolled his eyes at her from his station by the monitors.

"Dr. Connor," Wilson Kudla said quietly. "Have you come to join our vigil?"

"Our?" She took a step sideways in order to see Kudla's disciples sitting cross-legged on the floor behind their leader. Their eyes were closed and their lips moved in silent unison, their habit when forced to chant outside their tent. *Small mercies,* Mac thought. "Who let you in here, Kudla?" she demanded, keeping it low.

"Are we not part of this mission? Do we not have the same clearance as the rest?"

Only because you didn't go anywhere, so no one thought to cancel it. Mac fumed, eyes flitting between the Wasted, who wasn't dead yet, and the insufferable Human at his side. "Of course," she gritted out between her teeth. "May I ask why you're here?"

He swept both arms around to include the Wasted, ceiling, and a portion of the deck in the gesture. "This is one of the Lost Souls. Those who cry to me from the past." His gaze sharpened. "I describe them most clearly in Chapter Thirteen."

"Chapter Thirteen," echoed the disciples in an ardent monotone.

Doug coughed in the background.

Mac forced a smile, the tightness in her jaw warning her the result was probably unpleasant. "I'll have to look that one up again." As if aware he was being deleted, Kudla routinely messaged fresh copies of his opus, *Chasm Ghouls: They Exist and Speak to Me.* "You shouldn't neglect your writing," she ground out. "There's nothing you can do to help here—at the moment, anyway."

"We're doing no harm." Kudla had a forgettable face that tended to park itself at vaguely preoccupied. Mac was startled to see him frown with determination. "We wish to stay."

Ready to have the guard haul them out, her curiosity got the better of her. "Why?"

"He should not be abandoned."

"The med staff—"

His narrow-set eyes actually flashed with outrage. "Would you wish no other companions while awaiting your destiny, Dr. Connor? I think not!"

She sent Doug a helpless glance and he mouthed, "It's okay."

It did keep the author and his disciples busy.

"Stay," Mac agreed. "But you won't touch him. Get rid of the candles. Obey every order you're given by Doug here, or those who replace him, and do not—" she stressed the word, "—engage the Wasted in conversation if he wakes. I'm to be called. These aren't negotiable, Kudla."

"Lost Soul," he corrected.

She sighed. "Call him what you want. Just don't interfere with his care. Understand me?"

He stood and half bowed, sweeping back the voluminous brown robe he affected. It would have looked dignified except the fabric was caught under his stool and he lost his balance, the disciples scrambling up to save him from a fall.

Mac sighed again.

Humans.

"Thank you for coming." Mac stroked through her 'screen, storing her work. For the first time in a while she was struck by the blue tinge of her fingers. *He brought it out in her,* she thought without resentment, watching Cayhill's approach.

He took his time, his eyes darting around the room. She let him.

It looked liked a hospital room. *Or pending morgue,* Mac reminded herself. The former captain of the *Uosanah* lay on his side, festooned with machinery more alive than he appeared to be.

Cayhill's eyes passed over Kudla and his disciples, now happily huddled together in one corner, touched on the orderly station, now empty, and stopped at the Wasted. "I thought it would be dead by now."

"Nothing we've done," Mac admitted, rising to her feet. There'd been no change, no breakthrough. The nearest possible help? *She was looking at him.*

Giving her a glare as if to imply this was all her fault—*true*—the *Joy's* head physician wandered around the room, hands hovering over various instruments. *Most appropriated from his medlab.* His path wove with seeming casualness closer and closer to the unconscious being, until finally, he halted by the bed. "What's wrong with him?" Almost reluctant.

"A Dhryn can undergo a second metamorphosis," Mac explained, moving to the other side. "The change from *oomling* to adult form? They all do that. The second, the Flowering, changes an adult into something more specialized."

He flinched back. "The feeders."

"Yes. But not in this case." She laid her hand on the blue-stained sheet. "This is the Wasting. I was told it happens when the second metamorphosis fails. Ordinary Dhryn shun such individuals, ignoring their existence even when a Wasted is driven by hunger to attack the living, or feed on the dead. They don't live long, regardless."

"I can see why." Cayhill gazed down at the alien. "The skin is degenerating at every point of stress. The resulting fluid loss—What are you doing for his pain?"

"Nie rugorath sa nie a nai." At his puzzled look, Mac realized she'd spoken in Dhryn. "'A Dhryn is robust or a Dhryn is not.' They have no medical databases, Dr. Cayhill. There's nothing we can do."

His pale eyebrows drew together. "That's absurd," he snapped. "At least get him off this bed and into a suspension chamber—take the pressure off skin and bone."

"Anything else?" she asked innocently.

Cayhill's frown deepened into suspicion. "Oh, no, you don't. I can't be involved in his care. I told the captain. I can't deal with alien patients, Dr. Connor. It's another specialty altogether. I'm not capable—"

"Not even the Dhryn are capable of dealing with this patient," Mac pointed out. "I could dissect him—hopefully figure out the percentage of the population that ends up this way and why. My team is researching his past, the life on his planet—hopefully they'll figure out how the Dhryn came to be as they are." She could no longer decipher his expression, but kept going. "This Dhryn believes he no longer exists, Cayhill. What he needs is someone who won't let him die." She took a deep breath. "Please."

His fingers reached out to the bed, but he continued to hold Mac's eyes with his. "Why do you care?"

The question echoed hers of Kudla, who watched all this from his corner. She chose to take it at face value, as honest rather than more probing after her hidden motivations or unresolved guilt.

The truth, then.

"I'm not like you, Dr. Cayhill," Mac said quietly. "My work deals with species, not individuals. I follow changes in populations over time, how they interact with others, their environments. Bear with me, please." This as he scowled his impatience. "I want you to understand something. The drives acting on living things—that's what I do. And right now, all around us, those drives are colliding. The result will be extinction. The only real question left is who goes first. I can imagine destroying the Dhryn." Mac looked down at the Wasted and shrugged. "But when I stand here, all I see is someone as trapped as we are."

Without a word, Cayhill took a scanner from the nearby table and passed it over the Dhryn. As abruptly, he stopped, closing the instrument in his fist as if the results offended him. "I won't put up with interference," he informed her almost fiercely. "Not even from you. I want that understood, Dr. Connor. If he's my patient, I'm in charge."

Mac carefully didn't smile. "Of course. Just let us know what you'll—"

"I have my own supplies and staff," he interrupted. "Let me get to work. For what good it will do."

With a nod, she went to the Wasted's head and leaned over his ear, purposefully speaking Dhryn. "You'd better listen to him, *Lamisah*. He'll make your life miserable if you die under his care."

When she straightened, Cayhill was staring at her, patentedly dismayed. "He doesn't speak Instella?"

"He does," she assured him. "And he seems used to Humans. But don't expect a typical doctor-patient conversation. Dhryn don't discuss biology, including their own bodies. If you need me, I'll be available. Anytime."

He stiffened. "I won't need you, Dr. Connor."

"If he needs me," she modified, very quietly.

Cayhill waited for a few seconds, as if to make sure she knew he wasn't giving in, then nodded.

"Dr. Connor! Dr. Connor!"

"I know I'm late," she told the Grimnoii shambling up behind her, making sure to give it room. The creatures managed to sound twice as large as they were, even inside a starship. *Useful technique,* Mac thought, remembering the packed corridors of Base in spring.

There'd been nothing more from Emily or Case in the mail from the courier. *Nothing personal,* she clarified. The detailed reports waiting in her imp had gone a long way to easing her alarm. Emily Mamani at full throttle could give Kammie lessons in data dumping. None of it came sorted or annotated or indexed, just an "Oh, right. Mac wanted updates," tossed her way, loaded with schematics and Em-only jargon and the occasional salacious cartoon.

Annoying and utterly normal.

"Normal's wonderful," she said out loud.

"Pardon?"

Mac shrugged an apology. "Talking to myself. Human thing." She glanced at the alien, recognizing the array of curved knives. Grimnoii facial features were sufficiently distinct to Human eyes to set them apart as individuals, but she found it quicker to tell them apart by their hardware. It would have helped if they had names, but Rumnor was the only Grimnoii on board who had—or would admit to—one. *For all she knew, the Sinzi required their staff to go nameless and Rumnor was a rebel.*

Equally likely, she reminded herself, *"Rumnor" wasn't a name at all, but a some kind of rank, like "pack leader" or "cider enabler."* About the only sign of precedence was that he tended to speak up first. But then, the others usually caroled in with their contribution pretty quickly.

Undeterred, Mac had applied her own mental labels to keep them straight. This one was Fy-Alpha, Fy-Beta's belt sporting barbed darts. The other Sinzi had Rumnor, plus the two Mac called Ureif's Alpha and Beta, fond of axes and spears respectively.

Not that she'd use the names to their melancholy faces. She was becoming more diplomatic. *When she remembered.*

"Is Fy already there?" Mac asked.

"Of course." This followed by a sigh so heavy and prolonged it implied the universe itself had ended yesterday and they'd been left behind. Mac, taking the hint, picked up the pace. "I bring her the latest newspackets through the gate plus more data from the planet."

More data? "Anything I should know?"

"Do you perform comparative studies on reconstructions of technological remains based on molecular analyses, Dr. Connor?"

"Every Tuesday," she said, straight-faced.

The Grimnoii shook his head ponderously. "You are a tricky one."

Since they met their escort to the meeting at this point, Mac was left to wonder if being "a tricky one" was a desirable reputation to have among well-armed aliens.

Their escort, a tall friendly woman named Elane, walked them to the by-now familiar tube door, coding the request to send them on their way. Another escort would await them at the other end. *Dump the tourists in the river and net them downstream.* Although Mac and Fy-Alpha would have fit within the same bolus, to her relief it had become practice for the weapon-festooned aliens to travel alone.

Plus crusty bits from their happily weeping eyes tended to stray.

The door closed after the Grimnoii and it was Mac's turn. "Have a nice trip," Elane told her as she stepped inside.

"See you later." Mac grinned, finding her balance despite the way her feet sank in at first. *Getting to be a pro at this.* The walls flowed together behind her and she turned to press her back against the far wall, waiting for the bolus to move. Today's scent was fresh cut wood, most likely a crew suggestion.

She felt her body press into the yielding surface and relaxed, ready for the odd sensation as the bolus dropped away and flipped over.

. . . *scurry* . . . *scurry* . . .

Only knowing she had to be able to hear stopped the scream in her throat. *Nothing.*

The bolus merrily swooped and whirled its way toward its destination. *Nothing.*

Mac took small, careful breaths, forcing herself to think instead of panic. *Panic was so much easier.* She ran her eyes over the rest of the inner surface, studying every pink centimeter. There were no dimples or other marks to imply something else was along for the ride. She was alone.

Except for her imagination.

"Bah." She didn't need false alarms.

At this rate, she'd be imagining she and Norris had brought the Ro's walker to the *Uosanah* in the first place. That they'd flown together, its telltale sounds conveniently masked by argument and accordion.

That they were on the Joy, not the derelicts.

"Stop that," Mac told herself, aghast. The Gathering had developed ways to detect the Ro and their walkers; Dhryn fabric screens disabled them.

Screens that hadn't worked on the Uosanah.

"New rule," she said, fighting to keep her voice steady. "No thinking in a bolus."

But she couldn't hold back one more.

Just because something was terrifying didn't make it stupid.

"Take a seat and wait over there, Dr. Connor. Thank you."

Mac didn't want to sit. She wanted nothing more than to jump up on the captain's long polished table and shout for them all to listen. *Stamping her feet.*

And having gained their attention, she wanted to insist this mass of civilized, responsible beings stop whatever they were arguing about—said argument having continued despite her arrival—and convince her she was wrong.

The Ro couldn't be on board.

Mac sighed. Being a civilized and responsible being herself, she walked over to the row of chairs indicated, now lining the transparent wall overlooking the bridge, and sat beside Mudge.

She took a quick census. The large room was doing its best to hold over thirty individuals, and Humans, despite the furnishings, were in the minority. Herself, Mudge, a member of the crew by the door, and the captain, standing at the shoulder of the Sinzi-ra at the far end of the table. *A waste,* thought Mac, noticing the chairs suited very few of the posteriors presently planted in them. From where she sat, she could see a bench with cushions, but it was occupied by someone's feet.

She felt sorry for Ureif, if he took his guests' comfort as personally as Anchen had.

If this was a meeting, she had to wonder at the agenda. Several were speaking at once—*okay, with grunting and one off-key whistle*—and the room's air was being overscented with mint to compensate for odors it was never intended to handle.

Mudge tapped the back of her hand. "When did these arrive?" he whispered.

She could wish he was less observant—or had better timing. "Ureif brought them."

"And? Any news?" His anxious whisper attracted frowns or their equivalent from those nearest. She leaned over and put her lips to his ear. "Not now, Oversight. What's going on?"

If she'd hoped for reassuring calm, it wasn't here. The voices and body language of all species in the room showed tension, if not worse.

He returned the favor, ducking and twisting his head. "There's been an incident reported, Norcoast. The Frow home world, Tersisee."

Oh, no. Mac looked for, and found, the Frow. *Se* Lasserbee and his lackeys were backed firmly—and securely—against the far wall. From the grips they'd latched on one another, no one was going to fall alone.

"The Trisulians," she whispered.

Representatives of that species sat to the left of Sinzi-ra Ureif, bodies and limbs wrapped in red leather, paired eyestalks fixed on the Frow. Their broad, haired, and faceless heads revealed nothing to a Human observer. The weapons slung on their backs gave reasonable indication these weren't diplomats or scientists. In fact, few here looked obviously academic. *Not that she'd any idea what that meant once you left bipedal motion behind.*

The purple beadlike tip of the uppermost eyestalk on the nearest Trisulian abruptly swiveled to point at Mac. The lower, being male and blind in this light, remained lidded.

As proof she wasn't the only one who noticed such things, everyone in the room fell silent and turned to look at Mac.

Moments like this, she thought glumly, *were why she really hated meetings.*

"Dr. Connor." Ureif rose, fingers lifting. Fy was at his right. "On behalf of everyone here, as well as the Inner Council of the Interspecies Union, may I express our gratitude for your courage and quick thinking. You have provided us all—" *did she imagine "all" was stressed,* "—with our first advantage against the Myrokynay, at great risk to yourself. Thank you."

Mudge elbowed her ribs and Mac shot to her feet. "Any of you would have done the same," she blurted.

"Not me. I'd have expired on the spot," rumbled a well-dressed Nerban, waving his proboscis at her, his single eye almost closed.

"Tell her! Tell Dr. Connor!" *Se* Lasserbee shouted, rocking his trio of support. Sparks flew, and those beings in range of the Frow moved away. From the look on the captain's face, she wasn't the only one hoping the ventilation system could keep up with the Nerban's sweat. *The things one had to worry about around aliens.* "Tell her!" the Frow shrieked. One clawed hand daringly freed itself to point at the Trisulians. "Confess your evil to our Hero!"

Okay, a completely new reason to hate meetings.

"It is common knowledge," said the Trisulian who'd looked at Mac, "that Frow are inclined to paranoia, particularly in their dealings with other species. They scream collusion over regular freight runs; now they rant about innocent tourists. We have, Sinzi-ra, matters of *nimscent*—of future significance—to discuss."

Tourists? Mac wondered if she'd heard the right word.

"Villains!"

"Dr. Connor," the Trisulian continued smoothly, her—*his,* Mac corrected, counting eyestalks—powerful voice overriding the now-incoherent protests of *Se* Lasserbee. "It has come to our attention you may have news of our liaison with your Ministry, Cinder. We are most anxious to know why her communiqués have stopped prematurely."

She bet they were. Mac's hands wanted to curl into fists. She put them behind her back, rubbing her thumb against the rings on her fingers.

"The only matter before us is whether your entire misbegotten species should be sanctioned at the highest level!" *Se* Lasserbee roared. "The highest level!"

For improper tourism? She knew better than to hope that was all it was.

Since the aliens were again shouting at one another, Mac turned to Mudge, standing beside her. "What happened?" she whispered.

"The Trisulians are accused of planting transmitters on Tersisee. Some disguised as harmless ornaments, others left hidden in tourist areas. When the Frow found them and began destroying them, the remainder activated." Mac gasped and Mudge shook his head gently. "It's all right. They were removed in time. But their Sinzi-ra did confirm they were sending the Ro signal—the one that summoned the Dhryn to Sol System. Outside the IU Consulate on Earth, only the Trisulians have that technology."

Mac stared at the three Trisulians, trying to imagine how they could sit there and protest. These had to have been senior staff from the warship at Haven—perhaps the commander. Surely they would have known about the attempt to eradicate the Frow.

She narrowed her eyes. It was difficult to be sure, given the abundant thick strands of red and gray flowing over their shoulders and chests, but she thought the upper third of their torsos were enlarged, beginning above the opening to their stomach, the *douscent*.

Pregnant.

More to the point, territorial.

Argument wasn't going to overrule that state of mind.

She'd seen the mammoth Trisulian ship, sitting like a boulder in the flow to and from the gate. They weren't alone—every species in this room represented another ship, had another viewpoint. Mac took a step forward and raised her voice one notch above the rest. *Helped having spent summers talking over the roar of a river.* "Have you compared our Ro walker to the one found on Earth?"

Another pause, this one incredulous. Then, "What did you say?"

She didn't bother looking for the speaker; she kept her eyes on the Sinzi. "This is the group studying the corpse I brought back, isn't it? Surely you'll want to check it against the Ministry's specimen." Mac also ignored the strangled *harrumph* from behind her—she wasn't planning to explain how she knew. For that matter, she and Mudge could be completely wrong. For now, she had the rest of the room thinking about something else, something that faced them all. *Good enough.* "Unless of course you've started exploring the remaining Dhryn ships," she went on, taking advantage of their silence, "and found more for yourselves."

Ureif's red-coated fingers gleamed as they made a complex knot in front of his chest.

That one meant "difficulty," Mac judged, and wasn't surprised. She'd guessed the result of her explorations would be a standstill, with everyone reconsidering the stakes. The newspackets and couriers must be flying through the gate.

Speaking of messages . . . Fourteen should have voiced an opinion by now. She tried to see past those in front of her, searching for him without success.

The Sinzi-ra spoke. "A helpful suggestion, Dr. Connor. We will obtain the required data."

"With due respect, Sinzi-ra," this from the Nerban. "We haven't settled where the examination will be conducted. Given the Humans possess their own specimen, why should they keep this new one?"

A few other suggestions were shouted or grunted. The Sinzi-ra unraveled his fingers and lifted their tips to his shoulders. "This is no longer a Human ship, but a declared consulate of the Interspecies Union. As such, it is the recognized venue for research and discourse that may impact more than one species along the transects. Do you wish to petition the Inner Council for a change to that policy? I will entertain a vote."

Checkmate, Mac thought with admiration.

The Sinzi-ra's offer produced, if not a mellower mood, then a more thoughtful one. The Frow, while continuing to glare across the table at the Trisulians— something they did quite effectively, since it involved lowering a shoulder ridge and extending their necks—stopped sparking. The Trisulians, for their part, oriented their eyestalks on Ureif, as if setting themselves apart from the rest of the room.

Mac was grateful for eyes that weren't so blatantly obvious.

The discussion resumed, this time about establishing an agenda to continue various aspects of the business at hand. Mac and Mudge sat down again.

A *harrumph.* She glanced at him. "What?"

"Nothing."

Mac frowned. *She knew that tone.* It was the one Mudge used to make her think she'd won an argument, when she hadn't come close. "Someone had to say something."

"And you did, Norcoast."

Same tone.

"If you're wrong about the Ministry, it doesn't matter. If you're right?" She shrugged. "What's the worst Hollans can do?"

"Before we get back to Earth, or after?"

"After," Mac leaned back with a shrug, "I don't plan to care."

- 18 -

BOTHER AND BIOLOGY

T HERE WAS ONLY ONE thing worse than a meeting where she was on
the spot, Mac decided, stifling a yawn. *A meeting where she wasn't.* The discussion had droned on for over an hour now and showed no signs of ending.
Good thing the corpse was in stasis.

"Stop fidgeting, Norcoast."

"I'm not—" she began to protest, when the door opened.

It was Fourteen. He waved an urgent summons but not, to Mac's astonishment, to her. Instead, Fy bowed graciously and left her place with Ureif without
a word of explanation, walking past everyone to join the Myg.

Trundling in her wake, Fy-Alpha nearly knocked over the poor Frow.

The discussion continued without pause, the Cey delegation holding forth on
the need for more derelicts to be brought to Myriam so everyone could explore
their own and was there going to be lunch?

No one was looking. Seeing her opportunity, Mac grabbed Mudge's wrist and
pulled him to follow the Grimnoii out the door, keeping them both low in case
Captain Gillis spotted the escape of his fellow Humans and tried to interfere.
He'd begun to glaze over, too.

Once the door closed between them and the meeting, Mac let out a *whoof* of
relief.

Mudge shook off her grip and straightened with a glower. "Do you even
know what dignity means, Norcoast?"

"If it means being stuck there when I could be working, I'm not interested."

Fourteen and Fy were deep in conversation, walking rapidly down another
corridor, Fy-Alpha in tow. "What's that all about?" Mac wondered.

"With him, it could be anything." At her look, he relented. "The Sinzi-ra
requested his help earlier. I presume something to do with the message traffic.
They're headed to the bridge," he nodded after them.

"While we're going back to Origins." Mac started walking to the tube door.
"I want to check on our guest."

"Surely you should be packing, Norcoast." Mudge hurried to keep up.

"Why?"

"The drop to Myriam."

Mac snorted. "I'm a little busy right now to help you get ready, Oversight. Get Sam."

"I don't think you understand. You're coming, too. You need to pack."

She stopped in the middle of the corridor to stare at him.

Mudge backed up a step. "Now, Norcoast, surely you expected it. Only military personnel will be boarding a derelict until any and all risk has been removed. Sinzi-ra Ureif and the captain were quite sensible about that. Quite firm, in fact. No one disagreed. Civilians—including you—won't be put in danger. Losing Dr. Norris . . ." He tsked sorrowfully. "Too high a price to discover the Ro have been with the Dhryn all along."

"That's what you think?" She gestured at the closed meeting room door. "What they think? That the walker came with the Dhryn?"

"What else?"

That she'd brought it with her? Facing Mudge's puzzled look, Mac couldn't bring herself to say it. He'd think she was certifiable, and everyone would agree.

Besides, she chided herself, *why would a walker hide all this time on the* Joy *and then sneak a ride to a dead Dhryn ship?*

To follow her? Despite Fy's belief that Mac was *"a nexus of interest,"* for the Ro, Mac couldn't see what the aliens would gain from a trip to the *Uosanah.* They had to realize she'd bring back any findings. *Why risk discovery in the tiny space of the lev?*

If the walker had been on board with them, it would have had to dodge around Norris like a dancer. *Or clung to the ceiling.*

Mac shuddered.

"Norcoast?" Mudge's puzzlement turned to concern. "You're safe now. A terrible ordeal. Terrible. But a good night's sleep . . . you'll be fine." Having come to his own conclusions about her hesitation—*and how to deal with it,* Mac smiled to herself—Mudge scowled ferociously. "Norris had no right taking you on that ship. None!"

"I don't need to board the *Uosanah* again, or any other ship," she assured him. "We have her captain. Once he regains consciousness, we can ask him what happened to them."

Mudge shook his head. "Conscious? I thought he was dead already. He certainly looked dead," he modified.

"He does that," Mac nodded. "And he probably won't last the night, which is why I can't leave. If he wakes, I may be the only one he'll answer." She smiled. "Besides, Oversight, I have my own quarters, with a nice new bed I haven't used yet."

Harrumph. "In that case, I'm staying, too." He wagged his forefinger under her nose. "I'm not letting you out of my sight again, Norcoast." His lower lip developed a slight quiver. "I should have been with you—"

She put her finger to his, stopping its movement. "I wish you had." She dropped her hand. "On the bright side—" *before either of them grew more emotional,* "—there should be a record of Norris allowing Base to have the schematics for his ship. Full surround imaging, Oversight. Except for the seats," she added.

His eyes popped open, concern forgotten. "You saw the exterior of the *Joy?*" With awe. "What was she like?"

"Big," Mac offered, pointing to the tube door. "Reminded me of coral."

"The wonders of technology are wasted on you, Norcoast," he muttered. "Simply wasted."

"Origins, please," she told the crew waiting by the controls. "What more do you want, Oversight?" she asked him as they settled inside the bolus. "You've been on the bridge—how many times?"

"It's not the same," he said with unusual petulance.

The bolus sucked them against its walls and bounced into the stream.

Mac gradually relaxed.

It wasn't the same, she echoed to herself.

She'd been rattled, that was all. *Not the first time.* At Base, late at night, she'd wake to that sound, paralyzed with fear until she found its source. Dried reeds in her garden. Sleet against the walls. A disoriented bat. There'd been a crab . . .

"Norcoast."

She focused on him. "Yes?"

"Your new rings."

Mae sighed. "They've made contact. It's a waiting game now." *She didn't bother with the rest.*

"That much success. Good." But he frowned.

She knew that look. "What?"

"You say this is secure. But I'm concerned how the Trisulians would know to ask you about Cinder."

Mac would have shrugged, but her shoulders were stuck fast. "They asked," she disagreed. "Nothing says they knew. Their culture thrives on secrets, layers of them. Who knows what . . . who has information to trade for influence. It wouldn't surprise me if they presume we're all like they are and act accordingly." *Hairy spies,* she thought. *Disguises would be a snap.*

"But you do have information they'd want."

She sent him a cautioning look, *although presumably any eavesdroppers here would have faces.* "I wouldn't call it 'information,' Oversight."

He might have persisted, but the bolus snapped to a stop. The door opened almost immediately and Elane greeted them with smile. "Good meeting, Mac?"

"As always," she answered, pulling free of the walls. Mudge did the same, and they staggered their way out together.

Mac could almost feel Mudge fussing as they walked into the Origins section. *Never a good sign.* "What now?" she asked once they were alone.

"You should eat something."

"Sleep. Eat. You're worse than my dad." Mac's stomach gurgled and she threw up her hands. "Fine. I'll eat."

He ducked his head so she only saw the corner of his smile. *Which meant he didn't see hers.*

"You call that eating? Bah."

"I call it efficient." Mac sipped through the straw, trying in vain to identify the taste of the warm, thick liquid. She waved her tall cup at him enticingly. "You could have had one, Oversight." The ship's version of e-rations had turned out to be a soup, packed with nutrients and sealed into a container suited for zero-g. *Perfect for the biologist on the move,* she thought, taking another sip. "I should take some of these home."

Shaking his head in disbelief, Mudge bit into his carrot—or facsimile—then continued working his way through the mass of salad on his plate. "I prefer to recognize what goes into my body, thank you very much. And you," he jabbed his loaded fork at her hovering 'screen, "should learn to relax."

Mac blinked. "I'm relaxing." They were sitting in the empty dining room, and had been for some time. She'd only opened her 'screen to check for new messages, been scrolling haphazardly through the list. *Nothing from Emily.* She'd marked Kammie's for later reading. "What makes you think I'm not?"

Mudge shook his head again. "Never mind."

"I can do small talk," she offered, giving him a wicked grin.

He held up his hands. "Save me. What's come in?"

Mac set her list between them, two-sided so Mudge could read it at the same time. "I'd expected something from the Ministry by now," she complained.

He leaned so she could see his frown past the display. "Why?"

"Hollans should realize I'd want to see their results."

Mudge's face disappeared behind rows of text. She could hear crunching. *Opinionated crunching.*

"Well, he should." Mac closed the display and put away her imp, aware she sounded petulant. *She had a right to be.* "We have to understand these walkers— what they are—what they're capable of—how to detect them—how to—" *be safe.* She took a long sip.

"I'm sure, Norcoast, the scientists busy with the specimen you and your friend obtained will provide a report when they're ready. Including any comparative results. Copied to those who will act on it."

She grimaced. "In other words, it's none of my business."

"I didn't say that." Mudge divided his remaining beans into neat rows. "There are, of course, ways to work within any system to obtain timely documentation." One bean was moved from one row to the next. "Protocols, etcetera."

Mac sorted that out, then beamed at him. "Great!"

A sheepish *harrumph.* "I'll do my best, Norcoast. I can't promise—"

"You'll be my hero," she interrupted. "No matter what."

Almost a smile. "Have a carrot."

"Thanks." She helped herself to two, eyeing his plate. *At the rate he chewed, even with her help this was going to take a while.* "You don't have to finish all that. Unless you're hungry." She made it sound unlikely.

"If you're ready to go, Norcoast," Mudge said dryly, "I'll meet you there when I'm done."

Mac looked around the empty room and felt a twinge of guilt. "No problem. I'm relaxing," she claimed, tipping her chair back to prove it. She took out her imp and rolled it from one hand to the other. Back and forth. "See?"

He *harrumphed.* "I see you'll give me indigestion. Go. Please."

She leaped to her feet, cup in hand. "You know where to find me."

Mac was steps away when Mudge called after her. "Norcoast. Remember what he is."

She nodded without turning around.

Mac walked into the Wasted's infirmary and stopped, astonished. The bed had been banished to a corner. In its place was a large wheeled platform, in turn supporting what looked like a miniature escape pod.

"The Lost Soul rests within," Kudla said helpfully. He and his disciples were the only ones in the room. They'd pulled chairs around a table and were, Mac blinked, playing cards. As ordered, the candles were gone. Now the room held dozens of knee-high brown statues of what appeared to be frogs, mouths open. *Didn't anyone check their luggage?* she thought wildly. "Take a look," he suggested, pointing at the pod.

She began to frown, but went to peer through one of its windows.

The Wasted was floating in midair, tubes connected to various parts of his anatomy. His body, bathed in a pinkish light, had lost more flesh, something Mac would have deemed impossible. Only the barely perceptible rise and fall of his torso hinted at life.

So much for shaking him awake, she thought.

"Where's Cayhill?"

"He and the Myg went to commune with the planet. I assured them we could help, but they weren't interested. Can you imagine?"

The disciples exchanged glances and shrugged at one another as if to show they certainly couldn't.

She could. "Where's the orderly?"

"The doctor said it was a waste of personnel and set up remote monitors instead. We," this with great dignity, "would not abandon the Lost Soul."

As the "Lost Soul" appeared unlikely to notice a fire, let alone the existence of other life in the room, Mac merely nodded and left.

She found Cayhill where she'd expected, leaning over the shoulder of the officer assigned to the new communications room. *The room she hadn't been able to use yet.*

"MacMacMacMacMac . . ." Five offspring warbled a greeting and scampered toward her from several directions. The sixth sat down on the floor, its eyes scrunched with effort. Just as Mac worried about the carpeting, it opened its eyes and let out a triumphant "Mac!" of its own, running to her.

Oh, good, she thought wryly. *Now they can all talk.*

"Dr. Connor." Cayhill studied her for a moment, then looked back at whatever engrossed the com-tech. "About time."

Mac settled warm bundles of offspring on shoulders and hips, resisting the urge to toss a couple his way. *The offspring didn't deserve it.* "He looks more comfortable. How long does he have?"

Cayhill glanced up again, this time with a frown. "What are you talking about?"

Was she in the wrong room? Even the com-tech was giving her an odd look. "Before he dies," Mac clarified. "The Wasted."

"Idiot!" Unensela breezed by Mac, heading for Cayhill. "About time you got here."

The offspring, perhaps feeling the tensing of every muscle in Mac's body, chose that moment to launch themselves toward the female Myg. She, now busy at the console, expertly shoved them aside with one foot.

"I'm guessing there's something you two want to tell me," Mac said firmly, walking around to the other side of the console to confront them. At their blank looks, she pointed to the wall behind which the Wasted floated in his pod. "About him."

"I'll take a break," offered the com-tech, beginning to rise. Unensela and Cayhill took a shoulder each and pressed the poor man back into his seat.

"Stay on it. We need this data." Cayhill nodded to the side, and Mac followed him.

"Dr. Connor," he told her in a low voice. "I found no signs of injury, beyond the old amputations and present skin damage. I found no signs of illness. My patient isn't sick. He's starving. There's no reason to believe with a proper course of nutrients—"

"With all due respect," Mac interjected, not bothering to keep her voice down, "You don't know what you're talking about. This isn't some malnourished infant, Dr. Cayhill. This is a failed metamorphosis."

"Says who?"

She stared at him. "Pardon?"

"You heard me." Cayhill did smug as well as any Myg of Mac's acquaintance. "You told me yourself there isn't a medical database for this species. I see no justification for invoking some—some species' superstition over normal diagnostic procedure. All indicators show my patient is suffering from a lack of certain key nutrients. Unensela has been assisting me to identify those, with the help of a team of paleoecologists on the planet."

Mac shook her head. "Dhryn metamorphosis is no superstition, Cayhill."

He lifted an eyebrow. "I didn't say it was. If you insist we assume this individual is indeed undergoing a fundamental reorganization of his physiology, my argument only becomes stronger. Developmental deficiencies arise in Humans if there is an insufficiency of particular nutrients during that growth period. We could be seeing this pattern in the patient. Thus his metamorphosis isn't flawed—it is incomplete." When she didn't look convinced, he continued, "You work with fish, don't you? Do they eat the same food at every stage of their growth?"

She had an immediate mental image of a salmon eft fastening its tiny mouth on the fin of an anchovy five times its size and looking wistful.

Mac chewed her lower lip for a moment. "Say I accept your hypothesis—for now," as his eyes gleamed triumphantly. "How are you going to discover what he needs? You may know all there is about Human nutrition—that's not the same as Dhryn, believe me." She pulled a nutrient bar from her pocket and pointed it at him. "To be blunt, these went right through."

Implying the Wasted's show of life after consuming the bars had had more to do with fearing the Ro than digestion or alien acts of kindness.

"The only data I've seen has come from modern colonies or Haven itself. They consumed highly synthesized materials. What about their natural diet?"

Natural diet? Mac clenched her artificial hand. "That would be us, Cayhill."

"Ah, but this one didn't eat Human when he had the chance, did he?"

Mac bowed her head for a moment, then looked up, all antagonism gone from her voice. "Listen to me, Cayhill. Make no mistake. The Dhryn consume every organic molecule on the worlds they take. We can't pull anything specific from that."

"Is that diet necessary for all forms of Dhryn, or just the Progenitors?"

"We don't know—" She paused, thinking it over. *Could he be right? What would it mean?* "I'll admit it's a good question, Cayhill, but it doesn't affect this Dhryn."

"You don't know," he said flatly, his face set and stern. *She'd seen that look.* "Why does that make me wrong?"

This had been a bad idea, Mac realized. " Dr. Cayhill, I want to thank you for all you've done," she began.

"I have it!" Unensela crowed. "ItItItItIt . . . Mac!" echoed the excited offspring, the sixth stuck on its first word. "Come. See this."

Mac followed Cayhill's rush to the communication console. The com-tech moved aside to let them all see the 'screen. "What do you have?"

The 'screen held an image of a collection of seeds, turning to show them from every side. From the scale below, most were larger than Mac's palm. She leaned closer. Their thick cases were scarred and burned, but intact.

"What am I looking at, Unensela?"

"These were found within the Dhryn havens of the southern hemisphere—the one our findings show was beginning to regenerate. They represent these major families of—" she began to rattle off a series of names.

Mac held up her hand to stop the list. "Not a botanist."

"Neither am I," Cayhill joined in. "But these look damaged."

"Idiot! They've been bathed in feeder goo and passed through a gut. You'd look a little rough yourself."

" 'Feeder goo?' " Mac repeated, raising an eyebrow.

"Not a biochemist," the Myg said archly.

"'Passed through a gut.' You're sure."

Unensela pointed at the names on the bottom of the image. "They are."

The Dhryn, moving across a dying landscape, consuming everything. Carrying inside them the seeds of the future, to be left where they would grow and one day again support the migration of the Dhryn . . . mutual adaptation . . .

Then, one day . . . agriculture . . .

"We get these seeds brought to the ship and feed them to . . ." Cayhill's voice turned sharp as Mac shook her head at him. "Why not?"

"They weren't digested. For all we know, the inner material is poisonous to the Dhryn."

"Irrelevant! Irrelevant!" Unensela jumped up and down. "It gives us a viable course of action." She pointed at a new image, showing lush, green-blue vegetation. Chemical formulae danced among the leaves.

Cayhill looked between the two, his face blank. "What?"

Mac looked at the Myg, whose grin widened to show all four yellowed teeth, gum ridge, and white forked tongue. "The analysis of these plants," she reluctantly explained, "has produced a reasonable reconstruction of their physiology and structure when grown. If—*if*—some Dhryn ate them whole as a food source, you might be able to work out a nutrient regime suited to a present-day Dhryn to try using substances available on board."

"Idiot. There is no 'might.' Yes!"

The offspring ran up Mac again, warbling "YesYesYes-Yes . . . Mac . . . Yes!"

Unensela beckoned the amused com-tech back to his machinery, the two of them immediately occupied sending messages to her collaborators on the planet. Cayhill stood gazing at Mac and the offspring, a question on his face. "They aren't mine," she informed him. "They just think they are."

"Still going to fire me?"

"Oh." The corner of her mouth twitched up. "That obvious?"

"I thought so."

They did have history. Mac rubbed the back of an offspring; the creature responded by digging its claws into her chest. "No," she said to both man and claws. "I know you won't let him die if you can help it. As for this idea of yours? If I had a better one, believe me, I'd say so." She glanced at the Myg. "Just keep in mind that Unensela and the rest of them deal with the Dhryn of the past. We know the current generation has been extensively modified—the modern diet may be part of that."

"There you are, Norcoast," Mudge exclaimed, hurrying through the door. "Is everything all right?" His look to Cayhill vowed memos otherwise. "How's the patient?"

"Not dead," Mac answered.

"I couldn't tell."

"Notnotnotnotnot . . . Mac!" In the midst of this random enthusiasm, two of the offspring leaped from her to Mudge, not quite tearing fabric, though she'd have some marks. *Bonus for the uniform.*

Mudge caught them on his arm, wincing as they made sure of their landing. "I imagine they'll enjoy having room to run around."

On Myriam. Mac's hands sought the ones still clinging to her. She'd forgotten the offspring were to leave the *Joy,* too. "I'm not so sure that's a good idea," she began. "The situation in-system isn't as stable as it might be and—"

"Irrelevant." Unensela breezed by Mac, Mudge, and the offspring. "Everything's set. We're packed. I must work with these people, find out more about the recent plant life. First, my good-byes to Fourteen. I shall break his hearts. It's his fault, sticking to his own bed the entire trip." She marched out of the room, but they could hear her as she went down the hall. "We could have had sex fifty-seven times by now . . . twice that if he'd keep in shape . . ."

Cayhill smothered a laugh. Mac shook her head. "I wouldn't doubt it."

"We should head to the hangar as well, Norcoast. It's time."

"I'll be back as soon as I can, Cayhill," she promised. "Good luck."

Already preoccupied with the names in the image, he grunted something noncommittal.

Mac made sure the offspring planned to stay with her for the trip, welcoming the distraction.

She hated good-byes.

The hangar being used by the Origins Team wasn't the one where Norris had kept his lev. This was far larger, wider, and populated by vessels that dwarfed those walking the suspended access way.

Yet Norris was present, Mac discovered. She, Mudge, and the offspring arrived at the departure platform as the captain of the *Annapolis Joy* stepped behind a podium placed there for his use. Beside him, looking as real as if he'd never left, stood Norris.

His simulacrum, she told herself, noticing the differences. The three-dimensional projection was accurate, but carefully positioned so the face gazed back at no one. The feet stood on another surface. By the clothing, this was an image Norris had supplied. *She'd have guessed he'd own a tux; just the thing for those academic fund-raisers.* He'd likely held court and awed the donors; Norcoast usually asked her to hide in the back.

Tuxedo, no 'screen hovering by a distracted, busy eye, a too-careful pose from smile to shoulders.

She focused on Gillis' somber face. This Norris wasn't the man she'd known. *This wasn't the man who'd died for her.*

"Like many species within the Interspecies Union," Gillis began, "Humans respect the remains of our dead. We are negotiating to recover those of Dr. Sigmund Eduardo Norris as soon as possible without risk to others. We leave no one behind."

Mac judged this as much a promise to the Origins Team and the shuttle crew, gathered around the podium with them, as to Norris.

Might not be having the desired impact on civilian scientists. Mirabelle and Lyle

looked more worried than reassured. She understood completely. The last time
they'd been at Sencor's research outpost on Myriam, their biggest concern had
been sandstorms and funding. Suddenly, they had the promise of the captain of
a dreadnought to stand by them in case of emergency. They had to wonder what
he was anticipating that to be.

Captain Gillis said a few more words. Mac and the others listened. She was
impressed. He didn't pretend to know Norris as more than a passenger, nor did
he dwell on the manner of his death. Instead, the captain read from Norris' cur-
riculum vitae, listing awards and accomplishments, inventions and discoveries—
defining his life by his work.

What Norris himself would have done, Mac decided, and her estimation of the
captain rose again.

She was, however, slightly disturbed to think he'd have done much the same
had it been her.

When the brief service was done, Gillis came over to her. "Not my favorite
part of the job, Dr. Connor," in a quiet voice.

Mac laid her hand on his arm, the nearest offspring reaching out to do the
same with a tiny paw. Gillis looked down and smiled. "You did it well," she assured him. "I found what you said—" She blanked and finished with more honesty than tact, "I didn't know his full name until now. Thank you."

He appeared pleased. She withdrew her hand and gathered in the offspring.

Gillis surveyed the group waiting to board, several lingering nearby for a
chance to talk to her. "Important to give them a chance to pay their respects."

Mac half smiled. "And they got your point, Captain. Though I can't say it
will make them happy to think they might need a warship."

"I wouldn't be either," he said soberly. "Perilous times, Dr. Connor."

"Mac."

His eyes smiled. "Mac. I'll leave you to your farewells." With a hint of a bow,
Gillis walked away.

She hefted the offspring into the crook of her arm, looking around for Mudge
and his load.

Lyle came up to her, eyes gleaming. "I can't believe we're finally heading
home," he said. "I won't believe it until I smell the dust."

Mac chuckled. "I know the feeling—although for me it would be cedar and
sea." She grinned. "Okay, and rotting fish, but don't spread that around."

He rolled his eyes, grinning back. "Trust me. I'll keep your secret." A more
considering look. "Charles says you two will be joining us shortly. Pleasant surprise. Thought they'd be keeping you busy with the derelicts for weeks yet."

Mac shrugged. "Politics."

"Should have guessed." The archaeologist's smile widened. "But if it gets you
downworld sooner, that's fine with me."

"Thanks, Lyle." She was touched. *They'd come a long way.* "You'd better go,"
she added, understanding why his eyes kept flicking to the loading platform.
Heading to the field.

She could feel the pull herself.

He leaned forward and kissed her on the cheek. "Will do. And you behave." Others came up even as Lyle left, swamping Mac with handshakes and kisses and hugs. The offspring clung to her, wide-eyed and excited, patting anyone who came close enough with their paws. Their claws they kept firmly planted in her and Mac began to worry if she'd get them off when the time came.

Out the corner of her eye, she could see Mudge doing his utmost to fend off such overt affection, nodding gravely to each well-wisher before they came too close and holding his pair of offspring to his chest like a shield.

The initial crush worked its way past; everyone was as anxious as Lyle to get on board. *Maybe they thought the captain would change his mind.* Mirabelle, having waited until now, came up and gave Mac a hug. "'Bye, Mac."

Mac shook her head. "Archaeologists," she complained. "I might see you tomorrow, you know."

The other woman didn't smile. "And you might not. Don't underestimate how we feel about you. We've been through so much together, Mac, and you've done—well, you've done more for us than we could say."

Mac scrunched her face. "I seem to remember making you work all hours on crazy questions."

Mirabelle laughed but there was a suspicious brightness to her eyes. "Crazy questions that made us—and our work—significant. Whatever we've accomplished to help all of us survive, Mac, we did through you. And we won't forget that."

Speechless, Mac watched the woman walk away. Mudge came over. "Glad to see they recognize your contribution, Norcoast," he said quietly.

She snorted, shifting offspring. "They need to get back to work. We all—" Mac stopped to pull off the one gumming her chin. "Where's Unensela?" She hadn't spotted the Myg during the ceremony or good-byes. "Is she already on board?" She wasn't in the line to enter.

"She is late." Two of the tall, shaggy Sthlynii approached, Therin and Naman, his—with their complex, overlapping families, Mac had yet to figure out if Naman was an uncle or son. *Maybe both.* Naman and the remaining two Sthlynii in Origins rarely spoke aloud to anyone but each other. They were, to Mudge's delight, expert memo writers. Therin blew out his tentacles with annoyance. "We maaaaaaay nooooot waaaaiit."

As if his voice had been a signal, the offspring dropped from Mac and Mudge to climb up the Sthlynii, disappearing within their thick tunics as if they'd done it before. *Into pockets,* she realized, as six big-eyed heads popped back out, paws holding what appeared to be candy to their mouths. "Yumyumyumyumyum-Mac!" they sang happily around the treat.

"That's bribery!" Mudge accused, his hands still raised as if holding the small creatures. He dropped them to his sides at Mac's grin. "Well, it is."

Therin's tentacles milled in what Mac had learned meant amusement. "We miss our younglings, Charles. Caring for these sweet beings—" his hands patted several purring lumps, "—is a privilege. We mind them for Unensela as often as we can."

Mudge swallowed whatever objection he thought he had, perhaps, like Mac, relieved the offspring would have someone responsible watching over them on Myriam.

Speaking of Unensela . . .

"There she is," Mudge said, then gave a sharp *harrumph.* "I knew it."

His tone warned Mac. Sure enough, two Mygs, not one, were walking down the accessway toward the loading platform. *No,* Mac squinted, *make that one walking and the other jumping from foot to foot as if avoiding hot coals.*

The shouting became audible as the couple closed on them.

"IDIOT! IDIOT! IDIOT!" This from Unensela, who shouted the word continuously without turning to look at Fourteen.

He was the one hopping—and babbling. "Please, Glorious One. Your eyes are hidden chips of wet agate. Your tongue—let me tell you about your tongue . . ."

"IRRELEVANT!"

Needless to say, everyone else in earshot stopped what they were doing. Well, except for Kudla and his disciples, clutching bags Mac hoped contained frog statuettes. They used the distraction to move to the head of the boarding line and enter the shuttle. *Presumably anxious to resume communing.*

She looked forward to his next book.

Meanwhile, they had a problem.

Fourteen had finally managed to stop Unensela. The tactic of falling flat on the floor in front of his ladylove was perhaps not original, but Mac gave him points for drama.

The focus of all this was less impressed. Unensela kicked him in the midsection. "You are without *strobis!*" she shrieked. Fourteen curled his arms around his abused middle and kept his mouth closed. "There is nothing I want from you! Nothing!"

Aliens. Mac sighed and stepped forward. Mudge gave her a horrified look. She made a face at him, then turned to the Mygs. "Do I have *strobis,* Unensela?"

Unensela stared at Mac "Irrelevant. You don't know our ways. Don't interfere. This—" another kick, "—is worthless."

They weren't, Mac noticed, *particularly hard kicks.* Nor was Fourteen complaining, as if any attention was better than none. *More telling,* she sniffed, *the air was free of Myg distress.* "Does my life have value to the whole?"

"Idiot." The female Myg's mouth turned sullen. "Of course it does. We would not all follow you if it didn't."

"Which would be why Arslithissiangee Yip the Fourteenth offered his allegiance to me last year, before you two met."

She might have sprouted a second head and startled the Myg less. *Unless that was in a brochure, too,* Mac chuckled to herself.

"You . . ." Unensela dropped to her knobby knees beside Fourteen. Her hands hovered over him. Perhaps wary of her mood, he remained in a defensive curl. "Is this true, Tickles?"

A cautious nod.

Unensela's hands covered her face and she dropped backward to land on her rump, the picture of misery. "All is lost!"

So much for that plan. Mac sighed. *She really should leave aliens alone.*

Mudge *harrumphed.* "I believe," he said in his "officious" voice, "there is some confusion here. If I may, Norcoast?"

"Please," she told him.

"'Tickles,'" he used the nickname with obvious relish, "vowed himself to Dr. Connor's service in lieu of any other suitable offering. At a time when his circumstances were, *ahem,* somewhat less complex. I believe, if you ask her, she will tell you his service is no longer required."

"Absolutely," Mac agreed, having no clue where Mudge was going.

Fourteen rose on one elbow, the aim of his tiny eyes shifting from Unensela to Mac and back. "You no longer need me, Mac?" he asked in a heart-wrenching voice. Beads of moisture dotted his eyelids. "It is because I failed you, isn't it? I will do better next time. I have been studying sabotage techniques in my spare time. And explosives. You will see! I will throw myself into danger's mouth for you!"

Wonderful. Mac glared at Mudge. His lips shaped the words "trust me." "Irrelevant!" he shouted, in a perfect imitation of Fourteen at his most obnoxious. *He'd heard enough of it,* she realized. "Insufficient! Insulting! Dr. Connor requires the ultimate sacrifice."

She did? While Mudge on a roll was a thing of beauty, as evidenced by the rapt attention of those around them, Mac was growing concerned by the direction this seemed to be going. *Was the man after revenge for all those practical jokes?*

Then she noticed Unensela, who had moved her hands just enough to give Fourteen a wistful look.

"'The ultimate sacrifice,'" Mac echoed, putting some gusto into it.

Fourteen clambered to his knees, dividing his earnest pleading look between Mudge, Unensela, and Mac, as if unsure who needed to be influenced most. "I would if I could," he exclaimed. "But I've no offspring of my own."

The offspring already present sucked candy noisily, seeming entertained by it all. Mac spared a moment to wonder at the sheer chaos that must be a Myg family night.

"You could have." Unensela's hands fell into her lap. "If you were free to devote the appropriate effort, that is." This with a sly look at Mac. *The scamp wasn't the least confused by the Human-Myg interface.*

Mac felt a certain sympathy for Fourteen. *Still, he was the one who'd rapturously compared Unensela's beady little eyes to wet agate.* "Oh, he's free to do whatever it takes," she proclaimed. "So long as *strobis* is maintained." One of the crew arrived and stood looking anxious in the background; when he saw she'd noticed, he waved and pointed to the shuttle. "Perhaps we could move this along? The captain," Mac added, "would like the shuttle to depart on schedule."

Fourteen rose to his feet, then gave a deep bow from the waist. He put both hands over his eyes. "I, Arslithissiangee Yip the Fourteenth, can never hope to repay you, Mackenzie Connor of Little Misty Lake, for saving my valued life, more than once. If service to your *strobis* is not enough, then I, Arslithissiangee Yip the Fourteenth, can only offer my firstborn offspring to you, Mackenzie Connor of Little Misty Lake."

"That's really more than I—"

Hands went down. A stern look. She closed her mouth.

Hands up. "But to fulfill this obligation, I, Arslithissiangee Yip the Fourteenth, however unworthy, must now apply to the inestimable, the glorious, the—"

The shuttle? Mac wanted to say, but restrained herself. The forks of Unensela's tongue were hanging out.

And growing pink.

"—brilliant Unensela to accept my allegiance, flesh, mind, and spirit, so long as I may live." His hands came down, one reaching out. "Will you accept?"

The brilliant Unensela took his hand and pulled herself up, pausing to brush at her coat. "Took you long enough." This with an affectionate push at Fourteen's chest.

Both Mygs, Mac thought, *looked remarkably smug.*

And the waiting member of the crew looked remarkably desperate.

"You'll make your grandsires very happy," she hazarded. "Now, sorry to rush you, but those heading to the planet should go—"

She was talking to thin air. Both Mygs turned and started walking toward the shuttle, arms around each other. Therin and Naman, with the offspring, followed behind.

Leaving her and Mudge alone.

"What just happened?" Mac asked, throwing her hands in the air. "Where's he going? He's supposed to stay on the *Joy*—he was working with Fy—he can't just go with her!"

"Think of it not as losing Fourteen's expertise, Norcoast," Mudge suggested, looking smug himself, "but of gaining their firstborn."

"That's not funny, Oversight."

"You should see your face right now."

"I am not adopting or otherwise accepting any child of theirs! What?" This as he shook his head and smiled. "They can't make me," she insisted, then sighed. "Can they?"

Mudge laughed. "Norcoast, don't you know the Myg life cycle?"

Mac eyed him suspiciously. "Beyond wanton enthusiasm and sloppy parental care? Not really." *Given that enthusiasm, she'd half expected to have the results joining the offspring in ruining her wardrobe.*

"The firstborn of any fertile pair is a *nimb.*" Mudge held out one hand and mimed putting something in it. "Myg literature variously refers to it as "the love lump," "the ideal gift," or more crudely as "proof the plumbing works." They aren't the most lyrical species."

"Lump of what?"

His cheeks turned pink. "I'll let you look that up. Suffice it to say, caring for one requires a jar, not a room and education."

Why that . . . "Fourteen knew perfectly well I'd assume—" Mac's outrage turned to reluctant admiration. "He got me, didn't he?"

Mudge whirled one finger in the air. "Welcome to my world, Norcoast."

Mygs might boast they had no external genitalia, but their bodies possessed a number of effective contact points to compensate for a lack of pinpoint accuracy. Mac hurriedly scrolled through the known, presumed—*and highly unlikely*—sexual positions involved, to the physiology of pregnancy.

The pre-*nimb*, it turned out, was a plug separating the birth channel from the lower digestive tract, its eventual connection to the outside world. A male Myg's sperm not only impregnated his partner, but began the process of crystallizing that plug into a *nimb*, which the female would pass before discharging her embryos. The embryos came packaged in membranous sacs of six each, completing their growth outside the mother's body. Birth was officially declared when a sac split and offspring began climbing and warbling on the nearest adult or facsimile.

The *nimb* itself received somewhat better treatment, being considered a family heirloom as each pair could produce only one. *Not to mention,* Mac realized, *it was the only product of a successful mating that stayed put.* The birth sac was traditionally stuck up in a tree or, in urban centers, hung on a hook outside the door. The hatched offspring were quite capable of finding and adopting their own surrogate parent, who apparently couldn't refuse.

She grinned, imagining Unensela packed and on her way to the spaceport, only to become a Myg-mom by walking down the wrong street.

Ambush by cuteness. Somehow it suited the Myg personality.

Mac poked her finger in the 'screen to find an image and found a catalog of display containers instead, ranging from ornate to obnoxious. Apparently, one did not bother to look directly upon the *nimb.*

No surprise. "That is not going on my desk," she stated.

Cayhill looked up. "What isn't?"

Mac closed her 'screen and stretched. "Fourteen's firstborn." She got up from the table and walked over to the pod.

"I don't want to know." Cayhill went back to his work.

"Good choice." Mac peered into the window. "How's it working?"

The physician had come up with an ingenious, if low-tech, way around their lack of experience with Dhryn anatomy. Rather than hunt for a blood vessel or internal organ, he'd simply fixed tubing inside the pod so one end, with a self-closing nipple, rested against the Wasted's partly open lips. The other end of the tube came out of the pod, where a bulb and clip arrangement allowed Cayhill to test-squeeze a drop of his latest concoction into the being's mouth. The idea was that a preferred taste would make the lips close on the nipple, then the Dhryn would either suck on its contents or they could force more in from outside.

For this to work, Cayhill had had to reduce the repeller field to minimum. Even that slight press against the sheets below had caused more skin to fracture, more blue fluid to leak out.

It had to work, Mac thought, appalled. The Wasted was now more skeleton than flesh.

After leaving the hangar, Mudge had headed for the bridge, gleeful at having been invited by Townee to watch the shuttle launch. Mac had returned here to find Cayhill trying one mixture after another. The source? Bins and carts loaded with the remnants of fresh vegetables and ornamental plants filled one side of the room. A workbench with extraction equipment was in the center, lines of fluid-filled vials at one end. Piles of shredded leaves littered the floor. She assumed a technician had helped dismember and extract. No one person could have made that much mess so quickly.

Though it smelled quite wonderful. *You just had to ignore the undertone of rotting Dhryn flesh.*

Mac watched as the next glistening drop formed at the nipple's tip, fell away to land on a cracked lip, then slid inside. *No response.*

"Which one was that?"

He checked the 'screen hovering over the pod. "Aloe and soy."

"Hand cream?"

A shrug. "Components fit the list." Cayhill pointed to the bench. "Bring me the next please, Dr. Connor. There."

Mac found the vial he wanted and brought it. She chewed her lower lip as he poured the liquid into the dispensing apparatus.

He glanced at her. "You have a comment?"

"He'll be dead before you can try all the combinations." *They all would.*

"If I were substituting," Cayhill agreed. "But I don't care about negative reactions." He squeezed to release a new drop. "Only to find a positive one. I'm adding a new pair of nutrient sources each time. Should be done with the lot in another hour."

So much for scientific method. Mac shrugged, willing to go along. "Why not do them all at once, then?"

"Some of these items are in short supply, but contain essentially the same elements as the rest. So I'm trying the abundant ones first."

Okay, some logic. "Let me help."

"Wait." His face lit with triumph. "Look!"

Mac pressed her nose to the window.

The Wasted's lips had fastened over the tube. She could see the muscles of his neck working as he swallowed. *Again.* She scarcely breathed. *Again.*

"Hold this," Cayhill ordered, thrusting the tube and bulb at her. He hurried to the table, his 'screen going with him. "I'll make more."

"Hurry," she advised. The swallows were coming faster; the level of liquid in the tube dropping apace.

A vibration rattled the pod and the Wasted's eyes cracked open. Mac fumbled for the com switch with her free hand. "It's okay," she said. "You're safe. You need to stay still. This is—" *Dhryn had no medical terms* "—a rescue pod." His eyes closed again. She couldn't tell if it meant comprehension or collapse.

"Move." Without waiting, Cayhill shouldered her aside. He sat a beaker of liquid on top of the pod and began tearing apart the bulb and clip. Mac helped, taping in place the funnel he'd brought in his pocket. Cayhill threw more than poured, somehow managing to add more liquid into the tube before the Wasted drained it.

Once they were sure the Dhryn was swallowing steadily, Mac leaned her back against the pod and surveyed the damage. Pale green liquid coated the side of the pod and puddled the floor. They both had streaks of it down their clothing. "Toss you for cleanup."

Cayhill frowned. "Call someone. I have to make more broth." He went to the table, his left foot leaving damp prints on the floor.

Mac looked inside. The Wasted had closed his eyes, but his fingers were now wrapped around the tube as if to make sure it stayed in his mouth. He swallowed regularly. "We could be killing him," she commented uneasily. *Or not helping at all.*

"Do we have a choice?" Cayhill gave her that unreadable look. "Sometimes you have to trust the patient."

An apology? Mac let it go. She filled her cheeks, then let the air out through her teeth. "I'll clean up." There was a bag of wipes and a vacuum mop by the door. She set to work on the pod, sniffing at the spill. "Is that tea?"

"Green tea. And macadamia nuts."

Herbivore? Fits the migration profile, she pondered as she cleaned the floor. A trip across most of a planet might take a couple of generations of ordinary Dhryn to accomplish on foot, even if the Progenitors could live that long. More rapidly moving prey would elude them.

She helped Cayhill pour—more carefully—another dose of broth into the tube. "We need something better than this," he decided. "Wait here."

Between looks at the Wasted, Mac moved on to sweeping up the discarded leaves and other debris from around the table, putting those into the bins. It was the closest thing to gardening she'd done in years, and she found herself enjoying the feel of stems and peel, the delirious smells of what grew.

Cayhill backed through the door, pulling something with him.

"Don't you ever ask for help?" inquired Mac.

She could read that look all right. *Annoyance.* "It's the middle of the night, Dr. Connor."

Sure enough, she glimpsed night-dim lighting in the corridor before he was through the door.

Time flew when tending aliens.

He wrestled what turned out to be a stand festooned with empty bags over to the pod. "We fill these," Cayhill announced, "connect them in sequence, and he can drink all he wants."

"What about the—ah—consequence?" Mac ventured.

A pitying look. "The catheter was the easy part."

For whom?

Working together, they produced enough broth to fill all but one bag. Once he'd checked the system for leaks, Cayhill declared himself satisfied. "Nothing to do now but wait, Dr. Connor," he finished.

And stood there looking at her.

Mac sighed, giving up her untouched bed. "I'll stay. I've reports to read."

His eyes strayed to the equipment attached to the pod. *Not about to let a mere biologist handle* his *patient,* Mac decided. "No, no," Cayhill said at last. "I should stay. You go."

"I won't touch anything," she promised. "You've hooked it all to remote monitors, right?" At his hesitant nod, Mac grinned. "Get some rest, or we can play cards. Kudla left his deck."

"Call me if there's the smallest change," said Cayhill hastily. "And watch for gunk in the tubing. The filters were coarse."

"Change, gunk, got it. Go." Mac let her grin fade. "And thank you, Doctor. Whatever happens."

Her gratitude seemed to startle him. "Whatever happens," he replied gruffly, "I expect to be notified without delay."

After Cayhill left, Mac amused herself by walking around the room a few times, straightening this and that. Noticing the bed had fresh sheets, she rolled it from the corner and positioned it alongside the pod, in case she needed a nap. She stared in at the Wasted, seeing no change at all. In case, she switched on the com so they could hear one another.

Out of excuses not to sit down and work, she stood in the middle of the empty room and closed her eyes to listen.

The barely heard, self-conscious hum of machines. A drip from within the pod. *Satisfied?*

Mac checked the door again, then stared up at the unblinking vid in the corner, hating to think this would be public record. *So she was obsessive.* It wasn't the first time.

Despite feeling a thorough idiot, she disconnected the handle from the vacuum mop and used it to carefully sweep the room, including pokes at the ceiling and finishing with a lunge under the pod.

Done, she positioned two chairs so she could sit in the one and see blue flesh through a window. The other was for her feet.

She pulled out her imp and set up her 'screen, looking first for updates from Mudge. Nothing. *Probably going to stay on the bridge till they kick him off,* she thought, glad he was happy.

There were a few notes from members of the Origins Team, mostly dealing with what had been left behind, or for when she came down. Mac shunted those to Mudge and looked for anything from a little farther afield.

Finally. She smiled as she called up a set of newly arrived vid messages, from the latest newspacket or courier. She didn't care which.

Mac settled deeper in her chair and cued the messages to play.

- CONTACT -

EMILY WAS STANDING outside, lit by sunshine, framed by intense blue. Her head was covered in a large fluffy mass, more like a growth of bright red hair than a hat; a scarf of the same improbable fabric traced the underside of her jaw and cheek. Her nose was distinctly pink and her breath left little puffs as she spoke. "Hi, Mac! Got your message. You sound the veteran spacer. Proud of you, girl.

"Guess where we are!" The image briefly tilted sideways, catching the ice-rimmed prow of the harvester lev, a flat expanse of sea beyond. "Two tries. Whoops! Wrong!"

"Tracer's working, Mac. It's working," this with passion, her face close. "I knew it would. I'm on its tail—or whatever. Sneaky bastard. It's been leading me around . . . playing some tricks . . . thinks it's clever. But I'm not going to lose it. Not now."

Quiet, intense. "You should be here, Mac. This is where the answers are. I feel it. Forget that ball of dirt. This is where we'll learn how to stop *Them*, once and for all."

The image tilted again, this time spinning in a circle as if Emily had grabbed the 'bot for a dance partner. Behind her, more blue sky and ice, frozen metal, distant others wrapped against the cold.

"C'mon home, Mac," she urged, becoming still. She brought the 'bot to her eyes, as if trying to see inside, turning the image into a confusion of lashes and dark, dilated pupils. "*They've* never been in a hurry before. *They've* never made mistakes. Something's started the clock. Not—not at noon. It's eleven. Mac, it's eleven. Remember that."

The 'bot swung up, as if she'd tossed it, then leveled out and returned to its original position. Emily tucked her chin into her scarf. "Gotta go, Mac. Can't leave the Tracer for long, not even with Casey-boy.

"Just . . . come home as soon as you can. Okay?"

Case was sitting, his back against a curved wall that might have been anywhere along the lev's inner hull. He'd tanned, or gained freckles; aged, by the fine lines beside his eyes and mouth. But he looked out from the image with assurance. "Hi, Mac. We've been at sea a while. Feels good, you know. Being out here. You likely expected that.

"Em's gadget is hauling us all over. Sing-li's always on the com getting clearances. Part of my job is warning civilian harvesters we're coming through. A couple learned the hard way Em isn't going to divert course. You ever been on one of these big harvs when it ramps up and over another lev? Whoot! Don't worry. No one's been hurt." A grin. "Maybe a few feelings. Handy having Earthgov and the IU on our side, that's for sure."

The young man rubbed one hand over his jaw, the grin disappearing. "I guess I'm the one to tell you. Em—I caught her taking 'fix. She laughed—boasted 'Sephe was getting it for her, that no one cares, long as she finds their monster. I think—I know she's right, Mac. Everyone's too quiet, too focused. Feels like we're in a whirlpool and don't know how long till the bottom.

"About Em . . . I don't want you to worry. I'm making her take supplements, got her promise not to up the dose. I've seen guys 'fix for weeks, Mac. They weren't good for much by the end, but they pulled their weight for the harvest."

Case's lips quirked sideways and his eyes glowed. "With or without, none of them could keep up to Emily, though. She's on the trail.

"Hope you're okay, Mac. As I said, don't worry. We'll find this thing. You can trust us."

Hard to tell if Hollans had aged. His wrinkles contrarily defied it. Instead of looking at the 'bot, he stared out over a wide patio, edged by trees; one hand rested on the stone wall that edged the terrace. He took a deep breath before speaking. "Dr. Connor. Mac. They told me what happened on the *Uosanah*. I never meant you or Sigmund to be in any danger. I want you to believe that." A pause. "I've spoken to Katie, his wife. Those things—doesn't matter how many times I do it, I never know what to say. But I made sure your family knew you were okay. The media's got more than I'd like about the whole business. No help for that now."

His fingers worked at the stone. "What you did . . . what you both did . . . I've decorated agents for less." A low laugh. "You know, I can picture your face right now. Don't worry, Mac, I'd never make you accept a medal.

"I'd like to know how you found out about the walker before we sent the specs to you, but I'm learning not to be surprised by anything you and your people accomplish. Dr. Mamani, for instance. She's already chasing whatever the Ro left in Castle Inlet. None of our sensors detect a thing. She's either crazy or our best shot. I'm inclined to the latter."

He turned to face the 'bot at last. "I hope you've had news from our mutual friend. I know you've heard about the mess with the Frow. 'Mess.' " Hollans made a face. "A tragedy, that's what's coming. Earthgov's expelled the Trisulian ambassador. We aren't the only ones. But you know being politically isolated will send the wrong message to the Trisulians. I feel like a voice shouting in an empty room. We should be finding them opportunities to colonize, maybe even the Dhryn worlds, if it comes to that. Help them believe their coming generation is safe. But you get politics within species as well as between. Anchen's conducting negotiations around the clock." He looked away again. "Maybe they'll work. Regardless, now every species in the IU knows the Trisulians tried to summon the Dhryn. It's not much of a step to realize the only way to end that threat is to eliminate the Dhryn themselves.

"So we're back to that, Mac. The Ro or the Trisulians. Both now hold the Dhryn over our heads." His voice became very quiet. "You know what I'm asking. You know, I hope, what you must do if you have the opportunity. What Nik must do.

"For all our sakes."

REBIRTH AND RESUMPTION

MAC CLOSED HER 'screen, hand trembling. The rest of her messages could wait.

It wasn't as if any of it was a surprise.

She'd known. Deep inside, in the place where nightmares festered while she was awake, she'd known Emily was expendable. And the Dhryn.

And everyone else.

So long as they stopped this.

It was hard to remember normal, to think about the way the IU had been before this fundamental threat to its very nature. *Not that she'd paid attention to it then,* Mac mocked herself.

She walked over to the pod, and put her hand on its cool surface. "It's not even your fault," she said.

Ureif had seen no circularity.

Numb, Mac walked to the lighting controls and accepted ship settings. The room dimmed to twilight, the shadows softening the edge of machine and pod, the aroma of crushed plants teasing at the senses, a pretense of life.

She climbed on the bed and laid down, rolling to face the Wasted through his windows. He no longer swallowed, the nipple stuck to a lower lip as if abandoned. Perhaps he was dying.

Perhaps he was lucky.

Mac closed her eyes and wept.

She'd dimmed the lights.

Mac squinted, opening her eyelids the barest amount possible.

The glow wasn't much, but it was right in her face.

For an instant, she believed it was a flaw in the pod, its internal lights jumped to some higher setting, ready for an autopsy.

Then, as she came fully awake, she realized it was something else entirely.

The Wasted was . . . *glowing*.

She slid from the bed, tiptoeing closer, and gasped. Her hands caught at the pod to keep her upright.

Okay. Not just glowing.

The creature inside the pod wasn't what she'd left there. It was no feeder, no normal adult . . .

Warm, golden eyes gazed back at her.

"*Lamisah*. What am I?"

Luminescence.

"I don't know," Mac breathed.

The Wasted had . . . changed. *Cayhill was right,* she thought. *An arrested metamorphosis, not a failed one.*

The Dhryn before her was still blue, but that blue was almost painfully vivid. What had been fractures in his skin were now connected into bands wrapping his torso and limbs in softly glowing white. His face and body had fleshed again, the body thicker than before, stronger. The eyes. The eyes were everything Mac remembered about Dhryn, warm, alive, vibrant.

With a beseeching look. "Can you release me, *Lamisah*? I no longer fit inside."

Her hand reached for the control and froze. *The voice!* It was higher pitched, with a different cadence.

It was no longer male.

"*Lamisah?*"

Mac shook off her paralysis, aware the being was right. He—she—now more than filled the inside of the pod. No matter what else, getting out was a priority.

First, Mac went to the door and locked it from the inside.

Then she went to the table and picked up the closest thing to a weapon she could find, a thin metal rod.

Aim for the eye.

Last, she went to the pod, pushed the release, and moved back.

There was an alarm. *Of course.* Lights in the room shot up to normal day, then strobed orange. No sound here, but doubtless abundant bells and shrieks elsewhere. *She didn't have long.*

The pod lid opened and fell back with a clang, knocking over Cayhill's stand of bags.

The *creature* sat up and smiled. "Thank you." He—she climbed out with ease, power and grace in every movement.

When she stood on the floor in front of Mac, it was on four sturdy legs, not two. The uppermost arms were now legs, the middle set thicker, more muscled. They'd regrown something almost like hands at their wrists but these were broad, almost webbed. *Feet.* At the moment, those middle arms were bent at the elbows and carried up against her midsection. When she bowed her head and shoulders back in gratitude, Mac saw the seventh limb, now muscular and with a three-digit hand.

And when she came upright again—taller now, and solid—and settled to regard her Human companion, skin and eyes aglow even against the brighter light, she was nothing less than glorious.

Mac dropped her would-be weapon.

"What are you?"

The delicate mouth smiled, as if they now shared a secret. "Hungry."

"Dr. Connor. This is the second door you've locked on me. This is my ship, you realize."

Mac winced. Captain Gillis sounded infinitely more reasonable and calm than Cayhill, who'd been first to arrive and shouted himself hoarse at her while waiting for the rest. "Sorry about that," she said "Hang on." She unlocked and opened it, but kept herself firmly in the way. "I wanted you to be here," she explained, trying not to look at Cayhill. *He deserved better.* "All of you," this with a nod to Ureif and Mudge.

Mudge looked as grim as she'd ever seen him. She'd expected that.

She'd expected the armed guards, too.

"If you'd come in, calmly." Now she did look at Cayhill, doing her best to plead with him without saying a word.

His face was flushed with rage, his eyes fierce. But he gave a curt nod.

Mac backed slowly, controlling the entry. Not that any of them wanted to run in—they'd seen on the vid, she was sure, what waited. A new kind of Dhryn.

Or maybe something else. Her heart hammered as she considered the possibilities.

She'd done her best to provide a suitable setting for the introductions. *Not that she'd had much to work with,* Mac reminded herself. She'd shoved the wheeled platform to one side, the bed with it. The worktable joined them, its mass of vials and equipment hidden under a sheet. That left the table and chairs, plus the bins. The bins of used plants were now out of the way. Along with the all-but-one empty bags.

She'd put the table in the middle, fished out a plant sufficiently intact—*in her opinion*—to serve as a centerpiece, and arranged the chairs on one side. There weren't enough, but the Dhryn didn't need a chair. Neither did she.

It no longer looked like a hospital room.

A point not lost on Cayhill, whose lips pressed tightly together. Then he saw his patient and wonder flooded his face. "I don't believe it."

The Dhryn raised her head in a bow. "I am told you are responsible for my current state." She indicated herself with her flexible limb, the movement as graceful as any Sinzi. "I would give you my name, Human-*erumisah,* but I do not exist."

"Erumisah" *was a rank earned through* grathnu. Mac supposed providing food qualified. "This is Gordon Matthew Cayhill," she introduced, having taken a judicious look at the ship's crew list.

"Ah." The Dhryn paused, as if considering how to clap without paired hands. Then she dropped what Mac thought of as her mid-legs to the floor, their flatter feet making a reasonable smack. "Most distinguished. I take the name Gordon Matthew Cayhill into my keeping."

"The captain of the *Annapolis Joy,* Michael—Rupert James Gillis." Mac hadn't found his middle names, so she made up a few. Gillis didn't even blink.

Another vigorous smack. "Outstanding. I am honored to take the name Michael Rupert James Gillis into my keeping."

"Charles Jean Mudge III. *Erumisah.*"

The Dhryn passed her golden gaze over Mac for an instant at this claim, but dutifully smacked the floor to acknowledge Mudge.

Mac then gestured to the Sinzi, feeling ridiculously formal. *Should have ordered pizza and beer,* she thought. But this was what she had. "Sinzi-ra Ureif." She watched the Dhryn closely. If there was an alien face she read as well as her own, it was Dhryn. Now, she thought she saw a flicker of recognition.

"Sinzi-ra Ureif."

Ureif tilted his head to bring his lower eyes more in line with the Dhryn, but didn't speak. *How much did he know?* Mac wondered. *About this Dhryn, a former ship captain from Cryssin Colony. And about the Wasting.*

"If you'd have a seat?"

The Dhryn moved to one end of the table, going down on her four larger legs. Seated, she was taller than any Human in the room. Intimidating by size, awe-inspiring by her very existence, but there was something gentle, something warm about her—*don't Humanize,* Mac warned herself. It was hard. The Dhryn even smelled good.

Mudge waited for the captain and Ureif to choose seats, but not for Cayhill. Mac tried to catch his eyes, but he seemed to deliberately avoid hers. Cayhill took the last seat without hesitation.

Mac felt better pacing anyway. "I assume you've all seen what happened?" she asked, nodded at the vid.

Now Mudge looked at her. "You took an unconscionable risk, Norcoast."

Before she could reply, the Dhryn leaned forward. "I would never harm my *lamisah,* Charles Jean Mudge III."

"You ate your crew."

Mac gritted her teeth, but the Dhryn nodded gravely. "They sustained me." There was no remorse or regret in the voice. *That which is Dhryn must survive. Even one who "did not exist."*

"What about us?"

"Mr. Mudge, please." Mudge subsided, with a scowl at Mac. The captain put his forearms on the table and leaned forward on them. "Dr. Connor. This is your party."

Really could use the beer. Mac nodded. "Thank you. I asked you here to meet the Progenitor."

"Is that what I am?" asked the Dhryn, sounding thoughtful.

"I believe so."

"But I do not exist."

"That was before—"

"Dr. Connor." Mac turned from the golden eyes to meet Ureif's topaz ones. "Use great care."

A warning from the former Sinzi-ra of Haven, or the Speaker of the IU Inner Council? Or both.

Regardless, it was excellent advice. The being was like a new student, intensely curious, soaking up information without discrimination. Mac had done her utmost to avoid saying anything beyond simple commands, "move here," and reassurances, "there's more food coming." *She could do more harm than good.* "Yes, Sinzi-ra. I concur. That's why I need all of you—" she paused, like the rest watching as the Dhryn, unself-conscious, reached across the table to the centerpiece, fastened her fingers on the closest leaf, and pulled the ragged mass to herself.

But once she had the plant, the Dhryn seemed puzzled. She stared at it, her fingers toying with the leaves. A piece came free. She put it into her mouth, her lips working. After a moment, her mouth opened. The piece was clearly intact. She pulled it out and held it toward Mudge, a *thrum* of distress rolling through the floor underfoot. "*Erumisah,* this will sustain me. Why can I not eat it? I must have it. I hunger."

Mudge *harrumphed,* but there was no denying the confused hurt in the Dhryn's voice. He looked at Mac, who tipped her head toward Cayhill. "Dr. Cayhill," Mudge coughed. "If you'd be so good as to examine your—patient?"

Cayhill went pale. *Probably dawned on him unconscious dying aliens were the easy part,* Mac decided. She walked over to the Dhryn and rested her hand on the being's shoulder. "He must look inside your mouth," she explained.

Seeing Mac there, *uneaten,* Cayhill stood and approached, taking a scope from his pocket. When nothing more alarming happened than the Dhryn opening her mouth, he shone the light inside.

And frowned.

Without warning, he pushed the scope between her lips. The Dhryn shied back like a draft horse stung by a fly. Cayhill reacted by throwing himself in the opposite direction. He collided with his own chair and spun around to dive behind Mudge who, like the captain, had jumped to his feet.

The Dhryn sat. She picked up another leaf. "I must have this," she insisted, as if nothing had happened.

"The esophagus is gone," Cayhill blurted. He rose to his feet, apparently reassured, but stayed behind Mudge.

"What do you mean?" the captain asked.

"It's sealed off. There's only the airway left."

Explaining why the Dhryn had stopped before finishing the last bag.

"What is an esophagus, *Lamisah?*"

"Something you need." Mac chewed her lower lip, considering the Dhryn.

The glowing white bands merged along the back, the entire area now appearing to pulse with every breath. *Like the puffer form,* she realized suddenly. *Display or support for a growing body mass?*

Later.

She laid her palm on the nearest band, feeling the membrane shudder delicately in response. The Dhryn did not object, merely turned her great head as far as possible to watch. Mac smiled at her, then kept examining the band. At the verge of band and blue skin, she spotted a small ridge on the blue and leaned in to see. A dimple, such as all Dhryn possessed, but this felt different. Without taking her eyes from it, Mac said, "Cayhill, I need your scope."

She didn't pay attention to the ensuing protest, but wasn't surprised to have Mudge pass her the device and stay close.

Magnified, the dimple became a tiny, lipless mouth; its opening, when she pressed gently, no greater than her fingertip. She aimed the scope along the blue skin. Sure enough, all of the dimples had been modified in the same way.

Mac stood up, her hand lingering on the Dhryn. "You can no longer feed yourself," she said, unable to keep the regret from her voice. *The end of individuality. Did the Dhryn feel it?*

"Then you are correct and this is a Progenitor," concluded Ureif, rising slowly to his feet. "Reliant on her people."

"I am hungry." There was overwhelming trust in the look the Dhryn gave Mac. "My *lamisah* will provide for me."

And she'd worried about adopting a Myg offspring.

Mac was nodding before she knew she'd made the decision. "Dr. Cayhill's broth. Some eyedroppers. We'll figure something out." *For now.*

"Dr. Connor. I think we need to discuss a few things first." Gillis' jaw was clenched.

She'd wondered how long it would take him to begin to see the problem of hosting a rapidly growing Dhryn Progenitor on his ship. *Let alone what the neighbors were going to say.*

"Wait, Captain. If you would." The Sinzi stood away from the table. He swept his fingers stiffly from his shoulders, then brought them together in that complex knot. Finally, he bowed deeply to the Dhryn. "I welcome you home at last, She Who Is Dhryn, on behalf of the Interspecies Union. The Consulate of the *Annapolis Joy* is at your service." The fingers trembled, setting up a chime from their rings. "May I say, I am humbled to bear witness to this epic congruence, your return through space and body to the birthplace of your kind. It is the pinnacle of my life." The Sinzi collected himself, saying more calmly, "Captain, I rely upon you to expedite suitable accommodations."

She really didn't like the sound of this. From his pallor, neither did Gillis. Mac licked her lips. "Sinzi-ra, forgive me, but surely this is the best place right now for our—guest. While she requires medical care." *And eyedroppers.*

"I must make an immediate announcement that She Who Is Dhryn will receive representatives from other species. She cannot do that in here." The topaz eyes seemed to glitter. "This ship will accommodate her needs, or we will move to another."

"I am hungry," the object of these lofty plans reminded them.

Mac looked at Mudge, whose dumbfounded expression likely mirrored her own.

Even Sinzi could be trapped by their own nature, she realized, feeling a sick foreboding. *Those representatives weren't going to be happy.*

Still, she thought more cheerfully, *looked like she'd have help with the eyedroppers.*

The new Progenitor's appetite proved unexpectedly useful. Not only did it keep the being herself preoccupied to the point of total compliance to everything around her, Mac thought some time later, but Cayhill had roused to oversee the entire project.

Probably because he finally had a patient who didn't talk back.

"Are you listening to me, Norcoast?"

Mac stifled a yawn and nodded. She could sum up Mudge's response to recent events—*he thought she'd lost her mind*—but it would be impolite to stop him now. *Not to mention impossible without help.* "The Sinzi-ra is confident," she pointed out. *Again.*

"And the captain is not. Nor is Earthgov, or the Ministry, or any level of government represented in this solar system. Or on their way!"

There had been a steady flow of traffic through the gate. *Not surprising.* What had been a surprise was how quickly and thoroughly the Sinzi-ra managed to disseminate word of the presence and condition of their new guest. *Even her family should know by now.*

There was a basic consideration that transcended the Sinzi rapture at the physical journey of this individual. There could be other Wasteds lurking in the holds of the derelict ships, individuals innocent of the crimes committed by the rest of their species, individuals who needed immediate rescue.

Though immediate was unlikely. Any rescue attempt was now being debated by the Inner Council, Ureif—or rather Filt—participating from here. They also debated the future of the Dhryn on the *Annapolis Joy.*

Good luck with that, she wished them.

"Norcoast!" His fist thumped down on the table.

She rested her fingers on top of it. "Peace, Oversight. It's done. Whatever happens now is out of our hands."

He *harrumphed* at this, then sighed. "You could have left the room."

"You," she pointed out, "could have stayed at the Trust."

Mudge wasn't ready to smile. "And I suppose you would have managed without me?"

"It would have been difficult." *Being dead.* She didn't say it; she didn't have to. She could see the memory passing over his face. Mac patted his fist, then rubbed her eyes. They were waiting on Captain Gillis, who'd left orders they weren't to go anywhere until he'd clarified a few things.

In her experience, that implied yelling.

Or, harder to ignore, "how did you get me into this," looks.

Since Gillis had left to produce accommodations for his now-illustrious guest that wouldn't offend the Sinzi but would satisfy his security staff, she shouldn't have to face either for a while. "What time is it?" she asked Mudge, yawning again.

"Too early for breakfast, too late for a night's sleep."

Mac got up and went to the transparent wall that separated Gillis' meeting room from the bridge. The tree kept its vigil to the side. The rest of the space was as incomprehensibly busy as before. "Can they see us?" She waved at one of the crew looking this way.

"Of course not." Mudge joined her. "Too distracting."

"There's Fy." Mac pressed her finger on the wall to indicate the Sinzi. "Is that the com?" Hard to tell, given the cluster of Humans, Grimnoii, and hovering 'screens.

"Yes. If it hadn't been for the new traffic, she'd be running checks on the gate station by now, but there hasn't been a break." At her impressed look, he preened ever so slightly. "Darcy keeps me up to speed."

As the station in question was little more than an orbiting box of monitoring equipment, connected remotely to the myriad other orbiting boxes that together coaxed the gate out of no-space, Mac thought the Sinzi should be quite happy to be able to work from the comfort of the ship. " 'Darcy,' is it?" she teased, looking for the woman in question.

Mudge *harrumphed.* "There's no need for that tone, Norcoast," he began, when the lighting on the bridge went red.

Several other things happened at once. A klaxon went off, varying in volume but impossible to ignore. The organized confusion on the bridge became frantic, with some personnel diving for seats and others moving out of their way. The captain appeared through his door, one hand brushing the tree trunk as if by habit. Guards came through every other door, weapons at the ready.

Including this room. Mac and Mudge whirled together at the sound of the door opening and heavy feet.

"What's going on?" she demanded, but the armored man shook his head.

"There'll be an announcement," he told them, taking up his station by the now-closed door.

To keep them in or . . .

Mac whirled to Mudge, her hand tight on his arm. "The Ro. The walker. It didn't come with the derelict—"

"What are you talking about?"

She was shaking. "It came with us," she shouted, desperate to be understood. "They're on the *Joy—*"

"No, they aren't." Mudge took hold of her shoulders, eyes intent on hers. He spoke deliberately, as if making sure she heard every word over the alarm. "You weren't the only one who thought of that possibility, Norcoast. Security's run constant checks, accounted for all sounds and mass within the ship. They mist the corridors and hangars at night, looking for signs. The *Joy's* clean. We're safe."

"Could have—told me—" she hiccuped fiercely.

"And have you supervise that, too?" He gave her a small shake, looking more worried than he sounded. "I'm sorry, Norcoast. I didn't want you to think about them anymore. I should have told you."

Mac hiccuped once more, and shut her mouth. She took a deep, slow breath through her nose, Mudge nodding encouragement, then let it out. "At least we weren't asleep in bed," she said faintly. She found herself wondering how much, if anything, of the captain of the *Uosanah* remained to help the Dhryn understand the alarm.

Mudge's hands squeezed her shoulders, then dropped away. "Shouldn't be long."

Sure enough, the wailing alarm stopped, leaving an expectant silence. The red lighting switched back to normal. Mac could see Gillis preparing to speak— he looked her way, perhaps remembering they were there. She began to relax.

Then she heard his voice, level and devastatingly calm.

"We have Dhryn incoming. A Progenitor ship has arrived through the transect gate. Repeat, we have Dhryn incoming.

"Battle stations."

- 20 -

RISK AND REUNION

*W*HICH PROGENITOR?
Mac turned to Mudge.

He took one look at her face, then grabbed her wrist and pulled her with him to the door control leading to the bridge. He had it open before the startled guard could do more than shout, the two of them stumbling down the stairs to the bridge floor.

Captain Gillis appeared to be one of those rare beings unaffected by sudden entrances or emergencies. *Or was at his best under pressure.* He greeted them with a gracious nod, waving away the guard. "Dr. Connor. Mr. Mudge. Good timing. If you'll join me?" He led the way to the com area, where Fy had taken over the controls of three consoles, her fingers flying through their displays with that inhuman speed. Mac averted her eyes, queasy enough.

Townee was there. She looked at them with a frown. "We're having difficulty establishing a link, sir. Their equipment isn't IU standard."

"Keep on it. Sinzi-ra. Any more coming through?"

Were they outnumbered?

"Not yet. There has been—maneuvering—on the part of ships in a direct line. I have asserted the need to avoid provocation at this point."

Who'd fire first?

Mac rubbed her thumb over the rings on her fingers.

Gillis might have been asking about the weather. "Show me."

The air above them darkened until she might have looked outside the ship, into space itself. *The ships were too small,* she thought, but that was to include present company.

They were otherwise accurately rendered. She found the Trisulian, now at the far side of the group from the *Uosanah.* Many ships were in motion relative to one another, *moving away,* she realized. The *Joy* was still, sitting above the dotted oval representing the event of the gate, between all the others and the oncoming Progenitor Ship.

"Enlarge."

The image of the Progenitor Ship grew larger. As it did, there were gasps. The silver hull had been *eaten* away; vast portions were little more than dribbles of what had been solid, but had somehow melted and then congealed. The rest was deformed and pitted. *A wonder the thing flew at all . . .*

Mac's pocket chirped.

To be accurate, the *salmon* in her pocket chirped.

She pulled it out with numb fingers, then looked up to see she had the full attention of those around her.

The chirping, now louder, became an arrhythmic clicking. One of Fy's fingers reached toward Mac, the tip beckoning. She offered the carving—*whatever it was*—and the finger wrapped around it, while the Sinzi's other fingers darted and danced furiously within the com system display.

A loud crackle, then a voice. "Do not fire. This is Nikolai Trojanowski, Ministry of Extra-Solar Human Affairs, attached to the IU Gathering. Do not fire. Our intentions are not hostile. Please send a shuttle with adjustable docking clamps to these coordinates. Repeating. This is Nikolai—"

Mac listened to the words, hearing the triumph as well as exhaustion, and smiled.

The man knew how to make an entrance.

Mac thudded her fist into her pillow. She considered the situation and thumped it again.

She'd been the image of a calm, cool professional.

"Of course, there have to be negotiations," she told the cowering bit of foam. "Yes, I quite understand that means delays." *Thump!* "Why should anything involving aliens ever—" *Thump!* be—"*Thump!*"—easy?!" *Thump!*

The pillow succumbed, coughing up fluff and going flat at one end.

She'd been exceptionally understanding.

But hadn't fooled Mudge. He'd hovered a little too overtly, offering her drinks and running interference when she'd tried—*time after time*—for some answers.

At least he'd recovered her salmon from Fy. Mac threw herself down on her stomach, then rolled over to stare at it on the clear shelf.

"Some salmon you are," she scolded. The device within the carving had been Sinzi, a little something they'd provided Nik in case he'd been taken aboard the Dhryn ship, with its pre-IU technology. He'd had its partner, ready to coordinate com signals or whatever at the right time. Fy had been very pleased.

Mac wondered what other little surprises a certain spy had left in her life.

She pulled the blanket to her chin and stretched out her toes, yawning. The new bed was as comfortable as she'd hoped, the room private and peaceful. *And clean, right to an apologetic hint of lilac.* The Frow, while not talkative, had been on duty in the ladderway, lifting her with their accustomed flare. The Dhryn was resting, having—according to Cayhill—consumed most of the ship's supply of raspberries and cashews, shells included, in a new broth. *The man was in his element with tubing and a perfusion pump.*

She eased her hips and shoulders, almost hissing with the delicious pain of relaxing muscles. Tense muscles. She needed a good run.

Or a certain spy.

Mac smiled wistfully, but pulled her thoughts firmly from *that* direction. *He'd get here when he did.*

She shut her eyes, let her mind drift, intent on that too-brief clarity between committed to sleep and committing it. This was when threads wove themselves together without effort, when intuitive leaps came like breath. She'd learned not to waste it.

She let her thoughts go where they would . . .

. . . *a Progenitor the size of a blue whale moved across a sere landscape, six powerful limbs churning their way forward. She was less massive than Her bulk suggested, much of Her body composed of immense sacs of gas lighter than the surrounding air. Around Her flew a ceaseless pulse of others, attracted to the glow of her skin, jostling to be next to offer their store of digested nutrients to Her body. Beside her marched others, stout and capable, well-organized. Their low voices communicated well across the landscape. These carried the youngest under their bodies, as well as seeds.*

There was laughter, at the beginning of the Great Journey. The triumph of a species moving how it could, when it must, in a world that relied on its passing for renewal.

Mac's eyes shot open. *It fit.* A body plan that would have worked for the Dhryn. Not that glut of a form, suited only to producing millions more *oomlings* than one world could sustain.

She tossed until she found a less comfortable position; she needed to think.

A reversion to type.

She felt rigid as the idea took hold. "Is that what you are?" she breathed. *They'd need to run the genetic material, see if the Joy's Progenitor was a match to the current form, but with a different sequence of genes active.*

But some would always be born. The "lost souls."

"They'd have to forbid biology," she whispered. "They'd have to create the myth of the Wasted, shun them, let them die. They'd need a diet that wouldn't support the final metamorphosis of the original Progenitor."

Had this been the terrible price the Dhryn had paid the Ro, for admission to space?

Or had oomlings been stolen, changed, their own kind unaware until it was too late?

What did it mean now?

Ureif promoted this one Dhryn for all the wrong reasons. Non-Sinzi would see that.

Could there be a right one? Could she be fertile? Could the original form of Dhryn be restored through her and those like her?

Should it?

Mac fell asleep before she had answers, dreaming of limbs become hands, of hands become mouths, of mouths counting to eleven and dripping with green, while *something* laughed.

Fourteen had sent her three hundred and fifteen messages.

"Must have cut into their time for sex," Mac commented, scrolling the list. "And me waiting for my nugget."

"Norcoast!"

She opened one at random. "He's groveling. But busy."

"Good."

Mac raised her eyebrow at Mudge. "Good he's groveling?"

"Good he's busy." Mudge took a sip of tea. "Keeps him out of trouble."

She *tsked* at him, but kept opening messages. No need to rush through brunch. Every reason to keep busy here, too. *No news.*

And presleep thoughts weren't for the light. *She needed data.*

Mac opened another. "Whoops."

Mudge paused, a cracker halfway to his lips. " 'Whoops?' "

"Wasn't meant for me. I hope. 'The pale forks of your writhing tongue flutter the tent of my passion?' " She slid her finger through the 'screen to close that one. "Hello." This as she skimmed the next message, then reread more slowly. "I'll be . . ." She read it again. "You wouldn't believe what they had for supper."

"I hope you appreciate, Norcoast, that there is very little as annoying as being a forced spectator to message reading. Particularly," Mudge waved today's carrot, "your message reading."

"Sorry," she said without looking away from the 'screen. Sorting the messages by topic didn't seem to work. *Typical Fourteen convolutions.* "Don't mind me."

"You can eat while you read," he fussed, pushing more vegetables on her plate.

"This is odd." Mac squinted at the display hovering between them. The list of messages showed as lines of simple text—*simple for someone else*—but those three hundred and fifteen lines now formed a perfect zigzag to the right. "See this?" For emphasis, she followed the pattern through the display with her finger.

It shouldn't have done anything.

But the display changed immediately. The text list disintegrated and reformed into an image—a vid recording. "Look! It's Fourteen." Mac moved the 'screen so Mudge could see as well.

And only Fourteen, his face so close no background showed. He wasn't moving or talking. "It's not working," Mac said.

"If it's a private message, Norcoast, he'll have encoded something to activate it, a way for you to control when it plays."

"Oh. Of course." Mac leaned toward the 'screen.

"You know what it is?" Mudge sounded surprised.

"I've an idea," she replied, giving him a wink, then said firmly, "External genitalia."

Fourteen's image animated into a smile. "Idiot! I have none!" Then the smile was gone. "I knew you'd find this, Mac. You're more clever than you think. Not as clever as I am, but that's why you need me.

"You asked me to uncover the purpose of those rushing to Myriam. A simple matter. Boring, boring, boring. The same rush when a new restaurant becomes the trend. Everyone wants to be seen there, even if they hate the food. Irrelevant. Boring scientists and those who want to be boring scientists. With boring messages and no sex. I ignore them all. So should you. Any data of substance is moving freely."

His hands came into view, hovering near his eyes. "The Trisulians. I found additional proof of their infamy, of their plot against the Frow. Revolting species, but if we eradicated species for their looks, where would you Humans be, hmm?

"I gave this to the Sinzi. Fy asked my help in deciphering messages intercepted after the Frow were safe. The Trisulians are resentful beings. They blame the Sinzi, not themselves."

Beads formed on his eyelids. "There have been those who answer, privately, secretly. Only I could have found them. Words of fear. What do we know beyond the systems connected by the transects? How do we know the Sinzi aren't able to travel beyond those limits? What if we are trapped, not freed, by the transects?"

His hands flattened over his eyes. "Words of distrust. That the Myrokynay and their history are an invention, that the Sinzi are the Ro, that the unseen walkers are simply more new technology they haven't shared; that the Dhryn are the Sinzi's pawns and always have been."

Fourteen's hands moved away. His tiny eyes glistened. His mouth worked. "Words, Mac, from only a few. But now the Sinzi produce a new kind of Dhryn and permit a Progenitor ship to join us here. The Ro couldn't have done better themselves. For many, it's a thin line between admiration and envy. There should be no denying the *strobis* of the Sinzi. Idiots.

"We cannot survive the loss of the Sinzi. Yet we may be their destruction.

"In this dark time, I have the comfort of my life's love, Mac, and I thank you for that. Look after Charlie.

"I fear for us all."

The image fragmented back to the list of harmless messages.

Mac closed the 'screen, surprised her hand was steady. *Surprised her plate held green-and-yellow vegetables.*

Surprised to be sitting still when everything inside screamed in denial.

"We have to warn the Sinzi," she told Mudge.

His head was half bent, his eyes shadowed and fixed on her. "To what purpose? They have no weapons, no fleet of warships. Their protection from the

Ro was in being scattered. One, maybe two per system; a homeworld that's little more than a stopover; the rest in perpetual transit. The Sinzi will be helpless if the IU turns on them."

"And without them, the transects will fail."

"There are those who might consider that the only way out—safety in isolation." His palm turned over on the table to rest open and empty.

Mac's lips tightened. "Until they discover the Ro are real after all."

A miserable *harrumph*. "Norcoast . . . what if . . ."

"Don't say it, Oversight." She reached out with both hands to take and hold his. "Don't think it. Trust me. I know the Ro are real. I've seen one—felt its voice burn inside me. Emily has, too."

His free hand came down on hers, pressing gently. "Then we must find one to show everyone else."

The corridor lighting was midday bright. There was a gentle breeze laced with cinnamon and no crush of impatient archaeologists to block it. The temperature, Human perfect, was doubtless set to keep the crew comfortable, regardless of activity. The *Annapolis Joy* was putting on her best inside face.

A shiver coursed down Mac's spine, raising gooseflesh on her real arm. *Could cut the tension with a knife,* she noted as she walked toward the Sinzi's quarters. She knew her reasons and it wasn't hard to guess why the crew she passed failed to smile. *Battle stations, then a Progenitor ship for a neighbor might do it.*

She didn't want to know why the Grimnoii ahead were standing in a clump in the midst of the corridor, instead of standing at attention by the Sinzi's door.

But she had to know. "Rumnor," she greeted, making sure to smile as she approached. "Anyone home?"

"Mac." For once, only he replied. The other three, Fy-Alpha and -Beta, plus another of Ureif's, continued to pace. *Pace wasn't the right word,* Mac decided, noticing the Grimnoii weren't picking up their feet, but rather slid each one forward in turn. *Slow-motion skating?*

They were polishing a circle in the already gleaming floor, but otherwise she couldn't see the point. She looked back at Rumnor.

"Sinzi-ra Fy is 'home,'" he answered, his expression more doleful than usual. "Ureif is—" He stopped.

"Ureif is . . . ?" she prompted.

The others halted, turning as one to look at her.

They'd always been large and carried more weapons than they had hands to use, but she'd never viewed Grimnoii as menacing. *Gloomy bears with allergies who drank too much, yes.*

Mac changed her mind. There was nothing but menace in their present posture and attention. Nothing but the clearest possible signal even to an alien that the wrong move or word would precipitate something she was unprepared to face.

The Sinzi's door opened. *Monitoring the hall?* Mac thought, inclined to be grateful. "Mac," Fy said, beckoning her within. "I am pleased to see you. Come in."

"Gotta go," Mac told the Grimnoii, walking confidently, if quickly, past.

When the door closed, she let out a relieved breath. "Thank you, Fy. The Grimnoii seem a little—tense—today."

"They have withdrawn their service." Fy touched fingers to shoulders—*mild distress.* "Now they protest."

The polished floor . . . *they wiped the Sinzi's scent away.* Mac sank into the nearest jelly-chair. "The Dhryn."

Fy took another chair, her fingers restless. "How can they not appreciate the congruence, Mac? Is it not the most obvious of joys? Do you not feel it?"

How could the Dhryn not know a Human needed water . . .

At least this Sinzi asked the question. "I can understand that a Sinzi would be affected by this Dhryn," Mac said, careful of every word and its impact on the mind behind those glittering eyes. *Minds.* "I've had practice. But I also understand why the Grimnoii protest. They are—concerned—that Sinzi enthusiasm here means less for the goal of protecting the IU and its species."

"Why?"

"I'm not qualified to explain it," she hedged.

"I have no other!" Fingers flashed, rings sliding like a river of gold and silver. "Consider me your student. Do your best."

"We're both in trouble," Mac muttered, then pursed her lips in thought. Her student was an engineer and an historian who studied technology. *Perhaps if she tried something surely familiar to both.*

Mac climbed from the chair to kneel in the sand before the Sinzi. She swept a patch flat with her hand, then drew a straight line in it. "The Grimnoii." She drew a second line, parallel to the first. "Humans." She drew three more then stopped. "The IU. What do you see?"

"I see failure," Fy said cooperatively. "Isolation. Stagnation."

Mac added an arrow to each of the lines, all at the same end. "And now?"

"Directionality. Purpose. But isolation and stagnation remain." A fingertip came down, as if the drawing were irresistible, and drew a complex spiral that crossed all the lines, then met itself. Fy withdrew her finger. "There. Complex, interwoven, interdependent. Is this not better?"

"That's not the question." Mac drew another straight line outside the rest, adding an arrow. "You must remember the components. The IU is made up of cultures who view their progress as linear and isolated, who appreciate the role of the Sinzi and Sinzi technology, but as aids to one thing." She drove a thick, deep furrow through the complex spiral, putting an arrow at the end. "Survival. Together, or apart."

Fy pulled herself back as if the line were threatening, then leaned forward again. Two fingers explored the air above the drawing. "Remarkable. But if true, we are fundamentally different in our understandings and approach. How do we ever communicate properly?"

The mild complaint made Mac smile. "We keep trying," she said. "It's easier when dealing with similar goals. Biology's helpful that way—living things have a great deal in common."

"Technology also." Fy nodded. "There are rarely protests against physics."

She'd fit in at Base. Mac laughed, returning to her seat. "So you get my point?"

"We shall see." The Sinzi tilted her head one way, then the other, as if her two minds considered Mac separately. Then she straightened. "The Grimnoii see Ureif's support of this Dhryn and the Progenitor ship as an indication that all Sinzi could move away from their—direction." Fy touched the heavy line. "They fear we make a different choice. That we would abandon them, in favor of the Dhryn."

Mac was impressed. "And not return. There would be no circularity."

The Sinzi shuddered, rings glinting. "No future. They must be so afraid." Her voice rose. "I must share this with Ureif."

Who probably knows and moves ahead anyway, Mac told herself, *gripped by the tighter connection, perhaps believing he sees the right course.* "He was Sinzi-ra to the Dhryn, Fy."

"He bound himself to your promise," Fy said, as if Mac should realize this by now. "It takes precedence. We must preserve the Interspecies Union."

Her head hurt. "That's part of my promise?"

"How will you get home if the transects fail?"

As this was a question she tried to avoid on the principle of there being no good answer, Mac let it go. "There's another problem, Fy." She took a deep breath and plunged. "It's come to my attention—" *there was a good euphemism for having a code-breaking, moral-free Myg in your pocket* "—that some within the IU believe—it's ridiculous, of course—but rumors spread. What I mean is, some believe the Sinzi are—" Mac stopped, staring at the graceful being across from her. *She couldn't say it.*

"They believe we are the Myrokynay?" Fy's fingers shivered in a Sinzi laugh. "Ah! I am learning your face, Mac. It opens like a flower when I surprise you."

Mac shook her head ruefully. "Consider me in bloom. You knew?" *Had Fourteen sent his message to the Sinzi as well?*

"The site at Hift has been the focus of debate and controversy long before I began to work on it, Mac. Some groups claim we found the inspiration for no-space technology elsewhere, moving it to Hift to hide other discoveries. Others claim there was no ancient technology to be found, that we planted clues to cover the theft of vital components from other species." A dismissive gesture. "And, yes, there have always been those who say we are the Myrokynay's descendants, that Hift was a long-lost outpost rediscovered. How else would we have known where to look? And so forth. My work, in part, laid those claims to rest. The devices at Hift were made of materials previously unknown to Sinzi."

"But they are materials used by the Ro?"

"That remains in question," Fy replied with an almost Human shrug. "We have had none to compare. The Chasm transect stations were replaced before this was a priority. I await an opportunity to examine samples from the ocean floor of Myriam."

Mac chewed her lower lip, then nodded. "I think there's something closer."

"No."

"That was pretty quick. You could at least think it over."

Darcy Townee snorted. "What I think, Dr. Connor, is that you should have had enough shuttle rides for one lifetime. And realized our current situation means no travel, no exceptions."

Fy rested a fingertip on Mac's shoulder. They'd contacted the consular hangar deck, to find they'd need the captain's authorization to release the Sinzi's tiny ship. The next step had been a trip to the bridge, only to find Gillis tied up in a meeting. *Probably looking at them through the wall right now,* Mac thought with irritation.

"Surely I may be permitted to take out my dart? I should inspect the transect station."

Among other things. The Sinzi-ra had been galvanized by Mac's suggestion she investigate the construction of the Progenitor's ship, so conveniently nearby.

Not that they had to specify all their stops.

Or all their reasons.

"That's not up to me, Sinzi-ra. I'm very sorry."

"Then get him." Mac pointed to the wall.

Townee gave her a very strange look. "I beg your pardon, Dr. Connor?"

"You heard me." She took a step and wrapped her hand around the tree trunk, not for support but as warning she was prepared to hold on and stay. "You're interfering with the business of the Sinzi-ra of Myriam. We're not leaving until you release the Sinzi-ra's dart, or get Captain Gillis in here to do so."

Standing beside her, Fy let her fingers swoop around in a gesture that, while impressive, Mac was reasonably sure meant nothing in particular. *Quick study.*

Townee, confronted by insubordinate behavior on her own bridge, by individuals she couldn't do more than sputter at, turned a dusky red. *Mudge could do it better,* Mac thought rather cheerfully.

They should have stopped by his quarters to collect him. *Nothing like officious moral support.*

"Dr. Connor. We are at alert. I will have you removed."

Mac tightened her grip, the artificial fingers indenting the bark. "You can try," she offered politely.

"My money's on the biologist."

She reacted to that voice before she named it, her heart thudding helplessly in her chest. *Handy tree,* she thought, holding on for dear life.

Nikolai Trojanowski stood at the top of the stairs leading to the meeting room, within the opening left by its sliding door. Captain Gillis and Ureif were with him, as well as Cayhill.

They'd invited Cayhill and not her?

Mac's resentment vanished in a flash of understanding. Cayhill was supporting Nik, his arm around the other man's waist, his shoulder under Nik's arm.
He'd been hurt.

She could still feel it.

That was how they came down the three wide stairs. Slowly. So slowly she
had time to loosen each finger in turn, then walk forward to meet them.

"We wish to leave this ship," Fy insisted, having come along also.

Mac was close enough to see the amused look Nik gave her. "You do?"

Close enough to see the crusts of burns on his skin, the way his clothes hung
loose, how Cayhill was keeping him upright.

She stifled a cry behind her hand, eyes filling with tears. Nik said something she couldn't hear, pushing free of Cayhill to reach for her. She hurried to
take his weight, inhaling sweat, sickness, and pain as she pressed her cheek
against his. His hand cupped her head, then slipped. Warned, she held tighter.
"Cayhill!"

"I've got him. Here." They eased Nik to the floor, Mac going down first to
support his head and shoulders. "I warned you," Cayhill snapped furiously at no
one in particular. "Get a stretcher up here, stat."

"Is he dead?" This from Fy.

Mac ignored everything but Cayhill, kneeling beside Nik. "How bad is he?"

He gave her a quick look, then resumed going over his new patient. "Until I
do a scan and blood work, I won't know. Doubt he's slept in days. Signs of dehydration. Those burns—healed, maybe, but look like radiation. Stayed on his feet
by will, nothing more."

"Here." Mac held her hand over Nik's lower left rib, drew it up and over to
his right side. "He was hurt here. In a fight. About a week ago. I don't know the
weapon."

Cayhill opened Nik's shirt, giving a short grunt at what he saw. "I do. Hand-
held disrupter. Doesn't look too bad. More direct or prolonged, though . . ." He
looked at her. "How did you know?"

Because she remembered the pain as if it had been hers . . . "We've been in touch."

The stretcher arrived. Mac hovered nearby, finding it strange to watch the
smooth practiced motions of Cayhill and his orderlies from her feet, not her
back. *As Nik had watched when she'd come on board.*

No one spoke to her. There'd been a look or two. A whisper to the captain.
The Sinzi stood by, Fy silenced by confusion if nothing else. Mac didn't have
room for her now.

He looked . . . spent.

When the stretcher left the bridge, Mac followed.

As he'd followed.

No one tried to stop her.

By the time Nikolai Trojanowski opened his hazel eyes, Mac had spent a lazy eternity reminding herself of the strong lines of his jaw, the shadows below cheekbone and eyebrow, pooled in the hollow at the base of his throat. She'd already met the wound on his body, now washed and sealed with the rest of his scars.

Yummy.

By the time his eyes focused and puzzled at the ceiling, she'd adjusted the fine chain around his neck, with its paired rings. Each time, she'd practiced what she'd say when he awoke, and changed her mind as often. She'd flushed and paled and finally settled to content.

So by the time his head finally turned on the pillow and those hazel eyes found her, she just smiled. "Took you long enough. Trust Cayhill." The physician hadn't asked anyone's permission before pumping Nik full of sedative as well as nutrients. *Crisis or no.*

But when Nik didn't smile, or speak, or do anything but look at her—his eyes like someone drowning—Mac understood. "I'm really here," she whispered. "I can prove it."

She took off her clothes. Careful of the tubes and healing wound, she slipped in beside him, and pressed her body along his. "There. I won't let go." She held him while he shook.

And held him after he stopped shaking.

Mac opened her eyes and found Nik looking down at her. "Took you long enough," he said, his hand resting flat and warm on her hip. His cracked lips twitched into a half smile. "I can't believe you got Cayhill to put me in your quarters."

"We've reached an understanding." His hand strayed and she frowned. "An understanding, Mr. Trojanowski, which included you resting."

That dimple.

"Define 'resting,' Dr. Connor."

She wanted nothing more than to stay like this, the door locked with them hidden inside, his arm, sleep-heavy, across her stomach. Mac admitted it, then drew her fingertips down the side of his face, smooth one way, catching in stubble the other. "No more rest," she said when Nik opened his eyes.

Their hazel darkened as he gazed at her. His arm lifted, but when she started to move away, it came down to hold her in place. "We need to talk," his breath warm on her cheek.

As meeting venues went, Mac thought, snuggling closer, *this had merit.* "Who starts?"

His hand captured hers; his fingers toyed with the rings she wore. "I see they made it." A question in his eyes.

She nodded. "And worked. Those three," she amended, touching the one exiled for safety to her artificial hand. "This—I'm guessing the Progenitor wanted a close look."

His expression could only be described as dumbfounded. "She imprinted a message?"

Mac winced. "Let's just say I appreciate Her situation."

A pause. "So you got most of what I wanted you to know."

And more. She tensed involuntarily.

"What's wrong?" A flash of concern. "Did the *lamnas* hurt you? Mac, I would never have tried them if I thought there was a risk."

Okay, a potential disadvantage to bed meetings. She made herself relax. "Have you ever received a *lamnas*?"

He shook his head slightly, his lips brushing her ear. *Distraction.* Mac wasn't entirely clear if that was a disadvantage or not. "Anchen and I practiced, but I couldn't make sense of what she tried to send me. I had to rely on her belief that another Human—you—would be able to detect words, if I concentrated on them."

If they hadn't been like this—the dim light, huddled together under a sheet— Mac might not have said it. *Not without a few beers.* But Nik deserved to know. "To be honest," she said, "your messages weren't just words."

His turn to tense, which under other circumstances she would have found intriguing. "What do you mean?"

"I—felt—what you were feeling."

"Oh." His lips curved beside her eye. "I suppose that explains the lack of small talk, even from you." His hand rose to cup her breast in its warmth. "I can't say I mind."

"Not just those feelings," she clarified. "And not just feelings. I received memories. Your memories. As if I'd been there. Been you."

He might have turned to stone. Mac pulled away reluctantly, sitting up and crossing one leg beneath so she could look at him. Nik's stricken expression as he stared back was more than she could bear. "It's okay," she said, feeling clumsy. "No one else knows."

"Anchen—she didn't say anything about memories."

Mac didn't flinch from the growing outrage on his face. *She'd feel the same.* "How could she know what would happen between Humans? And how do we know she'd make that distinction at all?" *Words, feelings, memories—what had to pass between the individuals inhabiting one body?*

Nik sat up, ripping free the tubing that had somehow stayed in place. *Not for want of trying,* Mac thought, tempted to smile despite everything else. "What memories?" he demanded harshly, eyes dark.

Anyone else, she'd doubt. Anyone else would recoil from her, from such exposure.

"Your worst," Mac admitted without fear. "At a guess."

"Oh." His face paled and she watched him swallow. "And you still . . ." A hand waved vaguely at the bed.

She frowned. "Why wouldn't I?"

"Gods, Mac." Nik took her in his arms, pressing his lips to her forehead before burying his face in the hollow where her neck met her shoulder.

The man was in a weakened state. She put up with it for another thirty seconds, then tapped him on the back. "Saving the known universe?"

Nik lifted his head, his anguished expression wiping whatever else she might have said from her mind. "We have to talk about this," he stated. "All of it. I have to explain—"

From somewhere, Mac found the strength to deny him. "Later," she promised, very gently. "If we live that long. If it still matters." Before he could argue, she tightened her arms around him once, then stood. "Right now, there's someone the Progenitor needs to meet."

"She isn't here."

Mac blinked. "I saw the ship—"

"A negotiated sacrifice." Nik eased his legs over the side of the bed, wincing only slightly. His hand rested on his stomach, where Cayhill had applied memskin over the almost-healed but tender wound. *Habit,* Mac decided, well able to imagine trying to get medical help from the Dhryn.

There must have been others. "Who else survived?" she asked, feeling guilty not to have given the rest of his companions a thought. Then what he'd said sank in. " 'Negotiated sacrifice?' "

The corner of his mouth deepened. "We came out better than expected. The *Impeci* 's crew of five made it, as well as the research staff other than Genny P'tool. A bit worn, but nothing worse. The Progenitor broke from hiding to come to us; we docked and so escaped most of the radiation. As for the sacrifice?" He shook his head. "I wouldn't have believed it, Mac. Another Progenitor had taken shelter in the same system. Both were starving. They discussed the situation through their Vessels and the other—well, I don't know what argument was used, but all the Dhryn, including the Progenitor, from the other ship agreed to be consumed in order for our Progenitor to survive."

Mac tilted her head. " 'Our' Progenitor?"

Nik looked up at her, his eyes like transparent green glass. "I learned a few truths myself." He rose to his feet with almost his usual grace. "I've come in the empty ship, with a skeleton Dhryn crew, to act as Her Vessel." He paused. "Skeleton crew. There's truth for you. How long can they fast? I never saw one eat. They were skin on bone, Mac. Haven Dhryn. None spoke Instella—whenever one looked my way I'd say *lamisah* and hope for the best."

Mac fastened on what caught her attention. "You're Her Vessel? What happened to the Dhryn Vessel?"

"He disappeared the second day we were on board," his face grim and set. "Along with all the Dhryn not directly engaged in operating Her ship. There was no explanation."

"No need." Mac wasn't sure if what she felt was sympathy for the being who had been Parymn Ne Sa Las, or admiration for Dhryn communal will to survive. *Likely both.* "She told me." She held up her hand and touched the fourth *lamnas.* "The Progenitor's running out of time."

Nik looked stunned, but didn't ask. *Just as well,* Mac thought. "That's why I'm here. She sent me to prepare the way. She's following, to meet with the IU and negotiate a truce through the Sinzi. While we rested, Ureif's been setting up the protocols."

"We need a shower," Mac announced bluntly. "Now." She took his arm in a firm grip and pulled him into the stall with her, turning on the sprays. Once sure they were surrounded by the noise of water, she burst out: "Are you trying to destroy the IU? To ruin any credibility the Sinzi have? Because you couldn't have found a better way to—" The rest was smothered by his mouth.

When the wet, passionate kiss ended—*too soon and not soon enough, under the circumstances*—Nik held her close. She felt his sigh. "There's risk on all sides, Mac. But you said it. She doesn't have much time left. None of the Dhryn do. And we need them to defeat the Ro."

Brain damage? Mac considered it, as well as the option of having Nik sedated. "The Dhryn are the Ro's weapon," she pointed out.

"A weapon that almost destroyed them."

She shut off the water. They stood toe-to-toe, dripping in unison, Nik waiting for her to speak. *Which might take a while,* Mac thought wildly.

As if sensing this, he reached out and plucked a towel from the rack. "Our Progenitor sent Brymn Las looking for an answer." He began drying her off, starting with her hair. "What is the minimum genetic diversity required in a population to respond to evolutionary stress? Could this number be predicted for a species? He discovered your work on evolutionary units in salmon. Which, Dr. Connor," the towel progressed downward, "I found riveting reading, given our situation."

Just her luck, Mac grumbled to herself, *to be toweled by a handsome man in a shower and have* him *want to talk salmon.* "Brymn Las was worried about his people," she said, taking the towel and her turn drying him.

Thoroughly.

He put his hands against the tile behind her head as she worked, eyes warm. "That wasn't why his Progenitor asked the question, Mac. She wanted to know if they'd killed enough Ro in the Chasm to doom that species—to finally be safe from them."

Mac dropped the towel. "The Chasm?" she breathed, staring up at him.

"The Chasm. It's been the puzzle all along, Mac. The key to solving it isn't how, but why those worlds were laid waste." His smile was faint, but triumphant. "And that it happened twice."

"Twice." Now she let him hear her skepticism. "Why didn't the Origins Team—or any other—find a result like that?"

"There was nothing to find. The Ro used the Dhryn to wipe the life from those worlds, Mac. What happened next? The Progenitor had stories, legends, bits of information passed down from the three Progenitors who made it to Haven. Who were taken to Haven," he corrected, nothing warm or calm in his eyes now. "From these, and what She learned from Brymn Las and others—including what we told Her Vessel—She pieced together the rest. They were changed by the Ro, used by them to destroy other life in the Chasm, including their own homeworld. But there's more."

"Go on."

"Ro attention was fixed on those empty worlds—why, no Dhryn knew. The Dhryn were preoccupied themselves, desperate to find food for their now-starving Progenitors. Some broke the Ro conditioning. Whether they then real-ized what they'd been made to do and rebelled, or whether they were simply trying to survive—it doesn't matter now. The Dhryn attacked every world in the Chasm again, this time obliterating the Ro. Or so they thought."

"They were wrong."

"Yes. My guess is that some Ro were in their ships. All they had to do was wait for the Dhryn to turn on one another. Rather than lose such a useful tool," his voice had an edge, "they collected the last three Progenitors and took them to Haven, locking them into one system. The Dhryn could do nothing but breed and wait. The Progenitors kept their dreadful secrets from the new gener-ations, hoping they'd done so much damage to the Ro that they'd never return for them, always afraid they would. They did their best to forget. And almost succeeded."

The defense of ordinary Dhryn: "We do not think of it." Mac shivered. "The Ro did return. The IU even helped, giving the Dhryn access to the Naralax."

"Just what the Ro wanted. Only this time, when the Dhryn rebel, they'll have allies. The IU."

She frowned with concern. "Who else knows all this?" The question of his sanity she kept to herself.

"The Sinzi-ra, the captain, the Inner Council, the Ministry. The decision makers." Nik's fingers traced her jaw, lingered on her lips. She gave a startled protest as he turned on the shower. "No one needs us quite yet," he assured her, his voice low and husky. "You remember how dry a Dhryn ship can be, don't you?" He leaned his head back until water ran over his closed eyes and burned skin. It streamed from his chin and down his chest, glistening on his shoulders.

"Definitely yummy," Mac murmured, following the drops with her hands.

Good thing she'd locked the door.

- CONTACT -

"**L**OOK!"

"This may be a tedious and menial posting, but those are insufficient to excuse failure to fully utilize the excellent protocols established and prepared for our use." The seniormost Imrya relished this opportunity to elaborate in a meaningful yet sensitive manner appropriate to the youth and inexperience of her younger compatriot. "To properly request my attention," she began, "you must first—"

But her younger compatriot wasn't listening. Instead, his nostrils were pressed to the viewport. "Have you ever seen anything so glorious?" he gasped. "I must record this. I must write at least a stanza—no, I will surely dedicate the rest of my days to an epic work worthy of this moment, this spectacle, this—*oof*—"

The seniormost Imrya, notepad in hand and having successfully deposed her younger compatriot from the only viewport on this side of the station using her ample rump, settled in to see what was worth a life—such moments coming rarely even to a species devoted to the pursuit of literary perfection.

Slivers of light were converging on the Naralax gate, a region of space both infamous and lately well-explored by playwrights. Other traffic gave way, as was the custom when encountering a Sinzi courier dart.

But so many darts. They had been flowing in from other gates for weeks now. None had questioned their movement. Frankly, Imrya weren't roused to attention by the hasty, too-brief messaging of other species. Any news of import required, to their way of thinking, a minimum of ten thousand words to properly introduce the topic. Anything less simply couldn't matter.

Yet the flow of information represented by so many darts at once was on a scale to grab even an Imrya by the wattle. The beauty of the small, sleek ships. The way they followed one another, in perfect sync and sequence.

The seniormost scribbled down adjectives as quickly as she could, hearing her younger compatriot vainly attempting to do the same.

Neither bothered to wonder where the darts were going.

That which is Dhryn must make the Great Journey.

That which is Dhryn must *move*. It is the Way.

As before, as before, as too many times, the Call is heard. Insistent . . . dominant . . . *demanding*.

That which is Dhryn resists . . . resists . . . then succumbs.

The Call is the only hope left.

INVESTIGATIONS AND INVASION

Mac might have locked the door to her quarters.
Didn't mean the universe would pay attention.

The com panel was flashing. Someone less patient was knocking. *There was probably mail on her imp marked "urgent!"*

Mac glanced at Nik as they dressed and was oddly comforted by his wry grin. "It's probably Oversight," she warned, smiling back.

He pointed to the abandoned tube on the bed. "My money's on Cayhill." He closed the neck fastener of the pale green crew fatigues left for him, then deftly checked its pockets, pulling out to show her, in order, an ident chip, an imp, and one of the palm weapons she'd last seen him use on Earth. At her look, he grinned. "I always leave spares behind."

She reached into hers and brought out imp, nutrient bars, and the little salmon. "I take mine with me."

The knocking, now more like hammering, stopped for a moment, then resumed. *Given there was no shipwide alarm, whoever it was could wait.*

"Speaking of Cayhill," she bent to pull on her shoes, "how do you feel?" This with a twinge of guilt. Somehow she doubted the physician had included certain activities as part of her promise to look after his patient. *Though she could testify that the patient was fully functional.*

"Afraid."

The word, however matter-of-fact his voice, made her look up in surprise. "Of Cayhill?" *This seemed unlikely.*

His face showed unfamiliar strain. "Of waking up in a few minutes. Of finding none of this was real. I know that's ridiculous."

Still shaky, despite the bravado. "If I were you," Mac replied lightly, "I'd be more afraid of Cayhill. You're likely to be grilled on our time together."

"And me not at my best." *That wicked dimple.*

Mac raised a noncommittal eyebrow. "I've no complaints."

With a laugh, Nik captured her hand and brought it quickly to his lips. "When you've had my best, love, you'll know the difference. Trust me."

She felt the rush of heat in her cheeks, and elsewhere. Words failed her. *Banter like this was Emily's turf.*

Nik reacted at once. He knelt, still holding her right hand and collecting her left, all amusement gone from his face. "Mac—" The hammering intensified. Nik sent the door a baleful look, then turned back to her. "I didn't mean—damn it, Mac, you know what happened was—" He stopped there.

Had words failed him, too?

Mac almost smiled. "I know," she told him, turning her hands to hold his. Then she did smile. "You do realize, Mr. Trojanowski, that as a scientist I can't accept any hypothesis without thorough experimentation."

His smile was every bit as wide as hers. "Of course, Dr. Connor."

The door actually creaked. "I'd better get that," Mac said. She had to tug her hands free and pretended to scowl at Nik. *Who didn't look the least repentant.*

Mac opened the door. "What is it, Over—" She stopped and stared at Rumnor. The Grimnoii tucked his—*yes, he'd been using a hammer*—into its sling and bowed slightly.

"The Sinzi-ra requests you attend Her Excellence, the Progenitor." As Nik came to stand by Mac's shoulder, the alien blinked slowly, yellow crystals raining on the floor. "Both of you."

"She's arrived?"

Wrong Dhryn. "In a sense," Mac cautioned, relieved to see at least one of the Grimnoii had returned to the Sinzi's service. *Or was spying.* She disliked the notion; she didn't avoid it. "The Progenitor has recently undergone metamorphosis. Remember?"

They hadn't had time for much more conversation, but she'd made sure Nik knew about the Wasted and the corpse of the Ro walker. Captain Gillis had provided him with a somewhat skewed version of the entire business. She'd eventually need to add all the details—*given Gillis hadn't thought to mention her being on the* Uosanah *in the first place*—but at least the Ministry's man on the spot was aware of the players.

And had no reason to berate her for taking risks. *There were,* Mac decided, *distinct benefits to being anonymously foolhardy.*

"Ah, yes," Nik said smoothly. "Please tell the Sinzi-ra we'll be there shortly. We're expected at the remains first, you see. To provide final identification." He pronounced this last with such intense melodrama it was all Mac could do not to react.

Rumnor seemed to find the emphasis convincing, for he nodded and left without argument.

"'Final identification?'" Mac asked, once the alien disappeared down the ladderway.

"Even modern, space-faring Grimnoii follow tradition," her companion informed her. "The perished must be named in order to rest. Those who could identify the dead are not impeded in any way." His expression turned grim. "And I want to see the enemy."

"It's a walker, not a Ro." Mac made a face. "What's left of it."

"You've seen it?" Nik raised a rakishly singed eyebrow. "Do you know where it's kept?"

"Yes. Wait. The com was flashing. Let me check. I'm trying to be better about messages." Mac slipped back into her quarters—*funny how pleasant memories warmed a room*—then pressed the button.

It was a sequence of voice messages: Mudge, Cayhill, Mudge, Cayhill, Cayhill, Mudge, and so forth. A nice "hope you feel better soon, Nik" from Court, whom she guessed knew the spy from his earlier sojourns aboard. More Mudge, Cayhill. Both men sounded terse, as if they suspected why they weren't being answered but hoped she didn't know they knew and so would answer her com regardless.

Nothing more urgent. Mac recorded a quick "we're heading out" reply to any and all, then rejoined Nik in the corridor.

"Not that way," he said when she started toward the ladderway. "Through here." He indicated the door through the bulkhead to the rest of the ship.

"We're not allowed—" she objected, then watched him key in the door code. "Okay, I'm not allowed."

Her spy grinned. "After you, Dr. Connor."

Captain Gillis' accommodating crew had done a superb job of transporting the Origins Team, despite the quirks that came with archaeologists. They'd risen to the occasion when more aliens were added to the mix, and relished the challenge when one of those aliens turned out to be a Flowering Dhryn. No requirement had seemed too great, not even the need for more rooms and a private hangar for the new Interspecies Consulate on board.

But they must have been hard-pressed to find secure autopsy space for the Ro walker. Mac surveyed the result with some dismay. *No way around it*. It was a tent, tucked against one wall of the Sinzi's hangar. "This was the best they could do?" she asked the nearest of five guards stationed between the cable supports.

He shrugged. "Handy to the scientists' transports, Dr. Connor."

In her experience, convenience for scientists was a secondary motivation. "And they don't have to be escorted through the *Joy*," she guessed.

A flash of teeth, but a carefully neutral, "I wouldn't know about that, Dr. Connor."

Nik was heading for the open flap, so Mac nodded good-bye to the guard and followed.

To be fair, it was quite a tent. Mac was inclined to envy. Beyond the flap was a nicely rigid doorframe, complete with transparent door. Through it, she could see what appeared to be a well-lit metal cage, its upper surface head-high. Nik produced some kind of ident to wave at the guard at the door, gesturing her to follow as he passed that barrier.

Mac made clucking noises with her tongue, then took a deep breath and followed.

If an intent focus and the carrying of small, blinking instruments were the hallmarks of scientists, then the inside of the tent was packed with them. Otherwise, there was nothing to distinguish this group from one of Anchen's outdoor gatherings. *Less ventilation.* Mac wrinkled her nose, attempting not to breathe through it.

The cage wasn't to keep something in—*not that she'd any doubt the corpse was exactly that*—but an all-species' access mechanism. Frow clambered across the top. Something for which Mac had no name was fastened to a horizontal bar by curved teeth, its trio of tentacles poking through at the stiffened black remains suspended within the cage. Mac quickly moved her eyes from the corpse. While underneath? She bent over to watch a Nerban on its back, working with apparent comfort, a face shield protecting its proboscis from drips.

Group insanity or interspecies' efficiency. She hadn't made up her mind.

Nik had stopped, his eyes wide with shock as he stared at the walker. *There hadn't been any way to prepare him,* Mac thought sympathetically. At least he didn't look about to vomit. She had a feeling his default ran more to fight than flight.

Not that there was anything wrong with flight.

Especially from a nightmare.

"Mac!" Fy came forward from where she'd been in conversation with a heavier-than-most Imrya, moving through the crowd with that unexpected speed. "I am pleased you are here. I have made the most remarkable discovery with the help of these fine—ah." This as she noticed Nik. "You have improved."

Nik bowed, almost as gracefully as a Sinzi. "Greetings, Sinzi-ra. My name is—"

"You are Nikolai." Fy brought her fingers up to form rings in front of her great eyes. "My apologies for not recognizing you sooner. I participate in your promise as I do in Mac's."

"Mac's?" Nik turned his head to give her a look that could best be described as appalled. *Answering the question of whether he knew what a Sinzi promise meant.*

Mac replied with a helpless shrug.

Aliens.

"Your discovery, Fy?" she asked brightly.

Fy launched herself back to a console beside the cage, leaving the two Humans to make their way through the cluster of researchers. As they did, Nik whispered urgently: "You made a promise with Anchen? Do you have any idea of the possible consequences?"

"You did it first," she shot back.

"I—" He closed his mouth but not, she was sure, because he didn't have more to say on the subject.

"Here, Mac. Nikolai. See?" Fy's delicate fingers were wrapped around a grotesque serrated hook, about the size of Mac's forearm. The dull black of its surface was scored by regular holes. *Sample cores,* she realized, even as a more primitive part of her mind gibbered at her to either throw up or run, whichever reaction came first. *Simultaneous might work.*

Instead, Mac reached back until her fingers found Nik's wrist. "What did you find?" Her voice sounded normal, given the background of alto grunts and tenor mutters, but she felt his hand cover hers.

"Remember our discussion—concerning the Hift artifacts? This—" a triumphant wave of the hook came close to landing on Mac's nose, "—this is of the same material!"

"It's a machine?" This quick and sharp from Nik. "Some kind of construct?"

"Machine, no." The Nerban now with Fy spoke up. His long eyelid was opened to its maximum to admit more light in the—to his kind—dim room. The eye itself lay hidden deep within the revealed cavity. Mac didn't know their features well enough to be sure if this was the individual from the meeting. *The silver-and-emerald bangle circling his proboscis was new.*

"Construct? Most definitely. The biological portion consists of conjoined body parts, no two of which came from the same source organism. Despite this, there appears an underlying logic to the result. The sum did have life, as the IU defines it. The technology, the tools, were melded into the flesh. If only it hadn't been so damaged, we'd know more."

And she'd be dead. Mac shuddered and let go of Nik. "Have you compared this one to the one found on Earth?" she asked. The man beside her stiffened in shock. *Right. Full briefing overdue.* "Buried by the earthquake," she told him quickly. "The Ro used the landslide to cover the tracks of whatever they put into the ocean. Em's on its trail." *News at six,* she thought inanely.

"Yes," the Nerban said. "The components are identical."

She'd expected a match. That didn't make it any more pleasant. Mac closed her eyes for an instant. *One of those things had been on Earth, on the slopes of Castle Inlet.*

How many more?

"Have you identified any of the components?" Nik asked. "The organisms."

"Others are working on that. It will be difficult. The genetic material is severely distorted. Mutations, damage, manipulation at the molecular level. For now, all I can say is we've found no match to existing species within the IU, but—"

"There she is!"

Mac hunched her shoulders, somehow knowing that shout boded nothing good.

The shout announced the Trisulian who surged through the rest. This one was wrapped in red leather but with a belt of scanning equipment and probes instead of a weapon. *Not pregnant,* Mac noted, belatedly counting only two eyestalks. Female. *And going to stay that way.* "You," the alien continued without pause. "You are Mr. Mac, Mr. Connor. I have a question."

Quiet spread outward from their little group. *She hated it when that happened.* Having no other option, Mac nodded. "What is it?"

"There are inexplicable marks." The Trisulian lifted the black limb she carried. "Here. And here."

Were they cutting off souvenirs?

Somehow, Mac kept her feet from moving backward and made herself examine the limb. Easy to see what had puzzled the Trisulian. "Oh. Those are mine." Without touching the limb, she held her left hand over the marks, spreading her fingers and thumb to show how each fit into one of the indentations. "It's a prosthesis," she said, wiggling the fingers in case the aliens mistook Human strength. "I was in a bit of a hurry."

"In a— What the—" Nik switched to English for a few choice and impassioned phrases before recovering to think of their audience. "Mac? You were there? On that ship?"

"You could say that," Mac hedged.

"Alone, Mr. Mac captured it. At great risk to herself."

Nik's response to this was thankfully lost as the Frow from atop the cage structure chose this moment to plunge almost to the floor. "You will treat Dr. Connor with the respect due her rank!" he shouted at Nik. Then he noticed the Trisulian and snapped his membranes threateningly. "How dare you approach Dr. Connor! How dare you be in this room! How dare you be on this ship!"

The Trisulian cowered behind her share of corpse, the Frow kept shouting—*the Nerban sweating*—while other aliens either paid rapt attention, ignored the fracas completely, or began to edge to the exit, all in their own unique ways.

Mac shook her head at Nik. "You could have waited," she mouthed.

He said something she couldn't hear over the din—*probably just as well*—then jerked his thumb at the door. She nodded.

Time to find somewhere else to cause an uproar.

"This is a closet."

"I know."

Mac put her back to a convenient shelf and sniffed. *Cleansers, even in space.* "Why are we in a closet?"

Nik had taken her by the hand—her real one—and marched her into the nearest corridor from the hangar, along it past several doors identical to this one, then in here. *He knew the layout of the ship remarkably well,* she decided.

Or it was a spy thing. The ability to hunt out closets. Doubtless useful.

"Ureif's waiting for us," she commented.

"I know that, too." Nik stood in front of the now-closed closet door, close enough to touch. He'd tried to cross his arms, but had winced and left them at his sides. She guessed his wounded abdomen didn't appreciate the pressure. Now he leaned his shoulders against the door. "You've been busy, Dr. Connor. Care to save me finding out in bits and pieces?"

Not accusing, she judged. *Truly curious.* And there were things he should be told. "How do you want it? The abridged 'things I want you to know' or the really long 'it's too late to argue with me even if you could' version?"

"How about the 'I trust you' version." *Almost that dimple.*

Ah. Mac fastened her eyes on his and began at the beginning, with Emily.

Nik was more than a patient listener, he had that rare talent of drawing confidences from others. *Handy in a spy*. She'd noticed that about him before. He became absorbed, as if he processed every word. She could see it now, in how the hazel of his eyes responded, growing darker or lighter, and in the expressive lines of his mouth.

Those lines had settled into conviction by the time Mac finished.

"Emily keeps repeating 'eleven,'" Nik echoed in a low voice, eyes hooded. "Could it be that simple?"

She stared at him. "It means something to you?"

"Maybe." Nik frowned in thought. "We've wondered all along—why so few attacks? Why no more? It's not the Dhryn's choice. The Progenitors starve waiting for the Ro to 'call' them to feed. Why the delay?"

"Not because we've scared them," she said bluntly. "Not because we can stop them."

"The Ro do seem to hold all the cards." Nik lifted his head. The closet light caught fire in his eyes. *If she didn't know better, she'd swear he looked triumphant.* "Why would they let the Dhryn die now, after all they've done to start them in motion?"

"You expect me to explain the Ro?" Mac snorted, but Nik only raised a challenging eyebrow. *He was going someplace with this*, she realized. *Play along.* "The Dhryn are tools," she said slowly. "You discard a tool once you finish a job. Or if you find a better one. Or if it's defective," she added, remembering a certain unloved power screwdriver and a cold, wet night trying to repair an autosampler. *The screwdriver had skipped perfectly over the waves.*

"Or you put it down, so you can pick up something else. After all, you only have two of these." Nik lifted his hands and wiggled the fingers at her.

"Your point being?"

"Assume the Ro aren't finished. What if they've put the Dhryn aside, not because they want to, or it's convenient, but because there simply aren't enough Ro to be everywhere or do everything that's necessary to control them. Not enough hands, Mac."

He liked the idea. Mac chewed her lip, wanting to like it, too. But she'd learned caution the hard way. "Go on," she prompted.

"After I heard what the Progenitor had to say, about the Dhryn turning on the Ro in the Chasm, how close they'd come to defeating them—it dawned on me we could be dealing with the survivors of that battle. Emily said the Ro abandoned a planetary existence millennia ago." Nik reached out and took her by the arms, his eyes aglow. "Mac. Those survivors could be the last of them. I think that's what Emily discovered. What if she's been trying to tell us how many Ro are left?"

"Eleven?" Mac's hands tightened on his wrists. "Gods. That simple? Poor Em." *It made a terrible sense.* Through the confused and distorted memories, the well-meant efforts to cure her obsession, she'd clung to that one bit of vital information. She'd tried to tell them.

Without context, without Nik's new information about the Dhryn, it would have been for nothing.

He'd kept talking, the words staccato quick and sure. "The Ro paid no attention to us until the Progenitor began searching out the truth. When She rediscovered enough to be concerned the Ro could return, when She contacted a Human—you, Mac—that's when they took notice." Nik's voice turned grim. "They tried to identify and silence Her. One ship. Remember? Maybe . . . maybe one Ro. While the rest moved on to bigger things, directing the Dhryn against entire planets. One at a time. Why? Did one of them need to be there?" He looked distinctly annoyed, that familiar crease beside his eyes. "Too many damned questions."

She stood on tiptoe to kiss his nose. "So I'll add mine. Why did the Ro strip the oceans from the hundreds of worlds in the Chasm?"

Nik got that look. *The one she'd learned meant something she wasn't going to like.* "What is it?"

"Are you sure they did?"

Mac frowned. "It happened."

"Yes, but was it intentional? Think about it, Mac. The Dhryn kill the Ro on those worlds. Without the Ro, their no-space technology fails—technology they could have located deep underwater. And then?"

"I don't like where this is going, Nik."

"If the Ro lived or hid in oceans before, they could be doing it again." Nik's eyes burned into hers; she had the feeling he didn't see her at all, caught by nightmare. *She shared it.* Then his expression smoothed into what Mac thought of as his public face, his noncommittal, do-what-it-takes, face. *She wanted to shake him.* "What cost do you think the IU would be willing to bear," he asked in a light, pleasant, how-are-you voice, "if it meant the Dhryn destroyed the last of the Ro before dying themselves? To end both threats? Would they vote to accept the cost of a world?"

Not their world. "Not Earth," Mac heard herself say. She let go of him, backing into the shelf. *Half a step—small closet.*

"A backwater planet," Nikolai Trojanowski reminded her, implacable, cool. "A transportable, adaptable intelligent species. A small price, isn't it? If the IU can trap so much as one Ro there? Better yet, get them all? Save the transect system. Save themselves?"

Mac glared. "You aren't serious. Nik. You can't possibly—"

"'Where on that scale,' Dr. Connor. Remember?" His mouth twisted abruptly, his voice losing its calm. "Oh, the IU would owe humanity. Those who survived would be compensated, resettled. Our species would gain a seat on the Inner Council. A brand new world."

Salmon, surging into the air, water falling from their silvered sides. The great trees leaning overhead, green and gold and mossed with life. A slug, crawling toward the taste of sex and food.

The shivered cry of eagles.

"There is no other world," Mac said, knowing it was the truth.

Not for them.

Not for her.

"There's no other world," Nik agreed. He opened his arms. When she stepped into them, he put his lips to her ear. "We'll need another way."

Nik took them to the nearest communications station. Once there, he dropped his ident in front of the crew. Whatever it said, the three didn't hesitate, immediately standing and moving well back from their console, letting Nik take their place.

She could use one of those. Mac considered it, then changed her mind. She'd seen the cost of that kind of power. She waited, silent, while her spy composed several missives. *If anyone could send secrets, it would be this man.*

Those secrets sat inside her like a meal her body already regretted. *Hollans would get more than he bargained for,* Mac thought. Fact and speculation. The former might be scattered; the latter fit too well. *Neither were comforting.*

"I can't set up a give and go with Earth," Nik said abruptly. "Have you been having equipment problems?"

"Not at our end, sir," answered one of the crew. "But there've been sporadic delays with incoming packets for the past few hours. Sinzi-ra Myriam is monitoring the gate."

Nik swiveled the chair to look at the crew. "Outgoing?"

Two of them glanced at the third, a woman with specialist bars on her arm. "From our side, outgoing reads nominal, sir," she replied.

Even Mac could hear the unspoken doubt in her voice. Nik rose to his feet, every line of his body tense. "Traffic is moving through the gate?" he demanded.

"Of course, sir." All three looked astonished by the very idea. *They were lucky,* thought Mac, who wasn't. "But until the incoming rate returns to normal," the specialist pointed out, "we won't know if outgoing messages are being delayed as well."

"We'll notify you once the problem's rectified, sir. Shouldn't be long."

Nik nodded. "Thank you." He turned to Mac. "Shall we go meet your guest?" Warm smile, easy tone. If she didn't know better, she'd think it was an ordinary day and he was proposing to visit a mutual friend. *A Human chameleon,* she decided enviously. Anyone looking at Nik would think nothing was wrong with the world.

Anyone looking at her? Mac snorted. *She didn't need a mirror.* The crew they'd encountered in the corridor had given her second glances. *Worried ones.* These three had been no different.

"Let's go," she agreed.

The length of corridor leading back to the hangar and beyond turned out to be consular space, bustling with activity. *None of it Grimnoii,* Mac noted. They found the Wasted's luxurious new quarters without difficulty—just a little early.

Crew were still installing slanted false walls. *Humans only.* Mac hoped it was convenience. *It didn't bode well if only the Sinzi and Humans could bear to be near a Dhryn.*

The Progenitor, they were told, was still holding court in her room in the Origins corridor.

"They'd better hope she doesn't grow too big for the door first," Mac muttered to Nik as they retraced their steps. "Gillis won't be happy if they cut into a permanent wall."

Nik chuckled and took her hand. "Mikey's not so bad."

"'Mikey?'" She gave him a sidelong look. *Captain Gillis?* "Do I want to know?"

"We went to school together." Nik grinned at whatever he saw in her face. "What? Did you think I never went? I did, you know. Learned to read. Math. How to torment the new teacher. All that."

"I never thought of your life before all this—" Mac waved at the corridor. *Tactful as always,* she chided herself and tried to cover it. "Were you one of those daring kids whose parents came to know the principal?"

"Orphan."

Could she be worse at this? "I'm sor—"

He silenced her fumbling apology with a quick kiss, making her blush and gathering far too much interest from passing crew. "Doesn't matter. I wasn't old enough to know them. Mining accident took most of the adults that year. As for the principal?" Nik paused. "I managed to stay off his scanner."

They reached the door to the Origins upper level and he keyed in the code. "You do know I have brothers," she commented as they went through the door. "No staying off theirs."

An inscrutable look. "Should I be worried?"

"Not about Owen," Mac grinned. "Blake? Now he'll be—"

"Norcoast!"

Easier to face than a furious Mudge?

"Oversight," she greeted warily, taking in his decidedly rumpled appearance. "Been here long?" "Here" being outside the closed and locked door to her empty quarters.

"No. I've spent most of the last hour getting past those infernal Frow!"

Oh, dear. Mac winced. "I'll speak to them. This is—"

But Mudge had already transferred his glare to Nik, his entire body shaking with rage. "As for you, Mr. Trojanowski, I would expect a man of your responsibilities to not only appear in timely fashion at scheduled meetings but to have a care for others. Your treatment of Dr. Connor has been nothing short of appalling. Appalling!"

"You're absolutely right, Charles," Nik said solemnly.

Mac coughed. "Could we discuss this on the way, please?" *Or never?*

"On the—" Mudge sputtered.

"We're late, right?" she said, her eyes pleading, *not now.*

Mudge *harrumphed* fiercely, but subsided. "You were late," this with emphasis, "an hour ago."

"Then we'd best be going." Nik waited for Mudge to lead. Mudge gave a meaningful glare at the ladderway and stayed where he was.

Mac shook her head and walked past them both.

Probably the best approach with the Frow, anyway.

The Frow had wisely chosen discretion, perhaps remembering Mac's reaction to their previous Mudge-tossing escapade. Their presence was a mere shuffling in the distance, a glow of alert eyes. She waved as she stepped off the ladder at the lower level, as much to remind them she was watching while the others climbed down, as to say thanks.

The guards at the door were still crew. While steps away, Mac felt the touch of Nik's fingers on her wrist and stopped. "I'm not sure we should mention the other Dhryn," he told them both. "Not until we understand the dynamics better."

Mudge *harrumphed*. "Which would make perfect sense, except it's too late. While you were recuperating, Ureif made sure Her Glory was fully apprised of the situation. And myself." This last with a somewhat smug look. Mac could well imagine Mudge wearing down all authority in reach to find out what was happening.

"'Her Glory?'" She raised an eyebrow.

"We've been informed that's the appropriate address by a non-Dhryn."

"Haven Dhryn don't acknowledge the existence of non-Dhryn," she pointed out. "How could there be such a thing?"

"Makes sense," Nik countered. "The necessities of interacting with the IU. Sinzi-ra Ureif dealt with colonial Dhryn, true, but he would have needed to communicate with the Progenitors if only through their *erumisah*." He looked ahead to the guarded door. "I might as well pull what rank I have as the Vessel for—for the other Progenitor." He rubbed one hand over his chin thoughtfully. "Her Glory was a ship's captain, right? Brymn Las was a traveled scholar. Makes you wonder about the early experiences of the other Progenitors, doesn't it?"

"They're likely diverse individuals," Mudge agreed. "It could be difficult to predict their behavior, should they begin to act outside the influence of the Ro."

"Late, remember?" Mac rolled her eyes and started for the door. Her companions hastened to follow.

There'd been some effort to improve the Dhryn's temporary quarters. Another of the work area walls—*the one to her precious communication equipment*—had come down. The communication gear itself was no longer in sight. The floor was half sand, with a pair of jelly-chairs, the remainder a soft red carpeting. On the carpet was an immense padded chaise lounge affair, also red. From its proportions, it hadn't come from the *Joy*. The thing was propped to support its occupant.

An occupant who hooted with delight at the sight of Mac. *"Lamisah!"* shouted Her Glory. The floor underfoot thrummed with whatever else she said.

"Please don't move," Cayhill said, hovering over the recumbent alien. The Dhryn bristled with curved tubes, as if a clear spray was shooting from her body in all directions. *The other way around,* Mac realized, tracing the tubes back to where they connected to an apparatus. *Perfusion pump,* she grinned to herself. *Knew it.*

Ureif had risen from his chair, fingers flowing in a graceful welcome. His blood-red rings matched the carpet perfectly. *Nice touch,* Mac thought, although she was reasonably sure that "red" wasn't the color to the Sinzi it was to her eyes.

Nik acknowledged the Sinzi-ra, but his attention was fixed on the Dhryn. From his expression, he was every bit as amazed as she'd expected. He nodded to the physician. "Dr. Cayhill."

Cayhill ran his eyes over Nik and grunted. "I see you've recovered. When you get around to my messages, Mr. Trojanowski, do pay attention to the one listing your nutritional requirements." He turned back to his task.

"You look wonderful," Mac told the Dhryn, ignoring Cayhill. And she did seem the image of health, her blue skin almost fluorescent, the glow from her bands soft and steady. There seemed no further increase in size; perhaps growth occurred in spurts. *Must not help Gillis sleep better.*

"I feel wonderful! These are wonderful beings! All is wonderful!" Each "wonderful" was accompanied by a heave on the lounge, producing a fluttering of the tubes that sent Cayhill into frenzied action.

"You know you must keep still, *Lamisah,*" Mac said in Dhryn.

"Where's the fun in that?" One golden eye winked at her. Her Glory, no longer bouncing, switched back to Instella without effort. "He is a marvel, my *erumisah* Gordon Matthew Cayhill."

The voice, the phrasing, was warm and friendly. Confident. Even charming. *All things the Wasted hadn't been.* Somehow Mac doubted this personality had belonged to the former captain of the *Uosanah.* Here was a new individual, suited to lead her kind.

Or, at the moment, four Humans and a Sinzi. Mac turned to introduce Nik. He shook his head slightly and she closed her mouth, glancing at Mudge who looked equally puzzled.

Without a word, Nik walked up to the massive Dhryn and knelt near her head.

For her part, Her Glory looked as confused as Mac felt. She leaned forward as if studying Nik, her mouth slightly open, lips working as if she spoke without sound. Then she suddenly reared up, her handed arm coming up before her face, her other limbs tensed. Cayhill scrambled to corral the tubes. "I taste Her! I taste Her!" shouted the agitated Dhryn. "Where is She!?"

It seemed clear Nik was in imminent danger of attack—*the Dhryn could smash his skull with that arm,* Mac realized—but he remained motionless and in reach. When Mudge moved forward, she stopped him. "Nik knows what he's doing," she whispered. *Hopefully.*

"My Progenitor has sent me, Her Vessel," Nik said in Instella, calm and collected. "I am to speak with you on Her behalf."

"You are not-Dhryn." But she eased back down and lowered her hand. Cayhill growled something under his breath and shot Mac a dirty look as he hurried to reinstall now-dripping tubes.

How could this be her fault? Mac thought indignantly.

"These are unusual times."

A forlorn *hoot*. "As I am proof." A long pause, in which gold eyes met hazel. "Speak, then, Vessel."

She could almost feel the tension ease from Nik's shoulders. "My Progenitor would have me tell you of the Great Journey," he began. "How That Which Is Dhryn was perverted by the Ro. And how That Which Is Dhryn must follow the path of the truth."

Mac held her breath, waiting for the Dhryn's reaction, but Her Glory must have been made of sterner stuff than others of her kind. She merely said, "Go on."

"These things and more you should hear before my Progenitor joins us."

The glow from the bands around her torso pulsed with more intensity. *A display?* wondered Mac. "She returns to Haven?" asked the Dhryn.

Guess no one thought to correct that small confusion, Mac winced. But Nik didn't blink. "She'll be here soon," he answered smoothly.

In Dhryn. "Will She ask for my flesh?" The warmth was gone from Her Glory's voice. Mac felt the vibration through the floor, saw it shake the fountain spray of tubing. "I am younger, stronger. More fit, more deserving. That Which Is Dhryn must survive." Louder. "I will ask for Her flesh! My *lamisah* will be my Vessel. She will demand it!"

No doubt about it. That imperative finger was aimed her way. Mac sighed inwardly. *Salmon researcher. Would no one remember?*

"I can't be your Vessel—" she began.

"Why not? He claims to be one."

Mac's eyes narrowed. *Her Glory was as new to this as they were.* "Do you even know what a vessel is?"

That was a pout. "I know what a Vessel does—speak for a Progenitor. You must speak for me! She cannot have my flesh!"

Nik rose to his feet. "Don't be afraid," he said, making an accurate guess at what was going on. "My Progenitor means you no harm. She seeks a truce, a way for All That Is Dhryn to survive. She offers the truth."

"Why will he not speak Dhryn?" Her Glory asked with disdain.

She had a few choices here, thought Mac, *most of them complicated.* She'd learned not to trust complicated, when it came to aliens.

Mac stepped closer. "Because Her Vessel has good manners. It's rude to speak any language but Instella in the presence of other species." This, in Instella, as firmly as she'd ever chastised a student. "These fine beings will not take you seriously unless you behave to your station."

She was acutely aware of those fine beings, and how they were, each in his own way, staring at her in disbelief.

Her Glory, meanwhile, began to hoot. "Ah, my excellent Vessel," she said *in Instella*. "Again you guide my path correctly. I apologize to all. But—" her head bent to regard Nik, "—I remain of decided appetite."

To his credit, the Ministry's liaison with aliens bowed gracefully and took this strange comment in stride. "I will convey your words, of course."

"Tell me what I should hear," Her Glory requested, her small mouth smiling. "But first, *erumisah*? I crave something. Perhaps what you called grapes? And those delightful little leaves."

"I'll arrange it." Cayhill went to the com and barked orders, presumably to the crew now assigned to liquefying Her Glory's diet. He'd done a magnificent job so far. *Not that they had a reference,* Mac told herself. *For all they knew, she was supposed to have turned orange by now.*

"Sit, Vessel. Be comfortable, as I am. Is this not a wonderful seat?" Her Glory made a tiny bounce, smiling at Mac. "Is everything not wonderful?"

The door opened and Fy slipped in, her fingers tightly knotted. *Distress or other strong emotion,* Mac guessed, looking to Ureif for clues. His fingers hung still. *Too still. Distress, then.*

Not wonderful.

Ureif swept one of his Human-like bows to Her Glory. "Please excuse us. We must confer."

Mac looked to Nik; he nodded to the Sinzi. "Come on," she told Mudge, and led the way to the corner where the two aliens now swayed in earnest consultation, their voices too low to hear.

"—was anticipated," Ureif was saying. When the two Humans came close, he made a welcoming gesture. "Great news. The Progenitor's ship has come through the gate."

Timing was everything. Mac resisted the impulse to look over at Her Glory. "What's the situation?"

Fy's fingers moved restlessly, silver and gold jingling down their lengths. "There is discord. Ships are moving without authorization. A small number have aimed themselves at the gate, but wait. More from fear of the Dhryn than from respect for protocol. I fear a collision, should they not resume orderly behavior."

"Are any moving to open vectors?" This from Mudge, whose face was pale and set. "The Trisulians have a formidable ship."

"At my request," Ureif said very quietly, "Captain Gillis has repositioned our two ships within thirty minutes of the gate mouth. None are closer. We have asked the arriving Progenitor to station Her ship alongside, toward the gate."

"So they'll have to go through the *Joy* and the other Dhryn to reach Her." Mudge sounded quite pleased by this. "Or She can leave through the gate before any weaponsfire could catch up."

"Of greater importance," Ureif corrected gently, "all must come to meet Her

Glory here. It forms the most exquisite congruence." Both Sinzi swayed back and forth at this.

Mudge was pleased. The Sinzi were patently ecstatic.

Mac couldn't believe it. "Did you learn nothing from the Gathering?" she snapped. "You've made us into a single target!"

"We are in communication with the Progenitor," Fy soothed. "If there are any hostile acts, we will warn Her."

Who warns us? Mac kept that to herself. "How? I thought their ships didn't have IU technology."

Fy managed a fair approximation of a Human smile. *She'd been practicing,* Mac judged. "Ah, but remember this Progenitor's ship carries a Human craft in its hold. Nikolai's ship remains inside, crewed by his associates. Now that we are within the same system, this gives us the means to communicate."

Maybe she was wrong.

Mudge was studying her. He *harrumphed* uneasily. "What is it, Norcoast?"

Maybe she wasn't. Mac shivered.

"There's some problem with newspackets," she told him, feeling her skin crawl. "Incoming are delayed. We couldn't set up a dedicated exchange at all."

Fy touched her fingertips together. "There is a great deal of traffic. I am not the most experienced, Mac. I suspect a flaw in my scheduling. I have asked for assistance."

Mudge was still looking at Mac, eyebrows lowering in a frown. In the background, she could hear Nik's steady, calm voice as he kept briefing the Dhryn.

Did he feel it, too? That time was running out.

She backed a step away without thinking, needing space, her feet sinking in the sand. "Something's not right." She hadn't meant to say it out loud, but once she did, she believed it.

Nik was at her side in a heartbeat. She held up her hand to silence him, to silence them all.

She held her breath and closed her eyes to listen.

Nothing. The shift of sand under a long toe. The whisper of fabric. The steady thud of Cayhill's pump.

Okay, she was an idiot. Relieved, Mac smiled as she opened her eyes and turned toward Nik.

The ceiling fell.

Scurry, scurry.

Spit! POP!

- CONTACT -

GILLIS PATTED HIS TREE. It wasn't his, technically, having been a gift to the *Annapolis Joy* on her official launch. Some publicist's bright notion; a touch of the home planet heading to the stars. The little thing had outlived its day-of-launch purpose to become the ship's mascot. He was well aware its trimmings wound up in their own pots in crew quarters. They'd have a forest at this rate. He should look into some birds.

"Status, Darcy."

Townee glanced up from the scan console as the captain approached. "She's behaving."

"Amazing. Show me." Gillis sank into his chair, staring as the display revealed the massive bulk of not one, but two Dhryn Progenitor ships. He whistled through his teeth. "Ouch."

The new arrival was more intact than the first, but heat had melted and scored her prow into lumps of black slag. Proof, if they needed any, that this ship had been the focus of the Ro attack at Haven. Otherwise, her hull reflected white and silver wherever Myriam's sun reached, its curves and dips familiar to anyone who'd studied the images captured in Sol System. Every ship had been identical; this was another of the same.

"Sir. There's something strange going on with the gate."

"End display," Gillis ordered, blinking as normal lighting was restored. "What is it?"

"We had nominal to heavy packet traffic up to a moment ago, sir. Incoming from all over the IU. Now—the only incoming packets are from Sol," the tech said. "I can't explain it, sir. If I didn't know better—"

"Go on."

"It's as if the transect itself's been modified, sir. What could do that?"

This drew looks from around the bridge. *Anxious ones.*

Townee walked to the station to check the readings for herself. After a few seconds, she turned to nod at Gillis. "Confirmed. In fact, now the Sol packets are slowing to a trickle. Damnedest thing."

"Sir!" This from the system-tech, her voice raised but calm. "We have a shipwide mass shift. The grav generators are compensating but—"

The scan-tech broke in: "Something's just—appeared—on the hull. Out of nowhere. Another aft. Sir, we've multiple contacts. I repeat, multiple contacts on the hull."

"Battle stations," Gillis snapped, surging to his feet. "Now!" The alarms began wailing.

"We've breaches," the system-tech reported, her voice shaking. "Repeat, multiple hull breaches. Fields holding—"

Spit! POP!

A hot spray struck Gillis in the face. He scrubbed it from his eyes with a startled curse. He realized it was blood when the screaming began.

Scurry, scurry . . .

- 22 -

SHOCK AND SACRIFICE

HER GLORY HEAVED herself off the chaise lounge with a roar, the tubes snapping away. Their liquefied contents flew in every direction, to strike and stick in glistening lines against surfaces, moving surfaces, crawling surfaces.

So many . . .

Mac froze as forklike footprints scarred the sand before her. *Scurry, scurry . . .*

A weapon fired near her head. The Dhryn retched and spat. *Settling the question of whether the acidic spit came from the stomach or somewhere else,* Mac helplessly noticed.

Something died. Someone shouted.

Spit! POP!

Her arm. *Something had her by the arm.* She came to life, screaming and struggling. "Let go of me!!!"

"Mac! Come on!"

Scurry . . .

Nik. It was Nik. Mac shut up and tried to think past the terror. There were Ro walkers here. *Now was not the time to even think she'd told them so.* They were on the ship.

They were in the room. *So many . . .*

Some were dead, hulking masses of darkness, steaming with acid burns or flame. The Dhryn moved like a great blue-and-white panther, circling the huddled Humans and Sinzi on all six legs . . . Something unseen ripped through her skin, blue pouring out. Nik fired and it fell to the sand, revealed in death. He swung and fired again, shouting as he did. "Charles, take her! We have to get out—" The words were overwhelmed by the shrill of the ship's alarm.

Mudge's face blocked the carnage. Mac focused on it, breathing in shuddering gasps. "Now, Norcoast," he said with remarkable patience. "I want you to take a step for me. I'll help you." His hands took hers and pulled gently, as if nothing mattered but that first step. "That's the way."

In a sense nothing else did. If she didn't move, she'd die. On some level, Mac understood and fought to move her foot, even as the rest of her did its best to shut down completely. *It would be so much easier, so much quieter.*

"Come, Norcoast. We have to get back. The salmon won't wait. You've work to do. I may not always approve but since when did you listen to me? Just take a step. One step."

Mudge was babbling.

Shocked, Mac took two steps before she realized it.

Then, as if that motion burst some inner dam, her feet were driving through the sand as she ran with Mudge to the door, his arm around her. "Nik!" she twisted to look back.

A hard shove from behind. "Here. Go! Go!"

She hit the wall of the corridor and spun around wildly. Nik and the guards stood in the open doorway, firing into the room methodically and quickly. *They knew to aim at the torn ceiling.*

Mac shuddered and looked away, numbly aware the corridor was intact. *Nothing to attack them here.* The two Sinzi stood nearby; they seemed shaken, but unscathed. The Dhryn paced behind the Humans still firing, as if she wished to take part. Mudge was with her. She reached a hand toward him. "Where's Cayhill?" she whispered.

Despite the ongoing alarm, the Dhryn must have heard the question. She turned her head to look at Mac, yellow mucus bubbling from her nostrils, then resumed pacing. *Dhryn tears.*

Mac didn't need the short, grim shake of Mudge's head.

The weaponsfire ended. While the guards closed and sealed the door, Nik came to Mac, weapon still in his hand, and leaned close to be heard. "Are you all right?" His eyes were like flint as they searched for wounds, his mouth tight.

"I couldn't move. I couldn't—" she flushed as her voice broke. With an effort, "I thought I could handle it."

"You warned us, remember?" He laid his free hand along her cheek. "You did just fine, Mac. Now we'd better get—"

"Sir. Head for your quarters and stay there," one of the guards ordered. "We have to report to stations." With that, the two ran off toward the main portion of the ship.

"We can't stay," Mac said, her voice that of a stranger. Her hand shook as she pointed to the Dhryn. "They want Her dead, they want the past dead. They know She's here. They'll keep coming."

"We participate in the promise," Ureif said solemnly. "Our dart rests in the consular hangar."

Nik looked at Mudge. "If Ro think at all like us, that was an advance group with a specific target. The rest will go after ship's systems, create chaos. We could have a window. Remove what they're after. They might back off."

"Dart's transect-capable," Mudge agreed, then *harrumphed* firmly. "It's the best choice. I'm familiar with the specs."

"So am I." Something seemed to pass between the two men, then Nik nodded. "Let's go, then."

Someone had to ask, Mac thought. She turned to Her Glory. "Can you climb a ladder?"

"The Dhryn are attacking!"

Mac bumped her head against the ladder rung for the second time. "No. The Ro are attacking, *Se* Lasserbee. And this Dhryn is on our side. We need to climb the ladder. Now." *And if the Frow didn't get out of their way within the next few seconds, she was going to let Nik shoot him somewhere.*

That wasn't her first choice, but the appeal was growing. The shipwide alarm had subsided to a background drone, hopefully implying the captain and his crew were taking charge. *That didn't mean they were safe.* "Now," she repeated, smacking her artificial hand against the ladder.

"We saw the dead one." This from a lackey, hanging head down near Mac. "Is that what attacks?"

Mac shuddered. "Yes. There could be more on the ship. Many more. It's not safe. You should be in your quarters. And we," she said firmly, "need to climb the ladder."

"We will take you to your quarters!" This with a snatch for her arms she narrowly avoided. "To safety!"

"No. They're chasing us. Do you understand? We can't stay on the ship."

"You are in danger?"

"Yes! We all are. Please. Get out of the way."

Two scampered down, past the lower level entrance. *Se* Lasserbee climbed above her. "Then we shall protect you," he announced, his hat bobbing with each movement. "It is our duty."

So long as they got out of the way, she thought with relief.

Mac waved to the rest to follow, then climbed to the next level and turned to watch. The muscles between her shoulders seemed permanently knotted. *Turtles had the right idea,* she assured herself, wishing for some body armor and the ability to pull in her head. *They were only guessing the Ro hadn't infiltrated the entire ship already.*

The only evidence in favor of that hypothesis was that they continued to breathe. *She'd take it.*

First up was Her Glory, who climbed the vertical ladder much the same way as Brymn had managed to swim—by using the power of her limbs to overcome mechanical deficiencies. Once she was safely off the ladder—requiring some contortions and a leaping skid much like the landing of an albatross—the rest followed. The Sinzi climbed as dexterously as any Frow, their beringed fingers perfectly adapted to grasp and release in rapid sequence. Mudge was next, then Nik, weapon still out, brought up the rear.

Not quite. Claws appeared around the doorframe, followed by the pointy tips of hats, followed by feet, followed by . . . *Oh, no.*

The Frow were coming with them.

"You should go to your quarters," she said desperately. "Please. It's not—we're not safe."

"Which is why we must attend you, Dr. Connor," *Se* Lasserbee informed her, slowly working his body through the opening. Luckily for the Frow, there were hand grabs to either side. The corridor, however, loomed as a slick wasteland, its walls broken only by closed, smooth doors.

They'd be helpless.

Nik touched her shoulder. "Mac. We have to go." He didn't wait for her answer, half jogging to the bulkhead door at the end of the corridor to input his code, the Dhryn moving easily by his side. *Ran like a grizzly.*

Fy and Ureif stayed with Mac, as if they wouldn't move until she did. Mudge waited, too. Muttering under her breath, with a last look back at the Frow—who had made it to the cling-to-handrail stage and were regarding the floor—she went to Nik.

He had the door unlocked, but motioned them all to wait. "I'm going to scout ahead," he explained, slipping through the opening.

He moved like a predator, she thought.

He paused before closing the door behind him to take one last look at her, his eyes full of everything they didn't need to say to one another. *That distraction could get them killed,* she realized with a chill, finally comprehending Nik's dread of loving her.

Biology always wins, she reminded herself. Her spy might be distracted, but she could—*almost*—pity anything that threatened her.

Her Glory sat abruptly, supporting herself on upper and lowermost legs, the middle two—*that had supported her bulk in movement*—tucked up. "I am hungry, *Lamisah.*"

Mac rested her hand on the Dhryn's upper shoulder. "I know," she said gently. "How long—?" *Can you survive* was the part she didn't say. They couldn't feed her now. Later was past a gulf Mac couldn't imagine.

The golden eyes held boundless warmth. "If you can endure my complaints, *Lamisah,* I believe I can endure my hunger quite a while."

Mac snuck a peek at the Frow. They'd made it to cluster in the first doorway, feet splayed and holding onto one another. *Se* Lasserbee, ever alert, saluted, the movement almost knocking them down.

The door opened and Nik stepped through, keeping his hand on the doorframe. One look at his grim-set face and Mac's heart lurched. "They've been," he said without preamble. "No way to know how long we have. Let's go." His hand lifted to beckon them forward; Mac stared at the bloody print it left on the wall. His eyes followed hers.

"Watch your step," he added.

Mac learned a great deal about herself over the next few minutes. She could put her foot into a pool of blood without hesitation. *There was no floor free of it.* She could step over body parts, black, red, or glistening with slime. *None were identifiable.* And she could think about survival. *The body looked after itself.*

Emily's room had been nothing like this.

The corridor beyond the door was a slaughterhouse. The violence of the walkers had left nothing remotely recognizable. Perversely, their corpses—for the crew hadn't died alone—were intact, obstacles to pass.

She learned a great deal about Nik and Mudge as well. The former led, weapon out, muscles taut and body poised for action, using himself to test the way. Mudge had methodically checked every pile of intestine and bone until finding a weapon of his own. Now, he followed behind, a solid comfort.

The aliens were silent, except for the mutters of distress from the Dhryn, whose body was too wide to avoid brushing against the walkers. The Sinzi's gowns soaked up blood and became streaked with slime and ash. They walked with Mac, a finger each on her shoulder as if needing to be sure they remained together.

Once they made it this far, the Frow fared better, their claws finding ready holds. *Was it easier for them?* Mac wondered numbly. She'd lost count of the number of times she'd walked on the bodies of dead and dying salmon, more intent on her footing than the savage toll. *But they'd left eggs behind. They'd found a way for their kind to survive.*

Unlike the *Annapolis Joy,* gutted from the inside.

The consular area was no better. Nik paused beside the com station to let them catch up. She didn't look into the door. "Not far to the hangar now," he said. There were deep, harsh lines beside his mouth, but his voice was steady. *You could take strength from it.* "Ship's systems are still functioning—I could call for backup. They won't know anyone's alive here."

Mudge *harrumphed.* "If there isn't anyone else alive, you'd reveal our location for nothing. I say keep going."

"And if there is," Mac said, surprising herself, "they'll live longer with us gone."

The low drone of ship's alarm suddenly stopped, leaving a dizzy emptiness behind. The lights flared, then died to a flicker lower than night mode. Runnels of slime continued to fluoresce for brief seconds, marking the ceiling and walls as well as the dead.

As Mac's eyes adjusted, she realized the soft glow from the Dhryn's torso now pooled around them all. Just beyond, in the shadows, random sparks marked each Frow. *Useful adaptations,* she thought, unable to stop herself from trying to understand, even in a universe falling apart.

"Magnificent," exclaimed Fy. Her fingers lifted toward the Dhryn. "Mac, have you seen anything to compare?"

"Humans cannot see as we do," Ureif said.

Fy's "Oh," was accompanied with a look to Mac. "My apologies."

"We can discuss eyes later," Mac suggested. *That word again.*

"Ready?" Nik didn't wait for an answer, but led the way into the dark.

Mac supposed it was too much to hope that darkness would matter to whatever eyes the Ro walkers used.

The Dhryn's glow, however faint, proved a mixed blessing. While it helped Mac plan her next step—*and made it possible to ignore the rest of the corridor*—she felt as if she traveled inside a spotlight. Nik, Mudge, and the Frow stayed well out of it, likely for that reason.

The entry to the hangar was damaged, as if forced from the outside. *Explaining why the ceiling had been intact.* Nik went ahead to scout.

Mudge came up to Mac. "How are you managing, Norcoast?"

"Better," she said honestly. "I guess you can get used to anything."

What little she could see of his expression looked aggrieved, as if she'd presented an application to hang laundry from his precious trees. "He shouldn't have involved you in all this. I've said it before."

"Nik?" Mac found herself smiling. "Come on, Oversight. Surely I get some of the credit." Then she lost her smile. "I'm just sorry I—"

A *harrumph*. "None of that. I knew what was ahead. Better than you did."

"I wouldn't doubt it," she replied.

Nik returned. "I heard something," he said quietly. "Could have been broken equipment giving way. Could have been them."

"Guide us, Vessel." Her Glory reared to tower over them all, incidentally lighting some things Mac didn't want to see. "I long to destroy more."

A gleam of teeth. "You may have your chance," Nik said. "But let's try to do this tight and secure, all right? Sinzi-ra, I want you to lead. You'll need to get your dart open and running. Don't look back or hesitate, no matter what happens."

"We honor the promise," Ureif said solemnly. Mac thought Fy looked a great deal less certain.

They started moving, but when Mac would have gone through the door in turn, Nik pulled her against him and found her mouth with quick bruising force. Mac licked her lips, tasting blood. She stared at him, wide-eyed, her hands trembling against his shoulders.

He'd kissed her like that once before.

It had been good-bye.

"Oh, no," she whispered. "No," this time louder. Her hands formed into fists and pounded his shoulders.

Nik caught her right fist in his hands and opened it, pressing a ring inside. "Made it while you slept," he said in that matter-of-fact tone she hated. "In case."

"No."

"We have our jobs to do, Mackenzie Connor. Go. Save your fish." *That dimple.* "And the rest of the planet, if you don't mind."

"How?" Her voice cracked.

"You'll think of something." He backed away. "Time to leave."

Mac could have closed the distance with a step. *Could hold him. Could beg.* Instead, with a bone-deep shudder, she nodded.

"Where on that scale . . ."

The hangar was better illuminated than the corridor, by virtue of emergency lighting tracing the paths to the launch bay. At first, Mac thought the place untouched, then she saw the bodies clustered around two areas, a dark gaping hole in the side of the hangar—*the source of the walkers?*—and the examination tent. The tent had collapsed, hiding whatever lay inside. *Small mercies,* she thought as they passed it, not wanting to see what remained of the busy scientists.

The dart was closest to the launch bay. *Fy's request?* Mac thought, aware of the irony. Easy to spot among the squared shapes of the *Joy's* shuttles—a slim bit of silver and black, its design like the curved tip of a Sinzi finger, its surface etched with intricate designs.

They hurried together across the floor, a desperate drum of footsteps in the silence. *Almost together,* Mac corrected, glancing up to see the Frow scuttling a parallel course underneath the meshed walkway overhead. The Sinzi arrived at the dart first, as planned. Fy placed her fingertips into six places on the lower surface. Seams widened within the design, pulled away from the dart's side to become a graceful stair that lowered itself to the hangar floor without a sound.

Spit! Pop!

From in front—*and above!*

"Hurry!"

She didn't know who shouted, or if they all did. Everyone moved. Fastest of all were the Frow, who dropped down on the dart, their claws moving faster than her eyes could follow. For the first time, she saw they had weapons. One fired toward the end of the dart, and a heaving mass of darkness slid down its far side.

Scurry, scurry . . .

Se Lasserbee shouted something incomprehensible, pointed aft. The other lackey tried to fire, then *split* along *ne's* middle, dark red splashing over the dart.

As the Frow fought, the Sinzi urged the Dhryn inside, despite her loud and vocal protests. Backs to the little ship, Nik and Mudge were firing at seeming random. With success—shapes formed and died.

Spit! Pop!

A hat drifted down beside her. Mac reached for it in horror.

"Get inside!" Nik shouted. "Move!"

Startled back to sanity, she ran up the stairs and began to go in, then stopped, having almost run into Her Glory's anguished face. "I can't move back, *Lamisah,*" the Dhryn cried. "It's too small inside."

Mudge had known the specs, Mac thought numbly.

Nik had kissed her good-bye.

She fought to see past the bulk of the Dhryn. The dart was meant for a pilot and one passenger—both Sinzi. Now, Her Glory took up most of the floor and one of the forward seats. There might be space in front of her for one small, folded Human-sized body. *That didn't take into account providing air.*

Mac whirled to find herself facing Ureif and Fy. "There must be another ship—"

"Only this one can travel the transect and take you home, Mac," Ureif said calmly. "We participate in the promise." He touched fingertips with Fy, making a shivering motion that sent several rings cascading from his fingers to hers. "Fy will ensure you travel safely, and that all know what has transpired."

Fy was silent and trembling, but she slipped past Mac to enter the dart, climbing over Her Glory's back. Ureif then touched his fingertips to Mac's cheek. "I, who once failed the Dhryn, now find circularity. Thank you."

Stunned, Mac watched Ureif go back down the stairs, for the first time showing the astonishing speed of his kind. He wrapped three long fingers around Nik's shoulders and pulled him toward the stairs. "You must honor your promise as well," the Sinzi insisted. "You must go home."

Nik's eyes were wild. "No! No!" But before he could struggle free, Mudge calmly stepped up, took careful aim with the butt of his weapon, and struck Nik's head with a short, quick blow.

Scurry, scurry . . .

Spit! Pop! Skitter!

Hearing walkers from all sides now, Mac ran down the stairs, Fy behind her. Mudge and the Sinzi were already dragging Nik to them. "Take him," Ureif ordered.

"We can all go!" Mac cried as she took Nik's arm and felt Fy take the other. They hurriedly backed up the stairs, pulling the half-unconscious man. "Oversight! Come on!"

Mudge smiled at her.

Then he turned, raised his weapon, and resumed firing into the emptiness of the hangar.

It was like swimming in a nightmare, feeling the current pulling her down, feeling the drag on her legs, the loss of light as she sank.

"Oversight?"

Even as her mouth shaped his name, Ureif activated the stair controls from outside. Fy tugged at Nik; Mac roused to help. Somehow they squeezed themselves inside, Her Glory helping as best she could.

Mac caught a last glimpse through the closing door.

She saw Ureif fall, fingers still outstretched as though to deny the walkers with his dying flesh.

She saw a small, fussy man be a hero.

Then the door snapped closed.

- 23 -

ESCAPE AND ENCOUNTER

MAC HELD NIK, HER GLORY held them both, and Fy—somehow Fy climbed over her alien cargo to reach the controls.

Could the Ro still stop them?

Was Oversight watching them leave him behind or was he already dead?

Mac pressed her face into Nik's hair. He groaned and tried to move. "Don't," she said huskily. "You'll kick Her Glory."

He stilled. "Who?" Just the word.

She knew what he meant.

"Fy's here. She's flying the dart."

"How did . . . ?"

Mac lightly kissed the side of his head. "Hopefully you aren't concussed. Oversight—" she took a breath, "—he seemed to know what he was doing." *Odd skill for a man prone to memos.*

"We are in the launch bay," Fy announced. "They have not attempted to stop us."

"Yet," rumbled the Dhryn. Mac could feel her voice against her side and through the deck. Not that she had much feeling left in her legs or rump. Her spy had significant weight.

Better to think about that.

"I hunger, my *lamisah*."

And there was the distraction of a starving Progenitor.

Unlike Norris' modified lev, the dart was silent, vibration-free except for its passengers. "Launching now," Fy announced.

Mac closed her eyes.

When she was still breathing a moment later, she opened them again. "Are we okay?"

"Seems that way," Nik whispered. Louder: "Sinzi-ra, we should learn what we can of the situation before leaving Myriam for Earth. Can you tell if the Ro are attacking other ships? The planet?"

Mac shifted in alarm. Nik's hand found her thigh and squeezed it gently. "I doubt they've gone after anything but the Dhryn."

"All Dhryn?" This from Her Glory. "We must stop them!"

"That's the plan," he said, his tone leaving no doubt of the outcome.

Making doubt her job, Mac realized.

"There are transmissions," Fy announced. "Garbled, confused. They do not follow emergency protocols." She sounded faintly offended.

As Mudge would be. Mac pressed her cheek against Nik's head, careful to avoid where he'd been struck. Her eyes were dry; the way they'd get late at night after trying to read too many reports.

"Keep at it. Any information would help."

"Distress calls. Human. I think for the *Annapolis Joy,* not because of other attacks. Newspackets—heading into the Naralax. None arriving."

"We can't worry about the rest of the IU," he pointed out, remarkably sensible, Mac thought, for someone currently crushed between an overhead bin, a woman, and a Dhryn. "What about the other Progenitor? Can you reach Cavendish?"

"Tucker Cavendish?" Mac whispered. She remembered the Ministry agent she'd first met on the way station. *A lifetime ago.* Tough, ex-military, face covered with implants. *A survivor.*

"Yes."

"*Lamisah.* My Vessel. I require the other Progenitor. You must negotiate with Her Vessel." A muscular shudder passed through the Dhryn's body.

And tried to pass through hers. Mac squirmed for breathing room, Nik trying to help. "You must stay calm," she urged. "Don't move."

Very faintly, in Dhryn. "Must I die, *Lamisah?*"

Mac stared into the eye near her head, saw her face in its large, figure-eight pupil. *The eye of a being who'd commanded a starship and knew the Interspecies Union,* she reminded herself, wary of underestimating Her Glory. "I don't know," she replied in the same language. "The not-Dhryn have reason to fear your kind."

A vibration through her flesh. "Sinzi-ra Ureif told me. Our Great Journey has been perverted by the Ro; That Which Is Dhryn used as a terrible weapon, aimed by their will. If we are freed from the Ro, *Lamisah,* will we still be feared?"

There was no time left for lies. "Yes. As long as That Which Is Dhryn is capable of consuming the lives of others, you will be feared."

"Mac," asked Nik quietly. "What's going on?"

The Dhryn switched to Instella. "My apologies, Vessel. I seek to understand how I, who was Wasted and doomed, can have value to That Which Is Dhryn. The Sinzi-ra spoke of circularity, of my being the future. My Vessel speaks of the fear of not-Dhryn, a fear which may demand our extinction. I require the wisdom of your Progenitor. I must know which of these paths to follow."

Instead of answering, Nik spoke to Fy. "Sinzi-ra. Have you raised Cavendish?"

"There is a difficulty."

Mac felt him tense. "Explain."

"The belief spreads that the Progenitor's ship brought the Ro. Several warships are moving to open vectors. Cavendish is broadcasting a denial, but his signal clearly comes from a Human source, causing further misunderstanding." Mac could hear the rings on Fy's fingers, as if the Sinzi made a gesture of exasperation. "I continue to signal the truth, that the Ro seek to prevent our truce with the Dhryn, but I fear there is more reflex than reason at work around us."

"How close are we to the Progenitor?"

"We have already passed beyond her ship. The gate is ahead."

The Dhryn rumbled distress.

"Turn around," Mac urged. "Take us back."

"We cannot remain here, Mac. The promise—"

Nik's hand tightened on her thigh. *My turn.* "Fy. The only safety lies in stopping the Ro for good. The Progenitor is the key to the promise. We have to save her, too."

"I require the other Progenitor," Her Glory said, adding her vote.

Votes wouldn't matter, Mac realized. *The Sinzi worked by achieving consensus, not majority.* Fy had to want this for her own reasons.

"Listen to me, Fy," she said. "I shared *grathnu* with this Progenitor, the first and only alien to do so." *As far as she knew, anyway.* "I am the Vessel for Her Glory, who I believe is the original form of Dhryn. You will move away from profound congruence unless you bring us together. The drawing in the sand, Fy. Sinzi join the lines. Please."

Another squeeze. *Approval or caution?*

Either applied.

Every second added distance, which added risk, but the three of them waited in silence to let Fy think it through.

"I, Faras, am unsure," the Sinzi said at last. "I, Yt, am not."

It had to be a talent, Mac thought bitterly. *She'd paralyzed the Sinzi's selves with one well-intentioned argument.*

She decided not to say anything else for a while.

Nik took over. "Consider the sundered connections, Sinzi-ra. I know of your work with the Hift artifacts, yet you have never been able to view working Myrokynay technology. What if, as we believe, the Progenitor's ship was built by the Ro? I am apart from the crew of my expedition and would return to them. Mac would return to the Progenitor who sought her out on Earth. Her Glory is apart from her kind and requires her Progenitor's council. Should these connections not be attached, one to the other?"

Mac could hear the tinkling of rings. Then Fy's voice, subdued but clear. "Are you sure you are not Sinzi, Nikolai?"

"Quite sure." She could hear the smile in his voice. "If we now understand one another, Fy, all credit goes to Anchen as my teacher and Mac as my guide."

The man was good, Mac noted, smiling herself.

While Fy retraced their path to the Progenitor's ship, Mac, Nik, and Her Glory rearranged themselves in the cramped space. *Lucky none of them was claustrophobic,* Mac thought. At least the air remained fresh.

The rearrangement was a precaution. Nik couldn't vouch for what they'd face when the hatch opened—it made sense that both Humans be at least able to walk. Mac had lost touch with her feet some time ago.

Her Glory stayed put, being quite comfortable as she was. Nik managed to prop himself up so Mac could rub life back into her legs, hissing as awakening nerves merrily fired their displeasure. Once she could move, Mac crawled on top of the Dhryn, leaving the area directly before the hatch to Nik. The glowing bands were cool, the blue skin warm. She did her best to avoid sticking a finger into any of the tiny mouths.

Not bad. Mac stretched, careful to keep her feet from the Sinzi's back. She watched Nik bring out his weapon, holding it concealed in his palm. "You expecting a problem?"

"They got on the *Joy.*"

No need to ask who "they" were. "They don't need to board a Progenitor's ship to destroy it," Mac pointed out. Based on the fragments recovered in Sol System, the working hypothesis was that the Ro had somehow moved portions of their technology from the Dhryn ships into no-space, opening them to vacuum.

They'd stripped their technology from Emily's flesh at the same time.

"No Hift materials were found in the wreckage," Fy offered. "It was a great disappointment."

Nik sat on the deck, easing his legs straight. He looked up at Mac where she leaned her chin on the Dhryn's forehead ridge. "The Ro attack on the Progenitor's ship at Haven fried quite a few systems, including what my people deduced were long-range communications. That's why they hadn't replied to our signals in the first place. We stopped the Dhryn from repairing them. A gamble, I admit. No way to know if that's how a Ro destruct signal is picked up and distributed throughout the ship."

Mac rose and fell with Her Glory's sigh. "Surely the proof is that the ship remains intact," the Dhryn suggested.

"Something of a comfort, yes."

Mac frowned. "Not really."

"What are you thinking?" he asked. The Dhryn shifted and tried to turn her head to see Mac, forcing her on her elbows to protect her nose.

"She was hidden from the Ro," Mac pointed out. "Now She's not."

Nik jerked his thumb aftward. *Fy was listening.*

Mac grimaced but nodded.

They'd know soon enough.

The Progenitor's ship remained intact. The Ro either couldn't, or didn't, destroy her.

Maybe they didn't have to, Mac thought with a shiver, looking around.

What had hummed with life and light now seemed filled with the silent desolation of a graveyard. *Worse,* she decided, following Nik. *A graveyard implied mourners.*

From inside the dart, their approach and entry into the Progenitor's great ship had had all the high drama—*for passengers at least*—of taking a lift to another floor. Once inside the ship, they'd stepped out into this dimly-lit hollow cave. The space resembled the busy holds of the *Annapolis Joy* or the *Uosanah* only in being big enough to hold shuttles and their like. There were no guides along the floor. No lines of waiting empty craft. *No crew.* Lighting from above failed against the black, anti-Ro fabric lining ceiling, floor, and angled wall. Behind them, the Sinzi dart glittered like exotic jewelry, dropped and abandoned on velvet.

"There's the *Impeci.*" Nik's quiet voice echoed into the distance. He pointed to an ordinary shuttlelike craft, larger than those on the *Joy.*

Mudge would have known the specs. Mac took a steadying breath. The Human ship looked normal. "What's wrong with it?"

"Nothing a thorough scrub and filter replace wouldn't solve. Without that, you'd need an evacsuit to survive the radiation inside for more than a few hours."

"Where is everyone?" Her Glory was subdued; her body hunched low over her legs. "I've been here before. There should be workers here. Those to greet us. Other ships."

"There were when I left," Nik said. Mac, hearing that slight edge, glanced at him. His face was expressionless. *Never a good sign.* "My people will be in their quarters. We set up a com relay there. That way." He pointed to a door, its frame askew with that characteristic Dhryn slant.

Just then, a side hatch opened on the *Impeci,* sending a wash of brighter light outward along with its ramp. A figure appeared, calling out even as he began to stumble in their direction. "Nik? Is that you?"

"What the hell—" Nik took off at a run. "Tucker!" She understood the horror in his voice as Cavendish drew close enough for her to see clearly.

No suit!

The man staggered more than walked. When the two met, Nik grabbed and held him. Mac and the two aliens hurried to join them.

Nik had had isolated burns, already healing. The face Cavendish turned to greet them with was a mass of weeping sores and hanging implants, as if the flesh beneath the skin was dissolving away. His eyes were the only thing sane within that madness. Sane and, when they fell on Her Glory, filled with wonder. "What are you?" he asked, his lips bleeding with the words, enunciating with care.

Because he'd lost most of his teeth, she realized with a sick shock. Mac eased her shoulder under Cavendish's other arm, helping to support his weight, careful of what she touched. "We have to get you home—"

"What were you doing in there? Where's your suit?" Nik interrupted furiously, though his hands were gentle. "I gave strict orders to stay away from the ship—"

"Had to . . . come back. Stay inside. She can't control . . . warned . . . us . . . stay in the ship." Cavendish gasped between each burst of words, but didn't stop. "She's running out of Dhryn. Feeders . . . entered our quarters. Took . . . took . . . we've lost a few. Rest of us . . . figured . . . better the radiation . . . wouldn't be long before we got off . . . share the suits. Now you're here." This with a trusting look.

From where she stood, Mac could see how Nik's free hand clenched into a tight fist, but when he answered, it was warm and reassuring. "You'll be fine, Tucker."

Others appeared at the hatch, walking down the ramp. One, two Humans, an Imrya. Then no more.

Was that all? Mac watched Nik mouth names as they approached, his face growing pale.

Only two wore protective gear. She suddenly remembered Nik's battle with Cinder, her mind now filling in the rest. *Cinder's sabotage—she'd gone after the suits.* None looked as gravely ill as Cavendish. Mac looked her question at Nik. "You stayed on the coms all the time I was gone, didn't you, Tucker?" he asked, his voice soft. To Mac, "Even in a suit, exposure adds up."

"Thought you might call," Cavendish said, then convulsed in a cough.

"There are medical supplies on my dart." Fy took over from Mac and Nik, using her fingers to form a slinglike seat for the ill Human. Cavendish leaned back in that support, his head lolling against the stained white of her gown. "Sinzi," he managed.

Though all from the *Impeci* had suffered radiation burns, the two remaining researchers, especially the Imrya, were in far better shape than the ship's pilot. He needed help to walk, and exhibited more burns to his skin. Mac guessed he'd traded shifts at the *Impeci's* com with Cavendish. He'd been the ship's pilot. Now, he couldn't stop looking over his shoulder.

A reflex she understood very well.

Grim-faced, Nik told them what had transpired on the *Annapolis Joy*. Mac watched the hope of rescue fade from the faces of those who'd been waiting for it. There was no protest, only quiet questions. *A measure of Nik's colleagues,* she judged.

While this went on, Cavendish and the pilot, Bhar Dass, were made as comfortable as possible in the Sinzi's tiny ship. Nik ordered the Imrya—*whose name Mac couldn't pronounce*—and her Human colleague, Fiora Parrish, to stay and care for them. "We may have to run for it," he told them when they protested. "I want you here, ready to go. We'll keep in touch." He showed them the remote links the Sinzi had provided. "You're sure you can use the com system?" This to the Imrya. "It's not quite IU standard."

The alien looked at the Sinzi, who nodded. "We Imrya are honored to be the first recipients of improvements by the gracious Sinzi. I am familiar with this system."

Nik didn't look surprised. "Monitor what's happening outside and keep us posted."

"Should I broadcast a detailed advisement not to fire on this ship, given the presence of the Sinzi-ra?" The Imrya clutched her recorder tightly, as if she'd like to mention the presence of that as well.

Hand over proof to those already worrying about a Dhryn/Sinzi connection? Mac touched Nik's sleeve; he met her eyes and nodded before turning back to the Imrya. "Given the situation, let's not get specific. Just say this is a nonhostile ship, under truce."

The pilot raised his head, his eyes haunted. "Is it?"

"We'll find out," Nik promised.

The tiles, colored and bright, hadn't changed. The soft green carpet, the woven silk panels in rainbow shades, the floor rising in great steps were familiar. But nothing bounced on the carpet, or slept within the paneled pens, or cooed sleepily. The tiles surrounded a crèche emptied of life.

Mac stepped back from the lookout with a sigh. The Dhryn with her seemed less affected. *Perhaps because these hadn't been her oomlings.*

More likely, she reminded herself, *this sacrifice was part of being Dhryn, too.*

"This way," Nik said, pointing down the right-hand tunnel.

These tunnels had their own ghosts. "Did you see any Wasted while you were here?" Mac asked as she rejoined Nik. *Not that they could feed the one they had.*

He shook his head.

The Progenitor must have consumed their faint flickers of life, too.

Fy trailed their small line, her attention repeatedly caught by this or that about the walls or exposed controls, holding up one of the recorders she'd attached to a belt before they'd left the dart. Mac supposed the Sinzi was happy, in the way a researcher could find joy with her subject.

She couldn't remember it.

"Almost there," Nik told her. His fingers laced with hers. "No sign of trouble yet."

"As if that's a good thing to say," she complained, only half joking.

They watched for Ro, even here, where the shroud material of the Dhryn should provide protection.

As for Dhryn . . . "Could the entire ship be this empty?"

Nik shrugged. "We couldn't estimate the minimum crew requirement to keep things running. A lot's automated, as you'd expect." A pause. "When I was on board, She was working Her way through one section at a time."

Spy School 101: Euphemisms for All Occasions, Mac said to herself, not fooled by his tone. "I'm sorry," she offered. "If it helps, I felt Her grief through the *lamnas.* She consumed Her own children first."

Another shrug, this sharp and tense. "Feeders don't discriminate. We'll need to be careful."

"The Mouths of the Progenitor do not think," Her Glory agreed, her voice full of warmth and longing. "They only provide."

Of course she'd want to find feeders. Nik's fingers tightened around hers. *Not the only one worried.* "Can they provide for you?" he asked the Dhryn, as casually as if he inquired after her favorite color.

"Among the many things I don't know, Vessel. This state—" a quiet hoot, "—is new to me as well." Her Glory paused. "I'm reassured Haven remains after all. Even in this form. Something of my old life."

"Have you reached accommodation with your other self?" This from Fy. *Understandable curiosity from someone having a little trouble in that department.*

"Accommodation?" The Dhryn appeared to consider the question as they walked, the taller Sinzi leaning over to listen. "Those memories have no taste, no power. I simply know what happened. We arrived at Haven to find it destroyed. We waited for nothing, hiding ourselves from the Ro, from all that were not-Dhryn. The time came when some chose to die. I know I chose to survive, despite having no purpose or value. For that, I await the judgment of the Progenitor."

As if on cue, a figure appeared ahead. Standing, Mac noticed with relief. Nik's other hand eased back to his side. *He'd been ready to fire.*

"You were told to stay in your ship, not-Dhryn. Why are you here?" A Dhryn voice, male, older, his Instella flawless. He stepped forward into the light. *Two hands missing—someone of importance.* As if in emphasis, his eye and ear ridges were traced in vivid turquoise, more of that color on his lips and in the silk banding his torso.

The effect would have been better, Mac decided, *if he hadn't needed strings to hold the bands around what was close to a match for a Wasted's body.* The strings had a second function, being beaded with the Dhryn version of imps. *Odd decoration,* she puzzled.

"Deruym Ma Nas," Nik greeted. "I've returned, as promised."

The Dhryn leaned forward, slight threat. His remaining hands, Mac noted, held weapons, though not pointed at them. *Yet.* "Which not-Dhryn are you?"

Something about the attitude of what was obviously a cloistered Haven Dhryn, albeit an educated linguist, stiffened Mac's spine. "You know perfectly well he's Her Vessel," she stated in Dhryn. "We come on urgent business for That Which Is Dhryn and the Progenitor expects us. I am Mackenzie Winifred Elizabeth Wright Connor Sol."

His stumps and hands came together in a startled clap of respect. "I didn't see you. Or—" Words in either language failed him as Deruym Ma Nas finally caught sight of Her Glory.

She was worth a look, Mac thought with poignant pride, easily half again the size of the Haven Dhryn, her body robust and full. The dulled lighting only emphasized the golden luminescence banding her torso. Her Glory needed no silks—*or were the brilliant silks of modern Dhryn an echo of what they'd lost?* she wondered abruptly.

"Deruym Ma Nas," Her Glory said in that warm, loving voice. "A most admirable name. I take it into my keeping, though I've none of my own to exchange." She held out her single hand. "Know me by this, *erumisah.*"

The other Dhryn rose in a bow, then brought his mouth close to her palm, lips working at the air above the skin. His eyelids lowered and he began to sway in what seemed ecstasy. *Or a seizure,* Mac cautioned herself.

Never assume with aliens.

An old rule, but a good one.

With Deruym Ma Nas as escort, their group moved quickly to the wide, downsloping ramp that led to the Progenitor's Chamber, more precisely as quickly as his frequent backward looks at Her Glory permitted. Mac glared at the Dhryn as he did it again, almost stumbling.

The lush carpet quieted their footfalls. There were more spirals of silver than she remembered along the black shroud lining the walls. *More names added.* She wished for time to try and read them. But time they didn't have.

They should be running.

It wasn't only fear, though Mac didn't understand her eagerness to reach their destination until they stopped in front of the vaultlike door to the Progenitor's Chamber.

It felt like coming home.

Did she think the Progenitor could fix things?

Make things right?

Bring back the dead?

Mac shook her head, hard. *The Progenitor was as endangered as the rest of them.* She followed Nik through the door, seeing Deruym Ma Nas glance up at the last minute. Curious, she did the same.

Before, the holes around the great door had been empty, inexplicable. Now, a pale feeder Dhryn squatted in those above, as if waiting for strays.

Mac dropped her gaze, her nerve endings remembering what her mind refused.

"This one will remain here." Deruym Ma Nas pointed at Fy.

The Sinzi's fingers clenched in shock. "But I must see the Progenitor!"

No surprise, Mac thought. *To a Sinzi, a physical meeting was paramount.*

Deruym Ma Nas, surprised or not, wasn't about to be swayed. "She does not have to see you. You are—" he paused and blinked one/two at the tall alien, as if lost for the right word, then settled for: "—unfamiliar."

Fy looked to Mac, who could only shrug, thinking of the days she'd spent waiting for the Progenitor to be ready to meet her first Human. "I'll ask," she offered.

"Isn't there a safer place to wait?" Nik didn't need to point at the lurking feeders.

"It is all right." The Sinzi made a graceful come-hither gesture toward the silver-sparked walls. "I would prefer to stay here. These appear the oldest engravings. I would be grateful for the opportunity to record them."

Nik looked uneasy. "Are you sure, Sinzi-ra?"

Mac had learned to read Fy's fear and saw it now, in the tremble of fingertip, the distracted focus of the topaz eyes. To the Sinzi's credit, she remained steadfast. "Will it matter where any of us are if the Progenitor chooses to feed?" She faced the Dhryn and lifted her recorder. "Deruym Ma Nas, may I have your permission?"

"You need none," he told her. "These walls are meant to be read by all who come here, throughout the generations." For an instant, Mac thought she detected something sad and resigned in Deruym Ma Nas' expression, before it returned to impatient. "We must go."

The Haven Dhryn disappeared within the archway, Her Glory with him.

Nik nodded to Mac, who began to walk with him after the Dhryn. She couldn't help glancing back at the Sinzi. The willowy alien stood in the black-walled corridor, watching them leave her. She appeared composed, but her fingers were locked around her recorder. The lower half of her gown was stiff with dried Human blood. "Fy," Mac suggested, "you might want to ignore what I said about moving slowly around aliens."

An almost Human smile. "I understand."

"Mac?"

"Coming."

Fifteen steps through the arched door itself. Mac counted each, smelling metal, feeling the chill. Then the passage. Nik and their guide—still the only normal adult Dhryn they'd seen—led the way. Her Glory and Mac followed them.

Mac lifted her face, knowing the reason for the rhythmic pulse of warm air over her skin. She sniffed, disturbed by a faint decay.

Then they were out, into that world where flesh and biology ruled.

- CONTACT -

HUMANS WERE FAMED for their ability to grow accustomed to any marvel, to take the strange in stride. It made them easygoing crewmates on alien ships, although a frustrating market to satisfy.

But not even Humans could grow used to this.

"Current count?" Hollans requested, sipping his tea. None of them left the Atrium these days. He had a cot near Telematics, took his meals within sight of the screens monitoring traffic through the transect.

And what traffic . . .

Day after day, Sinzi had been pouring into Sol System through every gate. Polite, noncommittal Sinzi, following protocol to the letter, requesting only a designated orbit for their ships to stay out of the way of whatever else moved to and from Earth.

Saying nothing else.

"Two hundred and fifty-three thousand, four hundred and two personal darts, five hundred and twelve liners." The tech consulted a smaller screen. "That accounts for the entire registered Sinzi liner fleet, sir. I don't have a reference for darts."

Hollans shook his head. There wasn't a species in the IU whose delegate hadn't hammered—or the equivalent—on his door, demanding to know what the Humans were doing. Not a species who wasn't desperately afraid the Sinzi were leaving its system for good, the transect gates on automated settings only. Traffic had virtually stopped.

The Sinzi were abandoning them to the Dhryn.

That was the latest.

"Sinzi-ra?" Hollans asked quietly, as he had so many times. "What are your people doing?"

Anchen, as she had each time before, smiled her perfect Human smile.

"They participate in the promise."

24

RETURN AND REACTION

THE LANDSCAPE HAD AGED. Mac stared out over a grayed blue, its surface puckered and wrinkled by furrows deep enough to hide a starship. There were no wide ponds of shining black, no frosting of new life. The few feeders lay flaccid, their arms tipped into drying puddles.

With the others, she rode that improbable hand to the incredible wall of flesh, hollowed by nostrils able to engulf a lev as well as barges. Mac's eyes dismissed what was irrelevant, seeking the face embedded in the wall.

And found it.

"Welcome, Mackenzie Winifred Elizabeth Wright Connor Sol." The same quiet, so-normal voice she remembered, with its familiar kind warmth. The same gold-and-black eyes.

No sequins. Perhaps the Progenitor spared her few remaining Dhryn that service. *Seemed a shame.*

"My previous Vessel told me you had served in *grathnu* again."

"What?" *Oh.* Mac held out her artificial arm. "Not quite. You know what happened to Brymn Las?"

Those eyes could become cold. "The Ro interfered with That Which Is Dhryn." The hand underfoot shook. "They must never do so again."

"That's what we hope," Nik said.

"Ah. My Vessel. Welcome. You have done well. Very well. I had no doubt."

Nik gave a deep bow. "Thank you. But, Progenitor—forgive my haste. We must leave this system at once. I'll explain as we travel."

"Of course." A soft hoot, higher-pitched than other Dhryn. "We already answer the Call, my Vessel." Her eyes moved to Her Glory. "Tell me, what is this?"

"Answer the Call?" Before Mac could do more than exchange looks of alarm with Nik, she felt a nudge against her back. From its direction, it had to be from Her Glory's hand. *Right, Vessel.* "Well," she began helplessly, "this is—"

"What do you mean—'answer the Call'?" Nik interrupted, stepping forward. Deruym Ma Nas drew his weapons and moved to block the Human's way.

"Do not threaten my Vessel," the Progenitor chided her *erumisah*. "And do not fear." This in a more gentle tone to Nik. "The empty ship receives the Call and responds; my Dhryn who crew her would otherwise never disobey me. We follow by my will."

Mac's heart pounded. *Not good,* she babbled to herself. *Not good.*

If Nik shared that choking fear; he didn't show it. "I urge you to reconsider, Progenitor." Calm, reasoned. "What we've done to your ship—it may not be enough to protect you from the Ro. We don't know."

"We will know, my Vessel," She replied, as calmly, as reasonably, "when I attack them. We will know when I scour the Ro and its contamination from whatever world it has chosen. The Call will end. If others answered? You, my Vessel, will speak for me to those Progenitors. We will protect them, too. To-gether, we will continue until there are no Ro left alive."

As the Progenitor spoke, feeder-Dhryn rose from Her surface, like pastel pet-als caught by Her breath. Some came so close Mac could see their oblong clear bodies, their boneless arms. *Their mouths . . .*

She froze in place; Her Glory heaved a wistful sigh.

Those eyeless faces seemed to acknowledge their Progenitor before all of them turned, using the fins on back and sides to stroke the air. They began mov-ing toward the walls and ceiling of the vast chamber. *Thousands,* Mac realized numbly. Far less than she remembered. *Far too many.* As they reached their desti-nation, they disappeared through holes in the walls she hadn't noticed in her first visit. *Doors—but to what?*

The Progenitor smiled. "I will destroy my enemy."

There were certain unavoidable ramifications to standing on a giant hand. *Of course, even if there'd been time,* Mac told herself, *tact had never been her strong suit.* "You know," she ventured, "this might not be the best plan."

Eyes of gold and black fixed on her. "It is my will." She sounded more sur-prised than upset.

"The Dhryn are not alone, Progenitor." Nik came to stand by Mac. "Others oppose the Ro. Let us bring warships from other species. End the threat of the Ro together."

"They are our enemy—"

"Don't you understand?" Mac couldn't stop herself. "This Call—it won't just be Ro on that planet! There'll be other life!"

Were they watching the catastrophe of the Chasm unfold again?

The vivid blue underlid flashed over the Progenitor's eyes, twice. *Stress.* Mac tensed, but the hand supporting them might have been carved from rock. When the great creature spoke, it was still in that reasoning-with-aliens tone. "Of course. The Ro require it."

"For what?" Nik asked, silencing Mac with a look. "Why do the Ro require other living things, Progenitor?"

The first frown. "We do not think of it."

The first evasion. For safety's sake, Mac only imagined stamping her foot. *They were close to something vital here, something that would finally make sense.*

Nik must have sensed it, too. "They interfered with That Which Is Dhryn," he pursued relentlessly. "Made you consume the life from worlds at their command. Why would they require life on those worlds, if they planned to remove it?"

For a moment, Mac didn't think the Progenitor would answer. Her small lips worked as she remembered Brymn's would do when he was disturbed. The breath moving past was deeper, with more force.

Was that a tremble in the hand?

She resisted the urge to grab Nik. *They'd only fall together.* "Please, Progenitor," she said gently. "We seek the truth."

"As do I," came the response. Mac discovered she'd been holding her breath. "Bear with me, *Lamisah*. The fragments I have gleaned from the past resemble *oomlings,* precious because they represent continuance, but these never Freshen to the wisdom of adulthood. The most whole are the gifts from my predecessor, and She from Hers." A sigh that shook the barren landscape below and whistled past the hand. "Yet they answer no more questions. My predecessors wished That Which Is Dhryn to survive the Ro—not understand them."

"Trust me when I say we must understand them to survive," Nik urged. "Let us try. Tell us, tell your *lamisah,* everything you can about living things and the Ro. You sent Brymn Las and your Vessel to Mackenzie Winifred Elizabeth Wright Connor Sol for that very reason." He put his hand on Mac's shoulder, pressed gently as if in warning. "She's here, now. Earth's foremost biologist. She can help."

Nothing like an unearned promotion, Mac winced to herself. She attempted to be positive. *Maybe salmon would have relevance.*

"That's me," she said brightly.

The Progenitor's gold-and-black eyes regarded her. "Will we need to find and kill them all?"

A perfectly reasonable question. Mac wished it wasn't the one going through her mind about the Dhryn. *Emily'd warned her.* "I'll need to know more about their life cycle," she evaded. "How many it takes to reproduce—to make *oomlings,*" this as the Progenitor looked perplexed.

"I make *oomlings.*" With a low hoot—*presumably at bizarre alien notions*— echoed by Deruym Ma Nas and Her Glory.

Obviously the topic of Dhryn sex, or possible lack thereof, wasn't going to help. Mac picked another tack. "What do Ro make?"

"Tools."

"Machines?" Nik suggested. "Ships. Devices?"

The Progenitor pursed Her lips for an instant. "Servants. Servants of flesh and bone. Such as attacked you, *Lamisah,* and poor Brymn Las. The ones who hide within shields. The ones we learned to keep away from our world."

Nik looked disappointed; he'd doubtless hoped for something, anything, new.

But Mac felt the stirrings of curiosity. "Why do the Ro make servants?"

"How else can they reach beyond their chambers?"

"Chambers?" *An expression for no-space?* "What do you mean?"

The hand moved away from the face and swiveled to give them a view of the Progenitor's vast cavern. "Chamber," She said with a gentle hoot, returning Her hand, and guests, to their original position.

More than living quarters, Mac thought. *The only place She can survive.* "The Ro have to stay there," she guessed.

"Where are their chambers?" asked Nik, his eyes almost glowing. "Within their ships? On the worlds they choose?"

"They are not like us. Their chambers have holes, doors, to many places at once, places that flow together. The stories claim a Ro must open such a door to begin a world. Once opened, That Which Is Dhryn can reach in to kill it." Her voice held immense satisfaction.

"Explaining why that opening to no-space might stay open," he mused, "but why for only so long? A failsafe . . ." He frowned. "I could see something set to grab an attacked Ro back inside—but why take away the oceans, too? We're missing something." He looked at Mac.

As if she'd know. She obligingly frowned back. "You said a Ro opens its chamber to 'begin a world.'" She pounced on the odd phrase. *Ominous was more like it.* "What does that mean?"

The hand trembled again. "I do not think of it. We do not think of it."

"You must, Progenitor," Nik insisted. "Time's running out."

No need for a reminder. Mac shuddered. They were on their way to the next target. *She was not going to think about where or what.*

As if in echo, the Progenitor said, "I do not think of it." Her lips began to quiver; Her eyes flashed blue.

Before Nik could press Her further, Deruym Ma Nas put away his weapons. "Rest," he rumbled in Instella. "Allow me to answer your Vessel, my Progenitor."

"My *erumisah* is wise." This with a breathlessness that had nothing to do with the pulses of air through the great nostrils.

"Do you know what the Ro are doing?" Nik asked him.

"We do not know," an emphasis, "anything beyond the evil nature of the Ro. My Progenitor has directed our search of the archives. I am," a graceful bow, "the Senior Archivist."

Mac spared a moment to wonder if he knew of her and Brymn's ruthless foraging through the oldest of the Haven Dhryn's textiles, then decided it couldn't matter now.

Sure enough, Deruym Ma Nas gave a forlorn hoot. "A meaningless title, since no others remain." He touched a few of the imps decorating his torso. "I keep their trust."

Mac blinked. He could easily have over a hundred of the devices on those strings. *The amount of data that implied?*

But they had no time. "Could we hear your informed speculation on the Ro, Deruym Ma Nas?" she asked courteously.

Judging from Nik's face, he'd settle for a wild guess, so long as it moved them closer.

You couldn't rush Dhryn. She'd learned that lesson.

In response, Deruym Ma Nas folded his arms, the severed wrists outward, in case they forgot his earned rank. "We discovered forty-nine references concerning the Ro and taste."

"Taste? What does—" Mac frowned and Nik subsided. "Taste," he echoed. "Please continue."

"I'm hungry," Her Glory whispered in Mac's ear. She patted the huge Dhryn, but kept her attention on the archivist.

"In these references to taste," Deruym Ma Nas continued, his eyes not leaving Nik, "there is commonality. Whether embroidered within fabrics, or placed into mosaic, even within the stories remembered by my Progenitor, each refers to the foul taste of the worlds contaminated by the Ro, of how this taste was deemed unfit for the Progenitors to share."

"Because this was your enemy," Nik guessed.

Human bias. As she shook her head, Mac abruptly grasped the import of what Deruym Ma Nas was trying to tell them. *The taste of what?* "The Ro used the Dhryn to remove the original life from chosen worlds," she thought out loud. "But when the Dhryn rebelled and attacked the Ro, those worlds still had a taste, but now so different the Progenitors couldn't consume it." Her voice rose with excitement. "Don't you see? It means those worlds didn't stay barren. The Ro had put life on them. Their kind of life."

"Why?"

"The oldest imperative of them all." *Did they feel the rightness of it?* "Individual survival isn't enough—your kind must continue. The Ro aren't adapted to no-space. Maybe nothing is." *Just passing through it with the Ro had made her sick; repeated trips had damaged Emily's mind.* "We know they came from a planet. Those who left it were committed to live in no-space. We've seen time flows differently there—they could have lost touch with their previous existence almost at once. They might have thought they could exist like that forever, only to discover they'd become impotent, damaged, maybe even dying.

"What would they do? Give up the future?" Mac shook her head. "Not the Ro I met. They could make biological machines, but that wouldn't be good enough. They'd want the real thing, to rebuild themselves. Time here would mean nothing to them. They had the tools. All they needed were living worlds to host their regeneration—fresh, sterile worlds, free of alien life to compete or contaminate. Then they find the Dhryn, the perfect—"

Stop right there, Mac thought, suddenly remembering where she was.

Too late.

"More Ro!" roared the Progenitor. "They used us to make more?"

Her hand spasmed, toppling them all. Nik threw his arm over Mac as they fell, holding them flat against the palm.

- CONTACT -

"**W**E HAVE INCOMING SHIPS, SIR," the transect technician reported, smoothly, professionally.

"Finally!" her supervisor burst out. "You'd think with the Sinzi here, everything would run like clockwork. But no, traffic's off and if we get one more complaint about missing newspackets, I'll—"

"Sir. Sending to your station." Only someone standing close by could have seen her hands tremble. Or someone who'd been there when the Dhryn had arrived.

"Got it." One look at the display and her supervisor reached for the emergency com control, then thought better of it and reached for the secure line to Earth.

"This is Venus Orbital," he announced. "We've unannounced warships coming through the Naralax Transect. Repeat, incoming warships. Species—?"

"Trisulian, sir. They aren't broadcasting idents, but I'd know those profiles in my sleep. Fifty, another group of twenty, still coming."

"Going by profile, the intruders are Trisulian," he sent. "Venus Orbital, standing by." He began punching in the codes to lock the facility behind blast doors, for all the good they'd do against ships capable of smashing planets to rubble.

The technician swiveled her chair to stare at him. "Standing by for what, sir?" she asked in a low, urgent voice. "What the hell's going on?"

Her supervisor looked up at her question.

"Let's hope it isn't war."

"The Trisulians are demanding the Sinzi immediately submit to their authority, disband the Inner Council of the IU, and relinquish all information on no-space technology and the transect system."

Hollans picked up his teacup. "Anything else?"

"Did you not hear me?" The Imrya ambassador was a remarkably succinct individual for his species. *Doubtless why he'd been posted so far from home.* "You must allow me to request the immediate deployment of the Imrya fleet here."

"And escalate what is currently rhetoric into a battle?" Hollans sipped his tea. "No, thank you, Ambassador."

"We must stop the Trisulians! We must protect the Sinzi!"

"Our forces were already en route to the gate."

"Forgive me, Mr. Hollans, but your forces wouldn't give an Ar pause. We've had peace between systems because the Sinzi were scattered, everywhere. Now too many are here, vulnerable to attack or capture. They have made themselves too tempting a target."

"Something I've told the Sinzi-ra," Hollans replied rather testily, "several times. We all have. They persist in providing no information whatsoever."

"Do they wish confrontation? To what end?"

Hollans put down his teacup. "I think it's something far more dangerous than that, Ambassador. I think the Sinzi seek a congruence, here. If that's the case, the Trisulians?" He lifted his hand and bent one finger down. "They're merely the first to accept the invitation."

25

PREDICAMENT AND PERIL

AN ETERNITY LATER, the shuddering ended, the hand stopped moving, and no one was dead. During that time, while waiting to fall, be thrown, or survive, Mac noticed the little things. The skin beneath her hands was warm, although loose and dry, no longer as elastic as she remembered. The smell? She wrinkled her nose and tried to keep her face away from the surface. The Progenitor's circulation was failing; the hand itself likely septic.

Really not a good thing to think about while on that hand.

Although Her Glory appeared content to stay prone, Deruym Ma Nas struggled to his feet almost at once. "The evil of the Ro has no limits," he exclaimed.

Which would sound more impressive, Mac decided, peering at him, *if he wasn't still shaking.*

She was surprised not to be. The combination earthquake-with-potential-plunge would once have had her gibbering with fear.

New standards.

"Your idea about the Ro," Nik whispered. "It fits, Mac. What we know so far; what we've guessed. Good work."

"Desperation," she whispered back.

In answer, he kissed her nose.

They rose to their feet, the hand having remained stable throughout this exchange. The process entailed what Mac considered a responsible amount of clinging to one another.

A shame to let go, she acknowledged as her fingers left Nik's sleeve.

"Please forgive me," the Progenitor said quietly. "I could take such dreadful news when I was strong. I could endure." Her eyes held inexpressible weariness. "Now, I fail. And That Which Is Dhryn fails with me."

She had a choice, Mac realized. Something that seemed to be happening all too often lately.

She hated having a choice.

Nik simply raised an eyebrow when she sent him a pleading look. *Up to her.*

Mac glowered but nodded.

"That Which Is Dhryn may not be failing," she told the Progenitor, stepping aside so Her Glory was no longer hiding half behind her.

The Progenitor's eyes glanced at Her Glory, who stood up literally ablaze with joy, then back to Mac. "What is this?"

Mac thought of the *lamnas*. The Progenitor had done Her stomach-turning utmost to convey not only her despair, but her need. *A need she understood.* "What you asked of me," she said. "The truth."

The Progenitor's lips quivered and Deruym Ma Nas lowered his body in warning. Nik looked poised to—*do what? Tackle the bear-sized alien and toss them both off the hand?*

Mac didn't see much future in that.

"Explain," the Progenitor said at last.

Mac coughed. *In for it now.* "You spoke of the Ro's interference, Progenitor," she said carefully. "They've done more to That Which Is Dhryn than you know. Without them, I believe you would be like this. A little bigger," she added, giving Her Glory a considering look.

Or a great deal bigger, she suddenly realized, *once the migration had ended and the Dhryn population entered a stationary rebuilding generation—a variability within the norm the Ro could have exploited.* "The Ro didn't just take you from your home world into space," Mac went on. "They didn't just find ways to control your behavior. They made changes to the Flowering itself."

"Continue," the Progenitor said, her small mouth turned down at the corners, yellow drops forming on her nostrils. Otherwise, she appeared reassuringly calm. "Why would they do this?"

Calm for how long? Mac swallowed. "The Ro wanted Progenitors who could produce more *oomlings*. They wanted as many feeders, Mouths, as possible. Those are their weapon. That meant Progenitors so large they could no longer move by themselves. They knew how to change the pattern of your growth and development." *Another piece snicked into place.* "And Ro technology produced food to sustain you. These ships? They were essential. Not just to bring you where the Ro Called, but because—as they made you—you can't live anywhere else."

When the hand didn't immediately tip, she relaxed very slightly and continued. "They could alter the Flowering process, too. Remember Brymn Las? He didn't become what you predicted, a Progenitor, because the Ro—" she forced the words past the memory, "—made sure he didn't."

She indicated the silent Dhryn at her side. "This is what I believe you both would have become without the Ro. The original form of Dhryn Progenitor."

"Where did she come from?" Still to Mac. *Protocol between Progenitors, or a refusal to acknowledge what stood before her?* Without knowing which, all Mac could do was press ahead. She noticed Nik taking advantage of the Progenitor's attention to turn slightly away and lift his wrist to his mouth, likely contacting those left behind. *Warning them the ship was on the move.*

Where was anyone's guess.

"Where?" This from the Progenitor, when Mac failed to answer immediately. Gentle, but insistent. "Our home world? A colony of Dhryn who escaped the Ro?" There was a distinct and growing excitement in her voice.

"A little closer," Mac said. "Her Glory was once captain of the Cryssin freighter, *Uosanah*. He Flowered into what you've been calling the Wasted."

Deruym Ma Nas scuttled as far away from Her Glory as the hand permitted. *Almost too far.*

"I do not wish to doubt you, *Lamisah*," responded the Progenitor graciously. "But this is not possible. The lost ones fail and die. It is the Way."

"It's the Ro's way," Mac countered. "All they had to do was make it possible for your bodies to synthesize certain substances, things once obtained from what you ate on your home world. Any Dhryn without this ability would starve to death on Haven or on board your ships." *The whole truth.* "They might survive a little longer by eating other Dhryn. That's why the Wasted attack their own kind. To save one? All we had to do was provide this Dhryn, who was dying, with food as close as possible to what would have been available to your ancestors. Look at her."

"I hunger," Her Glory offered, less than helpfully.

The Progenitor's eyes shifted to her. "As do I, little one."

Before this could become a negotiation about who should eat whom, Mac jumped back in. "The point is, the diet you've been producing for yourselves on Haven—" *however clever the fungus,* "—was part of the Ro's plan. It couldn't meet the needs of any Dhryn born who reflected the original type. That was one way they've controlled your population. Any Dhryn whose body threw off their conditioning and reverted to the ancestral form would starve to death at Flowering instead of becoming a Progenitor. Wasted." *Had some Progenitor known to call them that?* "You would continue to produce the kind of Dhryn that suited the Ro."

"They came—they came and touched the *oomlings* until we found ways to keep them out." Deruym Na Mas had risen to a more conciliatory posture and was watching Mac intently. "Is that why, Mackenzie Winifred Elizabeth Wright Connor Sol?"

Why did everyone think she understood the damned Ro? Mac shrugged. "I don't know. They could have been making further modifications. They might have been monitoring something about you. Or—" She hesitated and looked to Nik. He nodded, still trusting her with this. *Great.* "Maybe the Ro were waiting for something. A sign your population was ready to migrate."

"The Great Journey. Even that they would pervert?"

"Especially that," Mac agreed.

"Have the Little One approach me."

Mac turned but Her Glory was already walking forward, her movement powerful yet graceful. Fit.

Could the Progenitor see it?

Her Glory stopped when she could walk no farther. She lifted her sole hand

and spread her strong, delicate fingers against the wall that was the Progenitor's cheek, then rose on four legs so their eyes met at the same level.

Gusts of warm air moved outward, cooler air returning. Nik stopped talking into his com, watching the new and the old. *Or rather,* Mac corrected herself, *the original and the perversion.*

Though to call the gracious Progenitor a perversion seemed as wrong as anything else. Especially when Her face, suspended in the wall like an image of who she really was, formed an expression of such kindness. "Can you speak so my Vessel can understand?"

The Progenitor had used Dhryn, but Her Glory didn't hesitate. "Yes," in Instella. "I ask your wisdom, She Who Lights the Way." Her luminescent bands shone more brightly, as if activated by emotion. They cast shadows on the great palm and attentive face. "I wish to know how I can serve That Which Is Dhryn."

The Progenitor squinted. "Commune with me. We shall sing the *Gnausa.*"

Deruym Ma Nas drew in his arms, leaning back in a Dhryn bow. *Just what they needed,* Mac thought. *Ro on the attack and a pause for another alien ceremony.*

She was not *providing a body part.*

And neither was Nik, decided Mac, having grown fond of his as well.

Singing implied voice, to a Human at least, but the Dhryn kept silent. *To Human ears,* Mac cautioned herself. She watched in fascination as Her Glory leaned forward, slowly, carefully, as if to offer the Progenitor a Human-style lover's kiss. She stopped a few centimeters short of contact. They remained thus, their lips parted, close but not touching.

A long minute passed. Then another.

Mac eased left for a better view.

Nothing.

Another minute. Two more. Deruym Ma Nas remained in his bow, although his limbs were now trembling with strain. He had a decidedly desperate look, as if he'd rather fall off the Progenitor's hand than stop bowing.

Mac glanced at Nik. He was studying Her Glory and the Progenitor. Catching her eye, he nodded toward the two, mouthing, "Look."

She dared step nearer and finally saw that something was passing between the open mouths. Moisture glistened on their lips and the surrounding flesh. *A fine spray?* Whatever it was, Her Glory's eyes had half closed in apparent rapture. The Progenitor's remained open and fixed on the other Dhryn.

This could take a while.

Mac walked over to Nik, careful to avoid the edge. "New to me," she whispered. "Have you seen anything like it before?"

Deruym Ma Nas' turquoise lips turned down in disapproval. *Haven Dhryn.* Mac smiled at him.

"No," Nik answered as quietly. "But when I agreed to be Her Vessel, She said it would be in spirit only, since Humans couldn't sing. Could be part of that process."

Mac turned to look outward, her shoulder against his. "Any idea where She's taking us?" *More exactly, where the Ro were leading them?*

"I had Fy contact the dart, to have Bhar check sensors. We're tractored to the other Dhryn, heading for the gate. From there?" She felt his shoulder move. "Any number of choices, Mac."

She sighed. "None of them good."

"No." A pause. "We've a couple of probes left on the *Impeci*. Once through the gate, we can at least let the IU know which system is under attack."

Mac reached into a pocket and brought out a nutrient bar. She snapped it in half. "Here."

Nik tapped his to hers. "Cheers, Dr. Connor."

She smiled. "Now you see the extent of my culinary skills."

"We won't starve." Nik's arm stole around her waist. "I can cook."

"Another experiment?" Mac leaned her head against him. Although her stomach objected, she ignored it, methodically chewing and swallowing the entire morsel.

Water would have been nice, but there was some on the dart. *They weren't desperate.*

Yet.

"Incredible, isn't She?" Nik murmured.

Mac gazed out at a vista holding all the beauty of a desert at twilight. "You should have seen Her whole." *Before She began to die.*

Before so many did.

She took an uneven breath and Nik's arm tightened. "You didn't see him fall," he said with that uncanny perception. "That's what you told me. That's what you need to remember."

"I feel appallingly selfish," Mac confessed. "Hoping for one among all the rest. With what's happening—"

Nik gathered her against him. "Then I'm selfish, too."

"Mac."

Didn't mind the sound of her name this way, breathed into her ear with such tenderness. Not about to wake up. But the sound . . . that was nice.

"I think they're about done. C'mon, Mac." The tenderness remained, but there was an added note of urgency that didn't intend to be ignored.

Mac opened her eyes, immediately realizing two things. First, she was tucked very comfortably within a nest composed of Nik's lap, arms, and body. Second, they were in . . . "This is the Progenitor's Chamber." She flushed and struggled to her feet. "You let me fall asleep on Her hand?"

In front of aliens?

"Guilty, though in my defense there was no 'letting' involved." Nik grinned unrepentantly as he stood. "Should I mention snoring? Guess not." This at her glare.

Mac rubbed her eyes. "What did I miss?"

"The Progenitors communed." Deruym Ma Nas sat nearby. His hands fussed with the strings holding his silks and the imps. He looked exhausted. *Not only the prolonged bow,* Mac judged. He was too thin, malnourished, and worn with care. "*Gnausa* is complete."

She looked at Her Glory. The large Dhryn leaned against the wall of the Progenitor. Glistening liquid streaked her jaw and upper chest, as it did the flesh beneath the Progenitor's mouth. Her bands glowed and her eyes were vivid gold. The Progenitor's eyes were closed, as if She slept.

"What is *Gnausa*?"

"It is how a Progenitor anoints Her Successor," Deruym Ma Nas told them. "No one else knows what passes between them." His lips moved and he folded his arms as if overcome by emotion. "But I—I can feel the result; I know I am in the presence of not one, but two of Those Who Light the Way." A hint of a bow to Mac and Nik. "An unexpected joy."

"Forgive me, but you don't seem joyful," Mac observed.

"After what you've revealed?" The archivist sighed. "I would like to believe there will be more accomplishments by That Which Is Dhryn to remember and record, but I am no fool, Mackenzie Winifred Elizabeth Wright Connor Sol. A Progenitor alone is doomed. A Successor without a future cannot save us."

Her Glory had been listening. Now, she came over to Deruym Ma Nas and bent to look the smaller Dhryn in the eye. "Despair cannot save us," she corrected.

This close, Mac could see that the liquid had spilled out of Her Glory's mouth—*which made sense, since the being could no longer swallow*—yet was viscous enough to stick to her skin. She looked closer. It was collecting in a maze of fine cracks in the thick blue. *Or had produced the cracks,* she realized, thinking of the potency of Dhryn spit. "How do you feel?" she ventured.

"Hungry." Her Glory smiled, as if asking Mac to share the humor in that admission. "Ambitious. Determined." She rose to her full height. "Is this not a glorious day? Who could not feel wonderful?" This as a shout that echoed far below.

"Hush. Leave me, Daughter." The Progenitor didn't open Her eyes. "I must rest before we reach our destination and defeat the Ro." There was no room for debate; as She spoke, Her hand moved away from Her face.

And so did they.

Fy was waiting for them within the long arched doorway. "May I see the Progenitor now?" she asked eagerly as Mac stepped from the hand.

"She fails," Her Glory said, her voice implacable. "I endure." She brushed by the Sinzi and headed up the ramp, Deruym Ma Nas following behind with a clatter of imps.

Move on. Survive. Mac understood the impulse. Part of her applauded it.

Part of her was already grieving. *No matter what happened next, the days of the Progenitor—Brymn's, hers—were numbered.*

Nik was shaking his head. "Blunt. I fear accurate." He touched the thick metal wall. "The ship will only last as long as there's crew."

Fy zipped around the two Humans, stopping in front of Nik. "I could examine the control systems," she said quickly, her fingers writhing. *Hopefully this was the excited anticipation of a scholar hoping to be set loose on the real thing,* though Mac didn't rule out a nervous twitch. "I would be willing—"

"We may need your help, Sinzi-ra," Nik assured her. "First, we need to check on the situation outside the ship. Anything new?"

Mac watched the two Dhryn, the old and the new. They'd stopped in the open, just beyond the arch. Deruym Ma Nas bowed to Her Glory and moved out of sight. Her Glory sat on the cushioned floor, her ridged back toward Mac, and began to rock from side to side.

What was she doing? Mac walked closer, curious.

Suddenly, a mass of tentacles appeared in one of the holes around the door, then three feeders dropped to where Her Glory sat, helpless and oblivious.

Mac let out a cry and broke into a run, *not that she had any idea what she could do.* "Mac! Wait!"

She slowed, not because of Nik's shout, but because the feeders had continued to drift downward until they rested on the floor before the Dhryn. Mac moved to the right-hand wall and edged forward to a good vantage point.

"You have the worst bloody reflexes—"

"Shhh." Mac grinned at Nik's fervent complaint as he hurried up beside her. "Look."

The feeders were not attacking Her Glory. *Far from it.* Instead, their tentacles were delicately exploring her face and chest. "I think they're after the liquid from the Progenitor," Mac whispered. The mouths at the ends of the tentacles stayed in no one place for long.

She noticed something else. Their clear bodies never stopped pulsating, but now each pulse spread a faint tinge of violet.

"They've friends," Nik cautioned as another pair joined the first three.

Fy's finger rested on Mac's shoulder. "Is this something to fear?"

Yes! Mac quelled the impulse and settled for a tight-lipped, "I don't know."

Her Glory had excellent hearing. "These are mine now, *Lamisah*. They will seek the Taste that I require. Which would," she added with the hint of a hoot, "include walnuts."

The violet was accumulating along the outer rim of each membrane; more drew a faint band across the ventral surface. *Perhaps coloration unique to each Progenitor,* Mac guessed.

Nik pressed his lips to her ear. She felt more than heard the words. "And us?"

He had his weapon out and ready. *He'd seen what a feeder could do to Human flesh.* She put her hand—*the new one*—over his, pressing it down. "Cayhill's work. Her Glory is herbivorous. Plants, Nik. We should be okay."

He resisted. " 'Should be' isn't good enough, Mac."

"There's only one way to know." She steeled herself to walk out there, but Nik beat her to it, heading for the Dhryn and her ghastly company.

"No. Wait!" She rushed after him, only to find Fy coming with her. "Oh, no. Not you," she declared, trying to grab some part of moving Sinzi. *It was remarkably difficult.* Mac wound up with an undignified handful of gown, said gown dragging her forward with it anyway.

Fortunately, the feeders scattered out of the way like jellyfish, their bodies bloating, membranes fluttering almost frantically. Her Glory hooted, her sides shaking. "You should see yourselves, *Lamisah!*"

Mac kept her eye on the feeders, now squeezing themselves back through the holes above the door. When the last tentacle disappeared from view, she looked back at the Dhryn. "I take it they were finished?"

Her Glory rose to her feet—*Her feet,* Mac corrected to herself, quite sure by this point the honorific was required. *Although she'd like to know more about the whole* oomling *production side of things.* "They will come with me. As will my *erumisah.*" She gestured grandly and Deruym Ma Nas scuttled back from where he'd been staying at a safe distance.

Someone not quite so sure, Mac thought.

"Come with you—where?" asked Nik.

"With you, of course. Deruym Ma Nas is right in one thing. I will need help. Your help. The help of the Interspecies Union."

Fy's fingers formed their complex knot. *Distress or confusion.* Mac sympathized "To do what?" the Sinzi inquired politely.

A one/two blink of warm golden eyes. "We shall destroy the Ro together. Then I shall restore That Which Is Dhryn to what we once were." Her Glory beamed at Mac. "Mac promised to help."

The Sinzi appeared paralyzed, then her head tilted, as if to let one set of eyes after the other study Mac's carefully noncommittal face.

Suddenly, her fingers shot upward, before gracefully lowering into circles through which she gazed at Mac. "I, Faras, participate in the promise! And I, Yt!"

Nik put one hand over his eyes and shook his head.

This, Mac told herself, *wasn't her fault.*

"I didn't promise," Mac insisted. "At least, I didn't promise what Her Glory thinks I did."

Nik raised one eyebrow. "Dare I ask?"

"It was more a 'that way to the washroom, I'll be here if you need me' kind of promise."

"That's not how She's interpreted it."

Mac slumped against the side of the dart. "I noticed."

"It could be worse," he said lightly, busy with his imp. It was preset to squeal its contents to a Ministry receiver when entering no-space. Something they were to do very soon, judging by the sensor data, so Nik was recording as much information as he could.

Other ships were on the move behind them; they wouldn't catch up. Starting position was everything in real-space travel. The only good news so far? The Imrya had caught signals from the *Annapolis Joy*. No specifics, not on unsecured channels, but Mac was willing to settle for knowing someone was alive. *For now.*

"Worse how?" Mac grumbled. "Fy wants in on it. Whatever it is."

"Worse if you'd promised the Progenitor."

"Oh." She dropped her head to stare at her feet. *Mistake.* The bottoms of her pants and boots were covered in dried blood and slime. She looked up again, breathing through her nose. *Mistake.*

The feeders had followed them to the vast hangar, rising to disappear into its darkness, only to reappear clothed as small silver ships. All five were now lined up between the *Impeci* and the Sinzi dart. Waiting, they'd been assured by Her Glory, for Her to enter Her chosen transport. At which point, they'd latch on to its hull and accompany Her.

Wherever She went.

Seeing the round doors on the lower half of the small things, Mac guessed where tentacles would protrude, allowing the feeders to digest their target, then suck up the result without leaving their casings.

"What are we going to do about them?" she nodded at the silent row.

This gained her a quick look.

A grim one. She straightened. "Nik? What did you do?"

"Let's just say I've prepared an option."

Her Glory was napping by the feeders, conserving Her strength. She'd stopped complaining about being hungry. *Not necessarily a good sign.* Deruym Na Mas sat nearby, nervously checking his imps, nervously checking his surroundings. He was having some difficulty imagining they were to travel outside the Progenitor's ship.

It didn't help that he'd believed the Progenitor's ship was still part of Haven.

Fy was inspecting the *Impeci*, wearing a Sinzi evacsuit from the dart. Meanwhile, those from the *Impeci*—the Imrya and Fiora, the pilot, Bhar, and Cavendish—remained inside her craft. It kept them away from the newest members of—*what were they anyway?* Mac wondered. *A merry band of adventurers? Or the walking dead, too stubborn to lay down?*

Not something Nik would do. She knew that about him. She didn't ask about his "option," trusting it would save them if the feeders couldn't find sufficient walnuts.

Wherever they went.

"Humans?"

It was the Imrya. Mac and Nik rose to their feet as she approached. "Cavendish," he said.

"Yes. He has expired." The alien lifted her recorder, then let it hang from its strap. "I find myself too full of words, Nikolai. A noble being."

Nik merely nodded. With an effort Mac could see, if no one else could, he fought back any reaction, focusing on the task at hand. "Let's get him on the *Impeci*. I want us all in place before transect. We don't know what's on the other side, or even if this ship will hold together." He went with the Imrya, the thorough professional.

Mac stayed where she was.

One less.

She felt ill. If they had to evacuate the Progenitor's ship, Cavendish, terminal and fading, had improved their chances by dying now. *You could never escape the math.* There had been too many of them for the dart.

There still were.

She leaned her head back against the swirled metal. They had the poisoned *Impeci*. The Dhryn could tolerate the radiation inside the Human ship. *That wasn't the problem.* Her Glory couldn't pilot it, not with only one hand.

Bhar, the *Impeci's* pilot, was slipping in and out of consciousness. Fy was needed to pilot the Sinzi dart. And Fiora knew as much as Mac about flying a starship. *Which was nothing.*

Leaving Nik, who knew too much.

He'd wear an evacsuit. Giving him a few hours of protection.

If that. He'd been exposed already.

"I hate this plan, Em," Mac muttered.

Sacrifice the Dhryn? For all they knew, Dhryn might be the only way to kill the Ro.

Sacrificing Nikolai Trojanowski? *Part of the job.*

"I hate the job, too," she said clearly and with emphasis.

"Why are you talking to the air? Does this serve a purpose?" Deruym Ma Nas shuffled closer. "What is that?" This last as Nik walked by them, his eyes straight ahead, carrying the wrapped form of Tucker Cavendish.

"Nie rugorath sa nie a nai." Mac switched to Instella. "A Human, Tucker Cavendish. Remember his name, Archivist."

"I will." He sat beside her. "I fear I will have more names to remember, Mackenzie Winifred Elizabeth Wright Connor Sol, than there are living Dhryn."

She looked at him. "What you do is important, Deruym Ma Nas. Remember that too."

"It is my value to That Which Is Dhryn," he agreed, then sighed. Mac felt a vibration of distress through the floor. "Is it true? Will the not-Dhryn help us? The Successor is certain. But I have doubts."

"You're her *erumisah*," she said carefully. "Doubt's part of your duty, isn't it?"

"To an extent." A small hoot. "I confess I lose my reasoned arguments within Her Light."

"Write them down," she suggested.

. . . Mac felt a vibration of distress through the floor. "Is it true? Will the not-Dhryn help us? The Successor is certain. But I have doubts."

"You're her—" she stopped there, understanding what had happened.

They'd gone through the gate.

The Dhryn looked confused. "Why do we repeat ourselves?"

"I'll explain later. Stay with Her Glory."

Mac started walking toward the *Impeci*. Nik was already coming back. From his intent expression, he'd felt it, too.

A shout from behind—Fiora, from the open door of the dart. "It's Earth! They've taken us home! We're saved!"

Mac didn't need to see the horror on Nik's face to know.

They weren't saved at all.

- CONTACT -

THE SINZI SHIPS HAD BEEN MOVING into position for days. Earthgov had maintained a politely interested view of these proceedings, there being little else to be done. Earth media, having more options, had launched sufficient remote probes to constitute a significant navigation threat to normal traffic, which was rerouted to other orbits.

However much a nuisance, it was the media who first realized what the Sinzi ships were doing. They were arranging themselves into an immense spiral, the narrow end pointing toward the Earth, the wider toward her Sun. The effect was dazzling, when the Moon didn't eclipse it, and the image became commonplace in homes across the system, complete with identifying logos and associated advertising.

Until problems with newspackets and other shipments made the headlines. The curious artistry of the Sinzi slipped from Human attention.

The arrival of the Trisulian fleet, with its threats, soon consumed it. But not, it seemed, the Sinzi, who refused to discuss the matter.

And so matters stood.

Until matters changed.

Hollans rose to his feet. "Say again."

"It's gone, sir."

"The Naralax Transect," he repeated, wondering what could be affecting the usually exemplary staff of Venus Orbital. *Some Trisulian gas?* "You're telling me it's gone."

"Yes, sir. The approach horizon, the gate—they don't register. It's gone, sir. Pending traffic's sitting in normal space. Yelling for answers."

"Let's get confirmation on that, Venus Orbital."

The voice on the com became somewhat shrill. "You don't think we'd call about something like this without making sure we weren't nuts? Sir." More calmly. "We've confirmation from all possible observation points. It's gone."

A slender fingertip rose before Hollans' eyes, claiming his attention. "I'll get back to you, Venus Orbital," he muttered, staring up at the Sinzi-ra for Earth.

"Sir?"

He closed the connection as Anchen took a seat at his gesture. "Did you hear that?" he said numbly. "The Naralax . . . gone?"

"It is not gone, Mr. Hollans." Two fingers inscribed a spiral through the air, rings tinkling. "We have moved it. Temporarily."

"Where?" Hollans gripped the edge of his desk, trying to understand. "Why?"

Anchen smiled. "Where? To Earth orbit. Why?" Her fingers formed loops before her eyes. "We participate in the promise."

- 26 -

HOME AND HORROR

OF THEM ALL, ONLY FY wasn't shocked. *Which was just as well*, Mac thought, since the Sinzi happily busied herself setting up a tactical display at Nik's hoarse request.

"What do you mean—we're in orbit?" The *Impeci*'s pilot, Bhar, had regained consciousness only to doubt he truly had. They'd made him comfortable in the dart's open hatch. "That's impossible," he insisted. "The gate's inside Venus' orbit. It takes almost a week to get to Earth."

"Apparently things have changed," Mac told him. She felt somewhat vindicated by this evidence the transects were not as foolproof as she'd been told. It brought the technology down to the level of a malfunctioning lev; something to be fixed.

Although there was the issue of crashing first.

The tactical display came to life outside the dart, a larger version of what might be generated by an imp. Earth was to one side, a breathtaking swirl of white over blue.

But like the others, Mac kept looking to the other side, where a rotating spiral of silver ships—*Sinzi ships*—dominated the polar sky.

"We are here." Enlarging the display, Fy put her fingertip on a pair of dots. They were within a cloud of similar dots exiting the base of the spiral.

Aimed at Earth.

"All That Are Dhryn," Her Glory rumbled.

Nik's eyes were fixed on the image, his hands clenched into fists. "I knew it," he accused. "The Sinzi will sacrifice Earth for the IU!"

"We participate in the promise—"

"Stop saying that!" Mac shouted at Fy. "This is our world. Our home! Don't you realize what you're doing to us? Why did you bring the Dhryn?"

"We did nothing but come to Sol and move the Naralax in congruence with Earth."

"Why?" Nik repeated, his voice no quieter than Mac's.

Fy's fingers were trembling. "Surely it is obvious—"

"What's obvious is you've betrayed us!" Her own hand shaking, Mac brushed tears from her cheeks. "I trusted you. We all did!"

"Wait," this sharply, from Her Glory. "Look."

The cloud of Dhryn was dispersing before their eyes; they weren't heading for the planet below.

Even as that relief hit, Mac gasped as she saw where they were going. "They—they aren't—"

Fy seemed to relax. "Yes. You see? As anticipated."

All that remained of the Dhryn turned to close on the spiral of Sinzi vessels.

"The Ro must have Called the Progenitors to eliminate the real threat to their plans," observed Her Glory. "We are too late."

"We're still in this," Nik said urgently. "Deruym Ma Nas. Tell the Progenitor—we must break away from the other Dhryn ships, now." The Dhryn looked startled, but ran for the nearest com panel—at least, Mac assumed that's what it was. "Fy," Nik continued, "show me system-wide tactical. Where are the Human ships?"

The display twinned under the Sinzi's direction, the second half showing from Earth inward. "Your fleet is gathered where the Naralax used to be," Fy said unnecessarily. "With a substantial number of Trisulian vessels. Together they approach your world. They will not reach it for another four days at maximum." A growing list of text appeared. Mac didn't try to read it. "Interesting. A substantial number of nongovernment newspackets are entering the gate from your world. I do not recognize the type."

"Media drones," Bhar volunteered. "I don't believe it."

"There's got to be something we can do." Nik yanked out his com and began spouting code and numbers into the device.

Spy stuff.

Mac was staring at Fy. "This won't accomplish anything," she objected. "You'll only die first. The Ro will use our worlds."

"The Sinzi go!" She glanced around at Bhar's hoarse cry. "They're running from the Dhryn."

They all looked. Sure enough, though a few Sinzi ships appeared to be holding position—*perhaps to control the transect gate*—the rest were now leaving the spiral. The result was like a flower opening.

And about as fast.

"You call that running?" Mac wanted to reach into the display and shove the tiny lights out of danger. The Progenitors were gaining every second. "Can't they go faster?"

"If they wish," Fy said calmly.

If she was being pursued by giant ships filled with feeders she'd wish a great deal harder, Mac thought, wondering what the Sinzi were up to—*and why it had to be in her corner of the universe.*

"If . . ." Nik closed his hand over his com. "You want the Dhryn to follow." Flat, sure, *that dangerous tone.* "Your people are bait. For what?"

"We promised to keep Anchen safe from the Ro, and to help Mac return home."

"How?" Mac burst out. "By dying?" The Progenitor ships in the display became haloed with a bright glitter. "Those are feeders." *She probably hadn't needed to point that out,* Mac realized, given there were five sitting on the deck behind them.

The first Sinzi ships disappeared within that glitter. Mac reached out blindly, finding warmth with one hand. It wasn't Human.

Her Glory.

Mac turned and stared into that alien face, those golden eyes. Only, for an instant, it wasn't alien at all, the grief in those eyes so real and familiar it was all she could do not to say his name and weep.

"The Progenitor has broken away as you suggested, Vessel," Deruym Ma Nas told Nik. From his tone, the Dhryn was thoroughly confused by the entire process. *Lucky.*

"Where's She going?" Mac asked, trying to find their dot among the many. *Away from the rest would be a positive step.*

The archivist sat down, as if exhausted by the trot to the com panel. *Which he could be,* Mac realized. "Our mission has not changed. The Progenitor hunts the Ro contamination," he told them. "It will be on the planet."

Nik's eyes caught and held Mac's. "Earth," he said.

Not a positive step.

- CONTACT -

THE TELEMATICS AREA of the Atrium was silent, except for technicians' low voices as they relayed information. Above them all, beyond the curve of atmosphere, Sinzi ran. Sinzi died. And when the rest of the Dhryn were finished, everyone knew they'd turn to follow the Progenitor already on course for Earth.

They'd done all they could for the Sinzi. Now it was time to save themselves.

Hollans turned to his aide. "Dee, do we have anything in range?"

Dee grimaced. "Nothing bigger than a docking shuttle. Unless you want to throw shipping crates at them." She checked the 'screen hovering by her ear. "The Sinzi—at least they're buying us time, sir. Evacuations are underway from every continent. How much damage we take depends on where that first Dhryn strikes."

They'd prepared for this—the way a desperate parent realizes she can carry only one child to safety through the fire and must let go of those other small fingers.

The Human species would survive another day, or however long the Ro left them.

"She hasn't said a word?"

Hollans looked over at the Sinzi-ra. Her great topaz eyes gazed at the display, her fingers quiet in their complex weaving, her gown impeccable. A dark red ring winked among the silver on her third left finger. He'd come to notice such things. "No," he answered. "But that doesn't mean silence."

Dee took a message and grabbed Hollans' arm even as she replied into her headset. Then, "Sir! It's Nik. Trojanowski!" Pure triumph. "He's back!"

"Patch him through. Now."

"Here."

"What's going on?" The familiar voice filled the area, drawing everyone's attention.

To the point. *Definitely Trojanowski.* "The Sinzi are being pursued by the Dhryn. Where are you?"

"On the Progenitor Ship heading for Earth. Don't shoot. She's our contact and free of Ro influence. She's after the Ro. Says there's one on Earth."

"We have no—" Hollans stopped as Anchen came up to him. "The Sinzi-ra is here," he said.

"Greetings, Nikolai," as if her kind wasn't in peril. "How is Mac?"

"Here and worried." Quick and sharp. "Sinzi-ra, what are your people doing?"

"What they must," she replied placidly. "Do you require assistance?"

A pause Hollans sympathized with, then a brisk: "Is Dr. Mamani still following the Ro device? We believe it's some kind of a mobile station—where a Ro interacts with real space. Vulnerable. If we can get to it, stop the Ro, that should stop the Dhryn."

Hollans made an urgent gesture to his aide. "We're sending you Dr. Mamani's current position now," he told Nik. "A force will meet you there."

"Have them stand by," came the surprising response.

"For what? You may have noticed time isn't something we have in great supply, Mr. Trojanowski."

"There's a threat, sir. We believe there's a Ro failsafe on the device. We'll need the Sinzi's help to disable it. Sinzi-ra Myriam, Fy, is on board. She'll pass along the details."

A threat—to Earth. Hollans relinquished his place at the com with a bow to Anchen.

To his aide, "Continue evacuation protocols."

- 27 -

CONSEQUENCE AND CHANGE

M AC HAD LISTENED carefully to Nik's plan. It had been as reasonable as anything else she'd heard lately.

She'd just modified it.

Which was why she was jamming her right foot into an evacsuit. The smell curling up from inside reminded her of dead salmon, which, under the circumstances, seemed almost pleasant. *Almost.*

"Tell me again why you're going instead of me, Dr. Connor."

Mac squinted at Bhar. The pilot was on his feet. *And leaning on the edge of the stairs to stay that way.* "Because I could push you down," she observed pleasantly.

"You're a civilian!"

"That's what I keep telling everyone," she agreed, pulling the wretched garment over her shoulders. "They never listen."

Nik, already in the other suit, sealed his visor. "Ready?" His voice came out with a tinny undertone, reminding her of Svehla in his scuba gear.

"Yes," she said, doing her best with the unfamiliar fasteners as she moved. "Bhar?"

"On my way, sir. Good hunting."

Mac hadn't asked about the *Impeci,* what it would be like. She didn't care. *They'd only be inside as long as it took to drop from orbit to Emily's last known position. Home.*

Fy was coming with them, as were the Dhryn. All the Dhryn. The Progenitor— both of them—were insistent. Mac eyed the five feeder pods now limpeted to the upper hull. *Probably should call ahead for walnuts.*

Among the elements Nik was coordinating as Sinzi died and they rushed to Earth?

Walnuts could wait.

The remaining Humans would trust themselves to the Imrya's skills with the Sinzi communication system and Earthgov's ability to track them. Fy had preset the dart to soft land on Earth. Mac wished them luck.

The *Impeci*—more specifically Her Successor—would find and destroy the Ro while the Progenitor waited in orbit. *She'd liked the plan.*

She wanted to like the plan, too, Mac told herself wearily. She nodded good-bye to Bhar and waved to the others.

A shame she couldn't.

Mac entered the contaminated ship after Nik, catching up to him in the wide opening that led to the ship's internal corridors. The *Impeci* seemed entirely harmless and ordinary; she could have been inside any overnight transit lev. *If she ignored the radiation warning that scrolled underfoot, its arrows pointing the way to safety.*

Outside.

Where safety was no more than one being's good intentions.

"Nik. Wait." Her voice echoed inside the visor. He pointed to the com control by her chin. Mac pushed it on, fumbling in her haste. "Nik," she repeated. "We can't leave yet. The Progenitor. She's— We can't trust Her."

His visor angled down so he could look at her, but she couldn't see enough of his face to read his expression. His tone was neutral. "She's promised to leave Earth alone."

"But I don't believe She can," Mac said urgently. "Her feeders—they won't let Her starve to death, not with a planetful of life in reach. You brought—" She swallowed hard. "I know you have the means on board."

"You know what you're asking, Mac?" Still that neutral voice.

Optimist, not idiot, Mac wanted to say. Instead, she snapped: "Of course I know," then regretted her temper. *It wasn't Nik's fault.* She put her gloved hand on his wrist in apology. "We must be able to stop Her, if it becomes necessary."

His glove covered hers. "Spy, remember? A certain level of mistrust's a job skill." More soberly. "I rigged charges when we first boarded, controlled from the *Impeci*. Two failsafes. One's here. Anything interrupts the signal from this ship, boom."

Mac shuddered inwardly. "The other?"

His hand moved to pat the biceps on his other arm.

Gods. "I really didn't want to know that."

"You might need to." A gesture forward. "Let's get going."

She'd—*almost*—prided herself achieving a level of ruthlessness she'd never imagined before.

Not in Nik's league.

The *Impeci's* bridge was small and straightforward. Once the Dhryn ripped out the chairs, there was room for all of them. Mac stayed back. Her role, if any, would come once they landed.

That had been the modification to the plan. Emily, and she supposed Case Wilson, had used the Tracer to pinpoint the location of the Ro chamber. Mac was the only other Human qualified to use the device; made sense to have her available.

That wasn't why Nik agreed to take her along.

The Ro had used the same technology to find her once. They had—*how had Fy put it?*—an interest in a certain salmon researcher.

Mac crossed her arms as best she could in the evacsuit. *There was,* she thought with no little irony, *distinct circularity to it all.* If she was Sinzi, she'd enjoy it.

The Tracer could find the Ro—Emily's hunt had proved that. What would happen next depended on luring the Ro from its chamber into the open.

So, like the Sinzi running not quite fast enough from the Dhryn, Mac was bait.

Once the Ro was exposed, Her Glory was more than willing to tackle the creature. *And probably could.* Though to Mac's unspoken relief, Nik had assured them that, if needed, reinforcements would be there.

But dealing with the Ro was only the first step. They had to seal the chamber's connection to no-space before it began draining Earth's oceans.

Fy believed it could be done.

They were, Mac decided, *leaping blind.*

"We're clear of the Progenitor," Nik announced. He cued the main screen. A mass of dim silver rushed by overhead, but Mac stared hungrily at their goal. Earth. Northern hemisphere. Pacific. *Home indeed.*

Deruym Ma Nas peered at the display. "What's that?"

Her Glory hooted. "Another world, Deruym Ma Nas."

"Are you sure? It looks too small," the archivist argued.

A louder hoot greeted that.

Fy came up to Mac. The Sinzi version of an evacsuit was a clear membrane, as if the being was coated with flexible glass. It silenced her rings, but not the restlessness of her fingers. "Mac, I have a difficulty."

Nik heard and frowned. *The man who knew the species.* Mac gave him a slight warning shake of her head, having a little more experience with this particular Sinzi. "What difficulty?"

"I must confer in more detail with Anchen—"

"The connection's open, Fy," Nik said, gesturing to the com panel. "But I thought you'd already discussed what needs to be done with the Sinzi-ra." Mac was likely the only one on board who could interpret his tone as: *don't need a problem, busy saving the world.*

Fy spun in a tight circle, fingers close to her body, then stopped as quickly, her neck bending to bring her face almost touching Mac's. "Instella is inadequate," she whispered miserably. "I must speak as Sinzi do, but that's not permitted in front of—"

"Aliens," Mac said helpfully, when the being faltered. The *Impeci* was plummeting to Earth, they were standing in evacsuits to survive even this brief exposure to the contaminated ship, and—*if she grasped the essentials*—the being who was to help save the planet was worrying over manners while her species faced near-extinction.

Somehow, Mac managed not to laugh, protest, or tear at her hair. Watching this exchange, Nik's frown turned into a look of serious concern and he pointed to the time. *Of which they had none.* "Tell you what, Fy," this as cheerfully as possible. "Close your eyes and pretend we aren't here."

Now Fy was frowning, too, although in a Sinzi the expression involved a painful-looking knot of fingers.

Plan B. Mac reached into the right side pocket of her evacsuit, pushed her hand through the sealant layer, and fumbled her way into the pocket of her coveralls. *Finally a real use for the damn thing.* "Hang on," she grunted, trying to snag her prize with two gloved fingers. *The world dies because she can't reach a stupid . . .* "There!" With that, she tugged free a blue-and-green envelope barred with gold. Her name appeared over its surface in moving letters of mauve. "By the authority of the Interspecies Union," Mac said glibly, "I demand you speak to Anchen in whatever language will save us." She brandished the envelope like a flag under the Sinzi's eyes. "Okay?"

There was a moment of complete silence on the bridge.

Then Fy bowed, almost as graciously as Ureif. "Okay." She walked over to the com, Nik easing out of her way, and called up a 'screen above the com. "Anchen," she said clearly. "Concerning the procedure to close the Myrokynay's no-space connections within the target area. I have additional thoughts, based on the likeliest materials of construction. We must—" the Instella stopped and something else began.

Mac had edged closer, curious. Now she winced and covered her ears, an action which made no difference whatsoever to the bedlam coming through the speakers inside her helmet. The two Dhryn merely looked startled. Nik waved at Mac, then pantomimed how to control the volume. Mac lifted her hand to do so, but waited.

The sound issuing from Fy's mouth was harsh to Human ears not because it was discordant, she realized, but because it was modulating so quickly and along such a scale it came across as static. *No, more than that.* Multiple tones implied a simultaneous conversation, as if Anchen's reply—perhaps more than Anchen's— in the same tongue overlapped Fy's. Certainly Fy's lips hadn't stopped moving.

They listened and spoke at the same time?

Jabulani would love this, Mac thought. Not to mention what it implied of the usual pace of information exchange between the Sinzi. *They must think we're snails.* The patience and skill required of any Sinzi who had to talk to another species—*no wonder they invented Instella.* They'd needed it so others could talk to them.

Finished, Fy's fingers closed her 'screen. She turned to Nik and Mac. "Anchen has studied the penetration of the consulate by the Ro. Their technology has not significantly advanced with time as has ours. We concur there is room for confidence our efforts will be successful. If the Ro opens its gate, that is. If it remains inactive, we can do nothing."

Great, up the odds. Still, Mac thought this a positive sign. Nik, however, had that expressionless *nothing good* look. "We'll get it to stick its head out," she insisted. "I'm not the only bait." She nodded at Her Glory.

Her Glory, perhaps fortunately, was preoccupied. She was watching the sensors. *Probably good someone was,* Mac thought.

Until the Dhryn's hand shot forward to adjust one control, then another. No haste, but not slow either. "We have new traffic, *Lamisah.*" The announcement was quiet and sure. "Coming through the gate."

Nik did something to the main screen, changing the display from the oncoming ball of ocean and cloud to a stream of code.

Fy let out a string of Sinzi, fingers moving more quickly than Mac could see. The Dhryn rumbled. While Nik, staring at the code, was muttering: "That's . . . that's . . . I don't believe it . . . how . . ."

All of which didn't help a certain biologist one iota.

"Would someone tell me what's going on?" Mac demanded.

- CONTACT -

EACH AND EVERY TRAFFIC controller, from the Antarctic spaceport to the Moon—and way stations between—reacted by locking down anything remotely near Earth orbit, including whatever sat in launch catapults. Although this meant a disruption in shipping likely to result in more than a few stale pastries, no one argued.

There wasn't room for more.

Ships differing in shape, size, and species were pouring from the gate held above the North Pole by the Sinzi. Hundreds. Thousands. There were no com calls. Protocol didn't exist. The only reason they didn't collide on arrival was that exiting from no-space somehow pushed existing matter aside.

That, and the fact that each ship immediately powered up to chase Dhryn.

"Even the Ar," Hollans observed, shaking his head in wonder. "Outstanding."

The Imrya ambassador was standing nearby. "Our fleet was the first through," he pointed out. "These others? Why, some do not have offensive capabilities! What can they hope to accomplish?"

"The same thing we all do, Ambassador," answered Hollans with a grim smile. "To save the Sinzi. To save the IU. Even an unarmed starship can be a weapon, if you have the will."

Anchen had been with consular staff, about to serve species-specific refreshments. Now she came up to the Human and Imrya, and gestured to the display. "You showed them our need and they have come." A deep bow to Hollans. "Thank you."

Hollans lost his smile. "You knew?"

With every military and government resource days away at the original gate, he'd pulled strings at every level, threatened, begged, and bribed, all to send every orbiting Human media packet and snoop satellite through the new gate, with their vid recordings of the Sinzi spiral—and the attack of the Dhryn. There hadn't been time to add explanations. He'd had to trust the images would be enough, even if the eyes seeing them wouldn't be Human.

"What you did? Of course. That any would answer?" A delicate shrug. "We had hope, nothing more. There comes a time, my friends, when actions speak past any differences of language or form. Observe."

Hollans followed the sweep of finger back to the display.

The spreading fountain of Sinzi vessels, the base already engulfed by Dhryn, slowed, then stopped. Before the Dhryn caught up to them, they began to move again, but this time inward, more and more quickly, the fountain collapsing back on itself.

Into the whirlpool of oncoming ships.

All two hundred and seventy Progenitors' ships slowed, then stopped, a decision echoed by the glittering clouds of tiny feeder ships. Then, as if unable to fathom anything but the Call to consume the Sinzi, every Dhryn turned and followed.

The minutes ticked by, positions shifting, the future becoming inevitable.

As the last Sinzi poured through the newcomers to safety, the display showed weaponsfire—a concentrated, targeted stream from every ship capable of it, at point-blank range.

Within minutes, the Great Journey was over. That Which Was Dhryn became nothing more than glowing debris.

Except for one.

A lone Progenitor's ship, with a slagged prow, still on course for Earth.

"Sinzi-ra Anchen?" Hollans asked diffidently. *There was no longer doubt who had planned this—who now would make the decision.*

"We await the final congruence," the Sinzi said. "Would you care for tea, Mr. Hollans?"

- 28 -

CONGRUENCE AND CONFRONTATION

MAC WAITED FOR THE OTHER SHOE to drop. Nik was busy on the com to Hollans, passing along congratulations and whatever else people said to one another during a victory celebration. *Victory,* she thought numbly. Her Glory, still at sensors, had showed no emotion as the IU destroyed Her kind. Deruym Ma Nas hadn't understood. *His Progenitors did.*

Unlike the Dhryn, Fy was visibly shaken. She hovered beside Mac and her fingers flowed up and down in short flutters, as if she tried to fly.

"Are you all right?" Mac asked at last.

"I'm in accord," Fy replied—*hopefully a yes.* "Other members of the IU now have proof we were as much at risk as they from the Dhryn. Their response—its result? I don't know the Human equivalent to how I feel, Mac. As you see, I cannot move slowly, as you've wisely suggested is appropriate. I shall never forget this moment. It will reshape what I am. Thus for all Sinzi."

Mac frowned. "I don't understand."

"Many of us died today." A fingertip rested on Mac's chest for an instant. "As you go where you're needed, so must we. The transects must be maintained and kept safe for all. My Faras-self is capable and will assume this task." A lift of two fingers, like a Human shrug. "Others will go to do the same."

"What of your research?" Mac asked.

"My Yt-self will continue." Fy's triangular mouth formed a passably Human smile. "She enjoys the hunt. To answer questions and seek new ones. To disturb the dust. Do not fear I'll—"

. . . "What of your research?" Mac asked—*again!*—then stared at the Sinzi. "What just—"

Her Glory shouted, "On intercept!"

There was always another shoe.

As if outside of panic, Mac considered the situation and snorted to herself. *Okay, with aliens, it could be more than two shoes. Or none.*

Life used to be so simple.

Nik was answering the Dhryn, his voice tense. "I see it. Fy—we'll need to sharpen our approach, get some speed."

"What is it?" Mac started to follow the Sinzi to her console, walking between the two Dhryn to reach Nik. "What's—"

A grip that would have broken her flesh arm. "It's them!" shrieked Deruym Ma Nas. "I saw them. I saw them before! I know that shape!"

Mac's eyes leaped to the main screen, no longer a *to-her* meaningless mass of codes. Instead, it showed a spire hanging in the darkness.

"So do I," she said numbly.

The Ro had stopped hiding.

- CONTACT -

CASE RAISED THE VIEWER TO HIS EYES, turning slowly to scan the sea ice. "What I thought. She's gone past the pressure ridge." He pointed to a line of heaved, upthrust white, the sleeve of his well-worn cold weather suit pressed flat by the biting wind. His hair stood straight.

Probably frozen. 'Sephe leaned her chin into her com, tucked inside the warmth of her hood. The former fisher had assured her this was spring. *Hadn't arrived as far as she could tell.* "This is Stewart. Inform Hollans Dr. Mamani isn't back yet. Does he want me to go and get her?"

She waited for the reply behind a dubious shelter of mem-fabric, hoping the answer would be no.

The Tracer had led them to this icy desolation. *According to Emily.* The Ro—or whatever they followed—had stopped. *According to Emily.* They'd been moving the harvester lev in steadily decreasing circles ever since. Now, the good doctor finally satisfied, they waited while she fine-tuned whatever it was. Which required peace and quiet. Without company.

According to Emily. Case hadn't argued. 'Sephe had learned to watch him for signals when Emily Mamani was pushing herself too far. Impossible to tell otherwise. The woman was driven.

So long as she went in the right direction, 'Sephe was happy. *She didn't want to follow her out on the ice.*

"Hollans here."

'Sephe straightened, the wind hitting her back. "Yes, sir."

"This isn't a conversation call. We're about to take out the hostile. Get Dr. Mamani back from wherever she's gone and stand by."

Before 'Sephe could acknowledge, there was a sudden *crack*, as if a whip had snapped across the sky. She looked up in time to see the rear of the harvester drop away.

"We're under attack!" she shouted, then ran for Case.

The sea exploded around them.

29

ENEMIES AND ENDS

"**T**HE TRUE BATTLE BEGINS!"

"Stay at your post!" Nik snapped at the aroused Dhryn. Her Glory subsided, but Mac could feel the vibration of her rage through the deck. "It's not our fight," he continued. "We're after the one on Earth. Monitor what's going on. How's the Progenitor?"

This brought an anguished moan from Deruym Ma Nas. Mac put her hand on his shoulder and bent to his ear. "Trust them, *Erumisah*," she said in Dhryn. "As She does."

Did the Progenitor know what Nik had left behind on Her ship? Did she understand what her lamisah *might do in the name of their own kind?*

Mac doubted any answer to those questions could remove the sick feeling from her stomach. She looked for a bright side. *Maybe it was the first sign of radiation poisoning.*

"The Ro do nothing," Her Glory rumbled. Then, "Aha! The Progenitor sends Her Mouths against them. We shall prevail!"

"Why don't they counterattack?" Fy pointed at the silent, motionless Ro ship.

Nik didn't look up from the *Impeci*'s controls. "I think they are," he said. "Looks like we were right—the autodestruct can't affect Her ship. But they'll—"

The display was erased by a blinding flash, then reset itself. Mac's visor compensated. The Dhryns' eyes, she noticed, were now protected by that blue inner lid. Fy had her fingers before her eyes and appeared in distress, but she had no time to check on her.

What was happening was before them all.

The Ro had fired on the Progenitor.

As Her great ship began to glow in wide bands—*almost mimicry*—Mac held onto Deruym Ma Nas, although the battered older Dhryn did nothing more than thrum his distress. *Finally understanding what he saw,* she thought, and held tighter.

She'd remembered the Ro ship as a towering splinter of bronze and light, accompanied by other, much smaller splinters. On the *Impeci's* screen, she saw the reality. The main splinter was not a single piece, but three identical shards, like immense crystal fingers. Those, like the smaller pieces, were connected by crisscrossing scaffolds, their tips toward the embattled Progenitor, as if whatever beam or power had been used originated from those ends.

All the while feeders swarmed over the Ro ship, fastening to its sleek surfaces, corroding through. Despite what she knew, Mac silently urged them on, but it was too little, too late.

The last Progenitor's ship lost its shape and reflection, turning dark as it was liquefied before their eyes. Fragments burst away. *Their contribution?* It didn't matter. She was gone.

Deruym Ma Nas curled into a massive ball of misery, eyes shut tight. But Her Glory began shouting at Nik. "Let me call them! They are mine now!"

At first, stung by grief, Mac couldn't understand what the Dhryn wanted so desperately.

Nik did.

"Stay back!" His weapon flashed out. "I won't let you send them against Earth!"

Mac stared at the screen. The dots that were the feeders now drifted aimlessly away from the Ro ship. *They might be mindless, but they reacted as if they knew their Progenitor was dead and they no longer had function.*

"Fool! I'll send them against our enemy! My Vessel, tell him!"

The Ro ship was tilting. *Aiming at them!*

"Nikolai. The other ships can't reach us before the Ro fire," Fy said quietly. *Why was everyone looking at her?*

"All I know," Mac told him, "is we can talk to Her Glory."

Nik whirled and punched a sequence of buttons. "Do it," he told the Dhryn over his shoulder, his eyes wild. "This should reach them."

Hadn't put down the weapon, Mac noticed.

Her Glory sat on Her four legs, and closed Her mouth. Before Mac could do more than frown with surprise, the Dhryn's sides began moving in and out.

If she'd thought the deck vibrated before, this was paramount to a quake. Mac tore her eyes back to the screen. "It's working!" she cried as dots began moving back to the Ro.

The Ro ship tipped further. Dots winked out in line with its sparkling prow. It continued to turn over, like an immense broom sweeping space clear.

"We're entering the atmosphere," Fy exclaimed.

The Ro ship was almost in line with them.

Nik looked at Mac and shook his head. "We're not going to make it."

Suddenly, a new voice screamed: "We take our vengeance!" The display filled with a black hull even as alarms rang through the small bridge.

"Damn Trisulian almost clipped us! Where'd she come from?" Nik demanded, hurrying back to the controls. The alarm fell away.

Fy's fingers were flying over her console, but it was Her Glory who answered. "Through the gate. They must have vectored in behind the Progenitor. There are more—"

On cue, the speaker blared again, this time with a familiar voice. "Sorry we're late. Got a bit crowded back there. Glad you've left us something to do."

"Welcome to the party, Captain." Nik's smile was a beautiful thing.

Captain Gillis?

Mac sagged against the conveniently still-comatose archivist. "The *Joy*—?" she whispered.

"We're battered and bloody, but we've teeth. The walkers left when you did. Thanks for that." The voice faded, then came back loud and clear. "We'll keep this guy busy. Good hunting. *Joy* out."

Nikolai Trojanowski shut off the display, then looked around the bridge. His head was up, his eyes bright and fierce. He held out his hand to Mac as she rose to her feet. He nodded to Fy. "Sinzi-ra," he said with a slight bow. "Put her down at the coordinates for Dr. Mamani. Mac? We need to change."

The air hit like a drug. Mac drew in a greedy gasp, coughed at the cold, then immediately took another, each feeling as though it went straight to her arteries.

"There!" Nik shouted, his arm raised to point.

Mac was busy looking the other way. "Ah, Nik?"

He turned and glanced up. The five feeders they'd brought were lifting free from the hull of the *Impeci,* their small craft noiseless and quick.

They weren't alone.

A dozen, maybe more, were overhead.

"Do not fear, *Lamisah!*" Her Glory boomed. "These shall drink only of the Ro!"

"Oh, good," Mac replied, for want of anything better to say.

Nik shrugged and pulled up his hood. "Let's go."

They'd only started walking when he touched her arm. "We're expected."

Mac followed his gesture. Coming behind them was a line of Ministry levs, large, black, and thoroughly reassuring.

Less reassuring was the plume of smoke beyond the levs, rising from a crashed hulk on the ice. "The harvester!" Mac gasped. "Emily!"

But she took only one step in that direction before Nik grabbed her. "She's not there, Mac. C'mon!"

"This way!" Her Glory was already on the move, her six legs churning. *Those padded feet were perfect for irregular ice,* Mac couldn't help but notice. Better traction than her borrowed boots, intended for a man half again her size.

It didn't matter. None of it mattered now. She could see their goal for herself: Emily, a dark slim line against the gray-blue ice, her attention on the Tracer.

They stumbled forward, levs landing all around them. Emily's hood was off. Mac saw the flash of pale as she twisted her head to check out the newcomers, then turned back to the machine.

"She's got it," Mac shouted to Nik as they ran. "She's found it!"

Armored figures began pouring from the levs. Some carried equipment. There were shouts, orders. Some at them. Nik slowed as someone claimed his attention. Several someones, like ice-white trees with topaz eyes. *Sinzi!*

Mac kept running, for these last few steps with one hand gripping the Dhryn beside her to take advantage of the larger being's power. Their breath puffed, out of sync.

A final slide and rush, and they arrived.

"Hi, Mac. About time you got here." Emily's lips pulled from her teeth in a predator's grin. Her eyes touched and dismissed the Dhryn. "I see we need to talk. Later. He's coming up." She drew a finger through the 'screen hovering above the console. "See?"

It felt so utterly normal that Mac stepped to the console without a second thought, her eyes reading the status. "The 'bots are under the ice," she said in wonder. And not in a straight line, as they'd used to scan the Tannu River, but closing in a circle like a net. "They've been reliable?"

"Good as your finny friends," boasted Emily. "Case helped with the mod. But can we focus on that, please?" "That" being something large and asymmetrical, rising slowly from the depths.

Not that slowly. "It's underneath us?" Mac shifted her feet.

"We're on top of it," Em countered cheerily. "Perfect! I admit, I was wondering how to get its attention. Seemed set on anchoring to the bottom here. Running into it with 'bots didn't seem to make any difference. But it began moving a moment ago. I should have known you'd bring the right bait." This time, she did look at the Dhryn, a long assessing look. "Interesting."

"Later," Mac reminded her. "Emily, we've a problem. This thing—" she pointed at their quarry. "It's capable of taking the ocean with it. Through some kind of no-space gate."

"Why?"

It was still rising. Mac could hear shouts across that ice and hoped that Nik and the Sinzi were ready with whatever they had.

If they had anything . . .

If the Ro ship had been destroyed . . .

If the feeders knew the difference between friend and foe . . .

Mac shrugged. In so many ways, the future might be measured in heartbeats. *Not her problem.*

"The Ro are trying to regrow themselves," she explained quickly. "Here. In the ocean. When they're stopped, they retrieve whatever they've done, including the water. We don't know if it's deliberate or a consequence—but that's why the Chasm worlds are dry, Em. The Dhryn killed the Ro, but their gate took away the water."

"We shall kill the Ro." Ice snapped as Her Glory spoke for the first time. Her hand rose to the feeders overhead.

Emily followed the gesture with her eyes and appeared transfixed. "Gods, Mac. What have you done?"

"Later," Mac said again. "Listen to me, Em. You, too." She smacked Her Glory on a broad shoulder. "We have to do this in the right order. The Ro has to come out first, hear me? We let the Sinzi do whatever they can. Then we—" *hold a meeting, ask its name, check its agenda, "*—then we kill it," she said, cold and sure.

Her species imperative.

"Which means we have to get out of the way!" Mac glanced at the readout. *The Ro was accelerating upward.* "Now would be good," she urged.

Her Glory was moving back. Emily shook her head, staying with the Tracer, her fingers reaching for its 'screen. "Just let me—"

"Em!" Mac reached for Emily and pulled with all her might.

The ice smashed open from below, blocks and crystal shooting in all directions. They were knocked flat.

And a huge writhing mass of *red* reached for the sky.

She'd expected a machine or some obscene blend like a walker. *Not this.* On her back beside Emily, Mac stared up into what was most definitely alive.

Not a tentacle, she decided. More like a rapidly growing tendril or root, pulsing wider every bit as quickly as it expanded in length. Transparent in places, with budlike protrusions also growing. Utter black in others. All of it in motion, yet she could swear she glimpsed stars within those patches of darkness.

~YOU WILL NOT INTERFERE WITH US~

The words tore into Mac's skin, cutting to the bone. She could hear Emily screaming.

The pain wasn't as important as the triumph. *They had the Ro!*

~WE CONTINUE~

Mac writhed, her back arching, but found her voice. "We'll stop you!"

~YOU ARE INSIGNIFICANT. YOU WILL END~

Agony!

~WE ARE WHAT WILL LIVE FOREVER~

The tendril seemed to reach the clouds.

There was a roar that shook the ice. Mac and Emily clung to one another.

Then, gently, it began to rain.

Green rain, the color of growing things, of spring.

The first drops struck the tendril and it flung itself from side to side, succeeding only in spreading the liquid.

More drops fell.

Great suppurating wounds appeared. The tendril flailed once more, then dropped to the ice with a heavy thud.

~WE MUST SUR~

And more drops fell.

Until nothing was left of the tendril but a pool of green liquid on the ice.

Then the mouths began to drink.

30

FRIENDS AND FINALES

MAC SPAT SNOW.

"You dead?" Emily asked, her tone one of idle curiosity.

Cold. And it felt like someone had pounded nails through her skin. Mac took a cautiously deep breath. "Nope. You?"

Emily Mamani rolled over on her stomach. Her dark eyes shone. There was snow in her hair. "Doesn't look like it."

"What about everyone else?"

The two biologists sat up and looked around.

Floating ice filled the hole torn by the Ro. Crystals were sifting into the cracks. The hole would be gone soon.

The ocean remained.

They'd done it. Mac said it to herself. *Didn't quite believe, yet.*

"Tracer's pooched," Emily commented. Sure enough, all that showed of the device was a bent support strut poking through the ice.

"Looks like it." They helped each other stand, the process complicated more by a tendency to giggle than the freshening wind. "What parts do you—"

"Mac!" She whirled at the voice and immediately lost her footing. It didn't help that Nik slipped as he tried to catch her. They fell to the ice laughing.

Emily leaned over to look down at them. "Gee, that's romantic."

"Get your own spy," Mac said, and proceeded to pay attention to her own.

There were details. *There were always details,* Mac fussed, holding Nik's hand. It wasn't that she didn't care, it was more that she viewed what was done as done.

Time to move on.

She could taste spring in the air, this close to the Arctic Circle.

But no, there were details. Which required standing in what the Ministry apparently viewed as a landing field. *She could tell them a thing or two about the seeming permanence of sea ice.* The levs were hovering, at least. The scattered clumps of people were taking their own chances.

Though a shot of hypothermia didn't seem to worry anyone at the moment.

The crew of the harvester were recovering from it. The few who'd been on board when the Ro attacked had landed in the icy water. They'd all been wearing survival skins beneath their gear. *Base regulations had their reasons,* Mac thought rather smugly.

"What's the situation?" Nik asked a newcomer, another of the armored anonymous in black.

The Sinzi had brought their own equipment. Mac had listened to the edges of that conversation. Something about transect gate management then the Sinzi ran out of words. She'd been mildly entertained by the ensuing charades, particularly as the Sinzi were wearing slim gloves over their muscular fingers, the *lamnas* adding odd lumps. They'd lost her well before the other Humans stopped nodding and looked mutely grateful.

The Sinzi weren't in danger of losing their role as no-space guardians any time soon, Mac thought. Although she suspected there'd be some hard discussions about consulting with their allies rather than simply maneuvering them into a desired location.

The Naralax Transect was as it had been, Sol's gate where it had been, to the relief of Venus Orbital and the now-quiet Trisulian armada.

She wasn't even going to ask. The Sinzi had put themselves at risk to prove a point. The Trisulians—they'd made a point as well. The Inner Council faced a hard decision. *If they asked her,* Mac thought, while profoundly hoping no one did, *she'd wait until after they'd all given birth.* No new mother in her experience had time to make trouble.

And there'd been enough suffering.

She found herself yawning and watched the cloud of breath condense.

Nik's hand abruptly tightened. "Mac. Wake up!"

"Wasn't asleep," she protested, shifting from foot to foot. *Maybe close.*

"You tell her," he ordered, shaking his head and grinning.

The newcomer tapped his left forefinger against his holster and Mac's eyes widened. "Sing-li?"

Up went the visor, revealing a huge grin. "Can't fool you, Mac. Nice having you back."

Her smile was so wide it hurt. "Nice to be back."

Sing-li glanced at Nik, then at her. "I see you're in good hands." *With a wink.*

She tried to scowl, but couldn't. "I think so," she grinned, tightening her arm around Nik's waist.

"The message?" Nik suggested. *She could hear his smile.*

"Delighted, sir. Dr. Connor," semiofficious, "a message for you has been relayed from Myriam." Another wink. "There's only one person I know who could sneak something personal directly here and this fast."

"Fourteen!" *Definitely awake now.* "What's he say?"

"It's not exactly from our talented Myg," Nik warned, his grip firming.

Mac stamped her boot on the ice. "Before I freeze, gentlemen?" she suggested.

Sing-li tried to compose his face into something more serious. *Didn't work,* Mac thought, waiting impatiently. "Here you go. 'There will be a full review of all upcoming projects in the Wilderness Trust before'—there's a line under 'before,' Mac—any such projects resume.' Signed Charles Mudge III.'" A pause. "Oh. Sorry, Mac. I didn't think it would make you cry. We can deal with him," almost grimly.

"Not crying." Mac burrowed her head into Nik's chest and hiccuped helplessly. "Laughing," she managed to say. *If there were some tears mixed in, that was her business.* Mudge was alive! "I can deal with Oversight, Sing-li. Trust me."

She had less to say when, shortly afterward, Nikolai Trojanowski was informed by another messenger that his ship had left orbit some time ago. Along with Her Glory, Deruym Ma Nas, several replete feeders, and one Sinzi.

They'd made it through the gate before the Sinzi removed it from Earth orbit.

Her spy hadn't seemed surprised.

"I hate these things."

"The clothes?" Emily gave her a critical look up and down. "Looks fine to me. Two has good taste."

Mac tugged at the rich blue jacket. "You know what I mean," she said darkly. "These things. These—" She waved wildly.

"Oh, and that's clear, Dr. Connor? C'mon. Get down."

Mac stepped from the platform in front of the Sinzi mirror. "While we're at it," she complained, "why do you get to wear normal clothes?" She looked at Emily with envy.

Emily Mamani wore coveralls, with useful pockets. And shoes that weren't going to trip her. *Not that she wasn't gorgeous,* Mac thought, trying to pin down exactly what gave the other woman that glow. Something in the face, perhaps. Freedom.

Purpose.

As represented by the necklace Emily now lifted between two gloved fingers. "Four down," she said, flipping past those red beads. "Three on the ship. One in the ice." The remaining beads were white. "Seven to go. Which makes eleven." She dropped the necklace savoring the word. "Didn't I tell you?"

"Yes, but you were nuts," Mac reminded her.

The Trisulian warship, with help from others from Myriam, had disabled the Ro ship—*if that's what you called something closer in function to a factory,* she thought. But it had already been crippled; the Progenitors, old and new, had had their revenge after all. Early reports described vast areas used to dismantle and rebuild living tissue, others as storerooms for completed walkers and other machines. The Ro themselves? They'd been physically bound to their ship as well as somehow existing outside of it. When the Sinzi terminated its no-space connection, three had reappeared. In pieces.

The chamber beneath the ice—what was left of it after the feeders had been called away by Her Glory—had been filled with preserved embryonic cells, all of the same basic pattern as the Ro themselves. Enough to saturate an ocean. Enough to restart their kind at the expense of any other.

The IU planned to waste no time tracking down the remaining Ro, fearing the beings would retreat before they could be found and destroyed. There would be no more negotiation. It had become apparent even to the idiot faction that the goals of the Myrokynay and the rest of the IU were mutually exclusive.

Survival depended on stopping the Ro while they still could.

Someone else's battle, Mac thought. Speaking of which. "When do you leave?" she asked Emily.

"The N'not'k await!" That wicked grin. "Don't worry, I'll stay long enough to catch your speech."

"I am not," Mac gritted her teeth, "giving a speech."

Emily ignored her. "Loved the last one, by the way. Did you know they'll be broadcasting to the IU?"

"Won't matter," Mac said, heading for the door. *Get it over with.* "Not giving a speech," she muttered. "Going to sit at the back and enjoy my supper. Two promised me shrimp. You," she jerked her thumb at Emily, "give a speech."

"Coward."

Mac stopped at the door and turned. "Behave. And be careful," she said. Before it could become emotional, she made herself frown. "Keep track of the field season. I'll have your gear at the station, but try not to arrive late next time."

Emily tapped her on the nose. "Careful's my middle name. But Mac?" She shook her head, her eyes warm yet strangely distant. "I won't be coming back. You can keep my stuff. Oh, I'll visit," this quickly as Mac's face must have shown her shock. "But I'm kind of popular right now, if you've noticed. Sencor's begged to renew my funding. There's that aquatic world out there. I'll be able to do what I want for some time." Her lips twisted to the side. "After I save the known universe."

"That first," Mac managed.

A hint of worry creased Emily's forehead. "You do understand, don't you? Fish really aren't my thing."

That word again.

Unfortunately, she did. "The Survivor Legend. You haven't given up."

"Never!" A quick hug and that dazzling smile. "It's still a puzzle, Mac. What happened to that one world, among all the rest. *Aie!* Now that we're getting a clearer picture—the mystery only deepens!" Emily laughed. "I'll stop. You don't want to be late for your speech."

"I'm not," Mac said clearly as she opened the door, "giving a speech."

They weren't all here. The realities of in-system space travel being what they were, it wouldn't have been possible to bring everyone. *Someone must have tried,* Mac thought as she surveyed the crowd on the Sinzi's vast patio. Her father and brothers; Emily's family. Hollans, of course, with a quite remarkable number of Ministry personnel. *In truly awful shirts.* She smiled to herself. Fourteen was here in spirit.

Her *nimb,* he'd informed her smugly, was waiting at Base. *Hopefully in a box.*

She counted alien species she recognized, getting into the forties before deciding "all of them" likely covered it—including the ones in the fountain she'd still never met in person. Most she didn't know. *Biospace.* She liked the word.

"Nice speech," Nik commented, his breath tickling her ear.

She gave him a suspicious look.

"No, really." *That dimple.* "Short, to the point. I think the Imrya, maybe a few others, expected more than 'Thank you for inviting me tonight. Support research. Enjoy the party.' But not me." He laid one hand over his heart. "''Twas pure Mac."

Mac sighed. "I hate these things. My mind goes blank. You, though?" She bumped her shoulder against his. "Even Blake was impressed. And that's saying something."

Nik had been more than eloquent. He'd stood before them all—vidbots and living eyes—to tell them exactly how close they'd come to disaster. Without naming names, or species, he'd made it plain that only courage and sacrifice had saved them when diplomacy faltered. The silence at the end had been more telling than any applause.

"I hope so. He kept grilling me. I think Owen and your father took notes. I've had easier interrogations, believe me."

"That's a good sign," Mac assured him. "Blake ignores people he doesn't like." She slipped her arm through his, watching as the groups below milled around the various bars and entertainments. Not at random. There were preferences. The weather being what it was, the staff had erected either heaters or chillers on poles throughout the expanse. The resulting pattern was quite fascinating. *She should make notes.*

Later. They'd found this quiet spot away from the rest. *They deserved it.*

"Do I intrude, Mac, Nikolai?"

"Of course not," Nik said immediately.

"Anchen!" Mac grinned with delight. "I wondered when we'd see you."

The gracious Sinzi bowed, her fingers spreading. "I waited. There were many demands on us all. Now, in the pause before departures, comes the right time to complete our promise."

A word that now made her nervous. "Please tell me this won't involve the entire civilized universe."

"Mac!" Nik looked horrified. "Sinzi-ra, there was wine with supper—"

"Giving a speech. Didn't drink," she informed him haughtily.

Anchen's fingers shivered in her laugh. "Always you speak your mind, Mac. I value this even more highly after our absence from one another. You are a joy to me, a nexus who will always be centered within my beings." This with a brush of those fingers through Mac's hair.

She restrained the urge to stick out her tongue at Nik. *Wine, indeed.* "So once I give you my gift, we're done?" *And safe?* "No more promises?" In case the Sinzi took that as a request, Mac hurriedly added, "which doesn't mean I'm suggesting one."

"You have already done so, Mac." Another bow. "I am honored to participate in your new promise."

Oh-oh. Mac glanced at Nik. He, for his part, was looking magnificently non-committal. *Which meant he knew something she didn't.* "What promise would that be?" she asked warily.

"The promise you made to Her Glory, in which Fy became the first partici-pant. Your Ministry's ship," this to Nik, "will be decontaminated and returned, Nikolai."

"You're sheltering the Dhryn." Mac chewed her lip and this notion for a mo-ment, then nodded. "Thank you."

"Shelter? No. Your promise was to help the Dhryn survive."

Mac could almost hear Brymn's anxious questions. *"How many of us must sur-vive . . . what is our evolutionary unit?"* "Ureif and I—we talked about a future for the species. I don't know if that's possible from one, Sinzi-ra."

"We will search the derelict ships for more survivors. Regardless, there are means to promote diversity," Anchen said with serene confidence. "Trust that we have seen the path taken by the Myrokynay and will tread more carefully, Mac. There is animosity toward the Dhryn, as well as gratitude for their help against the Ro. Her Glory wishes to continue to provide this help while we Sinzi undertake our portion."

"Your portion?"

Nik spoke. "The Sinzi have begun the restoration of Myriam."

Mac blinked. "Pardon?"

"Water is the first concern," Anchen replied, perhaps thinking Mac's shocked expression meant she required specifics. "We will work with experts on that world, including your colleagues. Technology will be in place soonest. The biology will follow apace. My understanding is that there have been caches of viable seeds recovered. Other species will have to be approximated or non-Dhryn substitutes found. The Dhryn will have a future, Mac. We participate in the promise."

The regeneration of an entire world. Unensela would be ecstatic. They'd all be. Her entire team.

She'd have to keep in touch.

"That's quite the promise," Mac ventured, beginning to smile.

"It attracts our interest, too. And now, I believe you have something for me?"

Mac reached into the pocket of her lovely jacket—*staff having realized the necessity of such things*—and drew out the salmon carving. "For your collection." She grinned at Nik, then offered it to the alien. "It's a well-traveled fish."

Anchen's fingertip wrapped around the tiny thing. Her mouth trembled, then smiled. "I'm overwhelmed. It shall have a place of honor."

Nik held out his hand. On the palm was a single *lamnas*. "Thank you," he said, his voice husky with emotion. "This is the last one."

Anchen didn't take the ring. "Surely you still need it?"

Mac felt a stir of worry. "Why?" Then, she looked at Nik and *knew*. "You're leaving." The words seem to come from someone else.

He met her eyes. Seeing the remorse in his, she took an involuntary step back. "You're leaving now. With Emily. To hunt the Ro."

"It's the job."

"You don't have to." Her hands were fists. "Someone else can go." Anchen looked from one Human to the other, but remained silent.

Nik closed the distance between them. "You could come with us, Mac." Low and intense. "Help finish your work."

"My work?" She paused in disbelief, then half smiled, as if to share a joke. "Don't you remember? I study salmon, Mr. Trojanowski."

"There you are, Norcoast!"

Mudge was climbing the stairs toward them, his cane banging every step. He looked flushed and irritated.

And alive.

"You shouldn't be out of bed," Mac told him.

"There's nothing wrong with me." He squinted at her through his good eye, the line from scalp to jaw over the other being covered with the Sinzi's wonderful bandaging. *He wouldn't lose it.*

Others on the *Joy* hadn't been so lucky.

Mudge looked from Nik to Mac. He *harrumphed* uneasily. "I'm interrupting—"

Mac swallowed and stood straighter. "No. What is it?"

"My lev to Vancouver's arrived early. I came to say good-bye." He hesitated and studied her face for an instant. "There's room, Norcoast," this in a gentle voice, "if you're ready to go home."

Home.

"Unless this is a bad time—"

"No," Mac said unsteadily, not looking at Nik. "It's the perfect time."

Time to return to who and what she was.

31

RESUMPTION AND REWARD

L ATE SEPTEMBER PAINTED the upper forest slopes with orange and yellow, poplar and tamaracks showing off their colors. Eagles and ravens gathered to argue over river shoals. Bears grew fat. And mice collected the velvet from antlers, in anticipation of the cold.

Deeper in the valleys, all remained green and lush, as if to belie winter's approach, while sleek-sided Coho sported heavy jaws and attitude as they rushed up the rivers to spawn.

"You're sure the scanner's in place?" Mac leaned out over the cliff, one hand on the edge.

A dizzying distance below, a Frow danced along the loose rock, humming to *ne-self.* "You worry too much, Mac," *ne* called up. "I've checked it twice."

She was sorely tempted to drop something. *The Frow would only enjoy catching it.* She grinned. Hadn't lost a tool since her latest grad student's arrival.

And once she'd let *Ne* Drysolee pitch *ne's* tent on the cliff face above the field station, she'd slept much better. *Something Mudge didn't need in a report.*

He'd been touchy since Fourteen's last visit. Mac winced slightly. *Though she did see his point.* The now child-sized offspring hadn't grasped that picking her flowers wouldn't go over well—and they'd picked quite a few before she'd noticed. *Including a number of small trees.* Mudge had produced so many forms for her to complete, she'd insisted on finishing at the restaurant. *On his bill.*

Mac got to her feet and headed for her tent. There was rain on the way as much as salmon. She'd left her coat off, the day having been warm and pleasant. One of those gifts.

"You expecting company?" Case asked, standing behind the console, wrench in hand. He'd come for the week to help install a modified version of the Mamani Tracer. *Twitchy in two days.* She wasn't sure if it was the Frow's fascination with his freckles or the cliffs.

"Not unless you've called a ride," she told him, glancing down the valley. It was a skim from Base. With Ty driving, by the look of it.

"Why would I do that? Because you're a slave driver and expect everyone to exist on food through a straw?" He chuckled as she pretended to scowl. "I'm used to it."

Ne Drysolee's two-pointed hat appeared above the cliff edge. "Perhaps they send us pizza, Case! Or ribs! Ribs, Mac!"

No matter the species, students always ganged up on her. Mac shook her head. "Don't even start. Help unload whatever it is, but don't waste time. They should be here today."

She ducked into her tent and retrieved her coat, catching sight of Wilson Kudla's latest on the box by her cot. She winced. *Dedicated to her; really should read the damn book,* she thought guiltily. *Later.*

Mac hunted and found the bag of moss she wanted sent back to her new garden. *No point wasting the ride.*

When she came out, however, Mac let the bag drop.

The skim had landed. Ty leaned against its side, grinning.

And Nikolai Trojanowski was walking toward her, wearing his suit and cravat, carrying his office over one shoulder.

No glasses. *Unless she counted the pair in her tent, tucked in the velvet case along with the one* lamnas *she'd never brought herself to view, having said good-bye enough for one lifetime.*

All she could think of was, "You do know it's going to rain." For proof, she lifted her coat.

He stopped just out of reach. "Hello, Mac."

What was she supposed to say now?

Case nonchalantly tossed his wrench over the cliff to keep *Ne* Drysolee occupied, then went to talk to Ty.

Fine, desert her.

"What are you doing here?" Mac blurted out.

Nik reached into his pocket and drew out an envelope, his eyes never leaving hers.

"Oh, no," she warned. "Don't you even think about it."

Paying no attention, he opened and held out a piece of ordinary mem-paper. "This is a formal complaint, Dr. Mackenzie Connor," in his most official voice. "I suggest you pay attention."

"Complaint?" She frowned. "From who? About what?"

"From the Oversight Committee of the Castle Inlet Wilderness Trust. To the Interspecies Consulate. Regarding the presence of unauthorized aliens within an Anthropogenic Perturbation Free Zone. Class Three."

"He's a registered student!" She snatched at the sheet and crumpled it into a ball. "Oversight's gone too far." *She'd even sent a new pot for his damn plant.* "You can just take this back and—"

Nik's eyes were smiling. "You didn't read it."

She muttered something anatomically unlikely, but opened the ball and gave its contents a quick glance.

Then a look.

Then a longer look.

"If that's okay with you, Dr. Connor?"

It was a request for a permanent on-site liaison from the consulate, to ensure any nonterrestrials interested in pursuing studies with the famed Dr. Connor would be supervised by someone knowledgeable. *In other words, watched like a hawk so they didn't break Oversight's rules.*

"This better not come out of my budget," she said, carefully not looking up. *Did he see her hands tremble?*

"Not at all."

"And this—liaison—stays out of the way."

"Absolutely. He'll even cook."

At this, Mac finally raised her eyes. "I thought you were gone," she said very quietly. She pointed up.

"I tried," Nik said just as quietly, stepping closer. "Then I realized it was time to come home."

Mac opened her arms to bring him the rest of the way.

Below, dorsal fins sliced the dark water, disappeared, rose again with a muscular heave. Rose-black bodies jostled for position, moving ever forward, seeking their future.

The salmon were back.

- CONTACT -

THE BEADS SLIPPED through slim fingers, one by one, the fingers at the end of smooth bare arms, skin a perfect match to the tanned olive tones of the woman's face and neck. Her fingers stopped at the lone white bead and her teeth flashed in a grim smile. "I'd say we have a lock. Everyone in place, Zimmie?"

Zimmerman checked his console then nodded. "You're sure?"

Emily Mamani let go of her necklace and stroked through the 'screen over the Tracer. "Oh, yes."

Riden IV's ocean wind was more howl than tropical breeze, the air hot, humid, and always in your face. Zimmerman had shed his armor the first week. The big man now worked barefoot, in shorts topped by a fanciful shirt. That shirt was plastered by sweat against his big frame. He'd take it off, but Emily had distracting ways of commenting on the view.

Not that she wasn't distracting herself.

She'd resumed singing in her not-quite Spanish language. He hid a relieved grin, knowing the signs of a successful hunt by now. *About time.* This planet gave him the creeps. The rest had been empty, lifeless. This—despite the sullen dark waves and barren islands—this was something else.

When they'd arrived, their team had conducted the usual assays, checking the results against those from an ill-fated Sencor survey. Something new had indeed appeared, right here, below where their lev hovered. Microscopic, colonial, all of a kind. Coating the rock of deep submerged ridges. Coming free to float beneath the surface. Sticking to the wave-scoured edges of the land.

And it wasn't alone.

"Call the bait," Emily said abruptly.

"You're sure?"

"It's time."

Zimmerman nodded and lifted his wrist to his mouth, spoke once, then lowered his arm. "Done." His hand dropped to the weapon belted over his shorts.

She noticed. "They're allies, now. Blame Mac."

"Right." He moved his hand away, his massive shoulders giving a self-conscious shrug. "Habit."

Emily's laugh blended with the wild wind. "We couldn't do this without Her help," she pointed out. "Nothing draws a Ro from its chamber but a Dhryn. I should know." Her finger-tip traced the necklace at her throat.

Six more Wasted had been found clinging to life in ships adrift at Haven. Two had survived and grown to full health. A tenuous, but promising beginning for their species.

As this was the end for another. There'd been no more ships, only dead worlds like Riden IV, each being prepared by an oblivious Ro. And only here had those preparations borne fruit.

"You'd think the Ro would get a clue," Zimmerman growled. "They must have noticed something was wrong by now."

" 'Now,' when it comes to our quarry, is a slippery thing," she said calmly, turning to look over the ocean, her shiny cap of black-and-white hair whipped by the wind. "We've been hunting for what . . . almost a year? In no-space, hardly time for a heartbeat. The Ro have taken advantage of what time does to us. It's their turn, Zimmie, to feel the other side of that knife." A chuckle. "Gotta love the irony. They built an entire world—a fleet of starships—all to keep their so-useful Dhryn safe and nearby. When the Dhryn turned on them the first time, they still saved as many possible. Even now, they blindly reach for the same tool, not noticing it's turned on them again."

A Sinzi dart drew near, surrounded by five smaller silver ships. "Keep in mind, my friend," she said quietly, "no one hunts the Ro with better reason than Her Glory. Not you. Not I. Now, to work."

She returned to the Tracer, her fingers moving rapidly through its hovering 'screen. Zimmerman watched the dart lower itself until ocean spray dotted its sides. Proof there was a Dhryn inside—otherwise, the Ro would react with one of its lightning attacks. *They'd lost a few levs discovering that detail.*

"It's on the move!" Emily shouted. "Get us up!"

He lunged for the controls, sending their lev to join the small fleet of others hovering overhead. The dart did the same.

"Catch of the day." She didn't need to point to the seething boil of water below. 'Bots were zipping from the water like chased fish. They circled once to locate the lev and began their return to their mistress. "Check the Sinzi have blocked the gate, then notify the team."

Zimmerman lifted his wrist again and spoke. The dart dipped once, as if in acknowledgment, then lifted out of the way.

He joined Emily at the rail. They watched as five larger-than-usual levs plunged down to fire their harpoons, cables playing out with a whine louder than the howling wind. The tips disappeared into the froth.

A froth suddenly stained with red.

Three of the cables snapped taut. The other lev crews released their failed harpoons and fired another round, this time hitting their target. All five began to strain upward. A dark shape gradually formed beneath the surface, huge and struggling. More harpoons, these without cables, launched into its midst.

"Messy," Zimmerman commented. Another detail they'd discovered: each of the Ro was somehow rooted into its chamber; much of that structure biological as well. A vulnerability exploited by the Dhryn feeders, but the IU wanted more of the technology left intact for study. *Messy worked.*

The struggle was over almost as soon as begun. More levs approached, sending down nets and divers. The limp shape shifted, but it was only the wind and waves; the cables held firm; the Ro was dead.

"Well," announced Emily. "That's done." She took the white bead in her fingers and pressed just so. Red flowed through it, until that bead matched its neighbors. "Eleven."

"How can we know that's all of them?" Zimmerman stared at the hideous shape being pulled from the sea.

"Here and now? I'm sure." Another shrug. "Anywhere else? Don't care. My job's done. And very well done." Emily slipped her arm around the big man's waist. "Time to find the party."

"There's a party?"

"There's always a party," Emily said, her tone vastly content. "With dancing." She laughed. "Don't look so worried. I'll behave. I promised Mac."

Zimmerman had scrunched up his forehead. Not so much a frown, as an indication of deep thought. "And after that?"

"Oh, that's when life gets interesting, Zimmie. What do you know about the Survivor Legend?"

Life coated rock, broke free to rise and float, struck an edge and stayed. It busied itself with sunlight and chemical reactions.

Bits failed. Bits survived. Of those, bits failed while others succeeded and grew and combined. Of those, some failed while others grew . . .

Without a caretaker's watchful eyes, the seeds of That Which Had Been Myrokynay became something else, many things else.

All new.